The Boston Composers Project

BOSTON AREA MUSIC LIBRARIES

Berklee College of Music

Boston College

Boston Conservatory

Boston Public Library

Boston University

Brandeis University

Harvard Musical Association

Harvard University, Hilles Library

Harvard University, Eda Kuhn Loeb Music Library

Longy School of Music

Massachusetts Institute of Technology

New England Conservatory of Music

Northeastern University

Tufts University

University of Massachusetts, Boston

Wellesley College

Boston Area Music Libraries

THE BOSTON COMPOSERS PROJECT

A Bibliography of Contemporary Music

Linda I. Solow
Editor

Mary Wallace Davidson
Brenda Chasen Goldman
Geraldine E. Ostrove
Associate Editors

The MIT Press
Cambridge, Massachusetts
London, England

This Project has been supported by grants from the National Endowment for the Humanities and the Massachusetts Council on the Arts and Humanities, and by the MIT Experimental Music Studio, the Council for the Arts at MIT, the MIT Information Processing Services, radio station WCRB, and the institutions and staff members of the Boston Area Music Libraries.

This book was printed on a Xerox9700 Laser Printer with Univers family fonts.

Library of Congress Cataloging in Publication Data
Main entry under title:

The Boston composers project.

    Includes indexes.
1. Music--Massachusetts--Boston Metropolitan Area--
20th century--Bio-bibliography.   I. Solow, Linda I.
II. Boston Area Music Libraries.
ML107.B7B67   1983   016.7817744'61   83-9922
ISBN 0-262-02198-6

To Mary Lou Little

CONTENTS

PREFACE

The Boston Composers Project, initiated in 1976, reflects a distinctive approach to documenting American contemporary music. It takes as its point of departure a suggestion made in 1966 by Paul Fromm:

> Just as university libraries take it as their responsibility to make available...the latest developments in any field of knowledge, so music libraries can undertake to offer to their communities an awareness of the contemporary state of music. This, of course, can be done only through the dissemination of new musical works--the true end-products of musical thinking.... And, on the other hand, just as university presses and university libraries make it their particular responsibility to preserve and disseminate the work done in their own scholarly communities, so music libraries...have a special responsibility for preserving and disseminating the work of the composers in their own communities.
>
> The great advantage possessed by each music library is its awareness of its own community, of the composers therein, and of the direction of the most vigorous and important work. In this country there are about 250 music libraries of major importance. I would propose that each music library adopt the most important composers living in its area in order to build up a catalog of scores that would constitute a total representation of these composers' works.(1)

While individual academic and public libraries have in fact been collecting materials--in some cases for many years--no coordinated national effort has emerged. By documenting the abundant musical creativity in the greater Boston area, we hope to stimulate renewed interest in Fromm's proposal and to encourage similar endeavors in other regions of the country.

The project has six objectives, devised to meet the needs of cultural historians, music researchers, librarians, performers, conductors, music directors and other planners of concert programs, and the musical public at large. These objectives are:

1. To document the current musical scene in the greater Boston area for both art music and jazz.

2. To assure that the musical works of composers in this area are collected and preserved.

3. To provide access to as many of these works as possible for consultation and listening.

4. To encourage the performance of works by Boston-area composers.

---

(1) "A Contemporary Role for American Music Libraries," *Perspectives of New Music*, 4 (1966): 141-142.

5. To provide information about all musical works of area composers, even works that may not be represented in local library collections.

6. To disseminate this information by publishing a combined bibliography and union catalogue of compositions.

Our aim in this book is to list every composition, published or unpublished, by every art music and jazz composer resident in the greater Boston area during the latter half of the 1970s. The choices of locale and musical genres were based on practical considerations. The Boston area supports an extremely active and wide-ranging musical community. Limiting our geographical scope enabled us to gather information largely through personal contact with the composers. This seemed essential if we were to complete the work in a reasonable time with the human and financial resources available. The selection of composers of art music and jazz was similarly practical.(2) We deemed it appropriate that this library-based project cover the types of music that are of greatest interest to our clienteles. This mode of selection from among the large population of Boston-area composers also allowed us to treat a manageable group in some depth rather than a large group superficially.

We have included as many composers as we could identify who were resident in the greater Boston area at some time between 1975 and 1980. Composers who left or died during that time are listed if resident for the five years prior to their departure or death. In order to qualify for listing, a composer must have had some music published, recorded, or performed publicly, or held a faculty appointment as a teacher of composition.

Some persons whose names came to our attention could not be located in the area, despite our best efforts. A few composers declined to be included. Others did not respond to requests for information or for comments on information we submitted to them for verification. This last group of composers are listed in the Appendix, together with as accurate a list of their works as we could compile.

This book captures the Boston Composers Project at two points: April 1, 1981, after which no names were added to the list of composers, and January 1, 1982, the closing date for the addition of bibliographic information to the data base.

The Boston Area Music Libraries (BAML) started in 1974 as an informal monthly discussion group chaired by Mary Lou Little, then Librarian of the Eda Kuhn Loeb Music Library at Harvard University. The sixteen libraries now comprising the group are widely disparate in size and character. Two house nationally known research collections. Of the others, modest collections outnumber the strong. The four conservatory libraries share some concerns that differ from those of the other institutions.

To help achieve the objectives of the Boston Composers Project, we enlisted the participation of several local institutions that are not members of BAML: three

---

(2) "Art music" and "jazz" are imprecise, even ambiguous, terms. But while not even mutually exclusive, they are commonly understood generalizations, and that is the sense in which they are used here.

public libraries, two FM radio stations, and an academic rare book and manuscript collection. The Brookline, Cambridge, and Newton public libraries have relatively large music holdings and/or sponsor contemporary music activities. Radio stations WCRB and WGBH both hold unique recordings of broadcasts they have aired of music by Boston area composers. Though their libraries are not open to the public, they have agreed to let qualified researchers use their sound recordings on the premises by appointment. The Houghton Library at Harvard University holds numerous manuscripts of works by composers in the project.

The relevant holdings of all participating libraries are identified in this volume. In addition, each academic and public library has agreed to serve as a resource library for designated composers in the project. Each resource library will maintain personal communications when possible, keep up-to-date records of its composers' works through an annual survey, and acquire, within the limits of its collection policy, all works of its composers in printed, photocopied, manuscript, or recorded form.

This bibliography lists works by 197 composers--161 in the section that comprises the main body of the book and 36 in the Appendix. The section for each composer is arranged as follows:

Composer Citation Number.

Biography. Date and place of birth and death; year moved to Boston area; post-secondary schools and academic degrees; teachers; musical pursuits other than composing; awards; books published; teaching positions; siglum for Boston area resource library to which queries may be directed. (This information was obtained primarily from the composers.)

Works List. Alphabetical listing of original works, followed by alphabetical listing of arrangements of other composers' works. Withdrawn works appear as brief entries. Arrangements made under contract for agencies such as publishing houses or motion picture companies are excluded, as are arrangements by others of listed works. For each work, the following information is provided, as applicable:

> Work citation number
> Filing title
> Title and date of composition (according to published score, if available; otherwise according to manuscript, information provided by the composer (sometimes including question marks), commercial or private recording, or other evidence; question marks in brackets supplied by editors)
> Duration (approximate, from information provided by composer, score, or recording)
> Medium (see note below)
> Genre
> Authors and sources of texts
> Contents (*vocal work*); or movement titles or number of movements (*instrumental work*)
> Commissioning agent; dedication; occasion or purpose for which composed; awards; revisions or variant versions; date, place, occasion, and performers of premiere
> Format (see note below)
> Availability note
> "In" note
> Publisher (*score*) or manufacturer and serial number (*sound recording*)
> Date and location of performance (*private sound recording*)
> Performers
> Rental note
> Library sigla

Medium of performance ("For:") The order of performance forces is: spoken parts, dancers, sung parts, instruments, special effects. For works scored for one through nine performers, forces required are written out in full, with the exception of string quartets (2 violins, viola, violoncello) and woodwind quintets (flute, oboe, clarinet, bassoon, horn). Instruments are listed in the composer's score order when known, otherwise in standard score order. Doublings are separated by a slash, as clarinet/saxophone.

Larger works are described by the closest applicable term for the ensemble. Excepting works for band, the specific instrumentation, when it could be ascertained, follows within parentheses in standard score order; for example,

2(&pic2)-2(&Ehn)-2(Ebc!)-2; 4-3-3-0; perc(3); str(no vla)

stands for:

> 2 flutes and 2 separate piccolo parts - 2 oboes and 1 separate English horn part - 2 clarinets, 1 doubling on E-flat clarinet - 2 bassoons; 4 horns - 3 trumpets - 3 trombones - no tuba; 3 percussionists; string sections of violins I and II, no violas, cellos, double basses

A string section may be identified by the exact number required:

5-4-4-3-2

Format, publication, and availability. Every known manifestation of the work except reissues of recordings is listed. The format terms "music" and "tape" are used when no more specific information is available. Manuscripts are identified but not described in detail. Names of publishers and record manufacturers appear in shortened form when possible. Unpublished works are identified as "available from composer" only with the composer's permission. Persons who wish to obtain such materials should contact the appropriate resource library, identified by the siglum in the biography section. Performers on recordings are listed when known. BAML library holdings are identified by sigla. Holdings of non-BAML libraries are listed only in the absence of a BAML citation.

ABBREVIATIONS

A	Alto (voice)	op.	opus
accord	accordion	org	organ
acl	alto clarinet	perc	percussion
afl	alto flute	perf. dir.	performance directions
amp	amplified	pf	piano
APNM	Association for	pf. red.	piano reduction
	the Promotion of	pf(4-hds)	piano (4-hands)
	New Music	pic	piccolo
arec	alto recorder	rec	recorder
arr.	arranged	reprod.	reproduction
asax	alto saxophone	S	Soprano (voice)
B	Bass (voice)	sax	saxophone
Bar	Baritone (voice)	sndr	snare drum
bar	baritone (instrument)	snino rec	sopranino recorder
barsax	baritone saxophone	srec	soprano recorder
bcl	bass clarinet	ssax	soprano saxophone
bdr	bass drum	str	strings
bfl	bass flute	T	Tenor (voice)
bgt	bass guitar	tamb	tambourine
brec	bass recorder	tamt	tamtam
bsax	bass saxophone	timp	timpani
btrb	bass trombone	tmblk	templeblock
cast	castanets	trec	tenor recorder
cbl	contrabass clarinet	tri	triangle
cbsn	contrabassoon	tsax	tenor saxophone
cel	celeste	vibra	vibraphone
cl	clarinet	vln	violin
cor	cornet	wch	windchimes
cym	cymbals	wdblk	woodblock
dr	drum	W.I.M.	Western International Music
Ebcl	E-flat clarinet	xylo	xylophone
Ebfl	E-flat flute		
ed.	edition		
Ehn	English horn		
elec	electric		
flghn	flugelhorn		
glock	glockenspiel		
gt	guitar		
harm	harmonica		
hdbells	handbells		
hp	harp		
hpsd	harpsichord		
kybd	keyboard		
mand	mandolin		
mar	marimba		
ms(s).	manuscript(s)		
Mz	Mezzo Soprano (voice)		
no(s).	number(s)		
nyp	not yet published		

PARTICIPATING LIBRARIES

A plus (+) following a siglum in an entry indicates that the work is found in a performance collection housed separately from the institution's main collection of music and sound recordings.

BC   Boston College
Bapst Library
140 Commonwealth Avenue
Chestnut Hill, MA 02167

BCM   The Boston Conservatory
Albert Alphin Music Library
8 The Fenway
Boston, MA 02215

Be   Berklee College of Music
Library
1140 Boylston Street
Boston, MA 02215

BkPL   Brookline Public Library
361 Washington Street
Brookline, MA 02146

BPL   Boston Public Library
Music Dept., Research Division
Copley Square
Boston, MA 02117

BrU   Brandeis University
Creative Arts Section
Goldfarb Library
Waltham, MA 02254

BU   Boston University
Music Library
Mugar Memorial Library
771 Commonwealth Avenue
Boston, MA 02215

CPL   Cambridge Public Library
449 Broadway
Cambridge, MA 02138

HMA   Harvard Musical Association
Library
57A Chestnut Street
Boston, MA 02108

HU   Harvard University
Eda Kuhn Loeb Music Library
Cambridge, MA 02138

HUh   Harvard University
Houghton Library
Cambridge, MA 02138

HUm   Harvard University
Morse Music Library
Hilles Library
59 Shepherd Street
Cambridge, MA 02138

L   Longy School of Music Library
1 Follen Street
Cambridge, MA 02138

MIT   Massachusetts Institute of Technology
Music Library, 14E-109
Cambridge, MA 02139

NEC   New England Conservatory
Harriet M. Spaulding Library
Idabelle Firestone Audio Library
33 Gainsborough Street
Boston, MA 02115

NFL   Newton Free Library
414 Centre Street
Newton, MA 02158

NU   Northeastern University
Dodge Library
360 Huntington Avenue
Boston, MA 02115

T   Tufts University Library
Medford, MA 02155

UMB   University of Massachusetts, Boston
Fine Arts Library
Dorchester, MA 02125

PARTICIPATING LIBRARIES

W   Wellesley College
           Music Library
           Wellesley, MA   02181

WCRB   WCRB Record Library
           750 South Street
           Waltham, MA   02154

WGBH   WGBH Record Library
           125 Western Avenue
           Allston, MA   02134

ACKNOWLEDGMENTS

To Jay K. Lucker, Director of Libraries at MIT, we offer special thanks. His active support of the Boston Composers Project has been a source of encouragement and a means to accomplishment.

Without the gracious participation of the composers represented in these pages, this book could not have come into being. No finer acknowledgment of their efforts could be made than for the users of this book to perform, listen to, and otherwise take an interest in their music.

PROJECT STAFF

Director: Linda I. Solow, *Massachusetts Institute of Technology*

Editorial Committee: Mary Wallace Davidson, *Wellesley College*, Brenda Chasen Goldman, *Tufts University*, Geraldine E. Ostrove, *New England Conservatory of Music*

Technical Editor: David F. Place, *Massachusetts Institute of Technology*

Research Associate: Helen Macarof

Research Assistant: Lise Foss

Computer Programmer: Michael Carnes

Consultants: Jay K. Lucker, *Director of Libraries, Massachusetts Institute of Technology*; Barry L. Vercoe, *Director, MIT Experimental Music Studio*

Associates: John Voigt, *Berklee College of Music*; Bettie Rose, *Boston College*; Cathy Balshone Becze, Reginald Didham, *Boston Conservatory*; Diane Ota, *Boston Public Library*; Francis L. Gramenz, Malloy M. Miller, *Boston University*; Ivy Anderson, Robert L. Evensen, *Brandeis University*; Barbara Kohl, *Brookline Public Library*; Natalie Palme, *Harvard Musical Association*; Michael Ochs, Holly Mockovak, Stephan Fuller, Robert J. Dennis, *Harvard University*; Nicholas Altenbernd, Roger Hale, Curtis Roads, Amelia Rogers, Helen W. Slotkin, Stephen D. Umans, *Massachusetts Institute of Technology*; Jean A. Morrow, Kenneth Pristash, Mary Ellen Sweeney, Julie Panciocco, Betty Burnett, *New England Conservatory*; Vivian A. Rosenberg, *Northeastern University*; Andrew Castiglione, *University of Massachusetts, Boston*; George C. Brown, *WCRB*; Jane Gottlieb, *American Music Center*.

The Boston Composers Project

BIBLIOGRAPHY

A1 JOHN C. ADAMS

Born November 28, 1947. Moved to Boston area 1966. *Education:* studied composition with Jacob Druckman, Alan Stout, Seymour Shifrin (Berkshire Music Center, Tanglewood, 1974); Leon Kirchner, Earl Kim, Ivan Tcherepnin, Tison Street (B.A., Harvard University, 1969). *Awards:* B.M.I. Award (1970), Margaret Grant Award (Tanglewood, 1974), University of Massachusetts Winds and Airs Award (1979). *Related activities:* member of the faculty of Boston Conservatory (1972--). BCM

WORKS

A1.1 Aria. (1979) Duration variable.
For: flute. 1 movement. *Dedicated to:* Daniel Riley. *First performed:* Apr. 1979; Boston Conservatory. Daniel Riley.
Score: reprod. of ms.; available from composer.
Cassette: recording of first performance.

A1.2 Band.
For: band.
Reel: May 14, 1973; Boston Conservatory. Boston Conservatory Wind Ensemble; Sterling Cossaboom, conductor. BCM
Reel: June 1, 1973; Boston Conservatory. Boston Conservatory Wind Ensemble; Sterling Cossaboom, conductor. BCM

[Canons]
A1.3 Seven Canons. (1968) 10'
For: clarinet and clarinet(bass).

Score: ms.; available from composer.
Score: reprod. of ms. BCM

A1.4 Chambers. (1974) 12'
For: saxophone, piano, instrumental ensemble(flute, oboe, clarinet, bassoon, percussion(2), harp, piano(4-hands)). 1 movement. *First performed:* 1975; Boston Conservatory. Laurence Adams, saxophone; Boston Conservatory Contemporary Ensemble, Joel Kabakov, conductor.
Score & parts: ms.; available from composer.
Score: reprod. of ms. BCM
Reel: Apr. 26, 1975. Laurence Adams, saxophone; Boston Conservatory Contemporary Ensemble, Joel Kabakov, conductor. BCM

Dolls and Dreams. *See* Study (Dolls and Dreams).

A1.5 Electric Wake. (1969)
For: Soprano(amplified), speaker(male)(amplified), string quartet(amplified), harp, celeste, piano, percussion. *Text:* poems adapted from *Talley Felt the Rain*, by Jeffrey Hamm. Honors thesis, Harvard University, 1969.
Score: reprod. of ms. HU

A1.6 Er Kommt. (1967) 7'
For: piano(played inside with mallet and pick). 1 movement. *First performed:* 1967; Boston. John Adams.
Score: ms.; available from composer.
Score: reprod. of ms. BCM
Reel: Apr. 23, 1974; Boston Conservatory. John Adams. BCM

A1.7 For Tomorrow. (1971) 20'
For: chamber orchestra. 1 movement.

Score: ms.; available from composer.
Score: reprod. of ms. BCM

A1.8 Genesis. (1970) 45'
For: choruses(SATB)(3), flute, string orchestras(2), organ. Cantata. *Text:* Bible, O.T., Genesis. 3 movements.
Score: ms.; available from composer.
Score: reprod. of ms. BCM

A1.9 Ibidem. (1974) 10'
For: piano(4-hands). *Movements:* Stars; Stone. *First performed:* 1974; Boston Conservatory. John Adams and Alfred Lee.
Score: ms.; available from composer.
Reel: Apr. 23, 1974; Boston Conservatory; in *Piano Works of John Adams.* John Adams and Alfred Lee. BCM
Reel: Apr. 26, 1975; Boston Conservatory; in *A Concert of New Music.* Jacqueline Gourdin and Harriet Lundberg. BCM
Reel: Nov. 18, 1978; Boston Conservatory. Boston Conservatory Piano Ensemble, Jacqueline Gourdin, director. BCM
Reel: Dec. 14, 1978; Boston Conservatory. Boston Conservatory Contemporary Ensemble, John Adams, director. BCM

A1.10 Kyrie and Sanctus.
For: chorus(SATB).
Vocal score: reprod. of ms. BCM

A1.11 Moment. (1967) 4'
For: piano. 1 movement. *First performed:* 1967; Boston Conservatory. John Adams.
Score: ms.; available from composer.
Score: reprod. of ms. BCM

[Pieces]
A1.12 Three Pieces. (1971) 8'
For: piano. *Contents:* Prelude; Reflections I; Reflections II. *First performed:* 1974; Boston Conservatory. Chandler Gregg.
Score: ms.; available from composer.

Reel: Boston Conservatory. Chandler Gregg. BCM

[Quartet, Strings]
A1.13 String Quartet. (1980) 25'
7 movements. *First performed:* 1980; Cambridge, Mass. Harvard Group for New Music.
Score & parts: ms.; available from composer.
Reel: recording of first performance.

A1.14 Quintet. (1981) 8'
For: woodwind quintet.
Score & parts: ms.; available from composer.

[Sonata, Piano]
A1.15 Sonata. (1970) 12'
4 movements. *First performed:* 1974; Boston Conservatory. Alfred Lee.
Score: ms.; available from composer.
Score: reprod. of ms. BCM
Reel: Apr. 23, 1974; Boston Conservatory; in *Piano Works of John Adams.* Alfred Lee. BCM

[Sonata, Violoncello and Piano]
A1.16 Sonata. (1979) 13'
3 movements. *Dedicated to:* Mark Simcox. *First performed:* 1979; Boston Conservatory. Mark Simcox, violoncello and Alfred Lee, piano.
Score: ms.; available from composer.
Cassette: Joel Moerschel, violoncello and Randall Hodgkinson, piano.

A1.17 Sonatina. (1977) 8'
For: piano. 3 movements. *First performed:* 1977; Arlington, Mass. Alfred Lee.
Score: ms.; available from composer.

[Songs]
A1.18 Five Songs. (1972) 15'
For: Soprano and piano. *Text:* John Adams. *First performed:* 1974; Lenox, Mass. Elizabeth Parcels, soprano and Barbara Kautzman, piano.
Score: ms.; available from composer.
Reel: Apr. 26, 1975; Boston Conservatory; in *A Concert of New*

Music. Elizabeth Parcells, soprano and Michael Dewart, piano. BCM
Cassette: recording of first performance.

A1.19 Study (Dolls and Dreams). (1966) 4'
For: violin and piano. 1 movement.
First performed: 1966; Lowell, Mass.
Score & part: ms.; available from composer.

A1.20 Trio. (1975) 18'
For: flute, violoncello, piano. 3 movements. *First performed*: 1975; Boston Conservatory. Alan Greenberg, flute; Michael Czitrom, violoncello; Peter Helms, piano.
Score & parts: ms.; available from composer.
Score: reprod. of ms. BCM
Reel: Sept. 3, 1975; Boston Conservatory. Alan Greenberg, flute; Michael Czitrom, violoncello; Peter Helms, piano. BCM
Reel: Daniel Riley, flute; Mark Simcox, violoncello; Alfred Lee, piano.

A1.21 Variations. (1976) 15'
For: piano and orchestra(2-2-2-2; 2-2-2-2; str). *Dedicated to*: Alfred Lee.
First performed: 1977; Buffalo, New York. Alfred Lee, piano; Buffalo Philharmonic Orchestra.
Score & parts: ms.; available from composer.
Cassette: recording of first performance.

A2 NICHOLAS ALTENBERND

Born May 22, 1946, in Yellow Springs, Ohio. Moved to Boston area 1975. *Education*: studied composition with Karel Husa and Robert Palmer (Cornell University, B.A., 1968, M.A., 1971). *Related activities*: pianist; Assistant to Music Director, Church of the Advent, Boston. MIT

WORKS

[Brass Fanfares]
A2.1 Four Brass Fanfares. (1963-69) 2' 30"
For: trumpets(2) and trombones(2) or trumpets(2), horn, trombone. *First performed*: 1969; Ithaca, N.Y.
Score & parts: ms. in composer's hand.

A2.2 Etude II. (1973) 6'
For: guitar.
Score: ms. in composer's hand.

A2.3 Happy Is He. (1979) 2' 30"
For: chorus(SATB). *Text*: Bible, O.T., Psalm 1. *Dedication*: To the memory of G. Harris Collingwood, Priest. *First performed*: Nov. 16, 1980; Church of the Advent, Boston. Church of the Advent Choir, Edith Ho, director.
Score: reprod. of ms.
Cassette: Jan. 16, 1982; Church of the Advent, Boston. Church of the Advent Choir, Edith Ho, director. MIT

[Preludes]
A2.4 Four Preludes. (1969)
For: guitar. *First performed*: Dec. 1969; Ithaca, N.Y. Nicholas Altenbernd.
Score: ms. in composer's hand.
Reel: recording of first performance.

A2.5 Sketch. (1967)
For: guitar and piano. *First performed*: May 15, 1967; Ithaca, N.Y. Nicholas Altenbernd, guitar and Joscelyn Godwin, piano.
Score: ms. in composer's hand.
Reel: recording of first performance.

A3 MARTIN AMLIN

Born June 12, 1953, in Dallas, Tex. Moved to Boston area 1977. *Education*: B.M. (Southern Methodist University); M.M., D.M.A. (Eastman School of Music); studied composition with Nadia Boulanger; piano with Frank Glazer. *Awards*: American Music Center Composer Assistance Program (1980); four Berkshire Music Center, Fellowships; four MacDowell Colony Fellowships. *Related activities*: pianist;

currently on the faculties of the Massachussetts Institute of Technology and Phillips Exeter Academy. MIT

WORKS

A3.1 The Black Riders. (1977) 10′
For: Mezzo Soprano, celeste, vibraphone, piano, harp. *Contents:* Prelude; Canto I; Interlude I; Canto II; Interlude II; Canto III; Postlude. *Text:* from *The Complete Poems* of Stephen Crane. *First performed:* 1979. Berkshire Music Center, Tanglewood, Mass. Rickie Weiner, mezzo soprano; Gretchen Saathoff, celeste; Mark Stingley, vibraphone; Margo Garrett, piano; Carrie Kourkemelos, harp.
Score: Seesaw, 1977.
Cassette: recording of first performance; available from the composer.

A3.2 Endless Ways. (1980-81) 15′
For: pianos(2). *Movements:* Recitativo-Fanfare; Le pas espagnol; "From Far, from Eve and Morning..." (Lullaby); Herbst; The Joyous New Tear (Dance Coda). *Texts:* movements 3 and 4 are preceded by texts from *A Shropshire Lad* by A.E. Housman and *Herbst* by Rainer Maria Rilke. *First performed:* Mar. 11, 1981; Harvard Musical Association. Adele Holevas and Martin Amlin.
Score: ms. in composer's hand.
Reel: available from composer.
Cassette: available from composer.

[Etudes]
A3.3 Six Etudes. (1973-80) 25′
For: piano. *Contents:* Thirds; Fourths; Fifths; Sixths; Sevenths; Tenths.
Dedication: "Sixths" to Nadia Boulanger "in memoriam." *First performed:* 1977; Rochester, N.Y. (selections only). Martin Amlin.
Score: ms. in composer's hand.
Score: reprod. of ms.

A3.4 L'Intrigue des accords oublies. (1977) 5′

For: harp. 1 movement. *First performed:* 1977; Rochester, N.Y. Kathy Bundock.
Score: ms. in composer's hand.
Score: Seesaw, 1977.
Reel: recording of first performance; available from composer.

A3.5 Israfel. (1980) 6′
For: Soprano, flute, piano, violin, violoncello. 1 movement. *Text:* from *The Complete Poems* of Edgar Allan Poe. *Dedication:* For the Phillips Exeter Academy Bicentennial, 1980-1981. *Commissioned by:* Phillips Exeter Academy. *First performed:* Oct. 5, 1980; Exeter, N.H. Rochelle Travis, soprano; Charles Forbes, violoncello; Michael Rosenbloom, violin; Douglas Worthen, flute; Martin Amlin, piano.
Score & parts: ms. in composer's hand.
Score & parts: reprod. of ms.
Cassette: recording of first performance; available from composer.

[Marias]
A3.6 The Three Marias. (1980) 7′
For: Soprano and piano. *Contents:* War (Maria Barreno); Among Joana's Papers (Maria da Horta); Despair (Maria Costa).
Dedicated to: Mimi Fulmer.
Commissioned by: Mrs. Robert Fulmer.
First performed: 1981. Mimi Fulmer.
Score: ms. in composer's hand.
Score: reprod. of ms.

A3.7 Quatrains from the Rubaiyat. (1977) 18′
For: Soprano and chamber orchestra(2(&pic)-2(&Ehn)-0-0; 2-1-0-0; perc(2), glock(2); hp; cel; str). 1 movement. *Text:* from *The Rubaiyat* of Omar Khayyam; English translation by Edward Fitzgerald. *First performed:* Nov. 11, 1980; Sanders Theatre, Harvard University. Judith Kellock, soprano; Pro Arte Chamber Orchestra of Boston, Larry Hill, conductor.
Score & parts: ms. in composer's hand.
Score & parts: reprod. of ms.
Reel: recording of first performance.

A3.8 Requiem. (1973) 5′
For: Alto, glockenspiel, chimes(tubular), vibraphone, piano. *Contents:* Exaudi; Dies irae; Rex tremendae; Pie Jesu; Libera me. *First performed:* 1973; Dallas, Tex. Celeste Mullen, alto; Ann Bidwell, percussion; Martin Amlin, piano.
Score: ms. in composer's hand.
Score: reprod. of ms. HU
Score: Seesaw, 1977.
Cassette: 1977; Berkshire Music Center, Tanglewood, Mass. Rickie Weiner, alto; Mark Stingley, percussion; Margo Garrett, piano.

[Songs on Texts of Anonymous Poets]
A3.9 Three Songs on Texts of Anonymous Poets. (1980) 10′
For: Soprano and piano. *Contents:* Aucassin et Nicolette; The Silver Swanne; Die Freude dieser Welt (Perpetuum mobile). *Dedicated to:* Rochelle Travis. *First performed:* 1981; Lenox, Mass. Rochelle Travis, soprano and Phillip Highfill, piano.
Score: ms. in composer's hand.
Score: reprod. of ms.
Cassette: recording of first performance; available from composer.

A4 THOMAS JEFFERSON ANDERSON, JR. (T.J.)

Born August 17, 1928, in Coatesville, Pa. Moved to Boston area 1972.
Education: B.M. (West Virginia State College, 1950); M.M.Ed. (Pennsylvania State University, 1951); Ph.D. (University of Iowa, 1958); studied composition with George Ceiga (1950), Scott Huston (1954), Richard Hervig (1957), Philip Bezanson (1958), Darius Milhaud (1964). *Awards:* MacDowell Colony Fellowships (1960, 1961, 1963, 1968), Copley Foundation Award (1964), Fromm Foundation Prizes (1964, 1971), Rockefeller Foundation grants (1969-1971), Yaddo Fellowships (1970, 1971), Danforth Foundation grants (1971-1972), National Endowment for the Arts Grants (1974, 1980), American

Music Center Composer Assistance Program, Mellon Foundation Grant.
Related activities: Judge, B.M.I. Student Composers Competition (1969, 1979); composer-in-residence, Atlanta Symphony Orchestra (1969-71); chairman of Honorary Advisory Committee, Black Music Center, Indiana University (1970-71); served on the faculties of Morehouse College, Tennesse State University, Langston University, West Virginia State College, Tufts University (1972; Fletcher Professor of Music, 1976-). T

WORKS

[Bagatelles]
A4.1 Five Bagatelles. (1963) 8′ 30″
For: oboe, violin, harpsichord.
Movements: Boca; Barcarolle; Burletta; Blues; Ballonchio. *Dedicated to:* Louise Clarkson. *First performed:* Mar. 15, 1963; University of Oklahoma. Leonard Klein, Catherine Paulu, Norman Paulu.
Score: American Composers Alliance, 1963.

A4.2 Beyond Silence. (1973) 15′
For: Tenor, clarinet, trombone, viola, violoncello, piano. Cantata. *Text:* Pauline Hanson. *First performed:* Oct. 2, 1973; Busch-Reisinger Museum, Harvard University. Scott MacAllister, tenor; Boston Musica Viva, Richard Pittman, conductor.
Score: American Composers Alliance, 1973. T

A4.3 Block Songs. (1972) 12′
For: Soprano/toys(chromatic pitch pipe, jack in the box, musical busy box).
Text: Pearl Cleage Lomax. *Dedicated to:* T.J., Janet, and Anita Anderson. *First performed:* Apr. 13, 1976; Busch-Reisinger Museum, Harvard University; Boston Musica Viva concert. Elsa Charlston, soprano and toys.
Score: American Composers Alliance, 1972.
Cassette: Oct. 29, 1976; New England Conservatory; in *ISCM/World Music*

Days, Program 10. Elsa Charlston, soprano and toys. NEC

A4.4 Chamber Symphony. (1968) 12'-14'
For: chamber orchestra. 1 movement.
Commissioned by: Thor Johnson.
Dedicated to: Thor Johnson and the Nashville Symphony Orchestra. *First performed:* Nov. 24, 1969; Nashville Symphony Orchestra, Thor Johnson, conductor.
Score: American Composers Alliance, 1969.
Parts: American Composers Alliance. Rental.
Disc: Composers Recordings CRI SD 258, 1970. Royal Philharmonic Orchestra, James Dixon, conductor. BrU BU HU MIT NEC T W

A4.5 Classical Symphony. (1961) 20'
For: orchestra. 3 movements.
Commissioned by: Oklahoma City Junior Symphony Orchestra. *First performed:* Apr. 22, 1961; Kansas City, Kan. Oklahoma City Junior Symphony Orchestra, T. Burns Westman, conductor.
Score & parts: American Composers Alliance, 1961. Rental.

A4.6 Connections, a Fantasy. (1966) 12'
For: violins(2), violas(2), violoncello.
Dedicated to: Darius Milhaud. *First performed:* Dec. 6, 1968; Nashville, Tenn. Blair String Quartet and Ovid Collins, viola.
Score: American Composers Alliance, 1967.

[Easy Pieces]
A4.7 Five Easy Pieces. (1974) 5'
For: violin, piano, Jew's harp. Written for the composer's children. *First performed:* May 18, 1974; Winchester Music Club, Winchester, Mass. Thomas Jefferson Anderson, III, violin; Janet Anderson, piano; Anita Anderson, African rattle.
Score: American Composers Alliance, 1974.

Score: in *Anthology of New Music*, Macmillan, 1977.

[Etudes and a Fancy]
A4.8 Five Etudes and a Fancy. (1964) 9'
For: woodwind quintet. *Movements:* Assimilation; Complements; Transference; Diversities; Recurrence; Fancy. *First performed:* Aug. 14, 1964; Aspen School of Music. Students, Harry Shulman, conductor.
Score: American Composers Alliance, 1967.
Parts: American Composers Alliance, 1967. Rental.

A4.9 Fanfare. (1976) 10'
For: trumpet and bands(4)(small).
Commissioned by: American Wind Symphony of Western Pennsylvania. First performed: May 30, 1976; Norfolk, Va. American Wind Symphony of Western Pennsylvania, Robert Boudreau, conductor.
Score: Peters, 1977.

A4.10 Horizons '76. (1975) 60'
For: Soprano and orchestra. *Contents:* A Song (Serenades, Introductions, Overture); F Natural (Interlude, Ritornello, Fantasia). *Text:* Milton Kessler. *Commissioned by:* National Endowment for the Arts for the United States Bicentennial.
Score: American Composers Alliance, 1975.
Parts: American Composers Alliance, 1975. Rental.

A4.11 In Memoriam Malcolm X. (1974) 10'
For: Soprano and orchestra. *Text:* Robert Earl Hayden. *Commissioned by:* Symphony of the New World for Betty Lou Allen. First performed: Apr. 7, 1974; Lincoln Center, New York City. Betty Lou Allen, mezzo soprano; Symphony of the New World, Leon Thompson, conductor.
Score: American Composers Alliance, 1974.

Parts: American Composers Alliance, 1974. Rental.

A4.12 In Memoriam Zach Walker. (1968) 4' 30"
For: band. *Dedicated to:* Coatesville High School Band. *First performed:* Apr. 27, 1969; Coatesville, Pa. Coatesville High School Band, Donald Suter, conductor.
Score: American Composers Alliance, 1968. T
Parts: American Composers Alliance, 1968.

A4.13 Intervals. (1970-71) 62'
For: orchestra(2(&pic)-2(&Ehn)-2(&bcl)-asax-tsax-2(&cbsn); 4-3-3-1; timp, perc(3); hp, pf/cel; str). 7 movements; played in part during intermission; may be performed using movements 1 and 7 only, under title Set VIII; movements 2 through 6 may also be performed separately. *Commissioned by:* Robert Shaw for the Atlanta Symphony.
Score: American Composers Alliance, 1970. T
Parts: American Composers Alliance, 1972. Rental.

A4.14 Introduction and Allegro. (1959) 8'-10'
For: orchestra. *First performed:* Oct. 11, 1959. Oklahoma City Symphony Orchestra, Guy Fraser Harrison, conductor.
Score: American Composers Alliance, 1959.
Parts: American Composers Alliance, 1959. Rental.

A4.15 Messages, a Creole Fantasy. (1979) 14'
For: orchestra. *Dedication:* To the family of Ila Marshall and David De Witt Turpeau. First performed: May 3, 1980. Atlanta Symphony, Robert Shaw, conductor.
Score: C. Fischer.
Parts: C. Fischer. Rental.

A4.16 Minstrel Man. (1977) 10'
For: trombone(bass)/percussion. Commissioned by and dedicated to: Thomas Everett. *First performed:* March 12, 1978; Brown University. Thomas Everett, bass trombone and percussion.
Score: Bote & Bock, 1978. T

A4.17 New Dances. (1960) 17'
For: chamber orchestra. *Movements:* Caccia; Can-Can; Counjai; Cachucha; Country Dance. *First performed:* Nov. 13, 1960. Oklahoma City Symphony Orchestra, Guy Fraser Harrison, conductor.
Score: American Composers Alliance, 1967.
Parts: American Composers Alliance, 1967. Rental.

A4.18 Personals. (1966) 15'
For: narrator, chorus(SATB), trumpets(2), horns(2), trombone, trombone(bass), tuba. Cantata. *Text:* Arna Bontemps.
Contents: Once More, Listening to the Wind and Rain; Darkness Brings the Jungle to Our Room; And Now the Downpour Ceases Let Us Dance by Metal Waters Burned: A Moment We Pause to Quench Our Thirst; Let Us Go Back into the Dusk Again.
Commissioned by: Fisk University, for its 100th anniversary. *First performed:* Apr. 28, 1966; Nashville, Tenn. Gladys Forde, narrator; Fisk University Choir; brass ensemble from the Nashville Symphony Orchestra, Robert Jones, conductor.
Score: American Composers Alliance, 1967. T
Vocal score: American Composers Alliance, 1967. Rental.
Parts: American Composers Alliance, 1967. Rental.

[Pieces]
A4.19 Six Pieces. (1962) 13'
For: clarinet and chamber orchestra(1(&pic)-1(&Ehn)-1(&bcl)-1; 1-1-1-1; timp, sndr; hp; str). *Movements:* Prologue; Liberamente; Dialogues; Ode;

Elegy; Epilogue. *Dedicated to:* Earl Thomas and the Oklahoma City Symphony Orchestra. First performed: Mar. 25, 1962. Earl Thomas, clarinet; Oklahoma City Symphony Orchestra, Guy Fraser Harrison, conductor.
Score: American Composers Alliance, 1966. T
Parts: American Composers Alliance, 1966. Rental.

A4.20 Play Me Something. (1979) 5" - 5'
For: piano(small hands). *Dedicated to:* Kathy Mortenson. *First performed:* Apr. 29, 1979; Weston, Mass. Music School at Rivers. Erick Fieleke.
Score: American Composers Alliance, 1979.

[Portraitures of Two People]
A4.21 Five Portraitures of Two People. (1965) 10'
For: piano(4-hands). *Movements:* Canvass; Contemplations; Capriciousness; Concordance; Candor. *Dedicated to:* Bill and Fay Bolcom. *First performed:* May 10, 1968; Nashville, Tenn. Enid Katahn and Lucien Stark.
Score: American Composers Alliance, 1967.

A4.22 Pyknon Overture. (1958)
For: orchestra. Doctoral thesis.

[Quartet, Strings, No. 1]
A4.23 String Quartet, No. 1. (1958) Doctoral thesis.

A4.24 Re-Creation: A Liturgical Music-Drama. (1978) 30'
For: speakers(3), dancer, violin, violoncello, trumpet, saxophone(alto), piano, drums. *Text:* Leon Forrest. *Commissioned by:* Richard Hunt. *First performed:* June 11, 1978; Chicago, Il. Meshack Taylor, Paul Butler, Terri Phillips, speakers; Ernest Snider, dancer; Elliott Golub, violin; Kenneth Slowik, violoncello; Paul Berliner, trumpet; Kenneth Soderblom, alto

saxophone; Vivian Taylor, piano; Warrick Carter, drums; T.J. Anderson, conductor.
Score: American Composers Alliance, 1978.

A4.25 Rotations. (1967) 15'
For: band. *Dedicated to:* Tennessee State University Band. *First performed:* 1969; Nashville, Tenn. Tennessee State University Band.
Score & parts: American Composers Alliance, 1967.

Set VIII. *See* Intervals.

A4.26 The Shell Fairy. (1976-77) 60'
For: voices (4), chorus, dancers, chamber orchestra. Operetta in 2 acts. *Libretto:* Sara S. Beattie; adapted from the story by Chester M. Pierce.
Score: American Composers Alliance, 1977.
Parts: American Composers Alliance, 1977. Rental.

A4.27 Soldier Boy, Soldier. (1981) 105'
For: voices(5), chorus, jazz sextet(saxophone(alto), trumpet, trombone, piano, electric bass, percussion), orchestra. Opera in 2 acts. *Libretto:* Leon Forrest. *Commissioned by:* Indiana University and the National Endowment for the Arts.

A4.28 Spirituals. (1979) 35'
For: chorus, chorus(children), Tenor, narrator, jazz quartet, orchestra. *Text:* Robert Earl Hayden. Visuals: Stanley Madeja. *Commissioned by:* Union United Methodist Church, Boston.
Score: American Composers Alliance, 1979.
Parts: American Composers Alliance.
Vocal score: American Composers Alliance.

A4.29 Squares, an Essay for Orchestra. (1965) 10'
Commissioned by: West Virginia State College for its 75th anniversary. *First performed:* Feb. 25, 1966; Chickasha,

Okla.; Third Annual Inter-American Festival of the Arts. Oklahoma City Symphony Orchestra, Guy Fraser Harrison, conductor.
Score & parts: American Composers Alliance, 1966.
Disc: Columbia M 33434, 1975. Baltimore Symphony Orchestra, Paul Freeman, conductor. BCM BrU HU MIT NEC T W

A4.30 Street Song. (1977) 8'
For: piano. *Dedicated to:* Vivian Taylor.
First performed: Mar. 4, 1979; Alice Tully Hall, New York City. Vivian Taylor.
Score: Bote & Bock, 1979.

A4.31 Swing Set. (1972) 12'
For: clarinet and piano. *Commissioned by:* Thomas Ayres. *First performed:* Feb. 18, 1973; University of Iowa. Thomas Ayres, clarinet and Carol Lesniak, piano.
Score: American Composers Alliance, 1972.

A4.32 Symphony in Three Movements. (1963) 15'
For: orchestra(2(pic)-2-2-2; 4-2-3-1; timp, perc; str). *Dedication:* To the memory of John F. Kennedy. *First performed:* Apr. 20, 1964; Oklahoma City, Okla.; Festival of 20th Century Music. Oklahoma City Symphony Orchestra, Guy Fraser Harrison, conductor.
Score: American Composers Alliance, 1964.
Parts: American Composers Alliance, 1964. Rental.

A4.33 This House. (1971) 5' 30"
For: chorus(TTBB) and pitch pipes(4)(chromatic). *Text:* T.J. Anderson; based on permutations of the word "Morehouse." *Dedicated to:* Wendell Whalum and the Morehouse College Glee Club. First performed: Mar. 11, 1972; Atlanta, Ga; Music Educators' National Conference, 23rd national biennial convention. Morehouse College Glee Club, Wendell Whalum conductor.

Vocal score: American Composers Alliance, 1971.

A4.34 Transitions, a Fantasy for Ten Instruments. (1971) 13' 30"
For: instrumental ensemble(flute, clarinet, bassoon, horn, trumpet, trombone, violin, viola, violoncello, piano). *Commissioned by:* Berkshire Music Center, Tanglewood and Fromm Foundation. First performed: Aug. 2, 1971; Lenox, Mass.; Tanglewood Festival of Contemporary Music. Charles Darden, conductor.
Score: American Composers Alliance, 1971. T

A4.35 Trio concertante. (1960) 9'
For: clarinet, trumpet, trombone, band. *First performed:* May 3, 1960; Langston Okla. Langston University Band, W.E. Sims, conductor.
Score: ms.

A4.36 Variations on a Theme by Alban Berg. (1977) 12'
For: viola and piano. *Dedicated to:* T. Samuel and Debbie Bruskin. *First performed:* Sept. 29, 1978; Longy School of Music. Marcus Thompson, viola and Seth Carlin, piano.
Score: American Composers Alliance, 1977. MIT

A4.37 Variations on a Theme by M.B. Tolson. (1969) 16'
For: Soprano, saxophone(alto), trumpet, trombone, violin, violoncello, piano. Cantata. *Text:* The Curator, Book I from *Harlem Gallery* and *Libretto for the Republic of Liberia* by M.B. Tolson. *Dedicated to:* Lois Anderson. *First performed:* May 26, 1970; Atlanta, Ga. Bernadine Oliphint, soprano; members of the Atlanta Symphony, T.J. Anderson, conductor.
Score: American Composers Alliance, 1969. Rental.
Disc: in *Spectrum; New American Music*, vol. 5, Nonesuch H71303, 1974. Jan De Gaetani, mezzo soprano; Al Regni, alto saxophone; Allan Dean, trumpet; John Swallow, trombone;

Jeanne Benjamin, violin; Fred Sherry, violoncello; Gilbert Kalish, piano. BCM BU HU MIT NEC T W

A4.38 Vocalise. (1980) 8' 30"
For: violin and harp. *Commissioned by:* Richard Hunt, for Jacques and Gail Israelivitch. First performed: Nov. 23, 1980; Webster College.
Score: American Composers Alliance,

A4.39 Watermelon. (1971) 6'
For: piano. *Dedicated to:* Dominique-Rene de Lerma. *First performed:* July 8, 1972; Bloomington, Ind. Hans Boepple.
Score: American Composers Alliance, 1971. T
Score: Bote & Bock, 1978. BPL BrU T

ARRANGEMENTS OF WORKS BY OTHER COMPOSERS

A4.40 Treemonisha.
For: opera cast and orchestra. Orchestration of the opera by Scott Joplin. *First performed:* Jan. 28, 1972; Atlanta, Ga. (concert version); Afro-American Music Workshop. Alpha Floyd, Seth McCoy, Joseph Bias, Louise Parker, Simon Estes, soloists; Atlanta Symphony, Robert Shaw, conductor.
Score & parts: American Composers Alliance.
Disc: in *Classic Rags and Ragtime Songs*, Smithsonian Collection N-001. T.J. Anderson, conductor (A Real Slow Drag). T

A5 THEODORE ANTONIOU

Born Feb. 10, 1938, in Athens, Greece. Moved to Boston area 1979. *Education:* studied violin, voice, composition (National Conservatory of Greece, Athens, 1947-58); composition with Jannis A. Papaioannou, Manolis Kalomiris (Hellenic Conservatory, Athens, 1956-61); conducting with Adolf Mennerich and composition with Guenter Bialas (Hochschule fuer Musik,

Munich, West Germany, 1961-65); composition with Josef Anton Riedl (Siemens Studio for Electronic Music, Munich, West Germany, 1965); composition with Pierre Boulez, Luciano Berio, Gyoergy Ligeti, Karlheinz Stockhausen (International Music Courses, Darmstadt, West Germany, 1963-65). *Awards:* Hellenic Conservatory Composition Prize (1961), Kassimatis Foundation Fellowship for Composition (University of Athens, 1961-63), Athens Technological Institute Honorary First Prize (1962), German Faculty Exchange for Composition (1963-65), Richard Strauss Prize (Munich, West Germany, 1964), Stuttgart, First Prize (1966), United States Department of State, Program for Leaders and Specialists (1966), Greek Ministry of Arts (First Prize in Composition, 1967), Kindler Foundation commission (1967), Fromm Foundation and Berkshire Music Center, Tanglewood commission (1969), Barcelona (Spain) Radio-Television, Premio Ondas (1970), Munich Radio Symphony Orchestra and Munich (West Germany) Olympic Games commission (1972), Koussevitzky Music Foundation (Library of Congress) commission (1974-75), National Endowment for the Arts Grants for composers (1975, 1977-78), Radio France Composition Prize for the Twentieth International Guitar Competition (1978), Guggenheim Grant (1979). *Related activities:* conductor; Director, The Summer Music Center, Greece; Artistic Director, Athens Center of Creative Arts; music consultant, Corfu Festival, Greece; co-organizer and director, Hellenic Week of Contemporary Music (1968, 1971); co-founder and Vice President, International Society of Contemporary Music, Greece and International Heinrich Schuetz Society, Greek Section; founder and Director, Hellenic Group of Contemporary Music, Athens, Greece; Director, Philadelphia Musical Academy New Music Ensemble, Philadelphia New Music Group, Alea II, Stanford, Calif.; composer-in-residence,

Stanford University (1969-70), Berkshire Music Center, Tanglewood (1969), University of Utah, Salt Lake City (1970, 1972); conductor, Philadelphia Musical Academy Symphony Orchestra (1970, 1975); founder and Director, Alea III, Boston (1979-); served on the faculties of the Philadelphia College of the Performing Arts (1970-79), Stanford University (1976), University of Pennsylvania (1978), Boston University (1979-). BU

WORKS

A5.1 Andorra.
Incidental music to the play by Max Frisch. *First performed:* May 10, 1962; Athens, Greece.

A5.2 Antigone.
Incidental music to the play by Jean Anouilh. *First performed:* Aug. 30, 1967; Athens, Greece.

Antiliturgy. *See* Revolution of the Dead.

A5.3 Antithesis, Op. 18a. (1962) 19'
For: orchestra(1-0-1-1; 0-1-0-0; perc; hp; str(string quartet and 2 groups of strings)). *Movements:* Prolog; Ison-Melos (Pedal-Melos); Episode A; Grammai-Choroi (Linien-Raeume); Episode B; Plana-Stigmata (Ebene-Punkte). *First performed:* Jan. 20, 1966; Hannover, West Germany.
Score & parts: Baerenreiter, 1962. Rental.
Study score: Baerenreiter, 1975. BU HU

A5.4 Aquarelle. (1958) 15'
For: piano. *First performed:* June 22, 1961; Athens, Greece.
Score: Modern, 1962. BU
Score: Modern, c1967. HU

A5.5 Atreides.
Incidental music to the play by V. Katsanis. *First performed:* 1964; Athens, Greece.

A5.6 Autopsy.
Incidental music. *Text:* G. Michaelidis.

First performed: Dec. 14, 1970; Athens, Greece.

A5.7 Bacchae: Chorodrama. (1980) 45'
For: chamber orchestra(1-0-2(&bcl)-0; 1-0-1-0; perc(2); pf, cel; tape; str(0-0-0-1-1)). Ballet. *First performed:* July 1981; Athens, Greece. Athens Experimental Ballet.
Score & parts: available from composer.

A5.8 Bacchae: Theater Music.
Incidental music to the play by Euripides. *First performed:* Apr. 14, 1976; Paris, France.

A5.9 Beggar's Opera.
Incidental music to the play by John Gay. *First performed:* Sept. 7, 1970; Athens, Greece.

A5.10 Birds.
Incidental music to the play by Aristophanes. *First performed:* Feb. 8, 1970; Nuremberg, West Germany.

A5.11 Cassandra: Sound-Action. (1969) 45'
For: dancers, actors, chorus(AB), tape, lights, projections, orchestra(3(afl)-2-2(&bcl)-2; 4-3-3-1; perc(4); pf; str). May be performed with orchestra alone. 25' Multi-media; ballet.
Commissioned by: Frankfurt (West Germany) State Radio and Television. Awarded Barcelona (Spain) Radio-Television, Premio Ondas (1970). *First performed:* Nov. 14, 1970; Barcelona, Spain.
Score: Baerenreiter, 1969.
Parts & tape: Baerenreiter, 1969. Rental.

A5.12 Cheironomiai: Conductor's Improvisation. (1971) Duration variable.
For: voices(unspecified)(8) or instruments(unspecified)(8) or orchestra. Aleatoric music. Composed for Erhard Karkoschka and the Stuttgart Ensemble. *First performed:* Oct. 31, 1971; Kassel, West Germany. Staatliche Hochschule fuer Musik und Darstellende Kunst (Stuttgart, West Germany) Ensemble

Neue Musik.
Score: Baerenreiter, 1974. BU HU
Study score: Baerenreiter, 1974.

A5.13 Chorochronos I. (1973) 45'
For: Baritone, narrator, percussion(4), trombones(4), tape, film, slides, light effects. To be performed in a planetarium. Concert version: percussion(4), trombones(4), tape. *Commissioned by:* Philadelphia May Festival. *First performed:* May 11, 1973; Philadelphia, Pa. Spyros Sakkas, baritone; Karry Hoenig, speaker; Philadelphia New Music Group, Theodore Antoniou, conductor.
Score: Baerenreiter, 1973.

A5.14 Chorochronos II. (1973) 18'
For: narrator(medium voice) and orchestra(1(&afl)-1-1(&bcl)-1; 1-1-1-0; perc(2); hp, pf, org(Hammond); str(1-1-1-1-1)). Cantata. *Contents:* God (Bible, O.T., Psalm 19); Time (T.S. Eliot); Cosmos (Bible, O.T., Genesis 1:31 and 2:1, Sacred Book of Egypt, Orphic Fragments, Brahman teaching); Death (Bible, N.T., John 19:40,41); Untitled (Pythagorean Epigram on the Temple of Delphi); Man; The Man (Brahmanas and Upanishads); Being (Lao-Tzu I). Written for the Southwest German Radio. *Dedicated to:* Dimitri Mitropoulos. *First performed:* Oct. 29, 1973; Reutlingen, West Germany. Spyros Sakkas, baritone; members of the Swabian Orchestra, Dimitri Agrafiotis, conductor.
Score: Baerenreiter, 1973. NEC
Study score: Baerenreiter, 1974.
Parts: Baerenreiter, 1973. Rental.
Reel: May 11, 1980; Boston University. Sanford Sylvan, baritone; Alea III, Theodore Antoniou, music director. BU
Cassette: Mar. 24, 1976; New England Conservatory; in *A Series of Twentieth-Century Innovations.* James Maddalena, baritone; NEC Contemporary Music Ensemble, Gunther Schuller, conductor. NEC

A5.15 Chorochronos III. (1975) 17'
For: narrator(medium voice), piano or percussion, tape, audience. *Contents:* God (Bible, O.T., Psalm 19); Time (T.S. Eliot); Cosmos (Bible, O.T., Genesis 1:3 and 2:1), Sacred Book of Egypt, Orphic Fragments, Brahman teaching); Death (Bible, N.T., John 19:40, 41); Untitled (Pythagorean Epigram on the Temple of Delphi); Man; The Man (Brahmanas and Upanishads); Being (Lao-Tzu I). Written for Spyros Sakkas. *First performed:* Jan. 26, 1977; RIAS, Berlin, East Germany. Spyros Sakkas, baritone and George Kouroupos, piano.
Score: Baerenreiter, 1975. BU HU NEC
Tape: Baerenreiter, 1975. HU

A5.16 Circle of Accusation: Chorodrama. (1975) 25'
For: orchestra(2(pic/afl)-1-2(bcl)-0; 2-2-2-1; perc(2); pf/org(Hammond); str(0-0-0-1-1)). *First performed:* Aug. 8, 1977; Lemesos, Cypress. Philadelphia New Music Group, Theodore Antoniou, conductor.
Score: Baerenreiter, 1975.
Parts: Baerenreiter, 1975. Rental.

A5.17 Circle of Thanatos and Genesis. (1977-78) 20'
For: Tenor, narrator, chorus, orchestra(2-2-2(&bcl)-2; 4-2-3-1; perc(4); hp, pf; str). Cantata. 2 movements.
Text: Takis Antoniou (Greek, English, or German). *First performed:* Jan. 24, 1981; Symphony Hall, Boston. Tanglewood Festival Chorus; Boston Symphony Orchestra, Seiji Ozawa, conductor.
Score: Baerenreiter, 1977.
Parts: Baerenreiter, 1977. Rental.

[Climate of Absence]
A5.18 Klima Tis Apussias (Stimmung der Abwesenheit) (Sense of Absence). (1968)
11' *For:* voice(medium) and orchestra(1-1-1-1; 0-0-0-0; perc; pf; str(one per part or orchestral)). *Text:* Odysseus Elytis (Greek in Roman

transliteration and English).
Commissioned by: Third Hellenic Week
of Contemporary Music. *First
performed:* Nov. 12, 1968; Munich,
West Germany. Spyros Sakkas,
baritone; Munich Studio for New Music,
Theodore Antoniou, conductor. Version
for medium voice and piano first
performed: Jan. 25, 1968; Paris, France.
Spyros Sakkas, baritone and George
Kouroupos, piano.
Score & parts: Baerenreiter, 1968.
Rental.
Study score: Baerenreiter, 1973. BU HU
Vocal score: Baerenreiter, 1968.
Disc: Columbia EMI/Odeon Greece
SCXG 59. Spyros Sakkas, baritone;
Hellenic Group for Contemporary
Music, Theodore Antoniou, conductor.
BU HU

A5.19 Clytemnestra: Sound-Action.
(1967) 25'
For: actress, dancers, tape,
instrumental ensemble(flutes(2), oboe,
trombones(3), tuba, percussion(2), harp,
double basses(4)). Stage work. *First
performed:* June 4, 1968; Kassel, West
Germany.
Score: Baerenreiter, 1968.
Parts & tape: Baerenreiter, 1968. Rental.

[Concertino, Op. 16b]
A5.20 Concertino. (1962) 13'
For: piano, string orchestra,
percussion(timpani, marimba,
vibraphone). 3 movements. Awarded
Athens Technological Institute Honorary
First Prize (1962). *First performed:* Dec.
16, 1962; Athens, Greece. George
Hadjinicos, piano; Lukas Foss,
conductor.
Score & parts: Baerenreiter, 1964.
Rental.
Study score: Baerenreiter, 1964. BU HU

[Concertino, Op. 21]
A5.21 Concertino. (1963) 15'
For: winds(9)(flute/piccolo, oboe,
clarinets(2), bassoons(2), horns(2),
trumpet), piano, percussion(timpani,
vibraphone, xylophone). 3 movements.

First performed: Dec. 4, 1973;
Philadelphia, Pa. Fran Faneli, piano;
Nick D'Amico, percussion; Philadelphia
New Music Group, Theodore Antoniou,
conductor.
Score & parts: Baerenreiter, 1964.
Rental.
Study score: Baerenreiter, 1973. BU HU

[Concerto, Percussion(2)]
A5.22 Double Concerto. (1977) 16'
For: percussion(2) and
orchestra(1(pic)-1-1(&bcl)-1; 1-1-1-1; hp,
pf; str(one per part or orchestral)). 3
movements. *First performed:* April 26,
1978; Philadelphia, Pa. Neil Grover and
Anthony Orlando, percussion;
Philadelphia College of the Performing
Arts Ensemble, Theodore Antoniou,
conductor.
Score: Baerenreiter, 1977.
Parts: Baerenreiter, 1977. Rental.
Reel: Aug. 12, 1978; Berkshire Music
Center, Tanglewood; in *Festival of
Contemporary Music.* James Saporito
and Patrick Hollenbeck, percussion;
Berkshire Music Center Orchestra,
Theodore Antoniou, conductor.
Reel: Oct. 19, 1978; Concert Hall,
Boston University; in *Omnibus: Music
of the 20th Century, Concert I.* Neil
Pregozen and Paul Pitts, percussion;
Boston University Repertory Orchestra,
Robert Sirota, conductor. BU

[Concerto, Violin]
A5.23 Violonkonzert: Op.28. (1965)
19'-22'
For: violin and orchestra(1-1-1-1;
1-1-1-1; perc(3), glock, xylo; hp, cel;
str). 3 movements. *Dedicated to:* Mano
Hadzidakis and the Experimental
Orchestra of Athens. Awarded Stuttgart
First Prize (1966). *First performed:* Aug.
16, 1965; Athens, Greece. Dimitris
Vraskos, violin; Athens Experimental
Music Chamber Orchestra, Manos
Hadzidakis, conductor.
Score & parts: Baerenreiter, 1965.
Rental.
Study score: Baerenreiter, 1973. BU HU
NEC

[Concerto, Violin, Trumpet, Clarinet]
A5.24 Triple Concerto. (1959) 20'
For: violin, trumpet, clarinet,
orchestra(2-2(&Ehn)-2-2; 4-2-2-l; perc;
pf/cel; str). 3 movements.
Score: available from composer.

A5.25 Dialogues. (1962) 11'
For: flute and guitar. 9 movements.
First performed: May 21, 1963;
Darmstadt, West Germany.
Score: Modern, 1962.

A5.26 The Do Quintet. (1978) 9'
For: horn, trumpets(2), trombone, tuba.
First performed: Apr.12, 1978;
Philadelphia, Pa. Chestnut Brass
Company.
Score: Baerenreiter, 1978.

A5.27 Drums of Snow.
Incidental music to the play by David
Pinner. *First performed:* 1970; Stanford,
Calif.

A5.28 The Eagle of Byzantium.
Music to the television film by
Magoulas. *First performed:* 1975;
Athens, Greece.

A5.29 Epilogue: After the Odyssey by
Homer. (1963) 10'
For: Mezzo Soprano, narrator, oboe,
horn, guitar, piano, percussion, double
bass. *Text:* Greek in Roman
transliteration (mezzo soprano) and
German or English (narrator). *Dedicated
to:* Professor Guenter Bialas. *First
performed:* Mar. 10, 1964; Munich, West
Germany.
Score & parts: Baerenreiter, 1964.
Rental.
Study score: Baerenreiter, 1974. BU HU

A5.30 Events I. (1967-68) 20'
For: violin, piano, orchestra(2(pic)-2-2-2;
4-2-3-1; hp, hpsd; timp, perc(3), glock,
mar, vibra; str). *Movements:* Symphonia;
Antithesis; Stichomythie; Happening;
Epilogos. *Commissioned by:* Hagen
Symphony Orchestra. *First performed:*
June 10, 1968; Hagen, West Germany.

Chara Tombras, piano; Spyros Tombras,
violin; Hagen Symphony Orchestra,
Berthold Lehmann, conductor.
Score & parts: Baerenreiter, 1974.
Rental.
Study score: Baerenreiter, 1974. BU HU

A5.31 Events II. (1969) 14'-15'
For:
orchestra(4(pic)-3(&Ehn)-3(&bcl)-3(&cbsn);
6-4-4-1; timp, perc(5), glock, vibra,
xylo; tape(optional); hp, pf; str).
Movements: Antitheta; Homonyma;
Antinoma. *Commissioned by:* Boston
Symphony Orchestra, Fromm
Foundation, Berkshire Music Center,
Tanglewood. *Dedicated to:* Gunther
Schuller. First performed: Aug. 30,
1969; Berkshire Music Center,
Tanglewood. Boston Symphony
Orchestra, Gunther Schuller, conductor.
Score & parts: Baerenreiter, 1969.
Rental.
Study score: Baerenreiter, 1973. BU HU

A5.32 Events III. (1969) 12'
For: tape, slides(optional),
orchestra(1-1-1-1; 0-0-0-0; perc(2); pf;
str(one per part or orchestral)).
Movements: Analoga; Paraloga. *First
performed:* Oct. 8, 1969; Barcelona,
Spain. Ars-Nova-Ensemble, Werner
Heider, conductor.
Score & parts: Baerenreiter, 1969.
Rental.
Study score: Baerenreiter, 1973. BU HU

A5.33 The First Step.
Music to the film by F. Mesthenaios.
First performed: 1962; Salonica,
Greece.

A5.34 Fluxus I. (1974-75) 16'
For:
orchestra(4(afl)-2(&Ehn)-2(&bcl)-2(&cbsn);
6-4-4-1; perc(4); hp,
pf/cel/org(Hammond); str). *Commissioned
by:* Koussevitzky Music Foundation
(Library of Congress). First performed:
Dec. 17, 1979; Basel, Switzerland. Basel
Radio Symphony Orchestra, Theodore
Antoniou, conductor.

Score: Baerenreiter, 1975.
Parts: Baerenreiter, 1975. Rental.

A5.35 Fluxus II. (1975) 18'
For: piano and chamber
orchestra(1(afl)-1(Ehn)-1-1; 1-1-1-0; perc;
str(one per part or orchestral)). *First
performed:* Apr. 4, 1976; Philadelphia,
Pa. Fran Faneli, piano; Philadelphia New
Music Group, Theodore Antoniou,
conductor.
Score: Baerenreiter, 1975.
Parts: Baerenreiter, 1975. Rental.

Games. *See* Jeux.

A5.36 Greek Folk Songs, I-V. (1961) 6'
For: chorus(SATB) and piano(optional).
Text: in German or English. *First
performed:* Mar. 28, 1963; Salonica,
Greece. University of Salonica Chorus,
Yannis Mandakas, conductor.
Vocal score: Baerenreiter, 1965.
Vocal score: G. Schirmer, 1978 (version
with piano).

A5.37 Greek Folk Songs, VI-X. (1961) 8'
For: chorus(SATB).
Vocal score: available from composer.

A5.38 The Hands.
Music to the film by J. Contes. *First
performed:* June 21, 1962; Berlin, East
Germany.

A5.39 Huts.
Incidental music. *Text:* Manthos Krispis.
First performed: Jan. 15, 1960; Athens,
Greece.

A5.40 Ich bin ein Gastarbeiter.
Music to the film by T. Laskoulas.
First performed: 1964; Munich, West
Germany.

A5.41 Inventions and Fugues. (1958) 15'
For: piano.
Score: available from composer.

A5.42 Jeux (Games): Op. 22. (1963)
13'-15'
For: violoncello and string orchestra. 5

movements. *First performed:* Jan. 8?,
1965; Hannover, West Germany. Werner
Taube, violoncello; Hannover Studio
Orchestra, Reinhard Petersen, conductor.
Score & parts: Baerenreiter, 1964.
Rental.
Study score: Baerenreiter, 1964. BU
Study score: Baerenreiter, 1973
[c1964]. HU

A5.43 The Jew of Malta.
Incidental music to the play by
Christopher Marlowe. *First performed:*
1970; Stanford, Calif.

A5.44 Juno and the Peacock.
Incidental music to the play by Sean
O'Casey. *First performed:* Oct. 16,
1969; Athens, Greece.

A5.45 Katharsis. (1968) 12'-14'
For: flute, tape, loudspeakers,
projections(optional), chamber
orchestra(0-1-2-0; 0-0-2-1; perc(2); pf,
org(Hammond); str(0-0-0-1-2)). *Text:*
Toulia S. Tolia; recited in Greek by
flute soloist and wind players.
Commissioned by: Third Hellenic Week
of Contemporary Music. *Dedicated to:*
E. Blum. *First performed:* Dec. 22,
1968; Athens, Greece. Eberhard Blum,
flute; Athens Group for New Music,
Theodore Antoniou, conductor.
Score: Baerenreiter, 1968.
Study score: Baerenreiter, 1973. BU
Parts: Baerenreiter, 1968. Rental.
Disc: Columbia EMI/Odeon Greece SCX
56. Eberhard Blum, flute; Hellenic Group
for Contemporary Music, Theodore
Antoniou, conductor. HU

A5.46 Kinesis ABCD, Op. 31. (1966) 12'
30"-15'
For: string ensemble(2 groups:
12-6-4-2). 4 movements. *Commissioned
by:* Athens Festival. *First performed:*
July 13, 1966; Athens, Greece. Zurich
Chamber Orchestra, Edmond De Stoutz,
conductor.
Score & parts: Baerenreiter, 1966.
Rental.
Study score: Baerenreiter, 1971. BU

Klima Tis Apussias. *See* Climate of Absence.

A5.47 Kontakion auf das Juengste, Op. 27. (1965) 12'
For: Soprano, Alto, Tenor, Bass, chorus(SSATB), string orchestra or Sopranos(2), Alto, Tenor, Bass, strings(5). *Text:* based on *The Last Judgement* by Romanos the Melodos; Greek in Roman transliteration. *Commissioned by:* International Heinrich Schuetz Society. *First performed:* May 7, 1965; Berlin, East Germany. Zdenka Hesky, soprano; Mechthild Brem, alto; Desmond Clayton, tenor; Franz Reuter-Wolf, bass; members of the Munich Chamber Ensemble, Fritz Buechtger, conductor.
Score: Baerenreiter, 1965. BU
Parts: Baerenreiter, 1965. Rental.

Laments. *See* Moirologhia for Jani Christou: Laments.

[Likes, Clarinet]
A5.48 Three Likes. (1973) 8'
Movements: Like an Overture; Like a Threnos; Like Variations. *First performed:* June 20, 1974; Graz, Austria. Eduard Brunner.
Score: Baerenreiter, 1974. NEC
Score: G. Schirmer, 1979.
Reel: Oct. 18, 1977; Boston University; in *Omnibus: Music of the 20th Century, Concert I*. Bruce Creditor. BU
Cassette: Dec. 2, 1976; New England Conservatory. Bruce Creditor. NEC

[Likes, Double Bass]
A5.49 Two Likes. (1976) 8'
Score: Baerenreiter, 1976.

[Likes, Oboe]
A5.50 Five Likes. (1969) 10'
Movements: Like a Dirge; Like a Study; Like a Diaulos; Like a Polymorphia; Like a Cadence. *Dedicated to:* Julien Singer. *First performed:* Oct. 23, 1969; Kassel, West Germany. Julien Singer.
Score: Baerenreiter, 1971. BU NEC
Score: G. Schirmer, 1979.

Cassette: May 14, 1980; New England Conservatory. Frederic Cohen. NEC

[Likes, Tuba]
A5.51 Six Likes. (1967) 8'
Movements: Like a Duet; Like a Study; Like a March; Like a Cackling; Like a Song; Like a Murmuring. *Dedicated to:* Y. Zouganelis. *First performed:* Mar. 31, 1967; Athens, Greece. Yannis Zouganelis.
Score: Baerenreiter, 1968. BU
Score: G. Schirmer, 1979.
Disc: Columbia EMI/Odeon Greece SCDG 62. Yannis Zouganelis. BU HU

[Likes, Violin and Sleigh Bells]
A5.52 Four Likes. (1972) 10'
Movements: Like a Lament; Like a Dance; Like a Hymn; Like a Fantasia. *Dedicated to:* Daniel Kobialka. *First performed:* Jan. 31, 1975; Berlin, East Germany.
Score: Baerenreiter, 1973. BU
Score: G. Schirmer, 1979.

A5.53 Lyrics. (1967) 15'-18'
For: violin and piano. *Movements:* Threnos (In Memory of Hans Kindler); Epigram; Elegy; Nomos; Hymn; Ode; Skolion. *Text:* Tassos Roussos (to be recited during performance or printed in program). *Commissioned by:* Kindler Foundation. *First performed:* Jan. 1, 1968; Washington D.C.
Score: Baerenreiter, 1968. BU HU

A5.54 Medea.
Incidental music to the play by Euripides. *First performed:* Aug. 2, 1976; Salonica, Greece.

A5.55 Melos, Op. 17. (1962) 14'
For: voice(medium) and orchestra(1(pic)-0-1-1; 0-1-1-0; timp, perc, mar, vibra; gt; str(one per part or orchestral)). Cantata. 5 movements. *Text:* after Sappho; Greek in Roman transliteration; English translation. *First performed:* Apr. 2, 1967; Athens, Greece. Spyros Sakkas, baritone; Athens Group for New Music,

Theodore Antoniou, conductor.
Score: Baerenreiter, 1964.
Study score: Baerenreiter, 1975. BU
Parts: Baerenreiter, 1964. Rental.
Vocal score: Baerenreiter, 1975.

A5.56 Meteorite.
Music to the film by Malamas. *First performed:* 1981; Salonica, Greece.

A5.57 Micrographies, Op. 24. (1964) 15'
For: orchestra(2(&pic)-2(&Ehn) -2(&bcl)-2(&cbsn); 6-3-3-1; perc(5); hp, pf, cel; str). Awarded Greek Ministry of Arts First Prize in Composition (1967). *First performed:* Mar. 4, 1968; Kassel, West Germany. Kassel State Theater Orchestra, Gerd Albert, conductor.
Score & parts: Baerenreiter, 1965. Rental.
Study score: Baerenreiter, 1968 (titled Mikrographien). BU HU

A5.58 Midsummer Night's Dream.
Incidental music to the play by William Shakespeare. *First performed:* Oct. 15, 1971; Athens, Greece.

Mikrographien. *See* Micrographies, Op. 24.

A5.59 Moirologhia for Jani Christou: Laments. (1970) 12'
For: voice(medium) and piano. *Text:* Greek folk poems in Roman transliteration. *First performed:* Oct. 1, 1970; Athens, Greece. Spyros Sakkas, baritone and Nelly Semitekolo, piano.
Score: Baerenreiter, 1970. BU

[Moirologhia for Jani Christou: Laments; Arr]
A5.60 Moirologhia for Jani Christou: Laments. (1970) 12'
For: voice(medium), piano, any combination of flute, clarinet, guitar, percussion(2), double bass).
Score: Baerenreiter, 1971. BU HU

A5.61 Music for Harp. (1965) 10'
First performed: Feb. 23, 1966; Munich,

West Germany.
Score: Modern, 1965.

[Musical Pictures]
A5.62 Eight Musical Pictures. (1953) 17'
For: voice and piano. *First performed:* 1957; Athens, Greece.
Score: ms.; available from composer.

A5.63 Nenikikamen (We Are Victorious). (1971) 25'
For: Baritone, Mezzo Soprano, narrator, chorus(mixed), orchestra(3-2(&Ehn)- 2(&bcl)-2(&cbsn); 4-3-3-1; perc(4); hp, pf; str). Cantata. *Text:* Toula S. Tolia; in Greek, German or English, and ancient Greek. *Commissioned by:* Munich Radio Symphony Orchestra and the City of Munich (West Germany) for the Olympic Games. *First performed:* Aug. 25, 1972. Hans Herbert Fiedler, speaker; Agnes Baltsa, mezzo soprano; Spyros Sakkas, baritone; Bavarian Radio Chorus; Bavarian Radio Symphony Orchestra, Theodore Antoniou, conductor.
Score: Baerenreiter, 1971.
Parts: Baerenreiter, 1971. Rental.

A5.64 News from the New World Discovered in the Moon.
Incidental music. *Text:* Ben Jonson. *First performed:* Nov. 30, 1978; Athens, Greece.

A5.65 Noh Musik. (1965) Duration variable.
For: musicians/actors(4). Stage work. *First performed:* Mar. 10, 1970; Stanford, Calif.
Score: Orlando, 1974.

A5.66 Oedipus.
Incidental music to the play by Sophocles. *First performed:* 1980; Athens, Greece.

A5.67 Oedipus at Colonus.
Incidental music to the play by Sophocles. *First performed:* 1975; Epidaurus, Greece.

A5 THEODORE ANTONIOU

A5.68 One Flew over the Cuckoo's
Nest.
Incidental music to the book by Ken
Kesey; text adapted by Wasserman.
First performed: Jan. 26, 1976; Athens,
Greece.

A5.69 OP Overture. (1966) 11'
For: tape, loudspeakers(3 groups),
orchestra(1-1-1(&bcl)-0; 2-2-2-1; perc(3);
pf(2); str).
Score & parts: Baerenreiter, 1966.
Rental.
Study score: Baerenreiter, 1971. BU HU

A5.70 Operetta.
Incidental music. *Text:* Gobrovich. *First
performed:* Sept. 29, 1972; Athens,
Greece.

A5.71 Oresteia.
Incidental music to the play by
Aeschylus. *First performed:* Feb. 24,
1976; Stanford, Calif.

A5.72 Overture. (1961) 12'
For: orchestra(3-2(&Ehn)-3-3; 4-2-3-1;
perc; hp, pf; str).
Score: ms.; available from composer.

A5.73 Parastasis. (1977) 22' 30"
For: percussion and tape. *First
performed:* Dec. 10, 1978; Philadelphia,
Pa. Anthony Orlando.
Score: Baerenreiter, 1978.
Tape: Baerenreiter, 1978.

A5.74 Parastasis II. (1978) 22' 30"
For: percussion, tape, dancer(optional),
instruments(2-8)(any combination of
flute/piccolo/flute(alto),
clarinet/clarinet(bass), horn, trombone,
harp, piano/organ(Hammond), viola,
double bass).
Score: Baerenreiter, 1978.
Tape: Baerenreiter, 1978.

A5.75 Parodies. (1970) 13'
For: voice/actor and piano. *Contents:*
Clouds; Cats and Peacocks; Dirge;
Gradji Bee i Bimba; Karawana;
Sea-horses and Flying Fish. *First

performed: Oct. 22, 1970; Munich, West
Germany. Spyros Sakkas, baritone and
Nelly Semitekolo, piano.
Score: Baerenreiter, 1972. NEC
Cassette: Dec. 2, 1976; New England
Conservatory. Spyros Sakkas, baritone
and Christopher O'Riley, piano. NEC

A5.76 Peace.
Incidental music to the play by
Aristophanes. *First performed:* July 22,
1967; Salonica, Greece.

A5.77 Periander. (1977-79) 100'
For: narrator, voices, dancers, actors,
chorus, tape, orchestra(2-2-2(&bcl)-2;
4-2-3-1; perc(3); hp, pf/cel; str). Opera.
Libretto: Yorgos Christodoulakis;
German translation by Peter Kertz.
Commissioned by: Munich State Theater
at the Gaertnerplatz.
Score & parts: Baerenreiter. Rental.
Vocal score: Baerenreiter. Rental.
Tape: Baerenreiter. Rental.

A5.78 Philoctet.
Incidental music. *Text:* Sophocles. *First
performed:* June 25, 1967; Epidaurus,
Greece.

A5.79 Protest I. (1970) 20'
For: tape and actors. *First performed:*
Sept. 30, 1970; Athens, Greece.
Tape: available from composer.

A5.80 Protest II. (1971) 15'
For: voice(medium), actors, tape,
synthesizer(ad lib.), lights,
orchestra(1-1-1(&bcl)-0; 1-1-2-1; perc;
pf, org; str(2-0-1-0-1)). *Commissioned
by:* Fourth Hellenic Week of
Contemporary Music. First performed:
Sept. 26, 1971; Athens, Greece. Athens
Group for New Music, Theodore
Antoniou, conductor.
Score & parts: Baerenreiter, 1971.
Rental.
Study score: Baerenreiter, 1971. BU
Tape: Baerenreiter, 1971.
Disc: Columbia EMI/Odeon Greece
SCDG 66. Hellenic Group for

Contemporary Music, Theodore
Antoniou, conductor. HU

A5.81 Quartetto giocoso, Op. 26. (1956)
12'-15'
For: oboe, violin, violoncello, piano.
Movements: Introduzione; Scherzino;
Notturno; Duettino; Ostinato; Perpetuo;
Rondoletto; Toccatina; Terzino; Finale.
First performed: June 8, 1968; Berlin,
East Germany. Athens Group for New
Music.
Score: Baerenreiter, 1968. BU HU

A5.82 Return of Benefactor.
Incidental music. *Text:* V. Goufas. *First
performed:* Apr. 26, 1961; Athens,
Greece.

A5.83 The Revolution of the Dead:
Antiliturgy. (1981) 22'
For: Soprano, Alto, Tenor, Bass,
chorus(SATB), orchestra(2-2-2-2; 2-3-3-0;
perc(2); hpsd, org; str).
Score: Baerenreiter, 1981.
Parts: Baerenreiter, 1981. Rental.

A5.84 Rhinoceros.
Incidental music to the play by Eugene
Ionesco. *First performed:* May 4, 1962;
Athens, Greece.

A5.85 Riders without Horses.
Incidental music. *Text:* V.
Andreopoulos. *First performed:* Apr. 26,
1961; Athens, Greece.

A5.86 Road to the Deep North.
Incidental music. *Text:* E. Bond. *First
performed:* Jan. 24, 1974; Athens,
Greece.

A5.87 Romeo and Juliet.
Incidental music to the play by
William Shakespeare. *First performed:*
Mar. 17, 1971; Athens, Greece.

A5.88 Scherzo. (1958) 8'
For: violin and piano. *First performed:*
Oct. 10, 1958; Athens, Greece.
Score: ms.; available from composer.

[School Songs]
A5.89 10 School Songs. 15'
For: chorus(SATB). *First performed:*
Mar. 10, 1968; Salonica, Greece.
Vocal score: available from composer.

A5.90 Schwerpunkt.
Music to the television film by F.
Fuertwangler. *First performed:* 1964;
Munich, West Germany.

Sense of Absence. *See* Climate of
Absence.

A5.91 Seven against Thebes.
Incidental music to the play by
Aeschylus. *First performed:* 1976;
Athens, Greece.

A5.92 Sonata. (1961) 9'
For: violin. *First performed:* Nov. 23,
1962; Athens, Greece.
Score: ms.; available from composer.

A5.93 Sonatina. (1958) 12'
For: violin and piano. *First performed:*
June 22, 1958; Athens, Greece.
Score & part: Ph. Nakas.

A5.94 Stichomythia I. (1976) 13'
For: flute and guitar. *Commissioned by:*
Philadelphia Guitar Society. *First
performed:* Nov. 17, 1978; Philadelphia,
Pa. Janet Ketcham, flute and Peter
Segal, guitar.
Score: Baerenreiter, 1976.

A5.95 Stichomythia II. (1977) 12'
For: guitar. Awarded the Radio France
Composition Prize for the Twentieth
International Guitar Competition (1978).
First performed: Mar. 13, 1979; Athens,
Greece. Kostas Kotsiolis.
Score: Baerenreiter, 1977.

Stimmung der Abwesenheit. *See*
Climate of Absence.

A5.96 Suite. (1960) 28'
For: oboe, clarinet, bassoon, horn,
trumpet, percussion, piano, double
bass. *First performed:* Jan. 16, 1967;

Athens, Greece.
Score & parts: ms.; available from composer.

A5.97 Summer of Anger.
Music to the film by R. Mourselas.
First performed: Jan. 8, 1962; Athens, Greece.

A5.98 Sunday's Walk.
First performed: Sept. 29, 1972; Athens, Greece.

A5.99 Syllables. (1965) 7'
For: piano. 7 movements. *First performed:* Apr. 5, 1967; Athens, Greece.
Score: Gerig.

A5.100 Synthesis. (1971) 11' 30"
For: oboe, percussion(bass drum and large variety of indefinite pitch intruments), organ(Hammond), double bass, synthesizers(4)(VSC-3 or SYNTHY A, played by performers) or tape(2- or 4-channel), conductor. *Dedicated to:* Guenther Becker and his group.
Score: Baerenreiter, 1972. BU HU
Tape: Baerenreiter, 1972.

A5.101 Telecommunications. (1970) 30'
For: tape. *First performed:* Sept. 30, 1970; Salonica, Greece.
Tape: available from composer.

A5.102 Threnos. (1972) 10'-12'
For: wind ensemble(minimum: 2-1-2(bcl)-2(cbsn); 2-2-3-1), percussion, piano, double bass. *Commissioned by:* Mario di Bonaventura, Hopkins Center Congregation of the Arts (Dartmouth College). *First performed:* Nov. 19, 1972; Tampa, Fla. Orchestra for New Repertory, Lukas Foss, conductor.
Score: Baerenreiter, 1972.
Parts: Baerenreiter, 1972. Rental.

A5.103 Trio. (1961) 15'
For: flute, viola, violoncello. *First performed:* Apr. 6, 1963; Munich, West Germany.
Score & parts: Modern.

A5.104 Verleih uns Freiden. (1971-72) 13' 30"
For: choruses(mixed)(3)(minimum of 24 voices. *Commissioned by:* International Heinrich Schuetz Society. *First performed:* Sept. 30, 1972; Kassel, West Germany. Netherlands Vocal Ensemble, Marinus Voorberg, conductor.
Vocal score: Baerenreiter.

We Are Victorious. *See* Nenikikamen.

A5.105 Die Weisse Rose. (1974-75) 22'
For: Baritone, narrators(2), chorus(mixed), chorus(boy), orchestra(4(afl)- 2(&Ehn)-2(&bcl)-2(cbsn); 6-4-4-2; perc(4); hp, pf/org(Hammond); str). Cantata. *Text:* Toula S. Tolia. *First performed:* Apr. 25, 1976; Philadelphia, Pa. Lisa A. Richette, Frank Ford, speakers; Spyros Sakkas, baritone; Philadelphia Musical Academy Boys Choir; Philadelphia Musical Academy Chorus; Philadelphia Musical Academy Orchestra, Theodore Antoniou, conductor.
Score & parts: Baerenreiter.
Vocal score: Baerenreiter.

A5.106 Wozzeck.
Incidental music to the play by Georg Buechner. *First performed:* July 30, 1972; Athens, Greece.

A6 REED ALDEN AUGLIERE

Born July 31, 1950, in Washington, D.C. Moved to Boston area 1975. *Education:* B.A., Political Science (Syracuse University, 1972); studied composition with William Thomas McKinley (New England Conservatory, M.M., 1978) and Francis Judd Cooke. *Related activities:* leader of Danger College (electric music/video improvisatory ensemble); President, The Future Research Company; author of monographs in 16th century musicology and American ethnomusicology; novelist; poet. BPL

WORKS

A6.1 Miniature. (1978) 15'
For: string quartet.
Score & parts: Future Research.

A6.2 New Moods. (1980) 45'
For: chorus(mixed) and
orchestra(unspecified).
Score & parts: Future Research.

A6.3 Una Nuova guitarra. (1981) 25'
For: orchestra(2-2-2-1; 1-2-2-0; perc(2);
str(10-8-6-4-0).
Score & parts: Future Research.

A6.4 Penetration. (1977) 9'
For: flute, clarinet, saxophone(alto),
piano. *First performed:* May 4, 1977;
New England Conservatory.
Score & parts: Future Research.

A6.5 Preludes. (1976) 8'
For: guitar.
Score: Future Research.

B1 JOHN BAVICCHI

Born April 25, 1922, in Boston.
Education: studied composition with
Carl McKinley, Francis Judd Cooke
(New England Conservatory, B.M., 1952);
Walter Piston (Harvard University,
1953-56). *Awards:* National Institute of
Arts and Letters Award (1960). *Related
activities:* conductor, Arlington-
Belmont Chorale and Arlington-Belmont
Chamber Chorus; member of the
faculty of Berklee College of Music
(1964-). Be

WORKS

[American Choruses]
B1.1 Three American Choruses, Op. 68.
(1975) 6'
For: chorus(SATB), trumpets(2), horn or
trumpet, trombone, tuba or
trombone(bass), piano(optional).
Contents: Ye Shall Proclaim (from the
Liberty Bell); Thank God I Am Here
(Sikorsky); What Is an American
(Pioneer Monument). *First performed:*
Mar. 14, 1976; Belmont, Mass.
Plymouth Congregational Church.

Arlington Philharmonic and Arlington
Chorus, John Bavicchi, conductor.
Score: Oxford, 1978. Be
Parts: Oxford, 1978.
Vocal score: Oxford, 1978.

B1.2 Band of the Year: An Overture for
Concert Band, Op. 66. (1974) 6'
1 movement. *Commissioned by:*
Massachusetts Music Education
Association. *First performed:* Apr. 15,
1975; Belmont, Mass. Belmont High
School Band, Jon Nicholson, conductor.
Score: Oxford, 1975. Be BPL
Parts: Oxford, 1975. BPL
Reel: Feb. 17, 1977; Boston
Conservatory. BCM

B1.3 Caroline's Dance, Op. 67. (1975) 5'
For: orchestra(2-1-2(&bcl)-1; 4-2-3-0;
timp, perc(3); str). 1 movement.
Commissioned by: Joseph Phelan.
Score & parts: BKJ, 1979. Also rental.

[Choruses, Op. 69]
B1.4 Two Choruses, Op. 69. (1975) 5'
For: chorus(mixed). *Contents:* There Was
a Lady (anon.); Psalm 98.
Vocal score: ms. in composer's hand
(also No. I separately).
Vocal score: Kjos, 1975.
Vocal score: in *Cambiata Contemporary
4-Part Music for Young Choruses*, Kjos,
1975 (No. 2). Be

B1.5 A Clarinet Handbook, Op. 47.
(1962) 14'
For: clarinets(2 and 3).
Score: BKJ, 1980. BPL

B1.6 A Concert Overture, Op. 29. (1957)
9'
For: orchestra. 1 movement.
Commissioned by: Civic Symphony
Orchestra of Boston. *First performed:*
Dec. 5,1957; John Hancock Hall, Boston.
Civic Symphony Orchestra of Boston,
Paul Cherkassky, conductor.
Score & parts: Oxford, 1960. Rental.
Reel: American Symphony Orchestra
League R 1587-88, 1959-60. American
Symphony Orchestra League, Guy
Taylor, conductor. Be HU

B1.7 Concertante for Flute, Clarinet and Wind Ensemble No. 2, Op. 65. (1972; 1975) 11'
1 movement. *Dedicated to:* Carole Epple and Barbara Brewer. *First performed:* May 5, 1976; Boston Conservatory. Boston Conservatory Wind Ensemble, John Corley, conductor.
Score & parts: ms. in composer's hand.
Score & parts: BKJ, 1981.
Reel: recording of first performance. BCM

B1.8 Concertante for Oboe, Bassoon and String Orchestra, Op. 44. (1961) 15'
3 movements. *Dedicated to:* Sherman Walt and Ralph Gomberg. *First performed:* Nov. 12, 1974; Erie, Pa. Erie Symphony Orchestra, Harold Bauer, conductor.
Score & parts: ms. in composer's hand.
Score & parts: BKJ, 1978.

B1.9 Concerto, Op. 11. (1954) 20'
For: clarinet and string orchestra. 3 movements. *Dedicated to:* Felix Viscuglia. *First performed:* May 4, 1958; New England Conservatory. Felix Viscuglia, clarinet; NEC Symphony Orchestra, Roger Voisin, conductor.
Score & parts: Oxford, 1960. Rental.
Pf. red: Oxford, 1967. Be BPL

B1.10 Corley's March, Op. 54. (1967) 4'
For: band. 1 movement. *Commissioned by and dedicated to:* John Corley. *First performed:* Jan. 30, 1968; Brunswick, Me. MIT Concert Band, John Corley, conductor.
Score: Oxford, 1971. MIT
Condensed score: Oxford, 1971. BPL
Parts: Oxford, 1971.

[Dialogues]
B1.11 Five Dialogues, Op. 7. (1952) 6'
For: clarinets(2). *Dedicated to:* Ronald White. *First performed:* Dec. 19, 1952; New England Conservatory. Henry Duckham and Anthony Fulginitti.
Score: Oxford, 1972. Be HMA HU

B1.12 Divertimento, No. 1, Op. 1 (Trio No. 1, Op. 1) . (1950) 9'
For: clarinet, trombone, violin. 3 movements. *First performed:* June 4, 1951; New England Conservatory. Eugene LaCritz, clarinet, Millard Neiger, trombone; Joanne Dempsey, violin.
Score & parts: ms. in composer's hand.
Score & parts: BKJ, 1975.

B1.13 A Duet Dozen, Op. 61. (1970) 6'
For: piano(4-hands). Children's music. *Dedicated to:* Clelia Goldings and Marlene Moy. *First performed:* Mar. 2, 1976; Acton, Mass. Alfa Radford and pupils.
Score: Oxford, 1975. BPL

[Duets]
B1.14 Six Duets, Op. 27. (1957) 11'
For: flute and clarinet. *Dedicated to:* Elinor Preble and Donna Klimoski. *First performed:* Apr. 25, 1957; Providence, R.I. Elinor Preble, flute and Donna Klimoski, clarinet.
Score: Oxford, 1962. Be BPL HMA HU
Reel: Nov. 16, 1966; Brookline Public Library.
Reel: Apr. 7, 1976; Berklee College of Music. Matthew Marviglio, flute and Daniel Klimoski, clarinet.

[Elizabethan Poems]
B1.15 Four Elizabethan Poems, Op. 3. (1951) 8'
For: chorus(SATB). *Contents:* Dawn (John Ford); Melancholy (John Fletcher); A Lament (William Drummond); Love Is a Sickness (Samuel Daniel). *First performed:* Feb. 28, 1952; New England Conservatory. NEC Chorus, Lorna Cooke deVaron, conductor.
Vocal score: ms. in composer's hand (Nos. 2-4).
Vocal score: Kjos, 1970 (No. 1).
Vocal score: BKJ, 1975 (Nos. 2-4).

B1.16 Fantasia on Korean Folk Tunes, Op. 53. (1966) 8'
For: orchestra(2-1-2(&bcl)-1; 2-2-3-1; timp, perc; str). 1 movement. *Dedicated to:* Paul Paradise. *First performed:* June

10, 1969; Lincoln School, Brookline, Mass. Musicians Union Orchestra, John Corley, conductor.
Score & parts: ms. in composer's hand.
Score & parts: BKJ, 1977.

B1.17 Fantasy for Concert Band, Op. 74. (1979) 9'
Dedicated to: John Corley. *First performed:* Jan. 28, 1980; Cleveland, Ohio. MIT Concert Band, Paul Husby, conductor.
Score & parts: BKJ, 1979. Also rental.

B1.18 Fantasy for Harp and Chamber Orchestra, Op. 36. (1959) 10'
1 movement. *Dedicated to:* John Owen Ward. *First performed:* Mar. 18, 1960; Cooper Union, New York City. Assunta Dell'Aquila, harp; Cooper Union Orchestra, Howard Shanet, conductor.
Score & parts: BKJ, 1979. Also rental.

B1.19 Fantasy for Organ, Op. 31. (1957) 6'
Dedicated to: Bartholomeus Kool. *First performed:* June 11, 1958; Wellesley Congregational Church, Wellesley, Mass. Jean White.
Score: BKJ, 1979.

B1.20 Fantasy for Piano, Op. 15. (1955) 9'
1 movement. *Dedicated to:* Tan Crone. *First performed:* June 4, 1960; Boston Center for Adult Education. Nicholas Van Slyck.
Score: reprod. of ms. NEC
Score: BKJ, 1979.
Reel: Dec. 14, 1972; Brookline Public Library. BkPL

B1.21 Farewell and Hail, Op. 28. (1957) 11'
For: Mezzo Soprano, trumpet, string orchestra. *Text:* Norma Farber.
Commissioned by: Norma Farber. *First performed:* Mar. 25, 1972; Hingham, Mass. Delores Fox, soprano; Hingham Civic Symphony, John Corley, conductor.
Score: reprod. of ms. NEC

Score & parts: ms. in composer's hand.
Score & parts: BKJ, 1980.

Festival Symphony. *See* Symphony No. 1.

B1.22 Fireworks: A Ballet, Op. 48. (1962) 20'
For: Baritone and orchestra(1-0-1-0; 1-0-0-0; timp, perc; str). 1 movement.
Commissioned by: Robert Joffrey.
Score & parts: ms. in composer's hand.

[Korean Folk Songs]
B1.23 Six Korean Folk Songs in a Contemporary Setting, Op. 35. (1959) 9'
For: Soprano and piano. *Text:* Korean, traditional. *Contents:* Miryang Arirang; Nohdle Kahngbyun; Pang ah Tahryung; Toraji Tahryung; Arirang; Pahgyun Pockpo. *Dedicated to:* Ann Myongsook Lee. *First performed:* May 9, 1960; Carnegie Recital Hall, New York City. Ann Myongsook Lee, soprano and Robert Sherwood, piano.
Score: Seesaw, 1971.

[Lithuanian Songs]
B1.24 Three Lithuanian Songs, Op. 40. (1960) 8'
For: Soprano and piano. *Text:* Stasys Santraras. *Contents:* Vysionos (Grapes); Rudenio duona (Autumn Bread); Dziaugsmus (Joy). Folksongs, Lithuanian. *Dedicated to:* Stasys Santraras. *First performed:* Mar. 20, 1960; South Boston High School. Corinne Curry, soprano and Trudi Van Slyck, piano.
Score: ms. in composer's hand.

[Miniatures]
B1.25 Four Miniatures, Op. 71. (1976) 10'
For: flute, oboe, clarinet, bassoon. *Dedicated to:* Anthony Garfield-Savage. *First performed:* Mar. 10, 1977; Berklee College of Music. Berklee College Faculty Quartet.
Score & parts: ms. in composer' hand.
Score & parts: BKJ, 1981.

B1.26 Mont Blanc Overture, Op. 72. (1977) 9'

For: orchestra(2-1-2-1; 4-2-3-0; timp, perc(3); str). *First performed:* June 20, 1980; Attleboro, Mass. Attleboro Civic Symphony Orchestra, D. Caron, conductor.
Score: Oxford, 1979. Be HU
Parts: Oxford, l979.

B1.27 Music for Horn and Piano, Op. 78. (1980) 7'
1 movement. *Dedicated to:* Lee Roberts.
Score & part: BKJ, 1980.

B1.28 Music for Mallets and Percussion, Op. 55. (1967) 5'
For: percussion(10)(glockenspiel, marimba, vibraphone, xylophone, timpani, drums(tenor(3) or tom-toms), drum(bass), cymbals, gong, woodblock, tambourines(2), triangle). l movement.
Dedicated to: Fred Buda. Written for the Berklee Percussion Ensemble of the Berklee College of Music. *First performed:* Feb. 3, 1969; Warwick, R.I. Members of the MIT Concert Band, John Corley, conductor.
Score: Oxford, 1973. BCM Be BPL HMA
Reel: Mar. 27, 1969; Brookline Public Library. BkPL
Reel: Dec. 3, 1975; Boston Conservatory. BCM
Reel: Dec. 16, 1976; Boston Conservatory. BCM
Reel: Apr. 15, 1980; Boston University. BU Percussion Ensemble, Thomas Gauger, conductor. BU
Disc: MIT Contemporary Music Series MITCMS 004, [1971?]. MIT Concert Band, John Corley, conductor. MIT

B1.29 Music for Small Orchestra, Op. 81. (1981) 15'
For: chamber orchestra(2-2-2-2; 2-2-0-0; timp; str). 1 movement. *Dedicated to:* Harold Bauer.
Score & parts: BKJ, nyp. Also rental.

B1.30 A Musical Sketch-Book, Op. 41. (1960) 9'
For: flute, oboe, clarinet, bassoon, piano. 6 movements. *Dedicated to:*

Helen Hughes.
Score: BKJ, 1980.

B1.31 Night Walk, Op. 26. (1956) 4'
For: Soprano and piano. *Text:* Frank Rooney. *Dedicated to:* Donna Jeffery.
First performed: Feb. 5, 1957; New England Conservatory. Donna Jeffery, soprano and John Moriarty, piano.
Score: ms. in composer's hand.
Score: BKJ, 1978.
Disc: Fassett Recording Studio, 1957. Recording of first performance. NEC

[Pieces]
B1.32 Three Pieces for String Quartet, Op. 2. (1950) 9'
Dedicated to: Mr. and Mrs. C. Morang.
First performed: Sept. 24, 1954; Harvard University. Francis Lanier and Phyllis Skoldberg, violins; Jean Comstock, viola; Hannah Sherman, violoncello.
Score & parts: ms. in composer's hand.
Score & parts: BKJ, 1974.

B1.33 Prelude and Dance, Op. 12. (1954) 4'
For: violin and piano. *Dedicated to:* Phyllis Skoldberg. *First performed:* Mar. 18, 1955; New England Conservatory. Ayrton Pinto, violin and Tan Crone, piano.
Score: BKJ, 1978. Be

B1.34 Prelude, Fugue and Coda, Op. 58. (1968) 4'
For: woodwind quintet. 4 movements.
Commissioned by: Pro Arte Woodwind Quintet. *First performed:* June 17, 1973; Stafford, England. Bavicchi Ensemble.
Score & parts: Seesaw, 1971.

[Preludes]
B1.35 Three Preludes for Unaccompanied Trombone, Op. 21. (1956) 6'
Dedicated to: Frank Montesanti. *First performed:* Dec. 13, 1966; Berklee College of Music. Samuel Burtis.
Score: Ensemble Publications, 1966. Be

BPL NEC
Reel: recording of first performance.
Be
Disc: Coronet 850 C 3107, [1974].
Alan Raph.

Psalm 98. *See* Choruses, Op. 69.

B1.36 Psalm 104, Op. 73. (1978) 25'
For: Soprano, Tenor, Bass,
chorus(SATB). 11 movements. *Dedicated
to:* Alfa Radford. *First performed:* Apr.
15, 1979; First Unitarian Church,
Belmont, Mass. First Unitarian Church
of Belmont Choir, John Bavicchi,
conductor.
Vocal score: Oxford, nyp.

[Psalms]
B1.37 Three Psalms, Op. 50. (1963) 12'
For: Soprano, Alto, Tenor, Bass,
chorus, trumpets(2), string orchestra.
Text: Bible, O.T., Psalms 47, 133, 98.
Commissioned by: Saint Cecilia Society.
First performed: Apr. 23, 1963; Jordan
Hall, Boston. Saint Cecilia Society,
William Seymour, conductor.
Score & parts: ms. in composer's hand.
Vocal score: Renfrew Press, 1963. W

[Quartet, Saxophones, No. 1]
B1.38 Saxophone Quartet No. 1, Op. 52.
(1965) 6'
For: saxophone(soprano),
saxophone(alto), saxophone(tenor),
saxophone(baritone). 1 movement.
Dedicated to: Joseph Viola. Written for
Joseph Viola and the Berklee
Saxophone Quartet. *First performed:*
Feb. 28, 1966; Vendome Hotel, Boston.
Berklee Saxophone Quartet.
Score: ms. in composer's hand. Be
Score & parts: Dorn, 1981.
Disc: Berklee BLP 102, 1973. Berklee
Saxophone Quartet, Joseph Viola,
director. BCM
Reel: Berklee Saxophone Quartet. Be

[Quartet, Saxophones, No. 2]
B1.39 Saxophone Quartet No. 2, Op. 59.
(1969) 9'
For: saxophone(soprano),
saxophone(alto), saxophone(tenor),

saxophone(baritone). *Dedicated to:*
Joseph Viola. *First performed:* July 11,
1970; Ogunquit, Me. Berklee Saxophone
Quartet.
Score & parts: Berklee.
Disc: Berklee LP 102, 1973. Berklee
Saxophone Quartet, Joseph Viola,
director. BCM

Quartet, Strings, No. 1. *See* Pieces.

[Quartet, Strings, No. 2]
B1.40 Quartet No. 2, Op. 6B. (1952) 12'
Score & parts: BKJ, 1975.

[Quartet, Strings, No. 3]
B1.41 String Quartet No. 3, Op. 42.
(1960) 21'
5 movements. *Commissioned by:*
Harvard Musical Association. *First
performed:* Oct. 19, 1962; Harvard
Musical Association. George Zazofsky
and Julius Shulman, violins; Earl
Hedberg, viola; Robert Ripley,
violoncello.
Score & parts: ms. in composer's hand.
Score & parts: reprod. of ms. HMA
Score & parts: BKJ, 1978.

[Quartet, Trumpets(2) and
Trombones(2)]
B1.42 Quartet No. 1 for Brass
Instruments, Op. 22. (1956) 14'
4 movements. *Dedicated to:* Roger
Voisin. *First performed:* Feb. 13, 1957;
Brookline Public Library. NEC Brass
Ensemble.
Score & parts: Oxford, 1971. Be BPL
HMA HU
Reel: recording of first performance.
BkPL
Reel: Dec. 13, 1966; Berklee College of
Music. Be

[Quintet, Woodwinds, Op. 43]
B1.43 Woodwind Quintet, Op. 43. (1961)
15'
4 movements. *Dedicated to:* New York
Woodwind Quintet. *First performed:*
May 19, 1963; Milwaukee, Wis.
Milwaukee Symphony Woodwind
Quintet.

Score & parts: ms. in composer's hand.
Score & parts: BKJ, 1980.

[Quintet, Woodwinds, Op. 64]
B1.44 Woodwind Quintet, Op. 64. (1973)
12'
4 movements. *Dedicated to:* Bavicchi
Ensemble. *First performed:* Apr. 27,
1976; Birmingham, England. Bavicchi
Ensemble.
Score & parts: ms. in composer's hand.
Score & parts: BKJ, 1979.

[Short Anthems]
B1.45 Four Short Anthems, Op. 76.
(1979) 8'
For: chorus(SATB). *Text:* Bible. *Contents:*
Unto Thee, O God; Choose You This
Day; God Our Hope; O Give Thanks
unto the Lord. *Dedicated to:* Alfa
Radford.
Vocal score: ms. in composer's hand.

[Short Poems]
B1.46 Five Short Poems, Op. 45. (1961)
10'
For: chorus(SSAA). *Contents:* Mr. Finney
(anon.); What a Dainty Life (John
Nabbes); Let Tomorrow Take Care of
Tomorrow (Charles Swain); Jenny
Kissed Me (Leigh Hunt); When Icicles
Hang by the Wall (William
Shakespeare). *Dedicated to:* Janet
Bavicchi. *First performed:* Feb. 6, 1965;
Buffalo, N.Y. Brookline High School
Chorus, William Seymour, conductor.
Vocal score: Oxford, 1968. Be

Short Sonata. *See* Sonata, Violin and
Piano, No. 3.

[Sonata, Clarinet, No. 1]
B1.47 Sonata, No. 1, Op. 20. (1956) 6'
For: clarinet. 3 movements. *Dedicated
to:* Felix Viscuglia. *First performed:*
Jan. 6, 1957; Boston Adult Education
Center. Andre Lizotte.
Score: ms. in composer's hand. Be
Score: Oxford, 1970. Be BPL HMA HU
Disc: Mark Educational Records, nyp.
Paul Drushler.

Reel: Dec. 13, 1966; Berklee College of
Music. David Mott. Be

[Sonata, Clarinet, No. 2]
B1.48 Sonata No. 2, Op. 38. (1959) 7'
3 movements.. *Dedicated to:* Donna
Klimoski. *First performed:* Sept, 2,
1960; Concord, Mass. Donna Klimoski.
Score: ms. in composer's hand. Be
Score: Oxford, 1973. Be BPL HMA HU

[Sonata, Clarinet and Piano]
B1.49 Sonata, Op. 57. (1969) 14'
4 movements. *Dedicated to:* Sherman
Friedland. *First performed:* Apr. 1,
1969; Plymouth, N.H. Sherman
Friedland, clarinet and Kenneth Wolf,
piano.
Score: ms. in composer's hand.

[Sonata, Piano]
B1.50 Sonata, Op. 37. (1959) 15'
3 movements. *Dedicated to:* Nicholas
Van Slyck. *First performed:* Nov. 28,
1962; Brookline Public Library. Frances
Burnett.
Score: reprod. of ms. NEC
Score: BKJ, 1979.

[Sonata, Pianos(2)]
B1.51 Sonata, Op. 9. (1953) 12'
3 movements. *First performed:* Jan. 13,
1954; Harvard University. Russell
Woollen and Nicholas Van Slyck.
Score: BKJ, 1979.

[Sonata, Violin and Piano, No. 1]
B1.52 Sonata No. 1, Op. 24. (1956) 16'
3 movements. *Dedicated to:* Ayrton
Pinto. *First performed:* Jan. 30, 1957;
Jordan Hall, Boston. Ayrton Pinto,
violin and John Moriarty, piano.
Score: BKJ, 1979.
Disc: Medea MCLP 1002, 196-. Daniel
Kobialka, violin and Myron Press,
piano. Be BU HU NEC

[Sonata, Violin and Piano, No. 2]
B1.53 Sonata No. 2, Op. 32. (1958) 10'
3 movements. *Dedicated to:* Adrienne
Rosenbaum. July 26, 1959; Isabella
Stewart Gardner Museum, Boston.

Giora Bernstein, violin and George
Zilzer, piano.
Score: BKJ, 1979.

[Sonata, Violin and Piano, No. 3]
B1.54 Sonata No. 3, Op. 39. (1960) 7'
For: violin and piano or harpsichord. 3
movements. *Commissioned by:* Daniel
Pinkham. *First performed:* Jan. 27,
1960; Buffalo, N.Y. Robert Brink, violin
and Daniel Pinkham, harpsichord.
Score: reprod. of ms. (titled Short
Sonata). NEC
Score: BKJ, 1979.
Disc: Composers Recordings CRI 138,
1960 (titled Short Sonata). Robert Brink,
violin and Daniel Pinkham, harpsichord.
BrU BU HU MIT NEC W

[Sonata, Violin and Piano, No. 4]
B1.55 Sonata No. 4, Op. 63. (1971) 15'
3 movements. *Commissioned by:*
Izidorius Vasyliunas. *First performed:*
Mar. 25, 1972; Carnegie Recital Hall,
New York City. Izidorius Vasyliunas,
violin and Vitanys Vasyliunas, piano.
Score: Oxford, 1974. BPL HU
Part: Oxford, 1974. HU

[Sonata, Violoncello and Piano, No.
1]
B1.56 Sonata No. 1 for 'Cello and
Piano, Op. 8. (1953) 12'
3 movements. *Dedicated to:* Corinne
Haller. *First performed:* May 13, 1953;
Harvard University. Corinne Haller,
violoncello and Jean Hersey, piano.
Score: BKJ, 1979.

[Sonata, Violoncello and Piano, No.
2]
B1.57 Sonata No. 2, Op. 25. (1956) 15'
4 movements. *Commissioned by:* Donald
Hoffman. *First performed:* May 3, 1957;
Harvard University. Judith Davidoff,
violoncello and Martin Boykan, piano.
Score: ms. Be
Score: BKJ, 1979.

B1.58 Sonatina. Op. 30. (1957) 8'
For: oboe and piano. 3 movements.
Dedicated to: Milton Hamilton. *First
performed:* Jan. 7, 1958; Jordan Hall,

Boston. Milton Hamilton, oboe and
William Brown, piano.
Score: Oxford, 1970. Be BP HU
Part: Oxford, 1970. HU

[Songs, Op. 6]
B1.59 Four Songs, Op. 6. (1952) 14'
For: Alto and chamber orchestra
(2-1-1(&bcl)-0; 2-0-0-0; str). *Contents:* To
Lorna (Eric Wilson Barker); In
Memoriam (Rose Nolfi); Lament
(Dorothy Berg); The Search (Marybelle
Tyree Schwertmann). *Dedicated to:*
Valentina Sobalvarro. *First performed:*
Dec. 17, 1952; Harvard University.
Valentina Sobalvarro, alto; members of
NEC Symphony Orchestra, Herbert
Blomstedt, conductor.
Score & parts: ms. in composer's hand.
Vocal score: reprod. of ms. NEC

[Songs, Op. 10]
B1.60 Three Songs, Op. 10. (1953) 10'
For: Mezzo Soprano and piano. *Text:*
Michael Drayton. *Contents:* Sonnet 61;
Sonnet 1; Sonnet 48. *Dedicated to:*
Valentina Sobalvarro. *First performed:*
May 9, 1954; Harkness Hall, Cambridge,
Mass. Valentina Sobalvarro, mezzo
soprano and Jean White, piano.
Score: ms. in composer's hand.

Songs, Op. 14. *See* Songs After
Sonnets of Conrad Aiken.

[Songs, Op. 17]
B1.61 Four Songs, Op. 17. (1955) 9'
For: Soprano and piano. *Text:* Alfred
Noyes. *Contents:* Autumn; Rain; Illusion;
Lamps. *Dedicated to:* Barbara Stahlman.
First performed: Jan. 13, 1956; New
England Conservatory. Barbara
Stahlman, soprano and John Moriarty,
piano.
Score: ms. in composer's hand.
Score: reprod. of ms. NEC

[Songs, Op. 80]
B1.62 Three Songs, Op. 80. (1981) 9'
For: Mezzo Soprano and piano.
Contents: This Place Was Formed
Divine (Herman James Elroy Flecker);
Felise (Algernon Swinburne); Go, Songs

(Francis Thompson). *Commissioned by:* Peter Papesch. *Dedicated to:* Barbara Papesch.
Score: ms. in composer's hand.

[Songs After Sonnets of Conrad Aiken]
B1.63 Four Songs After Sonnets of Conrad Aiken, Op. 14. (1954) 10'
For: Soprano and piano. *Dedicated to:* Christina Cardillo. *First performed:* Sept. 2, 1960. Linda Sanford, soprano and Trudi Van Slyck, piano.
Score: ms. in composer's hand.
Score: reprod. of ms. NEC

B1.64 Spring Festival Overture, Op. 56. (1968) 5'
For: band. *Commissioned by:* Canton High School Band and Walpole High School Bands. *First performed:* July 3, 1970; Boston Common. Metropolitan District Commission Band, John Corley, conductor.
Score & parts: BKJ, 1978.

[Suite, Band]
B1.65 Suite No. 3, Op. 60. (1969) 16'
Movements: Allegro molto; Andantino (Hommage a Bartok); Scherzo (Hommage a Piston); Con fuoco.
Written for the MIT Concert Band.
Dedicated to: John Corley. *First performed:* Feb. 3, 1970; Atlanta, Ga. MIT Concert Band, John Corley, conductor.
Score & parts: Oxford, 1977. Rental.
Disc: MIT Contemporary Music Series MITCMS 004, [1971?]. MIT Concert Band, John Corley, conductor. MIT
Reel: March 15, 1979; Boston Conservatory. BCM

[Suite, Clarinet Choir]
B1.66 Suite No. 2, Op. 46. (1961) 11'
For: clarinet choir or wind ensemble 4 movements. *Dedicated to:* Rosario Mazzeo. *First performed:* Nov. 15, 1966; Eugene, Ore. University of Oregon Clarinet Choir, Robert G. Cunningham, conductor.
Score & parts: ms. in composer's hand.

Reel: Apr. 12, 1973; Berklee Concert Hall, Berklee College of Music; in *An Evening of Chamber Works.* John Bavicchi, conductor. Be
Reel: Dec. 20, 1977; Boston Conservatory. BCM

[Suite, Orchestra]
B1.67 Suite No. 1, Op. 19. (1955) 22'
5 movements. *First performed:* Apr. 16, 1961; Sanders Theatre, Harvard University. Cambridge Civic Symphony, John Bavicchi, conductor.
Score & parts: Oxford, 1964. Rental.

B1.68 Summer Incident, Op. 34. (1959) 20'
For: chamber orchestra(2-2-2-2; 2-0-0-0; timp, perc; pf). Ballet. 1 movement.
Commissioned by: New England Civic Ballet. *First performed:* Nov. 17, 1959; Boston University. New England Civic Ballet.
Score & parts: ms. in composer's hand.

[Symphony No. 1]
B1.69 Festival Symphony Op. 51. (1964-65) 25'
For: band. *Commissioned by:* MIT Concert Band. *First performed:* Nov. 6, 1965; Massachusetts Institute of Technology. MIT Concert Band, John Corley, conductor.
Score & parts: Oxford, 1966. Rental.
Disc: MIT Contemporary Music Series MITCMS 004, [1971?]. MIT Concert Band, John Corley, conductor. MIT

B1.70 Symphony No. 2, Op. 70. (1975-77) 16'
For: brass ensemble(horns(4), trumpets(4), trombones(4), tuba), timpani, percussion(4)(glockenspiel, marimba, vibraphone, xylophone). 4 movements. *First performed:* May 28, 1976; Massachusetts Institute of Technology, Boston Brass Choir, John Corley, conductor.
Score & parts: ms. in composer's hand.
Reel: Apr. 27, 1978; Boston Conservatory. BCM

B1.71 Theme with Variations, Op. 75. (1979) 4'
For: flute. *Dedicated to:* Matthew Marvuglio. *First performed:* Dec. 2, 1979; Newton, Mass. Matthew Marvuglio.
Score: BKJ, 1980.

There Was a Lady. *See* Choruses, Op. 69.

B1.72 To the Lighthouse, Op. 16. (1955) 5'
For: Soprano, horn, piano. *Text:* Norma Farber. *Dedicated to:* Norma Farber. *First performed:* Apr. 30, 1956; College Club. Boston. Norma Farber, soprano; Paul Keaney, horn; Helen Keaney, piano.
Score & parts: Seesaw, 1971.

B1.73 Tobal, Op. 5. (1952) 11'
For: orchestra. 1 movement. *Dedicated to:* Beverly Ann Lewis.
Score & parts: BKJ, 1978. Also rental.

B1.74 Toccata, Op. 23. (1956) 5'
For: piano. 1 movement. *Dedicated to:* John Moriarty. *First performed:* Oct. 28, 1956; Jordan Hall, Boston. John Moriarty.
Score: reprod. of ms. NEC
Score: Seesaw, 1971. Be

[Trio, Alto, Violin, Violoncello]
B1.75 Trio No. 4, Op. 18. (1955) 9'
Dedicated to: Kraft & Elias.
Score & parts: Seesaw, 1971.

Trio, Clarinet, Trombone, Violin. *See* Divertimento, No. 1, Op. 1.

[Trio, Flute, Oboe, Violoncello]
B1.76 Trio No. 9, Op. 79. (1980) 12'
3 movements. *Dedicated to:* Diane Gold.
Score & parts: ms. in composer's hand.

[Trio, Flute, Viola, Violoncello]
B1.77 Trio No. 6, Op. 49. (1962) 12'
3 movements. *Dedicated to:* Elinor Preble. *First performed:* Nov. 21, 1963; Brookline Public Library. Elinor Preble, flute; Donald Clauser, viola; Carole

Procter, violoncello.
Score & parts: BKJ, 1980.

[Trio, Piano, Clarinet, Viola]
B1.78 Trio, No. 2, Op. 4. (1951) 16'
3 movements. *Dedicated to:* Felix Viscuglia. *First performed:* Jan. 12, 1952; New England Conservatory. William Shisler, viola; Felix Viscuglia, clarinet; Jean Hersey, piano.
Score & parts: BKJ, 1979.

[Trio, Piano, Clarinet, Violin]
B1.79 Trio No. 5, Op. 33. (1958) 13'
For: violin, clarinet, piano or harp. 3 movements. *Dedicated to:* Elizabeth Bayer.
Score & parts: BKJ, 1979 (version for piano, titled Trio No. 4).
Disc: Composers Recordings CRI 138, 1960 (titled Trio No. 4). Matthew Raimondi, violin; David Glazer, clarinet, Assunta Dell'Aquila, harp. BrU BU HU MIT NEC W

[Trio, Piano, Clarinet, Violoncello]
B1.80 Trio No. 3, Op. 13. (1954) 18'
3 movements. *Dedicated to:* Ronald and Jean White. *First performed:* Mar. 17, 1955; Brookline Public Library. Harold Zilch, violin; Ronald White, clarinet; Jean White, piano.
Score & parts: BKJ, 1979.

[Trio, Piano and Percussion(2)]
B1.81 Trio No. 7, Op. 62. (1970) 12'
4 movements. *Commissioned by:* Allen Barker.
Score & parts: Seesaw, 1971.

[Trio, Piano, Violin, Violoncello]
B1.82 Trio No. 8, Op. 77. (1980) 16'
3 movements. *Commissioned by:* Welsh Arts Council for University College (Cardiff, Wales).
Score & parts: ms. in composer's hand.

B2 LARRY THOMAS BELL

Born January 17, 1952, in Wilson, N.C. Moved to Boston area 1980. *Education:* B.M. (Appalachian State University, 1974); M.M. (Juilliard School, 1976);

studied composition with Gregory Kosteck, Donald Erb, Mario Davidovsky, Vincent Persichetti; piano with Richard Lucht and Alan Kindt. *Awards:* Composer's Conference (Johnson, Vt.) awards (1972, 1973), North Carolina Music Teachers Association Awards (1972, 1973), BMI Award (1973), Alexander Gretchaninoff Memorial Prize in Composition (Juilliard School, 1976), American Academy and Institute of Arts and Letters, Charles Ives Scholarship (1977), Marian Freschl Prize for Vocal Composition (Juilliard School, 1980), Guggenheim Grant (1981), MacDowell Colony Fellowship (1981). *Related activities:* member of the faculties of the Juilliard School (1979-) and Boston Conservatory. BCM

WORKS

B2.1 Caprice. (1979) 6'
For: violoncello. 1 movement.
Dedicated to: Scot Williams. *First performed:* Apr. 1980; Juilliard School. Scot Williams.
Score: reprod. of ms.
Reel: May 1980; Juilliard School. Scot Williams.

B2.2 Continuum. (1972) 8'
For: chamber orchestra(1(&pic)-1(&Ehn)-1(bcl)-1(&cbsn); 0-0-0-0; perc(2); hp, pf; str(8-6-5-4-2)). 1 movement. *First performed:* Aug. 1973; Johnson State College. Composer's Conference Chamber Players, Efrain Gaigai, conductor.
Score & parts: reprod. of ms.
Reel: recording of first performance.
Reel: May 1980; Juilliard School. Juilliard Orchestra, Richard Fletcher, conductor.

B2.3 Domination of Black. (1971) 3' 30"
For: Sopranos(2), Alto, Tenor, Bass.
Text: Wallace Stevens. *First performed:* Apr. 17, 1980; Juilliard School. Daureen Podensky and Lynn Yakes, sopranos; Anna Sofas, alto; Jeffrey Thomas, tenor; Greer Grimsley, bass.

Vocal score: reprod. of ms.
Reel: recording of first performance.

B2.4 Eclogue. (1973) 10'
For: saxophones(alto)(2), saxophone(tenor), saxophone(bass). 1 movement. *First performed:* May 1978; Alice Tully Hall, New York City. John Ingram and George Lowery, alto saxophones; Kenneth Hitchcock, tenor saxophone; Mathew Balensuela, bass saxophone.
Score: reprod. of ms.
Reel: recording of first performance.

B2.5 Mirage. (1971) 8'
For: flute and piano. 1 movement. *First performed:* Aug. 1972; Johnson State College. Karl Kraber, flute and Robert Miller, piano.
Score: reprod. of ms.
Reel: recording of first performance.

B2.6 Novelette. (1970) 6'
For: string quartet. 1 movement. *First performed:* Apr. 17, 1980; Juilliard School. Cavatina String Quartet.
Score & parts: reprod. of ms.
Reel: recording of first performance.

[Quartet, Strings]
B2.7 String Quartet No. 1. (1973) 11'
1 movement. *First performed:* May 1976; Juilliard School. Juilliard String Quartet.
Score: reprod. of ms.
Reel: recording of first performance.
Reel: May 1980; Juilliard School. Cavatina String Quartet.

B2.8 Reality Is an Activity of the Most August Imagination. (1976) 4' 30"
For: Soprano and piano. *Text:* Wallace Stevens. *First performed:* May 17, 1980; Juilliard School. Judith Malafronte, soprano and Larry Bell, piano.
Score: reprod. of ms.
Reel: recording of first performance.

B2.9 Variations. (1974) 10'
For: piano. 1 movement. *First*

performed: May 1974; Appalachian
State College. Larry Bell.
Score: reprod. of ms.
Reel: recording of first performance.
Reel: Nov. 1974; Juilliard School. Larry
Bell.

B3 HAMPARTZOUM BERBERIAN

Born May 25, 1905, in Adana, Turkey.
Moved to Boston area 1962. *Education:*
Athens National Conservatory (1930);
studied with Yale Bustundy, Die
Economidis, Dimitri Mitropoulos.
Awards: Lebanon, First Order of Cedar
(1956), Zareh Noubar Cultural Trust
Fund (First Prize, 1958), Armenian
General Benevolent Union Central
Committee of America Award (1973),
Asa Boyan Humanity Award (1976), St.
Sahag St. Mesrob, Medal (1979).
Related activities: violinist; conductor;
Assistant Dean, Music School of
Nicosia, Cyprus (1930-32); musical
director, Armenian General Benevolent
Union. BPL

WORKS

B3.1 Anonymous. (1961) 5' 30"
For: Soprano and piano. 1 movement.
Text: Misak Medzarents. *First
performed:* 1971; Boston. Nayiri
Berberian, soprano, and unidentified
pianist.
Score: ms. in composer's hand.
Reel: recording of first performance.

B3.2 Areknazan. (1940) 125'
For: voices and
orchestra(2(&pic)-2(&Ehn)-2-2; 4-3-3-1;
perc; hp; str). Opera in 4 parts. *Text:*
Hovhannes Toumanian. *First performed:*
Feb. 22, 1941; Aleppo, Syria. Serpouhie
Berberian, soprano, and others.
Score & parts: ms. in composer's hand.
Vocal score: ms. in compsoser's hand.

B3.3 Armenian Church. (1935) 17' 30"
For: chorus(SATB) and
orchestra(2(&pic)-2(&Ehn)-2-2; 2-3-2-0;
timp, perc; hp; str). Oratorio. 1
movement. *Text: Hayerkoutouin* by

Vahan Tekeyan. *Dedicated to:* The first
Catholicos Karekin, on his 80th
Birthday, his 60th Literary Jubilee, his
50th Ordination in Priesthood. *First
performed:* June 13, 1946. Hampartzoum
Berberian, conductor.
Music: Catholicosate of Cilicia,
Lebanon, 1950.
Parts: available from composer.
Vocal score: Nahmad, 1958. *Reels.*

B3.4 Armenian Maiden. (1938) 3' 30"
For: voice and piano. *Text:* Kamar
Katiba. *First performed:* 1938; Aleppo,
Syria. Serpouhie Berberian, soprano,
and unidentified pianist.
Score: Editions Hamber, 1938.
Reel: available from composer.

B3.5 Ascension Day (Hoy Nar). (1935) 8'
For: chorus(SATB) and
orchestra(2(&pic)-2-2-2; 0-1-1-0; timp,
perc; str). 2 movements. *Text:* Father
H.P. Sarhadian. *First performed:* May
1935; Aleppo, Syria. Nayiri Choral
Group and Nayiri Orchestra,
Hampartzoum Berberian, conductor.
Parts: available from composer.
Vocal score: in *Nayirian Choral*, A.G.B.U.
Zareh Noubar Cultural Fund, 1958. *Reel.*

[Ballade, Chorus and Orchestra]
B3.6 Ballade. (1931) 9' 30"
For: chorus(SATB) and
orchestra(2(&pic)-2(&Ehn)-2-2; 3-3-2-0;
timp, perc; hp, str). 2 movements. *Text:*
Yeghishe Charentz. *First performed:*
1933; Beirut, Lebanon. Hampartzoum
Berberian, conductor.
Parts: available from composer.
Vocal score: Nahmad, 1958. *Reel.*

[Ballade, Voice and Piano]
B3.7 Ballade. (1943) 6'
1 movement. *Text:* Azat Vshdouni. *First
performed:* 1943; Aleppo, Syria.
Serpouhie Berberian, soprano, and
unidentified pianist.
Score: Editions Hamber, 1948. *Reel.*

B3.8 The Beautiful Peasant. (1929) 5'
30"
For: chorus(SATB) and piano. 2

movements. *Text:* Father H.P. Sarhadian.
First performed: 1929; Athens, Greece.
Nayiri Choral Group, Hampartzoum
Berberian, conductor.
Vocal score: Editions Hamber, 1932.
Reel.

B3.9 Bejingo. (1935) 5′
For: chorus(SATB). 1 movement. *Text:*
Tchitouni. *First performed:* 1935;
Aleppo, Syria. Nayiri Choral Group,
Hampartzoum Berberian, conductor.
Vocal score: ms. in composer's hand.
Reel.

B3.10 The Birth of Vahakn. (1971) 4′
30″
For: chorus(SATB) and orchestra(1-1-1-1;
0-1-0-0; timp, perc; str). 1 movement.
Text: Zareh Melkonian. *First performed:*
1972; Detroit, Mich. Vahakn Choral
Group.
Music: ms. in composer's hand.
Reel: Hampartzoum Berberian,
conductor.

B3.11 The Blond Maiden. (1936) 4′
For: voice and piano. *Text:* Naghash
Hovnatan. *First performed:* 1936; St.
Joseph University, Beirut, Lebanon.
Emanuel Elmadjian, tenor, and
unidentified pianist.
Score: Editions Hamber, 1936. *Reel.*

B3.12 Caprice. (1926) 6′ 30″
For: violin and piano. 1 movement.
First performed: June 19, 1927; Athens,
Greece. Hampartzoum Berberian, violin
and Maro Manoukian, piano.
Music: ms. in composer's hand.

B3.13 Concerto for Violin and
Orchestra. (1950) 36′
For: violin and
orchestra(2(&pic)-2(&Ehn)-2(&bcl)-2;
4-3-1-1; timp, perc, xylo; hp; str). 3
movements. *Dedication:* To my son
Hratch. *First performed:* Feb. 16, 1951;
American University, Beirut, Lebanon.
Hratch Berberian, violin. *Parts.*
Pf. red & part: Berberian Music

Publication Committee, 1974. HU NEC
Reel.

B3.14 Concerto for Violoncello and
Orchestra. (1949) 34′
For: violoncello and
orchestra(2(&pic)-2(&Ehn)-2(&bcl)-2;
4-3-1-1; timp, perc, xylo; hp; str). 3
movements. *Dedication:* To my son
Vahe. *First performed:* Apr. 30, 1950;
American University, Beirut, Lebanon.
Vahe Berberian, violoncello. *Parts.*
Pf. red & part: A.G.B.U. Alex
Manoogian Cultural Fund, 1975. *Reel.*

B3.15 The Cross. (1948) 5′
For: chorus(SATB). 1 movement. *Text:*
Yeghishe Tourian. *First performed:*
1948; Antelias, Lebanon.
Antelias-Armenian Seminary Chorus,
Hampartzoum Berberian, conductor.
Vocal score: ms. in composer's hand.

B3.16 Dance. (1934) 8′
For: violin, violoncello, piano. 1
movement. *First performed:* Oct. 7,
1934; American University, Beirut,
Lebanon. Onnig Surmelian, violin; Vahe
Berberian, violoncello; Michelle
Tcheskinoff, piano.
Music: ms. in composer's hand.

B3.17 Dance. (1940) 9′
For: violin, violoncello, piano. 1
movement. *First performed:* Apr. 8,
1943; American Univeristy, Beirut,
Lebanon. Hratch Berberian, violin; Vahe
Berberian, violoncello; Michelle
Tcheskinoff, piano.
Music: ms. in composer's hand.

[Dance rustique, Piano]
B3.18 Dance rustique. (1936) 7′ 30″
2 movements. *First performed:* London,
England. Philip Colman.
Score: ms. in composer's hand.

[Dance rustique, Violin and Piano]
B3.19 Dance rustique. (1936) 8′ 30″
1 movement. *First performed:* Apr.
1940; American University, Beirut,
Lebanon. Hratch Berberian, violin and

Michelle Tcheskinoff, piano.
Score: ms. in composer's hand. *Reel.*

B3.20 Dances of Van. (1928) 6' 30"
For: chorus(SATB) and orchestra(1-1-1-1;
2-0-0-0; timp, perc; str). 2 movements.
First performed: 1928; Athens, Greece.
Nayiri Choral Group and Nayiri
Orchestra, Hampartzoum Berberian,
conductor.
Music: ms. in composer's hand. *Reel.*

B3.21 Dolavo. (1930) 7'
For: Tenor and chorus(SATB). 1
movement. *Text:* Tchitouni. *First
performed:* 1931; Nicosia, Cyprus.
Hampartzoum Berberian, conductor.
Music: ms. in composer's hand. *Reel.*

Fete rustique. *See* Maralo: Fete rustique.

B3.22 Golden Dream. (1931) 5'
For: Soprano, Tenor, piano. 2
movements. *Text:* Mihran Damadian.
First performed: American University,
Beirut, Lebanon. Serpouhie Berberian,
soprano; Emanuel Elmadjian, tenor;
unidentified pianist.
Music: Editions Hamber, 1931. *Reel.*

Hoy Nar. *See* Ascension Day (Hoy Nar).

B3.23 Introduction and Variation. (1932)
9' 30"
For: violin and piano. 2 movements.
First performed: Dec. 15, 1932; Nicosia,
Cyprus. Hampartzoum Berberian, violin
and Eleni Atanasiadis, piano.
Music: ms. in composer's hand. *Reel.*

B3.24 It Is Raining My Son. (1932) 5'
For: voice and piano. *Text:* Vahan
Tekeyan. *First performed:* 1932;
American University, Beirut, Lebanon.
Serpouhie Berberian, soprano, and
unidentified pianist.
Score: Editions Hamber, 1933.
Reel: available from composer.

B3.25 Lamp of the Illuminator. (1935) 6'
30"
For: Soprano, chorus(SATB),
orchestra(2(&pic)-2-2-2; 2-0-0-0; timp,

perc; hp; str). 2 movements. *Text:*
Hovhannes Toumanian. *First performed:*
Mar. 1935; Aleppo, Syria. Serpouhie
Berberian, soprano, and others.
Vocal score: in *Nayirian Songs*, Editions
Hamber, 1954. *Reel.*

B3.26 Love. (1950) 5'
For: voice and piano. 1 movement.
Text: Zareh Melkonian. *First performed:*
1972; Detroit, Mich. Violet Tcholakian,
soprano, and unidentified pianist.
Score: ms. in composer's hand. *Reel.*

B3.27 Love Song. (1979) 5' 30"
For: Soprano, Tenor, piano. *Text:* Sylva
Gaboudikian.
Score: ms. in composer's hand.

B3.28 The Loveliest of Roses. (1970) 7'
30"
For: Mezzo Soprano, chorus(SATB),
orchestra(1-1-1-1; 0-1-0-0; timp; str). 2
movements. *Text:* traditional. *First
performed:* Nov. 15, 1970; Carnegie
Hall, New York City. Antranig Choral
Group and Antranig Orchestra,
Hampartzoum Berberian, conductor.
Vocal score: Erevan Choral Society,
1980. *Reel.*

B3.29 Lullaby. (1949) 8' 30"
For: violoncello and piano. 1
movement. *First performed:* June 9,
1950; American University, Beirut,
Lebanon. Vahe Berberian, violoncello
and Michelle Tcheskinoff, piano.
Score: ms. in composer's hand.

B3.30 Maiden of the Hills. (1927) 5' 30"
For: chorus and piano. 2 movements.
Text: Father H.P. Sarhadian. *First
performed:* 1927; Athens, Greece. Nayiri
Choral Group, Hampartzoum Berberian,
conductor.
Music: Editions Hamber, 1933. *Reel.*

B3.31 Maralo: Fete rustique. (1933) 8'
For: chorus(SATB). 2 movements. *First
performed:* 1933; American University,
Beirut, Lebanon.
Vocal score: ms. in composer's hand.
Reel.

B3.32 My Heart. (1937) 4'
For: voice and piano. *Text:* H. Arekentz.
First performed: 1943; Aleppo, Syria.
Aghavni Guibinian, soprano, and
unidentified pianist.
Score: Editions Hamber, 1937.

B3.33 Native Village. (1947) 8' 30"
For: Soprano and piano. *Text:*
Yeghivart. *First performed:* Nov. 1947;
American University, Beirut, Lebanon.
Serpouhie Berberian, soprano, and
unidentified pianist.
Score: in *Nayirian Songs*, Editions
Hamber, 1954. *Reel.*

B3.34 Ode to Antranig, the Hero. (1979)
8'
For: Mezzo Soprano and
orchestra(2(&pic)-2(&Ehn)-2-2; 4-3-3-1;
timp, perc; str). 1 movement. *Text:*
Alexander Kludjian.
Music: ms. in composer's hand.

B3.35 Plough Song. (1940) 7'
For: chorus(SATB). 2 movements. *Text:*
Tchitouni. *First performed:* 1941;
Aleppo, Syria. Nayiri Choral Group.
Parts: available from composer.
Vocal score: in *Nayirian Choral*, A.G.B.U.
Zareh Noubar Cultural Fund, 1958.

B3.36 Prayer on the Threshhold of
Tomorrow. (1977) 23'
For: Mezzo Soprano, chorus(SATB),
orchestra(2(&pic)-2(&Ehn)-2-2; 2-3-3-0;
timp, perc; str). Cantata. 8 movements.
Text: Hayerkoutouin by Vahan Tekeyan.
First performed: Dec. 14, 1980; Holy
Trinity Armenian Church, Cambridge,
Mass. Yerevan Choral Society.
Parts: available from composer.
Vocal score: A.G.B.U. Alex Manoogian
Cultural Fund, 1978.
Cassette: recording of first
performance.

B3.37 Rejoice. (1963) 7'
For: piano. 1 movement.
Score: ms. in composer's hand.

B3.38 Rejoice O Mather. (1951) 4' 30"
For: Mezzo Sopano and piano. 1
movement. *Text:* Canticle. *First
performed:* 1951.
Score: Editions Hamber, 1962.
Reel: available from composer.

B3.39 Requiem Aeternam. (1972) 95'
For: chorus(SATB) and
orchestra(2(&pic)-2(&Ehn)-2-2; 4-3-3-1;
timp, perc; str). *Text:* Yeghishe
Charentz. *First performed:* Apr. 25,
1977; Detroit, Mich. Cantata Academy
of Metropolitan Detroit, Hampartzoum
Berberian, conductor.
Parts: available from composer. Rental.
Vocal score: Berberian Music Publishing
Committee, 1975. HU NEC
Reel: recording of first performance.
Cassette: recording of first
performance.

B3.40 Rivulet. (1945) 5'
For: chorus(SATB). 2 movements. *Text:*
V. Krikorian. *First performed:* 1945;
Aleppo, Syria. Nayiri Choral Group,
Hampartzoum Berberian, conductor.
Vocal score: ms. in composer's hand.
Reel.

B3.41 Sacrament of Vartanantz. (1951)
27'
For: Soprano, Alto, Tenor, Bass,
chorus(SATB),
orchestra(2(&pic)-2(&Ehn)-2-2; 4-3-3-1;
timp, perc; hp; str). Cantata. 4
movements. *Text: Hayerkoutouin* by
Vahan Tekeyan. *First performed:* Feb. 1,
1951; Antelias, Lebanon. Hampartzoum
Berberian, conductor.
Parts: available from composer.
Vocal score: Berberian Music Publication
Committee, 1974. HU NEC
Reel: recording of first performance.

B3.42 Sail. (1940) 7'
For: Soprano and piano. 1 movement.
Text: Antranik Dzarougian. *First
performed:* 1940; Aleppo, Syria.
Serpouhie Berberian, soprano, and
unidentified pianist.
Score: ms. in composer's hand. *Reel.*

B3.43 Sardarabad. (1972) 6'
For: chorus and orchestra(1-1-1-1;
0-1-1-0; timp, perc; str). March. 1
movement. *Text:* Barouir Sevag. *First
performed:* Dec. 1972; Carnegie Hall,
New York City. Antranig Choral Group
and Antranig Orchestra.
Music: ms. in composer's hand. *Tape.*

B3.44 Secret Love. (1931) 5' 30"
For: voice and piano. *Text:* Vahan
Tekeyan. *First performed:* 1931;
American University, Beirut, Lebanon.
Serpouhie Berberian, soprano, and
unidentified pianist.
Score: Editions Hamber, 1933.
Reel: available from composer.

B3.45 Serenade. (1931) 4'
For: voice and piano. 1 movement.
Text: Mihran Damadian. *First
performed:* 1932; Beirut, Lebanon.
Serpouhie Berberian, soprano, and
unidentified pianist.
Score: Editions Hamber, 1931.

B3.46 Shepherds Song. (1935) 6'
For: voice and piano. *Text:* Leylani.
First performed: 1936; Beirut, Lebanon.
Serpouhie Berberian, soprano, and
unidentified pianist.
Score: ms. in composer's hand.

B3.47 Shoghig. (1939) 135'
For: voices, chorus, orchestra. Opera in
4 acts. *Text:* Hovhannes Toumanian.
First performed: July 17, 1939; Aleppo,
Syria. Serpouhie Berberian, soprano,
and others.
Score & parts: ms. in composer's hand.
Vocal score: ms. in composer's hand.

B3.48 Song of the Pilgrim. (1924) 4'
30"
For: chorus(SATB) and piano. 1
movement. *First performed:* 1924;
Athens, Greece.
Vocal score: ms. in composer's hand.

B3.49 Song of the Troubadour. (1933)
5'
For: voice and piano. *Text:* Kaspar
Ipekian. *First performed:* Nov. 1933;

Beirut, Lebanon. Serpouhie Berberian,
soprano, and unidentified pianist.
Score: in *Nayirian Songs*, Editions
Hamber, 1954.

B3.50 Song of Troubadour. (1971) 8'
For: voice and piano. *Text:* Sylva
Gaboudikian. *First performed:* Dec. 2,
1973; Town Hall, New York City.
Score: ms. in composer's hand. Tape.

[Songs for Elementary and High
School Students]
B3.51 Fifty-six Songs for Elementary
and High School Students. (1953-60)
For: chorus(unison).
Vocal score: ms. in composer's hand.

[Songs for Kindergarten]
B3.52 Twenty Songs for Kindergarden.
(1953-60)
For: chorus(unison).
Vocal score: ms. in composer's hand.

[Songs of the Troubadour]
B3.53 Eight Songs of the Troubadour.
(1947) 38'
For: voice and piano. *Text:* Sayat-Nova.
First performed: Apr. 1948; Beirut,
Lebanon.
Score: (printed in Lebanon).
Reel: available from composer.

B3.54 Souvenir. (1926) 5'
For: violin and piano. 1 movement.
First performed: June 19, 1927; Athens,
Greece. Hampartzoum Berberian, violin
and Maro Manoukian, piano.
Score: ms. in composer's hand.

B3.55 Surmeli Djan. (1970) 8'
For: chorus(SATB) and orchestra(2-2-2-2;
1-1-1-0; timp, perc; str). 2 movements.
Text: traditional. *First performed:* Nov.
15, 1970; Carnegie Hall, New York City.
Antranig Choral Group and Antranig
Orchestra, Hampartzoum Berberian,
conductor.
Music: ms. in composer's hand. *Tape.*

B3.56 Teeter. (1934) 95'
For: voices, chorus, orchestra. Opera in
3 acts. *Text: The Child in the Nature*

and *The Butterfly of the Village* by Peniamin Jirair. *First performed:* May 5, 1934; Beirut, Lebanon.
Score & parts: ms. in composer's hand.
Vocal score: ms. in composer's hand. *Reel.*
Cassette: recording of first performance.

B3.57 To Her. (1926) 4′
For: voice and piano. Song. *Text:* Tlgadentzi. *First performed:* 1933; Athens, Greece. Serpouhie Berberian, soprano, and unidentified pianist.
Score: Editions Hamber, 1933.
Reel: available from composer.

B3.58 To My Varoujnag. (1935) 4′
For: voice and piano. 1 movement. *Text:* Daniel Varoujan. *First performed:* Feb. 1935; Aleppo, Syria. Serpouhie Berberian, soprano, and unidentified pianist.
Score: in *Nayirian Songs*, Editions Hamber, 1954.

B3.59 Winds of the Emerald Hills. (1939) 4′
For: voice and piano. *Text:* Hovhannes Shiraz. *First performed:* Nov. 7, 1939; Serpouhie Berberian, soprano and unidentified pianist.
Score: in *Nayirian Songs*, Editions Hamber, 1954.
Tape: available from composer.

B3.60 The Wine. (1962) 5′ 30″
For: voice and piano. 1 movement. *Text:* Hovhannes Shiraz. *First performed:* 1967; Montreal, Canada. Edmond Bezazian, baritone, and unidentified pianist.
Score: ms. in composer's hand. *Tape.*

B3.61 Words to My Son. (1951) 8′ 30″
For: chorus(SATB) and orchestra(2(&pic)-2(&Ehn)-2-2; 2-3-2-0; timp, perc; str). 2 movements. *Text:* Sylva Gaboudikian. *First performed:* Mar. 12, 1951; American University, Beirut, Lebanon. Hampartzoum Berberian, conductor.

Parts: available from composer.
Vocal score: in *Nayirian Choral*, A.G.B.U. Zareh Noubar Cultural Fund, 1958. *Reel.*

B3.62 Your Eyes. (1934) 3′ 30″
For: voice and piano. *Text:* Sybil. *First performed:* 1934; Beirut, Lebanon.
Score: Editions Hamber, 1934.
Reel: available from composer.

B3.63 Your Seven Sunlights. (1945) 4′ 30″
For: chorus(SATB). 1 movement. *Text:* Maro Markarian. *First performed:* 1945; Aleppo, Syria. Nayiri Choral Group, Hampartzoum Berberian, conductor.
Vocal score: ms. in composer's hand.

B3.64 Zil, Zil. (1970) 4′
For: voice and piano. 1 movement. *Text:* A. Khengoian. *First performed:* Dec. 2, 1973; Town Hall, New York City.
Score: ms. in composer's hand. *Reel.*

B4 ARTHUR VICTOR BERGER

Born May 15, 1912, in New York City. *Education:* studied composition with Vincent Jones (New York University, B.S., 1934); Walter Piston (Harvard University, M.A., 1936); Darius Milhaud, Nadia Boulanger (Paris, France, 1937-39). *Awards:* John Knowles Paine Travelling Fellowship (Harvard University, 1937-39), Fulbright Fellowship (1960), National Institute of Arts and Letters Award (1960), National Institute of Arts and Letters (member, 1972), Guggenheim Grant (1975-76), Council of Learned Societies Fellowship, Longy School of Music Fellowships. *Related activities:* music critic for *Boston Evening Transcript* (1934-37), *Sun* (New York, 1943-47), *New York Herald Tribune* (1946-53); editor of *The Musical Mercury* (1934-37), *Listen* (1943-44); co-founder of *Perspectives of New Music;* author of *Aaron Copland* (1953); contributor of articles to various journals; served on the faculties of Mills College (1939-41),

North Texas State Teachers College, Brooklyn College of The City University of New York, Juilliard School, Brandeis University (1953-80). BrU

WORKS

[Bagatelles]
B4.1 Three Bagatelles. (1946) 6'
For: piano. *Dedicated to:* Virgil Thomson. *First performed:* Feb. 20, 1948; WNYC-FM, New York City. Edmund Haines.
Score: E.B. Marks, 1948. BrU HU HUm
Disc: Decca DL 10.021, 1960. Sylvia Marlowe, harpsichord. BrU W

B4.2 Boo Hoo at the Zoo: Tails of Woe.
For: chorus(2-part). *Text:* Joyce Mullan.
Vocal score: Shawnee, 1978.

B4.3 Chamber Music for 13 Players. (1956) 9'-12'
For: instrumental ensemble(flute, oboe, clarinet, bassoon, horn, trumpet, harp, celeste, violins(2), viola, violoncello, double bass). *First performed:* Apr. 4, 1960; Los Angeles, Calif. Unidentified chamber ensemble, Robert Kraft, conductor.
Score & parts: Peters. Rental.
Disc: Columbia MS 6959, 1967. Columbia Chamber Ensemble, Gunther Schuller, conductor. BCM BU HU NEC
Disc: Composers Recordings CRI SD290, 1972. Reissue of Columbia MS 6959. BrU BU HU MIT NEC W

B4.4 Composition. (1976)
For: piano(4-hands).
Score: Association for the Promotion of New Music, 1977. BrU
Score: Mobart, 1980, NEC T
Reel: Oct. 15, 1979; Boston; Dinosaur Annex concert. Scott Wheeler and Rodney Lister. WGBH

[Concerto, Chamber Orchestra]
B4.5 Chamber Concerto. (1959; rev. 1978)
For: orchestra(2(pic)-1-1-1; 1-1-0-0; perc,

glock; hp; cel, pf; str(no 2nd vlns)). 2 movements. *Commissioned by:* Fromm Foundation. *First performed:* May 13, 1962; New York City. Unidentified orchestra, Ralph Shapey, conductor. Revised version (incorporates 1969 revision titled Movement) first performed: Apr. 12, 1979; New York City. Manticae Chamber Orchestra, Thomas James, conductor.
Score: Bomart, 1979. BrU HU NEC
Parts: Bomart.

B4.6 Duo for Oboe and Clarinet. (1952) 8'
1 movement. Commissioned for Locust Valley Festival, Long Island, N.Y. *First performed:* Sept. 7, 1952; Long Island, N.Y.; Locust Valley Festival. William Arrowsmith, oboe and David Glazer, clarinet.
Score: Peters, 1955. BPL BrU HU MIT T

[Duo, Oboe and Clarinet; Arr.]
B4.7 Duo. (1957) 8'
For: clarinet and piano. *First performed:* June 2, 1957; Brandeis University. David Wood, clarinet and Martin Boykan, piano.
Score & part: Henmar, 1979. BrU

[Duo, Violin and Piano, No. 1]
B4.8 Duo No. 1. (1948) 13'
First performed: Oct. 22, 1949; Town Hall, New York City. Joseph Fuchs, violin and Leo Smit, piano.
Score: Association for the Promotion of New Music. BrU
Score: American Composers Alliance.
Score: Boelke-Bomart, 1976. T
Reel: Oct. 15, 1979; Boston; Dinosaur Annex concert. Janet Packer, violin and Scott Wheeler, piano. WGBH

[Duo, Violin and Piano, No. 2]
B4.9 Duo No. 2. (1950) 12'
First performed: Oct. 19, 1951; Town Hall, New York City. Fredell Lack [violin?].
Score: Association for the Promotion of New Music. BU
Score: Boelke-Bomart, 1977. NEC T
Part: Boelke-Bomart, 1979. NEC

Disc: in *Music for a Twentieth Century Violinist,* Desto DC 6435-6437, 1974. Paul Zukofsky, violin and Gilbert Kalish, piano. BU HU NEC W

[Duo, Violoncello and Piano]
B4.10 Duo for 'Cello and Piano. (1951) 10'-12'
2 movements. *Commissioned by:* League of Composers for Lado. *First performed:* Nov. 17, 1952; Town Hall, New York City. Bernard Greenhouse, violoncello and Anthony Makas, piano.
Score: American Composers Alliance.
Score: Association for the Promotion of New Music. BrU
Disc: Columbia ML 4846, 1954. Bernard Greenhouse, violoncello and Anthony Makas, piano. BrU BU HU W
Disc: Columbia AML 4846. Reissue of Columbia ML 4846.
Reel: Oct. 15, 1979; Boston; Dinosaur Annex concert. Thomas Flaherty, violoncello and Rodney Lister, piano. WGBH

B4.11 Entertainment Piece. (1940)
For: dancers(3) and piano. Ballet.

[Episodes]
B4.12 Two Episodes. (1933) 4'
For: piano.
Score: Lawson-Gould.
Disc: in *New Music for Piano,* RCA Victor LM 7042, 1966. Robert Helps. MIT W
Disc: in *New Music for Piano,* Composers Recordings CRI SD 288, 1972. Reissue of RCA Victor LM 7042. BCM BrU MIT NEC NU W

B4.13 Fantasy. (1942) 6'
For: piano. *First performed:* Mar. 13, 1949; New York City. Harvey Siegel.
Score: American Composers Alliance.

B4.14 Garlands. (1945) 2'
For: voice (medium) and piano.
Score: American Composers Alliance.

B4.15 Ideas of Order. (1952) 12'
For: orchestra(2(&pic)-2-2(&bcl)-2;

2-2-2-0; timp; hp; str). 1 movement.
Commissioned by and dedicated to: Dimitri Mitropoulos. *First performed:* Apr. 11, 1953; Carnegie Hall, New York City. New York Philharmonic, Dimitri Mitropoulos, conductor.
Score & parts: Peters. Rental.
Study score: Peters, 1956. BPL BrU BU HU NEC
Disc: Jan. 22, 1954; Symphony Hall, Boston. Boston Symphony Orchestra, Charles Munch, conductor. MIT
Cassette: Oct. 19, 1972; New England Conservatory. NEC Symphony Orchestra, Gunther Schuller, conductor. NEC

B4.16 Intermezzo. 2' 5"
For: harpsichord.
Score: in *American Composers of Today,* E.B. Marks, 1965. NEC
Disc: Decca DL 10.021, 1960. Sylvia Marlow. BrU W

[Inventions, One-Part, Piano]
B4.17 Three One-Part Inventions. (1954) 10'
Dedicated to: Charles Rosen and Jacques Monod. *First performed:* Oct. 16, 1954; Town Hall, New York City. Charles Rosen.
Score: American Composers Alliance.
Score: Bomart. BrU HU
Cassette: Nov. 22, 1976; New Conservatory. Russell Sherman. NEC

[Inventions, Two-Part, Piano]
B4.18 Four Two-Part Inventions. (1948-49) 10'
First performed: Feb. 6, 1951; Town Hall, New York City. Stanley Lock.
Score: American Composers Alliance.

Movement, 1969. *See* Concerto, Chamber Orchestra.

B4.19 Partita. (1947) 9'
For: piano. *Movements:* Prelude; Aria; Capriccio; Intermezzo; Serenade. Material of last movement from his Serenade for String Orchestra. *First performed:* Mar. 18, 1948; Sarah

Lawrence College. Leo Smit.
Score: American Composers Alliance.
Score: Bomart, 1980. MIT
Disc: in *American Music,* New Editions
NE 1, 195-. Bernhard Weiser. BrU HU
HUm NEC

[Pieces, Piano]
B4.20 Five Pieces. (1969) 13′ 30″
Dedicated to: Robert Miller. *First
performed:* Oct. 11, 1968; New York
City. Robert Miller.
Score: Peters, 1969. NEC
Score: Henmar, 1975. BrU HU
Disc: AR Deutsche Grammophon 0654
088, 1971. Robert Miller. BrU HU MIT
NEC W
Disc: New World NW 308, 1980.
Reissue of AR Deutsche Grammophon
0654 088. MIT T W

[Pieces, Pianos(2)]
B4.21 Three Pieces. (1961) 8′
For: pianos(prepared)(2). *First
performed:* Columbia University. Robert
Miller and Lawrence H. Smith.
Score: ms. in composer's hand (No. 2).
HUh
Score: Bomart, 1977. BrU BU
Disc: Columbia MS 6959, 1967. Paul
Jacobs and Gilbert Kalish. BCM BU HU
NEC
Disc: Composers Recordings CRI SD
290, 1972. Reissue of Columbia MS
6959. BrU BU HU MIT NEC W

[Pieces, String Orchestra]
B4.22 Three Pieces. (1945) 10′
Contents: Prelude; Aria; Waltz. *Dedicated
to:* Alexei Haieff, Charles Jones,
Donald Fuller, respectively. *First
performed:* Jan. 26, 1946; Town Hall,
New York City. American Chamber
Ensemble, Harold Kohon, conductor.
Score: Associated, 1950. BPL BU HU
Score: Bomart, 1978. BrU HU

[Pieces, String Quartet]
B4.23 Three Pieces. (1945) 10′
First performed: Mar. 3, 1946;
Washington, D.C. Gordon Quartet.
Music: Associated.

Poems of Yeats. *See* Words for Music,
Perhaps.

B4.24 Polyphony. (1956) 15′
For: orchestra(2(pic)-2(Ehn)-2(bcl)-2;
4-2-2-0; timp, perc; hp; cel; str).
Commissioned by: Louisville Orchestra.
First performed: Nov. 17, 1956;
Louisville, Ky. Louisville Orchestra,
Robert Whitney, conductor.
Score: American Composers Alliance.
Score: Mobart, 1976. BrU
Disc: Louisville Orchestra 58-4, 1958.
Louisville Orchestra, Robert Whitney,
conductor. BrU BU HU HUm NEC W

Psalm 92. *See* Tov l'hodos.

[Quartet, Strings]
B4.25 String Quartet. (1958) 25′
6 movements. *Dedicated to:* Eugene
Lehner. *First performed:* Jan. 26, 1962;
New York City. Lenox Quartet.
Score: American Composers Alliance.
Score: Bomart, 1978. BrU
Disc: Composers Recordings CRI 161,
1962. Lenox Quartet. BCM BrU BU HU
MIT NEC W

[Quartet, Woodwinds]
B4.26 Quartet in C Major. (1941) 10′
For: flute, oboe, clarinet, bassoon. 3
movements. *Commissioned by:* Pierre
Monteux for performance of first desk
players of the San Francisco
Symphony. *Dedicated to:* Aaron
Copland. *First performed:* Mar. 5, 1941;
Oakland, Calif. San Francisco
Woodwind Quintet.
Score: Arrow, 1946. BCM BrU HU NEC
Score: Peters, 1961. BU HU MIT W
Parts: Peters, 1961. HU MIT NEC T W
Study score: McGinnis & Marx.
Disc: Columbia ML 4846, 1954. Fairfield
Wind Ensemble. BrU BU HU W
Disc: in *The Avant Garde String Quartet
in the U.S.A.,* Vox SVBX 5307, 1977.
Dorian Quintet. BCM BU MIT NEC W
Reel: Oct. 31, 1977; Boston University.
Doriot Anthony Dwyer, flute; Ralph
Gomberg, oboe; Harold Wright, clarinet;
Sherman Walt, bassoon. BU
Cassette: Oct. 7, 1969; New England

Conservatory; in *An Evening of Contemporary Music*. Members of the NEC Scholarship Woodwind Quintet. NEC
Cassette: Oct. 27, 1975; New England Conservatory; in *Contemporary American Music for the Flute*. John Heiss, flute; Peggy Pearson, oboe; William Wrzesien, clarinet; Philip Long, bassoon. NEC *Cassettes*: [Various subsequent performances by students or faculty at New England Conservatoary.] NEC

B4.27 Rondo. (1945) 3'
For: piano. *First performed:* 1945; Town Hall, New York City. Reah Sadowsky.
Score: Merrymount, 1949. BrU HU
Score: Mercury.

B4.28 Septet. (1965-66) 12'
For: flute, clarinet, bassoon, violin, viola, violoncello, piano. *Commissioned by:* Elizabeth Sprague Coolidge. *First performed:* Nov. 25, 1966; Library of Congress, Washington, D.C. Contemporary Chamber Ensemble, Arthur Weisberg, conductor.
Score:˙Henmar, 1978. BrU MIT W
Parts: Peters, 1978. Rental.
Disc: AR Deutsche Grammophon 0654 088, 1971. Contemporary Chamber Ensemble, Arthur Weisberg, conductor. BrU HU MIT NEC W
Disc: New World NW 308, 1980. Reissue of AR Deutsche Grammophon 0654 088. MIT W
Reel: May 23, 1975. WGBH

B4.29 Serenade Concertante. (1944; rev. 1951) 9' 18"
For: violin, flute, oboe, clarinet, bassoon, chamber orchestra(0-0-0-0; 2-1-0-0; str). *Commissioned by:* Columbia Broadcasting System for introduction by Bernard Hermann in its *Introduction to Music* series. *First performed:* Oct. 24, 1945; Rochester, N.Y. Unidentified orchestra, Howard Hanson, conductor.

Score & parts: Peters. Rental.
Study score: Peters, 1958. BPL BrU BU HU NEC UMB
Disc: MGM E 3245, 1957. Brandeis Festival Orchestra, Izler Solomon, conductor. BCM BU HU NEC
Disc: Composers Recordings CRI 143, 1961. Reissue of MGM E 3245. BrU BU HU MIT NEC W

Serenade for String Orchestra. *See* Partita.

[Songs]
B4.30 Five Songs for Tenor and Piano. (1979)
Contents: Ode (Horace); Sonnet (Rainer Maria Rilke); Le bois amical (Paul Valery); Piazza Novona Giuseppe Belli); When I am Dead (Christina Georgina Rossetti). *Dedicated to:* Ellen [Berger] *First performed:* May 4, 1980; Sanders Theatre, Harvard University; Fromm Foundation concert. Paul Sperry, tenor and Margo Garrett, piano.

Tails of Woe. *See* Boo Hoo at the Zoo.

B4.31 Tov l'hodos. (1946)
For: chorus(SATB). *Text:* Bible, O.T., Psalm 92.
Vocal score: A. Berger, 1951. BrU
Vocal score: G. Schirmer, 1951. BrU
Cassette: May 7, 1971; New England Conservatory; in *A Festival of New England Composers, Past and Present*. NEC Chorus, Lorna Cook Varon, conductor. NEC

B4.32 Trio for Guitar, Violin, Piano. (1972)
1 movement. *First performed:* [April 23, 1973?]; Brandeis University. Stanley Silverman, guitar; Jeanne Benjamin, violin; Robert Miller, piano.
Score: Bomart, 1974. BPL BrU HU MIT

[Trio,Violin, Violoncello, Piano]
B4.33 Trio for Violin, Cello & Piano. (1980)

B4.34 Words for Music, Perhaps. (1940)
7'
For: Soprano or Mezzo Soprano and
piano. *Text: Words for Music, Perhaps*
by William Butler Yeats. *Contents:*
Crazy Jane on the Day of
Judgement; His Confidence; Girl's Song.
Dedicated to: Esther. *First performed:*
Mar. 20, 1941; San Francisco, Calif.;
Composers Forum. Esther Berger,
singer.
Score: American Composers Alliance.

[Words for Music, Perhaps; Arr.]
B4.35 Words for Music, Perhaps. (1940)
7'
For: Soprano or Mezzo Soprano, flute,
clarinet, violoncello. *Text: Words for
Music, Perhaps* by William Butler Yeats.
Contents: Crazy Jane on the Day of
Judgement; His Confidence;
Girl's Song. *First performed:* Sept.
1949; Saratoga Springs, N.Y.; Yaddo
Festival.
Score: reprod. of ms. HU
Score: New Music Edition, 1950. BrU
BU HU NEC W
Reel: Oct. 15, 1979; Boston; Dinosaur
Annex concert. Barbara Winchester,
soprano; Nan Washburn, flute; Diane
Heffner, clarinet; Thomas Flaherty,
violoncello. WGBH

B5 RAN BLAKE

Born April 20, 1935, in Springfield,
Mass. Moved to Boston area 1968.
Education: B.A. (Bard College, 1960);
Lenox School of Jazz (summers,
1957-60); Columbia University (1960-62);
studied composition and improvisation
with Ray Cassarino (1953-56), Willis
Laurence James (1957-60), Oscar
Peterson (1958), William J. Russo
(1960-62), Mary Lou Williams (1960-64),
Gunther Schuller (1960-67), Mal Waldron
(1962-63). *Related activities:* pianist;
arts critic for the *Bay State Banner*
1974-); advisor to the Massachusetts
Council on the Arts and Humanities
(1979-80); member of the faculty of
Hartford Conservatory (1972-75) and

New England Conservatory (1967-).
NEC

WORKS

B5.1 Aftermath. (1960) 1' 1"
For: piano. Third stream music. *First
performed:* June 14, 1960; Bard
College.
Score: in his *A Collection of Third
Stream Compositions*, Margun, 1979. NEC
Lead sheets: Margun, nyp.
Disc: in *Wende*, Owl Records OWL 05,
1977.
Cassette: Sept. 26, 1976; New England
Conservatory; in *Stoneciphering*. Ran
Blake. NEC

B5.2 Alderson Penitentiary. (1974) 5'
For: clarinet(bass) and piano. *First
performed:* Dec. 15, 1974. Bruce
Henderson, bass clarinet and Ran Blake,
piano.
Lead sheets: Margun, nyp.

B5.3 Alexander Panagoulis. (1980)
For: piano. *First performed:* June 16,
1980; Paris, France.
Lead sheets: Margun, nyp.

B5.4 All about Ronnie. 2' 30"
For: piano. After the work by Joe
Greene.
Disc: in *Breakthru*, Improvising Artists
IAI 373842, 1976. Ran Blake. MIT NEC

[All about Ronnie; Arr]
B5.5 All about Ronnie. 7' 16"
For: voice, harp, piano. After the work
by Joe Greene.
Cassette: Sept. 26, 1979; New England
Conservatory; in *Out of the Past*.
Dominque Eade, voice; Andrea Stern,
harp; Ran Blake, piano. NEC

B5.6 All or Nothing at All. 4' 25"
For: piano. After the work by Arthur
Altman.
Disc: in *The Blue Potato*, Milestone
MSP 9021, 1969 (date recorded). Ran
Blake. BU NEC

B5.7 All the Things You Are. 2′ 28″
For: piano. After the work by Jerome
Kern.
Disc: in *Breakthru*, Improvising Artists
IAI 373842, 1976. Ran Blake. MIT NEC

B5.8 Allende. (1979)
For: piano. *First performed:* May 1979;
Jordan Hall, Boston. Ran Blake. Earlier
improvisation titled Death of Allende
and the Massacre at Munich.
Music: Margun, nyp.
Disc: in *Portfolio of Ran Blake*, Owl
Records, nyp.
Cassette: Mar. 23, 1975; New England
Conservatory; in *Dreams, Duets,
Dualities* (earlier improvisation). NEC

B5.9 Alone Together. 3′ 21″
For: saxophone(tenor) and piano. After
the work by Arthur Schwartz.
Disc: in *Rapport*, Arista Novus AN
3006, 1978. Ricky Ford, tenor
saxophone and Ran Blake, piano. NEC

Amelia Lehrfield. *See* Personalities.

[Arline, Instrumental Ensemble]
B5.10 Arline. (1963) 6′ 10″
For: instrumental ensemble(flutes(2),
clarinets(2), saxophone(alto),
saxophone(tenor), saxophone(baritone),
trumpets(4), trombones(4), tuba,
percussion, piano, violoncellos(2),
double bass). Third stream music. Arr.
by Hankus Netsky for flute, clarinet,
saxophones(alto)(2), saxophones(tenor)(2),
saxophone(baritone), trumpets(4),
trombones(4), tuba, percussion, piano,
violoncellos(2), double bass. *First
performed:* Apr. 1963.
Lead sheets: MJQ (original version and
arrangement).
Disc: in *Third Stream Today*, Golden
Crest NEC 116, 1979 (arrangement).
Members of NEC Third Stream
Department, Hankus Netsky, conductor.
NEC T
Cassette: Mar. 23, 1975; New England
Conservatory; in *Dreams, Duets,
Dualities* (arrangement). Members of
NEC Third Stream Department, Hankus

Netsky, conductor. NEC
Cassette: Sept. 26, 1979; New England
Conservatory; in *Out of the Past*
(arrangement). Members of NEC Third
Stream Department, Hankus Netsky,
conductor. NEC

[Arline, Piano]
B5.11 Arline. (1963) 3′ 17″
Third stream music.
Score: MJQ, 1963.
Score: in his *A Collection of Third
Stream Compositions*, Margun, 1979. NEC
Disc: in *Wende*, Owl Records OWL 05,
1977.
Cassette: Mar. 23, 1975; New England
Conservatory; in *Dreams, Duets,
Dualities*. Betci Buchman. NEC
Cassette: Sept. 26, 1976; New England
Conservatory; in *Stoneciphering*. Ran
Blake. NEC

[Arline, Saxophone(Tenor) and Piano]
B5.12 Arline. (1963) 4′ 12″
Third stream music.
Disc: in *Rapport*, Arista Novus AN
3006, 1978. Ricky Ford, tenor
saxophone and Ran Blake, piano. NEC

B5.13 Awakening. (1979)
For: piano and orchestra. Written in
collaboration with Larry Livingston.
First performed: May 2, 1979; New
England Conservatory; in Portfolio of
Doktor Mabuse. Ran Blake, piano; NEC
Symphony Orchestra, Larry Livingston,
conductor.
Music: Margun, nyp.
Cassette: recording of first
performance.

B5.14 The Ballad of Hix Blewitt. 1′ 23″
For: piano. After the work by George
Russell.
Disc: in *Rapport*, Arista Novus AN
3006, 1978. Ran Blake. NEC

B5.15 Bella ciao. 2′ 27″
For: piano. Traditional.
Disc: in *The Blue Potato*, Milestone
MSP 9021, 1969 (date recorded). Ran
Blake. BU NEC

[Bella ciao; Arr.]
B5.16 Bella ciao.
For: voice and piano. Traditional.
Dedicated to: Charlie Caccamesi of the
Back Bay Shoes.
Cassette: Sept. 26, 1979; New England
Conservatory; in *Out of the Past*. Eleni
Odoni, voice and Ran Blake, piano.
NEC

B5.17 Biko. (1977) 1' 38"-2' 21"
For: piano. Third stream music. *First
performed:* Oct. 27, 1977; New England
Life Hall, Boston. Ran Blake.
Lead sheets: Margun, nyp.
Disc: in *Rapport*, Arista Novus AN
3006, 1978. Ran Blake. NEC
Disc: in *Take One; Third Stream Jazz*,
Golden Crest CRS 4176, 1978. Ran
Blake. NEC
Disc: in *Take Two; Third Stream Jazz*,
Golden Crest CRS 4177, 1978. Ran
Blake. NEC

B5.18 Billie Holiday. 5' 50"
For: piano.
Cassette: Dec. 15, 1974; New England
Conservatory; in *Deep Song; the
1945-50 Decca Repertoire of Billie
Holiday*. Ran Blake. NEC

Bird Blues. *See* Manhattan Memories.

B5.19 Birmingham, USA. (1963) 4' 25"
For: piano. *First performed:* Town Hall,
New York City. Ran Blake.
Lead sheets: Margun, nyp.
Cassette: ESP-Disk' 1011, 1965 (date
recorded). Ran Blake. NEC
Cassette: Sept. 26, 1979; New England
Conservatory; in *Out of the Past*. Ran
Blake. NEC

B5.20 Blue Gardenia. 6' 32"
For: saxophone(alto) and piano. After
the work by Bob Russell.
Disc: in *Film Noir*, Arista Novus AN
3019, 1980. Daryl Lowery, alto
saxophone and Ran Blake, piano. NEC

B5.21 Blue Monk. 4' 40"
For: voice and piano. After the work
by Thelonious Monk.

Cassette: in *The Newest Sound Around*,
RCA Victor LPM/LSP 2500, 1962. Jeanne
Lee, voice and Ran Blake, piano. NEC

B5.22 Blue Potato. (1959) 2' 36"
For: piano. Third stream music.
Lead sheets: MJQ, 1959.
Disc: in *The Blue Potato*, Milestone
MSP 9021, 1969. Ran Blake. BU NEC

[Blue Potato, Instrumental Ensemble]
B5.23 Blue Potato.
For: instrumental
ensemble(flutes(2)/piccolo, oboe,
clarinets(2), bassoons(2), trumpets(3),
trombones(2), tuba, drums). Third
stream ensemble. Arr. by Joshua
Pruden. *First performed:* 1960; Bard
College. Bard Jazz Lab.
Lead sheets: MJQ, 1959.
Cassette: Feb. 4, 1976; New England
Conservatory; in *Cross-Stylizations*.
Members of NEC Third Stream
Department, Hankus Netsky, conductor.
NEC

[Blue Potato, Percussion(3)]
B5.24 Blue Potato.
Third stream music. Arr. by Christopher
Rathbun.
Lead sheets: MJQ, 1959.
Cassette: Mar. 23, 1975; New England
Conservatory; in *Dreams, Duets,
Dualities*. Christopher Rathbun, Alex
Skorupski, Er Wu. NEC

Blue Power. *See* Police. Blue Power.

B5.25 Blues for Mary Lou. (1977)
For: piano. *First performed:* Oct. 27,
1977; New England Life Hall, Boston.
Ran Blake.
Lead sheets: Margun, nyp.

B5.26 Blues for Wheatleigh. (1962) 3'
8"
For: piano. *First performed:* Sept. 26,
1976; New England Conservatory; in
Stoneciphering. Ran Blake.
Music: MJQ.
Disc: in *Wende*, Owl Records OWL 05,
1977.

Cassette: recording of first performance. NEC

B5.27 Le Boucher. (1980) 1' 45"
For: piano.
Lead sheets: Margun, nyp.
Disc: in *Film Noir*, Arista Novus AN 3019, 1980. Ran Blake. NEC T

[Breakthru, Instrumental Ensemble]
B5.28 Breakthru.
For: instrumental ensemble(saxophones(5), trumpets(4), trombones(3), tuba, drums, piano, guitar, double bass). Third stream music. Arr. by Bruce Henderson.
Lead sheets: MJQ.
Cassette: Mar. 23, 1975; New England Conservatory; in *Dreams, Duets, Dualities.* Members of NEC Third Stream Department. NEC

[Breakthru, Instruments(8)]
B5.29 Breakthru.
For: clarinet, oboe, saxophones(2), trombone, piano, guitar, drums. Third stream music. Arr. by Anthony Coleman.
Cassette: Feb. 4, 1976; New England Conservatory; in *Cross-Stylizations.* Members of NEC Third Stream Department. NEC

[Breakthru, Piano]
B5.30 Breakthru. (1959) 4"
Third stream music. *First performed:* 1959; Lenox School of Jazz. Ran Blake.
Score: in his *A Collection of Third Stream Compositions*, Margun, 1979. NEC
Score: MJQ.
Disc: in *Breakthru*, Improvising Artists IAI 373842, 1976. Ran Blake. MIT NEC
Cassette: Feb. 4, 1976; New England Conservatory; in *Cross-Stylizations.* Jaki Byard. NEC
Cassette: Sept. 26, 1976; New England Conservatory; in *Stoneciphering.* Ran Blake. NEC

[Breakthru, Saxophone(Tenor) and Piano]
B5.31 Breakthru. (1959) 3'

Third stream music.
Lead sheets: MJQ.
Disc: in *Rapport*, Arista Novus AN 3006, 1978. Ricky Ford, tenor saxophone and Ran Blake, piano. NEC
Disc: in *Third Stream Today*, Golden Crest NEC 116, 1979. Ricky Ford, tenor saxophone and Ran Blake, piano. NEC T

[Breakthru, Voice and Piano]
B5.32 Breakthru. (1959)
Third stream music. *Text:* Marty Yaseen.
Cassette: Feb. 4, 1976; New England Conservatory; in *Cross-Stylizations.* Marty Yaseen, voice and Ran Blake, piano. NEC

B5.33 Brindle. (1971) 1' 25"
For: piano. *First performed:* Apr. 20, 1966; Columbia University. Ran Blake.
Lead sheets: Margun, nyp.
Disc: in *Realization of a Dream*, Owl Records OWL 012, 1978.

Cadillac Joe. *See* Personalities. Cadillac Joe.

B5.34 Cancao do sol.
For: voice and piano. After the work by Milton Nascimento.
Cassette: Sept. 26, 1979; New England Conservatory; in *Out of the Past.* Eleni Odoni, voice and Ran Blake, piano. NEC

B5.35 El Cant dels ocells.
For: voice and piano. Traditional.
Cassette: Sept. 26, 1979; New England Conservatory; in *Out of the Past.* Eleni Odoni, voice and Ran Blake, piano. NEC

B5.36 Cart and Riders. (1964) 2' 15"
For: piano. *First performed:* 1964. Ran Blake.
Lead sheets: Margun, nyp.
Disc: in *Portfolio of Ran Blake*, Owl Records, nyp.

B5.37 Charles Caccamesi. (1979)
For: piano. *First performed:* Oct. 11,

1979; Bismarck Junior College.
Lead sheets: Margun, nyp.

B5.38 Chicken Monster. (1964) 2' 15"
For: piano. *First performed:* Apr. 26,
1970; Old West Church, Boston.
Lead sheets: Margun, nyp.
Disc: in *Portfolio of Ran Blake*, Owl
Records, nyp.

B5.39 Chicago. 3' 45"
For: piano. After the work by Fred
Fisher.
Disc: in *The Blue Potato*, Milestone
MSP 9021, 1969 (date recorded). Ran
Blake. BU NEC

B5.40 Chowder Society. (1981) 5'
For: piano. *First performed:* Feb. 20,
1981; Church of the Covenant, Boston.
Ran Blake.
Lead sheets: Margun, nyp.
Cassette: recording of first
performance.

B5.41 Chromatics. (1981) 8' 30"
For: pianos(2). Written in collaboration
with Jaki Byard. *First performed:* 1981;
Verona, Italy. Ran Blake and Jaki
Byard.
Lead sheets: Margun, nyp.
Disc: in *Ran Blake/Jaki Byard Duo*; Soul
Note SN 1022, 1981. Ran Blake and
Jaki Byard.
Cassette: May 1981; Verona, Italy. Ran
Blake and Jaki Byard.

Church on Russell Street. *See* Church
on Wooster Street.

[Church on Wooster Street, Piano]
B5.42 Church on Wooster Street. (1959)
3' 12"
Written for the Church of God in
Christ, Hartford, Conn. *First performed:*
1959; Lenox School of Jazz. Originally
titled Church on Russell Street.
Score: MJQ, 1959.
Disc: in *The Newest Sound Around*, RCA
LPM/LSP 2500, 1962 (titled Church on
Russell Street). Ran Blake. NEC

[Church on Wooster Street, Piano,
Guitar, Drums]
B5.43 Church on Wooster Street. (1959)
Cassette: Sept. 26, 1979; New England
Conservatory; in *Out of the Past*. Ran
Blake, piano; Paul Meyers, guitar; Jon
Hazilla, drums. NEC

B5.44 Claude Chabrol. (1979)
For: piano. *First performed:* Oct. 12,
1979; Northwestern University. Ran
Blake.
Lead sheets: Margun, nyp.

B5.45 Crystal Trip. 6' 15"
For: piano. *First performed:* Feb. 22,
1966; New York City. Ran Blake.
Lead sheets: Margun.
Disc: in *Crystal Trip*, Horo Records
H206, 1977. Ran Blake.

B5.46 Curtis. (1979)
For: electric bass, piano, drums, or
piano. *First performed:* Sept 26, 1979;
New England Conservatory; in Out of
the Past. Paul Meyers, electric bass;
Ran Blake, piano; Jon Hazilla, drums.
Lead sheets: Margun, 1979 (version for
piano).
Cassette: recording of first
performance. NEC

Darryl Williams. *See* Suite for Darryl
Williams and Shirley Simmons.

Death of Allende and the Massacre at
Munich. *See* Allende.

[Death of Edith Piaf, Piano]
B5.47 Death of Edith Piaf. (1977) 7' 20"
First performed: Nov. 19, 1977;
Philadelphia, Pa. Ran Blake.
Lead sheets: Margun, nyp.
Disc: in *Realization of a Dream*, Owl
Records OWL 012, 1978.

[Death of Edith Piaf, Voice and
Piano]
B5.48 Death of Edith Piaf.
Cassette: Sept. 26, 1979; New England
Conservatory; in *Out of the Past*. Eleni
Odoni, voice and Ran Blake, piano.
NEC

B5.49 Death Therapy. (1979)
For: piano. *First performed:* Nov. 4,
1979. Jonathan Swift's Pub, Cambridge,
Mass.
Lead sheets: Margun, nyp.

B5.50 Deathwatch. (1976)
For: piano. *First performed:* Sept. 26,
1976; New England Conservatory; in
Stoneciphering. Ran Blake.
Lead sheets: Margun, nyp.
Cassette: recording of first
performance. NEC

B5.51 Doktor Mabuse. (1978) 4' 7"
For: piano and drums. *First performed:*
June 6, 1978; Bogota, Columbia.
Lead sheets: Margun, nyp.
Disc: in *Film Noir*, Arista Novus AN
3019, 1980. Ran Blake, piano and
George Schuller, drums. NEC T

B5.52 Duke Dreams. (1981)
For: piano. *First performed:* May 29,
1981; Padua, Italy. Ran Blake.
Lead sheets: Margun, nyp.
Disc: in *Duke Dreams:
Ellington/Strayhorn Legacy*, Soul Note
SN 1027, 1981. Ran Blake.

B5.53 East Wind. (1958) 3' 10"
For: piano. Third stream music. *First
performed:* June 14, 1960; Bard
College. Ran Blake.
Score: in his *A Collection of Third
Stream Compositions*, Margun, 1979. NEC
Lead sheets: Margun, nyp.
Disc: in *Wende*, Owl Records OWL 05,
1977.

B5.54 Elwyn Avery. (1979)
For: clarinet, trombone, piano.
Cassette: Sept. 26, 1979; New England
Conservatory; in *Out of the Past*. John
Wulp, clarinet; Daniel Walker,
trombone; Ran Blake, piano. NEC

B5.55 Epilogue.
For: oboe.
Cassette: Feb. 4, 1976; New England
Conservatory; in *Cross-Stylizations*.
Hankus Netsky. NEC

B5.56 Epistrophy Blues. (1976)
For: piano. *First performed:* Nov. 19,
1977; Philadelphia, Pa. Ran Blake.
Lead sheets: Margun, [1979?].

B5.57 Eric. (1964) 3' 20"
For: piano. *First performed:* Sept. 20,
1964; Town Hall, New York City.
Lead sheets: Margun, nyp.
Disc: ESP-Disk' 1011, 1965 (date
recorded). Ran Blake. NEC

B5.58 Eve. 3' 20"
For: piano. After the music by Alfred
Newman for the film, *All about Eve*.
Disc: in *Film Noir*, Arista Novus AN
3019, 1980. Ran Blake. NEC

B5.59 Evil Blues. 3' 4"
For: voice and piano.
Cassette: in *The Newest Sound Around*,
RCA Victor LPM/LSP 2500, 1962. Jeanne
Lee, voice and Ran Blake, piano. NEC

B5.60 Ezz-thetic. 7' 14"
For: guitar, drums, piano. After the
work by George Russell.
Cassette: Sept. 26, 1979; New England
Conservatory; in *Out of the Past*. Paul
Meyers, guitar; Jon Hazilla, drums; Ran
Blake, piano. NEC

B5.61 Fables of Faubus. 3' 27"
For: piano. After the work by Charlie
Mingus.
Disc: in *The Blue Potato*, Milestone
MSP 9021, 1969 (date recorded). Ran
Blake. BU NEC

B5.62 Falanga. (1968) 40"
For: piano. *First performed:* June 28,
1968; Chicago, Ill. Ran Blake.
Lead sheets: Margun.
Disc: in *Crystal Trip*, Horo Records
H206, 1977. Ran Blake.

B5.63 Field Cry. (1957) 1' 45"
For: piano. Third stream music. *First
performed:* June 14, 1960; Bard
College. Ran Blake.
Score: in his *A Collection of Third
Stream Compositions*, Margun, 1979. NEC

Disc: in *Wende*, Owl Records OWL 05, 1976.

B5.64 Florence De Lannoy. (1976) 9'
For: piano. *First performed:* Sept. 15, 1976; Boston Center for Adult Education. Ran Blake.
Lead sheets: Margun.
Disc: in *Realization of a Dream*, Owl Records OWL 012, 1978.
Cassette: Sept. 26, 1976; New England Conservatory; in *Stoneciphering*. Ran Blake. NEC

B5.65 Floriano. (1977) 2' 10"
For: piano. *First performed:* June 18, 1977; Rome, Italy. Ran Blake.
Lead sheets: Margun, nyp.
Disc: in *Crystal Trip*, Horo Records H 206, 1977. Ran Blake.

B5.66 Frog Fountain and Aunt Jane. (1980) 2' 10"
For: piano. *First performed:* 1980; Paris, France. Ran Blake.
Lead sheets: Margun, nyp.
Disc: in *Portfolio of Ran Blake*, Owl Records, nyp.

B5.67 Garden of Delight. (1980) 2' 47"
For: trumpet and piano.
Lead sheets: Margun, nyp.
Disc: in *Film Noir*, Arista Novus AN 3019, 1980. Ran Blake, piano and Ted Curson, trumpet. NEC T

B5.68 Garvey's Ghost. 2' 16"
For: piano. After the work by Max Roach.
Disc: in *The Blue Potato*, Milestone MSP 9021, 1969 (date recorded). Ran Blake. BU NEC

B5.69 Glaciation. (1964) 55"
For: piano. *First performed:* Feb. 18, 1964; New York City. Ran Blake.
Lead sheets: Margun, nyp.
Disc: in *Open City*, Horo Records HDP 7-8, 1977.

B5.70 Go. (1956)
For: piano or third stream group. *First performed:* Nov. 22, 1957; Bard College.

Ran Blake, piano, and others.
Lead sheets: MJQ, 1956.

B5.71 God Bless the Child. 3' 47"
For: piano. After the work by Billie Holiday.
Disc: in *The Blue Potato*, Milestone MSP 9021, 1969 (date recorded). Ran Blake. BU NEC

B5.72 Good Mornin' Heartache. 3' 30"
For: piano. After the work by Irene Higginbotham.
Cassette: ESP-Disk' 1011, 1965 (date recorded). Ran Blake. NEC

B5.73 Green Ribbon.
Lead sheets: Margun, nyp.

B5.74 Grey December. 3' 10"
For: piano. After the work by Frank Campo.
Disc: in *Breakthru*, Improvising Artists IAI 373842, 1976. Ran Blake. MIT NEC

B5.75 Helder Camara. (1979)
For: piano. *First performed:* Dec. 11, 1979; McGill University. Ran Blake.
Lead sheets: Margun, nyp.

B5.76 How 'bout That. (1970)
For: piano. Third stream music.
Score: in his *A Collection of Third Stream Compositions*, Margun, 1979. NEC
Lead sheets: Margun, nyp.

B5.77 How 'bout That--Take 2. (1970) 2' 49"
For: piano. Third stream music. *First performed:* Jan. 28, 1972. Ran Blake.
Score: Margun.
Lead sheets: Margun, 1977.
Disc: in *Wende*, Owl Records OWL 05, 1977.

B5.78 How 'bout That--Take 3. (1970) 2' 10"
For: piano. Third stream music.
Disc: in *Wende*, Owl Records OWL 05, 1977.

B5.79 If Dreams Come True. 2' 23"
For: piano. After the work by Edgar

Sampson and Benny Goodman.
Disc: in *Breakthru*, Improvising Artists
IAI 373842, 1976. Ran Blake. MIT NEC

B5.80 Interrogation at Logan Airport.
(1972) 4' 53"
For: piano. *First performed:* Feb. 29,
1972. Ran Blake.
Lead sheets: Margun, nyp.
Disc: in *Portfolio of Ran Blake*, Owl
Records, nyp.

B5.81 Jada. 3' 20"
For: piano. After the work by Bob
Carleton.
Cassette: Nov. 14, 1976; New England
Conservatory; in *An Adaptation of
Favid Ud-din Attar's Conference of the
Birds*. Ran Blake. NEC

B5.82 Jean Jacques. (1980) 1' 2"
For: piano. *First performed:* Jan. 1981;
Paris, France. Ran Blake.
Lead sheets: Margun, nyp.
Disc: in *Portfolio of Ran Blake*, Owl
Records, nyp.

B5.83 Jim Crow. (1963) 3' 3"
For: piano. Third stream music. *First
performed:* Feb. 18, 1964.
Score: in his *A Collection of Third
Stream Compositions*, Margun, 1979. NEC
Lead sheets: Margun, nyp.
Disc: in *Wende*, Owl Records OWL 05,
1977.

B5.84 Jinxey's. (1962) 2' 30"
For: piano. Third stream music. *First
performed:* Aug. 1976; Dimension
Sound Studio, Boston.
Score: MJQ, 1962.
Score: in his *A Collection of Third
Stream Compositions*, Margun, 1979. NEC
Disc: in *Wende*, Owl Records OWL 05,
1977.

B5.85 Just a Closer Walk with Thee. 2'
4"-2' 42"
For: piano. Third stream music. After
the work by Thomas A. Dorsey.
Disc: in *Take One; Third Stream Jazz*,

Golden Crest CRS 4176, 1978. Ran
Blake. NEC
Disc: in *Take Two; Third Stream Jazz*,
Golden Crest CRS 4177, 1978. Ran
Blake. NEC

B5.86 Just a Gigolo.
For: guitar and piano. After the work
by Leonello Casucci.
Cassette: Sept. 26, 1979; New England
Conservatory; in *Out of the Past*.
Christopher Brooks, guitar and Ran
Blake, piano. NEC

B5.87 Key Largo.
For: electric bass, drums, piano. After
the work by Bennett Lester (Benny)
Carter and Karl Suessedorf.
Disc: in *Film Noir*, Arista Novus AN
3019, 1980. Paul Meyers, electric bass;
Jon Hazilla, drums; Ran Blake, piano.
NEC

B5.88 Klanwatch. (1981)
For: piano. *First performed:* May 20,
1981; Church of the Covenant, Boston.
Ran Blake.
Lead sheets: Margun, nyp.
Cassette: recording of first
performance.

B5.89 Kojo No Tsuki.
For: guitar and piano. After the work
by Rentaro Taki.
Cassette: Sept. 26, 1979; New England
Conservatory; in *Out of the Past*.
Christopher Brooks, guitar and Ran
Blake, piano. NEC

B5.90 Last Wave. (1980)
For: piano. *First performed:* Jan. 15,
1980; Paris, France. Ran Blake.
Lead sheets: Margun, nyp.

B5.91 Laura. 5' 6"
For: voice and piano. After the work
by David Raksin.
Cassette: in *The Newest Sound Around*,
RCA Victor LPM/LSP 2500, 1962.
Jeanne Lee, voice and Ran Blake,
piano. NEC

[Laura, Guitar and Piano]
B5.92 Laura. 3' 6"
After the work by David Raksin.
Cassette: Sept. 26, 1979; New England
Conservatory; in *Out of the Past*.
Christopher Brooks, guitar and Ran
Blake, piano. NEC

[Laura, Piano]
B5.93 Laura. 3' 59"
After the work by David Raksin.
Cassette: Nov. 14, 1976; New England
Conservatory; in *An Adaptation of
Favid Ud-din Attar's Conference of the
Birds*. Ran Blake. NEC

B5.94 Let's Stay Together.
For: piano. After the work by Billy
Mitchell, Al Green, Al Jackson.
Cassette: Mar. 23, 1975; New England
Conservatory; in *Dreams, Duets,
Dualities*. Ran Blake. NEC

B5.95 Little Girl Blue.
For: piano. After the work by Richard
Rodgers.
Cassette: Mar. 23, 1975; New England
Conservatory; in *Dreams, Duets,
Dualities*. Ran Blake. NEC

B5.96 Lonely Woman. 5'
For: piano. After the work by Ornette
Coleman.
Cassette: ESP-Disk' 1011, 1965 (date
recorded). Ran Blake. NEC

B5.97 Love Isn't Everything. 1' 20"
For: voice and piano.
Cassette: in *The Newest Sound Around*,
RCA Victor LPM/LSP 2500, 1962.
Jeanne Lee, voice and Ran Blake,
piano. NEC

B5.98 Lover Man. 5'
For: voice and piano. After the work
by Jimmy Davis, Ram Ramirez, Jimmy
Sherman.
Cassette: in *The Newest Sound Around*,
RCA Victor LPM/LSP 2500, 1962.
Jeanne Lee, voice and Ran Blake,
piano. NEC

B5.99 Lush Life. 9' 55"
For: piano. After the work by Billy
Strayhorn. *Dedication:* This performance
is dedicated to the composer and Fritz
Lang.
Cassette: Apr. 20, 1977; New England
Conservatory; in *Something To Live for;
the Music of Billy Strayhorn*. Ran Blake.
NEC

B5.100 A Man and a Woman.
For: piano. After the original by
Francis Lai.
Cassette: Sept. 26, 1979; New England
Conservatory; in *Out of the Past*. Ran
Blake. NEC

B5.101 Manhattan Memories. 4' 5"
For: piano. *Movements:* Bird Blues;
Bebopper (H. Gordon); Drop Me off in
Harlem (Duke Ellington and Nick Kenny).
First performed: Dec. 1975; Oslo,
Norway (Bird Blues). Ran Blake.
Music: Pablo, nyp (Bird Blues).
Disc: in *Breakthru*, Improvising Artists
IAI 373842, 1976. Ran Blake. MIT NEC

B5.102 Mera Dil Yeh Pukare. 2' 45"
For: piano. After the work by Hemant
Kumar.
Cassette: Apr. 11, 1979; New England
Conservatory; in *East-West; a Concert
Blending Musical Traditions....* Ran
Blake. NEC

B5.103 Merci bon Dieu.
For: voice and piano. After the work
by Franz Casseus.
Cassette: Sept. 26, 1979; New England
Conservatory; in *Out of the Past*. Eleni
Odoni, voice and Ran Blake, piano.
NEC

B5.104 Miguel Balle. (1977) 3'
For: piano. *First performed:* June 1977;
Paris, France. Ran Blake.
Lead sheets: Margun, nyp.
Disc: in *Realization of a Dream*, Owl
Records OWL 012, 1978.

B5.105 Moonlight on the Ganges. 2'
45"-3' 1"

For: piano. Third stream music. After the work by Sherman Myers.
Disc: in *Take One; Third Stream Jazz*, Golden Crest CRS 4176, 1978. Ran Blake. NEC
Disc: in *Take Two; Third Stream Jazz*, Golden Crest CRS 4177, 1978. Ran Blake. NEC
Cassette: Sept. 26, 1979; New England Conservatory; in *Out of the Past*. Ran Blake. NEC

B5.106 Never Can Say Goodbye.
For: piano. After the work by C. Davis.
Cassette: Mar. 23, 1975; New England Conservatory; in *Dreams, Duets, Dualities*. Ran Blake. NEC

B5.107 Never on Sunday. 2' 49"
For: piano. After the work by Manos Hadzidakis.
Disc: in *The Blue Potato*, Milestone MSP 9021, 1969 (date recorded). Ran Blake. Bu NEC

B5.108 Night. (1959)
For: piano. *First performed:* 1959. Ran Blake.
Lead sheets: MJQ, 1959.

B5.109 No Good Man. 3'
For: piano. After the work by Irene Higginbotham.
Disc: in *Breakthru*, Improvising Artists IAI 373842, 1976. Ran Blake. MIT NEC

B5.110 No More. 4' 35"
For: voice and piano. After the work by Toots Camarata.
Cassette: Mar. 27, 1978; New England Conservatory; in *No More; Dedicated to the Memory of Billie Holiday*. Wendy Shermet, voice and Ran Blake, piano. NEC

B5.111 Ol' Man River. 4' 35"-6' 25"
For: piano. Third stream music. After the work by Jerome Kern.
Disc: in *Take One; Third Stream Jazz*, Golden Crest CRS 4176, 1978. Ran Blake. NEC
Disc: in *Take Two; Third Stream Jazz*, Golden Crest CRS 4177, 1978. Ran Blake. NEC
Cassette: Nov. 7, 1977; New England Conservatory; in *Dualities*. Ran Blake. NEC

B5.112 Olivier Messiaen. (1979)
For: piano. *First performed:* Oct. 12, 1979; Northwestern University. Ran Blake.
Lead sheets: Margun, nyp.

B5.113 On Green Dolphin Street. 2' 45"
For: piano. After the work by Bronislaw Kaper.
Cassette: ESP-Disk' 011, 1965 (date recorded). Ran Blake. NEC

B5.114 Open City. (1977) 13' 40"
For: piano. *First performed:* 1977; Rome, Italy. Ran Blake.
Lead sheets: Margun.
Disc: in *Open City*, Horo Records HDP 7-8, 1977.

B5.115 Parkers Mood. 3' 4"
For: piano. After the work by Charlie Parker.
Disc: in *Breakthru*, Improvising Artists IAI 373842, 1976. Ran Blake. MIT NEC

[Personalities]
B5.116 Three Personalities. (1964-68) 2' 17"
For: piano. Third stream music.
Contents: Votichenko; Cadillac Joe; Amelia.
Score: in his *A Collection of Third Stream Compositions*, Margun, 1979. NEC
Lead sheets: Margun, nyp.
Disc: in *Wende*, Owl Records OWL 05, 1977.

[Personalities. Amelia]
B5.117 Amelia Lehrfield. (1964)
For: piano. Third stream music. *First performed:* 1964; Riverside Church, New York City.
Score: in his *A Collection of Third Stream Compositions*, Margun, 1979. NEC
Lead sheets: in *Three Personalities*, Margun, nyp.

Disc: in *Wende*, Owl Records OWL 05, 1977.

[Personalities. Cadillac Joe]
B5.118 Cadillac Joe. (1966)
For: piano. Third stream music. *First performed:* Apr. 20, 1966; Columbia University. Ran Blake.
Score: in his *A Collection of Third Stream Compositions*, Margun, 1979. NEC
Lead sheets: in *Three Personalities*, Margun, nyp.
Disc: in *Wende*, Owl Records OWL 05, 1977.
Cassette: Sept. 26, 1976; New England Conservatory; in *Stoneciphering*. Ran Blake. NEC

[Personalities. Cadillac Joe; Arr.]
B5.119 Cadillac Joe.
For: instrumental ensemble(flute, saxophones(4), trumpet, trombone, piano, double bass, drums). Third stream music. Arr. by Richard Eisenstein.
Music: Margun, 1976.
Cassette: Mar. 23, 1975; New England Conservatory; in *Dreams, Duets, Dualities*. Members of NEC Third Stream Department, Mark Harvey, conductor. NEC

B5.120 Pinky. 4' 1"-6' 50"
For: flute, electric bass, piano, drums(optional). After the work by Alfred Newman. *Dedicated to:* Sarah Vaughan.
Disc: in *Film Noir*, Arista Novus AN 3019, 1980. John Heiss, flute; Paul Meyers, electric bass; Ran Blake, piano; Jon Hazilla, drums. NEC
Cassette: Sept. 26, 1979; New England Conservatory; in *Out of the Past*. John Heiss, flute; Paul Meyers, electric bass; Ran Blake, piano. NEC

[Pinky, Voice and Piano]
B5.121 Pinky. 8' 10"
After the work by Alfred Newman.
Cassette: Dec. 4, 1979; New England Conservatory; in *Mabuse and Other Film Noir*. Mae Arnette, voice and Ran Blake, piano. NEC

B5.122 Pireas and Romiosyni. 13' 9"
For: piano, voice, clarinet, saxophone(tenor), saxophone(alto). Third stream music. After *Never on Sunday* by Manos Hadzidakis and *Romiosyni* by Mikis Theodorakis. Written in collaboration with Eleni Odoni.
Disc: in *Third Stream Today*, Golden Crest NEC 116, 1979. Ran Blake, piano; Eleni Odoni, voice; Eric Thomas, clarinet; Sam Matthews, tenor saxophone; Bruce Henderson, alto saxophone. NEC
Cassette: Mar. 23, 1975; New England Conservatory; in *Dreams, Duets, Dualities*. Ran Blake, piano; Eleni Odoni, voice; Eric Thomas, clarinet; Sam Matthews, tenor saxophone; Bruce Henderson, alto saxophone. NEC

B5.123 Police.
For: piano. *Movements:* Link Macdougal; Four Flashbacks (On a Quiet Vermont Day; Incident on Avenue Queen Sophie; Incident on 128th Street; Incident at Logan); Blue Power. *Dedicated to:* Clay Who Didn't Survive.
Cassette: Sept. 26, 1976; New England Conservatory; in *Stoneciphering* (omits Link Macdougal and Incident at Logan). Ran Blake. NEC

[Police. Blue Power]
B5.124 Blue Power. (1970)
For: piano. *First performed:* 1970; Jordan Hall, Boston.
Lead sheets: Margun, nyp.
Cassette: Jan. 30, 1978; New England Conservatory; in *Now Is the Time*. Ran Blake. NEC

B5.125 Porgy.
For: piano. After the work by George Gershwin.
Cassette: Sept. 26, 1979; New England Conservatory; in *Out of the Past*. Ran Blake. NEC

Portfolio of Doktor Mabuse. *See* Awakening; Vradizai; You Stepped out of a Dream.

53

B5.126 Prelude. (1981)
For: pianos(2). Written in collaboration with Jaki Byard. *First performed:* May 1981; Verona, Italy. Ran Blake and Jaki Byard.
Lead sheets: Margun, nyp.
Disc: in *Ran Blake/Jaki Byard Duo*, Soul Note SN 1022, 1981. Ran Blake and Jaki Byard.
Cassette: May 1981; Verona, Italy. Ran Blake and Jaki Byard.

B5.127 Present Tense. (1980) 1' 23"
For: piano. *First performed:* Jan. 1981; Paris, France.
Lead sheets: Margun, nyp.
Disc: in *Portfolio of Ran Blake*, Owl Records, nyp.

B5.128 Racial Vertigo. (1976) 1'
For: piano. *First performed:* Oct. 1, 1976; York College of The City University of New York. Ran Blake.
Lead sheets: Margun, nyp.
Disc: in *Realization of a Dream*, Owl Records OWL 012, 1978.

[Rage and Isolation, Instruments(7)]
B5.129 Rage and Isolation. (1979)
For: flute, oboe, piano, guitars(2), viola, drums.
Cassette: Sept. 26, 1979; New England Conservatory; in *Out of the Past*. Abby Rabinovitz, flute; Hankus Netsky, oboe; Ran Blake, piano; Christopher Brooks and Paul Meyers, guitars; Virginia Haines, viola; Jon Hazilla, drums. NEC

[Rage and Isolation, Piano]
B5.130 Rage and Isolation. (1979)
Lead sheets: Margun, nyp.

B5.131 Realization of a Dream. (1968 [?])
For: piano. *First performed:* June 26, 1968 [?]; Lenox School of Jazz. Ran Blake.
Lead sheets: Margun, nyp.
Disc: in *Realization of a Dream*, Owl Records OWL 012, 1978.

B5.132 Rejeanne Padovani. (1979)
For: piano. *First performed:* Dec. 11, 1979; McGill University.
Lead sheets: Margun, nyp.

B5.133 Requiem for Lennie. (1980)
For: piano. *First performed:* Oct. 30, 1980; Berlin, Germany. Ran Blake.
Music: Margun, nyp.

B5.134 Requiem for Mingus. (1980)
For: piano.
Cassette: Oct. 20, 1980; New England Conservatory; in *An Evening of the Music of Charles Mingus*. Ran Blake. NEC

B5.135 'Round Midnight. 8' 16"
For: piano. Third stream music. After the work by Thelonious Monk.
Cassette: Nov. 12, 1975; New England Conservatory; in *Misterioso; Third Stream Recompositions of the Blue-Note Repertoire of Thelonious Monk*. Ran Blake. NEC

B5.136 Rumanische Fantasie. 3' 55"
For: piano. After the work by Josef Solinski.
Cassette: Mar. 12, 1981; New England Conservatory; in *Jewish Music; New Sounds from an Ancient Tradition*. Ran Blake. NEC

B5.137 Season in the Sun. 2' 25"
For: voice and piano.
Cassette: in *The Newest Sound Around*, RCA Victor LPM/LSP 2500, 1962. Jeanne Lee, voice and Ran Blake, piano. NEC

[Seeds]
B5.138 Three Seeds. (1969) 7' 27"
For: piano. Suite. *Movements:* Regis Debray; Che Guevera; Malcom X. *First performed:* June 24, 1969; Belmont, Mass. Ran Blake.
Lead sheets: MJQ, 1959.
Disc: in *The Blue Potato*, Milestone MSP 9021, 1969. Ran Blake. BU NEC

B5.139 Shadows.
For: piano.
Lead sheets: MJQ, 1959.

B5.140 Silent Night. 4' 50"-5' 1"
For: piano. Third stream music. After the work by Franz Gruber.
Disc: in *Take One; Third Stream Jazz*, Golden Crest CRS 4176, 1978. Ran Blake. NEC
Disc: in *Take Two; Third Stream Jazz*, Golden Crest CRS 4177, 1978. Ran Blake. NEC

B5.141 Silver Fox. (1959) 3' 38"
For: piano. Third stream music. *First performed:* June 14, 1960; Bard College. Ran Blake.
Score: in his *A Collection of Third Stream Compositions*, Margun, 1979. NEC
Lead sheets: Margun, nyp.
Disc: in *Wende*, Owl Records OWL 05, 1977.

B5.142 Sirod. 2' 2"-3' 11"
For: piano. Third stream music. After the work by John Mehegan.
Disc: in *Take One; Third Stream Jazz*, Golden Crest CRS 4176, 1978. Ran Blake. NEC
Disc: in *Take Two; Third Stream Jazz*, Golden Crest CRS 4177, 1978. Ran Blake. NEC

[Sister Tee, Piano]
B5.143 Sister Tee. (1961) 4' 30"
Third stream music. *First performed:* Feb. 13, 1968; Choate School. Ran Blake.
Lead sheets: Margun, nyp.
Cassette: ESP-Disk' 1011, 1965 (date recorded). NEC

[Sister Tee, Voice and Piano]
B5.144 Sister Tee. (1961) 6' 14"
Third stream music. *Text:* Ran Blake.
Disc: in *Third Stream Today*, Golden Crest NEC 116, 1979. John West, voice and piano. NEC T
Cassette: Apr. 14, 1976; New England Conservatory. John West, voice and piano. NEC

B5.145 Sleep Secrets. (1979)
For: piano. *First performed:* June 13, 1979; New York City. Ran Blake.
Lead sheets: Margun, nyp.

B5.146 Sleepy Time Gal. 4' 45"
For: piano. After the work by Ange Lorenzo and Richard Whiting.
Cassette: ESP-Disk' 1011, 1965 (date recorded). Ran Blake. NEC

B5.147 Smoke after Smoke. (1967) 3'
For: piano. *First performed:* June 9, 1967; Italy. Ran Blake.
Lead sheets: Margun.
Disc: in *Portfolio of Ran Blake*, Owl Records, nyp.

B5.148 Solitaire. 3' 7"
For: piano. After the work by William J. Russo.
Disc: in *Rapport*, Arista Novus AN 3006, 1978. Ran Blake. NEC

B5.149 Sonata.
For: pianos(2). Written in collaboration with Jaki Byard.
Lead sheets: Margun, nyp.

B5.150 Sontagism. (1966) 1' 13"-1' 24"
For: piano. Third stream music. *First performed:* Feb. 22, 1966; New York City.
Lead sheets: Margun, nyp.
Disc: in *Take One; Third Stream Jazz*, Golden Crest CRS 4176, 1978. Ran Blake. NEC
Disc: in *Take Two; Third Stream Jazz*, Golden Crest CRS 4177, 1978. Ran Blake. NEC

B5.151 Sophisticated Lady. 2' 36"
For: piano. After the work by Duke Ellington.
Disc: in *Breakthru*, Improvising Artists IAI 373842, 1976. Ran Blake. MIT NEC

B5.152 Soul on Ice. (1959) 3' 38"
For: piano.
Lead sheets: MJQ, 1959.
Disc: in *The Blue Potato*, Milestone MSP 9021, 1969. Ran Blake. BU NEC

B5.153 Spinning Wheel. 2'
For: piano. After the work by David Clayton-Thomas.
Disc: in *Breakthru*, Improvising Artists IAI 373842, 1976. Ran Blake. MIT NEC

B5.154 Spiral Staircase. (1976) 4' 29"
For: oboe(optional), guitar(electric), piano, drums. *First performed:* July 22, 1976; Old West Church, Boston.
Lead sheets: Margun, nyp (version without oboe).
Disc: in *Film Noir*, Arista Novus AN 3019, 1980. Hankus Netsky, oboe; Paul Meyers, guitar; Ran Blake, piano; Jon Hazilla, drums. NEC

B5.155 Stars Fell on Alabama. 2' 18"
For: piano. After the work by Frank Perkins.
Disc: in *The Blue Potato*, Milestone MSP 9021, 1969 (date recorded). Ran Blake. BU NEC

B5.156 Stoneciphering. (1964) 1' 31"-2' 8"
For: piano. Third stream music. *First performed:* Mar. 23, 1964; Columbia University.
Lead sheets: Margun, nyp.
Disc: in *Take One; Third Stream Jazz*, Golden Crest CRS 4176, 1978. Ran Blake. NEC
Disc: in *Take Two; Third Stream Jazz*, Golden Crest CRS 4176, 1978. Ran Blake. NEC
Cassette: Sept. 26, 1976; New England Conservatory; in *Stoneciphering*. Ran Blake. NEC

B5.157 Stratusphunk. 3' 50"
For: piano. After the work by George Russell.
Cassette: ESP-Disk' 1011, 1965 (date recorded). Ran Blake. NEC

B5.158 Streetcar Named Desire. 5' 17"-8' 10"
For: piano, saxophone(alto), electric bass, drums. After the work by Alex North.
Disc: in *Film Noir*, Arista Novus AN 3019, 1980. Ran Blake, piano; Daryl Lowery, alto saxophone; Paul Meyers, electric bass; Jon Hazilla, drums. NEC
Cassette: Apr. 16, 1980; New England Conservatory; in *Offerings in Time*. Ran Blake, piano; Daryl Lowery, alto saxophone; Paul Meyers, electric bass; Jon Hazilla, drums. NEC

B5.159 Suite for Darryl Williams and Shirley Simmons. (1979)
For: piano. *Movements:* The Shooting; Medical Verdict; There's Been a Change in My Life/ Hubert Powell; The Aftermath and Prognosis. *First performed:* Nov. 20, 1979; Jordan Hall, Boston; in World Music for Peace. Ran Blake.
Lead sheets: Margun, nyp (titled Darryl Williams).
Cassette: recording of first performance. NEC

B5.160 Summer Soft. 10' 10"
For: drums and piano. After the work by Stevie Wonder.
Cassette: Nov. 29, 1978; New England Conservatory; in *You and I; a Concert Inspired by the Music of Stevie Wonder*. Ran Blake, piano and Curtis Warner, drums. NEC

B5.161 Summertime. 3' 30"
For: voice and piano. After the work by George Gershwin.
Cassette: in *The Newest Sound Around*, RCA Victor LPM/LSP 2500, 1962. Jeanne Lee, voice and Ran Blake, piano. NEC

B5.162 Tea for Two. 2' 45"
For: piano. After the work by Vincent Youmans.
Disc: in *Breakthru*, Improvising Artists IAI 373842, 1976. Ran Blake. MIT NEC

B5.163 There'll Be Some Changes Made. 1' 45"
For: piano. After the work by W.B. Overstreet.
Cassette: ESP-Disk' 1011, 1965 (date recorded). Ran Blake. NEC

B5.164 They've Soared Up High. 5' 28"
For: voice, piano, violin. After the
work by Mikis Theodorakis.
Cassette: Mar. 23, 1975; New England
Conservatory; in *Dreams, Duets,
Dualities*. Eleni Odoni, voice; Ran
Blake, piano; Andrew Jones, violin.
NEC

[Thursday, Instrumental Ensemble]
B5.165 Thursday. (1959)
For: instrumental ensemble(clarinet,
saxophones(alto)(3)/oboe,
saxophones(tenor)(2),
saxophone(baritone), trumpets(3),
trombones(2), percussion, piano,
violoncello, double bass). Third stream
music. Arr. by Anthony Coleman.
Cassette: Mar. 23, 1975; New England
Conservatory; in *Dreams, Duets,
Dualities*. Members of NEC Third
Stream Department. NEC

[Thursday, Piano]
B5.166 Thursday. (1959) 3' 33"
Third stream music.
Score: MJQ, 1959.
Score: in his *A Collection of Third
Stream Compositions*, Margun, 1979. NEC
Disc: in *Wende*, Owl Records OWL 05,
1977.
Cassette: Sept. 26, 1976; New England
Conservatory; in *Stoneciphering*. Ran
Blake. NEC

[Thursday, Saxophone(Tenor), Piano,
Double Bass]
Third stream music.
Lead sheets: MJQ.
Disc: in *Rapport*, Arista Novus AN
3006, 1978. Ricky Ford, tenor
saxophone; Ran Blake, piano; Rufus
Reid, double bass. NEC

B5.167 Touch of Evil. (1979) 4' 51"
For: third stream group or piano.
Lead sheets: Margun, nyp.
Disc: in *Film Noir*, Arista Novus AN
3019, 1980. Ran Blake, piano; members
of NEC Third Stream Department. NEC
T
Cassette: Sept. 26, 1979; New England
Conservatory; in *Out of the Past*.

Christopher Brooks, guitar; Frank
London, Spencer Macleish, Ingrid
Monson, trumpets; Thomas Regis and
George Schuller, drums; Paul Meyers,
double bass; Ran Blake, piano. NEC
Cassette: Dec. 4, 1979; New England
Conservatory; in *Mabuse and Other
Film Noir*. Ed Jackson, alto saxophone;
Spencer Macleish and Ingrid Monson,
trumpets; Joe Link, drums; Thomas
Regis, congas; Gregory Silberman,
piano. NEC

B5.168 Turncoat. (1964)
For: piano. *First performed:* Sept. 20,
1964; Town Hall, New York City.
Lead sheets: Margun, nyp.
Disc: in *Portfolio of Ran Blake*, Owl
Records, nyp.

B5.169 Until Dawn. (1978) 2' 4"-2' 10"
For: piano. Third stream music.
Lead sheets: Margun, nyp.
Disc: in *Take One; Third Stream Jazz*,
Golden Crest CRS 4176, 1978. Ran
Blake. NEC
Disc: in *Take Two; Third Stream Jazz*,
Golden Crest CRS 4177, 1978. Ran
Blake. NEC

[Vanguard, Instrumental Ensemble]
B5.170 Vanguard. (1953)
For: clarinet, saxophone(soprano),
saxophone(tenor), trumpets(2), tuba,
drums, piano, piano(electric), double
bass (arr. by Victor Comer) or clarinet,
saxophone(tenor), bassoon, trumpets(2),
trombones(2), percussion, drums, piano,
double bass (arr. by Bruce Henderson).
Third stream music.
Cassette: Mar. 23, 1975; New England
Conservatory; in *Dreams, Duets,
Dualities*. Members of NEC Third
Stream Department, Victor Comer,
conductor. NEC
Cassette: Feb. 4, 1976; New England
Conservatory; in *Cross-Stylizations*.
Members of NEC Third Stream
Department, Bruce Henderson,
conductor. NEC

[Vanguard, Piano]
B5.171 Vanguard. (1953; 1958) 3' 33"

Third stream music.
Score: MJQ, 1958.
Score: in his *A Collection of Third
Stream Compositions*, Margun, 1979. NEC
Cassette: Mar. 23, 1975; New England
Conservatory; in *Dreams, Duets,
Dualities*. Manny Williams. NEC
Cassette: ESP-Disk' 1011, 1965 (date
recorded). NEC
Cassette: Feb. 4, 1976; New England
Conservatory; in *Cross-Stylizations*. Jaki
Byard. NEC
Cassette: Sept. 26, 1976; New England
Conservatory; in *Stoneciphering*. Ran
Blake. NEC

[Vanguard, Saxophone(Alto) and
Piano]
B5.172 Vanguard. (1953) 5' 8"
Third stream music.
Disc: in *Rapport*, Arista Novus An
3006, 1978. Anthony Braxton, alto
saxophone and Ran Blake, piano. NEC

[Vanguard, Trombone]
B5.173 Vanguard. (1953)
Third stream music.
Cassette: Sept. 26, 1979; New England
Conservatory; in *Out of the Past*.
Norman McWilliams. NEC

B5.174 Vertigo. (1980)
For: piano. *First performed:* Jan. 16,
1980; Paris, France. Ran Blake.
Lead sheets: Margun, nyp.

B5.175 Vota No. (1967) 1' 45"
For: piano. *First performed:* Nov. 10,
1867; Philadelphia, Pa. Ran Blake.
Lead sheets: Margun, nyp.
Disc: in *Crystal Trip*, Horo Records H
206, 1977.

B5.176 Vradiazi. 2' 12"-3' 17"
For: piano. Third stream music. After
the work by Mikis Theodorakis.
Disc: in *The Blue Potato*, Milestone
MSP 9021, 1969 (date recorded). Ran
Blake. NEC
Disc: in *Take One; Third Stream Jazz*,
Golden Crest CRS 4176, 1978. Ran
Blake. NEC

Disc: in *Take Two; Third Stream Jazz*,
Golden Crest CRS 4177, 1978. Ran
Blake. NEC

[Vradiazi, Orchestra]
B5.177 Vradiazi.
After the work by Mikis Theodorakis.
Written in collaboration with Michael
Linn.
Cassette: May 2, 1979; New England
Conservatory; in *Portfolio of Doktor
Mabuse*. NEC Symphony Orchestra. NEC

[Vradiazi, Voice and Piano]
B5.178 Vradiazi. 4' 48"
After the work by Mikis Theodorakis.
Disc: in *Rapport*, Arista Novus AN
3006, 1978. Eleni Odoni, voice and Ran
Blake, piano. NEC
Cassette: Sept. 26, 1979; New England
Conservatory; in *Out of the Past*. Eleni
Odoni, voice and Ran Blake, piano.
NEC

[Wende, Instrumental Ensemble]
B5.179 Wende. (1955) 5' 27"
For: instrumental ensemble(flute,
clarinet, saxophone(alto), horn, trumpet,
trombones(2), tuba, percussion(2),
double bass). Third stream music.
Lead sheets: MJQ, 1955.
Disc: in *Third Stream Today*, Golden
Crest NEC 116, 1979 (arr. by Albin
Zak). Members of NEC Third Stream
Department, Albin Zak, conductor. NEC
T
Cassette: Mar. 23, 1975; New England
Conservatory; in *Dreams, Duets,
Dualities* (arr. by Albin Zak). Members
of NEC Third Stream Department, Albin
Zak, conductor. NEC

[Wende, Piano]
B5.180 Wende. (1955) 3' 38"
Third stream music.
Score: in his *A Collection of Third
Stream Compositions*, Margun, 1979. NEC
Score: MJQ.
Disc: in *Wende*, Owl Records OWL 05,
1976. Ran Blake.
Cassette: Jan. 30, 1978; New England

Conservatory; in *Now Is the Time*.
Gregory Silberman. NEC

[Wende, Voice and Instruments(3)]
B5.181 Wende. (1955) 3′ 22″
For: voice, piano, guitar(electric),
double bass. Third stream music. *Text:*
Richard Rodney Bennett and Dominique
St. John.
Lead sheets: MJQ, 1955.
Disc: in *Rapport*, Arista Novus AN
3006, 1978. Chris Connor, voice; Ran
Blake, piano; Jerome Thomas, guitar;
Rufus Reid, double bass. NEC

[Wende, Voice and Piano]
B5.182 Wende.
Third stream music. *Text:* Jezra Kaye.
Lead sheets: MJQ, 1955.
Cassette: Sept. 26, 1976; New England
Conservatory; in *Stoneciphering*. Elena
Odoni, voice and Ran Blake, piano.
NEC

B5.183 What Are You Doing the Rest
of Your Life. 2′ 50″
For: piano. After the work by Michel
Legrand.
Disc: in *Breakthru*, Improvising Artists
IAI 373842, 1976. Ran Blake. MIT NEC

B5.184 When Swing Gets Blue. 4′ 51″
For: voice and piano.
Cassette: in *The Newest Sound Around*,
RCA Victor LPM/LSP 2500, 1962.
Jeanne Lee, voice and Ran Blake,
piano. NEC

B5.185 Where Flamingos Fly. 4′ 17″
For: piano.
Cassette: in *The Newest Sound Around*,
RCA Victor LPM/LSP 2500, 1962.
Jeanne Lee, voice and Ran Blake,
piano. NEC

B5.186 Whirlpool. (1981)
For: piano. *First performed:* Feb. 1981;
Italy. Ran Blake.
Lead sheets: Margun, nyp.

B5.187 Wish I Could Talk to You Baby.
4′ 58″-8′ 40″
For: piano. After the work by Leon
Sylvers, III.
Disc: in *Breakthru*, Improvising Artists
IAI 373842, 1976. Ran Blake. MIT NEC
Cassette: Nov. 14, 1976; New England
Conservatory; in *An Adaptation of
Favid Ud-din Attar's Conference of the
Birds*. Ran Blake. NEC

B5.188 You Go to My Head. 4′ 3″
For: saxophone(tenor) and piano. After
the work by J. Fred Coots.
Disc: in *Rapport*, Arista Novus 3006,
1978. Ricky Ford, tenor saxophone and
Ran Blake, piano. NEC

B5.189 You Stepped out of a Dream. 3′
47″
For: piano. After the work by Nacio
Herb Brown.
Disc: in *Breakthru*, Improvising Artists
IAI 373842, 1976. Ran Blake. MIT NEC

[You Stepped out of a Dream, Oboe
and Piano]
B5.190 You Stepped out of a Dream. 4′
24″
After the work by Nacio Herb Brown.
Casette: Feb. 4, 1976; New England
Conservatory; in *Cross-Stylizations*.
Hankus Netsky, oboe and Ran Blake,
piano. NEC

[You Stepped out of a Dream,
Orchestra]
B5.191 You Stepped out of a Dream.
After the work by Nacio Herb Brown.
Written in collaboration with Daryl
Lowery.
Cassette: May 2, 1978; New England
Conservatory; in *Portfolio of Doktor
Mabuse*. NEC Symphony Orchestra. NEC

B5.192 You've Changed. 2′ 45″-3′ 9″
For: piano. Third stream music. After
the work by Carl Theodore Fischer.
Disc: in *Take One; Third Stream Jazz*,
Golden Crest CRS 4176, 1978. Ran

Blake. NEC
Disc: in *Take Two; Third Stream Jazz*,
Golden Crest CRS 4177, 1978. Ran
Blake. NEC

B6 PETER HERBERT BLOOM

Born February 2, 1949, in Boston.
Education: A.B., Philosophy (Boston
University); Baroque Performance
Institute (Oberlin Conservatory, 1978,
1979); M.M. (New England Conservatory,
1981); studied with Betty Bang Mather;
Karl-Heinz Zoeller, Gertrud Zoeller
(Mozarteum, Salzburg); studied
composition with Bruce Fithian (Longy
School of Music); early transverse
flute with Sandra Miller, David Hart,
Robert H. Willoughby, Carol Epple;
modern flute with James Pappoutsakis
and Carol Epple. *Related activities:*
member of the North Shore
Philharmonic Orchestra (1976-80);
currently on the faculty of the
Cambridge Center for Adult Education.
BU

WORKS

B6.1 Canonic Encore. (1973)
For: flute and guitar. *Dedicated to:* Jean
Cavallaro.
Score: ms.

B6.2 Crab God the Moon. (1974)
For: Soprano and piano. *Text:* Peter
Bloom.
Score: ms.

B6.3 Fantasy. (1974)
For: trumpet. Written for Mark S.
Harvey.
Score: ms.

B6.4 From the Drawer. (1979)
For: Tenor, flute/piccolo, clarinet, horn,
bassoon. *Text:* Constantine Cavafy.
First performed: May 10, 1979; Longy
School of Music. Bruce Fithian, tenor,
and others.
Score & parts: ms.

B6.5 Jowls of Winter; a Cantata. (1975)
For: Soprano, Bass, chorus(SATB),
instrumental ensemble(trumpets(2), horn,
trombone, tuba, percussion(3),
violoncello, double bass, electronic
effects(created with musique concrete
devices such as electric trains, music
boxes, and the like)).
Score & parts: ms.

B6.6 Rhapsody. (1976)
Dedicated to: Dr. Bernard Berman.
Score: ms.

B7 DAVID JOHN BOROS

Born May 17, 1944, in New York City;
died 1975. *Education:* studied
composition with David Lewin, Henri
Lazarof (University of California, Los
Angeles); Seymour Shifrin (University
of California, Berkeley, B.A., 1966 and
Brandeis University); Martin Boykan,
Arthur Berger (Brandeis University,
M.F.A., 1970); Goffredo Petrassi (Rome,
Italy). *Awards:* Weisner Award for
Creative Arts (University of California,
Berkeley, 1966), Fulbright-Hays grant
(1968-69). *Related activities:* pianist;
served on the faculty of Brandeis
University (1973-75). BrU

WORKS

B7.1 Anecdote of the Jar and Piano
Interlude. (The Pleasures of Merely
Circulating). (unfinshed) 10' 45"
For: chorus, clarinet(bass), piano,
double bass. *Text:* Wallace Stevens.
Contents: Anecdote of the Jar; Piano
Interlude, (The Pleasures of Merely
Circulating).
Disc: Composers Recordings CRI SD
379, 1977. David Satz, bass clarinet;
Martin Boykan, piano; Alan Nagel,
double bass; Brandeis Chamber Chorus,
James D. Olesen, conductor. BrU BU
HU MIT NEC W

[Fables]
B7.2 Three Fables. (1968)
For: Tenor, clarinet, bassoon, violin,

violoncello, piano. *First performed:* 1968; Brandeis University.

Piano Interlude. *See* Anecdote of the Jar.

The Pleasures of Merely Circulating. *See* Anecdote of the Jar.

B7.3 Trio. (1966)
For: violin, violoncello, piano. *Dedicated to:* Henri Lazarof. *First performed:* [1967?]; Brandeis University. Nancy Cirillo, violin; Madeline Foley, violoncello; Martin Boykan, piano.

B7.4 Waltz. (1968)
For: piano. *Dedication:* To my parents. *First performed:* [1969]; Brandeis University. George Fisher.
Score: ms. in composer's hand.

B7.5 Wedding Music. (1968) 6' 55"
For: piano. *Dedication:* For Irving and Winnie. *First performed:* [1969];
Brandeis University. George Fisher.
Score: ms. in composer's hand.
Disc: Composers Recordings CRI SD 379, 1977. George Fisher. BrU BU HU MIT NEC W

B7.6 Yet Once Again. (1970) 7' 35"
For: flute. *Dedicated to:* Connie Boykan.
First performed: 1971; Rome, Italy. Constance Boykan.
Disc: Composers Recordings CRI SD 379, 1977. Constance Boykan. BrU BU HU MIT NEC W

B8 ROGER BOURLAND

Born December 13, 1952, in Evanston, Ill. Moved to Boston area 1976.
Education: studied composition with Les Thimmig (University of Wisconsin, Madison, B.M., 1976); William Thomas McKinley, Donald Martino (New England Conservatory, M.M., 1978); Gunther Schuller (Tanglewood, 1978); John Harbison (Massachusetts Institute of Technology, 1978-79); Earl Kim, Leon Kirchner (Harvard University, M.A.,

1981). *Awards:* Koussevitzky International Award for Best Composition (1978), New England Conservatory, Composition Award (1978), ASCAP Grant to Young Composers (1979), Wesley Weyman Trust Grant (1979), John Knowles Paine Travelling Fellowship (Harvard University). *Related activities:* conductor, electronic music, film music. HU

WORKS

B8.1 Achaian Etude. (1974) 2'
For: clarinet(bass), trumpet, organ.
Score: ms.

B8.2 Alba. (1974) 8'
For: Soprano, flute, flute/piccolo, clarinet, clarinet(bass), percussion(4), harp, viola, violoncello. *First performed:* Oct. 27, 1974; University of Wisconsin, Madison. Les Thimmig, conductor.
Score & parts: ms. Tape.

B8.3 Allegory. (1977) 7'
For: Soprano and piano. *Text: Prelude to the Palace of Art* by Alfred, Lord Tennyson. *First performed:* Mar. 9, 1978; New England Conservatory. Kristin Samuelson, soprano and Nicholas Underhill, piano.
Score: ms. Tape.

B8.4 Beowulf, A Pageant. (1979) 20'
For: flute, violin, violoncello. 2 movements. *First performed:* Feb. 16, 1979; Harvard University.
Score: ms. Tape.

[Cellianos]
B8.5 Three Cellianos. (1973) 6'
For: violoncello and piano.
Score: ms.

B8.6 Chamber Concerto. (1977) 20'
For: instrumental ensemble(flute, clarinet, saxophone(soprano), bassoon, trumpet,piano, marimba, vibraphone, violin, violoncello, double bass). *First performed:* Mar. 7, 1978; New England

Conservatory. Roger Bourland, conductor.
Score & parts: ms.
Cassette: recording of first performance. NEC

B8.7 Chassau. (1974) 2' 30"
For: guitar.
Score: ms.

B8.8 Clarina. (1978) 6'
For: clarinets(3). *First performed:* Feb. 16, 1979; Harvard University.
Score: ms. Tape.

B8.9 A Clarinet Rhapsody. (1979) 11'
For: clarinet and orchestra(2-2-0-2; 2-0-0-0; str). *First performed:* Sept. 30, 1979; University of Southern California. John Strickler, conductor.
Score & parts: Margun.

[Clouds]
B8.10 Three Clouds. (1975) 12'
For: chamber chorus(SATB). *Text:* Roger Bourland. *First performed:* Feb. 16, 1975; University of Wisconsin, Madison. Christopher McGahn, conductor.

B8.11 The Death of Narcissus. (1980) 7'
For: flute, clarinets(2), bassoon, piano, violin, violoncello, double bass. *First performed:* Apr. 13, 1980; Sanders Theatre, Harvard University. Harvard-Radcliffe Ensemble Society, Jonathan Cohler, conductor.
Score: ms.
Tape.

B8.12 Diary. (1972) 10'
For: guitar. *First performed:* Mar. 12, 1973; University of Wisconsin, Madison.
Score: ms.

B8.13 Dickinson Madrigals. (1980) 10'
For: Soprano, Mezzo Soprano, Alto, Tenor, Bass. *First performed:* Old Cambridge Baptist Church; *Composers in Red Sneakers, Concert 1.* Nalin

Mukherjee, conductor.
Vocal score: E.C. Schirmer. *Tape.*

[Duets]
B8.14 Three Duets. (1973) 8'
For: violin and piano; clarinet and piano; flute and piano. *First performed:* Nov. 16, 1973; University of Wisconsin, Madison.
Score: ms.

Epiphany. *See* Soliloquy IX.

B8.15 Etude poetique. (1979) 7'
For: violoncello. *Commissioned by:* Alea III. *First performed:* Apr. 2, 1979; Institute of Contemporary Art, Boston. Freya Oberle.
Score: ms. Tape.

[Evening Studies]
B8.16 Two Evening Studies. (1974) 5'
For: piano.
Score: ms.

B8.17 Farewell Celebration. (1979) 11'
For: violin, viola, violoncellos(2). *First performed:* May 19, 1979; Harvard University.
Score: ms. Tape.

Fire from Fire. *See* Soliloquy I.

From Hamlet. *See* Soliloquy V.

From the Plains. *See* Soliloquy II.

B8.18 Garden Abstract. (1976) 8'
For: Sopranos(2), Mezzo Sopranos(2), Altos(2). *Text:* Hart Crane. *First performed:* Oct. 20, 1977; New England Conservatory. Thomas Toscano, conductor. Winner of New England Conservatory, Composition Award.
Vocal score: ms.
Cassette: recording of first performance. NEC
Cassette: May 14, 1978; New England Conservatory; in *Commencement Concert.* Thomas Toscano, conductor. NEC

B8.19 Ides, Book I. (1974) 8'
For: piano. *First performed:* Oct. 27, 1974; University of Wisconsin, Madison. Glenn Holmer.
Score: ms. Tape.

B8.20 Ides, Book II. (1975) 13'
For: piano. *First performed:* Mar. 12, 1976; University of Wisconsin, Madison. Janet [Shimon?].
Score: ms.
Cassette: Dec. 9, 1976; New England Conservatory; in *Premiere*. Nicholas Underhill. NEC

B8.21 Ides, Book III. (1977) 10'
For: piano. *First performed:* Apr. 14, 1978; University of Iowa. Robert Rowe.
Score: ms. *Tape.*

Incandescent Afternoon. *See* Soliloquy VI.

B8.22 Initiale. (1977) 4'
For: Soprano and piano. *Text:* Rainer Maria Rilke. *First performed:* Mar. 9, 1978; New England Conservatory. Kristin Samuelson, soprano and Nicholas Underhill, piano.
Score: ms. *Tape.*

B8.23 ....in the sky vaults, a song... (1975) 9'
For: Soprano, flute, English horn, clarinet, percussion(2), pianos(2), harp, viola. *Text:* Roger Bourland. *First performed:* Mar. 12, 1976; University of Wisconsin, Madison. Roger Bourland, conductor.
Score & parts: ms. *Tape.*

B8.24 Jabberwocky. (1973) 7'
For: speakers(2), oboe, clarinet, bassoon. *Text:* Lewis Carroll.
Music: ms.

B8.25 Keeja. (1975) 15'
For: pianos(2). *First performed:* Oct. 21, 1975; University of Wisconsin, Madison. Roger Bourland and Robert Rowe.
Score: ms. in composer's hand.

Cassette: Nov. 17, 1977; New England Conservatory; in *Premiere*. NEC

B8.26 Laredo Variations. (1973) 6'
For: horn, trumpet, snare drum, piano.
Score: reprod. of ms.

[Magical Places]
B8.27 Three Magical Places (Portrait of Monet). (1979) 10'
For: harp. *First performed:* Mar. 15, 1979; Harvard University. Susan Allen.
Score: ms.
Disc: Opus One, nyp. *Tape.*

Meditation. *See* Soliloquy VIII.

B8.28 Movements. (1977) 14'
For: brasses(5).
Score & parts: ms.

Musettes & Memoirs. *See* Soliloquy IV.

B8.29 Nascent Fire. (1976) 8'
For: orchestra(3-3-4-3; 4-3-2-2; hp(2), pf; str).
Score: ms.

[New Hymns]
B8.30 Twelve New Hymns. (1980) Duration variable.
For: chorus(SATB). *Vocal score.*

Ocean. *See* Soliloquy III.

[Olden Pieces]
B8.31 Four Olden Pieces. (1974)
For: Soprano, Alto, Tenor, Bass; Tenors(2); voices; Soprano, Alto, Tenor, Bass. *Vocal score.*

B8.32 Orchestral Set I. (1978) 16'
For: orchestra(2-2-2-2; 4-2-2-1; perc; hp; str).
Score: ms.

B8.33 Personae. (1978) 10'
For: violoncello and double bass. *First performed:* Feb. 16, 1979; Harvard University.
Score: Margun. nyp.

[Pictures]
B8.34 Three Pictures. (1975)
For: Soprano, organ, percussion. *First performed:* Mar. 12, 1976; University of Wisconsin, Madison. Unidentified soprano; Yollanda Ionesa, organ; James Latimer, percussion.

[Pieces for Tuesday]
B8.35 Three Pieces for Tuesday. (1974) 5'
For: voice, piano, guitar.
Score: ms.

[Poems]
B8.36 Three Poems. (1974) 7'
For: chorus(SATB). *Text:* Ezra Pound, Lewis Carroll, Roger Bourland.
Vocal score: ms.

Poems (Five). *See* Soliloquy VII.

[Pollock Paintings]
B8.37 Seven Pollock Paintings. (1978) 20'
For: flute, clarinet, saxophone(soprano), clarinet(bass), tam-tam, violin, viola, violoncello, double bass. Winner of Koussevitzky International Award for Best Composition (1978). *First performed:* July 17, 1978; Berkshire Music Festival, Tanglewood, Mass. Patricia Handy, conductor.
Score & parts: Margun, 1980. HU NEC
Tape.

Portrait of Monet. *See* Magical Places.

Postcard Sonatas. *See* Soliloquy X.

B8.38 Rape/Pianoforte. (1974) 15'
For: actors(7) and piano.
Score: ms. in composer's hand.

B8.39 The Red Cliff. (1977) 2'
For: Soprano and piano. *Text:* Andrew Hoyem. *First performed:* Mar. 9, 1978; New England Conservatory. Kristin Samuelson, soprano and Nicholas Underhill, piano.
Score: ms. *Tape.*

[Small Pieces]
B8.40 Five Small Pieces. (1973-74) 12'
For: piano.
Score: ms.

B8.41 Soliloquy I: Fire from Fire. (1976) 10'
For: saxophone(soprano). *First performed:* Mar. 12, 1976; University of Wisconsin, Madison. Les Thimmig.
Score: ms. *Tape.*

B8.42 Soliloquy II: From the Plains. (1976) 6'
For: horn. *First performed:* Aug. 2, 1976; University of Wisconsin, Madison. John Zirbel.
Score: ms. *Tape.*

B8.43 Soliloquy III: Ocean. (1976) 6'
For: flute. *First performed:* Oct. 14, 1976; New England Conservatory. Kathi Edelman.
Score: ms.
Cassette: recording of first performance. NEC
Cassette: Mar. 6, 1978; New England Conservatory; in *Premiere.* NEC

B8.44 Soliloquy IV: Musettes & Memoirs. (1976) 11'
For: oboe. *First performed:* Dec. 13, 1976; State College, Pa. Monte Bedford.
Score: ms. *Tape.*

B8.45 Soliloquy V: From Hamlet. (1977) 5'
For: Mezzo Soprano.
Score: ms.

B8.46 Soliloquy VI: Incandescent Afternoon. (1977) 8'
For: violoncello. *First performed:* Mar. 9, 1978; New England Conservatory. Phoebe Carrai.
Score: ms. *Tape.*

B8.47 Soliloquy VII: Five Poems. (1977) 7'
For: double bass. *First performed:* Mar. 19, 1978; Hirshberg Gallery, Boston.

Michael Gorajec.
Score: ms. *Tape.*

B8.48 Soliloquy VIII: Meditation. (1977) 5'
For: bassoon. *First performed:* Mar. 19, 1978; Hirshberg Gallery, Boston. Janet Grice.
Score: ms.

B8.49 Soliloquy IX: Epiphany. (1977) 10'
For: clarinet. *First performed:* Mar. 9, 1978; New England Conservatory. Robert Cohen.
Score: ms. *Tape.*

B8.50 Soliloquy X: Postcard Sonatas. (1977) 9'
For: harp. *First performed:* Mar. 19, 1978; Hirshberg Gallery, Boston. Faye Seaman.
Score: ms. *Tape.*

B8.51 Soliloquy XI. (1978) 6'
For: trumpet.
Score: ms.

B8.52 Song. (1972) 5'
For: flute and guitar. *First performed:* Dec. 17, 1972; Omaha, Neb.
Score: ms.

B8.53 Suite. (1974) 6'
For: clarinet(bass), trumpet. violoncello.
Music: ms.

B8.54 Sweet Alchemy. (1980)
For: orchestra(2-2-2-2; 2-0-2-0; perc; pf; str). *Commissioned by:* Alea III. *First performed:* May 11, 1980; Boston University. Theodore Antoniou, conductor.
Score & parts: ms.
Reel: recording of first performance. BU

B8.55 Three for Five. (1976) 10'
For: violins(2), violas(2), violoncello.
Music: ms.

B8.56 A Wedding. (1979) 3'
For: string quartet.
Music: ms.

B8.57 Windquill. (1973) 8'
For: piccolo, flute, oboe, clarinet(contrabass), bassoon. *First performed:* Dec. 9, 1973; University of Wisconsin, Madison.
Score & parts: ms. *Tape.*

B9 HAYG BOYADJIAN

Born May 15, 1938, in Paris, France. Moved to Boston area 1958. *Education:* studies in music at New England Conservatory (1965-66) and Brandeis University (1967-69); B.A., Economics (Northeastern University, 1967); studied composition with Beatriz Balzi (Liszt Conservatorio, Argentina, 1949-58) and Seymour Shifrin. *Awards:* MacDowell Colony Fellowship (1980). BPL

WORKS

B9.1 Armenian Song. (1969) 2'
For: Soprano and piano.
Score: ms. in composer's hand.

B9.2 Balance. (1977) 9'
For: oboe. *Dedicated to:* Patricia Morehead. *First performed:* July 1978; Rockport, Me. Patricia Morehead.
Score: ms. in composer's hand.

B9.3 The Blossom. (1975) 1' 20"
For: Mezzo Soprano and piano. *Text:* William Blake. *First performed:* Sept. 30, 1979; Hirshberg Gallery, Boston. Emmily Romney, mezzo soprano and Darryl Rosenberg, piano.
Score: ms. in composer's hand.
Reel: Jan. 6, 1979; Follen Church, Lexington, Mass
Cassette: Jan. 6, 1979; Follen Church, Lexington, Mass.

B9.4 Canticles of a Memory. (1973) 4'
For: violoncello and piano.
Score: ms. in composer's hand.

B9.5 Capriccioso No. 1. (1972) 1' 10"
For: piano. *First performed:* Oct. 25, 1973; Emmanuel Church, Boston. Cameron Grant.
Score: ms. in composer's hand.

Disc: Cameron Grant.
Tape: Cameron Grant.

B9.6 Capriccioso No. 2. (1975-76) 1' 30"
For: piano.
Score: ms. in composer's hand.

B9.7 Capriccioso No. 3. (1981) 1' 30"
For: organ.
Score: ms. in composer's hand.

B9.8 Contours. (1974) 6'
For: clarinet and piano. *First performed:* Mar. 20, 1977; Lexington, Mass. Lawrence Scripp, clarinet and Kenneth Ziegenfuss, piano.
Score: ms. in composer's hand.
Reel: Sept. 30, 1979; Hirshberg Gallery, Boston.
Cassette: Sept. 30, 1979; Hirshberg Gallery, Boston.

B9.9 Dialogues. (1980) 15'
For: clarinets(2). 8 movements. *First performed:* May 9, 1981; Music School at Rivers, Weston, Mass. (2nd and 3rd movements). Gordon Smith and Myron Aronwitt.
Score: ms. in composer's hand.

B9.10 Discourses. (1975) 12'
For: clarinet and violoncello. *Dedicated to:* Deborah Thompson and Lawrence Scripp. *First performed:* Jan. 23, 1976; South Shore Conservatory of Music, Hingham, Mass. Lawrence Scripp, clarinet and Deborah Thompson, violoncello.
Score: ms. in composer's hand.

B9.11 Duo No. 1. (1970) 6' 30"
For: flute and piano. *First performed:* Apr. 2, 1972; School of the Museum of Fine Arts, Boston. Christopher Krueger, flute and Robert Wieder, piano.
Score: ms. in composer's hand.

B9.12 Duo No. 2. (1972) 4' 30"
For: flute and piano. *First performed:* Apr. 2, 1976; South Shore Conservatory of Music, Hingham, Mass. Paul Fried, flute and Robert Wyatt, piano.
Score: ms. in composer's hand.

B9.13 Elegy. (1979) 4'
For: piano. *First performed:* June 1, 1980; Music School at Rivers, Weston, Mass. Jocelyn MacArthur.
Score: ms. in composer's hand.

B9.14 Episodes. (1972-73) 12'
For: flute, oboe, violin, viola, violoncello, piano.
Score & parts: ms. in composer's hand.

B9.15 Fantasy. (1981) 4'
For: organ.
Score: ms. in composer's hand.

B9.16 Fusion. (1973) Duration variable.
For: string quartet, trumpet(optional), trombone(optional), slides. *First performed:* May 1, 1974; Salem State College. Janet Packer and Beth Cohen, violins; David Schreiber, viola; Deborah Thompson, violoncello; Richard Garick, trumpet; Gary Shaw, trombone.
Score & parts: ms. in composer's hand.

B9.17 Mobile. (1977-78) 12'
For: flute, harp, violoncello. *First performed:* May 30, 1981; Follen Church, Lexington, Mass. Christopher Krueger, flute; Susan Allen, harp; Thomas Rutishauser, violoncello.
Score & parts: ms. in composer's hand.
Tape: recording of first performance.

B9.18 Movement No. 1. (1971) 2' 30"
For: piano. *First performed:* Oct. 25, 1973; Emmanuel Church, Boston. Cameron Grant.
Score: ms. in composer's hand.
Disc: Cameron Grant.
Tape: Cameron Grant.

B9.19 Movement No. 2. (1972) 4'
For: piano.
Score: ms. in composer's hand.

B9.20 Movement No. 3. (1973) 5' 30"
For: piano.
Score: ms. in composer's hand.

B9.21 Movement No. 4. (1974) 8' 30"
For: piano. *Dedicated to:* Darryl
Rosenberg. *First performed:* Apr. 2,
1976; South Shore Conservatory of
Music, Hingham, Mass. Darryl
Rosenberg.
Score: ms. in composer's hand.
Tape: Feb. 3, 1978; Jordan Hall, Boston.
Beatriz Balzi.

B9.22 Movement No. 5. (1975-76) 5'
For: piano.
Score: ms. in composer's hand.

B9.23 Murmurs of the C. (1981) 12'
For: flute, violoncello, piano. *Dedicated
to:* Deborah Nathan and the St. Germain
Trio.
Score: ms. in composer's hand.

B9.24 Noche. (1975-77) 3'
For: Mezzo Soprano and piano. *Text:*
Gabriela Mistral. *First performed:* Sept.
30, 1979; Hirshberg Gallery, Boston.
Emmily Romney, mezzo soprano and
Darryl Rosenberg, piano.
Score: ms. in composer's hand.
Reel: Jan. 6, 1979; Follen Church,
Lexington.
Cassette: Jan. 6, 1979; Follen Church,
Lexington, Mass.

B9.25 Nocturne No. 1. (1976) 9' 30"
For: violoncello. *First performed:* Mar.
20, 1977; Lexington, Mass. Deborah
Thompson.
Score: ms. in composer's hand.
Reel: Feb. 17, 1980; Cary Library,
Lexington, Mass. Bruce Coppock.
Cassette: Feb. 17, 1980; Cary Library,
Lexington, Mass. Bruce Coppock.

B9.26 Nocturne No. 2. (1977) 6'
For: violoncello. *First performed:* Feb.
17, 1980; Cary Library, Lexington,
Mass. Bruce Coppock.
Score: ms. in composer's hand.
Reel: recording of first performance.
Cassette: recording of first
performance.

[Quintet, Brasses]
B9.27 Brass Quintet. (1978) 15'
For: horns(2), trumpet, trombone,
trombone(bass).
Score & parts: ms. in composer' hand.

[Quintet, Woodwinds]
B9.28 Woodwind Quintet. (1980) 20'
4 movements.
Score & parts: ms. in composer's hand.

B9.29 Scythe Song. (1972) 2' 30"
For: Mezzo Soprano and piano. *Text:*
Andrew Lang. *First performed:* Jan. 6,
1980; Follen Church, Lexington, Mass.
Diana Cole, mezzo soprano and James
Busby, piano.
Score: ms. in composer's hand.
Reel: recording of first performance.
Cassette: recording of first
performance.

[Sonata, Piano]
B9.30 Sonata No. 1. (1980-1981) 15'
Score: ms. in composer's hand.

[Sonata, Piano(4-Hands)]
B9.31 Sonata. (1980) 15'
3 movements. *Dedicated to:* Angel
Ramon Rivera. *First performed:* May
10, 1981; Music School at Rivers,
Weston, Mass. (1st movement). Paula
Martin and Frank de la Pointe. May 30,
1981; Follen Church, Lexington, Mass.
(2nd movement). Darryl Rosenberg and
Leslie Amper.
Score: ms. in composer's hand.

[Sonata, Viola]
B9.32 Sonata. (1978-79) 14'
2 movements. *Dedicated to:* Stephan

Spackman. *First performed:* Apr. 22, 1980; St. Andrews University, St. Andrews, Scotland. Stephan Spackman. *Score:* ms. in composer's hand.

[Sonata, Violin]
B9.33 Sonata. (1975) 15'
First performed: Sept. 30, 1979; Hirshberg Gallery, Boston. Sofia Vilker. *Score:* ms. in composer's hand.
Reel: recording of first performance.

B9.34 Song Cycle on Poems of William Blake. (1977-78) 15'
For: Soprano, flute, clarinet, percussion, piano, violin, violoncello, double bass. *Contents:* To the Muses; A Poison Tree; Songs of Experience-Introduction; The Tyger; The Fly; Songs of Experience-Earth's Answer.
Score: ms. in composer's hand.

B9.35 Songs from a Dozen Fantasies from Dunkin Donuts. (1980-81) 8'
For: Baritone and piano. *Text:* Tony Fusco. *Dedicated to:* Robert Four.
Score: ms. in composer's hand.

B9.36 Suite for Brass Quintet. (1979) 14'
For: trumpets(2), horn, trombone, tuba or trombone(bass). *First performed:* Sept. 30, 1979; Hirshberg Gallery, Boston. Cambridge Symphonic Brass Quintet.

B9.37 Symphonia. (1980-81) 15'
For: string orchestra.
Score & parts: ms. in composer's hand.

B9.38 Triaco. (1976) 7'
For: flute. *First performed:* Sept. 30, 1979; Hirshberg Gallery, Boston. Andrea Mason.
Score: ms. in composer's hand.
Tape: recording of first performance.

B10 MARTIN BOYKAN

Born April 12, 1931, in New York City. Moved to Boston area 1947. *Education:* studied composition with Walter Piston (Harvard University), Paul Hindemith (University of Zurich and Yale University), Aaron Copland (Berkshire Music Festival, Tanglewood). *Awards:* Bohemians Prize (New York Musicians Club, Harvard University, 1951). *Related activities:* pianist; member of the faculty of Brandeis University (1956-). BrU

WORKS

B10.1 Concerto for 13 Players. (1971) 24'
For: instrumental ensemble(flute, clarinet, clarinet(bass), bassoon, horn, trombone, violin, viola, violoncello, double bass). *First performed:* 1971; Sanders Theatre, Harvard University. Boston Symphony Chamber Players.
Score & parts: Mobart. BrU
Score & parts: Association for the Promotion of New Music. Rental.
Cassette: Feb. 15, 1977. New England Conservatory. NEC Contemporary Music Ensemble, Gunther Schuller, conductor. NEC

B10.2 Duo. (1951) 10'
For: violin and piano. 2 movements.
First performed: 1951; Harvard University.
Score: ms.

B10.3 Elegy. (1979) 15'
For: Soprano, flute, clarinet, violin, violoncello, double bass, piano. 3 movements. *First performed:* Feb. 1981; Sanders Theatre, Harvard University. Elsa Charlston; Boston Musica Viva, Richard Pittman, conductor.
Score & parts: nyp.

B10.4 Psalm 126. (1975) 6'
For: chorus(SATTB).
Vocal score: Mobart, 1975.

[Quartet, Strings (1950)]
B10.5 String Quartet (1950).
First performed: 1950; Harvard

University. Juilliard String Quartet.
Music: ms.

[Quartet, Strings, No. 1]
B10.6 String Quartet. (1967) 19' 30"
4 movements. *First performed:* 1967;
Brandeis University. Brandeis String
Quartet.
Score & parts: New Valley Music Press,
1968. BPL BrU HU
Disc: Composers Recordings CRI SD
338, 1975. Contemporary Quartet. BrU
HU MIT NEC

[Quartet, Strings, No. 2]
B10.7 String Quartet No. 2. (1974) 17'
4 movements. *Dedication:* To my friend
and colleague, Seymour Shifrin. *First
performed:* 1976; Brandeis University.
American String Quartet.
Score: Mobart, 1976. BrU HU
Study score: Mobart, 1980.
Parts: Mobart, 1976.
Disc: Composers Recordings CRI SD
401, 1978. Pro Arte Quartet BrU HU
MIT NEC W

B10.8 Sonata. (1950) 15'
For: flute and piano 3 movements.
First performed: 1951; Harvard
University. Winner of Bohemians Prize
(New York Musicians Club, Harvard
University), 1951.
Score: ms. HU

B10.9 Trio. (1975) 14'
For: violin, violoncello, piano. 1
movement. *Commissioned by:* Fromm
Foundation, for the Wheaton Trio. *First
performed:* Wheaton College. Wheaton
Trio.
Study score: Mobart, 1978. BrU
Parts: Mobart, 1978.

B11 MARTIN BRODY

Born July 8, 1949, in Chicago, Ill.
Moved to Boston area 1979. *Education:*
B.A. (Amherst College, 1972); M.M.,
M.M.A., D.M.A. (Yale University, 1975,
1976, 1981); studied composition with
Donald Wheelock, Lewis Spratlan,
Yehudi Wyner, Robert Morris, Seymour

Shifrin, Barry Vercoe. *Awards:* Watson
Foundation Grant (1972), Massachusetts
Council on the Arts and Humanities,
Artist Fellowship Program (1978), Mt.
Holyoke College Faculty Grant (1978).
Related activities: cellist; pianist;
researcher in music theory; currently
on the faculty of Wellesley College. W

WORKS

B11.1 Concertino da camera. (1977-78)
7'
For: chamber orchestra(2-2(Ehn)-2-2;
2-2-2-1; perc(2); pf; str). 1 movement.
Commissioned by: Lewis Spratlan.
Dedicated to: Lewis Spratlan and the
Amherst-Mt. Holyoke Chamber
Orchestra. *First performed:* Apr. 1978;
South Hadley, Mass. Amherst-Mt.
Holyoke Chamber Orchestra.
Score: reprod. of ms.

B11.2 Duo. (1976) 6' 30"
For: flute and piano. 1 movement.
Commissioned by and dedicated to:
Jonathan Drexler and Gary Smart. *First
performed:* June, 1977; Los Angeles,
Calif. Jonathan Drexler, flute, and Gary
Smart, piano.
Score: reprod. of ms.

B11.3 Lucky Pierre, A Picaresque.
(1976) 14'
For: saxophone(soprano), violin, viola,
violoncello. 1 movement. *First
performed:* Aug. 1977; Composers'
Conference, Johnson, Vt.
Score: reprod. of ms.

B11.4 Moments musicaux. (1980-81) 5'
30"
For: piano and tape(computer). 1
movement. *Commissioned by and
dedicated to:* David Evans. *First
performed:* Feb. 13, 1981; New Haven,
Conn. David Evans.
Score: reprod. of ms.
Reel: Feb. 13, 1981; Wellesley College.
David Evans. W

B11.5 Music. (1977) 8'
For: violoncellos(2). 1 movement. *First

performed: May, 1977; Brandeis University. Martin Brody and Deborah Sherr.
Score: reprod. of ms.
Reel: Feb. 13, 1981; Wellesley College. Martin Brody and Deborah Sherr. W

B11.6 Nocturnes. (1979) 7'
For: flute. 1 movement. *Dedicated to:* Zorah Tucker. *First performed:* Feb. 24, 1980; Wellesley College. Christopher Krueger.
Score: reprod. of ms.
Reel: recording of first performance. W
Cassette: recording of first performance. MIT

B11.7 Pastorale Revisions. (1974) 3' 30"
For: flute and organ. 1 movement. *Commissioned by and dedicated to:* Jonathan Drexler. *First performed:* fall, 1974; New Haven, Conn. Jonathan Drexler, flute, and unidentified organist.
Score: reprod. of ms.

[Rituals]
B11.8 Three Rituals. (1977) 9'
For: chorus(SSAA) and violin.
Movements: Navajo; Zuni; Apache. *Text:* from *Technicians of the Sacred*, translated by Jerome Rothenberg and William Stanley Merwin. *Commissioned by:* Catharine Melhorn. *Dedicated to:* Catharine Melhorn and the Mt. Holyoke Coro. *First performed:* Mar. 1978; Midwestern tour. Linda Laderach, violin; Mt. Holyoke Coro.
Score: reprod. of ms.

B11.9 Saxifrage. (1975) 6'
For: piano. 1 movement. *Commissioned by and dedicated to:* Robert Weirich. *First performed:* Apr. 1976; New Haven, Conn. Robert Weirich.
Score: reprod. of ms. W
Cassette: Oct. 26, 1980; Wellesley College. Robert Weirich. W

B11.10 Turkish Rondo. (1980) 3' 30"
For: tape(computer). Created at the Massachusetts Institute of Technology

Experimental Music Studio. *First performed:* July 1980; Loeb Drama Center, Harvard University.
Reel: recording of first performance.

B12 ROSLYN BROGUE

Born February 16, 1919, in Chicago, Ill.; died August 1, 1981, in Beverly, Mass. *Education:* A.B. (University of Chicago, 1937); A.M. (Radcliffe College, 1943); Ph.D. (Harvard University, 1947). *Awards:* Phi Beta Kappa (1947), Brookline Library Music Association Composers Award, (1965), Ann Louise Barrett Fellowship (Wellesley College), Dorothy Bridgman Atkinson Fellowship, Georgina Holmes Thomas Fellowship (Radcliffe College). *Related activities:* teacher of classics, literature, music; harpsichordist, pianist, violinist, poet, author; Research assistant, Byzantine Studies, Dumbarton Oaks Foundation, Harvard University (1942-50); served on the faculties of the Cambridge School, Weston, Mass. (Latin, Greek, English), Harvard University Summer School (English for foreign students, 1951-61), Boston University, Tufts University (1962-75). T

WORKS

B12.1 Adoramus Te. (1938)
For: chorus(SATB). Motet. *First performed:* 1938; Chicago, Ill. St. James Methodist Church Choir.
Vocal score: reprod. of ms. T

After the Provencal. *See* Permutations.
Five Songs of Courtly Love.

B12.2 Allegretto. (1948) 4'
For: flute and piano. *First performed:* 1957; WBUR-FM, Boston. Cynthia Crain, flute and Tahouhi Chorbajian, piano.
Score & part: ms. T
Score & part: Music for Woodwinds, 1948. T

B12.3 Andante and Variations. (1954-56) 17' 30"

For: harpsichord and orchestra(2(&pic)-2-2(cl in A)-2; 4-0-0-0; str).
Score: ms. T
Score: reprod. of ms. T

B12.4 Arabesque. (1955) 3' 30"
For: violoncello and piano. *First performed:* 1955; WBUR-FM, Boston. Harold Sproul, violoncello and Allen Barker, piano.
Score: ms. T
Score: reprod. of ms. T

B12.5 The Baite. (1961)
For: Tenor or Bass Baritone, violoncello, harpsichord. *Text:* John Donne. *First performed:* Dec. 16, 1973; Tufts University. Luther Enstad, tenor; Robert Yaffe, violoncello; Janice Richardson, harpsichord.
Score: ms. T
Score: reprod. of ms. T

B12.6 Childing. (1957) 10'
For: Soprano, flute, violoncello, harp. *Text:* Salem Slobodkin. *First performed:* May 25, 1958; WBUR-FM, Boston. Martha Bentley, soprano; Cynthia Crain, flute; Harold Sproul, violoncello; Eleanor Hansen, harp.
Score & parts: ms.
Score & parts: reprod. of ms. T

B12.7 Christus factus est. (1938)
For: chorus(SATB). Motet. *First performed:* 1938; Chicago, Ill. St. James Methodist Church Choir.
Vocal score: reprod. of ms. T

B12.8 Come, Lovely and Soothing Death. (1960) 6' 07"
For: Soprano and Alto or Sopranos(2) or chorus(women) and harpsichord or piano. *Text:* from *When Lilacs Last in the Dooryard Bloom'd* by Walt Whitman. *First performed:* Jan. 17, 1961; Brookline Public Library. Roslyn Brogue, soprano; Mary Frances Dunlevy, mezzo soprano; Livia Rabinek, piano.
Score: ms. T
Score: reprod. of ms. T
Reel: recording of first performance.

Darest Thou Now O Soul. *See* Song of Exploration. Darest Thou Now O Soul.

B12.9 Duo lirico. (1952) 5'
For: violin and harpsichord. *Dedicated to:* Robert Brink and Daniel Pinkham. *First performed:* 1952; Boston Conservatory. Robert Brink, violin and Daniel Pinkham, harpsichord.
Score & parts: ms. T
Score & parts: reprod. of ms. T

[Elegies]
B12.10 Four Elegies. (1962)
For: Soprano and harpsichord or piano. *Contents:* Ayre, Fain Would I Change That Note (Tobias Hume); Song, How Many Times Do I Love Thee (Thomas Lovell Beddoes); Song, If Thou Wilt Ease Thine Heart (Thomas Lovell Beddoes); As by Water (T.S. Merwin). *First performed:* Oct. 23, 1962; Boston Conservatory; Fenway Concert. Delores Fox, soprano and Roslyn Brogue, harpsichord.
Score: ms. T
Score: reprod. of ms. T
Score: in *Poems New and Old*. T

B12.11 Equipoise. (1972)
For: saxophone(alto), piano, harpsichord. *First performed:* May 6, 1972; Tufts University. Lorenzo Lepore, clarinet; Virginia Armstrong, piano; Roslyn Brogue, harpsichord.
Score & part: Dorn, 1974. T *Tape.*

B12.12 Equipoise II. (1974)
For: flutes(2), clarinet, violoncello, dancers(optional). *Choreography:* Rosalind Pierson. *First performed:* Apr. 19, 1974; Mount Holyoke College. Esther Salmi and Erica Verrillo, flutes; Lorenzo Lepore, clarinet; Billie Miller, violoncello; Nancy Caplan, Christopher Howard, Rosalind Pierson, dancers.
Score & parts: ms. T *Tape.*

A Fantasy on the Chanson Mille regretz. *See* Quartet for Piano and Strings.

Juggler. *See* Permutations. Juggler.

Love Songs (After the Provencal). *See*
Permutations. Five Songs of
Courtly Love.

[Madrigals]
B12.13 Three Madrigals. (1959)
For: Soprano, Alto, Tenor, Bass, piano
or harpsichord. *Contents:* Song (John
Donne); Hippopotamus (T.S. Eliot); The
Sunne Rising (John Donne).
Vocal score: ms. (Nos. 1 and 3). T
Parts: ms. (Nos. 2 and 3). T

B12.14 Mass. (1937-39)
For: chorus(SATB). *First performed:*
1939; Chicago, Ill. Church of St.
Thomas Apostle Choir.
Vocal score: reprod. of ms.

Mille regretz. *See* Quartet for Piano
and Strings.

Ode. *See* Song of Exploration. Ode;
Arr.

An Old Entertainment for Amusing
Oneself Now. *See* Permutations. Five
Songs of Courtly Love.

B12.15 Parade. (1954) 1'
For: recorder or clarinet and keyboard.
Dedicated to: Narcissa Williamson.
Score: ms. T
Score: reprod. of ms. T

[Permutations]
B12.16 Four Permutations. (1958-62)
For: Soprano, flute, violoncello,
harpsichord. *Contents:* Five Songs of
Courtly Love (Salem Slobodkin); Speed,
We Say (Muriel Rukeyser); A
Valedication: Of Weeping (John Donne);
Juggler (Richard Wilbur). *Dedicated to:*
Martha Bentley.
Score: in *Poems New and Old*. T

[Permutations. Five Songs of Courtly
Love]
B12.17 Five Songs of Courtly Love, or,
An Old Entertainment for
Amusing Oneself Now. (1958) 12' *For:*
Soprano, flute, harpsichord. *Text:* Salem

Slobodkin. *Contents:* Overture; Aria;
Pastorale; Serenade; Rhapsody.
Dedicated to: Martha Bentley. *First
performed:* Feb. 16, 1959; Cambridge
School, Weston, Mass. (under title
Love Songs (After the Provencal)).
Martha Bentley, soprano; Karl Kraber,
flute; Roslyn Brogue, harpsichord.
Sketches: ms. T
Score & part: ms. T.
Score & part: reprod. of ms. T

[Permutations. Juggler]
B12.18 Juggler. (1962)
For: Soprano, violoncello, harpsichord.
Text: Richard Wilbur. *Dedicated to:*
Martha Bentley.
Score: ms. T
Score: reprod. of ms. T

[Permutations. Speed, We Say]
B12.19 Speed, We Say. (1961)
For: Soprano, flute, violoncello,
harpsichord. *Text:* Muriel Rukeyser.
Dedicated to: Martha Bentley. *First
performed:* Feb. 11, 1962; New York
City. Martha Bentley, soprano; Lee
Steelman, flute; Charles Forbes,
violoncello; Roslyn Brogue, harpsichord.
Score & parts: ms.
Score: reprod. of ms. T
Score: ms. T

[Permutations. A Valediction: Of
Weeping]
B12.20 A Valediction: Of Weeping.
(1962)
For: Soprano and harpsichord or piano.
Text: John Donne. *Dedicated to:* Martha
Bentley. *First performed:* July 20, 1962;
Boston University. Delores Fox,
soprano and Roslyn Brogue,
harpsichord.
Score: ms. T
Score: reprod. of ms. T

B12.21 Quartet for Piano and Strings:
A Fantasy on the Chanson Mille
regretz. (1948; rev. 1949) 21'
For: piano, violin, viola, violoncello.
First performed: 1954; WBUR-FM,
Boston (later version). Dorothy Bales,

violin; Ann Elmquist, viola; Harold Sproul, violoncello; Allen Barker, piano.
Score & parts: ms. (both versions). T
Score & parts: reprod. of ms. (later version). T

B12.22 Quartet for Strings. (1951) 15' 30"
1 movement. Winner of Brookline Library Music Association Composers Award 1965. *First performed:* Oct. 20, 1958; New York City. Max Pollikoff and Paul Wolfe, violins; Walter Trampler, viola; Alexander Kouguell, violoncello.
Score & parts: ms. T
Score & parts: reprod. of ms. T
Reel: Apr. 21, 1965; Brookline Public Library.

B12.23 Quintet for Organ and Winds. (1945) 14'
For: oboe, clarinet, trumpet, trombone, organ.
Score: ms. T
Parts: reprod. of ms. T

B12.23.5 Quintet for Winds. (1971)
For: woodwind quintet. *First performed:* May 9, 1972; Tufts University. [Tufts] University Woodwind Quintet.
Score & parts: reprod. of ms. T
Score: ms. T

B12.24 Quodlibet. (1953) 10'
For: flute, violoncello, harpsichord.
First performed: 1953; Museum of Fine Arts, Boston. Arthur Loeb, recorder; Barbara Watson, violoncello; Roslyn Brogue, harpsichord.
Score & parts: ms. T
Score & parts: reprod. of ms. T

B12.25 Sinfonia missae. (1949) 24'
For: organ. *Movements:* Prelude; Offertory; Communion; Postlude.
Score: ms. T
Score: reprod. of ms. T

B12.26 Sonatina. (1957) 4'
For: flute, clarinet, harpsichord. First performed; 1957; WBUR-FM, Boston. Cynthia Crain, flute; Louis Visco, clarinet; Roslyn Brogue Henning, harpsichord.
Score & parts: ms.
Score & parts: reprod. of ms. T
Score: ms. T

B12.27 Song of Exploration. (1959-60) 14'
For: Soprano, flute, clarinet, violoncello, harpsichord. Cantata. *Text:* from *Leaves of Grass* by Walt Whitman. *Contents:* Darest Thou Now O Soul; Passage to India (Aria I, Aria II); Ode; Recitative and Epode. *Commissioned by:* Society for Vocal Chamber Music, New York City. *First performed:* Apr. 18, 1961; Jordan Hall, Boston. Dorothy Renzi, soprano; Lee Steelman, flute; Louis Visco, clarinet; Laurence Lesser, violoncello; Roslyn Brogue Henning, harpsichord.
Score & parts: ms. T
Score & parts: reprod. of ms. T

[Song of Exploration. Darest Thou Now O Soul]
B12.28 Darest Thou Now O Soul. (1959) 3' 48"
For: Soprano, clarinet, violoncello. *Text:* from *Leaves of Grass* by Walt Whitman. *First performed:* Apr. 2, 1960; New York City. Dorothy Renzi, soprano; Charles Russo, clarinet; Seymour Barab, violoncello.
Sketches: ms. T
Score & parts: reprod. of ms. T

[Song of Exploration. Darest Thou Now O Soul; Arr]
B12.29 Darest Thou Now O Soul. 3' 48"
For: Soprano and organ. *Text:* from *Leaves of Grass* by Walt Whitman. *First performed:* 1960; Albuquerque, N.M. Flora Roussos, soprano.
Score: ms. T
Score: reprod. of ms. T

[Song of Exploration. Ode; Arr.]
B12.30 Ode. (1960)
For: Soprano and organ. *Text:* from *Leaves of Grass* by Walt Whitman.
Score: ms. T
Score: reprod. of ms. T

Songs of Courtly Love. *See*
Permutations. Five Songs of Courtly
Love.

B12.31 Sonnet: From the Portuguese.
(1959) 2' 24"
For: Soprano and piano. *Text:* Elizabeth
Barrett Browning. *Dedicated to:* Dorothy
Renzi. *First performed:* June 14, 1960;
WGBH-FM and WGBH-TV, Boston.
Dorothy Renzi, soprano and Roslyn
Brogue Henning, piano. Also titled
When Our Two Souls.
Sketches: ms. T
Score: ms. T
Score: reprod. of ms. T

Speed, We Say. *See* Permutations.
Speed, We Say.

[Suite, Orchestra]
B12.32 Suite for Small Orchestra.
(1947) 12' 15"
For: orchestra 2(pic)-2-2-2; 4-2-2-0;
timp; str). *First performed:* Apr. 29,
1946; Jordan Hall, Boston. Civic
Symphony Orchestra of Boston, Paul
Cherkassky, conductor.
Score: ms. in composer's hand. T
Score: ms. T
Score: reprod. of ms. T
Parts: reprod. of ms.

[Suite, Recorders(4)]
B12.33 Suite. (1949) 8'
First performed: June 1950;
Amsterdam, The Netherlands.
Amsterdams Blokfluit Ensemble, Kees
Otten, conductor.
Score: reprod. of ms. T

[Trio, Oboe, Clarinet, Bassoon]
B12.34 Trio. (1946) 9'
First performed: May 4, 1948; Women's
City Club, of Boston. Ethel Durant,
oboe; Warren Hatch, clarinet; Norman
Sherman, bassoon.
Score & parts: ms. T
Score & parts: Music for Woodwinds,
1948. T

[Trio, Violin, Clarinet, Piano]
B12.35 Trio. (1953) 12'
3 movements. *Dedicated to:* Ervin
Henning. *First performed:* 1953;
WBUR-FM, Boston. Ann Elmquist, violin
(1st and 2nd movements), Robert Brink,
violin (3rd movement); Louis Visco,
clarinet; Allen Barker, piano.
Score & parts: ms. T
Score & parts: reprod. of ms. T

A Valediction: Of Weeping. *See*
Permutations. A Valediction: of
Weeping.

When Our Two Souls. *See* Sonnet:
From the Portuguese.

B13 MARJORIE L. BURGESS

Born January 28, 1915, in Boston.
Education: diploma program (Berklee
College of Music); studied composition
and arranging with Eleanor C.
Kerr-Smith, Gertrude Price Wollner,
John La Porta, James Progris, Frederick
T. Pease, John Bavicchi, Bert Konowitz.
Related activities: pianist;
organist-choirmaster, Unitarian Church
of Melrose, Mass; served on the
faculties of various high schools and
adult education programs in the Boston
area. Currently composer, conductor,
arranger for Creative Arts for Kids,
Reading, Mass. W

WORKS

A-Caroling (Louisburg Square). *See*
Cityscapes. A-Caroling.

Along the Esplanade. *See* Cityscapes.
Along the Esplanade.

B13.1 Animal Gourmets. (1978)
For: piano and narrator(optional). Suite.
Text: Carolyn Baldwin. *Contents:* A
Robin, Two Bluejays, and a Crow; The
Lion; The Horse; Rabbits; The Koala;
The Bull Frog; The Sea Gull; The
Kitten; The Mole; The Giraffe; The

Elephant; The Squirrel; The Owl.
Score: Willis, 1979. W

B13.2 Autumn Song. (1974)
For: piano and speaker(optional).
Dedicated to: Louise H. Olsen.
Score: Willis, 1980. W

B13.3 Barn Dance. (1981)
For: piano. *Dedicated to:* Carol Fieleke.
Score: Emerson, 1981. W

B13.4 Benediction.
For: chorus(SAA) and organ.
Vocal score: reprod. of ms. W

B13.5 Blue Waltz. (1974)
For: piano. *Dedicated to:* Alice M.
Hamlet. Originally titled Blue Waltz for
Louis.
Score: Willis, 1980. W

[Blue Waltz for Louis; Arr.]
B13.6 Blue Waltz.
For: flute and piano.
Score: Emerson, 1977. W

B13.7 Bon Appetit.
For: piano and narrator(optional). *Text:*
Carolyn Baldwin.
Score: reprod. of ms. W

B13.8 Brotherhood. (1970)
For: voice or chorus(SATB) and piano.
Text: anon.
Score: reprod. of ms. W

B13.9 Chamomile. (1977)
For: piano and narrator(optional).
Variations. *Text:* Carolyn Baldwin.
Score: Emerson, 1977. W

Chicken Feathers. *See* Prisms. Chicken
Feathers.

B13.10 A Child Is Born.
For: chorus(SSATB), piano or organ,
flute or bells or guitar obbligato.
Christmas music. *Dedicated to:* Francis
Hood.
Vocal score: Emerson, 1974. W
Vocal score: Willis, nyp (to be

published under title, See the Lovely
Child Is Sleeping).

Chinese Folk Festival. *See* Cityscapes.
Chinese Folk Festival.

B13.11 Cityscapes.
For: piano. *Movements:* Along the
Esplanade; Chinese Folk Festival; Sand
Garden; Flaherty Way; Coronation of
the Moon; Harvard Square; Louisburg
Square (A-Caroling); Skating on Frog
Pond; Swan Boats.
Score: Emerson, 1980. W

[Cityscapes. A-Caroling]
B13.12 A-Caroling (Louisburg Square).
(1980)
For: piano. *Dedicated to:* Donna
Burgess-Warren.
Score: Emerson, 1980.

[Cityscapes. Along the Esplanade]
B13.13 Along the Esplanade.
For: piano. *Dedicated to:* John Richard
McNally.
Score: Willis, 1980. W

[Cityscapes. Chinese Folk Festival]
B13.14 Chinese Folk Festival.
For: piano. *Dedicated to:* Ella Solimine.
Score: Willis, nyp.

[Cityscapes. Coronation of the Moon]
B13.15 Coronation of the Moon. (1980)
For: piano. *Dedicated to:* Eric Fieleke.
Score: Emerson.

[Cityscapes. Flaherty Way]
B13.16 Flaherty Way (South Boston).
(1980)
For: piano. *Dedicated to:* Dorothy and
Richard Cadogan.
Score: Emerson, 1980.

[Cityscapes. Harvard Square]
B13.17 Harvard Square.
For: piano. *Dedicated to:* A. Ramon
Rivera.
Score: Willis, 1980. W

[Cityscapes. Sand Garden]
B13.18 Sand Garden.

For: piano. *Dedicated to:* Dianne
Goolkasian Rahbee.
Score: Emerson.

[Cityscapes. Skating on Frog Pond]
B13.19 Skating on Frog Pond.
For: piano. *Dedicated to:* Michele
Fanton.
Score: Willis, nyp.

[Cityscapes. Swan Boats]
B13.20 Mourning Dove. (1980)
For: piano. *Dedicated to:* Susan
Belmonte. Earlier titles, Swan Boats;
Public Gardens.
Score: Emerson.

B13.21 Cloud Palace.
For: piano. *Dedicated to:* Sylvia
Griffith.
Score: [Emerson Music, 1981?] W
Score: Willis, nyp.

B13.22 Cloud Pictures.
For: piano.
Score: Schmitt, 1975. W

Coronation of the Moon. *See*
Cityscapes. Coronation of the Moon.

B13.23 Dance of the Chimney Sweep.
For: piano. *Dedicated to:* Frank and
Donna Burgess.
Score: Willis, 1980. W

B13.24 Dust Rag or Housewife's Drag.
For: voice and piano, or chorus(SSA).
Written by Marjorie L. Burgess and her
students: Edna Beaton, Muriel Casey,
Dorothea Monohan, Rosemand Wentzel.
Score: Emerson, 1974 (version for
voice and piano). W
Vocal score: Emerson, 1974 (version for
chorus(SSA)). W

Flaherty Way. *See* Cityscapes. Flaherty
Way.

B13.25 Gift of Spring.
For: chorus(SAB) and organ or piano.
Text: Carolyn Baldwin.
Vocal score: Emerson, 1977.

B13.26 The Great Morris Rag.
For: piano.
Score: Emerson, 1974.

B13.27 Halleluia.
For: piano. Blues. *Dedicated to:* Louis.
Score: Emerson, 1977. W

Harvard Square. *See* Cityscapes. Harvard
Square.

B13.28 How Do I Love Thee. (1976)
For: voice and piano. *Text:* Elizabeth
Barrett Browning. *Dedicated to:* Ruth
Dechert.
Score: reprod. of ms. W
Score: Emerson, 1976.

B13.29 Humdinger. (1977)
For: piano or pianos(2). *Dedicated to:*
Earl Burgess.
Score: Emerson, 1977 (version for
piano). W
Score: Willis, 1981 (version for piano). W
Score: Emerson, 1977 (version for 2
pianos). W

B13.30 I Am Five and a Half.
For: Mezzo Soprano. *Text:* anon.
Score: reprod. of ms. W

B13.31 I Thank You God.
For: voice and organ or piano; or
chorus(SATB). *Text:* Edna Herbert.
Score: reprod. of ms. W

I'm Growing Far From You. *See*
Summer Secrets.

[Inventions]
B13.32 Three Inventions. (1974)
For: piano. *Movements:* Pearls for
Nancy; Nancy's Dream; Nancy's Lace.
Score: reprod. of ms. W

B13.33 Kangaroo Troop. (1980)
For: piano. *Dedicated to:* Arthur Houle.
Score: Emerson, 1980. W

The Kitty-Cat Bird. *See* Prisms for
Piano. The Kitty-Cat Bird.

B13.34 Loneliness. (1976)
For: voice and piano. *Text:* Yvonne Graham.
Score: reprod. of ms. W

Louisburg Square. *See* Cityscapes. A-Caroling.

B13.35 Loving You in Vain. (1964)
For: voice and piano. *Text:* Edna Herbert.
Score: reprod. of ms. W

B13.36 Lullaby. (1974)
For: voice and piano. *Text:* Isaac Watts.
Score: Emerson, 1974. W

B13.37 May Peace Dwell within Our Hearts.
For: chorus(SATB). Hymn.
Score: reprod. of ms. W

B13.38 May We Take the Time to Know.
For: voice and organ or piano. *Text:* Donna Burgess-Warren.
Score: Emerson, 1972.

B13.39 Mosquito.
For: piano(4-hands). *Dedicated to:* Nancy Oliva.
Score: Willis, 1980. W

B13.40 Mountain Laurel.
For: piano. *Dedicated to:* Maxwell Norman Gordon.
Score: Willis, nyp.

Mourning Dove. *See* Cityscapes. Swan Boats.

 B13.41 Music a la mode.
For: piano. *Movements:* Voyage of a Leprechaun; Winter Snow; Alhambra; Lullaby for Samantha; Hay; Scottish Festival; Lydian Lark; Lilliput March; Shepherd's Return; Dorian Romp.
Dedicated to: Eileen Dudek; Susan Adams; Susan Sladen; Doris McNally; Maurice Flannery; Bella Ratray; Donna Burgess; Roger La Rocca; Joyce-Anne Creen; Frank Lynn.

Score: Emerson, 1972. W
Score: G. Schirmer, 1972.

B13.42 Music from an Elfin Hill.
For: piano. *Commissioned by: Clavier.*
Dedicated to: Frances A. Ho **od.**
Score: Willis, 1980.
Score: Clavier 20 (Jan. 1981):39-40 (reprint of the above). W

B13.43 My Wish. (1976)
For: voice and piano. *Text:* Carliss St.
Score: reprod. of ms. W

B13.44 Pantomine Rag
For: piano. *Dedicated to:* Donna and Frank [Burgess].
Score: Emerson, 1977. W

B13.45 A Party for My Ghoul Friend.
For: piano. *Dedicated to:* Nancy and Samantha Burgess.
Score: Willis, 1979. W

B13.46 Pea Soup.
For: pianos(2). Blues. *Dedicated to:* Bert Konowitz.
Score: Emerson, 1972? W

[Pea Soup; Arr.]
B13.47
For: flute, saxophone(alto), saxophone(tenor), trumpet, drums, guitar, piano, double bass. *First performed:* July 17, 1981; Berklee College of Music. Faculty group.
Score: Emerson. W *Tape.*

B13.48 Penny Candy. (1979)
For: piano. Ragtime music. *Dedicated to:* Alice Proctor.
Score: Emerson, 1979. W

B13.49 Prayer for Peace.
For: voice and organ or piano; or chorus(SATB). *Text:* Donna Burgess-Warren.
Vocal score: [Emerson? n.d.] W

B13.50 Prayer in Spring.
For: chorus(SAB) and piano. *Text:* Robert Frost (1st verse); Carolyn

Baldwin (2nd verse).
Vocal score: reprod. of ms. W

B13.51 Prisms.
For: piano. *Movements:* Rhapsody on Top of Old Smokey; Round and Around; Senior Cricket Hop; The Kitty-Cat Bird; Greensleeves; Three Blithe Mice; Mary and Her Little Lamb; Chicken Feathers; The Gnome and the Tailor; Mimir; Come to the Fair.
Score: Boston, 1979. W

[Prisms. Chicken Feathers; Arr]
B13.52 Chicken Feathers.
For: flute and piano. *Dedicated to:* Charles Abbott and Norman Shin.
Score: Emerson, 1977. W

[Prisms. Chicken Feathers; Arr]
B13.53 Chicken Feathers.
For: chorus(SATB), flute, piano, guitar, drums, double bass. *Dedicated to:* Charles Abbott and Norman Shin.
Score & parts: Emerson, 1977. W

[Prisms. The Kitty-Cat Bird]
B13.54 The Kitty-Cat Bird. (1976)
For: Soprano and piano. *Text:* Theodore Roethke. *Dedicated to:* Ruth Dechert. For later version, for piano, see Prisms.
Score: Emerson. W

[Psalm 23]
B13.55 Twenty Third Psalm. (1977)
For: chorus(SAB) and piano. *Dedicated to:* Farmington High School Chorus.
Vocal score: Emerson, 1977. W

[Psalm 24]
B13.56 Twenty Fourth Psalm. (1970)
For: chorus(SATB). *Dedicated to:* Gertrude Price Wollner.
Vocal score: Emerson. W

Public Gardens. *See* Cityscapes. Swan Boats.

B13.57 Quiet Hour.
For: voice and organ or piano; or chorus(SATB).
Vocal score: reprod. of ms. W

B13.58 Reflections of a Troll.
For: piano and narrator(optional). *Text:* Carolyn Baldwin. *Dedicated to:* Nancy Burgess.
Score: Willis, 1980. W

B13.59 The Road Not Taken.
For: Baritone [and piano?] *Text:* Robert Frost. Sketch: reprod. of ms. W

Sand Garden. *See* Cityscapes. Sand Garden.

B13.60 Screen Door Rag.
For: piano.
Score: Schmitt, 1975. W

See the Lovely Child Is Sleeping. *See* A Child Is Born.

Skating on Frog Pond. *See* Cityscapes. Skating on Frog Pond.

B13.61 Summer Secrets.
For: piano. Jazz dance music. Originally titled I'm Growing Far From You.
Score: [Emerson? n.d.] W

B13.62 Summer Shadows. (1976)
For: piano. *Dedicated to:* Frank Lynn.
Score: Emerson, 1976. W

[Summer Shadows; Arr.]
B13.63 *For:* chorus(SATB) and piano. *Text:* Carolyn Baldwin. *First performed:* Farmington High School Chorus, Farmington, N.H.
Vocal score: Emerson, 1979. W

B13.64 Sweet William.
For: piano. Ragtime music; waltz.
Score: Emerson, 1975. W

B13.65 To Win A Colleen.
For: chorus(SSAA) or chorus(SATB).
Text: Marjorie L. Burgess.
Vocal score: Emerson, 1953 (version for SSAA). W
Vocal score: Emerson, 1974 (version for SATB). W

B13.66 Topaz.
For: piano. *Dedicated to:* Sylvia White.
Score: Willis, 1980. W

B13.67 Village Bells.
For: piano. *Dedicated to:* Eleanor
Kerr-Smith.
Score: Willis, 1981. W

B13.68 Waltz for Donna.
For: piano.
Score: Emerson, 1974. W

B13.69 Waltz for Freddy. (1976)
For: voice and instruments(unspecified).
Text: Edna Beaton.
Lead sheets: Emerson, 1976. W

We Thank You God. *See* I Thank You
God.

B13.70 Wedding March.
For: organ.
Score: Emerson, 1976. W

B13.71 Wedding Recessional.
For: organ.
Score: Emerson, 1977. W

B13.72 Winifred. (1964)
For: voice and piano. *Text:* Donna
Burgess-Warren.
Score: [Emerson?], 1964. W
Lead sheets: reprod. of ms. W

[Winifred; Arr.]
B13.73 Winifred.
For: piano.
Score: reprod. of ms; available from
composer.

B13.74 The Winter Time Is O'er. (1974)
For: voice or chorus(SATB) and piano.
Hymn. *Dedicated to:* Alice Procter.
Score: Emerson, n.d., (version for
voice). W
Vocal score: Emerson, 1974 (version for
chorus). W

B13.75 Wishes for a New Born Child.
(1972)
For: voice and piano. *Text:* George
Starbuck Galbraith.

B13.76 The World Stands Out on Either
Side. (1970)
For: chorus. Hymn *Text:* Edna St.
Vincent Millay.
Vocal score: reprod. of ms. W

ARRANGEMENTS

B13.77 Take Me Out to the Ball Game.
For: piano. Variations. Original by
Albert Von Tilzer.
Score: Emerson, n.d. W

C1 CURT CACIOPPO

Born September 23 1951, in Ravenna,
Ohio. *Education:* B.M. (Kent State
University, 1973); M.A. (New York
University, 1976); M.A., Ph.D. (Harvard
University, 1979, 1980). *Awards:*
American Society of University
Composers Award, Francis Booth Prize
(Harvard University), Massachusetts
Council on the Arts and Humanities,
Artist Fellowship Program in
Composition (finalist), Presser
Foundation grant. *Related activities:*
pianist; founder of chamber ensemble
Libramentum; toured with Bach Society
Orchestra; analyst of early music;
researcher in native American music;
currently on the faculty of Harvard
University. HU

WORKS

C1.1 Alla primavera. (1974; rev. 1978)
9'
For: voices, chorus(SATB), flute,
clarinet, bassoon, piano, harpsichord,
violin, viola, violoncello. Madrigal.
Text: G. Leopardi. *Dedicated to:* Gustave
Reese. Awarded the Francis Booth Prize
(Harvard University). *First performed:*
Mar. 1978; Harvard University. Curt
Cacioppo, conductor.
Score: Mobart, 1978. HU
Score: Association for the Promotion
of New Music.
Parts: Association for the Promotion
of New Music. Rental.
Vocal score: Association for the
Promotion of New Music. Rental.

Reel: 1978; Harvard University. Curt Cacioppo, conductor.

C1.2 Amen to Peace. (1970) 5'
For: chorus(SATB) and organ. *Text:* Agnus Dei (English translation).
Dedication: To the students slain at Kent State University, May 4, 1970.
Vocal score: ms. in composer's hand.
Disc: May 1970. Kent State University Chorale, Clayton Krehbiel, conductor.
Tape: May 1970. Kent State University Chorale, Clayton Krehbiel, conductor.

C1.3 Eclogue: Symphony for Piano. (1980) 27'
1 movement. Doctoral thesis. *First performed:* Mar. 1980; Harvard University; Fromm Foundation concert. Ira Braus.
Score: reprod. of ms. HU
Score: Association for the Promotion of New Music.
Reel: 1980; Harvard University. Ira Braus. HU

C1.4 Fugue & Chorale. (1979) 3'
For: piano.
Score: ms. in composer's hand.

C1.5 Introit. (1973) 3'
For: string orchestra. 1 movement.
Score & parts: ms. in composer's hand.

[Introit; Arr.]
C1.6 Introit.
For: piano(4-hands).
Score: ms. in composer's hand.

C1.7 Klavierstueck. (1976) 7'
For: piano. 1 movement. *Dedication:* To my wife. Winner of American Society of University Composers Award (1976).
First performed: Mar. 1977; Urbana, Ill.; American Society of University Composers Convention. Arthur Maddox.
Score: Mobart, 1978. HU
Score: Association for the Promotion of New Music.
Reel: recording of first performance.
Reel: 1979; Harvard University. Ira Braus.

C1.8 Largo. (1979) 8'
For: string orchestra and timpani(obbligato). 1 movement.
Dedicated to: Albert G. *First performed:* Mar. 1980; Sanders Theatre, Harvard University. Bach Society Orchestra, James Ross, conductor.
Score: Association for the Promotion of New Music.
Parts: Association for the Promotion of New Music. Rental.
Reel: recording of first performance.

[Largo; Arr.]
C1.9 Largo.
For: violins(2), violas(2), violoncellos(2).
Score & parts: Association for the Promotion of New Music.

C1.10 Linus. (1970) 10'
For: Alto, violin, viola, violoncello, piano. 1 movement. *Text:* Curt Cacioppo. *First performed:* Jan. 1970; Kent, Ohio.
Score & parts: ms. in composer's hand.
Vocal score: ms. in composer's hand.
Reel: recording of first performance.

C1.11 Music for Oboe and Piano. (1977) 10'
1 movement.
Score: ms. in composer's hand.

C1.12 Of Dark and Bright. (1972) 4'
For: horn. 1 movement. *First performed:* winter, 1978; Harvard University. James Ross.
Score: Association for the Promotion of New Music. HU
Reel: recording of first performance.

C1.13 Preludes on Pawnee Themes. (1981) 10'
For: piano. 9 movements.
Score: Association for the Promotion of New Music, nyp.

C1.14 Red Bird. (1981) Duration variable.
For: guitar and continuo(optional).
Score: Association for the Promotion of New Music, nyp.

C1.15 To a Child. (1981) 15'
For: Soprano and chamber
orchestra(2(pic)-2(Ehn)-2(bcl)-2; 2-2-0-0;
timp(2), perc; hp; pf; str). *Text: To a
Child Dancing in the Wind*, by William
Butler Yeats.
Score: Association for the Promotion
of New Music, nyp.
Parts: Association for the Promotion
of New Music. Rental.

C2 MICHAEL PAGE CARNES

Born May 15, 1950. *Education:* studied
composition with John Bavicchi
(Berklee College of Music, B.A., 1977);
Theodore Antoniou, John Thow, David
Del Tredici (Boston University, M.M.,
1980); Gunther Schuller; R.M. Van Dijk.
Awards: Margaret Lee Crofts
Fellowship (Tanglewood, 1980). *Related
activities:* currently with the
Experimental Music Studio,
Massachusetts Institute of Technology
and Analogic Corporation, Wakefield,
Mass. MIT

WORKS

C2.1 Anima. (1979) 12'
For: harp, piano, violoncellos(4). *First
performed:* Apr. 1980; Boston
University. Boston University Collegium
in Contemporary Music.
Score: ms. in composer's hand.
Score: reprod. of ms; available from
composer.
Reel: available from composer.
Cassette: available from composer.

C2.2 Brown Mountain Lights. (1975-76)
4'
For: piano.
Score: ms. in composer's hand.
Score: reprod. of ms; available from
composer.

[Concerto, Marimba]
C2.3 Marimba Concerto. (1981)
For: marimba and chamber
orchestra(1(pic)-1-1(in A)-1(cbsn);
2-0-0-0; perc(2) hp; str). *Movements:*
Lento; Comedy; Variation. *Commissioned*

by: Richard Flanagan.
Score: ms. in composer's hand.
Score: reprod of ms; available from
composer.

C2.4 Etc. (1981)
Film music. Written for comedy film
Not Manhattan produced by William
Rose. Winner of prize in Houston
International Film Festival.
Music: available from composer.

C2.5 Fantasy Music I. (1981) 5' 30"
For: flute and tape(computer)(2-channel).
Dedicated to: Frances Carnes. *First
performed:* Massachusetts Institute of
Technology. Wendy Stern.
Music: available from composer.

C2.6 Fantasy Music II. (in progress) 6'
For: harpsichord and
tape(computer)(2-channel). *Commissioned
by:* Joyce Lindoff.

C2.7 From Winter. (1979) 8'
For: Soprano and piano. *Text:* Michael
Carnes. *First performed:* May 25, 1980;
Sanders Theatre, Harvard University.
Elizabeth Van Ingen, soprano and
Martin Amlin, piano.
Score: ms. in composer's hand.
Score: reprod. of ms; available from
composer.
Reel: available from composer.
Cassette: available from composer.

C2.8 Masque. (1978) 14'
For: trumpet and piano. *Contents:*
Soliloquy; Juggler; Rhapsody; The
Fugitive. Winner of Boston University
Undergraduate Composition Prize
(Second Prize). *First performed:* Oct.
25, 1979; Boston University; in
Omnibus: Music of the 20th Century.
Thomas Cook, trumpet and Myron
Romanul, piano.
Score: ms. in composer's hand.
Score: reprod. of ms; available from
composer.
Reel: available from composer.
Reel: recording of first performance.
BU
Cassette: available from composer.

C2.9 Nocturnes. (1980-81) 9'
For: Soprano, tape(computer)(4-channel), orchestra(1(pic)-1-2(in A/Bb) -2(cbsn); 2-1-1-1; perc(2); hp, pf; str). *Contents:* Night (Walter de la Mare); The Eye (Robert Creeley); Lost (Carl Sandburg); I Stood upon a High Place (Stephen Crane); The Dark Hills (Edwin Arlington Robinson). *Dedicated to:* Margaret Lee Crofts.
Score: ms. in composer's hand.
Score: reprod. of ms; available from composer.

[Preludes]
C2.9.5 Five Preludes. (1975-76) 6'
For: guitar. *First performed:* May 1976; Berklee College of Music. Michael Carnes.
Score: ms. in composer's hand.
Score: reprod. of ms; available from composer.
Reel: available from composer.
Cassette: available from composer.

[Quartet]
C2.10 Recorder Quartet. (1976) Honorable Mention, Delius Festival Composition Contest (1977).
Score: ms. in composer's hand.
Score: reprod. of ms; available from composer.

[Quintet]
C2.11 Brass Quintet. (1979) 11'
For: trumpet in C, trumpet, horn, trombone, tuba. *First performed:* Apr. 1980; Boston University. Boston University Collegium in Contemporary Music.
Score: ms. in composer's hand.
Score: reprod. of ms; available from composer.
Reel: available from composer.
Cassette: available from composer.

C2.12 Ruminations--Old Lady's Winter Words. (1980) 12'
For: Soprano, clarinet, bassoon, harpsichord, viola. *Text:* Theodore Roethke. *First performed:* Aug. 3, 1980; Berkshire Music Center, Tanglewood.

Laurie Stewart Otten, soprano; Mark Berge, clarinet; Cynthia Bally, bassoon; Joyce Lindoff, harpsichord; Rachel Fagerberg, viola; Jahja Ling, conductor.
Score: ms. in composer's hand.
Score: reprod. of ms; available from composer.
Reel: available from composer.
Cassette: available from composer.

C2.13 Tears. (1980) 11'
For: chorus, voices, chamber orchestra(horns, strings, piano, synthesizer). *Text:* Walt Whitman. *First performed:* May 15, 1980; Longy School of Music. Longy Chamber Singers and Longy Orchestra, Tom Hall, conductor.
Score: ms. in composer's hand.
Score: reprod. of ms; available from composer.
Reel: available from composer.
Cassette: available from composer.

C2.14 A Whitman Portrait. (1979-80) 16'
For: orchestra(2(pic)-1(Ehn)-2(Ebcl, bcl)-sax(ssax, tsax)-2; 2-2-1-1; perc(3); hp, cel, pf; str).
Score: BU

C3 ALASTAIR K. CASSELS-BROWN

Born 1927 in Chiswick, London, England. *Education:* B.A., M.A. (Oxford University, 1948, 1952, Mus.D. (University of Toronto, 1972); studied composition with Hugo Norden (Toronto, Ont.); Fellow of the Royal College of Organists (1950). *Awards:* American Guild of Organists Composition Contest/Horn Club of Los Angeles Commission (shared Second Prize, 1962), Massachusetts Council on the Arts and Humanities, Artist Fellowship Program (Finalist, 1977). *Related activities:* organist, choirmaster, Cathedral of St. John the Divine, New York City (1955-57), Grace Church, Utica, N.Y. (1957-65), Hamilton College (1965-67); founder and director of the Utica Choral Society (1957-67); chairperson, Diocesan Music

Commission, Episcopal Diocese of Massachusetts (1977-80); organ recitals in the United States, Canada, and Europe (1966, 1979, 1980); leader of workshops in liturgical music; served on the faculties of Wellington College, England (1950-52), St. George's School, Newport, R.I. (1952-55), Choir School, Cathedral of St. John the Divine, New York City (1955-57), Hamilton College, (1965-67), Episcopal Divinity School, Cambridge, Mass. (1967-). HU

WORKS

[Canticles]
C3.1 Two Canticles. (1977) 5'
For: chorus(unison) and keyboard. *Texts: International Consultation On English Texts.*
Vocal score: Hinshaw, 1978, 1979.

C3.2 Chiltern Idyll. (1948) 9'
For: chamber orchestra(2-2-2-2; 2-1-0-0; timp; str). 1 movement. *First performed:* 1951; Hamburg, West Germany. BAFO Radio Orchestra.
Score & parts: ms.

C3.3 The Christ Child Lay in Mary's Lap. (1955) 3'-4'
For: chorus(SATB) and organ. Carol.
Text: G.K. Chesterton.
Vocal score: Gray, 1956.

[The Christ Child Lay in Mary's Lap; Arr.]
C3.4 The Christ Child Lay in Mary's Lap.
For: guitars. Carol.
Score: in *Trial Music*, Episcopal Church, Diocese of Massachusetts, 1969.

[Concerto]
C3.5 Little Concerto. (1961) 7'
For: flute, oboe, piano, string quartet, double bass(ad lib.). *Dedicated to:* Martin Katahn; Utica Chamber Players. *First performed:* 1961; Hamilton College. Utica Chamber Players.
Score & parts: ms.
Reel: recording of first performance.

[Concerto, Violoncello]
C3.6 Cello Concerto. (1953) 21'
For: violoncello and orchestra (2-2-2-2; 4-2-3-1; timp, perc; str). *Dedicated to:* Karen (Killilea). *First performed:* 1964. Donna Magendanz, violoncello; Utica Symphony Orchestra, Joseph Henry, conductor.
Score & parts: ms.

[Concerto, Violoncello; Arr.]
C3.7 Violin Sonata, No. 2. (1953) 21'
For: violin and piano. *Commissioned by:* George Szpinalski. *First performed:* 1953; Jordan Hall, Boston. *Score:* mss.

C3.8 Eucharistic Setting. (1975)
For: chorus(unison) and keyboard. *Text: International Consultation on English Texts. Contents:* Lord, Have Mercy; Kyrie Eleison; Holy God; Glory to God in the Highest; Holy, Holy, Holy, Lord God of Power and Might; Christ, Our Passover.
Vocal score: in *Hymns I*, Church Pension Fund, 1976.
Cassette: Catacomb Cassettes C83, C113.

C3.9 Fanfare. (1976) 1'30"
For: brass ensemble(trumpets(6), trombones(4), tuba or tubas(2)). *First performed:* 1976; Boston College; consecration of Bishop Coburn of Massachusetts.
Score & parts: ms.

C3.10 Fantasia. (1957) 7'
For: string quartet.
Score & parts: ms.

C3.11 Fear No More the Heat o' the Sun. (1947) 5'
For: chorus(SSATTB). *Text:* William Shakespeare.
Vocal score: ms.

[Folk-Song Arrangements]
C3.12 Thirty Folk-Song Arrangements. (1976-79) 105'
For: chorus(mixed) and keyboard. *Commissioned by:* Episcopal Church, Standing Commssion on Church Music.
Vocal score: in *Hymn Supplement II*

and *Hymn Supplement III* Church
Pension Fund, 1976, 1979.

C3.13 Forest Idyll. (1949) 10'
For: chamber orchestra(2-2-2-2; 2-2-1-0;
timp, perc(2); cel, hp(ad lib.); str). 1
movement. *First performed:* 1955;
Providence, R.I. Rhode Island
Philharmonic Orchestra , Francis
Madeira, Francis Madeira, conductor.
Score & parts: ms.
Reel: 1955; Providence, R.I. Rhode
Island Philharmonic Orchestra, Francis
Madeira, conductor.

C3.14 From the Divide. (1972) 35'
For: Soprano, Tenor, narrator, chorus,
orchestra(2(&pic)-2(&Ehn)-2(&bcl)-
2(&cbsn); 4-3-3-1; timp, perc(2), xlyo;
str). Cantata. 25 movements. *Text:* Hans
Juergensen.
Score: ms. in composer's hand.

C3.15 Jeu de cloches. (1962) 10'
For: horns(12) and organ. 1 movement.

[Jeu de cloches; Arr.]
C3.16 Jeu de cloches. (1976) 10'
For: brass ensemble)(trumpets(6),
trombones(4), tuba). 1 movement. *First
performed:* 1976; Boston College;
consecration of Bishop Coburn of
Massachusetts.
Score & parts: ms.
Reel: recording of first performance.

C3.17 A Lass and a Lackey. (1955) 120'
For: voices(8), chorus, piano. Musical
comedy. *First performed:* 1955;
Newport, R.I. Newport Players Guild.

C3.18 My Song Is Love Unknown.
(1948) 21'
For: Alto, chorus, orchestra(2-2-2-2;
4-2-3-1; timp, perc; str). Cantata. *Text:*
Samuel Crossman. *First performed:*
1953; Newport, R.I. Newport Music
Society.

[My Song Is Love Unknown; Arr.]
C3.19 My Song Is Love Unknown.
(1976) 21'

For: Alto, chorus, chamber
orchestra(2-1-0-0; 2-0-0-0; org;
str(1-1-1-1-0)). Cantata. *First performed:*
Episcopal Divinity School, Cambridge,
Mass. Unidentified alto; Cambridge
Motet Choir and Church of the
Redeemer Choir, Chestnut Hill, Mass.

[Pieces]
C3.20 Three Pieces. (1945) 8'
For: violoncello and piano. *Contents:*
Elegy; Sonnet; Dance.
Score: ms.

C3.21 Praise the Lord, O My Soul.
(1953) 4'
For: chorus(SATB) and organ. Anthem.
Text: from the Bible, O.T., Psalm 104.
Dedicated to: Marian Van Slyke.
Vocal score: Gray, 1955.
Reel: 1956; Cathedral of St. John the
Divine, New York City.

C3.22 Quartet, Strings, A Minor. (1949)
28'
Score & parts: ms.

C3.23 Serenade to Indestructible
Beauty. (1957) 15'
For: Baritone and piano. Song cycle.
Text: Carl Sandburg. *Contents:* The
Harbor; Fog; Sunsets; Nocturne in a
Brickyard; Wind Song. *Dedicated to:*
Rosemarie [Langath Cassels-Brown].
First performed: 1967; Hamilton
College. McKinley Collings, baritone
and Alastair Cassels-Brown, piano.
Score: ms.
Reel: May 1977; Episcopal Divinity
School, Cambridge, Mass. Richard
Brown, baritone and Alastair
Cassels-Brown, piano.

C3.24 Siva. (1977) 15'
For: tape. 1 movement. Composed in
the Bregman Electronic Music Studio,
Dartmouth College.

C3.25 Sonata, Violin, No. 1. (1946) 22'
For: violin and piano. 3 movements.
First performed: 1947; Oxford
University, England. Fred Hare, violin

and Alastair Cassels-Brown, piano.
Score & part: ms.

Sonata, Violin, No. 2. *See* Concerto,
Violoncello; Arr.

C3.26 Sredni Vashtar.
For: Soprano, Mezzo-Soprano, Alto,
Tenor, Bass, chamber
orchestra(1-1-2(bcl)- 0; 0-0-2-0; perc(3),
xyl; str(1-1-1-1-0)). Opera. *Libretto:*
Richard Adams. *Commissioned by:*
Richard Adams.

C3.27 Te Deum. (1953) 5'
For: chorus(SATB) and organ. Canticle.
Text: from the *Book of Common Prayer,*
1928. *Dedication:* To my mother.
Score: Gray, 1956.

C4 ROBERT CEELY

Born January 17, 1930, in Torrington,
Conn. Moved to Boston area 1965.
Education: studied composition with
Francis Judd Cooke (New England
Conservatory, B.M., 1954); Roger
Sessions, Milton Babbitt (Princeton
University, 1957-58); Darius Milhaud,
Leon Kirchner (Mills College, M.A.,
1961). *Awards:* Roy Dickinson Welch
Fellowship in Music (Princeton
University, 1957-58), Fromm Foundation
Commission (1969), Hobart College
Bicentennial Award (1971). *Related
activities:* worked at the Studio di
Fonologia, Milan, Italy (1963-64);
founder of BEEP (1965); participant in
R.A. Moog Company seminar to help
design Moog Synthesizer; music
director, Robert College, Istanbul,
Turkey (1961-63); technical supervisor,
Modern Language Center (Harvard
University (1965-66); director, Electronic
Music Studio, New England
Conservatory (1966-);
composer-in-residence, Northeastern
University (1975). NEC

WORKS

C4.1 Beyond the Ghost Spectrum.
(1969) 12'

For: tape and instrumental
ensemble(flute, oboes(2), clarinet(in A),
clarinet (bass), bassoon, trumpet, horn,
trombone(bass), violin, violoncello,
double bass, percussion(2). Ballet.
Commissioned by: Berkshire Music
Center, Tanglewood and the Fromm
Foundation. *Dedicated to:* Paul Fromm.
First performed: July 23, 1969;
Berkshire Music Center, Tanglewood.
Berkshire Music Festival Ensemble,
Michael Tilson Thomas, conductor.
Score: American Composers Alliance,
1969. NEC
Parts: American Composers Alliance,
1969.

C4.2 Bleve. (1976)
For: tape. Film music.
Film: National Fire Protection
Association, 1976.

C4.3 Bottom Dogs. (1981) 12'
For: double basses(4). 9 movements.
Commissioned by: National Endowment
for the Arts. *Dedication:* To the Times
Square Basstet in memory of Bill
Rhein. *First performed:* Apr. 14, 1981;
New England Conservatory; in
Enchanted Circle. Times Square Basstet.
Score: American Composers Alliance,
1981. NEC
Cassette: recording of first
performance. NEC

C4.4 Coition. (1966-67) 4' 7"
For: tape.
Score: American Composers Alliance,
1967.
Reel: 1966-67; BEEP; in
Coition-Intuition-Fruition
(Work-in-Progress).

C4.5 Composition for 10 Instruments.
(1963) 10'
For: instrumental
ensemble(piccolo/flute, clarinet,
contrabassoon, trumpet, horn,
trombone(bass), harp, violin,
violoncello, double bass). 1 movement.
Dedication: To my wife, Jonatha (a mia
moglia). *First performed:* Mar. 13, 1969;
New England Conservatory. Unidentified

student ensemble, Richard Pittman, conductor.
Score: reprod. of ms. (titled Music for Ten Instruments). NEC
Score & parts: American Composers Alliance, 1963.

C4.6 Elegia. (1963) 5' 5"
For: tape. Realized at the Studio di Fonologia, Milan, Italy.
Score: American Composers Alliance, 1963.
Disc: Composers Recordings CRI SD 328, 1974. BrU BU HU MIT NEC W

C4.7 Flee/Floret/Florens. (1977) 8' 6"
For: Sopranos(4), Altos(4), Tenors(4), Basses(3). Motet. *Contents: Flee* (adapted from *Truth* by Geoffrey Chaucer); *Florens vigor ulciscendo* (attributed to Philippe de Vitry); *Floret cum vana gloria* (attributed to Philippe de Vitry). *Dedicated to:* Lorna Cooke deVaron and the NEC Chamber Singers. First performed: May 8, 1980; New England Conservatory. NEC Chamber Singers, Lorna Cooke deVaron, director.
Vocal score: American Composers Alliance, 1978. NEC
Cassette: recording of first performance. NEC

C4.8 La Fleur, les fleurs. (1975) 25' 8"
For: tape. 3 movements.
Score: American Composers Alliance, 1975.
Disc: BEEP 1001; 1975. BU NEC

C4.9 Frames. (1978) 11'
For: tape(computer). *First performed:* Sept. 1978; Edinburgh, Scotland.
Score & tape: American Composers Alliance, 1978.
Cassette: Apr. 14, 1981; New England Conservatory; in *Enchanted Circle.* NEC

C4.10 Hayati. (1966) 8'
For: tape. Realized at BEEP.
Reel: American Composers Alliance, 1966.

C4.11 Hymn. (1968) 5' 57"
For: violoncello and double bass.
Commissioned by: Buell Neidlinger for his recital. *Dedication:* For Buell and Jay. *First performed:* Jan. 7, 1970; New England Conservatory. Edward J. Humeston, III, violoncello and Buell Neidlinger, double bass.
Score: American Composers Alliance, 1969. NEC
Disc: BEEP 1001, 1975. Fred Sherry, violoncello and Buell Neidlinger, double bass. BU NEC
Cassette: recording of first performance. NEC
Cassette: Feb. 2, 1973; New England Conservatory. Collage. NEC

C4.12 Incendio. (1975)
For: tape. Film music.
Film: National Fire Protection Association, 1975.

C4.13 Kyros (Theatrical Documentary). (1969) 20' 8"
For: viola, tape, film(8mm), slide projectors(2). *Commissioned by and dedicated to:* Steve Wilkes. *First performed:* May 1969; New England Conservatory. Steve Wilkes.
Score: American Composers Alliance, 1969.

C4.14 Logs. (1968) 4' 9"
For: double basses(2). 7 movements.
Commissioned by: Buell Neidlinger.
Dedicated to: Buell Neidlinger and Bill Rhein. *First performed:* Dec. 9, 1968; New England Conservatory. Buell Neidlinger and William Rhein.
Score: American Composers Alliance, 1969. NEC
Disc: BEEP 1001, 1975. Buell Neidlinger and Donald Palma. BU NEC
Cassette: Apr. 14, 1981; New England Conservatory; in *Enchanted Circle.* Members of Times Square Basstet. NEC

C4.15 Lullaby. (1979) 8'
For: Soprano and trombone. *Text:*

George Gascoigne.
Score: American Composers Alliance,
1979. NEC

C4.16 MITSYN Music. (1968) 8' 03"
For: tape. Realized at BEEP. *First
performed:* May 9, 1971; New England
Conservatory.
Score: American Composers Alliance,
1968.
Disc: Composers Recordings CRI SD
328, 1974. BrU BU HU MIT NEC W
Cassette: recording of first
performance. NEC
Cassette: Apr. 14, 1981; New England
Conservatory; in *Enchanted Circle*. NEC

C4.17 Modules. (1967) 10'
For: flute, saxophone(alto), violin, viola,
double bass, piano, percussion. *First
performed:* May 1968; Jordan Hall,
Boston.
Score: American Composers Alliance,
1968. NEC
Parts: American Composers Alliance.
Rental.

Music for Ten Instruments. *See*
Composition for 10 Instruments.

C4.18 Piano Piece. (1980)
Commissioned by and dedicated to:
Rebecca LaBrecque. *First performed:*
Apr. 14, 1981; Jordan Hall, Boston; in
Enchanted Circle. Rebecca LaBrecque.
Score: American Composers Alliance,
1980. NEC
Cassette: recording of first
performance. NEC

C4.19 Rerap. (1966) 9' 8"
For: tape. Realized at BEEP.
Reel: American Composers Alliance.

C4.20 Rituals. (1974-76) 11'
For: flutes(40). *Dedicated to:* John
Heiss. *First performed:* Dec. 13, 1976;
New England Conservatory. NEC Flute
Band, John Heiss, conductor.
Score & parts: American Composers
Alliance, 1976. NEC
Parts: American Composers Alliance,
1976. Rental.

Cassette: recording of first
performance. NEC

C4.21 Roundels. (1981) 16'
For: band and tape. *Movements:* Book
1; Interlude; Book 2; Interlude; Book 3;
Interlude. *Dedicated to:* Frank L. Battisti
and the NEC Wind Ensemble. *First
performed:* Oct. 22, 1981; New England
Conservatory. NEC Wind Ensemble;
Frank L. Battisti, conductor.
Score: American Composers Alliance,
1981. NEC
Parts: American Composers Alliance,
1981. Rental.
Tape: available from composer.
Cassette: recording of first
performance. NEC

C4.22 Slide Music. (1973) 8'
For: trombones(4). *Commissioned by:*
Thomas Everett for the Boston
Trombone Quartet. *First performed:*
Aug. 1974; Wellesley College. Boston
Trombone Quartet.
Score: American Composers Alliance,
1973. NEC
Reel: 1976. WGBH
Cassette: May 8, 1975; New England
Conservatory; in *An Evening of
Contemporary Music*. Richard
Chamberlain, Thomas Foulds, Peter
Harvey, Mark Lenz. NEC
Cassette: Feb. 29, 1976; New England
Conservatory; American Society of
University Composers, 11th Annual
Conference. Thomas Everett, Nathaniel
Gurin, Robert Moir, Donald Sanders.
NEC

C4.23 Spectrum. (1961) 3' 56"
For: flute, oboe, clarinet(bass),
violoncello. Film music.
Score & parts: American Composers
Alliance, 1981.
Film: John McKee Films, 1961.

C4.24 Stratti. (1963) 3' 43"
For: tape.
Score: American Composers Alliance,
1963.
Disc: BEEP 1001, 1975. BU NEC

C4.25 Trio. (1953) 9'
For: violin, viola, violoncello. 3
movements. *First performed:* Aug.
1955; Berkshire Music Center,
Tanglewood.
Score & parts: American Composers
Alliance, 1953. NEC

[Variations, Piano]
C4.26 Piano Variations. (1981) 22'
Theme and twenty-six variations.
Dedicated to: Thomas Stumpf. *First
performed:* fall, 1981. Thomas Stumpf.
Score: American Composers Alliance,
1981.

C4.27 Vonce. (1966) 7' 47"
For: tape. *First performed:* Nov. 1967;
New England Conservatory.
Score: American Composers Alliance,
1966.
Disc: BEEP 1001, 1975. BU NEC

C5 BASIL CHAPMAN

Born January 13, 1944, in Cape Town,
South Africa. Moved to Boston area
1969. *Education:* Licentiate (Royal
School of Music and Trinity College of
Music, London, England); Artists
Diploma (University of South Africa);
B.M., M.M. (New England Conservatory);
studied composition with John Heiss,
Donald Martino, Robert Ceely; clarinet
with Gino Cioffi and Peser W.
Hadcock; chamber music with Harold
Wright, Gunther Schuller, Rudolph
Kolisch. *Related activities:* clarinetist;
conductor; member of the faculties of
Longy School of Music and South
Shore Conservatory of Music. L

WORKS

C5.1 Caprice. (1972) 2'
For: clarinet. *First performed:* Sept.
1972; New England Conservatory. Basil
Chapman.
Score: Dorn, 1981.

C5.2 Flurries. (1972-73) 2' 30"
For: woodwind quintet. 1 movement.

First performed: 1975; WGBH-FM.
Boston Chamber Ensemble.
Score & parts: Dorn, 1981.

C5.3 Impressions. (1975) 6' 20"
For: trumpet and tape. *Dedicated to:*
Jay Rizzetto. *First performed:* Mar.
1975; WGBH-FM; Performer/Composer
Series.
Score & tape: Pasquina, 1976.

[Movements]
C5.4 Two Movements. (1972)
For: orchestra. *First performed:* 1972;
New England Conservatory. NEC
Symphony Orchestra, Tibor Pusztai,
conductor.
Score & parts: ms.
Tape: recording of first performance.

C5.5 Ode. (1974) 6' 20"
For: tape and clarinet(bass). *First
performed:* May 9, 1974; New England
Conservatory. Basil Chapman.
Choreography: Martha Gray Dance
Collective.
Score & tape: Dorn, 1981.
Cassette: in *Musica Maximus*; recording
of first performance. NEC

C5.6 Pieces for the California Brass.
Quintet. (in progress)
For: brasses(5).

[Quartet, Strings]
C5.7 String Quartet for Low Voices.
(1975) 5' 30"

[Quartet, Violin, Viola, Violoncello,
Double Bass]
C5.8 Solo String Quartet. (1973)
Score & parts: ms; available from
composer.

[Pieces]
C5.9 Three Pieces. (1971-72) 4' 30"
For: clarinet. *First performed:* May
1972; New England Conservatory. Basil
Chapman. Has been choreographed by
Martha Gray Dance Collective.
Score: Dorn, 1981.
Cassette: Mar. 15, 1973; New England

Conservatory; in *An Evening of New Music*. Basil Chapman. NEC

C5.10 Wind Band Piece No. 1, Part 1. (1973) 4' 30"
Dedicated to: Frank Battisti.
Score & parts: ms; available from composer.

C5.11 Wind Band Piece No. 1, Part 2. (1975) 5'
Score & parts: ms; available from composer.

C6 PETER CHILD

Born May 6, 1953, in Great Yarmouth, England. Moved to Boston area 1976. *Education:* B.A. (Reed College, 1975); studied composition with Seymour Shifrin, Arthur Berger, Martin Boykan (Brandeis University, Ph.D., 1981); Jacob Druckman (Berkshire Music Festival, Tanglewood). *Awards:* Watson Foundation Grant (1975-76), Remis Fellowship (Brandeis University, 1977-79), Bernstein Fellowship (Tanglewood, 1978), Margaret Grant Award (Tanglewood, 1978), East and West Artists Composition Competition (First Prize, 1979), WGBH-Boston Musica Viva Recording Prize (1980), Boston Musica Viva commission (1981). *Related activities:* member of the faculty of Brandeis University (1979-). BrU

WORKS

[Brief Impressions for Computer]
C6.1 Three Brief Impressions for Computer. (1979) 4'
3 movements. Realized at the Experimental Music Studio, Massachusetts Institute of Technology. *First performed:* July 27, 1979; Massachusetts Institute of Technology. *Disc:* Composers Recordings, nyp. *Reel:* Feb. 13, 1981; Wellesley College. W

C6.2 Duo for Flute and Percussion. (1979) 15'

Movements: Prelude; Two-Part Invention; Caprice; Fantasy. *Dedicated to:* Daniel Druckman. *First performed:* Mar. 16, 1980; New York City. Patricia Spencer, flute and Daniel Druckman, percussion.
Score: Mobart, 1981.
Parts: Mobart, 1981. Rental.

C6.3 Heracliti reliquiae (Fragments of Heraclitus). (1978) 10'
For: Soprano, flute/piccolo, oboe, clarinet, violin, violoncello. *Text:* Heraclitus. *Contents:* The Lord Whose Is the Oracle at Delphi; The Bacchae; Sibylla. *First performed:* Feb. 16, 1979; Waltham, Mass. Barbara Winchester, soprano; Randolph Bocsman, flute; Barbara Knapp, oboe; David Satz, clarinet; Maynard Goldman, violin; Lynn Nowels, violoncello; David Hoose, conductor.
Score: Association for the Promotion of New Music, 1981.
Parts: Association for the Promotion of New Music. Rental.

C6.4 Landscapes. (1977) 10'
For: Mezzo Soprano and piano. Song cycle. *Text:* T.S. Eliot. *Contents:* New Hampshire; Virginia; Usk; Rannoch, by Glencoe; Cape Ann. *First performed:* May 19, 1977; Waltham, Mass. Barbara Winchester, mezzo soprano and David Evans, piano.
Score: ms. in composer's hand.

C6.5 Sonata for Piano. (1977) 6'
1 movement. *First performed:* Apr. 3, 1980; New York City. Robert Pollock, piano.
Score: Association for the Promotion of New Music. 1981.

C6.6 Tape.intervention. (1981) 10'
For: horn, oboe/English horn, viola, violoncello, tape(computer). 1 movement. Realized at the Experimental Music Studio, Massachusetts Institute of Technology. *Dedicated to:* David Hoose. First performed: May 19, 1981; Alice Tully Hall, New York City. Jean Rife, horn; Frederic Cohen, oboe; Marcus

Thompson, viola; Lisa Lancaster,
violoncello; David Hoose, conductor.
Score & parts: ms. in composer's hand.
Tape.

C7 TIMOTHY VINCENT CLARK

Born November 29, 1949. Moved to
Boston area 1973. *Education:* studied
composition with Conrad Aiken (Paris
American Academy); Nadia Boulanger
(Fontainbleau School, France); Pierre
Revel (Conservatoire National Superieur
de Musique, Paris, France); Walter
Aschaffenburg, Richard Hoffmann
(Oberlin Conservatory, B.M., 1971);
Arthur Berger, Martin Boykan, Harold
Shapero, Seymour Shifrin, (Brandeis
University, Ph.D., 1981). *Awards:*
National Endowment for the Arts
Grant, (1979-80) and Massachusetts
Council on the Arts and Humanities,
Artist Fellowship Program (1981-82).
Related activities: pianist, performance
coach, conductor, teacher; member of
the faculty of Harvard University (197-
). HU

WORKS

C7.1 Cantata semplice. (1980) 25'
For: Baritone, chorus(SSAA), horn,
percussion, piano, violin, viola,
violoncello.
Score: ms. in composer's hand.

C7.2 Compass. (1973) 20'
For: piano, percussion,
instruments(8)(flute, oboe, clarinet,
horn, trombone, violin, viola,
violoncello). *Commissioned by:* Norfolk
Consortium, Norfolk, Va.
Score & parts: ms. in composer's hand.

C7.3 Convolutions. (1972) 20'
For: pianos(2). *Dedicated to:* Walter
Aschaffenburg. *First performed:* May
15, 1972; Oberlin Conservatory. Joyce
Squassoni and Timothy Clark.
Score: ms. in composer's hand.
Tape: available from composer.

C7.4 Epivariants (on a Space of
Webern). (1978) 23'
For: pianos(2). *First performed:* Mar. 9,
1980; Sanders Theatre, Harvard
University; Fromm Foundation concert.
Christopher Kies and Arlene Pepe Kies.
Score: ms. in composer's hand.
Tape: available from composer.

C7.5 Fresco Hung with Caricatures. (in
progress)
For: piano(4-hands).
Score: ms. in composer's hand.

C7.6 Gestures: Igor Stravinsky in
memoriam. (1971) 12'
For: chamber orchestra. *Commissioned
by:* Oberlin College Contemporary
Chamber Ensemble. First performed:
November 12, 1971; Oberlin
Conservatory. Oberlin College
Contemporary Chamber Ensemble,
David Aks, conductor.
Score & parts: ms. in composer's hand.
Tape: available from composer.

C7.7 Landscape in Three Lights. (1972)
15'
For: Soprano and instrumental
ensemble(flute, clarinet, bassoon, horn,
harp, piano, harpsichord, tape, violin,
viola, violoncello, slides). *Text:* David
Young. *First performed:* Apr. 11, 1972;
Oberlin Conservatory.
Score & parts: ms. in composer's hand.
Tape: available from composer.

C7.8 Lento. (1973) 6'
For: piano.
Score: ms. in composer's hand.

C7.9 Man & Woman. (1970) 12'
For: organ. *First performed:* Apr. 1970;
Oberlin Conservatory.
Score: ms. in composer's hand.
Tape: available from composer.

C7.10 Petite valse de la bonne bourse.
(1981) 45"
For: piano.
Score: ms. in composer's hand.

C7.11 Schenker. (1972) 7′
For: piano. *Dedicated to:* Gregory
Proctor. *First performed:* May 14, 1972;
Oberlin Conservatory. Robert Black.
Score: ms. in composer's hand.
Tape: available from composer.

[Sketches]
C7.12 Four Sketches. (1969) 10′
For: Soprano, oboe, piano. *First
performed:* Mar. 6, 1969; Oberlin
Conservatory. Susan Silverstein,
soprano; Nancy Vitt, oboe; Kathleen
Keasey, piano.
Score: ms. in composer's hand.
Tape: available from composer.

C7.13 Sonatine classique. (1976) 12′
For: piano. *First performed:* May 10,
1976; Brandeis University. Timothy
Clark.
Score: ms. in composer's hand.
Tape: available from composer.

C7.14 "S.S." and "A..h..Be.ge." [i.e.
Seymour Shifrin and Arthur
Berger]. (1980) 6′ *For:* piano(4-hands).
First performed: Apr. 25, 1980;
Brandeis University ("A..h..Be.ge."). Vicki
Jane Kanrek-Clark and Timothy Clark.
Score: ms. in composer's hand.
Tape: available from composer.

[Trio, Piano, Flute, Violoncello]
C7.15T Trio. (1969) 10′
First performed: Dec. 10, 1969; Oberlin
Conservatory.
Score & parts: ms. in composer's hand.
Tape: available from composer.

[Trio, Violin, Viola, Violoncello]
C7.16 String Trio. (1970) 12′
Score: ms. in composer's hand.

[Vues du meme endroit]

C7.17 Quatre vues du meme endroit.
(1970) 10′
For: horns(5). *First performed:* Apr.
1970; Oberlin Conservatory. Steven
Couch (pre-recorded tape).
Score: ms. in composer's hand.
Tape: available from composer.

C7.18 The Waking. (1968) 10′
For: chorus(TBB), flute, horn, harp. *Text:*
Theodore Roethke. *First performed:*
May 5, 1968; Oberlin Conservatory.
Score: ms. in composer's hand.
Tape: available from composer.

C8 ROBERT DAVID COGAN

Born February 2, 1930, in Detroit, Mich.
Moved to Boston area 1963. *Education:*
B.M., M.M. (University of Michigan,
1951, 1952); Conservatoire Royal de
Bruxelles (1952-53); Berkshire Music
Center, Tanglewood (1953); M.F.A.
(Princeton University, 1956); Staatliche
Hochschule fuer Musik, Hamburg, West
Germany (1958-61); studied composition
with Ross Lee Finney, Philipp Jarnach,
Roger Sessions, Nadia Boulanger,
Aaron Copland. *Awards:* Chopin
Fellowship (Kosciusko Foundation),
Fulbright Fellowship, Guggenheim Grant,
MacDowell Colony Fellowship,
Reemtsma Foundation Grant. *Related
activities:* co-author of *Sonic Design:
The Nature of Sound and Music* (1976)
and *Sonic Design: Practice and
Problems* (1981); author of *A Music
Spectrum Picture Book: Photos/Theory* (in
progress); co-editor of the journal,
Sonus; served on the faculties of New
England Conservatory (1963-),
Berkshire Music Center, Tanglewood
(1969-70), State University of New
York, College at Purchase (1969-70),
IBM Watson Research Center (1979).
NEC

WORKS

C8.1 A Birthday Song. (1979)
For: Soprano. *Text:* Charles Olson.
Dedicated to: Earl Kim on his 60th
birthday. *First performed:* 1979;
Cambridge, Mass. Joan Heller.
Score: reprod. of ms; available from
composer.

[Compositions]
C8.2 Two Compositions for String Trio.
(1956-59) 9′
For: violin, viola, violoncello. *First

performed: 1957; Rothschild Foundation, New York City (Composition II). 1961; Staatliche Hochschule fuer Musik, Hamburg, West Germany (Compositions I and II).
Score: reprod. of ms; available from composer.

C8.3 Dr. Faustroll Thinking. (in progress) 20′
For: tape. 5 movements.

[Dr. Faustroll Thinking. Level 1, Dr. Faustroll, Slidewhistle Virtuoso]
C8.4 Dr. Faustroll, Slidewhistle Virtuoso, Level 1. (1976)
For: tape. *First performed:* Nov. 19, 1978; New England Conservatory; in Robert Cogan Fifteen Year Retrospective Concert.
Cassette: recording of first performance. NEC

[Dr. Faustroll Thinking. Level 2, Dr. Faustroll Remembering Berlioz]
C8.5 Dr. Faustroll Remembering Berlioz. (1976)
For: tape. *First performed:* Nov. 19, 1978; New England Conservatory; in Robert Cogan Fifteen Year Retrospective Concert.
Cassette: recording of first performance. NEC

C8.6 Fantasia. (1951) 8′
For: orchestra(3-2-3-2; 4-3-3-1; timp, perc; hp; str). *First performed:* Nov. 1954; Severance Hall, Cleveland, Ohio. Cleveland Orchestra, Leopold Stokowski, conductor.
Score & parts: E.B. Marks.

C8.7 A Man Equals a Man.
Incidental music.
Score: reprod. of ms.

C8.8 No Attack of Organic Metals. (1971) 12′
For: organ and tape. *Written for and dedicated to:* Martha Folts. *First performed:* 1972. Martha Folts.
Score: reprod. of ms; available from

composer.
Tape: available from composer.
Disc: in *A Sonic Experience with Martha Folts at Harvard*, Delos DEL 25448, n.d. Martha Folts.

Phrases from Whirl...ds I. *See* Whirl...ds I II. Whirl...ds I. Phrases, Voice(s); Whirl...ds I II. Whirl...ds I. Voice(s) and Instruments.

C8.9 Purgatory. (in progress)
Stage work after William Butler Yeats.

C8.10 Quartet, Strings.

Red Allen Hock It.
See Whirl...ds I II. Whirl...ds II; Whirl...ds I II. IIa.

C8.11 Songs.
Text: Ezra Pound.
Score: reprod. of ms.

C8.12 Sounds and Variants. (1959-61) 8′
For: piano. *First performed:* 1964; New York City; Donnell Library Composer's Forum. David Del Tredici.
Score: reprod. of ms; available from composer.
Cassette: Nov. 18, 1980; New England Conservatory; in *Enchanted Circle.* David Hagan. NEC

C8.13 Spaces and Cries. (1963-64) 12′
For: trumpets(2), horn, trombone, tuba. *First performed:* 1964; New York City; Donnell Library Composers' Forum. Metropolitan Brass Quintet.
Score: reprod. of ms; available from composer.
Cassette: Nov. 19, 1978; New England Conservatory; in *Robert Cogan Fifteen Year Retrospective Concert.* NEC Scholarship Brass Quintet. NEC

C8.14 Utterances: An Open Ended Folio for Solo Voice. (1977-) 9′-15′
For: Soprano. Aleatoric music (segments selected and ordered by the performer according to composer's directions). *Text:* William Bronk. *Written*

for and dedicated to: Joan Heller.
Version for voice and tape incomplete.
First performed: Nov. 19, 1978; New
England Conservatory; in Robert Cogan
Fifteen Year Retrospective Concert.
Joan Heller.
Score: reprod. of ms; available from
composer.
Disc: in *New Events: Boston Composers
of the '70s,* Spectrum SR 128, 1980.
Joan Heller. NEC
Cassette: recording of first
performance. NEC

C8.15 Whirl...ds I II. 40'
For: voices(4),
instruments(unspecified)(44), projections.
Score: reprod. of ms; available from
composer.

[Whirl...ds I II. Whirl...ds I]
C8.16 Whirl...ds I. (1968-69) 18'
For: voices(2) and
instruments(unspecified)(44). Aleatoric
music (segments are selected and
ordered by the performers according to
composer's directions). *Text:* Robert
Cogan. *Commissioned by:* Kosciuszko
Foundation for the Centennial of New
England Conservatory. *Dedicated to:*
New England Conservatory of Music.
Version for 2 voices and 15
unspecified instruments titled
Whirlwinds Ia. *First performed:* 1969;
Symphony Hall, Boston. Jan De Gaetani
and Susan Stevens, sopranos; members
of the NEC Symphony Orchestra,
Gunther Schuller, conductor.
Score: reprod. of ms.; available from
composer.
Perf. dir: reprod. of ms; available
from composer. NEC
Reel: May 9, 1975. WGBH

[Whirl...ds I II. Whirl...ds I. Phrases,
Voice(s)]
C8.17 Phrases from Whirl...ds I.
(1968-69) 8'
For: voices(1 or 2). Aleatoric music
(contains twelve of the sixty-one vocal
phrases of the work Whirl...ds I,
selected by lottery from the whole).
Score: reprod. of ms; available from

composer.
Disc: in *New England Conservatory of
Music Faculty Composers,* Golden Crest
NEC 119, 1979. Joan Heller, soprano.
NEC
Reel: Dec. 5, 1976; Collage. WGBH
Cassette: Feb. 29, 1976; New England
Conservatory; American Society of
University Composers 11th Annual
Conference. Joan Heller, soprano. NEC
Cassette: Feb. 28, 1978; New England
Conservatory; in *An Evening of 20th
Century Music.* Kristen Samuelson,
soprano. NEC
Cassette: Nov. 19, 1978; New England
Conservatory; in *Robert Cogan Fifteen
Year Retrospective Concert.* Kristen
Samuelson, soprano and Thomas
Samuelson, baritone. NEC

[Whirl...ds I II. Whirl...ds I. Phrases,
Voice(s) and Instruments]
C8.18 Phrases from Whirl...ds I.
(1968-69) 8'
For: voices(1 or 2) and
instruments(unspecified)(3-6). Aleatoric
music (contains twelve of the
sixty-one vocal phrases of the work
Whirl...ds I, selected by lottery from
the whole). First performed; 1980;
Washington, D.C.; Contemporary Music
Forum. Marilyn Di Reggi, soprano and
members of Contemporary Music
Forum.
Score: reprod. of ms; available from
composer.
Disc: in *New England Conservatory of
Music Faculty Composers,* Golden Crest
NEC 119, 1979. Joan Heller, soprano.
NEC.

[Whirl...ds I II. Whirl...ds II]
C8.19 Whirl...ds II: Red Allen Hock It.
(1969) 18'-22'
For: voices(amplified)(2) and
projections(optional). *Dedicated to:* Pozzi
Escot. *First performed.* 1970; University
of Colorado, Boulder; American Society
of Aesthetics. Jane Bryden and Joan
Heller, sopranos.
Score: reprod. of ms; available from
composer.
Cassette: May 8, 1971; New England

Conservatory; in *A Festival of New England Composers Past and Present*. Jane Bryden and Joan Heller, sopranos. NEC.
Cassette: Nov. 19, 1978; New England Conservatory (performed simultaneously with Whirl..ds I II. Whirl...ds IIa); in *Robert Cogan Fifteen Year Retrospective Concert*. Joan Heller and Kathy Wright, sopranos.

[Whirl...ds I II. Whirl...ds IIa]
C8.20 Whirl...ds IIa: Red Allen Hock It. (1969) 18'-22'
For: chorus(playing glass jars, metal cans, round cardboard boxes, bull horns). Aleatoric music (the distribution among the voices of the original 2-voice work is made by the conductor). *Text:* Gerard Manley Hopkins, Rainer Maria Rilke, John Howard Griffin, Oscar Lewis. *First performed:* May 6, 1970; New England Conservatory. Betsy Watson, soprano; Elsa Jean Davidson, alto; Manuel Medeiros, tenor; Joshua Jacobson, bass; NEC Chorus, Lorna Cooke deVaron and James Walker, conductors.
Score: reprod. of ms; available from composer.
Cassette: recording of first performance. NEC
Cassette: Nov. 19, 1978; New England Conservatory (performed simultaneously with Whirl...ds I II, Whirl...ds II); in *Robert Cogan Fifteen Year Retrospective Concert*. NEC Chamber Singers, Lorna Cooke deVaron and James Pajak, conductors. NEC

C9 EDWARD COHEN

Born June 9, 1940. *Education:* studied composition with Irving Fine (Brandeis University, B.A., 1961); Max Deutsch (Paris, France, 1963-65); Seymour Shifrin, Luigi Dallapiccola (University of California, Berkeley, M.A., 1965).
Awards: Wechsler Prize in Composition (Brandeis University, 1961), De Lorenzo Prize in Composition (University of California, Berkeley, 1962), George Ladd Prix de Paris (University of California, Berkeley, 1963); commissions from the Fromm Foundation (1976), Brandeis University Department of Music, Martin Weiman Fund (Brandeis University).
Related activities: pianist; conductor; served on the faculties of Brandeis University (1966-77), Harvard University (1974-75), Massachusetts Institute of Technology (1977-). MIT

WORKS

C9.1 Cantata. (1963-69) 20'
For: voices, chorus, orchestra.

C9.2 Elegy. (1977) 16'
For: Soprano, flute, oboe, clarinet, violin, viola, violoncello. *Contents:* Eurydice; Leda. *Text:* Hilda Doolittle. *Commissioned by:* Fromm Foundation for Berkshire Music Center, Tanglewood. *First performed:* Aug. 1977; Berkshire Music Center, Tanglewood. Mikki Shiff, soprano; Berkshire Music Center Players.
Score: Mobart, 1977.

C9.3 Madrigal. (1967) 10'
For: flute, trumpet, viola, clarinet(bass), double bass. *First performed:* Apr. 1967; Brandeis University. Unidentified performers; David Epstein, conductor.
Score: Mobart, 1978. HU

C9.4 Nocturne. (1969-73) 10'
For: chamber orchestra(1-1-1-1; 1-2-1-0; timp; hp, pf; str). *Commissioned by:* Brandeis University Department of Music and the Martin Weiman Fund (Brandeis University). *First performed:* May 11, 1973; New England Conservatory; A Festival of Contemporary Music. NEC Symphony Orchestra, Gunther Schuller, conductor.
Score: Mobart, 1973.
Cassette: recording of first performance. NEC

An Otter. *See* Portraits. An Otter.

[Portraits. An Otter]
C9.5 An Otter. (1974)
For: chorus(men), clarinet, clarinet(bass), horns(2), trumpet, piano. *Text:* Kallimachos. *First performed:* Nov. 1975; Brandeis University. Unidentified performers; Edward Cohen, conductor. *Score:* in his *Two Portraits*; Mobart, 1974.

[Portraits. A Sailor]
C9.6 A Sailor. (1974)
For: Soprano, viola, violoncello, organ. *Text:* Kallimachos. *First performed:* Mar. 1974; Brandeis University. Beverly Morgan, soprano; Robert Koff, viola; Mark Maimone, [violoncello?] Louis Bagger, [organ?]
Score: in his *Two Portraits*; Mobart, 1974.

C9.7 Prelude and Serenade. (1963)
First performed: May 1963; University of California, Berkeley.

C9.8 Psalm 19. (1964)
For: Baritone and string quartet. *First performed:* June 1964; New York City.

[Quartet, Strings]
C9.9 String Quartet. (1963)
First performed: July 1963; Goucher College. Claremont Quartet.

C9.10 The Ruin. (1980) 15'
For: Soprano, violin, piano. *Text:* anon.; translated from Anglo-Saxon by Michael Alexander. *First performed:* Oct. 4, 1980; New York City. Judith Kellock, soprano; Rose Mary Harbison, violin; Edward Cohen, piano.

A Sailor. *See* Portraits. A Sailor.

C9.11 Serenade for a Summer Evening. (1976) 6'
For: voices(6), flutes(2), clarinet, clarinet(bass), violin, viola. *Text:* e.e. cummings. *Dedication:* For Marjorie. *First performed:* May 1976; Brandeis University. Unidentified performers; Edward Cohen, conductor. *Score:* Mobart, 1976.

C9.12 Sextet. (1961)
First performed: Mar. 1961; Brandeis University.

C9.13 Song Cycle. (1962)
For: Tenor and instruments(7). *First performed:* May 1962; University of California, Berkeley.

[Songs]
C9.14 Three Songs. (1975) 10'
For: Sopranos(2), viola, violoncello. *Text:* William Shakespeare, Robert Herrick. *First performed:* May 1975; Brandeis University. Catherine Bowers, soprano; Beverly Morgan, soprano; unidentified instrumentalists; Edward Cohen, conductor. *Score:* Mobart, 1975.

C9.15 Stone and Earth. (1978) 9'
For: Mezzo Soprano and string orchestra. *Text:* Henry Vaughn. *First performed:* Dec. 1978; Massachusetts Institute of Technology. Mary Ann Sego, mezzo soprano; MIT Symphony Orchestra, David Epstein, conductor. *Score:* Mobart, 1979.

C9.16 Trio. (1964) 5'
For: flute, violin, violoncello.

C10 JOHN COOK

Born 1918 in England. *Education:* Christ's College (Cambridge, England) and Royal College of Music (London, England). *Related activities:* conductor, Old Vic Theatre Orchestra (1946-49); organist and choirmaster, Holy Trinity Church (Stratford-on-Avon, England, 1949-[54?]) and St. Paul's Cathedral (London, Ont., 1954- [62?]); music director, Stratford Shakespeare Festival (Stratford, Ont., 1954-[67?]); organist and choirmaster, Church of the Advent (Boston, 1962-[68?]); member of the faculty of the Massachusetts Institute of Technology (1965-). MIT

WORKS

All Is in the Hands of God. *See* Variations on Alles ist an Gottes Segen.

C10.1 Author of Light. (1956) 3'
For: chorus(SATB). *Text:* Thomas Campion. *First performed:* 1956; First St. Andrews Church Choir, London, Ont.
Vocal score: Oxford.

C10.2 Christ Is Our Cornerstone. (1954) 4'
For: chorus and organ. *Text: Hymns Ancient and Modern. Commissioned by:* Diocese of Coventry. *First performed:* Nov. 1954; Coventry, England.
Vocal score: Novello.

C10.3 Concerto. (1955) 20'
For: trumpet, strings, percussion(3)(timpani, snare drum, tenor drum, bass drum, xylophone, cymbal). 4 movements. *Dedicated to:* James Ford. *First performed:* Dec. 1955; London, Ont. James Ford, trumpet; London Civic Symphony.
Score: ms. in composer's hand.

C10.4 Eclogue. (1958) 8'
For: orchestra. *Commissioned by:* Benjamin Award Foundation. *First performed:* May 1958; Wilmington, N.C.
Score & parts: ms. in composer's hand.

C10.5 Fanfare. (1951) 4' 33"
For: organ. *Text:* Bible, O.T., Psalm 81. *Dedicated to:* Pageant-master, Christopher Ede. Based on music written for the Festival of Britain Pageant at Hampton Court.
Score: Novello, 1952. MIT
Disc: Virtuoso TPLS 13022, 1968. BU HU
Disc: Vista VPS 1046, 1977. George Thalben-Ball. MIT
Disc: Westminster WST 17154. William Teague.
Disc: Wicks 8320-9785. Frederick Swann.

C10.6 Flourish and Fugue. (1959) 12'
For: organ. *Commissioned by and dedicated to:* Marilyn Mason. *First performed:* Aug. 1959; Cathedral of St. John the Divine, New York City. Marilyn Mason.
Score: Gray, 1962.
Disc: in *A Sacred Adventure*, University of Michigan, Ann Arbor, Mich. Marilyn Mason.

C10.7 Flourish for Those Who Have Failed. 7'
For: chorus(mixed), percussion, brasses(9)(horns(2), trumpets(3), trombones(3), tuba). *Text:* Walt Whitman.
Vocal score: Canadian Music Centre.

C10.8 Invocation and Allegro giojoso. (1952) 6'
For: organ. 2 movements.
Score: Novello.

C10.9 Mr. Purcell's Wedding March. (1951) 4'
For: organ.
Score: Novello.
Reel: in *Wedding Music* (excerpts). MIT

C10.10 Paean on Divinum mysterium. (1953) 5'
For: organ. 1 movement.
Score: Novello.

C10.11 Passacharlia. (1980) 5'
For: organ. *Commissioned by:* Canadian College of Organists. *Dedication:* In memory of Charles Peaker.
Score: Thompson, nyp.

C10.12 The Royal Regiment Ceremonial. (1959)
For: band. 1 movement. *Commissioned by:* Royal Regiment of Canada in commemoration of the regiment's centennial.
Score: Canadian Music Centre, 1962. MIT
Parts: Canadian Music Centre.

C10.13 Scherzo, Dance and Reflection. (1963) 12'
For: organ. 1 movement. *Dedicated to:*

Barrie Cabena. *First performed:* 1964; Coventry Cathedral, Coventry, England. Barrie Cabena.
Score: Gray, 1965. MIT

C10.14 Songs for the Merchant of Venice. (1955) 15'
For: chorus(SATB). *Contents:* Tell Me Where Is Fancy Bred (William Shakespeare); Hymn to Diana (Ben Jonson); Spring, the Sweet Sporting (Thomas Nashe). *Commissioned by:* Stratford Shakespeare Festival, Stratford, Ont. *Dedicated to:* Tyrone Guthrie; Tanya Moiseivitch; Gordon Scott, respectively. Written for a performance of Shakespeare's *The Merchant of Venice.* First performed: June 1955; Stratford, Ont.; Stratford Shakespeare Festival.
Vocal score: Novello, 1958. MIT

C10.15 Studies in Form of a Sonata. (1956) 25'
For: organ. *Movements:* Prelude; Fugue; Scherzo; Ostinato; Finale. *Dedicated to:* Healey Willan. *First performed:* London, Ont. Barrie Cabena. *Score:* Novello, 1958. HU MIT NEC

C10.16 A Suite of Psalms. (1960) 20'
For: speakers and orchestra(2-2-2-2; 4-2-0-0; timp, perc; str). *Movements:* Andante, un poco sostenuto (Psalm 139:1-11); Scherzo of Praise (Psalms 132 and 150); Dance of the King's Daughter (Psalm 45); Hymn of Sion (Psalm 122); Meditation (Psalm 84); Passacaglia of Creation (Psalm 104); Epilogue (Psalm 133). *Text:* Bible, O.T., Psalms. *Commissioned by:* Stratford Shakespeare Festival, Stratford, Ont. *First performed:* June 1960; Stratford, Ont.; Stratford Shakespeare Festival. Members of the Stratford Shakespeare Festival Company.
Score & parts: Canadian Music Centre. *Score:* ms. in composer's hand. MIT

C10.17 Variations on Alles ist an Gottes Segen: All Is in the Hands of God.
(1960) *For:* organ. *Dedication:* A joke

for Eric Harrison. *First performed:* Oct. 19, [1960?]; Windsor, Ont. Barrie Cabena.
Score: Gray, 1967. BPL MIT

C11 FRANCIS JUDD COOKE

Born December 28, 1910, in Honolulu, Hawaii. Moved to Boston area 1939. *Education:* B.A. (Yale University, 1933); studied composition with Charles Martin Loeffler (Medfield, Mass.) and Sir Donald Francis Tovey (University of Edinburgh, Mus. B., 1937). *Awards:* Mus. Doc. (New England Conservatory, 1974). *Related activities:* organist and choirmaster, First Parish Church, Lexington, Mass.; served on the faculties of New England Conservatory (1939-70), Yale University (1959-61), Wellesley College (1975-80). W

WORKS

C11.1 Anthem: Eye Hath Not Seen. (1943) 5'
For: Soprano, Tenor, Bass, organ. *Text:* from the Bible, N.T.
Score & parts: ms.

[Anthem: Eye Hath Not Seen; Arr]
C11.2 Anthem: Eye Hath Not Seen. (1956)
For: chorus(SATB) and organ. *Text:* from the Bible, N.T.
Vocal score: reprod. of ms.

C11.3 Hieland Rhaem: A Scottish Rhapsody. (1972) 5'
For: clarinet and piano. *First performed:* Apr. 13, 1980; Lexington, Mass. Diana Haffner, clarinet and Ellen Polansky, piano.
Score: ms.

C11.4 I Will Give Praise. (1960) 5'
For: chorus(SATB) and organ. *Text:* Bible, O.T., Psalm 30 and Bible, O.T., Psalm 69.
Vocal score: reprod. of ms.

C11.5 Joyously Sing Nowell. (1977) 5'
For: chorus(SATB) and organ. *Text:*

Francis Judd Cooke and others.
Vocal score: reprod. of ms.

C11.6 Incidental Music to King Nicolo.
(1955)
For: flute, oboe, clarinet or saxophone,
bassoon, trumpet, percussion, piano,
violoncello, double bass. *Text:* Frank
Wedekind. *First performed:* 1955;
Lincoln, Mass.
Parts: ms.

[Pieces]
C11.7 Three Pieces. (1971) 6'
For: violin and piano. *Contents:* Intrada;
Cavatina; Rigadoon. *Dedicated to:*
Dorothy Mackintosh. *First performed:*
Feb. 17, 1980; Lexington, Mass. Robert
Koff, violin and Rosalind D. Koff,
fortepiano.
Score: ms.
Reel: 1972; Lexington, Mass. Robert
Koff, violin and Francis Judd Cooke,
piano.

C11.8 Quintet. (1964) 25'
For: violin, viola, violoncello, double
bass, piano. *Movements:* Fantasia;
Notturno. *Commissioned by:* Harvard
Musical Association.
Score & parts: ms.
Reel: Feb. 1967; New England
Conservatory.

C11.9 Roque Island March. (1959) 6'
For: orchestra(2(&pic)-2(&Ehn)-2(in A)(bcl
in A)-2(&cbsn); 4-3-3-1; timp, xylo; hp;
str). *First performed:* 1960; Honolulu,
Hawaii. Honolulu Symphony Orchestra,
George Barati, conductor.
Score & parts: ms.
Disc: 1960. Honolulu Symphony
Orchestra, George Barati, conductor.

[Roque Island March; Arr.]
C11.10 Roque Island March. 6'
For: piano(6-hands).
Score: ms.

C11.11 Sonata for Piano and Horn.
(1967) 20'
3 movements. *Dedicated to:* Willem

Valkenier. *First performed:* Aug. 18,
1967; Castle Hill, Ipswich, Mass. David
Ohanian, horn and Liora Sarch, piano.
Score: ms.
Reel: 1968; London, BBC. Barry
Tuckwell, horn and Margaret Kitchen,
piano.

C11.12 The Spacious Firmament. (1944)
6'
For: chorus(SATB) and organ.
Vocal score: reprod. of ms.

C12 RICHARD CORNELL

Born August 18, 1946, in Boston.
Education: studied piano with Nicholas
Van Slyck and Evelyn Zuckerman
(Longy School of Music, Piano
Diploma, 1972); composition with
Nicholas Van Slyck (Longy School of
Music/Emerson College, B.M., 1972);
William Thomas McKinley, Donald
Martino (New England Conservatory,
M.M., 1980); conducting with Charles
Bruck. *Awards:* fellowships and
scholarships (New England
Conservatory, 1976-79). *Related
activities:* pianist; conductor; music
director, Framingham (Mass.) North High
School (1971-73); founder and
conductor of the Longy Chamber
Orchestra (1973-75); assistant
conductor, Worcester Chorus (1976-77);
conductor, NEC Repertory Chorus
(1976-77); author of *Exploring Music
Careers* (1976) and *391 Ways to Explore
Arts and Humanities Careers* (1976);
member of the faculties of Longy
School of Music (1973-) and Berkshire
Music Center, Tanglewood (1981). L

WORKS

[Duos]
C12.1 Five Duos. (1980) 5'
For: flute and clarinet.
Score: ms.

C12.2 Landscape. (1978) 12'
For: string orchestra. 1 movement.
Score: ms. in composer's hand.

C12.3 Lord, Now Let Thy Servant
Depart in Peace. (1980) 5′
For: chorus(SATB). Canticle. *Text:* Bible,
N.T., Luke 2:29-32. *Dedication:* In
memory of M.L. Plummer. *First
performed:* Apr. 4, 1981; Emmanuel
Church, Boston. Emmanuel Church
Choir, Craig Smith, conductor.
Vocal score: ms.

C12.4 Orion's Quarry. (1980) 12′
For: trombone and trombone
ensemble(5 to 20). *Movements:* Hyades;
Pleiades; Aldebaran. *First performed:*
Apr. 12, 1980; Boston Conservatory.
Ron Barron, Roy Campbell, Timothy
Van Dam, Albert Jussaume, Glen
Walant.
Score & parts: ms.
Cassette: Dec. 3, 1981; New England
Conservatory. Robert Blossom; NEC
Trombone Choir, Michael Walters,
conductor. NEC

[Part-Songs]
C12.5 Two Part-Songs on Children's
Texts. (1978) 5′
For: chorus(SATB). *Text:* traditional.
Contents: The Bat; The Crocodile.
Dedicated to: Eric Darling and Janice
Darling. *First performed:* May 15, 1980;
Longy School of Music. Longy
Chamber Singers, Tom Hall, conductor.
Vocal score: ms.

C12.6 Peregrinations. (1978) 8′
For: flute and piano. *Movements:* Larus;
Sterna. *First performed:* Mar. 24, 1979;
Claremont, N.H. Sharon Zuckerman,
flute and David Arsenault, piano.
Score: ms.
Cassette: Apr. 11, 1980; New England
Conservatory. Sharon Zuckerman, flute
and David Arsenault, piano.

C12.7 Phantasy. (1979) 7′
For: clarinet and piano. 1 movement.
First performed: Apr. 1979; Longy
School of Music. Basil Chapman,
clarinet and Richard Cornell, piano.
Score: ms.
Cassette: Oct. 15, 1979; New England
Conservatory; in *Monday Night*

Composers Series. Basil Chapman,
clarinet and Richard Cornell, piano. NEC

[Poems]
C12.8 Three Poems from Sea Drift.
(1981) 18′
For: Baritone, chorus(SATB),
orchestra(2(pic)-2(Ehn)-2(bcl)-2; 2-2-3-0;
timp, cym(s); hp; str). *Text:* Sea Drift
from *The Leaves of Grass* by Walt
Whitman. *Movements:* To the
Man-O-War Bird; On the Beach at
Night; After the Sea Ship.
Commissioned by: The Concord Chorus,
Tom Hall, conductor. *First performed:*
Jan. 23, 1982; Concord, Mass. Sanford
Sylvan, baritone; The Concord Chorus,
Tom Hall, conductor.
Score & parts: reprod. of ms.
Vocal score: reprod. of ms.

[Preludes]
C12.9 Three Preludes. (1977-78) 10′
For: piano. First performed; Mar. 6,
1979; Longy School of Music. Margaret
Baltz.
Score: ms.

C12.10 Quartet. (1977) 12′
For: flute, clarinet, violin, piano. 1
movement.
Score & parts: ms.

[Quartet, Strings]
C12.11 String Quartet. (1979) 13′
2 movements. First performed; Apr. 25,
1980; Longy School of Music. Julia
Prins and Sue Rabut, violins; Scott
Woolweaver, viola; Karen Kaderavec,
violoncello.
Score & parts: ms.
Cassette: recording of first
performance.
Cassette: Feb. 4, 1980; New England
Conservatory; in *Monday Night
Composers Series*. Robin Davis and Sue
Rabut, violins; Scott Woolweaver,
viola; Karen Kaderavec, violoncello.
NEC
Reel: April 25, 1980; in *Longy New
Music Program*. Julie Prinsen and Sue
Rabut, violins; Scott Woolweaver,
viola; Karen Kaderavec, violoncello. L

[Songs]
C12.12 Two Songs on Texts of Yeats.
(1978) 10'
For: Soprano and lute. *Text:* William
Butler Yeats. *Contents:* The Falling of
the Leaves; The Sorrow of Love. *First
performed:* Dec. 3, 1978; Institute for
Contemporary Art, Boston. Linda Terry,
soprano and Robert Aldridge, guitar.
Score: ms.
Cassette: Oct. 30,1978; New England
Conservatory. Linda Terry, soprano and
Robert Aldridge, guitar. NEC

[Trio]
C12.13 String Trio. (1981) 14'
For: violin, viola, violoncello. 2
movements. *Dedicated to:* Vaener Trio.
Score & parts: ms.

C13 SILVIO COSCIA

Born November 27, 1899, in Milan,
Italy; died September 15, 1977, in
Watertown, Mass. Moved to Boston
area 1968. *Education:* Milan
Conservatory of Music. *Awards:*
Knighted by the Italian government for
contributions in the field of music.
Related activities: pianist, horn player,
author, vocal coach and teacher;
arranger with the Goldman Band
(1920s); co-principal horn, Metropolitan
Opera Orchestra, New York City
(1930-64); served on the faculty of
New England Conservatory (1968-75).
Also composed under the names
Sylvius C. and G.J. Sylvius. NEC

WORKS

C13.1 Un Addio (Farewell). (1964) 4'
For: Soprano or Tenor and piano. *Text:*
Contessa Lara.
Score: mss. in composer's hand. NEC
Score: reprod. of ms. NEC

C13.2 Alla bimba mia: Romanza. (1918)
For: Tenor or Baritone and piano. *Text:*
Carlo Coscia.
Score: mss. in composer's hand. NEC

C13.3 Allegro appassionato in C.
(1935?) 7'
For: viola or violin and piano, or
violin violoncello, piano. *Dedication:* To
Mr. J[ohn] DiJanni.
Score: reprod. of mss. NEC

[Alouette Scherzo Overture, Band]
C13.4 Alouette Scherzo Overture. (1959)
3' 30"
Variations on the French Canadian folk
song "Alouette." *First performed:* Aug.
23, 1959; Central Park Mall, New York
City; Giuseppi Creatore Memorial
Concert.
Score: ms. in composer's hand. NEC
Condensed score & parts: ms. in
composers hand. NEC
Condensed score & parts: Baron, 1962.

[Alouette Scherzo Overture,
Orchestra]
C13.5 Alouette Scherzo Overture. 3'
30"
For: orchestra(2(pic)-2-2-2; 4-2-3-1;
timp, perc; hp; str). Variations on the
French Canadian folk song "Alouette."
First performed: Mar. 1, 1960;
Trans-Canadian Radio Network. Halifax
Symphony Orchestra.
Score & parts: ms. in composer's hand.
NEC
Score & parts: Baron, 1962.
Condensed score: ms. in composer's
hand. NEC
Condensed score: Baron, 1962. NEC

Amore ed odio. *See* Love and Hate.

C13.6 Andante religioso.
For: organ.

[Andante religioso, Piano Trio]
C13.7 Andante religioso. (1940)
For: violin, violoncello, piano or
harmonium.
Part(violin): ms. in composer's hand.
NEC

[Andante religioso, Strings]
C13.8 Andante religioso.
For: string quartet or string orchestra.

Score: mss. in composer's hand (2 versions with string orchestra). NEC
Parts: ms. in composer's hand (version with string quartet, subtitled Prayer). NEC

C13.9 Ave Maria, C major. (1957)
For: voice(medium high) and orchestra(3-2-2-2; 4-3-3-1; timp; hp, cel; str). *Text:* Roman Catholic liturgy. *Dedicated to:* Renata Tebaldi.
Score & parts: ms. in composer's hand. NEC
Score & parts: Baron, 1957. NEC
Vocal score: ms. in composer's hand. NEC
Vocal score: Baron, 1957. NEC

C13.10 Bacio morto (Dead Kiss). (1923)
For: Tenor or Baritone and piano. *Text:* Ada Negri.
Score: ms. in composer's hand. NEC
Score: reprod. of ms. NEC

C13.11 The Ballad Singer (Il cantastorie). (1964)
For: Baritone or Bass and piano. *Text:* Thomas Hardy.
Score: ms. in composer's hand. NEC
Score: reprod. of ms. NEC

C13.12 Batto a la chiusa imposta. 2'
For: voice(high), voice(medium high), voice(medium) or voice(low), piano. *Text:* Giosue Carducci. *Dedicated to:* Virginia (version for high voice); Richard Tucker (version for high voice titled, Cuore batti, and version for medium high voice).
Score: mss. in composer's hand (versions with high voice, titled Cuore batti, with medium voice, and with low voice). NEC
Score: reprod. of mss. (versions with high voice, titled Cuore batti, with medium voice, and with low voice). NEC
Score: Baron, 1958 (version with high voice published under title Cuore batti). NEC

[Beglio occhi lucenti, High Voice]
C13.13 Begli occhi lucenti (Lovely Eyes Shining Brightly).
For: voice(high) and string orchestra or piano. *Text:* anon., 17th century.
Score & parts: reprod. of ms. NEC
Vocal score: ms. in composer's hand (subtitled Beautiful Eyes). NEC

[Begli occhi lucenti, Low Voice]
C13.14 Begli occhi lucenti (Lovely Eyes Shining Brightly).
For: voice(low) and string orchestra or piano. *Text:* anon. 17th century. Written for Cesare Siepi. *First performed:* Hunter College. Cesare Siepi, bass and unidentified pianist.
Sketches: ms. in composer's hand (version with string orchestra). NEC
Score & parts: ms. in composer's hand. NEC
Vocal score: ms. in composer's hand (version with voice and piano). NEC
Vocal score: Ricordi, 1953. NEC

[Begli occhi lucenti, Medium High Voice]
C13.15 Begli occhi lucenti.
For: voice(medium high) and string orchestra or piano. *Text:* anon., 17th century.
Score & parts: ms. in composer's hand (version for voice and string orchestra). NEC
Score: mss. in composer's hand. NEC
Vocal score: ms. in composer's hand. NEC
Vocal score: reprod. of ms. NEC

[Begli occhi lucenti, Medium Low Voice]
C13.16 Begli occhi lucenti.
For: voice(medium low) and piano. *Text:* anon., 17th Century.
Score: ms. in composer's hand. NEC

[Begli occhi lucenti, Medium Voice]
C13.17 Begli occhi lucenti (O Beautiful Eyes).
For: voice(medium) and piano. *Text:* anon., 17th century.
Score: ms. in composer's hand. NEC
Score: reprod. of ms. NEC

C13.18 Bimba mia.
For: voice(high) and piano. *Text:* Carlo Coscia.
Score: ms. in composer's hand. NEC

C13.19 Il Brindisi. (1916)
For: Bass or Baritone and piano. *Text:* Giuseppe Parini.
Score: ms. in composer's hand. NEC

C13.20 Cantam le allodole.
For: voice(high) or voice(medium) and piano.
Score: mss. in composer's hand (version for high voice incomplete). NEC

Il cantastorie. *See* The Ballad Singer.

C13.21 Color Suite for Band in Three Moods. 10'
Movements: Andantino con licenza (Grey Hour); Valse Minuet (Blue); The Black Knight's Ride. *First performed:* Aug. 20, 1961; Central Park Mall, New York City; Giuseppe Creatore Memorial Concert.
Condensed score & parts: ms. in composer's hand. NEC
Condensed score & parts: Baron, 1962.

[Concert or Examination Studies]
C13.22 Five Concert or Examination Studies.
For: horn and piano.
Score & part: Baron.

C13.23 Concert Suite in Three Character Moods. 12'
For: horns(4), or horns(3) and trombone. 3 movements.
Score & parts: Baron, 1953.
Score: reprod. of ms. NEC
Parts: ms. in composer's hand. NEC

C13.24 Concertino. 15'
For: horn and orchestra(1(pic)-1-2-1; 0-1-1-0; timp, perc; pf or hp; str). 3 movements.
Score & parts: ms. in composer's hand. NEC
Score & parts: Baron, 1953.

Pf. red: ms. in composer's hand. NEC
Pf. red: Baron, 1953. NEC

C13.25 Concerto Phantasy. (1956) 15'
For: oboe and orchestra(2-0-2-2; 2-2-2-1; timp, perc; pf; str). *Dedication:* To my friend William Arrowsmith, first oboe of Metropolitan Orchestra.
Score & parts: ms. in composer's hand. NEC
Score & parts: Baron, 1957.
Pf. red: ms. in composer's hand. NEC
Pf. red: Baron, 1957. NEC
Part(oboe): reprod. of ms. NEC

Cuore batti. *See* Batto a la chiusa imposta.

C13.26 Czardas.
For: instruments(treble)(2) and piano.
Score: ms. in composer's hand. NEC

Dance Child. *See* Danza fanciulla.

[Dances of Different Nations]
C13.27 Six Dances of Different Nations: Suite No. 1. 15'
For: band. *Movements:* Gavotte Louis 15th; Dance Moresque; Lilliputians March; Tarantella; Hellas Dance; Siguedilla. *First performed:* Aug. 21, 1960; Central Park Mall, New York City. American Federation of Musicians Local 802 Symphonic Band.
Condensed score & parts: ms. in composer's hand. NEC
Condensed score: Baron, 1962. NEC
Parts: Baron, 1962.

[Dances of Different Nations. Siguedilla; Arr.]
C13.28 Siguedilla. (1953) 4'
For: voice(high) and piano.
Score: mss. in composer's hand. NEC
Score: reprod. of ms. NEC

C13.29 Danza fanciulla (Dance Child). (1950)
For: Tenor or voice(medium) and piano. *Text:* Silvio Coscia.
Score: mss. in composer's hand (both versions). NEC

Score: reprod. of ms. (version for medium voice). NEC

C13.30 Dark Hour. 3′
For: voice(high) or voice(low) and piano. *Text:* Paul Marie Verlaine.
Score: mss. in composer's hand (2 versions for high voice). NEC
Part(piano): mss. in composer's hand (2 versions for low voice). NEC

[Dark Hour; Arr.]
C13.31 Dark Hour. 3′
For: voice, string quartet, piano. *Text:* Paul Marie Verlaine.
Parts: ms. in composer's hand (strings). NEC

C13.32 De parla.
For: voice(high) and piano.
Score: ms. in composer's hand. NEC

Dead Kiss. *See* Bacio morto.

[Desiderio dell'oblio, High Voice]
C13.33 Desiderio dell'oblio. (1954) 3′
For: voice(high) and orchestra(2-1(&Ehn)-2-2; 4-2-2-1; timp, perc; str). *Text:* Nicolaus Lenau. *Written for and dedicated to:* Madame Antonietta Stella Trepiccioni.
Score & parts: ms. in composer's hand. NEC
Vocal score: ms. in composer's hand. NEC
Vocal score: Baron, 1958.

[Desiderio dell'oblio, Low Voice]
C13.34 Desiderio dell'oblio (Desire of Oblivion). (1954) 3′
For: voice(low) and piano. *Text:* Nicolaus Lenau.
Score: ms. in composer's hand. NEC

[Desiderio dell'oblio, Medium High Voice]
C13.35 Desiderio dell' oblio. (1954) 3′
For: voice(medium high) and orchestra. *Text:* Nicolaus Lenau.
Score & parts: Baron. Rental. NEC
Vocal score: Baron. NEC

[Desiderio dell'oblio, Medium Voice]
C13.36 Desiderio dell'oblio. (1954) 3′
For: voice(medium) and piano. *Text:* Nicolaus Lenau. *Dedication:* A Virginia.
Score: ms. in composer's hand. NEC
Part(voice): ms. in composer's hand. NEC

C13.37 Di verdi prati: Aria senza parole. (1954) 4′
For: voice(low) and orchestra(2(pic)-1-2-1; 2-2-1-0; timp; str). *Text:* Giuseppe Valdengo.
Score & parts: ms. in composer's hand. NEC
Score: ms. in composer's hand. NEC
Vocal score: ms. in composer's hand. NEC
Vocal score: reprod. of ms. NEC
Part(voice): ms. in composer's hand. NEC

[Dormi, dormi, High Voice]
C13.38 Dormi, dormi (Lullaby). 3′ 30″
For: voice(high) or voice(low) and orchestra(2-1-2-2; 2-1-0-0; tri; hp, cel or pf; str). *Text:* Michelangelo Buonarroti. *Written for and dedicated to:* Renata Tebaldi.
Sketches: ms. in composer's hand .(version for low voice). NEC
Score & parts: mss. in composer's hand (versions for high and low voice, subtitled Lullaby). NEC
Score & parts: Baron, 1957 (versions for high and low voice, subtitled Lullaby). NEC
Vocal score: mss. in composer's hand (version for high voice and 3 versions for low voice, subtitled Lullaby). NEC
Vocal score: Baron, 1957 (version for high voice). NEC

[Dormi, dormi, Low Voice]
C13.39 Dormi, dormi (Sleep, Sleep). 3′ 30″
For: voice(low), string quartet, piano. *Text:* Michelangelo Buonarroti.
Parts: ms. in composer's hand (strings). NEC

[Dormi, dormi, Medium Voice]
C13.40 Dormi, dormi (Sleep, Sleep).
For: voice(medium) and piano. *Text:*
Michelangelo Buonarroti.
Score: ms. in composer's hand. NEC
Score: reprod. of mss. NEC

[Dramatic Elegy, Band]
C13.41 Dramatic Elegy.
Dedication: To the memory of my
beloved teacher, academician Professor
Carlo Gatti.
Condensed score & parts: ms. in
composer's hand. NEC
Condensed score & parts: Baron, 1967.

[Dramatic Elegy, Orchestra]
C13.42 Dramatic Elegy.
For: orchestra(3(pic)-2-2-2; 4-3-3-1;
timp, perc(2); hp; str). 3 movements.
Score & parts: ms. in composer's hand.
NEC
Condensed score: ms. in composer's
hand. NEC
Condensed score: reprod. of mss. NEC
Parts: reprod. of ms. NEC

Drinking Song Ballad. *See* Love and
Hate.

[Duets, Horns]
C13.43 22 Duets: Character Sketches.
Score: King, 1976. NEC

[Duets, Trumpets]
C13.44 20 Original Duets for Trumpet.
Score: Fox.

[Easy Progressive Melodic Studies]
C13.45 126 Easy Progressive Melodic
Studies.
For: horn.
Score: ms. in composer's hand. NEC

C13.46 Ecce homo. 5'
For: band. Symphonic poem inspired
by Rubens' painting of The Crucifixion.
First performed: Aug. 21, 1960; Central
Park Mall, New York City. American
Federation of Musicians Local 802
Symphonic Band.
Condensed score & parts: ms. in

composer's hand. NEC
Condensed score & parts: Baron.
Parts: reprod. of ms. (incomplete). NEC

[Ecce homo; Arr.]
C13.47 Ecce homo. 5'
For: orchestra(3(pic)-2(&Ehn)-2(&bcl)-2;
4-2-3-1; timp, perc(4); hp; str).
Symphonic poem inspired by Rubens'
painting of The Crucifixion. *First
performed:* Feb. 11, 1962; Brooklyn
Museum, Brooklyn, N.Y. American
Symphony of New York.
Score & parts: ms. in composer's hand.
NEC
Score: Baron, 1962. NEC
Condensed score: ms. in composer's
hand. NEC
Condensed score: Baron, 1962. NEC
Parts: Baron, 1962.

C13.48 Elegy. (1930)
For: violin, violoncello, piano.
Score: reprod. of ms. NEC

C13.49 Epicedial March. 6'
For: band. Symphonic poem.
Dedication: To the heroes of U.S.A.
Armed Forces. *First performed:* Aug.
26, 1962; Central Park Mall, New York
City; Giuseppe Creatore Memorial
Concert.
Condensed score & parts: ms. in
composer's hand. NEC
Condensed score & parts: Baron, 1962.

C13.50 Epicedium pro heroes. (1947) 7'
For: violin, violoncello or horn, piano.
Score & parts: ms. in composer's hand.
NEC

C13.51 The Exorcism: Faust in the
Forest. (1939) 12'
For: orchestra(2(pic)-2(Ehn)-2-2; 4-3-3-1;
timp, perc(4); str). Symphonic poem;
ballet.
Score: reprod. of ms. NEC
Score: Margun. Rental. NEC
Parts: Margun. Rental.
Condensed score: ms. in composer's
hand. NEC
Condensed score: reprod. of mss. NEC

Farewell. *See* Un Addio.

Faust in the Forest. *See* The Exorcism: Faust in the Forest.

C13.5.1.5 Il Fiore del pensiere.
For: voice and piano.
Score: ms. in composer's hand. NEC

C13.52 Fire Dance. (1968) 2'
For: band.
Score: ms. in composer's hand. NEC
Condensed score & parts: mss. in composer's hand. NEC
Condensed score: reprod. of ms. NEC

[Fire Dance; Arr.]
C13.53 Fire Dance. 2'
For: flutes(2), oboe, clarinet, bassoon, trumpets(2), trombone, piano.
Score: ms. in composer's hand (incomplete). NEC
Parts: ms. in composer's hand. NEC

C13.54 Fra l'erba in una triste primavera.
For: voice(medium) and piano.
Score: ms. in composer's hand (incomplete). NEC

C13.55 Gloria.
For: chorus(SATB) and organ. *Text:* Roman Catholic liturgy.
Vocal score: ms. in composer's hand. NEC

C13.56 Gypsy Serenade: a Magyar Character Piece.
For: violin and piano.
Score: ms. in composer's hand. NEC

[I Come Tomorrow, High Voice]
C13.57 I Come To-morrow.
For: voice(high) and piano. *Text:* anon., 16th century, German. Written for Cesare Siepe.
Score: ms. in composer's hand. NEC
Score: reprod. of ms. NEC
Score: Ricordi. NEC

[I Come Tomorrow, Low Voice]
 C13.58 I Come Tomorrow (Verro domani).
For: voice(low) and piano. *Text:* anon.,

16th century, German. Written for Cesare Siepi.
Score: ms. in composer's hand (incomplete). NEC
Score: reprod. of ms. NEC
Score: Ricordi, 1961. NEC

[I Come Tomorrow, Medium Voice]
 C13.59 I Come Tomorrow (Verro domani).
For: voice(medium) and orchestra. *Text:* anon., 16th century, German. Written for Cesare Siepi.
Score: ms. in composer's hand. NEC
Vocal score: ms. in composer's hand. NEC
Vocal score: reprod. of ms. NEC

[Idyl, Band]
C13.60 Idyl. 5'
Symphonic poem based on native American themes. *First performed:* Aug. 1963; Central Park Mall, New York City. Symphonic Band of New York.
Condensed score & parts: ms. in composer's hand. NEC
Condensed score & parts: Baron, 1963-64. NEC

[Idyl, Orchestra]
C13.61 Idyl. 5'
For: orchestra(2(pic)-2(Ehn)-2-2; 4-2-2-1; timp, perc(3); hp; str). Symphonic poem based on native American themes.
Score & parts: Baron.

C13.62 In Old Naples. 7' 30"
For: orchestra(2(pic)-2(Ehn)-2-2; 4-2-3-1; timp, perc(4), glock; hp, pf; str). Symphonic poem. Version for band titled Neapolitan Day.
Score: reprod. of ms. NEC
Condensed score: reprod. of mss. NEC

C13.63 Intermezzo: A Story of a Life. 5'
For: orchestra(3(pic)-2(Ehn)-2(&bcl)-2; 4-3-3-1; timp, perc(4); hp; cel; str).

C13.64 Kindly Loving.
For: voice(high) and orchestra. *Text:* Nicholas Breton.
Score: Baron. Rental.

Vocal score: ms. in composer's hand.
NEC
Vocal score: reprod. of ms. NEC
Vocal score: Baron, 1959. NEC

C13.65 Lento elegiaco.
For: trumpet and organ or piano.
Score & part: Baron.

C13.66 Little Scherzo Overture. 4' 30"
For: orchestra(2(pic)-2-2-2; 4-2-3-1;
timp, perc(2); hp; str).

C13.67 Lord's Prayer. (1964)
For: voice(high) and orchestra(2-2-2-2;
4-3-2-1; timp, perc; hp or pf; str). *Text:*
Bible, N.T., Matthew 6:9-13.
Score: mss. in composer's hand. NEC
Vocal score: ms. in composer's hand.
NEC

C13.68 Love and Hate.
For: voice(high) or voice(medium high)
and piano. *Text:* J.J. Lauridsen.
Score: ms. in composer's hand
(versions for high voice, one
incomplete). NEC
Score: ms. in composer's hand (version
for medium high voice subtitled Amore
ed odio). NEC

C13.69 Love and Hate (Drinking Song
Ballad).
For: voice(medium) and piano. *Text:* J.J.
Lauridsen.
Score: ms. in composer's hand. NEC
Score: reprod. of mss. NEC
Part(voice): ms. in composer's hand
(with parallel title Amore ed odio).
NEC

C13.70 Love Me Little, Love Me Long.
1'
For: voice(high or medium high) and
piano or orchestra(2(pic)-2-2-2; 4-2-2-0;
timp; str) or voice(medium) and piano.
Text: anon. *Dedicated to:* Patrice
Munsel.
Score & parts: ms. in composer's hand
(version for medium high voice). NEC
Vocal score: mss. in composer's hand
(both versions). NEC

Vocal score: Baron, 1958. (version for
medium high voice). NEC

Lovely Eyes Shining Brightly. *See*
Beglio occhi lucenti.

Lullaby. *See* Dormi, dormi.

C13.71 Madrigal.
For: Baritone, chorus(TB), piano. *Text:*
anon.; from *The Oxford Book of English
Verse.*
Vocal score: ms. in composer's hand.
NEC

C13.72 March-Polka of the Clowns. 2'
30"
For: band. *First performed:*
Steeplechase Pier, Coney Island, New
York City; Concerts by the Sea.
Symphonic Band of New York.
Condensed score & parts: ms. in
composer's hand. NEC
Condensed score & parts: Baron, 1962.

C13.73 Marinka.
For: voice(high) or voice(medium) and
piano. *Text:* Silvio Coscia.
Score: mss. in composer's hand (both
versions). NEC
Score: reprod. of ms. (version for
medium voice). NEC

C13.74 Mattutino nostalgico (Nostalgic
Dawn). 4'
For: voice(high) or voice(medium) and
piano. *Text:* E. del Greco.
Score: mss. in composer's hand (both
versions). NEC

C13.75 Meditation. 5'
For: band.
Score: ms. in composer's hand. NEC
Condensed scores & parts: mss. in
composer's hand. NEC
Condensed score: Baron, 1967. NEC
Parts: Baron, 1967.

C13.76 Mephisto Serenade: Musical
Sketches, Suite in Three Moods.
For: band. *Movements:* Mephisto
Serenade; Night Blackness; Poignancy.

Score: ms. in composer's hand. NEC
Condensed score & parts: ms. in composer's hand. NEC
Condensed score: reprod. of ms. NEC

C13.77 The Modern French Horn Player: An Appendix to All Methods.
For: horn or horn and piano.
Score: Baron, 1947. NEC

[Modern Studies in Different Styles]
C13.78 Twelve Modern Studies in Different Styles.
Score: Baron, 1953. NEC

C13.79 Neapolitan Day. 7' 30"
For: band. Symphonic poem based on Roman folk themes. *Movements:* Morning; Pastoral; Carnival. Version for orchestra(2(pic)-2(Ehn)-2-2; 4-2-3-1; timp, perc(4), glock; hp, pf; str) titled In Old Naples.
Score: ms. in composer's hand (version for concert band). NEC
Score: ms. in composer's hand (version for Venice band). NEC
Condensed score & parts: ms. in composer's hand (version for Venice band). NEC
Condensed score & parts: Baron, 1967 (version for Venice band).
Condensed score: reprod. of mss. (versions for orchestra). NEC
Condensed score: Baron (version for concert band). NEC
Part(oboe II): ms. in composer's hand (version for concert band). NEC
Parts: reprod. of ms. (version for concert band). NEC

Never, Never. *See* Nunca, nunca.

Nostalgic Dawn. *See* Mattutino nostalgico.

[Nunca, nunca, High Voice, Piano]
C13.80 Nunca, nunca: Cancion triste. 3'
For: voice(high) or voice(medium) and piano. *Text:* B. Hubner. Sketch: ms. in composer's hand (version for high voice). NEC
Score: mss. in composer's hand (both versions). NEC

Score: reprod. of mss. (both versions). NEC

[Nunca, nunca; Arr.]
C13.81 Nunca, nunca: Never Never. 3'
For: voice(high), viola or violin, piano.
Text: B. Hubner.
Score & part: ms. in composer's hand. NEC
Part(viola): reprod. of ms. NEC

C13.82 O viso dolce (O Sweet Visage). 3' 30"
For: voice(high) or voice(low) and piano. *Text:* Giosue Carducci.
Score: mss. in composer's hand (both versions). NEC
Score: reprod. of mss. (both versions). NEC

C13.83 Occhi dolorosi.
For: voice(high) and piano. *Text:* Silvio Coscia.
Score: ms. in composer's hand. NEC
Score: reprod. of ms. NEC
Score: Baron, 1959. NEC

C13.84 October: Romanza.
For: voice(low) and piano. *Text:* L. Stecchetti.

C13.85 The Old Music Box. 3'
For: band.
Condensed score & parts: ms. in composer's hand. NEC
Condensed score: Baron, 1967. NEC
Parts: Baron, 1967.

On the Borderland. *See* Prelude Impromptu No. 1.

C13.86 Once Upon a Time: A Love Story for Young and Grown-Up Children.
For: voice(high) and piano. *Text:* Silvio Coscia.
Score: ms. in composer's hand. NEC

C13.87 Oriental Serenade.
For: violin, violoncello, piano.
Score & parts: ms. in composer's hand. NEC

Prayer. *See* Andante religioso, strings.

C13.88 Prelude Impromptu No. 1 in D Minor (On the Borderland) .
For: piano. *Dedication:* To Sylvana.
Score: ms. in composer's hand. NEC
Score: reprod. of ms. NEC

C13.89 Prelude Impromptu No. 2 in E Major. 8'
For: piano.
Score: ms. in composer's hand. NEC
Score: reprod. of ms. NEC

[Prelude Impromptu No. 3]
C13.90 Prelude Impromptu in C Minor. 7' 30"
For: piano.
Score: mss. in composer's hand. NEC
Score: reprod. of ms. NEC

C13.91 Prelude Impromptu No. 4 (Selene). 10'
For: piano.
Score: ms. in composer's hand. NEC
Score: reprod. of ms. NEC

C13.92 Prelude No. 1, F Major: Organ Imitation. 3' 30"
For: band. *First performed:* Aug. 1, 1962; Belle Isle, Detroit, Mich. Detroit Concert Band.
Condensed score & parts: ms. in composer's hand. NEC
Condensed score: Baron, 1962.
Parts: Baron, 1962. NEC

C13.93 Prelude No. 2, B Flat Minor: A Story of Life, Romantic and Passional. 5'
For: band. *First performed:* July 26, 1962; Prospect Park, Brooklyn, N.Y. Goldman Band.
Condensed score & parts: ms. in composer's hand. NEC
Condensed score & parts: Baron, 1962.

C13.94 Prelude No. 3, G Minor. 5'
For: band. *First performed:* Aug. 1964; Central Park Mall, New York City.
Condensed score & parts: ms. in

composer's hand. NEC
Condensed score & parts: Baron, 1964.

C13.95 Primavera. (1916) 2' 30"
For: voice(medium) or voice(low) and piano. *Text:* Enrico Panzacchi.
Sketches: ms. in composer's hand (version for low voice). NEC
Score: mss. in composer's hand (version for medium voice). NEC

[Quartet, Trombones(4)]
C13.96 Untitled.
Condensed score & parts: ms. in composer's hand. NEC

[Quintet, Brasses, C Minor]
C13.97 Brass Quintet: Suite in Three Moods. 5'
For: trumpets(2), horn, trombone, tuba.
Movements: Satanic Serenade; Night Blackness; Poignancy.
Score: ms. in composer's hand. NEC
Score: reprod. of ms. NEC
Score & parts: Baron.

[Quintet, Brasses, F Major]
C13.98 Brass Quintet: Old Style Religious Dramatic Madrigal and Fugue. 5'
For: trumpets(2), horn, trombone, tuba.
Score & parts: Baron. NEC

C13.99 Recitativo and Fugue. 9' 30"
For: horn and organ or piano.
Dedicated to: Gunther Schuller.
Parts: ms. in composer's hand. NEC
Part(horn): Baron, 1963. NEC.

C13.100 Request.
For: Soprano or Tenor and piano.
Score: ms. in composer's hand. NEC
Score: reprod. of ms. NEC

C13.101 Requiem. (1940)
For: chorus(men) and organ.
Vocal score: mss. in composer's hand (titled Requiem aeternam). NEC
Parts: ms. in composer's hand (titled Requiem aeternam). NEC

Romance. *See* Waltzer.

C13.102 Romanza: A Romantic Song.
For: horn or trombone or bassoon or violoncello and piano.
Score & parts: Baron, 1948. NEC

Romanza. *See also* Alla bimba mia.

Satanic Minuet. *See* Trio-Suite. Satanic Minuet; Arr.

Selene. *See* Prelude Impromptu No. 4.

Siguedilla. *See* Dances of Different Nations. Siguedilla.

C13.103 Septet for Winds.
For: flute, oboe, clarinet, bassoon, trumpet, horn, trombone.
Score & parts: reprod. of ms. NEC
Score & parts: Baron, 1953. NEC
Condensed score: ms. in composer's hand. NEC

C13.104 Sketches.
Music: ms. in composer's hand. NEC

Sleep, Sleep. *See* Dormi, dormi.

[A Star, Piano]
C13.105 A Star.
Dedicated to: Sylvana.
Score: Baron, 1948. NEC

[A Star, Strings]
C13.106 A Star: Lullaby.
For: string quartet or string orchestra.
Condensed score & parts: Baron, 1948. NEC

[A Star, Winds]
C13.107 A Star. 3'
For: flute, oboe, clarinets(2), horn, bassoon.
Parts: ms. in composer's hand. NEC

Studies. *See* Concert or Examination Studies; Easy Progressive Melodic Studies; Modern Studies in Different Styles.

Suite No. 1. *See* Dances of Different Nations.

C13.108 Swedish Rhapsody. (1971)
For: band. *Dedicated to:* John Rosene.
Sketches: ms. in composer's hand. NEC
Condensed score: mss. in composer's hand. NEC
Condensed score: reprod. of ms. NEC

C13.109 The Tartars.
Sketches: ms. in composer's hand. NEC

C13.110 Those Piccolos and Tubas. 2'
For: band.
Score: ms. in composer's hand. NEC
Condensed score & parts: mss. in composer's hand. NEC
Condensed score: Baron, 1967. NEC
Parts: Baron, 1967.

To a Star. *See* A Star.

[Trio, Piano and Strings]
C13.111 Trio in mi minore
For: violin, violoncello, piano. 1 movement.
Score & parts: ms. in composer's hand.

[Trio, Piano and Winds]
C13.112 Trio.
For: flute or violin, horn or violoncello or bassoon, piano.
Score & parts: Baron, 1955. NEC
Parts: ms. in composer's hand. NEC

C13.113 Trio-Suite. 16'-17'
For: violin, violoncello, piano.
Movements: Appassionata; Romanza; Satanic Minuet; Epilogue.
Score & parts: mss. in composer's hand. NEC
Score & parts: reprod. of ms. NEC

[Trio-Suite. Satanic Minuet; Arr]
C13.114 Satanic Minuet. 2' 30"
For: band.
Score: ms. in composer's hand. NEC
Condensed score & parts: ms. in composer's hand. NEC
Condensed score: mss. in composer's hand. NEC
Condensed score: reprod. of ms. NEC

Verro domani. *See* I Come Tomorrow.

C13.115 Vien l'April.
For: voice(high) and piano.
Score: ms. in composer's hand. NEC

C13.116 Visione erocia. 10'
For: orchestra(2(pic)-2-2-2; 4-3-3-1;
timp, perc(4); hp; str). Symphonic poem.

C13.117 Vous desirez savoir. (1944)
For: voice and piano. *Text:* Sully
Prud'homme.
Score: reprod. of mss (versions for
high voice, medium low voice,
baritone). NEC
Score: mss. in composer's hand
(versions for high, medium low, low
voices). NEC

C13.118 Waltzer (Romance).
For: piano.
Score: ms. in composer's hand (version
in B flat major). NEC
Score: mss. in composer's hand
(versions in C major). NEC

ARRANGEMENTS OF WORKS BY OTHER COMPOSERS

C13.119 Ave Maria.
For: Soprano or Tenor and piano.
Original by R. Monetti.
Score: reprod. of ms. NEC

C13.120 Coscia's Collection of 27
Duets for French Horn.
Original by various composers.
Score: Baron.

[Fugues]
C13.121 3 Fugues: Trio.
For: brasses(3) or woodwinds(3).
Original by Wilhelm Friedemann Bach.
Score & parts: ms. in composer's hand.
NEC
Score & parts: reprod. of ms. NEC
Score & parts: Baron.

[Pieces]
C13.122 Six Pieces.
For: brasses(4) or woodwinds(4).
Original by Piotr Ilyich Tchaikovsky.
Score & parts: ms. in composer's hand.

NEC
Score & parts: Baron.
Score: reprod. of ms. NEC

C13.123 Prelude and Fugue in F Major.
Prelude and Fugue in D Minor. 6' 40"
For: woodwinds(4) or brasses(4).
Original by Johann Sebastian Bach.
Score & parts: ms. in composer's hand.
NEC
Score & parts: reprod. of ms. NEC
Score & parts: Baron. NEC

C13.124 Prelude and Fugue in G Minor.
Prelude and Fugue in G Major. 7'
For: woodwinds(4) or brasses(4).
Original by Johann Sebastian Bach.
Score & parts: ms. in composer's hand.
NEC
Score & parts: Baron.

C14 JOHN CROTTY

Born 1950 in Philadelphia, Pa. Moved
to Boston area 1980. *Education:* B.M.,
M.M. (University of Michigan); studied
composition with Samuel Adler
(Eastman School of Music). *Related
activities:* pianist; theorist; currently on
the faculty of Boston University. BU

WORKS

Compendium. *See* Ghost Variations.

[Concerto]
C14.1 Piano Concerto. (1980) 30'
For: piano and orchestra(2(&pic)-3-2(&
Ebcl)-3; 6-3-4-0; timp, perc, vibra, xylo;
cel; str). 3 movements.
Score: ms. in composer's hand.

C14.2 An Enclosed Garden. (1979) 10'
For: Mezzo Soprano and piano. *Text:*
from the Bible. Song cycle (4 songs).
First performed: Mar. 1980; Rochester,
N.Y. Jaqueline Kadrmas, soprano and
Terri Adler, piano.
Score: ms. in composer's hand.

C14.3 Ghost Variations. (1979) 12'
For: violin, violoncello, piano.

Originally titled Compendium.
Score & parts: ms. in composer's hand.

C14.4 Puer natus. (1979)
For: chorus(SATB) and organ.
Vocal score: Lawson-Gould, nyp.

C14.5 Sommerset Carol. (1979)
For: chorus(SATB) and organ.
Vocal score: Lawson-Gould, nyp.

D1 JOHN GENNARO DAMIAN

Born January 7, 1946, in Albany, N.Y.
Moved to Boston area 1971. *Education:*
B.A. (Berklee College of Music).
Awards: Harris Stanton Award (Berklee
College of Music) in guitar
performance. *Related activities:*
guitarist; member of Boston New
Music Ensemble; musical director of
Rubber- Tellie String Quartet (the
Rubber-Tellie is a "tactiley played,"
sculptured instrument invented by the
composer); performer with wide variety
of groups from Howard McGee Quintet
to Collage; author of *Alternate Sources
for Improvisation* (in progress);
currently on the faculty of Berklee
College of Music. Be

WORKS

[Adagio]
D1.1 3 Adagio. (1980)
For: guitar.
Score: available from composer.

D1.2 Bird Study. (1977)
For: instrument(unspecified) and tape.
First performed: Oct. 18, 1977; Institute
of Contemporary Art, Boston.
Perf. dir: available from composer

[Cinderella. Selections]
D1.3 Excerpts from Cinderella. (1977)
For: violin, guitar, vibraphone, double
bass. Operetta. *First performed:*
People's Theatre, Cambridge, Mass.
Parts: available from composer.
Perf. dir: available from composer.

D1.4 Do Not Fold, Bend, Spindle, or
Mutilate. (1975)
For: instruments(unspecified)(4). *First
performed:* June 9, 1976; Stone Soup
Gallery, Boston.
Score & parts: available from
composer.

D1.5 Doreen & Alice. (1975)
For: voices and
instruments(unspecified(4) without
winds. *First performed:* May 26, 1976;
Stone Soup Gallery, Boston.
Score & parts: available from the
composer.

D1.6 Guitar Preludes. (1981)
For: guitars(2).
Score: available from composer.

D1.7 Just a Taste. (1974)
For: flugelhorn and jazz band. *First
performed:* May 17, 1974; Berklee
College of Music
Score: Berklee, 1975.
Parts: ms; available from composer.
Disc: Berklee Records. Unidentified jazz
band, Herb Pomeroy, conductor.
Reel: Be

D1.8 Kuckucks UHR (Cuckoo Clock).
(1977)
For: instruments(unspecified)(5), one of
which functions as soloist and dances.
First performed: Apr. 25, 1977.
People's Theatre, Cambridge, Mass.
Perf. dir: available from composer.

D1.9 Meditations on a Ground Bass.
(1978)
For: guitars(4). *First performed:* Apr.
13, 1978; Berklee College of Music
Score & parts: available from
composer.
Reel: Be

D1.10 Mimetal. (1976)
For: instruments(unspecified)(2 or more).
First performed: Apr. 25, 1977;
People's Theatre, Cambridge, Mass.
Perf. dir: available from composer.

D1.11 Module Systems No. 1. (1981)
For: marimbas(2).
Score & parts: available from composer.

D1.12 Piece for Dancer with Ropes. (1978)
For: dancer and instruments(unspecified)(4).
Perf. dir: available from composer.

[Quartet, Saxophones, No. 1]
D1.13 Saxophone Quartet No. 1. (1973)
First performed: Nov. 15, 1973; Berklee College of Music.
Score & parts: available from composer.
Reel: Be

[Quartet, Saxophones, No. 2]
D1.14 Saxophone Quartet No. 2. (1973)
First performed: Nov. 15, 1973; Berklee College of Music.
Score & parts: available from composer.
Reel: Be

D1.15 Radio Tune. (1979)
For: instruments(unspecified)(5). *First performed:* Apr. 2, 1979; Emmanuel Church, Boston.
Perf. dir: available from composer.

D1.16 Rubbertellie for Prizes I. (1977)
For: instruments(unspecified)(4) and audience. *First performed:* Feb. 19, 1977; Institute of Contemporary Art, Boston.
Perf. dir: available from composer.

D1.17 Rubbertellie for Prizes II. (1977)
For: instruments(unspecified)(4) and audience. *First performed:* Feb. 19, 1977; Institute of Contemporary Art, Boston.
Perf. dir: available from composer.

D1.18 Rubbertellieboy Meets R2D2. (1978)
For: rubbertellie, saxophone(soprano), vibraphone, double bass. Opera in 3 acts. *First performed:* Feb. 19, 1978;

Intitute of Contemporary Art, Boston.
Perf. dir: available from composer.

D1.19 Sonata for Violoncello Pft.
3 movements.
Score: available from composer.

D1.20 A Temple in Brooklyn. (1981)
For: instruments(unspecified)(2) and toys.
Perf. dir: available from composer.

D1.21 Water Muzak. (1976)
For: instruments(unspecified)(4) and tape. *First performed:* Apr. 25, 1977; People's Theatre, Cambridge, Mass.
Parts & tape: available from composer.

D2 AVRAM DAVID

Born June 30, 1930, in Boston.
Education: B.A., M.A., D.M.A. (Boston University, 1955, 1956, 1964); Berkshire Music Center, Tanglewood; Brandeis Summer Institute (1960); Kranichsteiner Musikinstitut, Darmstadt, West Germany (1961, 1966); studied composition with Pierre Boulez, Roslyn Brogue, Francis Judd Cooke, Harold Shapero, Karlheinz Stockhausen; piano, philosophy of performance and composition with Margaret Chaloff. *Awards:* BMI Award (First Prize, 1958), Royaumont Concours (Second Prize, 1965), fellowships at Boston University (1956-58), Brandeis University (summer, 1960), Carpenter Center, Harvard University (1965-66), National Endowment for the Arts Grant (1975). *Related activities:* pianist and teacher. BPL

WORKS

D2.1 Alleluia, Op. 61, No. 3. (1970) 5'
For: chorus(SSATTB). 1 movement.
Vocal score: ms. in composer's hand.
Reel: Apr. 18, 1973; Boston Conservatory. BCM

D2.2 Alleluia, Sanctus, Gloria Deo, Op. 75. (1972) 10'

For: chorus(SATB). 3 movements.
Vocal score: ms. in composer's hand.

D2.3 Almighty God, Op. 40. (1968) 8'
For: Soprano or trumpet. 1 movement.
Score: ms. in composer's hand.

D2.4 Anagram, Op. 71. (1971) 4'
For: piano. 1 movement.
Score: ms. in composer's hand.

D2.5 Antiphony.
For: brasses and strings. Withdrawn.

D2.6 Augmentation Canon, Contrary
Motion, Cancrizans, Op. 76. (1972) 2'
30"
For: trumpets(4). 1 moyement. *First
performed:* Apr. 28, 1972; New England
Conservatory. Charles A. Lewis, Jr.,
Ray Mase, Steven Schiller, Peter
Voisin.
Score: ms. in composer's hand.
Cassette: recording of first
performance.
Reel: May 16, 1972; Boston; in *A
Concert of Music by Avram David*.
Charles Lewis, Ray Mase, Steven
Schiller, Avram David, trumpets.

D2.7 Ave Maria, Op. 61, No. 1. (1970)
4'
For: Soprano and Altos(2). 1
movement.
Vocal score: ms. in composer's hand.

D2.8 Ave Maria, Op. 61, No. 2. (1970)
4'
For: Soprano, Altos(2), violins(2),
violas(2), violoncellos(2). 1 movement.
Score: ms. in composer's hand.

[Bagatelles]
D2.9 Eight Bagatelles, Op. 52. (1969) 7'
For: piano. *Contents:* Pre-chord;
Insistence; Contemplation; Recitative;
Simplicity; Declaration; Chorale;
After-Chord.
Score: ms. in composer's hand.
Tape: Apr. 18, 1973; Boston
Conservatory. BCM

D2.10 Bells, Op. 51. (1969) 5'
For: piano. 1 movement.
Score: ms. in composer's hand.

D2.11 Book of Fragments, No. 1, Op.
15. (1964) 14'
For: piano. 41 fragments. *First
performed:* Apr. 8, 1964; Brookline
Public Library; Brookline Library Music
Association Composers Workshops.
Avram David.
Score: Margun.
Tape: recording of first performance.
BkPL

D2.12 Breakthrough, Op. 110. (1974-81)
8'
For: piano. 3 movements.
Score: ms.

The Breath of God, Op. 73. *See* Sonata,
Guitar.

The Call. *See* Sonata, Trumpet, No. 2.

D2.13 Canonic Sonata, Op. 6. (1957) 10'
For: trumpets(3). 1 movement.
Score: ms. in composer's hand.

[Canons, Piano]
D2.14 Two-Part Canons, Op. 104B. (in
progress)
Score: ms. in composer's hand.

[Canons, Strings and Woodwinds]
D2.15 Fourteen Two-Part Canons, Op.
111. (1974-1981) 12'
For: violin, viola, violoncello,
flute(alto), clarinet(in A), bassoon.
Score: ms. in composer's hand.

D2.16 Canzona, Op. 3. (1954) 4'
For: trumpet, violin, viola, violoncello.
1 movement. *First performed:* Nov. 2,
1958; WBUR-FM broadcast, Boston
University. Don Ellis, trumpet; Avram
David, conductor.
Score: ms.
Tape: 1957; Boston University. Don
Ellis, trumpet; Avram David, conductor.

[Chamber Concerto No. 1]
D2.17 First Chamber Concerto, Op. 13. (in progress)
For: instrumental ensemble(flute, oboe, clarinet, clarinet(bass), bassoon, horn, trumpet, trombone, vibraphone, piano, violin, viola, violoncello, double bass). 1 movement.
Score: ms. in composer's hand.

D2.18 Chamber Concerto No. 2, Op. 90. (in progress)
For: clarinet, horn, trumpet, trombone, guitar, vibraphone, violin, violoncello. 1 movement.
Score: ms. in composer's hand.

D2.19 Chamber Concerto No. 3, Op. 93. (in progress)
For: flute, clarinet(bass), percussion, piano, voice(nigh), violin, violoncello, double bass. 1 movement.
Score: ms. in composer's hand.

D2.20 Clusterpiece, Op. 18. (1965; rev. 1975) 6'
For: piano. 1 movement. *Dedicated to:* Mme. Margaret Chaloff.
Score: ms.

Concerto, Chamber Instruments, No. 1[-3]. *See* Chamber Concerto No. 1 [-3].

D2.21 Concerto for Solo Clarinet, Op. 112. (1981) 23'
1 movement.
Score: ms. in composer's hand.

D2.22 Counterpoints, Op. 87. (1970-73) 12'
For: string quartet. 7 movements.
Score: ms. in composer's hand.

D2.23 Creation for Eight Instruments, Op. 19. (1966) 10'
For: flute, clarinet, trumpet, vibraphone, piano, guitar, violin, double bass. 1 movement.
Score: ms. in composer's hand.

D2.24 Designs, Op. 104c. (in progress)
For: piano.
Score: ms. in composer's hand.

D2.25 Duo, Op. 42. (1968) 6'
For: high voice and piano. 1 movement. *First performed:* May 5, 1968; Boston. Patricia Mairs Lockheimer, soprano and Michael Dewart, piano.
Score: ms. in composer's hand.
Tape: recording of first performance.

D2.26 Duo, Op. 85. (1972) 8'
For: violin and viola. 3 movements.
Score: ms. in composer's hand.

D2.27 Duo, Op. 97. (1974) 5'
For: trumpets(2). 3 movements.
Score: ms. in composer's hand.

D2.28 Duo, Op. 109. (1977) 10'
For: flutes(2). 3 movements.
Score: ms. in composer's hand.

D2.29 Duo Concertant, Op. 7. (1958) 20'
For: flute and clarinet. 7 movements. Winner of BMI Award (First Prize, 1958).
Score: ms. in composer's hand.
Reel: Feb. 25, 1959; Brookline Public Library.

D2.30 Eden, Op. 26. (1967) 8'
For: flute. 1 movement.
Score: ms. in composer's hand.

D2.31 Electronic Piece, Op. 70. (1970) 7'
For: tape. 1 movement. *Dedicated to:* Harry Brorby. *First performed:* May 13, 1970; Boston Conservatory.
Tape: recording of first performance.
Tape: May 16, 1971; Boston Conservatory. BCM

D2.32 Electronic Study, No. 1, Op. 70A. (1970) 11'
For: tape. 1 movement. *Tape.*

D2.33 Electronic Study, No. 2, Op. 70B. (1972) 4'
For: tape. 1 movement. *Tape.*

D2.34 Emanations from the Silence, Op. 77. (1972) 5'
For: string quartet. 7 movements.
Score: ms. in composer's hand.

D2.35 ESRAJ Symphony, Op. 84. (1971-73) 26'
For: orchestra(1(&pic)-2-0(Ehn)-0(bcl)-2; 3-3-3-1; timp, chimes; str). *Movements:* Prologue; Antiphony; Apotheosis.
Score: ms. in composer's hand.
Reel: May 30, 1972; Boston Conservatory (Prologue). BCM
Reel: June 1, 1973; Boston Conservatory (Apotheosis). BMC

D2.36 Essence, Op. 27. (1967) 8'
For: piano. 3 movements.
Score: ms.

D2.37 The Expected Moment, Op. 30. (1967) 7'
For: piano. 1 movement.
Score: ms. in composer's hand.

D2.38 Expression, Op. 81. (1966-71) 12'
For: violin. 1 movement.
Score: ms. in composer's hand.

D2.39 Factorial Seventeen, No. 1, Op. 10. (1961-62) 10'
For: piano, violin, flute.
17 movements. Can be performed as solo, duet, or trio by any or all of the above instruments. *First performed:* May 25, 1969; Boston Conservatory. Kenneth Sarch, violin.
Parts: ms. in composer's hand.
Reel: recording of first performance.

D2.40 Factorial Seventeen, No. 2, Op. 11. (1962-63) 8'
For: piano. *First performed:* May 11, 1967; Boston. Michael Dewart.
Score: ms. in composer's hand.
Reel: Mar. 26, 1968; Brookline Public Library. BkPL
Cassette: Mar. 9, 1981; New England

Conservatory; in *Enchanted Circle.* Michael Dewart. NEC

D2.41 For Clarinet.
Withdrawn.

D2.42 For Yves Klein.
For: chorus and orchestra. Withdrawn.

D2.43 Fugue for String Trio, Op. 1. (1948-49) 4'
For: violin, viola, violoncello.
Score: ms.

[Fugues]
D2.44 Four Fugues for String Trio, Op. 91A. (in progress)
For: violin, viola, violoncello.
Score: ms. in composer's hand.

Hexagram. *See* Sonata, Flute, No. 1.

D2.45 Hommage to Kenny Dorham, Op. 88. (1973) 4'
For: piano. 1 movement. *Dedicated to:* Kenny Dorham.
Score: ms. in composer's hand.

D2.46 Hommage to Marcel Duchamp, Op. 49. (1968) 5'
For: piano. 1 movement.
Score: Margun.

D2.47 Illumination, Op. 65. (1969) 10'
For: piano. 1 movement.
Score: ms. in composer's hand.

D2.48 Into the Night Air, Op. 55. (1969) 3'
For: trumpet. 1 movement. *Dedicated to:* Duke Ellington.
Score: ms. in composer's hand.

D2.49 Intonements, Op. 68. (1971) 8'
For: chorus(SSATBB). 5 movements.
Vocal score: ms. in composer's hand.
Reel: May 16, 1971; Boston Conservatory. BCM

D2.50 Introduction and Allegro, Op. 5. (1956-58) 15'
For: orchestra(2-2-3-2; 4-3-3-0; timp; str). 1 movement. *First performed:* Nov.

20, 1958; Jordan Hall, Boston. Civic
Symphony Orchestra of Boston, Paul
Cherkassky, conductor.
Score: ms. in composer's hand.

D2.51 Invention, Op. 87A. (1973) 3'
For: organ. 1 movement.
Score: ms.

[Invocations]
D2.52 Seven Invocations, Op. 53.
(1969-71) 22'
For: piano. *Movements:* Annunciation;
Transformation; Ascension; Revelation;
Renewal; Transcendance;
Transfiguration. *Dedicated to:* Mme.
Margaret Chaloff.
Score: ms. in composer's hand.

D2.53 IOAI, Op. 34. (in progress)
For: piano, oboe, bassoon, double
bass, percussion. 24 movements.
Parts: ms. in composer's hand.

D2.54 Judgement, Op. 105. (1978) 6'
For: piano. 3 movements. *Dedicated to:*
T.J. Anderson.
Score: ms. in composer's hand.

D2.55 Kyrie eleison, Op. 39. (1968) 8'
For: chorus(SATBB). 1 movement.
Vocal score: ms. in composer's hand.

D2.56 The Light-Giver, Op. 45. (1968) 8'
For: piano. 1 movement. *First
performed:* Mar. 2, 1968; Harvard
University. Avram David.
Score: ms. in composer's hand.
Tape: recording of first performance.

D2.57 Lyric Prelude, Op. 25. (1967) 8'
For: clarinet. 1 movement. *First
performed:* May 16, 1971; Boston.
William Lipman.
Score: ms. composer's hand.
Tape: recording of first performance.

D2.58 M.S.C. Fantasy, Op. 83. (1972) 15'
For: piano. 1 movement.
Score: ms. in composer's hand.
Reel: Apr. 18, 1973; Boston
Conservatory. BCM

D2.59 Megamelodic Sonata, Op. 103A.
(1977) 20'
For: organ. 29 melodies.
Score: ms. in composer's hand.

D2.60 Melody, Thirty-two Variations,
and Six Contrapuntal Interludes,
Op. 59. (1969-70). 35' *For:* piano.
Score: ms. in composer's hand.

D2.61 Memento, Op. 32. (1967) 4'
For: piano. 1 movement. *Dedicated to:*
Serge Chaloff.
Score: ms. in composer's hand.

[Miniatures]
D2.62 Three Miniatures, Op. 104A.
(1977) 4'
For: piano. 3 movements.
Score: ms. in composer's hand.

D2.63 Mirrors, Op. 44A. (1968) 35'
For: piano. 5 movements.
Score: ms. in composer's hand.

D2.64 Mirrors, Op. 44B. (1968) 35'
For: piano(quarter-tone). 5 movements.
Score: ms. in composer's hand.

[Moments]
D2.65 Eleven Moments, Op. 12.
(1962-63) 3'
For: piano.
Score: ms. in composer's hand.

D2.66 Motet, Op. 68A. (1971) 6'
For: chorus(SSATBB). *Text:* Bible, O.T.,
Isaiah 53:6, Bible, N.T., Romans 3:23,
10; Bible, N.T., John 1:29. 1 movement.
Vocal score: ms. in composer's hand.

D2.67 Motet, Op. 99. (1974) 12'
For: trumpets(2), horn, trombone,
trombone(bass). 1 movement.
Score & parts: ms. in composer's hand.

[Movements, Op. 36]
D2.68 Three Movements, Op. 36. (in
progress)
For: string quartet.
Score: ms. in composer's hand.

[Movements, Op. 56]
D2.69 Three Movements, Op. 56. (in progress)
For: organ.
Score: ms. in composer's hand.

[Neoclassic Pieces]
D2.70 Three Neoclassic Pieces, Op. 4. (1955) 14'
For: piano. *First performed:* Mar. 19, 1958; Brookline Public Library; Brookline Library Music Association Composers Workshop. Martin Boykan.
Score: ms. in composer's hand.
Tape: recording of first performance. BkPL

D2.71 Opusarch, Op. 79. (1972) 8'
For: violin. 1 movement. *Dedicated to:* Kenneth Sarch. *First performed:* May 13, 1970; Boston. Kenneth Sarch.
Score: Margun.
Tape: recording of first performance.
Tape: May 16, 1971; Boston. Kenneth Sarch.

D2.72 Paeans for Carl Ruggles, Op. 37. (in progress)
For: trumpets(2), cornet, horns(2), trombones(2), tuba.
Score: ms. in composer's hand.

D2.73 Page after a Sonata, Op. 35A. (1968) 2'
For: piano. 1 movement.
Score: ms. in composer's hand.

D2.74 Pater noster, Op. 86. (1972) 5'
For: chorus(SATB). *Text:* Bible, N.T., Matthew 6:9-13.
Vocal score: ms. in composer's hand.
Reel: Apr. 18, 1973; Boston Conservatory. BCM

D2.75 Pater noster, Op. 89. (1970-73) 8'
For: piano. 1 movement.
Score: ms. in composer's hand.

D2.76 Piano Piece, Op. 65A. (1970-79) 4'
1 movement.
Score: ms.

[Pieces, Op. 9]
D2.77 Three Pieces. (1959) 8'
For: piano. *Dedicated to:* Mme. Margaret Chaloff. *First performed:* Aug. 3, 1960; Brandeis University. Stephen Pruslin.
Score: ms. in composer's hand.
Reel: recording of first performance.

[Pieces, Op. 62]
D2.78 Three Pieces. (1969) 5'
For: piano.
Score: ms. in composer's hand.

[Pieces, Op. 65B]
D2.79 Four Pieces. (1968-75) 8'
For: piano. *Movements:* Theme; Toccata; Structure; Statement.
Score: ms. in composer's hand.

[Pieces, Op. 80]
D2.80 Three Pieces. (1971) 8'
For: piano.
Score: ms. in composer's hand.

[Portraits]
D2.81 Six Portraits, Op. 41. (1968) 10'
For: piano.
Score: ms. in composer's hand.

[Preludes]
D2.82 Three Preludes, Op. 47. (1968) 10'
For: piano.
Score: ms. in composer's hand.

D2.83 Processional, Op. 57. (1968) 6'
For: trumpets(2), trombones(3), organ, viola. 1 movement.
Score: ms. in composer's hand.

D2.84 Prologue, Twelve Pieces and Epilogue, Op. 60. (1969-70) 21'
For: piano. 14 movements.
Score: ms. in composer's hand.
Reel: May 16, 1971; Boston Conservatory. BCM

D2.85 Psalm I, Op. 83A. (1973) 4'
For: chorus(SATB).
Vocal score: ms. in composer's hand.

[Quartet, Percussion(4)]
D2.86 Percussion Quartet, Op. 43.

(1968) 20'
For: percussion(1-4)(vibraphones(2),
marimbas(2), orchestra bells(3),
xylophones(2), claves(4), woodblocks(9),
guiros(2), crotales, small tom-tom,
medium tom-tom, large tom-tom,
timpani(4), conga drums(2), bass
drums(2), gong, medium gong, small
gong, almglocken(12), iron pipe,
anvils(2), maracas(4), large suspended
Chinese cymbal, medium-to-large
suspended Chinese cymbal, triangles(3),
large suspended cymbal,medium
suspended cymbal, almglocken(6),
brakedrums(5), medium tambourine,
large tambourine). Can be performed in
quartet, trio, duo or solo versions. 17
versions are possible. *First performed:*
May 25, 1969; Boston. Michael
Christoforo.
Parts: ms. in composer's hand.
Tape: recording of first performance.
Tape: Apr. 18, 1973; Boston
Conservatory. Unidentified percussion
duo, Arthur Press, conductor. BCM

[Quartet, Strings, No. 1]
D2.87 String Quartet No. 1, Op. 66.
(1970) 12'
7 movements.
Score: ms. in composer's hand.

[Quartet, Strings, No. 2]
D2.88 String Quartet No. 2, Op. 67.
(1970-71) 45'
30 movements. *First performed:* Dec.
22, 1978; First and Second Church,
Boston. Concord String Quartet.
Score & parts: Margun.
Reel: recording of first performance.
Reel: Mar. 28, 1971; Boston
Conservatory. BCM

[Quartet, Strings, No. 3]
D2.89 String Quartet No. 3, Op. 72.
(1971) 22'
1 movement. *First performed:* Apr. 18,
1973; Boston Conservatory. Gabrielli
Quartet.
Score: ms. in composer's hand.
Reel: recording of first performance.
BCM

[Quartet, Strings, No. 4]
D2.90 String Quartet No. 4, Op. 102.
(1976) 24'
7 movements.
Score: ms. in composer's hand.

[Quartet, Strings, No. 5]
D2.91 String Quartet No. 5, Op. 108. (in
progress)
1 movement.
Score: ms. in composer's hand.

[Quintet, Strings]
D2.92 String Quintet, Op. 50. (1968-69)
15'
For: string quartet and double bass. 1
movement. *First performed:* May 4,
1969; Boston. Violone Ensemble.
Score: ms. in composer's hand.
Reel: recording of first performance.
BCM

[Quintet, Woodwinds]
D2.93 Wind Quintet, Op. 20. (1966-67)
16'
For: woodwind quintet. 13 movements.
Score: ms. in composer's hand.

D2.94 Reflexion 400, Op. 23. (1967) 10'
For: bassoon. 1 movement. *First
performed:* May 11, 1967; Boston. Allan
Grzyb.
Score: ms. in composer's hand.
Reel: Feb. 18, 1969; Jordan Hall,
Boston. John Miller.

[Romanzas]
D2.95 Three Romanzas, Op. 92.
(1973-74) 14'
For: piano. 3 movements.
Score: ms.

D2.96 Saturn 1, Op. 21. (1967) 14'
For: drum(bass). 34 movements. *First
performed:* May 11, 1967; Boston.
Stomu Yamash'ta.
Score: ms. in composer's hand.
Reel: recording of first performance.
Reel: May 16, 1972; Boston. Stephen
Shaw.

D2.97 Soliloquy for Contrabass, Op. 48. (1968) 6'
For: double bass. 1 movement. *Dedicated to:* William Rhein. *First performed:* Apr. 18, 1973; Boston. William Rhein.
Score: ms. in composer's hand.
Tape: recording of first performance.

[Sonata, Flute, No. 1]
D2.98 Sonata No. 1: Hexagrams, Op. 16. (1965) 20'
3 movements.
Score: ms. in composers hand.

[Sonata, Flute, No. 2]
D2.99 Sonata No. 2, Op. 22. (1967) 10'
1 movement.
Score: ms. in composer's hand.

[Sonata, Flute, No. 3]
D2.100 Sonata No. 3, Op. 46. (1968) 12'
6 movements.
Score: ms. in composer's hand.
Reel: May 13, 1970; Boston. Sadako Yokoyama.

[Sonata, Guitar]
D2.101 The Breath of God, Sonata in Five Movements, Op. 73. (1971-72) 23'
For: guitar. *Dedication:* To the guitar, 'The Breath of God.' *First performed:* June 17, 1975; Totnes, England. Albin Zak.
Score: ms. in composer's hand.
Reel: recording of first performance.
Reel: Sept. 19, 1975; Boston. Albin Zak.

[Sonata, Horn]
D2.102 Sonata, Op. 101. (1976-77) 14'
3 movements. *Dedicated to:* Gunther Schuller. *First performed:* Aug. 6, 1978; Berkshire Music Center, Tanglewood. Robert Ward.
Score: Margun, 1981. NEC
Reel: recording of first performance.

Sonata, Organ, Op. 103A. *See* Megamelodic Sonata, Op. 103A.

[Sonata, Piano, No. 1]
D2.103 Sonata I, Op. 35. (1967-68) . 17'

1 movement. *Dedicated to:* Mme. Margaret Chaloff. *First performed:* May 5, 1968; Boston. Michael Dewart.
Score: ms. in composer's hand.
Cassette: Mar. 9, 1981; New England Conservatory; in *Enchanted Circle.* Michael Dewart. NEC

[Sonata, Piano, No. 2]
D2.104 Sonata II, Op. 38. (in progress) 25 movements.
Score: ms. in composer's hand.

[Sonata, Piano, No. 3]
D2.105 Sonata III, Op. 100. (1974-76) 40'
1 movement.
Score: ms. in composer's hand.

[Sonata, Piano, No. 4]
D2.106 Sonata IV, Op. 104. (in progress)
5 movements. *Dedicated to:* Leslie David.
Score: ms. in composer's hand.

[Sonata, Piano, No. 5]
D2.107 Piano Sonata V, Op. 106. (1979-81) 35'
9 movements. *Dedicated to:* Christopher O'Riley.
Score: ms. in composer's hand.

[Sonata, Saxophone]
D2.108 Sonata in a Single Movement, Op. 29. (1967) 10"
For: saxophone(tenor).
Score: ms.

[Sonata, Trumpet, No. 1]
D2.109 Sonata No. 1, Op. 17. (1965-66) 8'
3 movements. *First performed:* Mar. 23, 1966; Boston. William Tower.
Score: ms. in composer's hand.
Reel: recording of first performance.

[Sonata, Trumpet, No. 2]
D2.110 Sonata No. 2: The Call, Op. 31. (1967) 12'
1 movement.
Score: Margun.

[Sonata, Trumpet, No. 3]
D2.111 Sonata No. 3, Op. 54. (1969-75) 12'
3 movements.
Score: ms. in composer's hand.

[Sonata, Trumpet, No. 4]
D2.112 Sonata No. 4, Op. 96. (1974) 12'
3 movements.
Score: ms. in composer's hand.

Sonata, Trumpets (3). *See* Canonic Sonata, Op. 6.

[Sonata, Viola]
D2.113 Sonata, Op. 69. (in progress)
Score: ms. in composer's hand.
Reel: May 16, 1971; Boston Conservatory (1st movement). BCM

[Sonata, Violin]
D2.114 Sonata, Op. 58. (1969) 16' 30"
3 movements. *Dedicated to:* Kenneth Sarch. *First performed:* May 13, 1970; Boston Conservatory. Kenneth Sarch.
Score: ms. in composer's hand.
Reel: recording of first performance.
Reel: May 16, 1971; Boston Conservatory. Kenneth Sarch. BCM

[Sonata, Violin and Piano]
D2.115 Sonata, Op. 64. (1969-70) 22'
7 movements. *Dedicated to:* Kenneth Sarch. *First performed:* May 16, 1972; Boston Conservatory. Kenneth Sarch, violin and Max Lifschitz, piano.
Score: ms. in composer's hand.
Tape: recording of first performance.

D2.116 Song of Truth, Op. 78. (1972) 11'
For: clarinet. 1 movement. *First performed:* May 16, 1972; Boston Conservatory. William Lipman.
Score: ms. in composer's hand.
Tape: recording of first performance.

[Studies]
D2.116.5 Seven Studies for String Trio, Op. 14. (1964) 8'
For: violin, viola, violoncello.
Score: ms. in composer's hand.

D2.117 The Sun, Op. 33. (1967) 10'
For: violin. 1 movement. *First performed:* Oct. 30, 1969; Carpenter Center for the Visual Arts, Harvard University. Kenneth Sarch.
Score: ms. in composer's hand.
Reel: recording of first performance.
Reel: May 16, 1971; Boston Conservatory.

Symphony, Op. 84. *See* ESRAJ Symphony, Op. 84.

D2.118 Symphony of Alleluias, Op. 103. (in progress)
For: chorus(SATB). 21 movements.
Vocal score: ms. in composer's hand.

D2.119 This Is My Rock, Op. 82; Five Songs on Texts by David McCord.
For: voice(high) and clarinet.
Score: ms. in composer's hand.

D2.120 Toccata, Op. 8. (1959) 15'
For: violin and piano. 1 movement.
Score: ms. in composer's hand.

D2.121 Tri-Canon, Op. 63. (1969) 5'
For: string quartet. 1 movement.
Score: ms. in composer's hand.

D2.122 Trio, Op. 2. (1951) 8'
For: trumpet, clarinet, violoncello. 1 movement.
Score: ms.

[Trio, Strings, No. 1]
D2.123 String Trio No. 1, Op. 74. (in progress)
For: violin, viola, violoncello. 5 movements.
Score: ms. in composer's hand.

[Trio, Strings, No. 2]
D2.124 String Trio No. 2, Op. 91. (1973) 23'
For: violin, viola, violoncello. 7 movements.
Score: ms. in composer's hand.

[Trio, Strings, No. 3]
D2.125 String Trio No. 3, Op. 98. (in

progress)
For: violin, viola, violoncello. 1 movement.
Score: ms. in composer's hand.

D2.126 Trope, Op. 95. (1974) 3'
For: piano. 1 movement. *Dedicated to:* Etienne Darbolle.
Score: ms. in composer's hand.

D2.127 The Unquestioned Answer, Op. 94. (1973) 3'
For: piano. 1 movement.
Score: ms. in composer's hand.

D2.128 Variations, Op. 107. (1979-80) 10'
For: viola and piano. 33 variations.
Score: ms. in composer's hand.

D2.129 Vision, Op. 28. (1967) 4'
For: tuba. 1 movement.
Score: ms. in composer's hand.

D2.130 Voices and Whirlwinds, Op. 24. (1967) 6'
For: clarinet. 1 movement. *First performed:* May 13, 1970; Boston. William Lipman.
Score: ms. in composer's hand.
Reel: recording of first performance.
Reel: May 16, 1971; Boston Conservatory.

D3 LYLE DAVIDSON

Born February 25, 1938, in Randolph, Vt. Moved to Boston area 1958.
Education: studied composition with Daniel Pinkham, Francis Judd Cooke (New England Conservatory, B.M., 1962, M.M., 1964); Arthur Berger (Brandeis University, 1964-66). *Related activities:* co-director of Evenings of New Music, New England Conservatory (1967-76); composer for various dance companies (1968-72); author and researcher in cognitive development and music from infancy to adulthood at Project Zero, Harvard University (1979-); member of the faculty of the New England Conservatory (1966-), Massachusetts

Institute of Technology (1971-73), Harvard University (1977-78). NEC

WORKS

D3.1 Along the Edge. (1967) 8'
For: chorus(SATB). *Text:* Richard Crashaw, John Donne, Robert Herrick, Gerard Manley Hopkins. *First performed:* May 7, 1971; New England Conservatory; in A Festival of New England Composers Past and Present. NEC Chorus, Lorna Cooke deVaron, conductor.
Vocal score: E.C. Schirmer, nyp.
Cassette: recording of first performance. NEC
Cassette: Dec. 10, 1980; New England Conservatory. NEC Chorus, Lorna Cooke deVaron, conductor. NEC

D3.2 As a Solid. (1968) 5'
For: tape. Dance music.
Tape: available from composer.

Centering. *See* Vermont Notebook for Christian Wolff.

D3.3 A Certain Gurgling Melodiousness. (1973) 8'
For: double bass. *First performed:* May 12, 1973; New England Conservatory; in A Festival of Contemporary American Music. Richard Fletcher.
Score: reprod. of ms.; available from composer.
Reel: Sept. 30, 1979; First and Second Church, Boston. Dinosaur Annex, Morton Cahn. WGBH
Cassette: recording of first performance. NEC

[Charlie Song Rag, Piano]
D3.4 Charlie Song Rag: Sometime Buster's Strut. (1979) 4'
Score: reprod. of ms.; available from composer.

[Charlie Song Rag, Piano(4-hands)]
D3.5 Charlie Song Rag: Sometime Buster's Strut. (1979) 4'
First performed: Sept. 30, 1979; First and Second Church, Boston. Dinosaur

Annex. Rodney Lister and Scott Wheeler.
Score: reprod. of ms.; available from composer.
Reel: recording of first performance. WGBH

D3.6 Chester. (1972) 9'
For: clarinet. *First performed:* Mar. 7, 1972; New England Conservatory; in An Evening of Contemporary Music. Chester Brezniak.
Score: reprod. of ms.; available from composer.
Cassette: recording of first performance. NEC

D3.7 Crystals. (1964) 5'
For: piano.
Score: reprod. of ms.; available from composer.

D3.8 Detours. (1968) 5'
For: strings(unspecified)(3). Aleatoric music; dance music. *Commissioned by:* Anne Tolbert for her dance company.
Score: reprod. of ms.; available from composer.

D3.9 Double Four Part I. (1971)
For: dancers(4) and harp. *Commissioned by:* Anne Tolbert for her dance company. *First performed:* Apr. 25, 1972; New England Conservatory. Anne Tolbert Dance Company; Martha Moor, harp.
Cassette: recording of first performance. NEC

D3.10 Divertimento. (1964) 7'
For: band.
Score & parts: available from composer.

D3.11 Dresden Amen. (1967) 6'
For: tape. *First performed:* Apr. 1966; Brandeis University.
Tape: available from composer.

D3.12 Embouchure. (1969) 18'
For: tape. Dance music; musique concrete. *Commissioned by:* Ina Hahn.

First performed: spring 1969; Loeb Theatre, Harvard University.
Tape: available from composer.
Cassette: Dec. 9, 1969; New England Conservatory; in *An Evening of Contemporary Music.*

D3.13 Fibonacci Rehearsed. (1967) 8'
For: tape. *First performed:* fall, 1965; Brandeis University.
Tape: available from composer.

D3.14 Furies of Complexity. (1981) 8'
For: Alto and trombones(3). *Text:* from *Byzantium*, by William Butler Yeats.
Score & parts: reprod. of ms.; available from composer.

D3.15 Greeley Ponds. (1973) 5' 30"
For: violoncello.
Score: available from composer.

D3.16 Kisses and Kazoos. (1977) Duration variable.
For: speakers(3) and tape(live). *Text:* valentine cards, etc. Written in collaboration with Joyce Mekeel and Paul Earls.
Perf. dir: reprod. of ms.; available from composer. *Tape.*

D3.17 March Detours. (1970) 10'
For: viola, violoncello, tape. *Commissioned by and dedicated to:* Jean Dane and Ronald Clearfield. First performed: fall 1970; New England Conservatory. Jean Dane, viola and Ronald Clearfield, violoncello.
Score & tape: reprod. of ms.; available from composer.
Cassette: Apr. 27, 1971; New England Conservatory; in *An Evening of Contemporary Music.* Jean Dane, viola and Ronald Clearfield, violoncello. NEC
Cassette: Nov. 9, 1971; New England Conservatory; in *An Evening of Contemporary Music.* Jean Dane, viola and Ronald Clearfield, violoncello. NEC

D3.18 Mass for Two Equal Voices. (1962) 10'
For: chorus(2-part) or voices(2).

Vocal score: reprod. of ms.; available from composer.

[Motets]
D3.19 Three Motets. (1963) 6'
For: chorus(SATB). *Text:* Richard Crashaw. *Contents:* Upon the Body of Our Blessed Lord, Naked and Bloody; Upon the Thorns Taken down From Our Lord's Head, Bloody; On the Still Surviving Marks of Our Saviour's Wounds.
Vocal score: reprod. of ms.; available from composer.

D3.20 Moveable Feast. (1973?) 60'
For: instruments(unspecified) and voices(unspecified). Written in collaboration with Joyce Mekeel and Paul Earls. *First performed:* Nov. 1973; Massachusetts College of Art. Student performers. *Perf. dir:* reprod. of ms.; available from composer.
Cassette: Mar. 7, 1974; New England Conservatory; in *An Evening of Contemporary Music*. NEC

D3.21 Phrase. (1968) 3'
For: trumpets in C(2). 1 movement.
Parts: E.C. Schirmer, 1977. Be BPL MIT NEC

D3.22 Quiet Hymns. (1978) 4' 30"
For: chorus(SATB). *Text:* from *Sounds of Silence* by Raymond John Baugham. *First performed:* Dec. 5, 1979; Church of the Covenant, Boston. Emerson Chamber Singers, Scott Wheeler, conductor.
Vocal score: reprod. of ms.; available from composer.
Cassette: recording of first performance; available from composer.

D3.23 Semandron. (1966) 6' 12"
For: tape. First performed; spring, 1966; Brandeis University.
Tape: available from composer.

D3.24 Stone. (1969) 6'
For: tape. Dance music; music concrete. *Commissioned by:* Ina Hahn

Dance Company.
Tape: available from composer.

D3.25 Vermont Notebook for Christian Wolff. (1969) Duration variable.
For: instruments(unspecified) and voices(unspecified). *Movements:* Centering; How Long; What Can Be Done; Anti-Pollution Campaign; Bubble Chamber; Gifts. *Dedication:* For Christian Wolff. *First performed:* 1970 [?] ; Museum of Fine Arts, Boston (Centering).
Perf. dir: reprod. of ms.; available from composer.

D3.26 Voices of the Dark. (1972) 9'
For: chorus(SATB), tape, instrument(bass)(optional). *Text:* Bible, O.T., Jeremiah 4:23-26.
Score & tape: E.C. Schirmer, 1973.
Cassette: Feb. 6, 1973; New England Consevatory; in *An Evening of Contemporary Music*. Unidentified chorus. NEC
Cassette: Apr. 1978; New England Conservatory. NEC Repertory Chorus, John Circe, conductor. NEC

D3.27 Wethersfield Quickstep. (1975) 9'
For: violin. *First performed:* Nov. 21, 1977; New England Conservatory; in Enchanted Circle. Janet Packer.
Score: reprod. of ms.; available from composer.
Cassette: recording of first performance. NEC

D3.28 Windhover. (1976) 9'
For: piano. *Commissioned by:* Rebecca LaBrecque. *First performed:* May 1976; Lincoln Center, New York City.
Score: reprod. of ms.; available from composer.
Cassette: Nov. 21, 1977; New England Conservatory; in *Enchanted Circle*. Rebecca LaBrecque. NEC
Cassette: Dec. 8, 1980; New England Conservatory; in *Enchanted Circle*. Alys Terrien-Queen. NEC

D4 KATHERINE K. DAVIS

Born 1892, in St. Joseph, Mo,; died April 20, 1980, in Concord, Mass. *Education:* B.A. (Wellesley College, 1914); studied composition with Stuart Mason (New England Conservatory, 1918) and Nadia Boulanger (1925). *Awards:* Billings Prize in Music (Wellesley College, 1914); honorary degree (Stetson University, 1967); ASCAP Awards (Standard) (1960-81). *Related activities:* co-founder of Concord Chorus (1944); arranger of numerous folk songs, carols, and melodies by Bach, Haydn, etc. and compiler of anthologies for teaching, issued by various publishers represented here (most held by W, excluded from the list of works below); served on the faculties of Concord Montessori School, Concord, Mass. (1921-22), and Shady Hill School, Philadelphia, Pa. (1923-30). W

WORKS

D4.1 All in the Morning.
For: chorus(SATB) and piano or organ.
Vocal score: Flammer, 1956. W

D4.2 All Together Sing.
For: chorus(unison). *Text:* Katherine K. Davis.
Vocal score: Broadman, 1975. W

D4.3 All Ye Saints Be Joyful.
For: chorus(SATB). Anthem. *Text:* from the Bible; adapted by Katherine K. Davis.
Vocal score: Remick, 1959. W

D4.4 Alleluia, Come, Good People. 1'
For: chorus(SSAA). *Text:* John Cowley.
Vocal score: Galaxy, 1941. W

D4.5 The Ardent Huntsmen.
For: chorus(TTBB). *Text:* John Cowley.
Vocal score: Boston Music, 1940. W

D4.6 Ballad by Abraham Lincoln.
For: chorus(SATB) and piano. *Text:* Abraham Lincoln.
Vocal score: Witmark, 1966. W

D4.7 Be Ye Kind, One to Another. 4' 30"
For: Alto or Baritone, chorus(SATB), piano or organ. Anthem. *Text:* Bible, N.T., Ephesians 4:32,31.
Vocal score: Galaxy, 1947. W

[Be Ye Kind, One to Another; Arr.]
D4.8 Be Ye Kind, One to Another. 4' 30"
For: Alto or Baritone and piano or organ. Anthem. Bible, N.T., Ephesians 4:32,31.
Vocal score: Galaxy, 1948. W

D4.9 Bethlehem Road.
For: chorus(SATB) and piano or organ.
Text: Katherine K. Davis
Vocal score: Alfred, 1971. W

[Bethlehem Road; Arr]
For: Baritone, chorus(SABar), piano or organ. *Text:* Katherine K. Davis
Score: Alfred, 1973. W

D4.10 Bless the Lord, O My Soul. 3'
For: chorus(SATB) and piano or organ. Anthem. *Text:* Bible, O.T., Psalm 103:1-4,11,13.
Vocal score: Galaxy, 1950. W

[Bless the Lord, O My Soul; Arr.]
D4.11 Bless the Lord, O My Soul. 3'
For: voice(low) and piano or organ. Anthem. *Text:* Bible, O.T., Psalm 103:1-4,11,13.
Score: Galaxy, 1952. W

D4.12 Boundless Love.
For: chorus(SATB) and keyboard. *Text:* Katherine K. Davis.
Vocal score: Sacred, 1978. W

D4.13 Brightest and Best of the Sons of the Morning.
For: chorus(SATB) and piano or organ.
Text: Reginald Heber.
Vocal score: Boston Music, 1952. W

D4.14 The Burial of a Queen. (1920)
For: violin and orchestra(2(pic)-2-2-2; 4-0-0-0; timp; pf; str). 1 movement.

After the poem by Alfred Noyes. *First performed:* June 1920; New England Conservatory. NEC Symphony Orchestra, Wallace Goodrich, conductor. *Score:* ms. W

The Butterfly. *See* Scenes from a Forest Ballet. The Butterfly.

[Carol of the Drum, Chorus(SA)]
D4.15 Carol of the Drum.
For: chorus(SA) and piano. Christmas music. *Text:* Czech Carol [i.e. Katherine K. Davis], transcribed by C.R.W. Robertson [i.e. Katherine K. Davis]. Later version titled The Little Drummer Boy.
Vocal score: Wood, 1941, 1957. W

[Carol of the Drum, Chorus(SSA)]
D4.16 Carol of the Drum.
For: chorus(SSA) and piano(optional). Christmas music *Text:* Czech Carol [i.e. Katherine K. Davis], transcribed by C.R.W. Robertson [i.e. Katherine K. Davis]. Later version titled the Little Drummer Boy.
Vocal score: Wood, 1941, 1960. W

[Carol of the Drum, Voice and Piano]
D4.17 Carol of the Drum.
Christmas music *Text:* Czech Carol [i.e., Katherine K. Davis], transcribed by C.R.W. Robertson [i.e. Katherine K. Davis]. Later version titled The Little Drummer Boy.
Score: Wood, 1941, 1959. W
Disc: [recorded by Gene Autry (1949) and others].

D4.18 The Cherubim Song.
For: chorus(SATB). *Text:* Eastern Orthodox liturgy. Anthem. *Dedicated to:* Giuliana Chorale.
Vocal score: Galaxy, 1960. W

D4.19 The Children of Bethlehem: A Christmas Cantata.
For: chorus(children), piano, flute(optional), percussion(optional).
Text: Katherine K. Davis. *Movements:* In Bethlehem; The Travelers; The Inn; The Glory of the Lord; The Shepherds Lo;

The Stable; Lullaby; The Angels.
Vocal score: Broadman, 1973. W

D4.20 Choristers of the Light. 2'
For: chorus(SATB). *Text:* Katherine K. Davis.
Vocal score: Galaxy, 1971. W

[Christ Is Risen Today, Chorus(SSA)]
D4.21 Christ Is Risen Today. 2'
Text: C.R.W. Robertson [i.e., Katherine K. Davis].
Vocal score: Galaxy, 1939. W

[Christ Is Risen Today, Chorus(SATB) and Piano]
D4.21.5 Christ Is Risen Today. 2' 30"
Text: C.R.W. Robertson [i.e., Katherine K. Davis].
Vocal score: Galaxy, 1954. W

[Christ Is Risen Today, Voice and Piano]
D4.22 Christ Is Risen Today. 2' 30"
Text: C.R.W. Robertson [i.e., Katherine K. Davis].
Vocal score: Galaxy, 1947. W

D4.23 The Church of God. 2'
For: chorus(SATB) and organ. *Text:* Katherine K. Davis.
Vocal score: Galaxy, 1965.

[The Church of God; Arr]
D4.24 The Church of God. 2'
For: chorus(SA) and organ. *Text:* Katherine K. Davis.
Vocal score: Galaxy, 1967. W

D4.25 Cider Through a Straw.
For: chorus(SAB) and piano. *Text:* traditional, American.
Vocal score: Boston Music, 1973. W

D4.26 Cinderella.
For: chorus(unison), voices, piano. Operetta in 3 acts. Based on folk-tunes, without spoken dialogue.
Vocal score: E.C. Schirmer, 1933. W

D4.27 Come Along, Sweet Liza Jane. 2' 20"
For: chorus(SATB) and piano. *Text:*

traditional, American (Appalachian).
Vocal score: Warner, 1975. W

Come, Singing Noel. *See* This Is Noel.
Come, Singing Noel; Arr.

D4.28 Comfort Ye. 4'
For: chorus(SATB) and piano or organ.
Anthem. *Text:* Bible, O.T., Isaiah 40:1,
49:13.
Vocal score: Galaxy, 1962. W

D4.29 The Divine Image. 2' 30"
For: Soprano and chorus(SATB). *Text:*
William Blake.
Vocal score: Galaxy, 1970. W

D4.30 The Drum: A Christmas Play with
Music.
For: chorus(SA), piano or organ,
handbells. *Text:* Katherine K. Davis.
Vocal score: Mills, 1966. W

D4.31 Easter Is a Song.
For: chorus(SA) and piano or organ.
Cantata. *Text:* Katherine K. Davis.
Contents: Gethsemene; The Cross; Night;
Night; Tale of Glory.
Vocal score: Witmark, 1967. W

[Easter Is a Song. Tale of Glory;
Arr.]
D4.31.5 Tale of Glory. 3' 16"
For: chorus(SAB) and piano or organ.
Text: Katherine K. Davis.
Vocal score: Witmark, 1967; Warner,
1973. W

D4.32 Fanfare for Palm Sunday.
For: chorus(SATB) and piano. Anthem.
Text: Bible, N.T., Matthew 21:9. For
later version for chorus(SA) and piano,
see Seasonal Anthems for Junior
Choir.
Vocal score: Wood, 1962. W

D4.33 The Firmament of Power.
For: chorus(SATB). Anthem. *Text:* Bible,
O.T., Psalms 150, 149, 145.
Vocal score: Witmark, 1967. W

[The Firmament of Power; Arr.]
D4.34 The Firmament of Power.
For: chorus(SAB) and piano or
organ(optional). Anthem. *Text:* Bible,
O.T., Psalms 150, 149, 145.
Vocal score: Witmark, 1967.
Vocal score: Warner, 1968.

D4.35 First Studies in Rhythm.
For: piano.
Score: Boston Music, 1920. W

D4.36 For All Men Everywhere. 3' 45"
For: chorus(SATB) and piano. *Text:*
Katherine K. Davis.
Vocal score: Piedmont, 1972. W

D4.37 From Far and Wide.
For: chorus(SATB) and piano or organ.
Text: Katherine K. Davis.
Vocal score: Remick, 1964.

[From Far and Wide; Arr.]
D4.38 From Far and Wide.
For: chorus(SAB) and piano or organ.
Vocal score: Remick, 1964. W

D4.39 Glory above the Heavens.
For: chorus(SATB) and organ. Anthem.
Text: Bible, O.T., Psalm 8:1-5.
Vocal score: Sacred, 1972. W

D4.40 Glory Be to God on High.
For: chorus(SATB) and organ. *Text:*
Theodore C. Williams.
Vocal score: Flammer, 1969. W

[Glory Be to God on High; Arr.]
D4.41 Glory Be to God on High.
For: chorus(SAB) and organ. *Text:*
Theodore C. Williams.
Vocal score: Flammer, 1970. W

[Glory in the Highest, Chorus(SA)]
D4.42 Glory in the Highest. 2'
Christmas music; anthem. *Text:* Bible,
N.T., Luke 2:14.
Vocal score: Galaxy, 1963. W

[Glory in the Highest, Chorus(SATB)]
D4.43 Glory in the Highest. 2'

Christmas music; anthem. *Text:* Bible, N.T., Luke 2:14.
Vocal score: Galaxy, 1963. W

[Glory in the Highest, Chorus(SSA) and Piano or Organ]
D4.44 Glory in the Highest. 2'
Christmas music; anthem. *Text:* Bible, N.T., Luke 2:14.
Vocal score: Galaxy, 1946. W

D4.45 God Adoring.
For: chorus(SATB) and piano or organ.
Text: Katherine K. Davis.
Vocal score: Flammer, 1960. W

D4.46 God Is in This Place.
For: chorus(SATB) and piano or organ.
Text: A.E.A. [i.e. Katherine K. Davis]
Vocal score: Sacred, 1971. W

D4.47 God So Loved the World. 3'
For: chorus(SATB). Christmas music; anthem. *Text:* Bible, N.T., John 3:16.
Vocal score: Galaxy, 1961. W

[Good Folk Who Dwell on Earth, Chorus(SAB)]
D4.48 Good Folk Who Dwell on Earth.
Text: John Cowley.
Vocal score: Wood, 1941, 1957. W

[Good Folk Who Dwell on Earth, Chorus(SSAA)]
D4.49 Good Folk Who Dwell on Earth.
Text: John Cowley. *Dedicated to:* Hollins College Chapel Choir, Arthur S. Talmadge, director, for the centennial anniversary of the founding of the college, 1942.
Vocal score: Wood, 1941. W

[Good Folk Who Dwell on Earth, Chorus(2-part)]
D4.50 Good Folk Who Dwell on Earth.
Text: John Cowley.
Vocal score: Wood, 1943. W

D4.51 Goosie, Goosie, Gander: A Mother Goose Setting in the Style of Mozart. 3' 30"
For: chorus(SATB) and orchestra.

Score & parts: Galaxy. Rental.
Vocal score: Galaxy, 1942. W

D4.52 Grant, We Beseech Thee, Merciful Lord.
For: chorus(SATB). Anthem. *Text: The Book of Common Prayer.*
Vocal score: Abingdon, 1972. W

D4.53 Great Is Our God. 2'
For: Soprano, chorus(SATB), piano or organ. *Text:* Katherine K. Davis.
Vocal score: Galaxy, 1967. W

D4.54 Hail His Coming, King of Glory.
For: chorus(SATB) and piano. *Text:* Katherine K. Davis.
Vocal score: Warner, 1972. W

D4.55 Harvest Song.
For: chorus(SAB) and piano or organ.
Text: adapted from W. Chatterton Dix. For earlier version for chorus(SA) and piano, see Seasonal Anthems for Junior Choir.
Vocal score: Wood, 1964. W

D4.56 Have You Seen the Star?
For: descant, chorus(SATB), piano. *Text:* Katherine K. Davis.
Vocal score: Warner, 1969. W

D4.57 He Is Born, Christ the King.
For: descant, chorus(unison), piano or organ. Carol. *Text:* Katherine K. Davis.
Vocal score: Flammer, 1961. W

D4.58 He Is Our King.
For: Soprano, chorus(SATB), piano or organ. Anthem. *Text:* Bible, O.T., Psalm 146:5,6. and Katherine K. Davis.
Vocal score: Flammer, 1967. W

D4.59 He Was Despised. 2'
For: chorus(SATB). Anthem. *Text:* Bible, O.T., Isaiah 53:3.
Vocal score: Piedmont, 1966. W

[Heavenly Father, Chorus(SAB)]
D4.60 Heavenly Father (Agnus Dei).
Text: H.N. Jahr.
Vocal score: Remick, 1940. W

[Heavenly Father, Chorus(SATB)]
D4.61 Heavenly Father (Agnus Dei).
Text: H.N. Jahr.
Vocal score: Remick, 1940. W

[Heavenly Father, Chorus(SSA)]
D4.62 Heavenly Father (Agnus Dei).
Text: H.N. Jahr.
Vocal score: Gamble Hinged, 1940. W

D4.63 Hide Thy Face from My Sins.
For: chorus(SSAA). Anthem. *Text:* Bible,
O.T., Psalm 51:9-12.
Vocal score: G. Schirmer, 1938. W

D4.64 Hi-Ho! The Sycamore Tree.
For: chorus(SATB) and piano. *Text:*
Katherine K. Davis.
Vocal score: Remick, 1962. W

D4.65 His Kingdom Is Begun.
For: chorus(SATB) and piano. *Text:*
William Cullen Bryant.
Vocal score: New Music (Oregon), 1977.
W

D4.66 The Holy Mountain.
For: Soprano, chorus(SATB), piano or
organ. *Text:* Katherine K. Davis, *Daye's
Psalter*; Bible, O.T., Isaiah.
Vocal score: Remick, 1959. W

D4.67 Honor and Praise.
For: chorus(SATB), trumpets(2)(optional),
organ. *Text:* Katherine K. Davis with
verses from Bible, O.T., Psalms 11 and
24. Written for the choirs of the
Harvey Browne Memorial Presbyterian
Church, Louisville, Ky., for the
dedication of a new sanctuary.
Vocal score: Witmark, 1966. W
Parts: Witmark, 1966. W

D4.68 Hornpipe
For: piano. 1 movement
Score: J. Fisher, 1956. W

D4.69 How Firm a Foundation. 3'
For: chorus(SATB) and keyboard. *Text:*
A Selection (1787) by John Rippon.
Vocal score: Galaxy, 1972. W

D4.70 How Lovely Are Thy Dwellings.
5'
For: voice(high) and piano or organ.
Text: Bible, O.T., Psalm 84:1-3.
Vocal score: Galaxy, 1952. W

D4.71 The Humble Shepherds.
For: chorus(TTBB). *Text:* Rhys Williams.
Dedicated to: Arthur Landers, and the
Phillips Exeter Academy Glee Club.
Vocal score: Boston, 1940. W

[The Humble Shepherds; Arr.]
D4.72 The Humble Shepherds.
For: chorus(SSAA). *Text:* Rhys Williams.
Vocal score: Boston, 1940. W

D4.73 I Gave My Love a Pretty Little
Ring. 1' 15"
Text: traditional, Norwegian; adapted by
Katherine K. Davis.
Vocal score: Birchard, 1953. W

[I Gave My Love a Pretty Little Ring;
Arr.]
D4.74 I Gave My Love a Pretty Little
Ring. 1' 15"
For: chorus(SAB). *Text:* traditional
Norwegian; adapted by Katherine K.
Davis.
Vocal score: Summy-Birchard, 1962. W

D4.75 I Got a Gal.
For: chorus(SATB) and piano. *Text:*
traditional, American; adapted by
Katherine K. Davis.
Vocal score: Warner, 1972. W

D4.76 I Have a Fawn. 2' 30"
For: voice(medium) and piano. *Text:*
Thomas Moore.
Score: Galaxy, 1966. W

D4.77 I Sing of a Maiden.
For: chorus(SATB). *Text:* traditional,
15th century.
Vocal score: E.C. Schirmer, 1933. W

D4.78 I Will Open My Eyes.
For: chorus(SATB) and piano or organ.
Anthem. *Text:* from the Bible; adapted

by Katherine K. Davis.
Vocal score: C. Fischer, 1972. W

D4.79 If I Were a Shepherd.
For: chorus(treble)(2-part) and piano or organ.
Vocal score: Boston Music, 1973. W

D4.80 If Ye Love Me, Keep My Commandments.
For: chorus(SATB). Anthem. *Text:* Bible, N.T., John 14:15, 16. For earlier version for chorus(SA) and piano, see Seasonal Anthems for Junior Choir.
Vocal score: Wood, 1964. W

D4.81 In the Bleak Midwinter.
For: chorus(SATB). *Text:* Christina Georgina Rossetti. *Dedicated to:* J.B.D.
Vocal score: E.C. Schirmer, 1933. W

[In the Bleak Midwinter; Arr.]
D4.82 In the Bleak Midwinter.
For: chorus(SSA). *Text:* Christina Georgina Rossetti. *Dedicated to:* J.B.D.
Vocal score: E.C. Schirmer.

D4.83 Indian Drum.
For: piano. *Dedicated to:* Frank Pilling.
Score: G. Schirmer, 1932. W

D4.84 Jazz Adoration.
For: chorus(SATB), piano, double bass(optional) or electric bass (optional), drums(3)(optional).
Vocal score: Alfred, 1972. W

D4.85 Jesu, the Very Thought of Thee.
For: Soprano, chorus(SATB), organ. Anthem. *Text:* Latin, 12th century, translated by Edward Caswell. For another version, for chorus(SA) and piano, see Seasonal Anthems for Junior Choir.
Vocal score: Wood, 1963. W

D4.86 Jesus Is His Name.
For: chorus(unison) and piano. *Text:* Katherine K. Davis.
Vocal score: Boston, 1972. W

D4.87 Jesus Sleeping in the Manger.
For: chorus(SA) and piano.
Vocal score: Summy, 1943. W

[Jesus Sleeping in the Manger; Arr.]
D4.88 Jesus Sleeping in the Manger.
For: chorus(SAB) and piano.
Vocal score: Summy, 1949. W

D4.89 Joy Has Filled the Sky.
For: descant, chorus(SATB), organ, handbells(6) or organ chimes.
Vocal score: Belwin, 1974. W

D4.90 The Lamb.
For: chorus(SA) and piano. *Text:* William Blake.
Vocal score: Galaxy, 1969. W

D4.91 The Land We Hold So Dear.
For: chorus(SATB), keyboard, flute(optional), recorder(optional), oboe(optional), trumpet(optional).
Dedicated to: First Church of Christ, Bedford, Mass. *First performed:* Apr. 19, 1975; Bedford, Mass; Bicentennial Service. First Church of Christ Choir.
Vocal score: Belwin, 1975. W

D4.92 Let All the World in Every Corner Sing. 3'
For: chorus(SATB) and piano. *Text:* George Herbert.
Vocal score: Warner, 1977. W

D4.93 Let Earthly Choirs Arise and Sing.
For: descant, chorus(unison), piano or organ. Anthem. *Text: The Assembly Praise Book.*
Vocal score: Broadman, 1962. W

D4.94 Let Not Your Heart Be Troubled.
For: chorus(SATB) and piano or organ. Anthem. *Text:* Bible, N.T., John 14:1-7.
Vocal score: Wood, 1940. W

[Let Not Your Heart Be Troubled; Arr.]
D4.95 Let Not Your Heart Be Troubled.
For: voice and piano. Anthem. *Text:*

Bible, N.T., John 14:1-7.
Vocal score: Wood, 1944. W

D4.96 Let Thy Mercies Come Also unto Me.
For: Alto and chorus(SSAA). Anthem.
Text: Bible, O.T., Psalm 114:41, 44.
Vocal score: Boston Music, 1940. W

D4.97 Let Thy Merciful Ears, O Lord, Be Open.
For: chorus(SATB). Anthem. *Text: The Book of Common Prayer.*
Vocal score: Abingdon, 1970.

D4.98 The Light of Heaven.
For: chorus(SATB) and piano or organ.
Vocal score: Alfred, 1972. W

D4.99 Listen in Your Heart.
For: chorus(unison) and keyboard. *Text:* Katherine K. Davis.
Vocal score: The Choristers Guild Letters, Choristers Guild, 1980. W

[The Little Drummer Boy, Chorus(SAB) and Piano]
D4.100 The Little Drummer Boy.
Christmas music. *Words and music by:* Katherine K. Davis, Henry Onorati, Harry Simeone. Earlier version titled Carol of the Drum.
Vocal score: Mills, Delaware, 1958. W

[The Little Drummer Boy, Choruses and Orchestra]
D4.101 The Little Drummer Boy.
For: chorus(SATB), chorus(children's), orchestra. Christmas music. *Words and music by:* Katherine K. Davis, Henry Onorati, Harry Simeone. Earlier version titled Carol of the Drum.
Disc: Columbia ML 6039; MS 66349, 1964. Temple University Choir; St. Francis de Sales Boychoir; Philadelphia Orchestra, Eugene Ormandy, conductor.

[The Little Drummer Boy, Voice and Piano]
D4.102 The Little Drummer Boy.
Christmas music. *Words and music by:* Katherine K. Davis, Henry Onorati,

Harry Simeone. This version became subject of a copyright dispute, 1959. Earlier version titled Carol of the Drum.
Score: Mill, Delaware, 1958. W
Disc: [recorded by Johnny Cash, Lou Rawls, Frank Sinatra, and others]

D4.103 Lonely Mountain.
For: chorus(SSA) and keyboard. *Text:* C.R.W. Robertson [i.e. Katherine K. Davis] .
Vocal score: Wood, 1953. W

Lord All Glorious, Lord Victorious. *See* The Road to Galilee. Lord All Glorious, Lord Victorious.

D4.104 Lord God of Sabaoth.
For: chorus(SABT). *Text:* John Cowley.
Vocal score: Summy-Birchard, 1950. W

D4.105 Lord Most Holy.
For: chorus(SSA). Anthem. *Text:* liturgical. *Dedicated to:* Concord Academy Choir.
Vocal score: Remick, 1956. W

D4.106 Love Is Born. (1972?)
For: chorus(SATB) and piano or organ.
Text: Katherine K. Davis.
Vocal score: ms. W

D4.107 Molly Alone.
For: chorus(SSA).
Vocal score: Remick, 1958. W

D4.108 Morning Madrigal.
For: chorus(SATB).
Vocal score: New Music (Kansas), 1974. W

D4.109 Morris Dance.
For: piano.
Score: G. Schirmer, 1928. W

A Mother Goose Setting in the Style of Mozart. *See* Goosie, Goosie, Gander.

D4.110 Musette.
For: piano. *Dedicated to:* Dora Lewis.
Score: G. Schirmer, 1928. W

D4.111 My Lord Hath Sent His Angel.
4'
For: voice and piano. *Text:* Bible, O.T.,
Daniel 6.
Score: Galaxy, 1956. W

[Nancy Hanks, Chorus(SATB) and
Piano]
D4.112 Nancy Hanks. 3' 30"
Text: Rosemary Carr Benet.
Vocal score: Galaxy, 1946. W

[Nancy Hanks, Chorus(SSA) and
Piano]
D4.113 Nancy Hanks. 3' 30"
Text: Rosemary Carr Benet.
Vocal score: Galaxy, 1945. W

[Nancy Hanks, Voice(High) and Piano]
D4.114 Nancy Hanks.
Text: Rosemary Carr Benet.
Score: Galaxy, 1941. W

D4.115 The Night Moth.
For: piano. 1 movement.
Score: Hatch, 1923. W

D4.116 Orientale. (1921)
For: orchestra(2-1-2-1; 2-2-2-0; timp;
str). *First performed:* May 2, 1921; St.
Joseph, Mo. St. Joseph Symphony
Orchestra, Hugh McNutt, conductor.
Score: ms. W

D4.117 Our God Is a Rock.
For: chorus(SATB) and piano or organ.
Text: Katherine K. Davis.
Vocal score: Birchard, 1949. W

D4.118 Out of Your Sleep Arise and
Wake.
For: chorus(SATB). *Text:* anon.,
15th-century carol.
Vocal score: E.C. Schirmer, 1934. W

D4.119 Pastorale.
For: organ. *Dedicated to:* Hamilton C.
Macdougall.
Score: Boston, 1918. W

D4.120 The Pixies.
For: piano. 1 movement.
Score: Hatch, 1923. W

D4.121 Poor Mary.
For: Soprano, chorus(SATB), piano or
organ. *Text:* John Cowley.
Vocal score: C. Fischer, 1945, 1961. W

[Poor Mary; Arr.]
D4.122 Poor Mary.
For: chorus(SSA) and piano. *Text:* John
Cowley.
Vocal score: C. Fischer, 1945. W

D4.123 Praise and Glory. 3'
For: chorus(SA) and piano or organ.
Dedicated to: K.K. Davis Choir, Patricia
Degen, Director, All Saints' Chapel,
Princeton, N.J.
Vocal score: Galaxy, 1965. W

[Praise and Glory; Arr]
D4.124 Praise and Glory. 3'
For: chorus(SATB), trumpet(optional),
keyboard.
Vocal score: Galaxy, 1979. W

D4.125 Praise the Lord Who Reigns
Above.
For: chorus(unison), trumpet, keyboard.
Text: Charles Wesley.
Vocal score: Broadman, 1968. W

D4.126 The Raising of Lazarus.
For: voice(medium) and piano. *Text:*
Bible, N.T., John 11:1, 3, 4, 17, 25,
41-44.
Score: C. Fischer, 1947. W

D4.127 Rejoice in the Lord.
For: chorus(SSA). Anthem. *Text:* Bible,
N.T., Philippians 4:4-7.
Vocal score: E.C. Schirmer, 1936. W

D4.128 Renew a Right Spirit within Me.
For: chorus(SA). Anthem. *Text:* Bible,
O.T., Psalm 51:9-10.
Vocal score: G. Schirmer.

[Renew a Right Spirit within Me;
Arr.]
D4.129 Renew a Right Spirit within Me.
For: Tenor and chorus(SATB). Anthem.
Text: Bible, O.T., Psalm 51:9-10.
Vocal score: G. Schirmer, 1938, 1962. W

D4.130 Riding to Jerusalem.
For: chorus(SATB), keyboard,
bells(optional). *Text:* Katherine K. Davis.
Vocal score: Galaxy, 1977. W

D4.131 The Road to Galilee. 37'
For: voices, chorus(SATB),
chorus(children), organ. Easter music;
oratorio. *Text:* Katherine K. Davis.
Vocal score: Galaxy, 1964. W

[The Road to Galilee. Lord All
Glorious, Lord Victorious]
D4.132 Lord All Glorious, Lord
Victorious.
For: chorus(mixed), Soprano or
chorus(unison), organ. Easter music.
Text: Katherine K. Davis.
Vocal score: Galaxy, 1966. W

D4.133 Russian Cradle Song.
For: piano. *Dedicated to:* Peggy Palmer.
Score: Presser, 1932. W

D4.134 Scenes from a Forest Ballet.
For: piano. 4 movements.

[Scenes from a Forest Ballet. The
Butterfly]
D4.135 The Butterfly.
For: piano.
Score: Hatch, 1922. W

D4.136 Seasonal Anthems for Junior
Choir.
For: chorus(SA) and piano. *Contents:*
Fanfare for Palm Sunday (Bible, N.T.,
Matthew 21:9); Harvest Song (W.
Chatterton Dix); How Bright Appears
the Morning Star (P. Nicolai); If You
Love Me, Keep My Commandments
(Bible, N.T., John 14:15, 16); Jesus, Son
of God Most High (T.B. Pollock); Jesu,
the Very Thought of Thee (Latin, 12th
century); Let All Mortal Flesh Keep
Silence (Liturgy of St. James); O Zion
That Bringest Good Tidings (Bible, O.T.,
Isaiah 10:9); Rejoice; Rejoice-Plainchant
(Latin, 9th century); This is a Day for
Singing (A.E.A. [i.e. Katherine K.
Davis]).
Vocal score: Mills, 1963. W

Seasonal Anthems for Junior Choir,
No. 1. *See also* Fanfare for Palm
Sunday.

Seasonal Anthems for Junior Choir,
No. 2. *See also* Harvest Song.

Seasonal Anthems for Junior Choir,
No. 4. *See also* If Ye Love
Me, Keep My Commandments.

Seasonal Anthems for Junior Choir,
No. 6. *See also* Jesu, the Very
Thought of. Thee.

D4.137 Shepherds, Awake!
For: chorus(SATB), chorus(SA), piano or
organ. *Text:* Katherine K. Davis.
Vocal score: Remick, 1938, 1967. W

D4.138 The Shepherds Came to
Bethlehem. 2'
For: Soprano, chorus(SATB), piano or
organ.
Vocal score: Galaxy, 1965. W

D4.139 The Shot Heard Round the
World. 2' 55"
For: chorus(SATB), trumpets(2)(optional),
organ. *Text: Concord Hymn* by Ralph
Waldo Emerson.
Vocal score: Warner, 1974. W

D4.140 Sicilienne.
For: piano. 1 movement. *Dedicated to:*
Sallie Kite.
Score: G. Schirmer, 1930. W

D4.141 Sing Gloria.
For: Soprano, Alto, chorus(SATB),
piano. *Text:* John Cowley.
Vocal score: Remick, 1952. W

D4.142 Song of the Magi.
For: descant, chorus(SATB), piano. *Text:*
Lon Woodrum.
Vocal score: Beacon Hill, 1974. W

[Songs for Young and Grown-up
Children]
D4.143 Four Songs for Young and
Grown-up Children.

For: voice and piano. *Text:* Katherine K. Davis and Burges Johnson (Clock). *Contents:* The Pop Corn Dance; The Piano; The Little Yellow Duster; Clock. *Dedicated to:* Miss "Bobby" Besler. *Score:* White-Smith, 1921. W

D4.144 Star at Christmas. 5'
For: chorus(SSA) and piano or organ. *Text:* Katherine K. Davis. *Dedicated to:* Lee Calder. *Score:* Galaxy, 1957. W

[Star at Christmas; Arr.]
D4.145 Star at Christmas. 4' 30"
For: voice(medium) and piano or organ. *Text:* Katherine K. Davis. *Dedicated to:* Lee Calder. *Vocal score:* Galaxy, 1957. W

D4.146 A Star Shone Out.
For: Soprano and chorus(SATB). *Text:* John Cowley. *Vocal score:* E.C. Schirmer, 1939. W

D4.147 The Stone Is Rolled Away.
For: chorus(SAB) and piano or organ. Easter music. *Text:* A.E.A. [i.e. Katherine K. Davis]. *Vocal score:* Flammer, 1963. W

Tale of Glory. *See* Easter Is a Song. Tale of Glory.

D4.148 Te Deum. 8'
For: Soprano, Alto, Tenor, Bass, chorus(SSATBB), organ. Canticle. *Text: The Book of Common Prayer. Vocal score:* Flammer, 1958. W

D4.149 Thank We the Lord.
For: Soprano, chorus(SATB), organ. *Text:* Bible, O.T., Psalm 145:9, 10; adapted by Katherine K. Davis. *Vocal score:* Piedmont, 1967. W

D4.150 Thanksgiving Song.
For: changing or treble voices; i.e., chorus(SAT) or chorus(SSA). *Text:* Katherine K. Davis. *Vocal score:* Warner, 1968. W

D4.151 This Is Noel.
For: Soprano, Baritone, chorus(SATB), oboe(optional), piano or organ(optional). *Text:* John Cowley. *Contents:* Come, Singing Noel; As Joseph Was A-Walking; The Shepherds; The Angels; The Three Kings; Mary's Lullaby; Come, Singing Noel. *Vocal score:* Remick, 1953. NU W

[This Is Noel. Come, Singing Noel; Arr.]
D4.152 Come, Singing Noel.
For: descant and chorus(SATB). *Text:* Katherine K. Davis. *Vocal score:* Remick, 1953. W

D4.153 Thou Art Our Wine and Bread. 3'
For: chorus(SATB). Anthem for Communion. *Text:* Katherine K. Davis. *Vocal score:* Galaxy, 1949. W

D4.154 To Him That Overcometh.
For: voice(high) and piano. *Text:* Bible, N.T., Revelations 2:7; 21:7; 2:26 and 28. *Dedicated to:* Jean Burrage Britton. *Score:* C. Fischer, 1967. W

D4.155 To Shepherds Fast Asleep. 3' 30"
For: chorus(SATB), chorus(SA), piano or organ. *Text:* C.R.W. Robertson [i.e. Katherine K. Davis]. *Vocal score:* Galaxy, 1963. W

D4.156 To the King of Glory.
For: chorus(SATB) and keyboard. Anthem. *Text:* Bible, N.T., Matthew 21:9; adapted by Katherine K. Davis. *Vocal score:* Hinshaw, 1978. W

D4.157 Treasure in Heaven.
For: voice(high) or voice(low) and piano. *Text:* Bible, N.T., Mark 10:17-24. *Score:* Row, 1951 (version for high voice). W
Score: Row, 1951 (version for low voice).

[Trust in the Lord, Chorus(SATB)]
D4.158 Trust in the Lord. 3'

For: chorus(SATB) and piano or organ.
Anthem. *Text:* Bible, O.T., Proverbs 3:5,
6. *Dedicated to:* Nancy Loring.
Vocal score: Galaxy.

[Trust in the Lord, Chorus(SSA)]
D4.159 Trust in the Lord. 3'
For: chorus(SSA) and piano or organ.
Text: Bible, O.T., Proverbs 3:5, 6.
Dedicated to: Nancy Loring.
Vocal score: Galaxy, 1944. W

[Trust in the Lord, High Voice]
D4.160 Trust in the Lord. 3'
For: voice(high) and piano or organ.
Text: Bible, O.T., Proverbs 3:5, 6.
Dedicated to: Nancy Loring.
Score: Galaxy, 1946. BPL W

[Trust in the Lord, Medium Voice]
D4.161 Trust in the Lord. 3'
For: voice(medium) and piano or organ.
Text: Bible, O.T., Proverbs 3:5, 6.
Dedicated to: Nancy Loring.
Score: Galaxy.

D4.162 Two Hundred Years Ago. 1' 48"
For: chorus(unison), piano,
piccolo(optional), handbells(optional),
tom-tom(optional), snare drum(optional).
Text: Katherine K. Davis.
Vocal score: Warner, 1974. W

D4.163 The Tyger.
For: chorus(SATB) and piano or organ.
Text: William Blake.
Vocal score: Galaxy, 1969. W

D4.164 The Unmusical Impresario.
For: Soprano, Mezzo Soprano, Alto,
Tenor, Bass, chorus, orchestra(1-1-2-1;
2-2-1-0; timp; str). Musical comedy in
1 act. *Text:* Katherine K. Davis and
Heddie Root Kent. *First performed:*
June 1954; Concord, Mass, Concord
Chorus.
Score & parts: G. Schirmer. Rental.
Vocal score: G. Schirmer, 1956. W

D4.165 Up on the Mountain.
For: chorus(TTBB) and piano(optional).
Text: H.N. Jahr. *Dedicated to:* Arthur

Landers, director, and the Phillips
Exeter Glee Club.
Vocal score: Boston, 1940. W

D4.166 We Are Thy Sons.
For: chorus(SATB) and organ. *Text:*
Katherine K. Davis.
Vocal score: New Music (Oregon), 1974.
W

D4.167 Where Men Are Free.
For: chorus(SATB), trumpet(optional),
piano. *Text:* Katherine K. Davis.
Vocal score: Lillenas, 1976. W

D4.168 Who Is Jesus?
For: narrator, chorus(children), piano.
Easter music; cantata. *Text:* from the
Bible; adapted Katherine K. Davis.
Contents: Jesus Was a Baby; Joseph
Was a Carpenter; How Is It That Ye
Sought Me? Jesus Heals; From From
Death to Life; Peace Be with You;
Easter Morning.
Vocal score: Broadman, 1974. W

D4.169 Who Is This Who Comes
A-Riding?
For: chorus(SATB), trumpet(obbligato),
organ. Anthem. *Text:* Katherine K.
Davis.
Vocal score & part: Remick, 1967;
Warner, 1968. W

D4.170 Who Was the Man.
For: chorus(unison) and piano or organ.
Text: Katherine K. Davis.
Vocal score: Choristers Guild. W

D4.171 Within Thy Love: A Prayer.
For: chorus(SSA) and piano. *Text:*
A.E.A. [i.e. Katherine K. Davis].
Vocal score: Remick, 1940, 1959. W

D4.171.5 A Wonderful Thing.
For: chorus(unison), piano, flute,
handbells(optional). Easter music; carol.
Text: Katherine K. Davis.
Vocal score: Warner, 1972. W

D4.172 The World Itself Keeps Easter
Day. 3'

For: Soprano and chorus(SSA). *Text:* J.M. Neale.
Vocal score: Galaxy, 1939. W

D4.173 You Spotted Snakes.
For: chorus(SSA). *Text: Fairy Chorus* from *A Midsummer-Night's Dream* by William Shakespeare.
Vocal score: G. Schirmer, 1938. W

D5 DAVID DEL TREDICI

Born March 16, 1937, in Coverdale, Calif. *Education:* studied composition with Seymour Shifrin, Arnold Elston (University of California, Berkeley, B.A., 1959); Earl Kim, Roger Sessions (Princeton University, M.F.A., 1964); piano with Bernhard Abramowitsch (1954-60) and Robert Helps (1959-63). *Awards:* Woodrow Wilson Award (1960), Hertz Award (1962), Guggenheim Grant (1966), Fromm Foundation commission (1964), Koussevitzky Music Foundation (Library of Congress) commission (1966), National Institute of Arts and Letters Award (1968), Naumburg Recording Award (1972), Brandeis University, Creative Arts Award (1973), National Endowment for the Arts Grants (1973, 1974), Pulitzer Prize in Music (1980), Atlantic Richfield Company grant (1981). *Related activities:* served on the faculties of Harvard University (1968-72), State University of New York, College at Buffalo (1972), Boston University (1973-). BU

WORKS

D5.1 Adventures Underground. (1971; rev. 1977) 23'
For: Soprano(amplified), folk group(saxophones(soprano)(2), mandolin, banjo(tenor), accordion), orchestra(2(pic2)-2-2(Ebcl)-2; 4-2-2-2; timp, perc(5); hp(2), cel; str(12-12-8-8-4)). *Text:* from *Alice's Adventures in Wonderland* by Lewis Carroll. *Contents:* The Pool of Tears; The Mouse's Tale. *Commissioned by:* Buffalo Philharmonic Orchestra, assisted by the New York State

Council on the Arts. *Dedicated to:* Michael Tilson Thomas. First performed: Apr. 13, 1975; Susan Davenny Wyner, soprano; Buffalo Philharmonic Orchestra, Michael Tilson Thomas, conductor.
Score & parts: Boosey & Hawkes, 197-. Rental.
Study score: Boosey & Hawkes, nyp.
Vocal score: Boosey & Hawkes, 197-.

D5.2 An Alice Symphony. (1969-76) 41'
For: Soprano(amplified), folk group(saxophone(soprano), saxophone(soprano)/ saxophone/tenor), mandolin, banjo(tenor), accordion), orchestra(2(pic2)-2-2(Ebcl)-1(cbsn); 4-2-2-1; timp, perc(5); str). *Text:* from *Alice's Adventures in Wonderland* by Lewis Carroll. *Contents:* Speak Gently/Speak Roughly; The Lobster Quadrille; 'Tis the Voice of the Sluggard; Who Stole the Tarts; Dream Conclusion.
Score & parts: Boosey & Hawkes, 198-? Rental.
Study score: Boosey & Hawkes, nyp.

[An Alice Symphony. Illustrated Alice]
D5.3 Illustrated Alice. (1975-76) 17'
For: Soprano(amplified), folk group(saxophone(alto)/ saxophone(soprano), saxophone(soprano/alto/tenor)), orchestra(2(pic2)-2-2-2(cbsn); 4-2-2-1; timp, perc(5); str). *Text:* from *Alice's Adventures in Wonderland* by Lewis Carroll. *Contents:* Speak Roughly/Speak Gently; Who Stole the Tarts; Dream Conclusion [i.e., excerpts of An Alice Symphony, performed in this order, under this title].
Earlier version for amplified soprano and orchestra, titled In Wonderland. Part II, withdrawn.
Commissioned by: Stern Grove Festival Association upon the occasion of the 500th Stern Grove Concert, Aug. 8, 1976. *Dedicated to:* Tison Street. *First*

performed: Aug. 8, 1976. Su Harmon, soprano; San Francisco Symphony Orchestra, David Del Tredici, conductor. *Score & parts:* Boosey & Hawkes, 197-. Rental.

[An Alice Symphony. In Wonderland]
D5.4 In Wonderland: A Scene with Lobsters. (1969; rev. 1974) 24'
For: Soprano(amplified), folk group(saxophones(soprano)(2), mandolin, banjo(tenor), accordion), orchestra(2(pic)-2-2(Ebcl)-2(cbsn); 4-2-2-1; perc(4); str). *Text:* from *Alice's Adventures in Wonderland,* by Lewis Carroll. *Contents:* The Lobster Quadrille; 'Tis the Voice of the Sluggard; Dream Conclusion [i.e., excerpts of An Alice Symphony, performed in this order, under this title]. Written with the assistance of a National Endowment for the Arts Grant. *Dedicated to:* Aaron Copland. *First performed:* July 29, 1975; Aspen Music Festival, Aspen, Colo. Susan Davenny Wyner, soprano; Aspen Festival Orchestra, Richard Dufallo, conductor.
Score & parts: Boosey & Hawkes, 197-. Rental.
Reel: Oct. 26, 1978; Boston University; in *Omnibus: Music of the 20th Century, Concert 2.* Rebecca McConnaughey, soprano; Harvey Pittel and Alan Bernstein, soprano saxophones; Richard Romiti, accordion; Robert Paul Sullivan, banjo; David Dyer, mandolin; Maurice Wright, synthesizer; Boston University Symphony Orchestra, David Del Tredici, conductor. BU

[An Alice Symphony. The Lobster Quadrille]
D5.5 The Lobster Quadrille. (1969; rev. 1974-75) 13'
For: Soprano(amplified)(optional), folk group(saxophones(soprano)(2), mandolin, banjo(tenor), accordion), orchestra(2(pic2)-2-2(Ebcl)-2(cbsn); 4-2-2-1; perc(4); str). *First performed:*

Nov. 14, 1969; London, England. London Symphony Orchestra, Aaron Copland, conductor.
Score & parts: Boosey & Hawkes, 197-. Rental.

All in the Golden Afternoon. *See* Child Alice. Part 3.

D5.6 Child Alice. (1977-) 110'
For: Soprano(amplified), voice(female)(optional), orchestra(3(pic2)-3(Ehn)-4(Ebcl, bcl)-3(cbsn); 4-4-3-1; timp, perc(5); hps(2), cel; str). *Text:* preface poems in *Alice's Adventures in Wonderland* and *Through the Looking Glass (Child of the Pure Unclouded Brow)* by Lewis Carroll. *Contents:* Part 1, In Memory of a Summer Day; Part 2, Quaint Evening [and] Happy Voices; Part 3, All in the Golden Afternoon.

[Child Alice. Part 1]
D5.7 In Memory of a Summer Day. (1977-80) 63'
For: Soprano(amplified) and orchestra(3(pic2)-3(Ehn)-4(Ebcl, bcl)-3(cbsn); 4-4-3-1; timp, perc(5); hps(2), cel; str). *Text: Child of the Pure Unclouded Brow,* in *Through the Looking Glass* by Lewis Carroll. *Contents:* Introduction; Simple Alice (Song); A Tale Is Told; Triumphant Alice (Marcia); Interlude; Ecstatic Alice (Aria); Postlude [included only when Part 1 is performed alone]. Awarded Pulitzer Prize in Music (1980). *Commissioned by:* St. Louis Symphony Orchestra in honor of its Centenary. *Dedicated to:* Leonard Slatkin. *First performed:* Feb. 23, 1980; St. Louis. Phyllis Bryn-Julson, soprano; St. Louis Symphony Orchestra, Leonard Slatkin, conductor.
Score & parts: Boosey & Hawkes, [1980?] Rental.
Study score: Boosey & Hawkes, nyp.

[Child Alice. Part 2]
D5.8 *For:* voice (female) (offstage)(optional) and orchestra(3(pic2)-3(Ehn)-4(Eb cl,

bcl)-3(cbsn); 4-4-3-1; timp, perc(5); hps(2), cel; str). *Contents:* Quaint Evening (in progress); Happy Voices.

[Child Alice. Part 2. Happy Voices]
D5.9 Happy Voices. (1980) 15'
For: voice(female)(offstage)(optional) and orchestra(3(pic2)-3(Ehn)-4(Ebcl, bcl)-3(cbsn); 4-4-3-1; timp, perc(5); hps(2), cel; str). 1 movement.
Commissioned by: Louise M. Davies for the San Francisco Symphony Orchestra, in celebration of the opening of the Louise M. Davies Hall. *Dedicated to:* Louise M. Davies, Edo de Waart, Milton Salkind. *First performed:* Sept. 16, 1980; San Francisco, Calif. San Francisco Symphony Orchestra, Edo de Waart, conductor.
Score & parts: Boosey & Hawkes, [1980?] Rental.
Study score: Boosey & Hawkes, nyp.

[Child Alice. Part 3]
D5.10 All in the Golden Afternoon. (1981) 32'
For: Soprano(amplified) and orchestra(3(pic2)-3(Ehn)-4(Ebcl, bcl)-3(cbsn); 4-4-3-1; timp, perc(5); hps(2), cel; str). *Text:* from *Alice's Adventures in Wonderland* by Lewis Carroll. *Contents:* Aria; Interlude (A Tale Is Told); Lullaby Cadenza; In Conclusion (Sunset). *Commissioned by:* Philadelphia Orchestra, assisted by an Atlantic Richfield Company Grant.
Dedicated to: Eugene Ormandy. *First performed:* May 8, 1981; Philadelphia, Pa. Benita Valente, soprano; Philadelphia Orchestra, Eugene Ormandy, conductor.
Score & parts: Boosey & Hawkes, [1981?] Rental.
Study score: Boosey & Hawkes, nyp.

D5.11 Fantasy Pieces. (1959-60) 6'
For: piano. 4 movements. *Dedicated to:* Stephanie Shehatovitch; Earl Kim; Jules Langert; Robert Helps. *First performed:* 1960; San Francisco, Calif. David Del Tredici.
Score: Boosey & Hawkes, 1970. BU HU MIT

Disc: Desto DC 7110(S), 1971. George Bennette. BrU BU HU MIT NEC

D5.12 Final Alice. (1975-76) 64'
For: Soprano(amplified), folk group(saxophones(soprano)(2), mandolin, banjo(tenor), accordion), orchestra(4(pic3)-4(Ehn)-4(Ebcl)-4(cbsn); 6-4-4-1; timp, perc(7); hps(2), cel; str(18-16-12-12-9)). *Text:* the last two chapters of *Alice's Adventures in Wonderland* by Lewis Carroll, and Victorian poems on which they are based. *Commissioned by:* Chicago Symphony Orchestra, assisted by the National Endowment for the Arts in honor of the United States Bicentennial. *First performed:* Oct. 7, 1976; Chicago, Ill. Barbara Hendricks, soprano; Chicago Symphony Orchestra, Sir Georg Solti, conductor.
Score & parts: Boosey & Hawkes, 197-. Rental.
Study score: Boosey & Hawkes, nyp.
Vocal score: Boosey & Hawkes, 197-.
Disc: Decca SXDL 7516, 1981. Barbara Hendricks, soprano; Chicago Symphony Orchestra, Sir Georg Solti, conductor.
Disc: London LDR 71018, 1981. Barbara Hendricks, soprano; Chicago Symphony Orchestra, Sir Georg Solti, conductor. BCM MIT W

Happy Voices. *See* Child Alice. Part 2.

D5.13 I Hear an Army. (1963-64) 13'
For: Soprano and string quartet. *Text:* XXXI from *Chamber Music* by James Joyce. *Commissioned by:* Fromm Foundation for the Berkshire Music Festival of Contemporary Music, Tanglewood. *Dedicated to:* Phyllis Bryn-Julson. *First performed:* Aug. 12, 1964; Berkshire Music Center, Tanglewood.
Study score: Boosey & Hawkes, 1974. BPL BU HU MIT W
Parts: Boosey & Hawkes, 1974. BU HU W
Disc: CRI SD 294, 1973. Phyllis Bryn-Julson, soprano; Composers String Quartet. BCM BrU BU HU HUm MIT NEC W

Reel: Nov. 22, 1977; Boston University; in *Omnibus: Music of the 20th Century, Concert 2.* Judith Kellock, soprano; Abraham Appleman and Elizabeth Field, violins; Steven Wedel, viola; Timothy Allcott, cello; David Del Tredici, conductor. BU

In Memory of a Summer Day. *See* Child Alice. Part 1.

In Wonderland. Part I. *See* An Alice Symphony. In Wonderland.

In Wonderland. Part II. *See* An Alice Symphony. Illustrated Alice.

D5.14 The Last Gospel. (1967) 13′
For: Soprano(amplified), chorus(SATB), rock group(saxophones(amplified)(2) and guitars(electric)(2)), orchestra(2(pic2),2-2(Ebcl)-1(cbsn); 4-2-2-1; perc; str). *Text:* Bible, N.T., John I: 1-18. *First performed:* June 15, 1968; San Francisco, Calif. San Francisco Symphony Orchestra, David Del Tredici, conductor.
Score & parts: Boosey & Hawkes. Rental.
Vocal score: Boosey & Hawkes.

The Lobster Quadrille. *See* An Alice Symphony. The Lobster Quadrille.

D5.15 Night Conjure-Verse. (1965) 18′
For: Soprano, Mezzo Soprano or Countertenor, instrumental ensemble (flute/piccolo, flute, oboe, clarinet, clarinet(bass)/clarinet, bassoon, horn, violins(2), viola, violoncello). *Text:* James Joyce. *Contents:* Simples; A Memory of the Players at Midnight.
Score & parts: Boosey & Hawkes. Rental.
Disc: CRI SD 243, 1970. Benita Valente, soprano; Mary Burgess, mezzo soprano; Marlboro Festival Players, David Del Tredici, conductor. BrU BU HU MIT NEC W

D5.16 Pop-Pourri. (1968) 28′
For: Soprano(amplified), Mezzo Soprano or Countertenor ad lib., chorus(SATB), rock group(saxophone(soprano), saxophone(soprano/tenor), guitar(electric), electric bass), orchestra(2(pic2)-2(Ehn)-2(bcl)-2(cbsn); 0-2-2-0; perc(3); str). *Text:* from *Alice's Adventures in Wonderland* and *Through the Looking Glass* by Lewis Carroll; Chorale from Cantata No. 60, by Johann Sebastian Bach; *Litany of the Virgin Mary* from the *Liber usualis* (optional). *Contents:* Chorale; Turtle Soup (A Song); Litany of the Blessed Virgin Mary; Chorale; Turtle Soup II; Chorale (with Fragments of Turtle Soup). *Commissioned by:* Men's Advisory Board of the Musical Arts Society of La Jolla, Calif. *Dedicated to:* R.J. Sullivan. *First performed:* July 28, 1968; La Jolla, Calif. Phyllis Bryn-Julson, soprano; La Jolla Musical Arts Society Orchestra, Milton Katims, conductor.
Score & parts: Boosey & Hawkes, 1974. Rental
Study score: Boosey & Hawkes, 1974. BU HU
Reel: Symphony Hall, Boston. HU

D5.17 Scherzo. (1960) 6′ 20″
For: piano(4-hands). *Commissioned by and dedicated to:* Milton Salkind and Peggy Salkind. *First performed:* 1960; Princeton University.
Score: Boosey & Hawkes, 1975. BCM BU HU MIT T
Disc: CRI SD 294, 1973. Robert Helps and David Del Tredici. BCM BrU BU HU MIT NEC W

D5.18 Soliloquy. (1958) 7′
For: piano. *Dedicated to:* Bernhard Abramowitsch. *First performed:* Aug. 1958; Aspen Music Festival, Aspen, Colo.
Score: Boosey & Hawkes, 1975. BU HU MIT

[Songs on Poems of James Joyce]
D5.19 Four Songs on Poems of James Joyce. (1958-60) 12′
For: voice and piano. *Text:* from

Chamber Music and *Pomes Penyeach* by James Joyce. *Contents:* Dove Song; She Weeps over Rahoon; A Flower Given to My Daughter; Monotone. These songs may be performed individually or as a group. They were not conceived as a song cycle. However, if all four songs are performed, the order in which they are printed is the composer's preference. *Dedicated to:* Ann Del Tredici; Miriam Abramowitsch; Noni; The memory of Martha Mood Lehmann. *First performed:* 1959; University of California (A Flower Given to My Daughter).
Score: Boosey & Hawkes, 1974. BPL BU HU HUm MIT NEC W

D5.20 Syzygy. (1966) 26'
For: Soprano, horn, bells, chamber orchestra(pic(afl)-1(pic)-2(Ehn2)- 2(cl in A, bcl)-2(cbsn); 0-2-0-0; str). *Text:* James Joyce. *Contents:* Ecce Puer; Nightpiece. *Commissioned by:* Koussevitzky Music Foundation (Library of Congress). *Dedicated to:* The memory of Serge and Natalie Koussevitzky. *First performed:* July 6, 1968; New York City; Koussevitzky Foundation Concert. Phyllis Bryn-Julson, soprano; Festival Chamber Ensemble, Richard Dufallo, conductor.
Score: reprod. of ms. MIT
Score & parts: Boosey & Hawkes, 1974. Rental.
Study score: Boosey & Hawkes, 1974. BPL BU HU MIT
Disc: Columbia MS 7281, 1969. Phyllis Bryn-Julson, soprano; Festival Chamber Ensemble, Richard Dufallo, conductor. BrU BU HU HUm MIT NEC
Reel: Nov. 1969; Harvard University; in *A Rehearsal of Syzygy.* HU

D5.21 Trio. (1959)
For: violin, viola, violoncello. 1 movement. *Dedicated to:* Seymour Shifrin.
Study score: E.C. Schirmer, 1974. BPL BU HU MIT NEC
Parts: E.C. Schirmer, 1974. BU HU MIT NEC

D5.22 Vintage Alice: Fantascene on A Mad Tea-Party. (1972) 28'
For: Soprano/narrator(amplified), folk group(saxophones(soprano)(2), mandolin, banjo(tenor), accordion, chamber orchestra(1(pic)-1-Ebcl-1; 2-1-1-0; timp, perc; str(5 or small orchestra)). 9 movements. *Text:* from *Alice's Adventures in Wonderland* by Lewis Carroll, and other Victorian material, compiled, adapted and developed by the composer. Includes parodies on *The Star*, by Jane Taylor and *God Save the Queen. Commissioned by:* Paul Masson. *Dedication:* With filial affection to my parents, Walter and Helen Del Tredici. *First performed:* Aug. 5, 1972; Saratoga, Calif; Music at the Vineyards. Claudià Cummings, soprano; David Del Tredici, conductor.
Score & parts: Boosey & Hawkes, 1979. Rental.
Study score: Boosey & Hawkes, 1979. BU HMA HU MIT NEC W

D6 NORMAN DELLO JOIO

Born Jan. 24, 1913, in New York City. Moved to Boston area [1972?]
Education: All Hallows Institute (1926-30); College of the City of New York (1932-34); Institute of Musical Art, New York City (1936); studied composition with his father Casimiro Dello Joio (1930-33), Bernard Wagenaar (Juilliard School, 1939-41), Paul Hindemith (Berkshire Music Center, Tanglewood and Yale University); organ with Casimiro Dello Joio (1930-33) and Pietro Yon (1934-39); piano with Gaston-Marie Dethier (1934-39). *Awards:* Elizabeth Sprague Coolidge Award for Services to Chamber Music (1937), Town Hall Composition Award (1943), Guggenheim Grants (1943, 1944), National Institute of Arts and Letters Award (1945), New York Music Critics Circle Award (1948, 1960), Pulitzer Prize in Music (1957), Emmy Award (1965). *Related activities:* organist, conductor, educator; musical director, Dance Players (1941-43); Chairman, Policy Committee, Contemporary Music

Project for Creativity in Music Education; delegate to the U.S.S.R., Rumania and Bulgaria, U.S. State Department, Cultural Exchange Program (1964); member of the Research Advisory Council, U.S. Office of Education (1965); served on the faculties of Sarah Lawrence College (1945-50), Mannes College of Music (1956-72), Boston University (Professor and Dean of The School for the Arts, 1972-79). BU

WORKS

D6.1 Adieu, Mignonne, When You Are Gone. (1954) 3' 30"-8' 30"
For: chorus(SSA) and piano. *Text:* Owen Meredith, 1st Earl of Lytton. *First performed:* Washington, D.C. Sigma Alpha Iota.
Vocal score: C. Fischer, 1955. BPL BU

D6.2 Air, for Strings. 4'
For: string orchestra.
Score: E.B. Marks, 1967. BU HU
Parts: E.B. Marks, 1967.
Disc: USAF 101878, 1978. United States Air Force String Orchestra, Lowell E. Graham, conductor. BCM

D6.3 Air Power. (1956-57)
For: orchestra(2-2-2-2; 4-3-3-1; perc(3); str). Film music for 22 television films (30 minutes each). *First performed:* Nov. 11, 1956 (initial broadcast); CBS-TV.
Score & parts: C. Fischer. Rental.

[Air Power. Suite]
D6.4 Air Power. (1956-57) 30'-40'
For: orchestra(2-2-2-2; 4-3-3-1; perc(3); str). *Movements:* Introduction; Frolics of the Early Days; Mission in the Sky; War Scenes. Based on music from the CBS television series. *First performed:* Sept. 1957; Philadelphia Orchestra, Eugene Ormandy, conductor.
Score & parts: C. Fischer. Rental.
Disc: Columbia ML 5214/MS 6029, 1957. Philadelphia Orchestra, Eugene Ormandy, conductor. BU HU HUm

D6.5 All Is Still.
For: Tenor, flute, oboe, clarinet, harp, violas, violoncellos, double bass. Stage work. *Score & parts.*

All Things Leave Me. *See* Love Songs. All Things Leave Me.

D6.6 America and Americans.
For: orchestra(2-2-2-2; 3-2-3-1; perc; str). Written for NBC-TV.
Score: ms.

D6.7 Anthony and Cleopatra. (1960) 16'
For: oboe, clarinet, horns(2), trombones(2), viola, percussion. Incidental music for the play by William Shakespeare. *First performed:* summer, 1960; Stratford, Conn.
Score: C. Fischer. Rental.

D6.8 Antiphonal Fantasy on a Theme of Vincenzo Albrici. (1966) 17'
For: organ, brass ensemble(horns(4), trumpets(3), trombones(3), tuba), strings(5)(violins(2), viola, violoncello, double bass). *Commissioned by:* Austin Organs, Inc. *Dedication:* To the memory of Paul Hindemith.
Score: E.B. Marks, 1966. BPL BU HU NEC
Parts: E.B. Marks, 1966. Rental.

D6.9 Aria and Toccata. (1952) 9'-12'
For: pianos(2). *First performed:* Oct. 14, 1953; New York City. Vera Appleton and Michael Field.
Score: C. Fischer, 1955. BPL BU

D6.10 Arietta. 3' 20"-4'
For: string orchestra.
Score: E.B. Marks, 1978. BPL HU
Parts: E.B. Marks, 1978. BPL

D6.11 As of a Dream.
For: narrator, chorus(mixed), voices, dancers(optional), orchestra. *Text:* based on poetry by Walt Whitman. *First performed:* May 18, 1979; Midland, Mich. Midland Center for the Arts Music Society.
Score: Associated, nyp.

D6.12 The Assassination: Two Fates Discuss a Human Problem. (1947) 4'
For: voice(low) and piano. *Text:* adapted from a poem by Robert Hillyer. *First performed:* Hartt College of Music. Lee Venora.
Score: C. Fischer, 1949. BU
Disc: Concert Hall D 6, 1950. John Druary, tenor and Peter Rogell, piano. HU

D6.13 Bagatelles. (1969) 5'
For: harp. 1 movement. *Commissioned by:* Hartt College of Music for the International Harp Competition, 1969.
Score: E.B. Marks, 1969. BPL BU

D6.14 Ballabili (Music for Dance). (1981) 27'
For: orchestra(3-3-3-2; 4-3-3-1; hp; str). 3 movements. *Commissioned by:* Greater Miami Opera Association. *First performed:* June 1981; Miami, Fla.

D6.15 Ballad. (1940)
For: string orchestra. Withdrawn.

A Ballad of the Seven Lively Arts. *See* Profile of a Composer. A Ballad of the Seven Lively Arts.

D6.16 Ballad of Thomas Jefferson. (1937)
For: voice and piano. Withdrawn.

D6.17 Blood Moon.
For: voices, chorus(mixed), orchestra. Opera in 3 acts. Withdrawn.

D6.18 The Bluebird. (1950) 4'-5'
For: chorus(SATB) and piano. *Text:* Joseph Machlis. *First performed:* State University of New York, College at Potsdam.
Vocal score: C. Fisher, 1952. BU

Bright Star. See Christmas Music. Bright Star (Light of the World).

D6.19 Caccia. 3'
For: band.
Score: E.B. Marks, 1978. HU
Parts: E.B. Marks, 1978.

D6.20 Capriccio on the Interval of a Second. (1969) 7'
For: piano. Commissioned for the third Van Cliburn International Piano Competition.
Score: E.B. Marks, 1969. BPL BU HU

D6.21 Choreography; Three Dances for String Orchestra. (1971) 9'
Commissioned by and dedicated to: American String Teachers Association on its 25th anniversary.
Score: E.B. Marks, 1972. BPL HU L
Parts: E.B. Marks, 1972. L

D6.22 Christmas Carol. (1962) 4'
For: chorus(SATB) and piano(4-hands). *Text:* G.K. Chesterton.
Vocal score: E.B. Marks, 1962. BPL BU HU

[Christmas Carol; Arr.]
D6.23 Christmas Carol. 4'
For: chorus(SSA) and piano. *Text:* G.K. Chesterton.
Vocal score: E.B. Marks, 1967. BPL BU HU

[Christmas Carol; Arr.]
D6.24 Christmas Carol. 4'
For: voice(high) and piano. *Text:* G.K. Chesterton.
Score: E.B. Marks, 1967.

[Christmas Carol; Arr.]
D6.25 Christmas Carol. 4'
For: voice(medium) and piano. *Text:* G.K. Chesterton.
Score: E.B. Marks, 1967. BU

D6.26 Christmas Music. (1962) 17'
For: chorus(mixed) and orchestra(1-1-2-1; 2-2-2-0; timp, perc, glock; str). Suite. *Contents:* Bright Star (Light of the World); God Rest Ye Merry, Gentlemen; Hark, the Herald Angels Sing; Holy Infants Lullaby; O Come, All Ye Faithful; Silent Night.
Score & parts: E.B. Marks.
Vocal score: E.B. Marks.

[Christmas Music; Arr.]
D6.27 Christmas Music. 17'

For: piano(4-hands).
Score: E.B. Marks, 1968. BU

[Christmas Music. Bright Star, Chorus]
D6.28 Bright Star (Light of the World).
2' 10"-3'
For: chorus(SA) and piano or chorus
(SATB) and piano(4-hands).
Vocal score: E.B. Marks, 1968 (both
versions).

[Christmas Music. Bright Star, Voice]
D6.29 Bright Star (Light of the World).
2' 10"-3'
For: voice(high) or voice(medium) and
piano.
Score: E.B. Marks, 1968 (version for
high voice).
Score: E.B. Marks, 1968 (version for
medium voice). BPL BU

[Christmas Music. God Rest Ye Merry,
Gentlemen]
D6.30 God Rest Ye Merry, Gentlemen.
2'
For: chorus(SATB) and piano(4-hands).
Vocal score: E.B. Marks, 1968.

[Chrismas Music. Hark, the Herald
Angels Sing]
D6.31 Hark, the Herald Angels Sing. 2'
For: chorus(SATB) and piano(4-hands).
Vocal score: E.B. Marks, 1968.

[Christmas Music. Holy Infant's
Lullaby, Chorus]
D6.32 Holy Infant's Lullaby. 3' 30"
For: chorus(SSA) and piano, or
chorus(SATB) and piano(4-hands) or
piano. *Text:* Norman Dello Joio.
Vocal score: E.B. Marks, 1962 (version
for chorus(SATB)). BU HU
Vocal score: E.B. Marks, 1967 (version
for chorus(SSA). T

[Christmas Music. Holy Infant's
Lullaby, Voice]
D6.33 Holy Infant's Lullaby. 3' 30"
For: voice(high) or voice(medium) and
piano. *Text:* Norman Dello Joio.
Score: E.B. Marks, 1967 (version for
medium voice). BPL BU

Score: E.B. Marks, 1968? (version for
high voice).

[Christmas Music. O Come, All Ye
Faithful]
D6.34 O Come, All Ye Faithful. 3'
For: chorus(SATB) and piano(4-hands).
Vocal score: E.B. Marks.

[Christmas Music. Silent Night]
D6.35 Silent Night. 2'
For: chorus(SATB) and piano(4-hands).
Vocal score: E.B. Marks.

D6.36 Colloquies. (1964)
For: violin and piano. Suite in 5
movements. *Commissioned by:* Ford
Foundation Concert Artist Program.
Dedicated to: Sidney Harth. *First
performed:* May 6, 1964; Carnegie Hall,
New York City. Sidney Harth, violin.
Score: E.B. Marks, 1964. BPL BU HU
Part: E.B. Marks, 1964. HU

D6.37 Colloquy. (1938)
For: violin and piano. Withdrawn.

D6.38 Colonial Ballads. 12'-14'
For: band. Variations on In dulci jubilo.
Score: Associated, 1979. HU
Parts: Associated, 1979.
Disc: Golden Crest ATH 5054, 1978.
West Texas State University
Symphonic Band, Gary Garner,
conductor. BU MIT

D6.39 Colonial Variants: 13 Profiles of
the Original Colonies
Based on an Ancient Tune. (1976) 27'
For:
orchestra(2(&pic)-2(&Ehn)-2(bcl)-2(cbsn);
4-3-3-1; timp, perc, glock, xylo; hp;
str). *Commissioned by:* Farmers Bank of
the State of Delaware. *First performed:*
May 27, 1976. Philadelphia Orchestra.
Score: Associated, 1978. BU HU
Parts: Associated, 1978. Rental.

D6.40 Come to Me, My Love. (1973)
4'-5' 15"
For: chorus(SATB) and piano. *Text:*
Echo by Christina Georgina Rossetti.

Vocal score: E.B. Marks, 1973. BU NU
Disc: Golden Crest ATH 5059, [1978 or 1979]. Boston University Choruses, Norman Dello Joio, conductor. HU

D6.41 Concert Music. (1944) 21'
For: orchestra(2(&pic)-2(&-Ehn) -2(&bcl)-2(&cbsn); 4-3-3-1; timp, perc(2), xylo; str). *First performed:* Jan. 4, 1946. Pittsburgh Symphony Orchestra, Fritz Reiner, conductor.
Score & parts: C. Fischer. Rental.

[Concertante, Band]
D6.42 Concertante for Wind Instruments. (1973) 9' 35"
2 movements. *Commissioned by and dedicated to:* North Hills High School Symphonic Band, Pittsburg, Pa., Warren Mercer, conductor. ·
Score: E.B. Marks, 1973. BCM BPL BU
Parts: E.B. Marks, 1973.
Disc: Golden Crest ATH 5054, 1978. West Texas State University Symphonic Band, Gary Garner, conductor. BU MIT
Reel: Nov. 18, 1976; Boston Conservatory of Music. BCM
Reel: Mar. 15, 1979. Boston Conservatory Wind Ensemble, John Corley, conductor. BCM

[Concertante, Clarinet and Orchestra]
D6.43 Concertante. (1949) 17'
For: clarinet and orchestra(2-2-2-2; 2-2-0-0; timp, perc(2), xylo; cel(optional); str). 2 movements.
Commissioned by: Artie Shaw. *First performed:* May 22, 1949; Chautauqua, N.Y. Artie Shaw, clarinet; Chautauqua Symphony Orchestra, Franco Autori, conductor.
Score & parts: C. Fischer. Rental.

[Concertante, Clarinet and Orchestra; Arr.]
D6.44 Concertante. 22'
For: clarinet and piano. 2 movements.
Score: C. Fischer, 1955. BPL BU
Disc: Orion ORS 79330, 1980. John Russo, clarinet and Lydia Walton Ignacio, piano. BU HU

[Concertino, Flute and Strings]
D6.45 Concertino. (1939)
Withdrawn.

[Concertino, Harmonica and Orchestra]
D6.46 Concertino.
Withdrawn.

[Concertino, Piano and Orchestra]
D6.47 Concertino. (1938)
Withdrawn.

[Concerto, Harp]
D6.48 Concerto. (1945) 20'
For: harp and orchestra(1-1-2-1; 2-0-0-0; timp, perc; str). Ballet (*Women's Song*).
First performed: Oct. 20, 1947; New York City. Little Orchestra Society, Thomas Scherman, conductor.
Score & parts: C. Fischer. Rental.
Disc: Columbia ML 4303, 1950. Edward Vito, harp; Little Orchestra Society, Thomas Scherman, conductor. BrU HU MIT

[Concerto, Pianos(2) and Orchestra]
D6.49 Concerto. (1941)
Withdrawn.

The Creed of Pierre Cauchon. *See* The Trial at Rouen. The Creed of Pierre Cauchon.

Dancing Sargeant. *See* Images. The Dancing Sergeant.

D6.50 Days of the Modern.
Withdrawn.

D6.51 Developing Flutist. (1972) 11'
For: flute and piano. Suite.
Score: E.B. Marks, 1972. BPL
Disc: in *Music for Flute and Piano by Four Americans,* Laurel-Protone LP 14, 1976. Leila Padorr, flute and Anita Swearengin, piano. WCRB

D6.52 Diversion of Angels. (1947-48; rev. 1955) 16'
For: orchestra(2-2-2-2; 4-3-3-1; perc; str). Ballet. *Choreography:* Martha Graham. *First performed:* Aug. 13,

1948; New London, Conn. Martha Graham. Originally titled Wilderness Stair. Concert version titled Serenade for Orchestra.
Score & parts: C. Fischer. Rental.

D6.53 Diversions. (1975) 8' 45"
For: piano. Suite. *Movements:* Preludio; Arietta; Caccia; Chorale; Giga. Version for organ titled Lyric Pieces for the Young Organist.
Score: E.B. Marks, 1975. BPL BU

D6.54 The Duke of Sacramento. (1942) 12'
For: pianos(2). Ballet. Withdrawn.

D6.55 Duo Concertato. (1945) 12'
For: violoncello and piano. *First performed:* Town Hall, New York City. Janos Scholz, violoncello.
Score: G. Schirmer, 1949. BU HU
Part: G. Schirmer, 1949. HU
Disc: Pelican LP 2010, 1979. Jeffrey Solow, violoncello and Albert Dominguez, piano. BU HU

The Dying Nightingale. *See* Love Songs. The Dying Nightingale.

D6.56 Epigraph. (1951) 7'
For: orchestra(2(&pic)-2-3-2; 4-3-3-1; timp, perc, glock; hp, cel; str).
Commissioned by: Mrs. Frederic H. Douglas in commemoration of her late brother, A. Lincoln Gillespie, Jr. for the Denver Symphony Orchestra. *First performed:* Jan. 29, 1952; Denver, Colo. Denver Symphony Orchestra, Saul Caston, conductor.
Score & parts: C. Fischer, 1958. Rental.
Study score: C. Fischer, 1958. BCM BPL BU HU UMB
Disc: American Recording Society ARS 31, 1953. Vienna State Symphony Orchestra, Hans Swarowsky, conductor.
Disc: Desto D 416/DST 6416, 1966. Reissue of American Recording Society ARS 31, 1953. BU HU

[Essays]
D6.57 Three Essays. (1974) 11'
For: clarinet and piano.
Score: E.B. Marks, 1974. BPL

[Evocations. Promise of Spring]
D6.58 Promise of Spring. (1970) 16'
For: chorus(SATB), chorus(children)(optional), orchestra(2(&pic)-2(&Ehn)-2(&bcl)-2(&cbsn); 4-3-3-1; timp, perc, glock, xylo; str). *Text:* based on *Spring* by Richard Hovey. *Commissioned by:* Tampa Arts Council for Generation '70.
First performed: Oct. 2, 1970; Tampa, Fla. Norman Dello Joio, conductor.
Score & parts: E.B. Marks, 1970. Rental.
Vocal score: E.B. Marks, 1970. BPL BU MIT
Choral part: E.B. Marks, 1970.

[Evocations. Promise of Spring; Arr.]
D6.59 Promise of Spring. 16'
For: chorus(SATB), chorus(children), band. *Text:* based on *Spring* by Richard Hovey.
Score & parts: E.B. Marks, 1970?
Vocal score: E.B. Marks, 1970. BPL

[Evocations. Visitants at Night]
D6.60 Visitants at Night. (1970) 16'
For: chorus(SATB) and orchestra(2(&pic)-2(&Ehn)-2(bcl)-2(cbsn); 4-3-3-1; timp, perc, glock, xylo; str).
Text: based on poem by Robert Hillyer.
Commissioned by: Tampa Arts Council for Generation '70. *First performed:* Oct 2, 1970; Tampa, Fla. Norman Dello Joio, conductor.
Score & parts: E.B. Marks, 1970. Rental.
Vocal score: E.B. Marks, 1970. BPL BU

Eyebright. *See* Love Songs. Eyebright.

D6.61 A Fable. (1946) 4'
For: Tenor, chorus(SATB), piano. *Text: The Mouse that Gnawed the Oak Tree Down* by Nicholas Vachel Lindsay. *First performed:* State University of New

York, College at Potsdam Chorus.
Vocal score: C. Fischer, 1947. BU HU

D6.62 Family Album. (1962) 7' 45"
For: piano(4-hands). *Movements:* Family
Meeting; Play Time, Story Time; Prayer
Time; Bed Time. *Dedication:* To G. and
V. and J. and N. Jr. *First performed:*
1962; CBS-Radio.
Score: E.B. Marks, 1962. BU

D6.63 Fantasia on a Gregorian Theme.
(1943) 6'-8'
For: violin and piano. 2 movements.
Score & part: C. Fischer, 1949. BPL BU

D6.64 Fantasies on a Theme by Haydn.
(1968) 14'
For: band. 3 movements. *Commissioned
by:* Michigan School Band and
Orchestra Association. *Dedication:*
Leonard Falcone, on his retirement as
Director of Bands at Michigan State
University. *First performed:* Jan. 17,
1969, Michigan State University Band.
Score: E.B. Marks, 1968. BPL BU NEC
Parts: E.B. Marks, 1968. NEC
Disc: Golden Crest ATH 5054, 1978.
West Texas State University
Symphonic Band, Gary Garner,
conductor. BU MIT

D6.65 Fantasy and Variations. (1961) 21'
25"
For: piano and
orchestra(2(&pic)-2-2(&bcl)-2; 4-3-3-1;
timp, perc; cel; str). *Commissioned by:*
Baldwin Piano and Organ Co. as part
of its centenary. *First performed:* Mar.
9, 1962; Cincinnati, Ohio. Lorin
Hollander, piano; Cincinnati Symphony
Orchestra, Max Rudolf, conductor.
Score & parts: C. Fischer, 1963. Rental.
Pf. red: C. Fischer, 1963. MIT
Disc: RCA Victor LM/LSC 2667, 1963.
Lorin Hollander, piano; Boston
Symphony Orchestra, Erich Leinsdorf,
conductor. BU HU MIT NEC

D6.66 From Every Horizon; a Tone
Poem to New York. 7' 30"-9'
For: band. *Commissioned by:* New York

Port Authority for a film of the same
title shown at the 1964 World's Fair.
Score: E.B. Marks, 1965. BPL BU HU
Parts: E.B. Marks, 1965.
Disc: Golden Crest ATH 5054, 1978.
West Texas State University
Symphonic Band, Gary Garner,
conductor. BU MIT

God Rest Ye Merry, Gentlemen. *See*
Christmas Music. God Rest Ye Merry,
Gentlemen.

D6.67 Greentree Thoroughbred. (1943)
Film music. Withdrawn.

Hark, the Herald Angels Sing. *See*
Christmas Music. Hark, the Herald
Angels Sing.

Heloise and Abelard. *See* A Time of
Snow.

D6.68 Here Is New York. (1957) 60'
For: orchestra. Film music. *First
performed:* Dec. 1957; CBS-TV. Includes
brief passages from New York
Profiles.
Score: C. Fischer. Rental.

[Here Is New York. Suite]
D6.69 Here Is New York. 35'
For: orchestra(2-2-2-2; 4-2-3-0; perc(3);
str). Based on music for CBS-TV.
Score & parts: C. Fischer. Rental.

Holy Infant's Lullaby. *See* Christmas
Music. Holy Infant's Lullaby.

D6.70 Homage to Haydn. (1968-69) 18'
For: orchestra(3-3-3-3; 4-3-3-1; timp,
perc, glock, xylo; str). 3 movements.
First performed: June 3, 1969; Little
Rock, Ark. Philadelphia Orchestra,
Eugene Ormandy, conductor.
Score & parts: E.B. Marks, 1969. Rental.
Disc: Louisville Orchestra LS 742, 1974.
Louisville Orchestra, Leonard Slatkin,
conductor. BrU BU HU NEC W

How Do I Love Thee? *See* Love Songs.
How Do I Love Thee?

Hymn to Saint Cecilia. *See* To Saint Cecilia.

D6.71 Hymn without Words. 9'
For: chorus and piano. 2 movements.
Vocal score: Associated, 1981.

[Images]
D6.72 Five Images. (1967) 7'-8'
For: orchestra(2(&pic)-2-2(&bcl)-2;
4-2-3-1; timp, perc, xylo; str). *Contents:*
Cortege; Promenade; Day Dreams; The
Ballerina; The Dancing Sargeant.
Score: E.B. Marks, 1967. BU
Parts: E.B. Marks, 1967. Rental.

[Images; Arr]
D6.73 Five Images. 8'
For: piano(4-hands). *Contents:* Cortege;
Promenade; Day Dreams; The Ballerina;
The Dancing Sargeant.
Score: E.B. Marks, 1967. BPL BU HU

[Images. The Dancing Sargeant]
D6.74 The Dancing Sargeant. 2'
For: orchestra(3-2-3-2; 4-2-4-2; str).
Score & parts: E.B. Marks.

[Images. The Dancing Sargeant; Arr.]
D6.75 The Dancing Sargeant. 2'
For: band.
Score & parts: E.B. Marks, 1980.

In dulci jubilo. *See* Colonial Ballads;
Variants on a Medieval Tune.

D6.76 A Jubilant Song. (1946) 6' 45"
For: chorus(SATB) and piano. *Text:*
adapted from Walt Whitman.
Commissioned by: G. Schirmer, Inc. for
the New York High School of Music
and Art. *First performed:* Columbia
University. New York High School of
Music and Art students.
Vocal score: G. Schirmer, 1946. BU L
NU
Disc: in *A Jubilant Song*, Columbia M
34134, 1976. Jo Ann Ottley, soprano;
Mormon Tabernacle Choir; Robert
Cundick, piano; Jerold D. Ottley,
conductor. BCM

[A Jubilant Song; Arr.]
D6.77 A Jubilant Song. (1946) 6' 45"
For: chorus(SSAA) and piano. *Text:*
adapted from Walt Whitman.
Vocal score: G. Schirmer, 1946.

D6.78 Lament. (1947) 4'
For: voice(medium) and piano. *Text:*
Chidiock Tichborn. Written on the eve
of the poet's execution. *First
performed:* Town Hall, New York City.
Manfred Hecht.
Score: in *Modern Art Songs*, C. Fischer,
1949. BU
Disc: Concert Hall D 6, 1950. John
Druary, tenor and Peter Rogell, piano.
HU
Reel: Jan. 23, 1978; Boston University.
Chloe Owen, soprano and Warren
Wilson, piano. BU

[The Lamentation of Saul, Baritone
and Orchestra]
D6.79 The Lamentation of Saul. (1954)
20'
For: Baritone and orchestra(3-3-3-2;
4-3-3-1; timp, perc; hp; str). *Text:*
adapted by the composer from the
play *David* by D.H. Lawrence. *Dedicated
to:* Elizabeth Sprague Coolidge
Foundation. *First performed:* Dec. 1962;
Baltimore, Md. Chester Ludgin, baritone;
Baltimore Symphony Orchestra.
Score & parts: C. Fischer, 1970. Rental.
Vocal score: C. Fischer, 1970. BU

[The Lamentation of Saul, Baritone,
Woodwinds, Strings]
D6.80 The Lamentation of Saul. (1954)
20'
For: Baritone, flute, oboe, clarinet,
viola, violoncello. *Dedicated to:*
Elizabeth Sprague Coolidge Foundation.
First performed: Aug. 1954; Pittsfield,
Mass.; Coolidge Foundation Concert.
Leonard Warren, baritone.
Score & parts: C. Fischer. Rental.
Vocal score: C. Fischer.

D6.81 Laudation. (1965) 5'
For: organ. 2 movements. *Commissioned
by:* Nita Akin and the Aeolian-Skinner

Organ Co. for the dedication of the new recital organ at Southern Methodist University, Tex.
Score: E.B. Marks, 1965. BU HU

D6.82 Leisure. 5'
For: chorus(SATB) and piano.
Vocal score: Associated, 1975. BU NEC

D6.83 The Listeners. (1955) 6'-7'
For: voice(medium) and piano. *Text:* Walter de la Mare. *First performed:* 1955; Juilliard School. Mack Harrell, baritone.
Score: C. Fischer, 1960. BPL BU
Disc: New World Records NW 300, 1978. William Parker, baritone and Dalton Baldwin, piano. BCM BU HU MIT NEC T W

The Louvre. *See* Scenes from The Louvre.

[Love Songs]
D6.84 Six Love Songs. (1949) 15'-20'
For: voice and piano. *Contents:* Eyebright (John Addington Symonds); Why So Pale and Wan, Fond Lover? (Sir John Suckling); Meeting at Night (Robert Browning); The Dying Nightingale (Stark Young); All Things Leave Me (Arthur Symons); How Do I Love Thee? (Elizabeth Barrett Browning).
Score: C. Fischer.

[Love Songs. All Things Leave Me]
D6.85 All Things Leave Me. (1949) 2' 30"-5'
For: voice(high) and piano. *Text:* Arthur Symons.
Score: C. Fischer, 1955. BCM BU

[Love Songs. The Dying Nightingale]
D6.86 The Dying Nightingale. (1949) 4'-4' 30"
For: voice(high) and piano. *Text:* Stark Young. *Dedication:* To Stark.
Score: C. Fischer, 1954. BCM BU

[Love Songs. Eyebright]
D6.87 Eyebright. (1949) 2'-2' 30"
For: voice(medium) and piano. *Text:*

John Addington Symonds.
Score: C. Fischer, 1954. BCM BU
Disc: in *The Art Song in America*, Duke University Press DWR 6417B, 1966. John Hanks, tenor and Ruth Friedberg-Erickson, piano. MIT

[Love Songs. How Do I Love Thee?]
D6.88 How Do I Love Thee? (1949) 2' 30"-3'
For: voice(high) and piano. *Text:* adapted from the poem by Elizabeth Barrett Browning.
Score: C. Fischer, 1954. BCM BU

[Love Songs. Meeting at Night]
D6.89 Meeting at Night. (1949) 2'
For: voice(high) and piano. *Text:* Robert Browning.
Score: C. Fischer, 1954. BCM BU
Disc: in *The Art Song in America*, Duke University Press DWR 6417B, 1966. John Hanks, tenor and Ruth Friedberg Erickson, piano. MIT

[*Love Songs. Why So Pale and Wan, Fond Lover?*]
D6.90 Why So Pale and Wan, Fond Lover? (1949) 1' 30"-2'
For: voice(medium) and piano. *Text:* Sir John Suckling.
Score: C. Fischer, 1954. BCM BU

D6.91 Lullaby. (1956)
For: chorus(unison) and organ or chorus(SATB) and organ(optional). Hymn. *Text:* Hush Thee, Princeling (Lullaby for the Christ Child) by Anna Elizabeth Bennett. *Commissioned by:* Albert Crist-Janer.
Vocal score: in *American Hymns Old and New*, Columbia University Press, 1980. BPL MIT W

D6.92 Lyric Fantasies. (1973) 17'
For: viola and string orchestra or viola, string quartet, double bass. 2 movements. *Dedicated to:* Michael Tree.
Score: Associated, 1975. HU MIT NEC
Parts: Associated, 1975. HU MIT
Pf. red: Associated, 1976. BPL BU HU NEC
Reel: Apr. 12, 1976; Boston University;

in *Omnibus: Music of the 20th Century, Concert 4*. Robert T. Karol, viola; Boston University Chamber Orchestra, Endel Kalam, conductor. BU

D6.93 Lyric Pieces for the Young. 14'-15'
For: piano. *Contents:* Boat Song; Prayer of the Matador; Street Cries; Night Song; The Village Church; Russian Dancer.
Score: E.B. Marks, 1971. BPL BU MIT T

[Lyric Pieces for the Young Organist]
D6.94 Five Lyric Pieces for the Young Organist. 9'
For: organ. Suite. *Contents:* Preludio; Arietta; Caccia; Choral; Giga. Version for piano titled Diversions.
Score: E.B. Marks, 1975. BPL BU

D6.95 Madrigal. (1947) 3' 30"
For: chorus(SATB) and piano. *Text:* adapted the from poem by Christina Georgina Rossetti. *First performed:* Town Hall, New York City. Collegiate Chorale.
Score: C. Fischer, 1947. BU HU

D6.96 Magnificat. (1941-42) 16'
For: orchestra(2(&pic)-0-2-0; 4-1-0-0; perc; pf; str). Winner of Town Hall Composition Award, 1943. *First performed:* 1942; Carnegie Hall, New York City. National Orchestral Association, Leon Barzin, conductor.
Score & parts: C. Fischer. Rental.

D6.97 Man From Independence. 4'
For: orchestra(2-2-3-1; 2-2-2-2; pf; str).
Score & parts: E.B. Marks.

D6.98 Mass. (1968) 21'
For: chorus(SATB), brass ensemble(horns(3), trumpets(3), trombones(2), trombone(bass), tuba), organ or piano. *Commissioned by:* Saint Mary's College (Notre Dame, Ind.) in commemoration of the 125th anniversary of the founding of the College.
Score: E.B. Marks, 1970. BPL BU HU

Parts: E.B. Marks, 1970. Rental.
Vocal score: E.B. Marks, 1970. BU

D6.99 Mass in Honor of the Blessed Virgin Mary. 19'
For: Cantor, congregation, chorus(SATB), organ, brass(optional)(horn, trumpets(2), trombone, tuba). *Commissioned by:* William M. Carrigan "with credit to the National Center for the Liturgy." *First performed:* Dec. 8, 1975; National Shrine of the Immaculate Conception, Washington, D.C.
Score & parts: Associated, 1975.
Vocal score: Associated, 1975. BPL BU HU NEC
Part(congregation): Associated, 1975.

D6.100 Mass in Honor of the Eucharist. 18'
For: Cantor, congregation, chorus(SATB), brass ensemble (horns(4), trumpets(3)(trombones(2), trombone(bass), tuba), organ, strings. *Commissioned by:* 41st International Eucharistic Congress Board of Governors, Philadelphia, Pa. *Dedicated to:* The Memory of Pope John XXII. *First performed:* Aug. 1976; Philadelphia, Pa. Unidentified 1,000-voice chorus.
Score & parts: Associated, 1976. Rental.
Vocal score: Associated, 1976. BPL BU
Part(congregation): Associated, 1976.
Disc: Golden Crest ATH 5059, [1978 or 1979]. Boston University Chorus; Max Miller, organ; Norman Dello Joio, conductor. HU

D6.101 Meditations on Ecclesiastes. (1955-56) 22'-24'
For: string orchestra. Ballet in 12 sections, based on Bible, O.T., Ecclesiastes 3:1-8. *Choreography:* There Is a Time by Jose Limon. Originally titled Variations on a Theme. Winner of Pulitzer Prize in Music, 1957. *First performed:* Dec. 17, 1957; Washington, D.C. (concert version). National Symphony Orchestra, Howard Mitchell, conductor.

Score & parts: C. Fischer. Rental. Also issued as ballet score with title, There Is a Time.
Study score: C. Fischer, 1959. BCM BPL BrU HU UMB
Disc: Composers Recordings CRI 110, 1957. Oslo Philharmonic Orchestra, Alfredo Antonini, conductor. BCM BrU BU HU HMA MIT NEC T W
Disc: Decca DL 10138/DL 710138, 1967. Princeton Chamber Orchestra, Nicholas Harsanyi, conductor. BU NEC
Disc: Golden Crest, nyp. Boston University Symphony, Joseph Silverstein, conductor.
Reel: Feb. 3, 1977; Hochschule der Kunste, Berlin, East Germany. Boston University Symphony, Joseph Silverstein, conductor. WCRB

Meeting at Night. *See* Love Songs. Meeting at Night.

D6.102 Mill Doors. (1939) 2' 30"-5'
For: voice(medium) and piano. *Text:* Carl Sandburg. *First performed:* Town Hall, New York City. M. Baumann, voice.
Score: C. Fischer, 1948. BU

D6.103 Music for Spoon River. (1941)
For: piano. Withdrawn.

D6.104 Music for the Young Pianist. (1964)
For: piano. Withdrawn.

D6.105 The Mystic Trumpeter. (1943) 12'-13'
For: Soprano, Tenor, Baritone, chorus(SATB), horn. Cantata. *Text:* adapted from Walt Whitman. *Dedicated to:* Robert Shaw and the Collegiate Chorale. *First performed:* Carnegie Hall, New York City. Collegiate Chorale, Robert Shaw, conductor.
Score: G. Schirmer, 1945. HU
Part(horn): G. Schirmer, 1945. Rental.
Vocal score: G. Schirmer, 1945. BPL BU

D6.106 New Born. (1946) 2'-3'
For: voice(medium) and piano. *Text:* from *No Boundary* by Lenore G. Marshall. *Dedication:* To Lenore. *First performed:* Town Hall, New York City. Nell Tangeman.
Score: C. Fischer, 1948. BU

D6.107 New York Profiles. (1949) 18'-20'
For: orchestra(2(&pic)-2(&Ehn)-2-2; 2-2-0-0; timp, xylo; str). Suite.
Movements: Prelude: The Cloisters; Caprice: The Park; Chorale Fantasy: The Tomb; Festival Dance: Little Italy.
Commissioned by: La Jolla Musical Arts Society. *Dedicated to:* Augustus L. Searle. *First performed:* Aug. 21, 1949; La Jolla, Calif. La Jolla Musical Arts Society Orchestra, Nikolai Sokoloff, conductor. Brief passages later used in Here Is New York.
Score & parts: C. Fischer, 1952. Rental.
Study score: C. Fischer, 1952. BPL BU HU UMB
Disc: Alco 1001, 1950. La Jolla Musical Arts Society Orchestra, Nikolai Sokoloff, conductor.
Disc: Composers Recordings CRI SD 209, 1966. Oslo Philharmonic Orchestra, Arthur Bennett Lipkin, conductor. BrU BU HU MIT NEC W

D6.108 Night Song. 2'
For: piano.
Score: in *American Composers of Today*, E.B. Marks, 1965. NEC

D6.109 Nocturne in E Major. (1946) 3' 5"
For: piano. *First performed:* 1949; Town Hall, New York City. Grace Gastagnetta.
Score: C. Fischer, 1950. BU
Disc: Golden Crest CRS 4111, 1972. Grant Johannesen. MIT NEC

D6.110 Nocturne in F-Sharp. 3' 1"
For: piano. *First performed:* 1949; Town Hall, New York City. Grace

Gastagnetta.
Score: C. Fischer, 1940. BU
Disc: Golden Crest CRS 4111, 1972.
Grant Johannesen. MIT NEC

D6.111 Note Left on a Doorstep. 2'
For: voice(medium) and piano. *Text:*
Lily Peter. *Dedicated to:* Lily Peter, the
writer of this lovely poem.
Score: E.B. Marks, 1969. BPL BU
Reel: Jan. 23, 1978; Boston University.
Chloe Owen, soprano and Warren
Wilson, piano. BU

D6.112 Notes from Tom Paine. (1975)
7'
For: chorus(SATB) and piano.
Commissioned by: J.C. Penney Co., Inc.
Vocal score: Associated.
Disc: in *A Bicentennial Celebration--200
Years of American Music*, Columbia M
33838, 1976. De Paur Chorus, Leonard
De Paur, conductor.

O Come, All Ye Faithful. *See* Christmas
Music. O Come, All Ye Faithful.

D6.113 O Sing unto the Lord. (1958) 4'
For: chorus(TTBB) and organ. *Text:*
Bible, O.T., Psalm 98. *Commissioned by:*
Yale University. *First performed:* New
Haven, Conn. Yale Glee Club.
Vocal score: C. Fischer, 1959. BU

D6.114 Of Crows and Clusters. 3'
For: chorus(SATB) and piano(optional).
Text: based on *Two Old Crows* by
Nicholas Vachel Lindsay.
Vocal score: E.B. Marks, 1972. BU
Disc: Golden Crest ATH 5059, [1978
or 1979]. Boston University Choruses,
Norman Dello Joio, conductor. HU

D6.115 On Stage. (1945) 15'
For: orchestra(2(&pic)-2(&Ehn)-2-2;
4-2-2-1; timp, perc, xylo; pf; str). Ballet
suite. *Movements:* Overture; Scene a
deux; Polka; Pas de deux; Waltz finale.
Commissioned by: Ballet Theatre. *First
performed:* Nov. 23, 1945; Cleveland,
Ohio.

Score & parts: G. Schirmer. Rental.
Pf. red: G. Schirmer, 1945. BPL

[On Stage; Arr.]
D6.116 On Stage.
For: piano(4-hands). Ballet suite.
Contents: Movements; Scene a deux;
Polka; Pas de deux; Waltz finale.
Score: G. Schirmer, 1955.

D6.117 The Poet's Song. 4'-5'
For: chorus(SATB) and piano. *Text:*
based on the poem by Alfred, Lord
Tennyson.
Vocal score: Associated, 1974. BU NEC
Disc: Golden Crest ATH 5059, [1978
or 1979]. Boston University Choruses,
Norman Dello Joio, conductor. HU

Prairie. *See* Sinfonietta.

D6.118 Prayers of Cardinal Newman.
(1960) 1' 20"
For: chorus(SATB) and organ or piano.
Text: from The Roman Missal,
translated by John Henry Cardinal
Newman. *Dedicated to:* Rev. Wilfred
Illies, Rev. Harold Pavelis, and the
Newman Choir of St. Cloud, Minn.
First performed: St. Cloud, Minn.
Newman Clubs.
Vocal score: C. Fischer, 1962. BPL BU
HU

D6.119 Prelude to a Young Dancer.
(1943) 4'
For: piano. *First performed:* Carnegie
Hall, New York City. Sidney Foster.
Score: G. Schirmer.

D6.120 Prelude: To a Young Musician.
(1943) 4'
For: piano. *First performed:* Carnegie
Hall, New York City. Sidney Foster.
Score: G. Schirmer, 1945. BU MIT NEC

[Profile of a Composer. A Ballad of
the Seven Lively Arts]
D6.121 A Ballad of the Seven Lively
Arts. (1958) 10'
For: piano and orchestra(2-2-2-2;
3-2-3-1; timp, perc, xylo; str). Film

music. *First performed:* Feb. 16, 1958; CBS-TV. Norman Dello Joio, piano. *Score & parts:* C. Fischer. Rental.

D6.122 Promise of Spring. *See* Evocations. Promise of Spring.

D6.123 Proud Music of the Storm. 15′ *For:* chorus(SATB), brasses(horns(3), trumpets(3), trombones(2), tuba), organ. *Text:* Walt Whitman. *Commissioned by:* Mr. & Mrs. J. Ralph Corbett, for 100th anniversary of the University of Cincinnati College-Conservatory of Music and for the dedication of its new home, the Corbett Center for the Performing Arts. *First performed:* Nov. 1967. *Score & parts:* E.B. Marks, 1967. Rental. *Vocal score:* E.B. Marks, 1967. BPL BU

D6.124 A Psalm of David. (1950) 25′-30′ *For:* chorus(SATB) and piano or chamber orchestra(0-0-0-0; 4-4-3-1; perc; str). *Text:* Bible, O.T., Psalm 51, Miserere mei, Deus. *Commissioned by:* State University of New York, College at Potsdam, Crane School of Music. *First performed:* 1951; State University of New York, College at Potsdam, Spring Festival. *Score & parts:* C. Fischer, 1951. Rental. *Vocal score:* C. Fischer, 1951. BPL BU HU T *Disc:* Concert Hall CHS 1118, 1952. State University of New York, College at Potsdam, Crane School of Music, Crane Chorus and Orchestra, Helen M. Hosmer, conductor. BU HU NEC

D6.125 Psalm of Peace. (1972) 16′ *For:* chorus(SATB), horn, trumpet, organ or piano. *Text:* Bible, O.T., Psalms. *Commissioned by:* Oratorio Society of Montgomery County, Bethesda, Md., for its 10th anniversary season. *Score & parts:* E.B. Marks, 1972. *Vocal score:* E.B. Marks, 1972. BPL BU

D6.126 The Psalmist's Meditation. (1978) 8′ 30″ *For:* chorus(mixed) and piano. 1

movement. *Text:* Bible, O.T., Psalm. *Commissioned by:* choral society of Hope, Mich. *First performed:* May 1979; Hope, Mich.

D6.127 Quartet for Bassoons. (1937) *For:* bassoons(4). Withdrawn.

D6.128 Quartet for Woodwinds. (1942) *For:* flute, oboe, clarinet, bassoon. Withdrawn.

[Quartet, Strings, Op. 1] **D6.129** String Quartet, Op. 1. (1974) *Disc:* Grenadilla GS 1023, [1977] Primavera String Quartet. HU

D6.130 Ricercari. (1946) 20′ *For:* piano and orchestra(2(&pic)-3-3-1; 4-3-3-0; timp, perc; str). 3 movements. *First performed:* Dec. 19, 1946. Norman Dello Joio, piano; New York Philharmonic, George Szell, conductor. *Score & parts:* C. Fischer. Rental. *Disc:* Concert Hall D 6, 1950. Germaine Smadja, piano; Concert Hall Symphony Orchestra, Henry Swoboda, conductor. HU *Reel:* Sept-Oct. 1959; Denver, Colo. Norman Dello Joio, piano; Denver Symphony, Saul Caston, conductor. HU

D6.131 The Ruby. 60′ *For:* voices and orchestra(3-3-3-2; 4-3-3-1; timp; cel; str). Opera in 1 act. *Libretto:* William Mass, adapted from *A Night at an Inn* by William Gibson (18th baron Dunsany). *First performed:* May 13, 1955; Indiana University School of Music. *Score & parts:* Ricordi. Rental. *Vocal score:* Ricordi. BPL BU HU *Reel:* May 1955. HU

D6.132 The Saintmaker's Christmas Eve. 35′ *For:* orchestra(3-3-3-2; 4-3-3-1; timp; cel; str). Film music for ABC-TV. *Score & parts:* Ricordi. Rental.

D6.133 Salute to Scarlatti. 9′ *For:* piano or harpsichord. 4

movements.
Score: Associated, 1981. HU

D6.134 Satiric Dances for a Comedy
by Aristophanes. (1974-75) 7'-9'
For: band. 3 movements. Originally
written for a production of a comedy
by Aristophanes for a performance by
the Boston University Theatre
Department, School for the Arts, in
1974. *Commissioned by:* Town of
Concord, Mass. and the Eastern
National Park and Monument
Association, in cooperation with the
United States National Park Service. In
commemoration of April 19, 1775.
First performed: July 17, 1975;
Concord, Mass. Concord Band, William
Toland, conductor.
Score: Associated, 1975. BPL BU HU
NEC
Parts: Associated, 1975.
Disc: Vogt L 2503, 1973. Concord Band,
William Toland, conductor. WCRB
Disc: Golden Crest ATH 5054, 1978.
West Texas State University
Symphonic Band, Gary Garner,
conductor. BU MIT
Disc: U.S. Coast Guard 8177. United
States Coast Guard Band, Lewis J.
Buckley, conductor. BU

D6.135 Scenes from The Louvre.
(1964?) 40'
For: orchestra. Film music. Winner of
Emmy Award, 1965. Written for
NBC-TV. *First performed:* Nov. 1964;
NBC-TV.
Score & parts: E.B. Marks.

[Scenes from The Louvre. Suite]
D6.136 Scenes from The Louvre. 10'
For: band. *Movements:* The Portals;
Children's Gallery; The Kings of France;
The Nativity Paintings; Finale.
Commissioned by: Baldwin-Wallace
College for the Baldwin-Wallace
Symphonic Band, Kenneth Snapp,
conductor. *First performed:* Mar. 13,
1966. Baldwin- Wallace Symphonic
Band, Norman Dello Joio, conductor.
Score: E.B. Marks, 1966. BPL BU HU

Parts: E.B. Marks, 1966. HU
Cassette: Dec. 9, 1972; New England
Conservatory. Massachusetts Youth
Wind Ensemble, Frank L. Battisti,
conductor. NEC

Seraphic Dialogue. *See* Triumph of St.
Joan Symphony.

D6.137 Serenade. (1947-48) 16'
For: orchestra(2(&pic)-2(&Ehn)-2(&bcl)-2;
4-3-3-0; timp, perc; hp, cel or pf; str).
First performed: Oct. 20, 1949;
Cleveland, Ohio. George Szell,
conductor. Ballet version titled
Diversion of Angels.
Score & parts: C. Fischer, 1963. Rental.
Study score: C. Fischer, 1963. BPL BU
HU UMB
Disc: American Recording Society ARS
36, 1953. Vienna State Symphony
Orchestra, Hans Swarowsky, conductor.
MIT NEC
Disc: Desto D 413/DST 6413, 1965.
Reissue of American Recording Society
ARS 36, 1953. BU HU MIT

D6.138 Sextet. (1941) 9'
For: recorders(3), violin, viola,
violoncello. *First performed:* 1943;
WNYC-FM, New York City. American
Music Festival.
Score & parts: Hargail.

Silent Night. *See* Christmas Music.
Silent Night.

D6.139 Sinfonietta. (1940) 20'
For:
orchestra(2(&pic)-2(Ehn)-2(&bcl)-2(cbsn);
4-3-3-1; timp, perc(2); str). Ballet.
Choreography: Prairie. *Commissioned by:*
Dance Players. *First performed:* 1941;
New York City (concert version).
Juilliard Orchestra; Edgar Schenkman,
conductor. *First performed:* 1942; New
York City (ballet version). Dance
Players.
Score & parts: G. Schirmer. Rental.

Somebody's Coming. *See* The Tall
Kentuckian. Somebody's Coming.

[Sonata, Piano, No. 1]
D6.140 Sonata No. 1. (1943) 12'-13'
3 movements. *Dedication:* To Sidney Foster in friendship and admiration.
First performed: Carnegie Hall, New York City. Sidney Foster.
Score: Hargail, 1947. HU

[Sonata, Piano, No. 2]
D6.141 Sonata No. 2. (1943-44) 12'-14'
3 movements. *First performed:* Carnegie Hall, New York City. Jorge Bolet.
Score: G. Schirmer, 1948. BPL HU MIT NEC

[Sonata, Piano, No. 3]
D6.142 Piano Sonata No. 3. (1948) 14'-16'
Movements: Theme & Variations; Presto e leggiero; Adagio; Allegro vivo e ritmico. The first and fourth movements, though somewhat shorter, are the same music as Variations, Chaconne and Finale for orchestra.
First performed: Carnegie Hall, New York City. Jorge Bolet.
Score: C. Fischer, 1948. BPL BrU HMA HU NEC
Disc: in *American Music*, Concert Disc M 1217/CS 217, 1960. Frank Glazer. BCM BrU
Disc: Music Library, MLR 7021, 195-. Del Purves.

[Sonata, Trumpet and Piano]
D6.143 Sonata. 12'
Commissioned by: International Trumpet Guild.
Score: Associated, 1981. HU MIT

[Sonata, Violin and Piano (1937)]
D6.144 Sonata in A.
Withdrawn.

[Sonata, Violin and Piano (1938)]
D6.145 Sonata. (1938)
Withdrawn.

[Sonata, Violoncello and Piano]
D6.146 Sonata. (1937)
Withdrawn.

D6.147 Un Sonetto di Petrarca. (1962) 3'
For: voice(high) and piano.
Score: E.B. Marks, 196-.
Score: in *New Vistas in Song*, E.B. Marks, 1964. BPL W
Reel: Jan. 23, 1978; Boston University. Chloe Owen, soprano and Warren Wilson, piano. BU

D6.148 Song of Affirmation; a Symphonic Cantata. (1952) 42'
For: Soprano, narrator, chorus(SATB), orchestra(2(&pic)-2-2-2; 4-3-3-1; timp, perc; str). *Text:* adapted from the poem *Western Star* by Stephen Vincent Benet.
Contents: Virgina (The First News of a Sweet Smelling Land); New England (There Were Human Beings Aboard the Mayflower, Not Merely Ancestors; The Star of the West (Americans Are Always Moving on). *Commissioned by:* Cornell College, Mt. Vernon, Iowa on the occasion of its first centennial.
First performed: May 1952; Cornell College, Mt. Vernon, Iowa.
Score & parts: C. Fischer, 1953. Rental.
Vocal score: C. Fischer, 1953. BPL BU T

D6.149 Song of the Open Road. (1952) 9' 51"
For: chorus(SATB), trumpet, piano. *Text:* Walt Whitman. *Commissioned by:* State University of New York, College at Potsdam, Crane School of Music.
Score: C. Fischer, 1963. BPL BU MIT T
Part(trumpet): C. Fischer, 1963.
Disc: Golden Crest ATH 5059, [1978 or 1979]. Boston University Choruses, Norman Dello Joio, conductor. HU

[Songs]
D6.150 Three Songs.
For: voice and piano. *Contents:* Lament; The Assassination; There Is a Lady, Sweet and Kind.
Score: C. Fischer.
Disc: Concert Hall D 6, 1950. HU

D6.151 Song's End. (1964?) 3'
For: chorus(SSA) and piano. *Text:* John Payne.
Vocal score: E.B. Marks, 1964.

D6.152 Songs of Abelard. (1969) 15'
30"-16'
For: Baritone(optional) and band.
Movements: Introduction; The Tryst;
Praise and Profanation; The Parting.
Commissioned by: Kappa Kappa Psi
National Fraternity and Tau Beta Sigma
National Sorority in honor of the 50th
Anniversary of the founding of Kappa
Kappa Psi. *First performed:* Aug. 22,
1969. Members of the Kappa Kappa Psi
National Fraternity and Tau Beta Sigma
National Sorority sponsored National
Intercollegiate Symphonic Band,
Norman Dello Joio, conductor. Earlier
version titled A Time of Snow.
Score: E.B. Marks, 1969. BPL BU HU
Parts: E.B. Marks, 1969.
Disc: Golden Crest 4186, 1980. Mary
Oderkirk, soprano; University of South
Florida Winds, James Croft, conductor.
BU
Reel: Nov. 2, 1978; Boston University.
Mac Morgan, baritone; Boston
University Wind Ensemble, Paul Gay,
conductor. BU

[Songs of Adieu]
D6.153 Three Songs of Adieu. (1962)
6'-6' 20"
For: voice(high) or voice(medium) and
piano. *Text:* Arthur Symons and John
Addington Symonds. *Contents:* After
Love; Fade, Vision Bright; Farewell.
Score: E.B. Marks, 1962 (version for
high voice). BCM BU HU
Score: E.B. Marks, 1962 (version for
medium voice).

[Songs of Chopin, Chorus(SA)]
D6.154 Three Songs of Chopin. (1963)
6'
For: chorus(SA) and orchestra(1-1-2-1;
2-2-1-0; timp, perc; str) or piano.
Contents: The Ring; The Lovers; The
Wish.
Vocal score: E.B. Marks.

[Songs of Chopin, Chorus(SATB)]
D6.155 Three Songs of Chopin. (1963)
6'
For: chorus(SA) and orchestra(1-1-2-1;

2-2-1-0; timp, perc; str) or piano.
Contents: The Ring; The Lovers; The
Wish.
Vocal score: E.B. Marks. BU

[Songs of Chopin, Orchestra]
D6.156 Three Songs of Chopin. (1963)
5' 30"
For: orchestra(1-1-2-1; 2-2-1-0; timp,
perc, glock; str). *Contents:* The Ring;
The Lovers; The Wish.
Score & parts: E.B. Marks, 1964. BU

[Songs of Chopin, Voice and Piano]
D6.157 Three Songs of Chopin. (1963)
6'
Contents: The Ring; The Lovers; The
Wish.
Score: E.B. Marks.

D6.158 Songs of Remembrance. 17'
For: Baritone and
orchestra(3(pic)-3(Ehn)-3(bcl)-3(cbsn);
4-3-3-1; timp, perc; hp; str). *Text:* John
Hall. Commissioned for: Saratoga
Performing Arts Festival. *First
performed:* Aug. 26, 1977; Saratoga,
N.Y.; Saratoga Performing Arts Festival.
Philadelphia Orchestra, Eugene
Ormandy, conductor.
Score & parts: Associated, 1979. Rental.
Vocal score: Associated, 1979. BrU BU

D6.159 Songs of Walt Whitman. 25'
For: Baritone, chorus(SATB),
orchestra(2(&pic)-2(&Ehn)-2(&bcl)-2(cbsn);
4-3-3-1; timp, perc(3), vibra, xylo; cel,
hp; str). Fourth movement has 3
optional brass choirs, each 3-3-3-0.
Text: adapted by the composer from
the poems of Walt Whitman. *Contents:*
I Sit and Look out upon the World;
The Dalliance of Eagles; Tears; Take
Our Hand. *Commissioned by and
dedicated to:* National Music Camp on
the occasion of the 7th International
Conference of the International Society
of Music Education, Interlochen, Mich.
Aug. 18-26, 1966.
Score & parts: E.B. Marks, 1966. Rental.
Vocal score: E.B. Marks, 1966. BPL BU
Vocal score: E.B. Marks, 1966 (No. 3). T

D6.160 Southern Echoes. 17'
For: orchestra(3(pic)-3(Ehn)-3(bcl)-3(cbsn);
4-3-3-1; timp, perc; str). Written for a
consortium of 20 orchestras of the
southeastern United States.
Score & parts: Associated. Rental.

D6.161 Stage Parodies, Piano Suite for
Young Players. (1974) 10'
For: piano(4-hands). *Contents:* The Actor;
The Writer; The Singer; The Dancer.
Score: Associated, 1975. BPL BU NEC

D6.162 Suite. (1941) 7'
For: piano. 4 movements. *First
performed:* Town Hall, New York City.
Abbey Simon.
Score: G. Schirmer, 1945. BPL BrU BU
HU NEC
Disc: Wardle TW 63, 1963. Gary
Towlen. BU
Reel: Mar. 18, 1976; Boston University.
Lenora Engdahl. BU

D6.163 Suite for the Young. 9'
For: piano. *Contents:* Mountain Melody;
Invention; Little Sister; Little Brother;
Lullaby; Echoes; Bagatelle; A Sad Tale;
Small Fry; Chorale Chant.
Score: E.B. Marks, 1964. HU MIT T

Sweet Sunny. *See* The Tall Kentuckian.
Sweet Sunny.

Symphonic Dances. *See* Variations,
Chaconne, and Finale.

D6.164 The Tall Kentuckian. 17'
For: voices, chorus(mixed),
orchestra(1-1-1-1; 3-3-3-1; timp, perc;
hp; str). Incidental music for the play
by Barbara Anderson. *First performed:*
June 15, 1953; Louisville, Ky. Louisville
Orchestra, Robert Whitney, conductor.
Score & parts: C. Fischer. Rental.

[The Tall Kentuckian. Somebody's
Coming]
D6.165 Somebody's Coming. 3'
For: chorus(SATB) and piano. *Text:*
Barbara Anderson.
Vocal score: C. Fischer, 1953. BU

[The Tall Kentuckian. Sweet Sunny]
D6.166 Sweet Sunny. 3'
For: chorus(SATB) and piano. *Text:*
Barbara Anderson.
Vocal score: C. Fischer, 1954. BU

D6.167 There Is a Lady Sweet and
Kind. (1946) 2'
For: voice(medium) and piano. *Text:*
anonymous. *First performed:* Leonard
Warren.
Score: C. Fischer, 1948. BU
Disc: Concert Hall D 6, 1950. John
Druary, tenor and Peter Rogell, piano.
HU
Disc: in *Cesare Valletti--Favorite Songs
from His Town Hall Recital. October 28,
1960*, RCA Victor LM/LSC 2540, 1961.
Cesare Valletti, tenor and Leo
Taubman, piano. BU
Reel: Jan. 23, 1978; Boston University.
Chloe Owen, soprano and Warren
Wilson, piano. BU

There Is a Time. *See* Meditations on
Ecclesiastes.

D6.168 Time of Decision. 32'
Film music. *Commissioned by:* David
Susskind for the television program
Talent Associates.
Score & parts: ms.

D6.169 A Time of Snow. (1969?) 35'
For: Baritone and chamber
orchestra(1-1-1-1; 1-1-1-1; timp, perc;
hp, pf; str). Ballet based on the story
of Heloise and Abelard. *Choreography:*
Martha Graham. Later version titled
Songs of Abelard.
Score & parts: E.B. Marks.

D6.170 To a Lone Sentry. (1943) 12'
For: chamber orchestra(1(pic)-0-1-0;
4-1-3-1; timp; str). *First performed:*
1946; New York City. Little Orchestra
Society, Thomas Scherman, conductor.
Score & parts: G. Schirmer.

D6.171 To Saint Cecilia, A Cantata.
(1958) 10'-15'
For: chorus(SATB) and piano or brass
ensemble(horns(3), trumpets(in C)(3),

trumpets(3), trombones(2), trombone(bass), tuba). *Text:* adapted by the composer from the poem, *A Song for St. Cecilia's Day* by John Dryden. *Commissioned by:* University of Kansas. *Dedicated to:* The Concert Band, University of Kansas, Clayton Krehbiel, conductor. *First performed:* Feb. 26, 1959; Kansas City, Kan.
Score & parts: C. Fischer, 1958. Rental.
Vocal score: C. Fischer, 1958. BPL BrU BU HU NEC T
Disc: in *Chorus, Organ, Brass and Percussion,* Kapp 9057/KCL 9057-S, 1961. Columbia University Chapel Choir with brass and percussion ensemble, Searle Wright, conductor.
Reel: Nov. 24, 1975; Boston University. Boston University Choruses, Joseph Huszti, conductor (titled Hymn to Saint Cecilia). BU

D6.172 The Trial at Rouen. (1955) 80'
For: voices, chorus, orchestra. Opera in 2 acts. *Libretto:* Norman Dello Joio. *First performed:* Apr. 8, 1956; NBC-TV; NBC Opera Theater. Elaine Malbin and Hugh Thompson, voices; members of Symphony on the Air, Peter Herman Adler, conductor. Later version titled The Triumph of St. Joan.
Score [& parts?]: G. Ricordi.
Reel: recording of first performance. HU

D6.173 The Trial at Rouen. The Creed of Pierre Cauchon]
The Creed of Pierre Cauchon. *For:* voice and orchestra.
Vocal score: Ricordi, 1957. BPL

[Trio, Clarinet, Horn, Bassoon]
D6.174 Trio for Woodwinds. (1941)
Withdrawn.

[Trio, Flute, Violoncello, Piano]
D6.175 Trio. (1944) 14'-15'
Commissioned by: Elizabeth Sprague Coolidge Foundation (Library of Congress). *First performed:* Mar. 1, 1944; New York City.

LeRoy-Foster-Scholz Trio.
Score & parts: C. Fischer, 1948. HU NEC

[Trio, Violin Violoncello, Piano]
D6.176 Trio. (1937)
Withdrawn.

D6.177 The Triumph of Saint Joan. (1949; rev. 1958-59)
For: voices, chorus, orchestra(2-2-2-2; 4-3-3-1; perc; str). Opera in 1 act. *Commissioned by:* Sarah Lawrence College through a grant from the Whitney Foundation (earlier version). Earlier version withdrawn; intermediary version titled The Trial at Rouen. Winner of New York Music Critics Circle Award, 1960. *First performed:* Apr. 16, 1959; New York City Opera (later version).
Score & parts: Deshon (later version).
Vocal score: Deshon (later version).

D6.178 The Triumph of St. Joan Symphony. (1951) 27'-30'
For: orchestra(2-3-2-2; 3-2-3-1; timp, perc, glock; str). Ballet. *Choreography:* Seraphic Dialogue by Martha Graham. *Movements:* The Maid; The Warrier; The Saint. *Commissioned by:* Louisville Orchestra. *First performed:* Dec. 5, 1951; Louisville, Ky. Martha Graham, dancer; Louisville Orchestra, Robert Whitney, conductor.
Score & parts: C. Fischer, 1954. Rental. Also issued with title, Seraphic Dialogue.
Study score: C. Fischer, 1954. BCM BPL BrU BU HU
Disc: Columbia ML 4615, 1952. Louisville Orchestra, Robert Whitney, conductor. BrU HU HUm MIT NEC W
Disc: Columbia CML 4615, 1968. Reissue of Columbia ML 4615, 1952.

D6.179 Vanity Fair. (1959) 35'
For: orchestra. Film music. *Commissioned by:* Talent Associates for dramatization of the novel by William Makepeace Thackeray. *First performed:* 1961; CBS-TV.
Score & parts: ms.

D6.180 Variants on a Mediaeval Tune. (1963) 11'-11' 40"
For: band. Variations on In dulci jubilo.
Commissioned by: Mary Biddle Duke Foundation for Duke University Band.
First performed: May 8, 1963; Duke University. Duke University Band.
Score: E.B. Marks, 1963. BCM BU HU NEC
Parts: E.B. Marks, 1963. NEC
Reel: Mar. 8, 1968. Boston Conservatory Concert Band; Herbert J. Philpott, conductor. BCM
Reel: Nov. 24, 1970. Boston Conservatory Concert Band; Herbert J. Philpott, conductor. BCM
Reel: Dec. 4, 1976; Boston University. Boston University Wind Ensemble. BU
Reel: March 27, 1977; Sanders Theatre, Harvard University. Metropolitan Wind Symphony, Rowland E. Sylvester, Jr., conductor. WGBH
Reel: Nov. 9, 1978. Boston Conservatory Wind ensemble; John Corley, conductor. BCM
Cassette: Nov. 9, 1978; New England Conservatory. NEC Repertory Wind Ensemble, Michael Walters, conductor. NEC
Cassette: Apr. 29, 1981; NEC Repertory Wind Ensemble, Michael Walters, conductor. NEC

D6.181 Variations and Capriccio. (1948) 12'-15'
For: violin and piano. *First performed:* Dec. 14, 1948; New York City. Angel del Reyes, violin.
Score & parts: C. Fischer, 1949. BU HU
Disc: Columbia ML 4845, 1954. Patricia Travers, violin and Norman Dello Joio, piano. BU HU
Disc: Columbia CML 4845, 1968. Reissue of Columbia ML 4845, 1954. BrU HU
Reel: Oct. 26, 1978; Boston University; in *Omnibus: Music of the 20th Century, Concert 2.* Elliot Markow, violin and Phillip Oliver, piano. BU

D6.182 Variations, Chaconne, and Finale. (1947) 21'
For: orchestra(2(&pic)-2(&Ehn)

-2(&bcl)-2(&cbsn); 4-3-3-1; timp, perc, xylo; str). Originally titled Three Symphonic Dances. Uses the same music as parts of Sonata, Piano, No. 3. *Dedicated to:* My father. Winner of New York Music Critics' Circle Award, 1948. First performed: Jan. 30, 1948. Pittsburgh Symphony, Fritz Reiner, conductor.
Score & parts: C. Fischer, 1950. Rental.
Study score: C. Fischer, 1950. BCM BPL BrU BU HU NEC UMB
Disc: Columbia ML 5263, 1958. Philadelphia Orchestra, Eugene Ormandy, conductor. BU HU

[Variations, Chaconne, and Finale; Arr.]
D6.183 Variations, Chaconne, and Finale.
For: orchestra(2-2-2-2; 2-2-1-0; timp, perc; str).
Score & parts: C. Fischer. Rental.

Variations on a Theme. *See* Meditations on Ecclesiastes.

D6.184 Vigil Strange. (1941) 9'-10'
For: chorus(SATB) and piano(4-hands).
Text: Walt Whitman. *First performed:* 1942; Greenwich House Music School.
Vocal score: Merrymount.

Visitants at Night. *See* Evocations. Visitants at Night.

D6.185 Western Star. (1946) Choral symphony. Withdrawn. Later version titled Song of Affirmation.

Why So Pale and Wan, Fond Lover? *See* Love Songs. Why So Pale and Wan, Fond Lover?

Wilderness Stair. *See* Diversion of Angels.

Women's Song. *See* Concerto, Harp.

D6.186 Years of the Modern. (1968) 15' 45"-16'
For: chorus(SATB), brass

ensemble(horns(3), trumpets(3), trombones(2), trombone(bass), tuba), percussion(timpani, glockenspiel, xylophone, bongo drums, snare drums, bass drums, chimes, hand cymbal, tam-tam, tambourine, woodblock). *Text:* adapted from poem by Walt Whitman. *Commissioned by:* Samuel S. Fels Fund for the 20th anniversary of the Singing City of Philadelphia.
Score & parts: E.B. Marks, 1968. Rental.
Vocal score: E.B. Marks, 1969. BPL BU HU

D7 DONALD E. DENNISTON

Born November 18, 1944, in Boston. *Education:* studied composition at Boston Conservatory and with Hugo Norden. *Related activities:* member of the Minnesota Composers Forum. BPL

WORKS

D7.1 And for All This..., Op. 22. (1977) 8'
For: chorus, woodwind quintet, harp.
Text: God's Grandeur by Gerard Manley Hopkins. *Commissioned by:* Church of the Covenant, Boston. *Dedicated to:* Jim Levinson and Louise Cochran. *First performed:* Jan. 11, 1981; Church of the Covenant, Boston and Sanders Theatre, Harvard University. Members of the Pro Arte Chamber Orchestra of Boston and Back Bay Chorale, Larry Hill, conductor.
Score & parts: ms.
Reel: recording of first performance.
Cassette: recording of first performance.

D7.2 Birthday Greetings: Fanfare, Op. 24. (1979) 2'
For: trumpets(4). *Dedicated to:* Daniel L. Fee.
Score: ms. in composer's hand.

D7.3 Capriccio, Op. 28. (1981) 2'
For: flute, violoncello, harpsichord. Written for Church of the Covenant, Boston, Arts Festival. *Dedication:* To

the memory of Checker. *First performed:* Apr. 4, 1981; Church of the Covenant, Boston. Brenda Kaufman, flute; Susan Randazzo, violoncello; David Schermer, harpsichord.
Score: ms. in composer's hand.
Cassette: recording of first performance.

D7.4 Celebration: Cosmic Hymn of Praise, Op. 18. (1974) 5'
For: chorus, trumpets(2), horn, trombone, tuba, percussion, organ.
Text: Bible, O.T., Psalm 150.
Commissioned by: Church of the Covenant, Boston. *Dedication:* To the Glory of God. *First performed:* June 2, 1974; Church of the Covenant, Boston. Larry Hill, conductor.
Score & parts: ms.
Reel: recording of first performance.
Cassette: recording of first performance.
Cassette: June 17, 1979; Walker Art Center, Minneapolis, Minn. Minnesota Composers Forum.

D7.5 Concerto, Op. 16a. (1970-71; rev.) 20'
For: orchestra(4-3-4-4; 4-4-4-1; timp, perc(6); hp, pf, cel; str). *Dedicated to:* Carlo Maria Giulini and the Chicago Symphony Orchestra.
Scoe: ms. (earlier version).
Score: ms. (later version).

D7.6 Evening Music, Op. 23. (1979) 25'
For: Tenor and orchestra(3-3-3-3; 4-3-0-0; timp, perc(5), hp, pf, cel; str).
Contents: The Night Wanderer (Douglas Shea); Instrumental Passage: The Evening Air; Night Has Fallen (Alfred, Lord Tennyson); Instrumental Passage: The Evening Star (Percy Bysshe Shelley). *Dedication:* In memory of Lord Benjamin Britten.
Score: ms. in composer's hand.

D7.7 Ode for Small Orchestra, Op. 12. (1970) 8'
For: chamber orchestra(1-1-1-0; 0-0-0-0; perc(2); hp, pf; str). *Dedication:* In

memory of Sir John Barbirolli.
Score: ms.

[Pieces, Op. 6]
D7.8 Six Pieces for Large Orchestra.
(1966) 10'
For: orchestra(4-4-4-4; 6-4-4-1; timp,
perc; hps(2), pf, cel; str). *Dedicated to:*
Mrs. Harry E. Cash.
Score: ms. in composer's hand.

[Pieces, Op. 17a]
D7.9 Six Pieces. (1973) 10'
For: orchestra(3-3-3-3; 4-3-3-1; timp,
perc(5); hp, pf, cel; str). *Dedicated to:*
Rouben Gregorian and David Callahan;
fourth piece in memory of Otto
Klemperer.
Score: ms.

[Pieces, Op. 27]
D7.10 Three Pieces. (1980)
For: organ. *Dedicated to:* David
Schermer. Written in homage to Leos
Janacek. *First performed:* June 28,
1981; Church of the Covenant, Boston
(2nd movement). David Schermer.
Score: ms. in composer's hand.

D7.11 A Poet's Song, Op. 19. (1975) 10'
For: chorus and orchestra(3-3-3-3;
4-3-3-1; timp, perc(5); hp, pf, cel; str).
Text: excerpts from *Leaves of Grass* by
Walt Whitman. *Dedication:* In
celebration of the American
Bicentennial, 1776-1976. To Stanislaw
Dyzbardis.
Score & parts: ms.

[Short Pieces]
D7.12 Three Short Pieces, Op. 25.
(1980) 3'
For: harpsichord. *Dedicated to:* David
Schermer. *First performed:* Apr. 19,
1980; Church of the Covenant, Boston.
David Schermer.
Score: ms. in composer's hand.

D7.13 Structures, Op. 3. (1965) 15'-20'
For: orchestra(3(&pic)-2(&Ehn)
-3(&bcl)-3(&cbsn); 4-4-4-1; timp, perc,
glock, vibra, xylo; hps(2), pf, cel; str).
1 movement. *Dedication:* To my mother

and father and Mrs. George Conroy.
Score: ms. in composer's hand. BPL

D7.14 Sun Song, Op. 11 (1968; rev.) 15'
For: Soprano, chorus(SATB),
orchestra(3(&pic)-2-(&Ehn)
-2(&bcl)-2(&cbsn); 4-3-3-1; timp, perc;
hp, pf, cel; str). 1 movement. *Text:*
Cantico de lo frato sole by St. Francis
of Assisi. *Dedication:* In memory of
Peter Brooks. Revised by Carlo Maria
Giulini. *First performed:* June 7, 1969;
Boston Conservatory (earlier version).
Christine Whittlesey, soprano; Boston
Conservatory Orchestra and Boston
Conservatory Chorus, Rouben Gregorian,
conductor. Later version first
performed Mar. 11, 1971; Elsa
Charlston, soprano; Chicago Symphony
Orchestra; Chicago Symphony Chorus,
Carlo Maria Giulini, conductor.
Score & parts: ms.
Vocal score: reprod. of ms. BCM BPL
Reel: recording of first performance
(earlier version). BCM

[Sun Song, Op. 11; Arr.]
D7.15 Sun Song. (1970)
For: Soprano, chorus(SATB), piano.
Text: Cantico de lo frato sole by St.
Francis of Assisi. Arranged in
collaboration with Robert LeClair and
John C. Adams.
Vocal score: reprod. of ms. BPL

D7.16 To Everything There Is a
Season, Op. 26. (in progress)
For: orchestra(2-2-2-2; 4-2-0-0; timp,
perc(2); hp; str). *Dedicated to:* Carlo
Maria Giulini.

D8 ROBERT DI DOMENICA

Born March 4, 1927, in New York City.
Moved to Boston area 1969. *Education:*
studied composition with Wallingford
Riegger and Josef Schmid. *Awards:*
Guggenheim Grant (1972-73). *Related
activities:* flutist (Metropolitan Opera
Orchestra, Modern Jazz Quintet),
conductor, teacher; member of the
faculty of the New England

Conservatory (1969- ; Dean, 1976-78).
NEC

WORKS

D8.1 Arrangements. (1979) 15'
For: Soprano, flute/piccolo/flute(alto),
clarinet/clarinet(bass), violin,
violoncello, piano, percussion, tape. 3
movements. *Text:* Johann Wolfgang von
Goethe; English translation by Michael
Hamburger. Work based on the music
of John Cage, Lester Young, Bela
Bartok. *Commissioned by:* Collage.
Dedicated to: The members of Collage.
First performed: Mar. 9, 1980; Sanders
Theatre, Harvard University. Joan
Heller, soprano; John Heiss, flute;
Robert Annis, clarinet; Ronald Knudsen,
violin; Joel Moerschel, violoncello;
Christopher Oldfather, piano; Frank
Epstein, percussion; Robert Di
Domenica, conductor.
Score & parts: Margun.
Tape: Margun. Rental.

D8.2 The Balcony. (1972)
For: Sopranos(2), Mezzo Sopranos(2),
Altos(2), Tenors(2), Baritones(2), Basses
(2), actors(8), chorus,
orchestra(0-0(&Ehn)-0(&Ebcl &bcl), ssax,
asax, tsax, barsax-1(&cbsn); 3-4-4-0;
timp(4), perc, glock, vibra, xylo; hp, gt;
str). Opera in 2 acts. *Libretto:* based on
the play by Jean Genet, English
translation by Bernard Frechtman. *First
performed:* May 9, 1975; New England
Conservatory (Scenes 1-3). NEC Opera
Theatre, David Bartholomew, director;
NEC Symphony Orchestra, Gunther
Schuller, conductor.
Score & parts: ms. in composer's hand.
Cassette: recording of first partial
performance. NEC

D8.3 Black Poems. (1976) 16'
For: Baritone, piano, tape. *Contents:*
Compensation (Paul Laurance Dunbar);
For Paul Lawrence Dunbar (Countee
Cullen); Pastourelle (Hayes); Finis
(Waring Cuney); Invocation (Johnson);
Adjeuration (Benjamin Franklin Wheeler);

Death of a Friend (Pauli Murray); Those
Winter Sundays (Robert Earl Hayden); I
Loved You Once (Dudley Randall); Song
(Holman); So? (James P. Vaughn).
Dedicated to: Daniel Windham and the
eleven poets. *First performed:* Apr. 2,
1977; New England Conservatory.
Daniel Windham, baritone and Leona Di
Domenica, piano.
Score: Margun.
Score: in *Auration; a Creative Writing
Effort of the New England Conservatory
of Music*, vol. 1, no. 1, Spring 1977
(Death of a Friend). NEC
Tape: Margun. Rental.
Cassette: recording of first
performance. NEC
Cassette: Nov. 21, 1977; New England
Conservatory; in *Enchanted Circle*.
Daniel Windham, baritone and Leona Di
Domenica, piano. NEC

[Concerto, Piano]
D8.4 Piano Concerto. (1963) 20'
For: piano and orchestra. Second
movement based on Alban Berg's
Violin Concerto.
Score and parts: ms. in composer's
hand.

D8.5 Concerto, Violin and Chamber
Orchestra. (1962) 20'
For: violin and chamber
orchestra(1-1-1-1; 0-0-0-0; str(1-1-1-1-1)).
4 movements.
Score & parts: MJQ, 1962.
Disc: in *New England Conservatory of
Music Faculty Composers*, Golden Crest
NEC-119, 1979. Eric Rosenblith, violin;
NEC Contemporary Music Ensemble,
Gunther Schuller, conductor. NEC T
Cassette: Mar. 3, 1970; New England
Conservatory; in *An Evening of
Contemporary Music*. Juan Ramirez,
violin; Richard Pittman, conductor. NEC
Cassette: Feb. 28, 1976; New England
Conservatory; American Society of
University Composers, 11th Annual
Conference. Eric Rosenblith, violin; NEC
Contemporary Music Ensemble, Gunther
Schuller, conductor. NEC

D8.6 Concerto, Wind Quintet, Strings and Timpani. (1964) 21'
Score & parts: E.B. Marks, 1964.

D8.7 Concord Revisited. (1978) 30'
For: piano, Soprano, Bass, tape, chamber orchestra(2(&pic)(afl)-2(Ehn)-2(&bcl)-2(&cbsn); 2-2-2(&btrb)-0; timp(3), perc, glock, vibra; hp(2), cel; 0-0-0-0-0). *Text:* from *The Scarlet Letter* by Nathaniel Hawthorne. *Contents:* Prologue; Emerson; Hawthorne; The Alcotts; Thoreau; Epilogue. *First performed:* May 7, 1981; New England Conservatory. Leona Di Domenica, piano; Larry Livingstone, conductor.
Score & parts: Margun. Rental.
Tape: Margun. Rental.

Death of a Friend. *See* Black Poems.

D8.8 The First Kiss of Love. (1960) 4'
For: Soprano and piano. *Text:* Lord George Noel Gordon Byron.
Score: Edition Musicus, 1960.
Cassette: May 9, 1975; New England Conservatory; in *A Program of American Songs.* Jacqueline Simpson, soprano. NEC
Cassette: Nov. 20, 1978; New England Conservatory; in *Enchanted Circle.* Barbara Winchester, soprano and Malcolm Peyton, piano. NEC

D8.9 Improvisations. (1974) 12'
For: piano. 4 movements. *First performed:* Mar. 18, 1975; New England Conservatory; in An Evening of Contemporary Music. Leona Di Domenica.
Score: Margun.
Disc: in *Leona Di Domenica in Live First Performances of the Solo Piano Music of Robert Di Domenica,* GM Records 2001-2002.
Cassette: recording of first performance. NEC
Cassette: Feb. 7, 1980; New England Conservatory; in *A Recital of Music by Robert Di Domenica.* Leona Di Domenica. NEC

[Movements]
D8.10 Four Movements for Piano. (1959) 8' 30"
First performed: Dec. 19, 1959; Donnell Library, New York City; Composer's Forum. Leona Di Domenica.
Score: Margun.
Disc: Leona Di Domenica in Live First Performances of the Solo Piano Music of Robert Di Domenica, GM Records 2001-2002.

D8.11 Music for Flute and String Orchestra. (1967) 17'
Dedicated to: Julius Baker. *First performed:* Nov. 16, 1980; Longy School of Music. Julius Baker, flute; Lyric Arts Ensemble, Thomas Toscano, conductor.
Score & parts: E.B. Marks. Rental.

[Quartet, Flute, Violin, Horn, Piano]
D8.12 Quartet. (1959) 11'
3 movements. *Dedicated to:* Matthew Raimondi and Gunther Schuller.
Score & parts: Margun, 1976. BPL NEC T
Cassette: Feb. 7, 1980; New England Conservatory; in *A Recital of Music by Robert Di Domenica.* Robert Stallman, flute; Eric Rosenblith, violin; David Hoose, horn; Leona Di Domenica, piano; Robert Di Domenica, conductor. NEC

[Quartet, Flute, Violin, Viola, Violoncello]
D8.13 Quartet. (1960) 16'
3 movements.
Score & parts: E.B. Marks. Rental.

[Quartet, Strings]
D8.14 String Quartet. (1960) 50'
Score & parts: ms. in composer's hand.

D8.15 Quintet. (1965) 22'
For: clarinet and string quartet. 4 movements. *Dedicated to:* Charles Russo. *First performed:* May 1971; New England Conservatory: in A Festival of New England Composers Past and Present. Composers String Quartet.

Score & parts: Margun, 1978. NEC
Cassette: recording of first
performance. NEC

D8.16 Saeculum aureum. (1967) 19'
For: flute, piano, tape.
Score: ms. in composer's hand.

D8.17 Sextet. (1957) 15'
For: woodwind quintet and piano
Score & parts: E.B. Marks, 1957. Rental.

[Short Pieces]
D8.18 Eleven Short Pieces. (1973)
For: piano. *Dedicated to:* Leona Di
Domenica. *First performed:* Mar. 18,
1975; New England Conservatory; in An
Evening of Contemporary Music. Leona
Di Domenica.
Score: Margun.
Disc: in *Leona Di Domenica in Live
Performances of the Solo Piano Music
of Robert Di Domenica*, GM Records
2001-2002.
Cassette: recording of first
performance. NEC
Cassette: Feb. 7, 1980; New England
Conservatory; in *A Recital of Music by
Robert Di Domenica*. Leona Di
Domenica. NEC

[Short Songs]
D8.19 Four Short Songs. (1975) 9'
For: Soprano, flute, clarinet, violin,
viola, violoncello, piano. *Text:*
Johannes Bobrowski; translated by Ruth
Mead and Matthew Mead. *Contents:* To
the Chassid Barkan; Lake Shore;
Always To Be Named; Village Music.
Commissioned by: Goethe Institut
(Boston) for the Boston Musica Viva.
First performed: Apr. 13, 1976; Longy
School of Music. Elsa Charlston,
soprano; Boston Musica Viva, Richard
Pittman, conductor.
Score & parts: Margun. Rental.
Cassette: Apr. 27, 1978; New England
Conservatory. Deborah Pfautsch,
soprano; NEC Contemporary Music
Ensemble, Larry Livingston, conductor.
NEC

D8.20 Sonata after Essays for Piano.
(1977) 30'
For: piano, Soprano, Baritone,
flute/flute(alto), tape. *Text:* from *The
Scarlet Letter* by Nathaniel Hawthorne.
Contents: Prologue; Emerson; Hawthorne;
The Alcotts; Thoreau; Epilogue.
Dedicated to: Charles Ives and the
authors he loved. *First performed:* Nov.
20, 1978; New England Conservatory; in
Enchanted Circle. Leona Di Domenica,
piano; Linda Gabriele, mezzo soprano;
David Ripley, baritone; Ellen Morris,
flute.
Score & parts: Margun. Rental.
Tape: Rental.
Disc: in *Leona Di Domenica in Live
First Performances of the Solo Piano
Music of Robert Di Domenica*, GM
Records 2001-2002.
Cassette: recording of first
performance. NEC

[Sonata, Flute and Piano]
D8.21 Sonata. (1957) 9'
Score & part: Editions Musicus, 1957.

[Sonata, Saxophone(Alto) and Piano]
D8.22 Sonata. (1968) 16'
4 movements. *Dedicated to:* Victor
Morosco.
Score & part: MJQ, 1968.

D8.23 Sonata, Violin and Piano. (1966)
27'
3 movements.
Score & part: ms. in composer's hand.
Cassette: Apr. 27, 1971; Jordan Hall,
Boston. Kenneth Sarch, violin and
Leona Di Domenica, piano.
Cassette: Feb. 7, 1980; New England
Conservatory; in *A Recital of Music by
Robert Di Domenica*. Eric Rosenblith,
violin and Leona Di Domenica, piano.
NEC

D8.24 Sonatina, Piano. (1958) 8'
3 movements.
Score: Edition Musicus, 1958. BU
Disc: in *Leona Di Domenica in Live
First Performances of the Solo Piano
Music of Robert Di Domenica*. GM

Records 2001-2002.
Cassette: Dec. 1, 1970; New England
Conservatory; in *An Evening of
Chamber Music.* Wendy Covell. NEC
Cassette: Feb. 7, 1980; New England
Conservatory; in *A Recital of Music by
Robert Di Domenica.* Leona Di
Domenica. NEC

D8.25 Songs from Twelfth Night. (1976)
6'
For: Tenor, flute, viola da gamba,
harpsichord. *Text:* from *Twelfth Night*
by William Shakespeare. 3 movements.
First performed: Nov. 6, 1977; New
England Conservatory. Richard Riley,
tenor; Susan Thomas, flute; Karen
Larsen, viola da Gamba; Daryl Bichel,
harpsichord.
Score & parts: ms. in composer's hand.

D8.26 Symphony. (1961) 18'
For: orchestra(3-2-2-2; 4-3-3-1; timp,
perc; str). 3 movements. *First
performed:* Nov. 15, 1972; New England
Conservatory. NEC Symphony
Orchestra, Gunther Schuller, conductor.
Tone row based on beginning of the
development section in the fourth
movement of Symphony No. 40 by
Wolfgang Amadeus Mozart.
Score & parts: E.B. Marks, 1961.
Reel: May 2, 1975. WGBH
Cassette: recording of first
performance. NEC

D8.27 Trio. (1966) 18'
For: flute, bassoon, piano. 3
movements.
Score & parts: ms. in composer's hand.
Cassette: May 4, 1975; New England
Conservatory. Ellen Morris, flute;
Masahito Tanaka, bassoon; Marilyn
Hixson, piano. NEC

D8.28 Variations on a Tonal Theme.
(1961) 4'
For: flute.
Score: Editions Musicus, 1961.

D8.29 Wind Quintet. (1963)
For: Soprano and woodwind quintet.
Score & parts: ms. in composer's hand.
Cassette: May 13, 1974; New England
Conservatory; in *Monday Night Concert
Series.* Cheryl Cobb, soprano; Stephanie
Jutt, flute; Sandra Apeseche, oboe; Ian
Greitzer, clarinet; Richard Sharp,
bassoon; Pamela Paikin, horn. NEC

D9 JOHN F. DUESENBERRY

Born October 10, 1950, in Boston.
Education: studied composition with
Joyce Mekeel, Allan W. Schindler, John
Goodman (Boston University, B.M.,
1974); Robert Stern (University of
Massachusetts, Amherst, M.M., 1978);
electronic music at the Computer
Music Workshop, Colgate University
(August 1979), Workshop in Computer
Music, Massachusetts Institute of
Technology (June-July, 1979), Boston
School of Electronic Music (Summer
1974). *Awards:* Boston University
Undergraduate Composition Prize (1974),
League-ISCM National Composers
Competition (Honorable Mention, 1974),
Massachusetts Council on the Arts and
Humanities, Artist Fellowship Program
in composition (1979). *Related
activities:* instructor, Boston School of
Electronic Music (1974-76) and director
(1978-79). BU

D9.1 Etude. (1979)
For: tape(2-channel). *First performed:*
Aug. 1979; 1st Annual Australian
Electronic Music Festival, La Trobe
University, Melbourne. *Tape.*

D9.2 Incidental Music for The Sleep of
Reason. (1975)
For: tape(2-channel). *Commissioned by:*
Boston Unversity Theatre Department.
First performed: Mar. 1975.

D9.3 Moduletude. (1979)
For: tape(computer). Generated at the
Experimental Music Studio,

Massachusetts Institute of Technology.
First performed: Aug. 1979;
Massachusetts Institute of Technology.
Tape. Disc: Opus One Records 60, 1980.

D9.4 Movement. (1974)
For: string quartet. *First performed:*
Apr. 1974; Boston University.
Score & parts: ms.

[Movements]
D9.5 4 Movements. (1976-77)
For: tape and piano(prepared). *First
performed:* Nov. 1977; University of
Massachusetts, Amherst. John
Duesenberry.
Score: ms. *Tape. Disc:* Opus One
Records 60, 1980. John Duesenberry.

D9.6 Phrase. (1977)
For: tape(synthesized)(2-channel; voice
of Carol Crawford). *Text:* Arthur
Rimbaud. *First performed:* Nov. 1977;
University of Massachusetts, Amherst.
Tape.
Disc: Opus One Records 60, 1980.

D9.7 Plath Poems. (1977-78)
For: chorus(women) and chamber
orchestra(woodwinds, brass, percussion,
violin, viola). *Text:* Sylvia Plath. *First
performed:* Apr., 1978; University of
Massachusetts, Amherst (4th
movement). University of
Massachusetts Group for New Music,
Charles Fussell, conductor.
Score: ms.

D9.8 6:02. (1974)
For: tape(2-channel). *First performed:*
1975; Berklee College of Music. *Tape.*

[Songs from A Season in Hell]
D9.9 3 Songs from A Season in Hell.
(1973)
For: Mezzo Soprano and piano. *Text:*
Arthur Rimbaud. *First performed:* Apr.
1974; Boston University. Mary Ann
Sego, mezzo soprano and John
Duesenberry, piano.
Score: ms.

D9.10 3:19. (1975)
For: tape(2-channel). *First performed:*
Nov. 1975; WGBH-FM, Boston; The
Composer's Show. *Tape.*

D9.11 Und fast ein Maedchen wars.
(1976)
For: Soprano, oboe, clarinet, bassoon,
violin, viola, violoncello. *Text:* Rainer
Maria Rilke.
Score & parts: ms.

[Variations, Interludes]
D9.12 3 Variations, 2 Interludes. (1976)
For: tape(2-channel). *First performed:*
Aug. 1976; Boston Conservatory.
Tape.
Disc: Opus One Records 60, 1980.

E1 PAUL EARLS

Born June 9, 1934, in Springfield, Mo.
Education: studied composition with
Bernard Rogers and Howard Hanson
(Eastman School of Music). *Awards:*
Rochester Philharmonic Orchestra
Recording Prize (1959), Guggenheim
Grant, Huntington Hartford Fellowship,
MacDowell Colony Fellowship, Mary
Duke Biddle Foundation grant, National
Endowment for the Arts Grant, Yaddo
Fellowship. *Related activities:* served
on the faculties of Southwest Missouri
State University, Chabot College,
University of Oregon, Duke University,
Massachusetts College of Art, Boston
University, Center for Advanced Visual
Studies at the Massachusetts Institute
of Technology (1969-). MIT

WORKS

E1.1 Alpha/Numeric 1: Prologue & Ten
Events. (1970)
For: chorus and audience. *Text:*
personal name phonemes. *First
performed:* May 1970; Duke University.
Perf. dir: MIT

E1.2 Alpha/Numeric: E. (1970)
For: instruments(unspecified)(3-7).
Aleatoric music. Based on encoded

personal data of the performers. *First performed:* May 1970; Duke University. *Perf. dir:* MIT

E1.3 Analogue (Lightworks, No. 1) . (1970)
For: tape(synthesized). *First performed:* May 1970; Duke University.
Tape: available from composer.

E1.4 And on the Seventh Day. (1959)
For: chamber orchestra. *First performed:* 1960; Rochester, N.Y. Eastman-Rochester Symphony Orchestra, Howard Hanson, conductor.
Score: reprod. of ms.; available from composer.
Disc: in *Music for Quiet Listening*, Mercury ERA 1003.

Aubade. *See* Summer, 1967.

E1.5 A Band of Solomon's Dukes. (1968)
For: band.
Score: reprod. of ms.; available from composer.

E1.6 The Bells. (1975)
For: Soprano, choruses(2), brasses, tape. *Text:* Edgar Allan Poe. *First performed:* Nov. 1976; University of Lowell. Su Harmon, soprano; University of Lowell Chorale, Edward Gilday, conductor.
Score: reprod. of ms. MIT

Brementown Musicians. *See* A Grimm Duo. Brementown Musicians.

E1.7 Brevis Mass. (1967; rev. 1971)
For: Sopranos(2), Mezzo Soprano, Alto, Tenor, chorus(SATB), chamber chorus (optional), organ or piano, flute, clarinet, trumpet, horn, trombone, double bass, percussion; earlier version accompaniment for piano, double bass, percussion. *Text:* Ordinary of the Mass, English and Latin. *Dedicated to:* Ruth Steese and the Penfield Choir. *First performed:* 1967; Rochester, N.Y.
Vocal score: Ione, 1974 (version for organ and percussion). BPL MIT NEC

E1.8 Brillo. (1973) Duration variable.
For: tape(live). Dance music. *Commissioned by:* Gus Solomons Jr. Dance Company. *First performed:* 1973; New York City. Gus Solomons Jr. Dance Company.
Score/perf. dir: available from composer.

E1.9 Cat Nap. (1979)
For: oscilloscope, laser, synthesizer, narrator, cat. Sounds generated from signals recorded from a sleeping cat. *Perf. dir.*
Tape: [1979?]. Dr. J. Allen Hobson, narrator.

E1.10 Centerbeam Music. (1977)
For: laser and tape. *Commissioned by:* Alcoa, United States Information Agency and others. Music and sound lines for collaborative sculpture created by the Center for Advanced Visual Studies, Massachusetts Institute of Technology for Documenta 6, Kassel, West Germany. *First performed:* June through October, 1977.
Tape: available from composer.

E1.11 Chabot. (1962)
For: voice or chorus(unison). *Text:* Leo Dodson. Alma mater for Chabot College. *First performed:* May 1962.
Score: MIT

Characters. *See* Divisions in Twelve.

Chestering. *See* CityRing. Chestering.

Chesterlay. *See* CityRing. Chesterlay.

E1.12 CityRing. (1975) 120'
For: bells(20), handbells(optional), bands(5-part), chorus(mixed)(optional), orchestra. *Contents:* Plaining the Common; Chesterlay; Chestering. *Commissioned by:* Boston 200 for opening of Boston's Bicentennial events. *First performed:* April 19, 1975: Boston City Hall. Arthur Fiedler, conductor.
Perf. dir: MIT

[CityRing. Chestering]
E1.13 Chestering. (1975)
For: handbells(optional), bands(5-part),
voices(optional). *Dedicated to:* William
Billings.
Score: Ione, 1975. MIT

[CityRing. Chesterlay]
E1.14 Chesterlay. (1975) 4'-6'
For: bands(5-part).
Score: Ione, 1975. MIT

[CityRing. Plaining the Common]
E1.15 Plaining the Common. (1975)
For: bells(20) and bands(5-part).
Dedicated to: Charles Ives.
Score: Ione, 1975. MIT

E1.16 Coronach for K,K,K. (1968) 6'
For: piano. 1 movement. *First
performed:* 1968; Donnell Library, New
York City; Composers Forum. Lalon
Parrot.
Score: reprod. of ms. NEC

De profundis. *See* Festive Church
Service. Out of the Depths.

E1.17 The Death of King Phillip. (1975)
For: speaker(male), Sopranos(2),
Tenors(2), Baritone, Bass,
dancer(female), chorus(SATB),
instrumental ensemble(flute/piccolo,
clarinet/clarinet(bass), trumpet, horn,
violoncello, accordion, harp, portative
organ, percussion), tape, electronics.
Opera. *Text:* based on the play by
Romulus Linney. Work supported in
part by a National Endowment for the
Arts grant. *First performed:* Mar. 26,
1976; Boston. New England Chamber
Opera Group, Philip Morehead,
conductor.
Score: reprod. of ms. MIT
Study score: reprod. of ms. MIT
Tape: available from composer.

E1.18 Dialogue: Music and... (1974)
For: multi-media.

[Dithyrambs]
E1.19 Five Dithyrambs. (1963)
For: tape. Musique concrete; dance
music. *First performed:* 1965; Honolulu,
Hawaii. Elsa Jordan, dancer.
Tape: available from composer.

E1.20 Divisions in Twelve. (1965; rev.
1966)
For: pianos(2) and tape. *Commissioned
by:* Iren Marik and John Ranck. *First
performed:* 1969; Duke University. Iren
Marik and John Ranck. Also performed
under title, Five Characters.
Score: reprod. of ms. MIT
Tape: available from composer.

The Dog and the Sparrow. *See* A
Grimm Duo. The Dog and the Sparrow.

E1.21 Dopplegaenger (Lightworks, No.
4). (1976)
For: oboes(1) and laser projections(for
oboe performance). *Commissioned by:*
Nora Post. Supported by a Center for
Creative and Performing Arts (State
University of New York, Buffalo) grant
and a New York State Council on the
Arts Meet the Composer Grant. *First
performed:* Oct. 1976; WBAI-FM, New
York City; in Evenings for New Music.
Nora Post.
Score: reprod. of ms. MIT

E1.22 Dreamstage (Lightworks, No. 5).
(1977)
For: synthesizer and laser.
Environmental media exhibition and
continuous music/laser event using the
physiological data of the human
dreaming brain as control signals for
processing music and light. Sponsored
by Roche Laboratories in conjunction
with Harvard Medical School,
Department of Neurophysiology. *First
exhibited:* April-May, 1977; Carpenter
Center for the Visual Arts, Harvard
University.

E1.23 E. E. by P.E.
For: piano.
Score: reprod. of ms. MIT

E1.24 Festive Church Service. (1963)
For: chorus(SATB), chorus(children),
organ, brasses, congregation.
Movements: Huguenot Variations; Nun
danket Fantasy; The Lord's Prayer; Out
of the Depths; Magnificat. *Text:* Bible,
N.T., Matthew 6:9-13; Bible, O.T., Psalm
130; Bible, N.T., Luke 1:46-55. *First
performed:* 1963; Berkeley, Calif. Earle
Blakes Lee, conductor.
Vocal score: available from composer.

[Festive Church Service. Huguenot
Variations]
E1.25 Huguenot Variations. (1963)
For: organ.
Score: in *Two Pieces for Organ*, Ione,
1974. HU MIT NEC

[Festive Church Service. The Lord's
Prayer]
E1.26 The Lord's Prayer. (1963)
For: Soprano or chorus(children) and
organ or brasses. *Text:* Bible, N.T.,
Matthew 6:9-13.
Vocal score: E.C. Schirmer, 1970. T

[Festive Church Service. Magnificat]
E1.27 Magnificat. (1963)
For: chorus(children) and organ or
brasses. Canticle. *Text:* Bible, N.T., Luke
1:46-55.
Score: available from composer.

[Festive Church Service. Nun danket
Fantasy]
E1.28 Nun danket Fantasy. (1963)
For: organ.
Score: in *Two Pieces for Organ*, Ione,
1974. HU MIT NEC

[Festive Church Service. Out of the
Depths]
E1.29 De profundis (Out of the Depths).
(1963)
For: chorus(SATB) and organ. *Text:*
Bible, O.T., Psalm 130.
Vocal score: Ione, 1970. T

E1.30 Flame Orchard. (1972)
For: tape. 3 movements. Music
modulates a field of flame. Written in
collaboration with Gyorgy Kepes,
William Walton, Mauricio Bueno.
Tape: available from composer.

E1.31 Flight. 150'
For: Sopranos(3), Tenor, Baritone, Bass
Baritone, Bass, chorus(SATB), chorus
(SSA), dancers, tape, film, chamber
orchestra(1(&pic)-1-1(Ebcl)-1(or bcl);
1-1-1-0; perc; pf; str). Stage work in 3
parts. *Text:* Evelyn Eaton.
Score: reprod. of ms. MIT

E1.32 Gamelan. (1971)
For: tape(synthesized). *First performed:*
Jan. 1971; Boston University.
Tape: available from composer.

E1.33 A Grimm Duo. (1976)
For: Soprano, Mezzo Soprano, Alto,
Tenor, Baritone, Bass, oboe, English
horn, horn, harp, harpsichord,
percussion, violin, tape. Chamber
operas. *Text:* based on fairy tales by
Jacob Grimm and Wilhelm Grimm.
Contents: The Dog and the Sparrow;
Brementown Musicians. Assisted by a
National Endowment for the Arts
Media Programs Grant. *First performed:*
Dec. 31, 1976; Old South Church,
Boston. New England Chamber Opera
Group, Philip Morehead, conductor.
Score.
Tape: available from composer.

[A Grimm Duo. Brementown
Musicians]
E1.34 Brementown Musicians. (1976)
For: Soprano, Alto, Tenor, Bass, harp,
oboe, violin, horn, tape. Chamber
opera. *Text:* based on the fairy tale by
Jacob Grimm and Wilhelm Grimm. *First
performed:* Dec. 31, 1976; Old South
Church, Boston. New England Chamber
Opera Group, Philip Morehead,
conductor.
Score: reprod. of ms. MIT
Videotape: available from composer.

[A Grimm Duo. The Dog and the Sparrow]
E1.35 The Dog and the Sparrow. (1976)
For: Mezzo Soprano, Baritone, harp, harpsichord, English horn, violin, horn, tape. Chamber opera. *Text:* based on the fairy tale by Jacob Grimm and Wilhelm Grimm. *First performed:* Dec. 31, 1976; Old South Church, Boston. New England Chamber Opera Group, Philip Morehead, conductor.
Score: reprod. of ms. MIT

E1.36 The Hindenburg. (1969)
For: tape(live). Processing of environmental sounds. Written in collaboration with Maurice Wright and Edgar Williams. *First performed:* 1969; Durham, N.C.
Tape: available from composer.

E1.37 Hold the Pickle. (1975)
For: tape. Collage of television food commercials. *First performed:* 1975; Massachusetts Institute of Technology; Food Show.
Tape: available from composer.

Huguenot Variations. *See* Festive Church Service. Huguenot Variations.

E1.38 Icarus: A Sky Opera. (1977; rev. 1981; in progress)
For: chorus(boy), narrator, oboe, harp, early music ensemble or folk ensemble. *Text:* libretto by Paul Earls incorporating the writings of Ovid, Friedrich Wilhelm Nietzsche, Gertrude Stein, A.E. Housman. *Contents:* Preparation for Lift-Off (Laser Patterns; Shawm Fanfare; Centerbeam: Song of the Minotaur; Whistle Trio and Narration); Lift-Off (Daedalus Sings from the Sky; Dawn, Part One; Canon; Icarus Sings from the Sky; Hoedown); Icarus Goes On (Dawn, Part Two; Icarus Patterns; What Is the Use?; Canon; All Those Brave Souls; Father, I Fly; Closing Speech). *First performed:* Sept. 8, 1978; Washington D.C. Columbus Boychoir of Princeton,

Donald Hanson, conductor; Alexander's Feast; Nora Post, oboe; Selim Earls, harp. Sky sculptures by Otto Piene. Later version first performed: Sept. 1981; Massachusetts Institute of Technology.
Score: reprod. of ms. MIT

[Icarus: A Sky Opera. What Is the Use?]
E1.39 What Is the Use of Being a Little Boy. (1977; rev. 1978)
For: chorus(boy). *Text:* Gertrude Stein.
Vocal score: reprod. of ms. MIT

E1.40 If. (1961)
For: chorus(children) and pianos(2). *First performed:* May 1961; Penfield, N.J. Penfield Elementary School Chorus; Ruth Steese, conductor.
Vocal score: reprod. of ms. MIT

E1.41 Inside. (1976-77)
For: band. Incorporates a poem by Patricia Goedicke. *First performed:* Apr. 1977. University of Lowell Wind Orchestra, Willis Traphagen, conductor.
Score: available from composer.

E1.42 The Jabberwocky. (1973-74)
For: Soprano, narrator, horn, tape(live). *Text:* Lewis Carroll. *First performed:* 1974; WQXR, New York City. Karen McBride, soprano; Selim Earls, narrator; Susan Graham, horn.
Score & part(narrator): reprod. of ms. MIT

E1.43 Joyce. (1971-72)
For: narrators(5) and tape. *First performed:* Jan. 1971; Boston University.
Score & tape: available from composer.

E1.44 Jubilee Ring.
For: all the carillons in Boston. Written for the 350th birthday of Boston, First Night 1980. *First performed:* Dec. 31, 1979; Boston.
Score: reprod. of ms. (version for keyboard carillon). MIT

E1.45 Kisses and Kazoos. (1977)
For: speakers(3) and tape(live). *Text:*
valentine cards, etc. Written in
collaboration with Lyle Davidson and
Joyce Mekeel. First performed: Feb.
1977. Massachusetts College of Art;
Eventworks Series.
Score/perf. dir: available from
composer.

E1.46 Laser Birds (Lightworks, No 6).
(1978)
For: laser and tape(live).
Perf. dir & tape: available from
composer.

E1.47 Laser Circus (Lightworks, No. 7).
(1980)
For: laser and tape.
Perf. dir & tape: available from
composer.

E1.48 Laser Loop, No. 1. (1971)
For: laser and tape. Written in
collaboration with Ted Kraynik.
Installed 1971 in permanent collection
of the Art and Science Museum, Tel
Aviv, Israel.
Perf. dir & tape: available from
composer.

E1.49 Let Me Live. (1970)
Stage work (collage).
Tape: available from composer.

Lightworks, No. 1. *See* Analogue.

Lightworks, No. 2. *See* Show and Tell.

Lightworks, No. 3. *See* Parhelion.

Lightworks, No. 4. *See* Doppelgaenger.

Lightworks, No. 5. *See* Dreamstage.

Lightworks, No. 6. *See* Laser Birds.

Lightworks, No. 7. *See* Laser Circus.

E1.50 Lincoln 'n Love. (1970)
For: tape. Environmental music for a
gallery. *First performed:* Feb. 1970;

Brandeis University.
Tape: available from composer.

E1.51 The Lobbyist. (1971-72)
For: tape(live). Processing of speech
into sustained pitches. *First performed:*
Jan. 1971; Boston University.
Perf. dir: available from composer.

E1.52 The Lord Zouches Maske. (1973)
55'
For: chorus(men) or chorus(women) or
chorus(mixed). Multi-media. Written in
collaboration with Robert Gronquist and
Larry Johnson. *First performed:* 1973;
Old West Church, Boston. Simmons
College Choir.
Perf. dir: available from Robert
Gronquist.

The Lord's Prayer. *See* Festive Church
Service. The Lord's Prayer.

E1.53 Love on Display. (1971) All day.
Environmental work; visual events by
Zeren Earls. *First performed:* Feb. 1971;
Kirkland [now Hamilton] College.
Perf. dir: available from composer.
Tape: available from composer.

E1.54 The Love Suicide at Schofield
Barracks. (1971)
For: tape. Incidental music to the play
by Romulus Linney. Music processed
from *Tristan und Isolde*, by Richard
Wagner.
Perf. dir: available from composer.
Tape: available from composer.

Magnificat. *See* Festive Church Service.
Magnificat.

E1.55 Mathematics of Encounter.
For: chorus and piano. *Text:* Isabella
Stewart Gardner. *Score.*

E1.56 Monday Music. (1970)
For: tape(synthesized). *First performed:*
Nov. 1970; Massaschetts Institute of
Technology.
Tape: available from composer.

E1.57 Mother. (1973)
For: tapes(cassette)(5) and dancers.
Commissioned by: New England
Dinosaur Dance Theatre. *First
performed:* May 1973; Cambridge,
Mass. New England Dinosaur Dance
Theatre.
Perf. dir: available from composer.
Tape: available from composer.

E1.58 Movable Feast [No. 1]. (1973)
60'
For: voices(unspecified) and
instruments(unspecified). Stage work;
aleatoric music. Written in
collaboration with Lyle Davidson and
Joyce Mekeel. *First performed:* Nov.
1973; Massachusetts College of Art.
Student performers.
Score & perf. dir: available from
composer.

E1.59 Movable Feast [No. 2]. (1974)
60'
For: voices(unspecified) and
instruments(unspecified). Stage work;
aleatoric music. Written in
collaboration with Lyle Davidson and
Joyce Mekeel. *First performed:* Mar. 7,
1974; New England Conservatory; An
Evening of Contemporary Music.
Student performers.
Score & perf. dir: available from
composer.
Cassette: recording of first
performance. NEC Movable Feast [No.
3] (1974) 60'

E1.60 Movable Feast [No. 3]. (1974)
60'
For: voices(unspecified) and
instruments(unspecified).
Stage work; aleatoric music. Written in
collaboration with Lyle Davidson and
Joyce Mekeel. *First performed:* Apr.
1974; Boston University. Student
performers.
Score & perf. dir: available from
composer.

E1.61 Music for a Wedding. (1968)
For: Tenor and organ. *Text:* compiled
by Rev. Banks Godfrey, Jr.
Score: available from composer.

[Music for a Wedding. Preparation]
E1.62 Preparation. (1968)
For: organ and tape(optional). Tape
sounds consist of vibraphone/celeste.

[Music for a Wedding. Song of Ruth]
E1.63 Song of Ruth. (1968; rev. 1969,
1970)
For: Tenor, finger cymbals, organ or
piano or tape. *Text:* Bible, O.T., Ruth
1:16-17.
Score: reprod. of ms. (version for tape).
MIT
Score: reprod. of ms.; in *Two Wedding
Songs* (version for piano). MIT
Score & tape: in *Two Wedding Songs*,
1970 (version for tape).
Disc: in *The American Art Song, Vol. 2*,
Duke University Press, [197-] 〈version
for organ, 1968).

[Music for a Wedding. Song of
Solomon]
E1.64 Song of Solomon. (1968; rev.
1969, 1970)
For: Tenor and organ or piano or tape.
Text: Bible, O.T., Song of Solomon
2:10-22.
Score: (version for organ, rev. 1969).
Score: reprod. of ms. (version for
piano, rev. 1969). MIT
Score & tape: in *Two Wedding Songs*
(version for tape, 1970).
Disc: in *The American Art Song, Vol. 2*,
Duke University Press, [197-]
(version for organ, 1968).

E1.65 Music with Harp. (1975)
For: harp and tape(live). For film
version, see The Tent.
Score & tape: available from composer.
Reel: Oct. 1975; Massachusetts
Institute of Technology.

E1.66 Name Your Zone. (1974)
For: instruments(unspecified). Aleatoric
music (of the performers' choice). *First
performed:* Mar. 7, 1974 (as part of his
Moveable Feast [No. 2]); New England
Conservatory; An Evening of
Contemporary Music. Student
performers.

Perf. dir: MIT
Cassette: recording of first
performance. NEC

E1.67 No Handouts for Mrs. Hedgepeth.
(1968)
Film music.

E1.68 Not a Covenant of Salt. (1969)
For: Tenor and piano. Song cycle. *Text:*
four poems by Isabella Stewart
Gardner. *First performed:* Nov. 1969;
Isabella Stewart Gardner Museum. John
Hanks, tenor and Paul Earls, piano.
Score: reprod. of ms. NEC

[Notables]
E1.69 Five Notables. (1967)
For: violin. *Contents:* Orations (GW);
Fable (MM); Figure (RB); Villanelle (IG);
Symphony with Conviction, Courage,
and Finality (LT). *Dedicated to:*
Rosemarie Beck Phelps. *First
performed:* 1968; Donnell Library, New
York City; Composer's Forum. Paul
Zukofsky.
Score: reprod. of ms. MIT NEC

Nun danket Fantasy. *See* Festive Church
Service. Nun danket Fantasy.

E1.70 Old C. (1973)
For: voices(4-16 parts) or
instruments(4-16 parts). Aleatoric music.
Based on variants of hymn tune, Old
Hundred. *First performed:* Oct. 1973.
California State University, Chico,
Choir, David Rothe, conductor.
Perf. dir & parts: available from
composer.

[Old C, Orchestra]
E1.71 Old C. (1976)
For: orchestra(any number of brasses,
percussion, strings). *First performed:*
Feb. 1977; University of Lowell.
University of Lowell Orchestra, Paul
Roby, conductor.
Score: available from composer.

[Old C, Tape]
E1.72 Old C. (1981)
For: tape(8-channel).

E1.73 Openings. (1975)
For: audience and brown
bags(prepared). From a student exercise
by Janis Bociz. *First performed:* Aug.
1975; Carpenter Center, Harvard
University.
Perf. dir: available from composer.

Out of the Depths. *See* Festive Church
Service. Out of the Depths.

E1.74 Parhelion (Lightworks, No. 3).
(1974) 9'
For: laser and tape. *First performed:*
May 1974; Massachusetts Institute of
Technology.
Tape: available from composer.

[Period Pieces]
E1.75 Three Period Pieces. (1975)
For: tape. *Movements:* Tango; Waltz;
Foxtrot. *Commissioned by:* MIT Alumni
Association. *First performed:* June
1975; Massachusetts Institute of
Technology.
Tape: available from composer.

Pieces for Organ. *See* Festive Church
Service. Huguenot Variations
and Festive Church Service. Nun danket
Fantasy.

Plaining the Common. *See* CityRing.
Plaining the Common.

E1.76 The Post-Easter Egg Hunt and
Roll. (1975)
For: oscillators(light-sensitive) and
candles. *First performed:* April 1975;
Institute for Contemporary Art, Boston.
Perf. dir: available from composer.

Preparation. *See* Music for a Wedding.
Preparation.

E1.77 Processional Music. (1971)
For: tape(synthesized), brasses,
percussion(optional). *First performed:*
June 1971; Massachusetts Institute of
Technology, Commencement. MIT
Concert Band, John Corley, conductor.
Score: available from composer.

Perf. dir: available from composer.
Tape: available from composer.

E1.78 Psalm 100. (1961)
For: chorus(SATB). *Text:* Bible, O.T.,
Psalm 100. *Dedicated to:* Zeren [
Earls]. *First performed:* Penfield, N.Y.
Penfield High School Chorus, Paul
Earls, conductor.
Score: Ostara Press, 1972. MIT

[Quartet, Strings]
E1.79 String Quartet No. 1. (1968)
First performed: 1968; Donnell Library,
New York City; Composer's Forum.
Score & parts: available from
composer.

E1.80 Reveille for a Rockinghorse Poet.
For: chorus. *Text:* Isabella Stewart
Gardner. *Vocal score.*

E1.81 Seats in Concert. (1973)
For: audience and chairs. *First
performed:* Oct. 1973; California State
University, Chico.
Perf. dir: available from composer.

E1.82 Selim's Aria. (1964)
For: tape. Musique concrete. *First
performed:* 1964; Eugene, Ore. *Tape.*

E1.83 Show and Tell (Lightworks, No.
2). (1970)
For: tape. Composed for *Audio Lumina,*
sculpture by Ted Kraynik. *First
performed:* Nov. 1970; Massachusetts
Institute of Technology. *Tape.*

E1.84 Slideface. (1971) 35'
For: slides and tape. Slides by John
Goodyear. *First performed:* Feb. 1971;
Kirkland (now Hamilton) College.
Perf. dir: available from composer.
Tape: available from composer.
Slides(35mm): available from composer.

E1.85 The Small Hour. (1964)
For: Soprano and piano. *Text:* Evelyn
Eaton. *First performed:* 1965; Eugene,
Ore. Exine Bailey, soprano and Paul

Earls, piano.
Score: available from composer.

Song of Ruth. *See* Music for a
Wedding. Song of Ruth.

Song of Solomon. *See* Music for a
Wedding. Song of Solomon.

E1.86 Springfield Mountain. (1961)
For: chorus)(children) and piano. *Text:*
traditional. *First performed:* 1961;
Penfield, N.Y. Penfield Elementary
School Chorus, Ruth Steese, conductor.

E1.87 Star. (1971)
For: Soprano and tape. Musique
concrete. *Text:* Ethel Casey. *First
performed:* 1971; Carnegie Recital Hall,
New York City. Ethel Casey, soprano.
Score: reprod. of ms. NEC
Tape: available from composer.

E1.88 Der Struwwelpeter oder, Lustige
Geschichten und drollige Bilder von Dr.
Heinrich Hoffmann. (1980) 15' *For:*
voices, pianos(2), whistler,
recorder(alto), organ, accordion, celeste.
Contents: Vorspruch; Der Struwwelpeter
Feuerzeug; Suppen-Kaspar;
Daumenlutscher; Fliegenden Robert.
Score: reprod. of ms. MIT

E1.89 Summer, 1967. (1969)
For: tape. Musique concrete. *First
performed:* Lucas Hoving Dance
Company under title, Aubade.
Tape: Peters. Rental.

E1.90 The Swan. (1975)
For: harp, violoncello, tape(live),
costumes(lighted).
Perf. dir: available from composer.

E1.91 The Tent. (1975)
Music for a film by Henry Darogovich.
Based on the composer's Music with
Harp. *Film.*

E1.92 Thru Sea & Sky. (1974)
For: tape(live). Processing of
environmental sounds. *First performed:*

1974; Jersey City State College.
Perf. dir: available from composer.
Tape: available from composer.

E1.93 Trine. (1968)
For: chorus(SATB) and clarinet(in C).
Contents: The Flying Geese (Terry
Bringle); Bible, O.T., Psalm 117; The
Song of the Stars (Algonquin). *First
performed:* 1969; Durham, N.C.
Vocal score: Ione, 1971. HU MIT T
Part: Ione, 1971.

E1.94 Trio/Duo. (1969)
For: violin, piano, tape. *First
performed:* Boston. Isabella Stewart
Gardner Museum. Paul Zukofsky, violin
and Gilbert Kalish, piano.
Score: reprod. of ms. NEC
Tape: available from composer.

E1.95 Twister. (1973)
For: chorus(women) and tape(live).
Movements: The Time; Procession;
Environments; Names; Twister Groups;
Tree Toad; Soup. Processing of
environmental sounds. *Commissioned
by:* Simmons College Glee Club, Robert
Gronquist, conductor. *First performed:*
1973; Simmons College. Simmons
College Glee Club, Robert Gronquist,
conductor.
Score: reprod of ms. MIT

E1.96 U.S. Air Weave. (1975)
For: woodwind ensemble, brasses(5),
tape, cassette choir, laser projections.
Score: available from composer.
Perf. dir: available from composer.

E1.97 Water Music. (1971)
For: tape(live). Processing of
environmental sounds.
Tape: available from composer.

Wedding Songs. *See* Music for a
Wedding. Song of Ruth
and Music for a Wedding. Song
of Solomon.

E1.98 Werk. (1972)
For: band and tape. *Commissioned by:*
MIT Concert Band. *First performed:*

1972. MIT Concert Band, John Corley,
conductor.
Condensed score & tape: MIT

What Is the Use of Being a Little Boy.
See Icarus: A Sky Opera. What Is
the Use?

E1.99 What's in a Name. (1972)
For: audience. Based on *Jackson Macl*,
by Robert Byrd.
Perf. dir: available from composer.

E1.100 Who-Ho-Ray.
For: tape. Music for a film by Stan
Vanderbeek. *Film.*

E1.101 Words of Isaiah. (1972) 14'
For: Bass Baritone and chamber
orchestra. Cantata. *Text:* Bible, O.T.,
Isaiah.
Score: available from composer.

ARRANGEMENTS OF WORKS BY OTHER COMPOSERS

E1.102 Bumble Bee. (1981)
For: tape. Original by Nikolai
Rimsky-Korsakov.
Tape: available from composer.

E1.103 Circus Musics. (1980)
For: tape.
Tape: available from composer.

E1.104 The Devils Trill. (1975)
For: violin and tape. Original from
Sonata, Violin and Continuo, G Minor
by Giuseppe Tartini.
Score & tape: available from composer.

E1.105 Glad Rag. (1974)
For: piano and tape(live). Original by
Scott Joplin.
Perf. dir.

E1.106 The Moonlight Sonata.
For: piano and tape(live). Original from
Sonata, Piano, No. 14, Op. 27, No. 2,
C-Sharp Minor by Ludwig van
Beethoven.
Perf. dir: available from composer.

E2 BARBARA J. ENGEL

Born May 25, 1950, in Cleveland, Ohio.
Moved to Boston area 1976. *Education:*
studied composition with Nadia
Boulanger (Ecoles d'Art Americaines,
Fontainebleau, France, 1971); Ross Lee
Finney, Leslie Bassett, Jack Fortner
(University of Michigan, B.A., History,
1972); B.M. (Hartt College of Music,
1976); piano with Joseph Howard,
Tirzah Mailkoff, Jean Casadesus, Alexander Lipsky, Watson Morrison, Jean
Poole Alderman; jazz improvisation
with Robert Smicrope. *Related
activities:* pianist; teacher of piano,
guitar, recorder; researcher and writer
of concert program notes for radio
broadcasts; served on the faculty of
Milton Academy Lower School
(1976-80); research assistant WGBH-FM,
Morning Pro Musica (1979-). W

WORKS

E2.1 Duet. (1968) 6'
For: flute and violoncello. *First
performed:* Dec. 1968; Ann Arbor, Mich.
Score: ms. in composer's hand.
Score: reprod. of ms.

E2.2 Fontainebleau. (1972) 2'-3'
For: piano. *Dedicated to:* Vivian Engel.
Score: ms. in composer's hand.

E2.3 Interpretation of e.e. cummings'
Poem No. 3 of *95 poems.* (1968) 1'
For: piano. Based on e.e. cummings.
Score: ms. in composer's hand.

E2.4 Prelude. (1973) 3'-4'
For: piano. *Dedicated to:* Cindy Taft.
Score: ms. in composer's hand.

E2.5 Prelude and Fugue. (1977) 6'
For: piano.
Score: ms. in composer's hand.
Score: reprod. of ms; available from
composer.
Cassette: Jan. 1981; Cleveland, Ohio.
Barbara Engel.

E3 DAVID M. EPSTEIN

Born October 3, 1930, in New York
City. Moved to Boston area 1965.
Education: A.B. (Antioch College, 1952);
studied composition with Francis Judd
Cooke, Carl McKinley, Felix Wolfes
(New England Conservatory, M.M., 1953)
Arthur Berger, Irving Fine (Brandeis
University, M.F.A., 1954); Roger
Sessions, Milton Babbitt, Edward T.
Cone (Princeton University, Ph.D, 1963).
Awards: Louisville Orchestra Award
(1953), BMI Award (1954), Fromm
Foundation Prize (1955), ASCAP Awards
(Standard, 1963-81), Arthur Shephard
Award (1964), Harvey Gaul Composition
Contest (1968?), Ford Foundation
Recording Grants (1971, 1977),
Rockefeller Foundation Commission
(1971), Boston Symphony Orchestra
Youth Concert Series commission
(1974), New York State Council on the
Arts commission (1974), Massachusetts
Council on the Arts and Humanities,
Artist Fellowship Program (1977).
Related activities: pianist; conductor of
the MIT Symphony Orchestra; guest
conductor of orchestras in Europe,
Israel and the United States; music
critic, *Musical America* (1957-62); music
director, Educational Broadcasting
Corporation, New York City (1962-64);
author of *Beyond Orpheus: Studies in
Musical Structure* (1979); served on the
faculties of Antioch College (1957-62)
and the Massachusetts Institute of
Technology (1965-). MIT

WORKS

E3.1 The Concord Psalter. (1979) 13'
For: chorus(SATB), piano, violoncello,
clarinet/clarinet(bass), trombone,
percussion. *Text:* Bible, O.T., Psalms.
Commissioned by and dedicated to: The
Concord Chorale, Phyllis Isaacson,
conductor. *First performed:* 1979;
Concord, N.H. Concord Chorale, David
Epstein, conductor.
Score: ms. in composer's hand.
Parts: ms.

E3.2 The Count Down Under. (1964)
For: orchestra. Film music. Produced by the United Nations.

E3.3 Excerpts from a Diary. (1953) 12'
For: Baritone and piano. *Text:* Walter Benton. 4 movements. *Commissioned by and dedicated to:* Rand Smith. *First performed:* 1954; Jordan Hall, Boston. Rand Smith, baritone and David Epstein, piano.
Score: C. Fischer, 1977. Rental.
Reel: 1954; Boston. Rand Smith, baritone and David Epstein, piano.

E3.4 Fancies. (1966) 9'
For: Soprano and clarinet. *Text:* Emily Dickinson. *Contents:* The Spider; The Leaves; I Heard a Fly Buzz When I Died; Papa Above! *Commissioned by and dedicated to:* Antonia Lavanne and David Glazer. *First performed:* 1966; New York City. Antonia Lavanne, soprano and David Glazer, clarinet.
Score: reprod. of ms. MIT
Score: C. Fischer, 1977. Rental.
Reel: Mar. 24, 1977; in *Music from M.I.T.* BkPL

[Fantasy Variations, Viola]
E3.5 Fantasy Variations. (1963) 15'
Commissioned by and dedicated to: Sylvia Rosenberg. *First performed:* Feb. 1979; Lexington, Mass. Marcus Thompson.
Score: MCA, 1971. MIT NEC
Reel: recording of first performance.

[Fantasy Variations, Violin]
E3.6 Fantasy Variations. (1963) 15'
Commissioned by and dedicated to: Sylvia Rosenberg. *First performed:* 1965; New York City. Sonya Monosoff.
Score: reprod. of ms. MIT
Score: MCA, 1971. MIT
Reel: 1969; New York City. Sonya Monosoff.

E3.7 Forms. (1963) 11'
For: saxophone, vibraphone, double bass. 1 movement. *Commissioned by:* New Music Trio. *Dedicated to:* Herb Harris. First performed: 1963; New York

City. New Music Trio.
Score: reprod. of ms. MIT
Score: C. Fischer, 1977. Rental.
Parts: C. Fischer, 1977. Rental.
Reel: 1963; New York City. New Music Trio.

E3.8 Frontiers. 12' 30"
For: flute, horn, violin, violoncello. Film music. *Commissioned by:* Utah (State). *First performed:* 1958.
Score & parts: C. Fischer, 1977. Rental.
Reel: 1958; New York City. Julius Baker, flute; Joseph Eger, horn; Dixie Eger; violin; David Soyer, violoncello.

E3.9 The Lament of Job. (1980) 12'
For: chorus(SATB), speakers(3), piano, violoncello, percussion. *Text:* Bible, O.T., Psalms. 1 movement. *Commissioned by:* Illinois Wesleyan University. *Dedicated to:* Illinois Wesleyan University Chorale. *First performed:* 1981; Bloomington, Ill. Illinois Wesleyan University Chorale, David Nott, conductor.
Score: ms. in composer's hand.
Parts: ms.

E3.10 Movement for Orchestra. (1952) 6' 30"
For: orchestra(2-2(Ehn)-2-2; 4-2-3-0; timp; str). Winner of Louisville Orchestra Award, 1953. *First performed:* 1954; Louisville, Ky. Louisville Orchestra.
Score: reprod. of ms. MIT
Score & parts: C. Fischer, 1952. Rental.
Reel: 1954; Louisville, Ky. Louisville Orchestra.

E3.11 Music for the Play Julius Caesar. (1957) 13' 30"
For: chamber orchestra(1-1-1-1; 1-1-1-0; timp, perc; pf; str). Incidental music to *Julius Caesar* by William Shakespeare. *Commissioned by:* Antioch Shakespeare Festival, Yellow Springs, Ohio. First performed: 1957; Antioch Shakespeare Festival, Yellow Springs, Ohio. Antioch Festival Orchestra.
Score & parts: C. Fischer, 1977. Rental.

Reel: 1957; Yellow Springs, Ohio.
Antioch Festival Orchestra.

E3.12 Night Voices. (1974) 13'
For: narrator, chorus(children)(optional),
orchestra2(pic)-2(Ehn)-2(bcl)-2; 2-2-2-1;
timp, perc(4), glock, mar, vibra, xylo;
hp; str). *Text:* Anne Merrick Epstein.
Contents: Owl; Mouse; Cricket; Stone.
Commissioned by: Boston Symphony
Orchestra Youth Concert Series, Harry
Ellis Dickson, music director. *First
performed:* Nov. 9, 1974; Symphony
Hall, Boston; Boston Symphony
Orchestra Youth Concerts at Symphony
Hall. Janet Bookspan, narrator; Boston
Boy Choir; Boston Symphony
Orchestra, David Epstein, conductor.
Score: C. Fischer, 1979. HU
Parts: C. Fischer, 1979. Rental.
Vocal score: C. Fischer, 1979. MIT
Disc: Candide CE 31116, 1979. Janet
Bookspan, narrator; Boston Boy Choir;
MIT Symphony Orchestra, David
Epstein, conductor. HU MIT NEC
Cassette: Candide CT 2257, 1979.
Simultaneous issue of Candide CE
31116.

E3.13 No Other Choice. (1964) 17'
For: flute, oboe, clarinet, horn,
violoncello. Film music. *Commissioned
by:* United Nations.
Score & parts: reprod. of ms.

[Pieces, Horn and Piano]
E3.14 Two Pieces. (1962) 7'
Commissioned by: Pamela Illott.
Score: Belwin, 1963.

[Quartet, Strings, 1952?]
E3.15 String Quartet. (1952?) 22'
4 movements. *First performed:* 1952;
New York City.
Score & parts: C. Fischer, 1977. Rental.
Reel: 1952; New York City.

[Quartet, Strings, 1971]
E3.16 String Quartet. (1971) 18'
4 movements. *Commissioned by:*
Philadelphia Quartet and the Rockefeller
Foundation. *First performed:* 1972;

Seattle, Wash. Philadelphia Quartet.
Score: C. Fischer. Rental.
Parts: C. Fischer, 1977. Rental.
Disc: Desto DC7148, 1974. Philadelphia
String Quartet. BU HU MIT W

E3.17 The Seasons: A Cycle. (1955) 12'
For: Soprano and piano. *Text:* Emily
Dickinson. *Contents:* There Came a
Wind Like a Bugle; These Are the Days
When Birds Come Back; The Sky Is
Low, the Clouds Are Mean; There's a
Certain Slant of Light; Of Bronze and
Blaze the North, Tonight! *Dedicated to:*
Earl Kim. *First performed:* 1956;
Princeton, N.J. Janice Harsanyi, soprano
and David Epstein, piano.
Score: reprod. of ms. MIT
Score: C. Fischer, 1977. Rental.
Disc: Desto DC7148, 1974. Jan De
Gaetani, soprano and Robert Freeman,
piano. BU HU MIT W

[Scenes]
E3.18 Five Scenes. (1955) 7'
For: chorus(SATB). *Text:* Chicago Poems
by Carl Sandburg. *Contents:* Fall in
Yellow; Nocturne in a Deserted
Brickyard; Fog; Wind-Scape; Uplands in
May. *First performed:* 1957; Antioch
College. Antioch College Chorus, David
Epstein, conductor.
Vocal score: Mercury, 1962. MIT
Reel: 1958; Yellow Springs, Ohio.
Antioch College Chorus.

E3.19 Sing to the Lord. (1973) 5'
For: chorus(SATB). *Text:* Bible, O.T.,
Psalm 150. *Commissioned by:* The
Union of American Hebrew
Congregations in honor of its
centennial anniversary, 5733/1973. *First
performed:* 1974; New York City.
Vocal score: MCA, 1973. MIT NEC

E3.20 Song of Isaiah. 10'
For: Soprano, violin, piano. *Text:* Bible,
O.T., Isaiah. *First performed:* 1953;
Jordan Hall, Boston. Anne English,
soprano; Rudolph Patmagrian, violin;
David Epstein, piano.
Score & parts: C. Fischer, 1977. Rental.

Reel: 1953; Boston. Anne English, soprano; Rudolph Patmagrian, violin; David Epstein, piano.

[Songs]
E3.21 Four Songs: A Cycle. (1959) 13'
For: Soprano, horn, string orchestra.
Text: Gerard Manley Hopkins and John Keats. *Contents:* Cuckoo; Strike, Churl; Spring and Fall; To a Young Child; Ode to Sleep. *First performed:* 1960; Antioch College. Nell Tangeman, soprano; Antioch Festival Orchestra, David Epstein, conductor.
Score: Mercury, 1964. BPL HU MIT NEC
Parts: Merrymount. Rental.
Reel: 1960; Yellow Springs, Ohio. Nell Tangeman, soprano; Antioch Festival Orchestra, David Epstein, conductor.

E3.22 Sonority-Variations. (1966) 15'
For: orchestra(3(pic)-3(Ehn)-(3bcl)-2; 4-3-3-1; timp, vibra, xylo; hp, pf/cel; str). *First performed:* 1969; Massachusetts Institute of Technology. MIT Symphony Orchestra, David Epstein, conductor.
Score & parts: MCA, 1971. Rental.
Study score: MCA, 1971. BPL HU MIT
Reel: 1969; Cambridge, Mass. MIT Symphony Orchestra, David Epstein, conductor.
Cassette: May 6, 1971; New England Conservatory; in *A Festival of New England Composers Past and Present*. NEC Repertory Orchestra, Richard Pittman, conductor, NEC

E3.23 Symphony No. 1. (1955) 20'
For: orchestra(2(pic)-2-3-2; 4-3-3-0; timp, perc(2), xylo; str). 3 movements.
Dedicated to: Irving Fine. Winner of Fromm Foundation Prize, Aspen Music Festival, 1955. *First performed:* 1955; Aspen Colo.; Aspen Music Festival. Aspen Festival Orchestra.
Score: reprod. of ms. MIT
Score & parts: C. Fischer, 1977. Rental.
Reel: 1955; Colo. Aspen Festival Orchestra.

[Trio, Piano and Strings]
E3.24 Trio. (1953) 25'

For: violin, violoncello, piano. 3 movements. Based upon European and Hebraic folk and religious music.
Dedicated to: Carl McKinley, Francis Judd Cooke, David Barnett. Winner of BMI Award, 1954. *First performed:* 1954; Aspen, Colo; Aspen Music Festival.
Score: reprod. of ms. MIT
Score: C. Fischer, 1953. Rental.
Reel: 1955; Aspen, Colo.

[Trio, Strings]
E3.25 String Trio. (1964) 13' 45"
For: violin, viola, violoncello. 4 movements. *Commissioned by:* Pacific String Trio. *First performed:* 1964; New York City. Pacific String Trio.
Score: reprod. of ms. MIT
Score & parts: MCA, 1969. MIT
Disc: Desto DC7148, 1974. Pacific String Trio. BU HU MIT W

[Variations, Piano]
E3.26 Piano Variations. (1961) 11'
Dedicated to: Anne [Epstein] *First performed:* 1962; New York City. Howard Lebow.
Score: reprod. of ms. MIT
Score: C. Fischer, 1977. Rental.
Reel: 1962; New York City. Howard Lebow.

E3.27 Vent-ures (1970) 12'
For: band. 3 moveements.
Commissioned by: Eastman Wind Ensemble. *First performed:* Dec. 11, 1970; Rochester, N.Y. Eastman Wind Ensemble, Donald Hunsberger, conductor.
Score & parts: C. Fischer, 1974. Rental.
Study score: C. Fischer, 1974. MIT
Disc: Desto DC7148, 1974. Eastman Wind Ensemble, Donald Hunsberger, conductor. BU HU MIT W

ARRANGEMENTS

E3.28 French Airs of the Early 18th Century.
For: Soprano and harpsichord or piano. Edited by Nell Tangeman.
Score: Boosey & Hawkes, 1962. BPL HU

E4 POZZI ESCOT

Born October 1, 1933, in Lima, Peru.
Moved to Boston area 1963. *Education:*
University of San Marcos
(mathematics); studied composition with
Andres Sas (Sas-Rosay Academy of
Music, Lima, Peru, 1949-53), William
Bergsma (Juilliard School, B.S., 1956,
M.S., 1957), Philipp Jarnach (Staatliche
Hochschule fuer Musik und Darstellende
Kunst, Hamburg, West Germany,
1957-61). *Awards:* Peru, Composer
Laureate (1956), Germany (Federal
Republic) Grants (1957-59), Hamburg
State Award (1960), Reemtsma
Foundation Grant (1960), MacDowell
Colony Fellowships (1962-65), Radcliffe
Institute Fellowships (1968-70), Ford
Foundation Grant, Outstanding
Educators of America Fellowships.
Related activities: co-author of *Sonic
Design: The Nature of Sound and Music*
(1976) and *Sonic Design: Practice and
Problems* (1981); co-editor of the
journal, *Sonus*; served on the faculties
of New England Conservatory (1964-67,
1980-81) and Wheaton College (1972-).
W

WORKS

E4.1 Ainu. (1970-71) 11'
For: chorus(mixed). *Text:* Latin and
Hebrew by Pozzi Escot. *Commissioned
by* Mid-America Chorale. *First
performed and exhibited:* Mar. 30 to
Apr. 18, 1971; Carpenter Center for the
Visual Arts, Harvard University; in
Seeing Music - Visual Aspect of 20th
Century Music Notation. New Graphic
Scores by 26 Composers.
Parts: Publications Contact
International, 1975. W

[Ainu; Arr.]
E4.2 Ainu. (1978) 8'
For: voice. *Text:* Latin and Hebrew by
Pozzi Escot. Written for singer Joan
Heller. *Dedicated to:* Lucie Pozzi-Escot.
Score: Publications Contact
International, [1979?].

E4.3 Canciones de mi pais. (1954)
For: Soprano and piano. Withdrawn.

E4.4 Cantata Roots. (1958)
For: Alto, chorus(mixed), orchestra.
Withdrawn.

E4.5 Concertino. (1956)
For: instruments(9). Withdrawn.

E4.6 Credo. (1958)
For: Soprano and string quartet.
Withdrawn.

Cristhos. *See* Trilogy. No. 2.

E4.7 Cuadros. (1949)
For: piano. Withdrawn.

E4.8 Differences, Group 1. (1960-61) 5'
For: piano. 3 movements (played twice,
in the following order: 1-2-3-3-1-2).
Commissioned by and dedicated to:
Howard Lebow. *First performed:* 1961;
Hamburg, West Germany. Robert Henry.
Score: Publications Contact
International, 1974. W
Cassette: Dec. 7, 1971; New England
Conservatory; in *An Evening of
Contemporary Music.* Anthony T. Rauche.
NEC

E4.9 Differences, Group 2. (1963) 5'-6'
For: piano. 3 movements. *Commissioned
by:* Carmen Moral. *First performed:*
1963; Donnell Library, New York City;
Composer's Forum. Howard Lebow.
Score: Publications Contact
International, 1974. W

E4.10 Eure pax. (1981) 7' 45"
For: violin. 5 movements.
Commissioned by: Nancy Cirillo.
Dedicated to: Claude Bourdet. *First
performed:* Mar. 1981. New York
University First National Congress on
Women in Music. Nancy Cirillo.
Score: Publication Contact International.
W
Disc: in *New Events II*, Spectrum SR
136, 1981. Nancy Cirillo.

Reel: Apr. 5, 1981; Wellesley College. Nancy Cirillo. W

E4.11 Fergus Are. (1975) 8'
For: organ and tape. *Movements:* Tangent Curve; Conjugate Diameter; Conjugate Hyperbole; Envelope; Center; Figures Similar; Inclination of Two Intersecting Planes to One Another. *Commissioned by:* Martha Folts. *Dedicated to:* Ireland. June 24, 1976; King's Chapel, Boston; American Guild of Organists Convention. Martha Folts. *Score:* Publications Contact International, 1976. W
Disc: Delos DEL 25448, 1980. Martha Folts.

E4.12 Interra. (1968) 13'
For: piano, film, tape, lights(spot). Collage. A piano recital of 13 preludes synchronized with 7 minutes of tape music (collage of the announcer from Dallas radio, Nov. 23, 1963; Magnificat by Johann Sebastian Bach; Survivor from Warsaw by Arnold Schoenberg; electronic music, the Swingle Singers performing Art of the Fugue by Johann Sebastian Bach) and a simultaneous visual performance of Opus 19, No. 6 for piano by Arnold Schoenberg. *Commissioned by:* John Felice. *First performed:* Feb. 10, 1970; New England Conservatory; in An Evening of Contemporary Music. Robert Jones. *Score:* Publications Contact International, 1974. W
Cassette: recording of first performance. NEC

E4.13 Interra II. (1980) 6'
For: piano(left hand) and tape(pre-recorded piano). 8 movements. *Commissioned by:* John Felice. *Dedicated to:* Basia. *First performed:* Oct. 13, 1980; New England Conservatory. John Felice
Score: Publications Contact International, 1980. W
Cassette: recording of first performance. NEC

[Lamentaciones]
E4.14 Dos lamentaciones. (1950) 3'
For: Mezzo soprano and piano. Withdrawn.

Lamentus. *See* Trilogy. No. 1.

E4.15 Little Symphony. (1954)
For: orchestra. Withdrawn.

E4.16 Metamorphosis. (1951) 4'
For: Soprano and instrumental ensemble. Withdrawn.

E4.17 Missa triste. (1981) 6' 30"
For: choruses(women)(3) and instruments(treble)(3)(optional). *Text:* Pozzi Escot. *Commissioned by:* Russell Sage College Women's Chorus. *Dedicated to:* Lucia. *First performed:* 1981; Russell Sage College. *Score & parts:* Publication Contact International, 1981. W
Cassette: recording of first performance.

[Movements]
E4.18 Three Movements for Violin and Piano. (1959-60) 5'
Dedicated to: Robert Henry and Daniel Thomas. *First performed:* 1963; Carnegie Recital Hall, New York City; International Society for Contemporary Music. Matthew Raimondi, violin and Paul Jacobs, piano.
Score: Publications Contact International, 1974. W

E4.19 Neyrac lux. (1978)
For: guitars(folk/classical/electric). 5 movements. *Commissioned by:* Harry Chalmiers. *Dedicated to:* Marius Emm. Pozzi-Escot. *First performed:* 1978; Boston College. Harry Chalmiers. *Score:* Publications Contact International, 1978. W
Score: Rocky, [1981?].
Disc: New Events: Boston Composers of the '70s, Spectrum SR 128, 1980. Harry Chalmiers. NEC

E4.20 Piezas infantiles I. (1942)
For: piano. Withdrawn.

E4.21 Piezas infantiles II. (1947)
For: piano. Withdrawn.

E4.22 Pluies. (1981) 5'
For: saxophone(alto) and
tape(pre-recorded saxophone). 4
movements. *Commissioned by:* William
Malone. *Dedicated to:* Ines Pozzi-Escot.
First performed: 1981; University of
Maryland.
Score: Dorn, nyp.
Cassette: recording of first
performance.

[Poems of Rilke]
E4.23 Three Poems of Rilke. (1959) 9'
For: narrator and string quartet. *Text:*
Rainer Maria Rilke. *Contents:* Der
Dichter; Schluss Stueck; Welt War in
dem Antlitz der Geliebten. *Dedicated
to:* Philipp Jarnach. *First performed:*
1965; Washington, D.C.; Inter-American
Music Festival. Hugo Weisgall, narrator;
Claremont Quartet.
Score: Publications Contact
International, 1974. W
Parts: Publications Contact
International, 1974.

[Portraits]
E4.24 Six Portraits. (1949)
For: piano. Withdrawn.

[Quartet, Strings, No. 1]
E4.25 Cuerteto de cuerda I. (1953)
Withdrawn.

[Quartet, Strings, No. 2]
E4.26 Cuerteto de cuerda II. (1953)
Withdrawn.

[Quartet, Strings, No. 3]
E4.27 Cuerteto de cuerda III. (1956)
Withdrawn.

E4.28 Sands. (1965) 11'-15'
For: instrumental
ensemble(saxophones(5), guitar(electric),
drums(bass(4), violins(17), double
basses(9). 3 movements. Earlier
version, for Alto, chorus(SATB),
orchestra, withdrawn. *Commissioned by:*

Instituto de Cultura y Bellas Artes de
Venezuela. *Dedicated to:* The city of
Caracas. *First performed:* May 1966.
Orquesta Sinfonica de Venezuela,
Gonzalo Castellanos, conductor.
Score: Publications Contact
International, 1975. W
Reel: Nov. 10, 1975; Lincoln Center,
New York City. New York Philharmonic
Orchestra.

E4.29 Sinfonia I. (1955)
For: string orchestra. Withdrawn.

E4.30 Sinfonia II. (1957)
For: orchestra. Withdrawn.

E4.31 Sonatina, No. 1. (1952)
For: piano. Withdrawn.

E4.32 Sonatina, No. 2. (1953)
For: piano. Withdrawn.

E4.33 Sonatina, No. 3. (1954)
For: piano. Withdrawn.

[Songs]
E4.34 Four Songs. (1955)
For: Soprano and piano. Withdrawn.

E4.35 Suite. (1943-48)
For: piano. Withdrawn.

[Trilogy. No. 1]
E4.36 Lamentus. (1962) 15'
For: Soprano, violins(2), violoncellos(2),
piano, percussion(3). *Text:* Pozzi Escot.
Contents: Sema elariis; Los gritos oh
Dios; Quien; El es un nino; Neam
amen. *Commissioned by:* Inter-American
Music Festival of Washington D.C. for
the 3rd Inter-American Music Festival.
Dedicated to: Stedman and Phyllis
Noble. *First performed:* 1964; Madrid,
Spain. Carmen Durias, soprano;
members of the Madrid Philharmonic
Orchestra.
Score: Publications Contact
International, 1974. W

[Trilogy. No. 2]
E4.37 Cristhos. (1963) 14'

For: violins(3), flute(alto), contrabassoon, percussion. *First performed:* 1963; Donnell Library, New York City; Composers Forum Group for Contemporary Music, Arthur Weisberg, conductor. Used under title Cristhos by Yugoslavian National Television in film *Razapeti* (1973).
Score: Publications Contact International, 1975. W
Parts: Publications Contact International, 1975.
Cassette: May 12, 1973; New England Conservatory; in *A Festival of Contemporary American Music.* Carl Roskott, conductor. NEC

[Trilogy. No. 3]
E4.38 Visione. (1964) 10'
For: double bass, flute/piccolo, flute(alto), saxophone(alto), Soprano, percussion, speaker(amplified). *Text:* Pozzi Escot, adapted from Arthur Rimbaud, Wassily Kandinsky, Gertrude Stein, Guenter Grass. *Commissioned by:* Hartt Chamber Players, Bertram Turetzky, conductor. *Dedicated to:* The six million of Treblinka, Dachau, Mauthausen, Buchenwald, Auschwitz, Belsec. *First performed:* 1964; New York City. Hartt Chamber Players, Bertram Turetzky, conductor.
Score & parts: Dorn.
Score: Publications Contact International, 1975. W

Visione. *See* Trilogy. No. 3.

E5 THOMAS GREGORY EVERETT

Born December 4, 1944, in Philadelphia, Pa. Moved to Boston area 1961.
Education: studied composition with Warren Benson and George Andrix (Ithaca College, B.S., 1966, M.S., 1969); Robert Ceely (New England Conservatory, 1972). *Awards:* American Music Center Composer Assistance Program (1980) and International Trombone Association Award (1980).
Related activities: bass trombonist; conductor; author of *Annotated Guide to Bass Trombone Literature* (1979);

associate editor of *Composer Magazine* and *Brass World Magazine*; Director of Bands, Harvard University (1971-); served on the faculties of the National Trombone Workshop, Nashville, Tenn. (1972-73), Brown University (1975-79), New England Conservatory (1973-). HU

WORKS

E5.1 Duos. (1966; rev. 1969) 8'
For: clarinet and trombone(bass). 2 movements. *First performed:* Aug. 1966; Ithaca, N.Y. (1966 version). James Trump, clarinet and Thomas Everett, bass trombone. Apr. 1, 1969 (1969 version); Neil Hartwick, clarinet and Thomas Everett, bass trombone.
Score & parts: reprod. of ms. (1969 version). HU
Score: Seesaw, 1978 (1969 version). HU
Parts: ms. in composer's hand (1966 version).
Parts: Seesaw (1969 version).
Reel: available from composer (both versions).

E5.2 Feowertig Nu. (1969) Duration variable.
For: band or instruments(unspecified)(any number and combination of winds, strings, percussion). 1 movement. *First performed:* Mar. 23, 1969; Batavia, N.Y. Batavia High School Concert Band, Thomas Everett, conductor.
Parts: Media, 1971. HU.
Reel: available from composer.

E5.3 Naturally "D". (1971) 3'-4'
For: trombone(bass) and piano(optional). 1 movement. *Dedication:* To my father. *First performed:* May 1971; Batavia, N.Y. Thomas Everett, bass trombone.
Score: reprod. of ms. HU
Part: Seesaw, 1979.
Reel: available from composer.

E5.4 Solo Piece for Violin. (1966) 2'
1 movement.
Score: ms. in composer's hand.

Three Comment. *See* Vietnam 70.

E5.5 Trio. (1967) 5'
For: trumpet, horn,trombone(with F attachment). 3 movements. *Dedication:* For Ray. *First performed:* May 1967; Ithaca, N.Y. Ray Brown, trumpet; Erwin Chandler, horn; Thomas Everett, bass trombone.
Score & parts: reprod. of ms. HU
Reel: available from composer.

E5.6 Vietnam 70. (1970) 6'
For: trombone(bass), saxophone(tenor), double bass, light effects(optional). 3 movements. *Dedication:* To those who died. *First performed:* Apr. 1970; Batavia, N.Y. Thomas Everett, bass trombone; Paul Stomper, tenor saxophone; Alan Dennis, double bass.
Parts: reprod. of ms. HU
Parts: Seesaw, 1979 (titled, Three Comment).
Reel: available from composer.

F1 PETER R. FARMER

Born October 14, 1941. *Education:* B.M. (Boston Conservatory, 1968); M.M. (University of Michigan, 1976); D.M.A. (University of Michigan). *Awards:* Brookline Library Music Association Composers Award (1972), MacDowell Colony Fellowships (1973, 1974).
Related activities: pianist, trumpet player, teacher of jazz improvisation and trumpet, music copyist, transcriber, arranger; currently on the faculty of Berklee College of Music. Be

WORKS

F1.1 Anecdotes before a Hymn. (1976) 3'
For: organ. 1 movement. *Commissioned by:* Bozeman-Gibson and Co. Organ Builders. *First performed:* Mar. 1978; Marine City, Mich.

F1.2 Ensemble. (1967)
Group composition under the direction of Karlheinz Stockhausen, Ferienkurze fuer neue Musik (Darmstadt, West Germany), summer, 1967. *First*

performed: Aug. 1967; Darmstadt, West Germany.

F1.3 Fantasy. (1976) 10'
For: violoncello and piano. 1 movement. *First performed:* 1978; Ann Arbor, Mich.; University of Michigan Composers' Forum. Eileen Benway, violoncello.

F1.4 Pastiche. (1972?)
For: flute and harpsichord. Awarded Brookline Library Music Association Composers Award (1972). *First performed:* 1972; Brookline Public Library.
Tape: recording of first performance. BkPL

F1.5 Sky Line High. (1975) 15'
For: trumpet, saxophone(alto), guitar, double bass, drums, orchestra. Jazz quintet and orchestra. Master's thesis. *First performed:* Feb. 1976; Ann Arbor, Mich. University of Michigan Symphony Orchestra.

F1.6 Sonata for 5 Brass Instruments. (1970) 5'
For: trumpets(2), horn, trombones(2). 3 movements. *First performed:* Aug. 1972; Berkshire Music Center, Tanglewood; Contemporary Music Festival. Student performers.

F1.7 Taking Charge. (1974)
Film music.

F1.8 Three Places in New England.
For: strings(6). *First performed:* 1970; Bennington, Vt.; Bennington Composer's Conference.

F1.9 Trio.
For: clarinet, cornet, bassoon. *First performed:* 1975; Ann Arbor, Mich.; University of Michigan Composers' Forum.

F1.10 Trio-Duo. (1977) 7'
For: clarinet, vibraphone, marimba. 1 movement. *First performed:* 1980; Ann

Arbor, Mich. Bruce Cohen, clarinet;
Dave Colson, percussion.

F2 MARTIN FARREN

Born July 10, 1942, in Lompoc, Calif.
Moved to Boston area 1973. *Education:*
studied composition with Stanworth
Beckler, Samuel H. Scott, Mary
Bowling (University of The Pacific);
Robert Schallenberg, Richard Hervig
(University of Iowa, Ph.D., 1971).
Awards: Georgia Council for the Arts
Grant (1972), National Endowment for
the Arts Grant (1972), Old Dominion
Award (Massachusetts Institute of
Technology, 1975). *Related activities:*
served on the faculties of Arkansas
Polytechnic College (1969-70),
University of Iowa (1971-72), California
State University, Fresno (1972-73),
Massachusetts Institute of Technology
(1973-78), University of Wisconsin,
Parkside (visiting composer, 1976). MIT

WORKS

F2.1 And a River Went out of Eden.
(1978) 10' 30"
For: string orchestra. *Movements:*
Prologue; Chaconne; Epilogue. *Dedicated
to:* Dalia Atlas and the Israel Pro
Musica Orchestra.
Score: reprod. of ms. MIT

F2.2 Augenmusik. (1977) Duration
variable.
For: performers(4) and audience.
Aleatoric music. *Commissioned by:*
William Parsons.
Perf. dir: in *Music for Citizens Band,*
vol. one; Will Parsons, 1978. MIT

F2.3 BODAFRE. (1968; rev. 1974) 3' 35"
For: Sopranos(2), Altos(2), Tenors(2),
Basses(2). 1 movement. *Text:* Bohumila
Groegerova; Josef Hirsal; Gerhard
Ruehm; Edward Lucie Smith; in English,
German, and Czech. *Dedicated to:*
Richard Hervig. *First performed:* 1968;
Iowa City. University of Iowa Center
for New Music Vocal Ensemble.

Score: reprod. of ms. MIT
Reel: recording of first performance.

F2.4 Collected Canons. (1974-77)
For: voices(2-4) and/or instruments(2-3).
Score: reprod. of ms. MIT

F2.5 da.. (1968; rev. 1970) 4' 33"
For: piano(8-hands) or
pianos(4-hands)(2). Aleatoric music.
Dedication: For Joan [Benjamin] *First
performed:* spring, 1968; University of
Iowa. August M. Wegner, William
Parsons, John Monick, Michael Lytle.
Score: reprod. of ms. MIT
Reel: recording of first performance.
Reel: Spring 1970; University of Iowa.
Arthur M. Wegner, William Parsons,
Donald Jenni, Michael Lytle.

F2.6 InMIS: In Paradisum. (1971) 2'
For: viola and chimes. *Dedication:* In
memoriam Igor Stravinsky. *First
performed:* spring, 1971; University of
Iowa; Composers Symposium Concert.
Unidentified violist and William
Parsons, chimes.
Score: reprod. of ms. MIT
Reel: May 1973; California State
University, Fresno.

F2.7 Magnum haereditatis mysterium.
(1976) 8'
For: Mezzo Soprano, trumpet,
trombone, tuba, vibraphone, celeste,
piano, violin, violoncello, double bass.
Commissioned by: University of
Wisconsin, Parkside, Lecture and Fine
Arts Committee for the Parkside
Contemporary Players, August M.
Wegner, director. *First performed:* Apr.
1976; University of Wisconsin,
Parkside. Parkside Contemporary
Players, August M. Wegner, director.
Score: reprod. of ms. MIT
Parts: ms. in composer's hand.

F2.8 Mix Well--Let Rise--When Double
in Bulk, Knead. (1967) Duration
unlimited,but not too long. *For:*
audience(4-part) and conductors(5).
Aleatoric music. *First performed:*
spring, 1967; Unitarian Universalist

Church, Iowa City, Iowa; the first
g.e.e.e.p. concert. The audience.
Score: reprod. of ms. MIT
Parts: ms. in composer's hand.
Reel: Winter 1967; University of Iowa;
the second g.e.e.e.p. concert. The
audience.

F2.9 music for clarinet and piano.
(1973) 6' 30"
Dedication: To my father, 1918-1972.
First performed: May 1973; California
State University, Fresno.
Score: reprod. of ms. MIT
Reel: recording of first performance.
Reel: Mar. 6, 1974; Brookline Public
Library. BkPL

F2.10 Music for December 23. (1973) 2'
30"
For: organ. *Dedication:* For Gerald and
Joann. *First performed:* Dec. 23, 1973;
Sacramento, Calif.
Score: reprod. of ms. MIT

F2.11 music for flute and piano. (1966)
3' 20"
1 movement. *First performed:* winter,
1966; University of Iowa. Patrick
Purswell, flute and Joan Purswell,
piano.
Score: reprod. of ms. MIT
Reel: recording of first performance.

F2.12 Musica Tridentina. (1974) 9' 40"
For: percussion(3) and tape. *First
performed:* 1976; Dekalb, Ill. Blackearth
Percussion Group.
Score: reprod. of ms. MIT
Reel: 1979; University of Cincinnati,
College Conservatory of Music.
Blackearth Percussion Group.

F2.13 Paean for Spring. (1962) 2'
For: handbells(English). *Commissioned
by:* First Methodist Church, Wesleyan
Bell Ringers, Santa Barbara, Calif.
Music: Crescendo (for American Guild
of English Handbell Ringers), 1973. MIT

F2.14 The Passage of Three Times.
(1975) 11'

For: string orchestra. *Movements:* On
Paths to Other Places; Among Celestial
Plains; Canticle. *Dedication:* For Patricia
Sparrow (1927-75)(2nd movement); In
memoriam Eric Satie (d. Aug 5,
1925)(3rd movement). *First performed:*
Dec. 11, 1976; Massachusetts Institute
of Technology. MIT Symphony
Orchestra, David Epstein, conductor.
Score: reprod. of ms. MIT
Parts: ms. in composer's hand.
Reel: recording of first performance.

F2.15 Soft Falls the Sounds of Eden.
(1977) 11'
For: piano. 1 movement. *Dedicated to:*
Michel Meynaud. *First performed:* Mar.
24, 1977; Brookline Public Library.
Martin Farren.
Score: reprod. of ms. MIT
Reel: recording of first performance.
BkPL

F2.16 Sonata for Bassoon and Piano.
(1963)
3 movements. *First performed:* Oct.
1963; University of The Pacific.
Marilyn Mayer, bassoon and Constance
Neville, piano.
Score & part: reprod. of ms.
Reel: recording of first performance.

F2.17 Sonata for Flute and Piano.
(1963)
2 movements. *First performed:* spring,
1964; University of The Pacific.
Unidentified flutist and Constance
Neville, piano.
Score: reprod. of ms. MIT
Reel: recording of first performance.

F2.18 while you were away for the
summer. (1975) 11' 20"
For: viola and piano. *Dedicated to:*
Marcus Thompson. *First performed:*
Oct. 1975; Mount Holyoke College.
Marcus Thompson, viola and Seth
Carlin, piano.
Score: reprod. of ms. MIT

F3 NANCY PLUMMER FAXON

Born November 19, 1914, in Jackson, Miss. Moved to Boston area 1946. *Education:* B.S. (Millsaps College, 1936); studied composition with Max Wald (Chicago Musical College, 1937-41); piano with Rudolf Ganz (Chicago Musical College, M.M., 1938); voice with Nelli Gardini (Chicago Musical College, M.M., 1941). *Awards:* National Composers Clinic (First Prize, 1941). *Related activities:* pianist and arranger of hymn tunes and folk songs for chorus, with or without optional instruments (excluded from the list of works below). W

WORKS

Adagio, Organ. *See* Miniature Suite. Adagio; Arr.

[Adagio, Piano]
F3.1 Adagio. (1939) 2'
1 movement.
Score: ms. in composer's hand.

Adagio espressivo. *See* Intermezzo; Arr.

F3.2 And David Said to Solomon His Son. (1968?) 1' 5"
For: chorus(SATB) and organ. Anthem.
Text: Bible, O.T., I Chronicles 28:20.
First performed: Trinity Church, Boston.
Vocal score: ms. in composer's hand.

F3.3 Andante. (1939) 1' 30"
For: carillon(30-bell). Written for the carillon at Wellesley College. *Dedicated to:* George Faxon.
Score: reprod. of ms.

F3.4 Benedicite omnia opera Domini (1979) 2'
For: chorus(SATB), congregation, organ. Canticle. *Commissioned by and dedicated to:* Clarence Snyder. *First performed:* 1979; Christ Church Christiana Hundred, Wilmington, Del.
Vocal score: reprod. of ms.

F3.5 Benediction (The Peace of God). (1942) 1'

For: chorus(SATB) and organ(optional).
Vocal score: reprod. of ms.

F3.6 Benedictus es, Domine. (1963) 2'
For: chorus(SATB) and organ. Anthem.
Commissioned by and dedicated to: Clarence Snyder and the Christ Church Christiana Hundred Choir, Wilmington, Del. *First performed:* 1963; Wilmington, Del. Christ Church Christiana Hundred Choir, Clarence Snyder, organ.
Vocal score: 1963.

F3.7 Christmas Fantasy. (1975) 40'
For: Soprano, chorus(SSAATTBB), orchestra(2-2-2-2; 2-3-2-0; timp, cym, bells; hp; str). *Text:* Magnificat and exerpts of 15 Christmas carols. Music based on the carol melodies, except for the Magnificat. *Commissioned by:* Fine Arts Chorale, Weymouth, Mass., for its 10th anniversary. *Dedicated to:* Peter Edwards and the Fine Arts Chorale. *First performed:* Dec. 1975; Weymouth, Mass. Fine Arts Chorale. *Reel:* 1975; Massachusetts Institute of Technology.

[Christmas Fantasy. Magnificat; Arr.]
F3.8 Magnificat from Christmas Fantasy. (1975) 4' 20"
For: Soprano and organ. *Dedicated to:* Eleanor Edwards.
Vocal score: reprod. of ms.

[Christmas Fantasy. Of the Father's Love Begotten; Arr.]
F3.9 Prelude on Divinum mysterium. (1976) 2' 15"
For: organ.
Score: reprod. of ms.

[Christmas Fantasy. Of the Father's Love Begotten and Unto Us a Boy Is Born; Arr.]
F3.10 Of the Father's Love Begotten and Unto Us a Boy Is Born. 5'
For: chorus(SSA) or chorus(TB), flute or violin Anthem.
Vocal score: reprod. of ms.

F3.11 Christmas Introit. (1962) 35'
For: chorus(SATB) and organ. Anthem.
Dedicated to: Rev. Theodore Parker

Ferris. *First performed:* 1962; Trinity Church, Boston.
Vocal score: reprod. of ms.

F3.12 A Christmas Litany. (1963) 2'
For: chorus(SATB) and organ. *Text:* Rev. Theodore Parker Ferris. Anthem.
Vocal score: Elkan-Vogel, nyp.

F3.13 A Christmas Prelude. (1942) 3'
For: organ. Variations on *Silent Night*. 1 movement. *Dedicated to:* George Faxon. *First performed:* 1942; St. Andrew's Church, Ann Arbor, Mich. George Faxon.
Score: reprod. of ms.

F3.14 Doxology on Vigiles et Sancti. (196-?) 1' 15"
For: chorus(unison), congregation, trumpets(2), trombones(2), timpani, organ. *Commissioned by:* George Faxon for Trinity Church. *First performed:* late 1960's; Trinity Church, Boston.
Score: reprod. of ms.

Divinum mysterium. *See* Christmas Fantasy. Of the Father's Love Begotten; Arr.

F3.15 Easter Canticle. (1968) 4' 15"
For: chorus(SATB), organ, trumpets(2), trombones(2), timpani. *Text:* Christ Our Passover Is Sacrificed for Us (Bible, N.T., I Corinthians 5:7-8 and 15:20-22; Bible, N.T., Romans 6:9-11). Music based on her Fanfare, Brasses and Timpani. *Commissioned by:* Trinity Church, Boston. *First performed:* Easter Sunday, 1968; Trinity Church, Boston.
Score & parts: ms.

F3.16 Easter Introit on Hymn 91 (Victory). (1965) 1' 10"
For: chorus, trumpets(2), trombones(2), timpani, organ. *Text:* from *Symphonia sirenum selectarum* (1695), translated by Francis Pott; *Victory* adapted by William H. Monk from a *Gloria* by Giovanni Pierluigi da Palestrina.
Vocal score: reprod. of ms.

F3.17 The Entrance into Jerusalem (Introit). (1947) 35"
For: chorus(SATBB). *First performed:* Palm Sunday, 1947; Church of the Advent, Boston. Church of the Advent Men and Boys Choir.
Vocal score: reprod. of ms.

F3.18 An Evening Prayer. 2' 30"
For: chorus(SATB). Motet. *Text:* St. Ambrose; translated by John Mason Neale. *Commissioned by:* Everett Titcomb.
Vocal score: reprod. of ms.
Vocal score: Wood, 1950.

[Fanfare, Brasses and Timpani]
F3.19 Fanfare. (1967) 1'
For: trumpets(2) and timpani. Basis for her Easter Canticle. *Commissioned by:* Trinity Church, Boston, for the 25th anniversary of Rev. Theodore Parker Ferris. *First performed:* 1967; Copley Plaza Hotel, Boston.
Score & parts: ms. in composer's hand.

[Fanfare, Brasses and Timpani; Arr.]
F3.20 Fanfare for Dr. Coburn, No. 1. (1976) 1'
For: trumpets(3), trombones(2), timpani. *Commissioned by:* Committee for the Installation of Bishop John Coburn. *First performed:* Sept. 1976; Boston College; installation of Bishop John Coburn.
Score & parts: ms. in composer's hand.

[Fanfare, Brasses, Timpani, Percussion]
F3.21 Fanfare for Dr. Coburn, No. 2. (1976) 35"
For: trumpets(6), trombones(4), timpani, drum(tenor) and/or drum(side). *Commissioned by:* Committee for the Installation of Bishop John Coburn. *Dedicated to:* Bishop John Coburn. *First performed:* Sept. 1976; Boston College.
Score & parts: ms. in composer's hand.

F3.22 Festival Mass. (1974) 7' 30"
For: chorus(SATB), trumpets(2), trombones(2), timpani, organ.

Commissioned by: Kenneth Starr. *First performed:* 1974; St. Patrick's Church, Boston.
Vocal score: reprod. of ms.

F3.23 Intermezzo. (1939) 2'
For: string quartet. 1 movement (unfinished work).
Score & parts: reprod. of ms.

[Intermezzo; Arr.]
F3.24 Adagio espressivo. (1939) 2'
For: organ. 1 movement.
Score: reprod. of ms.
Score: in *Anthology of Organ Music,* C. Fischer, 1966.
Disc: in *The Organ of the Mother Church,* Aeolian-Skinner AS 313(SD), [1959?] , *King of the Instruments* series, vol. 13. Ruth Barrett Philps, organ of the First Church of Christ Scientist, Boston.

Introit. *See* Christmas Introit; Easter Introit; The Entrance into Jerusalem (Introit); This Is the Victory (Introit).

F3.25 Lament. (1938) 1' 30"
For: voice(low) and piano. 1 movement.
Text: Mavis Douglas.
Score: reprod. of ms.

F3.26 Lament of the Women Following after Joseph of Arimathea. (1965) 3'
For: chorus(SA) and string quartet.
Commissioned by: Clarence Snyder for television broadcast, Wilmington, Del., Good Friday, 1965. *First performed:* 1965; Wilmington, Del.; television broadcast.
Vocal score: ms. in composer's hand.
Vocal score: reprod. of ms.

[Lament of the Women Following after Joseph of Arimathea; Arr.]
F3.27 Lament of the Women Following after Joseph of Arimathea. (1965) 3'
For: chorus(SA), organ, violin(optional). Organ part arranged by George Faxon.
Score & part: reprod. of ms.
Part(violin): ms. in composer's hand.

F3.28 Lead, Kindly Light. (1972) 2' 30"
For: chorus(SSATTBB) and organ. Anthem. *Text:* Cardinal John Henry Newman. *Commissioned by and dedicated to:* Dr. Theodore Parker Ferris. First performed: Nov. 1972; Trinity Church, Boston; funeral of Rev. Theodore Parker Ferris.
Vocal score: reprod. of ms.

Litany. *See* A Christmas Litany.

F3.29 Lord, in This Thy Mercy's Day. (1963) 3'
For: Soprano or Mezzo Soprano, violin, organ or piano. Anthem. *Text:* Isaac Williams. Commissioned by and dedicated to: Rev. A. Vincent Bennett. *First performed:* 1963; Christ Church, Fitchburg, Mass. Nancy Plummer Faxon, soprano; Emily Faxon, violin; George Faxon, organ.
Score & part: ms. in composer's hand.

[Lord, in This Thy Mercy's Day; Arr.]
F3.30 Lord, in This Thy Mercy's Day. (1963) 3'
For: Soprano and organ. Anthem. *Text:* Isaac Williams.

Magnificat from Christmas Fantasy. *See* Christmas Fantasy. Magnificat; Arr.

F3.31 Miniature Suite. (1939) 10'
For: orchestra(2-0-3(in A(2), in C)-0; 1-0-0-0; str(4-4-3-2-0)). 4 movements.
Score & parts: ms. in composer's hand.

[Miniature Suite. Adagio; Arr.]
F3.32 Adagio. 2' 30"
For: organ.
Score: reprod. of ms.

F3.33 Missa brevis. (1948) 4' 40"
For: chorus(SATTBB) and organ. Written for George Faxon and the Men and Boys Choir of the Church of the Advent Boston.
Vocal score & parts: reprod. of ms.

Of the Father's Love Begotten. *See* Christmas Fantasy. Of the Father's Love Begotten; Arr.

Of the Father's Love Begotten and Unto Us a Boy Is Born. *See* Christmas Fantasy. Of the Father's Love Begotten and Unto Us a Boy Is Born; Arr.

The Peace of God. *See* Benediction (The Peace of God).

F3.34 Prelude. (1963) 1' 30"
For: violin and organ or piano. 1 movement. *Commissioned by:* Rev. A. Vincent Bennett. *Dedication:* For Emily Faxon and her father. *First performed:* 1963; Christ Church, Fitchburg, Mass. Emily Faxon, violin and George Faxon, organ.
Score & part: reprod. of ms.

Prelude on Darmstadt. *See* Prelude on We Love the Place O God (Darmstadt, 1698).

F3.35 Prelude on Dies irae. (1969) 2' 30"
For: organ. 1 movement. Written for George Faxon. *First performed:* 1969; Longwood Gardens, Kennett Square, Pa. George Faxon.
Score: ms. in composer's hand.

Prelude on Divinum mysterium. *See* Christmas Fantasy. Of the Father's Love Begotten; Arr.

F3.36 Prelude on We Love the Place O God (Darmstadt, 1698). 2'
For: organ. *Commissioned by:* McLaughlin & Reilly.
Score: in *Gloria Deo: Eight Organ Works by Contemporary Composers*, McLaughlin, 1963.

F3.37 Rhapsody. (1941) 10'
For: orchestra(2-2-2-2; 2-2-2-0; timp, pf; str). 1 movement. *Dedicated to:* My husband, George. National Composers Clinic Prize (First), Chicago, 1941.
Score: reprod. of ms.

F3.38 Romans XII. (1950) 10'
For: Soprano, Baritone, chorus(SSAATTBB). Motet.

Commissioned by: Gordon College. *First performed:* Jan. 1951. Gordon College Choir, Charles Matheson, conductor. *Vocal score:* reprod. of ms.

F3.39 Scherzo for Right Hand and Pedal. (1963) 2' 30"
For: organ. *Commissioned by:* Clarence Snyder. *First performed:* fall, 1963; Longwood Gardens, Kennett Square, Pa. Clarence Snyder.
Score: reprod. of ms.

F3.40 Sonata Fantasy.
For: organ. 1 movement. *Commissioned by and dedicated to:* Kenneth Starr. *First performed:* 1977; Cathedral of Notre Dame, Paris, France. Kenneth Starr.
Score: reprod. of ms.

F3.41 Song for a Big Evening. (1970) 2' 45"
For: chorus(SSSAA) and piano. *Text:* Phyllis McGinley. *Commissioned by:* Clarence Snyder. *Dedication:* In memory of Maryellen Snyder. *First performed:* 1970; Wilmington, Del. Unidentified women's chorus, Clarence Snyder, conductor.
Vocal score: reprod. of ms.

[Suite, Chorus and Piano]
F3.42 Suite. (1953) 6' 30"
For: chorus(women, unison, SSA) and pianos(2). *Text:* from the *New Yorker* by Ruth Lambert Jones. *Contents:* Distinction; Tokens; Lament; Process. *Commissioned by:* Bradford College for its 150th Anniversary Concert, June 1953. *First performed:* June 1953; Bradford College. Bradford College Chorus, Ellwood Hill, conductor; pianists unidentified.
Vocal score: reprod. of ms.

[Suite, Trumpets(2) and Organ]
F3.43 Suite. (1965) 8' 30"
3 movements. *Commissioned by:* Mrs. Roger Voisin. *Dedicated to:* Roger and Peter Voisin. *First performed:* Feb. 14, 1965; Symphony Hall, Boston; in

Boston Symphony Orchestra Organ Series. Peter Voisin and Roger Voisin, trumpets; George Faxon, organ.
Score & parts: reprod. of ms.

F3.44 Surely the Lord. (1943) 2′
For: chorus(SATB) and organ. Anthem.
Text: Bible. *Commissioned by and dedicated to:* Bradford Wright for the 100th anniversary of Grace Church, Newton, Mass. *First performed:* 1973; Grace Church, Newton, Mass.
Vocal score: reprod. of ms.

F3.45 Te Deum laudamus. (1948) 5′ 30″
For: chorus(SATBB), organ, trumpets(2)(optional), trombones(2)(optional), timpani(optional). Canticle. Written for George Faxon and Church of the Advent Men and Boys Choir. *First performed:* 1948; Church of the Advent, Boston. Church of the Advent Men and Boys Choir, George Faxon, organ.
Score & parts: reprod. of ms.

F3.46 This Is the Victory (Introit). (1968) 25′
For: chorus(SSAATTBB). Anthem.
Commissioned by: Rev. Theodore Parker Ferris. *First performed:* 1968; Trinity Church, Boston.
Vocal score: ms. in composer's hand.

F3.47 Toccata. (1956) 3′ 10″
For: organ. 1 movement. *Commissioned by:* George Faxon. *First performed:* 1956; Riverside Church, New York City; American Guild of Organists national convention. George Faxon.
Score: Gray, 1958.

Vigiles et Sancti. *See* Doxology on Vigiles et Sancti.

F4 ALAN JOHN FELICE (JOHN)

Born June 5, 1938, in St. Catharines, Ont. Moved to Boston area 1966.
Education: A.R.C.T., Piano (Royal Conservatory of Toronto, 1956); studied composition with John Beckwith, Sam Dolin, John Weinzweig (University of

Toronto, B.M., 1960); Robert Cogan (New England Conservatory, M.M., 1968); piano with Pierre Souvarin.
Related activities: pianist; assistant stage manager and pianist, Canadian Opera Company (1963); served on the faculties of the National Ballet School, Toronto, Ont. (1963-66) and New England Conservatory (1968-). NEC

WORKS

F4.1 An American Ceremony for Solo Clarinet 1973. (1973) 18′
Written for Stephen Bates. *First performed:* Mar. 8, 1973; Washington, D.C. Stephen Bates.
Score.
Cassette: Dec. 4, 1973; New England Conservatory; in *An Evening of Contemporary Music.* Stephen Bates. NEC

An American Ritual for Solo Oboe....1975. *See* Hawkins.

F4.2 Andante and Allegretto. (1964) 2′
For: piano. *First performed:* Sept. 1965; Toronto, Canada. John Felice. *Score.*

F4.3 Angel Cloud. (1979) 15′
For: flutes(2), trumpet, euphoniums(2), violin. Written for Jacqueline De Voe, Rosemary Vecere, Dana Oakes, Peter Cirelli, Jeff Whittsett, Mike Prince. To be performed with A Night Ritual. *First performed:* Apr. 18, 1979; Harvard-Epworth United Methodist Church, Cambridge. Jacqueline De Voe and Rosemary Vecere, flutes; Dana Oakes, trumpet; Peter Cirelli and Jeff Whittsett, euphoniums; Mike Prince, violin.

F4.4 ANnotation '74. (1974) 15′
For: voice, flute, oboe, trumpet, double bass. *Text:* John G. Neihardt. Written for Alan Nagel. *First performed:* Mar. 14, 1975; New England Conservatory. Kristin Samuelson, voice; Edward A. Schultz, flute; David Hawkins, oboe; Scott Fessler, trumpet; Alan Nagel, double bass. *Score.*

F4.5 .... Before You Travel On .....1981...for Solo Flute. (1981) 8'
Written for Les Roettges.

A Birthday Recognition, 1984 I. *See* Trio 1980.

F4.6 A Birthday Recognition, 1984 II. (1980) 4'
For: pianos(2)(left hands). Written for Laurent Levy. *First performed:* Oct. 13, 1980; New England Conservatory. John Felice and Laurent Levy.
Cassette: recording of first performance. NEC

F4.7 Brief Encounter. (1978) 3'
For: piano. Written for Hilary Matzinger. *First performed:* Nov. 18, 1980; New England Conservatory; in Enchanted Circle. David Hagan.
Cassette: recording of first performance. NEC

F4.8 Chamber Music 1979. (1979) 12'
For: voice, flute, clarinet, bassoon, trumpets(2). *Text: Chamber Music* by James Joyce. Written for John Crelan. *First performed:* June 16, 1979; Emmanuel Church, Boston. Robert Hancock, voice; Anne Chatoney Shreffler, flute; Randall Ment, clarinet; James R. McFadden, bassoon; Scott Fessler and Thomas Scheibels, trumpets.

F4.9 Chamber Music 1980. (1980)
For: voice, flutes(3), bassoon, horn, trumpets(2), viola. *Text: Chamber Music* by James Joyce. *First performed:* June 21, 1980; Sanders Theatre, Harvard University. Robert Hancock, voice; Amy Flemming, Anne Chatoney Shreffler and Priscilla Call, flutes; unidentified bassoonist; Sara Menis, horn; Scott Fessler and Jonathan Knight, trumpets; Scott Jessup, viola.

F4.10 Chamber Music 1981. (1981) 15'
For: speaker, clarinet, flutes(2),

trumpets(2), double bass. 1 movement. *Text: Chamber Music* by James Joyce. *Commissioned by:* John Crelan. *First performed:* June 16, 1981; Jordan Hall, Boston; Bloomsday Concert. John Shreffler, speaker; Corey O'Brien, clarinet; Anne Chatoney Shreffler and Jacqueline De Voe, flutes; Scott Fessler and Jonathan Knight, trumpets; Jack Hill, double bass.

[Circumnavigation; Version A]
F4.11 Circumnavigation. (1980) 8'
For: flutes(2) and instruments(unspecified). Written for Jacqueline De Voe. *Dedicated to:* Jackie Devoe and Rosie Vecere. *First performed:* Mar. 3, 1981; New England Conservatory. Jacqueline De Voe and Rosemary Vecere, flutes; Pam Ambrose, violoncello; Karen Leopardi and Robert West, clarinets; Lucy Mackall, bassoon.

[Circumnavigation; Version B]
F4.12 Circumnavigation. (1980) 8'
For: violoncello and woodwind ensemble(flutes(5), clarinets(2), bassoons(3)). Written for Jacqueline De Voe. *Dedicated to:* Jackie Devoe and Rosie Vecere. *First performed:* Mar. 9, 1981; New England Conservatory; in Enchanted Circle. Jacqueline De Voe, Rosemary Vecere, Les Roettges, Nan Vlad, Anne Chatoney Shreffler, flutes; Karen Leopardi and Robert West, clarinets; Lucy Mackall, Leo Kenen, James R. McFadden, bassoons; Pam Ambrose, violoncello.
Cassette: recording of first performance. NEC

David '69. *See* Trio: David '69.

F4.13 DUO 1979. (1979) 9'
For: clarinet and viola. Written for Robert West and Scott Jessup. To be performed with Triock. First performed: Dec. 7, 1979; New England

Conservatory. Robert West, clarinet and Scott Jessup, viola.

For a Shaking Foot That Is No More. *See* Triod '73 (for a shaking foot that is no more).

F4.14 From Deep Within. (1975) 8' 30"
For: voice, flute, piano. *Text:* James Joyce. Written for Kristin Samuelson and Edward A. Schultz. *First performed:* Feb. 8, 1976; Harvard-Epworth United Methodist Church, Cambridge. Kristin Samuelson, voice; Edward A. Schultz, flute; John Felice, piano. *Score. Tape.*

F4.15 from Quasimodo Sunday. (1973) 6'
For: double bass. Plain chant. 1 movement. *Written for and dedicated to:* Alan Nagel. *First performed:* Mar. 14, 1974; New England Conservatory. Alan Nagel.
Score: Yorke, 1974. BPL NEC T

F4.16 A Ghtowening. (1975) 8'
For: piano(left hand or right hand).
Score.

Happiness Is...1970. *See* Trio: Happiness Is...1970.

F4.17 Hawkins--an american ritual for solo oboe....1975. (1975) 9'
For: oboe and speakers(2)(optional).
Text: John G. Neihardt. Written for David Hawkins. *First performed:* Apr. 16, 1975; New England Conservatory. David Hawkins, oboe; Lary Prince and Edward A. Schultz, speakers. *Score.*

F4.18 In Memoriam: September 5th 1877. (1977)
For: voice, trumpets(4), pianos(2).
Withdrawn.

In Nomine. *See* Trio: In Nomine.

In Protest...I. *See* Trio: In Protest...I.

F4.19 Interlude 1979. (1979) 12'
For: flute, clarinet, trumpet, trombone,

piano, viola. *Text: The Indian's Night Promises to Be Dark*, a speech given in 1853 by Seattle, Indian Chief of the Duquamisk and Duamisk tribes. *Dedicated to:* Anne Chatoney, Dana Oakes, Robert Couture, Robert West, Scott Jessup. *First performed:* Oct. 8, 1979; New England Conservatory. Anne Chatoney Shreffler, flute; Robert West, clarinet; Dana Oakes, trumpet; Robert Couture, trombone; John Felice, piano; Scott Jessup, viola.
Cassette: recording of first performance. NEC

F4.20 Lavertations 74. (1974) 10'
For: congregation(speaking) and organ.
Text: John G. Neihardt. Written for Lavert Stuart. *First performed:* Apr. 24, 1974; Old West Church, Boston. *Score.*

F4.21 Merton for a While. (1979) 8'
For: Tenor, bassoon, instruments(unspecified)(in audience).
Text: Thomas Merton. Written for April Forbell. *First performed:* Mar. 7, 1979; New England Conservatory. Paul Forrest, tenor and April Forbell, bassoon.
Cassette: Apr. 9, 1979; New England Conservatory; in *Enchanted Circle*. Paul Forrest, tenor and April Forbell, bassoon. NEC

F4.22 The Nightingale and the Rose. (1972) 12'
For: clarinet and tape(pre-recorded clarinet). Written for Dean Rhodes.
Score.

F4.23 A Night Ritual. (1978) 15'
For: flute and voice. *Text:* John G. Neihardt. Written for Anne Chatoney and Kristin Samuelson. *First performed:* Nov. 15, 1978; New England Conservatory. Anne Chatoney Shreffler, flute and Kristin Samuelson, voice.
Cassette: recording of first performance. NEC

F4.24 Night Spaces. (1974) 6'
For: harp. Written for Judy Loman.
First performed: Nov. 1975; Radio

Canadia; CBC Celebrity Series. Judy Loman. *Score. Tape.*

October 1968. *See* Trio: October 1968.

F4.25 On Either Side [E,K,] 1980. (1980) 10'
For: pianos(2) and trumpets(2)(optional). Written for John Felice and Donald Lafferty. *First performed:* Sept. 12, 1980; New England Conservatory. John Felice and Donald Lafferty, pianos; Scott Fessler and Jonathan Knight, trumpets.
Cassette: recording of first performance. NEC

F4.26 One Thousand, Two Hundred. (1974) 8' 30"
For: speaker and piano. *Text: Boston Globe*, June 1974. Written for Carol Commune and Kristin Samuelson. *First performed:* Feb. 18, 1975; New England Conservatory. Kristin Samuelson, speaker and Carol Commune, piano. *Score.*
Cassette: Sept. 21, 1981; New England Conservatory; in *Enchanted Circle*. John Shreffler, speaker and John Felice, piano. NEC

F4.27 Prelude, Recitative & Toccata. (1969-70) 6' 30"
For: harpsichord. *Written for and dedicated to:* Betsy Goldberg. Score.

F4.28 Quartet. (1968) 12'
For: flute, horn, piano, violin. Written for Robert Thistle. *First performed:* Feb. 11, 1968; New England Conservatory. Jonathan Landell, flute; Robert Thistle, horn; John Felice, piano; Ann T. Danis, violin. *Score. Tape.*

F4.29 A Quiet Beginning. (1975) 12'
For: flute, horn, trumpet. Written for Susan Graham. *First performed:* Feb. 18, 1975; Jordan Hall, Boston. Edward A. Schultz, flute; Susan Graham, horn; Tim Morrison, trumpet. *Score. Tape.*

F4.30 Quiring. (1977) 7'
For: trumpets(4). Written for Thomas Scheibels. May be performed with VONnotation. First performed: May 2, 1977; New England Conservatory. *Score.*

F4.31 A Reverence for the Sun. (1975) 8'
For: speaker and trumpet. *Text:* Scott Momaday. Written for Scott Fessler. *First performed:* May 2, 1977; New England Conservatory; in Enchanted Circle. Kristin Samuelson, speaker and Lary Prince, trumpet. Score.
Cassette: recording of first performance. NEC

F4.32 Rosa Amoris. (1960) 10'
For: Soprano and piano. 4 movements. *Text:* Oscar Wilde. *First performed:* Aug. 1965; Toronto, Canada. Vera Longly, soprano and John Felice, piano. *Score.*

F4.33 Sacred Ashes--Ancestral Voices. (1976) 18'
For: English horn, trumpets(3), winds(14 or more), percussion(3)(gong, bells, vibraphone). Written for David Gaylin. *First performed:* Mar. 25, 1976; New England Conservatory. Mike Duncan, English horn; Bruce Hall, Lary Prince, Thomas Scheibels, trumpets; NEC Wind Ensemble, David Gaylin, conductor. Score. Tape.

F4.34 Sextet. (1967) 5'
For: horn, trumpet, trombone, violin, viola, double bass.

F4.35 Sextet 1981. (1981) 8'
For: speaker/conductor, horn, trumpet, trombone, violin, viola, double bass. *Text:* John Shreffler. Written for Steve Adams.

[Songs]
F4.36 Five Songs on Poems by Emily Dickinson. (1963) 7'
For: Soprano and piano. *Text:* Emily Dickinson. *First performed:* Apr. 1965; Toronto, Canada. *Score.*

F4.37 Speech Is the Twin of My Vision. (1975) 16'
For: voice and piano. *Text:* Walt Whitman. Written for Kristin Samuelson. *First performed:* Feb. 18, 1976; New England Conservatory. Kristin Samuelson, voice and John Felice, piano. *Score. Tape.*

F4.38 Sunyata I. (1979) 8'
For: piano. Written for Jocelyn Lopatin. *First performed:* Nov. 18, 1980; New England Conservatory; in Enchanted Circle. David Hagan.
Cassette: recording of first performance. NEC

F4.39 Sunyata II. (1979) 8'
For: trombone, harp, piano. Written for Robert Couture and Judy Saiki. *First performed:* Mar. 16, 1979; New England Conservatory. Robert Couture, trombone; Judy Saiki, harp; John Felice, piano.

Sur le nom Martha N. Folts. *See* Trio: Sur le nom Martha N. Folts.

F4.40 To the King. (1978) 6'
For: piano.

F4.41 Torn Page. (1979) 4'
For: flute and harpsichord. Written for Priscilla Call. *First performed:* Mar. 16, 1979; New England Conservatory. Priscilla Call, flute and John Felice, harpsichord.

F4.42 Triatro. (1972) 8'
For: piano. Written for Anthony Rauche. *First performed:* Apr. 27, 1972; New England Conservatory. Anthony Rauche. *Score. Tape.*

F4.43 Trio: David '69. (1969) 22'
For: instrumental ensemble(flute/piccolo/alto flute, clarinet(in A), harpsichord, pianos(2), violin, vibraphone/cymbals/gong, instruments(unspecified) in audience(12)). Written for David Seaton. *First performed:* Oct. 7, 1969; New England Conservatory; in An Evening of

Contemporary Music. Nancy Joyce, flute; David Seaton, clarinet; Paul Patton, harpsichord; Dennis Giauque and Robert A. Glover, pianos; Ann T. Danis, violin; William Wiley, vibraphone.
Score.
Cassette: recording of first performance. NEC

F4.44 Trio espressivo. (1969) 8'
For: harpsichords(2). Written for Betsy Goldberg. *First performed:* 1971; New England Conservatory. Rodney Lister and James Winn.
Cassette: Oct. 17, 1972; New England Conservatory; in *An Evening of Contemporary Music*. Rodney Lister and James Winn. NEC

F4.45 Trio: Happiness Is...1970. (1970) 14'
For: horns(2), violin, viola, violoncello, piano, vibraphone(optional). Written for Ann T. Danis. *First performed:* Jan. 26, 1971; New England Conservatory; in An Evening of Contemporary Music. Kathleen Vaught and Bruce Wilhjem horns; Ann T. Danis, violin; Judy Wolper, viola; Ruth E. Trexler, violoncello; Eric Culver, piano.
Score.
Cassette: recording of first performance. NEC

F4.46 Trio: In nomine 1331. (1971) 12'
For: piano. Written for Robert A. Glover. *First performed:* Feb. 1972; New England Conservatory. Robert A. Glover.
Score.
Cassette: Mar. 7, 1972; New England Conservatory; in *An Evening of Contemporary Music*. Robert A. Glover. NEC

F4.47 Trio: In nomine 1970. (1970) 11'
For: horn and piano. Written for Kathleen Vaught. *First performed:* Apr. 24, 1970; New England Conservatory. Kathleen Vaught, horn and John Felice, piano.
Score.
Cassette: Nov. 9, 1971; New England

Conservatory; in *An Evening of Contemporary Music*. Ray Wagner, horn and Rodney Lister, piano. NEC

[Trio: In nomine 1971]
F4.48 Trio: In nomine. (1971) 10'
For: flute, clarinet, harpsichord. Written for Linda Works and Dean Rhodes.
First performed: Mar. 10, 1971; New England Conservatory. Linda Works, flute; Dean Rhodes, clarinet; John Felice, harpsichord.
Score.
Cassette: May 9, 1971; New England Conservatory; in *A Festival of New England Composers Past and Present*. Linda Burlingame, flute; Dean Rhodes, clarinet; John Felice, harpsichord. NEC

F4.49 Trio: In Protest...l. (1968) 7'
For: flute, horn, piano, trumpet(off stage), instruments(unspecified) in audience.   Written for Mary Biscoe.
First performed: Apr. 12, 1968; New England Conservatory. Amy Landers, flute; Mary Biscoe, horn; John Felice, piano; Lee Stevens, trumpet.
Score.
Cassette: Mar. 31, 1975; New England Conservatory. Edward A. Schultz, flute; Susan Graham, horn; Ron Willis, piano; Bo Winiker, trumpet, and others. NEC

F4.50 Trio: Lirico for Flute and Harpsichord. (1969) 8'
Written for Linda Works. *First performed:* Nov. 15, 1969; New England Conservatory. Linda Works, flute and John Felice, harpsichord. *Score.*

F4.51 Trio: Lirico for Viola and Harpsichord. (1969) 6'
Written for Ann Drinan. *First performed:* Feb. 18, 1970; Wis. Ann Drinan, viola and Betsy Goldberg, harpsichord. *Score.*

[Trio: Lirico, Violoncello and Harpsichord]
F4.52 Trio: Lirico for Cello and Harpsichord. (1969) 6'
Written for Andrea Hart. *First*

performed: Mar. 8, 1969; New England Conservatory. Andrea Hart, violoncello and Dennis Giauque, harpsichord.
Score.
Cassette: Apr. 8, 1970; New England Conservatory. Adrienne Hartzell, violoncello and Dennis Giauque, harpsichord.

F4.53 Trio (1968). (1968) 8'
For: flute, clarinet, trumpet. Written for Jonathan Landell. *First performed:* Mar. 8, 1968; New England Conservatory. Jonathan Landell, flute; Ellen Polansky, clarinet; Lee Stevens, trumpet. *Score.*
Tape.

F4.54 Trio 1980. (1980) 13'
For: clarinet, viola, piano(players also speak). *Text:* John Shreffler. *Contents:* A Birthday Recognition 1984 l for Piano Left Hand; Soliloquy for Clarinet; Monologue for Viola. Movements performed simultaneously. Written for Robert West, Scott Jessup, John Felice. *First performed:* Oct. 13, 1980; New England Conservatory. Robert West, clarinet; Scott Jessup, viola; John Felice, piano.
Cassette: recording of first performance.

F4.55 Trio: October 1968. (1968) 9'
For: clarinet, horn, piano. Written for Mary Biscoe and David Seaton. *First performed:* Oct. 22, 1968; Jordan Hall, Boston. David Seaton, clarinet; Mary Biscoe, horn; John Felice, piano.
Score.
Cassette: Nov. 15, 1978; New England Conservatory. Randall Ment, clarinet; Rebecca Burkhardt, horn; Suzanne Dewart, piano. NEC

F4.56 Trio: 7133 '71. (1971) 4'
For: tape(piano, pre-recorded). Written for Paul Patton. *First performed:* Nov. 14, 1971; New England Conservatory. Paul Patton. *Score.*

F4.57 Trio: 68/69. (1969) 18'
For: flute, clarinet(E-flat), clarinet,

clarinet(in A), oboe, English horn, trumpet(muted), violin, vibraphone.

F4.58 Trio: Sur le nom Martha N. Folts. (1971) 8'
For: harpsichord. Written for Martha Folts. *First performed:* Apr. 1974; Ames, Iowa. *Score.*

F4.59 Triock. (1979?) 16'
For: Soprano, flute/piccolo, bassoon. *Text:* from Zen liturgy. Written for James R. McFadden. May be performed with DUO 1979. First performed: Dec. 7, 1979; New England Conservatory. Joan Heller, soprano; Priscilla Call, flute; James R. McFadden, bassoon.

F4.60 Triod '73 (for a shaking foot that is no· more). (1973) 6'
For: piano. Written for Dennis Giauque. *First performed:* May 4, 1973; San Francisco, Calif. Dennis Giauque. *Score.*

F4.61 VONnotation 77. (1977) 10'
For: voice and piano(optional). Written for Celia Von Mering. May be performed with Quiring. *First performed:* May 2, 1977; New England Conservatory; in Enchanted Circle. Celia Von Mering, voice and John Felice, piano.
Score.
Cassette: recording of first performance. NEC

F5 ANTHONY J. FERRAZANO (ANTHONY ZANO)

Born June 4, 1937, in Worcester, Mass. *Education:* New England Conservatory (1954-56); Boston Conservatory (1956-57); Boston University (1958-63); Forest Conservatory, Sussex University, Sussex England (Mus.D., 1963); studied composition with William Tesson (1954), Roland Nadeau (1955), Walter Piston (1955), Margaret Mason (1955-56), Wei-Wing Lee (1956), Rouben Gregorian (1956-57), Francis Findlay (1959), Hugo Norden (1960-62). *Related activities:* pianist; teacher; arranger; organized New England Trio (1966);

author of *Mechanics of Modern Music* (Berben Editions); served on the faculties of New York School of Music (1959), Worcester Polytechnic Institute (1961), Schenectady Conservatory of Music (1966-67); staff musician, RCA, New York City (1975-78). BPL

WORKS

F5.1 Addition. (1957) 10'
For: clarinet, double bass, piano. 1 movement.

F5.2 Atonement. (1968) 20'
For: orchestra(2-2-2-2; 4-2-3-1; perc; str). 1 movement.
Score & parts: ms. in composer's hand.

F5.3 Concert in the Round Overture. (1967) 10'
For: orchestra(2-2-2-2; 4-2-3-1; perc; str). 1 movement. *Dedicated to:* Worcester Orchestra, Harry Levenson, conductor. *First performed:* Nov. 26, 1967; Worcester, Mass.
Score & parts: ms. in composer's hand.

F5.4 Dance Moderato. (1962) 10'
For: string orchestra. 1 movement.
Condensed score: ms. in composer's hand.

F5.5 Departure. (1958) 8'
For: clarinet and piano. 1 movement.
Score.

F5.6 Dispersion. (1969)
For: jazz ensemble. 1 movement.
Score & parts: ms. in composer's hand.

F5.7 Evening Star. (1968) 4'
For: chorus(SATB). 1 movement. *Text:* Edgar Allan Poe.
Vocal score & parts: ms. in composer's hand.

F5.8 Gathering Place. (1959) 10'
For: jazz ensemble. 3 movements.
Commissioned by: Balmore Records.
First performed: Apr. 27, 1960; New York City.

Score & parts: Balmore Music.
Disc: Balmore Records SL 381.

F5.9 Hail Holy Queen. 3'
For: chorus(SATB). 1 movement.
Condensed score: ms. in composer's hand.

F5.10 Hale Recollections. (1967) 20'
For: flute, clarinet, piano.
Score & parts: ms. in composer's hand.

F5.11 He Who Comes from Above.
(1971) 10'
For: chorus(SATB) and orchestra(2-2-2-2; str) or piano. *Text:* Bible, N.T., John 3:31.
Score & parts: ms. in composer's hand.

F5.12 Intimo. (1966) 15'
For: clarinet, piano, double bass. 1 movement. *Score.*

F5.13 Jazz Sonata. (1958) 20'
For: double bass and piano. 3 movements.
Score & part: ms. in composer's hand.

F5.14 Laudi Vergine Maria. (1959) 8'
For: chorus(SATB). *Text:* Dante.
Vocal score: ms. in composer's hand.

F5.15 Mass. (1967) 30'
For: chorus(SATB) and piano or organ or flutes(2), oboes(2), clarinets(2), bassoons(2).
Score: ms. in composer's hand.

F5.16 Night Prelude. (1976) 5'
For: piano.
Score: ms. in composer's hand.

F5.17 Preconception. (1971) 5'
For: double bass and piano.
Score & part: ms. in composer's hand.

F5.18 Prelude. (1958) 10'
For: double bass and piano. 1 movement. *Score.*

[Quartet, Strings, No. 1]
F5.19 String Quartet No. 1. (1956) 25'
3 movements.
Score & parts: ms. in composer's hand.

[Quartet, Strings, No. 2]
F5.20 String Quartet No. 2. (1967) 30'
3 movements.
Score & parts: ms. in composer's hand.

F5.21 Restatements. (1966) 10'
For: clarinet, double bass, piano.
Score & parts: ms. in composer's hand.

F5.22 Scherzo. 8'
For: trumpets(2) and piano.
Score & parts: ms. in composer's hand.

[Sonata, Clarinet and Piano]
F5.23 Clarinet Sonata. (1958) 20'
3 movements.
Score: ms. in composer's hand.

[Sonata, Flute and Piano]
F5.24 Flute Sonata. (1958) 15'
3 movements.
Score: ms. in composer's hand.

F5.25 The Soul's Season. (1967) 5'
For: chorus(SATB). *Text:* Henry David Thoreau.
Vocal score: ms. in composer's hand.

F5.26 Stillness. (1966) 8'
For: strings(unspecified). 1 movement.
Score & parts: ms. in composer's hand.

F5.27 Symphonic Suite. (1963) 38'
For: orchestra(2-2(&Ehn)-2-2; 4-2-3-1; perc; str). 6 movements.
Score: ms. in composer's hand.

F5.28 Symphony No. 1. (1959) 30'
For: orchestra(1-1-1-1; 0-2-2-0; str).
Movements: Allegro; Andante; Passacaglia; Interference.
Score: ms. in composer's hand.

F5.29 Symphony No. 2. (1960) 35'
For: orchestra(2-2-2-2; 0-2-3-1; perc;

str). 4 movements.
Score: ms. in composer's hand.

F5.30 Vita brevis, ars longa. (1966) 20'
For: flute, clarinet, violoncello, double
bass, piano. 1 movement.
Score & parts: ms. in composer's hand.

F6 THOMAS E. FLAHERTY

Born July 26, 1950, in Cambridge,
Mass. *Education:* studied composition
with Arthur Berger, Martin Boykan,
Seymour Shifrin (Brandeis University,
B.A., 1972); Buelent Arel, Billy Jim
Layton (State University of New York,
Stony Brook, M.A., 1976); violoncello
with Bernard Greenhouse and Timothy
Eddy (State University of New York,
Stony Brook, M.M., 1978). *Awards:*
Lado Scholarship (1971), New York
State Council on the Arts Meet the
Composer Grants (1978, 1979),
Massachusetts Council on the Arts and
Humanities, Artist Fellowship Program
(Finalist, 1978, 1979). *Related activities:*
member of the faculty of Scripps
College. BrU

WORKS

F6.1 Break, Break, Break. (1975) 4'
For: chorus(SSA) and piano. *Text:*
Alfred, Lord Tennyson.
Vocal score: available from composer.

F6.2 Conversation. (1975) 5'
For: flute and oboe. *First performed:*
June 22, 1976; New York City. Robin
Peller, flute and Mark Hill, oboe.
Score: available from composer.
Reel: Sept. 30, 1979; First and Second
Church, Boston; Dinosaur Annex
Concert. Nan Washburn, flute and
Barbara Knapp, oboe. WGBH

F6.3 Duo. (1978) 7'
For: violin and violoncello.
Score: available from composer.

F6.4 Music. (1976) 14'
For: orchestra(2-2-2-2; 4-3-3-0; perc(4);
str). *First performed:* Apr. 12, 1977.

State University of New York, Stony
Brook University Orchestra, David
Lawton, conductor.
Score & parts: available from
composer.

F6.5 Nocturne. (1981) 10'
For: chamber orchestra(2-2-2-2; 2-2-2-0;
pf; str). *First performed:* Apr. 12, 1981;
Sanders Theatre, Harvard University.
Pro Arte Chamber Orchestra of Boston,
Newell Hendricks, conductor.
Score & parts: available from
composer.

F6.6 Tetralogue. (1974) 10'
For: violins(2), violas(2), violoncellos(2),
pianos(2). *First performed:* Apr. 25,
1975; Stony Brook, N.Y. Rebecca
LaBrecque and George Fisher, pianos;
Anne Marie de Zeeuw and Ginette
Chang, violins; Douglas Anderson and
Marion Weinkiper, violas; Sarah Carter
and Martha Calhoun, violoncellos; Carol
Catwood, conductor.
Score & parts: available from
composer.

F6.7 Variations. (1973) 4'
For: piano. *First performed:* Nov. 8,
1978; Stony Brook, N.Y. George Fisher.
Score: available from composer.

F7 JAMES FORTE

Born September 19, 1936, in Boston.
Related activities: music director of the
Robbins Library Concert Series,
Arlington, Mass.; founder and chairman,
Arlington Alive (arts council of
Arlington, Mass.); manager,
Northeastern University Symphony
Orchestra; director, Northeastern
University Music Department Concert
Series; chairman of the Executive
Board, Massachusetts State Arts
Lottery Advisory Committee. NU

WORKS

F7.1 Adagio. (1967)
For: orchestra.

Score: reprod. of ms.; available from composer.

F7.2 And the Day after I Die. (1969)
For: chorus(SATB). *Text:* James Forte.
Vocal score: reprod. of ms.; available from composer.

F7.3 Bless the Lord. (1965)
For: Soprano, chorus(SATB), trumpet, organ. Cantata. *Text:* Bible, O.T., Psalm 130. *Commissioned by:* Church of the Covenant, Boston for their 100th anniversary celebration. *First performed:* 1965; Church of the Covenant, Boston. Church of the Covenant Choir, Allen Huszti, organist and conductor.
Score & parts: reprod. of ms.; available from composer.
Reel: available from composer.

F7.4 Blow Winds. (1966)
For: chorus(SATB). *Text: Out of the Cradle Endlessly Rocking* by Walt Whitman.
Vocal score: reprod. of ms.; available from composer.

F7.5 The Declaration of God. (1969)
For: chorus(SATB). *Text: The Mystery of Death* by Kirpal Singh.
Vocal score: reprod. of ms.; available from composer.

F7.6 Duo, Violin and Piano. (1974)
Commissioned by: Theodore Leutz. First performance: Apr. 28, 1974; Boston Conservatory of Music. Theodore Leutz, violin and Alfred Lee, piano.
Score & part: reprod. of ms.; available from composer.
Reel: available from composer.

For Those Who Must Journey into Eternity. *See* Sinfonia.

[A Holiday Cantata (Title to be announced)] (1973)
F7.7 *For:* Soprano, Alto, Tenor, Bass, chorus, orchestra.
Commissioned by: Hartford National

Bank and Trust Co.
Score: reprod. of ms.; available from composer.

F7.8 The Holy Child, A Dramatic Cantata. (1968)
For: Soprano, chorus(SATB), orchestra. *Commissioned by:* Boston Conservatory Chorus and Boston Conservatory Orchestra, Rouben Gregorian, conductor, for the Prudential Center's first Christmas Program. *First performed:* Dec. 18, 1968; Prudential Center, Boston. Boston Conservatory Chorus and Boston Conservatory Orchestra, Rouben Gregorian, conductor.
Score & parts: reprod. of ms.; available from composer. BCM
Reel: Dec. 18, 1968; Boston Conservatory. BCM
Reel: Dec. 25, 1968; broadcast, WCRB-FM, Boston. BCM
Reel: Dec. 25, 1969. BCM

F7.9 Homeland, A Chamber Cantata. (1970) 50′
For: Soprano, chamber chorus(SATB), orchestra. *Text:* based on Navaho texts from *Navajo Wildlands. Commissioned by:* Boston Conservatory Chorus and Boston Conservatory Orchestra, Rouben Gregorian, conductor. *First performed:* Dec. 16, 1970; St. Clement's Shrine, Boston. Boston Conservatory Chorus and Boston Conservatory Orchestra, Rouben Gregorian, conductor.
Score & parts: reprod. of ms.; available from composer. ˙BCM
Vocal score: reprod. of ms.; available from composer. BCM
Reel: Dec. 16, 1970; Boston Conservatory. BCM

In Memoriam. *See* Sonata, Piano, No. 3.

F7.10 Incline Thine Ear. (1965)
For: chorus(SATB). *Text:* Bible, O.T., Psalm 86. *First performed:* Apr. 27, 1975. Brockton Choral Society, Sterling P. Cossaboom, conductor.
Vocal score: reprod. of ms.; available

from composer.
Reel: available from composer.

F7.11 Music for Harp. (1965)
Score: reprod. of ms.; available from composer.

F7.12 Prelude, Flute Unaccompanied. (196-)
Score: ms.; available from composer.

F7.13 Prelude to Shakespeare's Play, Romeo and Juliet. (196-)
For: recorders(3) and viole da gamba(5). Incidental music.
Score & parts: reprod. of ms.; available from composer.

F7.14 Quartet, Strings, No. 1. (1952)
Score & parts: reprod. of ms.; available from composer.

F7.15 Quartet, Strings, No. 2. (1966)
Score: reprod. of ms.; available from composer.

F7.16 Quartet, Strings, No. 3. (1968)
First performed: May 17, 1973; Boston Conservatory. Members of the Boston Conservatory String Ensemble, Rouben Gregorian, conductor.
Score & parts: reprod. of ms.; available from composer.
Reel: available from composer.

F7.17 Quintet, Piano, Woodwinds & Strings. (1967?)
For: flute, clarinet, violin, violoncello, piano.
Score & parts: reprod. of ms.; available from composer.

Romeo and Juliet. *See* Prelude to Shakespeare's Play, Romeo and Juliet.

Short Works for Piano. *See* Works, Piano. Selections.

F7.18 Sinfonia, for Those Who Must Journey into Eternity. (1971-72)
For: string orchestra. *Commissioned by:* Boston Conservatory Chamber Orchestra, Rouben Gregorian, conductor.

First performed: Apr. 29, 1972; New Bedford, Mass. (1st movement). Boston Conservatory Orchestra, Rouben Gregorian, conductor.
Score & parts: reprod. of ms.; available from composer.
Reel: Apr. 30, 1972; Boston Conservatory (1st movement). BCM
Reel: Apr. 29, 1974; Boston Conservatory (1st movement). BCM

[Sonata, Double Bass, Piano]
F7.19 Sonata. (1976)
Commissioned by: Robert Olsen.
Score: reprod. of ms.; available from composer.

F7.20 Sonata, Piano, No. 1. (1969)
Score: reprod. of ms.; available from composer.

F7.21 Sonata, Piano, No. 2. (1971)
Commissioned by: Paul Caponigro. *First performed:* Mar. 31, 1971; Boston Conservatory. Lee Colby Wilson.
Score: reprod. of ms.; available from composer.
Reel: Mar. 31, 1971; Boston Conservatory. BCM

F7.22 Sonata, Piano, No. 3, In Memoriam. (1973)
First performed: May 1974; Boston Conservatory. Lee Colby Wilson.
Score: reprod. of ms.; available from composer.
Reel: May 23, 1974; Boston Conservatory. BCM

[Songs]
F7.23 Three Songs. (1966)
For: Soprano and piano. *Contents:* On Wings of Death (after Rabindranath Tagore); Autumn Night (James Forte); White Blossoms (James Forte).
Score: reprod. of ms.; available from composer.

F7.24 They That Dwell in the Fields of Rushes. (1969)
For: chorus(SATB). *Text:* adapted from the Egyptian by James Forte.

Vocal score: reprod. of ms.; available from composer.

F7.25 Tidings. (1972)
For: piano. *First performed:* 1980; Lexington, Mass. Claire Harkrider.
Score: reprod. of ms.; available from composer.
Reel: available from composer.

F7.26 We Meet But to Part. (1969)
For: chorus(SATB). *Text:* Kirpal Singh and James Forte.
Vocal score: reprod. of ms.; available from composer.

F7.27 Who Lives in Love. (1981)
For: chorus(boy)(SA) and organ. *Text:* Bible, N.T., John. *First performed:* May 23, 1981; Somerville, Mass. Boston Archdiocesan Choir, Theodore Marier, director.
Vocal score: reprod. of ms.; available from composer.
Reel: available from composer.

[Works, Piano. Selections]
F7.28 Short Works for Piano. (1965-)
Contents: Prelude; In the Presence of His Company; Sometime for Piano; Stupa; Largo; Chorale I; Chorale II; In Memory of Martin Luther King; Prelude No. 1; Prelude No. 2; Prelude No. 3; Slow Andante; Interlude; Adagio; Some Earth; French Overture; Chaconne; Ostinato.
Score: reprod. of ms.; available from composer.

F8 HERBERT FROMM

Born in Kitzingen, Germany. *Education:* M.A. (State Academy of Music, Munich, West Germany); studied composition with Walter Courvoisier and Paul Hindemith. *Awards:* D.H.L. (Hon., Lesley College) and Ernest Bloch Award (1945). *Related activities:* organist, Temple Israel, Boston; author of *Herbert Fromm On Jewish Music: A Composer's View, The Key O See, Travel Journal, Seven Pockets.* BPL

WORKS

F8.1 Adath Israel: Friday Eve Service. (1943) 35'
For: cantor, voices(mixed), organ. *Text: Union Prayer Book,* (rev. ed.), Bible, O.T., Psalms 95:1-7, 97, 98. *Contents:* Organ Prelude; L'cho Dodi; Adonoy Moloch; Shiru Ladonoy; L'chu N'ran'noh; Bor'chu; Sh'ma Yisroel; Mi Chomochoh; V'shom'ru; Yism'chu; Grant Us Peace; May the Words I; May the Words II; Kiddush; Torah Service; Let Us Adore; Vaanachnu; Adon Olom; Benediction.
Dedication: Grant us peace; to Alfred and Paul Fromm.
Vocal score: Transcontinental, 1943. BPL NEC

[Adath Israel. Grant Us Peace; Arr]
F8.2 Grant Us Peace. (1943) 2' 30"
For: voice(high) or voice(medium) and organ or piano. *Dedicated to:* Alfred and Paul Fromm.
Score: Transcontinental 1943 (versions for high and medium voice).
Disc: Unicorn.

F8.3 Ahavat Olam. 3'
For: cantor, chorus, organ.
Commissioned by: Temple Anshe Emet, Chicago.
Vocal score: Ethnic Music, 1974.

Al Hannissim. *See* Festival Song. Al Hannissim.

F8.4 Anthem of Praise. (1960)
For: tenor, chorus(SATB), trumpet, organ. *Commissioned by:* Trinity Church, Boston. *Dedicated to:* George Faxon. *First performed:* 1961; Trinity Church, Boston. George Faxon, organ; Roger Voisin, trumpet; Trinity Church Choir, Herbert Fromm, conductor.
Music: Transcontinental, 1961.

Aria. *See* Psalm Cantata. Aria.

F8.5 Atonement Music. (1947) 45'
For: cantor, chorus(mixed), organ. 23 pieces. *Text: Union Prayer Book* (rev.

ed.). *First performed:* 1948; Temple Israel, Boston. Herbert Fromm, organ and conductor.
Vocal score: Transcontinental, 1948. BPL BU NEC

[Atonement Music. Pesah Lanu Sha-ar]
F8.6 Pesah Lanu Sha-ar.
For: cantor and organ. *Text: Union Prayer Book* (rev. ed.).
Disc: in *Music from the Synagogue,* Musical Heritage Society MHS 1775, 1975.

[Atonement Music. A Servant unto Thee]
F8.7 A Servant unto Thee. 3'
For: chorus(SATB) and organ or piano.
Vocal score: Transcontinental, 1948.

[Atonement Music. V'al Kulom]
F8.8 V'al Kulom.
For: cantor and organ. *Text: Union Prayer Book* (rev. ed.).
Score: Transcontinental.
Disc: in *Music from the Synagogue,* Musical Heritage Society MHS 1775, 1975.

F8.9 Avodat Shabbat, Sabbath Eve Service. (1960)
For: cantor, chorus, organ. 17 movements. *First performed:* Feb. 26, 1960; New York City. Arthur Wolfson, cantor; Robert Baker, organ; Temple Emanu-El Chorus, Herbert Fromm, director.
Score: Transcontinental, 1960.

F8.10 Balak: A Cantata Based on a Biblical Theme. (1979) 42'
For: Soprano, Tenor, Bass, narrator, chorus(SATB), orchestra(2(pic)-2-2-2(cbsn); 3-3-3-0; timp, perc(2); hp(2)(second optional); str). 16 movements. *Text:* Bible, O.T., Numbers.
First performed: Nov. 9, 1980; Jordan Hall, Boston. Alex Zimmer, narrator; Elisabeth Phinney, soprano; Donald Sullivan, tenor; R. Farris, bass; Chorus Pro Musica and NEC Symphony Orchestra, Samuel Adler, conductor.

Score & parts: ms.
Vocal score: ms.
Tape: recording of first performance.

F8.11 The Banner of Love: A Secular Cantata. (1968) 25'
For: Soprano, Tenor, chorus(women), orchestra(2-1-1-(& bcl)-1; 2-1-1-0; perc; hp, cel; str). 4 movements. *Text:* Jehuda Halevi. *First performed:* Apr. 1, 1970; Temple Ohabei Shalom, Brookline. Jeanette Coran, soprano; Frank Hoffmeister, tenor; Samuel Adler, conductor.
Score: ms.

Baruch Haba. *See* Partita on Baruch Haba.

F8.12 Birthday Canon. (1957) ·
For: voices and pianos(2). Written for the one hundredth anniversary of the Brookline Public Library.
Score & parts: reprod. of ms. BkPL

F8.13 Chag Ha-matsot. (1967) 15'
For: flute, violoncello, harpsichord. Suite on Passover melodies.
Commissioned by: United Church Press.
Score: Transcontinental, 1967.
Disc: United Church Press.

F8.14 Chamber Cantata. (1965)
For: Soprano, Alto, Tenor, Bass, flute, oboe, clarinet, bassoon, horn, piano, viola, violoncello. 2 movements. *Text:* Jehuda Halevi, translated by Nina Salaman. *Dedicated to:* The memory of Dr. Josef Freudenthal (1903-1964). *First performed:* May 6, 1966; Temple Israel, Boston. Jeanette Coran, soprano; Jean Harper, alto; Donald Sullivan, tenor; Stephen H. Dimmock, bass; Herbert Fromm, conductor.
Score & parts: Transcontinental, 1966. Rental.
Vocal score: Transcontinental, 1966. BPL

F8.15 Chemdat Yamin: The Day of Delight; Sabbath Morning Service. (1964) 50'
For: cantor, voices, chorus, organ or orchestra. *Contents:* Organ Prelude;

Psalm 5:1-5, 8; Borechu; Shema; Ve-ohavto; Mi Chomochoh; Tsur Yisroel; Ke-dushah; Silent Devotion and Yihyuh le-Rotson; Se-u She-orim; Shema and Lecho Adonoy; Gad'lu Ladonoy and Hodu al Erets; Toras Adonoy-Ets Chayim; Olenu and Vaanachnu; Yigdal. *Commissioned by:* The Temple, Cleveland, Ohio, David Gooding, music director. *First performed:* Apr. 30, 1965; Temple Ohabei Shalom, Brookline, Mass. Temple Ohabei Shalom Chorus and Orchestra, Herbert Fromm, conductor. *Vocal score:* Transcontinental, 1964. BPL

F8.16 Children's Concert.
For: chorus(SATB) and piano.
Vocal score: Jewish Education Committee, 1954. BU

F8.17 Concerto. (1952) 22'
For: flute and string orchestra. 4 movements. *First performed:* 1954; Dallas, Tex. Samuel Adler, conductor.

F8.18 The Crimson Sap. (1956) 21'
For: voice(medium) and piano. Song cycle. *Text:* Jean Harper. *Contents:* I Shall Not Sing of Hearts; Cut Me a Twig; A Golden Band; Love for the Ankle Bone; Come Away with Me; The Devil Has a Forked Tongue; A Veil Is over the Moon; I Was Sick; I Am the Fever; Some Are Now Secret. *First performed:* 1956; Brookline Public Library. Jean Harper, mezzo soprano and Herbert Fromm, piano.
Score: C. Fischer, 1956. BPL NEC
Disc: Music Library 7112, 1965. Margot Blum, mezzo soprano.

[The Crimson Sap. I Was Sick]
F8.19 I Was Sick in the Stretches of My Limbs.
For: voice(medium) and piano. *Text:* Jean Harper.
Cassette: Nov. 9, 1975; Boston Conservatory. BCM

The Day of Delight. *See* Chemdat Yamin.

F8.20 Days of Awe: Sonata. (1967) 18'
For: organ. 4 movements. *First performed:* Dec. 4, 1967; St. Paul's Cathedral, Boston. Lois Jungas.
Score: Transcontinental, 1968.

[Days of Awe: Sonata. Organ Prelude]
F8.21 Organ Prelude for High Holidays. (1964) 3'
Score: Transcontinental, 1965.

Elegy. *See* Shakespeare Songs.

[European Folk-songs]
F8.22 Thirty European Folk-songs in New Settings. (1932)
For: voices and piano.

[European Folk-songs. Selections]
F8.23 Three Folksongs from Thirty European Folksongs in New Settings. (1932) *For:* voices and piano. *Contents:* Paradise (Brittany); Dana Fetching Water (Bulgaria); The Raven (Russia).
Reel: Nov. 18, 1964; Brookline Public Library; in *New Music*. BkPL

Fancy. *See* Shakespeare Songs.

F8.24 Fantasy for Organ. (1953) 10'
Also version for pianos(2).
Score: ms.

F8.25 Fantasy for Piano. (1971) 12'
3 movements.
Disc: Lyrichord LLST 7241, 1972. Eugene List. BU

Fantasy for Two Pianos. *See* Fantasy for Organ.

F8.26 Festival Cantata. (1973) 20'
For: cantor, chorus, flute, bassoon, trumpet, horn, timpani, percussion, harp, organ. Written for the dedication of the new sanctuary of Temple Israel, Boston. *First performed:* 1973; Temple Israel, Boston. Herbert Fromm, conductor.

[Festival Songs]
F8.27 Two Festival Songs. (1958) 7'
For: cantor, chorus(SATB), organ.
Contents: Shoshanas Ya-akov; Al
Hannissim.
Vocal score: Transcontinental, 1958.

[Festival Songs. Al Hannissim]
F8.28 Al Hannissim, a Chanukkah
Anthem.
For: chorus(mixed).
Vocal score: Transcontinental, 1954. BU

[Festival Songs. Shoshanas Ya-akov]
F8.29 Shoshanas Yaakov, a Purim Song.
For: chorus(mixed).
Vocal score: Transcontinental, 1955. BU

Friday Eve Service. *See* Adath Israel.

Grant Us Peace. *See* Adath Israel. Grant
Us Peace.

Hanukkah Madrigal. *See* Madrigals.
Hanukkah.

F8.30 High Holiday Anthems. (1978) 9'
For: cantor, chorus, organ. *Text: Union
Prayer Book. Contents:* B'yom Din (On
Judg ment Day); All the World; Eli
Tsion. *Commissioned by:*
Transcontinental.
Music: Transcontinental, 1979.

F8.31 How Can I Sing? (1977) 5'
For: chorus(SATB) and organ. *Text:
Sabbath Prayerbook.*
Score: Transcontinental, 1977.

F8.32 Hymns and Songs for the
Synagogue.
For: voice or chorus(unison). *Contents:*
Sweet Hymns and Songs (Anim
Z'miroth); The Sabbath Bride; Rock of
Plenty (Tsur Mishelo); Unto the Hills
(Psalm 121); Praise to the Living God
(Yigdal); Praise Ye the Lord; Let Us
Praise Our God; O Holy Sabbath; All
Living Souls; Hashivenu (School Song);
Am Yisrael Chai; Shevuos Song.
Music: American Conference of
Cantors, Sacred Music Press, 1961. BPL

F8.33 In Memoriam. (1963) 3'
For: organ.
Score: Transcontinental, 1963.

I Was Sick. *See* The Crimson Sap. I
Was Sick.

F8.34 The Kiddush. (1953)
For: cantor, chorus, organ. 4
movements (4 settings of the same
text for different occasions).
Vocal score: Transcontinental, 1953.

F8.35 Let All Mortal Flesh Keep Silent.
(1938) 12'
For: organ.
Score: ms.
Disc: in *Twentieth Century American
Organ Music*, Lyrichord LLST 7191,
1968. Robert Noehren. BU

F8.36 Light Is Sown: A Cantata. 28'
For: chorus(SATB) and orchestra. *First
performed:* 1943; Jordan Hall, Boston.
Score: ms.

Lullaby. *See* Shakespeare Songs.

F8.37 Ma-ariv: Cantata. (1977)
For: Baritone, chorus, orchestra(2-2-2-2;
2-2-2-2; timp, perc; hp; str). 4
movements. *First performed:* 1977;
Sanders Theatre, Harvard University.
David Evitts, baritone; Harvard
University Choir, James Yannatos,
conductor.
Vocal score: Transcontinental, 1977.

[Madrigals]
F8.38 Six Madrigals. (1950) 22'
For: chorus(SATB) and
chorus(SSAATTBB). *Contents:* Sabbath
(Day of Rest); Purim (Feast of Lots);
Hanukkah (Feast of Lights); The Ninth
of Ab (Day of Mourning); Passover
(Feast of Liberation); Sukkoth (Harvest
Festival). Hebrew words, with English
translation by Jean Harper.
Score: Transcontinental, 1951. BPL BU
Disc: Golden Crest CR 4093. Eastman
Singers, Samuel Adler, conductor.
Disc: Unicorn (Hanukkah).

[Madrigals. Hanukkah; Arr.]
F8.39 Hanukkah Madrigal (Mi Y'mallel).
For: chorus(SATB).
Score: Transcontinental, 1967, BU

[Madrigals. Sabbath; Arr.]
F8.40 Sabbath Madrigal (R'tzeh).
For: chorus(SATB).
Score: Transcontinental.

F8.41 Maise fun a Pastuchl, or
Shepherd's Story. (1938) 4'
For: voice(medium) and piano. *Contents:*
Shepherd's Story; Messiah Song.
Score: Transcontinental, 1938.

F8.42 May the Words.
Disc: Unicorn Recording of Hebrew
Music.

F8.43 Memorial Cantata. (1973) 22'
For: Tenor, chorus, orchestra(3-2(&
Ehn)-2(&bcl)-2; 4-3-3-1; timp, perc; hp;
str(0-0-1-1-1). *Text:* Bible, O.T.: II
Samuel, Job, Apocrypha, Ecclesiastes;
Ben Sirach.
Score: Transcontinental, 1973. BU HU

[Motets]
F8.44 Five Motets. (1979) 15'
For: chorus and organ. *Text:* Bible, O.T.
Commissioned by: Massachusetts Music
Teachers Association. *First performed:*
Harvard Memorial Church, Harvard
University. John R. Ferris, conductor.
Vocal score: ms.

F8.45 New Year's Prayer.
For: chorus(SATB).
Vocal score: Transcontinental.

F8.46 Old Little Man.
For: chorus(SATB) and piano.
Vocal score: Jewish Education
Committee, 1954. BU

[Opening Anthems]
F8.47 Five Opening Anthems for the
Synagogue. (1971) 12'
For: cantor, chorus(SATB), organ. *Text:*
Bible, O.T., Psalms. *Contents:* Mah Tovu;
Psalm 122; Psalm 5; Psalm 36; L'cha

Dodi. *Dedicated to:* Annette F. Jacob
(Mah Tovu).
Score: Transcontinental, 1971. BPL BU

Organ Pieces. *See* Pieces, Organ.

Organ Prelude. *See* Prelude, Organ;
Days of Awe: Sonata. Organ Prelude.

[Palestine Poems]
F8.48 Three Palestine Poems. (1938) 7'
For: voice and organ or piano.
Contents: Legend; There I Saw Here;
Cradle Song.
Score: Transcontinental, 1946.
Reel: Nov. 18, 1964; Brookline Public
Library. BkPL

F8.49 Partita on Baruch Haba. 15'
For: organ.
Score: E. C. Schirmer, 1962. HU

[Partita on Baruch Haba; Arr.]
F8.50 Partita.
For: pianos(2).
Reel: Nov. 13, 1958; Brookline Public
Library. BkPL

Pesah Lanu Sha-ar. *See* Atonement
Music. Pesah Lanu Sha-ar.

[Pieces, Organ]
F8.51 Two Organ Pieces. 6'30"
Contents: Mornings Will I Seek Thee;
Processional.
Score: in *Organ Music for Worship*,
Wallan, 1964.

[Prayers (1968)]
F8.52 Seven Prayers. (1968) 16'
For: voice(medium) and organ or piano.
Text: Jean Harper, adapter and
translator. *Contents:* Baruch Adonai
bayom (Praised Be the Lord by Day);
Sim Shalom (A Prayer for Peace);
Ribono Shel Olam (A Shepherd's
Prayer); Tsur Yisrael I (Rock of Israel);
Ata Hu (You Are God); Tsur Yisrael II
(Rock of Israel); Avinu Malkenu (Our
Father, Our King). *Dedication:* For
Cantor Alex Zimmer (Sim Shalom).
Vocal score: Transcontinental, 1969. BPL

[Prayers (1979)]
F8.53 Three Prayers (Hebrew). (1979) 8'
For: voice(high) and organ. *Text: Union Prayer Book* (rev. ed).
Score: ms.

[Prelude, Organ]
F8.54 Organ Prelude (after a Chassidic Melody). (1953)
Dedicated to: Eve and Ernest Simon, June 28, 1953.
Score: reprod. of ms. BU

Prelude, Organ. *See also* Days of Awe: Sonata. Organ Prelude.

[Proverbs]
F8.55 Four Proverbs: the Wisdom of Solomon. (1975) 10'
For: chorus(SATB) and piano. *Text:* Bible, O.T., Proverbs. *First performed:* May 6, 1975; Hancock Hall, Boston. Newton High School Concert Choir, Herbert Fromm, conductor.
Vocal score: ms.

F8.56 Psalm 23. 3'
For: chorus(SATB). English words.
Vocal score: Transcontinental, 1949.
Disc: VQR CSRV 2296, 19--. BCM

F8.57 Psalm 24. (1962) 10'
For: chorus(SATB) and orchestra(0-2-2-2; 2-2-2-0; str). *Commissioned by:* St. Paul's Cathedral, Boston. *First performed:* Oct. 14, 1962; St. Paul's Cathedral, Boston. St. Paul's Cathedral Choir and Temple Israel Chorus, Lois Juhgas, conductor.
Music: Transcontinental, 1964.

F8.58 Psalm 98. 2'
For: cantor, chorus(SATB), organ.
Commissioned by: Temple Emanu-El, Dallas, Tex.
Vocal score: Transcontinental, 1964.

F8.59 Psalm Cantata. (1962) 20'
For: Soprano, chorus(SATB), viola, orchestra(2-2-2-2;2-2-0-0; hp; str). 3 movements. *Text:* Bible, O.T., Psalms.
Score: Transcontinental, 1963.

[Psalm Cantata. Aria]
F8.60 Aria, from Psalm Cantata.
For: voice and viola.
Reel: Nov. 18, 1964. Brookline Public Library. Mary Sindoni, singer. BkPL

[Psalm Settings]
F8.61 Two Psalm Settings.
Text: Bible, O.T., Psalm 92 and Bible, O.T., Psalm 121.
Music: Hope, 1976.

[Psalms]
F8.62 Four Psalms (Using Sephardic Intonations). (1971)
For: voice(high) and organ or piano.
Text: Bible, O.T., Psalms 1, 121, 42, 140. *First performed:* 1970; Toronto, Canada.
Score: Transcontinental, 1971. BPL

[Quartet, Strings, No. 1]
F8.63 String Quartet.
7 movements.
Study score: Boosey & Hawkes, 1961. BPL BU HU
Parts: Boosey & Hawkes, 1961.
Disc: Lyrichord LL 203, LLST 7203, 1968. Pro Arte Quartet. BU HU

[Quartet, Strings, No. 2]
F8.64 String Quartet No. 2 (The Song of Songs). (1977) 20'
For: Soprano, Tenor, string quartet.
First performed: 1978; New York City.
Music: Transcontinental.

Sabbath Eve Service. *See* Avodat Shabbat.

Sabbath Madrigal. *See* Madrigals. Sabbath; Arr.

Sabbath Morning Service. *See* Chemdat Yamin.

F8.65 Sacred Choruses. (1948) 7'
For: chorus(SATB) and organ. *Contents:* All the World (I. Zanwill); Benediction; Psalm 121.
Score: Row, 1948. BPL

Sea change. *See* Shakespeare Songs.

A Servant unto Thee. *See* Atonement Music. A Servant unto Thee.

[Shakespeare Songs]
F8.66 Six Shakespeare Songs. (1965) 22'
For: chorus(SATB), chorus(SSATBB), chorus(TTBB). *Text: Cymbeline* (Act 4, Scene 2); *Merchant of Venice* (Act 3, Scene 2); *A Midsummer Night's Dream* (Act 2, Scene 2); *The Tempest* (Act 1, Scene 2); *Love's Labours Lost* (Act 5, Scene 2); *The Tempest* (Act 2, Scene 2) by William Shakespeare. *Contents:* Elegy; Fancy; Lullaby; Sea Change; Winter; Stephano's Song.
Vocal score: E. C. Schirmer, 1965. BPL
Vocal score: E.C. Schirmer, 1965 (published separately). T
Disc: Lyrichord LLST 7241, 1972. North Texas State University Choir, Frank McKinley, conductor. BU

Shepherd's Story. *See* Maise fun a Pastuchl.

F8.67 Shir Hama-alos. 2' 30"
For: voice and piano. *Text:* traditional.
Score: The Cantors Assembly of America, 1967.

F8.68 Shofar Service. (1948) 4'
For: chorus and organ. *Dedicated to:* Rabbi Joshua Loth Liebman.
Vocal score: Transcontinental, 1948.

[Short Hebrew Anthems]
F8.69 Six Short Hebrew Anthems. (1966) 11'
For: Alto or Baritone, cantor, chorus, organ, flute. *Text:* traditional; Bible, O.T., Proverbs, 31. *Contents:* Anim Z'mirot (Pleasant Songs); Al Tira, Ya-akov (Fear Not, O Jacob); Tsur mishelo Achalnu (God, Our Rock); Adir Hu (Yemenite Passover Song); Moladeti (My Land of Home); Eshet Chayil (A Woman of Valor).
Score: Transcontinental, 1966. BPL NU

Shoshanas Ya-akov. *See* Festival Songs. Shoshanas Ya-akov.

F8.70 Silent Devotion. (1963) 2'
For: organ.
Score: Transcontinental, 1963.

Sonata for Organ. *See* Days of Awe.

F8.71 Sonata for Piano, Based on a Sephardic Hymn. (1977) 15'
3 movements.
Score: Transcontinental, 1978.

[Sonata, Violin and Piano]
F8.72 Sonata in G. (1949; rev. 1953) 22'
4 movements. *First performed:* Mar. 1, 1950; Harvard University. Robert Ritzenhein, violin and Martin Boykan, piano.
Score & part: Boosey & Hawkes, 1954. BPL BU
Reel: Nov. 14, 1956; Brookline Public Library; in *New Music.* Elaine Pinkerton, violin and Martin Boykan, piano. BkPL

F8.73 Song of Miriam. (1944) 5'
For: Baritone or Mezzo Soprano, chorus(SSA), piano, triangle(optional), tambourine(optional). *Text:* Bible, O.T., Exodus 15:20-21 (adapted). Winner of the Ernest Bloch Award, 1945.
Score: C. Fischer, 1946. BPL
Disc: Unicorn.

[Songs of Worship]
F8.74 Five Songs of Worship. Revised Edition. (1946) 12'
For: voice(medium) and organ or piano.
Contents: Angels of Peace; Invocation, Lamentation of David; Sabbath Joy, Sabbath Queen.
Score: Transcontinental, 1946.

Stephano's Song. *See* Shakespeare Songs.

F8.75 The Stranger: A Dramatic Cantata. (1956) 25'
For: voices(3), chorus, orchestra(2-2-2-2; 2-2-2-2; timp, perc; str). *Text:* based on a parable by Benjamin Franklin. *First performed:* 1957; New York City. Schola Cantorum of New York, Hugh Ross, conductor.

F8.76 Studies. (1981?) 10'
For: organ. Based on hymns and chants of the Synagogue.
Score: ms.

F8.77 Suite on Hebraic Motifs. (1959) 18'
For: organ. *Contents:* Psalm; Hassidic Interlude; Out of the Depths; Pastorale; Cantillation; Song of Praise.
Score: Transcontinental, 1959.

F8.78 Transience: A Cantata. (1966) 12'
For: Tenor, chorus(mixed), flute, oboe, clarinet, bassoon, horn, harp, violoncello). *Text:* Robert Herrick.
Commissioned by: Lesley College. *First performed:* 1966; Lesley College, Cambridge, Mass.
Score: ms.`
Disc: Lyrichord LLST 7241, 1972. Grant Williams, tenor; North Texas State University Choir, Frank McKinley, conductor. BU

[Trio, Piano, Violin, Violoncello]
F8.79 Trio. (1980-81) 22'
4 movements.
Score: ms.

V'al Kulom. *See* Atonement Music. V'al Kulom.

F8.80 Vayechulu. 2' 30"
For: cantor, chorus, organ.
Music: Transcontinental, 1954.

F8.81 Veshamru. 2' 30"
For: cantor, chorus, organ.
Music: Transcontinental, 1960.

F8.82 We Worship.
For: chorus(mixed).
Disc: Unicorn.

Winter. *See* Shakespeare Songs.

The Wisdom of Solomon. *See* Proverbs.

F8.83 Yemenite Cycle. (1962) 12'
For: voice(medium), flute, harp, percussion. 4 movements. *First performed:* May 18, 1962; Temple

Israel, Boston. Herbert Fromm, conductor.
Music: Israeli Music Publishers, 1977.
Reel: Jan. 16, 1963; Brookline Public Library. BkPL

F8.84 Yidgal. (1973)
For: voices(2), chorus(SATB), piano or organ.

Yigdal. *See also* Chemdat Yamin (last movement).

F8.85 Yom zeh l'Yisrael. (1973) 3'
For: chorus and organ. *Text: Union Prayer Book* (rev. ed).
Music: Transcontinental, 1973.

F9 EUGENIA FROTHINGHAM

Born 1908 in Boston. *Education:* Diploma (New England Conservatory, 1935); studied composition with A. Tillman Merritt, Walter Piston (Harvard University); Nadia Boulanger; Frederick Shepherd Converse; Warren Story Smith; studied piano with Isidor Philipp. *Related activities:* teacher and violinist. W

WORKS

F9.1 Along the Way. (1966?) 4' 25"
For: violins(2). 1 movement.
Score: reprod. of composer's ms. W

F9.2 Briefly. (1963?) 4' 15"
For: violins(2). 1 movement. *First performed:* Glen Ellyn, Ill. Evelyn Aukerman and Mary Elizabeth Leaton
Music: reprod. of composer's ms.; available from composer. Rental.
Cassette: W

Fantasy. *See* Meditation and Fantasy.

F9.3 Idyll. (1980) 5'
For: oboe and piano. 1 movement.
Dedicated to: Natalie B. Lombard. *First performed:* 1980; Boston University. Nancy Fish, oboe and Mr. Fish, piano.
Score: reprod. of ms. W
Reel & cassette.

F9.4 Meditation and Fantasy. (1951) 8'
For: piano. 2 movements.
Score: Axelrod Music, 1951. BU NEC W
Score: Shawnee.

F9.5 Octet. (1979)
For: oboes(2), clarinets(2), bassoons(2), horns(2). 2 movements. *First performed:* members of the Little Orchestra of Cambridge, Rachael Worby, conductor.
Score: reprod. of ms. W
Cassette: available from composer. Rental.

F9.6 Overture. (1935) 8'
For: orchestra(2-2-2-2; 4-3-3-0; timp, cym; str). 1 movement. *First performed:* 1937?; Sanders Theatre, Harvard University. Unidentified orchestra, Alexander Theiman, conductor.
Music: reprod of ms.; available from composer. Rental.

F9.7 A Pond. (1966?) 2' 30"
For: violins(2). Withdrawn.

F9.8 Scherzo. (1935) 6'
For: orchestra(2-2-2-2; 4-3-3-0; timp, cym; str). *First performed:* 1934; New England Conservatory. NEC Symphony Orchestra, Wallace Goodrich, conductor.
Score & parts: ms. in composer's hand. Rental.

F9.9 Scottish Fantasy. (1959) 4'
For: violin and piano. 1 movement.
First performed: 1959; Winsor School Auditorium, Boston. Natalie B. Lombard.
Score & part: ms. in composer's hand. Rental.
Score: reprod. of ms. W

F9.10 Simplicity. (1963) 4' 30"
For: violins(2) and piano. 1 movement.
First performed: 1964; Boston Conservatory. Sarah Scriven, violin, and others.
Score: reprod. of ms. W
Cassette: 1979; Chatauqua, N.Y. Evelyn Aukerman, violin and Eugenia Lombard, piano. W

F9.11 Soliloquy. (1973) 5'-6'
For: English horn and orchestra(2-2-2-2; 2-2-1-2; timp; str). 1 movement. *First performed:* 1975; Arlington, Mass. Arlington Philharmonic, John Bavicchi, conductor.
Score: reprod. of ms. W
Cassette: Dupage Symphony Orchestra. W

F9.12 Sonatina. (1954)
For: piano. 3 movements. *First performed:* Connecticut College. Eugenia Lombard.
Score: Rental.

F9.13 Sunrise. (1966? or 1974?) 2' 25"
For: violins(2). 1 movement.
Score: reprod. of ms. W
Cassette: W

F9.14 A Thought. (1974) 4'
For: orchestra(2-2-2-2; 2-2-0-0; timp; str). 1 movement. *First performed:* 1975; Fairfield University. Fairfield University Orchestra, Frederic DeHaven, conductor.
Score: reprod. of ms. W
Cassette: W

F9.15 Vocalize. (1979) 3' 30"
For: voice and piano. 1 movement.
Dedicated to: Natalie Lombard. *First performed:* 1981; Bentwood Hall, Pocasset, Mass. Natalie B. Lombard, voice and Lynne Talley, piano.
Music: reprod. of ms. Rental.
Cassette: recording of first performance.

F9.16 Wanderings. (1979) 5'
For: oboe or English horn and orchestra(2-2-2-2; 2-2-1-0; timp; str). 1 movement. *First performed:* 1979; Peabody School Auditorium, Cambridge, Mass. Little Orchestra of Cambridge, Rachael Worby, conductor.
Score: reprod. of ms. W
Cassette: recording of first performance.

G1 GREGORY MARK GARGARIAN

Born September 11, 1949, in Detroit, Mich. *Related activities:* clarinetist; percussionist; music consultant to Computer Arts Society, U.S. (1972-75) and Boston Danceworks (1976-). MIT

WORKS

G1.1 Alternative to Violence. (1976) Duration variable.
For: percussion, bells, buzzers, bicycles. Structured outdoor event.

G1.2 Ein Auge, offen. (1975) 4' 48"
For: voice, guitar, percussion. *Text:* Paul Celan.

G1.3 Brass Landscapes. (1975) 7' 30"
For: trumpets(8) and trombones(8).

G1.4 Chamber Music. (1974) 23'
For: voices(5) and instruments(unspecified)(33), (divided into 5 groups). *Text:* from *Finnegan's Wake* by James Joyce.

G1.5 Commuter. (1978) 9'
For: violins(3), saxophone(tenor), trombone(tenor), percussion(2).

G1.6 Composition. (1979) 7' 30"
For: viola and double bass. 3 movements.

G1.7 Computer for Six Strings. (1974) 9'
For: violins(4), guitar(electric), electric bass. Computer music. Score generated on DEC 10 system, Eastern Michigan University.

G1.8 Copertino: Flights, Rapts and Ecstasies. (1980) 47'
For: tape(electroacoustic). Written in collaboration with Karl Malik for a film by Milton Cohen. [*First?*] *performed:* 1980; Cape Cod, Mass.

G1.9 Dance Music. (1975) 7'
For: dancers(7) with tap shoes,

castanets, finger cymbals. [*First?*] *performed:* Michigan.

G1.10 Decadence-Control. (1974) 2'
For: carillon.

G1.11 Easy Studies. (1978) 8'
For: clarinet and string quartet. 1 movement (18 studies). *First performed:* 1978; University of Massachusetts, Boston.

G1.12 Equator Music. (1978) Duration variable.
For: musicians(unspecified)(5, 7, 9, 11...). Aleatoric music. Takes place around a circle across which the musicians move. The choreography conducts the music and vice versa.

G1.13 Fanfare. (1975) 23"
For: trumpets(3), horns(3), trombones(3).

Flights, Rapts and Ecstasies. *See* Copertino.

G1.14 Flute Landscapes. (1979) Duration variable.
For: flutes(4) or any of the same four instruments. Aleatoric music. *First performed:* 1979; Institute of Contemporary Art, Boston.

G1.15 For Four Pianos. (1973; rev. in progress) 5'

G1.16 For Miriam, For Piano. (1975; rev. 1977-) 6'

G1.17 Interludes. (1976) 1' 40"
For: dancer/narrator, tape, violin, harp, trombone, double bass. *Choreography:* Susan Rose. [*First?*] *performed:* 1976; University of Michigan.

G1.18 Knock Yourself Out. (1974)
For: tape. Musique concrete. Written in collaboration with Karl Malik. *First performed:* 1974; Ann Arbor, Mich.

G1.19 Migrations: Composition for 4 Groups of 3 Instruments. (1977) 12'
For: percussion, clarinet, viola; or

percussion, flute/piccolo, trombone; or percussion, violin, trumpet/flugelhorn; or percussion, oboe/English horn, double bass; or instrumental ensemble(all of the above); or percussion(4).

G1.20 SAT:AM. (1976)
For: tape. Generated at the New England Conservatory Analog Music Synthesis Studio. [*First?*] *performed:* New England Conservatory.

G1.21 Sequenza. (1974)
For: tape(electroacoustic). Sound consists of Arabic lute recorded and electronically processed. *First performed:* Ann Arbor, Mich.

G1.22 Sinewaves. (1975) 15′
For: tape. Dance music. *First performed:* Institute for Contemporary Dance, Boston. Members of Caligan Mergi.

G1.23 Sound Cycles. (1980) 20′
For: tape(electroacoustic). Sound consists of violin and voice recorded and electronically processed. *Text:* Foundations of Modern Art by Amedee Ozenfant.

[Studies]
G1.24 Nine Studies for String Quartet. (1976) 5′

G1.25 Temperaments. (1977) 6′
For: tape(computer). Dance music; film music. Sound synthesized using MITSYN at the Speech Group, Massachusetts Institute of Technology. *First performed:* University of Massachusetts, Boston. Used in part as soundtrack for computer-animated film by Kenneth Kahn, 1978.

G2 PAUL GAY

Born August 23, 1936, in Brunswick, Me. Moved to Boston area 1954. *Education:* studied with Leland Proctor, Roland Nadeau, William Tesson, Francis Judd Cooke (New England Conservatory, B.M.); Hugo Norden (Boston University, M.M.); conducting with Pierre Monteux; trombone with Denis Wick. *Related activities:* served as trombonist with the Boston Symphony Orchestra, Boston Pops, Boston Ballet, Boston Opera Company; served as conductor of the New Hampshire Philharmonic and the New England Repertory Orchestra; currently conductor of the Indian Hill Chamber Orchestra and Boston University Wind and Brass Ensembles. BU

WORKS

G2.1 Academic Ceremonial Music. (1963) 6′
For: brass ensemble and percussion. *Movements:* Fanfare and Ceremonial Music; Convocation Fanfare; Prologue to an Academic Ceremony. *First performed:* 1968; University of Lowell. University of Lowell Brass Ensemble, Paul Gay, conductor.
Score & parts: ms. in composer's hand. *Reel:* Nov. 6, 1979; Boston University; in *A Program Commemorating the Visit of Pope John Paul II*. Boston University Brass Ensemble, Paul Gay, conductor. BU

G2.2 At the Big Rock. 4′
For: guitar or piano. *Dedicated to:* Jerry Gay.
Score: ms. in composer's hand.

G2.3 Bacchanalian Alarum. (1972) 4′
For: trumpets(3). 1 movement. *Dedicated to:* Roger Voisin. *First performed:* Horticultural Hall, Boston, in conjunction with Boston Symphony Orchestra's Centennial celebration. Boston University Trumpet Ensemble. *Score & parts:* King, 1980.

G2.4 The Cage. (1976)
For: horn, trombone, tuba. 1 movement. *Commissioned by:* Hal Janks. *Score & parts:* ms. in composer's hand. *Score & parts:* reprod. of ms. BU

G2.5 Chorale. (1975) 4'
For: trombones(3). 1 movement. *First performed:* South Shore Conservatory, Hingham, Mass. Ars Antiqua Trombone Ensemble.
Score & parts: King, 1979.
Reel: May 1, 1978; Emmanuel Church, Boston. Boston University Trombone Ensemble, Paul Gay, conductor. BU

G2.6 Concerto. 20'
For: piano and orchestra(2(pic)-2(Ehn)-2(bcl)-2; 4-3-3-1; timp, perc(3); str). 3 movements. *First performed:* 1975; Manchester, N.H. (1st movement). Arthur Houle, piano; New Hampshire Philharmonic, Paul Gay, conductor.
Score & parts: ms. in composer's hand.

G2.7 Elterephenie. (1978) 7'
For: instrumental ensemble(flute, oboe, clarinet, saxophone(alto), bassoon, horn, trumpets(2), trombone, tuba, percussion(3), piano). 1 movement.
Score & parts: ms. in composer's hand.
Score & parts: reprod. of ms. BU
Reel: Mar. 7, 1978; Boston University. Boston University Wind Ensemble, Paul Gay, conductor. BU

[Isometrics]
G2.8 Three Isometrics. 9'
For: violin and piano.
Score: ms. in composer's hand.

[Lyric Poems of Love]
G2.9 Three Lyric-Poems of Love. (1974) 10'
For: string orchestra. *First performed:* Peterboro, N.H. New Hampshire Philharmonic, Paul Gay, conductor.
Score & parts: ms. in composer's hand.

G2.10 Metal Music. (1969) 9'
For: brass ensemble and percussion. *First performed:* 1970; University of Lowell. University of Lowell Brass Ensemble.
Score & parts: ms. in composer's hand.

[Movements for Brass Trio]
G2.11 Three Movements for Brass Trio.

10'
For: trumpet, horn, trombone. *First performed:* University of New Hampshire. Natalo Paella, David Allan, Paul Gay.
Score & parts: King, 1977.
Reel: "recorded for CBC." Atlantic Brass Ensemble.

G2.12 North of Boston. (1958)
For: jazz band.
Score & parts: ms. in composer's hand. NEC
Tape: New England Conservatory Jazz Band.

[Pieces]
G2.13 Four Pieces. (1959-61) 15'
For: flute and piano.
Score: ms. in composer's hand.

G2.14 Profiles of North Atlantic Sea Birds.
For: woodwind quintet. *Movements:* Puffin; Sandpiper; Great Heron.
Score & parts: ms. in composer's hand.

[Quintet, Brasses]
G2.15 Brass Quintet. (1980) 10'
For: trumpets(2), horn, trombone, tuba. 3 movements. *Commissioned by:* Jay Rizzetto.

G3 VICTORIA M. GLASER

Born September 11, 1918, in Amherst, Mass. Moved to Boston area 1931.
Education: studied composition with Walter Piston, A. Tillman Merritt, Nadia Boulanger (Harvard University, B.A., 1940, M.A., 1943); piano with Frederick Tillotson and Margaret M. MacDonald (Longy School of Music, 1938-40); flute with Georges Laurent; voice with Bernard Barbeau (New England Conservatory); American Guild of Organists (choirmaster certificate).
Awards: Gedok Festival (Mannheim, West Germany, Honorable Mention, 1961), Brookline Library Music Association Composers Award (1963).
Related activities: flutist; choral conductor and arranger; author of

Training for Musicianship (1972); served on the faculties of Dana Hall School (1944-59), New England Conservatory (1957-), Longy School of Music (1976-). NEC

WORKS

A "Bach" Fugue on Happy Birthday to You. *See* Birthday Fugue.

G3.1 Biblical Song. (1963)
For: Soprano and organ. *First performed:* 1963; Follen Community Church, Lexington, Mass.
Score: available from composer.

G3.2 Birthday Fugue (A "Bach" Fugue on Happy Birthday to You). (1960) 3'
For: orchestra(2(&pic)-2-2-2; 4-3-2-1; timp, perc; str) or (1-1-2-1; 2-1-1-0; timp, sndr; str). *First performed:* Oct. 22, 1960; Brookline High School, Brookline, Mass.; Boston Symphony Orchestra Youth Concert Series. Harry Ellis Dickson, conductor.
Score & parts: available from composer.
Disc: 1965.
Reel: 1967.

[Carols]
G3.3 Three Carols. (1972) 6'
For: chorus(SAB), recorder, handbells, guitar, harpsichord. *Commissioned by:* NEC Youth Chamber Singers. First performed: Nov. 1972; Boston Public Library; dedication of new wing of the Boston Public Library. NEC Youth Chamber Singers.
Vocal score: Religious Arts Guild, Unitarian Universalist Association, 1972.

G3.4 Epithalamion. (1978)
For: violin and violoncello. Written for the marriage of Theodora Parker and Steven Colburn.
Score: available from composer.

[French Songs]
G3.5 Two French Songs. (1974)

For: chorus. *Commissioned by:* Buckingham School Glee Club. *First performed:* May 1974. Buckingham School Glee Club and unidentified performers from the Belmont Hill School.
Vocal score: available from composer.

Gallery (for Young Musicians). *See* On Seven Winds.

G3.6 Homeric Hymn. (1961) 1'
For: chorus(SSAA). *Text:* Homer; translation by Andrew Lang.
Vocal score: Associated, 1971.

G3.7 An Idyll Song. (1955) 45"
For: chorus(SSAA) and piano.
Vocal score: E.C. Schirmer, 1959. T

G3.8 Jazz Pastorale. (1977) 5'
For: flutes(2), snare drum, cymbal, piano, double bass. 1 movement.
Score: available from composer.

G3.9 Music for Carol of the Mice (from the Wind in the Willows). (1940)
For: chorus. *Text: Wind in the Willows* by Kenneth Grahame. Written for the Radcliffe College Choir. *Vocal score.*

G3.10 Music for Orchestra. (1962) 8'
For: orchestra(1(pic)-1-2-1; 2-1-2-0; perc, pf; str). 3 movements. *First performed:* Jordan Hall, Boston. NEC Youth Orchestra.
Score & parts: available from composer.

G3.11 On Seven Winds. (1980)
For: chorus(SA), recorder, hand drum, snare drum, piano. 7 movements. Written for the centennial celebration of the Dana Hall School. Earlier version titled Gallery (for Young Musicians). *First performed:* May 22, 1981; Dana Hall School. *Score & parts.*

[Quartet, Strings]
G3.12 String Quartet. (1943)
Score & parts: available from composer.

Rilke Sonata. *See* Sonata for Piano with Three Performers.

G3.13 Sonata for Flute and Violin. (1961) 3'
Winner of Gedok Festival (Mannheim, West Germany, Honorable Mention).
First performed: WNYC-FM, New York City.
Score: available from composer.

G3.14 Sonata for Piano with Three Performers (Rilke Sonata). (1979)
For: piano(4-hands) and piano(prepared).
First performed: 1979; New England Conservatory Preparatory Division.
Score: available from composer.

G3.15 Suite for Harpsichord. (1963) 5'
Winner of Brookline Library Music Association Composers Award, 1963.
First performed: Feb. 1963; Brookline Public Library. Jean Poole Alderman.
Score: available from composer.

ARRANGEMENTS OF WORKS OF OTHER COMPOSERS

[Airs, 1973]
G3.16 Three Airs. (1973) 4'
For: trumpet and organ. Original by Georg Philipp Telemann.
Score & part: Gray, 1973.

[Airs, 1981]
G3.17 Three Airs. (1981)
For: trumpet and organ. Original by Georg Philipp Telemann.
Score & part: Gray, 1981.

G3.18 Concerto for Trumpet and Strings (Finale). (1963) 4'
For: oboes(2), clarinets(2), horns(2), bassoons(2). Original by Georg Philipp Telemann.
Score & parts: available from Caleb Warner, Lexington, Mass.

G3.19 Salagadool Minchacaboola. (1958) 1'
Arranged under the pseudonym A. Copenhagen for Walt Disney Enterprises.
Score: Hansen, 1958.

G4 JOHN GOODMAN

Born April 7, 1937, in Kansas City, Mo. Moved to Boston area 1964. *Education:* B.S., Speech (Northwestern University, 1959); studied composition with Elliott Carter, Quincy Porter (Yale University, M.M., 1963); Gardner Read (Boston University, D.M.A., 1968). *Related activities:* served on the faculties of New England Conservatory, Emmanuel College, Boston University·(1969-). BU

WORKS

G4.1 Academic Processional for Antiphonal Brass Quintets. (1969) 5'·
First performed: 1969; Boston University.
Music: ms. in composers hand.

[Bagatelles]
G4.2 Seven Bagatelles. (1962) 12'
For: flute, clarinet, harp, marimba, double bass. *First performed:* 1963; Yale University.
Music: ms. in composer's hand. *Tape.*

Chinese Poems. *See* Songs of Parting.

G4.3 Concerto for Piano and Orchestra. (1968) 21'
2 movements. *First performed:* Feb. 9, 1969; Boston University. Donald Kidd, piano; Boston University Symphony Orchestra, Walter Eisenberg, conductor.
Music: ms. in composer's hand. BU *Tape.*

G4.4 Esther. (1961) 9'
For: Soprano and piano. Cantata. *First performed:* 1962; Yale University. Neva Pilgram, soprano and Irwin Gage, piano.
Score: ms. in composers hand. *Tape.*

G4.5 Fantasy for Piano. (1977) 15'
First performed: Mar. 31, 1978; Southeastern Massachusetts University. Eleanor Carlson.

Score: ms. in composers hand.
Reel: Oct. 19, 1978; Boston University; in *Omnibus: Music of the 20th Century, Concert I.* Eleanor Carlson. BU

G4.6 Fantasy for Violin and Piano. (1978) 15′
First performed: Apr. 3, 1978; Institute of Contemporary Art, Boston. Mary Crowder Hess, violin and John Goodman, piano.
Music: ms. in composer's hand. *Tape.*

G4.7 Goodbye Arnold. (1961)
Opera in one act.

G4.8 Kaddish. (1967) 9′
For: Soprano, chorus, trumpets(3), violoncello. *First performed:* Feb. 1967; Boston University. Christine Macomber, soprano; James Rives Jones, conductor.
Music: ms. in composer's hand. *Tape.*

G4.9 Lyric Pieces for Piano, Book 1. (1951-59)

G4.10 Lyric Pieces for Piano, Book 2. (1960-79)

[Madrigals on Poems of William Shakespeare]
G4.11 Four Madrigals on Poems of William Shakespeare. (1981) 12′
For: Sopranos(2), Alto, Tenor, Bass.
Contents: O Mistress Mine; Winter; Fear No More; Sigh No More. *First performed:* Apr. 26, 1981; Boston University. Boston University Vocal Ensemble, Robert Gartside, conductor.
Music: ms. in composer's hand.

Miscellaneous Songs. *See* Songs.

[Poems of Emily Dickinson, Mezzo Soprano and Piano]
G4.12 Fourteen Poems of Emily Dickinson. (1977) 30′
Contents: Because I Could Not Stop for Death; There's a Certain Slant of Light; Hope; I Heard a Fly Buzz When I Died; I Years Had Been from Home; My Life Closed Twice; Of All the Souls That

Stand Create; The Sky Is Low, the Clouds Are Mean; Much Madness; Title Divine Is Mine; The Heart Asks Pleasure First; Safe in Their Alabaster Chambers; I Never Saw a Moor. *First performed:* Oct. 18, 1977; Boston University; in Omnibus: Music of the Twentieth Century, Concert I. Maeda Freeman, mezzo soprano and John Goodman, piano.
Music: ms. in composer's hand.
Reel: recording of first performance. BU

[Poems of Emily Dickinson, Soprano and Piano]
G4.13 Four Poems of Emily Dickinson. (1959) 9′
For: Soprano or Alto and piano.
Contents: What Inn Is This; The Lightning Is a Yellow Fork; I Taste a Liquor Never Brewed; A Wife at Daybreak. *First performed:* 1959; Northwestern University. Mary Beth Piel, soprano and John Goodman, piano.
Music: ms. in composer's hand.

[Preludes, Piano]
G4.14 Twenty four Preludes for Piano. (1951-61)

[Quartet, Strings]
G4.15 String Quartet. (1965) 20′
First performed: Feb. 1967; Boston University.
Music: ms. in composer's hand. *Tape.*

G4.16 Rhapsody. (1961) 9′
For: violoncello and piano. *First performed:* 1963; Yale University. Jean Schweibert, violoncello and John Goodman, piano.
Music: ms. in composer's hand. *Tape.*

G4.17 Sonata for Piano. (1965) 15′
3 movements. *First performed:* 1965; Boston University. Donald Kidd.
Music: ms. in composer's hand. *Tape.*

G4.18 Sonata for Violin and Piano. (1959; rev. 1974) 18′

3 movements. *First performed:* 1959; Northwestern University. Sandra Sizer, violin and John Goodman, piano. Feb. 12, 1981 (rev. version); Boston University. Carole Lieberman, violin and John Goodman, piano.
Music: ms. in composer's hand. *Tape.*

G4.19 Sonatina for Oboe and Piano. (1966) 9'
3 movements. *First performed:* Feb. 1967; Boston University.
Music: ms. in composer's hand. *Tape.*

G4.20 Sonatina for Piano. (1961) 10'
4 movements. *First performed:* 1961; Yale University. Raymond Bills.
Music: ms. in composer's hand. *Tape.*

[Songs]
G4.21 Miscellaneous Songs. (1951-79)

[Songs from The Princess of Alfred Tennyson]
G4.22 Three Songs from The Princess of Alfred Tennyson. (1965) 12'
For: Soprano and piano or Soprano, harp, winds. *First performed:* 1965; Boston University. Christine Macomber, soprano and John Goodman, piano.
Music: ms. in composer's hand. *Tape.*

G4.23 Songs of Parting; 8 Chinese Poems. (1963) 24'
For: Soprano, Tenor, flute, clarinet, oboe, bassoon, violin, viola, violoncello, double bass. *First performed:* 1963; Yale University. Melinda Kessler, soprano; Eugene Cramer, tenor; Thomas Kirchbaum, conductor.
Music: ms. in composer's hand. *Tape.*

G4.24 Trio for Flute, Viola and Bassoon. (1962)

G4.25 Trio for Violin, Cello and Piano. (1974) 14'
4 movements. *First performed:* Nov. 1974; Boston University. Anthony Martin, violin; Margaret Cording, violoncello; Elizabeth McCrae, piano.
Music: ms. in composer's hand. *Tape.*

G5 WILLIAM GOTTSHALL

Born November 13, 1955, in Sellersville, Pa. Moved to Boston area 1975. *Education:* studied composition with Don Sebesky, Jeronimas Kacinskas, John Bavicchi, William Maloof (Berklee College of Music, B.M., 1978); arranging with Don Sebesky, Bob Chestnut, Michael Treni. *Related activities:* arranger of jazz, popular music, musical comedies. BPL

WORKS

[Advent Hymns for Children]
G5.1 Three Advent Hymns for Children. (1979) 3' 45"
For: voice and piano. *Contents:* What Can I Give Him?; The Little Birds Praise You; How Far Is It to Bethlehem.
Vocal score: ms. in composer's hand; available from composer.

Andante. *See* Song of the Mockingbird.

G5.2 Arise, My Love. (1977) 3' 20"
For: chorus(SATB). *Text:* Bible, O.T., Song of Solomon 2:10-13. *First performed:* Nov. 23, 1980; Church of the Covenant, Boston. Church of the Covenant Choir, Martin Mullvain, conductor.
Vocal score: ms. in composer's hand; available from composer.

G5.3 Behold, My Servant. (1977) 1' 40"
For: chorus(SATB). Motet. *Text:* Bible, N.T., Matthew 12:18, 21.
Vocal score: ms. in composer's hand; available from composer.

G5.4 Brookline Bossa Nova. (1975) 2' 35"
For: trumpet, trombone, saxophone(alto), saxophone(tenor), rhythm section.
Score & parts: ms. in composer's hand; available from composer.

[Fugue, A-Flat]
G5.5 Four-Part Fugue in A-Flat. (1977)

1' 30"
For: trumpets in C(2) and trombones(2).
1 movement.
Score: ms. in composer's hand;
available from composer.

[Fugue, G Major]
G5.6 Three-Part Fugue in G Major.
(1976) 1' 20"
For: piano. 1 movement.
Score: ms. in composer's hand;
available from composer.

G5.7 Now Every Child That Dwells on
Earth. (1976) 1' 40"
For: trumpets(2), horn, trombone, tuba.
Christmas carol..
Condensed score & parts: ms. in
composer's hand; available from
composer.

G5.8 O Mistress Mine. (1977) 2' 30"
For: chorus(SATB), oboe, harpsichord,
violoncello. Song. *Text: Twelfth Night*,
Act 2, Scene 3 by William
Shakespeare.
Score: ms. in composer's hand;
available from composer.

G5.9 Prelude to a Journey at Sea.
(1978) 10' 45"
For:
orchestra(2(&pic)-2(&Ehn)-2(bcl)-2(&cbsn);
4-3-3-1; timp, perc(3), xylo; str). 1
movement.
Score: ms. in composer's hand;
available from composer.

G5.10 The Scout Jamboree. (1976) 3'
75"
For: flute, trumpet in C, violin, double
bass. *Movements:* Farewell to the Folks;
The March to the Campside; Bivouac.
Score: ms. in composer's hand;
available from composer.

G5.11 Seasonal Country Sketches. 5' 5"
For: flutes(2), trumpet, horn, piano,
violin. *Movements:* Summer; Autumn;
Winter; Spring.
Score: ms. in composer's hand;
available from composer.

G5.12 Simple and Free. (1975) 2' 45"
For: voice and piano. *Text:* William
Gottshall and Michael Scheip.
Score: ms. in composer's hand;
available from composer.

G5.13 Sonata. (1978) 9' 15"
For: piano. 3 movements. *First
performed:* Apr. 4, 1981; Church of the
Covenant, Boston. David Schermer.
Score: ms. in composer's hand;
available from composer.

G5.14 Song of the Mockingbird. (1976)
2'
For: flute and piano. 1 movement.
Also titled Andante. *First performed:*
Apr. 19, 1980; Church of the Covenant,
Boston. Church of the Covenant Art
Festival. Suellan Hershman, flute and
David Schermer, piano.
Score: ms. in composer's hand;
available from composer.

G5.15 Thumbing to Ontario. (1972) 3'
45"
For: voice and piano. *Text:* William
Gottshall.
Score: ms. in composer's hand;
available from composer.

G5.16 Wedding Air. (1975) 1' 50"
For: flute and piano. 1 movement. *First
performed:* May 28, 1977; Hatfield, Pa.
Rebecca Baum, flute and Mary Baum,
piano.
Score: ms. in composer's hand;
available from composer.

G5.17 Whispering Moonlight. (1974) 2'
35"
For: voice and piano. *Text:* Michael
Scheip.
Score: ms. in composer's hand;
available from composer.

ARRANGEMENTS OF WORKS BY OTHER COMPOSERS

G5.18 Beneath It All. (1975; rev. 1976)
3' 33"
For: trumpet, flugelhorn,

saxophone(alto), saxophone(tenor), saxophone(baritone), trombone, rhythm section. Jazz music. Original by Gary Anderson.
Score & parts: ms. in composer's hand; available from composer.

G5.19 Daahoud. (1977) 2' 45"
For: jazz band. Original by Clifford Brown.
Score & parts: ms. in composer's hand; available from composer.

G5.20 Don't You Worry 'bout a Thing. (1977) 2' 36"
For: trumpets(2), saxophone(tenor), rhythm section. Jazz music. Original by Stevie Wonder.
Score & parts: ms. in composer's hand; available from composer.

G5.21 I Love to Tell the Story. (1981) 2' 45"
For: piano. Original by William G. Fischer. *First performed:* Mar. 15, 1981; Church of the Covenant, Boston. David Schermer.
Score: ms. in composer's hand; available from composer.

G5.22 Lucky Southern. (1975) 3' 11"
For: trumpet, trombone, saxophone(alto), saxophone(tenor), rhythm section. Jazz music. Original by Keith Jarrett.
Score & parts: ms. in composer's hand; available from composer.

G5.23 Melodie. (1977) 3' 33"
For: string quartet, double bass. Original by Sergei Rachmaninoff.
Score: ms. in composer's hand; available from composer.

G5.24 Minority. (1976) 2' 48"
For: trumpet, trombones(2), saxophone(alto), saxophone(baritone), rhythm section. Jazz music. Original by Gigi Gryce.
Score & parts: ms. in composer's hand; available from composer.

G5.25 Nardis. (1975) 1' 53"
For: trumpet, trombone, rhythm section. Jazz music. Original by Miles Davis.
Score: ms. in composer's hand; available from composer.

G5.26 The Shadow of Your Smile. (1977) 2' 25"
For: voice(male) and jazz ensemble(flutes(2), clarinets(2), clarinet(bass), trumpets(4), trombones(3), rhythm section). Original by Johnny Mandel.
Score & parts: ms. in composer's hand; available from composer.

G5.27 Sometimes in Winter. (1977) 4' 40"
For: jazz band. Original by Steven Katz.
Score & parts: ms. in composer's hand; available from composer.

G5.28 Too Close for Comfort. (1979) 3' 10"
For: jazz band. Original by Jerry Bock, Larry Holofcener, George Weiss.
Score: ms. in composer's hand; available from composer.

G5.29 When I Needed a Neighbor. (1980) 1' 40"
For: organ. Original by Sydney Carter.
Score: ms. in composer's hand; available from composer.

G6 ROUBEN GREGORIAN

Born September 23, 1915, in Tifliz, Russia. Moved to Boston area 1952. *Education:* Armenian Central College, Tabriz, Iran; Teheran Conservatory, Teheran, Iran; Ecole Normal de Musique, Paris, France; Conservatoire National de Musique, Paris, France; studied composition with Rudolph Urbanec and Arthur Honegger. *Awards:* Asa Boyan Humanity Award (1977), Man of the Year (Armenian Prelacy, New York City, 1978), Honorary citizen (State of Maine), two Iran Ministry of Education Awards, Symphonia Fraternity of America (Honorary member). *Related activities:* violinist; founding member of Komitas String Quartet; conductor, Teheran Symphony (1948-51), Portland (Maine) Symphony (1959-62), Boston Women's Symphony (1964-65); director, Komitas Choral Society of Boston (1955-); guest conductor, Boston Pops (annually); member of the faculty of Boston Conservatory (1952-). BCM

WORKS

G6.1 Armenian Divine Liturgy. (1960-78)
For: Soprano, Alto, Tenor, Bass, chorus(SATB), orchestra(3(pic)-2-2(&bcl)-2; 4-3-3-1; timp, perc; hp; str).
Text: based on version by Komitar Vardapet.
Score & parts: ms; available from composer.
Vocal score: ms; available from composer.

[Choral and Solo Songs]
G6.2 12 Choral and Solo Songs. (1954-56)
For: chorus(mixed). *Text:* Folksongs, Armenian.

[Concerto, Horn]
G6.3 Horn Concerto. (1974) 18'
For: horn and orchestra(2-2(&Ehn)-2-2; 4-2-3-1; timp, perc; str). *First performed:* 1967; Symphony Hall, Boston. Boston Pops.
Score & parts: ms.; available from composer.

G6.4 Easter Cantata. (1954) 15'
For: Soprano, Tenor, chorus(mixed), string orchestra.

G6.5 Gol Aman Gol. (1945) 6'
For: Soprano, chorus(SATB), string orchestra, harp. *First performed:* 1965; Boston Conservatory.
Score & parts: ms.; available from composer.

G6.6 Hega Orchestral Fantasie. (1958) 6'
For: orchestra(3-2-2-2; 4-2-3-1; timp,

perc; pf; str). Based on music of American Indians (Maine). *Dedicated to:* Portland (Maine) Symphony. *First performed:* 1962; Portland, Me. Portland Symphony Orchestra.

G6.7 Iranian Folk Songs. (1942)
For: voice, chorus, piano.
Music: Iranian Ministry of Education.

[Iranian Folk Songs]
G6.8 Two Iranian Folk Songs. (1954)
For: chorus.
Vocal score: Kjos.

G6.9 Iranian Suite. (1948) 18'
For: orchestra(3-2-2-2; 4-3-2-1; timp, perc; hp; str). Symphonic poem. 5 movements.
Score & parts: ms.; available from composer.

G6.10 Nairy Symphonic Suite. (1956) 12'
For: orchestra(3-2-2-2; 4-3-2-1; timp, perc; hp; str). 3 movements.

G6.11 Nocturne. (1953)
For: Soprano and string orchestra(2-2-2-2; 2-0-0-0; hp; str) or piano. *First performed:* 1954; Boston. Agnes Hagopian, soprano; Boston Pops.

Nocturne for Piano. *See* Scherzo and Nocturne.

[Pieces]
G6.12 Violin and Piano Pieces. (1952) 8'
Movements: Caprice; Varak.

[Quartets, Strings]
G6.13 Two String Quartets. (1948)
Based on folk themes. 4 movements.

G6.14 Recueil de chansons rustiques iraniennes. (1951)
For: chorus(SATB). *Contents:* Rawid-Xan; Hey Yar; Lay Lay; Dast be Dasmalom; Dam kil; Simay Can; Ay sar Kotal; Massom Massom; Doxtare Boyer-Ahmadi; Page Leyli; Korawim; Darebe Can; Aziz Cun.

Vocal score: Gregorian Institute of America, 1951. BCM
Vocal score: Iranian Ministry of Education, 1952.

G6.15 Scherzo and Nocturne. (1940) 4'
For: piano.
Score: Gregorian Institute of America, 1950.
Reel: Dec. 1, 1967; Boston Conservatory. Alfred Lee.

[Songs]
G6.16 Five Songs.
For: Soprano and piano. *Contents:* To Biow; Varan Baraneh; Dey Balal; Darineh Jan-aziz Joo; Badiur.
Score: ms.; available from composer.

[Suite, String Orchestra, No. 1]
G6.17 Suite. (1948) 15'
4 movements.

[Suite, String Orchestra, No. 2]
G6.18 Second Suite. (1981) 15'
5 movements.
Score & parts: available from composer.

G6.19 Symphony. (1964) 35'
For: orchestra(3-2(&Ehn)-2(&bcl)-0; 4-4-3-1; timp, perc; hp; str).
Score & parts: ms; available from composer.

G6.20 Tatragoms Bride. (1952) 12'
For: orchestra(3-2(&Ehn)-2-2; 4-3-3-1; timp, perc; str). Symphonic poem. *First performed:* 1955; Boston. Boston Pops.

G7 ROBERT GRONQUIST

Born October 15, 1938, in Aurora, Ill. Moved to Boston area 1973. *Education:* degrees from the University of Illinois and the University of California, Berkeley. *Awards:* National Endowment for the Humanities Grant and Aspen Music Festival Grant. *Related activities:* harpsichordist; conductor; served as Director of Choirs, Smith College and Director of Choral Music, Trinity College; editor of performing editions of Renaissance and Baroque choral music; contributor of articles to *Musical Quarterly*, *Notes*, *Gradiva*; currently on the faculty of Simmons College. NEC

WORKS

G7.1 Barekhu. (1980) 1' 30"
For: chorus(mixed). *First performed:* 1980; Simmons College. Simmons College Chorale.
Vocal score: ms.

G7.2 Invocation. (1977) 4'
For: chorus(women) and piano.
Vocal score: ms.

G7.3 The Lord Zouches Maske. (1973) 55'
For: chorus(men) or chorus(women) or chorus(mixed). Multi-media. Written in collaboration with Paul Earls and Larry Johnson. *First performed:* 1973; Old West Church, Boston. Simmons College Chorale.
Perf. dir: available from composer.

G7.4 Mass. (1971) 12'
For: chorus(mixed) and organ.
Vocal score: ms.

G7.5 Psalm. (1972) 5'
For: voices and tape. *First performed:* Hartford, Conn.
Score: ms.

G7.6 Quittez pasteurs. (1973) 2' 30"
For: chorus(SATB), piccolo or recorder(optional), drums. *First performed:* Hartford, Conn.
Vocal score: Kerby.

G7.7 Relavation. (1970) 40'
For: chorus(mixed). Multi-media. Written in collaboration with Robert Morris; electronic score by Morton Subotnick. *First performed:* Hartford, Conn.
Perf. dir: available from composer.

G7.8 This Endris Night. (1973) 4'
For: chorus(SATB). *First performed:*

Hartford, Conn.
Vocal score: Kerby.

G8 LANCE F. GUNDERSON

Born May 4, 1946, in Portsmouth, N.H.
Moved to Boston area 1964. *Education:*
Professional Diploma (Berklee College
of Music, 1970); B.A., Extension
Studies (Harvard University, 1978);
Aspen Music Festival (1972-75); Banff
Centre for the Arts (summer, 1973);
studied composition with Charles
Jones, George Russell, Michael
Tchiakowski; classical guitar with Oscar
Ghiglia, Alirio Diaz, J. Duarte; jazz
guitar with Jim Hall; sitar with Brian
Silver. *Related activities:*
artist-in-residence, Haystack School of
Crafts (1980-81); served on the
faculties of Berklee College of Music
(1973-80), Winsor School (1980),
Peabody School (1981). Be

WORKS

G8.1 Azure Skies. (1970) 5′
For: flute and guitar. 2 movements.
Commissioned by: EMI. *Dedication:* To
the classical music tradition of India.
First performed: 1971; Finlandia
Concert Hall, Helsinki, Finland. Heikki
Sarmanto Quartet.
Score: Fazer, 1972.
Disc: EMI Odeon E 5062-3406, 1971.
"Other compositions [chiefly solo and
chamber music for guitar] available
from [the composer]."

H1 REGINALD W. HACHE

Born November 26, 1932, in Waterville,
Me. Moved to Boston area 1950.
Education: studied composition with
Leland Proctor and Ivan Waldbauer;
orchestration with Richard Arnell; piano
with Miklos Schwalb (New England
Conservatory, B.M., 1954, M.M., 1958,
A.D., 1960). *Awards:* Pi Kappa Lambda
Annual Competition for Seniors and
Graduates (New England Conservatory,
First Prize, 1957), New England

Conservatory Concerto Competition
(winner, 1958, 1960). NU

WORKS

H1.1 Concerto. (1978) 20′
For: piano and orchestra. 3 movements.
First performed: 1978; Northeastern
University. Northeastern University
Symphony Orchestra.
Score & parts: ms.

H1.2 Fantasy 1984. (1975) 6′
For: piano. 1 movement.
Score: ms.

H1.3 Images of the Freedom Trail.
(1981) 15′-20′
For: pianos(2). *Movements:* Fanueil Hall;
4th of July at the Esplanade; The
Swan Boats in the Commons; Old
Haymarket Square; The Graveyard at
King's Chapel; Boston at Dawn.
Commissioned by: Eastern Public Radio.

H1.4 Rhapsody. (1977) 7′
For: violin and piano. 1 movement.
First performed: 1977.
Score: ms.
Reel: 1977; Robbins Library, Arlington,
Mass. Dorothy Bales, violin and
unidentified pianist.
Reel: Feb. 10, 1977; Northeastern
University. Dorothy Bales, violin and
Reginald Hache, piano. NU

H1.5 Scarlet Letter. (1979)
Incidental music. 17 episodes. Written
for a WGBH-FM, Boston production of
the book by Nathaniel Hawthorne.
Music: ms.

H1.6 Sonata. (1980)
For: piano. 4 movements.
Score: ms.

H1.7 Song Cycle. (1975) 8′
For: Soprano and piano. *Contents:* The
Crazy One; Goodby Er Howdy Do; The
Horseman.
Score: ms.
Reel: 1975; Robbins Library, Arlington,

Mass. Phyllis Kaplan, soprano and unidentified pianist.

[Suite, Piano]
H1.8 Piano Suite. (1976) 16'
Movements: Prelude; Minuet; Nocturne; Ragtime; Dirge; Scherzo; Fugue 1975.
First performed: 1976.
Score: ms.
Reel: 1976; Robbins Library, Arlington, Mass. Reginald Hache.
Reel: Feb. 10, 1977; Northeastern University. NU

H1.9 Symphonic Movement. (1980)
For: orchestra. 1 movement.
Music: ms.

H1.10 Treasure Island. (1978)
Incidental music. 20 episodes. Written for a WGBH-FM, Boston production of the book by Robert Louis Stevenson.

H1.11 [Variations, Piano]
Piano Variations for Ballet. (1975) 10'
Score: ms.
Reel: 1976; Robbins Library, Arlington, Mass. Northeastern University Dance Group; Reginald Hache, piano.

ARRANGEMENTS OF WORKS BY OTHER COMPOSERS

H1.12 Children's Corner Suite.
For: pianos(2). Original by Claude Debussy.
Score: ms.
Reel: Feb. 10, 1977; Northeastern University. Reginal Hache and Roland Nadeau. NU

H1.13 Entertainer.
For: pianos(2). Original by Scott Joplin.
Score: ms.

H1.14 Fugue B-Flat Minor.
For: pianos(2). Original from *The Well-Tempered Clavier I* by Johann Sebastian Bach.
Score: ms.

H1.15 Fugue C-Sharp Minor.
For: pianos(2). Original from *The*

Well-Tempered Clavier I by Johann Sebastian Bach.
Score: ms.

H1.16 Fugue D Major.
For: pianos(2). Original from *The Well-Tempered Clavier II* by Johann Sebastian Bach.
Score: ms.

H1.17 Gypsy Music.
For: pianos(2). Original from *Carmen* by Georges Bizet.
Score: ms.

H1.18 Pictures at an Exhibition.
For: pianos(2). Original by Modest Mussorgsky.
Score: 1980.

The Well-Tempered Clavier. *See* Fugue B-Flat Minor; Fugue C-Sharp Minor; Fugue D Major.

H2 JOHN HARBISON

Born December 20, 1938, in Orange, N.J. *Education:* B.A. (Harvard University, 1960); studied composition with Roger Sessions and Earl Kim (Princeton University, M.F.A, 1963). *Awards:* Brandeis University, Creative Arts Award (1971), National Institute of Arts and Letters Award (1972), Fromm Foundation commission (1973), Koussevitzky Music Foundation (Library of Congress) commission (1973), National Endowment for the Arts Composer/Librettist Fellowship (1974), Naumburg Chamber Music Awards (1974, 1978), Boston Symphony Orchestra Centennial commission (1981), Kennedy Center Friedheim Award (1981). *Related activities:* jazz pianist; violist; conductor; composer-in-residence at Reed College (1968-69), American Academy, Rome (1981), Santa Fe Chamber Festival (1981); director of the Cantata Singers (1969-73, 1980-); member of the faculty of the Massachusetts Institute of Technology (1972-). MIT

WORKS

H2.1 Amazing Grace. (1972) 10′
For: oboe. Variations. *First performed:*
Jan. 1975; Carnegie Recital Hall, New
York City. Philip West.
Score: reprod. of ms. MIT

H2.2 Autumnal. (1964) 15′
For: Mezzo Soprano and piano. *Text:*
Emily Dickinson, Charles Pierre
Baudelaire, Rainer Maria Rilke. *First
performed:* Mar. 1966; Brandeis
University. Patricia Stedry, mezzo
soprano and Martin Boykan, piano.
Score: reprod. of ms. MIT

Bermuda Triangle. *See* December Music.
Bermuda Triangle.

H2.3 Cantata I. (1965)
Withdrawn.

H2.4 Cantata II. (1967)
Withdrawn.

H2.5 Cantata III. (1968)
Withdrawn.

H2.6 (Chinese - German) Book of Hours
and Seasons. (1973-75) 15′
For: Mezzo Soprano, flute, violoncello,
piano. *Text:* Johann Wolfgang von
Goethe. *Contents:* Dem Aufgehenden (To
the Rising Full Moon); Immer und
ueberall (Always and Everywhere);
Jahreszeiten kommen wieder (The
Seasons Come Again); Mich aengstigt
das Verfaengliche (Theorizing Is Hateful
to Me); Um Mitternacht (At Midnight).
First performed: Nov. 13, 1977; Longy
School of Music. Seraphim Concert.
D'Anna Fortunato, mezzo soprano;
Seraphim.
Score: reprod. of ms. MIT
Reel: recording of first performance.
MIT

[Concerto, Piano]
H2.7 Piano Concerto. (1978-80)
For: piano and
orchestra(2(pic)-2-2(bcl)-2; 2-2-2-1;

perc(2); hp; str). 2 movements.
Commissioned by: Robert Miller. *First
performed:* May 1980; Alice Tully Hall,
New York City. Robert Miller, piano;
American Composers Orchestra,
Gunther Schuller, conductor.
Score & parts: Associated, 1980. Rental.
Pf. red: Associated, 1980.
Disc: Composers Recordings CRI SD
440, 1981. Robert Miller, piano;
American Composers Orchestra,
Gunther Schuller, conductor. MIT NEC
W
Reel: May 1980; Robert Miller, piano;
American Composers Orchestra,
Gunther Schuller, conductor. MIT

[Concerto, Violin]
H2.8 Violin Concerto. (1980) 28′
For: violin and orchestra(2-2-2-2;
2-2-2-1; timp, vibra; hp; str). 3
movements. *Dedicated to:* Rose Mary
Harbison. *First performed:* Jan. 24,
1981; Emmanuel Church, Boston. Rose
Mary Harbison, violin; Emmanuel
Chamber Orchestra, Craig Smith,
conductor.
Score & parts: Associated, 1980. Rental.
Reel: recording of first performance.
MIT

H2.9 Confinement. (1965) 15′ 15″
For: instrumental ensemble(flute,
oboe/English horn, clarinet/clarinet(bass),
saxophone(alto), trumpet, trombone,
percussion, piano, violin, viola,
violoncello, double bass). *Text:* based
on *Devotions* by John Donne. *First
performed:* Feb. 1967; Carnegie Recital
Hall, New York City. Contemporary
Chamber Ensemble, Arthur Weisberg,
conductor.
Score: reprod. of ms. MIT
Score & parts: Associated. Rental.
Disc: in *Spectrum: New American
Music*, vol. III; Nonesuch H 71221,
1969. Contemporary Chamber Ensemble,
Arthur Weisberg, conductor. BCM BrU
BU HU MIT NEC W

[December Music. Bermuda Triangle]
H2.10 Bermuda Triangle: Final Part,

December Music. (1970) 7' 25"
For: saxophone(tenor),
violoncello(amplified), organ(electric).
Commissioned by: New York Camerata.
First performed: Apr. 1973; Carnegie
Recital Hall, New York City. Albert
Regni, tenor saxophone; Helen Harbison,
amplified violoncello; Robert D. Levin,
electric organ.
Score & parts: Associated, 1978. Rental.
Disc: Composers Recordings CRI SD
313, 1973. Albert Regni, tenor
saxophone; Helen Harbison, amplified
violoncello; Robert Levin, electric
organ. BrU BU HU MIT NEC W

[December Music. Parody-Fantasia]
H2.11 Parody-Fantasia, from December
Music. (1968) 7'
For: piano. *Movements:* Preamble;
Take-Offs; Flights; Arrivals; Games;
Post-Mortem. *First performed:* Dec.
1969; Carnegie Recital Hall, New York
City. Ursula Oppens.
Score: reprod. of ms. MIT
Score: McGinnis & Marx, 1980. HU MIT
Disc: in *Pleskow, Harbison, Johnson;*
Composers Recordings CRI SD 293,
1972. Robert Miller. BrU BU HU MIT
NEC W

[December Music. Preludes]
H2.12 Four Preludes. (1967) 7'
For: flutes(3); or flute, clarinet, violin;
or flute and oboes(2). *First performed:*
Apr. 1969; Harvard University.
Score: McGinnis & Marx, 1973. MIT W
Reel: Mar. 6, 1974; Brookline Public
Library. BkPL
Reel: Feb. 24, 1980; Wellesley College.
Nancy Hall, Ann Palik, Suzanne Stumpf,
flutes. W
Cassette: Feb. 24, 1980; Wellesley
College. Nancy Hall, Ann Palik, Suzanne
Stumpf, flutes. MIT

H2.13 Diotima. (1976) 22'
For:
orchestra(3(pic)-2-3(Ebcl,cbcl)-2(cbsn);
4-3-3-1; timp, perc; hp, cel; str). Based
on poem by Friedrich Hoelderlin.
Commissioned by: Koussevitzky Music
Foundation (Library of Congress).

Dedication: To the memory of Serge
and Natalie Koussevitzky. *First
performed:* Mar. 8, 1977; Symphony
Hall, Boston. Boston Symphony
Orchestra, Joseph Silverstein,
conductor.
Score: reprod. of ms. MIT
Score & parts: Associated, 1977. Rental.
Reel: Mar 12, 1977; Symphony Hall,
Boston. Boston Symphony Orchestra,
Joseph Silverstein, conductor. MIT

Dumb Shows. *See* Winter's Tale. Dumb
Shows.

H2.14 Elegiac Songs. (1974) 21'
For: Soprano and chamber
orchestra(2-2-2(ssax)-2; 2-0-0-0; perc;
str). *Text:* Emily Dickinson.
Commissioned by: Fromm Foundation.
Dedicated to: Jan DeGaetani and Paul
Fromm. *First performed:* 1975; Carnegie
Recital Hall, New York City; Jan De
Gaetani, mezzo soprano; Contemporary
Chamber Ensemble, Arthur Weisberg,
conductor.
Score & parts: Associated, 1974. Rental.
Reel: recording of first performance.
MIT

H2.15 The Flower-Fed Buffaloes. (1976)
20'
For: Baritone, chorus(mixed), clarinet,
saxophone(tenor), violin, violoncello,
double bass, piano, percussion.
Contents: Preamble; The Flower Fed
Buffaloes (Nicholas Vachel Lindsay);
Enrich My Resignation (Stephen Crane);
Depths (Michael Fried); Above Pate
Valley (Gary Snyder); The Amaranth
(Nicholas Vachel Lindsay). *Commissioned
by:* New York State Bar Association.
First performed: Feb. 1978; Harvard
University; Fromm Foundation Concert.
David Evitts, baritone; Emmanuel
Church Choir of Boston; Speculum
Musicae, John Harbison, conductor.
Score: reprod. of ms. HU
Score & parts: Associated, 1978. Rental.
Disc: Nonesuch H 71366, 1979. David
Evitts, baritone; Emmanuel Church Choir
of Boston; Speculum Musicae, John
Harbison, conductor. MIT NEC

H2.16 Full Moon in March. (1977) 32'
For: Soprano, Mezzo Soprano, Tenor,
Baritone, flute, oboe, clarinet(bass),
violin, viola, violoncello, piano,
percussion. Opera in one act. *Text:*
adapted from the play by William
Butler Yeats. *First performed:* May
1978; Sanders Theatre, Harvard
University. Cheryl Cobb, soprano;
D'Anna Fortunato, mezzo soprano; Kim
Scown, tenor; David Arnold, baritone;
Boston Musica Viva, Richard Pittman,
conductor.
Score & parts: Associated, 1979. Rental.
Libretto: MIT
Reel: recording of first performance.
MIT
Reel: Apr. 30, 1979. Musica Viva,
Richard Pittman, conductor. WGBH

[Harp Songs]
H2.17 Three Harp Songs. (1975) 8'
For: Tenor and harp. *Contents:* August
Was Foggy (Gary Snyder); Falling
Asleep (Michael Fried); Poem (Ian
Hamilton) *Dedicated to:* Wassily
Leontief. *First performed:* Nov. 13,
1977; Longy School of Music;
Seraphim Concert. Karl Dan Sorensen,
tenor and T. Kathleen Moreno, harp.
Score: reprod. of ms. MIT
Reel: recording of first performance.
MIT WGBH

H2.18 Incidental Music for
Shakespeare's The Merchant of Venice.
(1971) 12'
For: string orchestra or string quartet,
double bass. 1 movement. Written for
the play by William Shakespeare.
Dedicated to: Klaus Liepmann. *First
performed:* Aug. 1973; Jaffrey, N.H.;
Monadnock Music Festival. James
Bolle, conductor.
Score: Associated, 1977. HU MIT NEC
W
Parts: Associated, 1977.
Reel: recording of first performance.
MIT

H2.19 Die Kuerze. (1970) 10'
For: flute/piccolo, clarinet/clarinet(bass),
violin, violoncello, piano. 3
movements. *Text:* third movement is a
wordless setting of the poem by
Friedrich Hoelderlin. *Dedicated to:*
Robert Levin. *First performed:* Feb.
1970; New York City; Composer's
Forum.
Score: reprod. of ms. MIT
Cassette: Mar. 2, 1971; New England
Conservatory. Robert Stallman, flute
David Satz, clarinet; Rose Mary
Harbison, violin; Maria Kyprie,
violoncello; Jerome Kuderna, piano;
John Harbison, conductor. NEC

H2.20 Moments of Vision. (1975) 15'
For: Soprano(with handbells), Tenor(with
handbells), recorder(sopranino/alto/bass),
crumhorn, hurdygurdy, dulcimer. *Text:*
Thomas Hardy. *Contents:* Prelude;
Moments of Vision; First or Last;
During Wind and Rain; Last Love-Word;
So, Time. *Commissioned by:* Naumburg
Foundation.
Score: reprod of ms. MIT

H2.21 Motetti di Montale. (1980) 56'
For: Mezzo Soprano and piano. *Text:*
Eugenio Montale. *Dedication:* Honoring
the poet on his 85th birthday. *First
performed:* Aug. 4, 1981; Sante Fe,
N.M.; Sante Fe Chamber Music Festival.
Janice Felty, mezzo soprano and
Edward Auer, piano.
Score: Associated, nyp.

H2.22 Music When Soft Voices Die.
(1966) 3'
For: chorus(mixed). *Text:* Percy Bysshe
Shelley. *First performed:* Apr. 1971;
Sanders Theatre, Harvard University.
Cantata Singers, John Harbison,
conductor.
Vocal score: Associated, 1975. MIT NEC
Reel: Feb. 27, 1976; New England
Consevatory. NEC Chamber Singers,
Lorna Cooke deVaron, conductor. WGBH
Cassette: Feb. 27, 1976; New England

Conservatory. NEC Chamber Singers, Lorna Cooke deVaron, conductor. NEC

H2.23 Nunc dimittis. (1979) 6'
For: Tenor, Bass, chorus, piano. *Text:* Bible, N.T., Luke ll:25-35. *Commissioned by:* Harvard Glee Club for its 100th anniversary. *Dedicated to:* Harvard Glee Club, Jameson Marvin, conductor.
Vocal score: reprod. of ms. MIT
Vocal score: Associated, 1980.

Parody-Fantasia. *See* December Music. Parody-Fantasia.

Preludes. *See* December Music. Preludes.

[Quintet, Piano and Strings]
H2.24 Piano Quintet. (1981) 23'
For: string quartet, piano. *Dedication:* To Georgia O'Keefe with gratitude from the artists, directors, and friends of the Sante Fe Chamber Music Festival. *First performed:* Aug. 10, 1981; Sante Fe, N.M.; Sante Fe Chamber Music Festival. Daniel Phillips and Ani Kavafian, violins; Walter Trampler, viola; Timothy Eddy, violoncello; Edward Auer, piano.
Score & parts: Associated, nyp.

[Quintet, Woodwinds]
H2.25 Quintet. (1978) 21' 45"
For: woodwind quintet. 5 movements. *Commissioned by:* Naumburg Foundation. Winner of the Naumburg Chamber Music Award. *First performed:* Apr. 1979; Jordan Hall, Boston. Aulos Quintet.
Score & parts: Composers Collaborative, 1979. Rental. MIT
Disc: Composers Recordings CRI SD 436, 1980. Aulos Quintet. MIT NEC T W
Cassette: Oct. 22, 1979; New England Conservatory; in *Contemporary American Music for the Flute.* John Heiss, flute; Frederic Cohen, oboe; Robert Annis, clarinet; Peter Schoenbach, bassoon; David Hoose, horn. NEC

H2.26 Samuel Chapter. (1978) 12'
For: Soprano, flute, clarinet, viola, violoncello, piano, percussion. *Text:* Bible, O.T., Samuel l:3. *First performed:* Oct. 1978; Pickman Auditorium, Longy School of Music. Joan Heller, soprano; Collage, John Harbison, conductor.
Score & parts: Associated, 1980. Rental.
Reel: Nov. 12, 1980; Emmanuel Church, Boston. Susan Larson, soprano; Christopher Krueger, flute; David Satz, clarinet; Emily Bruell, viola, Shannon Snap, violoncello; Lesley Amper, piano; Neil Grover, percussion; Craig Smith, conductor. MIT
Reel: Oct. 11, 1980; Boston University; Alea III concert. Elizabeth Van Ingen, soprano; and others; Theodore Antoniou, conductor. BU

H2.27 Serenade for Six Players. (1968) 11'
For: flute/piccolo, clarinet, clarinet(bass), violin, viola, violoncello. 2 movements. *First performed:* May 1969; Reed College. Portland Group for New Music.
Score: reprod. of ms. MIT
Score & parts: Associated. Rental.
Reel: 1976; Roger Sessions Festival, Amherst College. Da Capo Chamber Players. MIT

H2.28 Shakespeare Series. (1965) 8'
For: Mezzo Soprano and piano. *Text:* from the *Sonnets* of William Shakespeare. *First performed:* Nov. 1965; Cambridge, Mass; Club 47 series. Janice Harsanyi, mezzo soprano and Mathilde McKinney, piano.
Reel: Mar. 1976; Brandeis University. Jan De Gaetani, mezzo soprano and Martin Boykan, piano. MIT

H2.29 Sinfonia for Violin and Double Orchestra. (1963) 9' 30"
For: violin and string orchestra(6-6-4-4-2 or 4-4-3-3-1). *Dedicated to:* Rose Mary Harbison. *First performed:* Mar. 1963; Harvard Memorial Church, Cambridge. Rose Mary Harbison, violin; Bach Society

Orchestra, Gregory Biss, conductor.
Score: reprod. of ms. MIT
Score: American Composers Alliance.
Reel: recording of first performance.
MIT

[Songs of Experience]
H2.30 Five Songs of Experience. (1971)
17' 50"
For: Soprano, Alto, Tenor, Bass,
chorus(mixed), string quartet,
percussion(2). *Text:* William Blake.
Contents: Introductions; Earth's Answer;
Ah! Sunflower; The Voice of the
Ancient Bard; A Divine Image.
Commissioned by: Emmanuel Church,
Boston, Craig Smith, music director.
First performed: Sanders Theatre,
Harvard University. Cantata Singers and
Ensemble, John Harbison, conductor.
Parts: Associated, 1975.
Vocal score: Associated, 1975. BPL BrU
HU MIT NEC
Disc: Composers Recordings CRI SD
313, 1973. Cantata Singers and
Ensemble, John Harbison, conductor.
BrU BU HU MIT NEC W

H2.31 Symphony No. 1. (1981) 24'
For: orchestra(3-3-3-3;4-2-3-1; perc(6);
hp; str). *Dedicated to:* The BSO on its
centennial celebration. *Commissioned
by:* Boston Symphony Orchestra
Centennial Commission.
Score: Associated, nyp.

H2.32 Trio. (1969) 7' 10"
For: violin, violoncello, piano. 1
movement. *Dedicated to:* Bentley
Layton, Helen Abrahamian, Robert D.
Levin. *First performed:* Apr. 1969;
Harvard University. Bentley Layton,
violin; Helen Harbison, violoncello;
Robert Levin, piano.
Score: reprod. of ms. MIT
Parts: ms. in composer's hand.
Disc: Composers Recordings CRI SD
313, 1973. Wheaton Trio. BrU BU HU
MIT NEC W

H2.33 Verses. (1964) 7' 10"
For: violin. Withdrawn.

H2.34 Winter's Tale. (1974) 92'
For: voices(10), chorus(mixed), tape,
orchestra. Opera in 2 acts. *Text:*
adapted from the play by William
Shakespeare. Supported by a National
Endowment for the Arts
Composer/Librettist Fellowship. *First
performed:* Aug. 1979. San Francisco
Opera, David Agler, conductor.
Score, parts, tape: Associated. Rental.
Vocal score: reprod. of ms. MIT
Vocal score: Associated.
Reel: recording of first performance.
MIT
Cassette: recording of first
performance. W

[Winter's Tale. Dumb Shows]
H2.35 Winter's Tale: Six Dumbshows.
(1974)
For: chamber ensemble. Withdrawn as
an independent work.

H3 MARK S. HARVEY

Born July 4, 1946, in Binghamton, N.Y.
Moved to Boston area 1968. *Education:*
A.B. (Syracuse University); Th.M.
(Boston University); doctoral studies
(Boston University); studied jazz'
composition and arranging with Jaki
Byard and George Russell (New England
Conservatory, special student). *Awards:*
Massachusetts Council on the Arts and
Humanities Artist Fellowship Program
(Finalist-Runner-up, 1980). *Related
activities:* trumpet player; leader of
various jazz and new jazz musical
ensembles in the Boston area; founder
of Jazz Coalition, Inc. and the Jazz
Celebrations Concert series; director of
Jazz/Arts Ministry, Emmanuel Church,
Boston; music advisor for
Massachusetts Council on the Arts and
Humanities; board member of the
Performing Artists Associates
Massachusetts Cultural Alliance and
Cambridge Arts Council; designated
"Grand Bostonian" during Jubilee 350
Celebration; member of the faculties
of Curry College, Wheelock College,
Massachusetts Institute of Technology,

Community Music Center of Boston.
MIT

WORKS

H3.1 Allelu Chant. (1970)
For: jazz
ensemble(trumpets(2),horn(optional),
trombones(2), saxophones(2)(optional),
guitar, double bass, percussion).
Score & parts: ms. in composer's hand.

[Allelu Chant; Arr.]
H3.2 Allelu Chant. (1981) 7'
For: chorus(SATB), guitar or
organ(optional), trumpet or saxophone.
First performed: May 10, 1981;
Forty-Fort, Pa. Forty-Fort United
Methodist Church Choir; Peter Calo,
guitar; Frank Edwards, organ; Mark
Harvey, trumpet.
Score & parts: ms. in composer's hand.

H3.3 Celebration in Jazz Form (for
Protestant Worship Service). (1967) 40'
For: voice, chorus, congregation, jazz
ensemble(trumpets(2), mellophone,
trombone, saxophone(alto),
saxophones(tenor)(2),
saxophone(baritone), piano, guitar,
double bass, conga drum, percussion).
12 movements. *Text:* Bible, hymnals,
Mark Harvey, Rev. Harvey Bates.
Commissioned by: Syracuse University,
Hendricks Chapel Board. *Dedicated to:*
Dean Charles Noble and the Hendricks
Chapel. *First performed:* April 30, 1967;
Syracuse, N.Y. Doris Mayes, voice;
Hendricks Chapel Choir; student jazz
ensemble; Mark Harvey, conductor.
Score & parts: ms. in composer's hand.

H3.4 Ceremonial March. (1968)
For: trumpet and organ.
Score: ms. in composer's hand.

[Ceremonial March; Arr.]
H3.5 Ceremonial March. (1980)
For: trumpets(4) and trombones(2).
Score & parts: ms. in composer's hand.

H3.6 Come Thou Long Expected Jesus.
(1971)
For: chorus(SATB) and organ. *Text:*
Anthem on *Hyfrydol*, by Rowland Hugh
Prichard.
Vocal score: ms. in composer's hand.

H3.7 Dream Cycle. (1979)
For: piano, guitar, percussion. Jazz trio.
Score & parts: ms. in composer's hand.

H3.8 Exchange Place. (1974)
For: piano. Film music; aleatoric music.

H3.9 Firewave Suite. (1979) 30'
For: jazz ensemble(trumpets(2), horn,
trombones(2),
saxophones(2)/flute/saxophone(soprano),
guitar, double bass, percussion(2)). 4
movements. *First performed:* Dec. 23,
1979; Emmanuel Church, Boston.
Aardvark, Mark Harvey, conductor.
Score & parts: ms. in composer's hand.

H3.10 Funk Dumplings. (1970)
For: trumpet, saxophone, piano, guitar,
double bass, percussion. Jazz sextet.
Score & parts: ms. in composer's hand.

H3.11 G.B.T. (1967)
For: trumpet, saxophone, guitar, double
bass, percussion. Jazz quintet.
Score & parts: ms. in composer's hand.

H3.12 Mass. (in progress)
For: soloist, chorus(SATB),
orchestra(2-1-1-1; 2-2-2-1; timp, perc(2),
vibra; str).
Score & parts: ms. in composer' hand.

H3.13 Meditations and Jubilee. (1981) 6'
For: trumpet, trombone,
saxophone(alto), saxophone(tenor).
Movements: Chorale and Passages;
Jubilee and Reflections. *Commissioned
by:* John Stautner and Kim Stautner for
their wedding. *First performed:* Sept.
12, 1981; Emmanuel Church, Boston.
Mark Harvey, trumpet; Robert
Pilkington, trombone; Arni Cheatham,
alto saxophone; David Tidball, tenor

saxophone.
Score & parts: ms. in composer's hand.

H3.14 A New Creation Suite. (1970) 25'
For: jazz ensemble(trumpet, horn, trombones(2), saxophone(alto)/flute/saxophone(soprano), saxophone(tenor)/flute/ saxophone(soprano), guitar, double bass, percussion(2)). Aleatoric music. 3 movements. *First performed:* Spring 1970; Old West Church, Boston. Mark Harvey Group.
Score & parts: ms. in composer's hand.

H3.15 People and Players Street Theater Company. (1970-71)
For: chorus(mixed) and instruments(8). 15 movements. Incidental music.

H3.16 The Phoenix. (1970)
For: trumpet, saxophone, guitar, double bass, percussion. Jazz quintet.
Score & parts: ms. in composer's hand.

H3.17 Potato Chip. (1971)
For: trumpet, saxophone, double bass, percussion. Jazz quartet.
Score & parts: ms. in composer's hand.

H3.18 Prayer for Peace. (1978)
For: voice or chorus, trumpet, trombone, saxophones(2), double bass(optional).
Score & parts: ms. in composer's hand.

H3.19 Preface to Uneasiness: The Stations of the Cross (A Music-Drama). (1968) 30'
For: actors, mimes, or speakers and instrumental ensemble(saxophone/flute, trumpet, horm, trombones(2), double bass, timpani, drums, organ). Oratorio. 8 movements. *Text:* Bible, N.T. and Rev. Frank Halse, Jr. *Commissioned by:* Syracuse University, University Religious Council. *Dedicated to:* The memory of Martin Luther King, Jr. *First performed:* Apr. 12, 1968; Syracuse, N.Y. Student ensemble and readers, Mark Harvey, conductor.
Score & parts: ms. in composer's hand.

H3.20 The Sandwich Seller. (1970)
For: jazz band.
Score & parts: ms. in composer's hand.

Save Us Lord. *See* The Wail Suite.
Save Us Lord.

H3.21 Secret Riots (of the Soul). (1980) 20'
For: narrator, flute, trumpet, trombone, double bass, percussion. Aleatoric music. *Text:* after *Portrait of the Artist as a Young Man* by James Joyce. *First performed:* June 21, 1980; Sanders Theatre, Harvard University. Jack Powers, narrator; Peter Bloom, baroque flute; Mark Harvey, trumpet; Tom Plsek, trombone; Ken Filiano, double bass; Craig Ellis, percussion.
Score & parts: ms. in composer's hand.

H3.22 A Set of Modern Fanfares. (1980)
For: trumpets(6) and trombones(4).
Contents: Intrada; Festival Fanfare; Jubilee Fanfare; Fanfare for the Common Bible. . *First performed:* May 1, 1980; Boston; Opening Day Jubilee 350 (Jubilee Fanfare). Mark Harvey, conductor. Apr. 1973; Boston (Fanfare for the Common Bible). Mark Harvey, conductor.
Score & parts: ms. in composer's hand.

H3.23 Sweet Child. (1974)
For: voice and guitar or piano. Christmas carol.
Score: ms. in composer's hand.

H3.24 3:30 Blues. (1980)
For: jazz ensemble(trumpets(4), saxophones(4), piano, double bass, percussion).
Score: ms. in composer's hand.

H3.25 The Wail Suite. (1980) 50'
For: poets(2)(optional) and jazz ensemble(trumpet, horn, trombones(2), saxophone(alto)/flute/saxophone(soprano), saxophone(tenor)/ flute/ saxophone(soprano), saxophone(baritone)/ flute/ saxophone(soprano), violin, guitar,

piano, double basses(2), percussion(2).
Text: poet's own works(optional).
Movements: Prelude and Chorale (Save
Us Lord); Lament and Great O God Art
Thy Things); Blues; Ballad. Lament is
an arrangement of the Dakota Indian
Hymn from the United Methodist
Hymnal. First performed: Dec. 21, 1980;
Boston. Aardvark, Mark Harvey,
conductor. Text: collective authorship
by Fine Arts Camp Workshop on Music
at Sky Lake.
Score & parts: ms. in composer's hand.

[The Wail Suite. Save Us Lord]
H3.26 Save Us Lord. (1964)
For: chorus(unison) or chorus(SATB) and
organ or piano. Text: collective
authorship by Fine Arts Camp
Workshop on Music at Sky Lake.
Vocal score: ms. in composer's hand.

ARRANGEMENTS OF WORKS BY OTHER COMPOSERS

H3.27 And the Glory. (1973)
For: brass ensemble(trumpets(4),
horns(2), trombones(4), tuba(optional)).
From the Messiah by George Frideric
Handel.
Score & parts: ms. in composer's hand.

H3.28 Christmas Medley. (1971)
For: trumpets(2) and trombones(2).
Movements: I Saw Three Ships;
Coventry Carol; Drummer Boy. Written
for City of Boston Lighting of
Christmas Trees Ceremony. First
performed: Dec. 1971; Boston Common.
Score & parts: ms. in composer's hand.

H3.29 Cristo redentor. (1973)
For: jazz ensemble(trumpets(2), horn,
trombones(2), saxophones(2), guitar,
double bass, percussion(2),
piano(optional)). Original by Duke
Pearson.
Score & parts: ms. in composer's hand.

H3.30 He Shall Feed His Flock. (1979)
For: Soprano(optional), trumpets(2),
trombones(2). From Messiah by George

Frideric Handel.
Score & parts: ms. in composer's hand.

H3.31 Help Me, Jesus. (1979)
For: jazz ensemble(trumpets(2), horn,
trombones(2), saxophones(2), guitar,
double bass, percussion(2)). Original by
Edward Bonnemere.
Score & parts: ms. in composer's hand.

H3.32 Jesu, Joy of Man's Desiring.
(1979)
For: Soprano(optional), trumpets(2),
trombones(2). From Cantata 147 by
Johann Sebastian Bach.
Score & parts: ms. in composer's hand.

H3.33 Let All Mortal Flesh Keep
Silence. (1973)
For: jazz ensemble(trumpets(2), horn,
trombones(2), saxophones(2), guitar,
double bass, percussion(2)). Based on a
14th century plainsong.
Score & parts: ms. in composer's hand.

[Passiontide Chorales]
H3.34 Two Passiontide Chorales. (1980)
For: trumpets(2) and trombones(2).
Movements: Sometimes I Feel Like A
Motherless Child; What Wondrous Love
Is This, O My Soul.
Score & parts: ms. in composer's hand.

H4 PETER PEABODY HAZZARD

Born January 31, 1949, in
Poughkeepsie, N.Y. Moved to Boston
area 1962. Education: Boston University
(1966-68); studied composition with
John Bavicchi and William Maloof
(Berklee College of Music, B.M., 1971);
conducting with Jeronimas Kacinskas.
Related activities: conductor; served as
assistant conductor, Arlington
Philharmonic and Melrose Orchestra;
currently on the faculty of Berklee
College of Music. Be

WORKS

H4.1 Allegro, Op. 24. (1972) 5'
For: pianos(2).
Score: Aviso.

Cantata No. 1. *See* Merlin.

Cantata No. 2. *See* Death of Faust.

H4.2 Canzona and Overture, Op. 27. (1972) 14'
For: band. *Dedicated to:* John Bavicchi and the Berklee Concert Band. *First performed:* Dec . 5, 1972; New England Life Hall, Boston. Berklee Concert Band, Peter Hazzard, conductor.
Score: reprod. of ms. Be
Score & parts: Aviso.
Reel: recording of first performance.
Reel: Feb. 11, 1974; Massachusetts Institute of Technology. MIT Concert Band, John Corley, conductor.

H4.3 Ceremonial Music, Op. 36. (1976) 6'
For: trumpets(2) and organ. *First performed:* Oct. 23, 1976; All Saints Church, Brookline, Mass.
Score & parts: Seesaw.

H4.4 Children's Circus. (1976) 15'
For: orchestra(3(&pic)-1(&Ehn)-2-2; 4-2-3-1; timp, perc; str). Children's guide to the instruments of the orchestra. *First performed:* June 4, 1976; Arlington Town Hall, Arlington, Mass. Arlington Philharmonic, Peter Hazzard, conductor.
Score & parts: Aviso.

H4.5 Concertante, Op. 30. (1974) 35'
For: clarinet, English horn, violin, violoncello, orchestra (4(&pic)-2-2-2; 4-2-3-1; timp, perc; pf; str). 3 movements. *First performed:* Mar. 14, 1975; Arlington High School, Arlington, Mass. Arlington Philharmonic, Peter Hazzard, conductor.
Score & parts: Aviso.

H4.6 Concerto for Clarinet and Band, Op. 43. (1978) 15'
3 movements. *Commissioned by:* Jacksonville State University Wind Ensemble. Written for Carl H.C. Anderson. *First performed:* Apr. 8, 1979; Carl H.C. Anderson, clarinet;

Jacksonville State University Symphonic Band, David L. Walters, conductor.
Score: reprod. of ms. Be
Score & parts: Aviso.
Reel: recording of first performance. Be
Reel: April 19, 1979; Boston Conservatory. Katherine Clinton, clarinet; Boston Conservatory Wind Ensemble, John Corley, conductor. BCM

The Crown of Manfred. *See* Incidental Music from The Crown of Manfred.

H4.7 Death of Faust, Op. 37: Cantata, No. 2. (1977) 25'
For: Tenor, Bass, chorus(SATB), band. 3 movements. *Text:* Peter Hazzard, after Johann Wolfgang von Goethe. Written for Brian O'Connell, the Berklee Concert Choir and Berklee Concert Band. *First performed:* Apr. 24, 1978; Berklee College of Music. Brian O'Connell, tenor; Thomas Russell Martin, bass; Berklee Concert Choir; Berklee Concert Band, Peter Hazzard, conductor.
Score & parts: Aviso. Be
Vocal score: Aviso.
Reel: recording of first performance. Be

H4.8 Elegy: A Symphonic Portrait, Op. 47. (1979) 30'
For: Soprano, narrator, chorus(men), band. *Text: Elegy Written in a Country Churchyard* by Thomas Gray. Adapted by Peter Hazzard and James Harper. *Contents:* The Churchyard; The Inhabitants; the Stonecutter's Epitaph. *Dedicated to:* Deanna Kidd. *First performed:* Apr. 28, 1978; Berklee College of Music. Deanna Kidd, soprano; Thomas Russell Martin, narrator; Berklee Faculty Men's Chorus; Berklee Concert Band, Peter Hazzard, conductor.
Score & parts: Aviso.
Vocal score: reprod. of ms. Be
Vocal score: Aviso.

Reel: recording of first performance.
Be

H4.9 Fanfare for December 9, 1901, Op. 32. (1975) 5'
For: band. *Dedication:* For my friend John Corley and the MIT Concert Band.
First performed: Dec. 5, 1975;
Massachusetts Institute of Technology.
MIT Concert Band.
Score: reprod. of ms. Be
Score & parts: Aviso.
Reel: recording of first performance.
Reel: Apr. 28, 1977; Boston Conservatory. Boston Conservatory Wind Ensemble, John Corley, conductor. BCM

H4.10 Fantasia on a Theme by Brahms, Op. 31. (1974) 6'
For: piano. *First performed:* Feb. 15, 1975; Newton, Mass.
Score: BKJ.

H4.11 A Festival Overture, Op. 40. (1977) 6'
For: band. *Dedicated to:* William Toland and the Concord Band. *First performed:* Mar. 11, 1978; Concord, Mass. Concord Band.
Score & parts: Aviso.
Score: reprod. of ms. Be
Reel: Dec. 5, 1978; Berklee College of Music. Berklee Concert Band, Peter Hazzard, conductor. Be

H4.12 Harwichport Interlude, Op. 18. (1971) 6'
For: orchestra(2-2-(&bcl)-0; ·1-1-1-0; timp, perc; str).
Score & parts: Seesaw.

H4.13 Impressions of Winter, Op. 28. (1972) 8'
For: chorus(SATB) and piano(4-hands).
Text: Peter Hazzard.
Vocal score: Aviso.

H4.14 Incidental Music from The Crown of Manfred, Op. 46. (1979) 12'
For: saxophones(5)(each doubling on all other woodwinds). *First performed:* Apr. 4, 1979; Berklee College of Music.

Reeds at Play.
Score & parts: Aviso.
Tape: Be

H4.15 Landmark Suite, Op. 49. (1980) 12'
For: band. *Movements:* Old Ironsides; Swan Boats; John Hancock Tower-Copley Square; Old North Church; Harvard Yard. *Commissioned by:* Metropolitan Wind Symphony. *First performed:* Apr. 17, 1981; Sanders Theatre, Harvard University. Metropolitan Wind Symphony.
Score & parts: Ludwig. Rental.

H4.16 Laughing Till It Hurt. (1968) 70'
For: piano, celeste, double bass, electric bass, guitar, organ, percussion. Film music.
Film: Wholesome Film Center.

H4.17 Majestic, Op. 22. (1971) 4'
For: trumpets(2) and organ. *First performed:* Nov. 8, 1976; Berklee College of Music.
Score: Seesaw.

H4.18 Mentor, Op. 12. (1971) 5'
For: trumpets(4), trombones(4), percussion(3), timpani.
Score & parts: Seesaw.

H4.19 Merlin: Cantata No. 1, Op. 21. (1971) 15'
For: Bass, chorus(SATB), orchestra(2(&pic)-2(Ehn)-2(&bcl)-2(&cbsn); 4-4-3-1; timp, perc; cel; str). *Text:* B. Howard. 2 movements.
Score & parts: Aviso.
Vocal score: Aviso (reduction for 2 pianos).

[Movements]
H4.20 Four Movements, Op 38. (1977) 8'
For: saxophones(4). *First performed:* Mar. 30. 1978; Berklee College of Music. Carl Myres Sax Quartet.
Score & parts: BKJ.
Reel: recording of first performance.
Be

231

H4.21 Music in Honor of Millbrook School, Op. 51. (1981) 12'
For: trumpets(2), horn, trombones(2), tuba. *Movements:* Intrada; In Memoriam; Anthem: Si monumentum requiris, circumspice; Fanfare for the Next Fifty Years. *Commissioned by:* Millbrook School for its 50th anniversary. *Dedicated to:* Lucy and Edward Pulling. *First performed:* Oct. 11, 1981; Millbrook, N.Y. Berklee Student/Faculty Brass Sextet.
Score & parts: Aviso, 1981.
Reel: recording of first performance.

H4.22 O Come Let Us Sing, Op. 29. (1973) 10'
For: chorus(SATB), flute, oboe, clarinets(2), horn, violoncello, timpani. *Text:* Bible, O.T., Psalm 95 and Bible, O.T., Psalm 96. *First performed:* Apr. 15, 1973; First Unitarian Church, Arlington, Mass. Arlington-Belmont Chorus, Peter Hazzard, conductor.
Score & parts: Aviso.
Vocal score: Aviso.

H4.23 Pagan Ritual, Op. 41. (1977) 8'
For: bassoons(3). *First performed:* Apr. 18, 1978; Berklee College of Music; 20th-Century Chamber Music. Concord Bassoon Trio.
Score & parts: BKJ
Reel: recording of first performance. Be

H4.24 Passacussion, Op. 16. (1971) 5'
For: percussion(6)(mallet instruments(5), timpani(4), percussion instruments(13).
Score: Seesaw.

[Pieces for a Young Violinist]
H4.25 Five Pieces for a Young Violinist, Op. 44. (1978) 6'
For: violin and piano.
Score & part: Aviso.

H4.26 Poet Plants a Forest in His Wife's Marimba, Op. 19. (1971) 3'
For: chorus(SATB). *Text:* Nancy Willard.
Vocal score: Seesaw.

H4.27 Portrait for Flute, Op. 45. (1978) 4' 30"
For: flute and piano. *First performed:* Mar. 1980; Hammond Castle, Gloucester, Mass. Kithara.
Score & part: Aviso.

H4.28 A Praise Book, Op. 6. (1971) 5'
For: chorus(SATB), trumpets(2), tuba, piano, percussion(3). *Text:* Nancy Willard. *First performed:* June 4, 1971; Millbrook, N.Y. Millbrook School Chorus, James Hejduk, conductor.
Score & parts: Seesaw.

[Preludes]
H4.29 Three Preludes, Op. 5 & 8. (1971) 6'
For: piano.
Score: Aviso.

[Quartet, Clarinets(4)]
H4.30 Clarinet Quartet, Op. 15. (1971) 6'
Movements: Dance; Chorale; Dance. *First performed:* Apr. 15, 1977; Jacksonville, Ala. Jacksonville State University Clarinet Quartet, Carl H.C. Anderson, conductor.
Score: reprod. of ms. Be
Score: Seesaw.
Reel: recording of first performance. Be

[Quartet, Percussion]
H4.31 Percussion Quartet, Op. 10. (1971) 3'
For: percussion(4)(16 instruments).
Score: Seesaw.

[Quartet, Trombones]
H4.32 Quartet for Three Trombones, Op. 34. (1975) 9'
For: trombones(3) and piano.
Score & parts: Aviso.

H4.33 Soliloquy and Sorcery, Op. 42. (1977) 6'
For: flute, oboe, clarinet, bassoon. *First performed:* Mar. 30; 1978; Berklee College of Music.
Score & parts: BKJ. *Reel:* Be

[Sonata, Clarinet]
H4.34 Sonata No. 3, Op. 39. (1977) 7'
First performed: Apr. 9, 1979;
Jacksonville State University. Carl H.C.
Anderson.
Score: Aviso.
Reel: recording of first performance.
Be

[Sonata, Clarinet and Marimba]
H4.35 Sonata No. 2, Op. 23. (1971) 11'
First performed: Apr. 10, 1973; Berklee
College of Music.
Score: reprod. of ms. Be
Score: Seesaw, 1977. HU ·
Reel: Jacksonville, Ala. Carl H.C.
Anderson, clarinet and Craig Bergler,
marimba. Be

[Sonata, Clarinets(2)]
H4.36 Sonata No. 4, Op. 50. (1981) 8'
Score: Aviso.

H4.37 Suite, Op. 26. (1972) 10'
For: English horn and string quartet.
First performed: Nov. 6, 1975;
Brookline Public Library.
Score & parts: Seesaw.

H4.38 Suite, Op. 26a. (1972) 10'
For: English horn and clarinets(4). *First
performed:* Dec. 4, 1972; Brookline
Public Library.
Score & parts: Seesaw.
Reel: Jacksonville, Ala. Jacksonville
Chamber Players. Be

H4.39 Te Deum, Op. 35. (1976) 15'
For: chorus(SATB), flutes(2), oboe,
English horn, clarinets(2), bassoons(2).
Text: Latin. *First performed:* Feb. 13,
1977; Unitarian Church, Belmont, Mass.
Arlington-Belmont Chorus, Peter
Hazzard, conductor.
Score & parts: Aviso.
Vocal score: Aviso.

H4.40 Te Deum, Op. 35a. (1976) 15'
For: chorus(SATB) and band. *Text:*
Latin.
Score & parts: Aviso.
Vocal score: Aviso.

H4.41 Tema nuovo e vecchio, Op. 48.
(1980) 14'
For: clarinet choir.
Score & parts: Aviso.

H4.42 Travelieder, Op. 33. (1975) 6'
For: Soprano and piano. *Text:* Ogden
Nash. *First performed:* May 2, 1975;
Berklee College of Music. Oksana
Iwaszczenko, soprano and Lucille Gaita,
piano.
Score: Aviso.
Reel: recording of first performance.
Be

H4.43 Voyage, Op. 13. (1971) 7'
For: flute, clarinet(bass), double bass,
percussion.
Score & parts: Seesaw.

H4.44 Weird Sisters, Op. 9. (1971) 6'
For: percussion(6) and timpani.
Movements: Clotho; Lachosis; Atropos.
First performed: Feb. 18, 1971; Berklee
College of Music. Berklee Percussion
Ensemble.
Score & parts: Seesaw.
Reel: Aug. 8, 1975; Berklee College of
Music. Berklee Percussion and Mallet
Ensemble, Ted Wolff and Dean
Anderson, directors. Be

ARRANGEMENTS OF WORKS BY OTHER COMPOSERS

H4.45 Loth to Depart. (1977) 5'
For: wind ensemble. Variations. Original
by Giles Farnaby. *First performed:* Dec.
6, 1977; Berklee College of Music.
Berklee Concert Band, Peter Hazzard,
director.
Score: Aviso.
Reel: recording of first performance.
Be

H5 JOHN C. HEISS

Born 1938 in New York City. *Education:*
B.A., Mathematics (Lehigh University,
1960); Columbia University (1960-62);
M.F.A. (Princeton University, 1967);
studied composition with Otto Luening,
Milton Babbitt, Peter Westergaard,

Edward T. Cone, Earl Kim, Darius Milhaud, Henry Cowell, Jack Beeson. *Awards:* Bowdoin College Contemporary Music Competition (Winner, 1971), Fromm Foundation Prize (1973), National Institute of Arts and Letters Award (1973), National Endowment for the Arts Grants (1974, 1975, 1981), Massachusetts Council on the Arts and Humanities, Artist Fellowship Program (1975, 1979), ASCAP Awards (Standard) (1975-81), Martha Baird Rockefeller Fund for Music Grant (1976), Guggenheim Grant (1978-79). *Related activities:* conductor; flutist; principal flute, Boston Musica Viva (1969-74); member of the faculty of New England Conservatory (1967-). NEC

WORKS

H5.1 Capriccio. (1976) 6' 30"
For: flute, clarinet, percussion. *Commissioned by:* National Endowment for the Arts. *Dedicated to:* Frank Epstein and Frank Heiss. *First performed:* Dec. 5, 1976; Boston. Collage, Frank Epstein, director.
Score: E.C. Schirmer, 1977.
Score: E.C. Schirmer, 1980. HU
Reel: recording of first performance. WGBH
Cassette: Dec. 15, 1977; New England Conservatory. NEC Contemporary Music Ensemble, John Heiss, conductor. NEC

Chamber Concerto. *See* Concerto, Flute and Instrumental Ensemble.

[Choral Songs]
H5.2 Three Choral Songs. (1963) 8'
For: chorus(children, 2-part), bassoon, piano. *Text:* Carl Sandburg. *Dedicated to:* Jean Scott. *First performed:* Jan. 1964; Bronxville, N.Y. Unidentified children's chorus, John Heiss, conductor.
Score: E.C. Schirmer, 1979.

Chorale. *See* Etudes for Solo Flute. Chorale.

[Concerto, Flute and Instrumental Ensemble]
H5.4 Chamber Concerto. (1977) 11'
For: flute and instrumental ensemble(oboe, clarinet, bassoon, trumpet, horn, trombone, percussion, violin, viola, violoncello). *First performed:* Apr. 1977; New York City. Speculum Musicae.
Score & parts: E.C. Schirmer, 1980. HU

[Concerto, Flute and Instrumental Ensemble; Arr]
H5.5 Chamber Concerto. (1977) 12'
For: flute, clarinet, percussion, piano. *Dedicated to:* James Pappoutsakis. *First performed:* Oct. 17, 1977; New England Conservatory. John Heiss, flute; William Wrzesien, clarinet; Frank Epstein, percussion; Christopher Kies, piano.
Score: E.C. Schirmer, 1979.
Cassette: recording of first performance. NEC
Cassette: Apr. 10, 1978. New England Conservatory; in *The Enchanted Circle* Katherine Kitzman, flute; Karl Herman, clarinet, Roland Valliere, percussion; Thomas Stumpf, piano; John Heiss, conductor. NEC

H5.6 Eloquy for Four Woodwinds. (1978) 4' 30"
For: flute, oboe, clarinet, bassoon. *First performed:* Aug. 22, 1978; Bennington College.
Score: E.C. Schirmer, 1979.
Cassette: Feb. 13, 1979; New England Conservatory. NEC Scholarship Woodwind Quintet. NEC

H5.7 Episode. (1980) 3'
For: violin. 1 movement. *Dedicated to:* Daniel Stepner. *First performed:* Dec. 3, 1980; New England Conservatory. Daniel Stepner.
Score: reprod. of ms.
Cassette: recording of first performance. NEC

H5.8 Etudes for Solo Flute. (1979) 20'
24 etudes. *First performed:* Oct. 22,

1979; New England Conservatory (5 etudes). John Heiss.
Score: ms. in composer's hand.
Cassette: recording of first performance. NEC

[Etudes for Solo Flute. Chorale]
H5.9 Chorale. (1979)
Cassette: Nov. 10, 1980; New England Conservatory. John Heiss. NEC

H5.10 From Infinity Full Circle. (1979) 8'
For: chorus(children) and piano. Cantata.
Text: John Greenleaf Whittier, Henry David Thoreau, Frederic William Farrar.
Commissioned by: Youth Pro Musica.
First performed: Mar. 1979; Boston. Youth Pro Musica.
Vocal score: E.C. Schirmer, 1979.
Part(chorus): E.C. Schirmer, 1979.

H5.11 Inventions, Contours, and Colors. (1973) 9'
For: instrumental ensemble(flute, clarinet, bassoon, trumpet, horn, trombone, tuba, violin, viola, violoncello, double bass). 1 movement.
Commissioned by: Berkshire Music Center, Tanglewood and Fromm Foundation. *Dedication:* For Gunther Schuller. *First performed:* Aug. 9, 1973; Berkshire Music Center, Tanglewood. Tonu Kalam, conductor.
Study score: Boosey & Hawkes, 1977. HU MIT NEC
Parts: Boosey & Hawkes, 1977. Rental.
Disc: Composers Recordings CRI SD 363, 1976. Speculum Musicae, Richard Fitz, conductor. BrU BU HU MIT NEC W
Cassette: Apr. 1, 1974; New England Conservatory. John Heiss, conductor. NEC
Cassette: May 6, 1974; New England Conservatory; in *An Evening of Contemporary Music.* John Heiss, conductor. NEC
Cassette: Dec.7, 1980; New England Conservatory. NEC Contemporary Music Ensemble, John Heiss, conductor. NEC

[Lyric Pieces]
H5.12 Four Lyric Pieces for Solo Flute. (1962) 7'
First performed: Aug. 1962; Aspen, Colo.; Aspen Music Festival. John Heiss.
Score: Southern-Tex, 1971. MIT NEC
Cassette: Oct. 15, 1973; New England Conservatory. Barbara Jacobson. NEC
Cassette: Oct. 27, 1975; New England Conservatory. John Heiss. NEC
Cassette: Feb. 28, 1978; New England Conservatory. Liza Korns. NEC
Cassette: Nov. 10, 1980; New England Conservatory. John Heiss. NEC

[Movements]
H5.13 Four Movements for Three Flutes. (1969) 13'
Dedicated to: Arlene [Heiss]. *First performed:* Oct. 1972; Donnell Library, New York City; Composer's Forum.
Score: Boosey, 1977. HU NEC T
Score: in *ASUC Journal of Music Scores,* vol. 2. BU HU MIT NEC
Disc: Composers Recordings CRI SD 321, 1974. John Heiss, Paul Dunkel, Trix Kout. BrU BU HU MIT NEC T W
Cassette: Oct. 17, 1969; New England Conservatory. John Heiss, Nancy Joyce, Robert Stallman. NEC
Cassette: May 2, 1977; New England Conservatory. Katherine Kitzman, David Bruskin, Mark McGinley. NEC
Cassette: Apr. 10, 1978; New England Conservatory; in *Enchanted Circle.* Katherine Kitzman, David Bruskin, Mark McGinley. NEC
Cassette: May, 8, 1978; New England Conservatory. Katherine Kitzman, David Bruskin, Mark McGinley. NEC

[Pieces Flute and Violoncello]
H5.14 Five Pieces. (1963) 8'
Dedicated to: David Shostac and Beverly Lauridsen. *First performed:* Feb. 11, 1963; Columbia University. John Heiss, flute and Andree Emelianoff, violoncello.
Score: E.C. Schirmer, 1980. HU MIT
Cassette: Apr. 29, 1971; New England

Conservatory. April Showers, flute and Bruce Coppock, violoncello. NEC

H5.15 Psalm 33. (1964) 4'
For: chorus(children) and piano. *First performed:* May 1973. Princeton High School Choir.
Vocal score: ms. in composer's hand.

H5.16 Quartet. (1971) 7'
For: flute, clarinet, violoncello, piano. Written for Boston Musica Viva. Winner of the Bowdoin College Contemporary Music Competition, 1971. *First performed:* Feb. 2, 1971; Boston. Boston Musica Viva, Richard Pittman, conductor.
Score: Bowdoin College Music Press, 1972. HU NEC
Disc: Composers Recordings CRI SD 321, 1974. Boston Musica Viva, Richard Pittman, conductor. BrU BU HU MIT NEC T W
Cassette: Apr. 27, 1971; New England Conservatory. Robert Stallman, flute; Thomas Hill, clarinet; Ronald Clearfield, violoncello; Robert Pace, piano; John Heiss, conductor. NEC
Cassette: May 2, 1977; New England Conservatory. Kathy Boyd, flute; Eric Thomas, clarinet; Laura Blustein, violoncello; Fred Hersch, piano. NEC

[Short Pieces, Piano]
H5.17 Four Short Pieces. (1961) 4'
4 movements. After Six Little Piano Pieces, Op. 19, by Arnold Schoenberg. *First performed:* spring, 1962; Columbia University. David Liadov.
Score: Boosey & Hawkes, 1975. BU HU NEC
Cassette: Feb. 10, 1970; New England Conservatory; in *An Evening of Contemporary Music.* Victor Rosenbaum. NEC
Cassette: Mar. 19, 1973; New England Conservatory. Glenn Plaskin. NEC
Cassette: Apr. 10, 1978; New England Conservatory; in *The Enchanted Circle.* Victor Rosenbaum. NEC
Cassette: Apr. 12, 1978; New England Conservatory. Victor Rosenbaum. NEC

[Short Pieces, Piano; Arr.]
H5.18 Four Short Pieces. (1962) 4'
For: chamber orchestra(2-2-2-2; 2-0-0-0; str). 4 movements. *First performed:* Apr. 1964; Columbia University. Columbia University Orchestra, John Heiss, conductor.
Score & parts: Media Press, 1972. NEC
Cassette: May 9, 1971; New England Conservatory; in *A Festival of New England Composers Past and Present.* NEC Symphony Orchestra, Gunther Schuller, conductor. NEC
Cassette: May 16, 1976; New England Conservatory. Youth Chamber Orchestra, Benjamin Zander, conductor. NEC

H6.19 Sonatina. (1962) 5'
For: flute and piano. *First performed:* Jan. 1974; Isabella Stewart Gardner Museum, Boston. John Heiss, flute and unidentified pianist.
Score: ms. in composer's hand.

[Songs]
H5.20 Two Songs. (1966) 3'-4'
For: Mezzo Soprano and piano. *Text:* James Joyce and Samuel Beckett.
Score: ms. in composer's hand.

H5.21 Songs of Nature. (1975) 15'
For: Mezzo Soprano, flute, clarinet, violin, violoncello, piano. *Contents:* from Thanatopsis (William Cullen Bryant); The Yellow Violet (William Cullen Bryant); The Sound of the Sea (Henry Wadsworth Longfellow); Men Say (Henry David Thoreau); If I Shouldn't Be Alive (Emily Dickenson); How Happy Is the Little Stone (Emily Dickinson). Written for Boston Musica Viva under a National Endowment for the Arts Grant. *Dedication:* To the memory of my father. *First performed:* Oct. 1975; Cambridge, Mass. Boston Musica Viva, Richard Pittman, conductor.
Score & parts: Boosey & Hawkes, 1978. NEC
Disc: in *New American Music for Chamber Ensembles*, Nonesuch H 71351,

1978. Boston Musica Viva, Richard
Pittman, conductor. BU BrU MIT NEC W
Cassette: Oct. 29, 1976; New England
Conservatory; in *ISCM World Music
Days 1976.* Boston Musica Viva, Richard
Pittman, conductor. NEC
Cassette: Dec. 5, 1979; New England
Conservatory. NEC Contemporary Music
Ensemble, John Heiss, conductor. NEC
Cassette: May 11, 1980; New England
Conservatory. NEC Contemporary Music
Ensemble, John Heiss, conductor. NEC

H6 W. NEWELL HENDRICKS

Born February 23, 1943, in Los
Angeles, Calif. Moved to Boston area
1973. *Education:* studied composition
with Peter Racine Fricker (Santa
Barbara, Calif.) and David Del Tredici
(Boston). *Related activities:* assistant to
the conductor, Pro Arte Chamber
Orchestra of Boston and member of
the faculty of Northeastern University
(1980-81). NU

WORKS

H6.1 Anthem: Daughters of Jerusalem.
(1968) 10′
For: Soprano, voices(men)(8), trumpet,
organ. *Text:* Bible, N.T., Luke 23:28-31.
Score & parts: available from
composer.
Reel or cassette: available from
composer.

H6.2 Anthem: The Silent Word. (1979)
3′
For: chorus(SSATB). *Text:* from *Ash
Wednesday* by T.S. Eliot.
Score & parts: available from
composer.
Reel or cassette: available from
composer.

H6.3 Cain. (1980) 120′
For: Sopranos(2), Mezzo Soprano,
Tenors(2), Baritone, Bass, chorus,
orchestra(2(pic)-2(Ehn)-2(asax)-2; 2-2-2-1;
perc(2); hp; str(6-6-4-3-2)). Opera in
three acts. *Libretto:* Robert W. Brown
after Cain by George Noel Gordon

(Lord) Byron.
Score & parts: available from
composer.

H6.4 Chacone. (1976) 7′
For: violin(baroque) and harpsichord.
Score & parts: available from
composer.
Reel: available from composer.

H6.5 Christmas Cantata. (1965) 30′
For: voices, chorus, chamber
orchestra(1(pic)-1-1(bcl)-0; 2-1-2-0; timp;
pf; str).
Score & parts: available from
composer.

[Concerto, Violin]
H6.6 Violin Concerto. (1974) 35′
For: violin and
orchestra(2(pic)-2-2(bcl)-2; 2-2-2-1; timp,
perc(2); hp, pf; str(6-6-3-3-2)). 3
movements.
Score & parts: available from
composer.
Reel & cassette: available from
composer.

Daughters of Jerusalem. *See* Anthem.

Emergence. *See* Incidental Music for
Emergence.

H6.7 Fugue and Postlude. (1968) 16′
For: violin, violoncello, horn, piano.
Score & parts: available from
composer.
Reel or cassette: available from
composer.

H6.8 Incidental Music for Emergence.
(1972) 30′
For: violin, double bass, horn,
clarinet/saxophone(tenor), percussion. To
the play by Larry Rinehart.
Score & parts: available from
composer.

H6.9 Incidental Music for Trojan
Women. (1979) 15′
For: chorus(women), clarinet,
violoncello, percussion.

H6.10 Journey of the Magi. (1981) 12'
For: Baritones(3) and chorus(SSATB).
Text: T.S. Eliot.
Score & parts: available from composer.
Reel & cassette: available from composer.

H6.11 Magadar Wind. (1970) 40'
For: Soprano, narrator, string quartet.
Text: Everett Barton.
Score & parts: available from composer.
Reel & cassette: available from composer.

H6.12 Mass. (1971) 30'
For: voices(men)(12).
Score & parts: available from composer.

H6.13 Odysseus' Theme. (1966) 12'
For: orchestra(3(pic)-2(&Ehn)-2-2; 4-2-2-0; timp; str). Overture.
Score & parts: available from composer.

H6.14 Prelude and Fugue. (1981) 12'
For: flute and piano.
Score & parts: available from composer.
Reel & cassette: available from composer.

[Quartet]
H6.15 French Horn Quartet. (1974) 12'
For horns(4).
Score & parts: available from composer.
Reel & cassette: available from composer.

H6.16 Quintet. (1972) 15'
For: clarinet and string quartet.
Score & parts: available from composer.
Reel & cassette: available from composer.

The Silent Word. *See* Anthenm.

H6.17 Sonata. (1967) 12'
For: violin and piano.
Score & parts: available from composer.
Reel & cassette: available from composer.

H6.18 Symphony on B. (1968) 30'
For: orchestra(3(pic)-2-2(tsax)-2; 4-2-2-0; timp, perc(2); accord; hp; str). 4 movements.
Score & parts: available from composer.
Reel & cassette: available from composer.

H6.19 Tessera. (1975) 20'
For: Baritones(2), piano, percussion.
Text: Robert W. Brown. *Contents:* Note 80; El Bab; AIAIA; Kur; The Death of Gilgamesh.
Score & parts: available from composer.
Reel & cassette: available from composer.

H6.20 Theme and Variations. (1973) 12'
For: harp.
Score & parts: available from composer.

H6.21 Thing of Fleet Will. (1967) 6'
For: Tenor, chorus(men)(4-part), harpsichord. *Text:* Everett Barton.
Score & parts: available from composer.

H6.22 Trio. (1965) 10'
For: violin, viola, horn. *Movements:* Anxiety; Egression; Peace.
Score & parts: available from composer.

Trojan Women. *See* Incidental Music for Trojan Women.

H6.23 Voyager. (1968) 12'
For: Tenor, flute/flute(alto), clarinet/clarinet(bass), horn, violin, viola, double bass. Cantata. *Text:* Everett Barton.

Score & parts: available from composer.
Reel & cassette: available from composer.

H7 JAMES A. HOFFMANN

Born October 2, 1929, in Manchester, N.H. Moved to Boston area 1964.
Education: studied composition with Carl McKinley, Francis Judd Cooke (New England Conservatory, B.M., 1951); Quincy Porter, Norman Lockwood (Yale University, B.M., 1952, M.M., 1953); Boris Blacher (Berlin, East Germany, 1956-57); Burrill Phillips (University of Illinois, D.M.A., 1963). *Awards:* Chadwick Medal (New England Conservatory, 1951), John Day Jackson Prize (Yale University, 1952), Woods-Chandler Prize (Yale University, 1953). *Related activities:* served on the faculties of Oberlin College (1959-62), San Jose State College (1963-64), New England Conservatory (1964- ; Chairman of Undergraduate Theoretical Studies, 1968-80); co-director of series Enchanted Circle (1975-). NEC

WORKS

H7.1 Carrousel. (1976) 10'
For: piano. *Dedicated to:* Donald Lafferty. *First performed:* May 2, 1977; New England Conservatory; in Enchanted Circle. Seth Carlin.
Score: reprod. of ms.; available from composer.
Cassette: recording of first performance. NEC

H7.2 Conversations. (1968) Duration variable.
For: instruments(unspecified)(any number). Aleatoric music.
Perf. dir: available from composer.

H7.3 Crosscurrents. (1979) 6'
For: bassoon and piano. *First performed:* Mar. 9, 1981; New England Conservatory; in Enchanted Circle. Leo Kenen, bassoon and John Felice, piano.
Score: reprod. of ms.; available from composer.
Cassette: recording of first performance. NEC

H7.4 Crystals. (1967) 5'
For: strings(3). *First performed:* Feb. 1968; New England Conservatory. Martha Kolden, violin; Tibor Pusztai, viola; Burr Van Nostrand, violoncello.
Score: reprod. of ms.; available from composer.

H7.5 Depth Charge. (1978) 12'-15'
For: contrabassoon, percussion, double bass. *Dedicated to:* Leo Kenen. *First performed:* Mar. 10, 1979; New England Conservatory. Leo Kenen, contrabassoon; Nicholas Baratta, percussion; Robert Skavronski, double bass.
Score: reprod. of ms.; available from composer.
Cassette: Apr. 9, 1979; New England Conservatory; in *Enchanted Circle*. Leo Kenen, contrabassoon; Nicholas Baratta, percussion; Robert Skavronski, double bass. NEC

H7.6 Diversion. (1964) 4'
For: oboes(2). 3 movements. *Dedication:* For Bill [William Hoffmann].
Score: reprod. of ms.; available from composer.

H7.7 February 25, 1978. (1978) Duration variable.
For: instruments(unspecified)(any number, sustained pitches). Aleatoric music.
Perf. dir: available from composer.

H7.8 The Flight of the Flute. (1974) 9'
For: flute. *Dedicated to:* Mary Ann [Hoffmann]. *First performed:* Feb. 14, 1975; New England Conservatory. Catherine E. Folkers.
Score: reprod. of ms.; available from composer.
Reel: 1976. WGBH
Cassette: Feb. 27, 1976; New England Conservatory; in *American Society of University Composers, 11th Annual*

Conference: Contemporary Chamber Music Concert I. Robert Stallman. NEC

H7.9 Follow the Leader. (1973) Duration variable.
For: instruments(treble)(any number). Aleatoric music. *Dedication:* To L.D. [Lyle Davidson]. *First performed:* Feb. 28, 1974; Museum of Fine Arts, Boston.
Score & perf. dir: reprod. of ms.; available from composer.

H7.10 Four to Go. (1973) Duration variable.
For: pianos(2, 8 hands). *Dedicated to:* NEC Extension Division. *First performed:* Feb. 2, 1974; New England Conservatory. Michael Arnowitt, Sanford Bottino, Piotr Gajewski, Susan Greenberg, Kevin Murphy.

H7.11 Hot Potatoes. (1980) 8'
For: trombone. *Dedication:* For Steve Adams and his trombone. *First performed:* Mar. 9, 1981; New England Conservatory; in Enchanted Circle. Steve Adams.
Score: reprod. of ms.; availabe from composer.
Cassette: recording of first performance. NEC

H7.12 I Don't Care. (1979) 10'
For: flute/violoncello and violin/piano. *Dedication:* For Sue [Susan Hoffmann] and Poppy.
Score: reprod. of ms.; available from composer.

H7.13 Joe's Piece. (1975) 12'
For: saxophone(soprano), saxophone(alto), saxophone(tenor), saxophone(baritone). *Dedicated to:* Joseph Maneri. *First performed:* Apr. 9, 1979; Boston; in Enchanted Circle. New Boston Saxophone Quartet.
Score & parts: reprod. of ms.; available from composer.
Cassette: recording of first performance. NEC

H7.14 Jupiter's Maze. (1972) Duration variable.
For: woodwind quintet. *Movements:* Prelude; Nocturne; Variations; Round; Scherzo; Ostinato; Chant; Canon; Recitative; Chorale; Cadenza; Postlude. Order and frequency of internal movements variable. *First performed:* Mar. 13, 1973; New England Conservatory; in An Evening of Contemporary Music. Ernestine Whitman, flute; Charles Miller, oboe; Roy D. Gussman, clarinet; Hymeld Gaignard, bassoon; David Pandolfi, horn.
Score & parts: reprod. of ms.; available from composer.
Cassette: recording of first performance. NEC
Cassette: May 12, 1973; New England Conservatory; in *A Festival of Contemporary American Music*. Lyle Davidson, coach. NEC

H7.15 Loop the Loop. (1980) 5'
For: violin.
Score: reprod. of ms.; available from composer.

H7.16 Machol. (1981) 4' 15"
For: saxophone(soprano). *Dedicated to:* Merryl Goldberg. *First performed:* May 14, 1981; Harvard Hillel. Merryl R. Goldberg.
Score: reprod. of ms.; available from composer.

H7.17 Pageant of the Quiet Path. (1976) 15'
For: violins(3)(5 stands). *Dedication:* For John, Michael, Susan [Hoffmann]. *First performed:* 1977; Emmanuel College, Boston. John Hoffmann, Michael Hoffmann, Susan Hoffmann.
Score & parts: reprod. of ms.; available from composer.
Cassette: May 2, 1977; New England Conservatory; in *Enchanted Circle*. John Hoffmann, Michael Hoffmann, Susan Hoffmann; Frances Lanier, coach. NEC

H7.18 Pink Peony and Spuds. (1977) 30'
For: narrator and orchestra. *Text:*
Rootabaga Stories by Carl Sandburg.
Dedication: To my mother and father [
Charlotte and Maurice Hoffmann]
Score & parts: reprod. of ms.; available
from composer.

[Pink Peony and Spuds; Arr]
H7.19 Pink Peony and Spuds. (1980) 30'
For: narrator and wind ensemble. *Text:*
Rootabaga Stories by Carl Sandburg.
Dedication: To my mother and father [
Charlotte and Maurice Hoffmann] *First
performed:* Feb. 26, 1981; New England
Conservatory. Mark Pearson, narrator;
NEC Wind Ensemble, Frank L. Battisti,
conductor.
Score & parts: reprod. of ms.; available
from composer.

H7.20 Resolution. (1978) Duration
variable.
For: voices(any number). *Text:* Solfege
syllables. *Dedication:* To a Happy New
Year in Theory 351, 352.

H7.21 Seesaw. (1980) 3' 30"
For: clarinet and clarinet(bass).
Dedicated to: Diego Pokropowicz. *First
performed:* Mar. 9, 1981; New England
Conservatory; in Enchanted Circle. Eric
Thomas, clarinet and Diego
Pokropowicz, bass clarinet.
Score: reprod. of ms.; available from
composer.
Cassette: recording of first
performance. NEC

[Songs]
H7.22 Four Songs. (1960) 7'
For: Soprano and piano. *Contents:* All
Day (James Joyce); To Fortune (Robert
Herrick, 1591-1674); To Musick (Robert
Herrick); Draw Gloves (Robert Herrick).
First performed: 1961; Oberlin, Ohio.
Score: reprod. of ms.; available from
composer.

H7.23 Sound Circuits. (1968) Duration
variable.
For: violins(3) or violas(3) or
violoncellos(3) or double basses(3).

Aleatoric music. *Dedication:* For John,
Michael, Susan [Hoffmann]. *First
performed:* Oct. 21, 1972; New England
Conservatory. Karen Harris, David Eure,
Marlene McDermott.
Score: reprod. of ms.; available from
composer.

H7.24 a time to dance. (1980?)
For: piano. Written for the left hand of
John Felice. *First performed:* Oct. 13,
1980; New England Conservatory. John
Felice.
Score: reprod. of ms.; available from
composer.
Cassette: recording of first
performance. NEC

[Variations on a Folk Tune]
H7.25 32 Variations on a Folk Tune.
(1978) 4'
For: piano.
Score: reprod. of ms.; available from
composer.

H7.26 Volleys. (1973) 10'
For: drums(11). *Dedicated to:* Frank
Epstein. *First performed:* Feb. 6, 1977;
Jordan Hall, Boston. Thomas James
Koch.
Score: reprod. of ms.; available from
composer.

H7.27 Vortices. (1968) 10'
For: flute, oboe, trumpet, percussion,
marimba, mandolin, violin. *First
performed:* Dec. 16, 1968; Jordan Hall,
Boston. Jan Gippo, flute; Peter
Bowman, oboe; Michael Goldberg,
trumpet; Paul Berns, percussion; Linda
Raymond, marimba; Robert Sullivan,
mandolin; Ann T. Danis, violin.
Score & parts: reprod. of ms.; available
from composer.
Reel: WGBH

H7.28 Windings. (1981) 12'
For: oboe, flute, clarinet, bassoon,
horns(2), trumpet, trombone, tuba. 1
movement. *Dedicated to:* Frederic
Cohen.
Score & parts: reprod. of ms.; available
from composer.

H7.29 Winter '78. (1978) 1'
For: piano. *Score.*

H8 ALFRED HOOSE

Born September 17, 1918, in Wheeling,
W. Va. Moved to Boston area 1950.
Education: B.A. (Hartt School of Music,
1950), M.M. (New England Conservatory,
1952); studied composition with Francis
Judd Cooke (Boston), Fred Lerdahl
(Cambridge, Mass.), Antonio Modarelli
(Wheeling, W. Va.), Hugo Norden
(Boston). *Related activities:* organist;
choral director; member of the faculty
of Boston State College (1965-). NEC

WORKS

H8.1 Allegro. (1952) 15'
For: violin and piano. *First performed:*
1953; Boston. Stanley Dombrowski,
violin and Cynthia Brown, piano.
Score & parts: ms. in composer's hand.

H8.2 Chaconne. (1977) 6'
For: organ. *First performed:* Apr. 1979;
First and Second Church, Boston.
Kenneth Grinnell.
Score: ms.
Cassette: recording of first
performance.

H8.3 Crossroads. (1980) 12'
For: Sopranos(2), Altos(2), Tenors(2),
Basses(2). *Contents:* Words (David
Graham Phillips); For a Yellow Cat at
Midnight (Jean Burden); One Black Crow
(Ann Bradshaw); Nota bene (Jean
Garrigue).
Vocal score: ms. in composer's hand.

[Crossroads; Arr.]
H8.4 Crossroads. 12'
For: piano. *Cassette.*

H8.5 Diversion. (1977) 12'
For: viola, piano, vibraphone, tom-tom.
Score: ms. in composer's hand.

H8.6 Glimpses. (1978) 11'
For: Soprano, flutes(2), bassoon,

trumpet, piano, percussion, violins(2). 8
songs. *Contents:* A Bitter Morning (J.W.
Hackett); Before the Descent (William J.
Higginson); Brooms (Charles Simic);
Through the Small Holes (Cor Van den
Heuvel); That Love Is All There Is
(Emily Dickinson); Pine Tree Tops (Gary
Snyder); Milkweed (James Arlington
Wright); A Drinking Song (William
Butler Yeats).
Score: ms. in composer's hand.

H8.7 The Lord Shall Build Up Sion.
(1977) 15'
For: chorus and instrumental
ensemble(flutes(2), oboes(2), English
horn, clarinets(2), bassoons(2), horns(2),
timpani, percussion, piano). *First
performed:* 1978. Arlington-Belmont
Chorale; members of the Arlington
Philharmonic, John Bavicchi, conductor.
Score & parts: ms.
Cassette: recording of first
performance.

H8.8 Missa brevis. (1951) 24'
For: chorus(SATB) and organ. *First
performed:* 1952; New England
Conservatory. George Butler, organ;
NEC Chorus, Lorna Cooke deVaron,
conductor.
Score & parts: ms. in composer's hand.
Tape: recording of first performance.

H8.9 Music for Viola, Clarinet and
Pianoforte. (1970) 12'-13'
First performed: 1974; Boston State
College. Annex Players.
Score & parts: ms. in composer's hand.
Cassette: recording of first
performance.

H8.10 Prelude and Postlude on an
Angers Melody. (1960) 8'
For: organ. *First performed:* 1961; Hartt
School of Music; 13th Annual Institute
of Contemporary American Music. John
Doney.
Score: ms.
Reel: 1961; Church of the Advent,
Boston. George Butler.

[Quintet, Winds]
H8.11 Wind Quintet No. 2. (1976) 14'
For: woodwind quintet. *First performed:*
1979; Boston State College. New
Boston Wind Quintet.
Score & parts: ms.
Cassette: recording of first
performance.

H8.12 Rights to Passage. (1974) 20'
For: Soprano, Alto, Tenor, Bass,
chorus(SATB), orchestra(2(&pic)-2(&Ehn)
-2(&bcl)-2; 4-3-3-1; timp, perc(3); hp;
str). Cantata. *Text:* Richard Dehman and
William D. Mundell.
Score: ms.

H8.13 Symphony. (1981) 19'
For: orchestra(2-2-2(bcl)-2(cbsn); 2-2-2-0;
timp, perc(2); str).
Score & parts: ms. in composer's hand.

H8.14 Trio. (1979) 13'
For: flute, viola, piano. *First
performed:* Apr. 1979; Boston State
College. Michele Sahm, flute; John
Englund, viola; Ann Taffel, piano.
Score: ms. in composer's hand.
Cassette: recording of first
performance.

H9 JOHN HUGGLER

Born August 30, 1928, in Rochester,
N.Y. Moved to Boston area 1964.
Education: studied composition with
Charles Warren Fox (Eastman School of
Music, B.M., 1950) and Dante Fiorillo
(New York City). *Awards:* Guggenheim
Grants (1962, 1969), Boston Symphony
Orchestra composer-in-residence (1964),
Horblit Award (Boston Symphony
Orchestra) (1967). *Related activities:*
member of the faculty of the
University of Massachusetts, Boston
(1965-). UMB

WORKS

[Bagatelles]
H9.1 Seven Bagatelles. (1953) 12'-13'
For: piano. *First performed:* 1963;
Pittsburgh, Pa. Rosemary Mackown.

Score: reprod. of ms.; available from
composer.

H9.2 Bittere Nuesse. (1975) 8' 30"-10'
30"
For: Soprano, flute,
clarinet/clarinet(bass), violin, viola,
violoncello. *Text:* Paul Celan. *Contents:*
In Gestalt eines Ebers; Eine Hand;
Psalm. *Commissioned by:* Goethe
Institut (Boston). Later version, without
soprano, titled Serenata. *First
performed:* 1975; Boston. Elsa
Charlston, soprano; Boston Musica
Viva, Richard Pittman, conductor.
Score: Peters, nyp.
Cassette: Oct. 29, 1976; New England
Conservatory; in *ISCM World Music
Days 1976, Program 10.* Elsa Charlston,
soprano; Boston Musica Viva, Richard
Pittman, conductor. NEC

H9.3 Cantata, Op. 50. (1959?) 5'
For: Soprano, Alto, Tenor, Baritone,
orchestra(3-0-3-3; 2-3-3-0; perc; str).
Text: Old Tom Again by William Butler
Yeats.
Score: Peters, 1964. MIT
Parts: Peters. Rental.

H9.4 Celebration. (1966) 7'
For: band. *Commissioned by:* Ford
Foundation. *First performed:* 1966;
Music Teachers National Association
conference. Ithaca High School Band,
Frank L. Battisti, conductor.
Score & parts: reprod. of ms.; available
from composer.

[Concerto, Flute]
H9.5 Flute Concerto. (1968)
For: flute and orchestra(2-2-2(bcl)-2;
4-3-3(btrb)-0; timp, perc; hp; str).
Score: reprod. of ms.; available from
composer.

[Concerto, Horn]
H9.6 Horn Concerto, Op. 17. (1957) 11'
For: horn and orchestra(2-2-2-0; 0-0-0-0;
timp, perc; str). *First performed:* 1957;
Oklahoma City, Okla. Harvey Garber,
horn; Oklahoma City Symphony
Orchestra, Guy Fraser Harrison,

conductor.
Score & parts: Peters. Rental.

[Concerto, Trumpet]
H9.7 Trumpet Concerto, Op. 72.
(1968-69)
For: trumpet and orchestra.
Commissioned by: Armando Ghitalla.
Score: reprod. of ms.; available from
composer.

[Concerto, Violin, No. 1]
H9.8 Violin Concerto. (1955)
For: violin and orchestra.
Score: reprod. of ms.; available from
composer.

[Concerto, Violin, No. 2]
H9.9 Violin Concerto, Op. 31. (1961) 14'
For: violin and orchestra(2-0-2-1;
0-3-3-1; timp, perc; hp; str).
Score & parts: Peters. Rental.

Contemplation of Desert Forms. *See*
Quartet, Strings, No. 7.

H9.10 "D" into Blossom, Op. 36. (1958)
6'
For: orchestra(3-2-2-1; 4-2-3-0; timp,
perc; hp; str).
Score & parts: Peters. Rental.

H9.11 Desert Forms, Op. 65. (1965) 7'
For: orchestra(3(arec)-0-2-2; 4-3-3-1;
timp, perc; hp; str). 1 movement.
Score & parts: Peters. Rental.

H9.12 Divertimento, Op. 32. (1960) 11' ·
For: viola and orchestra(3-0-2-1;
0-2-3-0; timp, perc; hp; str(no viola)). 5
movements. *First performed:* 1961;
New York City; Music in the Making.
Walter Trampler, viola; unidentified
orchestra, Howard Shanet, conductor.
Score & parts: Peters. Rental.

H9.13 Duo. (1953) 7'
For: trombone and piano. *First
performed:* 1955 or 1956; Phillips
Gallery, Washington D.C. Byron
McCulloh, trombone and Walter Hartley,
piano.

Score: reprod. of ms.; available from
composer.

H9.14 Ecce homo, Op. 30, a Fantasy
for Mixed Instrumental Groups within a
Large Orchestra. (1959) 15'
For: orchestra(4(pic4)-4-3-3;
0(optional4)-3-3-1; timp, perc; hp, pf;
str(no double bass)). *First performed:*
May 13, 1973; New England
Conservatory; A Festival of
Contemporary American Music. NEC
Repertory Orchestra, Richard Pittman,
conductor.
Score & parts: Peters. Rental.
Reel: recording of first performance.
UMB
Cassette: recording of first
performance. NEC

H9.15 Elaborations. (1967) 12'
For: saxophone(alto) and orchestra. 3
movements. Written for Don Sinta.
Score: reprod. of ms.; available from
composer.

H9.16 Elegy Op. 2. (1952) 6'
For: orchestra(2-2-2-2; 2-3-3-0; timp,
perc; str). Written in memory of
Federico Garcia Lorca. *First performed:*
1952; Oklahoma City, Okla. Oklahoma
City Symphony Orchestra, Guy Fraser
Harrison, conductor.
Score: Peters, 1966. BPL BU HU L MIT
NEC T UMB
Parts: Peters. Rental.

H9.17 Music for 13 Instruments, Op.
75. (1971) 5' 30"
For: instrumental ensemble(flutes(2),
oboe, clarinets(2), clarinet(bass),
bassoon, contrabassoon, horns(2),
trumpet, trombone, violoncello).
Commissioned by: Boston Musica Viva.
First performed: October 6, 1971;
Busch-Reisinger Museum, Harvard
University. Boston Musica Viva, Richard
Pittman, conductor.
Score & parts: Peters. Rental.
Reel: recording of first performance.
UMB

Cassette: recording of first performance. NEC

H9.18 Music (in 2 Parts), Op. 62. (1963) 9'-10'
For: piano, timpani, percussion(9), brass ensemble(horns(4), trumpets(7), trombones(4), tubas(2)). 1 movement with epilogue. *First performed:* 1964; Ithaca College Wind Ensemble, Robert Prins, conductor.
Score & parts: Peters. Rental.

H9.19 Music (in 2 Parts), Op. 63. (1964) 6'
For: flute, clarinets(2), trumpets(2), timpani, percussion, piano, violin, double bass. *Commissioned by:* Horace Mann School, New York City. *First performed:* 1965; Horace Mann School, New York City.
Score & parts: Peters. Rental.
Cassette: May 9, 1971; New England Conservatory; in *A Festival of New England Composers Past and Present.* Instrumental ensemble, Gunther Schuller, conductor. NEC

H9.20 Music (in 2 Parts), Op. 64. (1965) 14'
For: orchestra(4-0-3-0; 4-4-3-0; timp, perc; hp; str). *First performed:* April 1, 1966; Symphony Hall, Boston. Boston Symphony Orchesra.
Score & parts: Peters. Rental.

H9.21 Opus 20. (1958) 12'
For: Soprano, clarinet, viola, violoncello, harp. 2 movements.
Score: reprod. of ms.; available from composer.

Opus 58. *See* Quintet, Brasses, No. 2.

H9.22 Quartet for Bassoon and String Trio. (1960) 8'
For: bassoon, violin, viola, violoncello.
Score: reprod. of ms.; available from composer.

H9.23 Quartet for Flute and String Trio. (1958) 7'-8'
For: flute, violin, viola, violoncello.

First performed: 1960; New School of Music, New York City; International Society for Contemporary Music Concert. Samuel Baron, flute; Galimir Trio.
Score: reprod. of ms.; available from composer.

H9.24 Quartet for Horn and String Trio. (1962?) 7'-8'
For: horn, violin, viola, violoncello.
Score: reprod. of ms.; available from composer.

H9.25 Quartet for Oboe and String Trio. (1961?) 7'-8'
For: oboe, violin, viola, violoncello.
First performed: 1961; Donnell Library, New York City; Composer's Forum (New York City). Henry Schumann, oboe; Matthew Raimondi, violin; Harry Zarazian, viola; Charles McCracken, violoncello.
Score & parts: reprod. of ms.; available from composer.

[Quartet, Strings, No. 1]
H9.26 String Quartet No. 1. (1951) Fragment only.

[Quartet, Strings, No. 2]
H9.27 String Quartet No. 2. (1952) 13'
Music: reprod. of ms; available from composer.

[Quartet, Strings, No. 3]
H9.28 String Quartet No. 3. (1954) 15'
Music: reprod. of ms; available from composer.

[Quartet, Strings, No. 4]
H9.29 String Quartet No. 4. (1956) 12'
Music: reprod. of ms; available from composer.

[Quartet, Strings, No. 5]
H9.30 String Quartet No. 5. (1959) 10'
First performed: 1961; Donnell Library, New York City; Composer's Forum (New York City). Matthew Raimondi, violin; and others.
Score & parts: reprod. of ms.; available from composer.

[Quartet, Strings, No. 6]
H9.31 String Quartet No. 6. (1960?) 10′
Music: reprod. of ms. available from composer.

[Quartet, Strings, No. 7]
H9.32 String Quartet No. 7
Contemplation of Desert Forms. (1962) 7′
First performed: 1966; Philadelphia, Pa. Ithaca String Quartet.
Music: reprod. of ms; available from composer.

[Quartet, Strings, No. 8]
H9.33 String Quartet No. 8. (1963) 8′
Music: reprod. of ms; available from composer.

[Quartet, Strings, No. 9]
H9.34 String Quartet No. 9. (1967) 14′
First performed: 1967; Donnell Library, New York City; Composer's Forum (New York City). Composers String Quartet.
Music: reprod. of ms.; available from composer.

[Quintet, Brasses, No. 1]
H9.35 Quintet for Brass Instruments. (1955) 15′
For: trumpets(2), horn, trombone(bass), tuba.
Score & parts: Chamber Music Library, 1963. BCM MIT NEC
Disc: Crystal 204, 1976. Cambridge Brass Quintet. HU MIT
Reel: Oct. 30, 1974; University of Massachusetts, Boston. Cambridge Brass Quintet. UMB.
Cassette: Nov. 30, 1970; New England Conservatory. NEC Scholarship Brass Quintet. NEC
Cassette: Mar. 15, 1977; New England Conservatory. NEC Scholarship Brass Quintet. NEC

[Quintet, Brasses, No. 2]
H9.36 Quintet No. 2 for Brass Instruments. (1961?) 7′
For: trumpets(2), horn, trombone(bass), tuba. 3 movements.

Music: reprod. of ms. available from composer.
Disc: Trilogy 1001, 1973. Iowa Brass Quintet (titled Opus 58).
Disc: Golden Crest, 197-. Tidewater Brass Quintet.

[Quintet, Brasses, No. 3]
H9.37 Quintet No. 3 for Brass Instruments, Op. 77. (1974; rev. 1977) 13′
For: trumpets(2), horn, trombone(bass), tuba.
Music: Margun, nyp.
Reel: Oct. 30, [1974]. University of Massachusetts, Boston. Cambridge Brass Quintet. UMB

H9.38 Sculptures, Op. 39. (1964) 14′
For: Soprano and orchestra(4-0-3-0; 4-6-6-0; timp, perc(4); pf; str). 5 movements. *Text:* Robinson Jeffers.
First performed: November 13, 1964; Symphony Hall, Boston. Bethany Beardslee, soprano; Boston Symphony Orchestra.
Score & parts: Peters. Rental.

H9.39 Serenata. (1978) 14′
For: flute, clarinet, clarinet(bass), violin, viola, violoncello. *Movements:* In Gestalt eines Ebers; Eine Hand; Psalm.
Commissioned by: Chamber Music Society of Baltimore. Earlier version, with soprano, titled Bittere Nuesse.
First performed: 1978; Baltimore, Md. Boston Musica Viva, Richard Pittman, conductor.
Music: reprod. of ms.; available from composer.

H9.40 Sinfonia for 13 Players. (1974) 14′
For: instrumental ensemble(flute, oboe, clarinet, bassoon, trumpet, trombone, piano, harp, percussion(2), violin, viola, violoncello). 1 movement. *Commissioned by:* Fromm Foundation. *First performed:* February 23, 1981; Sanders Theatre, Harvard University. Collage, Gunther Schuller, conductor.
Music: Margun, nyp.

[Sonata, Piano]
H9.41 Piano Sonata. (1957) 11'
First performed: 1961; Donnell Library,
New York City; Composer's Forum.
Richard Wortach.
Score: reprod. of ms.; available from
composer.

[Songs, Op. 74]
H9.42 Seven Songs, Op. 74. (1972)
18'-20'
For: Soprano and orchestra(2-2-2-2;
4-3-3-0; timp, perc; hp; str). *Text:*
Edward Leavenworth. *Contents:* The Nun
of Art; Five Fingers; Five Stars;
Profane Cantata; Memorial to a Red
Creek Man; Excerpts from Armageddon;
Quiet; I, Theseus. *Dedicated to:* Bethany
Beardslee. *First performed:* 1980;
Sanders Theatre, Harvard University.
Bethany Beardslee, soprano; Pro Arte
Chamber Orchestra of Boston, Richard
Pittman, conductor.
Score & parts: Peters. Rental.

H9.43 Symphony in 3 Movements.
(1980) 20'
For: orchestra(2-2-2-2; 4-3-3-3; timp,
perc; hp; str).
Score & parts: Peters, nyp.

H9.44 Variations, Op. 73. (1969) 14'
For: orchestra(2(pic)-2-2-2; 4-3-3-0;
timp, perc; hp; str).
Score & parts: Peters. Rental.

H10 NICHOLAS D. HUMEZ

Born March 11, 1948, in Cambridge,
Mass. *Education:* B.A., English (Harvard
University, 1969); studied piano with
Chester Cook and Roberta Humez.
Related activities: vocal performer;
co-founder of Cantores Sine (now Vox
Humana Quartet); Trustee, Friends of
Music at Guilford (Vt.), Inc. HU

WORKS

H10.1 Alice, Op. 45. (1978)
For: voices, flute, clarinet, violin,
violoncello. *Text:* Alice's Adventures in
Wonderland by Lewis Carroll. Incidental

music. *First performed:* July 23, 1978;
Guilford, Vt. Silvia Pippin, flute;
Eleanor Thomas, clarinet; Linda
Feigenbaum Hecker, violin; Paul Butler,
violoncello; Kent Bailey, double bass;
Singers of the Monteverdi Players,
Zeke Hecker, oboe and music director.
Score & parts: reprod. of ms.; available
from composer.

[Alice. Suite]
H10.2 Suite from Alice, Op. 45a. (1979)
For: Soprano, Tenor, chamber
orchestra(1-0-0-0; 2-2-0-0-;
str(1-1-1-1-1)). 9 movements. Arranged
by Zeke Hecker. *Text:* from Alice's
Adventures in Wonderland by Lewis
Carroll. *First performed:* Aug. 1979;
Guilford, Vt. Evelyn McLean, soprano;
Don McLean, tenor; Jerry Bellows,
conductor.
Score: reprod. of ms.; available from
composer.

Ask Us Not the Word. *See* Choral
Album I, Op. 44. Ask Us Not the
Word.

Aus tiefer Not. *See* Choral Album I,
Op. 44. Aus tiefer Not.

H10.3 A voi presenti. (1966)
For: Soprano, violin, violoncello. *Text:*
anon.
Score: reprod. of ms.; available from
composer.

H10.4 B-Fragment to J. Holan's Minuet.
(1979)
For: keyboard. *Score.*

H10.5 Birthday Organum. (1972)
For: piano.
Score: reprod. of ms.; available from
composer.

H10.6 Brief Recessional: Two Steps to
the Bar.
For: organ. Version for harpsichord or
piano in Keyboard Booklet No. 2. *First
performed:* June 1972; Old North
Church, Boston. Nicholas Humez.

Score: reprod. of ms.; available from composer.

Camptown Races. *See* Kyrie "Camptown Races."

[Canons]
H10.7 Four Canons. (1975)
For: organ.
Score: reprod. of ms.; available from composer.

H10.8 Cantata No. 1: Zwischen Berg, Op. 29. (1970)
For: Soprano, Tenor, oboe, violin, organ. 6 movements. *Text:* attributed to Ludwig Senfl and Josquin Desprez.
First performed: Aug. 1970; Guilford, Vt. Jan Gilewski, soprano; Rod Parke, tenor; Zeke Hecker, oboe; Linda Feigenbaum Hecker, violin; Joseph Elliot, organ.
Score & part: reprod. of ms.; available from composer.

H10.9 Cantata No. 2: Es warb ein schoener Jungling, Op 42. (1977)
For: Soprano, Tenor, flute, keyboard. 7 movements.
Score: reprod. of ms.; available from composer.

Cantique. *See* Verbe egal au tres haut.

[Choral Album I, Op. 44. Ask Us Not the Word]
H10.10 Ask Us Not the Word. (1972)
For: chorus(SATB). *Text:* Eugenio Montale; translated by Alice Coggeshall.
Vocal score: reprod. of ms.; available from composer.

[Choral Album I, Op. 44. Aus tiefer Not]
H10.11 Aus tiefer Not. (1970)
For: chorus(SATB). Chorale. *Text:* Bible, O.T., Psalm 130:1-3 (German versification). *First performed:* Oct. 11, 1970; Boston, Mass. Old North Singers; Douglas Davidson, conductor.

Vocal score: reprod. of ms.; available from composer.

[Choral Album I, Op. 44. Christ Our Passover]
H10.12 Christ Our Passover. (1972)
For: Soprano and chorus(SATB). Anthem. *Text:* Bible, N.T., I Corinthians 5:7-8.
Vocal score: reprod. of ms.; available from composer.

[Choral Album I, Op. 44. Cry. What Shall I Cry?]
H10.13 Cry. What Shall I Cry? (1966)
For: chorus(TTBB). Anthem. *Text:* Bible, O.T., Isaiah 40:6, 8.
Vocal score: reprod. of ms.; available from composer.

[Choral Album I, Op. 44. Doleo super te]
H10.14 Doleo super te. (1977)
For: chorus(STTB). Motet. *Text:* Bible, O.T., II Samuel 1:26-27.
Vocal score: reprod. of ms.; available from composer.

[Choral Album I, Op. 44. The Great God Bummer]
H10.15 The Great God Bummer (Fuguing Tune). (1969)
For: chorus(STTB). *Text:* Alex Humez.
Vocal score: reprod. of ms.; available from composer.

[Choral Album I, Op. 44. Judge Me, O God]
H10.16 Judge Me, O God. (1973)
For: chorus(STTB). Anthem. *Text:* Bible, O.T., Psalm 43:1, 3.
Vocal score: reprod. of ms.; available from composer.

[Choral Album I, Op. 44. O Heav'nly Father]
H10.17 O Heav'nly Father. (1972)
For: chorus(SATTB). Anthem. *Text:* Book of Common Prayer.
Vocal score: reprod. of ms.; available from composer.

[Choral Album I, Op. 44. Oculus non vidit]
H10.18 Oculus non vidit (second setting). (1968)
For: chorus(SATB). Motet. *Text:* Bible, N.T., I Corinthians 2:9.
Vocal score: reprod. of ms.; available from composer.

[Choral Album I, Op. 44. Personent hodie]
H10.19 Personent hodie. (1964)
For: chorus(SAATTB). Motet. *Text: Piae cantiones.*
Vocal score: reprod. of ms.; available from composer.

[Choral Album I, Op. 44. Qui autem docti]
H10.20 Qui autem docti. (1973)
For: chorus(SATB). Motet. *Text:* anon.
First performed: June 29, 1975; Brattleboro, Vt. Guilford Chamber Singers.
Vocal score: reprod. of ms.; available from composer.

[Choral Album I, Op. 44. Rejoice in the Lord Alway]
H10.21 Rejoice in the Lord Alway. (1965)
For: chorus(SAB) or chorus(STB). Anthem. *Text:* Bible, N.T., Philippians 4:4-7.
Vocal score: reprod. of ms.; available from composer.

[Choral Album I, Op. 44. Rings]
H10.22 Rings. (1970)
For: Tenors(2), Bass, violoncello. *Text:* Alex Humez. *Dedicated to:* Alice and David Humez. *First performed:* Dec. 19, 1970; Lincoln, Mass. Alex Humez and Nicholas Humez, tenors; David E. Humez, bass; unidentified violoncellist.
Score: reprod. of ms.; available from composer.

[Choral Album I, Op. 44. The Shadows Lengthen]
H10.22.5 The Shadows Lengthen. (1971)
For: chorus(SA) and piano. Anthem. *Text:* Book of Common Prayer.

Commissioned by and dedicated to: John Nicholls.
Vocal score: reprod. of ms.; available from composer.

[Choral Album I, Op. 44. Sicut erat in principio]
H10.23 Sicut erat in principio. (1964)
For: chorus(SATB). Motet.
Vocal score: reprod. of ms.; available from composer.

[Choral Album I, Op. 44. To a Northeast Airlines Junior Clerk]
H10.24 To a Northeast Airlines Junior Clerk. (1971)
For: chorus(SATB). *Text:* Philip Boswell.
Vocal score: reprod. of ms.; available from composer.

[Choral Album I, Op. 44. Ursus in tabernam]
H10.25 Ursus in tabernam. (1976)
For: chorus(STTB). *Text:* Alex Humez.
Vocal score: reprod. of ms.; available from composer.

[Choral Album I, Op. 44. Veni Creator Spiritus]
H10.26 Veni Creator Spiritus. (1965)
For: chorus(TTB). Motet. *Text: Liber usualis.*
Vocal score: reprod. of ms.; available from composer.

[Choral Album I, Op. 44. Wherefore Do the Wicked Live?]
H10.27 Wherefore Do the Wicked Live? (1966)
For: chorus(TTBB). Anthem. *Text:* Bible, O.T., Job 21:7; Bible, O.T., Psalm 71:1, 4.
Vocal score: reprod. of ms.; available from composer.

[Choral Album I, Op. 44. Who Fathoms the Eternal Thought?]
H10.28 Who Fathoms the Eternal Thought? (1963)
For: chorus(SATB). *Text:* John Greenleaf Whittier.
Vocal score: reprod. of ms.; available from composer.

[Choral Album I, Op. 44. Yankee Church Rounds]
H10.29 Two Yankee Church Rounds. (1972)
For: chorus(TTT) or chorus(BBB). Anthem. *Contents:* Break Thou the Arm (Bible, O.T., Psalm 10:14-17); Let Them Be Confounded (Bible, O.T., Psalm 26:1 and Bible, O.T., Psalm 35:4, 6).
Vocal score: reprod. of ms.; available from composer.

H10.30 Choral Response. (1963)
For: chorus(SATB). *Text:* Nicholas Humez.
Vocal score: reprod. of ms.; available from composer.

Christ Our Passover. *See* Choral Album I, Op.44. Christ Our Passover.

H10.31 Concerto for Five Instruments, Op. 21. (1968)
For: violin, violoncello, clarinet, horn, piano. 4 movements. *Dedicated to:* Thomas Bassett and his four children.
Score & parts: reprod. of ms.; available from composer.

H10.32 Conductus a 4. (1962; rev. 1965)
For: instruments(unspecified)(4).
Score: reprod. of ms.; available from composer.

Cry. What Shall I Cry? *See* Choral Album I, Op. 44. Cry. What Shall I Cry?

[Cummings Songs]
H10.33 Three Cummings Songs, Op. 4. (1965)
For: voice, oboe, piano. *Text:* e.e. cummings. *Contents:* Buy Me an Ounce; Love is the Every Only God; A Pretty Day.
Score: reprod. of ms.; available from composer.

Dance Suites, Op. 6. *See* Suite Nos. 1-3.

H10.34 The Dancing Princesses, Op. 48. (1979)
For: flute, oboe/English horn, clarinet, violin, viola, violoncello, piano. Ballet. *Choreography:* Kathleen Keller, after Jacob Grimm and Wilhelm Grimm. Excerpts arranged for harpsichord or piano in Keyboard Booklet No. 3. *First performed:* Mar. 2, 1979; Brattleboro, Vt. Silvia Pippin, flute; Shawn Nordell, oboe and English horn; Kathryn Issa, clarinet; Peggy James, violin; Linda Feigenbaum Hecker, viola; Peter Caldwell, violoncello; Eleanor Adams, harpsichord; Zeke Heller, conductor.
Score & parts: reprod. of ms.; available from composer.

[The Dancing Princesses. Polonaise]
H10.35 Polonaise from the Dancing Princesses, Op. 48b. (1980)
For: chamber orchestra(1-2-0-0; 2-0-0-0; str(1-1-1-1-1)). *First performed:* Aug. 31, 1980; Guilford, Vt. Jerry Bellows, conductor.
Score & parts: reprod. of ms.; available from composer.

[The Dancing Princesses. Suite]
H10.36 Suite No. 18: The Dancing Princesses, Op. 48a. (1979)
For: piano. 7 movements.
Score: reprod. of ms.; available from composer.

H10.37 Darest Thou Now, O Soul. (1969)
For: Tenors(2). *Text:* Walt Whitman.
First performed: June 1969; Cambridge, Mass. Ross Faneuf and Nicholas Humez.
Score: reprod. from ms.; available from composer.

[Death Will Come, and She Will Have Your Eyes]
H10.38 Secular Motet: Death Will Come, and She Will Have Your Eyes, Op. 30. (1971)
For: chorus(SATB) and piano. *Text:* Cesare Pavese, translated by Alice

Coggeshall.
Vocal score: reprod. of ms.; available from composer.

H10.39 The Detective's Dilemma, Op. 39. (1976)
For: Soprano, Tenors(2), flute, oboe, horn, violoncello, piano. *Text:* Alex Humez. *First performed:* Oct. 23, 1976; Brattleboro, Vt. Susan Middleton, soprano; Alex Humez and Nicholas Humez, tenors; Antonia Cimino, flute; Zeke Hecker, oboe; Judith Levine, horn; David Runnion, violoncello; Mitchell Davis, piano.
Score & parts: reprod. of ms.; available from composer.

Doleo super te. *See* Choral Album I, Op. 44. Doleo super te.

H10.40 Duet for Suzaphone and Piccolo. (1963)
Score: reprod. of ms.; available from composer.

Easy Suites for Two Instruments Each, Op. 49. *See* Suite Nos. 19-21.

H10.41 English Mass, Op. 38. (1976)
For: chorus(STTB). 6 movements. *Text:* Book of Common Prayer.
Vocal score: reprod. of ms.; available from composer.

Es warb ein schoener Jungling. *See* Cantata No. 2: Es warb ein schoener Jungling.

H10.42 Estampie. (1964)
For: piano.
Score: reprod. of ms.; available from composer.

H10.43 Expansion Canon a 3. (1971)
For: organ.
Score: reprod. of ms.; available from composer.

H10.44 Fanfare for L----- H-----. (1965)
For: trumpets(3). *Commissioned by:* Louise T. Cavalieri. *First performed:* spring 1965; Lexington, Mass.

Score: reprod. of ms.; available from composer.

H10.45 Fanfare for the Pilgrim to Paradise. (1965)
For: instruments(unspecified)(9).
Score: reprod. of ms.; available from composer.

H10.46 Fanfare Sol La La Re Ut. (1978)
For: recorderss(alto)(2) and recorder(tenor). *Dedicated to:* Ross A. Faneuf. *First performed:* Feb. 22, 1979; Gorham, Me. Anne Emerson and Venita Winkler, alto recorders; Lois Libby, tenor recorder.
Score: reprod. of ms.; available from composer.

H10.47 Fantasia on a Theme by Hildebrand. (1963) .
For: piano.
Score: reprod. of ms.; available from composer.

H10.48 Fantasia on Sanctorum meritis. (1964)
For: violin and organ.
Score: reprod. of ms.; available from composer.

[For Behold, My Brother Esau and My Father Peradventure]
H10.49 Recitative and Aria: For Behold, My Brother Esau and My Father Peradventure.
(1965) *For:* Bass, violoncello, harpsichord. *Text:* Bible, O.T., Genesis 27:11-12.
Score: reprod. of ms.; available from composer.

Fuguing Tune. *See* Choral Album I, Op. 44. The Great God Bummer; Proportion.

The Great God Bummer. *See* Choral Album I, Op. 44. The Great God Bummer.

H10.50 Greenaway Garden, Op. 53. (1981)
For: Mezzo Soprano, flute, oboe, horn,

viola, violoncello. Song cycle. *Text: Marigold Garden* by Kate Greenaway. *Contents:* Little Girlie, Tell to Me; In My Little Greenhouse; The King Said He Liked Apples; Oh Roses Shall Be for Her Carpet; Baby Mine over the Land; If You Were a Little Boy; Four Princesses; A Lord Was There; When You and I Grow Up, Polly; They Saw It Rise; What Did She See. *First performed:* Sept. 6, 1981; Guildford, Vt. Diana Stugger, mezzo soprano; Sandra Miller, flute; Zeke Hecker, oboe; Dean Grittelman, horn; Linda Feigenbaum Hecker, viola; Chris White, violoncello; Jerry Bellows, conductor. *Score:* reprod. of ms.; available from composer.

The Helmsman. *See* Quartet, Strings, No. 2.

Horn Trio. *See* Sonata No. 14.

H10.51 Interlude on 1 cps. (1965) *For:* trumpet and oscillator(pure-tone). *Score:* reprod. of ms.; available from composer.

H10.52 It's Useless Trying to Carry an Umbrella. (1972) *For:* chorus(TTBB). *Vocal score:* reprod. of ms.; available from composer.

[Joyous Dances] *For:* trumpet, piano, violins(2), violoncello. *Score:* reprod. of ms.; available from composer.

Judge Me, O God. *See* Choral Album I, Op. 44. Judge Me, O God.

[Keyboard Booklet No. 1] **H10.53** First Keyboard Booklet: Eight Preludes and Fugues, Op. 25. (1966-69) *For:* harpsichord or piano. *Contents:* I Will Give Praise; Victoria; Wa boo jer dow; Ann's (First) Keyboard Piece; Ex post facto; Ann's Second Keyboard

Piece; Heroic; Veni Creator Spiritus. *Score:* reprod. of ms.; available from composer.

[Keyboard Booklet No. 2] **H10.54** Second Keyboard Booklet: Seven Preludes and Fugues Plus Recessional, Op. 46. (1969-78) *For:* harpsichord or piano. *Contents:* King Kong; Tritone; St. Valentine; Le Tambourin; Bourgeois Syncopations; On a Theme from Sonata No. 13; Western Wynde; Brief Recessional, Two Steps to the Bar (for version for organ, see Brief Recessional: Two Steps to the Bar). *Score:* reprod. of ms.; available from composer.

H10.55 Keyboard Booklet No. 3: Nine Preludes and Fugues, Op. 54. (1978-81) *For:* harpsichord or piano. *Contents:* from The Dancing Princesses; Christ lag in Todesbanden; The Skyhawk; Trinidad; Duodecimi toni; Levesque ne porte pas ses lunettes; The Recursive; Romanesca & Ricercar; Innsbrueck. *Score:* reprod. of ms.; available from composer.

H10.56 Kyrie "Camptown Races." (1980) *For:* chorus(STTB). *Dedicated to:* John Hetland. *Vocal score:* reprod. of ms.; available from composer.

[Latin Cheers] **H10.57** Three Latin Cheers. (1963) *For:* chorus(SATB). *Text:* Nicholas Humez. *Vocal score:* reprod. of ms.; available from composer.

H10.58 Let My Prayer Come up into Thy Presence. (1966) *For:* Bass and organ. *Text:* Bible, O.T., Psalm 141:2. *First performed:* summer, 1966; Lexington, Mass. Thomas Meier, bass and unidentified organist. *Score:* reprod. of ms.; available from composer.

H10.59 The Life of Bongo Bill (Acts I and II), Op. 33. (1972)
For: Sopranos(3), Tenors(2), Bass, chorus(chamber), piano, guitar, banjo, dulcimer, recorders, percussion, harpsichord(optional). Chamber opera.
Text: Alex Humez; Sanskrit and Hittite texts translated by Alex Humez.
Chorus parts: reprod. of ms.
Disc: Titanic Ti 6, 1976. Nini Evans, Deborah Fahnestock, Susan Middleton, sopranos; Alex Humez, Nicholas Humez, Peter Hunsberger, tenors; Cantores Sine Nomine Remnant; David Humez, percussion. W

[The Life of Bongo Bill. Act III]
H10.60 Act III (of The Life of Bongo Bill, Op. 36) (1973)
Text: Alex Humez. *Music. Tape.*

[Memorial Songs]
H10.61 Four Memorial Songs, Op. 31. (1972)
For: Tenor, chorus(SATB), piano. Anthems. *Contents:* Into Thy Hands (Book of Common Prayer); Jesus Said (Bible, N.T., John 14:1-3); I Heard a Voice from Heaven (Bible, N.T., Revelations 14:13); I Will Not Leave You Comfortless (Bible, N.T., John 14:18, 19, 27). *Dedication:* In memory of Charlessie McKinnon Humez.
Vocal score: reprod. of ms.; available from composer.

H10.62 Missa prima, Op. 1. (1963)
For: chorus(SATB). 6 movements. *First performed:* May 23, 1965; Lexington, Mass. First Parish Choir, Francis Judd Cooke, director (Sanctus).
Vocal score: reprod. of ms.; available from composer.

H10.63 Missa sanctorum meritis, Op. 17. (1968)
For: chorus(SATB). 6 movements.
Vocal score: reprod. of ms.; available from composer.

H10.64 My Beloved Spake. (1978)
For: Tenor and Bass. *Text:* Bible, O.T., Song of Solomon 2:10, 7:6. *Dedicated*

to: Kathleen FitzGerald and Keith Stavely. *First performed:* Aug. 1978; Newton, Mass. Nicholas Humez, tenor and Alex Humez, baritone.
Score: reprod. of ms.; available from composer.

[New Madrigals]
H10.65 Three New Madrigals, Op. 5. (1965)
For: chorus(SATB). *Contents:* Under the Bamboo Tree (T.S. Eliot); A Spring Madrigal (C.W. Gleason); The Way to Hump a Cow (e.e. cummings).
Vocal score: reprod. of ms.; available from composer.

O Heavn'ly Father. *See* Choral Album I. Op. 44. O Heaven'ly Father.

H10.66 Oculus non vidit (first setting). (1964)
For: Soprano and Tenor. *Text:* Bible, N.T., I Corinthians 2:9; Bible, O.T., Psalm 71:1.
Score: reprod. of ms.; available from composer.

Oculus non vidit (second setting). *See* Choral Album I, Op. 44. Oculus non vidit.

H10.67 Partita No. 1, Op. 9. (1966)
For: organ. 6 movements. *Dedicated to:* Francis Judd Cooke. *First performed:* spring 1967; Lexington, Mass. Francis Judd Cooke.
Score: reprod. of ms.; available from composer.

H10.68 Partita No. 2, Op. 26. (1969)
For: organ. 7 movements.
Score: reprod. of ms.; available from composer.

H10.69 Pentatonic Kyrie. (1964)
For: chorus(SATB).
Vocal score: reprod. of ms.; available from composer.

Personent hodie. *See* Choral Album I, Op. 44. Personent hodie.

H10.70 Piece for Keyboard and Empty Corridor. (1961)
Score: reprod. of ms.; available from composer.

[Plainsong Fantasias]
H10.71 Three Plainsong Fantasias, Op. 3. (1965)
For: guitar or organ. *Contents:* Hostis Herodes; Ut queant laxis; Sanctorum meritis. *First performed:* May 23, 1965; Lexington, Mass. (Hostis Herodes). Francis Judd Cooke, organ.
Score: reprod. of ms.; available from composer.

Polonaise from The Dancing Princesses. *See* The Dancing Princesses. Polonaise.

Preludes and Fugues. *See* Keyboard Booklet Nos. 1-3.

[Profane Plainsongs]
H10.72 Three Profane Plainsongs. (1966)
For: Tenor.
Score: reprod. of ms.; available from composer.

H10.73 Proportion (Fuguing Tune). (1980)
For: chorus(SATB). *Text:* Isaac Watts.
Vocal score: reprod. of ms.; available from composer.

H10.74 Quant Theseus, Hercules et Jazon. (1975)
For: Tenor and piano. *Text:* Guillaume de Machaut. *First performed:* July 1975; W. Brattleboro, Vt. Nicholas Humez, tenor and unidentified pianist.
Score: reprod. of ms.; available from composer.

[Quartet, Strings, No. 1]
H10.75 String Quartet No. 1, Op. 8. (1966)
Score & parts: reprod. of ms.; available from composer.

[Quartet, Strings, No. 2]
H10.76 String Quartet No. 2, The Helmsman, Op. 12. (1967; rev. 1968)

4 movements. *First performed:* June 29, 1975; Brattleboro, Vt. Linda Feigenbaum Hecker and Leslie Straley, violins; Don Becker, viola; David Tasgal, violoncello.
Score & parts: reprod. of ms.; available from composer.

[Quartet, Strings, No. 3]
H10.77 String Quartet No. 3, Op. 20. (1968)
4 movements. *First performed:* June 23, 1974; Brattleboro, Vt. Linda Feigenbaum Hecker and Gudrun Gay, violins; Mariana Webster, viola; Tim Merton, violoncello.
Score & parts: reprod. of ms.; available from composer.

[Quartet, Strings, No. 4]
H10.78 String Quartet No. 4, Op. 37. (1974)
4 movements.
Score: ms.

Qui autem docti. *See* Choral Album I, Op. 44. Qui autem docti.

[Quintet, Brasses]
H10.79 Brass Quintet No. 1, Op. 16. (1967)
For: trumpets(2), horn, trombone, tuba. 5 movements.
Score & parts: reprod. of ms.; available from composer.

H10.80 Railroad Song from Thespis. (1976)
For: Baritone and piano. *Text:* Sir William Schwenck Gilbert.
Score: ms.

Recitative and Aria. *See* For Behold, My Brother Esau and My Father Peradventure.

Rejoice in the Lord Alway. *See* Choral Album I, Op. 44. Rejoice in the Lord Alway.

H10.81 Requiem Mass, Op. 28. (1970)
For: Soprano, Tenor, chorus(SATB),

organ. 7 movements.
Vocal score: reprod. of ms.; available from composer.

H10.82 Requiem Trium Vocum, Op. 52. (1979-81)
For: chorus(SAB). *Contents:* Introit and Kyrie; Domine Jesu Christe; Sanctus/Benedictus; Pie Jesu; Agnus Dei/Lux aeterna; Libera me; In paradisum. *Dedication:* In memory of Theodore Badger, Harold T. Handley, Gabriel Randolph (first three movements, respectively).
Vocal score: reprod. of ms.; available from composer.

[Rhapsody No. 1]
H10.83 Premiere Rhapsodie, Op. 11. (1966)
For: trumpet or oboe and piano.
Score & part: reprod. of ms.; available from composer.

[Rhapsody No. 2]
H10.84 Deuxieme Rhapsodie, Op. 27. (1969)
For: violin and piano.
Score & part: reprod. of ms.; available from composer.

[Rhapsody No. 3]
H10.85 Troisieme Rhapsodie. (1979)
For: recorder(soprano).
Score: reprod. of ms.; available from composer.

[Rhapsody No. 4]
H10.86 Quatrieme Rhapsodie. (1980)
For: flute and harpsichord. *Dedicated to:* Dorothy Rice and Miriam Kallus.
Score & part: reprod. of ms.; available from composer.

Rings. *See* Choral Album I, Op. 44. Rings.

H10.87 Rondeau paysan. (1978)
For: violin. *Dedicated to:* John S. Diggs.
Score: reprod. of ms.; available from composer.

Sanctorum meritis. *See* Fantasia on Sanctorum meritis; Missa Sanctorum meritis; Plainsong Fantasias.

H10.88 Scurrilous Glee.
For: chorus(TTB). *Text:* traditional expletives.
Vocal score: reprod. of ms.; available from composer.

Secular Motet: Death Will Come. *See* Death Will Come, and She Will Have Your Eyes.

The Shadows Lengthen. *See* Choral Album I, Op. 44. The Shadows Lengthen.

Sicut erat in principio. *See* Choral Album I, Op. 44. Sicut erat in principio.

Solo Sonatas, Op. 23. *See* Sonata Nos. 5-9.

H10.89 Sonata No. 1, Op. 7. (1966)
For: trumpet and piano. 3 movements.
Score: reprod. of ms.; available from composer.

H10.90 Sonata No. 2, Op. 13. (1967)
For: recorder(soprano) and harpsichord. 3 movements. *First performed:* Feb. 8, 1968; Gorham, Me. Anne Emerson, recorder and Charlotte Zax, piano.
Score: reprod. of ms.; available from composer.

H10.91 Sonata No. 3, Op. 19. (1968)
For: oboe, violin, harpsichord. 3 movements. *First performed:* spring, 1968; Waltham, Mass. Zeke Hecker, oboe; Linda Feigenbaum Hecker, violin; Joseph Elliot, harpsichord.
Score & parts: reprod. of ms.; available from composer.

H10.92 Sonata No. 4, Op. 22. (1968)
For: flute and harpsichord. 3 movements. *First performed:* Sept. 23, 1978; North Shrewsbury, Vt. Miriam Kallus and Masanobu Ikemiya, flutes;

Dorothy C. Rice, harpsichord; Bettina Roulier, viola da gamba.
Score: reprod. of ms.; available from composer.

H10.93 Sonata No. 5 (from Five Solo Sonatas, Op. 23). (1968)
For: oboe. 3 movements. *Dedicated to:* Zeke Hecker. *First performed:* spring, 1969; Cambridge, Mass. Zeke Hecker.
Score: reprod. of ms.; available from composer.

H10.94 Sonata No. 6 (from Five Solo Sonatas, Op. 23). (1968)
For: violin. 4 movements.
Score: reprod. of ms.; available from composer.

H10.95 Sonata No. 7 (from Five Solo Sonatas, Op. 23). (1968)
For: trumpet. 3 movements.
Score: reprod. of ms.; available from composer.

H10.96 Sonata No. 8 (from Five Solo Sonatas, Op. 23). (1968)
For: clarinet. 3 movements.
Score: reprod. of ms.; available from composer.

H10.97 Sonata No. 9 (from Five Solo Sonatas, Op. 23). (1968)
For: violoncello. 3 movements.
Score: reprod. of ms.; available from composer.

H10.98 Sonata No. 10 (Treble Sonata), Op. 35. (1973)
For: oboe (or other treble C-instrument) and piano. 4 movements. *Dedicated to:* Zeke Hecker. *First performed:* Sept. 23, 1978; North Shrewsbury, Vt. (3rd movement). Masanobu Ikemiya, flute and Dorothy C. Rice, piano.
Score: reprod. of ms.; available from composer.

H10.99 Sonata No. 11, Op. 40. (1976)
For: recorder(alto) and piano or harpsichord. 4 movements. *Dedicated to:* Alex Humez.

Score: reprod. of ms.; available from composer.

H10.100 Sonata No. 12, Op. 34. (1972?)
For: viola, violoncello, keyboard. 3 movements.
Score: ms.

H10.101 Sonata No. 13, Op. 41. (1977)
For: flute, violoncello, piano. 4 movements. *Dedicated to:* Antonia Cimino.
Score & parts: reprod. of ms.; available from composer.

H10.102 Sonata No. 14 (Horn Trio), Op. 50. (1980)
For: violin, horn, piano. 4 movements. *Dedicated to:* Masanobu Ikemiya.
Score & parts: reprod. of ms.; available from composer.

["Song of Songs" Songs]
H10.103 Five "Song of Songs" Songs. (1980)
For: Alto and Tenor. *Text:* Bible, O.T., Song of Solomon. *Contents:* My Beloved Spake (2:10, 7:6); A Garden Enclosed (1:11, 2:6, 4:12, 7:10); Stay Me With Flagons (2:5, 4:14-15, 6:4); Many Waters Cannot Quench Love (8:7); Set Me as a Seal (8:6).
Score: reprod. of ms.; available from composer.

H10.104 A Song on Song (Oblong). (1975)
For: Tenor and piano. *Text:* Alex Humez. *First performed:* July 1975; West Brattleboro, Vt. Nicholas Humez, tenor and unidentified pianist.
Score: reprod. of ms.; available from composer.

H10.105 Songbook I, Op. 51. (1980)
For: voice(medium) and piano. *Contents:* Le bouquet ultime (Jenny Holan); Huswifery (Edward Taylor); Berceuse (W.H. Auden); Last Poem (Alex Humez, after A. Desnos); It May Not Always Be So (e.e. cummings); Two Singing Commercials (entr'acte to Joseph

Timko's opera *Peri Massone*): The Green Mountain Bookstore and The Brattleboro Public Market (Alex Humez); Si je cuidois (attributed to J. Maillard). *First performed:* Nov. 7, 1980; Brattleboro, Vt. (Nos. 6 and 7). Nicholas Humez, tenor and Rebecca Graber, piano.
Score: reprod. of ms.; available from composer.

Suite from Alice. *See* Alice. Suite.

[Suite No. 1]
H10.106 Three Dance Suites, Op. 6. No. 1. (1965)
For: flute, oboe, clarinet. 7 movements.
Score & parts: reprod. of ms.; available from composer.

[Suite No. 2]
H10.107 Three Dance Suites, Op. 6. No. 2. (1965)
For: flute, oboe, clarinet, violin. 7 movements.
Score & parts: reprod. of ms.; available from composer.

[Suite No. 3]
H10.108 Three Dance Suites, Op. 6. No. 3. (1965; rev. 1967)
For: psaltery. 7 movements and 2 interludes.
Score & parts: reprod. of ms.; available from composer.

H10.109 Suite No. 4, Op. 10. (1966)
For: violoncello. 5 movements.
Score: reprod. of ms.; available from composer.

[Suite Nos. 5-9]
H10.110 Five Suites, Op. 14. (1967)
For: flute and violoncello. Suite No. 5 is rescored from a suite for trumpet and euphonium; No. 8 from Three Dance Suites, Op. 6 and Sonata No. 2.
Score: reprod. of ms.; available from composer.

H10.111 Suite No. 10, Op. 18. (1968)
For: guitar and psaltery. 4 movements.
Dedicated to: Sally Thorpe and

Hopkinson Smith. *First performed:* spring, 1968; Cambridge, Mass. Hopkinson Smith, guitar and Sally Thorpe, psaltery.
Score: reprod. of ms.; available from composer.

H10.112 Suite No. 11, Op. 24. (1968)
For: recorders(soprano)(2). 6 movements.
Score: reprod. of ms.; available from composer.

H10.113 Suite No. 12, Op. 32. (1972)
For: recorder(soprano), recorder(alto), recorder(tenor). 4 movements.
Score: reprod. of ms.; available from composer.

[Suite No. 13]
H10.114 Five Suites for Solo Instruments, Op. 47. No. 13. (1978)
For: recorder(alto). 6 movements.
Dedicated to: Alex Humez. *First performed:* Feb. 22, 1979; Gorham, Me. Anne Emerson.
Score: reprod. of ms.; available from composer.

[Suite No. 14]
H10.115 Five Suites for Solo Instruments, Op. 47. No. 14. (1978)
For: bassoon. 4 movements. *Dedicated to:* Louise T. Cavalieri.
Score: reprod. of ms.; available from composer.

[Suite No. 15]
H10.116 Five Suites for Solo Instruments, Op. 47. No. 15. (1978)
For: horn. *Dedicated to:* Judy Levine.
Score: reprod. of ms.; available from composer.

[Suite No. 16]
H10.117 Five Suites for Solo Instruments, Op. 47. No. 16. (1978)
For: violin. 4 movements. *Dedicated to:* Wallace Dailey. *First performed:* Oct. 4, 1980; Cambridge, Mass. Wallace Dailey.
Score: reprod. of ms.; available from composer.

[Suite No. 17]
H10.118 Five Suites for Solo
Instruments, Op. 47. No. 17. (1978)
For: English horn. 5 movements.
Dedicated to: Shawn Nordell.
Score: reprod. of ms.; available from
composer.

Suite No. 18. *See* The Dancing
Princesses. Suite.

[Suite No. 19]
H10.119 Trivia: Three Easy Suites for
Two Instruments Each, Op. 49. No. 19.
(1979) *For:* oboe and violin. 6
movements. *Dedicated to:* Zeke and
Linda Hecker.
Score: reprod. of ms.; available from
composer.

[Suite No. 20]
H10.120 Trivia: Three Easy Suites for
Two Instruments Each, Op. 49. No. 20.
(1979) *For:* recorder(soprano) and
recorder(alto). 5 movements. *Dedicated
to:* Jenny Holan.
Score: reprod. of ms.; available from
composer.

[Suite No. 21]
H10.121 Trivia: Three Easy Suites for
Two Instruments Each, Op. 49. No. 21.
(1979) *For:* violins(2). 5 movements.
Dedicated to: John and Matthew Dunne.
Score: reprod. of ms.; available from
composer.

H10.122 Symphony No. 1, Op. 15.
(1967)
For: orchestra. 4 movements.
Score: reprod. of ms.; available from
composer.

To a Northeast Airlines Junior Clerk.
See Choral Album I, Op. 44. To
a Northeast Airlines Junior Clerk.

Treble Sonata. *See* Sonata No. 10.

Trio, Flute, Violoncello, Piano. *See*
Sonata No. 3.

Trio, Horn, Violin, Piano. *See* Sonata
No. 14.

Trio, Oboe, Violin, Harpsichord. *See*
Sonata No. 3.

Trio, Viola, Violoncello, Keyboard. *See*
Sonata No. 12.

Trivia: Three Easy Suites for Two
Instruments Each. *See* Suite
Nos. 19-21.

H10.123 Turtles, Op. 43. (1977)
For: Sopranos(2), Tenors(2), Bass,
chorus, flute, oboe, English horn, piano.
Chamber opera. *Libretto:* Alex Humez
and Kathleen Fitzgerald. *First
performed:* Oct. 28, 1977; Brattleboro,
Vt. Pat Lemon, Susan Middleton,
sopranos; Alex Humez, Nicholas Humez,
tenors; Ross Faneuf, bass; members of
the Guilford Chamber Singers.
Score & parts: reprod. of ms.; available
from composer.

H10.124 Ulysses 'twixt Scylla and
Charybdis. (1979)
For: Baritones(3). *Text:* Nicholas Humez.
First performed: Dec. 16, 1979; Harvard
Business School, Boston. Ross Faneuf,
Alex Humez, Nicholas Humez.
Score: reprod. of ms.; available from
composer.

H10.125 Unter der Linden. (1972)
For: Soprano, recorder(soprano),
harpsichord. *Text:* Walther von der
Vogelweide. *First performed:* June 29,
1975; Brattleboro, Vt. Evelyn McLean,
soprano; Gudrun Gay, recorder; Joseph
Elliot, harpsichord.
Score & parts: reprod. of ms.; available
from composer.

Ursus in tabernam. *See* Choral Album I,
Op. 44. Ursus in tabernam.

[Variations]
H10.126 Five Variations on a Theme of
Betsy Howard. (1966)

For: piano. 5 movements.
Music: ms.

Veni Creator Spiritus. *See* Choral Album I, Op. 44. Veni Creator Spiritus; Keyboard Booklet No. 1.

[Verbe egal au tres haut]
H10.127 Cantique: Verbe egal au tres haut. (1981)
For: chorus(SATB). *Text:* Jean Baptiste Racine.
Vocal score: reprod. of ms.; available from composer.

H10.128 Westminster West. (1980)
For: chorus(SATB). *Text:* Jenny Holan.
Vocal score: reprod. of ms.; available from composer.

Wherefore Do the Wicked Live? *See* Choral Album I, Op. 44. Wherefore Do the Wicked Live?

Who Fathoms the Eternal Thought? *See* Choral Album I, Op. 44. Who Fathoms the Eternal Thought?

Yankee Church Rounds. *See* Choral Album I, Op. 44. Yankee Church Rounds.

Zwischen Berg. *See* Cantata No. 1.

H11 LESLIE H. HURWITZ

Born 1928 in Boston. *Education:* B.M. (Eastman School of Music); M.M. (University of Frankfurt, West Germany); New England Conservatory; studied composition with Howard Hanson (Eastman School of Music); David Diamond (Rochester N.Y.), Ervin Henning (Boston); piano with Jerome Diamond, Jose Iturbi, George MacNabb (Eastman School of Music); Isidor Philipp (Paris, France); organ with Helmut Walcha (Frankfurt, West Germany). *Awards:* National Teachers Award (1969). *Related activities:* music educator; theorist; currently on the faculty of Longy School of Music. L

WORKS

H11.1 Arguments Over a Well-Known Theme. (1978) 10'
For: piano. Children's music.
Movements: Haydn; Mozart; Sturm und Drang; Chopin; Baroque; Chromatics; Contemporary. *First performed:* May 1978; Arlington, Mass. *Score. Tape.*

H11.2 Sonatine antique. (1978) 10'
For: flute. Children's music. 5 movements. *Dedication:* To my young flute-playing friends. *Score.*

H11.3 Toccatina. (1980) 3'
For: piano. 1 movement. *Score.*

J1 LEON JANIKIAN

Born June 23, 1947, in Cambridge, Mass. *Education:* studied composition with Carmine Pepe (Mark Hopkins College, B.A., 1969), Philip Bezanson, Charles Fussell, Robert Stern, Frederick Tillis (University of Massachusetts, Amherst, M.M., 1975); clarinet with Felix Viscuglia. *Related activities:* free-lance musician; owner of Sound Techniques Recording Studio. BPL

WORKS

J1.1 Anoush Hovig. (1971)
For: voice and piano.
Score: ms.

J1.2 Cadences. (1972)
For: piano.
Score: ms.

J1.3 Chalumeau. (1971)
For: clarinet.
Score: ms.

J1.4 Elements. (1980)
For: percussion.
Score: ms.

J1.5 Krikor Lousavoritch. (1979)
Ballet.
Score: ms.

J1.6 New Music for the Armenian Divine Liturgy. (1980)
Score: ms.

[Pieces]
J1.7 15 Pieces (1972)
For: piano.
Score: ms.

J1.8 Preludes and Fugues. (1970)
For: harpsichord.
Score: ms.

[Quartet, Strings]
J1.9 String Quartet. (1974)
Music: ms.

[Quintet, Brasses, No. 1]
J1.10 Brass Quintet No. 1. (1976)
Music: ms.

[Quintet, Brasses, No. 2]
J1.11 Brass Quintet No. 2. (1977)
Music: ms.

J1.12 Sinfonietta (1975)
For: voice and chamber orchestra.
Dedicated to: Philip Bezanson. Written in partial fulfillment of requirements for M.M., University of Massachusetts, Amherst.
Music: reprod. of ms.

J1.13 Suite for Band. (1973)
Music: ms.

J1.14 Suite for Oboe and Marimba. (1974)
Music: ms.

J1.15 Symphony. (1973)
For: band.
Music: ms.

J2 GLORIA JASINSKI

Born April 18, 1956, in New York City. Moved to Boston area 1975. *Education:* B.M. (Berklee College of Music, 1978). *Related activities:* music teacher in Boston area schools; currently private instructor in piano and music theory. BkPL

WORKS

J2.1 Fugue for Brass Quartet. (1977) 1' 15"
For: trumpets(2) and trombones(2).
Score: ms. in composer's hand.

J2.2 Fugue for Brass Trio. (1977) 2'
For: trumpets(2) and trombone.
Score: ms. in composer's hand.

J2.3 Motet. (1977) 1' 55"
For: chorus(SATB). *Text:* Bible, O.T., Song of Solomon 2:11-13.
Vocal score: ms. in composer's hand.

[Pieces, Piano and Flutes(2)]
J2.4 Three Pieces for Chamber Ensemble. (1978) 3' 40"
3 movements.
Score: ms. in composer's hand.

[Pieces, Piano, Woodwinds, Strings]
J2.5 Two Pieces for Chamber Ensemble. (1978) 3'
For: flute, clarinets(2), piano, double basses(2). 2 movements.
Score: ms. in composer's hand.

J2.6 Sonata for Solo Piano. (1978) 8' 30"
3 movements.
Score: ms. in composer's hand.

J2.7 Suite. (1979) 8'
For: orchestra(2(&pic)-2(&Ehn)-2(&bcl)-2(&cbsn); 4-3-3-1; timp, perc(2), glock, mar, vibra, xylo; str). 3 movements.
Score: ms. in composer's hand.

[Themes]
J2.8 Three Themes for Woodwind Trio. (1979) 3' 10"
For: flutes(2) and clarinet.
Score: ms. in composer's hand.

J3 KEVIN JONES

Born January 11, 1952, in St. Louis, Mo. Moved to Boston area 1979. *Education:* studied composition with James Sellars and Merrill Ellis (North Texas State University). *Awards:* North Texas State University Student Composer's Award (1973, 1974, 1975), Dallas New Arts Festival (Featured Composer, 1975). *Related activities:* conductor; stage director; multi-media performer; founder and director, Sonic Arts Theater Performance Ensemble (1974-78). NU

WORKS

J3.1 Adios Amigos, So Long, Farewell. (1979) 15'
For: tape(electroacoustic). Dance music; musique concrete. 1 movement. *Choreography:* Theresa Reeves. *First performed:* 1979; Theresa Reeves.
Reel or cassette: available from composer.

J3.2 Ahh. (1975) 3'
For: tape(electroacoustic). 1 movement. Musique concrete. Realized at the North Texas State University Electronic Music Center. *First performed:* 1975.
Reel or cassette: available from composer.

J3.3 Dialogue. (1973) 5'
For: chorus(SATB). 1 movement. *Text:* Kevin Jones.
Score: available from composer.

J3.4 Dialogue II. (1974) 8'
For: speakers(male)(2) and speakers(female)(2). 1 movement. *Text:* Kevin Jones. *First performed:* Oct. 28, 1974. Members of the Sonic Arts Theater.
Score: available from composer.
Reel or cassette: available from composer.

J3.5 Dialogue III. (1975) 8'
For: speakers(male)(3) and speakers(female)(2). 1 movement. *Text:* Kevin Jones. *First performed:* May 23, 1975. Members of the Sonic Arts

Theater.
Score: available from composer.
Reel or cassette: available from composer.

J3.6 Dialogue IV. (1976) 10'
For: speakers(male)(4) and speakers(female)(3). 1 movement. *Text:* Kevin Jones. *First performed:* Dec. 9, 1976. Members of the Sonic Arts Theater.
Score: available from composer.
Reel or cassette: available from composer.

[Eine Fiktion. Functional]
J3.7 Functional. (1976) 15'
For: Soprano and tape. Opera excerpt. *Text:* Kevin Jones. *Commissioned by:* American Institute of Musical Studies. Act 3 of a collectively composed work. *First performed:* Aug. 1976; Graz, Austria.
Score & tape: available from composer.

Functional. *See* Eine Fiktion. Functional.

J3.8 Gradient. (1975-76) 5'
For: tape. 1 movement. Realized at the Brown University Studio and the North Texas State University Electronic Music Center. *First performed:* 1976.
Reel or cassette: available from composer.

J3.9 Moment. (1978) 8'
For: Soprano. Dance music. 1 movement. *Text:* Kevin Jones. *Choreography: Continuing* by Theresa Reeves. *First performed:* Dec. 7, 1978. Lynn Yakes.
Score: available from composer.
Reel or cassette: available from composer.

[Quartet, Strings]
J3.10 String Quartet. (1977-78) 12'
1 movement. *First performed:* Apr. 24, 1978; North Texas State University. Gloria Lucey and Jim Hargrave, violins; Maurice Hood, viola; Paul Kirkpatrick, violoncello.
Score & parts: available from

composer.
Reel or cassette: available from composer.

J3.11 Snap Shot. (1980-81) 20'
For: Soprano, Tenor, speaker(male), speaker(female), clarinet, clarinet(bass), piano, violin, viola, violoncello, percussion(tom-toms(4), drums(brake)(4), cymbal, triangle, claves, wood blocks(3). 1 movement. *Text:* Kevin Jones.
Score: available from composer.

J3.12 Song. (1978) 3'
For: Soprano, flute, clarinet. *Text: Chamber Music #20* by James Joyce.
First performed: Apr. 24, 1978; Bunny Hodges, [soprano?]; Sharon Richardson, [flute?]; Bob Price, [clarinet?].
Score: available from composer.
Reel or cassette: available from composer.

[Texts]
J3.13 Four Texts. (1974) 3'
For: tape(electroacoustic). Dance music.
Text: Kevin Jones. Pre-recorded voice and computer-generated sound realized at the Sonic Arts Studio. *First performed:* 1974. Theresa Reeves, dancer.
Reel or cassette: available from composer.

J3.14 Voce-voce. (1977-78) 25'
For: Soprano/actress, conductor/actor, speakers(female)(2), chamber orchestra(1-0-1-0; 0-1(or euphonium or bass coronet)-1-0; perc; str(1-1-1-1-0). Chamber opera in 1 act. *Libretto:* Kevin Jones. *First performed:* Apr. 24, 1978; Bunny Hodges, soprano; Bruce Balentine, conductor; members of the Sonic Arts Theater, Kevin Jones, director.
Score: available from composer.
Reel or cassette: available from composer.

K1 JERONIMAS KACINSKAS

Born April 17, 1907, in Vidukle, Lithuania. Moved to Boston area 1949. *Education:* State Conservatory of Music, Prague, Czechoslovakia; studied composition with Jaroslav Kricka and Alois Haba; conducting with Pavel Dedecek. *Related activities:* conductor; organist; director of the Radio Orchestra, Kaunas and Vilna, Lithuania (1938-41) and of the State Philharmonic Orchestra and State Opera, Vilna, Lithuania (1941-44); organist and choir director, Displaced Persons Camp, Augsburg, Germany (1945-49) and St. Peter's Lithuanian Church, Boston (1949); director, Melrose Symphony Orchestra, Melrose, Mass. (1960-69); served on the faculties of the State Conservatory of Music, Klaipeda, Lithuania (1931-38) and Berklee College of Music (1968-). Be

WORKS

Black Ship. *See* Juodas Laivas (Black Ship).

[Choral Songs]
K1.1 Six Choral Songs. (1925-47) 22'
For: chorus(SATB). *Contents:* Esi Dangau (B. Brazdzionis); Berzas; Lietuves Takeliai (J. Baltrusaitis); Jau Saulute Leidzias (traditional); Gintarelis (L. Andriekus); Zvanguciai (J. Aistis). *First performed:* June 8, 1975; Arlington, Mass. Arlington Chamber Chorus, Jeronimas Kacinskas, conductor.
Vocal score: ms. in composer's hand; available from composer.
Reel: Dec. 7, 1977; Berklee College of Music (Songs 1, 2, and 4). Berklee Concert Choir; Brian O'Connell, conductor.

K1.2 Haec dies. (1981) 5'
For: chorus(SATB) and organ or piano.
Text: Liber usualis, antiphon.
Vocal score: available from composer.

K1.3 In Lithuania. (1980) 6'
For: flute, violin, viola, violoncello.
First performed: Oct. 25, 1980;
Chicago, Ill. Matthew Marruglio, flute;
Berklee String Trio.
Score & parts: ms.; available from
composer.

K1.4 Introduction and Toccata. (1977) 7'
For: violin. *First performed:* Nov. 20,
1977; Lithuanian Citizens Club, Boston.
Izidorius Vasyliunas.
Score: ms; available from composer.
Reel: Apr. 18, 1978; Berklee College of
Music; in *A Concert of 20th Century
Music*. Izidorius Vasyliunas. Be

K1.5 Juodas Laivas (Black Ship). (1975)
50'
Opera in 1 act. *First performed:* May
8, 1976; Chicago, Ill. Lithuanian Opera
Company.
Score & parts: available from Lithuanian
Opera Company, Chicago.

K1.6 Lento. (1957) 8'
For: orchestra. *First performed:* Nov.
16, 1958; Symphony Hall, Boston.
Boston University Orchestra, Jeronimas
Kacinskas, conductor. *Score & parts.*

[Lithuanian Folk Songs]
K1.7 Three Lithuanian Folk Songs.
(1977) 8'
For: Soprano, clarinet, string quartet,
piano. *First performed:* Nov. 20, 1977;
Lithuanian Citzens Club, Boston. Birute
Aleksaite and others.
Score & parts: available from
composer.

K1.8 Lithuanian Trio. (1980) 8'
For: flute, clarinet, viola. 3 movements.
First performed: Oct. 25, 1980;
Chicago, Ill.
Score & parts: available from
composer.
Reel: Dec. 9, 1980; Boston
Conservatory of Music. Boston
Conservatory Chamber Ensemble,
William Gross, director. BCM

[Miniatures]
K1.9 Four Miniatures. (1957) 14'
For: flute, clarinet, violoncello. *First
performed:* May 3, 1959; Boston Center
for Adult Education.
Score & parts: available from
composer.
Score & parts: Vasyliunas, 1966. BPL
Reel: Mar. 9, 1960; Brookline Public
Library. BkPL

K1.10 Missa in honorem immaculati
cordis Beatae Mariae Virginis. (1952)
40'
For: Soprano, Alto, Tenor, Bass,
chorus(mixed), organ, brasses(7). *First
performed:* Mar 24, 1963; Jordan Hall,
Boston. St. Peter's Lithuanian Choir and
Belmont Community Chorus, John
Bavicchi, conductor.
Score & parts: available from
composer.
Score: G.I.A., 1952. BPL

K1.11 Mistery of Redemption. (1946-54)
80'
For: orchestra. 6 movements. *First
performed:* Oct. 12, 1952; Carnegie
Hall, New York City (1st movement).
Members of the NBC Symphony
Orchestra and the New York
Philharmonic, Jeronimas Kacinskas,
conductor.
Score: available from composer.

K1.12 Nonet. (1932) 45'
For: woodwind quintet, violin, viola,
violoncello, double bass. 4 movements.
First performed: 1932; Panevezys,
Lithuania.

K1.13 Oi Tai Buvo. 3'
For: chorus(SATB). *Text:* traditional.
Vocal score: available from composer.
Reel: Dec. 2, 1980; Berklee College of
Music. Berklee Concert Choir, Brian
O'Connell, conductor. Be

[Quartet, Saxophones, No. 1]
K1.14 Saxophone Quartet No. 1. (1969)
14'
For: saxophone(soprano),

saxophone(alto), saxophone(tenor), saxophone(baritone). 4 movements. *First performed:* Jan. 7, 1969; Ogunquit, Me. Berklee Saxophone Quartet.
Score: in *The Berklee Saxophone Quartet,* Berklee, 1972. BCM Be
Disc: in *The Berklee Saxophone Quartet,* Berklee Records LP 102, 1972. Berklee Saxophone Quartet. BCM Be

[Quartet, Saxophones, No. 2]
K1.15 Saxophone Quartet No. 2. (1976) 30'
For: saxophone(soprano), saxophone(alto), saxophone(tenor), saxophone(baritone). 4 movements. *First performed:* Nov. 20, 1977; Lithuanian Citizens Club, Boston. Berklee Saxophone Quartet.

[Quartet, Strings] (1930)
K1.16 String quartet No. I. (1930) Withdrawn.

[Quartet, Strings] (1932)
K1.17 String Quartet in Quarter-Tones. (1932)
Withdrawn.

[Quintet, Piano and Strings]
K1.18 Quintet. (1978) 24'
For: string quartet, piano. 4 movements. *First performed:* Oct. 27, 1979; Lithuanian Cultural Center, Brooklyn, N.Y. Berklee String Quartet.
Score & parts: available from composer.
Reel: Apr. 9. 1980; Berklee College of Music. Diane Wheeler and Julia Harghiner, violins; Todd Sagar, viola; Barbara Wood, violoncello; Stephany King Plsek, piano. Be

[Quintet, Woodwinds]
K1.19 Woodwind Quintet. (1968) 9'
1 movement. *First performed:* 1968; Boston. Fine Art Quintet.
Score & parts: available from composer.

K1.20 Reflections. (1966) 16'
For: piano. 4 movements. *First*

performed: Nov. 1, 1967; Brookline Public Library. Kenneth Wolf.
Score: available from composer.

K1.21 Septet. (1966)
For: clarinet, bassoon, horn, violin, viola, violoncello, piano. *First performed:* Dec. 10, 1967; Jordan Hall, Boston.
Score & parts: available from composer.

K1.22 Sonata for Violin and Piano. (1974) 22'
3 movements. *First performed:* Sept. 30, 1975; New England Conservatory. Izidorius Vasyliunas, violin and Vitanys Vasyliunas, piano.
Score: available from composer.
Reel: Mar. 10, 1977; Berklee College of Music. Be

K1.23 Song to the Light. (1947) 8'
For: orchestra. *First performed:* 1948; Augsburg, West Germany. Augsburg Symphony Orchestra, Jeronimas Kacinskas, conductor. *Score & parts.*

K1.24 Symphonic Fantasy No. I. (1941) Withdrawn.

K1.25 Symphonic Fantasy No. 2. (1960) 16'
For: orchestra. *First performed:* Apr. 10, 1960; Sanders Theatre, Harvard University. Cambridge Civic Symphony, Jeronimas Kacinskas, conductor.
Score & parts: available from composer.

K1.26 Te luci ante. (1977) 6'
For: chorus(SATB) and chamber orchestra. *First performed:* Nov. 20, 1967. Berklee Concert Choir and Orchestra, Brian O'Connell, conductor.
Score & parts: available from composer.

K1.27 Transcendental Expression. 16'
For: band. *First performed:* Dec. 10, 1967; Massachusetts Institute of Technology. MIT Concert Band, John

Corley, conductor.
Score & parts: MIT

Trio. *See* Lithuanian Trio.

K1.28 Triptic. (1968) 18'
For: Soprano and
orchestra(2-2(Ehn)-2(bcl)-2; 4-2-3-1; timp,
perc; str). 3 songs. *First performed:*
Sept. 1, 1968; Lincoln Center, New
York City. New York Symphony
Orchestra, Vytautas Marijosius,
conductor.
Score: available from composer.

K1.29 Vilniaus Suita. (1960) 15'
For: orchestra. 2 movements
(unfinished). *First performed:* Nov. 25,
1962; School, Chicago, Ill. Chicago
Lyric Opera Orchestra, Jeronimas
Kacinskas, conductor.
Score & parts: available from
composer.

K2 MINUETTA KESSLER

Born September 5, 1914, in Gomel,
Russia. *Education:* studied composition
with Howard Brockway and Ivan
Langstroth (Juilliard School); piano with
Gladys McKelvie Egbert (Royal College
and Royal Academy of Music, London,
England, Licentiate, 1929); Ernest
Hutcheson, Ania Dorfman, Helena
Augustin, Victor Biart (Juilliard School).
Awards: Composers, Authors, and
Publishers Association of Canada
Prizes (1946, 1947), Calgary (City) key
(1951), Alberta Outstanding Woman
Composer and Musician (1955),
Brookline Library Music Association
Composers Award (1957), National
Federation of of Music Clubs,
American Women Composers Contest,
Best Program Award (1975), Sigma
Alpha Iota (Honorary Member, 1979).
Related activities: pianist; teacher;
founder of the New England Jewish
Music Forum (1957), Boston Juilliard
Alumni Association (1961), Concerts in
the Home (1964), Friends of Young
Musicians (1966); President, New
England Pianoforte Teachers

Association (1965-67), President,
Massachusetts Music Teachers
Association (1979-81); hosted program
on WNYC-AM and FM, New York City;
contributor of articles to the *Christian
Science Monitor, Clavier, European Piano
Teachers Journal*; served on the
faculties of the Juilliard School and
the Longy School of Music. BPL

WORKS

Alberta Concerto. *See* Concerto, Piano.

K2.1 Alberta with Love, Op. 98. (1980)
For: voice and piano. *Text:* Minuetta
Kessler. *Contents:* We Celebrate Alberta;
I Love Alberta; Only in Alberta; Wide
Open Spaces in Alberta; Beauty in
Alberta; Alberta's Open to You.
Dedication: For the 75th Anniversary of
Alberta, Canada. *First performed:* July
1980; Alta., Canada. Richard A.
Livingston, bass baritone and Minuetta
Kessler, piano.
Score: Musical Resources, 1980.

K2.2 Baby Ballads of Today, Op. 25.
(1947) 17'
For: voice(medium), voice(high), piano.
Text: Minuetta Kessler. *Contents:* The
Three Pigs; Little Red Riding Hood; The
Wolf and the Fox; Johnny and the
Tree; The Wolf and the Goats; The Ant
and the Cricket; Cinderella. *First
performed:* Feb. 20, 1980; Belmont,
Mass. (Movements 1-5) Jennifer
Patterson, soprano; John Oliver,
baritone; Minuetta Kessler, piano.
Score: reprod. of ms.; available from
composer.
Disc: in *Childhood Cameos*, AFKA S
4663, 1980 (Movements 1-5).
Unidentified singer and Minuetta
Kessler, piano.
Reel: Mar. 13, 1981; Belmont, Mass.
(Movements I and 4). Leslie Holmes,
soprano and Minuetta Kessler, piano.
WCRB

K2.3 A Baby Is a Precious Thing, Op.
103. (1980)
For: Soprano and piano or Soprano,

Baritone, piano. *Text:* Minuetta Kessler.
First performed: Feb. 20, 1980;
Belmont, Mass. Jennifer Patterson,
soprano; John Oliver, baritone;
Minuetta Kessler, piano.
Score: available from composer.
Disc: in *Childhood Cameos*, AFKA S
4663, 1980. Jennifer Patterson, soprano;
John Oliver, baritone and Minuetta
Kessler, piano.
Reel: Mar. 13, 1981; Belmont, Mass.
Leslie Holmes, soprano and Minuetta
Kessler, piano. WCRB

K2.4 Baby's Music Box, Op. 19. (1945)
13' 3"
For: voice(medium) or voice(high) and
piano. *Text:* Minuetta Kessler. *Contents:*
Making Music on the Floor; Baby's
Toes; Teeth in November; Baby's Tear;
Peek-a-Boo; Happy Birthday; My Nose
Is Running; Sleepy Land; Take a Step.
Dedication: To my son, Ronald Kessler.
Winner of the National Federation of
Music Clubs, American Women
Composers Contest, Best Program
Award (1975). *First performed:* Feb. 13,
1973; Northeastern University. Susan
Stone, soprano and Minuetta Kessler,
piano.
Score: Musical Resources, 1947. BPL
Disc: in *Childhood Cameos*, AFKA S
4663, 1980. Unidentified singer and
Minuetta Kessler, piano.
Reel: Mar. 13, 1981; Belmont, Mass.
(Movements 1, 5, 8). Leslie Holmes,
soprano and Minuetta Kessler, piano.
WCRB
Cassette: Feb. 21, 1981. (movements 1,
5, 8). Leslie Holmes, soprano and
Minuetta Kessler, piano.

K2.5 Ballet Sonatina, Op. 20, No. 2.
(1946) 6' 30"
For: piano. 3 movements. *Dedication:*
With affection and admiration to my
dear friend Hilde Somer. Winner of
Composers, Authors and Publishers
Association of Canada Prize (1947).
Originally titled Sonatina. *First
performed:* Sept. 25, 1946; Wesley
United Church, Calgary, Alta., Canada.

Minuetta Kessler.
Score: reprod. of ms.
Score: Musical Resources, 1980. BPL
Disc: AFKA SK 288, 1979. Minuetta
Kessler. L WCRB WGBH
Tape: Feb. 14, 1956; Brookline Public
Library. Minuetta Kessler. BkPL
Tape: June 13, 1973; WGBH-FM, Boston.
Minuetta Kessler.
Videotape: June 3, 1979; WBZ-TV,
Boston; in *Woman 79*. Minuetta Kessler.

K2.6 Beginning Piano for Adults, Op.
90. (1978)
Score: available from composer.

K2.7 Bicentennial Sonata, Op. 78. (1975)
20'
For: piano. 4 movements. Originally
titled Sonata for Piano. *First
performed:* Feb. 26, 1977; Belmont,
Mass. Minuetta Kessler.
Score: Musical Resources, 1975. BPL
Tape: Mar. 24, 1977; Robbins Library,
Arlington, Mass. Minuetta Kessler.
WCRB

K2.8 The Blessing of the Sabbath
Candles, Op. 37. (1955) 1' 15"
For: Soprano and organ or piano. *First
performed:* 1956.
Score: reprod. of ms.

K2.9 The Boston Red Sox, Op. 58.
(1964) 2' 30"
For: pianos(2). Written for television
program, *Why Women Compose*. *First
performed:* Oct. 7, 1964; WHDH-TV,
Boston. Roland Nadeau and Minuetta
Kessler.
Score: Musical Resources, 1981.
Videotape: recording of first
performance.

K2.10 But We Shall Bloom, Op. 22.
(1946) 5' 30"
For: chorus(SATB) and organ or piano.
Text: Haim Guri.
Vocal score: reprod. of ms.; available
from composer.

Cantata for Yom Kippur. *See* Kol Nidre.

K2.11 Caprice, Op. 71. (1971) 2' 15"
For: piano. Originally titled Fantasette
No. 2. *Dedicated to:* Andrew Gordon.
First performed: Jan. 24, 1973; New
England Life Hall, Boston. Andrew
Gordon.
Score: Musical Resources, 1981.

K2.12 Cat 'n' Mouse Tales, Op. 85.
(1977-80)
For: piano. *Movements:* A Mouse in the
House; A Curious Cat; A Midnight
Encounter. Originally titled A Mouse in
the House.
Score: Willis, 1981.

[Christmas Carols]
K2.13 Three Christmas Carols in a
Concert Arrangement, Op. 40. (1957)
For: piano. *Movements:* Joy to the
World; Good King Wenceslas; The First
Nowell.
Score: Musical Resources, 1981.

K2.14 Cinnamon Stick, Op. 83, No. 1.
(1977)
For: piano. *Dedicated to:* Parwane
Parsa.
Score: available from composer.

K2.15 Clowns, Op. 99, No. 2. (1980)
For: piano.
Score: available from composer.

Color Pieces. *See* More Color Pieces,
Op. 50, No. 2; Primary Colors, Op.
50, No. 1.

K2.16 Confirmation Prayer, Op. 37, No.
2. (1957) 2' 10"
For: Tenor and organ or piano. Sacred
music, Jewish. *Text:* Minuetta Kessler.
Written for son Ronald Kessler's Bar
Mitzvah. *First performed:* 1956; Beth El
Temple Center, Belmont, Mass. Cantor
Jacob Seully, tenor and unidentified
organist.
Score: Transcontinental, 1957.

[Confirmation Prayer; Arr.]
K2.17 Confirmation Prayer, Op. 37, No.
2. (1957) 2' 10"
For: Tenor, chorus(SATB), organ. Sacred

music, Jewish. *Text:* Minuetta Kessler.
Vocal score: ms. in composer's hand;
available from composer.

[Concerto, Piano]
K2.18 Alberta Concerto, Op. 24. (1947)
23'
For: piano and
orchestra(2(pic)-2-2(bcl)-1; 4-3-3-1; timp,
perc, glock; str). 4 movements. *First
performed:* Nov. 20, 1947; CBC,
Montreal, Canada. Minuetta Kessler,
piano; CBC Symphony Orchestra.
Score & parts: Musical Resources, 1947.
Rental. BPL
Pf. red: Musical Resources, 1947. BPL
Reel: June 13, 1973 (2nd movement of
version for solo piano). Minuetta
Kessler. WGBH

K2.19 Country Scenes, Op. 29. (1948) 4'
30"
For: piano. *Movements:* Early in the
Morning; Watching a Sunset; Rustic
Dance.
Score: Musical Resources (Movements 1
and 2).
Score: Willis, 1981 (Movement 3).

K2.20 A Day in the Park, Op. 30. (1948)
For: piano. *Movements:* Let's Go to the
Park; Swinging; Sandpile; See-Saw; The
Slide; Come Home!
Score: Willis, 1981.

K2.21 Dedication Offering, Op. 102.
(1980) 10'
For: Baritone, chorus(SSATB), flute,
organ. Sacred music, Jewish.
Commissioned by and dedicated to: Beth
El Temple Center, Belmont, Mass. on
the occasion of its 25th anniversary.
First performed: Oct. 17, 1980; Beth El
Temple Center, Belmont, Mass. Cantor
Boris Greisdorf, baritone; Constance
Boykan, flute; James David Christie,
organ; unidentified chorus.
Score: Musical Resources, 1980.

K2.22 Easy Piano Pieces, Op. 88. (1978)
Text: Minuetta Kessler. 18 movements
(some with words).
Score: Boston, 1978.

[Easy Piano Pieces, Op. 95]
K2.23 The Improper Grasshopper: And Other Easy Piano Pieces, Op. 95 (Easy Piano Pieces Book II). (1979)
Text: Minuetta Kessler.
Score: Boston, 1979.

Easy Piano Pieces, Op. 97. *See* Jewish Easy Piano Pieces, Op. 97.

K2.24 Etude brilliante, Op. 28: (Hora). (1948) 2'
For: piano. Folk dance music, Jewish. *Dedicated to:* Ania Dorfman. *First performed:* June 29, 1949; CBC, Vancouver, B.C., Canada. Minuetta Kessler. *Score:* Transcontinental, 1973.
Reel: June 13, 1973; WGBH-FM, Boston. Minuetta Kessler. WGBH
Videotape: May 26, 1979; WHDH-TV, Boston; in *Good Day Show*. Minuetta Kessler.

Fantasette No. 2. *See* Caprice, Op. 71.

K2.25 Fantasette, Op. 17. (1943) 2' 13"
For: piano.
Score: reprod. of ms.
Score: Musical Resources, 1981.

Fantasy, Op. 87. *See* Lake O'Hara Fantasy, Op. 87.

Fantasy, Op. 93. *See* Lake McArthur Fantasy, Op. 93.

K2.26 Fantasy, Op. 96. (1979) 7'
For: clarinet and piano. *Dedicated to:* Giora Fiedman. *First performed:* Feb. 21, 1981; International Institute, Boston. John Breda, clarinet and Minuetta Kessler, piano.
Score: Musical Resources, 1980.

K2.27 Free Men All, Op. 16, No. 2. (1942)
For: voice and piano. *Text:* Morris C. Shumiatcher. *First performed:* Jan. 28, 1942; Calgary, Alta., Canada. Colin Bray, voice and Minuetta Kessler, piano.

Score: ms. in composer's hand; available from composer.

Give My Country Life. *See* My Canada, Op. 91.

K2.28 God's Canopy of Love, Op. 60. (1965) 3' 20"
For: voice and piano. Sacred music, Jewish. *Text:* Minuetta Kessler. Written for son Ronald Kessler's wedding. *First performed:* Sept. 11, 1965; Beth El Temple Center, Belmont, Mass. Jeanette Coran, soprano and unidentified pianist.
Score: reprod. of composer's ms.; available from composer.

K2.29 Grant Us Peace, Op. 76. (1975)
For: Bass Baritone, chorus(SATB), organ. Sacred music, Jewish. *Text:* Gates of Prayer from *The New Union Prayerbook. First performed:* June 4, 1980; Temple Israel, Boston. Cantor Boris Greisdorf, bass baritone and others.
Vocal score: Musical Resources, 1980.

K2.30 Hear My Prayer, Op. 63. (1967) 2' 15"
For: chorus(SATB) and organ. Anthem. *Text:* Bible, O.T., Psalms. *Dedication:* To my daughter Jean, on the occasion of her Bat Mitzvah. First performed: Jan. 16, 1976; Temple Sinai, Brookline, Mass. Sandra Evans, soprano; Mary Ann Valaitis, alto; William Cushman, tenor; Juergen Keller, baritone; unidentified organist.
Vocal score: Transcontinental, 1967.

K2.31 Hunting Hoodlebabes, Op. 14, No. 3. (1940) 5' 25"
For: voice and piano. *Text:* Morris C. Shumiatcher. *First performed:* Feb. 20, 1980; Belmont, Mass. John Oliver, baritone and Minuetta Kessler, piano.
Score: Musical Resources, 1981.
Disc: in *Childhood Cameos* AFKA S 4663; 1980. John Oliver, baritone and Minuetta Kessler, piano.

K2.32 I Had a Love, Op. 72. (1972) 2'
45"
For: voice(medium) or voice(high) and
piano. *Text:* Minuetta Kessler. *First
performed:* Feb. 26, 1978; Belmont,
Mass. Jennifer Patterson, soprano and
Minuetta Kessler, piano.
Score: available from composer.

K2.33 I Looked at a Tulip, Op. 34.
(1951)
For: voice and piano *Text:* Marks
Levine.
Score: reprod. of ms.; available from
composer.

I See Your Face. *See* It's Only Fantasy,
Op. 32, No. 2.

The Improper Grasshopper. *See* Easy
Piano Pieces, Op. 95.

K2.34 In Memorium: Martin Luther King,
Op. 106. (1978)
For: chorus(SATB) and organ or piano.
Text: Minuetta Kessler.
Vocal score: reprod. of ms.; available
from composer.

K2.35 Introduction and Allegro, Op. 62.
(1966) 5'
For: violin, violoncello, piano.
Dedicated to: The Chromatic Club. *First
performed:* Feb. 11, 1966; The College
Club, Boston. Ruth Rabinovitz, violin;
Alan Copeland, violoncello; Minuetta
Kessler, piano.
Score & parts: Musical Resources, 1981.

K2.36 It's Only Fantasy, Op. 32, No. 2.
(1951)
For: voice(medium or voice(high) and
piano. Originally titled I See Your
Face. *First performed:* Feb. 25, 1979;
Belmont, Mass. Sara Hoff, mezzo
soprano and Minuetta Kessler, piano.
Score: Musical Resources, 1981.

K2.37 Jewish Easy Piano Pieces, Op.
97.
Text: Minuetta Kessler. *Movements:*
Rosh Hashana; Yom Kippur; Succoth;
Simchat Torah; Chanuka; Purim; Pesach;

Yom Ha-atz-ma-ot; Rosh Chodesh;
Israeli Dance; T'Fillah; Sabbath Candles;
Hora. *Dedication:* With gratitude to my
Aunt Naomi and Uncle Lazar Weiner.
Score: Transcontinental, 1980.

K2.38 Join Your Country, Op. 16, No.
1. (1942)
For: voice and piano. *Text:* Morris C.
Shumiatcher. *First performed:* Jan. 28,
1942; Calgary, Alta, Canada. Colin Bray,
voice and Minuetta Kessler, piano.
Score: ms. in composer's hand;
available from composer.

K2.39 Kiddy City, Op. 51. (1961) 42'
For: voices(children), chorus(children),
orchestra. Operetta. *Libretto:* Minuetta
Kessler. *Commissioned by:* Belmont
PTA, Belmont, Mass. Written for the
5th and 6th grades of Belmont's Winn
Brook School. *First performed:* May 9,
1969; Belmont, Mass. Members of the
5th and 6th grades of the Winn Brook
School; Members of the Winn Brook
Orchestra, John E. Mainez, conductor.
Score: Musical Resources, 1961. BPL
Parts: available from composer.
Libretto: available from composer.

K2.40 Kiddy Kidoodle Land, Op. 33.
(1950)
For: voice, narrator, piano. Television
program. *Script:* Minuetta Kessler.
Contents: Kiddy Kidoodle Land; The
Adventures of Nicky in Whiztown; The
Magic of Makebelieve; It's Fun to Use
Magic; The Great Bombo; Exactly
Where I'm Needed.
Score & parts: reprod. of ms.; available
from composer.

K2.41 Kol Nidre: The Sacrifice of the
Innocents, Op. 70, No. 1. (1970) 30'
For: chamber chorus, organ or piano,
trumpets(2)(optional),
trombones(2)(optional), horn(optional),
percussion(optional). Cantata. *Text:*
Minuetta Kessler. *Contents:* We
Remember; Adagio; Six Million
Innocent Victims; We Await; A New
Way to Live; Be Not a Ruler Over Us,
God; Where Were You, O God; Now,

Today in Soviet Russia; Israel Calls;
See! Out of Ashes; God Is Where You
Let Him in. Originally titled Cantata for
Yom Kippur; also titled Kol Nidre
Cantata. *First performed:* Oct. 8, 1970;
Beth El Temple Center, Belmont, Mass.
Doris Aharonian and Yvonne Crockett,
sopranos; Elizabeth Barton, alto; Phillip
Morrison, tenor; David Elgart, bass;
Rabbi Earl Grollman, narrator; Alpha
Morrison, organ; Cantor Jacob Seully,
conductor.
Vocal score: Musical Resources, 1970.
Parts: Musical Resources, 1970.

K2.42 Lake McArthur Fantasy, Op. 93.
(1979) 8'
For: flute and piano. *Dedicated to:*
Constance Boykan. *First performed:*
Feb. 25, 1979; Belmont, Mass.
Constance Boykan, flute and Minuetta
Kessler, piano.
Score & part: Musical Resources, 1979.
NEC

K2.43 Lake O'Hara Fantasy, Op. 87.
(1977) 9'
For: oboe and piano. *Dedicated to:*
Patricia Morehead. *First performed:*
May 23, 1978; Robbins Library,
Arlington, Mass. Patricia Morehead,
oboe and Minuetta Kessler, piano.
Score & part: Musical Resources, 1979.
BPL
Disc: AFKA SK 288, 1979 (titled
Fantasy). Patricia Morehead, oboe and
Minuetta Kessler, piano. WGBH WCRB
Tape: recording of first performance.

K2.44 Lake O'Hara's Magic Circle, Op.
55. (1961) 1' 15"
For: voice and piano. *Text:* Minuetta
Kessler. *First performed:* Feb. 25, 1979;
Belmont, Mass. Sara Hoff, mezzo
soprano and Minuetta Kessler, piano.
Score: Musical Resources, 1980.

K2.45 The Lighting of the Sabbath
Candles, Op. 37, No. 4. (1955)
For: Soprano and organ. *Text:* from *The
Union Prayer Book. First performed:*

1956.
Score: reprod. of ms.; available from
composer.

K2.46 Little Red Ridinghood, Op. 94.
(1979) 40'
For: dancers(6 or more) and piano. 2
acts. *Commissioned by:* MJT Dance
Company, Marjie Topf, artistic director.
First performed: Pine Manor College.
MJT Dance Company, Marjie Topf,
artistic director; Minuetta Kessler,
piano.
Score: available from composer.
Videotape: May 3, 1979; WBZ-TV,
Boston; in *Woman 79* (opening of Act
II).
Videotape: May 26, 1979; WHDH-TV,
Boston; in *Good Day Show* (opening
scene).

K2.47 Love Everlasting, Op. 86. (1978)
For: Soprano and piano. *Text:* Minuetta
Kessler. Written for the wedding of
daughter Jean Kessler. *First performed:*
Feb. 26, 1978; Belmont, Mass. Jennifer
Patterson, soprano and Minuetta
Kessler, piano.
Score: available from composer.

K2.48 Love's Garland, Op. 14, No. 2.
(1940)
For: voice and piano. *Text:* Morris C.
Shumiatcher. Originally titled Queen of
All My Heart.
Score: Musical Resources, 1981.

K2.49 The Magic of Musicland, Op. 43.
(1958)
Television program. *Script:* Minuetta
Kessler. *First performed:* WHDH-TV,
Boston; in *Dateline Boston.* Minuetta
Kessler. *Libretto:* available from
composer.

K2.50 May the Words of My Mouth,
Op. 46, No. 1. (1958) 2' 46"
For: Tenor, Soprano, organ. *Text:* Bible,
O.T., Psalm 19:14.
Score: reprod. of ms.; available from
composer.

K2.51 May the Words of My Mouth, Op. 74, No. 1. (1974)
For: chorus(SATB) and organ or piano. *Text:* Bible, O.T., Psalm 19:14.
Vocal score: ms.; available from composer.

K2.51.5 Meditation and May the Words, Op. 74, No. 2. (1975) 2' 15" *For:* chorus(SATB) and organ. *Text:* Bible, O.T., Psalm 19:14.
Vocal score: Transcontinental, 1981.

K2.52 Memories of Tevye, Op. 35. (1953) 30'
For: dancers, clarinet, clarinet(bass), violoncello, percussion or dancers and piano. Ballet sonatina. Based on the character Tevye by Sholom Aleichem. Originally titled A World Passed By. *First performed:* Feb. 25, 1953; Calgary, Alta., Canada. Calgary Ballet, directed by Olga Valda; Minuetta Kessler, piano.
Score & parts: Musical Resources.

[Memories of Tevye; Arr.]
K2.53 Memories of Tevye, Op. 35.
For: piano. *Movements:* Overture; Wedding. Originally titled A World Passed By. *First performed:* May 19, 1956; Belmont, Mass. Minuetta Kessler.
Score: ms.; available from composer.

K2.54 Mid-Point Reflections, Op. 100. (1980)
For: piano. *Commissioned by:* Sandra Hudson. *Dedication:* For the 50th birthday of John Hudson. *First performed:* Mat. 19, 1981; Peasant Stock Restaurant, Somerville, Mass. Minuetta Kessler.
Score: Musical Resources, 1980.

K2.55 More Color Pieces, Op. 50, No. 2. (1965)
For: piano. *Movements:* Pink; Yellow; Ochre; Burgundy; Olive Green. Original version comprised of first three movements only.
Score: Musical Resources, 1981.

A Mouse in the House. *See* Cat 'n' Mouse Tales, Op. 85.

K2.56 My Canada, Op. 91. (1979)
For: voice(medium) and piano. *Text:* Morris C. Shumiatcher. Original version titled Give My Country Life. *First performed:* Feb. 25, 1979; Belmont, Mass. Sara Hoff, mezzo soprano and Minuetta Kessler, piano.
Score: available from composer.

K2.57 The Naughty Necklace, Op. 79. (1975)
For: dancers and piano. Ballet. Based on a libretto by Lorraine Michele.
Score: ms. in composer's hand; available from composer.

K2.58 New York Suite, Op. 21. (1942) 17'
For: piano. *Movements:* In the Subway; The Bowery; Fifth Avenue Bus; Cloisters; Times Square Fugue.
Dedicated to: John M. Williams. Winner of Composers, Authors and Publishers Association of Canada Prize (1946). *First performed:* Apr. 14, 1945; Central United Church, Calgary, Alta., Canada. Minuetta Kessler.
Score: reprod. of ms., 1946.
Score: Musical Resources, 1980.
Reel: Nov. 18, 1964; Brookline Public Library. BkPL

[New York Suite; Arr]
K2.59 New York Suite, Op. 21.
For: piano and orchestra(2(&pic)-2-1(cl in A(2))-1(&cbsn); 2-2-0-1; timp, perc; pf; str). *Movements:* In the Subway; The Bowery; Fifth Avenue Bus; Cloisters; Times Square Fugue. *First performed:* Jan. 24, 1982. Belmont Orchestra.
Score & parts: Musical Resources. Rental.

K2.60 Nocturne, Op. 99, No. 1. (1980)
For: piano. *Dedicated to:* Wendy Liu.
Score: available from composer.

K2.61 Peace and Brotherhood through Music, Op. 48. (1967) 12' 30"
For: voices, chorus(SATB), organ or piano. Cantata. *Text:* Minuetta Kessler.
Contents: Seek the Music of Peace; Add Another Voice; Let Us Raise Our

Voices to God; Thousands of Years; The Music of Souls; Music Kindles the Flame of Brotherhood; Let Us Raise Our Voices to God. *First performed:* Feb. 26, 1960; Beth El Temple Center, Belmont, Mass. Beth El Temple Center Choir, Rabbi Earl Grollman, narrator; Cantor Jacob Seully, soloist; unidentified organist.
Vocal score: Transcontinental, 1967.
Libretto: Transcontinental.

K2.62 Pieces of Chocolate, Op. 61, No. 1. (1965, 1979)
For: piano. *Movements:* Vanilla; Orange Cream; Butternut Crunch; Pineapple Delight; Peanutbutter Marshmallow; Raisin Clusters; Coffee Cream; Twin Almond; Peppermint; Nougat; Peanut Brittle; Cherry Cordial; Caramel; Cinnamon Sticks; Hazelnut Clusters; Maple Walnut; Ginger; Raspberry Cream; Brazilnut Kumquat; Pecan Stuffed Date Creams. Parts of original version, titled Three Pieces of Chocolate, now titled Savory Sweet, Op. 61, No. 2.
Score: ms.; available from composer.

K2.63 Playful Squirrels, Op. 56. (1961)
For: piano. 12 movements. Earlier version titled Twelve Rote Pieces.
Score: Willis, 1981.

K2.64 A Prayer for Peace, Op. 82. (1976)
For: voice(medium) and piano. *Text:* adapted from the poem *With Marie at the Western Wall* by Asenath Petrie. Original version titled With Marie at the Western Wall. *First performed:* Feb. 25, 1979; Belmont, Mass. Sara Hoff, mezzo soprano and Minuetta Kessler, piano.
Score: available from composer.

K2.65 Prelude, Op. 15. (1941) 1'
For: piano.
Score: Musical Resources, 1981.

K2.66 Primary Colors, Op. 50, No. 1. (1960, 1981)

For: piano. *Movements:* The Blue Piece; The Red Piece; The Yellow Piece. Original version titled Two Color Pieces.
Score: Musical Resources, 1981.

[Psalm 2]
K2.67 The Twenty-third Psalm, Op. 46, No. 2. (1958) 2' 30"
For: chorus(SATB) and organ or piano.
Vocal score: reprod. of ms.; available from composer.

Queen of All My Heart. *See* Love's Garland, Op. 14, No.2.

Rote Pieces. *See* Playful Squirrels, Op. 56.

Rustic Dance. *See* Country Scenes, Op. 29.

K2.68 Savory Sweet, Op. 61, No. 2. (1965-80)
For: piano. *Movements:* Caramel; Cinnamon Sticks; Maple Walnut; Raspberry Creme; Brazilnut Kumquat. Originally part of Pieces of Chocolate, Op. 61, No. 1.
Score: Willis, 1980.

K2.69 Scherzetta, Op. 68. (1969)
For: flute, clarinet, violins(2), violoncello, piano. 1 movement. *First performed:* May 7, 1970; Belmont, Mass. Members of the Belmont High School Orchestra.
Score & parts: Musical Resources, 1981.

K2.70 The Secret of Death, Op. 52, No. 5. (1975)
For: Soprano, Bass, piano. *Text:* from *The Prophet* by Kahlil Gibran. *First performed:* Feb. 23, 1975; Belmont, Mass. Susan Stone, soprano; Boris Greisdorf, baritone; Minuetta Kessler, piano.
Score: ms.; available from composer.

K2.71 Shades of Grey, Op. 92. (1978)
For: dancers and piano. *Dedicated to:* Marjie J. Topf. *First performed:* May 4,

1979; Pine Manor College. Marjie Topf, dancer and Minuetta Kessler, piano.
Score: available from composer.

K2.72 Sharples Sonata, Op. 20, No. 1. (1946) 14' 30"
For: piano. 4 movements. *Dedicated to:* Mr. and Mrs. H.H. Sharples of Calgary, Alta., Canada. First performed: June 29, 1949; CBC Trans-Canada Network, Vancouver, B.C., Canada. Minuetta Kessler.
Score: available from composer.

K2.73 Show Me the Way, Op. 69. (1970)
For: Tenor and organ. *Text:* Minuetta Kessler. *Dedicated to:* Eric W. Seder. *First performed:* Apr. 11, 1970; Beth El Temple Center, Belmont, Mass. Cantor Jacob Seully, tenor and unidentified organist.
Score: reprod. of ms.; available from composer.

K2.74 Sonata concertante, Op. 38. (1957; rev. 1974) 18'
For: violin and piano. 3 movements. *Dedicated to:* Marylou Speaker. Original version titled Sonata for Violin and Piano. *First performed:* Jan. 23, 1972; Wheelock College. Marylou Speaker, violin and Minuetta Kessler, piano.
Score & part: Musical Resources, 1974. BPL
Disc: AFKA SK 288, 1979. Marylou Speaker, violin and Minuetta Kessler, piano. L WCRB WGBH
Tape: Mar. 24, 1977; Robbins Library, Arlington, Mass. Priscilla Hallberg, violin and Minuetta Kessler, piano. WCRB

K2.75 Sonata for Clarinet and Piano, Op. 83. (1978) 16' 15"
4 movements. *Dedication:* For my daughter Jean. *First performed:* Feb. 26, 1978; Belmont, Mass. Charles Condello, clarinet and Minuetta Kessler, piano.
Score & part: Musical Resources, 1978.
Disc: AFKA SK 288, 1979. William

Wrzesien, clarinet and Minuetta Kessler, piano. L WCRB WGBH

Sonata for Piano. *See* Bicentennial Sonata, Op. 78.

Sonata for Violin and Piano. *See* Sonata concertante, Op. 38.

[Sonata, Violoncello and Piano]
K2.76 Sonata for Cello and Piano, Op. 54. (1961) 20' 4"
4 movements. *Dedicated to:* Mary Fraley Johnson. Winner of the National Federation of Music Clubs, Northeastern District, American Women Composers Contest, Best Program Award (1975). *First performed:* Nov. 15, 1961; Brookline Public Library. Mary Fraley Johnson, violoncello and Minuetta Kessler, piano.
Score: Musical Resources, 1974. BPL
Tape: recording of first performance. BkPL

Sonatina. *See* Ballet Sonatina, Op. 20, No. 2.

[Songs of Western Canada, Op. 27]
K2.77 Three Songs of Western Canada, Op. 27. (1947) 6' 20"
For: voice(medium) and piano. *Text:* Minuetta Kessler. *Contents:* The Mountains; My Land; The Prairies; The Oesa Waterfall. *First performed:* Feb. 25, 1979; Belmont, Mass. Sara Hoff, mezzo soprano and Minuetta Kessler, piano.
Score: reprod. of ms.
Score: Musical Resources, 1980.

K2.78 Spanish Rhapsody, Op. 89. (1978)
For: piano. *Dedicated to:* Sharon Ostroger.
Score: Musical Resources, 1980.

K2.79 Stand on Guard, Op. 67. (1968) 2' 40"
For: voice(medium) and piano. *Text:* Minuetta Kessler. *Dedicated to:* Chloe Owen. *First performed:* Feb. 26, 1978; Belmont, Mass. Jennifer Patterson,

soprano and Minuetta Kessler, piano.
Score: available from composer.

K2.80 Suite No. 1 Piano, Op. 53. (1959)
14'
For: piano. *Movements:* Prelude;
Minuet; Eccossaise; Intermezzo;
Mazurka; March. *Dedicated to:* Anna
Wolf. *First performed:* Sept. 29, 1959.
Calgary, Alta, Canada. Minuetta Kessler.
Score: Musical Resources, 1961
(movements also available separately).

K2.81 That Precious Blanket, Op. 36.
(1955)
For: voice and piano. *Text:* Minuetta
Kessler. *First performed:* Feb. 23, 1978;
Belmont, Mass. Jennifer Patterson,
soprano and Minuetta Kessler; piano.
Score: reprod. of ms.
Disc: in *Childhood Cameos*; AFKA S
4663, 1981. Jennifer Patterson, soprano
and Minuetta Kessler, piano.

K2.82 This Too Shall Pass, Op. 45.
(1958?) 2' 15"
For: voice and piano. *Text:* Lazarus
Aaronson.
Score: reprod. of ms.; available from
composer.

K2.83 Thou Shalt Love the Lord, Op.
59. (1965)
For: chorus(SATB) and organ or piano.
Text: Bible, O.T., Deuteronomy 6:5-8;
11:20; Bible, O. T. Numbers 15:40.
Vocal score: available from composer.

K2.84 Thought Is a Bird of Space, Op.
52, No. 1. (1961) 22' 52"
For: voices(4), chorus(SATB), piano.
Cantata. *Text:* adapted from *The
Prophet* by Kahlil Gibran. *Contents:* On
Talking; On Joy and Sorrow; On Death.
Written for the Belmont Community
Chorus, John Bavicchi, conductor. *First
performed:* Mar. 27, 1962; Boston
Conservatory. Jeanette Coran, soprano;
Donna Klimoski, alto; Wesley
Copplestone, tenor; Stephen H.
Dimmock, bass; Anne Haugen, piano;
Belmont Community Chorus, John

Bavicchi, conductor.
Vocal score: Musical Resources, 1961.
BPL

K2.85 Through Mothers, Op. 49. (1960)
For: voice and piano. *Text:* Minuetta
Kessler. *Dedication:* To my Mother.
First performed: Feb. 25, 1979;
Belmont, Mass. Sara Hoff, alto and
Minuetta Kessler, piano.
Score: available from composer.
Tape: Mar. 13, 1981; Belmont, Mass.
Leslie Holmes, soprano and Minuetta
Kessler, piano. WCRB

K2.86 Toccata, Op. 64. (1967)
For: piano.
Score: ms. available from composer.

K2.87 The Trees Are Weeping, Op. 81.
(1976)
For: voice(medium) and piano. *Text:*
Susan Brenner. *First performed:* Feb.
25, 1979; Belmont, Mass. Sara Hoff,
mezzo soprano and Minuetta Kessler,
piano.
Score: available from composer.

K2.88 Trilogy, Op. 52. (1963) 14' 32"
For: voice(high) and piano. *Text:* from
The Prophet by Kahlil Gibran. *Contents:*
Of Love; Born Together; Speak to Us
of Children. Winner of the National
Federation of Music Clubs,
Northeastern District, American Women
Composers Contest Best Program
Award (1975). *First performed:* Feb. 24,
1964; Boston Conservatory. Jeanette
Coran, soprano and Minuetta Kessler,
piano.
Score: reprod. of ms.; available from
composer.
Tape: June 13, 1973. Jeanette Coran,
soprano and Minuetta Kessler, piano.
WGBH
Tape: Mar. 24, 1977. Robbins Library,
Arlington, Mass. Susan Stone, soprano
and Minuetta Kessler, piano. WCRB
Tape: Mar. 13, 1981; Belmont Mass.
Leslie Holmes, soprano and Minuetta
Kessler, piano. WCRB

K2.89 Trio No. 1, Op. 39. (1957) 13'
For: violin, violoncello, piano. 3
movements. Winner of Brookline
Library Music Association Composers
Award (1957). Winner of the National
Association of Music Clubs,
Northeastern District, American Women
Composers Award Contest Best
Program Award (1975). *First performed:*
Feb. 12, 1958; Brookline Public Library.
Richard Elias, violin; Judith Rosen,
violoncello; Minuetta Kessler, piano.
Score & parts: Musical Resources, 1957.
BkPL
Tape: May 22, 1975; Robbins Library,
Arlington, Mass. Susan Gottschalk,
violin; Margaret Gonyea Brundage,
violoncello; Minuetta Kessler, piano.
WCRB

K2.90 Twin Almonds, Op. 83, No. 2.
(1977)
For: piano.
Score: available from composer.

K2.91 Variations on a Jewish Lullaby,
Op. 104 (Under der Kinds Veegele).
(1981)
For: flute and harp. *Text:* traditional.
Dedicated to: Donna Hieken and Ruth
Saltzman. *First performed:* Jan. 23,
1981; Providence, R.I. Donna Hieken,
flute and Ruth Saltzman, harp.
Score: Musical Resources, 1981.

K2.92 Victory Hora, Op. 65 (Hora
Nitsachon). (1967) 3'
For: piano. *Dedication:* To the heros
who defended Israel in May 1967. *First
performed:* Jan. 23, 1972; Wheelock
College. Minuetta Kessler.
Score: available from composer.

[Victory Hora; Arr]
K2.93 Victory Hora, Op. 65 (Hora
Nitsachon). (1967)
For: chorus(SATB) and piano. *Text:*
Minuetta Kessler; translated into
Hebrew by Nachum Glatzer. *Dedication:*
To the heros who defended Israel in
May 1967. *First performed:* Apr. 1,
1973; Belmont High School, Belmont,
Mass. Zamir Chorale, Joshua Jacobson,

conductor; Minuetta Kessler, piano.
Vocal score: Transcontinental, 1967.

K2.94 V'Ohavto, Op. 37, No. 3 (Thou
Shalt Love the Lord) . (1956) 3'
For: voice(high) and organ. *Text:*
adapted from Bible, O.T., Deuteronomy
6:5-8; 10:20; Bible, O.T., Numbers 15:40.
Score: reprod. of ms.; available from
composer.

With Marie at the Western Wall. *See* A
Prayer for Peace, Op. 82.

K2.95 With Minuetta Kessler in
Musicland, Op. 44. (1958)
For: voice and piano. *Text:* Minuetta
Kessler. *Contents:* Music; A Cup of
Music Tea; The Wedding Ring. *First
performed:* Feb. 26, 1978; Belmont,
Mass. Jennifer Patterson, soprano and
Minuetta Kessler, piano.
Score: available from composer.
Tape: Mar. 13, 1981; Belmont, Mass.
Leslie Holmes, soprano and Minuetta
Kessler, piano. WCRB

A World Passed by. *See* Memories of
Tevye.

K2.96 You Are My Lucky Four-Leaf
Clover, Op. 14, No. 1. (1940)
For: voice and piano. *Text:* Morris C.
Shumiatcher.
Score: Musical Resources, 1981.

K3 EARL KIM

Born January 6, 1920, in Dinuba, Calif.
Moved to Boston area 1967. *Education:*
studied composition with Arnold
Schoenberg (University of California,
Los Angeles, 1940-41); Ernest Bloch,
Roger Sessions (University of
California, Berkeley, 1947-52). *Awards:*
Brandeis University, Creative Arts
Award, George Ladd Prix de Paris
(University of California, Berkeley),
Guggenheim Grant, Ingram-Merrill Grant
in Composition, Koussevitzky Music
Foundation (Library of Congress)
commission, Massachusetts Council on
the Arts and Humanities Artist

Fellowship Program in composition, National Institute of Arts and Letters Award, Naumburg Chamber Music Award. *Related activities:* pianist; conductor; composer-in-residence, Berkshire, Marlboro and Dartmouth music festivals and the Seminar for Advanced Studies in Music (Princeton University); served on the faculties of Princeton University (1952-67) and Harvard University (James Edward Ditson Professor of Music, 1967-). HU

WORKS

[Bagatelles]
K3.1 Two Bagatelles. (1948-50) 5'
For: piano. 2 movements. *First performed:* 1951; Berkeley, Calif. Bernhard Abramowitsch, piano.
Score: in *New Music for the Piano*, Lawson-Gould, 1954.
Score: British and Continental, 1967.
Disc: in *New Music for the Piano*, RCA LM/LSC 7042, 1966. Robert Helps. HU NEC NU W
Disc: Composers Recordings CRI SD288, 1972 (reissue of RCA Victor LM/LSC 7042, 1966). BCM BU HU MIT NEC W
Cassette: Nov. 22, 1976; New England Conservatory. Russell Sherman. NEC

K3.2 Caprices. (1980) 13'
For: violin. *Commissioned by:* National Endowment for the Arts.
Score: Composers Collaborative.

[Concerto, Violin]
K3.3 Violin Concerto. (1979) 22'
For: violin and orchestra(3(pic)-2-2(bcl)-2; 3-3-3-0; perc; hp, cel; str). 1 movement.
Commissioned by: National Endowment for the Arts. *Dedicated to:* Itzhak Perlman. *First performed:* 1979. Itzhak Perlman, violin; New York Philharmonic, Zubin Mehta, conductor.
Score & parts: Composers Collaborative, 1979. Rental.

Dead Calm. *See* Exercises en Route. Dead Calm.

K3.4 Dialogues. (1959) 12'
For: piano and orchestra(2-2-2-2; 2-2-2-0; perc; str). 1 movement. *First performed:* 1959; Princeton, N.J. Earl Kim, piano; Princeton Symphony, Nicholas Harsanyi, conductor.
Score & parts: Composers Collaborative. Rental.

Duet. *See* Narratives. Duet.

Earthlight. *See* Narratives. Earthlight.

Eh Joe. *See* Narratives. Eh Joe.

K3.5 Exercises en Route. 29' 18"
For: Soprano, flute/piccolo, oboe, clarinet, percussion(2), violin, violoncello. Stage work. *Text:* Samuel Beckett. *Contents:* Dead Calm; Gooseberries, She Said, Rattling On; They Are Far Out. These pieces may be performed together or separately.
Score & parts: Composers Collaborative. Rental.
Reel: 1969; Cambridge, Mass; in *A Rehearsal of 'Exercises en Route'* (work in progress).... Bethany Beardslee, soprano; Earl Kim, conductor. HU

[Exercises en Route. Dead Calm]
K3.6 Dead Calm. (1961?) 6'
For: Soprano, piccolo, oboe, clarinet, percussion(2), violin, violoncello. *Text:* Addenda No. 1 from *Watt* by Samuel Beckett. *First performed:* 1969; Princeton, N.J. Bethany Beardslee, soprano, and others.
Score & parts: Composers Collaborative. Rental.

[Exercises en Route. Gooseberries, She Said]
K3.7 Gooseberries, She Said. (1965?) 6'
For: Soprano, flute, oboe, clarinet, percussion, violoncello. *First performed:* 1973; Brandeis University. Benita Valente, soprano, and others.

Score & parts: Composers
Collaborative. Rental.

[Exercises en Route. Rattling On]
K3.8 Rattling On. (1967?) 11′ 18″
For: Soprano, flute, oboe, clarinet,
percussion, violin, violoncello. *First
performed:* 1971; Sanders Theatre,
Harvard University. Benita Valente,
soprano, and others.
Score & parts: Composers
Collaborative. Rental.

[Exercises en Route. They Are Far
Out]
K3.9 They Are Far Out. (1963?) 6′
For: Soprano, percussion(2), violin,
violoncello.
Score & parts: Composers
Collaborative. Rental.

K3.10 Footfalls. (in progress) 22′
For: voices(female)(2) and chamber
orchestra. Opera in 1 act. *Text:
Footfalls* by Samuel Beckett.

Gooseberries, She Said. *See* Exercises
en Route. Gooseberries, She Said.

K3.11 Letters Found near a Suicide.
(1954) 6′
For: voice(high to medium) and piano.
Text: by Frank S. Horne from *The
Poetry of the Negro* edited by Langston
Hughes and Arna Bontemps. *Contents:*
To All of You; To Wanda; To Tellie.
First performed: 1954. Bethany
Beardslee, soprano and Earl Kim, piano.
Score: in *New Vistas in Song*, E.B.
Marks, 1964. HU W
Score: British and Continental Music
Agencies, 1967.
Cassette: May 5, 1971; New England
Conservatory; in *A Festival of New
England Composers Past and Present.*
Jean Hakes, soprano and Robert Helps,
piano. NEC

Lines. *See* Narratives. Lines.

Melodrama. *See* Narratives. Melodrama.

Monologues. *See* Narratives.
Monologues.

K3.12 Narratives. (1973-78) 73′ 30″
For: actress/speaker(female), actor,
soprano(high), trumpets(2),
trombone(alto), piano, violins(2),
violoncellos(2), television, lights.
Text: from *Happy Days, Lessness,
Enough, Act Without Words 1* by
Samuel Beckett. *Contents:* Monologues;
Melodrama 1; Eh Joe; Melodrama 2;
Duet; Earthlight. *First performed:* 1979;
Loeb Drama Center, Cambridge, Mass.
Irene Worth, actress; Jane Bryden,
soprano; Ariel Chamber Ensemble,
Martha Potter, music director.

[Narratives. Duet]
K3.13 Duet. (1978) 6′
For: trombone(alto) and violoncello.
Text: from *Act Without Words* by
Samuel Beckett.

[Narratives. Earthlight]
K3.14 Earthlight. (1973) 15′ 3″
For: Soprano(high), piano, violin(con
sordino), lights(3 light boxes with 3
operators). *Text:* from several works by
Samuel Beckett. *Commissioned by:*
Koussevitzky Music Foundation (Library
of Congress). *Dedicated to:* The
Memory of Serge and Natalie
Koussevitzky. *First performed:* 1973;
Sanders Theatre, Harvard University.
Merja Sargon, soprano; Earl Kim, piano;
Martha Potter, violin.
Score: Mobart, 1978. HU MIT NEC T
Parts: Mobart, 1978.
Mutes and light boxes: available from
composer. Rental.
Disc: New World Records NW 237,
1977. Merja Sargon, soprano; Earl Kim,
piano; Martha Potter, violin. BCM BU
HU HUm MIT NEC T W

[Narratives. Eh Joe]
K3.15 Eh Joe. (1974)
For: speaker(female), actor, trumpets(2),
trombone, violins(2), violoncellos(2),
television camera, screen(9x12),
projection equipment. A television play.

Actors are televised on a large screen.
Supported by a grant from the
National Endowment for the Arts. *First
performed:* 1975; Sanders Theatre,
Harvard University. Lois Smith, actress,
and others.
Score & parts: Mobart.
Score & parts: Composers
Collaborative.

[Narratives. Lines]
K3.16 Lines. (1978) 8'
For: Soprano(high). *Text:* from *Lessness*
by Samuel Beckett.
Score: Composers Collaborative.

[Narratives. Melodrama 1]
K3.17 Melodrama 1. (1974) 6'
For: voice(woman) and piano. *Text:*
from *Happy Days* by Samuel Beckett.
Score: Composers Collaborative.

[Narratives. Melodrama 2]
K3.18 Melodrama 2. (1977) 10'
For: speaker(female), violins(2), piano.
Score: Composers Collaborative.

[Narratives. Monologues]
K3.19 Monologues. (1976) 12'
For: piano, violin, violoncello.
Commissioned by: Naumburg Foundation
for the Francesco Trio. Winner of
Naumburg Chamber Music Award. *First
performed:* 1977; Library of Congress,
Washington, D.C. Francesco Trio.
Score: Composers Collaborative.

Rattling On. *See* Exercises en Route.
Rattling On.

K3.20 The Road.
For: Baritone and piano. Song cycle.
Withrawn.

K3.21 Sonata, Violin and Piano.
Withdrawn.

K3.22 Sonata, Violoncello and Piano.
Withdrawn.

They Are Far Out. *See* Exercises en
Route. They Are Far Out.

K4 LEON KIRCHNER

Born January 24, 1919, in New York
City. Moved to Boston area 1961.
Education: studied composition with
Arnold Schoenberg (University of
California, Los Angeles, B.A., 1940),
Roger Sessions, Ernest Bloch
(University of California, Berkeley).
Awards: M.A. (Hon.), D.M. (Hon.), George
Ladd Prix de Paris (University of
California, Berkeley, 1942), Guggenheim
Grants (1948, 1949), New York Music
Critics Circle Award (1949, 1959),
National Institute of Arts and Letters
Award (1950), Naumburg Foundation
Award, Naumburg Recording Award,
Naumburg Chamber Music Award,
Koussevitzky International Award for
Best Composition (1958), American
Academy of Arts and Sciences
(member, 1962), National Institute of
Arts and Letters (member, 1962),
Pulitzer Prize in Music (1967), Center
for Advanced Study in the Behavioral
Sciences Fellowship (1974), National
Music Award (1976), Brandeis
University, Creative Arts Award (1977),
Walter Channing Cabot Fellow (Harvard
University, 1978). *Related activities:*
pianist; conductor; guest conductor or
soloist with the orchestras of New
York, San Francisco, Pittsburgh,
Minneapolis, Philadelphia, Boston,
Buffao, and others;
composer-in-residence, American
Academy in Rome (1973); soloist and
composer-in-residence at the Aspen,
Berkshire, Marlboro music festivals and
at many colleges and universities;
composer/performer on television
channels NBC, CBS, and NET, New
York City; served on the faculties of
the University of California, Berkeley
(1946-48), University of Southern
California (1950-54), Mills College
(1954-61), Harvard University (1961- ;
Walter Bigelow Rosen Professer, Jan.
1, 1966-); director of the Harvard
Chamber Players (1973-) and the
Harvard Chamber Orchestra (1978-). HU

WORKS

[Concerto, Piano, No. 1]
K4.1 Piano Concerto No. 1. (1953)
25'-30'
For: piano and orchestra(3-3-3-3;
4-3-3-1; timp, perc; cel; str). 3
movements. Winner of Naumburg
Recording Award. *Commissioned by:*
UNESCO and the Koussevitzky Music
Foundation (Library of Congress). *First
performed:* Feb. 23, 1956; New York
City. Leon Kirchner, piano; New York
Philharmonic, Dimitri Mitropoulos,
conductor.
Score: Associated, 1978. HU
Score & parts: Associated. Rental.
Disc: Columbia ML 5185, 1957. Leon
Kirchner, piano; New York Philharmonic,
Dimitri Mitropoulos, conductor. BrU BU
HU HUm MIT NEC T W
Disc: New World NW 286, 1977.
Re-issue of Columbia ML 5185, 1957.
BCM BrU BU HU HUm MIT NEC T W

[Concerto, Piano, No. 2]
K4.2 Piano Concerto No. 2. (1963) 30'
For: piano and orchesta(2(&pic)-2(&Ehn)
-2(&bcl)-2(&cbsn); 4-3-3-1; timp, perc(5),
glock, xylo; str). 2 movements.
Commissioned by: Leon Fleisher through
the Ford Foundation. *Dedicated to:* Leon
Fleisher. *First performed:* Oct. 28, 1963;
Seattle, Wash. Leon Fleisher, piano;
Seattle Philharmonic Orchestra, Leon
Kirchner, conductor.
Score: Associated, 1967. BPL BrU HU
HUm MIT NEC NU UMB
Parts: Associated. Rental.
Reel: Oct. 1963; Seattle, Washington.
Leon Fleisher, piano; Seattle
Philharmonic Orchestra, Leon Kirchner,
conductor. HU
Reel: Mar. 8, 1968; Harvard University.
Luise Vosgerchian, piano;
Harvard-Radcliffe Orchestra, Leon
Kirchner, conductor. HU

[Concerto, Violin, Violoncello, Wind
Ensemble, Percussion]
K4.3 Concerto. (1960) 18' 20"
For: violin, violoncello, wind
ensemble(flute/piccolo, oboe, clarinet,

bassoon, contrabassoon, horn,
trumpets(2), trombones(2)), percussion
(timpani, glockenspiel, xylophone,
celeste). 2 movements. *Commissioned
by:* Chamber Music Society of
Baltimore. *First performed:* 1960;
Baltimore, Md. Robert Gerle,
violoncello and others; Leon Kirchner,
conductor.
Score: Associated, 1962. BPL BrU HU
UMB
Score: ms. (pp.4-5 in composer's hand).
HUh
Parts: Associated. Rental.
Disc: Epic BC 1157/LC 3830, 1962.
Tossy Spivakovsky, violin; Aldo
Parisot, violoncello; Leon Kirchner,
conductor. BCM BU HU HUm NEC W
Reel: Marlboro, Vt.

K4.4 Dawn. (1943-46) 8'
For: chorus and organ. *Text:* Federico
Garcia Lorca. *First performed:* 1946;
Berkeley, Calif. Leon Kirchner,
conductor.

K4.5 Duo, Violin and Piano. (1947) 9'
40"
First performed: 1947; Berkeley, Calif.
Miriam Zunser, violin and Leon
Kirchner, piano.
Score: Mercury, 1950. BPL HU
Disc: Medea MCLP 1002, [196-]
Daniel Kobialka, violin and Myron
Press, piano. BU HU NEC
Reel: n.d.; Berklee College of Music.
Daniel Kobialka, violin and Myron
Press, piano. Be

K4.6 Fanfare for Brass Trio. (1965) 2'
For: trumpets(2) and horn. 1 movement.
First performed: 1965; Marlboro, Vt.;
Marlboro Music Festival.
Score & parts: Associated, 1974. BPL
HU NEC T
Reel: Oct. 25, 1979; Boston University;
in *Omnibus: Music of the Twentieth
Century, Concert I.* Julia Cohen and
Steven Matera, trumpets; Mark
Knowles, horn. BU.

Flutings. *See* Lily. Flutings.

Henderson. *See* Lily.

K4.7 Letter. (1943)
For: Soprano and piano. *Text:* S.
Alexander. *First performed:* 1946;
Berkeley, Calif.

K4.8 Lily. (1973-76) 90'
For: Sopranos(2), Mezzo Sopranos(2),
Tenor, Bass Baritones(2), orchestra
(2(&pic)-2(&Ehn)-2(&bcl)-2(&cbsn);
4-3-3-1; timp, perc(3), vibra; pf/cel; str),
projections; tape. Opera. *Text:* Leon
Kirchner, adapted from *Henderson, the
Rain King* by Saul Bellow.
Self-contained segment of larger
theatrical work titled Henderson.
Commissioned by: Fromm Foundation
and New York State Opera. *First
performed:* Apr. 14, 1977; New York
City. New York City Opera, Leon
Kirchner, conductor.
Score & parts: Associated. Rental.
Vocal score: Associated, 1978-79.

[Lily. Selections]
K4.9 Lily. (1973) 22' 29"
For: Soprano, tape, instrumental
ensemble(flute, oboe, clarinet, bassoon,
horn, percussion, piano/celeste,
violins(2), viola). Chamber version of
the opera.
Disc: Columbia M 32740, 1974. Diana
Hoagland, soprano; Columbia Chamber
Soloists, Leon Kirchner, conductor. BU
HU MIT NEC W

[Lily. Flutings]
K4.10 Flutings.
For: flute and percussion(optional).
First performed: Marlboro Vt.; Marlboro
Music Festival. Paula Robison, flute.
Score & part: Associated, 1980.
Cassette: Oct. 22, 1979; New England
Conservatory; in *Contemporary American
Music for the Flute.* John Heiss, flute
and Frank Epstein, percussion. NEC

K4.11 Little Suite. (1949)
For: piano. *Movements:* Prelude; Song;
Toccata; Fantasy; Epilogue. *Dedication:*
For Gertrude.

Score: Mercury, 1950. BrU HU NEC
Cassette: Nov. 11, 1981; New England
Conservatory. Eliane Lust. NEC

K4.12 Music for Orchestra. (1969) 13'
For: orchestra(2(&pic)-2(&Ehn)
-2(&bcl)-2(&cbsn); 4-3-3-1; timp,
perc(4-5), glock, vibra, xylo; pf/cel; str).
Commissioned by: New York
Philharmonic in celebration of its 125th
anniversary. *First performed:* Oct. 16,
1969; New York City. New York
Philharmonic, Leon Kirchner, conductor.
Study score: Associated, 1970. BrU
HMA HU MIT NEC T W
Parts: Associated. Rental.
Reel: Symphony Hall, Boston.

K4.13 Of Obedience. (1950)
For: Soprano and piano. *Text:* Walt
Whitman. *First performed:* 1950; Los
Angeles, Calif.

K4.14 Piece. (1946)
For: piano and orchestra.

[Quartet, Strings, No. 1]
K4.15 String QuartetNo. 1. (1949) 20'
19"
4 movements. *Dedicated to:* Roger
Sessions. Winner of New York Music
Critics Circle Award. *First performed:*
Mar. 1950; New York City.
Score: Mercury, 1950. BPL BrU BU HU
Disc: Columbia ML 4843, 1955.
American Art Quartet. BCM BrU BU HU
HUm MIT W
Disc: Columbia Special Products AML
4843, 1974. Reissue of Columbia ML
4843. T
Disc: Composers Recordings CRI SRD
395, 1978. Reissue of Columbia ML
4843. BrU BU HU MIT NEC T W

[Quartet, Strings, No.2]
K4.16 String Quartet No. 2. (1958) 19'
3 movements. *Commissioned by:*
University of Michigan for the Stanley
Quartet. Winner of New York Music
Critics Circle Award.
Study score: Associated, 1963. Be BPL
HU HUm MIT UMB

Parts: Associated, 1963. HU NEC
Disc: Columbia M 32740, 1974. Lenox
Quartet. BU HU MIT NEC W

[Quartet, Strings, No. 3]
K4.17 Quartet No. 3. (1967) 16′ 28″
For: string quartet and tape. 1
movement. Winner of the Pulitzer Prize
in Music (1967). *Commissioned by:*
Beaux Arts Quartet under a Naumburg
Foundation grant. *First performed:* Jan.
27, 1967; New York City. Beaux Arts
Quartet.
Score: Associated, 1971. BCM BPL BrU
HU MIT NEC W
Disc: Columbia MS 7284, 1970. Beaux
Arts Quartet. BrU BU HU HUm NEC W
Disc: in *The Avant Garde String Quartet
in the U.S.A.,* Vox SVBX 5306, 1973.
Concord String Quartet. BCM BU HU
MIT NEC W
Reel: Nov. 23, 1976; Museum of Fine
Arts, Boston. Collage. WGBH
Reel: Nov. 1969; Cambridge, Mass.
Beaux Arts Quartet. HU

K4.18 The Runner. (1950)
For: Soprano and piano. *Text:* Walt
Whitman. *First performed:* 1950; Los
Angeles, Calif.

K4.19 Sinfonia. (1951) 19′
For: orchestra(2(&pic)-2(&Ehn)
-2(&bcl)-2(&cbsn); 4-3-3-1; tam-tam; hp,
pf, cel; str). 2 movements.
Commissioned by: Richard Rodgers and
Oscar Hammerstein, II for the League
of Composers. Winner of Naumburg
Foundation Award (1951). *First
performed:* Jan. 1952; New York City.
Study score: Mercury, 1955. BPL BrU HU
UMB
Reel: Symphony Hall, Boston.

K4.20 Sonata concertante. (1952) 19′
For: violin and piano. 1 movement.
Commissioned by: Fromm Foundation.
First performed: Nov. 30, 1952; New
York City. Tossy Spivakovsky, violin
and Leon Kirchner, piano.
Score: Mercury, 1955. HU
Disc: Epic LC 3306, 1956. Eudice
Shapiro, violin and Leon Kirchner,

piano. BU HU HUm
Disc: Desto DC 7151, 1973. Jaime
Laredo, violin and Ruth Laredo, piano.
BU HU
Reel: Jan. 24, 1978; WGBH-FM, Boston.
Syoko Aki, violin and Lisa Goldman
WGBH

[Sonata, Piano]
K4.21 Piano Sonata. (1948; rev. 1960)
15′ 37″; 16′ 30″
3 movements. *Dedicated to:* Edward
Steuermann. *First performed:* Mar.
1949; New York City.
Score: Bomart, 1950. BPL BrU MIT
Score: Bomart, 1961. BPL HU T
Disc: Educo Records 3081 (1960
version). BU
Disc: Epic BC 1262/LC 3862, 1962. Leon
Fleisher. HU
Disc: Composers Recordings CRI SD
461, 1981. Robert Taub. BrU MIT W
Reel: Nov. 28, 1962; Brookline Public
Library. BkPL
Reel: Oct. 20, 1976; Boston University.
Nanette Kaplan. BU
Reel: Jan. 24, 1978; WGBH-FM, Boston;
in *Leon Kirchner and Friends.* Lisa
Goldman. WGBH.

K4.22 The Times Are Nightfall. (1943)
For: Soprano and piano. *Text:* Gerard
Manley Hopkins. *First performed:* 1946;
Berkeley, Calif.

K4.23 Toccata. (1955; rev.) 14′
For: orchestra(1-1-1-0; 1-1-1-0; perc,
xylo; cel; str). 1 movement.
Commissioned by: Enrique Jorda.
Dedicated to: Milton Feist. *First
performed:* Feb. 16, 1956; San
Francisco, Calif.
Study score: Associated, 1962 (rev.
version). Be BPL BrU HU MIT NEC UMB
Parts: Associated. Rental.
Disc: Louisville Orchestra LS 683, 1968.
Louisville Orchestra, Jorge Mester,
conductor. BCM BrU BU HU HUm MIT
NEC W

K4.24 Trio. (1954) 15′
For: violin, violoncello, piano. 2
movements. *Commissioned by:* Elizabeth

Sprague Coolidge Foundation (Library of Congress) for the 50th anniversary of the Coleman Chamber Series of Pasadena, Calif. First performed: Nov. 1954; Pasadena, Calif. Henri Temianka, violin; Lucien Laporte, violoncello; Leon Kirchner, piano.
Score: ms. HU
Score & parts: Associated, 1964. BPL BrU HU HUm MIT NEC
Disc: Epic LC 3306, 1956. Nathan Rubin, violin; George Neikrug, violoncello; Leon Kirchner, piano. BU HU HUm

K4.25 Words from Wordsworth. (1968)
For: chorus(mixed). 1 movement.
Dedicated to: G. Wallace Woodworth.
Vocal score: Associated, 1968. BPL
Vocal score: in *The AMP Contemporary Choral Collection for Mixed Chorus Associated, 1969. HU* W
Vocal score: in *Words and Music: The Composer's View,* Harvard University Department of Music, 1972. BPL HU MIT NEC W

K5 SHIRISH KORDE

Born 1945. Moved to Boston area 1965. *Education:* studied composition with Herb Pomeroy (Berklee College of Music, B.M., 1969), Robert Cogan (New England Conservatory, M.M., 1971), Ron Nelson (Brown University, 1973-74); saxophone and flute with Joseph Viola; flute with Nicholas Caiazza and Charlie Mariano; conducting with Jeronimas Kacinskas; doctoral candidate in American music and composition (Brown University, 1973-76). *Awards:* Uganda Ministry of Education Fellowship (1965-69), University of East Africa and Uganda Museum Research Fellowship (1971), Carnegie Mellon Foundation Research Grant (1977), Fuller Foundation Tri-College Electronic Music Grant (1977), College of the Holy Cross, Research Grants (1977-80), National Endowment for the Humanities Grant (1978), Massachusetts Council on the Arts and Humanities, Artist Fellowship in Composition (1979), New

York State Council on the Arts Meet the Composer Grant (1980). *Related activities:* conductor, flutist, saxophonist, lecturer; artist-in-residence, Groton Center for the Arts; currently editor of *Sonus;* member of the faculties of the College of the Holy Cross (1976-) and New England Conservatory of Music (1980-). NEC

WORKS

K5.1 Chants of Time. (1977) 17'
For: Soprano, flute, clarinet, violin, viola, guitar, percussion.
Music: ms.

[Concerto, Instrumental Ensemble]
K5.2 Chamber Concerto. (1980) 12'
For: instruments(10). *Commissioned by:* Barbara Kolb for Music New to New York Series. *First performed:* Feb. 1980; New York City. Music New to New York Series, Bruce Hangen, director.
Disc: Spectrum Records, nyp.

K5.3 Constellations for Saxophone Quartet. (1974) 9' 30"
For: saxophone(soprano), saxophone(alto), saxophone(tenor), saxophone(baritone). 1 movement.
Commissioned by: Boston Saxophone Quartet. *Dedication:* For Sanjit. *First performed:* 1975; Brown University; Nineteen Mile Festival of Contemporary Music. Boston Saxophone Quartet.
Score: Dorn, 1979. NEC
Disc: in *New Events: Boston Composers of the '70s,* Spectrum SR 128, 1980. Boston Saxophone Quartet. NEC
Cassette: Nov. 15, 1978; New England Conservatory. Robert Patton, soprano saxophone; Donald Bodio, alto saxophone; Richard Hermann, tenor saxophone; William Perlich, baritone saxophone. NEC

K5.4 Constellations for Wind Ensemble. (1979) 9' 30"
Music: ms.

K5.5 Hexachords for Solo Flute.
First performed: 1970; New England
Conservatory.

K5.6 Hexachords for Violin. (1970) 7'
Music: ms.

K5.7 In Memoriam--John Coltrane.
(1972) 10'
For: jazz orchestra. *First performed:*
1976; Berklee College of Music. Berklee
Faculty Concert Jazz Orchestra.
Music: ms.

K5.8 Mirrors, Canons and Inventions.
(1972) 14'
For: flute, clarinet, harp, percussion.
First performed: Apr. 1972; Boston
University. Boston University Collegium
in Contemporary Music Ensemble.
Music: ms.

K5.9 Mosaics. (1968) 12'
For: orchestra. 1 movement.
Music: ms.

[Pieces]
K5.10 Five Pieces. (1967) 14' 30"
For: piano. *First performed:* Mar. 1971;
New England Conservatory. Anthony
Rauche.
Music: ms.

K5.11 Prelude, Canon and Fugue. (1967)
9'
For: string quartet. 3 movements.
Music: ms.

K5.12 Prisms. (1972) 14'
For: instrumental groups(5).
Music: ms.

[Quartet, Strings, No. 1]
K5.13 String Quartet No. 1. (1969) 8'
2 movements. *First performed:* Dec.
1970; Brookline Public Library. Boston
Conservatory String Quartet.
Music: ms.

[Quartet, Strings, No. 2]
K5.14 String Quartet No. 2. (1980) 19'

3 movements. *Commissioned by:* Groton
Center for the Arts Resident String
Quartet. *First performed:* June 1980;
Groton Center for the Arts. Groton
Center for the Arts Resident String
Quartet.
Music: ms.

[Sketches]
K5.15 Three Sketches. (1971) 12'
For: woodwind quintet. *First performed:*
Apr. 1971; Museum of Fine Arts,
Boston. NEC Scholarship Woodwind
Quintet.
Score & parts: Dorn, 1981.

K5.16 Solo. (in progress)
For: clarinet(bass) and tape(computer).
Commissioned by: Kenneth Radnofsky.

[Sonata, Violin and Piano, No. 1]
K5.17 Sonata. (1967) 22'
3 movements. *First performed:* 1969;
Berklee College of Music; New Music
Series. John Boykan, violin and
Elizabeth Courtney, piano.
Music: ms.
Reel: May 1, 1969; Berklee College of
Music. Boden Boika, violin and Denise
Gerolimatos, piano. Be

[Sonata, Violin and Piano, No. 2]
K5.18 Violin Sonata No. 2. (1968) 19'
3 movements. *First performed:* Mar.
1974; Queens College of the City
University of New York. Andrew
Gottlieb, violin and unidentified pianist.
Music: ms.

K5.19 Spaces-Circles-Prisms.
First performed: 1979.

[Spectra, Brasses and Tape]
K5.20 Spectra. (1973) 12'
Music: ms.

[Spectra, Trombone and Tape]
K5.21 Spectra. (1973) 12'
Commissioned by: Tom Plsek. *First
performed:* May 1974; Berklee College

of Music; International Trombone Association Concerts. Tom Plsek.

K5.22 Tape Study. (1975) 3'
For: tape.
Music: ms.

K5.23 Tape Study No. 2. (1978) 7' 30"
For: tape. *First performed:* Nov. 1978; Clark University.
Music: ms.

［Work, Orchestra］
K5.24 Work for Symphonic Orchestra. (in progress)
Commissioned by: Indian Hill Chamber Orchestra.

［Work, Pianos(2) and Percussion(2)］
K5.25 Work for 2 Pianos and 2 Percussionists. (in progress)
Commissioned by: Suzanna Waldbauer and Ivan Waldbauer.

［Work, Saxophone and Piano］
K5.26 Work for Saxophone and Piano. (in progress)
Commissioned by: Phil I. Delibro.

L1 JOHN LA PORTA

Education: B.M., M.M. (Manhattan School of Music, 1956, 1957); studied composition with Ernst Toch and Alexei Haieff; clarinet with Herman Pade, William Dietrich, Joseph Gigiotti, Leo Russianhoff; flute with Robert Morris; jazz improvisation with Lennie Tristano. *Awards:* ASCAP Awards (Pop) (1966-82). *Related activities:* teacher of clarinet, saxophone, theory, composition, improvisation (1948-); member of All American Youth Orchestra; performed with and arranged for Bob Chester, Woody Herman, Charlie Mingus, Herb Pomeroy; musical director of the Composers' Workshop (1952-54) and the Jazz Foundation of America; co-founder of the National Association of Jazz Educators; Assistant Music Director, Newport Youth Band and Newport International

Youth Band; Director, Boston Youth Band (1964-65); member of the Berklee Faculty Saxophone Quartet; author of *Developing Sight Reading Skills* (1967), *Developing the School Jazz Ensemble* (1968), *A Guide to Improvisation* (1968), *A Guide to Jazz Phrasing and Interpretation* (1972), *Ear Training Phase 1* (1973), *Tonal Organization of Improvisational Techniques* (1977), *Jazz Ear Training* (1980); member of the faculties of the National Stage Band Clinics (1958-), Manhattan School of Music, Berklee College of Music (1962-). Be

WORKS

L1.1 Absentee. 4' 57"
For: saxophone(alto)/clarinet, piano, double bass, drums. Jazz quartet.
Music: Circle, 1956.
Disc: in *Conceptions*, Fantasy 3-228, 1957. John La Porta, alto saxophone/clarinet; Wally Cirillo, piano; Wendell Marshall, double bass; Clem de Rosa, drums.

L1.2 Advance.
For: jazz band. *Commissioned by:* Long Island Jazz Foundation.
Score & parts: Berklee, 1965.

L1.3 Adventures in Time, Opus One.
For: jazz group.
Reel: Jan. 11, 1972; Berklee College of Music. Berklee Jazz Percussion Ensemble. Be

L1.4 The Aging Process.
For: instruments(unspecified)(2). Jazz duo.
Score: in his *14 Jazz-Rock Duets*, Kendor, 1981.

L1.5 AHTYAH. (1978)
For: instruments(unspecified)(2). Jazz duo.

L1.6 Andalusian Reflections. (1967) 3' 55"
For: saxophone(soprano),

saxophone(alto), saxophone(tenor), saxophone(baritone). Jazz quartet.

L1.7 Another Round of Blues. (1972) 4' 25"
For: jazz band.

L1.8 At Peace.
For: jazz band.
Score & parts: Berklee, 1962.

L1.9 Augmentation. (1955)
For: instruments(unspecified)(2). Jazz duo.

L1.10 Baby Gnu. 4' 15"
For: trumpet, trombone, saxophone(alto), saxophone(tenor), saxophone (baritone), piano, guitar, double bass, drums. Jazz nonet.

L1.11 Barton Bag. (1968) 8' 10"
For: jazz band. *First performed:* 1968; National Summer Jazz Camps.

L1.12 Bas Relief. (1979) 5'
For: jazz band. Written for the Herb Pomeroy Orchestra.

L1.13 Bird in Hand.
For: instruments(unspecified)(2). Jazz duo.
Score: in his *14 Jazz-Rock Duets*, Kendor, 1981.

L1.14 Bird in Retrospect. (1979) 7'
For: jazz band. Written for the Herb Pomeroy Orchestra. *Dedicated to:* Charlie Parker.

Bird's World. *See* Moods, Jazz Quartet.

L1.15 Blue. (1953) 4' 12"
For: trumpet, trombone, saxophone(alto)/clarinet, saxophone(tenor), saxophone(baritone), piano, double bass, drums. Jazz octet.

L1.16 Blue Tail. 6' 22"
For: trumpet, trombone, saxophone(alto), saxophone(tenor), saxophone (baritone), piano, guitar, double bass, drums. Jazz nonet.

Disc: in *Eight Men in Search of a Drummer*, Music Minus One, 1960.

L1.17 Blues Backstage. 5'
For: jazz band.
Disc: Century, 1961 (Stan Kenton Clinic at Southern Methodist University).

L1.18 Blues Chorale.
For: jazz band.
Score: Berklee. Be
Score & parts: Colin, 1957.
Disc: in *Sound of the Guitar*, Roost (S) 2246, 1961. Johnny Smith, guitar.

L1.19 Blues in D. (1968) 4' 10"
For: trumpet, saxophone(tenor)/clarinet, piano, double bass, drums. Jazz quintet.

L1.20 Blues Part Time. (1980) 4' 25"
For: trumpet, saxophone(tenor)/clarinet, piano, double bass, drums. Jazz quintet.

L1.21 Blues-Way Up. (1961) 4' 25"
For: trumpet, saxophone(tenor)/clarinet, piano, double bass, drums. Jazz quintet.

L1.22 Boomerang. (1979) 4' 25"
For: trumpet, saxophone(tenor)/clarinet, piano, double bass, drums. Jazz quintet.

L1.23 Boston Bound.
For: jazz band.
Score & parts: Berklee, 1962.

L1.24 Brief Encounter. (1978)
For: instruments(unspecified)(2). Jazz duo.

L1.25 Bright Blues in G. (1969) 4' 30"
For: trumpet, saxophone(tenor)/clarinet, piano, double bass, drums. Jazz quintet.

L1.26 Bright Journey.
For: jazz band. Written for the National Summer Jazz Clinics.
Music: Kendor, 1966.
Score & parts: Berklee, 1967.

L1.27 Bright Spot. (1957) 5'
For: saxophone(alto) and jazz ensemble(strings, harp, oboe, piano, double bass, drums). Written for Charlie Parker.

Bright Yellow. *See* Series II.

Bright-Eyed Blue. *See* Moods, Jazz Quartet.

L1.28 The Brighter Side. (1955)
For: instruments(unspecified)(2). Jazz duo.

L1.29 Buzzin'. 3' 46"
For: saxophone(alto), piano, double bass, drums. Jazz quartet.
Music: Earl Music, 1958.
Disc: in *The Most Minor*, Everest DBR 5037, SDBR 1037, 1959. John La Porta, alto saxophone; Jack Reilly, piano; Richard Carter, double bass; Charles Perry, drums.

L1.30 The C. T. Calypso.
For: jazz band.
Reel: July 13, 1978; Berklee College of Music. Breather Brothers Band. Be

Call It What You Will. *See* Series III.

L1.31 Cape Ann Tri-Umvirate. (1977) 5' 45"
For: flugelhorn, saxophone(alto), trumpet, jazz band. Written for the Herb Pomeroy Orchestra.

L1.32 Caprice. (1966) 4' 15"
For: saxophone(soprano), saxophone(alto), saxophone(tenor), saxophone(baritone). Jazz quartet.

L1.33 Chance Acquaintance. 1' 15"
For: trumpet and saxophone(alto). Jazz duo.
Score: Chaz-Mar.
Disc: in *Three Moods*, Debut, DLP 122, 1955. Unidentified trumpet and John La Porta, alto saxophone.

L1.34 Change Over.
For: jazz band.
Score & parts: Berklee, 1963.

L1.35 Changing Moods. (1971) 3' 40"
For: saxophone(soprano), saxophone(alto), saxophone(tenor), saxophone(baritone). Jazz quartet.
Reel: Feb. 10, 1971; Berklee College of Music. Berklee Faculty Saxophone Quartet. Be

L1.36 Chapter and Verse.
For: jazz band.
Score & parts: Kendor, 1960.

L1.37 Charlston Boy. 4' 55"
For: trumpet, trombone, saxophone(alto), saxophone(tenor), saxophone (baritone), piano, guitar, double bass, drums. Jazz nonet.
Disc: in *Eight Men in Search of a Drummer*, Music Minus One, 1960.

L1.38 Chorale. (1957) 4' 55"
For: trumpet, trombone, saxophone(alto)/clarinet, saxophone(tenor), saxophone(baritone), piano, double bass, drums. Jazz nonet.

L1.39 Color Blind.
For: jazz band.
Music: Kendor, 1960.

L1.40 Concertina for Clarinet. 3' 44"
For: trumpet, trombone, saxophone(alto)/clarinet, saxophone(baritone), piano, double bass, drums. Jazz septet. *First performed:* Cooper Union, New York City. Composers' Workshop Series.
Disc: in *Conceptions*, Fantasy 3-228, 1957. Louis Mucci, trumpet; Sonny Russo, trombone; John La Porta, alto saxophone/clarinet; Sol Schlinger, baritone saxophone; Wally Cirillo, piano; Wendell Marshall, double bass; Clem de Rosa, drums.

L1.41 Conversation Piece. (1954)
For: instruments(unspecified)(2). Jazz duo.

L1.42 Cookin'. (1954)
For: instruments(unspecified)(2). Jazz duo.

L1.43 Course of Events. (1969) 4' 30"
For: jazz band. Written for Sylvester Sample. *First performed:* Aug. 1969; Illinois Wesleyan University.
Reel: Jan. 11, 1972; Berklee College of Music. Berklee Jazz Percussion Ensemble, John La Porta, director. Be

L1.44 Cradle. 6' 10"
For: trumpet, trombone, saxophone(alto), saxophone(tenor), saxophone (baritone), piano, guitar, double bass, drums. Jazz nonet.
Disc: in *Eight Men in Search of a Drummer*, Music Minus One, 1960.

L1.45 Crash Course. (1978) 5' 15"
For: clarinet/saxophone(tenor), trumpet, piano, double bass, drums. Jazz quintet.

L1.46 A Daily Priority. (1978)
For: instruments(unspecified)(2). Jazz duo.

L1.47 Dante Inferno.
For: jazz band.
Score & parts: Kendor.

L1.48 Day of Reckoning. (1977)
For: instruments(unspecified)(2). Jazz duo.

L1.49 Debut. (1957) 4' 5"
For: jazz band. Written for the John La Porta Jazz Orchestra.

L1.50 Diction.
For: saxophone(alto), piano, double bass, drums. Jazz quartet.
Disc: in *The Most Minor*, Everest DBR 5037, SDBR 1037, 1959. John La Porta, alto saxophone; Jack Reilly, piano; Richard Carter, double bass; Charles Perry, drums.

L1.51 Diversion. (1979) 4' 5"
For: trumpet, saxophone(tenor)/clarinet, piano, double bass, drums. Jazz quintet.

Don't Fight It. *See Series II.*

L1.52 Double Counter. (1953)
For: instruments(unspecified)(2). Jazz duo.

L1.53 Double or Nothing. (1977) 3' 20"
For: jazz band. Written for the Herb Pomeroy Orchestra.

L1.54 Double Time. (1954)
For: instruments(unspecified)(2). Jazz duo.

L1.55 Down Boy. (1946)
For: jazz band. Written for Woody Herman.

L1.56 Down Home Some. (1976) 4' 10"
For: trumpet, saxophone(tenor)/clarinet, piano, double bass, drums. Jazz quintet.

L1.57 Down Nassau Way.
For: instruments(unspecified)(2). Jazz duo.
Score: in his *14 Jazz-Rock Duets*, Kendor, 1981.

L1.58 Duke Jam. 4'
For: jazz band.

L1.59 Early Dues. 4' 50"
For: trumpet, trombone, saxophone(alto), saxophone(tenor), saxophone(baritone), piano, guitar, double bass, drums or jazz band. Jazz nonet.
Score & parts: Colin, 1959 (version for jazz band).
Disc: in *Eight Men in Search of a Drummer*, Music Minus One, 1960.

L1.60 Echonitus. 4' 25"
For: trumpet, saxophone(alto), saxophone(tenor), saxophone(baritone)/clarinet, piano, double bass, drums. Jazz septet.
Disc: in *Jazz Composers' Workshop*,

Savoy, 1955-56. Charlie Mingus and others.

L1.61 Elasticity. (1973) 5' 10"
For: jazz band. *First performed:* 1973; National Summer Jazz Camps.

L1.62 En Masse. (1946)
For: jazz band. Written for Woody Herman.

L1.63 En Rapport. 5' 5"
For: trumpet, trombone, saxophone(alto)/clarinet, saxophone(baritone), piano, double bass, drums. Jazz septet.
Music: Circle, 1956.
Disc: in *Conceptions*, Fantasy 3-228, 1957. Louis Mucci, trumpet; Sonny Russo, trombone; John La Porta, alto saxophone/clarinet; Sol Schlinger, baritone saxophone; Wally Cirillo, piano; Wendell Marshall, double bass; Clem de Rosa, drums.

L1.64 En Route. (1977)
For: instruments(unspecified)(2). Jazz duo.

L1.65 Escape. (1980) 5' 10"
For: jazz band. Written for the Herb Pomeroy Orchestra.

L1.66 Essay for Clarinet (Alone).
Jazz solo.
Score: Kendor, 1979.
Reel: Jan. 6, 1971; Berklee College of Music. John La Porta. Be
Reel: Dec. 15, 1977; Berklee College of Music. John La Porta. Be

L1.67 Essellobee.
For: jazz band. *Commissioned by:* National Summer Jazz Clinics.
Score & parts: Berklee, 1966.

L1.68 Eternal Question? (1978)
For: instruments(unspecified)(2). Jazz duo.

L1.69 Excursions. (1971) 3' 40"
For: saxophone(soprano), saxophone(alto), saxophone(tenor), saxophone(baritone). Jazz quartet.

L1.70 F.D. and Company. (1978)
For: instruments(unspecified)(2). Jazz duo.

L1.71 Fancy Free. (1957) 4' 15"
For: trumpet, trombone, saxophone(alto)/clarinet, piano, double bass, drums. Jazz sextet.

L1.72 Fantasy in Blue. (1957) 4' 25"
For: trumpet, saxophone(tenor)/clarinet, piano, double bass, drums. Jazz quintet.

L1.73 Ferme La Porta. 4' 54"
For: clarinet, piano, double bass, drums. Jazz quartet.
Disc: in *Conceptions*, Fantasy 3-228, 1957. John La Porta, clarinet; Wally Cirillo, piano; Wendell Marshall, double bass; Clem de Rosa, drums.

L1.74 Fifth Avenue Doll. (1977)
For: instruments(unspecified)(2). Jazz duo.

L1.75 Figure Eights. (1980) 4' 10"
For: trumpet, saxophone(tenor)/clarinet, piano, double bass, drums. Jazz quintet.

L1.76 Five over Five. (1967) 5' 15"
For: trumpet, saxophone(tenor)/clarinet, piano, double bass, drums. Jazz quintet.

L1.77 Flamencan Sketch. (1967) 4' 26"
For: jazz band. Written for the Jimmy Mosher/Paul Fontaine Jazz Orchestra.

L1.78 Flight. (1958) 3' 45"
For: trumpet, trombone, saxophone(alto)/clarinet, saxophone(tenor), saxophone(baritone), piano, double bass, drums. Jazz octet.

L1.79 Flotsam and Jetsam. 4' 30"
For: jazz band.

Disc: Nippon, 1981. Herb Pomeroy Orchestra.

L1.80 Fluid Drive. 3' 20"
For: saxophone(alto)/clarinet, trumpet, piano, double bass, drums. Jazz quintet.
Disc: Debut DLP 10, 1954 (date recorded). John La Porta, alto saxophone /clarinet; Louis Mucci, trumpet; Wally Cirillo, piano; Richard Carter, double bass; Eddie Shaughnessy, drums.

L1.81 Fore Front.
For: jazz band.
Score & parts: Berklee, 1964.

L1.82 Four Other Brothers.
For: jazz band.
Score & parts: Berklee, 1962.

L1.83 4468 Road. (1965) 7' 16"
For: jazz band. Written for the Jimmy Mosher/Paul Fontaine Jazz Orchestra. Later version for rock group included in his Series IV.
Reel: Jan. 11, 1972; Berklee College of Music. Berklee Jazz Percussion Ensemble, John La Porta, director. Be

L1.84 The Fourth Dynasty.
For: jazz band.
Score & parts: Barnhouse, 1965.

L1.85 Fourth Estate. 4' 35"
For: trumpet, trombone, saxophone(alto), saxophone(tenor), saxophone (baritone), piano, guitar, double bass, drums. Jazz nonet.
Disc: in *Eight Men in Search of a Drummer*, Music Minus One, 1960.

L1.86 Frankie and Johnny.
For: instruments (unspecified)(2). Jazz duo. Traditional.
Score: in his *14 Jazz-Rock Duets*, Kendor, 1981.

L1.87 Fringe Area. 3' 45"
For: saxophone(alto)/clarinet, trumpet, piano, double bass, drums. Jazz quintet.

Disc: Debut DLP 10, 1954 (date recorded). John La Porta, alto saxophone /clarinet; Louis Mucci, trumpet; Wally Cirillo, piano; Richard Carter, double bass; Eddie Shaughnessy, drums.

L1.88 From Another Place. (1977)
For: instruments(unspecified)(2). Jazz duo.

L1.89 From Brownie's Bag. (1979) 4' 55"
For: trumpet, saxophone(tenor)/clarinet, piano, double bass, drums. Jazz quintet.

L1.90 From Here to There. (1978)
For: instruments(unspecified)(2). Jazz duo.

L1.91 The Great John L. (1952) 7' 12"
For: jazz ensemble(trumpets(2), trombone, saxophone(alto), saxophone(tenor), saxophone(baritone), piano, guitar, double bass, drums). *First performed:* Carnegie Recital Hall, New York City; in Jazz Composers' Workshop Series.

L1.92 Growing Pains. (1957) 5' 35"
For: trumpet, trombone, saxophone(alto)/clarinet, saxophone(tenor), saxophone(baritone), piano, double bass, drums. Jazz octet.

L1.93 Growth of an Idea. (1949) 3' 55"
For: jazz band.

L1.94 Hail and Farewell.
For: jazz band.
Score & parts: Berklee, 1966.

L1.95 Happy Go Lucky. (1947) 4' 35"
For: jazz band. Written for Artie Shaw.

L1.96 The Happy Trio.
For: jazz band.
Score & parts: Berklee, 1967.

L1.97 Harangue. 1'
For: trumpet and saxophone(alto). Jazz duo.

Score: Chaz-Mar.
Disc: in *Three Moods*, Debut DLP 122, 1955. Unidentified trumpet and John La Porta, alto saxophone.

L1.98 Harvest Time. 4' 10"
For: trumpet, saxophone(tenor)/clarinet, double bass, drums. Jazz quartet.

L1.99 Image. (1964)
For: jazz band. Written for Jimmy Mosher/Paul Fontaine Jazz Orchestra.

L1.100 In a Dream World. (1954) 3' 25"
For: trumpet, trombone, saxophone(alto)/clarinet, saxophone(tenor), saxophone(baritone), piano, double bass, drums. Jazz octet.

L1.101 In a Roundabout Way. (1978) 4' 35"
For: trumpet, saxophone(tenor)/clarinet, piano, double bass, drums. Jazz quintet.

L1.102 In Random Tandom. (1976) 5' 15"
For: trumpet, saxophone(tenor)/clarinet, piano, double bass, drums. Jazz quintet.

L1.103 In Search of. (1978)
For: instruments(unspecified)(2). Jazz duo.

L1.104 In Transition. (1978) 18'
For: jazz band. Written for the Herb Pomeroy Orchestra.

L1.105 Induction. (1950)
For: jazz band. Written for the Stan Kenton Orchestra.

L1.106 Informal Opus. (1953)
For: instruments(unspecified)(2). Jazz duo.

L1.107 Interplay.
For: instruments(unspecified)(2). Jazz duo.
Score: in his *14 Jazz-Rock Duets*, Kendor, 1981.

L1.108 Into Somewhere. (1977)
For: instruments(unspecified)(2). Jazz duo.

L1.109 Introducing the Band.
For: jazz band.
Score & parts: Berklee, 1962.

L1.110 Introducing the Saxophone Quartet. (1966) 5' 15"
For: speaker, saxophone(soprano), saxophone(alto), saxophone(tenor), saxophone(baritone). Jazz music.

L1.111 Invention on Lady Bird. (1977)
For: instruments(unspecified)(2). Jazz duo. After the work by Tadd Dameron.

L1.112 Le Jazz. (1959) 4' 35"
For: trumpet, trombone, saxophone(alto)/clarinet, saxophone(tenor), saxophone(baritone), piano, double bass, drums. Jazz octet.

L1.113 Jazz Allegro. (1957) 5' 12"
For: trumpet, trombone, saxophone(alto)/clarinet, saxophone(tenor), saxophone(baritone), piano, double bass, drums. Jazz octet.

L1.114 Jazz Concerto. 5'
For: saxophone(alto) and jazz band.
Commissioned by: Marshall Richard Brown for the Newport Jazz Festival, 1958.
Score: Earl Music.
Disc: in *Newport 1958*, Columbia CS 8073, 1959. Andy Marsala, alto saxophone; Newport International Youth Band, Marshall Richard Brown, conductor.

L1.115 The Kangaroo. (1957) 4' 30"
For: trumpet, saxophone(tenor)/clarinet, piano, double bass, drums. Jazz quintet.

L1.116 La-Porta-thority. 4' 5"
For: trumpet, saxophone(alto), piano, double bass, drums. Jazz quintet.
Disc: in *Klook's Clique*, Savoy MG 12065, 1957. Donald Byrd, trumpet;

John La Porta, alto saxophone; Ronnie Ball, piano; Wendell Marshall, double bass; Kenneth Spearman Clarke, drums.

Latin American Meeting Place. *See Series III.*

L1.117 Linear Independence. (1949) 5'
For: jazz band.

L1.118 Listen to Me. (1953) 4' 20"
For: trumpet, trombone, saxophone(alto)/clarinet, saxophone(tenor), saxophone(baritone), piano, double bass, drums. Jazz octet.

L1.119 Little Fantasy. 48'
For: trumpet and saxophone(alto). Jazz duo.
Music: Circle, 1956.
Disc: in *Conceptions*, Fantasy 3-228, 1957. Louis Mucci, trumpet and John La Porta, alto saxophone.

L1.120 Lonely Lament.
For: jazz band.
Score & parts: Berklee, 1963.

L1.121 Lonely Lullaby. (1977)
For: instruments(unspecified)(2). Jazz duo.

L1.122 Lou's Tune. 1' 25"
For: trumpet and saxophone(alto). Jazz duo.
Music: Circle, 1956.
Disc: in *Conceptions*, Fantasy 3-228, 1957. Louis Mucci, trumpet and John La Porta, alto saxophone.

L1.123 Lyric Mood.
For: jazz band.
Score & parts: Berklee, 1964.

L1.124 Lyrical Interplay. (1972)
For: instruments(unspecified)(2). Jazz duo.

L1.125 Madame Bird. (1977)
For: instruments(unspecified)(2). Jazz duo.

L1.126 Magical Moments. (1979) 3' 30"
For: trumpet, saxophone(tenor)/clarinet, piano, double bass, drums. Jazz quintet. *Dedicated to:* Bill Evans.

Main Street. *See Series III.*

Major Scene. *See Series II.*

L1.127 Man to Man. (1974) 5' 10"
For: jazz band. *Written for and first performed:* 1972; Oakton, Va. Bands of Tommorrow All Star-Concert.
Score: Berklee, 1971. Be

Mark V. *See Series IV.*

L1.128 Mid-Century Event. (1957) 5'
For: jazz band. *Commissioned by:* Oyster Bay High School. *First performed:* 1957; New England Life Hall, Boston.

L1.129 Miles Apart. (1957) 5' 12"
For: trumpet, saxophone(tenor)/clarinet, double bass, drums. Jazz quintet. *Dedicated to:* Miles Davis.

L1.130 Miniature for Alto Saxophone. (1956) 4' 10"
For: trumpet, trombone, saxophone(alto)/clarinet, saxophone(tenor), saxophone(baritone), piano, double bass, drums. Jazz octet.

L1.131 Miniature for Baritone Saxophone. (1956) 4' 40"
For: trumpet, trombone, saxophone(alto)/clarinet, saxophone(tenor), saxophone(baritone), piano, double bass, drums. Jazz octet.

L1.132 Miniature for Trombone. (1957) 3' 50"
For: trumpet, trombone, saxophone(alto)/clarinet, saxophone(tenor), saxophone(baritone), piano, double bass, drums. Jazz octet.

L1.133 Miniature for Trumpet. (1956) 4' 25"
For: trumpet, trombone,

saxophone(alto)/clarinet,
saxophone(tenor), saxophone(baritone),
piano, double bass, drums. Jazz octet.

L1.134 A Minor Affair. 5' 5"
For: trumpet, trombone,
saxophone(alto), saxophone(tenor),
saxophone(baritone), piano, guitar,
double bass, drums or jazz band. Jazz
nonet.
Score & parts: Colin, 1957 (version for
jazz band).
Disc: in *Eight Men in Search of a
Drummer*, Music Minus One, 1960.

Minor Blues Bag. *See* Series III.

L1.135 Minor Incident.
For: jazz band.
Score & parts: Barnhouse, 1965.

L1.136 Minor Reflections. (1977)
For: instruments(unspecified)(2). Jazz
duo.

L1.137 Minor Relief. 4' 40"
For: trumpet, trombone,
saxophone(alto), saxophone(tenor),
saxophone(baritone), piano, guitar,
double bass, drums. Jazz nonet.
Disc: in *Eight Men in Search of a
Drummer*, Music Minus One, 1960.

Minor Rhythm. *See* Moods, Jazz
Quartet.

L1.138 Minority Leader.
For: jazz band.
Score & parts: Berklee, 1965.

L1.139 Montage. (1970) 10' 15"
For: jazz band. 3 movements. Written
for the National Summer Jazz Camps.

Montuno Mix. *See* Series II.

[Moods, Jazz Band]
L1.140 Three Moods. 10' 25"
For: saxophone(alto) and jazz band.
Written for the Jazz Foundation of
America. *First performed:* 1957;

Hempstead, N.Y.
Disc: Audio-House Fidelity, 1960 (Stan
Kenton Clinics).

[Moods, Jazz Quartet]
L1.141 Three Moods. 10' 10"
For: saxophone(alto)/clarinet, guitar,
double bass, drums. *Movements:*
Bright-Eyed Blue; Minor Rhythm; Bird's
World.
Music: Chaz-Mar, 1955.
Disc: in *Three Moods*, Debut DLP 122,
1955. John La Porta, alto
saxophone/clarinet; Joseph Barry
Galbraith, guitar; Richard Carter, double
bass; Charlie Berry, drums.

L1.142 Moon Ain't What She Used to
Be. 5'
For: jazz band. Written in memory of
Johnny Richards. *First performed:* Apr.
23, 1969; New England Life Hall,
Boston; John La Porta, conductor.
Reel: Jan. 11, 1972; Berklee College of
Music. Berklee Jazz Percussion
Ensemble, John La Porta, director. Be

L1.143 More or Less. 4' 22"
For: jazz band.
Score & parts: Berklee, 1963.
Disc: Century, 1965 (University of
Connecticut Summer Jazz Clinic
Concert Series).

L1.144 The Most Minor. 4' 9"
For: jazz band. *Commissioned by:*
Marshall Richard Brown.
Disc: Coral, 1956 (date recorded).
Newport Youth Band, Marshall Richard
Brown, conductor.

[The Most Minor; Arr.]
L1.145 The Most Minor. 4'
For: saxophone(alto), piano, double
bass, drums. Jazz quartet.
Music: Earl Music, 1958.
Disc: in *The Most Minor*, Everest SDBR
1037, 1959. John La Porta, alto
saxophone; Jack Reilly, piano; Richard
Carter, double bass; Charles Perry,
drums.

L1.146 Mother's Invention.
For: jazz band. Written for Thad Jones.
Score & parts: Kendor, 1976.

L1.147 Moving Out.
For: jazz band.
Score & parts: Kendor, 1959.

L1.148 Mr. A. and Company. (1976) 4' 25"
For: trumpet, saxophone(tenor)/clarinet, piano, double bass, drums. Jazz quintet.

L1.149 My Gin. (1949) 4' 10"
For: jazz band.

L1.150 Nature's Driving Force. (1979) 4' 15"
For: saxophone(tenor)/clarinet, trumpet, piano, double bass, drums. Jazz quintet.

L1.151 Netherworld.
For: instruments(unspecified)(2). Jazz duo.
Score: in his *14 Jazz-Rock Duets,* Kendor, 1981.

L1.152 New Day. (1979) 4' 12"
For: saxophone(tenor)/clarinet, trumpet, piano, double bass, drums. Jazz quintet.

L1.153 New Venture. (1957) 4' 25"
For: jazz band. *Commissioned by:* Buddy De Franco.

L1.154 Nightly Vigil. 1' 20"
For: trumpet and saxophone(alto). Jazz duo.
Music: Circle, 1956.
Disc: in *Conceptions,* Fantasy 3-228, 1957. Louis Mucci, trumpet and John La Porta, alto saxophone.

L1.155 Non-Alcoholic. (1946) 3' 30"
For: jazz band. Written for the Woody Herman Orchestra.
Disc: Columbia CL 592, 1946 (date recorded; many re-issues). Woody Herman Orchestra.

L1.156 Novellette. (1952)
For: instruments(unspecified)(2). Jazz duo.

L1.157 Oasis. (1979) 5' 20"
For: trumpet, saxophone(tenor)/clarinet, piano, double bass, drums. Jazz quintet.

L1.158 The Old Man's Touch. 4' 5"
For: saxophone(alto)/clarinet, trumpet, piano, double bass, drums. Jazz quintet.
Disc: Debut DLP 10, 1954 (date recorded). John La Porta, alto saxophone/clarinet; Louis Mucci, trumpet; Wally Cirillo, piano; Richard Carter, double bass; Eddie Shaughnessy, drums.

L1.159 On a Theme by B.G. (1977)
For: instruments(unspecified)(2). Jazz duo.

On Past Reflection. *See Series IV.*

L1.160 On Stage Blues.
For: jazz band.
Score & parts: Kendor, 1956.

L1.161 On the Move.
For: jazz band.
Score & parts: Berklee, 1964.

L1.162 One Man's Jazz Journey. (1977) 4' 12"
For: jazz band. *Commissioned by:* Berklee College of Music for its graduation concert, A Tribute to Woody Herman. *First performed:* May 13, 1977; Berklee College of Music. John La Porta, conductor.
Reel: recording of first performance. Be

L1.163 Only as a Last Resort. (1965)
For: instruments(unspecified)(2). Jazz duo.

L1.164 A Pair of Aces. 5' 15"
For: jazz band. *Commissioned by:* Farmingdale High School Jazz Band.
First performed: Newport Jazz Festival.

Farmingdale High School Jazz Band, Marshall Richard Brown, conductor.

L1.165 A Pantoscopic Vision. (1956) 5'
For: jazz band. Written for the Stan Kenton Orchestra.

L1.166 Pastel. 3' 30"
For: jazz band.
Disc: Century, 1961 (Stan Kenton Clinics at Southern Methodist University).

L1.167 Pastorale.
For: instruments(unspecified)(2). Jazz duo.
Score: in his *14 Jazz-Rock Duets*, Kendor, 1981.

The Pent Up Minority. *See* Series III.

Pentatonic Contrasts. *See* Series IV.

L1.168 Phillie's Willie. (1946) 4' 15"
For: jazz band. *Dedicated to:* Bill Harris.
First performed: Woody Herman Orchestra.

Play Time. *See* Series II.

A Present Day Scene. *See* Series IV.

L1.169 The Principal Is the Thing.
For: jazz band.
Score & parts: Berklee, 1962.

L1.170 Pure and Simple. (1978)
For: instruments(unspecified)(2). Jazz duo.

[Quartet, Saxophones, No. 1]
L1.171 First Saxophone Quartet. (1965) 12' 2"
For: saxophone(soprano), saxophone(alto), saxophone(tenor), saxophone(baritone). Jazz quartet. 3 movements.

[Quartet, Saxophones, No. 2]
L1.172 Second Saxophone Quartet. (incomplete) 3' 45"

For: saxophone(soprano), saxophone(alto), saxophone(tenor), saxophone(baritone). Jazz quartet. 1 movement.

L1.173 Quarto. 3' 15"
For: saxophone(alto)/clarinet, trumpet, piano, double bass, drums. Jazz quintet.
Disc: Debut DLP 10, 1954 (date recorded). John La Porta, alto saxophone/clarinet; Louis Mucci, trumpet; Wally Cirillo, piano; Richard Carter, double bass; Eddie Shaughnessy, drums.

L1.174 Quintet. (1959) 4' 10"
For: trumpet, trombone, saxophone(alto), double bass, drums. Jazz quintet.

L1.175 R.T. and Company. (1976)
For: instruments(unspecified)(2). Jazz duo.

L1.176 Reap the Harvest. 4' 50"
For: jazz band.
Disc: in *Pramlatta's Hips*, Shiah HP 1, 1980. Herb Pomeroy Orchestra.

L1.177 Remember Mingus. 7' 40"
For: jazz band.
Disc: in *Pramlatta's Hips*, Shiah HP 1, 1980. Herb Pomeroy Orchestra.

L1.178 Remembrance of Times Past.
For: instruments(unspecified)(2). Jazz duo.

L1.179 Reminiscence of the Past. (1979) 4' 10"
For: trumpet, saxophone(tenor)/clarinet, piano, double bass, drums. Jazz quintet.

L1.180 Resting Place for a Traveling Musician.
For: jazz group.
Reel: Jan. 11, 1972; Berklee College of Music. Berklee Jazz Percussion Ensemble. Be

L1.181 Reunion. 4' 5"
For: jazz band.
Disc: Nippon, 1981. Herb Pomeroy Orchestra.

L1.182 Rhapsody.
For: trumpet and jazz band. Written for Doc Severenson.
Score & parts: Kendor, 1965.

L1.183 Richochet. (1976) 4' 35"
For: trumpet, saxophone(tenor)/clarinet, piano, double bass, drums. Jazz quintet.

L1.184 Riff Song.
For: jazz band.
Score & parts: Kendor, 1954.

L1.185 Right around Home. 4' 10"
For: saxophone(alto)/clarinet, trumpet, piano, double bass, drums. Jazz quintet.
Disc: Debut DLP 10, 1954 (date recorded). John La Porta, alto saxophone/clarinet; Louis Mucci, trumpet; Wally Cirillo, piano; Richard Carter, double bass; Eddie Shaughnessy, drums.

L1.186 Rock Invention for Lefty and Righty. (1979) 4' 15"
For: percussion(2) and jazz band. Written for the National Summer Jazz Camps.

L1.187 Roots. (1957) 4' 55"
For: trumpet, trombone, saxophone(alto)/clarinet, saxophone(tenor), saxophone(baritone), piano, double bass, drums. Jazz octet.

L1.188 Rotation. (1966) 5' 15"
For: jazz band. Written for the Jimmy Mosher/Paul Fontaine Jazz Orchestra.

L1.189 Running Commentary.
For: instruments(unspecified)(2). Jazz duo.
Score: in his *14 Jazz-Rock Duets*, Kendor, 1981.

L1.190 Saby's Lament. (1976) 4' 55"
For: trumpet, saxophone(tenor)/clarinet, piano, double bass, drums. Jazz quintet. *Dedicated to:* Swedish Music Guild. *First performed:* June 1976; Stockholm, Sweden.

L1.191 Salt Lake Mix. (1971) 4' 35"
For: trumpet, saxophone(tenor)/clarinet, piano, double bass, drums. Jazz quintet.

L1.192 Searching.
For: saxophone(alto), piano, double bass, drums. Jazz quartet.
Disc: in *The Most Minor*, Everest DBR 5037, SDBR 1037, 1959. John La Porta, alto saxophone; Jack Reilly, piano; Richard Carter, double bass; Charles Perry, drums.

L1.193 September Days. (1978)
For: instruments(unspecified)(2). Jazz duo.

L1.194 September Morn. (1978)
For: instruments(unspecified)(2). Jazz duo.

L1.195 A Sequential Journey. (1978)
For: instruments(unspecified)(2). Jazz duo.

L1.196 Serenade. 3' 10"
For: saxophone(soprano), saxophone(alto), saxophone(tenor), saxophone(baritone). Jazz quartet.

L1.197 Series II. (1968-69)
For: rock group. *Contents:* Bright Yellow; Don't Fight It; Major Scene; Montuno Mix; Play Time.
Parts: Berklee.
Disc: Berklee.

L1.198 Series III. (1968-69)
For: rock group. *Contents:* Call It What You Will; Latin American Meeting Place; Main Street; Minor Blues Bag; The Pent Up Minority.
Parts: Berklee, 1971.
Disc: Berklee, 1971.

Reel: n.d.; Berklee College of Music (Nos. 1, 2, 4). Be

L1.199 Series IV. (1968-69)
For: rock group. *Contents:* Pentatonic Contrasts; A Present Day Scene; Mark V; 4468 Road; On Past Reflection. For earlier version of No. 4, see 4468 Road.
Parts: Berklee, 1971.
Disc: Berklee, 1971.
Reel: n.d.; Berklee College of Music (Nos. 1, 3, 4). Be

L1.200 Seven Four Shout.
For: jazz band.
Score & parts: Berklee, 1966.

L1.201 Shouting Friends. 5'
For: jazz band.
Disc: Century, 1965 (University of Connecticut Summer Jazz Clinic Concert Series).

L1.202 Small Blue Opus. 5' 14"
For: trumpet, trombone, saxophone(alto)/clarinet, saxophone(baritone), piano, double bass, drums. Jazz septet.
Disc: in Conceptions, Fantasy 3-228, 1957. Louis Mucci, trumpet; Sonny Russo, trombone; John La Porta, alto saxophone/clarinet; Sol Schlinger, baritone saxophone; Wally Cirillo, piano; Wendell Marshall, double bass; Clem de Rosa, drums.

L1.203 Soliloquy. (1955) 4' 12"
For: jazz band. *Dedication:* In memory of Anna Otto.

L1.204 Solstice. (1980) 3' 30"
For: jazz band. Written for the Herb Pomeroy Orchestra.

L1.205 Some Changing Times 5/4. (1962)
For: instruments(unspecified)(2). Jazz duo.

L1.206 Sometimes It Takes a While. (1976) 4' 5"

For: trumpet, saxophone(tenor)/clarinet, piano, double bass, drums. Jazz quintet.

L1.207 Sonny Speaks. (1946) 3' 20"
For: jazz band.
Disc: Capitol 1170, 1950 (date recorded; many re-issues). Woody Herman Orchestra.

L1.208 Sound the Drum. 4' 10"
For: jazz band.
Disc: Audio-House Fidelity, 1960 (Stan Kenton Clinics).

L1.209 South to Caracas.
For: jazz band.
Score & parts: Berklee, 1964.

[Spanish Rhapsody, Jazz Band]
L1.210 Spanish Rhapsody.
Commissioned by: York High School, York, Pa.
Score & parts: Berklee, 1966.

[Spanish Rhapsody, Jazz Quartet]
L1.211 Spanish Rhapsody. 5' 5"
For: saxophone(soprano), saxophone(alto), saxophone(tenor), saxophone(baritone).
Score & parts: Berklee, 1972. BCM
Disc: Berklee Records LP 102, 1972. Berklee Faculty Saxophone Quartet. BCM Be
Reel: Nov. 7, 1967; Berklee College of Music. Arrangers' Workshop, John La Porta, director. Be
Reel: Feb. 10, 1971; Berklee College of Music. Berklee Faculty Saxophone Quartet. Be
Reel: Dec. 4, 1979. Boston Conservatory Chamber Ensemble, Pasquale Prencipe, director. BCM

L1.212 Spin Off. (1979)
For: instruments(unspecified)(2). Jazz duo.

L1.213 Spring Is! (1976) 3' 30"
For: jazz band. Written for the Thad Jones/Mel Lewis Orchestra.

L1.214 Spring Ritual. (1978) 10' 22"
For: jazz band. Written for the Herb Pomeroy Orchestra.

L1.215 Spring Serenade. (1956) 5' 30"
For: jazz band. Written for the Stan Kenton Orchestra.

L1.216 Spur of the Moment. 4' 30"
For: trumpet, saxophone(alto), saxophone(tenor), saxophone(baritone)/ clarinet, piano, double bass, drums. Jazz septet.
Disc: in *The Jazz Composers' Workshop*, Savoy, 1955-56. Charlie Mingus and others.

L1.217 Star Light. (1977)
For: instruments(unspecified)(2). Jazz duo.

L1.218 Star Loss. (1977)
For: instruments(unspecified)(2). Jazz duo.

L1.219 The Steel Drum Man.
For: instruments(unspecified)(2). Jazz duo.
Score: in his *14 Jazz-Rock Duets*, Kendor, 1981.

L1.220 Stellar Visions. (1977)
For: instruments(unspecified)(2). Jazz duo.

L1.221 Stellar World. (1980) 3' 55"
For: trumpet, saxophone(tenor)/clarinet, double bass, drums. Jazz quartet.

L1.222 Stretto. (1968) 6' 15"
For: jazz band. *First performed:* 1968; National Summer Jazz Camps.

L1.223 Strolling Along. (1978) .
For: instruments(unspecified)(2). Jazz duo.

L1.224 Study in G Major. (1980) 4' 35"
For: trumpet, saxophone(tenor)/clarinet, piano, double bass, drums. Jazz quintet.

L1.225 Sugar and Spice. (1972) 5' 5"
For: trumpet, saxophone(tenor)/clarinet, piano, double bass, drums. Jazz quintet.

L1.226 Summer Jazz Camps. (1973) 5' 10"
For: jazz group.

L1.227 Summer Social Ammenities. (1973) 4' 45"
For: trumpet, saxophone(tenor)/clarinet, piano, double bass, drums. Jazz quintet.

L1.228 Summit Conference. 4' 50"
For: saxophone(alto) and jazz band.
Commissioned by: Marshall Richard Brown for the Newport Jazz Festival, 1958.
Music: Earl Music.
Disc: in *Newport 1958*, Columbia CS 8073, 1959. Andy Marsala, alto saxophone; International Youth Band, Marshall Richard Brown, conductor.

L1.229 Sunday Morning Muse. (1979) 4' 50"
For: trumpet, saxophone(tenor)/clarinet, piano, double bass, drums. Jazz quintet.

L1.230 Sweet Bird. (1977)
For: instruments(unspecified)(2). Jazz duo.

L1.231 That Comfortable Groove. (1955)
For: instruments(unspecified)(2). Jazz duo.

L1.232 That Lonely Place.
For: jazz band.
Score & parts: Kendor, 1955.

L1.233 Theme and Variations on the Blues. (1957) 35' 10"
For: trumpet, trombone, saxophone(alto)/clarinet, saxophone(tenor), saxophone(baritone), piano, double bass, drums. Jazz octet. Theme and 12 variations. *First performed:* Hofstra College; Contemporary Music Festival.

L1.234 This Hectic Life. 3' 30"
For: trumpet, saxophone(alto)/clarinet, piano, double bass, drums. Jazz quintet.
Disc: Debut DLP 10, 1954 (date recorded). Louis Mucci, trumpet; John La Porta, alto saxophone/clarinet; Wally Cirillo, piano; Richard Carter, double bass; Eddie Shaughnessy, drums.

L1.235 A Timely Respite. (1976)
For: instruments(unspecified)(2). Jazz duo.

L1.236 Times Passing Parade. (1977)
For: instruments(unspecified)(2). Jazz duo.

L1.237 Togetherness.
For: instruments(unspecified)(2). Jazz duo.
Score: in his *14 Jazz-Rock Duets*, Kendor, 1981.

L1.238 Tread Mill. (1979) 3' 50"
For: trumpet, saxophone(tenor)/clarinet, piano, double bass, drums. Jazz quintet.

L1.239 Trial and Error. (1952)
For: instruments(unspecified)(2). Jazz duo.

L1.240 El Trio. (1981) 5' 30"
For: jazz band. Written for the Herb Pomeroy Orchestra.

L1.241 Triplets, You Say? 55"
For: trumpet and saxophone(alto). Jazz duo.
Music: Circle, 1956.
Disc: in *Conceptions*, Fantasy 3-228, 1957. Louis Mucci, trumpet and John LaPorta, alto saxophone.

L1.242 Trocadero. (1942)
For: jazz band. Film music.

L1.243 True to Myself.
For: jazz band. Written for Thad Jones.
Score & parts: Kendor, 1976.

L1.244 Try Again. (1945)
For: jazz band. Written for Woody Herman.

L1.245 Two, as One, in Three.
For: instruments(unspecified)(2). Jazz duo.
Score: in his *14 Jazz-Rock Duets*, Kendor, 1981.

L1.246 Two by Two.
For: jazz band.
Score & parts: Colin, 1958.

L1.247 Two Party Campaign. 1' 20"
For: trumpet and saxophone(alto). Jazz duo.
Score: Chaz-Mar.
Disc: in *Three Moods*, Debut DLP 122, 1955. Unidentified trumpet and John La Porta, alto saxophone.

L1.248 Two's Aloud, Three's a Crowd. (1972)
For: instruments(unspecified)(2). Jazz duo.

L1.249 Two's Company. (1952)
For: instruments(unspecified)(2). Jazz duo.

L1.250 Under Reuben's Eye. (1956) 5' 12"
For: trumpet, saxophone(tenor)/clarinet, piano, double bass, drums. Jazz quintet.

L1.251 Under Sunny Skies. (1972) 4' 5"
For: jazz band.

L1.252 Variations on a Ballad. (1978)
For: instruments(unspecified)(2). Jazz duo.

L1.253 Variations on a Theme by Green. (1980) 3' 30"
For: jazz band. Written for the Herb Pomeroy Orchestra.

L1.254 Walkathon. 3' 30"
For: jazz band. Film music.

L1.255 Wash Day. 44"
For: trumpet and saxophone(alto). Jazz duo.
Music: Circle, 1956.
Disc: in *Conceptions*, Fantasy 3-228, 1957. Louis Mucci, trumpet and John La Porta, alto saxophone.

L1.256 Welcome Back Jack.
For: jazz band.
Score & parts: Colin, 1958.

L1.257 Well Spring. (1979) 3' 55"
For: trumpet, saxophone(tenor)/clarinet, piano, double bass, drums. Jazz quintet.

L1.258 When the Saints Go Marching In.
For: instruments(unspecified)(2). Jazz duo. Traditional.
Score: in his *14 Jazz-Rock Duets*, Kendor, 1981.

L1.259 Will Wail. 4' 10"
For: trumpet, saxophone(alto), piano, double bass, drums. Jazz quintet.
Disc: in *Klook's Clique*, Savoy MG 12065, 1957. Donald Byrd, trumpet; John La Porta, alto saxophone; Ronnie Ball, piano; Wendell Marshall, double bass; Kenneth Spearman Clarke, drums.

L1.260 Winning Ways.
For: instruments(unspecified)(2). Jazz duo.
Score: in his *14 Jazz-Rock Duets*, Kendor, 1981.

L1.261 Young's World. (1956) 4' 35"
For: trumpet, trombone, saxophone(alto)/clarinet, saxophone(tenor), saxophone(baritone), piano, double bass, drums. Jazz octet.

ARRANGEMENTS OF WORKS BY OTHER COMPOSERS

L1.262 All the Things You Are.
For: saxophone(alto), double bass, guitar, drums. Jazz quartet. Original by Jerome Kern.
Disc: in *Three Moods*, Debut DLP 122, 1955. John LaPorta, alto saxophone; Richard Carter, double bass; Joseph Barry Galbraith, guitar; Charles Perry, drums.

L1.263 Don't Blame Me.
For: jazz group. Original by Jimmy McHugh.
Disc: in *Three Moods*, Debut DLP 122, 1955. John La Porta, alto saxophone; Richard Carter, double bass; Joseph Barry Galbraith, guitar; Charles Perry, drums.

L1.264 Just in Time.
For: jazz band. Original by Jule Styne.
Score & parts: Kendor.

L1.265 Prelude No. 4.
For: saxophone(soprano), saxophone(alto), saxophone(tenor), saxophone(baritone). Jazz quartet. Original by Johann Sebastian Bach.
Reel: n.d.; Berklee College of Music. Berklee Faculty Saxophone Quartet. Be

L1.266 Serenity. (1979) 4' 30"
For: jazz band. Original by Joe Henderson. Arranged for the Herb Pomeroy Orchestra.

L1.267 Speak Low.
For: jazz group. Original by Kurt Weill.
Reel: Nov. 7, 1967; Berklee College of Music. Arrangers' Workshop, John La Porta, director. Be

L1.268 Yesterday's Blues. 4' 10"
For: jazz band. Original by Jerome Kern.
Score & parts: Berklee, 1965.
Disc: Century 1965 (University of Connecticut Summer Jazz Clinics Concert Series).
Reel: Jan. 6, 1971; Berklee College of Music. Phil Wilson Blues Band. Be

L2 OTTO E. LASKE

Born April 23, 1936, in Oels, Silesia. Moved to Boston area 1966. *Education:* attended Internationales Musikinstitut and Internationale Ferienkurse fuer neue

Musik (Darmstadt, West Germany, 1960-66); studied composition with Theodore W. Adorno (Goethe University, Frankfurt, West Germany, Ph.D., Philosophy, 1966); Robert Cogan (New England Conservatory, M.M., 1968); Milton Babbitt, Roger Sessions (Berkshire Music Center, Tanglewood and Ipswich Summer School); sonology, computer science, cognitive psychology with G.M. Koenig (Instituut voor Sonologie, Utrecht, The Netherlands, 1970-75); further studies with H.A. Simon (Carnegie-Mellon University, 1975-77), and at Boston University. *Awards:* Volkswagenwerk Fellowship (1965-66), Fulbright Fellowship (1966-68), Berkshire Music Center, Tanglewood, Associate Fellow in Composition (1967), Pi Kappa Lambda (member, 1968), International Gaudeamus Music Week (Finalist, 1970), Deutsche Forschungsgemeinschaft Fellowship (1971-74), La Biennale di Venezia commission (1981), Schola Cantorum (Stuttgart, West Germany) commission (1981). *Related activities:* author of monographs and journal articles; co-editor, *Interface: Journal of New Music Research*, (1970-75) and *Sonological Reports* (1970-75); co-founder, New England Computer Music Association, Inc. (1981); served on the faculties of the Staatliche Hochschule fuer Musik und Darstellende Kunst, Stuttgart, West Germany; Instituut voor Sonologie, Utrecht, The Netherlands, (1970-75); McGill University; University of Illinois, Urbana; University of Pittsburgh (Andrew Mellon Fellow, 1975-76). MIT

WORKS

L2.1 Cantus. (1970/77) 11′
For: violin. Computer music. Computer-generated score. *First performed:* 1981; Staatliche Hochschule fuer Musik und Darstellende Kunst, Stuttgart, West Germany.
Score: ms. in composer's hand.

L2.2 De Aegypto. (1965) 9′
For: Tenor, vibraphone, xylophone, harp, horn, viola, percussion(2). *Text:* Ezra Pound.
Score: ms. in composer's hand.

[Duets, Violoncello and Piano]
L2.3 Two Duets. (1965) 2′ 30″
First performed: 1968; New England Conservatory.
Score: ms. in composer's hand.

[Fascinants]
L2.4 Quatre fascinants. (1972/81) 6′
For: Altos(3) and Tenors(3). Computer music. *Text:* Rene Char. Computer-generated score.
Score: ms. in composer's hand.

L2.5 How Time Passes. (1967/69) 16′
For: instrumental ensemble(oboe, English horn, bassoon, horns(2), trumpets(2), trombones(2), tuba, piano).
Score & parts: ms. in composer's hand.

L2.6 Ils sont heureux. (1969) 3′
For: Baritone, trombone, piano. *Text:* Guillevic. *First performed:* 1973; Oslo Konservatoriet, Oslo, Norway.
Score: ms. in composer's hand.

L2.7 Klage. (1968) 4′ 30″
For: Alto and violoncello. *Text:* Otto Laske. *First performed:* 1961; Donnell Library, New York City; Composer's Forum.
Score: ms. in composer's hand.

L2.8 Kyrie eleison. (1968) 9′
For: chorus(36 voices). International Gaudeamus Music Week (Finalist, 1970).
Vocal score: ms. in composer's hand.

L2.9 Mediations. (1981) 11′ 30″
For: tape and loudspeakers(2). Computer music. Computer-generated score and sound. *First performed:* 19981; Staatliche Hochschule fuer Musik und Darstellende Kunst, Stuttgart, West Germany.
Tape: available from composer. Rental.

L2.10 Message to the Messiah. (1978) 25'
For: tape and loudspeakers(2). *First performed:* 1979; Chicago, Ill.
Tape: available from composer. Rental.

L2.11 Monologue interieur. (1968) 3'
For: horn and viola. *First performed:* 1968; New England Conservatory.
Score: ms. in composer's hand.
Cassette: Apr. 21, 1976; New England Conservatory. NEC Contemporary Music Ensemble, Gunther Schuller, conductor. NEC

L2.12 Motet. (1964) 2' 30"
For: chorus(mixed). *First performed:* 1965; Darmstadt, West Germany.
Vocal score: ms. in composer's hand.

L2.13 Nachtstuecke. (1981) 13'
For: chorus(mixed). Computer music.
Text: Otto Laske. Computer-generated score.
Vocal score: ms. in composer's hand.

L2.14 Perturbations. (1981) 12'
For: flute, clarinet, violin, viola, violoncello, piano, percussion(2). Computer music. Computer-generated score. *First performed:* 1981; Denton, Tex.
Score & parts: ms. in composer's hand.
Tape: available from composer. Rental.

L2.15 Piano Piece No. 1. (1967/77) 5' 30"
First performed: 1969; Donnell Library, New York City; Composer's Forum.
Score: ms. in composer's hand.

L2.16 Piano Piece No. 2. (1969) 6' 30"
Score: ms. in composer's hand.

[Quintet, Woodwinds]
L2.17 Woodwind Quintet. (1967/72) 6' 30"
First performed: 1976; Pittsburgh, Pa. Pittsburgh New Music Ensemble.
Score & parts: ms. in composer's hand.

L2.18 Radiation. (1966) 6'
For: instrumental ensemble(clarinet, clarinet(bass), saxophone(soprano), saxophone(tenor), trumpets(2), trombones(2), violin, viola, violoncello, percussion(2)). *First performed:* 1967; Berkshire Music Center, Tanglewood.
Score & parts: ms. in composer's hand.

L2.19 Song. (1965) 3'
For: Soprano and piano. *Text:* Edna St. Vincent Millay. *First performed:* 1969; Donnell Library, New York City; Composer's Forum.
Score: ms. in composer's hand.

L2.20 Structure I. (1971) 7' 25"
For: tape and loudspeakers(4). Musique concrete.
Tape: available from composer. Rental.

L2.21 Structure II. (1972) 11' 30"
For: tape and loudspeakers(4). *First performed:* 1972; Geertekerk, Utrecht, The Netherlands.
Tape: available from composer. Rental.

L2.22 Structure III, No. 1. (1972) 8'
For: tape and loudspeakers(4). *First performed:* 1973; Geertekerk, Utrecht, The Netherlands.
Tape: available from composer. Rental.

L2.23 Structure III, No. 2. (1972) 5'
For: tape and loudspeakers(4). *First performed:* 1973; Geertekerk, Utrecht, The Netherlands.
Tape: available from composer. Rental.

L2.24 Structure IV. (1973) 17' 30"
For: tape and loudspeakers(4). Computer music. *First performed:* 1974; Bourges, France.
Tape: available from composer. Rental.

L2.25 Structure V. (1974) 18'
For: tape and loudspeakers(4). Computer music.
Tape: available from composer. Rental.

L2.26 Structure VI. (1974) 19' 30"
For: tape and loudspeakers(4). *First performed:* 1975; Kunsttiendaagse, Amsterdam, The Netherlands.
Tape: available from composer. Rental.

L2.27 Structure VII. (1974) 17'
For: tape and loudspeakers(4). Musique concrete. *First performed:* 1977; Pittsburgh, Pa.
Tape: available from composer. Rental.
Cassette: Nov. 15, 1978; New England Conservatory. NEC

L2.28 Structure VIII. (1975/82) 14' 30"
For: tape and loudspeakers(4). Computer music. *First performed:* 1977; Kunsttiendaagse, Amsterdam, The Netherlands.
Tape: available from composer. Rental.

L2.29 Structure IX. (1975/81) 12' 30"
For: tape and loudspeakers(4). Computer music. *First performed:* 1978; Los Angeles, Calif.
Tape: available from composer. Rental.

[Studies, Piano]
L2.30 Four Studies. (1964) 6' 30"
First performed: 1965; Darmstadt, West Germany.
Score: ms. in composer's hand.

L2.31 Terpsichore. (1980) 13' 30"
For: tape and loudspeakers(2). Computer-generated score/sound.
Commissioned by: Massachusetts Dance Ensemble. *First performed:* 1980; Queens College of The City University of New York.
Tape: available from composer. Rental.

L2.32 Time Points, No. 1. (1966) 4' 30"
For: string quartets(2). *First performed:* 1968; Bennington College, Vt.
Score: ms. in composer's hand.

L2.33 Time Points, No. 2. (1966) 6' 30"
For: string quartets(2). *First performed:* 1969; Donnell Library, New York City; Composer's Forum.
Score: ms. in composer's hand.

L2.34 Transitions. (1967) 5'
For: clarinet(bass), guitar, percussion, dancers(3).
Score: ms. in composer's hand.

L2.35 Tristus est anima mea. (1968) 2' 5"
For: chorus(mixed). Dance music. *First performed:* 1971; Utrecht, The Netherlands.
Vocal score: ms. in composer's hand.

L2.36 Vienne la nuit sonne l'heure. (1968) 4'
For: clarinet, violoncello, percussion. *First performed:* 1968; Rochester, N.Y.
Score: ms. in composer's hand.

L3 HENRY LASKER

Born 1909 in Boston; died 1976.
Education: studied composition with Walter Piston and Hugo Leichtentritt (Harvard University, M.A). *Awards:* elected to Boston University Collegium of Distinguished Alumni (1974); member of Phi Beta Kappa; Teacher of the Year (Newton, Mass.), Newton North High School auditorium named Henry Lasker Auditorium (posthumously). *Related activities:* author of *Teaching Creative Music in Secondary Schools* (1971); served on the faculties of Newton North High School (33 years), Bridgewater State Teachers College, Newton Creative Arts Center, Newton, Mass.; lecturer at Northeastern University and Harvard University. (NFL)

L3.1 Beauty and the Beast.
For: narrator, Sopranos(2), Mezzo Soprano, Tenor, Baritone, Bass, voices(male)(4), orchestra. Opera. Libretto by Henry Lasker. *Dedicated to:* Gertrude Lasker.

L3.2 Have a Heart.
For: orchestra. Ballet. *First performed:* Jordan Hall, Boston. Russokoff Dance Ensemble.

L3.3 Jack and the Beanstalk.
For: Soprano, Mezzo Soprano, Tenor, Baritone, Bass, orchestra. Children's opera. Libretto by Henry Lasker. *Dedicated to:* Gertrude Lasker.
Score & parts: Frank Music.

Disc: in *Henry Lasker (1909-1976)*, Mark Records MC 5465 (excerpt of performance in June 1958 by soloists and members of the Boston Symphony Orchestra). NFL

L3.4 The Lord Is My Shepherd.
For: voice and organ. *Text:* Bible, O.T., Psalm 23. *Commissioned by:* Massachusetts Institute of Technology. *First performed:* Massachusetts Institute of Technlogy.

L3.5 The Oath of Hippocrates.
For: Baritone, chorus, orchestra. Cantata. *Commissioned by:* Newton, Mass. for its Centennial. *Dedicated to:* Physicians everywhere. *First performed:* Boston College. John Horner, baritone; Newton North High School Choir; Newton South High School Choir; Newton Symphony Orchestra, Michel Sasson, conductor.
Disc: in *Henry Lasker (1909-1976)*, Mark Records MC 5465 (excerpt). NFL

L3.6 On Stage Everybody.
For: voices and orchestra. Musical comedy. *Lyrics:* Alfred Sherman.

L3.7 Power of Industry.
Ballet. *First performed:* Symphony Hall, Boston. Boston Pops, Arthur Fiedler, conductor.

L3.8 Rotogravure.
Musical comedy. *Lyrics:* Alfred Sherman.

L3.9 Trio.
For: flute, oboe, bassoon. *First performed:* Harvard University. Members of the Boston Symphony Orchestra.

L4 THOMAS OBOE LEE

Born September 5, 1945, in Peking, China. *Education:* B.A. (University of Pittsburgh, 1972); studied composition with William Thomas McKinley, Gunther Schuller (New England Conservatory, M.M., Jazz Composition, 1974, M.M.,

Composition, 1976); Betsy Jolas (Berkshire Music Center, Tanglewood, 1976); Earl Kim (Harvard University, Ph.D., 1981); theory and analysis with Robert Cogan, Donald Martino, Ernst Oster; jazz with Jaki Byard, Nathan Davis, Thad Jones, George A. Russell; flute with James Walker. *Awards:* Notre Dame Intercollegiate Jazz Festival (Best Flute Soloist, 1970, 1971, 1972), Berkshire Music Center, Fellowship (1976), Koussevitzky Tanglewood Composition Prize (1976), Massachusetts Council on the Arts and Humanities, Artist Fellowship Program (1977), Bohemians Prize (New York Musicians Club, Harvard University, 1979), Berkshire Music Center, Tanglewood and Fromm Foundation Commission (1981), MacDowell Colony Fellowship (1981), Stroud Festival International Composers Competition (First Prize, 1981), Collage commission (1982), Yaddo Fellowship (1982). *Related activities:* jazz flutist; served on the faculties of Berklee College of Music (1973-79) and Swarthmore College (1979-80). HU

WORKS

L4.1 After a Lecture by John Cage. (1977)
For: piano.
Score: ms. in composer's hand.

L4.2 Aperture. (1974)
For: string quartet. *First performed:* May 9, 1974; New England Conservatory. Student performers.
Score & parts: ms.
Cassette: recording of first performance. NEC

L4.3 Birthday Piece. (1977)
For: piano.
Score: ms.

L4.4 C.C.--Duo for Cabot and 'Cello. (1980-1981)
For: violoncello and piano. Winner of Stroud Festival International Composers Competition (First Prize, 1981). *First*

performed: Oct. 14, 1981; Stroud, England. Timothy Hugh, violoncello and Robert Lochaert, piano. *Score & part.*

L4.5 The Cockscomb. (1981) 12'
For: actress/singer, violin, trumpet, double bass, piano, percussion(2). 1 movement. *Text: Made to Order* by Barbara Kuehn. *Commissioned by:* Berkshire Music Center, Tanglewood and Fromm Foundation. *First performed:* Aug. 4, 1981; Berkshire Music Center, Tanglewood. Tanglewood Fellows, Theodore Antoniou, conductor. *Music:* ms.

L4.6 Departed Feathers. (1980)
For: string quartet. *Commissioned by:* Kronos String Quartet. *First performed:* May 11, 1981; Mills College. Kronos String Quartet. *Score & parts.*

L4.7 Departed Feathers I. (1980)
For: jazz group. Withdrawn.

L4.8 Departed Feathers II.
For: jazz group. Withdrawn.

Dragonfly. *See* Libelle (Dragonfly).

[Fireflies]
L4.9 29 Fireflies. (1977)
For: piano. *First performed:* Apr. 13, 1978; Berklee College of Music. Michael Dewart.
Score: ms.

L4.10 Libelle (Dragonfly). (1977-79)
For: harp. *First performed:* Apr. 13, 1978; Berklee College of Music. Susan Allen.
Reel: May 18, 1978; WGBH-FM Boston, *Morning Pro Musica.* Susan Allen. WGBH

L4.11 The Mad Frog. (1974)
For: oboe, clarinet(bass), harp. *First performed:* Dec. 4, 1974; New England Conservatory. Roger Jannotta, oboe; Carl Atkins, bass clarinet; Susan Allen, harp.

Score & parts: Margun.
Cassette: recording of first performance. NEC

L4.12 New Sheep '55.
For: jazz group. Withdrawn.

L4.13 1956, Year of the Monkey.
For: jazz group. Withdrawn.

L4.14 Nobody.
For: jazz group. Withdrawn.

L4.15 Octopus Wrecks. (1979-81)
For: trumpets(2), horn, trombone, tuba, double basses(3). *First performed:* Apr. 30, 1981; Old Cambridge Baptist Church, Cambridge, Mass. NEC Chamber Wind Ensemble, Fredric Cohen, conductor.
Score & parts: Margun.

L4.16 Phantasia for Elvira Shatayev. (1981)
For: Soprano and chamber orchestra(2(pic)-2-1-2; 2-1-2-1; 0-0-0-0; perc(2); hp; pf; str(9-9-6-4-2)). *First performed:* Dec. 25, 1981; Sanders Theatre, Harvard University. Judith Kellock, soprano; Pro Arte Chamber Orchestra of Boston. *Score & parts.*

L4.17 Photograph, 1920. (1978)
For: Mezzo Soprano, clarinet/clarinet(bass), violin, viola, violoncello. *First performed:* May 19, 1979; Harvard University. *Score & parts.*

L4.18 Piece for Viola. (1976)
For: saxophone(soprano), saxophone(alto/soprano), saxophone(tenor/baritone), saxophone(tenor). *First performed:* Apr. 13, 1978; Berklee College of Music. Gregory Badolato, tenor saxophone; Berklee College of Music, members of the Saxophone/Woodwinds Department. *Score & parts:* Dorn.

L4.19 Pro Vitor.
For: jazz group. Withdrawn.

L4.20 The Rabbit.
For: jazz group. Withdrawn.

L4.21 The Sensuous Gargoyle. (1975)
For: violin and piano. *First performed:*
Jan. 29, 1976; New England
Conservatory. Mary Crowder Hess,
violin and Rebecca LaBrecque, piano.
Score: ms.
Cassette: recording of first
performance. NEC

L4.22 710 Filbert Street.
For: jazz group. Withdrawn.

L4.23 Six at the Top Means.
For: jazz group. Withdrawn.

L4.24 Sour Mash. (1976-78)
For: saxophone(alto) and piano. *First
performed:* Feb. 3, 1980; Swarthmore
College. Kenneth Radnofsky, alto
saxophone and Michael Dewart, piano.
Score: Dorn, 1980.

L4.25 Tennessee Sour Mash (1976)
For: violoncello and piano. Withdrawn.

L4.26 Wakefield.
For: jazz group. Withdrawn.

L5 FRED LERDAHL

Born 1943 in Madison, Wis. Moved to
Boston area 1971. *Education:* studied
composition with James Ming
(Lawrence University, 1961-65); Earl
Kim, Milton Babbitt (Princeton
University, 1965-68); Arthur Berger
(Berkshire Music Center, Tanglewood,
1964); Roger Sessions (Berkshire Music
Center, Tanglewood, 1966); piano with
Robert Helps. *Awards:* Koussevitzky
International Award for Best
Composition (1966), Fulbright
Fellowship (1969), National Institute of
Arts and Letters Award (1971),
Guggenheim Grant (1974-75), Naumburg
Recording Award (1977). *Related
activities:* pianist; co-author with
linguist, Ray Jackendoff, of *A
Generative Theory of Tonal Music*
(forthcoming) and journal articles on

this subject; Composer-in-Residence,
Marlboro Music Festival (1967-68);
served on the faculties of the
University of California, Berkeley
(1969-71), Harvard University (1971-79),
Columbia University (1979-). HU

WORKS

L5.1 Aftermath: A Dramatic Work.
(1973) 25'-30'
For: Soprano, Mezzo Soprano, Baritone,
instrumental ensemble(flutes(2), oboe,
clarinets(2), horn, percussion(2), harp,
strings). *First performed:* May 1973;
Harvard University; Fromm Foundation
concert.
Score: Mobart, 197-. HU

L5.2 Chords. (1974) 15'
For: orchestra(in 3 groups: flutes(3),
trumpets(3), percussion(3), violas(3);
clarinets(3), bassoons(3), horns(3),
percussion, violoncellos(3); oboes(3),
trombones(3), double basses(3)).
Commissioned by: Berkshire Music
Center, Tanglewood and Fromm
Foundation. *First performed:* Aug. 1974;
Berkshire Music Center, Tanglewood.
Berkshire Music Center Orchestra.
Score: Mobart, 197-. HU

L5.3 Eros: Variations. (1975) 23'
For: Mezzo Soprano, flute(alto),
piano(electric), percussion(2), harp,
guitar(electric), electric bass, viola. 21
continuous variations. *Text:* Coitus,
from *Lustra* by Ezra Pound.
Commissioned by: Koussevitzky Music
Foundation (Library of Congress). First
performed: Feb. 1977; New York City.
Beverly Morgan, mezzo soprano;
Chamber Music Society of Lincoln
Center.
Score: Mobart, 1978. HU
Disc: Composers Recordings CRI SD
378, 1978. Beverly Morgan, mezzo
soprano; Collage, Fred Lerdahl,
conductor. BrU BU HU MIT NEC W

[Etudes]
L5.4 Six Etudes. (1977)
For: flute, viola, harp. *Commissioned*

by: Orpheus Trio.
Study score: Mobart, 1981. MIT

L5.5 Piano Fantasy. (1964) 4' 5"-7'
First performed: Oct. 1964; Lawrence University. Fred Lerdahl.
Score: Finell Music Services.
Disc: Composers Recordings CRI SD 319, 1974. Robert Miller. BrU BU HU MIT NEC W

[Quartet, Strings, No. I]
L5.6 First String Quartet. (1978) 22'
Commissioned by: Joslyn Art Museum, Omaha, Neb., for the Juilliard String Quartet. *First performed:* Mar. 1979; Omaha, Neb. Juilliard String Quartet.
Score: Mobart, 1978. HU

[Quartet, Strings, No. 2]
L5.7 Second String Quartet. (1980) 22'
Commissioned by: National Endowment for the Arts, for the Pro Arte Quartet.
Music: Finell Music Services.

[Trio, Violin, Viola, Violoncello]
L5.8 String Trio. (1965-66; rev. 1967) 11' 25"-14'
First performed: July 1966; Berkshire Music Center, Tanglewood (earlier version). 1967; Princeton University (later version). Matthew Raimondi, violin; Jean Dupouy, viola; Michael Rudiakov, violoncello.
Music: Mobart.
Disc: Composers Recording CRI SD 319, 1974. Matthew Raimondi, violin; Jean Dupouy, viola; Michael Rudiakov, violoncello. BrU BU HU MIT NEC W

L5.9 Wake. (1968) 16'
For: Soprano, percussion(3: tom-toms(6), conga drums(2), suspended cymbals, maracas; marimba, bongos(4), suspended cymbals(4), tamtams(2), templeblocks(5), crash cymbals(2); xylophone, woodblocks, bass drum, crotales(4), maracas), harp, violin, viola, violoncello. 1 movement. *Text:* e.e. cummings; arranged from Book I, Chapter 8 of *Finnegan's Wake*, by James Joyce. *First performed:* Aug. 14,

1968; Marlboro Music Festival. Bethany Beardslee, soprano; Fred Lerdahl, conductor.
Score: Mobart, 197-. HU
Parts: Mobart. Rental.
Disc: AR Deutsche Grammophon 0654 083, 1971. Bethany Beardslee, soprano; members of the Boston Symphony Chamber Players, David Epstein, conductor. MIT NEC W
Disc: New World, nyp. Reissue of AR Deutsche Grammophon 0654 083, 1971.

L5.10 Waltzes. (1981) 10'
For: instrumental ensemble.
Commissioned by: Festival of Two Worlds, Spoleto (Italy) and Spoleto Music Festival U.S.A.

L6 ERIK LINDGREN

Born December 15, 1954, in Harrisburg, Pa. Moved to Boston area 1972. *Education:* studied composition with T.J. Anderson (Tufts University B.A., 1976); Alfred Nieman (Guildhall School of Music, London, England, 1974-75); Donald Jenni and Richard Hervig (University of Iowa, Iowa City, M.A., 1977); electronic music with Peter Lewis (1976-77); piano with Birgette Wild (1974- 75) and John Simms (1976-77). *Related activities:* pianist; publisher; composer of popular electronic music and songs. T

WORKS

L6.1 Changes. (1980) 10'
For: clarinet, piano, percussion, guitar(bass)(optional). *Dedicated to:* Monovogue. *First performed:* 1980; The Underground, Boston. Chris Jepperson, clarinet; Erik Lindgren, electric piano; Michel Biard, percussion; Digney Fignus, guitar.
Score & parts: reprod. of ms.; available from composer.
Reel: recording of first performance.

L6.2 Cloud 9. (1977) 10'
For: flute, oboe, clarinet, bassoon,

percussion ensemble, string orchestra.
Score & parts: reprod. of ms.; available from composer.
Reel: 1977; University of Iowa. John Floreen, conductor. Available from composer.

L6.3 Fantasy. (1979) 8'
For: piano(4-hands). *Dedicated to:* Jane Lindgren.
Score: reprod. of ms.; available from composer.

L6.4 Flight. (1976) 10'
For: flute. *First performed:* 1976; University of Iowa. Pat Fry.
Score: American Composers Alliance.
Reel: recording of first performance; available from composer.

L6.5 Grown-Up Children's Pieces. (1972) 9'
For: piano. *Movements:* Mesmirations; Montmartre; The Day the Dinosaures Came into This World and Challenged the Vegetable Kingdom; Erik's Attire.
First performed: May 27, 1973; Trinity Lutheran Church, Camp Hill, Pa. Erik Lindgren.
Score: American Composers Alliance.
Reel: 1976; Tufts University. Erik Lindgren. Available from composer.

L6.6 Homage to Brian Izen. (1977) 8'
For: trombones(2). *First performed:* 1977; University of Iowa. Frank Jaeckle and Chris White.
Score: American Composers Alliance.
Reel: recording of first performance; available from composer.

L6.7 Intergalactic Insights. (1974-75) 12'
For: piano. 3 movements. *First performed:* 1976; Tufts University. Erik Lindgren.
Score: American Composers Alliance.
Reel: recording of first performance; available from composer.

L6.8 Introduction and Rag. (1973) 6'
For: piano. *First performed:* July 28, 1974; Trinity Lutheran Church, Camp Hill, Pa. Erik Lindgren.

Score: American Composers Alliance.
Reel: 1976; Tufts University. Erik Lindgren. Available from composer.

L6.9 Kyrie eleison. (1974) 3'
For: Soprano, Alto, Tenor, Bass. *First performed:* July 28, 1974; Trinity Lutheran Church, Camp Hill, Pa. Eleanor Hamm, soprano; Mary Jane Nelson, alto; Bob Smith, tenor; Doug Durante, bass.
Vocal score: American Composers Alliance.
Reel: 1976; Tufts University. Alice Honner, soprano; Lee Fesman, alto; George McGovern, tenor; Paul Ritterhoff, bass. Available from composer.

L6.10 Music for String Quartet. (1978) 15'
4 movements.
Score & parts: reprod of ms.; available from composer.

[Pieces, Piano]
L6.11 Two Pieces. (1976) 12'
Score: American Composers Alliance.

L6.12 Prelude and Fantasia. (1976) 9'
For: trumpets(2), horn, trombone, tuba.
First performed: 1977; University of Iowa. Ray Smith and Herb Blauel, trumpets; Tom Hundemer, horn; James Lindholm, trombone; Dan Troxell, tuba, John Floreen, conductor.
Score & parts: American Composers Alliance.
Reel: recording of first performance; available from composer.

L6.13 Quartet. (1976) 18'
For: clarinet, violin, violoncello, piano.
4 movements. *First performed:* 1976; Tufts University. Lonice Thomas, clarinet; Daniel Abbott, violin; Carol Sheats, violoncello; Erik Lindgren, piano; James Ritchie, conductor.
Score: reprod. of ms.; available from composer.
Reel: recording of first performance; available from composer.

L6.14 Radio Soul. (1978) 6'
For: piano. *Dedicated to:* Brian
Goodspeed.
Score: reprod. of ms.; available from
composer.

[Rags]
L6.15 Two Rags. (1974) 5'
For: piano. *Movements:* Winthrop House
Rag; Back to the Piano Rag (to be
played with back to piano).
Score: American Composers Alliance.

L6.16 Revelation. (1980) 10'
For: chorus(SATB) and orchestra(0-0-0-0;
2-1-2-1; electronic ensemble; perc; pf,
org; str). *Text:* adapted from Bible,
N.T., Revelations. Commissioned for
the Northfield Mt. Hermon Centennial.
Score & parts: reprod. of ms.; available
from composer.

L6.17 Seasons. (1977-78) 10'
For: violin, violoncello, percussion.
Movements: Winter; Spring; Summer;
Fall. *Dedicated to:* Lee Fesman.
Score & parts: reprod. of ms.; available
from composer.

[Seasons. Winter; Arr.]
L6.18 Winter. (1977) 3'
For: viola, violoncello, celeste.
Score: reprod. of ms.; available from
composer.

L6.19 Tides. (1981) 10'
For: flute, oboe, clarinet, bassoon,
vibraphone, piano, synthesizer(Arp
string), tape.
Score & parts: reprod. of ms.; available
from composer.
Tape: available from composer.

L6.20 Tonal Piano Music. (1972-74)
9 movememts.
Score: American Composers Alliance.

L6.21 Trio. (1975) 18'
For: flute, clarinet, piano. 3
movements. *Dedicated to:* Roky
Erickson, Tommy Hall, and the

thirteenth floor elevators. *First
performed:* 1976; Tufts University.
Betsy Sheehan, flute; Thomas Kazior,
clarinet, Richard Skarnes, violoncello.
Score: reprod. of ms.; available from
composer.
Reel: recording of first performance;
available from composer.

Winter. *See* Seasons. Winter; Arr.

ARRANGEMENTS OF WORKS BY OTHER COMPOSERS

L6.22 Le Piege de Meduse. (1975) 4'
For: orchestra(1(&pic)-1-2-2(&cbsn);
cor-3-0-1; perc(2); str(6-6-4-2-2)).
Movements: Quadrille; Valse; Pas vite;
Mazurka; Un'peu vif; Polka; Quadrille.
Original by Erik Satie.
Score & parts: reprod. of ms; available
from composer.

L7 J. RODNEY LISTER

Born May 31, 1951, in Ft. Payne, Ala.
Moved to Boston area 1969. *Education:*
studied composition with Malcolm
Peyton (New England Conservatory,
B.M., 1973), Donald Martino (Berkshire
Music Center, Tanglewood, 1973), Peter
Maxwell Davies (1973-75), Arthur
Berger, Harold Shapero (Brandeis
University, M.F.A, 1977). *Awards:*
Bernstein Fellowship (Tanglewood,
1973), Charles M. Cox Trust Grant
(1980), Wesley Weyman Trust Grant
(1980). *Related activities:* pianist;
conductor; music coordinator, Dinosaur
Annex. NEC

WORKS

L7.1 Adam Lay Ybounden. (1974) 3'
For: chorus(children), recorders, piano.
Text: anon.; early English. *Dedicated to:*
Sir James Barrie JM Sch., ILEA,
London. First performed: Dec. 1974;
London, England. Sir James Matthew
Barrie Junior School students.
Score: American Composers Alliance.

L7.2 Agreeably of Love. (1973) 4'
For: Soprano and piano. *Text:* W.H.
Auden. *Dedicated to:* Barbara
Winchester and Malcolm Peyton. *First
performed:* May 1976; WGBH-FM,
Boston. Barbara Winchester, soprano
and Malcolm Peyton, piano.
Score: American Composers Alliance.

L7.3 Alex--Berceuse du chat. (1978) 12'
For: clarinet, violin, piano. 1
movement. *Dedication:* To Janet &
Kathy with love. *First performed:* Aug.
1978; London, England. Kathy Matasy,
clarinet; Janet Packer, violin; Rodney
Lister, piano.
Score: American Composers Alliance.
Reel: Sept. 30, 1979; First and Second
Church, Boston; Dinosaur Annex
concert. Ian Greitzer, clarinet; Janet
Packer, violin; Rodney Lister, piano.
WGBH

L7.4 The Bell Doth Tolle. (1973) 6'
For: Bass and instruments(4). *Text:*
George Herbert. *Contents:* The Knell;
Affliction. *Dedication:* In memoriam
Marion Tronerud. *First performed:* May
24, 1973; New England Conservatory; in
An Evening of Music by New England
Conservatory Composers. Peter Bugel,
bass; Deanna Dalrymple, oboe; Ray
Cutler, trombone; Marc Parmet,
vibraphone; Deborah Collins, viola.
Score: ms. in composer's hand.
Cassette: recording of first
performance. NEC

L7.5 Bird Song. (1978) 2'
For: Soprano, clarinet, violin, double
bass. 1 movement. *Text:* William
Shakespeare. *Dedicated to:* Toby,
Michaela, and Adam. *First performed:*
winter 1979; Isabella Stewart Gardner
Museum, Boston. Dinosaur Annex.
Score: American Composers Alliance.

L7.6 The Bluejays Lullaby. (1980) 3'
For: Soprano, clarinet, violin, double
bass. 1 movement. *Text:* Peter Soyez
Beagle. *Dedicated to:* Arthur Berger.
First performed: Mar. 1980; Emerson
College. Robin Lloyd, soprano; Ian

Greitzer, clarinet; Janet Packer, violin;
Morton Cahn, double bass.
Score: American Composers Alliance.

L7.7 The Breaking. (1975) 10'
For: Countertenor, Tenor, Baritone,
instruments(5). *Text:* George Herbert. 3
movements. *Dedicated to:* G.A.
Ffrench-Beytaugh. *First performed:*
spring 1975; London, England.
Score: ms. in composer's hand.

A Certain World. *See* Though the Night
is Gone.

L7.8 A Christmas Prayer: Hommage to
T. Tertius Noble. (1975) 4'
For: chorus(SATB). *Text:* Gerard Manley
Hopkins. *Dedication:* For Roderick
Swanston and the Choir of Christ
Church, Lancaster Gate, London. *First
performed:* Dec. 1978; First and Second
Church, Boston. Emerson College Choir,
Scott Wheeler, conductor.
Vocal score: reprod. of ms. NEC
Vocal score: American Composers
Alliance.

L7.9 Come All Ye Fair and Tender
Ladies: Folksong Settings No. 1. (1979)
5'
For: Mezzo Soprano and viola. *Text:*
Appalachian folksong. *Dedicated to:*
D'Anna and David. *First performed:*
May 1979; Isabella Stewart Gardner
Museum, Boston. Laurel Stavis, mezzo
soprano and David Allcott, viola.

L7.10 Engendered in the Eyes. (in
progress) 8'
For: voice(medium) and harp. *Text:*
William Shakespeare. *Contents:* Lullaby I
(in progress); Tell Me Where Is Fancy
Bred; Take O Take Those Lips Away;
Lullaby II.
Score: American Composers Alliance.

L7.11 The Foil. (1973) 3'
For: chorus(mixed). *Text:* George
Herbert. *First performed:* spring 1975;
London, England. Choir of Christ
Church, Lancaster Gate, Roderick

Swanston, choirmaster.
Score: ms. in composer's hand.

Folksong Settings No. 1. *See* Come All Ye Fair and Tender Ladies.

Folksong Settings No. 2. *See* The Truth Sent from Above. Folksong Settings No. 2.

Folksong Settings No. 3. *See* The Truth Sent from Above: Folksong Settings No. 3.

L7.12 From the Sea and the Mirror. 4'
For: Mezzo Soprano, clarinet, violin, piano. 1 movement. *Text:* W.H. Auden. *Dedicated to:* Martin. *First performed:* Aug. 1980; Dartington Hall Summer School, England. Susan Anderson, mezzo soprano; John Mchoy, clarinet; Rupert Borden, violin; unidentified pianist; Rodney Lister, conductor.

L7.13 Hymn. (1978) 4'
For: Soprano, Tenor, instruments(5).
Text: Christopher Smart.
Music: ms. in composer's hand.

L7.14 I Will Not Leave You Comfortless. (1976) 5'
For: chorus(mixed), handbells, organ. 1 movement. *Text:* Bible, N.T., John and Bishop Myles Coverdale. *Dedicated to:* Nine O'Clock Choir, Church of the Advent, Boston. *First performed:* Whitsunday, 1976; Boston. Church of the Advent Nine O'Clock Choir.
Vocal score: American Composers Alliance.

L7.15 The King of Love My Shepherd Is. (1978) 4'
For: chorus(mixed). 1 movement. *Text:* George Herbert. *Dedication:* For Laurel & the Social Harp. *First performed:* spring, 1978; First and Second Church, Boston. Emerson College Choir, Steven Wilson, conductor.
Vocal score: American Composers Alliance.

L7.16 The Lesson. (1977)
For: Mezzo Soprano, clarinet, clarinet(E-flat), clarinet(bass), crotales, piano. 1 movement. *Text:* Robert Lowell. *Dedicated to:* D'Anna. *First performed:* spring, 1978; First and Second Church; Boston. D'Anna Fortunato, mezzo soprano; Dinosaur Annex.
Score: reprod. of ms. NEC
Score: American Composers Alliance.

L7.17 A Little Cowboy Music. (1980) 6'
For: clarinet, piano, violin, double bass. 1 movement. *Commissioned by and dedicated to:* Toby Armour. *First performed:* Apr. 1980; Somerville, Mass. Dinosaur Annex.
Score: American Composers Alliance.

L7.18 Mary Sings. (1974) 5'
For: Alto and instruments(6). 1 movement. *Text:* For the Time Being by W.H. Auden. *First performed:* May 1976; Old South Meeting House, Boston. Dinosaur Annex.
Score: American Composers Alliance.

L7.19 Music for a While. (1971) 6'
For: flute, oboe, piano. 1 movement. *Dedicated to:* Conrad Michael Pope. *First performed:* Nov. 9, 1971; Jordan Hall, Boston; in An Evening of Contemporary Music. David Hart, flute; Deanna Dalrymple, oboe; Margit Rahkonen, piano.
Score: American Composers Alliance.
Cassette: recording of first performance. NEC

L7.20 My World and Welcome to It, Book I. (1973) 5'
For: double bass. *Movements:* Les adieux; L'absence. *Dedicated to:* Alan Nagel. *First performed:* May 1973; Walden Pond, Mass. Alan Nagel (Les adieux). Aug. 1973; Aspen, Colo. Alan Nagel (L'absence).
Score: American Composers Alliance.

L7.21 Nowe Welcome, Somor. (1975) 4'
For: Countertenor or Alto and

instruments(5). 1 movement. *Text:* Geoffrey Chaucer. *Dedicated to:* Eleanor. *First performed:* winter, 1977; Waltham, Mass.
Score: American Composers Alliance.

L7.22 Nuns Fret Not. (1973) 12'
For: Soprano, flute, clarinet, trumpet, vibraphone, harp, viola, double bass. *Text:* William Wordsworth. *Contents:* Nuns Fret Not; Composed on Westminster Bridge: September 3, 1802; The World Is Too Much with Us; London, 1802; Mutability. *Dedicated to:* Malcolm Peyton. *First performed:* March 27, 1973; New England Conservatory; in An Evening of Contemporary Music. Joyce Fields, soprano; David Hart, flute; John Colbert, clarinet; Mark Schubert, trumpet; Mark Belair, vibraphone; Susan Page, harp; Linda Walton, viola; Alan Nagel, double bass; Rodney Lister, conductor.
Cassette: recording of first performance. NEC
Cassette: May 12, 1973; New England Conservatory; in *A Festival of Contemporary American Music.* Rodney Lister, conductor. NEC

L7.23 Ritornello. (1970) 4'
For: flute and piano. Withdrawn.

[Sacred Songs]
L7.24 Three Sacred Songs. (1976-77) 6'
For: Soprano and violin. *Contents:* Untitled (anon., fourteenth century); Untitled (W.H. Auden); Generosity (Christopher Smart). *Dedication:* To Max; In memoriam Benjamin Britten, December 4, 1976; To Virgil Thomson for his 80th Birthday (25 November 1976). *First performed:* Apr. 1977; First and Second Church, Boston. Barbara Winchester, soprano and Janet Packer, violin.
Score: reprod. of ms. NEC
Score: American Composers Alliance.

L7.25 The Second, Part III. (1974) 8'
For: Bass and instruments(9). 1 movement. *Text:* Walt Whitman. *First*

performed: spring, 1976; Waltham, Mass.
Score: American Composers Alliance.

L7.26 The Shepherd. (1974) 3'
For: chorus(children)(unison), recorders, percussion, piano. 1 movement. *Text:* William Blake. *Dedication:* Sir James Barrie JM Sch/homage to Virgil Thomson. *First performed:* spring, 1977; First and Second Church, Boston. Cambridge Chorale, Rodney Lister, conductor.
Score: American Composers Alliance.

L7.27 The Shepherds. (1975) 4'
For: Soprano and instruments(6). *Text:* John Milton. *First performed:* May 1976; Old South Meeting House, Boston. Dinosaur Annex.
Score: American Composers Alliance.

L7.28 Such Beauty as Hurts to Behold. (1981) 4'
For: voice(medium) and piano. 1 movement. *Text:* Paul Goodman. *Dedicated to:* K.C.
Score: American Composers Alliance.

L7.29 Sweet Was the Song. (1973) 3'
For: Soprano, Alto, instruments(5). 1 movement. *Text:* from *Lute Book* by W. Ballet. *First performed:* May 1973; Old South Meeting House, Boston. Dinosaur Annex.
Score: American Composers Alliance.

L7.30 Taller To-day. (1974) 6'
For: Soprano and instruments(10). *Text:* W.H. Auden. *Dedicated to:* Cathy. *First performed:* May 1976; WGBH-FM, Boston. Barbara Winchester, soprano; Dinosaur Annex, Rodney Lister, conductor.
Score: American Composers Alliance.

L7.31 Tango alla canonica. (1977) 4'
For: instruments(unspecified)(4). 1 movement. *Dedication:* In memoriam James Waring. *First performed:* fall, 1977; Isabella Stewart Gardner Museum, Boston.

Score: reprod. of ms. NEC
Score: American Composers Alliance.

L7.32 Thank God It's Friday. (1975) 2'
For: chorus(children), recorder, percussion, piano. 1 movement. *Text:* Christopher Smart. *Dedication:* For Barbara (Lippett) & her new school.
Score: American Composers Alliance.

L7.33 Though the Night Is Gone: A Certain World, Book II. (1980) 10'
For: Baritone and piano. *Text:* W.H. Auden. *Contents:* Lullaby; As I Walked out One Evening. *Commissioned by:* Sanford Sylvan. *Dedicated to:* Sanford Sylvan and David Breitman.
Score: American Composers Alliance.

L7.34 The Truth Sent from Above: Folksong Settings No. 2. (1980) 3'
For: clarinet, violin, double bass. *Text:* English Christmas carol. *Dedicated to:* Larry Killian.
Score: American Composers Alliance.

L7.35 The Truth Sent from Above: Folksong Settings No. 3. (1981) 3'
For: chorus(unison) and piano. *Text:* English Christmas carol. *Dedicated to:* Nine O'Clock Choir, Church of the Advent, Boston.
Vocal score: American Composers Alliance.

L7.36 When God Lets My Body Be. (1979) 4'
For: chorus(mixed). 1 movement. *Text:* e.e. cummings. *Dedicated to:* Lorna Cooke deVaron.
Vocal score: American Composers Alliance.

L7.37 The Wuggly Ump. (1977) 8'
For: chorus(women), recorders, percussion, piano. 1 movement. *Text:* Edward Gorey. *Dedicated to:* Scott. *First performed:* spring, 1977; First and Second Church, Boston. Cambridge Chorale, Rodney Lister, conductor.
Vocal score: American Composers Alliance.

ARRANGEMENTS OF WORKS BY OTHER COMPOSERS

L7.38 Prelude and Fugue in D major. (1978) 10'
For: clarinet(E-flat), clarinet(in A), clarinet(bass), marimba, violin, viola, violoncello. Original from *The Well-Tempered Clavier*, Book II by Johann Sebastian Bach. *Dedicated to:* Barbara and Vance. *First performed:* May 1979; Isabella Stewart Gardner Museum, Boston. Dinosaur Annex.
Score: American Composers Alliance.

L8 GREGORY LIVINGSTON

Born February 25, 1951, in Suffern, N. Y. Moved to Boston area 1969. *Education:* studied composition with Avram David and double bass with William Rhein (Boston Conservatory, B.M., 1974). *Related activities:* principal double bass, Boston Civic Symphony; currently on the faculty of Brown Junior High School, Newton, Mass. BCM

WORKS

L8.1 Festival March, Op. 4. (1979) 2'
For: band. *First performed:* Aug. 1979; Newton, Mass. Newton Creative Arts Center Band, Gregory Livingston, conductor.
Score: ms. in composer's hand.

L8.2 Going Out Tune, Op 3. (1979) 2' 5"
For: jazz ensemble(saxophones(alto)(2), saxophone(tenor), saxophone(baritone), trumpets(4), trombones(2), guitar, double bass, piano, drums). *First performed:* Mar. 1979; Newton, Mass. Newton North High School Jazz Ensemble, Gregory Livingston, conductor.
Score: ms. in composer's hand.

L8.3 Pastorale, Op. 5. (1980) 3' 5"
For: saxophone(tenor) and piano. *First performed:* Aug. 1980; Newton, Mass. Lisa Stern, saxophone and Gregory

Livingston, piano.
Score: ms. in composer's hand.

L8.4 Prologue, Op. 2. (1973) 3' 25"
For: trumpets(2), horn, trombone, tuba, timpani. *First performed:* May 11, 1973; Boston Conservatory. Avram David, conductor.
Score: ms. in composer's hand.
Reel: recording of first performance. BCM

[Short Pieces]
L8.5 Five Short Pieces, Op. 1. (1973) 10'
For: double bass and piano.
Movements: Waltz; Pastorale; Andante cantabile; Elegy; Untitled.
Score: ms. in composer's hand.

L9 RUTH LOMON

Born November 8, 1930, in Montreal, Que. Moved to Boston area 1960.
Education: Licentiate (McGill University, Montreal, Que); Licentiate (Conservatoire de Musique de Quebec); studied composition with Carl McKinley, Francis Judd Cooke (New England Conservatory); Witold Lutoslawski (Dartington, England); piano with Miklos Schwalb. *Awards:* Yaddo Fellowship (1977) and Helene Wurlitzer Foundation of New Mexico grant (1978).
Related activities: pianist and duo pianist; teacher of piano, theory and composition. W

WORKS

L9.1 Celebrations; Nimbus and the Sun God. (1978) 16' 45"
For: harps(2). *Dedicated to:* Susan Allen.
First performed: Nov. 5, 1978; Massachusetts Institute of Technology. Susan Allen (live and pre-recorded).
Score: reprod. of ms. W
Reel & cassette: recording of first performance.
Reel & cassette: Feb. 17, 1980; Lexington, Mass.

[Concerto, Bassoon]
L9.2 Bassoon Concerto. (1978-79)
For: bassoon and orchestra(2(pic)-1-2(&bcl)-0; 2-2-2-1; timp, perc, vibra, xylo; hp, cel; str). 3 movements.
Score: reprod. of ms. W
Part(bassoon): reprod. of ms.; available from composer.

L9.3 Dialogue. (1964) 6'
For: harpsichord and vibraphone.
Score: reprod. of ms.; available from composer.

L9.4 Dust Devils. (1976) 7' 40"
For: harp. *Movements:* The Whorl; The Eye; The Jinn. *Commissioned by:* Phyllis Whitman. *First performed:* June 22, 1977; Emmanuel College; American Harp Society meeting. Susan Allen.
Score: Arsis, 1976. W
Disc: 1750 Arch, nyp. Susan Allen.
Reel & cassette: Nov. 11, 1978; Massachusetts Institute of Technology. Susan Allen.

L9.5 Equinox. (1978) 4' 30"
For: trumpets(2) and trombones(2).
Commissioned by: First Parish Church Unitarian Universalist. *First performed:* Mar. 26, 1978; Lexington, Mass. Jay Rizzetto and Wayne King, trumpets; Nathaniel Gurin and Roy Campbell, trombones.
Score & parts: reprod. of ms. W
Reel & cassette: recording of first performance.

Erinnyes. *See* The Furies.

L9.6 The Fisherman and His Soul.
For: Soprano, Alto, Tenor, Bass, chamber orchestra(woodwinds and strings). Chamber opera. *Text:* based on the fairy tale by Oscar Wilde.
Score: ms. in composer's hand.

L9.7 The Furies (Erinnyes). (1977) 10'
For: oboe, oboe d'amore, English horn.
Dedicated to: Patricia Morehead. *First performed:* Mar. 15, 1978; Rhode Island

College. Patricia Morehead and tape.
Score: reprod. of ms. W
Reel & cassette: Mar. 23, 1978;
Arlington, Mass. Patricia Morehead and
tape.
Reel & cassette: Mar. 29, 1978; Longy
School of Music. Patricia Morehead
and tape.

L9.8 Masks. (1980) 15'
For: piano. *Movements:* Changing
Woman; Dancer; Spirit; Clown; Talking
Power. *Text:* Inspired by five
ceremonial masks from the Navajo
Yeibichi night chants. *First performed:*
Apr. 13, 1980; Lexington, Mass. Ruth
Lomon.
Score: reprod. of ms. W
Reel & cassette: Nov. 1980; studio. Ruth
Lomon.
Reel & cassette: June 10, 1981; London
University, England. Ruth Lomon.

L9.9 Phase I. (1969) 5' 30"
For: violoncello and piano. *Dedicated
to:* Glynis Lomon. *First performed:*
Nov. 10, 1974; Massachusetts Institute
of Technology. Glynis Lomon,
violoncello and Mark Engler, piano.
Score: reprod. of ms. W
Reel & cassette: Feb. 2, 1975;
Bennington College. Glynis Lomon,
violoncello and Mark Engler, piano.

L9.10 Phase II. (1975) 5' 30"
For: Soprano, violoncello, piano. *Text:*
Manahatta and *Oh Living Always,
Always Dying* by Walt Whitman.
Dedicated to: R.M. Weiner. *First
performed:* 1975; Sigma Alpha Iota,
The Friends House, Boston. Catherine
Wise Randall, soprano; Glynis Lomon,
violoncello; Mark Engler, piano.
Score: reprod. of ms. W
Reel & cassette: recording of first
performance.

L9.11 Requiem. (1977) 35'
For: Soprano, chorus(SATB), flute,
clarinet, clarinet(E-flat/bass), bassoon,
trumpets(2), trombones(2). *Text:* Latin
Requiem Mass and Ruth Lomon.

Contents: Requeim aeternam; Kyrie; Dies
irae; Offertorium; Sanctus; Hosanna;
Benedictus; Agnus Dei; Libera me; Les
baux; The Mammoth Head; Interregnum;
One Revolution; Cancrizans; Black
Mesa; Incantation. *Dedicated to:* Vera
Lemere Finnie. *First performed:* Mar.
26, 1978; Lexington, Mass. (sections
for chorus and brass). Wayne King and
Jay Rizzetto, trumpets; Roy Campbell
and Nathaniel Gurin, trombones; First
Parish Church Unitarian Universalist
Choir, Francis Judd Cooke, director.
Score: reprod. of ms. W
Parts: for Requiem aeternam, Kyrie,
Sanctus, Hosanna, Benedictus. W
Reel & cassette: recording of first
performance.

[Requiem. Songs for a Requiem]
L9.12 Songs for a Requiem. (1977)
For: Soprano, flute, clarinet,
clarinet(bass), bassoon. *Text:* Ruth
Lomon. *Contents:* Les baux; The
Mammoth Head; Interregnum; One
Revolution; Cancrizans; Black Mesa;
Incantation.
Score: reprod of ms. W

L9.13 Rondo. (1959) 5'
For: piano. *First performed:* 1960; New
England Conservatory. Ruth Lomon.
Score: reprod. of ms. W

L9.14 Shapes.
For: guitar, violin, violoncello, piano.
Score: reprod. of ms.; available from
composer.

L9.15 Solstice. (1978) 5' 30"
For: trumpets(2) and trombones(2).
Score: reprod. of ms.; available from
composer.

[Songs after Poems by William
Blake]
L9.16 Five Songs after Poems by
William Blake. (1962) 8'
For: Alto and viola. *Text:* from *Songs
of Experience* (Nos. 1-4) and *Satiric
Verses and Epigrams* (No. 5), by
William Blake. *Contents:* The Sunflower;

The Fly; The Sick Rose; The Clod and the Pebble; Injunction. *First performed:* 1963; New England Conservatory. Myra Fronmeyer, alto and William Hibbard, viola.
Score: Arsis, 1980. W
Reel & cassette: recording of first performance.

L9.17 Soundings. (1975) 7'
For: piano(4-hands). *Dedicated to:* Iris Graffman Wenglin. *First performed:* Feb. 11, 1976; WGBH-FM, Boston. Ruth Lomon and Iris Graffman Wenglin.
Music: Arsis. 1975.
Reel: recording of first performance.
Reel & cassette: May 15, 1978; Brookline Public Library. Ruth Lomon and Iris Graffman Wenglin.

L9.18 Toccata and Fugue. (1961) 5'
For: piano. *First performed:* 1961; New England Conservatory. Ruth Lomon.
Score: reprod. of ms. W

L9.19 Trio.
For: horn, violoncello, piano.
Score: reprod. of ms.; available from composer.

L9.20 Triptych. (1978) 7'
For: pianos(2). *Dedicated to:* Elaine Quick. *First performed:* June 17, 1979; Lexington, Mass. Ruth Lomon and Iris Graffman Wenglin.
Score: reprod. of ms. W
Reel & cassette: recording of first performance.
Reel & cassette: Nov. 1980; studio. Ruth Lomon and Iris Graffman Wenglin.

L10 HARRIET AGDA LUNDBERG

Born February 28, 1944, in Brooklyn, N.Y. Moved to Boston area 1968.
Education: B.M. (Indiana University, 1966); M.M. (Boston Conservatory, 1969); studied composition with Hugo Norden; piano with Marie Bono.
Awards: Delta Omicron Triennial Composition Competition (Carson-Newman College, Second Place, 1978). *Related activities:* pianist;

accompanist; teacher; member of the faculty of Boston Conservatory (1970-)
W

WORKS

[Anthems]
L10.1 Two Anthems. (1974) 5'
Text: Bible, O.T., Psalm 98 and Bible, O.T., Jeremiah 7:23. *For:* Soprano and organ or piano. *Contents:* O Sing unto the Lord and Thus Saith the Lord of Hosts.
Score: reprod. of ms.; available from composer.

L10.2 Enigmas. (1976) 6'
For: piano. 3 movements. *Dedicated to:* Sister Mary Roy Weiss. *First performed:* Oct. 1980; Fisk House, Boston. Harriet Lundberg.
Score: reprod. of ms.; available from composer.

L10.3 In the Beginning. (1980)
For: piano and piano(4-hands). *Score.*

L10.4 Intaligo with Trees and People. (1980) 6'
For: narrator, flute, harp, viola. 1 movement. *Text:* Claire Keyes. *First performed:* 1981; Winthrop, Mass. Claire Keyes, narrator; Laura Montgomery, flute; Judith Ross, harp; Dale Hall, viola.
Score & parts: reprod. of ms.; available from composer.
Cassette: recording of first performance.

L10.5 Intrada, Chorale and Scherzo. (1976) 6'-7'
For: trumpets(2), horn, trombone, tuba. 3 movements.
Score & parts: reprod. of ms.; available from composer.

L10.6 Introduction, Theme, Variations and Fantasy. (1975) 15'-18'
For: piano. 1 movement.
Score: reprod. of ms.; available from composer.

L10.7 Journals: Cycle of Five Songs. (1974) 10'
For: Soprano and piano. *Text:* Henry David Thoreau and John Muir. *Contents:* Again It Rains; In this Fresh Evening; Last Year's Grasses; Now the Storm; How Deeply with Beauty. *First performed:* 1976; Boston Conservatory. Vicky Casey, soprano and Jacqueline Gourdin, piano.
Score: reprod. of ms.; available from composer.

L10.8 Matinee. (1980) 5'
For: carillon. 1 movement.
Score: reprod. of ms.; available from composer.

L10.9 Monologues. (1977) 10'-11'
For: harp. 3 movements.
Score: reprod. of ms.; available from composer.

[Movements]
L10.10 Three Movements.
For: string orchestra. Suite.
Score: reprod. of ms.; available from composer.

L10.11 Music for a Threesome. (1977) 10'-12'
For: flute, clarinet, bassoon. 3 movements. Awarded Delta Omicron Triennial Composition Competition, (Carson-Newman College), Second Place, (1978).
Score & parts: reprod. of ms.; available from composer.

[Pieces]
L10.12 Eleven Pieces. (1978) 13'
For: piano. *Contents:* Prologue; March in Five; Elegy; Whim; Quasi Waltz; Aubade; Fantasy; Quasi March; Pastorale; Hommage; Epilogue. *First performed:* Oct. 1980; Fisk House, Boston (selected pieces). Harriet Lundberg.
Score: reprod. of ms.; available from composer.

L10.13 Quaternion. (1979) 5'
For: saxophone(alto). 4 movements.
Score: reprod. of ms.; available from composer.

[Quintet, Woodwinds]
L10.14 Woodwind Quintet. (1975)
Score.

L10.15 Serenade. (1979) 15'
For: flute, clarinets(2), bassoon, viola, harp. 1 movement.
Score & parts: reprod. of ms.; available from composer.

L10.16 Sonatine. (1980) 12'-13'
For: flute and piano. 3 movements.
Score: reprod. of ms.; available from composer.

[Songs]
L10.17 Two Songs of Thought. (1975) 6'
For: voice(high) and piano. *Contents:* The Passing (Emma Maud McLaughlin); Flute (Marjorie Strauss). *First performed:* 1976; Belmont, Mass. Beatrice Werlin, soprano and Harriet Lundberg, piano.
Score: reprod. of ms.; available from composer.

L10.18 Symphony. (1973-74)
For: orchestra(2(&pic)-2(Ehn)-2-2; 4-3-3-1; timp, perc(3), xylo; hp; str(16-12-12-10-8)). 4 movements. *Score.*

L11 SALLY LUTYENS

Born October 31, 1927, in Syracuse, N.Y. Moved to Boston area 1962. *Education:* studied with Paul Boepple (special studies, University of Southern California); piano with Claude Frank (Bennington College, 1945-49). *Related activities:* member of the faculty of the Cambridge School, Weston, Mass.; established music program and member of the faculty at the College of The Atlantic. W

WORKS

L11.1 Auguste. (1980) 75'-80'
For: Mezzo Soprano, Tenors(2),
Baritone, Bass, chorus(SATB),
instrumental ensemble(oboe, English
horn, flute(bass), clarinet(bass),
contrabassoon, side drum, celeste,
strings(5)). Chamber opera in 5 scenes.
Libretto: Sally Lutyens, based on a
short story by Henry Miller.
Score & parts: reprod. of ms.; available
from composer.
Vocal score.

L11.2 The Burning Babe. (1979) 10'
For: chorus(SATB) and piano. *Text:*
Robert Southwell. *Commissioned by:*
Chorus Pro Musica. *First performed:*
Dec. 1979; Old South Church, Boston.
Chorus Pro Musica.
Vocal score: reprod. of ms.; available
from composer.
Reel: recording of first performance.

[Duino Elegy]
L11.3 Sixth Duino Elegy. (1977) 15'
For: Tenor, flute, violoncello. *Text:*
Rainer Maria Rilke.
Score & parts: reprod. of ms.; available
from composer.
Reel: Wayne Rivera, tenor; Donald
Palumbo, piano; unidentified
violoncellist (study tape).

L11.4 Encore. (1970) 6'
For: piano.
Score: reprod. of ms.; available from
composer.
Reel.

L11.5 From: Phaedra. (1980) 12'
For: Alto, flute, violin, viola,
violoncello, piano. *Text:* Jean Baptiste
Racine.
Score & parts: reprod. of ms.; available
from composer.

L11.6 From the Notebooks of Leonardo
da Vinci. (1976) 12'
For: Soprano and chorus(SATB).
Score: reprod. of ms.; available from
composer.

L11.7 From the Poems of Alfred Starr
Hamilton. (1976) 10'-12'
For: Soprano and piano. 6 songs. *First
performed:* May 1979; Hirshberg
Gallery, Boston. Virginia Sheppard,
soprano and Donald Palumbo, piano.
Score: reprod. of ms.; available from
composer.
Reel: recording of first performance.

L11.8 From the Poems of Katherine
Hoskins. (1980) 12'
For: Soprano and piano. 4 songs. *First
performed:* May 1981. Isabella Stewart
Gardner Museum, Boston. Elena
Gambulos, soprano and Donald
Palumbo, piano.
Score: reprod. of ms.; available from
composer.
Reel: recording of first performance.

L11.9 The Light Princess. (1978) 60'
For: Soprano, Mezzo Soprano, Alto,
Tenor, Baritones(2), Bass, instrumental
ensemble(flute, clarinet, bassoon,
guitar, vibraphone, piano, strings(5)).
Chamber opera in one act, 7 scenes.
Libretto: Sally Lutyens, based on text
by George MacDonald. *Commissioned
by:* Newport Music Festival. *First
performed:* Aug. 1979; Newport, R.I.
Elena Gambulos, soprano; Valerie
Walters, mezzo soprano; Sally
Williams, alto; Wayne Rivera, tenor; J.
Scott Brumit and Rene De La Garza,
baritones; Richard Crist, bass.
Score & parts: reprod. of ms.; available
from composer.
Vocal score: reprod. of ms.; available
from composer.
Reel or cassette: recording of first
performance.

L11.10 The Minister's Black Veil. (1976)
38'
For: Soprano, Tenor, Bass,
choruses(SATB)(2), instrumental
ensemble(flute, saxophone(soprano),
English horn, bassoon, piano, bells,
side drums). Chamber opera in one act,
five scenes. *Libretto:* Sally Lutyens,
based on the short story by Nathaniel

Hawthorne. *First performed:* Nov. 1976; Old South Church, Boston. Elisabeth Phinney, soprano; Wayne Rivera, tenor; Richard Crist, bass; Chorus Pro Musica. *Score & parts:* reprod. of ms.; available from composer. *Vocal score:* reprod. of ms.; available from composer. *Tape:* soloists and piano (study tape). *Reel:* recording of first performance.

L11.11 Missa brevis. (1977; 1981) 30' *For:* voices, chorus(SATB), horns(2), trumpets(2), trombones(2). *First performed:* Mar. 1980; Old South Church, Boston (Kyrie, Gloria). Chorus Pro Musica. *Score & parts:* reprod. of ms.; available from composer. *Vocal score:* reprod. of ms.; available from composer. *Reel:* tape of first performance.

L11.12 Nonsense Songs. (1977) *For:* chorus(SATB). 3 movements. *Text:* Sally Lutyens. *Vocal score:* reprod. of ms.; available from composer.

M1 EDWARD J. MADDEN

Education: University of New Hampshire; studied composition with Hugo Norden and Gardner Read (Boston University). *Awards:* Brookline Library Music Association Composers Award. *Related activities:* arranger and conductor. Be

WORKS

Air Varie. *See* A Gentle Air (Air Varie).

M1.1 Anthem of Heritage. (1965) 6' *For:* chorus(SATB) and orchestra(2-2-2-2; 4-3-3-1; timp, perc; str) and/or band. 1 movement. *Text:* William Seymour. *First performed:* Dec. 1962; Brookline, Mass. Brookline High School Chorus and Brookline High School Orchestra. *Score & parts:* mss. in composer's hand

(orchestral and band versions). *Score & parts:* C. Fischer (orchestral and band versions). Rental. *Vocal score:* C. Fischer.

M1.2 Cakewalk. (1958) 3' *For:* band. 1 movement. *First performed:* winter 1958; Boston University. Boston University Symphonic Band. *Music:* Fillmore, 1963.

M1.3 Colonial Rhapsody. (1957) 7' *For:* band. 1 movement. *First performed:* spring 1957; Rochester, N.H. Spaulding High School Band, Edward Madden, conductor. *Condensed score:* E.B. Marks, 1958. *Disc:* Pepper JWP 111775, 1976. Central Michigan University Band.

M1.4 Concertante. (1978) 9' *For:* violin, flute, clarinet, piano. 2 movements. *First performed:* Mar. 1978; Brookline, Mass. *Score & parts:* ms. in composer's hand. *Reel:* Mar. 1978; Pine Manor College.

M1.5 Concerto for Jazz Ensemble and Symphonic Band. (1975) 20' *For:* jazz ensemble(saxophones(5), trumpets(4), trombones(4), rhythm(3)) and band. 4 movements. *Commissioned by:* Arizona State University Concert Band. *Dedicated to:* Dr. Richard Strange. *First performed:* May 1975; Tempe, Ariz. Arizona State University Jazz Ensemble and Arizona State University Concert Band. *Score & parts:* reprod. of ms. *Reel:* May 1975; Arizona State University.

M1.6 Divertimento. (1961) 10' *For:* piano, violin, violoncello. *Movements:* Abstraction; Air; Humoresque. Winner of the Brookline Library Music Association Composers Award. *First performed:* Apr. 4, 1961; Brookline Public Library. *Reel:* recording of first performance.

M1.7 The Eve of St. Agnes. (1971) 12′ 30″
For: piano and band. 1 movement.
Text: after the poem by John Keats.
Commissioned by: University of Tennessee at Martin Symphonic Wind Ensemble. *Dedicated to:* Robert Fleming, Director UTM Bands. *First performed:* Mar. 2, 1971; Martin, Tenn. University of Tennesee at Martin Symphonic Wind Ensemble.
Score & parts: ms.
Reel: May 1975; Arizona State University. Arizona State University Concert Band, Robert Fleming, conductor.
Reel: Nov. 9, 1978; Boston Conservatory. Boston Conservatory Wind Ensemble, John Corley, conductor. BCM

M1.8 Fantasia on a Folk Theme. 6′ 20″
For: band. 1 movement. *First performed:* Apr. 1961; Boston University.
Score: Colombo, 1968. BPL
Disc: Colombo Educational Reference Library, 1968.

M1.9 Fantasy on a Bell Carol. (1968) 4′
For: band. 1 movement. *Commissioned by:* Carl Fischer, Inc.
Score & parts: C. Fischer, 1970.
Condensed score: C. Fischer.
Disc: C. Fischer, 1970.

M1.10 Flutes, Flutes, Flutes. (1964) 5′
For: flutes(3 or multiples) and band. 1 movement. *First performed:* 1965; Brookline, Mass. Brookline High School Band, Edward Madden, conductor.
Condensed score & parts: C. Fischer, 1968.
Disc: C. Fischer, 1968.

M1.11 A Gentle Air (Air Varie). 3′
For: violin or viola or violoncello and piano. *Commissioned by and dedicated to:* Committee of the Alaska Biennial Competition, Fairbanks, Alaska. *First performed:* May 20, 1979; Fairbanks, Alaska. Contestants in the Alaska Biennial Competition.

Score & parts: ms. in composer's hand.
Reel: recording of first performance.

M1.12 Glory: Music for the 20th Century Mass. (1974) 15′
For: congregation, Soprano, Alto, Tenor, Bass, chorus(SATB)(optional), trumpets(2), trombones(3)(optional), rhythm section(drums, guitar, double bass)(optional), piano, organ(optional).
Text: International Commission on English Translation (1973). *Contents:* Kyrie; The Nicene Creed; Sanctus; The Lord's Prayer; Christ Our Passover; Gloria. *Commissioned by:* Trinity Church, Boston. *First performed:* Mar. 24, 1974; Trinity Church, Boston. Trinity Church Choir; George Faxon, organ; and others; Edward Madden, conductor.
Music: reprod. of ms.
Cassette: recording of first performance.

M1.13 The Gospel Truth. (1973) 3′ 33″
For: band. 1 movement. *First performed:* Jan. 1973; Brookline, Mass. Brookline High School Band, Edward Madden, conductor.
Condensed score & parts: E.B. Marks.

M1.14 March Festivo. (1974) 4′ 15″
For: band. 1 movement. *Commissioned by:* South Eastern Massachusetts School Band Master Association. *First performed:* Mar. 18, 1973; Southborough, Mass. Festival Band of SEMSBA members.
Condensed score & parts: C. Fischer.
Disc: C. Fischer.
Reel: Carnegie Hall, New York City. Carnegie-Mellon Symphonic Band, Richard Strange, conductor.

M1.15 March Symphonique. (1961) 3′ 30″
For: band. 1 movement. *First performed:* spring, 1961; Boston University. Boston University Concert Band, Lee Chrisman, conductor.
Score: E.B. Marks, 1969. BPL
Condensed score & parts: E.B. Marks, 1969.

Disc: Crest Records, 1968. North Hill High School Symphonic Band Pittsburgh, Pa.
Disc: 1970 Massachusetts All State Band, Frank L. Battista, conductor.
Reel: 1963; WGBH-TV, Boston. Boston University Wind Ensemble, Edward Madden, conductor.

M1.16 Our Eternal King.
For: chorus(SATB) and organ. 1 movement. *Text:* Edward Madden. *First performed:* 1972; Trinity Church, Boston. Trinity Church Choir; George Faxon, organ; Edward Madden, conductor.
Vocal score: C. Fischer.

M1.17 Our Own Thing. 3' 30"
For: band, guitar(optional), guitar(bass)(optional), drums(optional).
First performed: Apr. 1968; Brookline, Mass. Brookline High School Band, Edward Madden, conductor.
Condensed score: E.B. Marks, 1969.

M1.18 Rock Movement. (1970) 7' (without solos)
For: band, guitar(optional), electric bass(optional), drums(optional). 1 movement. *First performed:* Jan. 1970; Brookline, Mass. Brookline High School Band.
Score & parts: E.B. Marks, 1971.
Condensed score: E.B. Marks, 1971. BPL
Disc: Crest Records, 1972. Jefferson High School Wind Ensemble, Bloomington, Minn.

M1.19 Sinfonia on Jewish Folksongs. (1962) 8'
For: band. 1 movement. *First performed:* Jan. 1963; Brookline, Mass. Brookline High School Band, Edward Madden, conductor.
Score & parts: ms.
Condensed score & parts: ms. Recording: Dec. 17, 1978; New London, Conn. U.S. Coast Guard Band.

[Soliloquies]
M1.20 Five Soliloquies. (1954-79) 12'

For: piano. *Commissioned by:* Committee of the Alaska Biennial Competition (No. 5). *First performed:* May 1979; Fairbanks, Alaska. Contestant in the Alaska Biennial Competition.
Score: ms.
Reel: May 20, 1979; University of Alaska, Fairbanks (No. 5).

M1.21 Symphonic Variations on a Theme by Purcell. 11' 30"
For: band. 3 movements. *Commissioned by:* North Hills High School Symphonic Band, Warren S. Mercer, conductor.
First performed: May 17, 1968; Pittsburgh, Pa. North Hills High School Symphonic Band, Warren Mercer, conductor.
Score & parts: Boston Music, 1973. BPL
Disc: Columbo Educational Reference Library, B.P. 136. Carnegie-Mellon Symphonic Band.
Disc: Silver Crest Custom C.U.W.E. 7, 1970. Cornell University Wind Ensemble, Maurice Stith, conductor. BU HU

M1.22 There Is Sweet Music Here. 2' 30"
For: voice(high) or voice(low) and piano. 1 movement. *Text: The Lotus Eaters* by Alfred, Lord Tennyson. *Commissioned by:* Committee of the Alaska Biennial Competition. *First performed:* May 1979; University of Alaska, Fairbanks. Contestant in the Alaska Biennial Competition.
Score: ms.
Reel: May 20, 1979; University of Alaska, Fairbanks.

M2 JOSEPH MAKHOLM

Born December 6, 1954, in Burlingame, Calif. Moved to Boston area 1977.
Education: B.A., Journalism (University of Wisconsin, Milwaukee, 1976); Wisconsin Conservatory of Music; Berklee College of Music; studied composition with Thomas Oboe Lee (Boston) and William Thomas McKinley

(New England Conservatory); piano with Adelaide Banaszynski; jazz piano with Charlie Banacos, Tony King, Ray Santisi; trombone with Bill Schaefgen and Rick Stepton; conducting with Leon Barzin, George Monseur, Attilio Poto. *Awards:* Elmhurst Jazz Festival (Elmhurst, Ill., Outstanding Jazz Piano Soloist, 1977). *Related activities:* jazz pianist; member of brass quintet; conductor; currently Assistant Conductor, Melrose Symphony Orchestra. BPL

WORKS

M2.1 Concord, New Hampshire, in August. (1980-81) 27'
For: piano. *Movements:* Jocose; Savage; Pastoral; Arcane; Majestic; Morose. *First performed:* Apr. 19, 1980; Church of the Covenant, Boston (Jocuse). Newell Hendricks.
Score: ms. in composer's hand.

M2.2 Divertimento. (1980) 10' 30"
For: trumpets(2), horn, trombone, tuba. 3 movements. *Dedicated to:* Jeff Makholm and Mercedes Ridao on the occasion of their wedding, 24 May 1980. *First performed:* May 24, 1980; Milwaukee, Wis. James Brus and Rich ¡Tanner, trumpets; John Havu, horn; John Foshager, trombone; Ron Brusky, tuba.
Score & parts: ms. in composer's hand.

[Fantasies]
M2.3 Four Fantasies after a Painting by R. J. Krutke. (in progress)
For: clarinet and piano. *Movements:* Black Lines in the Sun; Aquatic Pulsations; The Monuments; Unity of the Winds. *First performed:* May 1, 1981; New England Conservatory. (Black Lines in the Sun). Terry Grissino, clarinet and Judy Cataldo, piano.
Score & parts: ms. in composer's hand.

[Quartet, Strings]
M2.4 String Quartet. (1980) 9' 30"
2 movements.
Score & parts: ms.

[References]
M2.5 Two References. (1981) 12'
For: trumpets(2), horn, trombone, tuba. *Movements:* Invocation; Latitude. *First performed:* Apr. 4, 1981; Church of the Covenant, Boston (Invocation). Don Mills and Scott Fessler, trumpets; Bob Moffitt, horn; Joseph Makholm, trombone; Pat Feig, tuba.
Score & parts: ms. in composer's hand.

M2.6 Untitled, Based on a Poem by Albert J. Bellg. (1979) 4'
For: piano.
Score: ms.

M3 JOSEPH GABRIEL MANERI

Born February 9, 1927, in New York City. Moved to Boston area 1970. *Education:* studied composition with Josef Schmid. *Related activities:* improviser on clarinet, saxophone, piano; performer of ethnic music and jazz; served on the faculties of Brooklyn Conservatory of Music (1964-65) and New England Conservatory (1970-). NEC

WORKS

M3.1 Adagio. (1957) 5'
For: string quartet.
Score & parts: Branch, 1957.

M3.2 And Death Shall Have No Dominion. (1977) 13'
For: Mezzo Soprano and piano. 1 movement. *Text:* Dylan Thomas. *Dedicated to:* Beverly Morgan in memory of Anna and Marion Radis. *First performed:* May 2, 1977; New England Conservatory; in Enchanted Circle. Beverly Morgan, mezzo soprano and Christopher Oldfather, piano.
Score: Margun.
Cassette: recording of first performance. NEC

[Concerto, Piano]
M3.3 Piano Concerto Called Metanoia. (1961-62) 23' 30"
For: piano and orchestra(2(&pic)-2(&Ehn)

-2(&bcl)-2(&cbsn); 4-3-2-1; timp, perc; str). *Commissioned by:* Erich Leinsdorf for the Boston Symphony Orchestra. *Score & parts:* Margun.
Cassette: Apr. 29, 1977; New England Conservatory (rehearsal). Rebecca La Brecque, piano; NEC Symphony Orchestra, Gunther Schuller, conductor. NEC

M3.4 Ephphatha, Be Thou Opened. (1972) 12' 30"
For: clarinet, trombone, tuba, piano.
First performed: Dec. 4, 1973; New England Conservatory; in An Evening of Contemporary Music. Thomas Hill, clarinet; Stanley Schultz, trombone; Mark Tetreault, tuba; Eric G. Schwartz, piano; Carl Roskott, conductor.
Score & parts: Margun.
Cassette: recording of first performance. NEC

[Fugue, Organ]
M3.5 Organ Fugue. (1953) 4' 30"
Score: Branch.

[Fugue, Strings]
M3.6 Double Fugue for String Quintet. (1954) 4'
For: violins(2), violas(2), violoncello.
Score & parts: Branch, 1954.

[Fugues, Piano]
M3.7 Ten Piano Fugues. (1952-53)
Score: Branch.

M3.8 Holy Land. Part I, Cain and Abel. (in progress)
For: voices, chorus, saxophones(soprano/alto/tenor)(2), orchestra. Oratorio.

M3.9 Maranatha. (1967-68) 15' 30"
For: woodwinds, brasses, percussion.
Commissioned by: Gunther Schuller.
First performed: 1968; Berkshire Music Center, Tanglewood. Stefan Minde, conductor.
Score & parts: Branch.
Reel: May 2, 1975. WGBH
Cassette: May 11, 1973; New England

Conservatory. Members of the NEC Symphony Orchestra, Gunther Schuller, conductor. NEC

Metanoia. *See* Concerto, Piano.

[Quartet, Strings]
M3.10 String Quartet. (1960) 8'
2 movements. *First performed:* 1960; Carnegie Recital Hall, New York City.
Score & parts: Branch, 1960-61.

M3.11 Rondo. (1957) 4'
For: piano. *First performed:* 1960; Carnegie Recital Hall, New York City.
Score: Branch, 1957.

[Sonata, Piano]
M3.12 Piano Piece Called Sonata. (1958-59) 6'
First performed: 1960; Carnegie Recital Hall, New York City.
Score: Branch, 1959.
Tape: NEC

M3.13 Theme and 3 Variations. (1958) 1'
For: piano. *First performed:* 1960; Carnegie Recital Hall, New York City.
Score: Branch, 1958.

M3.14 Trio. (1959) 5'
For: piano, drums, double bass. *First performed:* 1960; Carnegie Recital Hall, New York City.
Score & parts: Branch, 1959.

M4 JOHN DAVID MANN

Born June 10, 1954, in Summit, N.J. Moved to Boston area 1975. *Education:* studied composition with Alfred Mann (Rutgers University, 1969-72), Peter Pindar Stearns (Mannes College of Music, 1973-74), Randall Thompson (1978); violoncello with David Finckel. *Awards:* BMI Award (1968), New Jersey State Council on the Arts Grant in Composition (1971, 1973). *Related activities:* cellist and recorder player. BPL

WORKS

M4.1 Anthem on the Ascension. (1980) 25'
For: voices, chorus(SATB), organ, percussion. *Text:* Bible, N.T., Gospel; Bible, N.T., Revelations; Bible, O.T., Psalm 23. *First performed:* May 4, 1980; New Jersey. Rutgers University Chorale, John Floreen, conductor.
Vocal score: reprod. of ms.; available from composer.

M4.2 Cantata. (1974) 35'
For: Mezzo Soprano and string quartet. *Text:* Anglo-Saxon Lord's Prayer; R. Buckminster Fuller.
Score & parts: reprod of ms.; available from composer.

M4.3 Chaconne. (1972) 23'
For: violoncello.
Score: reprod. of ms.; available from composer.

[Dances]
M4.4 Two Dances. (1977) 15'
For: chamber orchestra(2-2-2-2; 1-0-0-0; perc; cel, hp; str). *Commissioned by:* Indiana Chamber Orchestra. *First performed:* 1977. Indiana Chamber Orchestra.
Score & parts: reprod. of ms; available from composer.

M4.5 Lamento. (1972) 8'
For: violoncellos(2).
Score: reprod. of ms; available from composer.

M4.6 Mass. (1981) 40'
For: chorus(SSATB).
Vocal score: reprod. of ms. (includes piano reduction for rehearsal); available from composer.

[Minuets]
M4.7 Two Minuets. (1971) 2'
For: violoncello.
Score: reprod. of ms.; available from composer.

[Poems]
M4.8 Four Poems. (1980) 25'
For: chorus(SSATB), flute, percussion. *Text:* from *The Tempest* (William Shakespeare); Honey and Salt (Carl Sandburg); Mass.
Vocal score: reprod. of ms. (includes piano reduction for rehearsal); available from composer.

M4.9 Prelude and Fugue. (1974) 18'
For: violoncello and piano. *First performed:* 1975; Indiana University. John David Mann, violoncello and Sherry Feintuck, piano.
Score & part: reprod. of ms.; available from composer.

M4.10 Requiem. (1976) 7'
For: double bass and dancers(4)(optional). Can be performed as a ballet or concert piece. *Commissioned by:* Adrian Mann. *First performed:* 1977; Indiana University. Adrian Mann.
Part: reprod. of ms.; available from composer.

[Sonata, Double Bass and Harp]
M4.11 Sonata in One Movement. (1968) 7'
For: double bass and harp or piano. *Commissioned by:* Adrian Mann. *First performed:* 1969; New School of Music. Adrian Mann, double bass and unidentified harpist.
Parts: reprod. of ms.; available from composer.

[Sonata, Flute and Viola]
M4.12 Duo Sonata. (1974) 16'
First performed: 1975; Indiana University. Ruth Condon, flute and Connie Whelan, viola.
Score: reprod. of ms.; available from composer.

M5 PAMELA J. MARSHALL

Born May 31, 1954, in Beverly, Mass. *Education:* studied composition with Samuel Adler, Warren Benson, Joseph

Schwantner (Eastman School of Music, B.M., 1976); Jacob Druckman, Betsy Jolas, Krzysztof Penderecki, Morton Subotnick (Yale University, M.M., 1980); horn with Verne Reynolds (Eastman School of Music), Paul Ingraham (Yale University), Charles Kavalovski. *Awards:* Delius Festival Composition Contest (First Prize, 1978), Belding Internship Grant for the Computer Music Workshop (Yale University, 1979), Francis Kellogg Prize (1980), MacDowell Colony Fellowship (1981). *Related activities:* teacher; music copyist; horn player; conductor and musical director; camp music counselor and accompanist. W

WORKS

M5.1 Arcanum. (1977) 12'-15'
For: violin. 1 movement. *First performed:* Oct. 12, 1978; New Haven, Conn. Sharan Leventhal.
Score: reprod. of ms. W
Reel: recording of first performance.

M5.2 Bewildered Chimes. (1978) 7'-9'
For: percussion(3)(chimes, woodblocks(2), templeblock, crotales(2 or 3), vibraphone, sizzle cymbal, suspended cymbal, tambourine, bongos, conga drums(2) or tom-tom, maracas, glockenspiel). 1 movement. *First performed:* May 1, 1979; New Haven, Conn. Warren Stein, Kevin Wilmering, George Mardinly.
Score: reprod. of ms. W
Reel: recording of first performance.

M5.3 Blessed and Holy. (1975)
For: chorus(SATB). *Text:* William Wordsworth; Bible, O.T., Daniel; Bible, N.T., Revelations.
Vocal score: reprod. of ms. W

M5.4 Blessing for a Good Journey. (1976) 6'
For: orchestra(2-2-2-2; 4-3-2-1; perc; hp; str). 1 movement. *Dedicated to:* Eastman Class of 1976. *First performed:* May 1976; Rochester, N.Y.

Members of the Rochester Philharmonic Orchestra.
Score & parts: reprod. of ms.; available from composer.
Reel: recording of first performance.
Reel: May 1976; recording of a reading session, Eastman School of Music. Eastman students.

M5.5 A Chill Wind in Autumn. (1978) 10'-12'
For: Mezzo Soprano or Tenor and orchestra(2-2-2-2; 4-0-0-0; perc; hp; str). 8 movements. *Text:* adaptations by Pamela Marshall of Tang dynasty poets Wang Wei, Li Po, Po Chu-i, Meng Hao-jan, Tu Fu, Wang Chien. *First performed:* Dec. 3, 1978; Sanders Theatre, Harvard University. New England Women's Symphony, Kay Gardner, conductor.
Score: reprod. of ms. W
Parts: reprod. of ms.; available from composer.

[A Chill Wind in Autumn; Arr.]
M5.6 A Chill Wind in Autumn. (1978) 10'-12'
For: Mezzo Soprano or Tenor and piano. 8 movements. *Text:* adaptations by Pamela Marshall of translations of Tang dynasty poets Wang Wei, Li Po, Po Chu-i, Meng Hao-jan, Tu Fu, Wang Chien. *First performed:* Oct. 4, 1979; New Haven, Conn. Thomas Crumb, tenor and Barbara Peterson, piano.
Score: reprod. of ms. W
Reel: recording of first performance.

M5.7 Dances for the Morning. (1975) 6'
For: harp. 4 movements. *First performed:* 1975; Rochester, N.Y. Kathy Bundock.
Score: Seesaw, 1976. W
Reel: recording of first performance.

M5.8 Fantasy-Variations on a Nova Scotian Ballad. (1978-80)
For: instrumental ensemble(flute/piccolo, oboe, clarinet, horn, trumpet, percussion, harp, string quartet, double bass).

Score: reprod. of ms. W
Parts: reprod. of ms.; available from composer.

M5.9 Fyr on Flode. (1975) 20'
For: Mezzo Soprano, oboes(2), horns(2), percussion, violins(2), viola, double bass. *Text:* Anglo-Saxon charms, translated by Robert Kay Gordon. *Contents:* Against a Wen; For a Sudden Stitch; Running Fire; Journey Spell. *First performed:* Jan. 21, 1976; Rochester, N.Y. Catherine Nesbit, mezzo soprano; Pamela Marshall, conductor. *Score & parts:* reprod. of ms. *Reel:* recording of first performance.

M5.10 Kaleidoscope-Departures. (1980) 5'
For: horn, trumpets(2), trombone, tuba. 1 movement. *Dedicated to:* Wall Street Brass Quintet. *First performed:* May 20, 1980; Paris, France. Wall Street Brass Quintet.
Score & parts: ms.

M5.11 Meadowlarks and Shawms. (1979) 6'
For: tape(computer). 1 movement. *First performed:* July 27, 1979; Massachusetts Institute of Technology. *Reel:* available from composer.

[Meadowlarks and Shawms; Arr.]
M5.12 Meadowlarks and Shawms. (1979) 6' 30"
For: English horn and tape(computer). 1 movement. *First performed:* Feb. 22, 1980; New Haven, Conn. Elizabeth Kieronski, English horn.
Score: reprod. of ms. W
Tape & part: reprod. of ms.; available from composer.
Reel: recording of first performance.

M5.13 Miniatures. 6'
For: horn. *Movements:* March; Motion; Lament; Song; Echoes. *First performed:* May 16, 1973; Rochester, N.Y. Pamela Marshall.
Score: Seesaw, 1976. W
Reel: recording of first performance.

M5.14 Nautilus. (1977; rev. 1979) 6'
For: woodwind quintet. 1 movement. *First performed:* Jan. 27, 1978; Wakefield, R.I. Cantilena Quintet.
Score: reprod. of ms. W
Parts: reprod. of ms.; available from composer.
Reel: Mar. 30, 1978; University of Massachusetts, Boston. Lunacharsky Wind Quintet.

M5.15 Starshine. (1981) 19'
For: orchestra(2-2-2-2; 4-2-2-1; timp, perc(2); str). *Movements:* Introduction, energico--Arcturus, the Guardian; Allegro moderato--When the Morning Stars Sing Together; Scherzo--Capella, the Goat; Adagio sostenuto--The Hoarfrost of Heaven; Deliberato--Rigel, the Lame Foot of the Hunter.
Score & parts: reprod. of ms.; available from composer.

M5.16 Symphonic Bells (1981)
For: orchestra(2-2-2-2; 2-2-2-0; timp; hp; str). 1 movement.
Score & parts: reprod. of ms.; available from composer.

M5.17 Toccata armonica. (1979) 10'
For: double bass, clarinets(2)/clarinets(bass)(2), horns(2), percussion. 1 movement. *Dedicated to:* Christian C. Kollgaard. *First performed:* Mar. 28, 1980; New Haven, Conn. Christian Kollgaard, double bass; Eric Mandat and Ed Johnson, clarinets; Penelope Britton and Jean Bennet, horns; Jay Yasen, percussion; Pamela Marshall, conductor.
Score: reprod. of ms. W
Reel: recording of first performance.

M5.18 Torrsong. (1977) 5'
For: clarinets (2), viola, xylophone. 1 movement. Winner of First Prize, Delius Festival Composition Contest, 1978. *First performed:* Feb. 28, 1978; Jacksonville, Fla. Peter Wright and Martin Kersich, clarinets; Elizabeth Kingston, viola; Brent Tarnow, xylophone.

Score: reprod. of ms. W
Reel: recording of first performance.

M5.19 Wander Bitter-Sweet. (1976) 10'
For: horn and string quartet. 1
movement. *First performed:* Feb. 25,
1976; Rochester, N.Y. Pamela Marshall,
horn; Susan Heerman and Linda Failing,
violins; Tracey Schopfer, viola; Lurene
Ekwurtzel, violoncello.
Score & parts: Seesaw, 1976. W
Reel: recording of first performance.
Reel: Apr. 7, 1976; Rochester, N.Y.
Pamela Marshall, horn; Susan Heerman
and Linda Failing, violins; Tracey
Schopfer, viola; Lurene Ekwurtzel,
violoncello.

M5.20 Watchmen for the Morning.
(1975) 5'
For: Mezzo Soprano or Baritone, horn,
piano. *Text:* Bible, O.T., Psalms.
Contents: Hear My Cry, O God (Psalm
61); Watchmen for the Morning (Psalm
130); The Floods Have Lifted up Their
Voice (Psalm 93); Lift up Your Heads,
O Ye Gates (Psalm 24). *First
performed:* Apr. 11, 1976; Rochester,
N.Y. Stanley Warren, tenor; Pamela
Marshall, horn; Martin Amlin, piano.
Score: Seesaw, 1976. W
Reel: recording of first performance.

M5.21 When Does the Bell Toll? (1981)
8'
For: actor/piano and actor/percussion. 1
movement.
Score: reprod. of ms. W

M5.22 Wind-blown Echoes. (1976)
For: chorus(SSAA). 1 movement. *Text:*
Pamela Marshall, based on *Science
News* coverage of the Viking missions
to Mars.
Vocal score: reprod. of ms. W

ARRANGEMENTS

M5.23 Christmas Songs. (1977)
For: voice and horns(2). *Text:*
traditional carols. *Contents:* Cradle
Hymn; Silent Night; Dona nobis pacem;

Tomorrow Shall Be My Dancing Day;
The Holly and the Ivy; Star in the
East; Awake My Soul; Rejoice My
Friends; Don't You Hear the Lambs;
Shepherds in Judea; Ring Christmas
Bells; God Rest Ye Merry Gentlemen.
First performed: Christmas 1977;
Boston subways. Jane Peppler, voice;
Ellen Donahue and Pamela Marshall,
horns.
Score: reprod. of ms.

[Christmas Songs]
M5.24 Two Christmas Songs (1980)
For: chorus(SSA) and horns(4). *Text:*
traditional carols. *Contents:* Shepherds
in Judea; Cradle Hymn. *First
performed:* Dec. 21, 1980; Ipswich,
Mass.
Vocal score: reprod. of ms.; available
from composer.
Parts: reprod. of ms.; available from
composer.

M5.25 Traditional Spirituals. (1978)
For: Soprano and orchestra. *Contents:*
City of Heaven; Didn't My Lord Deliver
Daniel?; Honor, Honor; Give Me Jesus.
Commissioned by: Plymouth
Philharmonic Orchestra. *First
performed:* Apr. 30, 1978; Plymouth,
Mass. Roberta Law, soprano; Plymouth
Philharmonic Orchestra, Rudolph
Schlegel, conductor.
Score: ms. Parts.

M6 DONALD MARTINO

Born May 16, 1931, in Plainfield, N.J.
Moved to Boston area 1969. *Education:*
studied composition with Ernst Bacon
(Syracuse University, B.M., 1952); Roger
Sessions, Milton Babbitt (Princeton
University, M.F.A., 1954); Luigi
Dallapiccola (Florence, Italy, 1954-56).
Awards: Kosciuszko Foundation
Scholarship (1953), National Federation
of Music Clubs Award (1953), BMI
Awards (1953, 1954), Kate Neal Kinley
Memorial Fellowship (University of
Illinois, 1954), Fulbright Fellowship
(1954-56), Pacifica Foundation Award

(1961), Brandeis University, Creative Arts Award (1963), Fromm Foundation commission (1964), Morse Fellowship (Yale University, 1965), National Institute of Arts and Letters Award (1967), Guggenheim Grants (1967, 1973), Naumburg Chamber Music Award (1973), National Endowment for the Arts Grant (1974), Pulitzer Prize in Music (1974), Classical Critics Citation (*Record World*, 1976), American Academy and Institute of Arts and Letters (member, 1981), Boston Symphony Orchestra Centennial commission (1981). *Related activities:* clarinetist; composer-in-residence, Berkshire Music Center, Tanglewood (1965-67, 1969; Koussevitzky composer-in-residence, 1973); lectureship, Harvard University (1971); served on the faculties of the Third Street Settlement, New York City (1956-57), Princeton University (1957-59), Yale University (1959-69), New England Conservatory (1969-81), Brandeis University (Irving Fine Professor of Music, 1980-). BrU

WORKS

Anyone Lived in a Pretty How Town. *See* Portraits. Anyone Lived in a Pretty How Town.

M6.1 Augenmusik: A Mixed Mediocritique. (1972) 10'
For: actress or dancer(female) or percussion(uninhibited female) and tape. 1 movement. *Dedicated to:* Sherry Dorn.
Perf. dir & tape: Ione, 1974. NEC

M6.2 B, A, B, B, IT, T. (1966) 4'
For: clarinet(with extensions). 1 movement. *Dedication:* To Milton B, A, B, B, IT, T (on your fifieth birthday).
First performed: May 21, 1966; New Haven, Conn. Donald Martino.
Score: Ione, 1970. BrU BU HU NEC
Disc: Advance FGR 17S, 1973. Phillip Rehfeldt. NEC
Cassette: Dec. 15, 1977; New England Conservatory. Lori Haddad. NEC

[Canoni enigmatici]
M6.3 Sette canoni enigmatici. (1955) 12'
For: violas(2) and violoncellos(2) or bassoons(2). Includes the original canons for unspecified instruments, the Italian verses and riddles which serve as clues for the resolution, and the resolutions by the composer for this instrumentation. May be combined with the composer's resolutions for clarinet quartet to make a version for mixed quartet. *Dedicated to:* Luigi Dallapiccola.
Score: Ione, 1974. NEC

[Canoni enigmatici; Arr.]
M6.4 Sette canoni enigmatici. (1962) 12'
For: string quartet. *Dedicated to:* Luigi Dallapiccola.
Score: Ione, 1974. NEC

[Canoni enigmatici; Arr.]
M6.5 Sette canoni enigmatici. (1966) 12'
For: clarinets(2), clarinet(alto)(E-flat) or basset horn, clarinet(bass). Includes the original canons for unspecified instruments, the Italian verses and riddles which serve as clues for the resolution, and the resolutions by the composer for this instrumentation. May be combined with the composer's resolution for 2 violas and 2 violoncellos (or bassoons) to make a version for mixed quartet. *Dedicated to:* Luigi Dallapiccola.
Score: Ione, 1974. HU NEC
Cassette: Mar. 18, 1980; New England Conservatory; in *The Enchanted Circle*. Eric Thomas and Diane Heffner, clarinets; David Satz, basset horn; Kenneth Weiner, bass clarinet. NEC

[Concerto, Clarinets(3)]
M6.6 Triple Concerto. (1977) 26'
For: clarinet, clarinet(bass), clarinet(contrabass), chamber orchestra(1(pic)-1(Ehn)-0-2(cbsn); 1-1-2-0; perc(2); cel/pf; str(1-1-1-1-1). 3 movements. *Commissioned by:* Group for Contemporary Music with grants from the New York State Council on the Arts, Mellon Foundation, National Endowment for the Arts. *Dedicated to:*

Milton Babbitt at 60. *First performed:* Dec. 18, 1978; Manhattan School of Music. Anand Devendra, clarinet; Dennis Smylie, bass; Les Thimmig, contrabass clarinet; Group for Contemporary Music, Harvey Sollberger, conductor.
Score: Dantalian, 1978.
Study score: Dantalian, 1978. BrU BU HU MIT NEC
Parts: Dantalian, 1978. Rental.
Pf. red: Dantalian, 1978. BU NEC
Disc: Nonesuch H 71372, 1980. Anand Devendra, clarinet; Dennis Smylie, bass clarinet; Les Thimmig, contrabass clarinet; Group for Contemporary Music, Harvey Sollberger, conductor. BrU BU MIT NEC T W
Cassette: Dec. 5, 1979; New England Conservatory. Anand Devendra, clarinet; Dennis Smylie, bass clarinet; Les Thimmig, contrabass clarinet; NEC Contemporary Music Ensemble, Larry Livingston, conductor. NEC

[Concerto, Piano]
M6.7 Concerto. (1965) 30'
For: piano and orchestra(3(pic)-2(Ehn)-3(bcl,cbcl)-3(cbsn); 4-3-3-1; timp, perc; hp; pf; str). 3 movements. *Commissioned by:* New Haven Symphony Orchestra under a grant from The William Inglis Morse Trust for Music. *First performed:* Mar. 1, 1966; New Haven, Conn. Charles Rosen, piano; New Haven Symphony Orchestra, Frank Brieff, conductor.
Score & parts: Ione, 1971. Rental.
Study score: Ione, 1971. BrU MIT NEC
Pf. red: Ione, 1971. HU NEC

[Concerto, Violoncello]
M6.8 Concerto. (1972) . 24'
For: violoncello and orchestra(3-3-3-3; 4-4-3-1; timp, perc(4); hp, cel, pf; str). 3 movements. *First performed:* Oct. 16, 1979; Cincinnati, Ohio. Joel Krosnick, violoncello; Philharmonia Orchestra (University of Cincinnati), Gerhard Samuel, conductor.
Score: Dantalian, 1978. BrU
Parts: Dantalian. Rental.
Study score: Dantalian, nyp.

Pf. red: Dantalian, nyp.
Part(violoncello): Dantalian, nyp.

[Concerto, Woodwind Quintet]
M6.9 Concerto for Wind Quintet. (1964) 15'
For: flute/piccolo(optional), clarinet, horn, oboe/English horn(optional), bassoon. 5 movements *Commissioned by and dedicated to:* Fromm Foundation and Berkshire Music Center, Tanglewood. *First performed:* Aug. 13, 1964; Berkshire Music Center, Tanglewood. Gunther Schuller, conductor.
Score: Ione, 1970. BrU BU HU MIT NET W
Disc: Composers Recordings CRI 230 USD, 1969. Contemporary Chamber Ensemble, Arthur Weisberg, conductor. BrU BU HU MIT NEC T W

Composition for Orchestra. *See* Contemplations.

M6.10 Contemplations. (1956) 16'
For: orchestra(2-2(Ehn)-2(bcl)-2(cbsn); 4-3-3-1; timp, perc(3); cel; str). 1 movement. *Commissioned by:* Paderewski Fund. Originally titled Composition for Orchestra. *First performed:* Aug. 1966; Berkshire Music Center, Tanglewood. Berkshire Music Center Orchestra, Gunther Schuller, conductor.
Score & parts: Dantalian. Rental.

M6.11 Fantasies and Impromptus. (1981) 28'
For: piano. 9 movements. *Commissioned by and dedicated to:* Koussevitzky Music Foundation (Library of Congress).
Score: Dantalian, 1981.

[Fantasy]
M6.12 Piano Fantasy. (1958) 5'
Selected for the Repertory List of the Kennedy Center-Rockefeller Foundation International Competition for Excellence in the Performance of American Music. *First performed:* 1960; Carnegie Recital Hall, New York City. William Masselos.

Score: Ione, 1970. BPL BrU BU HU MIT NEC
Cassette: Mar. 24, 1976; New England Conservatory. Vivian Taylor. NEC
Cassette: Nov. 22, 1976; New England Conservatory. Russell Sherman. NEC
Cassette: Mar. 18, 1980; New England Conservatory; in *The Enchanted Circle.* Thomas Stumpf. NEC

M6.13 Fantasy-Variations. (1962) 12'
For: violin. Selected for the Repertory List of the Kennedy Center-Rockefeller Foundation International Competition for Excellence in the Performance of American Music.
Score: Ione, 1970. BPL BrU BU HU MIT NEC
Disc: Advance FGR 6c, [1969]. Daniel Kobialka. BU HU MIT
Disc: Composers Recordings CRI 240 USD, 197-. Paul Zukofsky. BCM BrU BU HU MIT NEC T W
Reel: Sept. 30, 1979; First and Second Church, Boston. Dinosaur Annex Concert. Janet Packer. WGBH
Cassette: Mar. 31, 1975; New England Conservatory. Eric Rosenblith. NEC

[Frammenti]
M6.14 Cinque frammenti. (1961) 5'
For: oboe and double bass. 5 movements. *Dedicated to:* Josef Marx and Bertram Turetzky.
Score: McGinnis & Marx, 1964. BPL BrU BU HU NEC
Disc: Advance FGR 1. Josef Marx, oboe and Bertram Turetzky, double bass. T

M6.15 From The Bad Child's Book of Beasts. (1952) 6'
For: voice(high) and piano. *Text:* Hilaire Belloc. *Contents:* The Lion, The Tiger; The Frog; The Microbe. *Dedication:* To my godchild little William Renz, January 20, 1952 and to my own little Christopher James, age 3, February 4, 1978. *First performed:* Feb. 10, 1952; Syracuse, N.Y. Loren Driscoll, tenor and Herbert Bliss, piano.
Score: Dantalian, 1978. BrU NEC
Cassette: Mar. 18, 1980; New England

Conservatory; in *The Enchanted Circle.* Thomas Toscano, tenor and Thomas Stumpf, piano. NEC

Grave. *See* Sonata, Clarinet and Piano. Grave.

M6.16 Harmonica Piece. (1954) 6'
For: harmonica. *Dedicated to:* John Sebastian.
Score: Dantalian.

M6.17 Impromptu for Roger. (1977) 3'
For: piano. 1 movement. *Dedicated to:* Roger Sessions. *First performed:* Nov. 21, 1977; Princeton University. Robert Miller.
Score: Dantalian, 1978. BU NEC W
Cassette: Oct. 23, 1979; New England Conservatory; in *The Enchanted Circle.* Claudia Stevens. NEC

M6.18 Mosaic for Grand Orchestra. (1967) 15'
For: orchestra(4-4-4-4; 4-4-4-1; perc(6); hp(2); elec gt; cel, pf, elec org; str).
Commissioned by: University of Chicago for the Chicago Symphony Orchestra. *Dedicated to:* University of Chicago on the occasion of its 75th anniversary. *First performed:* May 1967; Chicago, Ill. Chicago Symphony Orchestra, Jean Martinon, conductor.
Score: Dantalian, 1978. BrU
Study score: Dantalian, nyp.
Parts: Dantalian, 1978. Rental.
Cassette: Nov. 17, 1971; New England Conservatory. NEC Symphony Orchestra, Gunther Schuller, conductor. NEC

M6.19 Notturno. (1973) 16'
For: instrumental ensemble(flute/piccolo/flute(alto), clarinet/clarinet(bass), violin/viola, violoncello, percussion(glockenspiel, marimba, vibraphone, xylophone, templeblocks, tamtams), piano).
Commissioned by: Naumburg Foundation for Speculum Musicae. *Dedicated to:* Speculum Musicae and the Naumburg Foundation. Winner of Pulitzer Prize in Music (1974). *First performed:* May 8,

1973; New York City. Speculum
Musicae.
Score: Ione, 1975. BrU HU MIT NEC T
W
Parts: Ione, 1975. Rental.
Disc: Nonesuch H 71300, 1974.
Speculum Musicae, Daniel Shulman,
conductor. BrU BU HU MIT NEC T W
Cassette: Mar. 18, 1980; New England
Conservatory; in *The Enchanted Circle*.
Lyric Arts Ensemble, Thomas Toscano,
conductor. NEC

M6.20 Paradiso Choruses. (1974) 29′
For: Sopranos(3), Mezzo Sopranos(4),
Tenors(3), Baritones(2), chorus(SATB),
tape, orchestra(3-3-3-4; 4-4-4-1; perc;
hp; pf, org; str). Oratorio. *Text: Divine
Comedy: Paradiso* by Dante and
Ordinary of the Mass (Latin).
Movements: Prelude--The Celestial
Ascent from the Mount of Purgatory;
Scene 1--The Sphere of the Ten
Heavens; Scene 2--The Beatific Vision,
Part 2, Part 3; Scene 3--Dante's
Affirmation of Faith. *Commissioned by:*
Paderewski Fund to honor Lorna Cooke
deVaron on the occasion of her 25th
year as director of the New England
Conservatory Chorus. *Dedicated to:*
Lorna Cooke deVaron and the
Paderewski Fund. Winner of Classical
Critics Citation (*Record World*), 1976
(Golden Crest recording). *First
performed:* May 7, 1975; New England
Conservatory. Elizabeth Parcells and
other soloists; NEC Chorus; NEC
Repertory Orchestra; members of the
NEC Opera Department; NEC Children's
Choir; Lorna Cooke deVaron, conductor.
Score: reprod. of ms. NEC
Study score: Dantalian, nyp.
Parts: Dantalian. Rental.
Vocal score: Dantalian, nyp.
Disc: Golden Crest NEC 114, 1975.
Recording of first perfomance. BrU BU
HU MIT NEC
Cassette: recording of first
performance. NEC

M6.21 Parisonatina al'dodecafonia.
(1964) 12′

For: violoncello. *Movements:* A Species
of Passacaglia; Scherzo in Rondo Form;
A Three-Part Song; Cadenza sul nome
Parisot. *Commissioned by and dedicated
to:* Aldo Parisot. *First performed:*
summer, 1965; Norfolk, Conn. Aldo
Parisot.
Score: Ione, 1966. BrU BPL HU NEC
Reel: Jan. 20, 1974; Boston
Conservatory. Luis Leguia. BCM
Cassette: May 8, 1971; New England
Conservatory; in *A Festival of New
England Composers Past and Present*.
Fred Sherry. NEC

M6.22 Pianississimo. (1970) 29′-34′
For: piano. 4 movements. *Commissioned
by and dedicated to:* Easley R.
Blackwood. Selected for the Repertory
List of the Kennedy Center-Rockefeller
Foundation International Competition
for Excellence in the Performance of
American Music, 1978. *First performed:*
Dec. 10, 1974; New England
Conservatory. Edward Wood.
Score: E.C. Schirmer, 1977. BPL BrU
NEC
Cassette: Dec. 10, 1974; recording of
first performance. NEC
Cassette: Feb. 28, 1976; New England
Conservatory; in *American Society of
University Composers 11th Annual
Conference*. Edward Wood. NEC

[Pious Pieces]
M6.23 Seven Pious Pieces. (1972) 16′
For: chorus(SATB) and organ(optional)
or piano(optional). *Text: His Noble
Numbers, or, His Pious Pieces* (1647
ed.) by Robert Herrick. *Contents:* To His
Ever-Loving God; Mercy and Love; His
Ejaculation to God; The Soule;
Eternitie; Teares/To Death/Welcome
What Comes; No Coming to God
without Christ. *Dedicated to:* Ernst
Bacon. *First peformed:* Mar. 31, 1976;
New England Conservatory. NEC
Chorus, Lorna Cooke deVaron,
conductor.
Vocal score: E.C. Schirmer, 1974. BPL
MIT NEC
Disc: New World NW 210, 1977. John

Oliver Chorale, John Oliver, conductor.
BCM BU HU HUm MIT NEC T W
Cassette: recording of first
performance. NEC

M6.24 Portraits: A Secular Cantata.
(1954) 40'
For: Mezzo Soprano, Bass,
chorus(SATB),
orchestra(2(&pic)-2(&Ehn)-2(&bcl)-2(&
cbsn); 4-3-2-1; timp, perc; str).
Movements: Prologue--I Sit and Look
Out (Walt Whitman); Ones Self (Walt
Whitman); I Shall Forget You (Edna St.
Vincent Millay); Anyone (e.e.
cummings); Somewhere I Have Never
Travelled (e.e. cummings); Humanity
(e.e. cummings). *Commissioned by:*
Paderewski Fund.
Score: Dantalian. Rental.
Parts: Dantalian, nyp.
Vocal score: Dantalian, nyp.

[Portaits. anyone lived in a pretty
how town; Arr.]
M6.25 anyone lived in a pretty how
town. (1954) 6'
For: chorus(SATB), piano(4-hands),
percussion(optional). *Text:* from *Poems,
1923-1954* by e.e. cummings.
Commissioned by: Paderewski Fund.
Vocal score: Ione, 1970. BPL HU MIT
NEC

[Quartet, Clarinet and Strings]
M6.26 Quartet. (1957) 23'
For: clarinet(Bb/A), violin, viola,
violoncello. 3 movements. Winner of
Pacifica Foundation Award (1961). *First
performed:* 1958; New York. Charles
Russo, clarinet and others.
Score: Ione, 1973. BPL BrU BU HU MIT
NEC

[Quartet, Strings, No. 2]
M6.27 Second String Quartet. (1952) 18'
Withdrawn.

[Quartet, Strings, No. 3]
M6.28 Third String Quartet. (1954) 30'
Withdrawn.

M6.29 Quodlibets. (1954) 8'
For: flute. *Movements:* Studio; Arietta;
Burla.
Score: McGinnis & Marx, 1961. BrU HU
MIT NEC W
Disc: Composers Recordings CRI 212,
1966. Samuel Baron. BrU BU MIT NEC
W

M6.30 Quodlibets II. (1980) 12'
For: flute. *Movements:* Intrade e
Scherzo; Canto sentimentale in eius
memoriam; Cadenza, Canzone e Coda.
Commissioned by and dedicated to:
Besse Welsh. *First performed:* Mar. 31,
1981; Carnegie Recital Hall, New York
City. Besse Welsh.
Score: Dantalian, 1981. MIT

[Rilke Songs]
M6.31 Two Rilke Songs. (1961) 5'
For: Mezzo Soprano and piano. *Text:*
from *Neue Gedichte*, II and *Das Buch
der Bilder*, II, ii by Rainer Maria Rilke;
English version by Jean Lunn. *Contents:*
Die Laute (The Lute); Aus einen
Sturmnacht VIII (On a Stormy Night
VIII). *Dedicated to:* Michael Kowal; in
memory of Robert Schumann. Selected
for the Repertory List of the Kennedy
Center-Rockefeller Foundation
International Competition for Excellence
in the Performance of American Music,
1979.
Score: Ione, 1970. BPL BrU BU HU NEC

M6.32 Ritorno. (1976) 13'
For: orchestra(1(&pic)-2(&Ehn)-2(&bcl)-2;
4-3-3-1; perc(4); hp; cel/pf;
str(12-10-8-6-4)). 1 movement.
Commissioned by: Plainfield Symphony
Society Auxiliary for the Plainfield
Symphony Bicentennial Concert, Edward
Murry, conductor. *Dedication:* To my
parents. *First performed:* Dec. 12, 1976;
Plainfield, N.J. Plainfield Symphony,
Edward Murray, conductor.
Score: Dantalian.
Study score: Dantalian, 1978. BrU BU
NEC T
Parts: Dantalian. Rental.

[Ritorno; Arr.]
M6.33 Ritorno. (1977) 15′
For: band.
Score & parts: Dantalian. Rental.

M6.34 Separate Songs. (1951) 6′
For: voice(high) and piano. *Contents:* All
Day I Hear the Noise of Waters (from
Chamber Music by James Joyce); The
Half-Moon Westers Low, My Love
(from *Last Poems* by A.E. Housman).
First performed: Feb. 10, 1952;
Syracuse, N.Y. Loren Driscoll, tenor
and Herbert Bliss, piano.
Score: Dantalian, 1978. BrU NEC

M6.35 A Set for Clarinet. (1954; rev.
1974) 9′
3 movements. *Dedicated to:* Art Bloom.
First performed: May 1954; Princeton
University. Arthur Bloom.
Score: McGinnis & Marx, 1957, 1974.
BPL BrU BU HU MIT NEC
Disc: Advance SD FGR 4, 1964. Phillip
Rehfeldt. BU
Disc: Advance FGR 15-S, 1972. Phillip
Rehfeldt. NEC
Disc: Composers Recordings CRI SD
374, 1977. Michael Webster. BrU BU HU
MIT NEC W
Cassette: Mar 11, 1979; New England
Conservatory. Melvin Warner. NEC

M6.36 Sinfonia. 15′
For: orchestra. Withdrawn.

[Sonata, Clarinet and Piano]
M6.37 Sonata. (1950-51) 13′
Movments: Allegro deciso; Grave;
Andante cantabile. *Dedicated to:*
Harwood Simmons. *First performed:*
Feb. 10, 1952; Syracuse, N.Y. Donald
Martino, clarinet and Herbert Bliss,
piano.
Score: Dantalian, 1979. BrU BU MIT
Part: Dantalian, 1979. MIT

[Sonata, Clarinet and Piano. Grave;
Arr.]
M6.38 Grave. (1950) 3′
Arranged for advanced beginner. *First
performed:* 1950; Syracuse, N.Y. Donald

Martino, clarinet and Alfred Heller,
piano.
Score & part: Dantalian, 1979.

[Songs]
M6.39 Three Songs. (1955; 1961) 9′
For: Bass or Soprano and piano. *Text:
Pomes Penyeach* from *Chamber Music*
by James Joyc e. *Contents:* Alone;
Tutto e sciolto; A Memory of the
Players in a Mirror at Midnight.
Dedicated to: Roy Lazarus.
Score: Ione, 1970 (version for bass).
BPL BrU BU HU NEC W
Score: Ione, 1970 (version for soprano).
BPL BU HU NEC
Cassette: May. 8, 1975; New England
Conservatory. Linn Jackson, bass and
Gait Sirguey, piano (No. 2). NEC

M6.40 Strata. (1966) 6′
For: clarinet(bass). *Movements:*
Postlude--To Muffin, in Memoriam.
Score: Apogee, 1967. BPL BU MIT NEC
Score: Ione, 1972. BrU
Cassette: Mar. 26, 1974; New England
Conservatory. Les Thimmig. NEC

M6.41 Suite of Variations on Medieval
Melodies. (1952; rev. 1954) 12′
For: violoncello. *Movements:* Minnelied
(Nu al'Erst by Walther von der
Vogelweide); Gregorian Sequence
(Victimae paschali by Wipo of
Burgandy); Troubadour Alba (Reis
glories by Giraut de Bornelh); Laude
(Gloria in cielo, 13th century); Estampe
(England, 13th century). *Dedicated to:*
Lewis Lockwood.
Score: Dantalian, 1978. BrU MIT NEC

M6.42 Trio. (1959) 12′
For: clarinet(in A), violin, piano.
Selected to represent the United States
at annual conference of the
International Society for Contemporary
Music, Amsterdam, Holland (1963). *First
performed:* 1960; Carnegie Recital Hall,
New York City. Stanley Drucker,
clarinet; Matthew Raimondi, violin;
Yehudi Wyner, piano.
Score: Ione, 1970. BrU BU HU MIT NEC

Disc: Composers Recordings CRI 240 USD, 197-. Arthur Bloom, clarinet; Paul Zukofsky, violin; Gilbert Kalish, piano. BCM BrU BU HU MIT NEC T W
Reel: Nov. 22, 1977; Boston University; in *Omnibus: Music of the 20th Century.* Deborah Goodwillie, clarinet; Sharan Levanthal; violin; Linda Jiorle, piano. BU
Cassette: Apr. 25, 1972; New England Conservatory. Dean Rhodes, clarinet; Juan Ramerez, violin; Robert Pace, piano. NEC

[Trio, Violin, Viola, Violoncello]
M6.43 String Trio. (1955) 30'
Withdrawn.

M7 JAMES McCULLOUGH

Born 1939, in Richmond, Va. *Education:* studied composition with Undine Smith Moore (Virginia State University, B.S., Music, 1962) and Daniel Pinkham (New England Conservatory, 1964-66); studies at Northeastern University (1974-77). *Related activities:* arranger, choral conductor, tenor, actor, opera stage director; co-founder of Amarilli Press; currently on the faculty of Boston State College, teaching children's literature. MIT

WORKS

M7.1 Apotheosis: Arise! to Atlanta's Dead Black Children. (in progress)
For: Soprano, Tenor, Baritone, chorus(SATB), orchestra (2(&pic)-2(&Ehn2)-1-1(cbsn); 4-3-3-1; perc(3); str). Based on play songs of black children from the Old South with additional text by James McCullough. *Dedicated to:* The black children slain in Atlanta, Ga.

M7.2 Beyond the Dark River. (1970) 4' 9"
For: tuba and violoncello. 1 movement. *Score & parts:* Amarilli Press, nyp.

M7.3 Black Knight of the Theban Legion: Saint Maurice of Brandenburg.

(1975-) 25' 41"
For: chorus(SATTBB) and orchestra(2(&pic)-2(&Ehn)-1-1(cbsn); 4-3-3-0; perc(2); str). Ballet in two acts: The Cathedral in Siena; Apotheosis at Brandenburg. *Text:* James McCullough. *Dedicated to:* William McCullough, Sr. *Score:* ms.

M7.4 Call Me Ishmael: A Symphony. (1980) 24' 17"
For: violoncello and orchestra(2(&pic)-1-1-1; 2-1-1-0; perc; str). 3 movements. *Dedicated to:* John Patrick Kearney.
Score & parts: Amarilli Press. Rental.

M7.5 Dark Structures. (1971) 21' 14"
For: trombones(5) and percussion. *Movements:* Fast; Blues. *Dedicated to:* Alfred Henderson, Jr.
Score & parts: Amarilli Press, nyp.

M7.6 Faces in the Water. (1971) 27' 12"
For: string orchestra. 4 movements. *Dedicated to:* Undine Smith Moore. *Score & parts:* Amarilli Press. Rental.

M7.7 The Handsome Drummer. (1974) 35' 58"
For: orchestra(2-2-1-1; 2-1-1-0; perc(2); str). Children's ballet; based on a story by Jacob Grimm and Wilhelm Grimm. *Movements:* That Black Night; Daybreak with My Drum; Dance of the Giants; On Top of the Glass Mountain; Fire and the Evil, Old Witch; The Princess of Silk and Gold; "Forget Me Not," She Cried; The Wedding of the True Bride.
Score & parts: Amarilli Press. Rental. *Libretto:* Amarilli Press. Rental.

M7.8 I Will Not Leave You Comfortless. (1979) 3' 29"
For: Tenor and chorus(SATB). *Text:* Bible, O.T., Psalms. *Dedicated to:* John Patrick Kearney.
Vocal score: Amarilli, nyp.

M7.9 Jimmie's House. (1973) 10' 9"
For: violoncello and double bass. 2

movements.
Score: ms.

M7.10 A Life Lesson. (1962) 3' 20"
For: chorus(SATB). 1 movement. *Text:*
James Whitcomb Riley. *Dedication:* To
my twin sister, Jean. *First performed:*
1962; Petersburg, Va. Virginia State
College Choir, A. Adkins, conductor.
Music: Marks, 1962.

M7.11 Loth to Depart. (1970) 4' 59"
For: guitar. 1 movement. *Dedicated to:*
Pepe Romero.
Score: Amarilli, nyp.

M7.12 O Pensive Dove. (1963) 3' 48"
For: chorus(SATB). 1 movement. *Text:*
New England folk hymn. *Dedicated to:*
Thomas Pantages. *First performed:*
1965; Boston University. Boston
University Choir, Max Miller, conductor.
Vocal score: J. Fisher, 1964. BPL

M7.13 Plead My Cause, O Lord. (1971)
4' 7"
For: Tenor and chorus(SATB). 1
movement. *Text:* from Bible, O.T.,
Psalm 35. *Dedicated to:* Robert Louis.
First performed: 1972; Old South
Church, Boston. Old South Church
Choir, Alfred Nash Patterson,
conductor.
Vocal score: Pro Art, 1971.

[Quartet, Strings, No. 1]
M7.14 String Quartet No. 1. (1969) 19'
57"
4 movements. *Dedicated to:* Roger
Burkhart.
Score & parts: Amarilli, nyp.

[Quartet, Strings, No. 2]
M7.15 String Quartet No. 2. (1976) 22'
48"
3 movements. *Dedicated to:* Edward
Sheehan.
Score: Amarilli, nyp. Rental.

[Quartet, Strings, No. 3]
M7.16 String Quartet No. 3. (1978) 17'
9"

3 movements. *Dedicated to:* David
Hansen.
Score: Amarilli, nyp. Rental.

[Quintet]
M7.17 Piano Quintet. (1972) 15' 37"
For: string quartet, piano. 4
movements. *Dedicated to:* Richard L.
Bowman.
Score & parts: Amarilli, nyp. Rental.

M7.18 Regatta. (1980) 5' 7"
For: double bass and wind
ensemble(piccolo, flutes(2),
oboes(2)/English horns(2), clarinets(4),
contrabassoon). 1 movement. *Dedicated
to:* Don Swinchoski.
Score & parts: Amarilli, nyp.

M7.19 Rest, Sweet Prince. (1972; rev.
1978) 14' 39"
For: clarinet and viola. 2 movements.
Dedication: To the memory of my
father.
Score: Amarilli, nyp.

[Songs]
M7.20 Five Songs. (1978-79) 14' 47"
For: Tenor and piano. *Text:* James
McCullough. *Contents:* Finding Home;
Give Me a Rainbow; She Was
Forbidden to Joy; Give Me a Big One;
I Want It All. *Dedicated to:* David
Milke.
Parts: Amarilli, nyp.

[Songs]
M7.21 Nine Songs. (1977) 17' 37"
For: Baritone and piano. *Text:* Langston
Hughes. *Contents:* Harlem Night Song;
Daybreak in Alabama; Morning After;
Litany; Sylvester's Dying Bed; Black
Maria; Still Here; Midnight Dancer; The
Negro Speaks of Rivers. *Dedicated to:*
Richard Frankie.
Parts: Amarilli, nyp.

M7.22 The Substance of All
Philosophy. (1969) 7' 7"
For: chorus(TTBB) and xylophone. *Text:*
Soeren Kierkegaard.
Vocal score: ms.

M7.23 This Little Light. (1971) 9' 17"
For: harp. *Movements:* Like Rays of
Light; Barcarolla. *Dedication:* For my
mother.
Score: Amarilli, nyp.

M8 THOMAS J. McGAH

Born April 7, 1938, in Waltham, Mass.
Education: B.A. (University of Lowell);
M.M. (Boston University); studied
composition and theory with Hugo
Norden. *Awards:* New York State
Council on the Arts Meet the
Composer Grant (1980). *Related
activities:* member of the faculty of
Berklee College of Music (1973-). Be

WORKS

M8.1 Aithra. (1970) 8'
For: violoncello and chamber
orchestra(2-1-1-0; 2-0-0-0; timp; hp; str).
Score: ms.
Parts: available from composer.

M8.2 Alleluia. (1976) 4'
For: chorus(SATB) and piano.
Vocal score: ms.

[Choruses from Alice in Wonderland]
M8.3 Two Choruses from Alice in
Wonderland. (1975) 5'
For: chorus(SATB) and woodwind
quintet. *Text:* from *Alice's Adventures
in Wonderland* by Lewis Carroll.
Contents: Turtle Soup; Jabberwocky.
First performed: Jan. 30, 1975.
Arlington-Belmont Chamber Chorus;
unidentified woodwind quintet.
Score: ms.
Parts: available from composer.

[Concerto, Flute, No. 1]
M8.4 Concerto. (1968) 25'
For: flute and orchestra(2-2-2(bcl)-2;
2-0-0-0; timp, perc; hp; str).
Score: ms.
Score & parts: available from
composer.

[Concerto, Flute, No. 2]
M8.5 Concerto. (in progress) 17'

For: flute and
orchestra(1(&pic)-2(Ehn)-2(bcl)-2; 2-2-2-0;
timp, perc, glock, xylo; hp; str).

M8.6 Cynosure. (1971) 5'
For: horns(2), trumpets(2), trombones(2),
tuba, timpani.
Score: ms.
Parts: available from composer.

M8.7 Design. (1966) 13'
For: brass ensemble(horns(3),
trumpets(3), trombones(3), tuba),
timpani, percussion. *First performed:*
Feb. 18, 1973; University of Lowell.
Score: ms.
Parts: available from composer.

M8.8 Divertimento for String Trio.
(1973) 5'
For: violins(2) and viola. *First
performed:* Mar. 24, 1973; Rhodes,
Greece.
Score: ms.; available from composer.

[Durrell Reflections]
M8.9 Four Durrell Reflections. (1976) 8'
For: clarinet and piano. *First
performed:* Feb. 5, 1981; Berklee
College of Music.
Score: BKJ.
Reel: recording of first performance; in
Faculty Composers' Concert. Be

M8.10 The Fanaid Grove. (1964) 4'
For: chorus(SATB).
Vocal score: ms.

[Fantasys on Chorale Melodies]
M8.11 Four Fantasys on Chorale
Melodies. (1977) 9'
For: violin and viola. *First performed:*
Mar. 25, 1978; Rhodes, Greece.
Score: ms.

M8.12 Five for Four. (1961) 8'
For: trumpets(2) and trombones(2).
Score: ms.

[Grecian Love Songs]
M8.13 Four Grecian Love Songs. (1979)
10'
For: Soprano, wind ensemble(flutes(2),

oboes(2), clarinet, clarinet/
clarinet(bass), bassoons(2), horns(2),
trumpets(2)), percussion(timpani,
glockenspiel, xylophone), celeste.
Contents: In Rhodes (Lawrence Durrell);
Snow in Summer (Asklepiades); To a
Handsome Man (Sappho); For Them to
Come (Constantine Cavafy). *First
performed:* Jan. 13, 1980; Sanders
Theatre, Harvard University. Pro Arte
Chamber Orchestra of Boston.
Score & parts: available from
composer.

M8.14 Greek Dance. (1975) 3' 30"
For: piano.
Score: ms.

M8.15 He's Goin' Away. (1977) 5'
For: chorus(mixed).
Vocal score: ms.

M8.16 Idee fixe. (1975) 3' 30"
For: guitar. *First performed:* Dec. 12,
1975; Berklee College of Music. Harry
Chalmiers.
Score: ms.
Reel: recording of first performance.
Be
Reel: Apr. 7, 1976; Berklee College of
Music. Harry Chalmiers. Be

M8.17 Impression. (1969) 4'
For: flute and piano.
Score: ms.

M8.18 Kroma. (1972) 20'
For: wind ensemble(piccolo, flutes(2),
oboes(2), clarinet(E-flat), clarinet (in A),
clarinet(bass), horns(4), trumpets(4),
trombones(3), tuba), timpani, percussion,
film(8mm)(2), film(16mm)(2), slide
projectors(2), overhead projectors(2),
tape. Multi-media. *First performed:*
Nov. 22, 1972; University of Lowell.
Score & parts: available from
composer.

M8.19 Metra. (1975) 8' 30"
For: violoncello and piano.
Score: ms.

M8.20 Phantasy. (1970) 7'
For: violin and piano. *First performed:*
May 30, 1973; Elmira College.
Score: ms.

M8.21 Poem. (1963) 5' 30'
For: flute and string orchestra. *First
performed:* Apr. 20, 1968; Boston
University.
Score: ms.
Parts: available from composer.

M8.22 Prelude and Aria. (1974) 8'
For: Soprano, wind ensemble(flute,
flute/piccolo, oboe, clarinet/
clarinet(alto), clarinet/clarinet(bass),
saxophone(alto), horns(2), trumpets(2),
trombones(2), tuba), timpani, percussion,
piano. *First performed:* Dec. 12, 1974;
University of Lowell.
Score: ms.
Parts: available from composer.

M8.23 Quarternary. (1972) 3'
For: flute. *First performed:* Mar. 28,
1977; Adams House, Harvard University.
Score: ms.
Reel: Mar. 26, 1974; Berklee College of
Music. Roger Jannotta. Be

[Quartet, Strings]
M8.24 String Quartet, No. 1. (1973) 30'
Score: ms.
Parts: available from composer.

[Quintet, Woodwinds]
M8.25 Woodwind Quintet. (1968) 12'
Score: ms.
Parts: available from composer.

[Rhodian Scenes]
M8.26 Four Rhodian Scenes. (1976) 25'
For: guitar, wind
ensemble(flute(2)/piccolo,
oboes(2)/English horn, clarinet,
clarinet/clarinet(bass), bassoons(2),
horns(2), trumpets(3), trombones(3),
tuba), timpani, percussion. Suite. 4
movements. *First performed:* Oct. 15,
1976. Arlington Philharmonic.
Score & parts: BKJ.

M8.27 Rumeurs et visions. (1975) 4'
For: oboe and piano. After Arthur
Rimbaud. *First performed:* Oct. 23,
1975; Brookline Public Library.
Score: ms.
Reel: Dec. 15, 1975; Berklee College of
Music.
Reel: Apr. 7, 1976; Berklee Recital Hall,
Berklee College of Music. Janice
Nicholson, oboe and David Degrand,
piano. Be

M8.28 Suite for Brass. (1971) 10'
For: brass ensemble(horns(3),
trumpets(3), trombones(3), tuba),
timpani, gong.
Score: ms.
Parts: available from composer.

M8.29 Suite for Clarinet Quartet. (1970)
9'
For: clarinets(2), clarinet(alto),
clarinet(bass).
Score: ms.
Parts: available from composer.

M8.30 Suite for Two Violins, Viola and
Piano. (1973) 13'
First performed: Feb. 23, 1974; Rhodes,
Greece.
Score: ms.

[Trio]
M8.31 Woodwind Trio. (1970) 4'
For: flute, clarinet, saxophone(alto).
First performed: Mar. 15, 1975; Berklee
College of Music.
Score: BKJ.
Reel: Mar. 26, 1974; Berklee College of
Music. Roger Jannotta, flute; Chris
Colclessor, clarinet; John McLaughlin,
alto saxophone. Be

M8.32 La Ville lumiere. (1970) 7'
For: piano. Suite.
Score: ms.

M9 DOUGLAS McGILVRA

Born October 21, 1945, in New York
City. Moved to Boston area 1970.
Education: studied composition with

Earl Kim (Harvard University, Ph.D.,
1975). *Awards:* Composer's Conference
(Bennington, Vt.) fellowship (1967),
Bohemians Prize (New York Musicians
Club, Harvard University) and George
Arthur Knight Prize (Harvard University,
1970-75), Massachusetts Council on the
Arts and Humanities, Artist Fellowship
Program (1979). *Related activities:*
pianist. CPL

WORKS

M9.1 Artes.
Recipient of George Arthur Knight Prize
(Harvard University), 1975. Written
under the pseudonymn Jack Grat.
Score: HU

M9.2 Ariel's Songs. (1980) 6'
For: Soprano, flute, clarinet, celeste,
viola, violoncello. *Text:* from *The
Tempest* by William Shakespeare.
Score & parts: Composer's
Collaborative. Rental.

M9.3 Baudelairescape. (1979-80) 25'
For: Soprano, flute, clarinet, trumpet,
violin, viola, piano/ celeste. *Text:* two
poems by Charles Pierre Baudelaire.
Score & parts: Composer's
Collaborative. Rental.

M9.4 Blake Texts. (1976-77) 20'
For: Soprano, flutes(3), pianos(2),
celeste. 10 songs. *Text:* from *Songs of
Innocence* and *Songs of Experience* by
William Blake. *First performed:* Apr.
1978; Sanders Theatre, Harvard
University; Fromm Foundation Concert.
Score & parts: Composer's
Collaborative. Rental.

M9.5 Cartouche. (1979-80) 20'
For: violin, violoncello, piano.
Score & parts: Composer's
Collaborative. Rental.

[Concerto, Violin]
M9.6 Violin Concerto.
Doctoral thesis.
Score: HU

M9.7 Flower Speech. (1981) 6'
For: Soprano, flute, clarinet, percussion, celeste, harp, violin, viola, violoncello. *Text:* from *The Winter's Tale* by William Shakespeare.
Score & parts: Composer's Collaborative. Rental.

M9.8 Intermezzo. (1981) 12'
For: flute, violin, piano. *Commissioned by:* New School of Music.
Score & parts: Composer's Collaborative. Rental.

M9.9 Intermezzos and Capriccios. Winner of the Bohemians Prize (New York Musicians Club, Harvard University), 1973. Written under the pseudonymn Brian Oaks.
Score: HU

[Songs, Soprano and Instruments(4)]
M9.10 Four Songs. (1980) 14'
For: Soprano, flute, clarinet, viola, piano. *Text:* Heinrich Heine, Richard Wilbur, d'Orleans, Paul Marie Verlaine.
Score & parts: Composer's Collaborative. Rental.

[Songs, Voice and Piano]
M9.11 Two Songs. (1964) 5'
Text: Friedrich Hoelderlin. *First performed:* 1964; Oberlin Festival of Contemporary Music.
Score: Composer's Collaborative. Rental.

M9.12 Songs with Words. (1979-80) 10'
For: Soprano, clarinets(3), mandolin, violin, viola, violoncello. *Text:* Samuel Beckett, Rainer Maria Rilke, Paul Marie Verlaine.
Score & parts: Composer's Collaborative. Rental.

M10 WILLIAM THOMAS McKINLEY

Born December 9, 1938, in New Kensington, Pa. Moved to Boston area 1973. *Education:* studied composition with Nikolai Lopatnikoff (Carnegie-Mellon University, B.F.A.); Mel Powell, Gunther Schuller (Yale University, M.M., M.M.A., D.M.A. program); Frederick Dorian; Yehudi Wyner. *Awards:* Minnesota Symphony 75th Anniversary Orchestra Prize; commissions from the Chicago Symphony Orchestra, Fromm Foundation, Naumburg Foundation, National Endowment for the Arts and others. *Related activities:* jazz pianist; member of the faculty of New England Conservatory (1973-). NEC

WORKS

M10.1 Arabesques. (1971)
For: violin. 10 movements.
Commissioned by and dedicated to: Paul Zukofsky.
Score: reprod. of ms. NEC

M10.2 Arabesques for Assorted Instruments. (1969-70) 9' 26"
For: instruments(unspecified). Aleatoric music. 8 movements. *Dedicated to:* Marlene. *First performed:* University of Chicago.
Score: reprod. of ms. NEC

Blues. *See* Piece, Piano, No. 22.

M10.3 Blues Lament: An Encore Piece.
For: clarinet and orchestra(2-2-2-2; 4-2-2-1; perc; str). *Commissioned by:* Richard Stoltzman.
Score: MMC.

M10.4 Cello Music: A Portfolio for Solo, 2, 3, and 4 Cellos. (1972)
For: violoncellos(1-4). *Contents:* Pristine Drops, Dances for 4 Cellos; Blue Expansion; Kinetic Haze; Solo Excursion; Time Steps; Solo Excursion 2-3; Solo Excursion 4-5; Dialogue 1; Static Flight; Triple; Solo Excursion 6; Winter Muse; Solo Excursion 7; Episode, A-C. *Commissioned by:* University of Wisconsin. *First performed:* University of Wisconsin.
Score: reprod. of ms. NEC

M10.5 Circular Forms for Grand Orchestra. (1970)

For: orchestra(3(pic)-2-3(bcl)-2;
3-3-2(btrb)-1; perc(6), glock, mar, xylo;
cel; tape; str(18-8-8-4)). 1 movement.
Commissioned by: University of
Chicago. *Dedication:* To my wife,
Marlene. *First performed:* University of
Chicago.
Score: reprod. of ms. NEC

M10.6 Composition I. (1972)
For: clarinet(bass). *Dedicated to:* Les.
First performed: University of
Wisconsin.
Score: reprod. of ms. NEC

M10.7 Concertino for Grand Orchestra,
Op. 71. (1976) 10'
For: orchestra(4-5(Ehn)-4(bcl)-3(cbsn);
4-2-2-1; timp, perc(4), glock, vibra,
xylo; cel, str(includes at least 4 double
basses with C extension)). 1 movement
Commissioned by: National Endowment
for the Arts. *First performed:* Aug. 16,
1977; Berkshire Music Center,
Tanglewood. Berkshire Center
Orchestra, Gunther Schuller, conductor.
Score: reprod. of ms. NEC
Score: Margun.
Parts: Margun. Rental.

M10.8 Concertino for Percussion
Ensemble. (1981)
Commissioned by: Dave Samuels.
Score & parts: MMC.

[Concerto, Clarinet]
M10.9 Concerto. (1976)
For: clarinet. *Dedicated to:* Richard
Stoltzman.
Score: reprod. of ms. NEC

[Concerto, Clarinet and Orchestra]
M10.10 Clarinet Concerto: A Symphony.
Funded by a grant from the National
Endowment for the Arts. *First
performed:* July 5, 1980; Boulder, Colo.
Richard Stoltzman, clarinet; Colorado
Festival Orchestra, Giora Bernstein,
conductor.
Score & parts: Margun.

[Concerto, Clarinet and Violin]
M10.11 Double Concerto: Lucy

Variations. (1981)
For: clarinet, violin, chamber
orchestra(2-2-2-2; 2-2-0-0; perc; hp; str
(6-4-4-4-2)). *Commissioned by:* Richard
Stoltzman.
Score & parts: MMC.

[Concerto, Oboe/English Horn/Oboe
d'Amore and Percussion]
M10.12 Concerto. (1978)
oboe/English horn/oboe d'amore and
percussion. *First performed:* Apr. 11,
1978; New England Conservatory.
Frederic Cohen, oboe, English horn,
oboe d'amore and Sara Tenney,
percussion.
Score & parts: MMC.
Cassette: recording of first
performance. NEC

[Concerto, Orchestra]
M10.13 Concerto for Grand Orchestra,
Op. 53. (1974) 18'
For: orchestra(8(pic8)-4-8(bcl8)-3(cbsn3);
4-3-2(btrb)-1; perc(6), glock, vibra, xylo;
gt(amplified), hp(2); cel, pf(2);
str(16-14-12-10-8)). 1 movement.
Dedication: To Tom. *First performed:*
Nov. 19, 1980; New England
Conservatory. NEC Symphony
Orchestra, Wolfgang Balzer, conductor.
Score: reprod. of ms. NEC
Score: MMC.
Cassette: recording of first
performance. NEC

[Concerto, Piano]
M10.14 Piano Concerto, No. 1, Op. 60.
(1974) 25'
For: piano and orchestra. 1 movement.
Dedicated to: Peter Serkin.
Score: reprod. of ms. NEC

[Concerto, Piano, Timpani, Double
Bass]
M10.15 Triple Concerto for Piano,
Contra Bass, Drums and Grand
Orchestra. (1970) 25'
For: piano, timpani, double bass,
orchestra(2-2-2(bcl)-2(cbsn); 2-2-2-1;
perc(5); str). 1 movement. *Commissioned
by and dedicated to:* Chicago Symphony
Orchestra. First performed: June 1971;

William Thomas McKinley, piano;
Chicago Symphony Orchestra, Irwin
Hoffman, conductor.
Score: reprod. of ms. NEC

[Concerto, Viola]
M10.16 Concerto for Viola and
Orchestra. (1977)
1 movement. *Commissioned by:*
National Endowment for the Arts.
Dedicated to: Sol Greitzer, New York
Philharmonic.
Score & parts: MMC.

[Concerto, Violoncello]
M10.17 Concerto for Cello and
Orchestra. (1976)
1 movement *Commissioned by:* National
Endowment for the Arts. *Dedicated to:*
Aldo Parisot.
Score: MMC.

M10.18 Eliot. (1972)
For: chorus(mixed)(at least 64 singers).
1 movement. *Text:* based on Burnt
Norton from *The Four Quartets* by T.S.
Eliot. *Dedicated to:* James Mack and
the University of Chicago Chorus.
Vocal score: reprod. of ms. NEC

M10.19 Etude No. 1. (1973)
For: harp. 1 movement. *First
performed:* 1975; Boston. Susan Allen.
Score: reprod. of ms. NEC
Score: Salvi.
Disc: 1750 Arch Records, nyp.

M10.20 Etude No. 2. (1974)
For: harp. 1 movement.
Score: reprod. of ms. NEC

M10.21 Extempora. (1968)
For: flute. *Dedicated to:* Irvin Gilman.
First performed: Albany, N.Y.
Score: reprod. of ms. NEC

M10.22 Fantasia concertante. 20'
For: string quartet. 1 movement.
Commissioned by: Sequoia String
Quartet and the Naumburg Foundation.
Dedicated to: Sequoia Quartet. *First
performed:* Alice Tully Hall, New York

City.
Score: reprod. of ms. NEC
Score & parts: Margun.
Disc: Delos, nyp.

M10.23 Fantasy. (1975)
For: piano.

M10.24 Fantasys and Inventions. (1972)
For: harpsichord.
Score: reprod. of ms. NEC

M10.25 For Les: 3 Pieces. (1972)
For: saxophone(soprano). *First
performed:* University of Wisconsin.
Score: reprod. of ms. NEC

M10.26 For One. (1970) 5'
For: clarinet. 1 movement. *Dedicated
to:* Richard Stoltzman. *First performed:*
New York Public Library at Lincoln
Center, New York City.
Score: MMC, 1980.
Cassette: May 10, 1981; New England
Conservatory. Edward Ferris. NEC

From a Private Monologue. *See* Piece,
Piano, No. 20 and Piece, Piano,
No. 21.

M10.27 From Opera: For 4 Players.
(1968)
For: flute/piccolo/flute(alto),
oboe/English horn, clarinet/clarinet
(bass)/saxophone(soprano), piano. 1
movement. *Dedicated to:* Paul and
Wilma Zonn. *First performed:* Yale
University.
Score: reprod. of ms. NEC

[From Opera No. 1]
M10.28 From Opera: Last Section
Revised. (1971)
For: piano.
Score: reprod. of ms. NEC

M10.29 From Opera No. 2.
For: clarinet and string quartet. *First
performed:* 1979; Syracuse, N.Y.;
Syracuse Chamber Music Society.
Richard Stoltzman, clarinet; Tashi.
Score & parts: MMC.

M10.30 Galaxy. (1973)
For: string quartet. 1 movement.
Dedication: To my wife.
Score: reprod. of ms. NEC

[Impromptus]
M10.31 Six Impromptus. (1978)
Commissioned by: National Endowment
for the Arts and Boston Musica Viva.
First performed: Nov. 21, 1978; Boston.
Boston Musica Viva, Richard Pittman,
conductor.
Score & parts: MMC.
Disc: Northeastern Records, nyp.
Reel: recording of first performance.
WGBH

[Interim Piece, No. 1]
M10.32 Interim Pieces. (1968)
For: clarinet(bass) and violin. *Dedicated
to:* Les and Shoko Aki. *First
performed:* Yale University.
Score: reprod. of ms. NEC

M10.33 Interim Piece, No. 2. (1974)
For: clarinet/clarinet(contrabass),
saxophone(soprano), violoncello. *First
performed:* University of Wisconsin.
Score: reprod. of ms. NEC

[Interludes, Oboe and Piano]
M10.34 Ten Interludes. (1971)
First performed: University of Illinois.
Score: reprod. of ms. NEC

[Interludes, Piano]
M10.35 11 Interludes. (1971)
Dedication: To my wife.
Score: reprod. of ms. NEC

M10.36 Interruptions. (1974) 10'
For: saxophone, flute, drums, double
bass, woodwind ensemble(24). Aleatoric
music. *Commissioned by:* University of
Wisconsin. *First performed:* University
of Wisconsin. William Thomas
McKinley and others, Frank Reynolds,
conductor.
Score: reprod. of ms. NEC
Parts: MMC.
Cassette: Feb. 17, 1977; New England
Conservatory. NEC Wind Ensemble,
Frank L. Battisti, conductor. NEC

Journeys. *See* Piece, Piano, No. 18.

M10.37 Little Sonata. (1973)
For: viola, clarinet, piano. *Dedicated to:*
Richard Stoltzman.
Score: reprod. of ms. NEC

Lucy Variations. *See* Concerto, Clarinet
and Violin.

Magical Visions. *See* Paintings No. IV.

[Movements]
M10.38 Three Movements. (1980)
For: wind ensemble. *Commissioned by:*
National Endowment for the Arts and
Frank L. Battisti. *First performed:* Dec.
11, 1980; New England Conservatory.
NEC Wind Ensemble, Frank L. Battisti,
conductor.
Score & parts: Margun. Rental.
Cassette: recording of first
performance. NEC

M10.39 October Night. (1976)
For: orchestra(2-3(Ehn)-3(bcl)-3(cbsn);
4-2-2-1; perc(3); str).
Score: reprod. of ms. NEC
Parts: MMC.

M10.40 Paintings, No. 1 for 7 Players.
(1972)
For: percussion(2), clarinets(2), bassoon,
violin, violoncello. *Movements:* Fancy;
Wheels; Cubes; Purple; Question.
Commissioned by: University of
Wisconsin. *First performed:* University
of Wisconsin. Les Thimmig, conductor.
Score: reprod. of ms. NEC
Music: MMC.

M10.41 Paintings, No. 2 for Double
Trio. (1974-75) 12'
For: flute, oboe, clarinet, violin, viola,
violoncello. *Movements:* Winter; Spring;
Summer; Autumn; Epilogue.
Commissioned by: Yale University. *First
performed:* Feb. 28, 1976; Jordan Hall,
Boston; American Society of University
Composers, 11th Annual Conference
NEC Contemporary Ensemble, Gunther
Schuller, conductor.
Score & parts: Margun, 1978. NEC

Disc: in *New England Conservatory of Music Faculty Composers*, Golden Crest NEC 119, 1979. Recording of first performance. NEC T
Cassette: recording of first performance. NEC

M10.42 Paintings, No. 3, Op. 70. (1976)
For: clarinet and string quartet.
Movements: Worlds; Dusk; Coins; Dust; March Day; Coda. *Commissioned by and dedicated to:* Richard Stoltzman.
Score: reprod. of ms. NEC
Music: MMC.

M10.43 Paintings No. IV: Magical Visions. (1978) 13'
For: flute/piccolo, clarinet, violoncello, piano, percussion. 1 movement.
Commissioned by: National Endowment for the Arts and Collage. *Dedicated to:* Frank Epstein of Collage. *First performed:* 1979; Boston. Collage, Gunther Schuller, conductor.
Score & parts: Margun. Rental.
Cassette: Feb. 29, 1980; New England Conservatory. NEC Contemporary Music Ensemble, Larry Livingston, conductor. NEC

M10.44 Paintings V. (1979-80) .
For: violin, viola, violoncello, flute, clarinet(bass), trumpet. *Commissioned by:* Pittsburgh New Music Ensemble, David Stock, conductor. *First performed:* Pittsburgh, Pa. Pittsburgh New Music Ensemble, David Stock, conductor.
Score: MMC.

M10.45 Paintings VI: To Hear the Light Dancing.
For: violin, viola, violoncello, flute, clarinet, piano, percussion, dancers(4). Ballet. *Commissioned by:* National Endowment for the Arts and Boston Musica Viva. *First performed:* May 2, 1981; Sanders Theatre, Harvard University. Boston Musica Viva, Richard Pittman, conductor.
Score & parts: MMC.
Disc: Northeastern Records, nyp.

[Piece, Piano, No. 16]
M10.46 Piano Piece 16. (1971)
1 movement.
Score: reprod. of ms. NEC

[Piece, Piano, No. 18]
M10.47 Piano Piece No. XVIII: Journeys. (1973)
1 movement.
Score: reprod. of ms. NEC

[Piece, Piano, No. 19]
M10.48 Piano Piece XVIV (i.e. XIX). (1973)
1 movement.
Score: reprod. of ms. NEC

[Piece, Piano, No. 20]
M10.49 Piano Piece, No. 20: From a Private Monologue. (1975)
1 movement.
Score: reprod. of ms. NEC

[Piece, Piano, No. 21]
M10.50 Piano Piece no. 21: From a Private Monologue. (1975)
1 movement.
Score: reprod. of ms. NEC

[Piece, Piano, No. 22]
M10.51 Piano Piece No. 22: Blues. (1975)
1 movement. *First performed:* 1977; Jordan Hall, Boston. Thomas Stumpf.
Score: reprod. of ms. NEC
Score: MMC.

[Piece, Saxophone(Tenor), No. 1]
M10.52 Solo Tenor Saxophone Piece, No. 1. (1974)
First performed: University of Wisconsin. Les Thimmig.

[Pieces, Horn]
M10.53 Three Pieces. (1980)
Dedicated to: Phil Meyers and Dale Cleavenger.
Score: MMC.

[Pieces, Oboe and Piano]
M10.54 Four Pieces. (1973)
First performed: University of

Wisconsin.
Score: reprod. of ms. NEC
Score: MMC.

[Pieces, Piano]
M10.55 Four Piano Pieces. (1971)
Dedication: To my wife.
Score: reprod. of ms. NEC

[Pieces, Piano, Saxophone(Soprano),
Violoncello]
M10.56 Six Pieces.
Music: MMC.

[Pieces, Soprano and Piano]
M10.57 Six Pieces. (1974)
First performed: University of Chicago.
Elsa Charlston, soprano and
unidentified pianist.
Score: MMC.

[Pieces, String Quartet]
M10.58 Six Pieces.
Commissioned by: National Endowment
for the Arts.
Score: MMC.

M10.59 Portraits. (1973)
For: viola. *Movements:* Autumn;
Weapons; Prayer; Granite; Clay; Silver;
Flowers; Ivory; Crystals. *First
performed:* California Institute of The
Arts. Jim Dunham.
Score: reprod. of ms. NEC
Score: MMC.

M10.60 Premises and Expositions.
(1968)
For: flute, oboe, clarinet, bassoon,
string quartet. *Commissioned by and
dedicated to:* Fromm Foundation. *First
performed:* 1968; Berkshire Music
Center, Tanglewood.
Score: reprod. of ms. NEC

M10.61 Progeny. (1971)
For: piccolo, flute, oboe, clarinet,
saxophone(soprano), clarinet(bass),
percussion, tape.
Score: reprod. of ms. NEC

M10.62 Quadruplum. (1970)
For: Soprano, piano, flute/piccolo,

violin, instrumental ensemble. 1
movement. *Commissioned by:* Fromm
Foundation. *Dedicated to:* Paul Fromm.
First performed: University of
Chicago. Ralph Shapey, conductor.
Score: reprod. of ms. NEC

M10.63 Quartet.
For: piano, saxophone(soprano), double
bass, drums. 1 movement.
Score: reprod. of ms. NEC

M10.64 Quintet. (1980) 20'
For: woodwind quintet. 1 movement.
First performed: Nov. 10, 1980; New
England Conservatory. John Heiss,
flute; Frederic Cohen, oboe; Robert
Annis, clarinet; Peter Schoenbach,
bassoon; David Hoose, horn.
Score: MMC, 1981.
Cassette: recording of first
performance. NEC

M10.65 Rhapsody. 15'
For: harp and band. *Commissioned by:*
American Harp Society. *First
performed:* Susan Allen, harp; Newton
High School Band.
Score & parts: Salvi.

M10.66 Rhapsody Fantasia.
For: clarinet(in A) and orchestra.
Commissioned by: National Endowment
for the Arts. *Dedicated to:* Richard
Stoltzman.
Score: MMC.

M10.67 A Short Symphony, Op. 103.
(1979)
For: brass ensemble(horns(4),
trumpets(4), trombones(4), tubas(4) and
percussion(3)). *First performed:* Nov. 14,
1979; New England Conservatory. NEC
Wind Ensemble, Frank L. Battisti,
conductor.
Music: MMC.
Cassette: recording of first
performance. NEC

M10.68 Sinfonia. (1976)
For: string quartet. 1 movement.
Dedication: To my wife Marlene and to

the spirit of the Baroque sinfonia.
Score: reprod. of ms. NEC

M10.69 Sonatas I. (1972)
For: pianos(2). 1 movement. *First
performed:* Stony Brook, N.Y. Rebecca
LaBrecque and unidentified second
pianist.
Score: reprod. of ms. NEC
Cassette: May 8, 1975; New England
Conservatory; in *An Evening of
Contemporary Music.* Cameron Grant and
James Winn. NEC

M10.70 Sonatas II. (1972)
For: pianos(2). 1 movement. *First
performed:* Stony Brook, N.Y. Rebecca
LaBrecque and unidentified second
pianist.
Score: reprod. of ms. NEC

M10.71 Sonatas III. (1972)
For: pianos(2). *Movements:* On the Eve;
Sunshine; Holidays. *First performed:*
Stony Brook, N.Y. Rebecca LaBrecque
and unidentified second pianist.
Score: reprod. of ms. NEC

[Songs]
M10.72 5 Songs. (1973)
For: Soprano, clarinet(bass), violoncello,
piano. *Dedication:* To my wife Marlene.
First performed: University of
Wisconsin.
Score: reprod. of ms. NEC

M10.73 Songs without Words, Op. 72.
(1976) 21'
For: flute. *First performed:* 1976; Longy
School of Music. Stephanie Jutt.
Score: reprod. of ms. NEC
Score: Margun, 1980. NEC
Cassette: Oct. 17, 1977; New England
Conservatory (Nos. 1-3, 7, 9, 20, 25,
27, 28). John Heiss. NEC

[Stages]
M10.74 Twelve Stages. (1971)
For: bassoon. *Movements:* Aria; Lai;
Talea; Time; Chanson; Organum;
Plainsong; Chant; Pretty; Maze;
Epilogue; Cadenza. *First performed:*

Jordan Hall, Boston.
Score: reprod. of ms. NEC

M10.75 Steps I - II. (1972)
For: clarinet(bass)/basset
horn/saxophone(soprano)/
saxophone(tenor) /clarinet(contrabass)
and tape. *Commissioned by:* University
of Wisconsin.
Reel: 1976.
Cassette: Mar. 26, 1974; New England
Conservatory; in *An Evening of
Contemporary Music.* Les Thimmig. NEC

M10.76 Studies. (1975)
For: violin, viola, violoncello.
Score: reprod. of ms. NEC
Score: MMC. NEC

M10.77 Symphony No. 1. (1977) 22'
For: orchestra(3-4-4-4; 4-2-2-1; perc; hp;
pf; str). 1 movement. Winner of the
Minnesota Symphony 75th Anniversary
Orchestra Prize. *Dedication:* To the
memory of Nikolai Lopatnikof. *First
performed:* Jan. 5, 1979; Minneapolis,
Minn. Minneapolis Symphony, Gunther
Schuller, conductor.
Score & parts: Margun. Rental.

M10.78 Symphony No. 2. (1978)
For: orchestra(6-2(Ehn)-4(in
A)(&bcl)-3(&cbsn); 4-4-4-2; timp, perc(2);
str(at least 4 double basses with C
string extension)). *Commissioned by:*
National Endowment for the Arts.
Dedication: To my wife.

M10.79 Tashi Quartet.
For: piano, clarinet, violoncello, violin.
Dedicated to: Tashi. *First performed:*
New York City. Tashi.

[Text Settings] ,
M10.80 Four Text Settings, Op. 109.
(1970) 17'
For: chorus(SATB). *Text:* Marlene Marie
Mildner McKinley. *Commissioned by:*
National Endowment for the Arts. *First
performed:* Apr. 4, 1981; Sanders
Theatre, Harvard University. John Oliver
Chorale, John Oliver, conductor.

Music: MMC.
Parts: Margun. Rental.

To Hear the Light Dancing. *See* Paintings VI: To Hear the Light Dancing.

M10.81 Trio.
For: violins(2) and viola. 1 movement. *Dedicated to:* Paul Zukofsky. *First performed:* University of Wisconsin. *Score:* reprod. of ms. NEC

M10.82 Trio and Poem. (1969)
For: Soprano, flute, piano, snare drum, double bass. 1 movement. *Text: I Am* by Marlene Marie Mildner McKinley. *First performed:* Yale University. *Score:* reprod. of ms. NEC

M10.83 Waves: A Study for Solo Viola. (1973)
1 movement.
Score: reprod. of ms. NEC

ARRANGEMENTS OF WORKS BY OTHER COMPOSERS

M10.84 Night and Day, I'll Go My Way by Myself, Goodbye. (1981)
For: clarinet and piano. *Commissioned by:* Richard Stoltzman. *First performed:* New York City.
Score: MMC.

M11 JOYCE MEKEEL

Born July 6, 1931. *Education:* B.M., M.M. (Yale University, 1959, 1960); studied composition with Nadia Boulanger (Conservatoire National de Musique, Paris, France, 1955-57) and Earl Kim (1960-62); harpsichord with Gustav Leonhardt (1957) and Ralph Kirkpatrick (1957-59). *Awards:* MacDowell Colony Fellowships (1963, 1964, 1974), Ingram-Merrill Grant in Composition (1964), Sigma Alpha Iota Inter-American Music Award (First Prize, 1965), Radcliffe Institute Fellowship (1968-1970), Boston University Research Grant (1971), Yaddo Fellowship (1974), National Endowment

for the Arts Grant (1975). *Related activities:* sculptor; environmental anthropologist; composer of incidental music for plays at the McCarter Theater, Princeton, N.J. (1961-64) and music for various dance companies (1967-71, 1979); served on the faculties of New England Conservatory (1964-70) and Boston University (1970-). BU

WORKS

M11.1 Alarums and Excursions. (1978) 22'
For: actress/Mezzo Soprano, flute, clarinet, violin, viola, violoncello, percussion. 1 movement. *Text:* Aeschylus, Emily Dickinson, August Stramm, and others. *Commissioned by and dedicated to:* Boston Musica Viva. *First performed:* October 1978; Longy School of Music. Boston Musica Viva, Richard Pittman, conductor.
Score: reprod. of ms. BU
Reel: Jan. 1980; WGBH-FM, Boston. Boston Musica Viva, Richard Pittman, conductor. WGBH
Disc: Northeastern Records, nyp. Boston Musica Viva, Richard Pittman, conductor.

M11.2 Birth History.
Withdrawn.

M11.3 Clique. (1960?)
For: piano(4-hands). Withdrawn.

M11.4 Corridors of Dream. (1972) 11' 30"
For: Mezzo Soprano, flute(alto), clarinet, viola, violoncello, harp, percussion. 1 movement. *Text:* Wassily Kandinsky, Manfred Peter Hein, Wolf Dietrich Schurre, August Stramm, Hans Magnus Enzensberger. *Commissioned by:* Goethe Institut (Boston) for the Boston Musica Viva. *First performed:* Dec. 1972; Busch-Reisinger Museum, Harvard University. Boston Musica Viva, Richard Pittman, director.
Score: ms. in composer's hand.
Disc: in *Premiere Performances*, Delos DEL 25405, 1975. Jan Curtis, mezzo

soprano; Boston Music Viva, Richard Pittman, director. BCM BU HU MIT NEC T W

M11.5 Dark Rime. (1965) 9'
For: Soprano and piano. 1 movement.
Text: Rainer Maria Rilke. *Dedicated to:* Bethany Beardslee. *First performed:* Mar. 1966; New York City; Composer's Forum. Bethany Beardslee, soprano and Yehudi Wyner, piano.
Score: ms. in composer's hand.

M11.6 Embouchure I. (1969)
For: tape. Written in collaboration with Lyle Davidson. *First performed:* Dec. 9, 1969; New England Conservatory; in An Evening of Contemporary Music.
Cassette: recording of first performance. NEC

M11.7 Embouchure II. (1972) 8'
For: trumpets(3) and trombones(3). *First performed:* May 1972; Boston University. Student performers.
Score & parts: ms. in composer's hand.

M11.8 Epiphanies (1960?)
For: piano. Withdrawn.

M11.9 Fertile Vicissitudes. (1981) 7'
For: oboe and harp. 1 movement.
Commissioned by and dedicated to: Peggy Pearson and Susan Allen. *First performed:* March 15, 1981; Longy School of Music. Peggy Pearson, oboe and Susan Allen, harp.
Score: ms. in composer's hand.
Score: reprod. of ms. W
Reel: Apr. 5, 1981; Wellesley College. Peggy Pearson, oboe and Susan Allen, harp. W

M11.10 Gifts of the Ebb Tide. (1965) 9'
For: piano. 1 movement. *Dedicated to:* Robert Helps. *First performed:* Mar. 1966; New York City. Robert Miller.
Score: ms. in composer's hand.
Reel: 1967; Jordan Hall, Boston. Robert Helps.
Reel: March 4, 1978; WGBH-FM,

Boston; in *Live Performance Series.* Richard Kessler. WGBH

M11.11 Grido. (1974?)
Withdrawn.

M11.12 Hommages. (1973) 9'-10'
For: trumpets(2), horn, trombone, tuba. 1 movement. *Commissioned by and dedicated to:* Empire Brass Quintet.
First performed: Feb. 1974; Isabella Stewart Gardner Museum, Boston. Empire Brass Quintet.
Score & parts: ms. in composer's hand.
Cassette: Mar. 20, 1977; New England Conservatory. Empire Brass Quintet. NEC

M11.13 Kisses and Kazoos. (1977)
For: speakers(3) and tape(live). *Text:* valentine cards, etc. Written in collaboration with Lyle Davidson and Paul Earls. *First performed:* 1977; Massachusetts College of Art; in Eventworks Series.

M11.14 Monotony of Absences.
For: flute(alto), clarinet, English horn, bassoon, harp. Withdrawn.

M11.15 Moveable Feast, No. 1. (1973) 60'
For: voices(unspecified) and instruments(unspecified). Stage work; aleatoric music. Written in collaboration with Paul Earls and Lyle Davidson. First performed: Nov. 1973; Massachusetts College of Art. Student performers.

M11.16 Moveable Feast, No. 2. (1974) 60'
For: voices(unspecified) and instruments(unspecified). Stage work; aleatoric music. Written in collaboration with Paul Earls and Lyle Davidson. *First performed:* Mar. 7, 1974; New England Conservatory. Student performers.
Cassette: recording of first performance. NEC

M11.17 Moveable Feast, No. 3. (1974) 60'
For: voices(unspecified) and instruments(unspecified). Stage work; aleatoric music. Written in collaboration with Paul Earls and Lyle Davidson. *First performed:* Apr. 1974; Boston University. Student performer.

M11.18 Nunc est cantandum. (1960)
For: voice and piano(prepared). Withdrawn.

M11.19 Phrases. (1960) 6'
For: Soprano and piano. 1 movement. *Text:* Gertrude Stein. *First performed:* 1960. Yale University, New Haven, Conn. Sheila Marks, soprano and Joyce Mekeel, piano.
Score: ms. in composer's hand.

M11.20 Planh. (1974) 13'
For: violin. 1 movement. *Commissioned by and dedicated to:* Nancy Cirillo. *First performed:* Mar. 1975; Alice Tully Hall, New York City. Nancy Cirillo.
Score: ms. in composer's hand.
Score: reprod. of ms. W
Disc: in *Premiere Performances*, Delos DEL 25405, 1975. Nancy Cirillo. BCM BU HU MIT NEC T
Reel: WGBH-FM, Boston; in *Live Performance Series*. Mary Crowder Hess. WGBH
Cassette: Mar. 11, 1975; New England Conservatory. Nancy Cirillo. NEC

M11.21 Rune. (1976) 6'
For: flute and percussion. 1 movement. *Commissioned by:* Boston Musica Viva. *Dedicated to:* Fenwick Smith and Dean Anderson. *First performed:* Mar. 1977; Longy School of Music. Fenwick Smith, flute and Dean Anderson, percussion.
Score: ms. in composer's hand.
Disc: Northeastern Records, nyp. Fenwick Smith, flute and Dean Anderson, percussion.
Reel: recording of first performance. WGBH
Reel: Mar. 4, 1978; WGBH-FM, Boston; in *Live Performance Series*. Fenwick Smith, flute and Dean Anderson,

percussion. WGBH
Cassette: Nov. 10, 1980; New England Conservatory. John Heiss, flute and Dean Anderson, percussion. NEC

M11.22 Scroll of Hungry Dreams. (1980) 6'
For: tuba. 1 movement. *Commissioned by and dedicated to:* Barton Cummings. *First performed:* May 1980; North Texas State University; Tubists Universal Brotherhood Association Convention. Barton Cummings.
Score: ms. in composer's hand.

M11.23 Serena. (1975) 10'
For: Mezzo Soprano, speaker, piano(prepared). 1 movement. *Text:* from *Joseph and His Brothers* by Thomas Mann and various other authors. *Commissioned by:* Fromm Foundation. *First performed:* Aug. 1975; Berkshire Music Center, Tanglewood. Beverly Morgan, mezzo soprano.
Score: ms. in composer's hand.
Reel: recording of first performance.
Reel: Mar. 4, 1978; WGBH-FM, Boston; in *Live Performance Series*. Judy Kellock, soprano; Maeda Freeman, speaker; Richard Kessler, piano. WGBH

M11.24 Shape of Silence: in Memoriam Theodore Roethke. (1969) 6'
For: flute. 1 movement. *Text:* Joyce Mekeel. *Commissioned by:* John Heiss. *Dedicated to:* Theodore Roethke. *Firs t performed:* Oct. 22, 1969; Busch-Reisinger Museum, Harvard University. John Heiss.
Score: Peters, 1981.
Cassette: Apr. 27, 1970; New England Conservatory. John Heiss. NEC
Cassette: Oct. 27, 1975; New England Conservatory. John Heiss. NEC
Cassette: Oct. 22, 1979; New England Conservatory. John Heiss. NEC

M11.25 Sigil. (1980-81)
For: actor, actress, instrumental ensemble(English horn, clarinet, contrabassoon, horns(2), tuba, violins(2), viola, violoncello), electronics (microphones(2), mixer, loudspeakers(4)).

1 movement. *Text:* Gertrude Stein, David Bohm, Giuseppe Ungarelli, Theodore Roethke, Albert Camus, Thomas Mann, Jose Luis Borges. *Dedicated to:* James Malcolm and Kathy Lenel. *First performed:* Dec. 5, 1981; Boston University. James Malcolm, actor; Kathy Lenel, actress; Boston University Collegium in Contemporary Music, Robert Sirota, conductor. *Score:* ms. in composer's hand. *Reel:* recording of first performance. BU

M11.26 Solo.
For: violin. Withdrawn.

M11.27 Spindrift. (1970)
For: string quartet. 1 movement. *Dedication:* For C.R. *First performed:* Nov, 1970; Boston University. Student performers.
Score & parts: ms. in composer's hand.

M11.28 String Figures Disentangled by a Flute. (1968) 9'-10'
For: flute and string orchestra. 1 movement. *Commissioned by and dedicated to:* James Pappoutsakis and the Boston Sinfonietta. *First performed:* Apr. 1969; Jordan Hall, Boston. James Pappoutsakis, flute; Boston Sinfonietta.
Score & parts: ms. in composer's hand.
Reel: 1973; Boston University. Boston Universty Orchestra. BU

M11.29 Tessera. (1981) 20'
For: harpsichord and instrumental ensemble(saxophone(soprano), English horn, contrabassoon, horn, trumpet, violins(2), viola, violoncello, double bass). Concerto in 1 movement. *Commissioned by and dedicated to:* Mark Kroll and Alea III, Theodore Antoniou, conductor.
Score: ms. in composer's hand.

M11.30 Toward the Source. (1975) 20'
For: chorus(mixed) and orchestra. 1 movement. *Text:* tombstones, town records, etc. *Commissioned by:* Concord

Bicentennial Committee. *Dedicated to:* The people of Concord past and present. *First performed:* Apr. 1975; Concord, Mass. Concord Symphony and Concord High School Chorus. *Score & parts.*
Reel: recording of first performance.

M11.31 Variations. (1960?)
For: piano. Withdrawn.

M11.32 Vigil. (1975-77) 10'-11'30"
For: orchestra. 1 movement. *First performed:* Oct. 19, 1978; Boston University; in Omnibus series. Boston University Repertory Orchestra, Robert Sirota, conductor.
Score & parts: ms. in composer's hand.
Disc: Louisville Orchestra LS 768, 1980. Louisville Orchestra, Jorge Mester, conductor. BU NEC
Reel: recording of first performance.

M11.33 Warning. (1960?)
For: speaker, piano, percussion. Withdrawn.

M11.34 Waterwalk. (1970) 6'
For: chorus(SATB). 1 movement. *Text:* Joyce Mekeel. *Commissioned by:* Boston University Chorus. *First performed:* Apr. 1970; Boston University. Boston University Chorus. *Vocal score:* ms. in composer's hand. *Reel:* recording of first performance. BU

M11.35 White Silence. (1965) 3'-4'
For: chorus(SATB). *Text:* translations from Japanese haiku by Joyce Mekeel. *First performed:* Aug. 1965; Minneapolis, Minn. *Vocal score:* Peters, 1966. BPL

M12 MARJORIE MERRYMAN

Born June 9, 1951. *Education:* B.A. (Scripps College, 1972); M.F.A., Ph.D. (Brandeis University, 1975, 1981); studied composition with Seymour Shifrin, Martin Boykan, Gail Kubik, Betsy Jolas. *Awards:* Phi Beta Kappa

Member, (1972); Scripps College Composition-Commission Prize, (1972), Remis Fellowship (Brandeis University, 1974-76); Berkshire Music Center, Fellowship, (1977). *Related activities:* served on the faculties of Massachusetts Institute of Technology (1976-77), Brandeis University (1975-79), Boston University (1979-). BU

WORKS

M12.1 Ariel. (1978) 8′
For: Soprano, clarinet, violoncello, percussion. *Commissioned by:* Diane Heffner. *First performed:* Feb. 1978; New England Conservatory.
Score: APNM.

M12.2 Laments for Hektor. (1977) 14′
For: Sopranos(2), Alto, flute, clarinet, horn, violin, violoncello, percussion, piano. *First performed:* May 1977; Brandeis University. Susan Larson, soprano, and others; David Hoose, conductor. Doctoral thesis.
Score & parts: APNM.

[Pieces, Piano]
M12.3 Three Pieces. (1975) 7′
First performed: Feb. 1976; Library and Museum for the Performing Arts, New York City. Rebecca LaBrecque.
Score: APNM.

M12.4 The River Song. (1981) 14′
For: Soprano and orchestra(2-2-2(bcl)-2; 2-2-2-0; timp, glock; str). *First performed:* Mar. 1981; Boston University; Omnibus Series. Theodore Antoniou, conductor.
Score & parts: APNM.

M12.5 Serenade for Six Instruments. (1974) 8′
For: flute, clarinet(bass), violin, violoncello, harp, piano. *First performed:* May 1974; Brandeis University. David Hoose, conductor.
Score & parts: APNM.

M13 MALLOY M. MILLER

Born May 6, 1917, in Duenweg, Mo.; died June 1981 in Boston. Moved to Boston area 1954. *Education:* B.A. (University of Denver); M.M., D.M.A. (Boston University); studied composition with Horace Tureman, Roy Harris, Nicolas Slonimsky; violin with Henry Ginsberg, Leon Sammetini, Richard Burgin. *Related activities:* violinist, conductor, teacher, administrator; interested in ethnic music, particularly of the Pueblo Indians of the Rio Grande Valley; violinist with the Denver Symphony Orchestra and the Central City Opera (1936-40); served on the faculties of the Pueblo, Colo. schools (1946-54) and Boston University (1954-81; Associate Dean, School for the Arts, 1966-1981). BU

WORKS

M13.1 Concertino. (1951) 14′
For: oboe and chamber orchestra(1-0-1-1; 1-1-1-0; timp; str). 3 movements. *First performed:* Apr. 1956; WGBH-TV, Boston. Boston University Chamber Orchestra, Russell Stranger, conductor.
Score & parts: ms. in composer's hand.

M13.2 Koshare. (1958-59) 27′
For: orchestra. Ballet. *Movements:* Introduction; Harvest; Dance; Eagle Dance; Corn Grinding Scene; Celebration Dance. *Commissioned by:* Pikes Peak Panorama Centennial Celebration. *First performed:* July 4, 1959; Colorado Springs, Colo. Koshare Indian Dancers, LaJunta, Colo.; Colorado Springs Symphony, Walter Eisenberg, conductor.
Score & parts: ms. in composer's hand.
Reel: recording of first performance.
BU

M13.3 Legend. (1940) 10′
For: viola and piano. *Commissioned by and dedicated to:* Robert Becker. *First performed:* Sept. 24, 1940; Denver, Colo. Robert Becker, viola and Esther

Alice Browning, piano.
Score & part: ms. in composer's hand.

[Movements]
M13.4 Two Movements. (1975) 16'
For: viola, harp, percussion. *Dedicated to:* Walter Trampler. *First performed:* May 1, 1978; Boston University. Walter Trampler, viola, and others.
Score & parts: ms. in composer's hand.
Reel: recording of first performance. BU

M13.5 Music for Richard III. (1967) 25'
For: trumpets(3), trombones(3), tuba, timpani(2), percussion(3). Incidental music to the play by William Shakespeare. *Commissioned by:* Boston University Theatre. *First performed:* 1967; Boston University Theatre.
Score & parts: ms. in composer's hand.
Reel: 1967. Boston University Theatre; recording of production.

M13.6 Music for Trojan Women. (1971) 20'
For: orchestra(2(pic)-2-2-0; 3-6-3-1; timp(2), perc(3); hp; str(4-0-0-0-2)). Incidental music to the play by Euripides. *Commissioned by:* Boston University Theatre. *First performed:* Apr. 28, 1971; Boston University Theatre. Boston University Symphony Players; Malloy Miller, conductor.
Score & parts: ms. in composer's hand.
Reel: Apr. 1971; Boston University Theatre. Boston University Symphony.

[Music for Trojan Women. Suite] (1973) 15'
M13.7 *For:* orchestra (2(pic) -2-2-0; 3-6-3-1; timp(2), perc(3); hp; str(4-0-0-0-2)). *Movements:* Captured Troy; The Gods; The Women and the Greeks; The Death of Astyanax; Troy Destroyed. *First performed:* Feb. 9, 1973; Boston University. Boston University Symphony Orchestra, Malloy Miller, conductor.
Score & parts: ms. in composer's hand.
Reel: recording of first performance.

M13.8 Ngoma--Invocation and Dance. (1955) 14'
For: timpani(4) and orchestra. *First performed:* June 1, 1956; Symphony Hall, Boston. Salvatore Rabbio, timpani; Boston Pops, Russell Stanger, conductor.
Score & parts: ms. in composer's hand.
Reel: Boston University. Thomas Gauger, timpani; Boston University Symphony Orchestra, Walter Eisenberg, conductor.

[Ngoma--Invocation and Dance; Band]
M13.9 Ngoma--Invocation and Dance. 14'
For: timpani(4) and band. *First performed:* Apr. 17, 1962; West Virginia University.
Score & parts: ms. in composer's hand.

[Ngoma--Invocation and Dance; Piano]
M13.10 Ngoma--Invocation and Dance. 14'
For: timpani(4) and piano(4-hands). *First performed:* May 12, 1960; Manhattan School of Music, New York City.
Score & parts: Music for Percussion, nyp.

M13.11 Ode. (1959) 12'
For: band. *First performed:* Apr. 28, 1959; Boston University. Boston University Symphonic Band.
Score & parts: ms. in composer's hand.
Reel: recording of first performance.

M13.12 Pastorale. (1956) 10'
For: flute(alto) and organ. *Commissioned by and dedicated to:* Phillip Kaplan and E. Power Biggs. *First performed:* 1958; Harvard University. Phillip Kaplan, alto flute and E. Power Biggs, organ.
Score & part: ms. in composer's hand.

[Pastorale; Arr]
M13.13 Pastorale. 10'
For: flute(alto) and piano. *First performed:* Nov. 27, 1960; New York Flute Club. Phillip Kaplan, alto flute and Edith Stearns, piano.
Score & part: ms. in composer's hand.

M13.14 Poem. (1946) 8'
For: violin and piano. *Dedicated to:*
Nicolas Slonimsky. *First performed:*
Nov. 16, 1960; Brookline Public Library.
Giora Bernstein, violin; George Zilzer,
piano. Work based on scales 7 and 12
from Nicolas Slonimsky's *Thesaurus of
Musical Scales and Melodic Patterns.*
Score & part: ms. in composer's hand.
Reel: recording of first performance.
BkPL

M13.15 Prelude for Percussion. (1956)
8' 30"
For: percussion ensemble(timpani(4),
glockenspiel, xylophone, tom-tom,
snare drum, bass drum, wood-block,
cymbals(2), suspended cymbal, whip,
tambourine, triangle). *Dedicated to:*
Charles Smith. *First performed:* Dec. 3,
1958; Manhattan Percussion Ensemble,
Leopold Stokowski, conductor. Used by
Paul Taylor Dance Co. and Les Grands
Ballets Canadiens as part of music for
dance, *Cloven Kingdom*, 1980.
Score & parts: Music for Percussion,
1960. BMC
Parts: reprod. of ms. HU
Disc: in *Sound Adventure*, Period SPL
743, 1958. Manhattan Percussion
Ensemble, Paul Price, conductor. BU
Disc: Orion ORS 7276, 1972. Reissue of
Period SPL 743, 1958. BU HU

Richard III. *See* Music for King Richard
III.

[Rituals]
M13.16 Two Rituals. (1963) 9'
For: percussion(5). *Commissioned by and
dedicated to:* Paul Price. *First
performed:* 1963; Philadelphia, Pa.
Score & parts: Music for Percussion,
1970. BCM NEC
Disc: 1970; in *Manhattan Music.*
Manhattan Percussion Ensemble, Paul
Price, conductor.
Reel: Nov. 7, 1980; Boston University.
Kristiana Koch, Jeffrey Lafferty,
Cornelius J. Larivee, James Lattini,
Gerald Scholl.

M13.17 Salute to the Air Force
Reserve. (1956) 7'
For: orchestra. *Commissioned by and
dedicated to:* United States Air Force
Reserve. *First performed:* 25, 1956;
Symphony Hall, Boston. Boston Pops,
Malloy Miller, conductor.
Score & parts: ms. in composer's hand.
Reel: June 23, 1961; Symphony Hall,
Boston. Boston Pops.

[Salute to the Air Force Reserve;
Arr.]
M13.18 Salute to the Air Force
Reserve. 7'
For: band.
Score & parts: ms. in composer's hand.

M13.19 Suite. (1950) 16'
For: orchestra. 3 movements. *First
performed:* Nov. 17, 1952; Worcester,
Mass. Worcester Orchestra, Francis
Findlay, conductor.
Score & parts: ms. in composer' hand.
Reel: 1953; Wichita, Kansas. Wichita
Symphony Orchestra, Lloyd Robertson,
conductor.

Trojan Women. *See* Music for Trojan
Women.

[Tyuonyi]
M13.20 Orchestral Sketch: Tyuonyi.
(1951) 9'
For: orchestra. 1 movement. *First
performed:* June 4, 1954; Symphony
Hall, Boston. Boston Pops, Francis
Findlay, conductor. Also used for
dance by the Koshare Indian Dancers,
LaJunta, Colo.
Score & parts: ms. in composer's hand.

[Tyuonyi; Arr.]
M13.21 *For:* band.
Score & parts: ms. in composer's hand.

M13.22 Variations for Orchestra. (1948)
15'
First performed: 1949; Pueblo, Colo.
Pueblo Symphony.
Score & parts: ms. in composer's hand.

M13.23 Variations for Violin and Percussion. (1972) 12'
For: violin and percussion(4). *Dedicated to:* Roman Totenberg. *First performed:* Nov. 25, 1974; Boston University. Roman Totenberg, violin; Boston University Percussion Ensemble, Thomas Gauger, conductor.
Score & parts: ms. in composer's hand.
Reel: Apr. 12, 1976; Boston University; in *Omnibus: Music of the 20th Century.* Roman Totenberg, violin; Paul Pitts, George Marinly, Neil Pregozen, Andrew Solomon; percussion, David Carney, conductor.

M13.24 Western Overture. (1954) 12' 30"
For: orchestra. *First performed:* June 3, 1955; Symphony Hall, Boston. Boston Pops, Malloy Miller, conductor.
Score & parts: ms. in composer's hand.

N1 HANKUS HOWARD NETSKY

Born May 11, 1955, in Philadelphia, Pa. *Education:* studied composition with Roland Leich (Carnegie Mellon University); William Thomas McKinley, Malcolm Peyton (New England Conservatory, B.M., 1976, M.M., 1978); studied oboe with Fernard Gillet, Frederic Cohen, Thomas Faye. *Related activities:* dance accompanist, music therapist, jazz performer; private teacher; served on the faculty of the New England Conservatory (1978-81). NEC

WORKS

N1.1 Arline, A Recomposition. 6' 10"
For: jazz band. Based on a piece by Ran Blake.
Disc: Golden Crest, 1978.

N1.2 Dwelling. (1978)
Commissioned by: Amy Zell Ellsworth, Dancentral, Cambridge, Mass.

[Dwelling. Solo]
N1.3 Solo from Dwelling.

For: piano.
Cassette: Mar. 6, 1978; New England Conservatory; in *Premiere.* Hankus Netsky. NEC

N1.4 Epilogue.
For: piano.
Cassette: Mar. 30, 1976; New England Conservatory; in *Premiere.* Robert Conway. NEC

[Headpieces]
N1.5 Three Headpieces.
For: oboe.
Cassette: Mar. 12, 1974; New England Conservatory; in *Musica Maximus.* Hankus Netsky. NEC

N1.6 Images I and II.
For: flute, saxophone(tenor), horn, trumpet, trombone, piano.
Cassette: Dec. 6, 1977; New England Conservatory; in *Premiere.* Hankus Netsky, conductor. NEC

N1.7 Meditation for Three Players.
For: flute, violin, violoncello.
Cassette: Jan. 30, 1975; New England Conservatory; in *Premiere.* Beth Watson, flute; Harris G. Shiller, violin; David Cleary, violoncello. NEC

N1.8 Steppin' Lively.
For: jazz band. Arranged by Steven Netsky.
Cassette: May 9, 1974; New England Conservatory. Prepared by Jaki Byard. NEC

N1.9 Welcoming. ..
For: violin and piano.
Cassette: Jan. 27, 1977. New England Conservatory; in *Premiere.* Harris G. Shiller, violin and Robert Conway, piano. NEC

N2 HUGO NORDEN

Born December 31, 1909, in Providence, R.I. *Education:* studied composition with Sebastian Matthews and Howard Thatcher (University of

Toronto, B.M., 1943, D.M., 1948); violin with Hugo Kontschak and Felix Winternitz. *Related activities:* violinist; author of *The Technique of Canon, Fundamental Harmony, Fundamental Counterpoint, Form: The Silent Language*; editor, Arthur P. Schmidt Co. (1943-58); served on the faculties of Boston Conservatory (1943-45, 1975-) and Boston University. BCM

WORKS

N2.1 Advice to Gentlemen. (1981) 12'
For: Soprano and violoncello. 5 songs.
Text: Bible, O.T., Ecclesiastes.
Reel: Feb. 1, 1982; Boston Conservatory. Lillian Lee, soprano and Gary Wedow, piano. BCM

[Bicinia]
N2.2 Four Bicinia. (1980) 10'
For: clarinet and viola.

N2.3 Chorale, Ennead & Fugue.
For: string orchestra.
Score & parts: ms.
Reel: May 24, 1970; Boston Conservatory. Boston Conservatory Chamber Orchestra, Rouben Gregorian, conductor. BCM

N2.4 Concertino for Violin and Orchestra. (1973) 18'
Reel: May 8, 1978; Boston Conservatory. Alfred Schneider, violin; Boston Conservatory Orchestra, Rouben Gregorian, conductor. BCM

[Concertino, Violin and Piano]
N2.5 Concertino in G, Op. 14.
For: violin and piano.
Score & part: Schmidt, 1951.

[Concertino, Violin and Piano; Arr.]
N2.6 Concertino in G, Op. 14.
For: clarinet and piano.
Score & part: Schmidt, 1951.

N2.7 Concerto for Flute and Orchestra. (1976) 20'
Reel: May 9, 1979; Boston Conservatory. Robin Lee, flute; Boston

Conservatory Orchestra, Rouben Gregorian, conductor. BCM

N2.8 Contrappunti lirici: Greenland's Icy Mountain. (1968) 15'
For: organ.
Score: ms.

N2.9 Contrapuncto accademico.
For: clarinet and wind ensemble.
Score & parts: ms.
Reel: Dec. 10, 1975; Boston Conservatory. M. Hammond, clarinet; Boston Conservatory Wind Ensemble, John Corley, conductor. BCM

N2.10 Elegy in Three Triangles.
For: woodwind quintet.
Reel: Nov. 23, 1980; Boston Conservatory. Cantilena Quintet. BCM

N2.11 Fantasia erotica. 15'
For: clarinet and piano.
Score & part: ms.

N2.12 Fantasia liturgica. (1973) 12'
For: clarinet and string quartet.
Score & parts: ms.

N2.13 Fuga canonica.
For: violins(2).
Score: Schmidt, 1946.

Greenland's Icy Mountain. *See* Contrappunti lirici: Greenland's Icy Mountain.

[Hymns for Lovers]
N2.14 Two Hymns for Lovers. (1970)
For: Soprano and piano.
Reel: Feb. 1, 1982; Boston Conservatory. Lillian Lee, soprano and Gary Wedow, piano. BCM

N2.15 Impromptu.
For: violin, violoncello, piano.
Score & parts: Humphries, 1961. NEC

N2.16 Lament and Dance. (1980) 7'
For: oboe and bassoon.

N2.17 Music in A. (1980) 22'
For: woodwind quintet. *Movements:*

Etude; Spiral Canon with Variations; Fugue; Epilogue. *Commissioned by:* Massachusetts Music Teachers Association. *First performed:* Nov. 23, 1980; Boston Conservatory. Cantilena Quintet.
Reel: recording of first performance. BCM

N2.18 Music in C. 15'
For: piano(4-hands). *Movements:* Fantasia; Fugue; Finale.
Score: ms.
Reel: Oct. 20, 1974; Boston Conservatory. Jacqueline Gourdin and Harriet Lundberg. BCM
Reel: Oct. 29, 1978; Boston Conservatory. Jacqueline Gourdin and Harriet Lundberg. BCM
Reel: Nov. 23, 1980; Boston Conservatory. Jacqueline Gourdin and Harriet Lundberg. BCM

[Partita, Organ]
N2.19 Partita on a Theme by Lowell Mason. (1974) 12'
Score: ms.

[Partita, Woodwind Quintet]
N2.20 Partita for Woodwind Quintet. 25'
Movements: Fanfare; Fugue; Theme with Variations; Andante tranquillo; Presto.
Reel: Nov. 23, 1980; Boston Conservatory. Cantilena Quintet. BCM

N2.21 Passacaglia. 12'
For: horn and piano.
Score & part: Chester.

N2.22 Pentad. (1972) 25'
For: viola and piano.
Score & part: ms.

[Pious Fugues]
N2.23 Two Pious Fugues.
Vocal score: reprod. of ms.

[Quartet, Strings]
N2.24 String Quartet in A Minor. (1972) 30'
Score & parts: ms.

N2.25 Solemne Musicke.
For: trumpets(2), trombone, tuba.
Score & parts: Boosey & Hawkes.

[Sonata, Double Bass and Piano]
N2.26 Sonata in A Minor for Contrabass and Piano. (1974) 15'
Score & part: ms.

[Sonata, Pianos(2)]
N2.27 Sonata for Two Pianos.
3 movements.
Reel: Oct. 29, 1978; Boston Conservatory. Jacqueline Gourdin and Harriet Lundberg. BCM
Reel: Nov. 23, 1980; Boston Conservatory. Jacqueline Gourdin and Harriet Lundberg. BCM

[Sonata, Violin and Piano, No. 1]
N2.28 Sonata in E Minor for Violin and Piano. (1946)
Score & part: Schmidt, 1948.

[Sonata, Violin and Piano, No. 2]
N2.29 Sonata in D Major for Violin and Piano. (1970) 20'
First performed: 1971; Rollins College. Alphonse Carlo.
Score & part: ms.

[Sonata, Violin and Piano, No. 3]
N2.30 Sonata in F Sharp Minor for Violin and Piano. (1975) 25'
Score & part: ms.

ARRANGEMENTS OF WORKS BY OTHER COMPOSERS

N2.31 Capricietto.
For: violin or clarinet and piano. Original by Rodolphe Kreutzer.
Score & part: Schmidt, 1952.

01 LINDA OSTRANDER

Born February 17, 1937, in New York City. Moved to Boston area 1968. *Education:* studied composition with Joseph R. Wood, Richard Hoffman (Oberlin College, B.M., 1958); Alvin Derald Etler (Smith College, M.A.,

1960); Gardner Read (Boston University, D.M.A., 1972); Benjamin B. Johnston (University of Illinois); piano with Emil Dannenberg and John Duke. *Awards:* Fatman Compostion Prize (Smith College, 1960), Radcliffe Institute Fellowship (1963-64), University Fellowship (University of Illinois (1964-65), Gilchrist-Potter Prize (Oberlin College, 1965-66), National Endowment for the Arts Grants (1969, 1977). *Related activities:* pianist; arts consultant; founding member, Massachusetts Group Piano Teachers Association; served on the faculties of Adelphi Suffolk College (1961-63), Southampton College (1963-64), Lesley College (1972-73), Bunker Hill Community College (1973-). W

WORKS

01.1 Chorale Preludes, Book I. (1964) 14'
For: organ. *Movements:* Lift up Your Heads; Lo, He Comes with Clouds Descending; Let All Mortal Flesh; Jesus Christ, Our Lord, Redeemer; We Sing the Glorious Conquest. *First performed:* 1964; Southampton, N.Y.
Score: ms.

[Choruses]
01.2 Two Choruses. (1978) 5'
For: chorus(women). *Text:* Lord George Noel Gordon Byron. *Contents:* When We Two Parted; Stanzas for Music.
Vocal score: reprod. of ms. (No. 1). W

01.3 Collage. (1972) 45'
For: slides and tape. *Movements:* Collage; Search; Holiday; [Untitled] .
First performed: 1973; Framingham, Mass. *Tape.*
Reel: recording of first performance.

01.4 Communion Service. (1964) 8'
For: chorus(SATB). *Text:* Mass.
Dedicated to: Rev. Hobart Jude Gary.
First performed: 1964; Southampton, N.Y. St. John's Church Choir.
Vocal score: reprod. of ms. W

01.5 Concertino for Conductor and Dancers. (1966) 6' 30"
For: dancers(5) and chamber orchestra(1-1-1-1; 1-2-2-1; perc; str(2-2-2-2-0). 3 movements. *Dedicated to:* Paul Vermel and the Maine State Ballet.
Score & parts: ms.
Score: reprod. of ms. W
Score: Pioneer.

01.6 Concerto Grosso No. 1. (1958) 15'
For: orchestra(3(pic)-3(Ehn)-3(&bcl)-3; 4-3-3-0; timp, perc(2), glock, mar, xylo; hp, cel, pf). 3 movements.
Score: reprod. of ms. W
Reel: 1958; Oberlin College (3rd movement). Oberlin College Orchestra, David Zinman, conductor.

01.7 Concerto Grosso No. 2. (1965) 20'
For: saxophone(alto)/saxophone(tenor), trumpets(2), horn, trombone, double bass, drums, piano and orchestra (1-1-1-1; 1-1-1-0; perc; cel; str).
Movements: Blue; Strict; Free; Solid.
Commissioned by: National Endowment for the Arts. *First performed:* 1969; Portland, Me. Portland Symphony Orchestra, Paul Vermel, conductor.
Score: reprod. of ms. W

01.8 Cycle for Six. (1969)
For: instruments(treble)(3), bassoon, xylophone, double bass. *Movements:* Introductions; Gestures; Developments; Trios; Return. *First performed:* May 1972; Boston University. Jeff Hollander Cook, conductor.
Score: reprod. of ms. W
Reel: recording of first performance.

01.9 Don't Tell the Scarecrow. (1967) 2'
For: chorus(SSA), flute, piano, loudspeakers(3). 1 movement.
Vocal score & cards: ms.
Vocal score: reprod. of ms. W

01.10 Duet.
For: piano(4-hands). *Movements:* Prelude; Dance; Variations. *First performed:* 1970; Boston University. Lily Siao Owyang and Rita Simo.

Score: reprod. of ms. W
Reel: 1972; Boston University. Judy Ross and John Goodman.

[Duets]
01.11 Three Trumpet Duets. (1956) 2'
Dedicated to: Fred Woodaman (my father). *First performed:* 1956; Oberlin College. Edward Tarr and second unidentified trumpeter.
Score: ms. in composer's hand.

01.12 11'25". (1970)
For: chamber orchestra. *Movements:* 6'55"; 4'30".
Score: ms.

01.13 Extrapolations. (1971) 8'
For: Soprano, recorder ensemble, percussion. *Contents:* Homage to Baude Cordier; Trouvere Song; Laude; Estampie. *First performed:* 1971; Boston University. Mary Jo Steffes, soprano; Mark Lutton, percussion; and others.
Music: ms. in composer's hand.

01.14 Five for Five. (1972) 5'
For: flute(alto), clarinet(E-flat), bassoon, trumpet, baritone. *Movements:* Fantasy, Pensively; Toccata I; Nocturne; Toccata II; Rhapsody.
Score: ms. in composer's hand.

01.15 From Here to There. (1965)
For: Baritone, violin, horn, bassoon, percussion(2), vibraphone. Song cycle.
Text: Dr. Seuss. *Contents:* Introduction; Wump; My Hat Is Old; Hello!; Ying; Yink; Zans; Good Night. *First performed:* 1965; Urbana, Ill.
Score & parts: ms.
Reel: recording of first performance.

01.16 Fun 'n' Games. (1966) 3' 40"
For: string quartet. *Movements:* Simon Says...; Crossword; Stoop Tag.
Score & parts: ms.
Score: reprod. of ms. W

01.17 Game of Chance. (1966) Duration variable.

For: instruments(unspecified). 1 movement. *First performed:* 1967; Isabella Stewart Gardner Museum, Boston. Cambridge Brass Quintet.
Score: reprod. of ms. W
Reel: 1977; Boston; Young Audiences concert. Cambridge Brass Quintet.

01.18 Gebrauchsmusik, or, TV '67. (1967) 4'
For: brasses(5). Written for Music in Maine Brass Quintet.
Score: ms.

01.19 Globe '66. (1966)
For: violin, horn, piano. *Movements:* Pearl Harbor: 25 Years After; Museum; Protest. *Dedicated to:* Hursheline Griffin, Steve Keckskemethy and Ralph Lockwood.
Score: reprod. of ms. W

01.20 Incident--Dialogue--Protest--Riot. (1972) 15'
For: orchestra(3-0-0-3; 0-2-2-0; timp(2), perc(4), metallophone(soprano, alto, bass), vibra; str). 4 movements.
Score: ms.

01.21 Introduction to the Piano. (1960)

01.22 Jazz Songs. (1977-81)
For: musicians(unspecified) or jazz ensemble. *Contents:* Thinking of You; Lonely Bossa; Where Is Love?; Boston Bossa; Nice Work; Love Theme; Linda's Blues; Fooling Around; Sometimes; Suddenly; How Many Times?; Hold Me Again; If I Could Be with You; Merry Christmas to You; You Can't Hardly Get There Anymore; When I'm Melancholy; High Road; Turn Around; Last Night.
Lead sheets(piano-vocal) or score: ms.

01.23 Loneliness. (1978) 3'
For: chorus(SSAA), percussion, piano, tape(white noise only).
Score: reprod. of ms. W

01.24 Mousike. (1972) 14'
15" *For:* speaker, oboe, vibraphone,

percussion(3). *Movements:* Invocation;
Dance; Evocation; Alea; Celebration.
First performed: 1972; Boston
University. Mary Ricker, speaker; James
Grush, oboe; Deborah Schwartz,
vibraphone; Lawrence Pim, Jonathan
Scully, Bonnie Seligson, percussion;
Theodore Nicholeris, conductor.
Score: reprod. of ms. W

[Movements, Flute, Viola, Harp]
01.25 Two Movements. (1973) 4'
Movements: Play; Dream. *Commissioned
by:* Young Audiences.
Score: ms. in composer's hand.

[Movements, Trumpets(2), Horn,
Trombone, Tuba]
01.26 Three Movements. (1978) 6'
Movements: Intrada; Intensities; 1-2-3,
1-2. *Commissioned by:* Young Audiences
and National Endowment for the Arts.
First performed: 1978. Cantabrigia
Brass Quintet.
Score: ms.

01.27 Mr. Lucky--Song Cycle. (1972) 11'
54"
For: voice(high) or voice(medium) and
piano. *Text:* Aaron Kramer. *Contents:*
Mr. Lucky and the Wind; Softly; The
Pier; The Night Watchman; Just Then a
Little Voice Said; Nightsong. *First
performed:* 1972; Boston University.
Hugh Carey.
Score: reprod. of ms. W
Reel: recording of first performance.

01.28 Music for an Exhibition of Prints
and Drawings
For: Soprano, Alto, Tenor, Bass, flute,
clarinet, bassoon, trumpet, trombone,
percussion, celeste. *Contents:* Questions;
Reflections; Protests. *First performed:*
Feb. 5, 1971; Boston University. Mary
Jo Steffes, soprano; Mary Ricker,
contralto; Charles Spinning, tenor; Jay
Giullembardo, bass; and
instrumentalists.
Score: reprod. of ms. W
Reel: 1971; Boston University.

01.29 Music for ETV
Program--Principles and Elements of
Design. 15'
For: horn, piano, violoncello.
Movements: Straight Lines; Curves;
Circles; Zig-zag. *Commissioned by:*
Maine ETV. *First performed:* 1967;
Orono, Me. Ralph Lockwood, horn and
piano.
Score: ms.

01.30 New Sounds for the Young
Pianist. (1961) 3'
First performed: 1962; Easthampton,
N.Y. Students of Joan Brill: Shelley
Brill, Philip Markowitz, Nan Marmon.
Score: in *Creative Piano: A Modular
Approach for the Adult Beginner,*
Houghton Mifflin, 1978.

01.31 Outside In--Series of 4 Children's
Musicals. (1979-81) 240'
For: voice, piano, flute. *Text:* Sara
Beattie. *Contents:* Faces; The Polka Dot
Dragon; The Wombies and the
Tromsees; The Grand Zazoo.
Score: ms.

[Pieces]
01.32 Four Pieces. (1956) 4'
For: chamber orchestra(1-1-0-0; 0-0-0-0;
perc(3); str). 4 movements. *First
performed:* 1956; Oberlin College.
Score: reprod. of ms. W

01.33 Praise the Lord. (1964) 1' 30"
For: chorus(unison) and organ. Anthem.
Text: Bible, O.T., Psalm. *First
performed:* 1964; Southampton, N.Y. St.
John's Church Choir, Linda Ostrander,
organ[?].
Vocal score: reprod. of ms. W

01.34 The Replacement. (1981) 5' 45"
For: tape(flute and piccolo
prerecorded). 1 movement. *First
performed:* Boston Mime Theatre.
Melinda Ostrander. *Tape.*
Reel: 1981. Melinda Ostrander.

01.35 Rounds. (1972)
For: brasses(5). 1 movement. *First*

performed: 1972; Boston University.
Score: reprod. of ms. W
Reel: 1972; Boston University.

01.36 Sci-Fi. (1979) 75'
Musical comedy. *First performed:* 1980;
Bunker Hill Community College.
Students.
Score: reprod. of ms. W

01.37 Sioux Songs--Song Cycle. (1969)
6'
For: voice(high) and piano. *Text:* Aaron
Kramer. *Contents:* All Winter Long; I
Know What's Coming; The Gods Grow
Impatient; You Have Forgotten; They've
Lost It. *First performed:* 1969; Boston
University.
Score: reprod. of ms. W

[Sonata, Piano]
01.38 Sonata No. 1. (1957)
3 movements. *First performed:* 1957;
Oberlin College; Contemporary Festival.
Linda Ostrander.
Score: reprod. of ms. W
Cassette: 1957; Oberlin, Ohio. Linda
Ostrander.

[Sonata, Violin and Piano]
01.39 Sonata. (1954-55) 12'
3 movements. *First performed:* 1956;
Oberlin College. Grace MacDonald and
Jean Mentzer.

01.40 Songs (on e.e. cummings). (1968)
2' 35"
Text: e.e. cummings. *Contents:* The
Cambridge Ladies; No Time Ago.
Score: reprod. of ms. W

[Songs on Poems of Emily
Dickinson]
01.41 Two Songs on Poems of Emily
Dickinson. (1965) 3'
For: Mezzo Soprano and piano.
Contents: A Certain Slant of Light; The
Sky Is Low.
Score: reprod. of ms. W

[Songs on Poems of Emily Dickinson;
Arr.]

01.42 Two Songs on Poems of Emily
Dickinson. (1978) 3'
For: chorus(SA) and orchestra. *Contents:*
A Certain Slant of Light; The Sky Is
Low. *First performed:* Feb. 11, 1979;
Sanders Theatre, Harvard University.
New England Women's Symphony, New
England Women's Chorus, Sonja Pryor,
conductor.
Score & parts: ms.
Vocal score: ms.
Reel: recording of first performance.
WGBH
Cassette: 1979; Sanders Theatre, Harvard
University.

[Songs on War]
01.43 Three Songs on War. (1955) 4'
50"
For: voice(high) and piano. *Contents:*
The Dragon (James Lewis); The Owl
(Edward Thomas); On Seeing a Piece
of Artillery Brought into Action
(Wilfred Owen).
Score: reprod. of ms. W

01.44 Sonnet to Sleep. (1955) 3' 50"
For: chorus(SSAA). *Text:* William
Drummond. *First performed:* 1970;
Boston University. Boston University
Women's Chorus, Edmund Ostrander,
conductor.
Vocal score: reprod. of ms. W
Vocal score: Plymouth.
Reel: 1970; Boston University.

01.45 Space Music I. (1967) 4' 30"
For: brasses(5) and trumpet. *Movements:*
Count-down; Blast-off!; Discovery.
Score & parts: ms.
Score: reprod. of ms. W

01.46 Space Music II. (1967) 7' 50"
For: string quartet and violin.
Movements: Explorer; Surveyor; Luna;
Lem; Recovery. *Commissioned by:* Music
in Maine.
Score & parts: ms.

01.47 Suite for Chamber Orchestra (No.
2) . (1960) 20'
For: chamber orchestra(1-1-1-1; 0-0-0-0;

perc(3); str). 4 movements. *First performed:* 1967; Portland, Me. Northeast Chamber Orchestra, Paul Vermel, conductor.
Score & parts: ms.
Score: reprod. of ms. W

01.48 Suite for Piano. (1957)
Movements: Sinfonia; Allemande; Sarabande; Minuet; Burlesca; Rondo.
First performed: Mar. 22, 1958; Oberlin College. Linda Ostrander.
Score: reprod. of ms. W

01.49 Tarot. (1971)
For: saxophone(alto), percussion, dancer, speaker, slides, lights, tape.
Movements: Patterns; Comments; Images; Rota. Multi media.
Commissioned by: Ken Dorn.
Score: reprod. of ms. W

01.50 Theater Piece on Sayings of Confucius. (1964) 20'
For: Baritone, actors, guitar(electric). 1 movement. *Text:* Confucius.
Score: reprod. of ms. W

01.51 Theme and Variations for Flute. (1979) 2' 45"
For: flute and piano. 1 movement.
Score: reprod. of ms. W

01.52 Theme and Variations for Piano. (1954) 6'
1 movement. *First performed:* 1955; Oberlin College. Linda Ostrander.
Score: ms. in composer's hand.

Theme and Variations for Strings. *See* Variations and Theme.

01.53 Three for Eight. 4' 35"
For: pianos(2)(8-hands). 3 movements.
First performed: 1969; Portland, Me; Federation of Music Clubs Concert.
Score: reprod. of ms. W
Score: in *Creative Piano: A Modular Approach for the Adult Beginner*, Houghton Mifflin, 1978.

01.54 Time Out for Tuba. (1979) 9' 30"
For: tuba and tape(4-channel).

Movements: Canon; Everything Comes Out Blue; Rondo. *Commissioned by:* Barton Cummings for national T.U.B.A. convention. *First performed:* May, 1980; Tex. Barton Cummings.
Score: reprod. of ms. W
Graphic score & reel: (1st movement).

01.55 Time Studies. (1970)
For: violin, oboe, trombone, percussion(2), tape. *Movements:* Abstraction; Interlude; Retrospective I; Retrospective II; Collage. *First performed:* Mar. 30, 1970; Boston University. Alan MacMillan, violin; Susan Stewart, oboe; Marshall Stith, trombone; Peter Carnevale and Mark Lutton, percussion.
Score: reprod. of ms. W
Reel: recording of first performance.

01.56 Tom Bombadil.
For: chorus(SATB) and instrumental ensemble. Song cycle. *Contents:* Old Tom Bombadil; Little Princess Mee; Bombadil Goes Boating; The Man in the Moon; Elven Song.
Score: reprod. of ms. W

[Trio, Flute, Clarinet, Bassoon]
01.57 Woodwind Trio. (1954) 4'
3 movements. *First performed:* 1954; Oberlin College.
Score & parts: ms.
Score: reprod. of ms. W

[Trio, Violin, Viola, Violoncello]
01.58 String Trio. (1971) 9' 30"
Movements: Sonata, Freely with Expression; Variations.
Score: reprod. of ms. W

[Trio, Violin, Violoncello, Piano]
01.59 Piano Trio. (1956)
First performed: 1962; Easthampton, N.Y. Barbara Gibson, violin; Hobart Jude Gary, violoncello; Linda Ostrander, piano.

01.60 Unto Us a Child Is Born. (1964) 1' 30"
For: chorus(SATB). 1 movement. *Text:*

Bible, O.T., Isaiah 9:6.
Vocal score: reprod. of ms. W

01.61 Variations and Theme. (1958) 12'
For: string quartet. 1 movement. *First performed:* Feb. 28, 1958; Oberlin College; Contemporary Festival. Lauren Jakey and Lillian Foote, violins; Gary Schnerer, viola; Nancy Meisel, violoncello.
Score: ms. W
Reel: 1958; Oberlin, Ohio.

01.62 Visions. (1972) 30' 55"
For: Soprano, Alto, Tenor, Bass, chorus, orchestra(1-1-1-1; 2-1-1-0; timp(4), perc(2), glock; pf; str). *Text:* Bible, O.T., Isaiah and Bible, O.T., Psalm 66. *Contents:* Hear, O Heavens; Ah, Sinful Nation; Stay Yourselves; Wash You, Make You Clean; They Shall Go into the Holes of the Rocks; Be Strong. Doctoral thesis (Boston University, 1972).
Score: reprod. of dissertation. W

01.63 Whispers of Heavenly Death. (1956) 10'
For: Soprano, Tenor, chorus, flute, viola, harpsichord. Cantata. *Text:* Walt Whitman.
Score: reprod. of ms. W

01.64 The Wish. (1972) 1' 30"
For: voice(high) and piano. Song. 1 movement. *Text:* 13th century canon.
Score: ms.

P1 MARTIN PEARLMAN

Born 1945 in Chicago, Ill. Moved to Boston area 1971. *Education:* studied composition with Karel Husa, Robert Palmer (Cornell University, B.A., 1967); Yehudi Wyner, Buelent Arel (Yale University, M.M., 1971); harpsichord with Gustav Leonhardt and Ralph Kirkpatrick. *Awards:* Fulbright Fellowship (1967-68), Bodky Award for Early Music Performance (1972), Festival of Flanders Competition Prize (Bruges, Belgium) (1974). *Related*

activities: harpsichordist; fortepianist; director, Banchetto Musicale; served on the faculties of Brandeis University and the University of Massachusetts, Boston. MIT

WORKS

P1.1 Etudes. (1978-79) 6'
For: harpsichord.
Score: ms. in composer's hand.

P1.2 Mask. (1971) 4' 30"
For: harpsichord. 1 movement. *First performed:* 1971; New Haven, Conn. Martin Pearlman.
Score: ms. in composer's hand.

P1.3 Music for Flute and Piano. (1969) 7' 30"
1 movement. *First performed:* 1969; New Haven, Conn. Jill Shires, flute and Martin Pearlman, piano.
Score: ms. in composer's hand.

P1.4 Scena. (1975) 5' 30"
For: harpsichord. 1 movement. *First performed:* 1975; Boston. Martin Pearlman.
Score: ms. in composer's. hand.

P1.5 Song, 3 Views. (1970) 16'
For: Soprano, Mezzo Soprano, Tenor, clarinet, piano, percussion. *Contents:* Ways to Eliminate the Castle (Gabor Brogyanyi); Commentary on the Blue Guitar (Wallace Stevens); Portrait of Picasso (Gertrude Stein); Epilogue: The Blue Guitar (Wallace Stevens). *First performed:* 1970; New Haven, Conn.
Score & parts: ms. in composer's hand.

P1.6 Trio for Solo Recorder. (1976) 4'
Score: ms. in composer's hand.

[Untitled work] (1977) 5'
 P1.7 *For:* recorder(alto).
Score: ms. in composer's hand.

P2 FREDERICK PEASE (TED)

Born May 17, 1939, in New York City.

Moved to Boston area 1961. *Education:* B.A., English (Cornell University, 1961); B.Mus.Ed. (Berklee College of Music, 1965); studied with Herb Pomeroy, Everett Longstreth, William Maloof. *Awards:* National Endowment for the Arts Jazz Fellowship (1975). *Related activities:* free-lance drummer (pop and jazz) and composer/arranger; adjudicator and clinician at various high school jazz festivals in Massachusetts (1970-); co-leader, composer, arranger, and drummer with the Berklee Faculty Concert Jazz Orchestra (1971-); author of *Jazz-Rock Theory* (1971); member of the faculty of Berklee College of Music (1964-). Be

WORKS

P2.1 Are You Ready? (1972)
For: jazz band. *First performed:* Oct. 3, 1972; Berklee College of Music. Berklee Faculty Concert Jazz Orchestra, Ted Pease and Larry Monroe, conductors.
Score: Berklee, 1974. Be
Parts: Berklee, 1974.
Score & parts: Berklee, 1980 (version for high school stage band).
Reel: recording of first performance. Be
Reel: Oct. 24, 1973; John Hancock Hall, Boston. Berklee Faculty Concert Jazz Orchestra, Ted Pease and Larry Monroe, conductors. Be
Reel: Nov. 10, 1977. Berklee Faculty Concert Jazz Orchestra, Ted Pease and Larry Monroe, conductors. Be

P2.2 Blues for a Bilious Bystander.
For: jazz band.
Score & parts: Berklee, 1980 (version for high school stage band).

P2.3 Blues in the Birdbath. (1973)
For: jazz band. *First performed:* Nov. 10, 1977. Berklee Faculty Concert Jazz Orchestra, Ted Pease and Larry Monroe, conductors. *Score & parts.*
Reel: recording of first performance. Be

P2.4 Boneshakers. (1972)
For: jazz band. Written and arranged in collaboration with Larry Monroe. *First performed:* Oct. 5, 1971; Berklee College of Music. Berklee Faculty Concert Jazz Orchestra, Ted Pease and Larry Monroe, conductors.
Score: Berklee, 1974. Be
Reel: recording of first performance. Be
Reel: July 13, 1972; Berklee College of Music. Berklee Faculty Concert Jazz Orchestra, Ted Pease and Larry Monroe, conductors. Be

P2.5 Cold Country Mornings. (1971)
For: jazz band. *First performed:* Oct. 5, 1971; Berklee College of Music. Berklee Faculty Concert Jazz Orchestra, Ted Pease and Larry Monroe, conductors.
Score: Berklee, 1974. Be
Parts: Berklee, 1974.
Score & parts: Berklee, 1980 (version for high school stage band).
Reel: recording of first performance. Be

P2.6 Cornerstone. (1970)
For: jazz ensemble(saxophones(5),trumpets(4), trombones(3)). Written for the Buddy Rich Band.
Music: Cathy Music.
Score: Berklee. Be

P2.7 Dusk to Dawn. (1974)
For: jazz band. *First performed:* Nov. 10, 1977. Berklee Faculty Concert Jazz Orchestra, Ted Pease and Larry Monroe, conductors.
Score & parts: Berklee.
Score & parts: Berklee, 1980 (version for high school stage band).
Reel: recording of first performance. Be

P2.8 Fender Bender. (1970)
Jazz nonet. *First performed:* Sept. 11, 1970; Berklee College of Music. Berklee Nine- Piece Jazz Ensemble, Ted Pease, conductor.
Score: Berklee. Be

Reel: recording of first performance.
Be
Reel: Dec. 16, 1970; Berklee College of Music; Arrangers Workshop. Ted Pease, conductor. Be

P2.9 G.F.P. (1966)
For: saxophone(alto)/saxophone(soprano), saxophone(tenor), saxophone (baritone), trumpet/flugelhorn, trombone, piano, double bass, drums. Jazz octet. *First performed:* Dec. 5, 1967; Berklee College of Music. Members of the Berklee Nine-Piece Jazz Ensemble, Ted Pease, conductor.
Reel: recording of first performance.
Be

P2.10 One More Time.
For: jazz band.
Score & parts: Berklee, 1980 (version for high school stage band).

P2.11 Pancakes. (1972)
For: jazz band. *First performed:* Oct. 3, 1972. Berklee Faculty Concert Jazz Orchestra, Ted Pease and Larry Monroe, conductors.
Score: Berklee, 1974. Be
Reel: recording of first performance.
Be

P2.12 Suite. (1975)
For: jazz band. *Movements:* Introduction; Movin' on Down; A Legacy of the Blues; Interlude and Finale: A Touch of the Brew. Work supported by a National Endowment for the Arts Jazz Fellowship. *Score & parts.*
Reel: in *Berklee Faculty Association Concert.* Be
Reel: Nov. 10, 1977. Berklee Faculty Concert Jazz Orchestra, Ted Pease and Larry Monroe, conductors. Be

P2.13 Wait 'til Next Year. (1971)
For: jazz band. *First performed:* Oct. 5, 1971; Berklee College of Music. Berklee Faculty Concert Jazz Orchestra, Ted Pease and Larry Monroe, conductors.
Score: Berklee. Be
Reel: recording of first performance.

Be
Reel: July 13, 1972; Berklee College of Music. Berklee Faculty Concert Jazz Orchestra, Ted Pease and Larry Monroe, conductors. Be

P2.14 When the Saints Go Marching In. (1971)
For: saxophone(alto), saxophone(baritone), trumpet, trombone, double bass, piano, drums. Jazz septet.
Score: reprod. of ms. Be
Score: in *Jazz-Rock Theory*, Berklee, 1971.

P2.15 Your Smile. (1971)
For: jazz band or jazz nonet. *First performed:* May 4, 1971; Berklee College of Music. Berklee Nine-Piece Jazz Ensemble, Ted Pease, conductor.
Score & parts: Berklee, 1980 (version for high school stage band).
Reel: recording of first performance.
Be

ARRANGEMENTS OF WORKS BY OTHER COMPOSERS

P2.16 Ain't Life Grand. (1969)
For: jazz ensemble(flute, saxophone(alto), saxophone(tenor), saxophone(baritone), trumpets(2), trombone, guitar, double bass, drums). Original by Bill Holman. *Score.*
Reel: Apr. 29, 1969. Berklee Ten-Piece Ensemble, Ted Pease, conductor. Be

P2.17 Django.
For: jazz band. Original by John Lewis. *First performed:* Oct. 24, 1973; John Hancock Hall, Boston. Berklee Faculty Concert Band. *Score.*
Reel: recording of first performance.
Be
Reel: Nov. 10, 1977. Berklee Faculty Concert Jazz Orchestra. Be

P2.17.5 Forget Me.
For: saxophone(alto)/saxophone(soprano), saxophone(tenor), saxophone (baritone), trumpet/flugelhorn, trombone, piano, double bass, drums. Jazz octet.

Original by Abe Laboriel. *First performed:* May 4, 1971. Members of the Berklee Nine-Piece Jazz Ensemble, Ted Pease, conductor. *Score.*
Reel: recording of first performance. Be

P2.18 George Gershwin Medley. (1964)
For: saxophone(alto), saxophone(tenor), saxophone(baritone), trumpets(2), trombone, guitar, double bass, drums. Jazz nonet.
Score: Berklee. Be

P2.19 Georgia on My Mind. (1964)
For: saxophone(alto), saxophone(baritone), trumpet, trombone, guitar, double bass, piano, drums. Jazz octet. Original by Hoagy Carmichael.
Score: Berklee. Be

P2.20 Grover Wailin'. (1972)
For: jazz band. Original by Johnny Mandel. *First performed:* July 13, 1972. Berklee Faculty Concert Jazz Orchestra, Ted Pease and Larry Monroe, conductors.
Score: Berklee. Be
Reel: recording of first performance. Be
Reel: Nov. 10, 1977. Berklee Faculty Concert Jazz Orchestra, Ted Pease and Larry Monroe, conductors. Be

P2.21 Here's That Rainy Day. (1968)
For: saxophone(alto), saxophone(baritone), trumpet, trombone, guitar, double bass, piano, drums. Jazz octet. Original by John D. Burke and James Van Heusen.
Score: Berklee. Be

P2.22 The Honk. (1969)
For: saxophone(alto), saxophone(baritone), trombone, guitar, double bass, drums. Jazz sextet. Original by T. Teixeira. *First performed:* Apr. 29, 1969. Members of the Berklee Ten-Piece Ensemble, Ted Pease, conductor.
Score: Berklee. Be
Tape: recording of first performance. Be

P2.23 I'm Gonna Go Fishin'. (1966)
For: saxophone(alto), saxophone(soprano)/flute, saxophone(soprano)/ saxophone(tenor), saxophone(baritone)/clarinet(bass), piano, English horn, bassoon, drums. Jazz octet. Original by Duke Ellington.
Score.
Reel: Dec. 16, 1970; Berklee College of Music; Arrangers Workshop. Ted Pease, conductor. Be

P2.24 Israel. (1964)
For: trumpet, trombone, saxophone(alto), saxophone(tenor), saxophone (baritone), guitar, double bass, drums. Jazz octet. Original by John E. Carisi. *First performed:* Dec. 5, 1967. Members of the Berklee Nine-Piece Jazz Ensemble, Ted Pease, conductor. *Score.*
Reel: recording of first performance. Be

P2.25 Killer Joe. (1973)
For: jazz band. Original by Benny Golson.
Score: Berklee. Be

P2.26 Lush Life. (1972)
For: jazz band. Original by Billy Strayhorn.
Score: Berklee. Be

P2.27 Make Me Understand. (1972)
For: jazz ensemble(saxophones(3), trumpets(2), trombone, piano, electric bass, vocals, drums). *Text:* Pam Oken. Original by Abe Laboriel. *First performed:* May 2, 1972. Berklee Nine-Piece Jazz Ensemble, Ted Pease, conductor. *Score.*
Reel: recording of first performance. Be

P2.28 My Ship. (1970)
For: saxophone(alto), saxophone(tenor), saxophone(baritone), flugelhorn, trombone, guitar, double bass, drums. Jazz octet. Original by Kurt Weill.
Score: Berklee. Be

P2.29 Nardis. (1971)
For: jazz band. Original by Miles Davis.
First performed: Oct. 5, 1971. Berklee Faculty Concert Jazz Orchestra, Ted Pease and Larry Monroe, conductors.
Score: Berklee. Be
Reel: recording of first performance. Be
Reel: Oct. 24, 1973; John Hancock Hall, Boston. Berklee Faculty Concert Jazz Orchestra, Ted Pease and Larry Monroe, conductors. Be
Reel: Nov. 10, 1977. Berklee Faculty Concert Jazz Orchestra, Ted Pease and Larry Monroe, conductors. Be

P2.30 Reminiscing. (1972)
For: jazz band. Original by Gigi Gryce; arranged in collaboration with Larry Monroe. *First performed:* July 13, 1972. Berklee Faculty Concert Jazz Orchestra, Ted Pease and Larry Monroe, conductors. *Score.*
Reel: recording of first performance. Be

P2.31 Satin Doll. (1965)
For: saxophone(alto)/flute, saxophone(tenor), saxophone(baritone), trumpets(2), trombone, guitar, double bass, drums. Jazz nonet. Original by Duke Ellington.
Score: Berklee. Be

P2.32 Sing with Me. (1972)
For: jazz ensemble(saxophones(3), trumpets(2), trombone, piano, electric bass, vocals, drums). Original by Abe Laboriel. *First performed:* May 2, 1972. Berklee Nine-Piece Jazz Ensemble, Ted Pease, conductor.
Score: Berklee. Be
Reel: recording of first performance. Be

P2.33 Up Up and Away. (1969)
For: jazz ensemble(saxophone(alto), saxophone(tenor), saxophone(baritone), trumpets(2), trombone, guitar, double bass, piano, drums). Original by Jimmy Webb.
Score: Berklee. Be

P2.34 Valdez in the Country. (1973)
For: jazz band. Original by Donny Hathaway. *First performed:* Oct. 24, 1973; John Hancock Hall, Boston. Berklee Faculty Concert Jazz Orchestra, Ted Pease and Larry Monroe, conductors.
Score: Berklee. Be
Reel: recording of first performance. Be

P2.35 Watermelon Man. (1969)
For: jazz ensemble(saxophone(alto), saxophones(tenor)(1 or 2), saxophone(baritone), trumpets(2 or 3), trombone/trombone(bass), guitar, double bass, piano, drums). Original by Herbie Hancock.
Score: Berklee. Be

P2.36 Yesterdays. (1967)
For: trumpet, trombone, saxophone(alto), saxophone(tenor), saxophone (baritone), guitar, double bass, drums. Jazz octet. Original by Jerome Kern. *First performed:* Dec. 5, 1967. Members of the Berklee Nine-Piece Jazz Ensemble, Ted Pease, conductor.
Lead sheets: Berklee. Be
Reel: recording of first performance. Be

P3 STEPHEN PEISCH

Born January 26, 1952, in Burlington, Vt. Moved to Boston area 1973. *Education:* studied composition and analysis with Robert Cogan (New England Conservatory, B.M., 1977, M.M., 1979); violin with Nancy Cirillo. *Related activities:* violinist, teacher, author of journal articles, record producer; member of the faculty of the Preparatory School, New England Conservatory (1978-). CPL

WORKS

P3.1 Clap. (1979) 1' 10"
For: percussion(4)(8 clapping hands, high and low woodblocks, bongos).

Score & parts: available from composer.

P3.2 Composition for Violin. (1979) 1' 45"
Score: available from composer.

P3.3 Distribution for N Instruments. (1979) Duration variable.
For: instruments(unspecified).
Score: available from composer.

P3.4 Flute Lyric. (1979) 1' 50"
For: flute.
Score: available from composer.

P3.5 Mekanique. (1979) 3' 50"
For: piano.
Score: available from composer.

[Pieces]
P3.6 3 Pieces for 10 Players. (1979) 5' 15"
For: instrumental ensemble(string quartet, double bass, flute, trumpet, horn, trombone, harp). 3 movements.
Score & parts: available from composer.

P3.7 Quintet. (1979) 2' 50"
For: violin, guitar, trumpet, trombone, percussion(bongos, temple blocks).
Score & parts: available from composer.

P3.8 White Block Eleven. (1979) 6' 45"
For: pianos(2).
Score: available from composer.

P4 C. ALEXANDER PELOQUIN

Born June 16, 1918, in Northbridge, Mass. *Education:* studied piano with Jesus Maria Sanroma (New England Conservatory, 1937-40); attended Berkshire Music Center, Tanglewood. *Awards:* ASCAP Awards (Standard) (1980, 1981), Caecilia Medal (Boys Town), Golden Bell Award (NBC), Rhode Island Governor's Award for Excellence in the Arts, honorary degrees from various institutions including Brown University. *Related activities:* conductor; pianist; teacher; contributor of articles to various journals and to the *New Catholic Encyclopaedia*; founder of the Peloquin Chorale, Providence, R.I.; director, Boston College University Chorale; organist and music director, St. Peter and Paul Cathedral, Providence, R.I. (1950-); member of the faculty of Boston College (1955-).
BC

WORKS

P4.1 Alleluia! In All Things!
For: voices(equal)(2) or chorus(2-part), organ, instruments(optional).
Commissioned by: St. Gertrude School of Music, Richmond, Va. *Dedicated to:* Frances Marie Reif. *First performed:* Sept. 15, 1972. St. Gertrude School of Music Choir.
Vocal score: G.I.A.

P4.2 Alleluia on a Byzantine Hymn. (1965) 1' 25"
For: chorus(SATB). *Text:* Bible.
Vocal score: McLaughlin, 1965.

Amen. *See* Triple Amen.

P4.3 An American Liturgy. (1975-76) 50'
For: chorus(SATB), congregation, chamber orchestra. *Commissioned by:* St. Michael Church, Independence, Ohio. *First performed:* June 1976; Independence, Ohio. St. Michael Church Choir and unidentified chamber orchestra.
Parts: G.I.A.
Vocal score: G.I.A., 1976.
Disc: Century-Advent.

P4.4 Angelic Acclamations. (1964) 4'
For: chorus(SAB) and organ. *Text:* Bible, N.T., Revelations 7:12.
Vocal score: McLaughlin, 1964.

P4.5 Ave Maria. (1955) 3'
For: chorus(SATB) and organ(optional).
Vocal score: World Library of Sacred Music, 1955. BPL

P4.6 Ave verum. (1961) 3'
For: chorus(SATB). *Text:* Roman liturgy.
Dedicated to: Walter Burke and the
Burke Family Singers.
Vocal score: McLaughlin, 1961.

Behold How Good It Is. *See* Psalm 132.

P4.7 The Bells. (1964) 10'
For: chorus(mixed), percussion, bells,
pianos(2), celeste, double basses(2).
Text: Edgar Allan Poe. *Commissioned
by:* Brown University for its
bicentennial. *First performed:* Brown
University. Peloquin Chorale, C.
Alexander Peloquin, conductor.
Score & parts: Boosey & Hawkes.
Vocal score: Boosey & Hawkes, 1964.
BPL HU

The Bread Is One. *See* Prayers for
Christian Unity. The Bread Is One.

P4.8 Canticle of Brother Sun. (1976)
For: cantor, chorus, congregation,
trumpets(2), trombones(2), glockenspiel,
harp, organ. *Text:* St. Francis of Assisi.
First performed: 1975; Staten Island,
N.Y.
Score & parts: North American Liturgy
Resources, nyp.
Vocal score: North American Liturgy
Resources, nyp.
Disc: North American Liturgy
Resources.

P4.9 Canticle of Simeon (Nunc
dimittis). (1976) 4'
For: Baritone, chorus(SATB), organ.
Text: Bible, N.T., Luke 2:29-32.
Commissioned by: Diocese of
Pittsburgh. *First performed:* Sept. 5,
1980; Pittsburgh, Pa. Robert
Honeysucker, baritone; Peloquin
Chorale, C. Alexander Peloquin,
conductor.
Vocal score: G.I.A.

P4.10 Carol Fantasy. (1971)
For: chorus(SATB) and organ or string
orchestra. Based on the *Coventry Carol*
and *Puer nobis nascitur. Commissioned*

by: Church of St. Dominic, Shaker
Heights, Ohio.
Score & parts: ms.
Vocal score: ms.

P4.11 Celebration of Presence, Prayer
and Praise. (1974) 15'
For: cantor, chorus(SATB), trumpets(3),
trombones(2), timpani, percussion,
organ. *Commissioned by:* Cardinal John
Cody. *First performed:* Aug. 1974;
Chicago, Ill. Cathedral of the Holy
Name Choir.
Score & parts: G.I.A.
Vocal score: G.I.A.

[Celebration of Presence, Prayer and
Praise. God Is in His Holy Place]
P4.12 God Is in His·Holy Place. (1974)
For: chorus(SATB), congregation,
trumpets(2)(optional), trombones(2)
(optional), timpani, organ.
Score & parts: G.I.A.
Vocal score: G.I.A.

Children's Liturgy. *See* Unless You
Become.

P4.13 Choral Precision: A Book of
Vocal Exercises. (1962)
For: chorus(SSA) or chorus(SATB) and
piano.
Vocal score: G.I.A., 1962.

[Choral Processionals]
P4.14 Four Choral Processionals.
For: chorus(TTB) or chorus(TTBB). *Text:*
Hymns of the Catholic Church. *Contents:*
Holy God We Praise Thy Name; The
God Whom Earth and Sea; O Mary of
All Women; Blessed Be Our God.
Vocal score: World Library of Sacred
Music, 1955. BPL

P4.15 Chorale. (1967) 4'
For: chamber orchestra(1-2-0-1; 1-2-2-0;
timp; str). Based on O Sacred Head,
Sore Wounded (O Haupt voll Blut und
Wunden). *First performed:* Palm Sunday
1967; in CBS-TV program, *In Praise of
the Lord.*
Score & parts: ms.

P4.16 Christ Is King. (1961) 3'
For: chorus(men), trumpets(2),
trombones(2), tuba, timpani, organ. *First
performed:* Easter 1963; Holy Cross
Cathedral, Boston. Boston College
University Chorale; Festival Orchestra,
C. Alexander Peloquin, conductor.
Score & parts: World Library of Sacred
Music.
Vocal score: World Library of Sacred
Music, 1961.

P4.17 Christ, the Light of the Nations.
(1967) 5' 20"
For: chorus(2-part), congregation,
instrumental ensemble(trumpets(3),
trombones(2), bongos(3), organ, double
bass). *Text: Church in the Modern
World* (Vatican II). *Commissioned by:*
Archbishop John Quinn. *First
performed:* Dec. 1967; San Diego, Calif.
Franciscan students of San Luis Rey
Mission.
Score & parts: G.I.A.
Vocal score: G.I.A.
Disc: in *Missa a la samba*, Gregorian
Institute Records M/S124, 197-.
American Brass Quintet; Peloquin
Chorale, C. Alexander Peloquin,
conductor.

P4.18 Christ the Priest; Complete
Ordination Liturgy. (1976) 40'
For: cantor, congregation, brasses,
percussion, organ. *Text:* Byzantine
liturgy and Roman liturgy. *First
performed:* June 1976; Fordham
University. Columbia University Chapel
Choir.
Vocal score: G.I.A., 1976.

Christmas Concerto. *See* Concerto,
Organ.

P4.19 Colony Fantasia. (1978) 8'
For: chorus(mixed) and
orchestra(1-1-1-1; 0-2-2-0; timp; str).
Text: traditional folksongs and hymns.
Contents: Maria zu Lieben; Freut euch
der Lebens; Grosse Gott (Holy God We
Praise Thy Name). *Commissioned by:* St.
Peter's Abbacy. *Dedicated to:* Thomas
Gerwing. *First performed:* July 18,

1978; Muenster, Sask.

Colony Fantasia. Holy God We Praise Thy
Name (Chorus(SATB), Congregation, Orchestra)]
P4.20 Holy God We Praise Thy Name.
4'
Text: Katholisches Gesangbuch, Vienna,
1774. *Dedicated to:* Theodore Marier.
Score & parts: G.I.A.
Vocal score: G.I.A.

Colony Fantasia. Holy God We Praise Thy
Name (Chorus(SATB), Congregation, Organ)]
P4.21 Holy God We Praise Thy Name.
4'
Text: Katholisches Gesangbuch, Vienna,
1774. *Dedicated to:* Theodore Marier.
Vocal score: McLaughlin, 1961.
Disc: in *Hymns Thru the Centuries*,
Gregorian Institute Records.

Common Mass of the Virgin Mary.
Love Song. *See* Mass of the Virgin
Mary. Love Song.

Communion Rite. *See* Lyric Liturgy.
Communion Rite.

[Concerto, Organ]
P4.22 Christmas Concerto. (1966) 15'
For: organ and chamber
orchestra(1-2-0-1; 1-0-0-0; timp; str).
Movements: March of the Magi;
Pastoral; Dance of the Shepherds.
Dedicated to: Daniel Durand. *First
performed:* Phoenix, Ariz. Daniel
Durand, organ; C. Alexander Peloquin,
conductor.
Score & parts: ms.

Contemplation. *See* Joy. Contemplation.

P4.23 A Creed for All Occasions.
(1978)
For: cantor, chorus(SATB), brasses,
timpani, organ. *Commissioned by:*
Diocese of Memphis. *First performed:*
Easter 1978; Memphis, Tenn.
Parts: G.I.A.
Vocal score: G.I.A.

Earthquake. *See* Freedom Songs.

P4.24 Ecce sacerdos. [1954?] 4′
For: chorus(SATB) and organ. *Text:*
Roman liturgy. *Dedicated to:* His
Excellency, the Most Rev. Russell J.
McVinney, D.D., Bishop of Rhode
Island. *First performed:* 1954;
Providence, R.I. Cathedral of SS. Peter
and Paul Choir, [C. Alexander
Peloquin, conductor?]
Vocal score: McLaughlin, 1954. BPL
Disc: Gregorian Institute Records, 1961.

[Ecce sacerdos; Arr.]
P4.25 Ecce sacerdos. (1954?) 4′
For: chorus(unison) and organ. *Text:*
Roman liturgy.
Vocal score: McLaughlin, 1954.

P4.26 Eucharist of Healing Ministry.
(1978) 15′
For: flute, percussion, organ, double
bass. Text: Roman liturgy. *Movements:*
Sanctus; Christ Has Died; Amen; Lamb
of God. *Commissioned by:* The Mercy
Hospital of Pittsburgh. *Dedicated to:*
Karen J. Clarke.
Parts: ms.

Faith, Hope and Love. *See* Lyric Liturgy.
Faith, Hope and Love.

P4.27 Fanfare. (1967) 2′
For: chamber orchestra(1-2-0-1;1-2-2-0;
timp; str). Based on the Gregorian
chant, Christus vincit. *Commissioned by:*
Columbia Broadcasting System . *First
performed:* Palm Sunday 1967; in
CBS-TV program, *In Praise of the Lord.*
Score & parts: ms.

P4.28 Festival Mass. (1966)
For: voice, chorus, organ, chamber
orchestra(1-1-0-0; 0-3-2-0; cel, org;
str(0-0-0-2-0)). *Commissioned by:*
Diocese of St. Augustine for the
celebration of the 400th anniversary of
the city. *First performed:* St.
Augustine, Fla. Barry College Tara
Singers and the Boston College
University Chorale; members of the
Jacksonville Symphony, C. Alexander
Peloquin, conductor.

Score & parts: G.I.A.
Vocal score: G.I.A, 1966.
Disc: in *Mass for Joy,* Gregorian
Institute Records GIA 113C, 196-.
Peloquin Chorale, C. Alexander
Peloquin, conductor. WCRB

P4.29 Freedom Songs.
For: Baritone, chorus(SATB), chamber
orchestra(1-1-0-0; 1-2-2-0; timp; hp, cel;
str(0-0-0-2-1)). *Text:* Thomas Merton.
Contents: Sundown; All the Way; The
Lord Is Good; Earthquake.
Commissioned by: Liturgical Conference
of Washington, D.C. *Dedicated to:* The
memory of Martin Luther King, Jr. *First
performed:* Aug. 19, 1968; Washington,
D.C. Ebenezer Baptist Choir of Atlanta.
Vocal score: G.I.A., 1968 (Earthquake
also available separately).
Disc: Oct. 30, 1970; University of
Connecticut, Storrs; 25th
All-Connecticut Music Festival. Jesse
Coston, baritone.

P4.30 Gaelic Blessing.
For: voice(medium), chorus(SATB), harp
or piano. *Text:* Irish, traditional. *First
performed:* Warren, R.I. Diane Harrison,
soprano and Anne Marguerite Michaud,
harp.
Vocal score: ms.

P4.31 Gathering Song.
For: voice, chorus, congregation,
percussion, organ. *Text:* Kenneth
Omernick. *First performed:* 1976;
Milwaukee, Wis. Priests; Theophane
Hytreck, organ.
Vocal score: G.I.A., 1974.

Give Praise to the Lord. *See* Psalm
117.

Gloria. *See* Lyric Liturgy. Gloria.

P4.32 Gloria in excelsis. (1976) 4′
For: cantor, chorus, congregation,
brasses, timpani, percussion, organ.
Commissioned by: Bishop Dozier. *First
performed:* Memphis, Tenn.

Score & parts: G.I.A.
Vocal score: G.I.A., 1976.

Gloria of the Bells. *See* Mass of the Bells. Gloria.

God Is in His Holy Place. *See* Celebration of Presence, Prayer and Praise. God Is in His Holy Place.

God Mounts His Throne. *See* Psalm 46.

P4.33 Hail Mary. (1954) 2'
For: chorus(mixed). *Text:* anon.
Vocal score: McLaughlin, 1954. BPL
Disc: in *Hymns Thru the Centuries,* Gregorian Institute Records.

P4.34 Happiness. (1978) 4'
For: voice, chorus(2-3-part), organ. *Text:* Speech delivered to educators in Chicago by Mother Teresa of Calcutta, India. *First performed:* Dec. 25, 1978; Providence, R.I. Peloquin Chorale, C. Alexander Peloquin, conductor.
Vocal score: G.I.A., 1978.

P4.35 Happy Holiday, O Welcome! (1954) 3'
For: chorus(mixed). *Text:* anon.
Dedicated to: Theodore Marier.
Vocal score: McLaughlin, 1954. BPL
Vocal score: G.I.A.

Have Mercy on Me. *See* Psalm 50.

P4.36 Hic est Michael. (1963)
For: chorus(SAB) and organ.
Commissioned for: 75th anniversary of the Church of St. Michael, Rochester, N.Y.
Vocal score: McLaughlin.

Holy God We Praise Thy Name. *See* Choral Processionals; Colony Fantasia. Holy God We Praise Thy Name.

P4.37 Hommage a Purcell. (1958) 4'
For: organ. *Commissioned by:* McLaughlin & Reilly. *Dedicated to:* Berj Zamkochian.
Score: McLaughlin, 1968.

Honey from the Rock. *See* Psalm 80.

How Lovely Is Your Dwelling Place. *See* Psalm 83.

Hymn of Triumph. *See* Psalm 149.

P4.38 L'Hymne de l'univers. (1967) 15'
For: Tenor, chorus(mixed), organ, instrumental ensemble(horns(2), trumpets(3), trombones(2), timpani, harp, organ, double bass). *Text:* Pierre Teilhard de Chardin. Written for closing Mass for EXPO 67, Montreal, Que. *Dedicated to:* Cardinal Emile Leger.
First performed: Oct. 1967; Montreal, Que. Robert Peters, tenor; Chorale de Vaudreuil.
Score & parts: ms.
Vocal score: ms.

P4.39 Hymnus angelorum. (1962) 4' 15"
For: chorus(men)(3-part), timpani, organ or piano. *Text:* Gloria in excelsis Deo from the Roman liturgy. *Commissioned by:* Berj Zamkochian. *First performed:* 1962; Catholic Memorial High School, Boston.
Vocal score: McLaughlin, 1962.

P4.40 I Am Forgotten. (1975) 2' 30"
For: voice and piano. *Text:* Hubert Van Zeller. *Dedicated to:* Lucien Olivier.
Score: ms.

P4.41 I Believe That My Redeemer Lives.
For: chorus(SATB) and organ. *Text:* Bible. *Commissioned by:* Margaret Peirce, London, Ont. *First performed:* Aug. 1971; Providence, R.I. Peloquin Chorale, C. Alexander Peloquin, organ.
Vocal score: G.I.A.

I Will Bless the Lord. *See* Psalm 33.

I Will Give Thanks to You, O Lord. *See* Psalm 94.

In Christ the Lord. *See* Prayers for Christian Unity. In Christ the Lord.

P4.42 In Kindness and in Truth. (1978) 6′
For: voice, chorus(mixed), organ. *Text:* *Bangor Antiphoner*, 7th century, Irish. *Dedicated to:* The Most Rev. Daniel P. Reilly, Bishop of Norwich, Conn. *First performed:* Norwich, Conn. Diocesan choir.
Vocal score: G.I.A, 1974.

P4.43 In Praise of the Virgin Mary: A Song Cycle.
For: chorus(mixed) and chamber orchestra(1-1-0-0; 0-2-2-0; timp; hp; cel, org; str(0-0-0-2-1)). *Text:* Roman liturgy. *Dedicated to:* Tara Singers of Barry College. *First performed:* 1966; St. Augustine, Fla.
Vocal score: McLaughlin, 1966.

[Indian Songs]
P4.44 Four Indian Songs. (1981) 15′
For: voices, chorus(SATB), flute, trumpet, trombone, xylophone, drum, harp, double bass. *Text:* Indian, North American. *Contents:* Medicine Song (Geronimo); Morning Song; Wedding Song; Eskimo Song (Iglulik).
Commissioned by: North American Liturgy Resources. *First performed:* Mar. 19, 1981; Phoenix, Ariz. Bach & Madrigal Society; All Saints Children's Choir; Southwest Brass Quintet, Desert Dancetheatre.
Score & parts: North American Liturgy Resources.
Vocal score: North American Liturgy Resources.
Disc: North American Liturgy Resources.

P4.45 Introit for All Saints Day. (1960) 3′
For: chorus(SATB). *Text:* Roman liturgy. *Dedicated to:* Henry Hokans. *First performed:* Nov. 1, 1960; Worcester, Mass.

P4.46 Jesus Christ Is Lord. (1978) 6′
For: voice, chorus(mixed),

orchestra(1-1-1-1; 4-3-2-1; timp; str). *Text:* Bible, N.T., Epistle of St. Paul to the Philippians. *Dedicated to:* Thomas O'Malley, S.J., president, John Carroll University. *First performed:* Nov. 1978; St. Ignatius Church, Newton, Mass. Boston College University Chorale; Festival Orchestra, C. Alexander Peloquin, conductor.

P4.47 Jesus Shepherd of Our Souls. (1976) 4′
For: chorus(SA) and organ. *Text:* from *Plymouth Praise* by Fred Kahn. *Dedicated to:* Elizabeth Walker.
Vocal score: G.I.A., 1974.

P4.48 Joy.
For: organ. Suite. *Movements:* Prelude; Dance; Interlude; Contemplation; Joy. *Commissioned by:* Sacred Music Press. *Dedicated to:* Berj Zamkochian, Marilyn Mason, Gerre Hancock. *First performed:* 1971.
Score: Sacred Music, 1971.

[Joy. Contemplation]
P4.49 Contemplation. 5′ 6″
For: organ. *Dedicated to:* Marilyn Mason.
Score: Sacred Music, 1971.
Disc: in *Missa a la samba*, Gregorian Institute Records GIA M/S 124, 197-. C. Alexander Peloquin, organ. WCRB

P4.50 Just Sitting There. (1981) 5′
For: Mezzo Soprano, chorus(SATB), organ or piano. *Text:* from *The Long Loneliness* by Dorothy Day. *Commissioned by:* James B. Welch. *First performed:* May 8, 1981; New York City. Welch Chorale.
Vocal score: North American Liturgy Resources.

Laudate Dominum. *See* Psalm 117.

P4.51 Litany. (1964) 4′
For: chorus(SATB) and organ(optional).

Dedicated to: Sister Claire Agnes.
Vocal score: G.I.A., 1964.

Liturgy of the Word. *See* Lyric Liturgy.
Liturgy of the Word; Lyric
Liturgy. Penitential Rite.

Lord, Every Nation. *See* Psalm 72.

Lord Jesus Come. *See* Lyric Liturgy.
Lord Jesus Come.

P4.52 The Lord of Life: A Liturgy.
(1980) 50'
For: celebrant, cantor, chorus(SATB),
congregation, chamber orchestra
(1-0-0-0; 2-2-2-0; timp, perc(2), hp, org;
str(0-0-0-1-1)). *Commissioned by:*
Cardinal Terence Cooke. *First
performed:* Oct. 5, 1980; St. Patrick
Cathedral, New York City. Peloquin
Chorale and St. Patrick Cathedral Choir.
Score & parts: G.I.A., nyp.
Vocal score: G.I.A., nyp.
Parts(congregation): G.I.A., nyp.

Lord, Send out Your Spirit. *See* Psalm
104.

Lord, You Have the Words. *See* Psalm
19.

P4.53 The Lourdes Hymn. 2'
For: chorus(SATB).
Vocal score: McLaughlin, 1958. BPL

The Lourdes Hymn. *See also* Partita on
the Lourdes Hymn.

P4.54 Love Is Everlasting. (1967) 9' 15"
For: cantor, chorus(SATB) or
chorus(equal voices), organ or brasses,
timpani, double bass. *Text:* from the
Bible, O.T., Daniel. *Dedicated to:* Bishop
James A. Hickey. *First performed:* June
1967; Seattle, Wash. Singers from the
Diocese of Seattle and members of
the Seattle Youth Orchestra, C.
Alexander Peloquin, conductor.
Vocal score: G.I.A., 1967. BPL
Disc: in *Mass for Joy*, Gregorian
Institute Records GIA 113C, 196-.

Peloquin Chorale, C. Alexander
Peloquin, conductor. WCRB

Love Song. *See* Mass of the Virgin
Mary. Love Song.

P4.55 Lyric Liturgy. (1974) 44' 46"
For: cantor, chorus(mixed),
congregation, brasses, timpani, organ.
Text: Roman liturgy. *Contents:* Lord
Jesus Come; Penitential Rite; Liturgy of
the Word; Alleluia, Offertory; Liturgy
of the Eucharist; Communion Rite
(Second Prayer); Faith, Hope and Love;
Gloria; Sacred Dance. *Commissioned by:*
St. Mary's Seminary, Cleveland, Ohio.
First performed: June 1974; Cleveland,
Ohio. Diocesan chorus.
Vocal score: G.I.A., 1973.
Disc: Gregorian Institute Records M/S
144, 197-. Robert H. Oldershaw,
celebrant; Stephen Szaraz, cantor;
Robert Plimpton, organ; Peloquin
Chorale and Orchestra; Boston College
University Chorale. WCRB

[Lyric Liturgy. Communion Rite]
P4.56 Communion Rite.
For: voices, chorus(SATB),
congregation, timpani, organ.
Vocal score: G.I.A, 197-.

[Lyric Liturgy. Faith, Hope and Love]
P4.57 Faith, Hope and Love.
For: Cantor, chorus(SATB),
congregation, organ.
Vocal score: G.I.A., 197-.

[Lyric Liturgy. Gloria]
P4.58 Gloria.
For: chorus(SATB), congregation,
brasses, percussion, organ, double
bass.
Score & parts: ms.
Vocal score: G.I.A., 197-.

[Lyric Liturgy. Liturgy of the Word]
P4.59 Liturgy of the Word.
For: Cantor, chorus(SATB),
congregation, organ.
Vocal score: G.I.A., 197- (also published
with Lyric Liturgy. Penitential Rite).

[Lyric Liturgy. Lord Jesus Come]
P4.60 Lord Jesus Come.
For: cantor, chorus(SATB), congregation, brasses, timpani, organ, double bass.
Vocal score: G.I.A., 197-.

[Lyric Liturgy. Penitential Rite]
P4.61 Penitential Rite and Liturgy of the Word.
For: cantor, chorus(SATB), congregation, organ.
Vocal score: G.I.A., 197-.

P4.62 March for Joyous Occasions.
For: organ.
Score: McLaughlin, 1958. BPL

P4.63 Mass for Joy. (1966) 6' 55"
For: chorus(SATB), trumpets(2), trombones(2), timpani, guitar, organ, double bass. *Dedicated to:* Youth of America. *First performed:* Dec. 1966; Providence, R.I. Peloquin Chorale.
Score & parts: G.I.A.
Vocal score: G.I.A., 1967. BPL
Disc: Gregorian Institute Records GIA 113C, 196-. Peloquin Chorale and Orchestra, C. Alexander Peloquin, conductor. WCRB

P4.64 Mass for Parishes. (1965) 15'
For: cantor, chorus(unison), congregation. *Commissioned by:* Stonehill College. *Dedicated to:* George Pelletier.
Vocal score: McLaughlin, 1965.

P4.65 Mass in English. (1963) 15'
For: chorus(mixed), congregation, trumpets(2)(optional), trombones(2)(optional), timpani(optional), organ. *Commissioned by:* Liturgical Conference of Washington, D.C., 1963. *First performed:* Aug. 1964; St. Louis, Mo. National Choir.
Vocal score: McLaughlin, 1964. BPL

P4.66 Mass of Resurrection. (1971-72) 30'
For: cantor, chorus(SATB), congregation. *Contents:* Processional; Lord Have Mercy; Psalm; Holy Holy; Acclamation; Lamb of God; I Believe That My Redeemer Lives; May the Angels Lead You. *Dedicated to:* William Campbell and the Fall River Singers.
Vocal score: G.I.A.

P4.67 Mass of the Bells. (1971-72) 20'
For: chorus(mixed), congregation, organ, chamber orchestra. *Contents:* Lord Have Mercy; Gloria of the Bells; Holy Holy Holy; Dying You Destroyed; Amen; Lamb of God.
Vocal score: G.I.A., 1972.
Cassette: G.I.A.

[Mass of the Bells. Gloria]
P4.68 Gloria of the Bells. (1972) 4'
For: Cantor, chorus(SATB), congregation, trumpets(2), trombones(2), percussion, organ. *Dedicated to:* Monsignor William Carey. *First performed:* Apr. 1972. Providence, R.I. Dennis Murphy, cantor; priests; C. Alexander Peloquin, organ.
Vocal score: in *Worship II*, G.I.A.
Cassette: in *Festival Mass*, Basement Records, 197-.

[Mass of the Virgin Mary. Love Song]
P4.69 Love Song from the Common Mass of the Virgin Mary.
For: chorus(SSA), congregation, chamber orchestra(1-1-0-0; 0-3-2-0; timp; hp; org; str(0-0-0-2-1)).
Vocal score: Summy Birchard.

P4.70 May the Lord Bless You. (1968) 1' 45"
For: Soprano, Alto, chorus, bongos, guitar or organ. *Text:* St. Francis of Assisi. *Dedicated to:* San Luis Rey Mission, Calif. *First performed:* Jan. 1968; Berchtesgaden, West Germany. Armed Forces Singers of Europe.
Vocal score: McLaughlin, 1968.
Disc: in issa a la samba, Gregorian Institute Records GIA M/S 124, 197-. Peloquin Chorale. WCRB

P4.71 Messe, Terre des hommes. (1967) 20'

For: chorus(mixed), horn, trumpet, timpani, organ, double bass.
Commissioned by: Eglise St. Jacques, Montreal, Que. Written for closing Mass at EXPO 67. *First performed:* Oct. 1967; Montreal, Que. Chorale de Vaudreuil.
Vocal score: G.I.A.

P4.72 Missa a la samba. (1970) 7' 52"
For: celebrant, cantor, chorus(SATB), percussion, organ.
Vocal score: G.I.A., 1970. BPL NU
Disc: Gregorian Institute Records, GIA M/S 124, 197-. American Brass Quintet; Peloquin Chorale. WCRB

[Missa a la samba; Arr]
P4.73 Missa a la samba.
For: voices(2 or 3), trumpet, double bass, bongos.
Score & parts: G.I.A., 197-.

[Missa a la samba; Arr]
P4.74 Missa a la samba.
For: chorus(unison), trumpet, double bass, bongos.
Score & parts: G.I.A., 197-.

P4.75 Missa Christus Rex. (1957-58) 35'
For: chorus(treble), chorus(men)(3-part), trumpets(3), timpani, organ.
Commissioned for: 50th anniversary of Archbishop Cicognani. *First performed:* 1958; Trinity College Chapel, Washington, D.C. Seminarians.
Score & parts: G.I.A.
Vocal score: G.I.A., 1958. BPL

[Missa Christus Rex. Kyrie and Gloria]
P4.76 Kyrie and Gloria from Missa Christus Rex. (1957-58) 6'
For: chorus(treble), chorus(men)(3-part), trumpets(3), timpani, organ.
Disc: in *Thirteen Centuries of Christian Choral Art*, Gregorian Institute Records E1-100, 197-.

P4.77 Missa Domini. (1962-63) 20'
For: chorus(men)(3-part), congregation, orchestra(1-1-1-1; 3-3-2-1; timp; str).
Commissioned by: Boston College for its centennial. *First performed:* Mar. 30, 1963; Holy Cross Cathedral, Boston. Boston College University Chorale, Festival Orchestra, C. Alexander Peloquin, conductor.
Score & parts: McLaughlin.
Vocal score: McLaughlin, 1963. BPL

P4.78 Missa nativitatis. (1960) 20'
For: chorus(treble)(2-part) and chamber orchestra(1-1-0-0; 0-0-0-0; timp; org; str). *Dedicated to:* Rev. Norman Leboeuf. *First performed:* Dec. 25, 1960; in NBC *Catholic Hour*. St. Bernard's Boys Choir, Pittsburgh, Pa.
Vocal score: G.I.A.

P4.79 Missa pentatonica. (1960) 15'
For: chorus(unison) and organ.
Dedicated to: Brother Basil, S.C., Basutoland, South Africa.
Vocal score: G.I.A.

P4.80 Missa Sancti Bernardi. (1956) 15'
For: chorus(mixed). *Dedicated to:* Alexander Bernard (died 1918 in France). *First performed:* [1956?]; Boys Town Chapel, Boys Town, Neb. Workshop Singers and Boys Town Choir.

P4.81 Motets for Benediction. (1955) 10'
For: voices(equal)(3). *Contents:* O Saving Victim; Hail Star of the Sea; Therefore We, Before Him Bending; Give Praise to the Lord. *Dedicated to:* The Men's Choir, Cathedral of Saints Peter and Paul, Providence, R.I.
Score: World Library of Sacred Music, 1955. BPL

P4.82 Mother. (1980) 15'
For: Soprano, Tenor, chorus, orchestra(1-1-1-1; 4-3-2-1; timp; str).
Text: Pope John Paul II. *Contents:* Her Amazement at Her Only Child; John Beseeches Her; Embraced by New Time. *Commissioned by:* Assumption College on the occasion of its 75th anniversary. *First performed:* Mar. 23, 1980; Worcester, Mass. Peloquin Chorale; Boston College Univeristy

Chorale; National Philharmonia of Boston, C. Alexander Peloquin, conductor.
Score & parts: ms.
Vocal score: ms.

My God, My God. *See* Psalm 22.

P4.83 Noel nouvelet. (1957)
For: chorus(SATB). *Dedicated to:* The Welch Chorale, New York City.
Vocal score: Flammer.
Disc: in *Christmas Carols and Noels,* Gregorian Institute Records. Peloquin Chorale.

Nunc dimittis. *See* Canticle of Simeon.

P4.84 O Blessed Trinity. (1956) 3'
For: chorus(unison) and organ. *Text:* Roman liturgy (Matins responsory, Trinity Sunday).
Vocal score: World Library of Sacred Music.

O Haupt voll Blut und Wunden. *See* Chorale.

O Sacred Head, Sore Wounded. *See* Chorale.

P4.85 Open the Door. (1970) 3' 56"
For: cantor, chorus, brasses, organ.
Text: Mickey Kenney. Written for St. Mary of the Bay, Warren, R.I. for the dedication of new church. *Dedicated to:* David Coffey.
Parts: G.I.A.
Disc: in *Missa a la samba,* Gregorian Institute Records, M/S 124, 197-. Lucien Olivier, cantor; Peloquin Chorale. WCRB

Ordination Liturgy. *See* Christ the Priest.

P4.86 Our Father. (1954) 2'
For: chorus(mixed). *Text:* Bible, N.T., Matthew 6:9-13. *Dedication:* In memory of my father. Used for several years by WEAM-AM, Providence, R. I., as sign-off.
Vocal score: McLaughlin, 1955. BPL

Disc: in *Hymns Thru the Centuries,* Gregorian Institute Records.

P4.87 Partita on the Lourdes Hymn. (1958) 10'
For: organ. 10 movements. *Dedicated to:* Flor Peeters, Belgium. *First performed:* 1959; Providence, R.I. C. Alexander Peloquin.
Score: McLaughlin, 1959. BPL

Penitential Rite. *See* Lyric Liturgy. Penitential Rite.

P4.88 Prayer.
For: chorus and organ.
Vocal score: G.I.A.

Prayer for Peace. *See* Prayers for Christian Unity. Prayer for Peace.

P4.89 A Prayer for Us. (1975) 8'
For: speaker, voice, chorus(mixed), congregation, brasses, percussion, organ. *Text: Book of Common Prayer* (1928); David B. Watermulder.
Commissioned by: Princeton Theological Seminary. *Dedicated to:* Robert Plimpton. *First performed:* May 1975; Bryn Mawr, Pa. Bryn Mawr Presbyterian Church Choir.
Score & parts: G.I.A.
Vocal score: G.I.A., 1975.

P4.90 Prayer of St. Francis. (1973) 3' 15"
For: chorus(SATB). *Text:* St. Francis of Assisi. *Dedicated to:* Irene Simas.
Vocal score: G.I.A.

[Prayers]
P4.91 Four Prayers. (1977) 10'
For: chorus(mixed) and organ. *Text:* Cardinal John Henry Newman; St. Bernard of Clairvaux; St. Augustine; Bible, N.T. *Contents:* Soul of Christ, Jesus!; Do Whatever He Tells; Sing Along the Road. *Commissioned by:* St. Dominic Church, Shaker Heights, Ohio. *First performed:* Shaker Heights, Ohio.
Vocal score: G.I.A.

[Prayers for Christian Unity]
P4.92 Four Prayers for Christian Unity.
For: chorus(mixed), brasses, timpani.
Contents: Psalm for Unity; Prayer for
Peace; In Christ the Lord; The Bread Is
One. *Commissioned by:* Liturgical
Conference of Washington, D.C. First
performed: Aug. 1965; Chicago, Ill.
Convention Choir.
Vocal score: G.I.A., 1965.

[Prayers for Christian Unity. The
Bread Is One]
P4.93 The Bread Is One. 2' 26"
For: chorus(SATB).
Vocal score: G.I.A.
Disc: in *Missa a la samba*, Gregorian
Institute Records M/S 124, 197-.
Peloquin Chorale, C. Alexander
Peloquin, conductor. WCRB

[Prayers for Christian Unity. In Christ
the Lord]
P4.94 In Christ the Lord.
For: chorus(SATB) and organ.
Vocal score: G.I.A.

[Prayers for Christian Unity. Prayer
for Peace]
P4.95 Prayer for Peace. (1965) 3' 55"
For: chorus(SATB) and congregation.
Vocal score: G.I.A.

P4.96 Promised Land. (1977) 50'
For: cantor, chorus(mixed),
congregation, orchestra(1-1-1-1; 2-2-2-0;
timp, perc, glock; str). *Contents:* The
Promised Land; Kyrie; Responsorial
Psalm; Alleluia; I Pray for My Friends;
Holy Holy; Acclamations; Lord's Prayer;
Amen; Lamb of God; Jesus Really
Lives (Dietrich Bonhoeffer); Gloria.
Commissioned by: Bishop James A.
Hickey of Cleveland, Ohio. *Dedication:*
To the memory of Amadeus Rappe,
first Bishop of Cleveland, Ohio. First
performed: Nov. 1977; Cleveland, Ohio.
Stephen Szaraz, cantor; diocesan
choirs; unidentifed orchestra, C.
Alexander Peloquin, conductor.
Score & parts: G.I.A.
Vocal score: G.I.A., 1977.

[Psalm 9. Why, O Lord, Do You
Stand Aloof?]
P4.97 Why, O Lord, Do You Stand
Aloof?
For: chorus(SATB). *Commissioned by:*
Liturgical Conference of Washington,
D.C. *First performed:* Aug. 27, 1964; St.
Louis, Mo. National Choir, C. Alexander
Peloquin, conductor.
Vocal score: G.I.A.

[Psalm 19. Lord, You Have the
Words]
P4.98 Lord, You Have the Words. (1971)
4'
For: chorus(SATB) and congregation.
Commissioned by: Gregorian Institute of
America.
Vocal score: in *Songs of Israel*, G.I.A.,
1972. BPL
Disc: in *Songs of Israel*, Gregorian
Institute Records, 1972.

[Psalm 22. My God, My God]
P4.99 My God, My God. (1971) 4'
For: Cantor, chorus(SATB),
congregation. *Commissioned by:*
Gregorian Institute of America.
Dedicated to: Robert Batastini.
Vocal score: in *Songs of Israel*, G.I.A.,
1972. BPL
Disc: in *Songs of Israel*, Gregorian
Institute Records, 1972.

[Psalm 24. To You, O Lord]
P4.100 To You, O Lord. (1972) 3'
For: chorus(SATB). *Commissioned by:*
Gregorian Institute of America.
Vocal score: in *Songs of Israel*, G.I.A.,
1972. BPL
Disc: in *Songs of Israel*, Gregorian
Institute Records, 1972.

[Psalm 33. I Will Bless the Lord]
P4.101 I Will Bless the Lord.
For: chorus(mixed) and congregation.
Commissioned by: Liturgical Conference
of Washington, D.C. *First performed:*
Aug. 27, 1964; St. Louis, Mo. National
Choir, C. Alexander Peloquin,
conductor.
Vocal score: McLaughlin, 1964.

[Psalm 34. Taste and See]
P4.102 Taste and See. (1971) 4'
For: chorus(SATB) and congregation.
Commissioned by: Gregorian Institute of
America.
Vocal score: in *Songs of Israel*, G.I.A.,
1972. BPL
Disc: in *Songs of Israel*, Gregorian
Institute Records, 1972.

[Psalm 46. God Mounts His Throne]
P4.103 God Mounts His Throne. (1971)
3'
For: cantor, chorus(SATB), congregation,
brasses, strings. *Commissioned by:*
Gregorian Institute of America.
Score & parts: ms.
Vocal score: in *Songs of Israel*, G.I.A.,
1972. BPL
Disc: in *Songs of Israel*, Gregorian
Institute Records, 1972.

[Psalm 50. Have Mercy on Me]
P4.104 Have Mercy on Me. (1971) 3'
For: Cantor, chorus(SATB),
congregation. *Commissioned by:*
Gregorian Institute of America.
Vocal score: in *Songs of Israel*, G.I.A.,
1972. BPL
Disc: in *Songs of Israel*, Gregorian
Institute Records, 1972.

[Psalm 72. Lord, Every Nation]
P4.105 Lord, Every Nation. (1971) 4'
For: chorus(SATB), congregation,
brasses, harp, timpani. *Commissioned
by:* St. Michael Church, London, Ont.
Score & parts: ms.
Vocal score: in *Songs of Israel*, G.I.A.,
1972. BPL
Disc: in *Songs of Israel*, Gregorian
Institute Records, 1972.

[Psalm 80. Honey from the Rock]
P4.106 Honey from the Rock. (1966)
For: chorus(SA), congregation,
trumpets(2), trombones(3), timpani,
organ. *Dedicated to:* Rev. Robert Ryan,
Director of Music, Archdiocese of
Detroit. *First performed:* Detroit, Mich.;
Choirboy Festival.

Vocal score: World Library of Sacred
Music, 1966.

[Psalm 83. How Lovely Is Your
Dwelling Place]
P4.107 How Lovely Is Your Dwelling
Place. (1964) 6'
For: Cantor, chorus(3-part),
congregation. *Dedicated to:* Rev. Richard
Wojcik, Chicago, Ill.
Vocal score: G.I.A.

[Psalm 94. I Will Give Thanks to
You, O Lord]
P4.108 I Will Give Thanks to You, O
Lord. (1964)
For: chorus(SATB), congregation, organ.
Commissioned by: Liturgical Conference
of Washington, D.C. *First performed:*
Aug. 1964; St. Louis, Mo. National
Choir, C. Alexander Peloquin,
conductor.
Vocal score: World Library of Sacred
Music.

[Psalm 98. Shout for Joy]
P4.109 Shout for Joy. (1970) 4' 28"
For: Cantor, chorus(SATB),
congregation, trumpets(3), trombones(2),
percussion, organ. *Dedicated to:* Dr.
Hollis Grant, director of St. Dunstan
Conference on Sacred Music. *First
performed:* Aug. 1970; Providence, R.I.
Gerre Hancock, organ; Peloquin Chorale;
workshop chorus.
Vocal score: in *Songs of Israel*, G.I.A.,
1972. BPL
Disc: in *Songs of Israel*, Gregorian
Institute Records, 1972.

[Psalm 100. We Are His People. 1st
version]
P4.110 We Are His People. (1971) 3'
For: chorus(SATB) and congregation.
Commissioned by: Gregorian Institute of
America.
Vocal score: in *Songs of Israel*, G.I.A.,
1972, BPL
Disc: in *Songs of Israel*, Gregorian
Institute Records, 1972.

[Psalm 100. We are His People. 2nd version]
P4.111 Psalm One Hundred. (1973) 5'
For: chorus(SATB), brasses, double bass, percussion, organ. *Commissioned by:* St. Dominic Church, Shaker Heights, Ohio. *First performed:* 1974; Lincoln Center, New York City. Boston College University Chorale; Robert Plimpton, organ.
Vocal score: G.I.A.

[Psalm 104. Lord, Send out Your Spirit]
P4.112 Lord, Send out Your Spirit. (1971) 4'
For: chorus(SATB) or congregation, trumpets(3), trombones(2), percussion, organ. *Commissioned by:* Gregorian Institute of America. *Dedicated to:* Rev. Robert Wallace, Toronto, Ont.
Vocal score: in *Songs of Israel*, G.I.A., 1972. BPL
Disc: in *Songs of Israel*, Gregorian Institute Records, 1972.

[Psalm 117. Laudate Dominum]
P4.113 Laudate Dominum: Give Praise to the Lord. (1959) 3'
For: chorus(mixed), trumpets(3), trombones(3), tuba, timpani, organ. Winner of Caecilia Medal (Boys Town).
Dedicated to: James B. Welch and the Welch Chorale, New York City. *First performed:* Aug. 1964; Boys Town, Neb. Workshop choir, Roger Wagner, conductor.
Vocal score: G.I.A., 1959.

[Psalm 118. This Is the Day]
P4.114 This Is the Day. (1971) 4'
For: cantor, chorus(SATB), congregation. *Commissioned by:* Gregorian Institute of America. *Dedicated to:* Cecilia Roy Kenny.
Vocal score: in *Songs of Israel*, G.I.A., 1972. BPL
Disc: in *Songs of Israel*, Gregorian Institute Records, 1972.

[Psalm 132. Behold How Good It Is]
P4.115 Behold How Good It Is.
For: cantor, chorus(2-part), congregation.
Vocal score: G.I.A.

[Psalm 136. Resurrection Psalm]
P4.116 Resurrection Psalm. (1971) 3'
For: cantor, chorus(SATB), congregation.
Vocal score: *Songs of Israel*, G.I.A., 1972. BPL
Disc: in *Songs of Israel*, Gregorian Institute Records, 1972.

[Psalm 138. Song of Hope]
P4.117 Song of Hope.
For: chorus(mixed), timpani, harp, chimes, double bass, organ. *Text:* Hubert Van Zeller. *Dedicated to:* Josephine Morgan. *First performed:* Aug. 1969; Manhattanville College. Workshop choir.
Score & parts: ms.
Vocal score: ms.

[Psalm 149. Hymn of Triumph]
P4.118 Hymn of Triumph. (1962) 5'
For: chorus(3-part) and organ or orchestra(1-1-1-1; 3-3-2-0; timp; str). *Commissioned by:* Boston College for its centennial. *First performed:* Mar. 1963; Holy Cross Cathedral, Boston. Boston College University Chorale and unidentified orchestra, C. Alexander Peloquin, conductor.
Score & parts: ms.
Vocal score: McLaughlin, 1962.

[Psalm 150. Symphony of Praise]
P4.119 Symphony of Praise. (1972) 4'
For: chorus(men)(3-part), congregation, orchestra(1-1-1-1; 3-3-2-0; timp; str). *Commissioned by:* Boston College for its centennial. *First performed:* Mar. 1963; Holy Cross Cathedral, Boston. Boston College University Chorale and unidentified orchestra, C. Alexander Peloquin, conductor.
Score & parts: McLaughlin.
Vocal score: McLaughlin.

P4.120 Receive the Holy Spirit. (1974) 3'
For: cantor, chorus(SATB), congregation, organ. *Text:* Roman liturgy. *Commissioned by:* St. Mary's Seminary,

Cleveland, Ohio. *Dedicated to:* Most Rev. Michael J. Murphy.
Vocal score: G.I.A.

P4.121 Rejoice in Hope. (1972) 5'
For: speaker, chorus(mixed), instrumental ensemble(horns(2), trumpets(2), trombones(2), percussion, harp, organ, double bass). *Text:* Bible, N.T. and Roman liturgy for Maundy Thursday. *Dedicated to:* Most Rev. Louis E. Gelineau for his ordination as Bishop. *First performed:* Jan. 1972; Providence, R.I. Rev. Charles Maher, speaker; Peloquin Chorale; unidentifed instrumental ensemble.
Score & parts: G.I.A.
Vocal score: G.I.A.

Responsorial Psalm for Christmas. *See* Today Is Born Our Savior.

Responsorial Psalms for the Entire Year. *See* Songs of Israel.

Resurrection Psalm. *See* Psalm 136.

Shout for Joy. See Psalm 98.

P4.122 Song of Daniel. (1965) 2' 50"
For: cantor, chorus(mixed), congregation, brasses, timpani, organ. *Commissioned by:* St. Michael Church, Buffalo, N.Y. *First performed:* Buffalo, N.Y.
Vocal score: G.I.A., 1965.
Disc: in *Mass for Joy*, Gregorian Institute Records GIA 113C, [1966?]. Peloquin Chorale and Orchestra, C. Alexander Peloquin, conductor. WCRB

[Song of Daniel; Arr.]
P4.123 Song of Daniel. (1965) 3' 30"
For: cantor, chorus(men)(4-part), congregation, trumpets(2), trombones(2), timpani, organ.
Score: G.I.A., 1965. BPL
Vocal score: G.I.A., 1965.

Song of Hope. *See* Psalm 138.

P4.124 Song of Thanksgiving. (1967) 4'
For: chorus(SATB) and organ. *Text:* Bible, O.T. Written for the celebration of the centennial of the confederation of Canada. *First performed:* Oct. 9, 1967; Calgary, Alta.
Vocal score: ms.

P4.125 Song of Zachary. (1965) 3' 15"
For: chorus(SATB). Canticle. *Text:* Bible, N.T., Luke 1:68-79. *Dedicated to:* Joseph Michaud, St. Bernard's Church, Pittsburgh, Pa.
Vocal score: G.I.A.

[Te Deum, English]
P4.126 Te Deum. (1976)
For: chorus(mixed), congregation, organ, orchestra. Canticle. *Text:* Roman liturgy. *Commissioned by:* Sisters of Charity of Seton Hill College to celebrate [the canonization of Elizabeth Ann Seton]. *First performed:* Greensburg, Pa. Workshop chorus, C. Alexander Peloquin, conductor.
Vocal score: G.I.A., 1976.

[Te Deum, Latin]
P4.127 Te Deum. (1964) 25'
For: chorus(SATB) and orchestra(2-2-2-2; 4-3-3-1; perc, glock; hp; pf(2), org; str). Canticle. *Text:* Roman liturgy. *Commissioned by:* St. Joseph College, Rensselaer, Ind. on the occasion of its Diamond Jubilee. *First performed:* Apr. 12, 1964; Rensselaer, Ind. Alverno College Chorus; St. Joseph College Chorus; members of the Gary Symphony Orchestra; Theophane Hytreck, organ.
Score & parts: World Library of Sacred Music.
Vocal score: World Library of Sacred Music, 1964.

Terre des hommes. *See* Messe, Terre des hommes.

This Is the Day. *See* Psalm 118.

To You, O Lord. *See* Psalm 24.

P4.128 Toccata. (1963) 6'
For: organ. *Dedicated to:* Berj
Zamkochian. *First performed:* Apr. 7,
1963; Symphony Hall, Boston. Berj
Zamkochian.
Score: McLaughlin.

P4.129 Today Is Born Our Saviour:
Responsorial Psalm for Christmas.
(1976) 4'
For: Soprano, chorus(mixed), harp,
chimes. Written for ABC-TV program in
honor of the American Bicentennial.
First performed: Dec. 25, 1976;
Providence, R.I. Laetita Blain, soprano;
Peloquin Chorale; Anne Marguerite
Michaud, harp; Everett Beale, chimes;
C. Alexander Peloquin, conductor.

P4.130 Triple Amen. (1965) 30"
For: chorus(mixed) and congregation.
Commissioned by: Liturgical Conference
of Washington, D.C. *First performed:*
Aug. 27, 1964; St. Louis, Mo. National
Choir, C. Alexander Peloquin,
conductor.
Vocal score: Summy Birchard.

P4.131 Turba Choruses from the
Passion of St. Matthew as Sung on
the Second Sunday of
the Passion. *For:* chorus(men)(3-part).
Text: Liber usualis. Dedicated to:
Russell Davis. *First performed:* 1958;
St. John's Seminary, Boston.
Vocal score: McLaughlin, 1958. BPL

P4.132 Unless You Become: A Full
Children's Liturgy. (1979) 45'
For: voice, narrator, chorus(SATB),
chorus(unison), instrumental
ensemble(flute, trumpets(2),
trombones(2), timpani, percussion,
glockenspiel, organ, double bass).
Commissioned by: National Shrine of
Our Lady of the Snows, Belleville, Ill.
First performed: Aug. 1979; Belleville,
Ill.
Score & parts: G.I.A.
Vocal score: G.I.A.
Parts(congregation): G.I.A.
Disc: Gregorian Institute Records. C.
Alexander Peloquin, conductor.

P4.133 Upon This Night. (1954)
For: chorus(SATB) and organ. *Text:*
Omer Goulet. *Dedication:* To my
mother.
Vocal score: McLaughlin, 1954. BPL
Vocal score: G.I.A.

We Are His People. *See* Psalm 100.

Why O Lord, Do You Stand Aloof? *See*
Psalm 9.

P4.134 Winter Is Past. (1975) 5'
For: narrator, chorus, harp. *Text:* Bible,
N.T., John and Bible, N.T., Luke. *First
performed:* Dec. 25, 1975. Elizabeth
White, narrator; Anne Marguerite
Michaud, harp; Peloquin Chorale.

P5 MALCOLM C. PEYTON

Born January 12, 1932, in New York
City. Moved to Boston area 1965.
Education: studied composition with
Roger Sessions and Edward T. Cone
(Princeton University, B.A., 1954,
M.F.A., 1956); Wolfgang Fortner, Aaron
Copland. *Awards:* Woodrow Wilson
Award (1955), Fulbright Fellowship
(1956), American Academy and Institute
of Arts and Letters, Academy Institute
Award (1980). *Related activities:* pianist;
served on the faculties of Princeton
University (1960-61) and New England
Conservatory (1965-). NEC

WORKS

P5.1 Adagio. (1954) 7'
For: string quartet.
Score: ms. in composer's hand.
Score: reprod. of ms.

P5.2 The Blessed Virgin Compared to
the Air We Breathe. (1973) 7'
For: chorus(SATB). *Text:* Gerard Manley
Hopkins. *Dedicated to:* Lorna Cooke
deVaron. *First performed:* Mar. 14,
1974; New England Conservatory. NEC
Concert Choir, Lorna Cooke deVaron,
conductor.
Vocal score: Mobart, 1977. NEC
Disc: Composers Recordings, nyp.

Cassette: recording of first performance. NEC
Cassette: Dec. 10, 1980; New England Conservatory. NEC Chorus, Lorna Cooke deVaron, conductor. NEC

Cello Piece. *See* Piece, Violoncello.

P5.3 Chamber Cantata. (1956-58) 29'
For: Soprano, Tenor, flute, oboe, clarinet, clarinet(bass), trumpet, horn, trombone. 2 movements. *Text: Chamber Music* by James Joyce. *First performed:* Oct. 1958; New York City. Shirley Emmons, soprano; Ray DeVoll, tenor; unidentified instrumentalists, Daniel Saidenberg, conductor.
Score: ms. in composer's hand.
Score & parts: reprod. of ms.
Reel: Apr. 1977; Susan Carlson, soprano; David Dusing, tenor; unidentified instrumentalists, Chris Carlson, conductor.

P5.4 Choruses from e.e. cummings. (1967) 7'
For: chorus(mixed) and chorus(spoken). 5 movements. *Text:* e.e. cummings.
Commissioned by: NEC Chorus. *First performed:* Apr. 1968; New England Conservatory. NEC Chorus, John Arterton, conductor.
Vocal score: Mobart, 1979. NEC
Cassette: May 7, 1971; New England Conservatory (3 movements). NEC Chorus, Lorna Cooke deVaron, conductor. NEC

P5.5 Concertine. (1980-) 18'
For: chamber orchestra(1-1-1(bcl)-1; 1-1-1-1; perc(3); pf; str(1-0-1-1-1)).
Movements: Fantasy in March Tempi; Interlude; (3rd movement in progress). Earlier version titled Fantasia, Interlude and.... *Commissioned by:* Collage. *First performed:* Feb. 23, 1981; Sanders Theatre, Harvard University. Collage, Gunther Schuller, conductor.
Score: ms. in composer's hand.
Score: reprod. of ms.
Score: APNM, nyp.
Parts: ms.

Parts: APNM, nyp. Rental.
Reel: recording of first performance.

[Concerto, Violin]
P5.6 Concerto. (1959) 12'
For: violin and orchestra(2-2-2-2; 2-2-2-0; str). 2 movements.
Commissioned by: Princeton Symphony.
First performed: Dec. 1960; Princeton, N.J. Joseph Kovacs, violin; Princeton Symphony, Nicholas Harsanyi, conductor.
Score: ms. in composer's hand.

P5.7 Fantasia, Interlude and... (1975) 8'
For: chamber orchestra. 2 movements. Later version titled Concertine. *First performed:* May 10, 1977; New England Conservatory. NEC Contemporary Music Ensemble, Gunther Schuller, conductor.
Score.
Cassette: recording of first performance. NEC

P5.8 The Lamb. (1962) 8'
For: chorus(SA), flute, oboe, English horn, strings. *Text:* William Blake. Companion piece to The Shepherd.
Score.

P5.9 Night. (1961) 7' 30"
For: chorus and organ. *Text:* William Blake.
Vocal score: ms. in composer's hand.

P5.10 Nocturnes. (1978) 6'
For: viola. *Movements:* Elegie; Berceuse.
First performed: May 1979; New York City. Lois Martin.
Score: APNM, 1981.
Cassette: Mar. 9, 1981; New England Conservatory; in *Enchanted Circle.* Virginia Haines. NEC

[Piece, Violoncello]
P5.11 Cello Piece. (1971) 4'
Dedicated to: Ronald Clearfield. *First performed:* Dec. 1971; New England Conservatory. Ronald Clearfield.
Score: Mobart, 1978.
Reel: Apr. 14, 1975. WGBH
Reel: Sept. 30, 1979; First and Second

Church, Boston; Dinosaur Annex.
Thomas Flaherty. WGBH
Cassette: Jan. 19, 1972; New England
Conservatory. Ronald Clearfield. NEC
Cassette: Apr. 25, 1972; New England
Conservatory. Ronald Clearfield. NEC
Cassette: May 8, 1975; New England
Conservatory. Bruce Coppock. NEC
Cassette: Dec. 15, 1977; New England
Conservatory. Sato Knudsen. NEC
Cassette: Apr. 5, 1979; New England
Conservatory. Thomas Flaherty. NEC

[Pieces, String Orchestra]
P5.12 Two Pieces for String Orchestra.
(1955) 11'
Commissioned by: Princeton Symphony.
First performed: 1956; Princeton, N.J.
Princeton Symphony, Nicholas Harsanyi,
conductor.
Score: ms. in composer's hand. *Score &
parts.*

P5.13 Quintet for Strings. (1953) 11'
For: violins(2), viola, violoncellos(2). 2
movements. *First performed:* Aug.
1953; Berkshire Music Center,
Tanglewood.
Score: ms. in composer's hand.
Score: reprod. of ms.

P5.14 Rondo. (1952) 5'
For: pianos(2). *First performed:* May
1952; Princeton, N.J. William Stewart
and Malcolm Peyton. *Score.*

P5.15 The Shepherd. (1962)
For: chorus(TB), horns, strings. *Text:*
William Blake. Companion piece to his
The Lamb. *Score.*

[Songs from Shakespeare]
P5.16 Four Songs from Shakespeare.
(1959) 12'
For: Mezzo Soprano, clarinets(2), violin,
viola, violoncello. *Text:* from the
Sonnets of William Shakespeare.
Contents: Music to Hear; Orpheus with
His Lute; Blow, Blow Thou Winter
Wind; Lo, in the Orient. *First
performed:* Mar. 1960; Carnegie Recital
Hall, New York City. Shirley Suddock,
mezzo soprano; unidentified

instrumentalists, Gustave Meier,
conductor.
Score: Mobart.
Cassette: Apr. 25, 1979; New England
Conservatory; in *Music about Music.*
Kimberly Bernhardt, mezzo soprano;
NEC Contemporary Ensemble, John
Heiss, conductor. NEC

P5.17 Songs from Walt Whitman. (1977)
18'
For: Mezzo Soprano, violin, piano.
Text: from *The Leaves of Grass* by Walt
Whitman. *Contents:* O Me! O Life!;
Roots and Leaves Themselves Alone;
Darest Thou Now O Soul; Scented
Herbage of My Breast; Warble for
Lilac-Time. *Dedicated to:* Bethany
Beardslee. *First performed:* Apr. 5,
1979; New England Conservatory.
Bethany Beardslee, mezzo soprano; Eric
Rosenblith, violin; Malcolm Peyton,
piano.
Score: Mobart, nyp.
Disc: Composers Recordings CRI SD
466, 1982. Bethany Beardslee, mezzo
soprano; Linda Quan, violin; Malcolm
Peyton, piano. NEC MIT W
Cassette: recording of first
performance. NEC
Cassette: March 9, 1981; New England
Conservatory; in *Enchanted Circle.*
Kimberly Bernhardt, mezzo soprano;
Kenneth Sugita, violin; Malcolm Peyton,
piano. NEC

P5.18 Sonnets from John Donne.
(1968-81) 8'
For: Bass Baritone, horn, trombone,
viola, violoncello, double bass. *Text:*
from *Holy Sonnets* by John Donne.
Contents: Why Are We by All Creatures
Waited On?; If Poysonous Minerals...;
As Due by Many Titles...; O to Vex
Me...; I Am a Little World...; What If
This Were the World's Last Night?;
This Is My Playe's Last Scene. *First
performed:* Mar. 1967; New England
Conservatory (Movements 2, 3, 7).
Jesse Coston, bass baritone;
unidentified instrumentalists, Malcolm
Peyton, conductor.
Score & parts: APNM.

Cassette: Apr. 5, 1979; New England Conservatory. Dinosaur Annex. NEC

P5.19 Suite. (1955) 8' 30"
For: clarinet. 4 movements. *First performed:* May 1955; Princeton, N.J.
Score: APNM.
Cassette: Nov. 20, 1978; New England Conservatory; in *Enchanted Circle*. Eric Thomas. NEC

P5.20 Warble Me Now. (1972) 2'
For: chorus(women). *Text:* Walt Whitman. *Vocal score.*

P6 DANIEL PINKHAM

Born June 5, 1923, in Lynn, Mass.
Education: studied composition with A. Tillman Merritt, Walter Piston, Archibald T. Davison, Aaron Copland, (Harvard University, A.B., 1943, A.M., 1944); Arthur Honegger, Samuel Barber (Berkshire Music Center, Tanglewood); Nadia Boulanger; harpsichord with Claude Jean Chiasson, Putnam Aldrich, Wanda Landowska; organ with E. Power Biggs, choral conducting with G. Wallace Woodworth; orchestral conducting with Stanley Chapple.
Awards: Fulbright Fellowship (1950), Ford Foundation Fellowship (1962), Litt. D. (Hon., Nebraska Wesleyan University, 1976), Mus. D. (Hon., Adrian College, 1977), Mus. D. (Hon., Westminster Choir College, 1979); American Academy of Arts and Sciences (member). *Related activities:* served on the faculties of Boston Conservatory, Simmons College, Boston University, Harvard University; currently on the faculty of New England Conservatory and music director of King's Chapel, Boston. NEC

WORKS

Acclamation. *See* Easter Set. Acclamation.

Alleluia. *See* Easter Set. Alleluia.

P6.1 Amens. 3'
For: Soprano, Alto, Tenor, Bass, tape.
Vocal score: Ione.
Tape: Ione.

P6.2 Angelus ad pastores ait. 2' 30"
For: chorus(SSA), trumpets(3)(optional), trombones(3), tuba. *Text: Liber usualis.*
First performed: Saint Cecilia Society, Theodore Marier, conductor.
Score & parts: King, 1959. BCM
Reel: Dec. 12, 1974. Boston Conservatory Chorale, William A. Seymour, conductor. BCM

Apollo's Revels. *See* The Garden of Artemis.

P6.3 Ascension Cantata. (1970) 11'
For: chorus(SATB), band, organ(ad lib.)
Text: Bible, O.T., Psalm 47:5 and Propers from the *Liber usualis.*
Commissioned by: Ohio State University, Columbus, Ohio. *Dedicated to:* Maurice Casey.
Score & parts: Ione, 1972. Rental.
Vocal score: Ione, 1972. BPL HU NEC

P6.4 Aspects of the Apocalypse. (1972) 7'
For: tape.
Tape: Ione, 1972.

P6.5 Ave Maria. 2'
For: Soprano and Alto. *Text:* Bible, N.T., Luke. *First performed:* Pine Manor Junior College. Edward Low, conductor.
Vocal score: Associated, 1962. BPL

P6.6 Ave verum Corpus. 2' 30"
For: Soprano, Alto, Tenor, Bass, organ(optional). Motet. *Text: Liber usualis. First performed:* King's Chapel, Boston. King's Chapel Choir.
Vocal score: E.C. Schirmer.

P6.7 Baptism Canon. (1974) 2'
For: chorus(treble)(3-part) and organ. Anthem. *Text:* Bible, N.T., Matthew 28:19. *Dedicated to:* David Bradford Osgood. *First performed:* 1974; King's

Chapel, Boston. King's Chapel Choir.
Vocal score: ms. in composer's hand.
NEC
Vocal score: Peters, 1977. BPL

Be Gracious to Me, O God. *See* The
Passion of Judas. Be Gracious to Me,
O God.

P6.8 Beggar's Opera.
Withdrawn.

P6.9 Behold, How Good and How
Pleasant; Psalm Motet V. (1966) 2'
For: chorus(SATB) and organ or
piano(optional). *Text:* Bible, O.T., Psalm.
Dedicated to: Hope and Dennis Ehn.
First performed: 1966.
Vocal score: ms. in composer's hand.
HUh
Vocal score: Peters, 1967. BPL

P6.10 Blessings. 16'
For: organ. *Movements:* Jacob Wrestles
with the Angel and Receives His
Blessing; The Lord Appears to Isaac
and Blesses Him; God's Blessing on
Mary and on the Fruit of Her Womb;
The Blessing Before the Throne of
God. *Commissioned by:* John Holtz for
the 1977 Hartt College of Music
International Contemporary Organ
Music Festival. *First performed:* June
6, 1977; Trinity College. John Holtz.
Score: E.C. Schirmer, 1977. BPL HU NEC
W

Bow Down Mountain. *See* Hymn No. 2.

P6.11 The Call of Isaiah.
For: Soprano, Alto, Tenor, Bass,
chorus(women) or chorus(men), organ,
timpani, percussion(ad lib.), tape.
Anthem. *Text:* Bible, O.T., Isaiah 6:1-9.
First performed: May 7, 1971; Jordan
Hall, Boston; in A Festival of New
England Composers Past and Present.
NEC Chorus, Lorna Cooke deVaron,
conductor.
Score: Ione, 1971. BPL HU T
Tape: Ione, 1971. BPL
Cassette: recording of first
performance. NEC

P6.12 Canticle of Praise. (1965) 13'
For: Soprano, chorus(SATB), brass
ensemble(trumpets(in C)(3), horns(2)
trombones(2), trombone(bass), tuba),
timpani, percussion(2)(glockenspiel,
vibraphone). 3 movements. *Text:* Bible,
N.T., Apocrypha: Song of the Three
Holy Children, 29-68. *Commissioned by:*
War Memorial Auditorium Dedication
Committee, Mayor John F. Collins,
Honorary Chairman. *First performed:*
Beverly Sills, soprano; G. Wallace
Woodworth, conductor.
Vocal score: Ione, 1965. MIT
Vocal score: Ione, 1968. BPL NEC T

P6.13 Cantilena and Capriccio. (1958) 6'
37"
For: violin and harpsichord.
Score: Ione, 1972. BPL BU
Parts: Ione, 1972.
Disc: Composers Recordings CRI 109, [
1972] Robert Brink, violin and Daniel
Pinkham, harpsichord. BrU BU HU MIT
NEC W
Cassette: Oct. 30, 1969; New England
Conservatory. Diane Mauser, violin and
Elizabeth Kulbach, harpsichord. NEC
Cassette: Jan. 25, 1972; New England
Conservatory. Eric Rosenblith, violin
and Blanche Winogron, harpsichord.
NEC

[Canzonets]
P6.14 Five Canzonets. (1958) 7'
For: chorus(SA). *Text:* Old English
nursery rhymes. *Contents:* The Nut Tree;
The Blossom; Daybreak; Calico Pie;
Spring. *First performed:* Pine Manor
Junior College. Edward Low, conductor.
Vocal score: Associated, 1960. BPL L
Reel: Sept. 23, 1973. Isabella Stewart
Gardner Museum. WGBH

Capriccio *See* Cantilena and Capriccio.

Carol. *See* Easter Set. Carol.

A Caroll or Himme for Christmas. *See*
The Sheepheards Song.

P6.15 Catacoustical Measures. (1964) 4'
30"

For: orchestra(3(&pic)-
2(&Ehn)-3(&bcl)-3(&cbsn); 4-4-4-1; timp,
perc; hp, cel, pf; str).
Score & parts: Peters. Rental.

Charm Me Asleep. *See* Songs on Old
English Texts. Charm Me Asleep.

P6.16 Christmas Cantata. (1957) 9' 30"
For: choruses(2)(double), brass choirs(2),
organ(optional). *Dedication:* For the NEC
Chorus, Lorna Cooke deVaron,
conductor. *First performed:* Dec. 1957;
Jordan Hall, Boston. NEC Chorus, Lorna
Cooke deVaron, conductor.
Vocal score: King, 1958. BPL BU HU
HUm NEC NU T
Disc: in *A Christmas Festival*, Angel
SF-36016, 1967. Roger Wagner Chorale,
Roger Wagner, conductor. NEC
Disc: Delta DRS69 676. HU
Disc: in *The Road Not Taken; 20th
Century Choral Music*, Northeastern
Records NR 103, 1980. Northeastern
University Choral Society, Jacobson,
conductor.
Reel: Dec. 12, 1972. Boston
Conservatory Chorale, William A.
Seymour, conductor. Boston
Conservatory Brass Ensemble, Sterling
Cossaboom, conductor.

[Christmas Cantata. Gloria; Arr.]
P6.17 Gloria.
For: trumpets(2), horn, trombone, organ.
Score: King.

P6.18 A Christmas Carol. (1948)
For: chorus(SATB). *Text:* Robert Hillyer.
Vocal score: ms. HU

P6.19 Christmas Eve. (1947) 2'
For: Soprano, Alto, Tenor, Bass. *Text:*
Robert Hillyer.
Vocal score: ms. in composer's hand.
HU
Vocal score: Ione.

P6.20 Come, Love We God. (1969)
For: chorus(SATB) and guitar or harp or
piano. *Text:* collected by Sir R. Shanne.
Vocal score: ms. in composer's hand.

HUh
Vocal score: Ione, 1970. BPL

P6.21 Company at the Creche. 8' 21"
For: Sopranos(2), Alto, Tenor, Baritone,
chorus(children), piano, glockenspiel.
Text: Norma Farber. *Contents:* Stork;
Dove; Caterpillar; Rooster; Spider;
Porcupine; Lion. *Commissioned by:*
United Methodist Church of
Worthington, Ohio.
Disc: in *Love Can Be Still*; Music on
Verses of Norma Farber, Northeastern
Records NR 201, 1981. Patti Dell and
Barbara Wallace, sopranos; Pamela
Gore, alto; Richard Conrad, tenor; Bryan
McNeil, baritone; Gary Wedow, piano;
Robert W. Cross, glockenspiel. NEC

[Concertante, Harpsichord, Guitar,
Chamber Orchrestra]
P6.22 Concertante. (1968) 12'
For: harpsichord, guitar, chamber
orchestra(0-0-0-0; 0-0-0-0; perc; str) or
organ. *Commissioned by:* Helen Keaney.
Score & parts: Peters, 1966, Rental.
NEC

Concertante, No. 1. *See* Concertante,
Violin, Harpsichord, String Orchestra.

Concertante, No. 2. *See* Concertante,
Violin and String Orchestra.

Concertante, No. 3. *See* Concertante,
Organ, Celeste, Percussion.

[Concertante, Organ, Brasses,
Percussion]
P6.23 Concertante. (1964) 12'
For: organ, trumpets(2), trombones(2),
percussion(2). *Movements:* Canzona;
Procession; Plaint. Written for the
dedication of the Peabody Memorial
Organ (Charles Fisk, builder), King's
Chapel, Boston. *First performed:* King's
Chapel, Boston. Leonard Raver, organ;
Daniel Pinkham, conductor.
Score: ms. in composer's hand. HUh
Score: Peters, 1966. BPL BU HU NEC
UMB
Parts: Peters, 1966. NEC

[Concertante, Organ, Celeste, Percussion]
P6.24 Concertante, No.3. (1962) 12'
For: organ, celeste, timpani, percussion(triangle, giant tamtam, small gong, medium gong, suspended cymbal, woodblock, snare drum, glockenspiel).
Movements: Aria; Scherzo; Elegy.
Commissioned by: American Guild of Organists, Boston Chapter for the dedication of the Peabody Memorial Organ (Charles Fisk, builder), King's Chapel, Boston.
Score: ms. in composer' hand. HU HUh
Score: reprod. of ms. NEC
Score: Peters, 1963. Be BPL BU HMA HU
Parts: Peters, 1963. Be BPL HMA NEC

[Concertante, Violin and String Orchestra]
P6.25 Concertante II.
Score & parts: Ione. Rental.

[Concertante, Violin, Harpsichord, String Orchestra]
P6.26 Concertante, No.1. (1954) 8'-9'
Movements: Introduction; Cantilena; Burlesca. *First performed:* Dec. 1954; Cambridge, Mass. Robert Brink, violin; Claude Jean Chiasson, harpsichord; Cambridge Festival Orchestra, Daniel Pinkham, conductor.
Score: American Composers Alliance, 1955. HU
Score: Ione. Rental.
Parts: American Composers Alliance.
Parts: Ione. Rental.
Disc: Composers Recordings, CRI 143, [1961] Robert Brink, violin; Claude Jean Chiasson, harpsichord; unidentified string orchestra; Izler Solomon, conductor. BrU BU HU MIT NEC W
Disc: MGM E 3245. Robert Brink, violin; Claude Jean Chiasson, harpsichord; MGM String Ensemble; Izler Solomon, conductor. BrU BU HU NEC

[Concertino, Organ and String Orchestra]
P6.27 Concertino. (1947) 12'
Movements: Intrada; Aria; Finale.
Dedicated to: E. Power Biggs.

Score: reprod. of ms. NEC
Score: American Composers Alliance.

[Concertino, Piano and Chamber Orchestra]
P6.28 Concertino in A for Small Orchestra and Obbligato Piano.
Score: American Composers Alliance. BPL
Score & parts: Ione. Rental.
Disc: Cambridge Festival Recordings XTV 14448. BCM

[Concerto, Celeste and Harpsichord]
P6.29 Concerto. (1955) 9' 27"
Movements: Prelude; Ricercare; Canzona.
Dedicated to: Henry Cowell. *First performed:* Nov. 1955; Columbia University. Edward Low, celeste and Daniel Pinkham, harpsichord.
Score: E.C. Schirmer, 1971. BPL BU HU
Disc: Composers Recordings CRI 109, [1972] Edward Low, celeste and Daniel Pinkham, harpsichord. BrU BU HU HU MIT NEC W

[Concerto, Organ and Chamber Orchestra]
P6.30 Organ Concerto. (1970) 21'
For: organ and chamber orchestra(0-0-0-0; 2-2-2-0; timp, perc(2); str).
Score & parts: Peters, 1970. Rental.

[Concerto, Violin]
P6.31 Violin Concerto.
For: violin and orchestra(1-2-0-0; 2-0-0-0; hp; str). *First performed:* Robert Brink, violin; unidentified orchestra, Daniel Pinkham, conductor.
Score: Ione.

Dancer, How You Dance. *See* Poems of Norma Farber. Dancer, How You Dance.

P6.32 Daniel in the Lion's Den. 22'
For: narrator, Tenor, Bass Baritone, pianos(2), timpani, percussion. *Text:* Bible, O.T.; Bible, N.T., Apocrypha; John Newton.
Score: E.C. Schirmer, 1973. HU
Vocal score: E.C. Schirmer, 1974. BPL HU NEC

P6.33 The Death of the Witch of Endor. (1981) 12' 30"
For: alto, harpsichord, percussion. *First performed:* Oct. 13, 1981; New England Conservatory; in Enchanted Circle. Pamela Gore, alto; Larry Phillips, harpsichord; John Grimes, percussion.
Cassette: recording of first performance. NEC

P6.34 The Descent into Hell. (1980) 20'
For: Soprano, Tenor, Bass Baritone, chamber chorus(SATB)(12), chorus(SATB), brass ensemble(trumpets(3), horns(2), trombones(3)), percussion(timpani, glockenspiel, triangle, syspended cymbal, crash cymbals, giant tamtam, tambourine, bass drum, dumbeg or other hand drum), organ, tape. Stage work. *Text:* Daniel Pinkham, based on a Greek narrative describing the Harrowing of Hell as found in The Apocryphal New Testament, translated by M.R. James. *Contents:* Introit; Scene in Hell. *Commissioned by:* West Virginia Wesleyan College on the occasion of its 90th birthday. *First performed:* Oct. 17, 1980; Buckhannon, W. Va. Caroline Dees, soprano; Larry R. Parson, tenor; Peter Infanger, bass baritone; The Concert Chorale; Daniel Pinkham, conductor.
Score: Ione, 1980. HU NEC
Parts: Ione, 1980. Rental.

Divertimento. *See* Duet; Arr.

P6.35 Duet. (1954; rev. 1956) 7'
For: recorder(soprano) or oboe and harpsichord or harp. *Movements:* Prelude; Aria; Dithyramb; Recessional. *Commissioned by:* American Recorder Society, Boston Chapter, Arthur Loeb, president.
Score: ms. in composer's hand (version for recorder and harpsichord, 1954). HUh
Score & parts: American Composers Alliance, 1957. HU
Score & parts: Ione, 1969. MIT NEC

[Duet; Arr.]
P6.36 Divertimento. 7'
For: recorder(soprano) or oboe, harpsichord or harp, string orchestra.
Score & parts: Ione. Rental.

P6.37 Duo.
For: violin and violoncello. *Movements:* Preamble; Variations. *Dedicated to:* Aaron Copland.
Score: reprod. of ms. L

P6.38 Easter Cantata. (1960) 11'-12'
For: chorus(mixed), brass ensemble(trumpets(4), horns(2), trombones(3), tuba(ad lib.)), timpani, percussion(2), celeste. 4 movements. *Text:* Bible, O.T., Psalm 68:18,32-34; Bible, O.T., Psalm 118:24; Bible, N.T., Matthew 28:5-7; Bible, N.T., John 20:13. *Dedicated to:* Herff Applewhite; Lorna Cooke deVaron; Warner Imig; Harold Schmidt.
Score & parts: Peters. Rental.
Vocal score: Peters, 1962. BCM BPL BrU BU HU HUm MIT NEC T W

Easter Canticle. *See* When God Arose.

P6.39 Easter Set. (1973) 7'
For: Sopranos, chorus(SATB), timpani, percussion, tape. Aleatoric music. *Contents:* Alleliua; Acclamation; Carol (Now Is the Hour of Darkness Past) by Isaac Watts. *Commissioned by:* Saint Mary's College (Notre Dame, Ind). *First performed:* 1973; Notre Dame, Ind. Unidentified performers, Daniel Pinkham, conductor.
Vocal score: Ione, 1975. BPL NEC
Tape: Ione.

[Easter Set. Acclamation]
P6.40 Acclamation. (1973)
For: Sopranos, chorus(SATB), timpani, percussion, tape.
Vocal score: Ione, 1975. NEC
Tape: Ione.

[Easter Set. Alleluia]
P6.41 Alleluia. (1973)
For: Sopranos, chorus(SATB), timpani,

percussion, tape.
Vocal score: Ione, 1975. HU NEC
Tape: Ione.

[Easter Set. Carol]
P6.42 Carol. (1973)
For: Sopranos, chorus(SATB), timpani,
percussion, tape.
Vocal score: Ione, 1975. NEC
Tape: Ione.

P6.43 Eclogue. (1968) 3'
For: flute, harpsichord, handbells(2).
Dedicated to: Eric Herz and Leonard
Raver. *First performed:* Eric Herz, flute;
Leonard Raver, harpsichord;
handbells(off-stage).
Score: Ione, 1971. BPL HU MIT NEC

[Elegies]
P6.44 Four Elegies.
For: Tenor, chorus(SATB), tape,
chamber orchestra(0-0(Ehn)-0-1;
1-0-0-0;org(chamber), str(one per part or
orchestral)). *Contents:* To His Dying
Brother, Master William Herrick (Robert
Herrick); Upon the Death of a Friend
(Richard Crashaw); Silence, and Stealth
of Days (Henry Vaughan); At the Round
Earth's Imagin'd Corners (John Donne).
Dedication: In Memoriam, Ralph A. Hall.
Score & parts: Ione.
Vocal score: Ione, 1979. NEC
Tape: Ione.

P6.45 Elegy. (1947) 2'
For: chorus(SATB). *Text:* Robert Hillyer.
Vocal score: ms. NEC
Vocal score: E.C. Schirmer, 1964. BPL
NEC
Disc: in *Modern American Madrigals*,
Composers Recordings CRI 102, 1956
(titled Folk Song: Elegy). The Randolph
Singers, David Randolph, conductor.
MIT NEC T W

P6.46 Elegy. (1949) 2'
For: voice and piano. *Text:* Robert
Hillyer. *Dedicated to:* Nell Tangeman.
Score: ms. in composer's hand. Huh
Score: reprod. of ms. NEC
Score: Ione, 1949.
Score: E.C. Schirmer, 1964. NEC

P6.47 An Emily Dickinson Mosaic.
(1961) 10'
For: chorus(SSAA) and chamber
orchestra(2-0-2-0; 0-0-0-0; perc; cel; str)
or piano. *Text:* Emily Dickinson.
Contents: The Brain Is Wider Than the
Sky; The Heart Is the Capital of the
Mind; The Mind Lives on the Heart; To
Be Alive; Exhilaration Is the Breeze;
Each Life Conveys to Some Centre.
Commissioned by: Mount Holyoke
College. *First performed:* 1961.
Score & parts: Peters. Rental.
Vocal score: Peters, 1963. BPL BU HU
HUm

P6.48 Envoi.
For: English horn, horns(2), strings.
Withdrawn.

[Epigrams]
P6.49 Seven Epigrams. (1944)
For: voice(medium) and piano. *Text:*
Robert Hillyer. *Dedicated to:* Isabel
French (Nos. 1, 6, 7).
Score: reprod. of ms. (Nos. 1, 6, 7).
NEC

P6.50 Epiphanies. 30'
For: organ. *Commissioned by:* House of
Hope Presbyterian Church, St. Paul,
Minn.
Score: E.C. Schirmer, 1980. HU NEC

P6.51 Etude. 3'
For: clarinet.
Score: Ione, 1969. BPL

P6.52 Evergreen. 3'
For: chorus(unison),
instruments(unspecified), tape(optional).
Text: Robert Hillyer.
Vocal score: Ione, 1974. NU

P6.53 Fanfare, Aria and Echo. (1962) 6'
For: horns(2) and timpani. *Dedicated to:*
Philip Nesbit and Joseph Rinello.
Score: reprod. of ms. NEC
Score: Peters, 1963. MIT NEC
Study score: Peters, 1963. BPL BU HU
NEC UMB

P6.54 A Fanfare of Praise. 9' 25"
For: chorus. *Contents:* Introit; Alleluia;
Psalm. *First performed:* Dec. 17, 1974;
New England Conservatory; in A
Program of American Religious Music
from Pilgrims to Present. NEC Chorus,
Lorna Cooke deVaron, conductor.
Cassette: recording of first
performance. NEC

P6.55 Fanfares. 9' 30"
For: Tenor, chorus(SATB),
chorus(unison)(optional) or congregation,
horn, trumpets(2), trombone, timpani,
percussion(2), organ. *Contents:* Prophecy;
Proclamation; Alleluia; Psalm.
Score & parts: Ione.
Vocal score: Ione, 1975. BU HU NU
Reel: Mar. 19, 1978; Sanders Theatre,
Harvard University. Kim Scown, tenor;
Masterworks Chorale, Allen Lannom,
conductor. WGBH

P6.56 Farewell, Vain World. 2'
For: Soprano, Alto, Tenor, Bass. *Text:*
Robert Hillyer.
Vocal score: Ione, 1964. BPL

P6.57 The Faucon. (1947) 3'
For: voice and piano. *Text:* anon.
Dedicated to: Janet Fairbank.
Score: reprod. of ms. HU NEC
Score: Row, 1949. BPL HU L NEC
Score: C. Fischer.

Fawn Bridge. *See* Poems of Norma
Farber. Fawn Bridge.

P6.58 Festival Magnificat and Nunc
dimittis. (1961) 5'
For: Soprano, Alto, Tenor, Bass;
optional organ or piano, horn,
trumpets(2), trombone. Canticles. *Text:*
Bible, N.T.
Score: Peters, 1963. BPL HU
Parts: Peters.
Vocal score: Peters.

Folk Song. *See* Elegy. (1947)

P6.59 For Evening Draws On. (1973) 6'
36"

For: English horn, organ, tape.
Dedicated to: John Holtz for the 1973
Hartt College of Music Contemporary
Organ Music Workshop, University of
Hartford.
Score: E.C. Schirmer, 1976. BPL NEC
Parts: E.C. Schirmer, 1976. BPL HU NEC
W
Tape: E.C. Schirmer.
Disc: Golden Crest NEC 114, 1975.
Kenneth Roth, English horn and Larry
Phillips, organ. BrU BU HU MIT NEC

P6.60 The Garden of Artemis or
Apollo's Revels: A Tableau Chantant
in the Antique Manner. (1948) 24' *For:*
Soprano, Alto, Baritone, chorus(women),
flute, clarinet, violin, viola, violoncello.
Chamber opera. *Text:* Robert Hillyer.
Dedicated to: Miss Fanny P. Mason.
First performed: Oct. 17, 1948; Sanders
Theatre, Harvard University. Nancy
Trickey, soprano; Eunice Alberts, alto;
Paul Tibbetts, baritone; Daniel Pinkham,
conductor.
Score: reprod. of ms. HU
Score: Ione.
Disc: Cambridge Festival Recordings,
XTV 144 48, n.d. BCM

Gloria. *See* Christmas Cantata. Gloria.

P6.61 Glory Be to God: Motet for
Christmas Day. (1955) 1' 30"
For: chorus(SATB)(2) and
organ(optional). *Dedicated to:* Alfred
Nash Patterson.
Vocal score: Ione, 1966. BPL NEC T
Disc: in *Sing unto the Lord a New
Song*, Composers Recordings CRI 191,
1964. Mid-America Chorale, John
Dexter, conductor. BCM MIT NEC W

P6.62 God Is a Spirit.
For: chorus(SATB) and organ.
Vocal score: Ione, 1966. BPL T

P6.63 Going and Staying. (1975) 2'
For: chorus(women), guitar(electric),
tape (or celeste or harp or orchestra
bells). *Text:* Norma Farber.
Commissioned by: Wayne State

University Women's Chorale, Douglas K. Belland, conductor.
Vocal score: ms. in composer's hand. NEC
Vocal score: reprod. of composer's ms. NEC
Vocal score: Ione, 1975.
Parts: Ione.

P6.64 Grace Is Poured Abroad: Psalm Motet VII. (1970) 2'
For: Soprano, Alto, Tenor, Bass, organ or piano. *First performed:* Aug. 16, 1970; Long Beach, Calif.
Vocal score: ms. in composer's hand. Huh
Vocal score: reprod. of ms. HUh
Vocal score: Peters.

Happy Is the Man. *See* The Passion of Judas. Happy Is the Man.

The Hatch. *See* Poems of Norma Farber. The Hatch.

P6.65 He Scatters the Snow. (1973) 7' 23"
For: clarinet and tape. *Text:* Bible, O.T., Ecclesiastes 43:17-18. *Dedicated to:* Philip Fields.
Score & perf. dir: Ione, 1974. NEC
Tape: Ione, 1974.
Reel: Oct. 11, [1977 or 1979?] Boston Musica Viva concert. William Wrzesien, clarinet. WGBH
Cassette: Jan. 24, 1975; New England Conservatory; in *Electric Weekend*. Bruce Creditor, clarinet. NEC

Heaven-Haven. *See* Poems of Gerard Manley Hopkins. Heaven-Haven.

P6.66 Henry Was a Worthy King. 2'
For: chorus(mixed). Madrigal. *Text:* Robert Hillyer.
Vocal score: Ione, 1963. NU

P6.67 The Hour Glass. 2'
For: voice(high) and piano. *Text:* Ben Jonson. *Dedicated to:* Eleanor Davis.
Score: E.C. Schirmer, 1964. NEC

P6.68 How Precious Is Thy Loving Kindness: Psalm Motet VI. (1967) 1'
For: Soprano, Alto, Tenor, Bass, organ or piano(ad lib.) *Text:* Bible, O.T., Psalm 36:7-9. *Dedicated to:* Carl Scovel.
Vocal score: ms. in composer's hand. NEC
Vocal score: Peters, 1968. BPL

P6.69 Hymn No. 1.
For: chorus(unison) and organ, or chorus(SATB) and organ(optional). *Text:* Why Sleepest Thou by Norma Farber.
Vocal score: reprod. of composer's ms. NEC

P6.70 Hymn No. 2. (1955)
For: chorus(unison) and organ, or chorus(SATB) and organ(optional). *Text:* Bow Down Mountain by Norma Farber. *Commissioned by:* Albert Crist-Janer.
Vocal score: reprod. of ms. NEC
Vocal score: in *American Hymns Old and New*, Columbia University Press, 1980. MIT NEC W

P6.71 I Have Preached Righteousness: Psalm Motet VIII. (1967) 1'
For: Soprano, Alto, Tenor, Bass, organ or piano.
Vocal score: Peters.

P6.72 I Saw an Angel. (1974)
For: Soprano, Alto, Tenor, Bass, chorus(SATB), tape.
Vocal score: Ione.

P6.73 I Was Glad.
For: chorus(mixed) and organ˙ or piano(optional). Anthem. *Text:* Bible, O.T., Psalm 122.
Vocal score: Associated, 1963. BPL
Vocal score: in *AMP Contemporary Choral Collection*, Associated, 1969. HU W

P6.74 If Ye Love Me.
For: chorus(SSA) and organ. Anthem. *Text:* Bible, N.T., John 14:15, 16, 18, 21.
Vocal score: E.C. Schirmer, 1964. BPL

P6.75 In grato jubilo.
For: Soprano, double bass, wind ensemble(flute, oboe, clarinet, bassoon, horn, trumpets(3), trombones(2)). *Text:* David Thompson Watson McCord. Written for retirement banquet of Serge Koussevitzky. *First performed:* Phyllis Curtin and members of the Boston Symphony Orchestra.

P6.76 In the Beginning of Creation. (1970)
For: chorus(mixed) and tape. Anthem. *Text:* Bible, O.T., Genesis 1:1-3. *First performed:* June 1970; Westminster Choir College.
Score: Ione, 1970. BPL HU NU T
Tape: Ione, 1970. NU
Cassette: May 7, 1971; New England Conservatory; in *A Festival of New England Composers Past and Present.* NEC Chorus, Lorna Cooke deVaron, conductor. NEC
Cassette: Apr. 18, 1978; New England Conservatory. NEC Repertory Chorus, John Cice, conductor. NEC

P6.77 In Youth Is Pleasure. (1953; rev. 1968)
For: chorus(unison) and guitar or piano, or voice(medium) and piano. *Text:* Robert Wever. *Dedicated to:* Hugues Cuenod.
Score: ms. in composer's hand (later version). NEC
Score: reprod. of ms. (earlier version). NEC
Score: Row, 1953 (earlier version). NEC
Score: Ione, 1968 (later version).

P6.78 International Geophysical Year.
For: horns(2), celeste, harpsichord, string orchestra. Withdrawn.

P6.79 Invention No. 1.
For: English horn, clarinet(bass), string orchestra. Withdrawn.

P6.80 Invention No. 2.
For: English horn, clarinet(bass), string orchestra. Withdrawn.

P6.81 Intreat Me Not to Leave Thee.
For: Sopranos(2) and strings. Withdrawn.

P6.82 Jonah. (1966)
For: Mezzo Soprano, Tenor, Bass Baritone, chorus(mixed), orchestra(3(pic)-3(Ehn)-3(bcl)-2(cbsn); 4-3-3(btrb)-1; timp, perc(6), glock, vibra; hp, cel; str). Cantata. *Commissioned by:* Paderewski Fund for 100th anniversary of the New England Conservatory.
Score: Ione, 1967. BPL NEC
Parts: Ione.
Vocal score: Ione, 1967. HU T

P6.83 Jubilate Deo (O Be Joyful in the Lord).
For: chorus(mixed), chorus(SSA), chorus(treble unison)(optional), organ. Canticle. *Commissioned by:* Trinity Parish, Southport, Conn., James H. Litton, organist and choirmaster.
Vocal score: Ione, 1966. BPL NEC T

P6.84 The King and the Shepherds. (1974)
For: chorus(SATB). Madrigal. *Text:* Robert Hillyer.
Vocal score: Ione, 1978.

P6.85 The Lamb. (1947)
For: voice(treble) or chorus (treble) and guitar or piano. *Text:* William Blake.
Vocal score: Ione, 1970. T

[The Lamb; Arr.]
P6.86 The Lamb. (1952)
For: voice(high) and piano. *Text:* William Blake. *Dedicated to:* Janet Hayes.
Score: reprod. of ms. NEC

P6.87 The Lament of David. 5'
For: chorus(mixed) and tape. Anthem. *Text:* Bible, O.T., 2 Samuel 1:19-28. *Dedicated to:* Lorna Cooke deVaron on the occasion of her 25th year as choral conductor of the New England Conservatory.
Vocal score: E.C. Schirmer, 1974. NEC
Tape: E.C. Schirmer.

P6.88 The Lamentations of Jeremiah. 11'
For: chorus(SATB) and instrumental ensemble(trumpets(2), horns(2), trombones(2), double bass, timpani, percussion(2)). Anthem. *Text:* Bible, O.T., Lamentations 1:1-5.
Score & parts: Peters. Rental.
Vocal score: Peters, 1966. BPL HMA HU UMB

P6.89 Land of White Alice. 15'
For: alto, chorus(TTBB), orchestra. Film music. Withdrawn.

P6.90 The Leaf. (1955)
For: chorus(SATB). Madrigal. *Text:* Robert Hillyer. *Dedicated to:* Vose Greenough.
Vocal score: reprod. of ms. NEC
Vocal score: Ione, 1963. NU

[Lenten Poems of Richard Crashaw]
P6.91 Three Lenten Poems of Richard Crashaw. (196-) 5'
For: chorus(women), string quartet(with double bass optional) or string orchestra, handbells or celeste or harp or keyboard with handbells(optional).
Contents: On the Still Surviving Marks of Our Savior's Wounds; Upon the Body of Our Blessed Lord, Naked and Bloody; O Save Us Then.
Score & parts: Ione. Rental.
Vocal score: Ione, 1965. BPL HU NEC

[Lenten Poems of Richard Crashaw; Arr.]
P6.92 Three Lenten Poems of Richard Crashaw. (196-) 5'
For: chorus(mixed) and orchestra.
Score & parts: Ione, 1965. Rental.
Vocal score: Ione, 1965.

P6.93 Lessons. (1971) 10'
For: harpsichord. 6 movements.
Commissioned by: Helen Keaney.
Score: Peters, 1973. BPL BU HMA HU MIT NEC T

P6.94 Let Us Now Praise Famous Men: Five Motets. (1966) 8'
For: chorus(SA) and instruments (unspecified)(optional)(doubling). *Text:* Bible, O.T., Ecclesiastes; Bible, N.T., Revelations. *Contents:* The Lord Brought Forth Moses; The Lord Exalted Aaron; David Played with Lions; Solomon Reigned in Days of Peace; The Prophet Elijah Rose.
Score: E.C. Schirmer, 1970. BPL T

P6.95 Letters from St. Paul. (1965)
For: voice(high) and organ or piano.
Text: Bible, N.T.
Vocal score: E.C. Schirmer, 1971. BPL

P6.96 Listen to Me: Five Motets. (1965) 5'
For: Soprano, Alto, oboe(optional), English horn(optional), violin(optional), viola(optional).
Score: Ione, 1965. T

P6.97 A Litany. (1961) 2'
For: Sopranos(2) and keyboard. *Text:* Phineas Fletcher.
Score: ms. in composer's hand. HUh
Score: Associated. L

P6.98 Little Brass Book.
For: brasses and percussion.
Movements: Tucket I; Tucket II; Tucket III; Tucket IV; Intrada.
Score: ms. in composer's hand (titled A Tacket). HUh
Score & parts: E.C. Schirmer, 1980. HU
Cassette: Oct. 13, 1981; New England Conservatory; in *Enchanted Circle* (Tucket I). David Washburn and Roger Zacks. NEC

P6.99 Liturgies. (1974; rev. 1975) 14'
For: timpani, organ, tape. 3 movements. *Dedicated to:* John Grimes.
First performed: June 7, 1974; Hartt College of Music. Judith Chilnick, timpani; Leonard Raver, organ; Daniel Pinkham, tape.
Score: E.C. Schirmer, 1976. BPL HU NEC W
Tape: E.C. Schirmer.
Disc: Golden Crest NEC 114, 1975. John Grimes, timpani and Larry Phillips, organ. BrU BU HU MIT NEC

P6.100 The Lord Has Established His Throne: Psalm Motet X. 1'
For: chorus(SATB) and organ or piano(optional).
Vocal score: Peters, 1975. BPL

P6.101 Love Came Down at Christmas. (1973) 2'
For: Soprano, Alto, Tenor, Bass, organ(optional). *Text:* Christina Georgina Rossetti.
Vocal score: Ione.

P6.102 Love Can Be Still. 5'
For: chorus(SSATB) and piano(optional).
Text: Norma Farber. *Contents:* Take Me Walking in Your Mind; After the Storm a Star; Love, Bone-Quiet, Said; Da Capo. *Commissioned by:* Kansas State University Concert Choir, Rod Walker, director.
Vocal score: Ione, 1978. NEC
Disc: in *Love Can Be Still; Music on Verses of Norma Farber*, Northeastern NR 201, 1981. Patti Dell and Barbara Wallace, sopranos; Pamela Gore, alto; Richard Conrad, tenor; Bryan McNeil, baritone; Gary Wedrow, piano. NEC
Cassette: Oct. 13, 1981; New England Conservatory; in *Enchanted Circle*. Patti Dell, Barbara Wallace, sopranos; Pamela Gore, alto; Richard Conrad, tenor; Bryan McNeil, baritone; Gary Wedow, piano. NEC

P6.103 Love's Yoke. (1980) 5' 40"
For: chorus. *Movements:* Solitary Shepherd's Song; We Love; Merrily, Cheerily.
Cassette: Apr. 21, 1981; New England Conservatory. NEC Recital Chorus, Johanna Hill Simpson, conductor. NEC

[Lyric Scenes]
P6.104 Three Lyric Scenes. (1948) 10'
For: voice and string quartet. *Text:* W.H. Auden.
Parts: reprod. of ms. NEC

[Lyric Scenes. Sing Agreeably of Love]
P6.105 Sing Agreeably of Love. (1948)

3'
For: voice and string quartet. *Text:* W.H. Auden.
Score: Row, 1949. BPL HU L
Parts: Row, 1949.

[Lyric Scenes. Sing Agreeably of Love; Arr]
P6.106 Sing Agreeably of Love. (1948)
For: voice and piano. *Text:* W.H. Auden.
Score: Row, 1949. BPL

Madrigal. *See* Piping Anne and Husky Paul.

[Madrigals]
P6.107 Six Madrigals.
Reel: Nov. 20, 1957; Brookline Public Library. BkPL

P6.108 Magnificat. (1968) 8'
For: Soprano, chorus(SA), oboes(2), bassoons(2), harp or piano. Canticle.
Score & parts: Peters. Rental.
Vocal score: Peters, 1969. BPL HU

P6.109 Man, That Is Born of a Woman.
For: Mezzo Soprano and guitar. *Text:* The Book of Common Prayer.
Score: E.C. Schirmer, 1971. BPL HU

P6.110 The Martyrdom of Saint Stephen.
For: chorus(mixed) and guitar or piano. Anthem. *Text:* Bible, N.T., Acts 7:55-60.
Vocal score: ms. in composer's hand. HUh
Vocal score: Ione, 1970. HU T

P6.111 Masks. (1977)
For: harpsichord, flute, oboe/English horn, clarinet, violin, violoncello, percussion.
Score and parts: Ione, nyp.
Cassette: Feb. 27, 1979; New England Conservatory; in *Enchanted Circle*. Maryse Carlin, harpsichord; John Heiss, flute; Frederic Cohen, oboe; Robert Annis, clarinet; Robert Brink, violin; Adrienne Hartzell, violoncello; Daniel Pinkham, conductor. NEC
Cassette: Oct. 13, 1981; New England

Conservatory; in *Enchanted Circle*. Wendy Young, harpsichord; instrumental ensemble; Daniel Pinkham, conductor. NEC

P6.112 Mass of the Good Shepherd.
For: chorus(unison) and organ.
Vocal score: Ione, 1970. BPL HU T

P6.113 Mass of the Word of God.
For: chorus(SATB), congregation, organ. Withdrawn.

P6.114 Memory, Hither Come.
For: Soprano and Alto. *Text:* William Blake. *Dedicated to:* Pine Manor Junior College Choral Society, Edward Low, conductor.
Vocal score: ms. in composer's hand. NEC
Vocal score: Composers Facsimile Edition, 1959. NEC
Vocal score: Ione, nyp.

P6.115 Men and the Moon. (1959-60) Written for CBS-TV documentary, *Reaching for the Moon*.
Score: ms. in composer's hand. HUh

P6.116 The Message.
For: chorus(SATB) and guitar or piano.
Text: Siegfried Sassoon.
Vocal score: Ione, 1973. BPL

P6.117 Miracles. 17'
For: flute and organ. 5 movements.
First performed: Doriot Anthony Dwyer, flute and Yuko Hayashi, organ.
Score: Ione, 1979. BU HU
Part: Ione, 1979.

P6.118 Mizma l'asaph.
For: chorus(men), flute, horn, guitar, double bass, vibraphone, percussion.
Score & parts: Ione.

Motets. *See* Let Us Now Praise Famous Men; Listen to Me.

[Motets, Chorus]
P6.119 Three Motets. 4' 30"
For: chorus(SSA), organ or piano, violoncello(optional), double bass

(optional), bassoon(optional). *Text:* Bible, O.T., Psalms 95:11-13, 113:1-3, 9:1-4.
Parts: Peters, 1979.
Vocal score: Peters, 1979.

[Motets, Voice]
P6.120 Two Motets.
For: Soprano or Tenor, flute, guitar.
Contents: Non vos relinquam orphanos; Te lucis ante terminum.
Score: Ione, 1971. HU

P6.121 Mourn for the Eclipse of His Light.
For: violin, organ, tape.
Score: Ione, 1980. HU
Tape: Ione, 1980.

P6.122 Musette.
For: viole da gamba(2) and tape; or violin or viola, violoncello, tape.
Parts: Ione, 1972. BPL HU
Tape: Ione, 1972. BPL

P6.123 Music, Thou Soul of Heaven. (1953; rev. 1977)
For: voice(medium) and piano. *Text:* University of Oxford. Christ Church College. Library. Manuscript (87), May 6, 1663. Anon. *Dedicated to:* Ned Rorem.
Score: Ione, 1978. BPL NEC

P6.124 My Heart Is Steadfast: Psalm Motet XI. 1' 30"
For: chorus(SATB) and organ or piano(ad lib.)
Vocal score: Peters.

P6.125 Narragansett Bay.
For: orchestra. Ballet. Withdrawn.

P6.126 Now the Trumpet Summons Us Again. 5'
For: voice(high) and orchestra(3-3-3-2; 4-3-3-1; timp, perc; hp; str) or chamber orchestra(0-0-0-0; 0-1-0-0; glock or cel(ad lib.); str) or instrumental ensemble(trumpet, glockenspiel or celeste (ad lib.); violins(5), viola, violoncello, double bass). *Text:* Inaugural Address of John Fitzgerald

Kennedy.
Score: Peters, 1965 (orchestral version).
BPL
Parts: Peters. Rental.
Pf. red: Peters. HMA
Cassette: May 8, 1975; New England
Conservatory. Lynn Hoffman, soprano.
NEC

Nunc dimittis. *See* Festival Magnificat
and Nunc dimittis.

O Be Joyful to the Lord. *See* Jubilate
Deo.

P6.127 O Beautiful! My Country. 8'
For: chorus(SATB) and piano(optional).
Contents: Take Warning, Tyrants (Philip
Morin Freneau); The Happy Flood (Anne
Bradstreet); The Promised Land (James
Russell Lowell).
Vocal score: E.C. Schirmer, 1976. BPL
BU HU NEC

P6.128 O Lord God, to Whom
Vengeance Belongeth: Psalm Motet I.
(1961) 2'
For: chorus(SATB) and organ or
piano(optional). *Text:* Bible, O.T., Psalm
94:1-2.
Vocal score: Peters, 1962. BPL NU T

P6.129 On the Dispute About Images.
(1969) 7'
For: Soprano, Alto, Tenor, Bass,
chorus(mixed), guitar or piano. *Text:*
Maximus of Tyre.
Vocal score: ms. in composer's hand.
HUh
Vocal score: Ione, 1974. BPL

P6.130 Open to Me the Gates of
Righteousness: Psalm Motet IV. 1'
For: chorus(SATB) and organ or
piano(optional).
Vocal score: Peters, 1966. BPL

P6.131 The Other Voices of the
Trumpet.
For: trumpet, organ, tape.
Score & tape: E.C. Schirmer, 1972. BPL
Disc: Crystal Records, 1980.

P6.132 Partita. (1958) 24'
For: harpsichord. *Movements:* Toccata,
Andante and Fugue; Three Inventions;
Interlude and Rondo; Fantasia; Scherzo
and Trio; Envoi. *Commissioned by:*
WGBH-TV, Boston. *Dedicated to:*
Melville Smith; Silvia Kind; Albert
Fuller; Sylvia Marlowe; David Fuller;
Claude Jean Chiasson.
Score: ms. in composer's hand. HUh
Score: Peters, 1964. BPL BU HMA HU
MIT NEC W
Disc: Cambridge Records CRS 412,
1962. Danniel Pinkham. HU HUm NEC W

P6.133 A Partridge in a Pear Tree.
For: Soprano or Tenor and piano. *Text:*
anon. *Dedicated to:* Janet Hayes.
Score: reprod. of ms. NEC
Score: Row, 1948. HU L NEC

P6.134 The Passion of Judas. (1976) 32'
For: Soprano, Mezzo Soprano, Tenor,
Baritone, Bass, narrator, chorus(mixed),
clarinet, harp, viola, double bass,
organ. Oratorio. *Text:* Bible, O.T.,
Psalms 1,15, 51. *Contents:* Psalm 1:
Happy Is the Man; Lection I; Tell Me
about the Mother of Judas; Lection II;
Choral; Lection III; Rescue of the
Innocents; Lection IV; Saint Judas;
Psalm 51: Be Gracious to Me.
Commissioned by: National Prebyterian
Church, Washington, D.C.
Score: E.C. Schirmer, 1978. HU NEC
Parts: E.C. Schirmer, 1978.

[The Passion of Judas. Be Gracious
to Me, O God]
P6.135 Be Gracious to Me, O God.
For: Soprano, Mezzo Soprano, Tenor,
Baritone, Bass, chorus(mixed). Anthem.
Text: Bible, O.T., Psalm 51: 1, 2, 5-8,
10-12; Amen.
Vocal score: E.C. Schirmer, 1978. NEC

[The Passion of Judas. Happy Is the
Man]
P6.136 Happy Is the Man.
For: chorus(mixed). Anthem. *Text:* Bible,
O.T., Psalm 1.
Vocal score: E.C. Schirmer, 1978. NEC

[The Passion of Judas. Who May Lodge in Thy Tabernacle?]
P6.137 Who May Lodge in Thy Tabernacle?
For: chorus(mixed) and organ. Anthem.
Text: Bible, O.T., Psalm 15:1-3, 5.
Vocal score: E.C. Schirmer, 1978.

P6.138 Pastoral XVII from Thirty Pastorals. (1944) 2'
For: voice and piano. *Text:* Robert Hillyer. *Dedicated to:* Isabel French.
Score: reprod. of ms. NEC

P6.139 Pastorale on the Morning Star. 2' 30"
For: organ.
Score: Highgate, 1963. BPL

P6.140 Pater noster.
For: chorus(mixed), woodwinds, organ.
Score: Ione, 1972. BPL

P6.141 Piping Anne and Husky Paul. (1955) 44"
For: chorus(SATB). Madrigal. *Text:* Robert Hillyer. *Dedicated to:* David Randolph.
Vocal score: reprod. of ms. NEC
Vocal score: E.C. Schirmer, 1964. BCM BPL NU
Disc: in *Modern American Madrigals*, Composers Recordings CRI 102, 1956 (titled Madrigal). The Randolph Singers, David Randolph, conductor. MIT NEC T W

P6.142 Pleasure It Is. (1973) 6'
For: voice or chorus(unison), instruments(optional), organ. *Contents:* Pleasure It Is (William Randolph Cornish); For Saturday (Christopher Smart); Christ Was the Word (16th century; sometimes attributed to Queen Elizabeth I); Hallelujah. *Dedicated to:* Alice Parker; Helen Willard; Nancy Joyce; David Carney.
Score: E.C. Schirmer, 1974. NEC

[Poems of Gerard Manley Hopkins]
P6.143 Eight Poems of Gerard Manley Hopkins. (1964) 15'
For: Baritone or Tenor Baritone and

viola. Song cycle. *Contents:* Jesus to Cast One Thought Upon; Spring; Heaven-Haven; Pied Beauty; Strike, Churl; Spring and Fall; Christmas Day; Jesu That Dost in Mary Dwell.
Commissioned by: Harvard Musical Association.
Score: ms. in composer's hand. HUh
Score: reprod. of ms. HMA
Score: E.C. Schirmer, 1970. BPL HMA HU NEC

[Poems of Gerard Manley Hopkins. Heaven-Haven; Arr]
P6.144 Heaven-Haven. (1947) 3'
For: Baritone or Tenor Baritone and piano.
Score: reprod. of ms. NEC
Score: Ione, nyp.
Cassette: May 8, 1975; New England Conservatory. Keith Kibler, baritone. NEC

[Poems of Norma Farber]
P6.145 Four Poems of Norma Farber. (1974-76)
For: chorus(mixed). *Contents:* The Hatch; Fawn Bridge; Dancer How You Dance; The Star and Pulsar Discovered.
Commissioned by: The Wall Chamber Choir, Fredric Woodbridge Wilson, director.
Vocal score: Ione, 1978. BU HU NEC

[Poems of Norma Farber. Dancer, How You Dance]
P6.146 Dancer, How You Dance. (1974)
For: Soprano and chorus(SATB).
Commissioned by: The Wall Chamber Choir, Fredric Woodbridge Wilson, director.
Vocal score: ms. in composer's hand. NEC

[Poems of Norma Farber. Fawn Bridge]
P6.147 Fawn Bridge. (1974)
For: chorus(SATB). *Commissioned by:* The Wall Chamber Choir, Fredric Woodbridge Wilson, director.
Condensed score: ms. in composer's hand. NEC

[Poems of Norma Farber. The Hatch]
P6.148 The Hatch.
For: chorus(SATB). *Commissioned by:*
The Wall Chamber Choir, Fredric
Woodbridge Wilson, director.
Vocal score: ms. in composer's hand.
NEC

[Poems of Norma Farber. The Star
and Pulsar Discovered]
P6.149 Star and Pulsar Discovered
Waltzing: N. Y. Times, Dec. 22, 1972.
For: Soprano, Alto, Tenor, Bass.
Commissioned by: The Wall Chamber
Choir, Frederic Woodbridge Wilson,
director.
Condensed score: ms. in composer's
hand. NEC

P6.150 Prelude. (1946) 30'
For: piano. *Dedicated to:* Dr. and Mrs.
A. LeRoy Johnson.
Score: reprod of ms. HU

P6.151 Prelude, Adagio and Chorale.
(1968) 7'
For: trumpets(2), horn, trombone, tuba,
chorus(unison)(optional). *Text:* Bible,
O.T., Psalm 134. *Commissioned by:*
Wykeham Rise, Washington, Conn.
Score & parts: Peters, 1969. HU NEC
Part(chorus): Peters, 1969.
Cassette: Oct. 13, 1981; New England
Conservatory; in *Enchanted Circle*. NEC
Scholarship Brass Quintet. NEC

P6.152 Prelude, Epigram and Elegy. 7'
For: band. *Commissioned by:*
Northeastern University.
Score & parts: Ione.

P6.153 Prelude for Flute and String
Trio. (1945)
Withdrawn.

P6.154 A Prophecy. (1968) 4'
For: organ. *Commissioned by:* Harvard
University. *Dedicated to:* E. Power
Biggs.
Score: Ione, 1971. BPL HU NEC

P6.155 Prothalamion.
For: oboe, horns(2), strings. Withdrawn.

P6.156 Psalm 42, Verse 11. (1955)
For: chorus(SATB). Withdrawn.

P6.157 Psalm 79(80).
For: Tenor and piano. *Dedicated to:*
Romolo de Spirito.
Score: reprod. of ms. NEC
Score: Composers Facsimile Edition,
1952. HU

P6.158 Psalm 94, Verses 1 & 2. (1955)
For: chorus(SATB). Withdrawn.

Psalm Motet, No. I. *See* Q Lord God.

Psalm Motet, No. II *See* Why Art Thou
Cast Down?

Psalm Motet, No. III. *See* Thou Hast
Loved Righteousness.

Psalm Motet, No. IV. *See* Open to Me
the Gates of Righteousness.

Psalm Motet, No. V. *See* Behold, How
Good and How Pleasant.

Psalm Motet, No. VI. *See* How Precious
Is Thy Loving Kindness.

Psalm Motet, No. VII. *See* Grace Is
Poured Abroad.

Psalm Motet, No. VIII. *See* I Have
Preached Righteousness.

Psalm Motet, No. IX. *See* Thou Hast
Turned My Laments into Dancing.

Psalm Motet, No. X. *See* The Lord Has
Established His Throne.

Psalm Motet, No. XI. *See* My Heart Is
Steadfast.

P6.159 Psalm Set. (1968) 7'
For: chorus(mixed), trumpets(2),
trombones(2), tuba(optional),

timpani(optional), or chorus(mixed) and organ or piano. *Contents:* Fanfare (Bible, O.T., Psalm 134); Benediction (Bible, O.T., Psalm 117); Jubilation (Bible, O.T., Psalm 47).
Score: ms. in composer's hand. HUh
Score & parts: Peters, 1969.
Vocal score: Peters, 1969. BPL HU

P6.160 Reaching for the Moon.
For: orchestra. Withdrawn.

P6.161 Rejoice in the Lord Alway. Withdrawn.

P6.162 The Reproaches. 18'
For: chorus(mixed) and organ(optional). Motet. *Text: Liber usualis;* English translation by J. Lunn. *Contents:* Ecce lignum crucis; Intonation; Popule meus; Quia e duxi te de terra Aegypti; Agios, O Theos; Quia eduxi te per desertum; Quid ultra; Ego propter te Hagellavi Aegyptum; Ego te eduxi de Aegypto; Ego ante te aperui mare; Ego ante te praeivi; Ego te pavi manna; Ego te potavi; [Untitled]; Ego dedi tibi; Ego te exaltavi; Intonation; Crucem tuam adoramus.
Vocal score: ms. in composer's hand. NEC
Vocal score: Composers Facsimile Edition, 1960.
Vocal score: Associated, 1965. BPL BU HU

P6.163 Requiem. (1962-63) 15'
For: Alto, Tenor, chamber chorus(SATB), trumpets(2), horns(2), trombones(2), double bass, or organ or piano. *Contents:* Requiem aeternam; Kyrie eleison; Absolve, Domine; Domine Jesu Christe; Sanctus; Agnus Dei. *Commissioned by:* Contemporary Music Society, Leopold Stokowski, president. *Dedication:* In memoriam W.W.P., 1926-1962. *First performed:* Museum of Modern Art, New York City. Betty Lou Austin, alto; Richard Conrad, tenor; members of the King's Chapel Choir; members of the New York Brass Quintet and three unidentified players, Daniel Pinkham,

conductor.
Score & parts: Peters. Rental.
Vocal score: Peters, 1963. BPL BU HMA HU NEC

P6.164 Revelations.
For: oboe, horns(2), celeste, strings. Withdrawn.

P6.165 Revelations. 7'
For: organ. *Movements:* Pastorale; Litany; Toccata. *Dedicated to:* William Self.
Score: ms. in composer's hand. NEC
Score: E.C. Schirmer, 1965. NEC

P6.166 Rondo.
For: oboe, horns(2), celeste, strings. Withdrawn.

P6.167 Sacred Service.
For: cantor or Baritone, Soprano, Alto, Tenor, chorus(SATB), organ.
Vocal score: Ione, 1967. HUh

P6.168 Safe in Their Alabaster Chambers. (1972) 7'
For: voice(medium) and tape. *Text:* Emily Dickinson.
Score: E.C. Schirmer, 1974. BPL HU
Reel: Sept. 23, 1973; Isabella Stewart Gardner Museum, Boston. WGBH

P6.169 Saint Mark Passion. (1965) 33'
For: Soprano, Tenor, Baritone, Bass, chorus(SATB), instrumental ensemble (trumpets(2), horns(2), trombones(2), timpani, percussion, harp, double bass), or organ or piano. Oratorio. *Text:* Bible, O.T. and Bible, N.T.
Commissioned by: St. Mark's School, Southboro, Mass., on the occasion of its 100th Anniversary.
Score & parts: Peters. Rental.
Vocal score: Peters, 1966. BPL HMA HU NEC

P6.170 Scherzo.
For: oboe, horns(2), celeste, strings. Withdrawn.

P6.171 See That Ye Love One Another. 3'

For: organ or guitar or harp and tape.
Score & tape: Ione (all versions).

P6.172 Serenade. 16'
For: violin and harpsichord or piano.
Written for the concerts of the
Brink-Pinkham Duo. *First performed:*
Nov. 15, 1951; St. John, New
Brunswick. Robert Brink, violin and
Daniel Pinkham, harpsichord.
Score: Row, 1961. HU NEC T

P6.173 Serenades.
For: trumpet and band.
Score: E.C. Schirmer, 1980. HU
Parts: E.C. Schirmer, 1980.
Cassette: Dec. 11, 1980; New England
Conservatory. NEC Wind Ensemble,
Frank L. Battisti, conductor. NEC

Set Me as a Seal. *See* Wedding
Cantata. Set Me as a Seal.

P6.174 The Seven Last Words of Christ
on the Cross. (1970)
For: Tenor, Bass Baritone, Bass,
chorus(mixed), organ, tape. *First
performed:* Feb. 19, 1971; Saint Norbert
College.
Score: reprod. of ms. HUh
Score: Ione, 1971. BPL HU T
Tape: Ione, 1971. BPL

P6.175 The Sheepheards Song: A Caroll
or Himme for Christmas. (1971) 4'
For: Soprano, chorus(mixed),
tape(optional). *First performed* Dec. 13,
1971; Harvard Memorial Church,
Cambridge, Mass.
Vocal score: ms. in composer's hand.
HUh
Vocal score: Ione, 1972. BPL

P6.176 The Shepherd's Symphony. 5'
For: instruments(melody), organ,
percussion(optional), tape. Aleatoric
music.
Parts: E.C. Schirmer, 1974. MIT NEC
Tape: E.C. Schirmer, 1974. MIT

[Short Pieces, Organ]
P6.177 Four Short Pieces for Manuals.

(1962) 6'
Contents: Prelude; Aria; Interlude;
Ostinato. *Dedicated to:* Ted Hallman;
Fritz Noack; John Fesperman; Max
Miller.
Score: ms. in composer's hand. HUh
Score: E.C. Schirmer, 1963. BPL NEC

[Short Pieces, Pianos(2)]
P6.178 Four Short Pieces. (1946)
Contents: Chorale; Interlude; Cantus
firmus; Finale. *Dedicated to:* Nadia
Boulanger. Version for string or
chamber orchestra withdrawn.
Score: reprod. of ms. HMA HU

P6.179 Signs in the Sun. 8'
For: organs(2).
Score: Peters.

P6.180 Signs of the Zodiac. (1965) 21'
For: speaker(optional) and
orchestra(2(&pic)-2(&Ehn)-2(&bcl)-2;
4-3-2(&btrb)-1; timp, perc; hp, pf/cel;
str). *Text:* David Thompson Watson
McCord. *Contents:* Aries, the Ram;
Taurus, the Bull; Gemini, the Twins;
Cancer, the Crab; Leo, the Lion; Virgo,
the Virgin; Libra, the Balance; Scorpio,
the Scorpion; Sagittarius, the Archer;
Capricornus, the Goat; Aquarius, the
Waterbearer; Pisces, the Fishes.
Commissioned by: Arthur Bennett Lipkin
for the Portland Symphony Orchestra.
First performed: Nov. 10, 1964;
Portland, Me. Portland Symphony
Orchestra, Arthur Bennett Lipkin,
conductor.
Score & parts: Peters. Rental.
Score: Peters, 1964. HU
Study score: Peters, 1964. BPL BU HMA
HU NEC UMB
Disc: Louisville Orchestra LS 673, 1967.
Louisville Orchestra, Robert Whitney,
conductor. BrU BU HU HUm NEC W

Sing Agreeably of Love. *See* Lyric
Scenes. Sing Agreeably of Love.

[Slow, Slow, Fresh Fount, Voice(Low)
and Piano]
P6.181 Slow, Slow, Fresh Fount. (1949)

2'
Text: Ben Jonson.
Score: ms. in composer's hand. HUh

[Slow, Slow Fresh Fount,
Voice(Medium) and Piano]
P6.182 Slow, Slow, Fresh Fount. (1949)
2'
Text: Ben Jonson. *Dedicated to:* Verna
Osborne.
Score: reprod. of ms. NEC
Score: Peters, 1961.

[Slow, Slow, Fresh Fount, Tenor and
Piano]
P6.183 Slow, Slow, Fresh Fount. (1949)
2'
Text: Ben Jonson. *Dedicated to:* Verna
Osborne.
Score: Peters, 1961. HU
Disc: in *Songs by American Composers,*
Desto D 411-412 (ST/AND SPL 411-412)
and DS 6411-6412, 1964. John
McCollum, tenor and Edwin Biltcliffe,
piano. MIT NEC W

P6.184 Sometimes the Soul.
For: chorus(SATB) and guitar or piano.
Text: Norma Farber.
Vocal score: E.C. Schirmer, 1970. BPL
HU T

P6.185 Sonata da Requiem. (1978) 5'
For: violin, viola da gamba, handbell.
Movements: Prelude; Variation and
Knell.
Score: Ione, nyp.
Cassette: Jan. 22, 1978; New England
Conservatory. Daniel Stepner, baroque
violin; Laura Jeppesen, viola da gamba;
Nancy Joyce Roth, handbell. NEC
Cassette: Oct. 13, 1981; New England
Conservatory; in *Enchanted Circle.*
Daniel Stepner, violin; Laura Jeppesen,
viola da gamba; John Grimes, handbell.
NEC

P6.186 Sonata No. 1. (1943; rev. 1964)
5'
For: organ, violins(2), viola(optional),
violoncello, double bass(optional), or
string orchestra. 1 movement.
Dedicated to: E. Power Biggs.

Score: E.C. Schirmer, 1952, 1966. BPL
HU NEC
Parts: E.C. Schirmer, 1952, 1966. HU
NEC

P6.187 Sonata No. 2. (1954; rev. 1964)
8'
For: organ, string quartet, double
bass(optional), or string orchestra.
Dedicated to: Oliver Daniel.
Score & parts: ms. in composer's hand
(earlier version). HUh
Score & parts: Ione, 1966 (later
version). HU NEC
Score: reprod. of ms. NEC

P6.188 Sonatina.
For: violin and harpsichord or piano.
Score: American Composers Alliance,
1952. HU

P6.189 A Song for the Bells. 3'
For: carillon or handbells. *Dedicated to:*
Laurence Apgar.
Score: reprod. of ms. (version for
carillon). HU
Score: Peters, 1952 (version for
carillon). BPL BU
Score: Peters, 1969 (version for
handbells). HU

P6.190 The Song of Jeptha's Daughter.
(1963)
For: Soprano and piano or Soprano,
Baritone, chorus(SSA), piano. Cantata in
9 movements. *Text:* Robert Hillyer.
Dedicated to: Alice Esty.
Vocal score: ms. in composer's hand.
HUh
Vocal score: Peters, 1966. BPL HMA HU
HUm NEC
Part(chorus): Peters, 1966. NEC
Reel: Sept. 23, 1973; Isabella Stewart
Gardner Museum, Boston. WGBH

[Songs from Ecclesiastes]
P6.191 Three Songs from Ecclesiastes.
5'
For: voice(high) and piano. Song cycle.
Text: Bible, O.T., Ecclesiastes. *Contents:*
Vanity of Vanities; Go Thy Way, Eat
Thy Bread with Joy; To Everything Is

a Season.
Score: E.C. Schirmer, 1963. NEC

P6.192 Songs of Innocence. (1947)
For: Soprano, flute, piano. *Text:*
William Blake. *Contents:* Prelude; Infant
Joy; The Lamb; Piping Down the
Valleys Wild. *Dedicated to:* Lois
Schaefer; Ned Rorem; Janet Hayes;
Nancy Trickey; Lois Schaefer.
Vocal score: reprod. of ms. NEC

P6.193 Songs of Peaceful Departure. 5'
For: chorus(mixed) and guitar or piano.
Vocal score: ms. in composer's hand.
HUh
Vocal score: Ione, 1970. T

[Songs on Old English Texts. Charm
Me Asleep]
P6.194 Nine Songs on Old English
Texts. Charm Me Asleep. (1977) 18' 30"
For: voice(medium) and guitar. *First
performed:* Dec. 31, 1978. Pamela Gore,
alto and Robert Paul Sullivan, guitar.
Score: reprod. of ms. NEC
Score: Ione, nyp.
Cassette: Feb. 1979; New England
Conservatory; in *Enchanted Circle.*
Charles Robert Stephans, baritone and
Frank Wallace, guitar. NEC

P6.195 Stabat Mater. (1964) 16'
For: Soprano, chorus(mixed),
orchestra(1-1-1-1; 1-1-1-0; timp, perc;
hp, cel; str), or organ or piano. 10
movements. Written for the Festival of
Contemporary American Music
sponsored by the Berkshire Music
Center in cooperation with the Fromm
Foundation. *First performed:* Berkshire
Music Center, Tanglewood. Frances
Riley, soprano; Tanglewood Festival
Choir; Fromm Fellowship Players;
members of the instrumental
department of the Berkshire Music
Center, Thomas Sokol, conductor.
Score & parts: Peters. Rental.
Vocal score: Peters, 1964. BPL HU NEC

Star and Pulsar Discovered Waltzing.
See Poems of Norma Farber. The Star
and Pulsar Discovered.

P6.196 Star-Tree Carol.
For: Soprano, Alto, Tenor, Bass. *Text:*
Robert Hillyer. *Dedicated to:* Theodore
Chanler.
Vocal score: Row, 1949. HU
Vocal score: C. Fischer.

P6.197 Structures.
For: timpani, percussion(11), celeste,
piano. Film score for documentary on
work of R. Buckminster Fuller.
Withdrawn.

P6.198 Suite. 10'
For: organ. *Contents:* Epitaph; Morning
Song; Toccata.
Score: E.C. Schirmer, 1964. BPL

P6.199 Symphony No. 1. (1961) 17'
For:
orchestra(3(pic)-2(&Ehn)-2(&bcl)-2(&cbsn);
4-3-3-1; timp, perc, glock; hp, cel, pf;
str). 3 movements. *Commissioned by:*
Broadcast Music, Inc. in celebration of
its 20th anniversary. *Dedicated to:* Carl
Haverlin.
Score & parts: Peters. Rental.
Study score: Peters, 1961. BPL BrU BU
HU NEC UMB

P6.200 Symphony No. 2. (1963) 26'
For: orchestra(2(&pic)-2(&Ehn)-2(&bcl)-2;
4-3-3-1; timp, perc(3); hp, pf; str).
Movements: Aria; Three Epigrams
(Energico, Con nostalgia; Lento);
Ballade; Envoy. *Dedicated to:* Michigan
Civic Orchestra Association. *First
performed:* Nov. 23, 1963.
Score & parts: Peters. Rental.
Study score: Peters, 1964. Be BPL HMA
HU HUm NEC UMB
Disc: Louisville Orchestra LOU 652,
1965. Louisville Orchestra, Robert
Whitney, conductor. BrU BU HU HUm
NEC W

A Tacket. *See* Little Brass Book.

P6.201 Te Deum.
For: chorus(SA) or chorus(TB), trumpets(3), organ. Canticle. *Text:* John Dryden.
Score: King.

P6.202 The Temptations in the Wilderness.
For: Baritone, organ, tape. Withdrawn.

P6.203 Thou Hast Loved Righteousness: Psalm Motet III. 3'
For: chorus(SATB) and organ or piano(optional).
Vocal score: Peters, 1964. BPL NU

P6.204 Thou Hast Turned My Laments into Dancing: Psalm Motet IX. (1973) 1'
For: chorus(SATB) and organ or piano(optional). *Text:* Bible, O.T., Psalm 30:11, 12. *Dedicated to:* Evelyn Hinrichsen, president, on the occasion of the 25th anniversary of C.F. Peters Corp.
Vocal score: ms. in composer's hand. NEC
Vocal score: Peters, 1975. BPL BU HU NEC

P6.205 Thy Statutes Have Been My Songs.
For: Soprano, Alto, Bass, organ.
Score: Ione, 1970. T

P6.206 Time of Times. (1975) 8'
For: chorus(SATB) and piano. *Text:* Norma Farber.
Vocal score: E.C. Schirmer, 1980.
Disc: in *Love Can Be Still; Music on Verses of Norma Farber*, Northeastern Records NR 201, 1981. Patti Dell and Barbara Wallace, sopranos; Pamela Gore, alto; Richard Conrad, tenor; Bryan McNeil, baritone; Gary Wedow, piano. NEC

P6.207 To Think of Those Absent. (1969)
For: chorus(SATB) and guitar or harp or piano. *Text:* Norma Farber.
Vocal score: ms. in composer's hand.

HUh
Vocal score: Ione, 1970. BPL

P6.208 To Troubled Friends. (1972) 18'
For: chorus(SATB), tape, string orchestra. *Text:* James Wright. *Contents:* To a Troubled Friend; Father; A Fit against the Country; Evening.
Vocal score: E.C. Schirmer, 1974. BPL

P6.209 Toccatas for the Vault of Heaven. (1972) 6'
For: organ and tape.
Score & tape: Ione.
Disc: Golden Crest NEC 114, 1975. Larry Phillips. BrU BU HU MIT NEC

P6.210 Transitions. (1979)
For: voice(medium) and bassoon. Song cycle. *Text:* Howard Holtzman. *Contents:* Grey; I Like the Light Diffused; Lullaby for a Shrouded Figure; Home Movies; Aubade; Near This Stone; So, One by One. *Commissioned by:* Pamela Gore and Linda Smith. *First performed:* Sept. 30, 1979; Carnegie Recital Hall, New York City.

[Transitions; Arr.]
P6.211 Transitions. (1979)
For: voice(medium) and piano. Song cycle. *Text:* Howard Holtzman. *Contents:* Grey; I Like the Light Diffused; Lullaby for a Shrouded Figure; Home Movies; Aubade; Near This Stone; So, One by One.
Score: s.l., s.n. NEC
Score: Ione, 1980. HU NEC
Cassette: Oct. 13, 1981; New England Conservatory in *Enchanted Circle*. Pamela Gore, alto and Gary Wedow, piano. NEC

[Trio]
P6.212 Brass Trio. (1970) 5'
For: trumpet, horn, trombone.
Dedication: To the memory of Walter Hinrichsen.
Score: ms. in composer's hand. HUh
Score: Peters, 1970. BCM BPL HU NEC
Study score: Peters.
Cassette: Apr. 8, 1970; New England Conservatory; in *An Evening of*

Contemporary Music. NEC
Cassette: Jan. 21, 1980; New England Conservatory; in *Enchanted Circle.* Robert Earl Nagel, Jr., trumpet; Paul Ingraham, horn; John Swallow, trombone. NEC

Tucket. *See* Little Brass Book.

P6.213 Variations. (1969) 11'
For: oboe, and organ. *Movements:* Prelude; Dithyramb; Scherzo; Fantasia; Nocturne; Finale. *Dedicated to:* Kenneth Roth.
Score: Peters, 1970. BPL HU NEC T
Part: Peters, 1970. NEC

[Voluntaries]
P6.214 Five Voluntaries for Organ Manuals. 6'
Score: E.C. Schirmer, 1971. BPL HU

P6.215 Wedding Cantata. (1956) 10'
For: Soprano, Tenor(optional), chorus(SATB), horns(2), celeste, strings. *Text:* Bible, O.T., Song of Songs. *Contents:* Rise Up, My Love; Many Waters; Awake, O North Wind; Epilogue: Set Me as a Seal. *Dedicated to:* Lotje and Arthur Loeb.
Vocal score: reprod of ms. HUh
Vocal score: Dow, 1959. NEC T
Vocal score: Peters, 1959. BPL

[Wedding Cantata. Set Me as a Seal; Arr.]
P6.216 Set Me as a Seal. 2
For: voice(high) and organ.
Score: Peters, 1975. BPL BU HU

P6.217 When God Arose: Easter Canticle. (1979) 6' 30"
For: Sopranos(2), Mezzo Soprano, Tenor, Baritone, chorus(SATB), timpani, percussion, glockenspiel, vibraphone, harpsichord, organ. 2 movements. *Text:* Bible, O.T., Psalm 76:9-10; Bible, N.T., Matthew 28:1-7; Bible, N.T., Colossians 3:1-4. *Commissioned by:* University of Oklahoma School of Music for the Contemporary Music Festival, 1980.

Dedicated to: Dennis Shrock.
Score: ms. in composer's hand. NEC

P6.218 When the Morning Stars Sang Together. (1971)
For: organ and tape. 1 movement.
Commissioned by: Elizabeth Travis Sollenberger for the Hartt College of Music Contemporary Organ Music Workshop, University of Hartford, 1972.
Score: Ione, 1972. BPL NEC
Tape: Ione, 1972. BPL

Who May Lodge in Thy Tabernacle? *See* The Passion of Judas. Who May Lodge in Thy Tabernacle?

P6.219 Why Art Thou Cast Down? Psalm Motet No. 2. 2'
For: chorus(SATB) and organ or piano(optional). *Text:* Bible, O.T., Psalm 42:11.
Vocal score: Peters, 1962. BPL NU T

Why Sleepest Thou. *See* Hymn No. 1.

P6.220 Witching Hour. (1975)
For: chorus(women), guitar(electric), tape. *Text: Fire Sleet and Candlelight* by Norma Farber. 1 movement. *Commissioned by:* Wayne State University Women's Chorale, Douglas K. Belland, conductor.
Vocal score: ms. in composer's hand. NEC
Vocal score: Ione, 1975.

ARRANGEMENTS OF WORKS BY OTHER COMPOSERS

P6.221 Behold, He Is My Salvation.
For: Soprano, Alto, Tenor, Bass, continuo. Original by William Selby.
Score: Ione.

[Choruses from the Medea of Euripides]
P6.222 Seven Choruses from the Medea of Euripides.
For: chorus(SATB) and percussion(optional). Original by Virgil Thomson, English translation of text by

Countee Cullen.
Vocal score: G. Schirmer, 1978. BPL

P6.223 Christ ist erstanden.
For: chorus(SATB). Original by Franz Peter Schubert.
Vocal score: Ione.

P6.224 Christe, adoramus te (Jesu, We Adore Thy Name).
For: Sopranos(2), Alto, Tenor, Bass, organ(optional). Original by Claudio Monteverdi.
Score: Row, 1949. BPL

P6.225 Forest Music.
For: string orchestra or chamber orchestra(0-2-0-1; 2-0-0-0; timp; str). Original by George Frideric Handel.
Score: Ione, 1972. BPL HU
Parts: Ione, 1972.

P6.226 Fugue or Voluntary.
For: organ. Original by William Selby.
Score: Ione, 1972.

P6.227 Hear, O Heavens.
For: Alto, Tenor, Bass, organ. Original by Pelham Humphrey.
Score: Ione.

P6.228 If Music Be the Food of Love.
For: Mezzo Soprano or Baritone and piano. *Text:* John Dryden. Original by Henry Purcell.
Score: reprod. of ms. HU

[L'Incoronazione di Poppea. Sinfonia and March]
P6.229 Sinfonia and March.
For: organ. Original by Claudio Monteverdi.
Score: Row, 1950. BPL

Medea. *See* Choruses from the Medea of Euripides.

P6.230 Music for a Merry Christmas. 39'
For: orchestra(3(or recs)-2(Ehn)-0-1; 2-2-2-0; timp, perc(2), glock; hp, cel/pf, org; str). *Contents:* Adeste fideles;

Angel Voices; All My Heart This Night Rejoices; The Birds; Coventry Carol; Deck the Halls; The First Nowell; God Rest You Merry Gentleman; Good King Wenceslas; Greensleeves; The Holly and the Ivy; In dulci jubilo; Joy to the World; March of the Kings; O Tannenbaum; Silent Night; Sing We Now Noel; Wassail; We Three Kings.
Score & parts: Peters, 1971. BPL

P6.231 O Lord, My God.
For: Alto, Tenor, Bass, organ or strings and continuo. Original by Pelham Humphrey.
Score: Ione.

P6.232 Passionsmusik ueber die Sieben Worte Jesu Christi
am Kreutz (Passion Music on the Seven Words of Jesus Christ on the Cross).
For: Sopranos(2), Tenor, Bass, chorus(SATB), viole da gamba(3) or violas(2), violoncello, continuo. Original by Augustin Pfleger, edited by Daniel Pinkham.
Score & parts: E.C. Schirmer, 1973. BPL

P6.233 Salve Regina.
For: chorus(SATB) and organ(optional). Original by Franz Peter Schubert.
Vocal score: Ione.

Sinfonia and March. *See* L'Incoronazione di Poppea. Sinfonia and March.

[Songs]
P6.234 Two Songs.
Original figured bass by Henry Purcell.
Score: Row, 1958. BPL

P6.235 Vom Himmel hoch da komm ich her.
For: Sopranos(2), Tenor, organ. Original by Johann Hermann Schein.
Score: Ione.

P6.236 The Ways of Zion Do Mourn.
For: Soprano or Mezzo Soprano and organ. Original by Michael Wise.
Score: Ione, 1966. T

P6.237 While I Listen to Thy Voice.
(1947)
Original by Henry Purcell. *Dedicated to:*
N.B.
Score: reprod. of ms. HU

P7 WALTER HAMOR PISTON

Born January 20, 1894, in Rockland,
Me.; died November 12, 1976, in
Belmont, Mass. Moved to Boston area
1905. *Education:* studied composition
with Archibald T. Davison (Harvard
University, 1919-24); Nadia Boulanger
(Paris, France), Paul Dukas (Paris,
France). *Awards:* John Knowles Paine
Travelling Fellowship (Harvard
University, 1924), Elizabeth Sprague
Coolidge Award for Service to
Chamber Music (1935), Guggenheim
Grant (1935), National Institute of Arts
and Letters (member, 1938), American
Academy of Arts and Sciences
(member, 1940), New York Music
Critics Circle Awards (1945, 1958,
1964), Pulitzer Prize in Music (1948,
1961), Naumburg Recording Award
(1953), American Academy of Arts and
Letters (member, 1955); Officier dans
l'Ordre des Arts et Lettres (1969).
Related activities: violinist; conductor;
author of *Principles of Harmonic
Analysis* (1933), *Harmony* (1941; 4th ed.
1978), *Counterpoint* (1947), *Orchestration*
(1955); served on the faculty of
Harvard University (1926-60; Walter W.
Naumburg Professor of Music, 1951-60).
Most manuscripts not located in the
Boston area can be found at the
Library of Congress. BPL

WORKS

P7.1 Bicentennial Fanfare. (1975)
For:
orchestra(2(&pic)-2(&Ehn)-2(&bcl)-2(cbsn);
4-3-3-1; timp, perc(4); str).
Commissioned by: Cincinnati Symphony
Orchestra, Thomas Schippers, music
director.
Score: ms. in composer's hand. BPL
Score: reprod. of ms. BPL

Bow Down Thine Ear, O Lord. *See*
Psalm and Prayer of David. Bow
Down Thine Ear, O Lord.

P7.2 Capriccio. (1963) 8'
For: harp and string orchestra.
Commissioned by: Broadcast Music, Inc.
on the occasion of its 20th
anniversary. *Dedicated to:* Nicanor
Zabaleta. *First performed:* Oct. 19,
1964; Madrid, Spain.
Score & parts: Associated, 1966. Rental.
Score: ms. in composer's hand. BPL
Score: reprod. of mss. BPL
Part(harp): ms. BPL
Pf. red: reprod. of ms. BPL
Pf. red: Associated, 1966. BPL HUm

P7.3 Carnival Song. (1938) 6'-8'
For: Tenor, Baritone, Bass, chorus(men),
brass ensemble(horns(4), trumpets(3),
trombones(3), tuba). *Text:* Lorenzo de'
Medici. *Dedicated to:* G. Wallace
Woodworth and the Harvard Glee Club.
First performed: Mar. 7, 1940;
Cambridge, Mass. Harvard Glee Club, G.
Wallace Woodworth, conductor.
Score & parts: Associated. Rental.
Score: ms. in composer's hand.
Score: Arrow, 1941. BU BPL HU HUm
Vocal score: Arrow, 1941. BPL
Vocal score: Associated, 1941. BPL
Disc: Victor 18013. Harvard Glee Club,
Boston Symphony Brass Ensemble, G.
Wallace Woodworth, conductor.
Disc: Harvard Glee Club F-H63, 1963
(date of recording). Harvard Glee Club,
Elliot Forbes, conductor. HUm
Disc: Fleetwood Records FLP 6001,
1964. Cornell University Glee Club;
Rochester Symphonic Brass Ensemble,
Thomas A. Sokol, conductor. HU

P7.4 Ceremonial Fanfare. (1969) 2'
For: brass ensemble(trumpets(4),
horns(6), trombones(4), tuba), timpani,
percussion(2). 1 movement.
Commissioned by: Metropolitan Museum
of Art for its 100th anniversary
exhibition, 1970.
Score & parts: Associated, 1971. BCM
BPL HU

Score: reprod. of ms. BPL
Reel: May 17, 1973; Boston
Conservatory. Boston Conservatory
Brass Ensemble, Sterling P.
Cossaboom, conductor. BCM

P7.5 Chromatic Study on the Name of
Bach. (1940) 4'
For: organ. *First performed:* Mar. 4,
1940; Hartford, Conn. William
Strickland.
Score: ms. in composer's hand.
Score: Gray, 1941. BPL HU NEC
Score: Gray, 1969. MIT
Disc: Psallite PET 144 280574. Kaete
van Tricht.
Disc: University [of Oklahoma]
Recordings 2, 1953. Mildred Andrews.
BU
Disc: in *20th Century American Organ
Music*, Lyrichord LL 191/LLST 7191,
1968. Robert Noehren. BU NEC

P7.6 Concertino. (1937) 14'
For: piano and orchestra(2(&pic)-2-2-2;
2-0-0-0; str). 1 movement.
Commissioned by: Columbia
Broadcasting System. *First performed:*
June 20, 1937; CBS-TV. Jesus Maria
Sanroma, piano; CBS Symphony
Orchestra, Walter Piston, conductor.
Score: ms. in composer's hand.
Score: Cos Cob, 1934. W
Score: Arrow, 1938. BPL HU HUm L
MIT NEC
Score: Associated, 1938. BPL
Pf. red: Arrow, 1939. BCM BPL HMA
HU HUm NEC
Pf. red: Associated, 1939. BPL L MIT
Disc: in *A Concert of American Music
in Schoenbrunn*, Vox PL 7750, 1952.
Alexander Jenner, piano; Vienna State
Academy Orchestra; William Strickland,
conductor. NEC
Disc: Composers Recordings CRI 180,
1964. Marjorie Mitchell, piano;
Goeteborg Symphony Orchestra,
William Strickland, conductor. BrU BU
HU MIT NEC W
Disc: Turnabout TV 34733, 1978. Gary
Steigerwalt, piano; Philharmonia
Virtuosi of New York, Richard Kapp,
conductor. MIT

Reel: n.d. HU
Reel: Feb. 10, 1960; Jordan Hall,
Boston. Jesus Maria Sanroma, piano;
NEC Orchestra, Walter Piston,
conductor. HU

[Concerto, Clarinet]
P7.7 Concerto. (1967) 15'
For: clarinet and
orchestra(2-2(&Ehn)-2(&bcl)-2; 2-2-0-0;
timp, perc(3); str). 1 movement.
Commissioned by: Mario di Bonaventura
for the Hopkins Center, Congregation
of the Arts, Dartmouth College. *First
performed:* Aug. 6, 1967; Dartmouth
College. Donald Wendlandt, clarinet;
Dartmouth Symphony Orchestra, Mario
di Bonaventura, conductor.
Score & parts: Associated. Rental.
Score: reprod. of ms. BPL
Study score: Associated, 1968. BPL BrU
BU HMA HU HUm MIT
Pf. red: Associated, 1968. BPL HU MIT
Pf. red: Muzyka, 1977.
Part(clarinet): Muzyka, 1977.

[Concerto, Flute]
P7.8 Concerto. (1971) 19'
For: flute and
orchestra(2-2(&Ehn)-2(&bcl)-2; 4-2-0-0;
timp, perc; hp; str). *Dedicated to:*
Doriot Anthony Dwyer. *First performed:*
Sept. 21, 1972; Symphony Hall, Boston.
Doriot Anthony Dwyer, flute; Boston
Symphony Orchestra, Michael Tilson
Thomas, conductor.
Score: ms. in composer's hand. BPL
Score: reprod. of mss. BPL
Score: Associated, 1978. BU HU MIT
NEC
Pf. red: reprod. of ms. BPL
Reel: Sept. 22-23, 1972; WGBH-FM.
Doriot Anthony Dwyer, flute; Boston
Symphony Orchestra, Michael Tilson
Thomas, conductor. HU

[Concerto, Orchestra]
P7.9 Concerto. (1933) 14'
For:
orchestra(3-2(&Ehn)-2(&bcl)-2(&cbsn);
4-3-3-1; timp, perc; pf; str). 3
movements. *First performed:* Mar. 8,
1934; Cambridge, Mass. Boston

Symphony Orchestra, Walter Piston, conductor.
Sketches: ms. in composer's hand.
Score: ms. in composer's hand.
Score: Cos Cob, 1934. BCM BPL BU HU HUm NEC
Score: Arrow, 1934. Reissue of Cos Cob edition. BPL HU
Study score: Cos Cob.
Study score: Arrow, 1934. Reissue of Cos Cob edition. BPL HU
Study score: Associated, 1934. MIT
Pf. red: ms. in composer's hand. BPL
Pf. red: reprod. of ms. BPL
Disc: Composers Recordings CRI SD 254, 1970. Polish National Radio Orchestra, William Strickland, conductor. BCM BrU BU HU MIT NEC W
Reel: n.d. New York Philharmonic, Leonard Bernstein, conductor. HU

[Concerto, Pianos(2)]
P7.10 Concerto. (1959) 19'
For: pianos(2) and orchestra(2(&pic)-2(Ehn)-2(bcl)-2(cbsn); 4-2-3-1; timp, perc; str). 3 movements.
Commissioned by and dedicated to: Melvin Stecher and Norman Horowitz.
First performed: July 4, 1964; Hanover, N.H. Melvin Stecher and Norman Horowitz, pianos; Dartmouth Community Symphony Orchestra, Mario di Bonaventura, conductor.
Score: ms. in composer's hand. BPL
Score: reprod. of ms. BPL
Pf. red: ms. in composer's hand. BPL
Pf. red: reprod. of ms. BPL
Pf. red: Associated, 1966. BPL

[Concerto, String Quartet, Wind Ensemble, Percussion(5)]
P7.11 Concerto. (1976) 11'
For: string quartet and instrumental ensemble(2(&pic)-2(&Ehn)-2(&bcl)-2; 2-2-2-0; timp, perc(4)). 1 movement.
Dedicated to: Portland Symphony String Quartet. *First performed:* Oct. 26, 1976; Portland, Me. Portland Symphony String Quartet; Portland Symphony Orchestra.
Score: ms. in composer's hand. BPL

Score: reprod. of ms. BPL
Score: Associated, 1978. Rental.
Disc: Composer's Recordings CRI SD 248(78), 1978. Emerson String Quartet; Juilliard Orchestra, Sixten Ehrling, conductor. BU MIT NEC W

[Concerto, Viola]
P7.12 Concerto. (1957) 23'
For: viola and orchestra (2(&pic)-2(&Ehn)-2(&bcl)- 2(&cbsn); 4-2-3-1; timp; hp; str). 3 movements.
Commissioned by and dedicated to: Joseph de Pasquale. Winner of New York Music Critics Circle Award, 1958.
First performed: Mar. 7, 1958; Symphony Hall, Boston. Joseph de Pasquale, viola; Boston Symphony Orchestra, Charles Munch, conductor.
Score & parts: Associated. Rental.
Score: reprod. of ms. BPL
Study score: Associated, 1965. BCM BrU BPL HU MIT NEC UMB
Pf. red: Associated, 1959. BPL HU
Disc: Louisville Orchestra LOU 633, 1963. Paul Doktor, viola; Louisville Orchestra, Robert Whitney, conductor. BrU BU HU HUm MIT NEC W
Reel: Mar. 8, 1958; Joseph de Pasquale, viola; Boston Symphony Orchestra, Charles Munch, conductor. HU

[Concerto, Violin, No.1]
P7.13 Concerto. (1939) 23'
For: violin and orchestra(3-3-3-3; 4-3-3-1; timp, perc; str). 3 movements.
Dedicated to: Ruth Posselt. *First performed:* Mar. 19, 1940; New York City. Ruth Posselt, violin; National Orchestra, Leon Barzin, conductor.
Sketches: ms. in composer's hand (3rd movement).
Score & parts: Boosey, 1948. Rental.
Score: ms. in composer's hand.
Pf. red: reprod. of ms. HU
Pf. red: Boosey & Hawkes, 1948. BPL HU HUm MIT NEC
Part(violin): Boosey & Hawkes, 1948. BPL HU HUm MIT NEC
Disc: Odeon 0 80 610, 196-. Hugo Kolberg, violin; Berlin Symphony

Orchestra, Otto Matzerath, conductor.
HU
Disc: Mace MXX 9089, 1970. Hugo
Kolberg, violin; Berlin Symphony
Orchestra, Otto Matzerath, conductor.
MIT NEC

[Concerto, Violin, No. 2]
P7.14 Concerto. (1960) 22′
For: violin and
orchestra(2(&pic)-2(&Ehn)-2(&bcl)-2(cbsn);
4-2-3-1; timp, perc; hp; str). 3
movements. *Commissioned by:* Joseph
Fuchs under a grant from the Ford
Foundation. *Dedicated to:* Joseph Fuchs.
First performed: Oct. 28, 1960;
Pittsburgh, Pa. Joseph Fuchs, violin;
Pittsburgh Symphony Orchestra, William
Steinberg, conductor.
Score: ms. in composer's hand. BPL
Score: reprod. of ms. BPL
Score: Associated, 1962. Rental. BPL
Pf. red: Associated, 1962. BPL NEC
Reel: Dec. 13, 1960; Joseph Fuchs,
violin; Detroit Symphony Orchestra,
Paul Paray, conductor. HU

[Counterpoints]
P7.15 Three Counterpoints. (1973)
For: violin, viola, violoncello. *Dedicated
to:* George Humphrey.
Score: ms. in composer's hand. BPL
Score & parts: Associated, 1975. BPL
BrU BU HMA HU MIT NEC

P7.16 Divertimento for Nine
Instruments. (1946)
For: flute, oboe, clarinet, bassoon,
string quartet, double bass. 3
movements. *Commissioned by:*
International Society for Contemporary
Music. *First performed:* May 18, 1946.
Score & parts: BMI, 1946. BPL HU HUm
Score: ms. in composer's hand.
Score: Associated, 1946. BPL BU MIT
Parts: Associated, 1946. BU MIT
Disc: in *The Boston Symphony Chamber
Players*, RCA Victor LM/LSC 6167,
1966. Boston Symphony Chamber
Players. BrU BU MIT NEC NU W
Reel: Apr. 22, 1960; Sanders Theatre,
Harvard University; in *A Concert of
Music by Walter Piston*. Doriot Anthony

Dwyer, flute; Ralph Gomberg, oboe;
Gino Cioffi, clarinet; Sherman Walt,
bassoon; Ruth Posselt and Richard
Burgin, violins; Joseph de Pasquale,
viola; Samuel Mayes, violoncello,
George Moleux, double bass; Walter
Piston, conductor. HU

P7.17 Duo for Viola and Violoncello.
(1949)
3 movements. *Commissioned by and
dedicated to:* Sven and Kurt Reher. *First
performed:* Feb. 13, 1950; Los Angelos,
Calif. Sven Reher, viola and Kurt Reher,
violoncello.
Score: reprod. of ms. BPL
Score: Associated, 1953. BPL HMA HU
W
Disc: Coronet LPS 1715, 1972. Irving
Ilmer, viola and Leopold Teraspulsky,
violoncello. HU
Reel: n.d. Joseph de Pasquale, viola
and Samuel Mayes, violoncello. HU
Reel: Oct. 27, 1972; Harvard Musical
Association. George Humphrey, viola
and Karl Zeise, violoncello. HU

P7.18 Duo for Violoncello and Piano.
(1972)
3 movements. *Dedicated to:* Luis Leguia
and Robert Freeman.
Score & part: reprod. of ms. BPL
Reel: Jan 31, 1975. Luis Leguia,
violoncello and Janet Roberts, piano.
BCM

P7.19 Fanfare for the Fighting French.
(1942)
For: brass ensemble(trumpets(4),
horns(3), trombones(3), tuba), timpani,
percussion(3). *First performed:* Oct. 23,
1942; Cincinnati, Ohio. Cincinnati
Symphony Orchestra, Eugene Goossens,
conductor.
Score: in *Ten Fanfares by Ten
Composers*, Boosey & Hawkes, 1944.
BPL
Study score: Boosey & Hawkes, 1959.
HU
Parts: Boosey & Hawkes, 1959. HU

P7.20 Fantasia. (1970) 16′
For: violin and

407

orchestra(2(&pic)-2(&Ehn)-2(&bcl)-2(cbsn);
4-3-3-1; perc; hp; str). *Commissioned by:*
Mario di Bonaventura for Salvatore
Accardo and the Hopkins Center,
Congregation of the Arts, Dartmouth
College.
Score & parts: Associated, 1975. Rental.
Score: ms. in composer's hand. BPL
Score: reprod. of ms. BPL
Study score: Associated, 1975. BPL BU
HU MIT NEC T
Pf. red: ms. in composer's hand. BPL
Pf. red: Associated, 1978. HU NEC

P7.21 Fantasy. (1952) 10'
For: English horn, harp, string
orchestra. *Dedicated to:* Louis Speyer.
First performed: Jan. 1, 1954;
Symphony Hall, Boston. Louis Speyer,
English horn; Bernard Zighera, harp;
Boston Symphony Orchestra, Charles
Munch, conductor.
Score & parts: Associated, 1955. BPL
HU NEC
Score: reprod. of ms. BPL
Pf. red: ms. in composer's hand.
Part(English horn): reprod. of ms. BPL
Reel: n.d. Boston Symphony Orchestra,
Charles Munch, conductor. HU

P7.22 Fugue on a Victory Tune. (1944)
For: orchestra. *Commissioned by:*
League of Composers. *First performed:*
Oct. 21, 1944; New York City. New
York Philharmonic, Artur Rodzinski,
conductor.
Score: ms. in composer's hand. BPL

P7.23 Fugue pour quatuor a cordes sur
un sujet de Fenaroli.
For: string quartet.
Score: ms. HU

P7.24 Improvisation. (1945)
For: piano.
Score: ms. in composer's hand.
Score: Delkas, 1946. BPL
Score: in *U.S.A.; Compositions for Piano
by Contemporary American Composers*,
Leeds, 1946-49. HU
Disc: in Vox 174, Vox 16070. Andor
Foeldes.

P7.25 The Incredible Flutist. \1938) 41'
For: dancers and
orchestra(2(&pic)-2&Ehn)-2(bcl)-2(cbsn);
4-3-3-1; timp, perc, glock; pf; str).
Ballet. Dance play by Hans Wiener, i.e.,
Jan Veen. *First perfomed:* May 30,
1938; Symphony Hall, Boston. Hans
Wiener Dancers Boston Pops, Arthur
Fiedler, conductor.
Score: reprod. of ms. BPL
Score: Associated, 1938.
Pf. red: ms. BPL
Pf. red: reprod. of ms. BPL
Disc: Louisville Orchestra LS 755, 1975.
Louisville Symphony Orchestra, Jorge
Mester, conductor. BrU BU HU NEC
UMB W

[The Incredible Flutist; Suite]
P7.26 The Incredible Flutist. (1938) 17'
For:
orchestra(2(&pic)-2(&Ehn)-2(bcl)-2(cbsn);
4-3-3-1; timp, perc, glock; pf; str).
Movements: Introduction; Siesta in the
Market Place; Entrance of the Vendors;
Entrance of the Customers; Tango of
the Merchants Daughters; Arrival of the
Circus; Circus March; The Flutist;
Minuet; Spanish Waltz; Sicilianna; Polka
Finale. *First performed:* Nov. 22, 1940;
Pittsburgh, Pa. Pittsburgh Symphony
Orchestra, Fritz Reiner, conductor.
Study score: Associated, 1938. BCM
BPL HMA T
Study score: Arrow, 1939. BPL BU HU L
MIT NEC NEC W
Part: reprod. of ms. (1st violin). BPL
Disc: RCA Victor M/DM 621. Boston
Pops, Arthur Fiedler, conductor.
Disc: RCA Camden CAL 145, n.d.
Boston Festival Concert Orchestra [
i.e., Boston Pops]. Reissue of RCA
Victor M/DM 621. BU
Disc: Urania URLP 7092, 1953. Berlin
Radio Symphony Orchestra, Arthur
Rother, conductor. BCM HU T
Disc: in *The Ballet*, RCA Victor LM
6113, 1954. Boston Pops, Arthur
Fiedler, conductor. BU
Disc: RCA Victor LM/LSC 2084, 1957.
Reissue of RCA Victor LM 6113, 1954.
Disc: in *Pop Concert U.S.A.*, Epic LC

3539/BC 1013, 1959. Cleveland Pops
Orchestra, Louis Lane, conductor.
Disc: Mercury MG 50206/SR 90206,
1959. Eastman-Rochester Symphony
Orchestra, Howard Hanson, conductor.
BCM HU HUm MIT W
Disc: Mercury MG 50423/SR 90423,
1965. Reissue of Mercury MG 50206/SR
90206, 1959. BU NEC W
Disc: Mercury SRI 75050, 1975. Reissue
of Mercury SR 50423/SR 90423, 1965.
BU MIT NEC
Disc: Columbia ML 6343/MS 6943,
1967, New York Philharmonic, Leonard
Bernstein, conductor. BU NU
Disc: Columbia MG 31155, 1972.
Reissue of Columbia ML 6343/MS 6943,
1967.
Disc: Turnabout QTVS 34670, 1976.
MIT Symphony Orchestra, David
Epstein, conductor. MIT

P7.27 Interlude. (1942)
For: viola and piano. *First performed:*
Sept. 4, 1943; New York City. Louise
Rood, viola and Irene Jacobi, piano.
Score: reprod. of ms. BPL
Score: in *Boletin latino-americano de
musica.* Suplemento musical 5.
Score: Boosey & Hawkes, 1952. BPL HU
MIT
Part(viola): Boosey & Hawkes, 1952.
BPL HU MIT

P7.28 Intermezzo.
For: band.
Score: ms. in composer's hand. BPL

P7.29 Lincoln Center Festival Overture.
(1962) 12'
For: orchestra(2(&pic)-
2(&Ehn)-2(&bcl)-2(&cbsn); 4-3-3-1; timp,
perc; hp(2); str). *Commissioned by:*
Eugene Ormandy. *First performed:* Sept.
25, 1962; Philadelphia, Pa. Philadelphia
Orchestra, Eugene Ormandy, conductor.
Score & parts: Associated, 1962. Rental.
Score: reprod. of ms. BPL
Study score: Associated, 1962. BCM
BPL BrU BU HU MIT NEC UMB

[New England Sketches]
P7.30 Three New England Sketches.
(1959) 17'-18'
For: orchestra(2(&pic)-
2(&Ehn)-2(&bcl)-2(&cbsn); 4-3-3-1; timp,
perc; hp(2); str). *Movements:* Seaside;
Summer Evening; Mountains.
Commissioned by: Worcester County
Musical Association. *Dedicated to:* Paul
Paray. *First performed:* Oct. 23, 1959;
Worcester, Mass. Detroit Symphony
Orchestra, Paul Paray, conductor.
Score & parts: Associated. Rental.
Score: reprod. of ms. BPL
Study score: Associated, 1964. BCM
BPL HMA HU MIT W

O Sing unto the Lord a New Song. *See*
Psalm and Prayer of David. O Sing
unto the Lord a New Song.

P7.31 Orchestra Piece. (1925)
For: orchestra.
Score: ms. in composer's hand.

P7.32 Partita. (1944)
For: violin, viola, organ. *Movements:*
Prelude; Sarabande; Variations; Burlesca.
Commissioned by: Elizabeth Sprague
Coolidge Foundation (Library of
Congress). *Dedicated to:* Elizabeth
Sprague Coolidge. *First performed:* Oct.
29, 1944; Library of Congress,
Washington D.C. Wolfe Wolfinsohn,
violin; Eugene Lehner, viola; E. Power
Biggs, organ.
Symphony & parts: Arrow, 1951. BPL
HU L
Score & parts: Associated, 1951. MIT
Disc: ASCAP PFCM CB 190, 1954.
Samuel Thaviu, violin; Kras Malno,
viola; V.W. Fillinger, organ. BCM HU
NEC W

P7.33 Passacaglia. (1943)
For: piano. *First performed:* Oct. 23,
1944; New York City. Shura
Cherkassky.
Sketches: ms. in composer's hand.
Score: Mercury, 1943. BPL HU MIT NEC
Disc: in *Piano Music in America*, vol. 2:

1900-1945, Vox SVBX 5303, 1976.
Roger Shields. MIT NEC W

[Pieces]
P7.34 Three Pieces. (1926) 9' 20"
For: flute, clarinet, bassoon. *Dedicated to:* K.N. *First performed:* May 8, 1926; Paris, France. G. Blanquart, Coste, M. Dherin.
Score & parts: ms. in composer's hand. HU
Score: in *New Music: A Quarterly of Modern Compositions*, vol. 6, no. 4, 1933. BPL BrU HU W
Study score: Associated, 1933. BCM BPL MIT NEC
Parts: Andraud, 1933. BPL
Parts: Associated, 1933. HU T
Parts: Associated, 1961. MIT NEC
Disc: in *American Woodwind Symposium*, Classic CE 2003-A, 1954. Members of the New Art Wind Quintet. BCM
Disc: in *Modernists*, Unicorn UNLP 1029, 1956. Members of the Berkshire Woodwind Ensemble. BrU HU
Disc: Lyrichord LL 158/LLST 7158, 1966. Members of the Soni Ventorum Wind Quintet. BCM BrU BU HU MIT NU
Disc: Golden Crest CRS/Q 4140, 1975. Bennington Trio. BCM
Reel: Oct. 27, 1972; Harvard Musical Association. Lois Schaefer, flute; Pasquale Cardillo, clarinet; Ernst Panenka, bassoon. HU
Reel: Nov. 3, 1977; Boston Conservatory. Boston Woodwind Trio. BCM
Reel: Mar. 12, 1979; Boston Conservatory. Boston Conservatory Flute Chamber Ensemble, William Grass, director. BCM
Cassette: Mar. 22, 1971; New England Conservatory. Christopher Krueger, flute; Thomas Hill, clarinet; Vincent Ellin, bassoon. NEC
Cassette: May 8, 1971; New England Conservatory; in *A Festival of New England Composers Past and Present*. Christopher Krueger, flute; Thomas Hill, clarinet; Vincent Ellin, bassoon. NEC

P7.35 Pine Tree Fantasy. (1965) 10'
For: orchestra(2(&pic)-2(&Ehn)-2(&bcl)-2(cbsn); 4-2-3-1; timp, perc(4); str).
Commissioned by: Mary Castleman Lipkin. *Dedicated to:* Arthur Bennett Lipkin. *First performed:* Nov. 16, 1965; Portland, Me. Portland Symphony Orchestra, Arthur Bennett Lipkin, conductor.
Score: ms. in composer's hand. BPL
Score: reprod. of ms. BPL
Study score: Associated, 1967. BCM BPL BU HU MIT
Parts: Associated. Rental.

P7.36 Prelude and Allegro. (1943) 12'
For: organ, string quartet, double bass. Written for the Busch-Reisinger Museum, Harvard University, Radio Recitals. *Dedicated to:* E. Power Biggs. *First performed:* Aug. 1943; CBS. E. Power Biggs, organ; Fiedler Sinfonietta, Arthur Fiedler, conductor.
Score: reprod. of ms. BPL
Score: Arrow, 1944. BPL BrU BU HU NEC W
Score: Associated, 1944. BPL MIT
Disc: RCA Victor 11-9262. E. Power Biggs, organ; Boston Symphony Orchestra, Serge Koussevitzky, conductor.
Disc: in *A Tribute to E. Power Biggs*, Columbia M4X 35180, 1979. E. Power Biggs, organ; Boston Symphony Orchestra, Serge Koussevitzky, conductor. BU
Reel: Jan. 10, 1969; Boston Symphony Orchestra, Erich Leinsdorf, conductor. HU

P7.37 Prelude and Fugue. (1934) 13'
For: orchestra(3-2(&Ehn)-2(&bcl)-2(&cbsn); 4-3-3-1; timp; hp; str). *Commissioned by:* League of Composers. *First performed:* Mar. 12, 1936; Cleveland, Ohio. Cleveland Orchestra, Rudolf Ringwall, conductor.
Study score: Cos Cob, 1937. BPL BrU HU L W

Study score: Associated, 1937. BCM
BPL MIT

P7.38 Psalm and Prayer of David.
(1958) 11'
For: chorus(SATB), flute, clarinet,
bassoon, violins(1 or 2), viola,
violoncello, double bass. *Text:* Bible,
O.T., Psalm 86 and Bible, O.T., Psalm
96. *Contents:* O Sing unto the Lord a
New Song; Bow Down Thine Ear, O
Lord. *Commissioned by:* Brandeis
University. *First performed:* May 9,
1959. Chorus Pro Musica, Alfred Nash
Patterson, conductor.
Score: ms. in composer's hand. BPL
Score: reprod. of ms. (version with
optional 2nd violin). BPL
Parts: Associated, 1959 (version with
optional 2nd violin). BPL
Vocal score: Associated, 1959. BPL HU
Disc: in *America Sings: 1920-1950*, Vox
SVBX 5353, 1977. Peabody
Conservatory Concert Singers, Gregg
Smith, conductor. W

[Psalm and Prayer of David. Bow
Down Thine Ear, O Lord; Arr.]
P7.39 Bow Down Thine Ear, O Lord.
For: chorus(SATB) and piano. *Text:*
Bible, O.T., Psalm 86.
Vocal score: Associated, 1959. BPL
Vocal score: in *Contemporary Settings of
Psalm Texts, for Mixed Chorus*,
Associated, 1969. W

[Psalm and Prayer of David. O Sing
unto the Lord a New Song; Arr.]
P7.40 O Sing unto the Lord a New
Song.
For: chorus(SATB) and piano. *Text:*
Bible, O.T., Psalm 96.
Vocal score: Associated, 1959. BPL

[Quartet, Piano and Strings]
P7.41 Quartet. (1964)
For: violin, viola, violoncello, piano. 3
movements. *Commissioned by:* Harvard
Musical Association. *First performed:*
Apr. 27, 1964; Harvard Musical
Association.
Score & parts: reprod. of ms. BPL HMA
Score & parts: Associated, 1974. BPL

BU HMA HU MIT NEC W
Reel: Oct. 27, 1972; Harvard Musical
Association. Robert Brink, violin;
George Humphrey, viola; Karl Zeise,
violoncello; Bruce Simonds, piano. HU

[Quartet, Strings, No.1]
P7.42 String Quartet No. 1. (1933)
3 movements. *Dedicated to:* Chardon
Quartet. *First performed:* Mar. 7, 1934.
Chardon Quartet.
Score: Cos Cob, 1934. BPL BU HU NEC
Score: Associated, 1934. BPL MIT
Study score: Arrow, 1934. BCM HMA
MIT W
Parts: ms. BPL
Parts: Cos Cob, 1934. HU MIT NEC
Disc: Columbia M/AM 388. Dorian
String Quartet.
Disc: ASCAP PFCM CB 157, 1954.
Juilliard String Quartet. NEC W

[Quartet, Strings, No. 2]
P7.43 String Quartet No. 2. (1935) 19'
46"
3 movements. *Dedicated to:* Chardon
Quartet. *First performed:* Mar. 16, 1935;
Cambridge, Mass. Chardon Quartet.
Study score: G. Schirmer, 1946. BCM
BPL BrU BU HMA HU MIT W
Parts: ms. in composer's hand. BPL
Parts: G. Schirmer, 1946. HU MIT
Disc: New World NW 302, 1979.
Budapest String Quartet. BU MIT NEC
W

[Quartet, Strings, No. 3]
P7.44 String Quartet No. 3. (1947)
3 movements. *Commissioned by:*
Harvard University. *Dedicated to:* Diran
Alexamian. *First performed:* May 1,
1947. Walden Quartet.
Score & parts: reprod. of ms. NEC
Study score: Boosey & Hawkes, 1949.
BCM BPL BrU BU HMA HU MIT UMB
W
Parts: Boosey & Hawkes, 1949. BPL
Reel: May 15, 1949; Los Angeles,
Calif. American Art Quartet. HU
Reel: 1953; Library of Congress,
Washington, D.C. Budapest String
Quartet. HU

[Quartet, Strings, No. 4]
P7.45 String Quartet No. 4. (1951)
4 movements. *Commissioned by:*
Elizabeth Sprague Coolidge Foundation
(Library of Congress). Elizabeth Sprague
Coolidge. *First performed:* May 16,
1952; Mills College. Hungarian String
Quartet.
Score: reprod. of ms. BPL L
Study score: Associated, 1953. BCM
BPL BrU BU HMA HU MIT NEC W
Parts: reprod. of ms. L
Parts: Associated, 1953. BPL NEC
Reel: 1953; Library of Congress,
Washington D.C. Budapest String
Quartet. HU

[Quartet, Strings, No. 5]
P7.46 String Quartet No. 5. (1962)
3 movements. Commissioned for the
Berlin Festival, 1962. New York Music
Critics Circle Award, 1964. *First
performed:* Oct. 8, 1962. Kroll Quartet.
Score: ms. in composer's hand. BPL
Score: reprod. of ms. BPL
Study score: Associated, 1963. BCM
BPL HU MIT UMB W
Parts: Associated, 1963. BPL HU
Disc: in *American String Quartets,* vol.
2: 1900-1950, Vox SVBX 5305, 1974.
Kohon Quartet. BU HU MIT NEC W

P7.47 Quintet for Flute and String
Quartet. (1942) 18'
4 movements. *Commissioned by:* League
of Composers. *First performed:* Dec. 9,
1942; New York City. Ruth Freeman,
flute; Budapest String Quartet.
Study score: Arrow, 1946. BCM BPL BU
HU W
Study score: Associated, 1946. BCM
MIT
Parts: ms. BPL
Parts: Arrow, 1946. BPL HU
Parts: Associated, 1946. MIT
Reel: n.d. Doriot Anthony Dwyer, flute;
Concord String Quartet. HU

P7.48 Quintet for Pianoforte and String
Quartet. (1949)
3 movements. *Commissioned by:*
University of Michigan. *Dedicated to:*

Stanley Quartet. *First performed:* Aug.
2, 1949; Ann Arbor, Mich. Joseph
Brinkman, piano; Stanley Quartet.
Score & parts: reprod. of ms. L
Score & parts: Associated, 1953. HU
MIT NEC W
Parts: reprod. of ms. BPL
Disc: WCFM LP 14, 1953. Earl Wild,
piano; Walden String Quartet. BrU HU
NEC
Disc: ASCAP PFCM CB 159, 1954.
Johanna Harris, piano; New Music
String Quartet. BCM HU NEC W
Disc: McIntosh Music MM 109, [
1956?]. Earl Wild, piano; Walden String
Quartet.
Disc: Heliodor H/HS 25027, 1966. Earl
Wild, piano; Walden String Quartet. BU
HUm W

P7.49 Quintet for Wind Instruments,
1956. (1956) 18'
For: woodwind quintet. 4 movements.
Commissioned by: Elizabeth Sprague
Coolidge Foundation (Library of
Congress). *First performed:* Jan. 24,
1957; Library of Congress, Washington
D.C. Boston Woodwind Quintet.
Study score: Associated, 1957. BCM
BPL BrU HU MIT NEC W
Parts: Associated, 1957. BCM BPL MIT
NEC
Disc: Boston B 407/BST 1005, 1958.
Boston Woodwind Quintet. BU HU HUm
Disc: Orion ORS 75206, 1975. Boehm
Quintette. HU MIT
Reel: May 2, 1957. HU
Reel: n.d. Members of the Boston
Symphony Orchestra. HU
Cassette: Feb. 2, 1977; New England
Conservatory. NEC Scholarship
Woodwind Quintet. NEC
Cassette: Apr. 30, 1979; New England
Conservatory. NEC
Cassette: Dec. 17, 1979; New England
Conservatory. NEC

P7.50 Ricercare. (1967) 11'
For: orchestra(2(&pic)-
2(&Ehn)-2(&bcl)-2(&cbsn); 4-3-3-1; timp,
perc(3); hp(2); str). *Commissioned by:*
New York Philharmonic in celebration

of its 125th anniversary. *Dedicated to:* Leonard Bernstein. *First performed:* Mar. 7, 1968; New York City. New York Philharmonic, Leonard Bernstein, conductor.
Score & parts: Associated. Rental.
Score: reprod. of ms. BPL
Study score: Associated, 1968. BPL BU HU MIT UMB
Cassette: Dec. 3, 1969; New England Conservatory. NEC Symphony Orchestra, Leon Barzin, conductor. NEC

P7.51 Salute.
For: trumpets(4) and drums(last 3 measures).
Score: ms. in composer's hand. BPL

P7.52 Serenata. (1956) 12'
For: orchestra(2-2-2-2; 4-2-0-0; timp; hp; str). 3 movements. *Commissioned by:* Louisville Philharmonic Society for the Louisville Orchestra. *Dedicated to:* Robert Whitney. *First performed:* Oct. 24, 1956. Louisville Orchestra, Robert Whitney, conductor.
Score & parts: Associated. Rental.
Study score: Associated, 1958. BCM BPL BrU BU HU MIT NEC UMB
Disc: Louisville Orchestra LOU 58-6, 1958. Louisville Orchestra, Robert Whitney, conductor. BU HU HUm MIT NEC W

P7.53 Sextet. (1964)
For: violins(2), violas(2), violoncellos(2). 3 movements. *Commissioned by:* Elizabeth Sprague Coolidge Foundation (Library of Congress). *First performed:* Oct. 31, 1964; Library of Congress, Washington D.C; Elizabeth Sprague Coolidge Centennial Concert.
Score: reprod. of ms. BPL
Study score: Associated, 1965. BCM BPL HU MIT UMB
Parts: Associated, 1965. HU

P7.54 Sinfonietta. (1940-41) 17'
For: orchestra(2-2-2-2; 2-0-0-0; str). 3 movements. *Commissioned by and dedicated to:* Bernard Zighera. *First performed:* Mar. 10, 1941; Jordan Hall, Boston; Zighera Concert. Zighera

Chamber Orchestra, Bernard Zighera, conductor.
Score: Boosey & Hawkes, 1942. BPL HU W
Study score: reprod. of ms. BPL

[Sonata, Flute and Piano]
P7.55 Sonata. (1930) 15'
3 movements. *Dedicated to:* Georges Laurent. *First performed:* Feb. 13, 1931; Boston. Georges Laurent, flute and Jesus Maria Sanroma, piano.
Score & part: Arrow, 1933. L W
Score & part: Associated, 1933. BPL BU HU MIT NEC
Score: Cos Cob, 1933. BPL
Disc: in *American Music for Flute*, Claremont Records CR 1205. Doriot Anthony Dywer, flute and Barbara Korn, piano. HU
Disc: Westminster XWN 19121/WST 17121, 1967. Julius Baker, flute and Anthony Makas, piano. MIT
Disc: in *Music for Flute and Piano by Four Americans*, Laurel Protone LP 14, 1976. Laila Padorr, flute and Anita Swearengin, piano. WCRB
Disc: Orion ORS 76242, 1976. Keith Brian and flute; Karen Keys, piano. HU
Disc: Composers Recordings CRI SD 394, 1978. Ingrid Dingfelder, flute and Anita Gordon, piano. BrU BU HU MIT NEC W
Reel: Oct. 27, 1972; Harvard Musical Association. Lois Schaefer, flute and Bruce Simonds, piano. HU
Reel: Jan. 28, 1975; Boston University. Doriot Anthony Dwyer, flute and Fredrik Wanger, piano.
Cassette: Jan. 22, 1973; New England Conservatory. Edward A. Schultz, flute and John Felice, piano. NEC

[Sonata, Piano]
P7.56 Sonata. (1926) 18'
First performed: May 5, 1926; Paris, France. Marcel Ciampi.
Score: ms. in composer's hand. HU

[Sonata, Violin and Piano]
P7.57 Sonata. (1939) 18'
3 movements. *First performed:* Apr. 20, 1939; Brunswick, Me. Jascha Brodsky,

violin and Frederick Tillotsin, piano.
Score & part: Associated, 1940. BPL
MIT NEC
Score: Arrow, 1940. BPL BU HU
Part: Arrow, 1940. BPL
Disc: Columbia MX 199. Louis Krasner,
violin and Walter Piston, piano.
Disc: Decca DL 9541, 1951. Joseph
Fuchs, violin and Artur Balsam, piano.
BU HU MIT

P7.58 Sonatina. (1945)
For: violin and harpsichord or piano. 3
movements. *Dedicated to:* Alexander
Schneider and Ralph Kirkpatrick. *First
performed:* Nov. 30, 1945. Alexander
Schneider, violin and Ralph Kirkpatrick,
harpsichord.
Score & part: Boosey & Hawkes, 1948.
BPL BU HU L MIT
Part: reprod. of ms. BPL
Disc: Columbia ML 4495, [1953?]
Alexander Schneider, violin and Ralph
Kirkpatrick, harpsichord. HU HUm MIT
W
Disc: in *Music for a 20th Century
Violinist*, Desto DC 6435-6437, 1974.
Paul Zukofsky, violin and Gilbert
Kalish, piano. BU NEC W
Reel: n.d. O. Pernel, violin and Melville
Smith, harpsichord. HU
Reel: Mar. 26, 1979; Boston University.
Max Hobart, violin and Mark Kroll,
harpsichord. BU
Cassette: Jan. 31, 1974; New England
Conservatory. Eric Rosenblith, violin
and Blanche Winogron, harpsichord.
NEC

P7.59 Souvenir. (1967)
For: flute, viola, harp.
Score: ms. in composer's hand. BPL

[Suite, Oboe and Piano]
P7.60 Suite. (1931)
Movements: Prelude; Sarabande;
Minuetto; Nocturne; Gigue. *Dedicated to:*
Dr. Augustus Thorndike. *First
performed:* Jan. 17, 1932; Boston Flute
Players Club. Fernard Gillet, oboe and
Jesus Maria Sanroma, piano.
Score: E.C. Schirmer, 1934. BPL HU L

Score: E.C. Schirmer, 1964. BPL MIT
Part: E.C. Schirmer, 1934. BPL NEC
Part: E.C. Schirmer, 1964. BPL MIT
Disc: Technichord T 1561. Louis
Speyer, oboe and Walter Piston, piano.
Disc: Coronet 850 C-3652. Wayne
Rapier, oboe and John Perry, piano. BU
Disc: Coronet LPS 1409, 1969. Wayne
Rapier, oboe and John Perry, piano. HU
NEC

[Suite, Orchestra, No. 1]
P7.61 Suite. (1929) 15'
For:
orchestra(3(pic)-2(&Ehn)-2(bcl)-2(&cbsn);
4-3-3-1; timp, perc; pf; str). 3
movements. *First performed:* Mar. 28,
1930; Symphony Hall, Boston. Boston
Symphony Orchestra, Walter Piston,
conductor.
Score: Cos Cob, 1930. BPL BU HMA HU
Score: Associated. BPL
Study score: Arrow, 194-, 1930. BCM
BPL HU MIT

[Suite, Orchestra, No. 2]
P7.62 Second Suite. (1947-48) 23' 30"
For:
orchestra(2&pic)-2(&Ehn)-2(&bcl)-2(cbsn);
4-3-3-1; timp, perc; str). *Movements:*
Prelude; Sarabande; Intermezzo;
Passacaglia and Fugue. *Commissioned
by:* Dallas Symphony Orchestra.
Dedicated to: Antal Dorati and the
Dallas Symphony Orchestra. *First
performed:* Feb. 1948. Dallas Symphony
Orchestra, Antal Dorati, conductor.
Score & parts: Associated, 1953. Rental.
Score: reprod. of ms. BPL
Study score: Associated, 1953. BCM
BPL BU HU

P7.63 Symphonic Piece. (1927)
For: orchestra(2(&pic)-
2(&Ehn)-2(&bcl)-2(&cbsn); 4-3-0-1; timp,
perc; hp(2); str). *Dedicated to:* Serge
Koussevitzky. *First performed:* Mar. 23,
1928; Symphony Hall, Boston. Boston
Symphony Orchestra, Serge
Koussevitzky, conductor.
Score: ms. in composer's hand. HU

P7.64 Symphonic Prelude. (1961) 10'
For:
orchestra(2(&pic)-2(&Ehn)-2(&bcl)-2(cbsn);
4-3-3-1; timp; hp(2); str). *Commissioned by:* Association of Women's Committees for Symphony Orchestras. *First performed:* Apr. 20, 1961; Cleveland, Ohio. Cleveland Orchestra, George Szell, conductor.
Score & parts: Associated, 1962. Rental.
Score: reprod. of ms. BPL

[Symphony No. 1]
P7.65 First Symphony. (1937) 28'
For:
orchestra(2(&pic)-2(&Ehn)-2(bcl)-2(cbsn);
4-3-3-1; timp; str). 3 movements. *First performed:* Apr. 8, 1938; Symphony Hall, Boston. Boston Symphony Orchestra, Walter Piston, conductor.
Sketches: ms. in composer's hand. BPL
Score: reprod. of ms. BPL
Study score: G. Schirmer, 1945. Rental.
BCM BPL BrU BU HU NEC W
Disc: Louisville Orchestra LS 766, 1979.
BrU NEC W

P7.66 Symphony No. 2. (1943) 26'
For: orchestra(2(&pic)-
2(&Ehn)-2(&bcl)-2(&cbsn); 4-3-3-1; timp, perc; str). 3 movements. *Commissioned by:* Alice M. Ditson Fund of Columbia University. Winner of New York Music Critics Circle Award, 1945. *First performed:* Mar. 5, 1944; Washington D.C. National Symphony Orchestra, Hans Kindler, conductor.
Score & parts: Associated, 1944. Rental.
Score: ms. in composer's hand. HU
Score: Arrow, 1944. BPL HU NEC W
Study score: Associated, 1944. BCM
BrU MIT UMB
Disc: American Recording Society ARS 1, 1953. American Recording Society Orchestra [i.e. Vienna Symphony Orchestra], Dean Dixon, conductor.
HUm NEC T W
Disc: American Recording Society ARS 112, [195-]. American Recording Society Orchestra [i.e. Vienna Symphony Orchestra], Dean Dixon, conductor. BCM HU W
Disc: Desto D 410/DST 6410, 1965.

Vienna Symphony Orchestra, Dean Dixon, conductor. BU HU
Disc: Deutsche Grammophon 2530 103, 1971. Boston Symphony Orchestra, Michael Tilson Thomas, conductor.
BCM BrU BU HU MIT NEC

P7.67 Symphony No. 3. (1947) 31'
For: orchestra(2(&pic)-
2(&Ehn)-2(&bcl)-2(&cbsn); 4-3-3-1; timp, perc(5), glock, xylo; hp(2); str). 4 movements. *Commissioned by:* Koussevitzky Music Foundation (Library of Congress). *Dedication:* To the memory of Natalie Koussevitzky. Winner of the Pulitzer Prize in Music, 1948. *First performed:* Jan. 9, 1948; Symphony Hall, Boston. Boston Symphony Orchestra, Serge Koussevitzky, conductor.
Score: reprod. of ms. BPL
Score: Boosey & Hawkes, 1951. BPL
BrU BU HU MIT W
Disc: Pierian Sodality X7V 15382, 1951. Harvard-Radcliffe Orchestra, Russell Stanger, conductor. HU
Disc: Mercury MG 40010, 1954. Eastman Rochester Symphony, Howard Hanson, conductor. BPL BrU BU HU HUm W
Disc: Mercury MG 50083, 1956. Reissue of Mercury MG 40010, 1954. HU MIT
Disc: Mercury SRI 75107, 1978. Eastman Rochester Orchestra, Howard Hanson, conductor. HU
Reel: 1959/60. Boston Symphony Orchestra, Charles Munch, conductor. HU

P7.68 Symphony No. 4. (1950) 23'
For: orchestra(2(&pic)-
2(&Ehn)-2(&bcl)-2(&cbsn); 4-3-3-1; timp, perc; hp(2); str). *Movements:* Piacevele; Ballando; Contemplativo; Energico. Commissioned for the centennial celebration of the University of Minnesota, 1951. Winner of the Naumburg Recording Award, 1953. *First performed:* Mar. 30, 1951; Minneapolis, Minn. Minneapolis Symphony, Antal Dorati, conductor.
Score & parts: Associated, 1953. Rental.
Score: reprod. of ms. BPL

Score: Associated, 1953. MIT NEC
Study score: Associated, 1953. BCM
BPL BrU BU HU NEC W
Disc: Columbia ML/AML 4992, 1955.
Philadelphia Orchestra, Eugene
Ormandy, conductor. BCM BrU BU HU
HUm L MIT NEC W
Reel: n.d. Boston Symphony Orchestra,
Charles Munch, conductor. HU
Reel: Feb. 8, 1980; Boston University.
Boston University Orchestra, Mario di
Bonaventura, conductor. BU

P7.69 Symphony No. 5. (1954) 23'
For: orchestra(2(&pic)-
2(&Ehn)-2(&bcl)-2(&cbsn); 4-3-3-1; timp,
perc; hp(2); str). 3 movements.
Commissioned by: Juilliard School. *First
performed:* Feb. 24, 1956; New York
City. Juilliard Orchestra, Jean Paul
Morel, conductor.
Score & parts: Associated, 1956. Rental.
Score: Associated, 1956. BPL NEC UMB
Study score: Associated, 1956. BCM
BPL BrU BU HU MIT W
Disc: Louisville Orchestra LOU/LS 653,
1965. Louisville Orchestra, Robert
Whitney, conductor. BrU BU HU HUm
MIT NEC W
Reel: Oct. 27, 1956; WGBH-FM, Boston.
Boston Symphony Orchestra, Charles
Munch, conductor. HU

P7.70 Symphony No. 6. (1955) 25'
For: orchestra(2(&pic)-
2(&Ehn)-2(&bcl)-2(&cbsn); 4-3-3-1; timp,
perc; hp(2); str). 4 movements.
Dedication: To the memory of Serge
and Natalie Koussevitzky in celebration
of the 75th season of the Boston
Symphony Orchestra. *First performed:*
Nov. 25, 1955; Symphony Hall, Boston.
Boston Symphony Orchestra, Charles
Munch, conductor.
Score & parts: Associated, 1957. Rental.
Score: reprod. of ms. BPL
Score: Associated, 1957. BPL NEC W
Study score: Associated, 1957. BPL BrU
BU HMA HU MIT UMB
Disc: RCA Victor LM 2083, 1957.
Boston Symphony Orchestra, Charles

Munch, conductor. BrU HU HUm MIT
NEC NU W
Disc: New World Records NW 286,
1977. Reissue of RCA Victor LM 2083,
1957. BCM BU HU HUm MIT NEC T W
Disc: RCA Gold Seal AGL1-3794, 1981.
Reissue of RCA Victor LM 2083, 1957.
Reel: Nov. 26, 1955. Boston Symphony
Orchestra, Charles Munch, conductor.
HU

P7.71 Symphony No. 7. (1960) 19'
For: orchestra(2(&pic)-
2(&Ehn)-2(&bcl)-2(&cbsn); 4-3-3-1; timp,
perc; hp(2); str). 3 movements.
Commissioned by: Philadelphia Orchestra
Association. *Dedicated to:* Eugene
Ormandy. Winner of the Pulitzer Prize
in Music, 1961. *First performed:* Feb.
10, 1961; Philadelphia, Pa. Philadelphia
Orchestra, Eugene Ormandy, conductor.
Score & parts: Associated, 1961. Rental.
Score: reprod. of ms. BPL
Score: Associated, 1961. BPL W
Study score: Associated, 1961. BCM
BPL BrU BU HU MIT UMB
Disc: Louisville Orchestra LS 746, 1975.
Louisville Orchestra, Jorge Mester,
conductor. BrU BU HU MIT NEC W

P7.72 Symphony No. 8. (1965) 20'
For: orchestra(2(&pic)-
2(&Ehn)-2(&bcl)-2(&cbsn); 4-3-3-1; timp,
perc(3); hp(2); str). 3 movements.
Commissioned by: Boston Symphony
Orchestra. *Dedicated to:* Erich Leinsdorf.
First performed: Mar. 5, 1965;
Symphony Hall, Boston. Boston
Symphony Orchestra, Erich Leinsdorf,
conductor.
Score & parts: Associated, 1966. Rental.
Score: ms. in composer's hand. BU
Score: reprod. of ms. BPL
Score: Associated, 1966. BrU
Study score: Associated, 1966. BPL BU
HU MIT NEC
Disc: Louisville Orchestra LS 746, 1975.
Louisville Orchestra, Jorge Mester,
conductor. BrU BU HU MIT NEC W
Reel: recording of first performance.
HU

P7.73 Toccata. (1948) 9'
For:
orchestra(2(&pic)-2(&Ehn)-2(bcl)-2(cbsn);
4-3-3-1; timp, perc(6); str). 1 movement.
Dedicated to: Charles Munch. *First
performed:* Oct. 14, 1948; Bridgeport,
Conn. L'Orchestre national de France,
Charles Munch, conductor.
Score: reprod. of ms. BPL
Score: Boosey & Hawkes, 1953. Rental.
BPL HU NEC

[Trio, No. 1]
P7.74 Trio. (1935) 17'
For: violin, violoncello, piano. 4
movements. *Commissioned by:* Elizabeth
Sprague Coolidge Foundation (Library
of Congress). *Dedicated to:* Elizabeth
Sprague Coolidge. *First performed:* Oct.
30, 1935; Library of Congress,
Washington, D.C. William Kroll, violin;
Horace Britt, violoncello; Frank
Sheridan, piano.
Score & parts: Arrow, 1938. BPL HMA
HU NEC W
Score & parts: Arrow, 1951. L
Score & parts: Associated, 1951. BPL
NEC
Score & parts: Cos Cob, 1951. MIT
Disc: Perspective PR 2004, 1954. New
York Trio.
Disc: Golden Crest CRS 4117, 1974.
Temple University Trio. BU HU MIT
Disc: Laurel LR 104, 1976. Western
Arts Trio. MIT NEC

[Trio, No. 2]
P7.75 Trio. (1966)
For: violin, violoncello, piano. 3
movements. Commissioned in memory
of Rembert Wurlitzer by his family.
Dedicated to: Balsam-Kroll-Heifetz Trio.
Score & parts: reprod. of ms. BPL
Score & parts: Associated, 1974. BPL
BU HU MIT W
Score: ms. in composer's hand. BPL

P7.76 Tunbridge Fair: Intermezzo. (1950)
4' 30"
For: band. *Commissioned by:* League of
Composers. *First performed:* June 16,
1950. Goldman Band, Walter Piston,
conductor.

Score: Boosey & Hawkes, 1951. BCM
BPL HU MIT NEC
Parts: Boosey & Hawkes, 1951. BCM
NEC
Disc: in *American Concert Band
Masterpieces*, Mercury MG 40006, 1954.
Eastman Wind Ensemble, Frederick
Fennell, conductor.
Disc: MG 50079, 1956. Reissue of
Mercury MG 40006, 1954.
Disc: Mercury SRI 75086, 1977. Reissue
of Mercury MG 40006, 1954. BCM
Disc: MIT Concert Band XTV 21867 &
G8-0L-0367, n.d. MIT Concert Band,
John Corley, conductor. MIT
Reel: Nov. 25, 1974; Boston
Conservatory. Boston Conservatory
Wind Ensemble, John Corley,
conductor. BCM
Reel: Mar. 26, 1977. Harvard University
Band, Thomas Everett, conductor.
WGBH
Reel: Mar. 30, 1977; Boston University.
Boston University Wind Ensemble, Paul
Gay, conductor. BU
Reel: Oct. 22, 1981; Boston
Conservatory. Boston Conservatory
Wind Ensemble, Peter Cokkinias,
conductor. BCM
Cassette: Apr. 25, 1974; New England
Conservatory. NEC Wind Ensemble,
Frank L. Battisti, conductor. NEC
Cassette: Dec. 9, 1975; New England
Conservatory. NEC Repertory Wind
Ensemble, Michael Walters, conductor.
NEC
Cassette: May 8, 1977; New England
Conservatory. Massachusetts Youth
Wind Ensemble, Thomas Everett,
conductor. NEC
Cassette: Nov. 10, 1977; New England
Conservatory. NEC Repertory Wind
Ensemble, Michael Walters, conductor.
NEC
Cassette: Nov. 6, 1979; New England
Conservatory. NEC Repertory Wind
Ensemble, Michael Walters, conductor.
NEC

P7.77 Variations. (1966) 16'
For: violoncello and orchestra
(2(&pic)-2(&Ehn)-2(&bcl)-2(&cbsn);
4-2-3-1; timp, perc(3); hp; str).

Commissioned by and dedicated to: Mstislav Rostropovitch. *First performed:* Mar. 2, 1967; Carnegie Hall, New York City. Mstislav Rostropovich, violoncello; London Symphony Orchestra, Gennady Rozhdestvensky, conductor.
Score & parts: Associated, 1968. Rental.
Score: reprod. of ms. BPL
Study score: Associated, 1968. BCM BPL BrU BU HU MIT UMB
Part(violoncello): reprod. of ms. BPL
Part(violoncello): Associated, 1968. BPL HU
Pf. red: reprod. of ms. BPL
Pf. red: Associated, 1968. BPL HU

P7.78 Variations on a Theme by E.B. Hill. (1963) 11'
For: orchestra(2-2(&Ehn)-2(&bcl)-2; 4-2-3-1; perc, timp; hp; str).
Commissioned by: Isaac Kibrick.
Dedication: To the memory of Herbert Kibrick. *First performed:* Apr. 30, 1960; Boston. Civic Symphony Orchestra of Boston, Kalman Novak, conductor.
Score: ms. in composer's hand. HUh
Score: reprod. of ms. BPL
Score: Associated, 1964. BCM BPL HU MIT
Parts: Associated, 1964. Rental. BCM

P7.79 Variations on a Theme by Eugene Goossens. (1944)
For: orchestra. One of ten variations by American composers written at the invitation of Eugene Goossens. *First performed:* Mar. 23, 1945; Cincinnati, Ohio. Cincinnati Symphony Orchestra, Eugene Goossens, conductor.
Score: ms. in composer's hand. BPL

ARRANGEMENTS OF WORKS BY OTHER COMPOSERS

Clair de lune. *See* Suite Bergamasque. Clair de lune.

P7.80 Promethee, Acte II, Scene I.
For: orchestra. Original by Gabriel Faure.

[Sonata, Piano, No. 14. Adagio sostenuto]
P7.81 Adagio Sostenuto from the Moonlight Sonata, Op. 27, No. 2.
For: orchestra. Original by Ludwig van Beethoven.

[Suite bergamasque. Clair de lune]
P7.82 Clair de lune. (1936)
For: orchestra(2-2-2-2; 2-2-0-0; timp, perc, glock; hp; str). Original by Claude Debussy.
Score: reprod. of ms. BPL

P8 STEPHANY KING PLSEK

Born June 18, 1949, in Brighton, Mass.
Education: B.M. (Berklee College of Music, 1974); studied composition with William Thomas McKinley (New England Conservatory, M.M., 1978) and Hugo Norden; piano with Margaret Chaloff.
Related activities: pianist/accompanist; member of the faculty of Berklee College of Music (1975-). Be WORKS

P8.1 Bass Solos. (1977)
For: double bass.
Score: reprod. of ms.; available from composer.

[Concerto, Piano]
P8.2 Piano Concerto. (in progress)
Score: reprod. of ms.; available from composer.

P8.3 Conversations. (1976)
For: clarinet.
Score: reprod. of ms.; available from composer.

[Quartet, Strings]
P8.4 String Quartet. (1976) 11'
1 movement. *First performed:* Oct. 14, 1976; New England Conservatory. Bradley Stewart and Harris Shiller, violins; Emily Bruell, viola; Barbara Wood, violoncello.
Score: reprod. of ms.; available from composer.

[Sonata, Piano]
P8.5 Piano Sonata. (1975 or 1976) 19'
3 movements. *First performed:* Nov.
20, 1976; New England Conservatory.
Stephany King Plsek.
Score: reprod. of ms.; available from
composer.

[Sonata, Violin and Piano]
P8.6 Violin and Piano Sonata. (1977)
Score: available from composer.

P8.7 Stereophonic Suite. (1978) 5'
For: trombone, trombone(bell only),
garden hose. 2 movements. *Dedicated
to:* Tom Plsek. *First performed:* 1979;
Emmanuel Church, Boston. Tom Plsek,
trombone.
Score: reprod. of ms.; available from
composer.

P8.8 Transformations I-VII. (1977-78)
20'
For: piano. *Dedicated to:* Margaret
Chaloff. *First performed:* Mar. 7, 1978;
New England Conservatory. Stephany
King Plsek.
Score: reprod. of ms.; available from
composer.

[Trio, Brasses]
P8.9 Brass Trio. (1977)
For: trumpet, trombone, horn.
Score & parts: available from
composer.

P8.10 Verbum. (1976 or 1977) 8'
For: trumpet and piano. 2 movements.
First performed: Jan. 27, 1977; New
England Conservatory. Gregory Hopkins,
trumpet and Stephany King Plsek,
piano.
Score: reprod. of ms.; available from
composer.

P9 THOMAS J. PLSEK (Tom)

Born October 8, 1947, in Waco, Tex.
Moved to Boston area 1972. *Education:*
B.M. (Texas Christian University, 1970);
M.M. (University of Houston, 1972).
Related activities: trombonist; founder
and director of the Boston New Music

Ensemble; organizer of Boston Sackbut
Week; currently artist-clinician for
Yamaha Corporation; member of the
faculty of the Berklee College of
Music (1972-). Be

WORKS

P9.1 Forms. (1979) 15'
For: instrument(unspecified). 1
movement. *First performed:* Apr. 2,
1979; Emmanuel Church, Boston. Boston
New Music Ensemble.
Score: reprod. of ms.; available from
composer.

P9.2 Ken/Keeping Still, Mountain. (1978)
1' 15"
For: instruments(unspecified). *Text: I
Ching.* Conceptual, improvisational
piece that included, as part of
performance, the destruction of the
score and parts by fire. *Dedication:* For
the Boston New Music Ensemble. *First
performed:* Oct. 31, 1978; Emmanuel
Church, Boston. Boston New Music
Ensemble.

P9.3 Logic Variations--A Theater Piece
for Five Musicians. (1975) 15'-20'
For: instruments(unspecified)(5). *First
performed:* May 2, 1975; Emmanuel
Church, Boston. Richard Allen, William
Elgart, Brian O'Connell, Tom Plsek,
John Voigt.
Perf. dir & parts: reprod. of ms.
Reel: Dec. 1, 1975; Berklee Recital Hall
(later version, titled Logic Variations
II). Richard Allen, Billy Elgart, Brian
O'Connell, Tom Plsek, John Voigt. Be

P9.4 The Lone Ranger Silver Atomic
Trombone Art Auction. (1976) 30'
For: trombone, instruments(unspecified),
conceptual artist. 1 movement.
Conceptual piece in which solo
trombonist determines material and
manner of usage. Written in
collaboration with John Voigt. *First
performed:* May 7, 1976; Emmanuel
Church, Boston. Tom Plsek, trombone;
Martha Conners-O'Connor, conceptual

artist; The John Voigt Group.
Music: available from composer.

P9.5 Nash Animals. (1972) 10'
For: Soprano or Tenor, flutes(2), oboe,
clarinet, bassoon, horn, trombone, tuba
or trombone(bass), percussion. *Text:*
Ogden Nash. *Contents:* The Fly; The
Termite; The Mules; The Octopus; The
Porcupine; The Germ. *First performed:*
1972; Houston, Tex.
Score & parts: reprod. of ms.; available
from composer.
Reel: Mar. 20, 1973; Berklee College of
Music. Be

P9.6 Reactions I. (1975) 15'-20'
For: conductor/composers(4) and
trombone ensemble(4 players minimum
in each of 4 groups, dispersed in large
outdoor area). 1 movement. *Dedicated
to:* Boston Sackbut Week. *First
performed:* May 1975; City Hall Plaza,
Boston.
Music: available from composer.

P9.7 Streets Whose Names Are Trees.
(1974) 4'
For: voice(woman), percussion, dancer.
1 movement. *Text:* Anita Barrows. *First
performed:* Mar. 26, 1974; Berklee
College of Music. Carla Bee, voice;
David Patt, percussion; Holly Whipple,
dancer.
Score: reprod. of ms.; available from
composer.
Reel: recording of first performance.
Be

P9.8 (SW) Radio Activity. (1980) 15'-20'
For: trombone and radio(short-wave).
Aleatoric music. *Dedicated to:* George
Norris. *First performed:* Feb. 27, 1980;
Berklee Performance Center. Tom
Plsek, trombone and short-wave radio.
Score: reprod. of ms.; available from
composer.

P9.9 Through the Sounding Glass.
(1981) Duration variable.
For: instruments(unspecified)(1-4), glass,
television monitor. Conceptual piece

using a large sheet of glass as a
loudspeaker, musicians (not heard
acoustically by audience), television
monitor. *Commissioned by:* DeCordova
Museum, Lincoln, Mass. *First
performed:* June 28, 1981; DeCordova
Museum, Lincoln, Mass. Malcolm
Goldstein, violin; John Voigt, double
bass; Mark Harvey, trumpet; Tom
Plsek, trombone.
Music: available from composer.

P10 LEILA PRADELL

Born in Boston. *Education:* B.A. (Boston
University, 1953); studied composition
with Francis Judd Cooke (New England
Conservatory, M.M.Ed., 1959) and Nadia
Boulanger (Fontainebleau Music School,
Fontainebleau, France); voice with
Gladys Miller, Eunice Alberts,
Professor von Schmeidel. *Related
activities:* has composed for the
Charles Playhouse, Boston;
composer-in-residence, Newton Public
Schools, Newton, Mass.; created
Contemporary Music for Children
Project (New England Conservatory);
founded the Boston Women's
Composers Organization; member of
American Women Composers and the
League of Women Composers;
currently on the faculty of the
Preparatory School, New England
Conservatory. NFL WORK

P10.1 Alaskan Song Cycle. (1972)
For: Soprano and piano. *Text:* Claire
Fejes. *First performed:* 1979; New
England Conservatory. Afrika Hayes,
soprano.
Score: ms.

Billy Goats Gruff. *See* Three Billy
Goats Gruff.

[Bridal Songs]
P10.2 Two Bridal Songs.
For: Soprano and piano. *Text:* Emily
Dickinson.
Score: ms.

P10.3 Carousel. (1978)
For: Soprano, chorus(children)(3-part),
string quartet, harp. Song cycle. *Text:*
Samuel Taylor Coleridge; Indian legend;
A. Keymbourg; Dag Hammarskjoeld.
First performed: 1978; Newton High
School, Newton, Mass.
Score & parts: ms.

P10.4 Diary of Athens.
For: piano. 6 movements. *First
performed:* May 1980; Rivers Music
School, Weston, Mass. Mark Saltzer.
Score: Boston, nyp.

P10.5 Don Quixote.
Incidental music. Withdrawn.

P10.6 Easter Vigil.
For: Bass Baritone and string quartet.
Text: Pope John Paul II. *First
performed:* 1980; Holy Cross Cathedral,
Boston. Jan Milun, bass baritone.
Score & parts: ms.

P10.7 The Elephant's Child.
For: voices(children) and piano.
Children's opera. *Text:* Rudyard Kipling.
Commissioned by: Newton Public
Schools Creative Arts Program,
Newton, Mass. Performed by children's
groups.
Vocal score: ms.

Four Musicians of Bremen. *See*
Musicians of Bremen.

P10.8 Fugue for Orchestra.
Withdrawn.

P10.9 A Game of Fifths.
For: piano and flute(optional). Suite. 3
movements.
Score: ms.

P10.10 The Gingerbread Man.
For: voices(children) and piano.
Children's opera; based on a folk tale.
Commissioned by: Newton Public
Schools Creative Arts Program,
Newton, Mass. Performed by children's
groups.
Score: ms.

P10.11 The Hobbit.
Incidental music. Withdrawn.

P10.12 June.
For: chorus(SA), Orff instruments,
piano. *Text:* John Hoyer Updike.
Score & parts: ms.

P10.13 Lament.
For: Soprano and piano. *Text:* Leila
Pradell. *First performed:* Oct. 18, 1981;
Museum of Our National Heritage,
Lexington, Mass. Mary Sindoni,
soprano.
Vocal score: ms.

[Musicians of Bremen]
P10.14 The Four Musicians of Bremen.
For: voices(children) and piano.
Children's opera; based on the folk
tale by Jacob Grimm and Wilhelm
Grimm. *Commissioned by:* Newton
Public Schools Creative Arts Program,
Newton, Mass. Performed by children's
groups.

P10.15 My World.
For: voice or chorus(unison) and piano.
Song. *Text:* E.A. Guest. *First performed:*
Newton Public Schools Chorus.
Score: ms.

P10.16 Nanushka.
For: Soprano, flute, horn, piano. Song
cycle. *Text:* Nan Whitcomb. *First
performed:* New England Conservatory,
Afrika Hayes, soprano.
Score: ms.

P10.17 Noah and the Ark.
For: voices(children) and piano.
Children's opera. *Commissioned by:*
Newton Public Schools Creative Arts
Program, Newton, Mass. Performed by
children's groups.
Score: ms.

P10.18 The Paint Box.
For: Soprano and piano. Song cycle.
Text: based on poems by children of
the Arab-Israeli conflict. *First
performed:* 1979; New England

Conservatory. Afrika Hayes, soprano.
Score: ms.

P10.19 The Pied Piper of Hamelin.
For: voices(children) and piano.
Children's opera; based on a folk tale.
Commissioned by: Newton Public
Schools Creative Arts Program,
Newton, Mass. Performed by children's
groups.
Score: ms.

P10.20 Rivers.
For: Soprano or Mezzo Soprano,
violoncello, piano. *Text:* Langston
Hughes. *First performed:* New England
Conservatory. Afrika Hayes, soprano.
Score & parts: ms.

P10.21 Roads Go Ever on.
For: chorus(SA) and piano. *Text:* J.R.R.
Tolkien.
Vocal score: ms.

P10.22 Selfish Giant.
For: voices(children) and piano.
Children's opera. *Text:* Oscar Wilde.
Commissioned by: Newton Public
Schools Creative Arts Program,
Newton, Mass. Performed by children's
groups.
Score: ms.

[Sonata, Piano]
P10.23 Sonata for Piano.
Withdrawn.

[Studies]
P10.24 Four Studies for Piano.
Score: ms.

P10.25 Three Billy Goats Gruff.
For: voices(children) and piano.
Children's opera; based on a folk tale.
Commissioned by: Newton Public
Schools Creative Arts Program,
Newton, Mass. Performed by children's
groups.

P10.26 Tomorrow.
For: Soprano, flute, horn,
strings(unspecified). *Text:* Kahlil Gibran.

First performed: New England
Conservatory. Afrika Hayes, soprano.
Parts: ms.

P10.27 Ugly Duckling.
For: voices(children) and piano.
Children's opera; based on a folk tale.
Commissioned by: Newton Public
Scnools Creative Arts Program,
Newton, Mass. Performed by children's
groups.
Score: ms.

P10.28 Where the Wild Things Are.
For: voices(children) and piano.
Children's opera. *Text:* Maurice Sendak.
Commissioned by: Newton Public
Schools Creative Arts Program,
Newton, Mass. *First performed:* 1981.
Score: ms.

P10.29 Winter Song Cycle.
For: chorus(children)(3-part), piano, Orff
instruments. *Text:* John Hoyer Updike;
Robert Frost; Leila Pradell. *Dedicated
to:* Anne Gombosi. *First performed:*
1978; Newton, Mass. Newton All-City
Chorus. *Score.*

ARRANGEMENTS

[Arrangements of Folk Songs]
P10.30 Thirty-Four Arrangements of
Folk Songs.
For: voice and Orff instruments.
Score: ms.

P11 ALICE McELROY PROCTER

Born 1915, in Albany, New York.
Moved to Boston area 1946. *Education:*
studied composition with Ross Lee
Finney, Werner Josten (Smith College,
B.A., 1935, M.A., 1936); Howard Hanson,
Bernard Rogers (Eastman School of
Music, Ph.D., 1940). *Related activities:*
compiler and editor of *Panorama: A
Collection of American Piano Music*
(1953); pianist; accompanist for the
Dedham Choral Society (1957-73);
teacher of piano to students in the
Upward Bound program; served on the

faculties of Southwestern State College, Weatherford, Okla. (1939-42), Milton Academy, Milton, Mass. (1962-78), Dedham Country Day School, Dedham, Mass. (1974-78). W

WORKS

Andante and Allegretto. *See* Concertino, String Orchestra. Andante and Allegretto; Arr.

P11.1 Andante and Allegro. (1963)
For: handbells. 2 movements. *Dedicated to:* Beacon Hill Bell Ringers.

P11.2 Andantino. (1952)
For: violoncello and piano. *Score & part.*

P11.3 The Ballad of Befana. (1970)
For: Mezzo Soprano, chorus(unison), piano. *Text:* Phyllis McGinley.
Vocal score: ms.

P11.4 Ballerina.
For: piano.
Score: ms.

P11.5 Ballet Music from Three White Feathers. (1936; rev. 1938)
For: string quartet, double bass, piano. Libretto: Emily Tompkins. *Movements:* Allegro robusto; Sarabande; Gavotte.
Score: ms.

P11.6 Ballet Suite from a Singspiel in 3 Acts. (1936)
For: chamber orchestra(1-1-2(in A)-2; 2-0-0-0; pf; str(5)).
Score: reprod. of ms.

P11.7 Banrigh Suite. (1936) 7'
For: chamber orchestra. 5 movements.
First performed: June 1936; Northampton, Mass. Smith College Orchestra, Werner Josten, conductor.

P11.8 Barefoot Days. (1947)
For: Mezzo Soprano and piano. *Text:* Rachel Lyman Field. *Dedicated to:* Werner Josten. *First performed:* Dec. 5, 1952; New England Conservatory.

Delores Baldyga, soprano and Elizabeth Gill, piano.
Score: ms.

P11.9 The Black Swan from Three White Feathers. (1936; rev. 1938)
For: Mezzo Soprano, string quartet, harp, piano. *Libretto:* Emily Tomkins.
Score & parts: ms.
Vocal score: ms.

P11.10 A Boy's Song.
For: voice and piano. *Text:* Henry Charles Beeching. *Dedicated to:* Werner Josten. *First performed:* Dec. 5, 1952; New England Conservatory. Delores Baldyga, soprano and Elizabeth Gill, piano.
Score: ms.

P11.11 Cake-Walk.
For: piano(right hand). 1 movement.
Dedicated to: Toney Jo Barry.
Score: ms.

P11.12 Caprice.
For: piano. 1 movement.
Score: ms.

P11.13 Castle Hill Suite. (1963)
For: handbells. *Movements:* Overture; Sarabande; Divertimento; Minuet; Finale.
Dedicated to: Marie Pereira.
Score: Gray, 1963.

P11.14 Chapel in the North. (1950)
For: piano(4-hands).
Score: ms.

[Christmas Lullaby, Chorus(SATB)]
P11.15 Christmas Lullaby. (1947)
For: chorus(SATB) and piano or organ.
Text: Janet Sprague Williams.
Vocal score: ms.

[Christmas Lullaby, Chorus(SSA)]
P11.16 Christmas Lullaby. (1947)
For: chorus(SSA) and piano or organ.
Text: Janet Sprague Williams. *Vocal score.*

[Christmas Lullaby, Mezzo Soprano and Piano]

P11.17 Christmas Lullaby.
Text: Janet Sprague Williams. *Dedicated to:* Barbie and the twins.
Score: ms.

P11.18 Cinderella. (1935)
For: voices, chorus(women), string quartet, piano. Operetta. *Libretto:* Emily Tomkins and Barbara Shelley.
Score & parts: ms.
Vocal score: ms.

P11.19 Concertino for String Orchestra. (1935) 5'
2 movements. *First performed:* June 1935; Smith College. Smith College Orchestra, Werner Josten, conductor.
Score & parts: ms.; available from composer.

[Concertino, String Orchestra. Andante and Allegretto; Arr.]
P11.20 Andante and Allegretto.
For: violin and piano.
Score & part: ms.

P11.21 Contemplation.
For: piano. *Dedication:* To Mother and Dad.
Score: ms.

P11.22 Country Dance.
For: piano(4-hands). 1 movement.
Score: reprod. of ms.

P11.23 Dance of the Red Skirt. (1950)
For: piano(4-hands).
Score: ms.

P11.24 Dance Suite. (1934)
For: piano. 3 movements.
Score: ms.

P11.25 Daydream.
For: piano. *Dedicated to:* Karen Rhodes.
Score: Elkan-Vogel, 1963.

[Easy Pieces]
P11.26 Five Easy Pieces. (1967)
For: piano. *Movements:* Wacky Song; Simple Waltz; Joyful Fling; Lullaby; Bib

Bells.
Score: ms.

[Easy Pieces]
P11.27 Nine Easy Pieces for the Piano.
For: piano. *Contents:* Prelude; Little March; Broken Music Box; Rocking Horse; Nonchalance; Touch and Go; Melody in 5/8; Reminiscence; Scherzo.
Score: reprod. of ms.

P11.28 Elegy.
For: organ, or flute and strings, or orchestra. 1 movement. *Dedication:* In memory of Samuel G. Trepp.
Sketches: ms. (versions for flute and strings (1947) and for orchestra (1950)).
Score: ms.

P11.29 Epiphany Hymn. (1966)
For: chorus(children) and piano. 1 movement. *Text:* Sally Burt. *Dedicated to:* St. Paul's Church Sunday School.

P11.30 Etude in F Minor. (1969)
For: piano. 1 movement. *Dedicated to:* Claude Frank.
Score: ms.

P11.31 Festive Overture. (1963)
For: handbells. *Dedicated to:* Charlotte Boynton Smith.
Score: Gray, 1964.

P11.32 Flute Prints. (1938)
For: flute, piano, string quartet.
Score & parts: ms.
Pf. red: ms. in composer's hand.

P11.33 Footsteps in the Night.
For: piano(4-hands).
Score: Oxford.
Score: Scribner's.

P11.34 Fragment. (1937)
For: piano. 1 movement.
Score: ms.

P11.35 From My Address Book: a Collection of 6 Short Pieces, Based on Zip Codes and Telephone Numbers. (1969) *For:* piano. *Movements:* 02186;

12771; 21163; 23185; 60615;
201-828-9352.
Score: ms.

P11.36 From Now On: A Folk Mass for
Our Time. (1968)
For: chorus(unison), piano or organ,
guitar. *Movements:* Kyrie; The Apostles'
Creed (spiritual); Eso Evnay (I Will Lift
Mine Eyes; Presentation of the
Offering; From Now On...; Amen (Negro
melody); Kumbaya (West African
Melody); The Lord's Prayer; Agnus Dei;
Gloria; Vine and and Fig Tree
(traditional). Written and arranged in
collaboration with Chip Harding, Bill
Schwartz, Susan Wales, Elisabeth Colt.
First performed: May 12, 1968; St.
Paul's Episcopal Church, Dedham, Mass.
Richard J. Griffin, conductor.
Score: ms.

P11.37 Fun for Two.
For: piano(4-hands). *Contents:* Country
Dance; Song of the Ranger; Coney
Island; When Johnnie Comes Marching
Home; Theme from the New World
Symphony (Antonin Dvorak); Ally Ally
in Free. *Dedicated to:* Johnny and Sue.
Score: Elkan Vogel, 1955.

P11.38 Fun to Play.
For: piano.
Score: in *Beginning Piano Book*, Pro-Art,
1955.

P11.39 Gaelic Song.
For: piano(4-hands). 1 movement.
Dedicated to: Judy and Jean Condon.
Score: ms.

P11.40 Halloween Piece. (1967)
For: piano. 1 movement. *Dedicated to:*
Debbie Fontana.
Score: ms.

P11.41 Happy Go Lucky.
For: piano(4-hands).
Score: Oxford.

P11.42 Hayride.
For: piano. 1 movement.
Score: reprod. of ms.

P11.43 Heyday. (1965)
For: piano(4-hands). 1 movement.
Dedicated to: Leslie, Linda, and Laurie
Dempsey.
Score: reprod. of ms.

P11.44 Holiday Bells.
For: piano(4-hands). *Dedicated to:*
Marcia and Joan.
Score: Elkan-Vogel, 1954.

P11.45 How Bright the Glory of the
Lord. (1970)
For: chorus(SATB) and piano. *Text:*
James F. McElroy
Score: ms.

P11.46 I Did Believe in Fairies. (1940)
For: Mezzo Soprano and piano. *Text:*
Fern Lewis.
Score: ms.

P11.47 Invention in E Major.
For: piano.
Score: reprod. of ms.

P11.48 Jaunt to Town.
For: piano. *Dedicated to:* Ellen Driscoll.
Score: Elkan-Vogel, 1968.

P11.49 Johnny Has a Girlfriend.
For: piano.
Score: Summy Birchard, 1959.

P11.50 The Jumping Cat.
For: piano.
Score: in *Scribner Music Library*, vol. 1,
Scribner, 1964.

P11.51 Lament. (1970)
For: violoncello and piano. 1
movement.
Score & part: ms.

P11.52 Lazy River.
For: piano(4-hands). *Dedicated to:* Helen
and John.
Score: ms.

P11.53 Let the Heart of Them Rejoice.
For: chorus(SATB) and piano. *Text:*
Bible, O.T., I Chronicles 16: 8-10. *First
performed:* Apr. 29, 1970. Dedham

Choral Society, Brian E. Jones, conductor.
Vocal score: ms.

P11.54 A Lively Journey.
For: piano(4-hands).
Score: Oxford.
Score: Scribner's.

P11.55 Lullaby.
For: piano(4-hands). *Dedicated to:* Gail and Joanne.
Score: Elkan-Vogel, 1951.

P11.56 March of the Moon Men.
For: piano(4-hands). *Dedicated to:* Pieter and David.
Score: Elkan-Vogel, 1965.

P11.57 Marionette.
For: piano.
Score: reprod. of ms.

P11.58 Melody in 5/8.
For: piano.
Score: in *Panorama: A Collection of American Piano Music,* American Music Publishing, 1953.

.Melody in 5/8. *See also* Easy Pieces; Small Piano Pieces.

P11.59 Merry Christmas. (1972)
For: handbells(23). 1 movement.
Dedicated to: Felix and Marie.
Score: reprod. of ms.

[Minuet, Handbells]
P11.60 Minuet. (1964)
Score: Flammer.

[Minuet, Piano(4-hands)]
P11.61 Minuet in F major.
Score: reprod. of ms.

[Minuet, Violin and Piano]
P11.62 Minuet.

P11.63 Music Box.
For: piano.
Score: ms.

P11.64 Music for Brass. (1971)
For: trumpets(2), horns(2), trombone, euphonium, tuba. 1 movement.
Instrumentation by John L. Procter.
Score & parts: ms.

P11.65 My Sweetheart of the Northland. (1930)
For: chorus(unison) or Soprano and piano. *Text:* Sherman Murphy.
Score: reprod. of ms.

P11.66 Nocturnal Stroll.
For: piano. *Dedicated to:* Sally Dana.
Score: ms.

P11.67 Oh, Fair Is the Wind. (1950)
For: Mezzo Soprano and piano.
Score: ms.

P11.68 On a Bright Sunny Morning.
For: piano(4-hands).
Score: ms.

P11.69 On the Road.
For: piano(4-hands). *Dedicated to:* Tina and Kathy Bird.
Score: Elkan-Vogel, 1965.

P11.70 One for You.
For: piano(4-hands).
Score: Oxford.

P11.71 Overture to a Singspiel in 3 Acts. (1936)
For: chamber orchestra(1-1-2(in A)-2; 2-1-0-0; perc; hp, pf; str(5)). Master's thesis.
Score: reprod. of ms.

P11.72 Pandora. (1939) 20'
For: orchestra(2-2(&Ehn)-2-2; 4-3-3-1; timp, perc, glock, xylo; hp; str). Ballet in 1 act. *First performed:* 1939. Rochester Civic Orchestra.
Score & parts: available from composer.

P11.73 Pentatone, Black Key & Pedal Study.
For: piano. *Dedicated to:* Ellen and

Anne Prescott.
Score: Boston, 1966.

[Pieces]
P11.74 Three Pieces. (1963)
For: handbells. *Dedicated to:* Raymond
Myrer and the Beacon Hill Bell Ringers.

P11.75 Pirate Pete.
For: piano. *Dedicated to:* Peter Massey.
Score: Summy Birchard, 1960.
Score: in *American Festival*, Book 3,
Summy Birchard, 1963.

P11.76 Pogo Stick.
For: piano. *Dedicated to:* Leslie Barry.
Score: Summy Birchard, 1957.
Score: in *Folio of Favorites for Young
Students*, Book 1a, Summy Birchard.

P11.77 Posse.
For: piano(4-hands).
Score: Oxford.
Score: Scribner's.

P11.78 Procession. (1964)
For: handbells. 1 movement. *Dedicated
to:* Dedham Bellringers.
Score: Flammer.

P11.79 Puppet Parade.
For: piano(4-hands). *Dedicated to:*
Russell and John.
Score: Elkan-Vogel, 1951.

P11.80 The Quiet Hillside.
For: chorus(SATB) and piano. *Text:* Rev.
James F. McElroy. *Dedicated to:*
Dedham Choral Society.
Vocal score: Elkan-Vogel, 1970.

P11.81 Rhapsody. (1976)
For: piano. 1 movement. *Dedicated to:*
Frank McKeithan.
Score: ms.

P11.82 Romance.
For: piano. 1 movement. *Dedicated to:*
Sandra Howlett.
Score: ms.

P11.83 Romance in Flats.
For: piano. 1 movement.
Score: reprod. of ms.

P11.84 Rondo.
For: piano.
Score: reprod. of ms.

P11.85 Rondo. (1971)
For: piano.
Score: ms.
Cassette: Feb. 11, 1979; Dedham, Mass.
Frank McKeithan.

P11.86 Saint Agnes. (1937)
For: chorus(women)(unison) and piano.
Text: Prudence Wagoner. School song.

P11.87 Sammy Sea Horse.
For: Mezzo Soprano and piano. *Text:*
Lydia Lyons Roberts. *Dedicated to:*
Evelyn Masson.
Score: ms.

P11.88 Scherzo. (1964)
For: piano. *Dedicated to:* Nicholas Van
Slyck.
Score: ms.

P11.89 Seanachas. (1937) 4'
For: orchestra(2(&pic)-2-3(in A)-2;
4-3-1(&btr)-1; timp, glock; hp, cel; str).
1 movement. *First performed:* Apr.
1937. Rochester Civic Orchestra,
Howard Hanson, conductor.
Score & parts: ms.

P11.90 Shadow Brook Blues.
For: piano. 1 movement.
Score: ms.

P11.91 Silently Came the Three
Shepherds. (1968)
For: chorus(SATB) and piano. *Text:* Rev.
James F. McElroy. *Dedicated to:*
Dedham Choral Society.
Vocal score: Elkan-Vogel, 1971.

Singspiel. *See* Ballet Suite from a
Singspiel in 3 Acts; Overture to a
Singspiel in 3 Acts.

[Small Piano Pieces]
P11.92 Seven Small Piano Pieces.
Contents: Prelude; March of the
Chess-men; Nonchalance; Touch and
Go; Melody in 5/8; Reminiscence;
Scherzo.
Score: ms.

P11.93 Song. (1963)
For: piano. *Dedicated to:* Jim Flaherty.
Score: ms.

P11.94 Song for Kathleen.
For: piano(4-hands).
Score: Elkan-Vogel.

P11.95 A Special Place. (1977)
For: piano. 1 movement.
Score: reprod. of ms.

P11.96 Spring Snow.
For: piano. *Dedicated to:* Anne Halladay.
Score: Summy Birchard, 1958.
Score: in *American Festival*, Book 2,
Summy Birchard, 1962.
Score: in *Folio of Favorites for Older
Students*, Book 2a, Summy Birchard,
1964.

P11.97 Squares Tonight.
For: piano(4-hands).
Score: Elkan-Vogel, 1957.

P11.98 Swan Boats.
For: piano(4-hands).
Score: reprod. of ms.

P11.99 Swing Tune.
For: piano(4-hands). *Dedicated to:* Sally
Ann and Jay Johnson.
Score: Elkan-Vogel, 1957.

P11.100 There Once Was a Puffin.
(1947)
For: Mezzo Soprano and piano. *Text:*
Florence Page Jaques.
Score: ms.

Three White Feathers. *See* Ballet Music
from Three White Feathers; The Black
Swan from Three White Feathers.

P11.101 The Tiny Bells Rang.
For: chorus(SATB) and piano. *Text:* Rev.
James F. McElroy. *Dedicated to:*
Dedham Choral Society. *First
performed:* Dec. 12, 1967. Dedham
Choral Society, Brian E. Jones,
conductor.
Vocal score: Elkan-Vogel, 1970.

P11.102 The Tired Soldiers. (1951)
For: piano(4-hands).
Score: ms.

P11.103 Transition Suite. (1936)
For: piano. *Movements:* Bridge; After
the Bridge.
Score: ms.

[Trio, Violin, Violoncello, Piano]
P11.104 Piano Trio.
1 movement. *Dedicated to:* Lucille and
Carol.
Score: ms.

P11.105 Tumblers.
For: piano. *Dedicated to:* Joanne
Hanson.
Score: Summy Birchard, 1958.

P11.106 Two Sides of a Coin.
For: piano.
Score: reprod. of ms.

[Untitled] (1936?)
P11.107 *For:* orchestra(2-2-2-2; 2-1-2-1;
perc; str).
2 movements completed. *Dedicated to:*
Paul Beckhelm.
Pf. red: ms.

P11.108 Veni Emmanuel. (1966)
For: chorus(SATB) and piano. *Text:*
Latin, 9th century. *First performed:*
Dec. 8, 1965; Dedham, Mass. Dedham
Choral Society, Brian E. Jones,
conductor.

P11.109 Village Dance.
For: piano(4-hands).
Score: Elkan-Vogel, 1955.

P11.110 Wind Elegy.
For: Soprano and piano. *Text:* Sara
Teasdale. *First performed:* Dec. 5,
1952; New England Conservatory.
Delores Baldyga, soprano and Elizabeth
Gill, piano.
Score: ms.

P11.111 Yehoing.
For: piano. *For:* Jock Sedgwick.
Score: ms.

P11.112 Youth Overture. (1954) 3'
For: chamber orchestra(1-1-2-0; 2-2-1-0;
perc; pf; str). 1 movement. *First
performed:* Apr. 1954; Dedham, Mass.
Dedham Youth Orchestra, Robert Kelley,
conductor.
Score: ms.
Score: reprod. of ms.
Pf. red: ms. *Parts.*

P12 KENNETH PULLIG

Born April 14, 1945, in Torrington,
Conn. Moved to Boston area 1971.
Education: B.S. (University of
Connecticut, 1967); studied composition
with Herb Pomeroy, John Bavicchi,
Jeronimas Kacinskas (Berklee College
of Music, B.M., 1975). *Awards:*
Massachusetts Council on the Arts and
Humanities, Artist Fellowship Program
(1979). *Related activities:* founder and
leader of Decahedron 1, jazz ensemble;
trumpet player; member of Cambridge
Symphonic Brass Ensemble (1973-);
staff arranger for Herb Pomeroy Big
Band; currently on the faculty of
Berklee College of Music. Be

WORKS

P12.1 Basically Bop. (1978) 10'
For: jazz ensemble(saxophone(alto),
saxophone(tenor), saxophone(baritone),
horn, trumpets(2), trombone, guitar,
piano, double bass, drums). *First
performed:* Nov. 8, 1978; Berklee
College of Music. Decahedron 1,
Kenneth Pullig, conductor. *Lead sheets.*
Reel: recording of first performance.

P12.2 Birdman's Blues. (1975?) 6'
For: jazz ensemble(saxophone(alto),
saxophone(tenor), saxophone(baritone),
trumpets(2), trombone, guitar, piano,
double bass, drums). *First performed:*
Mar. 31, 1977; Berklee College of
Music. Gregg Badolato, tenor
saxophone; Bill Brinkley, guitar;
Decahedron 1, Kenneth Pullig,
conductor. *Lead sheets.*
Reel: recording of first performance.
Be

P12.3 Blue Dolphy Road. (1973) 10'
For: jazz ensemble(saxophone(alto),
saxophone(tenor), saxophone(baritone),
trumpets(2), horn, trombone, guitar,
piano, double bass, drums). *First
performed:* Nov. 8, 1978; Berklee
College of Music. Decahedron 1,
Kenneth Pullig, conductor. *Lead sheets.*
Reel: recording of first performance.
Be

P12.4 Chorale for Brass.
For: trumpets(2), horn, trombone,
trombone(bass).
Score: reprod. of ms. Be

P12.5 Departations.
For: jazz ensemble(saxophone(alto),
saxophone(tenor), saxophone(baritone),
trumpets(2), trombone, guitar, piano,
double bass, drums). *First performed:*
Mar. 31, 1977; Berklee College of
Music. Mike Dooner, piano; Bob Siebel,
trumpet; Decahedron 1, Kenneth Pullig,
conductor. *Lead sheets.*
Reel: recording of first performance.
Be
Reel: Nov. 14, 1977. Out Group,
Kenneth Pullig, conductor. Be
Reel: Nov. 6, 1980. Decahedron 1,
Kenneth Pullig, conductor. Be

P12.6 Dialogue '76. (1976) 17'
For: trombone(bass), Soprano, flute,
clarinet, trumpet, horn, piano(4-hands),
vibraphone. *Text:* Robert V. Jason.
Commissioned by: Lamar Jones. *First
performed:* Apr. 7, 1976; Berklee
College of Music. Lamar Jones, bass
trombone; Mary McDonald, soprano;

Matthew Marvuglio, flute; Daniel Klimoski, clarinet; John Schnell, trumpet; Brian Holmes, horn; Michael Dewart and Suaznne Dewart, piano; Phillipe Saisse, vibraphone; Kenneth Pullig, conductor. *Music.*
Reel: recording of first performance. Be

P12.7 Different Shades of Blue. (1980) 4'
For: jazz band. *Commissioned by:* Herb Pomeroy Big Band.

P12.8 Fantasy, the Planet Earth. (1979) 45'
For: chorus(SATB) and jazz band. *Text:* Kenneth Pullig. *First performed:* May 3, 1979; Berklee College of Music. Decahedron 1 and others, Kenneth Pullig, conductor. *Lead sheets.*
Reel: recording of first performance. Be

P12.9 Four-Part Fugue.
For: trumpet in C, trumpet, trombones(2).
Score: reprod. of ms. Be

P12.10 Friends. 6'
For: jazz ensemble(saxophone(alto), saxophone(tenor), saxophone(baritone), trumpets(2), trombone, guitar, piano, double bass, drums). *First performed:* Nov. 22, 1977; Center, Berklee College of Music. Decahedron 1, Kenneth Pullig, conductor. *Lead sheets.*
Reel: recording of first performance. Be

P12.11 Goodby Mr. M. (1979) 12'
For: jazz ensemble(saxophone(alto), saxophone(tenor), saxophone(baritone), trumpets(2), horn, trombone, guitar, piano, double bass, drums) or jazz band. *First performed:* Nov. 14, 1979; Berklee College of Music (version for jazz ensemble). Decahedron 1, Kenneth Pullig, conductor. *Lead sheets.*
Reel: recording of first performance. Be

P12.12 Jazz Suite. (1980) 15'
For: trumpets(2), horn, trombone, trombone(bass). *Movements:* Waltz Improvisation; Ballad; Blues Variants. *Music.*
Cassette: Mar. 1980; WGBH-FM, Boston; *Morning Pro Musica.* Cambridge Symphonic Brass Ensemble. WGBH

P12.13 Lullaby and Jazz Extension. (1980) 12'
For: jazz ensemble(saxophone(alto), saxophone(tenor), saxophone(baritone), trumpets(2), trombone, guitar, piano, double bass, drums). *First performed:* Nov. 6, 1980; Berklee College of Music. Decahedron 1, Kenneth Pullig, conductor. *Lead sheets.*
Reel: recording of first performance. Be

P12.14 Marche oblique. (1976) 4'
For: trumpets(2), horn, trombone, trombone(bass).

P12.15 Motet.
For: chorus(SATB).
Vocal score: reprod. of ms. (includes piano reduction). Be

P12.16 Octet. (1974)
For: jazz ensemble(saxophone(soprano), saxophone(alto), saxophone(tenor), saxophone(baritone), trumpets(2), trombone, tuba).
Score: reprod. of ms. Be

P12.17 1625 Swingrama Ave. (1976) 6'
For: jazz ensemble(saxophone(alto), saxophone(tenor), saxophone(baritone), trumpets(2), horn, trombone, guitar, piano, double bass, drums). *First performed:* Nov. 22, 1977; Berklee College of Music. Decahedron 1, Kenneth Pullig, conductor. *Lead sheets.*
Reel: recording of first performance. Be
Reel: Nov. 14, 1979; Berklee College of Music. Decahedron 1, Kenneth Pullig, conductor. Be

P12.18 The Other Side. (1974) 13'
For: jazz ensemble(saxophone(alto), saxophone(tenor), saxophone(baritone), trumpets(2), horn, trombone, guitar, piano, double bass, drums). *First performed:* Nov. 8, 1978; Berklee College of Music. Decahedron 1, Kenneth Pullig, conductor. *Lead sheets.*
Reel: recording of first performance. Be

P12.19 Prelude (for a Crucifixion). (1973)
For: jazz ensemble(saxophone(alto), saxophone(tenor)/(soprano), saxophone(baritone), trumpets(2), trombones(2), percussion).
Score: reprod. of ms. Be

P12.20 Promenade. (1975) 2'
For: trumpets(2), horn, trombone, trombone(bass).

P12.21 Requiem. (1974) 9'
For: jazz ensemble(saxophone(alto), saxophone(tenor), saxophone(baritone), trumpets(2), horn, trombone, guitar, piano, double bass, drums). *First performed:* Nov. 8, 1978; Berklee College of Music. Decahedron 1, Kenneth Pullig, conductor. *Lead sheets.*
Reel: recording of first performance. Be

[Short Pieces]
P12.22 Three Short Pieces.
For: flute, clarinet, trumpet in C, trombone.
Score: reprod. of ms. Be

P12.23 Silvio's Sanctorum. (1976) 10'
For: jazz ensemble(some or all of saxophones(3), trumpets(2), horn, trombone, guitar, piano, double bass, drums). *First performed:* Nov. 22, 1977; Berklee College of Music. Decahedron 1, Kenneth Pullig, conductor. *Lead sheets.*
Reel: recording of first performance. Be

P12.24 Soliloquy. (1974)
For: string orchestra(6-6-6-4-2).
Score: reprod. of ms. Be

P12.15 Sonata for Trumpet [in C] and Pianoforte. (1974) 15'
3 movements.
Score: reprod. of ms. Be

P12.26 Song for Spooner. (1975) 7'
For: jazz ensemble(saxophone(alto), saxophone(tenor), saxophone(baritone), trumpets(2), horn, trombone, guitar, piano, double bass, drums).

P12.27 Sounds for Kira. (1980) 6'
For: jazz ensemble(saxophone(alto), saxophone(tenor), saxophone(baritone), trumpets(2), trombone, guitar, piano, double bass, drums). *First performed:* Nov. 6, 1980; Berklee College of Music. Decahedron 1, Kenneth Pullig, conductor. *Lead sheets.*
Reel: recording of first performance. Be

P12.28 Suite No. 1. (1973) 20'
For: jazz ensemble(saxophone(alto), saxophone(tenor), saxophone(baritone), trumpets(2), trombone, guitar, piano, double bass, drums). *Movements:* Migraines; Mutations; Machinations.
First performed: Dec. 12, 1974; Brookline Public Library. Decahedron 1, Kenneth Pullig, conductor. *Lead sheets.*
Reel: Mar. 31, 1977; Berklee College of Music. Decahedron 1, Kenneth Pullig, conductor. Be

P12.29 Suite No. 2. (1977) 43'
For: jazz ensemble(some or all of saxophones(3), trumpets(2), horn, trombone, guitar, piano, double bass, drums). *Movements:* Introductorials; Dance of the Modalitiles; Siebel in Megopolis; For Those No Longer with Us; For Those Here, Forward. *First performed:* Nov. 22, 1977; Berklee College of Music. Decahedron 1, Kenneth Pullig, conductor. *Lead sheets.*
Reel: recording of first performance.

Be
Reel: Nov. 14, 1979; Berklee College of Music. Decahedron 1, Kenneth Pullig, conductor. Be

P12.30 Sus Tense. (1978) 8'
For: jazz ensemble(saxophone(alto), saxophone(tenor), saxophone(baritone), trumpets(2), horn, trombone, guitar, piano, double bass, drums). *First performed:* Nov. 8, 1978; Berklee College of Music. Decahedron 1, Kenneth Pullig, conductor. *Lead sheets.*
Reel: recording of first performance. Be

P12.31 Synapse. (1975) 25'
For: jazz ensemble(saxophone(alto), saxophone(tenor), saxophone(baritone), trumpets(2), trombone, guitar, piano, double bass, drums). *Movements:* Present Tense; Fantasy; Synapse, Ganglions on Parade. *First performed:* May 6, 1975; Berklee College of Music. Decahedron 1, Kenneth Pullig, conductor. *Lead sheets.*
Reel: Mar. 31, 1977; Berklee College of Music. Decahedron 1, Kenneth Pullig, conductor. Be

P12.32 Thinking of You. (1974) 7'
For: jazz ensemble(saxophone(alto), saxophone(tenor), saxophone(baritone), trumpets(2), trombone, guitar, double bass, piano, drums). *First performed:* Nov. 14, 1977; Berklee College of Music. Out Group, Kenneth Pullig, conductor. *Lead sheets.*
Reel: recording of first performance. Be

P12.33 Los Tostados. (1978) 13'
For: jazz ensemble(saxophone(alto), saxophone(tenor), saxophone(baritone), trumpets(2), horn, trombone, guitar, piano, double bass, drums). *First performed:* Nov. 8, 1978; Berklee College of Music. Decahedron 1, Kenneth Pullig, conductor. *Lead sheets.*
Reel: recording of first performance. Be

P12.34 Trio.
For: trumpet, saxophone(soprano), saxophone(tenor).
Score: reprod. of ms. Be

P12.35 Vectorial.
For: orchestra(2(pic)-2(Ehn)-2(&bcl)-1(&cbsn); 4-3-3-1; timp(3), perc(3); str).
Score: reprod. of ms. Be

P12.36 Yardbird's Skull.
For: chorus(SATB), trumpets in C(2), horn, trombone(bass). *Text:* Owen Dodson.
Score: reprod. of ms. Be

R1 DIANNE GOOLKASIAN RAHBEE

Born February 9, 1938, in Somerville, Mass. *Education:* diploma program (Juilliard School, 1957-60); Diploma (Mozarteum, Salzburg, Austria, 1969); studied composition with John Heiss (Boston); piano with Alton Jones, Antoine Louis Moeldner, David Saperton, Lily Dumont, Russell Sherman, Veronica Jochum Von Moltke; orchestration with Vittorio Giannini; literature with Hugo Weisgall. *Related activities:* pianist; piano teacher; member of the New England Pianoforte Teachers Association, Massachusetts Music Teachers Association, The National Guild of Pianists, American Women Composers, International League of Women Composers. W

WORKS

R1.1 Abstracts, Op. 7. (1970-81) 10'
For: piano. *Movements:* Nocturne for the Left Hand Alone; [6 untitled movements]; Prologue or Epilogue; Floating Clouds. *First performed:* Oct. 18, 1981; Museum of Our National Heritage, Lexington, Mass. Vivian Taylor. Originally titled Musical Moments, Op. 7.
Score: Composer, 1981.

[Abstracts, Op. 7. No. 1]
R1.2 Nocturne for Left Hand Alone,
Op. 9 [*sic*]. (1970) 2'
For: piano(left-hand).
Score: reprod. of ms. W

[Abstracts, Op. 7. Nos. 2-9]
R1.3 Musical Moments, Op. 7. (1980) 8'
For: piano. 8 movements.
Score: reprod. of ms. W

R1.4 Essay No. 1. (1972) 1' 30"
For: piano. *First performed:* 1972;
Boston. Unidentified student performer.
Score: Carousel. W

R1.5 Essays, Op. 4. (1980) 10'
For: piano. 12 movements. *First
performed:* 1980.
Score: Musicalligraphics. W

R1.6 Expressions, Op. 8. (1980) 8'
For: piano. 9 movements. *First
performed:* 1980; Boston. Originally
titled Musical Expressions, Op. 8.
Score: Composer, 1981. W

[Expressions, Op. 8. Two Jokes]
R1.7 Two Jokes, Op. 10. (1970) 3'
For: piano. *Movements:* Harlequin Waltz;
Scherzo. *First performed:* 1970; Boston.
Score: reprod. of ms. W

Jokes, Op. 10. *See* Expressions, Op. 8.
Two Jokes.

Musical Moments, Op. 7. *See* Abstracts,
Op. 7.

Nocturne for Left Hand Alone, Op. 9.
See Abstracts. Op. 7. No. 1.

R1.8 Phantasie Variations, Op. 12.
(1980) 5'
For: piano. *Commissioned by and
dedicated to:* Phyllis Alpert Lehrer.
First performed: June 7, 1981; Museum
of Our National Heritage, Lexington,
Mass. Phyllis Alpert Lehrer.
Score: Composer, 1981. W

R1.9 Pictures, Op. 3. (1980) 8'
For: piano. 11 movements. *First*

performed: 1980.
Score: Musicalligraphics. W
Score: Boston Music, nyp.

[Preludes]
R1.10 Three Preludes, Op. 5. (1979) 6'
For: piano. *Dedicated to:* Sylvia
Griffith; Marjorie Burgess; Alberto
Ginastera. *First performed:* Oct. 18,
1981; Museum of Our National
Heritage, Lexington, Mass. Vivian
Taylor.
Score: Composer, 1980. W

[Quartet, Strings]
R1.11 String Quartet Improvisation.
(1973) Duration variable.
First performed: 1974; Belmont, Mass.
Score: reprod. of ms. W

[Quartet, Strings, Op. 2]
R1.12 String Quartet Satz, Op. 2. (1973)
5'
Dedicated to: Alfred Rahbee. *First
performed:* 1974; Belmont, Mass.
Score & parts: ms. in composer's hand.

R1.13 Question, Op. 11. (1980) 2'
For: piano.
Score: reprod. of ms. W

R1.14 Tarantella. (1972) 1'
For: piano(4-hands). *First performed:*
1972; Boston; in New England
Pianoforte Teachers Association
Recital.
Score: Carousel. W

[Trio]
R1.15 Flute Trio. (1981) 4'
For: flutes(3) or oboes or clarinets in
any combination. *Dedicated to:* John
Heiss. *First performed:* June 1981;
Belmont, Mass.
Score: ms. in composer's hand.

R2 GARDNER READ

Born January 2, 1913, in Evanston, Ill.
Moved to Boston area 1948. *Education:*
studied composition with Howard
Hanson, Bernard Rogers (Eastman
School of Music, B.M., 1936, M.M.,

1937); Jean Sibelius (Finland, 1938-39); Ildebrando Pizzetti (Rome, Italy, 1939); Aaron Copland (Berkshire Music Center, Tanglewood, 1941); conducting with Vladimir Bakaleinikoff and Paul White. *Awards:* MacDowell Colony Fellowships (1936, 1937, 1946, 1950), American Composers Contest (New York Philharmonic Symphony Society, First Prize, 1937), Cromwell Traveling Fellowship (1938-39), Juilliard Publications Awards (1938, 1941), Berkshire Music Center, Fellowship (1941), Paderewski Fund Competition (First Prize, 1943), Composers Press Publication Award (1948), Huntington Hartford Fellowships (1960, 1965), D.M. (Hon., Doane College). *Related activities:* guest conductor of various orchestras (1943-); host of radio show *Our American Music* (1953-60); author of *Thesaurus of Orchestral Devices* (1953), *Music Notation: A Manual of Modern Practice* (1964; 2nd ed., 1969), *Contemporary Instrumental Techniques* (1976), *Modern Rhythmic Notation* (1978), *Style and Orchestration* (1979); served on the faculties of the St. Louis Institute of Music (1941-43), Kansas City Conservatory of Music (1943-45), Cleveland Institute of Music (1945-48), Boston University (1948-78; Professor Emeritus, 1978), University of California, Los Angeles (Visiting Professor, 1966). BU

WORKS

The Admirable Crichton. *See* Incidental Music for Barrie's The Admirable Crichton, Op. 98.

L'aio de rosto. *See* Chants d'Auvergne, Op. 117a, No. 1, L'Aio de rosto.

All Day I Hear. *See* Songs for a Rainy Night, Op. 48 and Op. 48a. No. 2, All Day I Hear.

R2.1 All Things Bright and Beautiful, Op. 5. (1930) 2'

For: chorus(SATB) and piano. Withdrawn.

R2.2 American Circle, Op. 52 (Music for a Dance) . (1940) 4'
For: piano. 1 movement. Versions for orchestra, Op. 52a, and piano, Op. 52c (titled Circle Dance), withdrawn.
Score: reprod. of ms. BU
Score: Summy, 1940. BU

R2.3 American Circle, Op. 52b. (1945) 4'
For: violin and piano. 1 movement.
Dedicated to: Louis Kaufman.
Score: reprod. of ms. BU

[American Folksongs]
R2.4 Three American Folksongs, Op. 97. (1955) 9'
For: chorus(SATB) and piano. *Text:* traditional. *Contents:* Star in the East; You Can Dig My Grave; Hop up, My Ladies.
Score: Presser, 1956.

[American Folksongs. No. 1, Star in the East]
R2.5 Star in the East, Op. 97, No. 1. (1955) 5'
For: chorus(SATB). *Text:* from *The Southern Harmony*.
Vocal score: Presser, 1956. BU
Vocal score: Lawson-Gould, 1979. BU

[American Folksongs. No. 2, You Can Dig My Grave]
R2.6 You Can Dig My Grave, Op. 97, No. 2.
For: chorus(SATB) and piano.
Vocal score: Presser, 1956. BU

[American Folksongs. No. 3, Hop up, My Ladies]
R2.7 Hop up, My Ladies, Op. 97, No. 3.
For: chorus(SATB) and piano. *Text:* Virginia folksong.
Vocal score: Presser, 1956. BU

[American Hymns]
R2.8 Two American Hymns, Op. 99. (1955-56) 6'
For: chorus(SATB).

Vocal score: reprod. of ms.; available from composer.

[American Hymns. New Day]
R2.9 New Day, Op. 99, No. 2. (1955) 2' 30"
For: chorus(SATB). *Text: This New Day* by Vail Read.
Vocal score: in *American Hymns Old and New;* Columbia University Press, 1980. BPL MIT W

An Ancient Dance. *See* Easy Pieces. No. 2, An Ancient Dance.

R2.10 And There Appeared unto Them Tongues as of Fire, Op. 134. (1975-76) 7' 30"
For: organ. 1 movement. *Dedicated to:* David Craighead. *First performed:* July 28, 1977; Hartford, Conn.; American Guild of Organists regional convention. David Craighead.
Score: reprod. of ms. BU
Score: Gray, 1978. BPL NEC

L' antoueno. *See* Chants d'Auvergne, Op. 117a. No. 5, L'Antoueno.

R2.11 Arioso elegiaca, Op. 91. (1951) 7' 25"
For: string orchestra. 1 movement. Later version for organ titled Elegiac Aria, Op. 91a. *Commissioned by:* Zimbler (String) Sinfonietta, 1951. *First performed:* Apr. 8, 1953; Boston. Zimbler (String) Sinfonietta.
Score: ms. in composer's hand.
Score: reprod. of ms. BU
Score: Henmar, 1971. Rental.
Reel: Chicago Strings, Francis Akos, conductor. BU

As I Walked Through the Meadows. *See* Songs for Baritone, Op. 68. No. 3, As I Walked Through the Meadows.

As White as Jade. *See* Songs to Sing. No. 2, As White as Jade.

At Bedtime. *See* A Sheaf of Songs, Op. 84 and Op. 84a. No. 1, At Bedtime.

An Auvergne Lullaby. *See* Chants d'Auvergne, Op. 117a. No. 9, Brezairola.

The Aztec Gods. *See* Los Dioses aztecas.

R2.12 Badinage, Op. 13. (1931) 6'
For: orchestra. Withdrawn.

Bailero. *See* Chants d'Auvergne, Op. 117a. No. 2, Bailero.

R2.13 A Bell Overture, Op. 72. (1946) 7' 30"
For: orchestra(3-3-3-3; 4-3-3-1; timp, perc; hp, pf; str). 1 movement.
Commissioned by: Mrs. Fred R. White for the Cleveland Orchestra, 1946. *First performed:* Dec. 22, 1946; Cleveland, Ohio. Cleveland Orchestra, Rudolf Ringwall, conductor.
Score & parts: available from composer.
Score: reprod. of ms. BU

Berceuse d'Auvergne. *See* Chants d'Auvergne, Op. 117a. No. 9, Brezairola.

Un berger, de dans sa cabane. *See* Chants d'Auvergne, Op. 117a. No. 7, Le Pastrassou (English) and Le Pastrassou (French).

R2.14 Boston Arts Festival Fanfare, Op. 106. (1958) 1'
For: orchestra. Withdrawn.

Brand. *See* Incidental Music for Ibsen's Brand, Op. 113.

Brezairola. *See* Chants d'Auvergne, Op. 117a. No. 9, Brezairola.

R2.15 By-Low, My Babe, Op. 138. (1978-79) 10' 30"
For: chorus(SATB), flute, English horn, harp. *Text:* early Anglo-Saxon traditional.
Vocal score: reprod. of ms. BU

R2.16 Canzone di notte, Op. 127. (1971) 9'
For: guitar. 1 movement. *Dedicated to:*

Angelo Gilardino.
Score: reprod. of ms. BU
Score: Berben, 1972. BPL BU HU MIT
NEC

Capriccio. *See* Sonata, Piano, Op. 27.
No. 3a, Capriccio.

Chant de fileuse. *See* Chants
d'Auvergne, Op. 117a. No. 3, Lo
Fiolaire.

Chant de moisson. *See* Chants
d'Auvergne, Op. 117a. No. 5,
L'Antoueno.

[Chants d'Auvergne, Op. 117]
R2.17 Chants d'Auvergne (Songs of the
Auvergne). (1962) 40'
For: chorus(SATB) and instrumental
ensemble. Texts: Old French traditional.
Contents: L'Aio de rosto; Bailero; Lo
Fiolaire; N'ai pas ieu de Mio;
L'Antoueno; Ound'onoren garda?; Le
Pastrassou; Malurous quo uno fenno;
Brezairola; Lo Calhe; Passo pel prat;
La-bas, de dans le bois; Obal, din lou
limouzi. *First performed:* Nov. 23, 1965.
Boston University Choruses; student
instrumentalists, James Vincent
Cunningham, conductor.
Score & parts: available from
composer.
Reel: recording of first performance.

[Chants d'Auvergne, Op. 117. No. 12,
La-bas, de dans le bois]
R2.18 O'er Yonder in the Wood. (1963)
2'
For: chorus(SATB). *Text:* Old French
traditonal; English translation by Vail
Read.
Vocal score: Boosey & Hawkes, 1965.
BU

[Chants d'Auvergne, Op. 117a. No. 1,
L'Aio de rosto]
R2.19 Plain Water (L'Eau de source).
(1962) 2'
For: chorus(SATB), piano, viola(ad lib.).
Text: Old French traditional; English
translation by Vail Read.

Vocal score: Canyon, 1968. BPL BU
Vocal score: Kerby, 1972.

[Chants d'Auvergne, Op. 117a. No. 2,
Bailero]
R2.20 Shepherd's Song. (1962) 7'
For: chorus(SATB) and piano. *Text:* Old
French traditional.
Vocal score: ms.; available from
composer.

[Chants d'Auvergne, Op. 117a. No. 3,
Lo Fiolaire]
R2.21 Song of the Spinner (Chant de
fileuse). (1962) 3'
For: chorus(SATB). *Text:* Old French
traditional.
Vocal score: Colombo, 1968. BU NEC

[Chants d'Auvergne, Op. 117a. No. 5,
L'Antoueno]
R2.22 Harvest Song (Chant de
moisson). (1962) 3' 30"
For: chorus(SATB). *Text:* Old French
traditional; English translation by Vail
Read.
Vocal score: reprod. of ms. BU
Vocal score: Lawson-Gould, 1970. BPL
BU HU

[Chants d'Auvergne, Op. 117a. No. 5,
L'Antoueno; Arr.]
R2.23 L'Antoueno. 5' 30"
For: chorus(SSAATBB). *Text:* Old French
traditional.
Vocal score: reprod. of ms. BPL

[Chants d'Auvergne, Op. 117a. No. 7,
Le Pastrassou (English)]
R2.24 A Shepherd Lone Lay Fast
Asleep (Un Berger, de dans sa cabane).
(1962) 6'
For: chorus(SATB), viola(ad lib.),
organ(ad lib.). *Text:* Old French
traditional; English translation by Vail
Read.
Score: J. Fischer, 1965. BU

[Chants d'Auvergne, Op. 117a. No. 7,
Le Pastrassou (French)]
R2.25 Un Berger, de dans sa cabane. 6'
For: chorus(SATB), viola(ad lib.),

organ(ad lib.). *Text:* Old French traditional.
Score: reprod. of ms. BU

[Chants d'Auvergne, Op. 117a. No. 9, Brezairola]
R2.26 An Auvergne Lullaby (Berceuse d'Auvergne). (1962) 3' 30"
For: chorus(SATB), horn(ad lib.), harp or piano. *Text:* Old French traditional; English translation by Vail Read.
Score: Canyon, 1968. BPL BU
Score: Kerby, 1972.

[Chants d'Auvergne, Op. 117a. No. 11, Passo pel prat]
R2.27 Come Through the Field (Viens par le pre). (1962) 4' 30"
For: chorus(SATB). *Text:* Old French traditional; English translation by Vail Read.
Vocal score: reprod. of ms. BU
Vocal score: Seesaw, 1971. BU

Chorale. *See* Polytonal Etudes, Op. 116. No. 4, Chorale.

Chorale and Fughetta. *See* In grato jubilo, Op. 83, Op. 83a, and Op. 83b. No. 1, Chorale and Fughetta.

R2.28 Chorale-Fantasia on Good King Wenceslas, Op. 50. (1938-41) 6'
For: organ. 1 movement. Versions for 4-hand piano, Op. 50a, and 2 pianos, Op. 18b, withdrawn.
Score: Gray, 1941. BU

[Chorale Preludes]
R2.29 Three Chorale Preludes, Op. 32. (1934) 8'
For: organ. Withdrawn.

[Chorale Preludes. Jesu, meine Freude]
R2.30 Chorale Prelude, Jesu, meine Freude, Op. 32, No. 2. (1934) 3'
For: organ.
Score: Summy, 1940.

[Chorale Preludes. Meditation on Jesu, meine Freude]
R2.31 Meditation on Jesu, meine

Freude, Op. 32, No. 2a. (1954) 3'
For: organ.
Score: Gray, 1955. BPL BU HU NEC

R2.32 A Christmas Ballad (The Storke), Op. 129. (1973) 5'
For: chorus(SATB). *Text:* from the flyleaf of Edward VI's prayer book.
Vocal score: reprod. of ms. BU
Vocal score: Lawson-Gould, 1975.

R2.33 Christmas Bells, Op. 4. (1929-31) 2'
For: Soprano and piano. Withdrawn.

R2.34 A Christmas Pastorale, Op. 124. (1966) 5' 30"
For: violin and organ. 1 movement. *Commissioned by:* Trinity Church, Boston. *Dedicated to:* Emily and George Faxon.
Score: reprod. of ms. BPL BU
Score: Seesaw, 1974. T

Christmas Plantation Song. *See* Spiritual: Christmas Plantation Song, Op. 63 and Op. 63a.

Circle Dance, Op. 52c. *See* American Circle, Op. 52.

Come Through the Field. *See* Chants d'Auvergne, Op. 117a. No. 11, Passo pel prat.

[Concerto, Piano, Op. 130]
R2.35 Concerto. (1973-78) 36'
For: piano and orchestra(2-2-2-2; 4-3-3-0; timp, perc; str). 4 movements. *Dedicated to:* David Burge.
Score & parts: available from composer.
Score: reprod. of ms. BU
Pf. red: reprod. of ms. (labelled Op. 130a). BU

[Concerto, Violoncello, Op. 55]
R2.36 Concerto. (1939-45) 30'
For: violoncello and orchestra(3-3-3-2; 4-3-3-0; timp, perc; hp; str). 1 movement. *First performed:* Oct. 14, 1975. Barry Sills, violoncello; New Haven Symphony Orchestra, Erich

Kunzel, conductor.
Score & parts: available from composer.
Score: reprod. of ms. BU
Pf. red: reprod. of ms. (labelled Op. 55a).

Da capo. *See* Songs to Sing. No. 3, Da capo.

R2.37 Dance of the Locomotives, Op. 57. (1942) 4'
For: piano. 1 movement.
Score: reprod. of ms. BPL BU
Score: Seesaw, 1971. BU

R2.38 Dance of the Locomotives, Op. 57a. (1944) 4'
For: orchestra(3-2-3-2; 4-2-3-1; timp, perc; pf; str). 1 movement. *First performed:* June 26, 1948. Boston Pops, Arthur Fiedler, conductor.
Score: Seesaw, 1971. BU
Reel: recording of first performance. BU

Day's End. *See* Piano Solos for Young People, Op. 79a. No. 5, Day's End.

R2.39 De profundis, Op. 71. (1946) 10'
For: horn or trombone and organ. Written for E. Power Biggs. *First performed:* Nov. 17, 1946. Harold Meek, horn and E. Power Biggs, organ.
Score & parts: King, 1958. BPL BU HU NEC

R2.40 De profundis, Op. 71a. (1947) 10'
For: organ. 1 movement.
Score: Leeds, 1947. BU

R2.41 Diabolic Dialogue, Op. 137. (1978-79) 5' 30"
For: timpani and double bass. 1 movement.

R2.42 Los Dioses aztecas (The Aztec Gods), Op. 107. (1959) 25'
For: percussion(6)(timpani(4), chimes, glockenspiel, xylophone, vibraphone, marimba, claves, cymbals(antique, pair, sizzle, suspended(3)), drums(large and small bass, snare(2), tenor), gongs(high and deep), maracas, rasper, sandpaper blocks, tambourines(large and small), templeblocks(5), thundersheet, tom-toms(3), triangles(large and small), woodblocks(3)). *Movements:* Xiuhtecuhtli: Dios del fuego (God of Fire); Mictecacihuatl: Diosa de los muertos (Goddess of the Dead); Tlaloc: Dios de la lluvia (God of Rain); Tezcatlipoca: Dios de la noche (God of Night); Xochipilli: Dios de la alegria y la danza (God of Pleasure and Dance); Coyolxauhqui: Diosa de la luna (Goddess of the Moon); Huitzilopochtli: Dios de la guerra (God of War).
Dedicated to: Paul Price and the Manhattan Percussion Ensemble. First performed: Mar. 8, ·1960. Manhattan Percussion Ensemble, Paul Price, conductor.
Score & parts: Cole, 1969. BPL BU HU NEC
Score: reprod. of ms. BU
Parts: reprod. of ms. NEC
Disc: Composers Recordings CRI SD 444, 1981. Paul Price Percussion Ensemble, Paul Price, conductor. BrU BU HU MIT NEC W
Reel: Apr. 19, 1960; Urbana, Ill. University of Illinois Percussion Ensemble, Jack McKenzie, conductor. BU

Dreaming. *See* Piano Solos for Young People, Op. 79.

R2.43 Driftwood Suite, Op. 54. (1942) 11'
For: piano. *Movements:* Driftwood; Jungle Gardens by Moonlight; Spider-Monkeys.
Score: reprod. of ms. BU

[Driftwood Suite, Op. 54. No. 3, Spider-Monkeys]
R2.44 Spider-Monkeys.
For: piano.
Score: reprod. of ms. BU

[Driftwood Suite, Op. 54a. No. 2, Jungle Gardens by Moonlight]

R2.45 Jungle Gardens by Moonlight. (1949) 5'
For: harp.
Score: reprod. of ms. BU
Score: Seesaw, 1971.

Dunlap's Creek. *See* Pennsylvaniana Suite, Op. 67a. Dunlap's Creek.

[Easy Pieces]
R2.46 Six Easy Pieces, Op. 77. (1947-48) 12' 30"
For: piano. Withdrawn.

[Easy Pieces. No. 1, March of the Tin Soldiers]
R2.47 March of the Tin Soldiers, Op. 77, No. 1. (1947-48) 3' 30"
For: piano.
Score: Volkwein, 1948. BPL BU
Score: Bradley, 1981 (published under title, The Toy Soldiers' March). BPL

[Easy Pieces. No. 2, An Ancient Dance]
R2.48 An Ancient Dance, Op. 77, No. 2. 2'
For: piano. *Dedicated to:* Jean Miller.
Score: J. Fischer, 1948. BPL BU

[Easy Pieces. No. 3, Tally-Ho!]
R2.49 Tally-Ho! Op. 77, No. 3. 1' 30"
For: piano.
Score: J. Fischer, 1964. BPL BU

[Easy Pieces. No. 4, On Parade]
R2.50 On Parade, Op. 77, No. 4. (1947-48) 2'
For: piano.
Score: Volkwein, 1948. BPL BU
Score: Bradley, 1981. BPL

[Easy Pieces. No. 5, An Old Court Dance]
R2.51 An Old Court Dance, Op. 77, No. 5. (1947-48) 1' 30"
For: piano. *Dedicated to:* Clement Miller.
Score: J. Fischer, 1948. BPL BU

[Easy Pieces. No. 6, Marionettes]
R2.52 Marionettes, Op. 77, No. 6. (1947-48) 2'

For: piano.
Score: Volkwein, 1948. BPL BU
Score: Bradley, 1981. BPL

L'eau de source. *See* Chants d'Auvergne, Op. 117a. No. 1, L'Aio de rosto.

Eccentric Dance. *See* Satirical Sarcasms, Op. 29.

R2.53 Elegiac Aria, Op. 91a. (1964) 7' 25"
For: organ. Earlier version for string orchestra titled Arioso elegiaca, Op. 91.
Score: J. Fischer, 1969. BPL HU NEC

R2.54 E.T.H.S. Senior Class Song, '32, Op. 18. (1932) 1'
For: chorus(unison) and piano. *Text:* Muriel Reeves. Versions for chorus and orchestra, Op. 18a, and unaccompanied chorus, Op. 18b, withdrawn.
Vocal score: in *E.T.H.S. Songbook*, 1932.

R2.55 Evanston High Song, Op. 2. (1929) 2'
For: Soprano or chorus(unison) and piano. Withdrawn.

R2.56 Fanfares for a Maske, Op. 104. (1958) 3'
For: horns(2), trumpets(2), trombone. Withdrawn.

R2.57 Fantasy, Op. 38. (1935) 10'
For: viola and orchestra(3-3-2-2; 4-3-3-1; timp, perc; hp; str). 1 movement. *Dedicated to:* Vladimir Bakaleinikoff. *First performed:* Apr. 22, 1937. Julia Wilkinson, viola; Rochester Civic Orchestra, Howard Hanson, conductor.
Score: reprod. of ms. BPL BU
Score: Associated, 1950. BU HU
Parts: Associated, 1950. BU
Pf. red: Associated, 1950 (published as Op. 38a). BPL NEC

Lo fiolaire. *See* Chants d'Auvergne, Op. 117a. No. 3, Lo Fiolaire.

The First Jasmines. *See* Songs to Children, Op. 76. No. 2, The First Jasmines.

R2.58 From a Lute of Jade, Op. 36. (1935-36) 8'
For: Mezzo Soprano and piano.
Contents: Tears (Wang Seng Ju); The River and the Leaf (Po Chu-i); Ode (Confucius).
Score: Composers Press, 1943. BPL BU NEC

R2.59 From a Lute of Jade, Op. 36a. 8'
For: Mezzo Soprano and chamber orchestra(2-2-2-2; 2-0-0-0; perc(2); hp, cel; str). *Contents:* Tears (Wang Seng Ju); The River and the Leaf (Po Chu-i); Ode (Confucius).
Score: reprod. of ms. BU
Score: Composers Press, 1943. BU

R2.60 Galactic Novae, Op. 136. (1977-78) 12' 30"
For: organ and percussion. 1 movement. *Commissioned by:* Leonard Raver. *First performed:* March 12, 1981; New York City. Leonard Raver, organ and Gordon Gottlieb, percussion.
Score: reprod. of ms.

A Game of Musical Chairs. *See* Hexadic, a Game of Musical Chairs, Op. 128.

Gavotte, Op. 12a. *See* Suite of Dances, Op. 12a. Gavotte.

Gavotte, Op. 21, No. 4a. *See* Suite, Op. 21. No. 4a, Gavotte.

R2.61 Geometric Systems, Op. 139. (1979) 9' 30"-41' 30"
For: instruments(unspecified). Withdrawn.

R2.62 The Golden Harp, Op. 93. (1952) 3' 45"
For: chorus(SATB). *Text:* from *The Sacred Harp. Commissioned by:* First Pittsburgh International Contemporary Music Festival, 1952.

Vocal score: Birchard, 1954. BU HU
Vocal score: Summy-Birchard, 1954. BPL
Vocal score: J. Fischer, 1965.
Vocal score: Lawson-Gould, 1980. BPL
Disc: ASCAP CB 160, 1954. BCM HU NEC

R2.63 The Golden Journey to Samarkand, Op. 41. (1936-39) 26'
For: voices, chorus, orchestra(4-3-4-3; 6-4-4-1; timp, perc(3); hp(2), cel; str). Withdrawn. Version for voices, chorus, piano, Op. 41a, also withdrawn.

Good King Wenceslas. *See* Chorale-Fantasia on Good King Wenceslas, Op. 50.

R2.64 Haiku Seasons, Op. 126. (1970) 20'
For: speakers(female)(2), speakers(male)(2), celeste, piano, harpsichord, harp, mandolin, percussion(3). *Text:* ancient Japanese poets (Basho, Issa, Buson, Shiki). *Contents:* Prelude; Spring; Summer; Autumn; Winter; Postlude. *First performed:* Apr. 1, 1971; Boston University. Gardner Read, conductor.
Score: reprod. of ms. BU

Harvest Song. *See* Chants d'Auvergne, Op. 117a. No. 5, L'Antoueno.

Hedda Gabler. *See* Incidental Music for Ibsen's Hedda Gabler, Op. 73.

R2.65 Hexadic, a Game of Musical Chairs, Op. 128. (1972) 25'
For: instruments(unspecified)(unduplicated and portable; woodwind, brass, plucked, or string). *First performed:* Jan. 25, 1973; Harvard, Mass. Annex Players.
Score: reprod. of ms. BU

R2.66 The Hidden Lute, Op. 132. (1975-79) 20'
For: Soprano, flute(alto), percussion, harp. *Text:* Po Chu-i. *Contents:* The Island of Pines; Sleeplessness; The

Ancient Wind.
Score & parts: available from composer.

Hop up My Ladies. *See* American Folksongs. No. 3, Hop up My Ladies.

I Hear an Army. *See* Songs for a Rainy Night, Op. 48. No. 3, I Hear an Army.

R2.67 Impromptu, Op. 42. (1936) 3'
For: piano. 1 movement. *Dedicated to:* Mrs. Edward MacDowell. Later version titled Intermezzo, Op. 42a.
Score: Summy, 1940. BU

[In grato jubilo, Op. 83. No. 1, Chorale and Fughetta]
R2.68 Chorale and Fughetta. (1949) 4'
For: chorus(SSA) and instrumental ensemble(flute, oboe, clarinet, bassoon, horn, trumpets(3), trombones(2), percussion, double bass). Cantata excerpt. Withdrawn.

[In grato jubilo, Op. 83a. No. 1, Chorale and Fughetta]
R2.69 Chorale and Fughetta. (1954) 4'
For: brass ensemble(horns(3), trumpets(3), trombones(3), baritones(2), tuba). Cantata excerpt.
Score: King, 1957. BCM BPL BU
Parts: King, 1957. BCM BU
Reel: Dec. 9, 1974; Boston Conservatory. BCM

[In grato jubilo, Op. 83b. No. 1, Chorale and Fughetta]
R2.70 Chorale and Fughetta. (1949) 4'
For: chorus(SATB) and brass ensemble. Cantata excerpt. Withdrawn.

R2.71 Incidental Music for Anderson's The Golden Six, Op. 105. (1958) 16'
For: instrumental ensemble(woodwinds, brasses, percussion, harp, organ). Withdrawn.

R2.72 Incidental Music for Barrie's The Admirable Crichton, Op. 98. (1955) 9'
For: woodwind quintet and piano. Music to the play by Sir James

Matthew Barrie. *Movements:* Overture & Introduction to Act I; Introduction to Act II; A Storm; Firelight Scene; Introduction to Act III; Dinner Exit, Act IV; Final Exit, Act IV.
Score: ms. in composer's hand. BU

R2.73 Incidental Music for Forsyth's Everyman, Op. 120. (1964) 9' 30"
For: voice(male) and woodwind quintet. Withdrawn.

R2.74 Incidental Music for Forsyth's Seven Scenes for Yeni, Op. 119. (1963) 3' 30"
For: voices(male), flute, trumpet, guitar. Withdrawn.

R2.75 Incidental Music for Harding's Kinderspiel, Op. 108. (1959) 7'
For: oboe, horn, percussion, organ, piano. Withdrawn.

R2.76 Incidental Music for Ibsen's Brand, Op. 113. (1961) 22'
For: Soprano, Tenor, instrumental ensemble(oboe, brasses, percussion, organ). Music to the play by Henrik Ibsen.
Score: ms. in composer's hand; available from composer.

R2.77 Incidental Music for Ibsen's Hedda Gabler, Op. 73. (1947) 11'
For: piano. Music to the play by Henrik Ibsen. *Movements:* Introduction to Act I; Introduction to Act II; Introduction to Act IV; Hedda's Dance, Act IV.
Score: reprod. of ms. BU

R2.78 Incidental Music for Lorca's The Shoemaker's Prodigious Wife, Op. 101. (1957) 20'
For: voices, flute, trumpet, guitar, percussion. Withdrawn.

R2.79 Incidental Music for Lorca's Yerma, Op. 115. (1961) 6'
For: flute, guitar, tom-tom. Withdrawn.

R2.80 Incidental Music for MacKaye's The Scarecrow, Op. 103. (1957-58) 5'

For: Tenor and instrumental ensemble(harpsichord, brasses, organ). Withdrawn.

R2.81 Incidental Music for Sister Gretchen's Pilate, Op. 114. (1961) 18'
For: flute, clarinet, trumpets, percussion. Withdrawn.

R2.82 Interior Motives, Op. 140. (1980) 8'-18'
For: piano(interior). Withdrawn.

R2.83 Intermezzo, Op. 42a. (1952) 3'
For: piano. Earlier version titled Impromptu, Op. 42.
Score: Summy-Birchard, 1959. BU HU NEC

[Intimate Moods]
R2.84 Six Intimate Moods, Op. 35. (1935-37) 13'
For: violin and piano. *Movements:* Serious; Whimsical; Amorous; Coquettish; Wistful; Hysterical.
Score & part: C. Fischer, 1947. BU

[Inventions]
R2.85 Four Inventions, Op. 28. (1934) 7'
For: piano. Withdrawn.

R2.86 Invocation, Op. 135. (1977) 8'
For: trombone and organ. 1 movement.
Commissioned by: Gordon College, for Jeffrey Price. *First performed:* Mar. 13, 1978; Trinity Church, Boston. Jeffrey K. Price, trombone and R. Rice-Nutting, organ.
Score: reprod. of ms. BU
Score & part: King, 1978. NEC
Score: Easton, 1978. HU

Ironical March. *See* Satirical Sarcasms, Op. 29.

Is It a Waltz? *See* Satirical Sarcasms, Op. 29.

It Is Pretty in the City. *See* A Sheaf of Songs, Op. 84. No. 4, It Is Pretty in the City.

R2.87 Jesous Ahatonhia ('Twas in the Moon of Wintertime), Op. 87. (1950) 4'
For: chorus(SATB) and organ. *Text:* St. Jean de Brebeuf and S.J. (Martyr).
Dedicated to: Boston University Chorus, James R. Houghton, conductor.
Vocal score: Birchard, 1950. BPL BU HU
Vocal score: Summy-Birchard, 1957.
Vocal score: Lawson-Gould, 1975.

Jesu, meine Freude. *See* Chorale Preludes. Jesu, meine Freude.

R2.88 Jeux des timbres, Op. 111. (1960-63) 10'
For: orchestra. Withdrawn.

Jungle Gardens by Moonlight. *See* Driftwood Suite, Op. 54a. No. 2, Jungle Gardens by Moonlight.

La-bas, de dans le bois. *See* Chants de'Auvergne, Op. 117. No. 12, La-bas, de dans le bois.

The Lamb. *See* A Sheaf of Songs, Op. 84 and Op. 84a. No. 3, The Lamb and Songs for Voice and Woodwind Quintet, Op. 84b.

R2.89 Legend Suite, Op. 7. (1930-31) 8'
For: piano. Withdrawn.

R2.90 Little Pastorale, Op. 40c. (1956) 2' 20"
For: organ. 1 movement. Earlier version for piano titled Petite pastorale, Op. 40.
Score: Galaxy, 1957. BU HU NEC

The Little Soldiers. *See* Marches for Children, Op. 95 and Op. 95a. No. 1, The Little Soldiers.

R2.91 The Lotus-Eaters, Op. 19. (1932) 15'
For: orchestra. Withdrawn.

Lullaby for a Dark Hour. *See* Songs for Baritone, Op. 68. No. 1, Lullaby for a Dark Hour.

Lullaby for a Man-Child. *See* Songs to Children, Op. 76. No. 1, Lullaby for a Man-Child.

R2.92 The Magic Hour, Op. 60. (1944) 4'
30"
For: chorus(SSA) and piano. 1
movement. *Text:* Nelle R. Eberhart.
Vocal score: J. Fischer, 1946. BU

March of the Tin Soldiers. *See* Easy
Pieces. No. 1, March of the Tin
Soldiers.

[Marches for Children, Op. 95]
R2.93 Two Marches for Children. (1953)
3'
For: piano. *Movements:* The Little
Soldiers; The Toy Parade.
Score: reprod. of ms. BU
Score: J. Fischer, 1958, 1959.

[Marches for Children, Op. 95. No. 1,
The Little Soldiers]
R2.94 The Little Soldiers.
For: piano.
Score: reprod. of ms. BU

[Marches for Children, Op. 95. No. 2,
The Toy Parade]
R2.95 The Toy Parade.
For: piano.
Score: reprod. of ms. BU

[Marches for Children, Op. 95a]
R2.96 Two Marches for Children, Op.
95a. (1954) 3'
For: piano(4-hands).
Score: J. Fischer, 1965.

[Marches for Children, Op. 95a. No. 1,
The Little Soldiers]
R2.97 The Little Soldiers.
For: piano(4-hands).

Score: J. Fischer, 1964. BPL
Score: J. Fischer, 1965. BU

[Marches for Children, Op. 95a. No. 2,
The Toy Parade]
R2.98 The Toy Parade.
For: piano(4-hands). Children's music

Score: J. Fischer, 1964. BPL
Score: J. Fischer, 1965. BU

Marionettes. *See* Easy Pieces. No. 6,
Marionettes.

A May Madrigal. *See* A Merry
Madrigal, Op. 39a.

Meditation on Jesu, meine Freude. *See*
Chorale Preludes. Meditation on
Jesu, meine Freude.

R2.99 A Merry Madrigal, Op. 39.
(1934-35) 2'
For: chorus(SSAA). *Text:* Old English
traditional.
Vocal score: FitzSimons, 1940. BU NEC

R2.100 A Merry Madrigal, Op. 39a.
(1964) 2'
For: chorus(SATB).
Vocal score: reprod. of ms. (titled A
May Madrigal). BU
Vocal score: FitzSimons, 1967. BPL BU
HU NEC

[Moods, Op. 79b]
R2.101 Two Moods for Band. (1956) 5'
30"
Earlier version titled Piano Solos for
Young People, Op. 79.
Score: Lawson-Gould, 1958. BU
Pf. red: Lawson-Gould, 1958. BU

The Moon. *See* Nocturnes, Op. 23 and
Op. 23a. No. 4, The Moon.

R2.102 Motion Picture Music, Op. 1;
Fifty Pieces for Piano or Organ.
(1928-30) 120'
Withdrawn.

R2.103 Motion Picture Music, Op. 1.
No. 45a, Under Western Skies. (1931) 3'
For: orchestra. Withdrawn.

R2.104 Mountain Sketches, Op. 11.
(1931-32) 15'
For: piano. Withdrawn.

R2.105 A Mountain Song, Op. 69.
(1946; rev. 1964)

For: chorus(SATB). *Text:* Frances Frost.
Vocal score: reprod. of ms., 1964
(labelled Op. 69a). BU
Vocal score: Elkan-Vogel, 1948. BPL BU
HU
Vocal score: J. Fischer, 1964 (published
as Op. 69a). BU

R2.106 Music, Op. 64a. (1947) 3' 30"
For: chorus(SSA) and piano. *Text:* Vail
Read. Version for chorus(SSA) and
piano, Op. 64, withdrawn.
Vocal score: C. Fischer, 1948. BCM BPL
BU HU

Music for a Dance. *See* American
Circle, Op. 52.

R2.107 Music for Chamber Winds, Op.
141. (1980) 6' 40"
For: woodwind quintets(2) and
percussion(suspended cymbal, bass
drum, snare drum, gong, glockenspiel,
tom-toms, triangle, woodblocks,
xylophone). 1 movement. *Commissioned
by:* Gordon College for The Chamber
Winds, Jeffrey Price, conductor.
Score & parts: available from
composer.
Score: reprod. of ms. BU

R2.108 Music for Piano and Strings,
Op. 47a. (1946) 21'
For: piano and string orchestra. Earlier
version titled Quintet, Op. 47. *First
performed:* Feb. 12, 1947. Leonard
Shure, piano; CBS Symphony Orchestra,
Daniel Saidenberg, conductor.
Score & parts: available from
composer.

New Day. *See* American Hymns. New
Day.

R2.109 Night Flight; A Tone Poem, Op.
44a. (1961) 6' 30"
For: orchestra(4-3-3-3; 4-3-3-1; timp,
perc; hp; str). 1 movement. Earlier
version, Op. 44 (1936-42), withdrawn.
Score: reprod. of ms. BCM
Score: Henmar, 1961. HU UMB
Study score: Henmar, 1961. BPL BrU BU

HMA MIT NEC
Disc: Louisville Orchestra 632, 1963.
Louisville Orchestra, Robert Whitney,
conductor. BrU BU HU W
Reel: BU

R2.110 Night of All Nights, Op. 62.
(1945) 4'
For: Soprano and piano. *Text:* Jesse
Stuart.
Score: in *Songs*, reprod. of ms. BU

Night Song. *See* Piano Solos for Young
People, Op. 79.

R2.111 Nine by Six: Suite, Op. 86.
(1950) 15'
For: flute/piccolo, oboe/English horn,
clarinet/clarinet(bass), bassoon, horn,
trumpet. 4 movements. *First performed:*
Apr. 27, 1951; New England
Conservatory.
Score & parts: reprod. of ms. BU
Score & parts: Peters, 1973. BrU HU
NEC T
Score & parts: Henmar, 1974. BPL MIT
Parts: reprod. of ms. NEC

R2.112 Nocturne, Op. 8, D Major. (1931)
4'
For: piano. Withdrawn.

Nocturne. *See* Songs for a Rainy Night.
Op. 48 and Op. 48a. No. 1,
Nocturne.

[Nocturnes, Op. 23]
R2.113 Four Nocturnes. (1933-34) 11'
For: Alto and piano. Withdrawn, but
published separately as Op. 23, Nos.
1-4. Version for Alto and chamber
orchestra titled Nocturnes, Op. 23b;
versions for chorus(SSA) and piano
published separately as Nocturnes, Op.
23a, No. 1-4.

[Nocturnes, Op. 23. No. 1, When
Moonlight Falls]
R2.114 When Moonlight Falls. (1942) 3'
For: voice(medium) and piano. *Text:*
Shoes of the Wind by Hilda Conkling.
Score: Galaxy, 1945. BU

[Nocturnes, Op. 23. No. 2, The Unknown God]
R2.115 The Unknown God. (1942) 2'
For: Alto and piano. Text: from The Collected Poems of George E. Russell.
Score: Associated, 1945. BPL BU

[Nocturnes, Op. 23. No. 3, A White Blossom]
R2.116 A White Blossom. (1942) 2' 30"
For: Alto and piano. Text: Vail Read.
Score: Summy-Birchard, 1960.

[Nocturnes, Op. 23. No. 4, The Moon]
R2.117 The Moon. (1942) 3' 30"
For: Alto and piano. Text: William Henry Davies.
Score: Associated, 1945. BPL

[Nocturnes, Op. 23a. No. 1, When Moonlight Falls]
R2.118 When Moonlight Falls. (1942) 3'
For: chorus(SSA) and piano. Text: Shoes of the Wind by Hilda Conkling.
Arranged by Vail Read.
Vocal score: Galaxy, 1942. BU NEC

[Nocturnes, Op. 23a. No. 2, The Unknown God]
R2.119 The Unknown God. (1942) 2'
For: chorus(SSA) and piano. Text: from The Collected Poems of George E. Russell.
Vocal score: Associated, 1946. BU

[Nocturnes, Op. 23a. No. 3, A White Blossom]
R2.120 A White Blossom. (1942) 2' 30"
For: chorus(SSA) and piano. Text: Vail Read.
Vocal score: Gray, 1945. BU NEC

[Nocturnes, Op. 23a. No. 4, The Moon]
R2.121 The Moon. (1942) 3' 30"
For: chorus(SSA) and piano. Text: William Henry Davies.
Vocal score: Associated, 1946. BU

[Nocturnes, Op. 23b]
R2.122 Four Nocturnes. (1934) 11'
For: Alto and chamber

orchestra(1-1-1-1; 1-0-0-0; hp; str).
Contents: When Moonlight Falls (Hilda Conkling); The Unknown God (George E. Russell); A White Blossom (D.H. Lawrence); The Moon (William Henry Davies. Version for Alto and piano, Op. 23, withdrawn, but published separately as Op. 23, Nos. 1-4. Versions for chorus(SSA) and piano published separately as Nocturnes, Op. 23a, Nos. 1-4.
Score & parts: available from the composer.
Score: reprod. of ms. BPL

R2.123 An Ocean Rhapsody, Op. 3. (1929-31) 13'
For: piano. Withdrawn.

O'er Yonder in the Wood. See Chants d'Auvergne, Op. 117. No. 12, La-bas, de dans le bois.

An Old Court Dance. See Easy Pieces. No. 5, An Old Court Dance.

On Parade. See Easy Pieces. No. 4, On Parade.

[Overture, No. 1]
R2.124 First Overture, Op. 58. (1943) 7' 30"
For: orchestra(3-3-3-3; 4-3-3-1; timp, perc; hp, pf; str). 1 movement.
Commissioned by and dedicated to: Dr. Fabien Sevitzky. Winner of Composers Press Publication Award (1948). First performed: Nov. 6, 1943; Indianapolis Symphony Orchestra, Fabien Sevitzky, conductor.
Score: reprod. of ms. BU
Score: Composers Press, 1949. BPL BrU BU HU MIT NEC
Parts: Composers Press. Rental.
Reel: Feb. 13, 1947; University of Rochester. Rochester Philharmonic Orchestra; Guy Fraser Harrison, conductor. BU

R2.125 The Painted Desert, Op. 22. (1932-33) 26'
For: orchestra. Withdrawn.

R2.126 Pan e Dafni, Op. 53. (1940) 10'
For: orchestra(2(&pic,
&afl)-2(&Ehn)-2(&bcl)-2(&cbsn);
4-3-2(&btrb)-1; timp, perc; hp; str). 1
movement.
Score & parts: available from
composer.
Score: reprod. of ms. BU

R2.127 Partita, Op. 70. (1946) 11' 25"
For: chamber orchestra(1-1-1-1; 1-1-1-0;
timp; str). 3 movements. *First
performed:* May 4, 1947. Eastman Little
Symphony, Frederick Fennell, conductor.
Score: reprod. of ms. BU
Reel: recording of first performance.
BU

R2.128 Passacaglia and Fugue in D
Minor, Op. 34. (1935-36) 12'
For: organ. 1 movement. Version for
orchestra, Op. 34a (1938), withdrawn.
Score: Manuscript Society, 1938. BPL
BU HU MIT
Score: Row, 1938. L
Score: Gray, 1948. NEC
Reel: Eastman School of Music. David
Craighead. BU

R2.129 Passacaglia and Fugue in D
Minor, Op. 34b. (1938-40) 12'
For: pianos(2). 1 movement.
Score: reprod. of ms. BPL BU NEC

Passo pel prat. *See* Chants d'Auvergne,
Op. 117a. No. 11, Passo pel prat.

Le Pastrassou. *See* Chants d'Auvergne,
Op. 117a. No. 7, Le Pastrassou
(English) and Le Pastrassou (French).

R2.130 Pennsylvaniana Suite, Op. 67.
(1946-47) 16'
For: orchestra(3-3-3-3; 4-3-3-1; timp,
perc; hp, pf; str). Based on tunes from
a collection of western Pennsylvania
folklore compiled by Jacob A.
Evanson. *Movements:* Dunlap's Creek;
I'm a Beggar; John Riley. *Commissioned
by:* Fritz Reiner. *First performed:* Nov.
21, 1947. Pittsburgh Symphony
Orchestra, Fritz Reiner, conductor.

Score: reprod. of ms. NEC
Score: Colombo, 1969. BPL BrU BU HU
MIT NEC
Parts: Belwin. Rental.
Reel: recording of first performance.
BU

[Pennsylvaniana Suite, Op. 67a.
Dunlap's Creek]
R2.131 Dunlap's Creek; a Folk-Hymn,
Op. 67a, No. 1. (1955-56) 4' 30"
For: band.
Score: reprod. of ms. BU
Score: Belwin, 1970. BPL BU
Score: Colombo, 1970. HU
Parts: Belwin, 1970.
Reel: Boston University. Boston
University Symphonic Band, Lee
Chrisman, conductor. BU

R2.132 Petite berceuse, Op. 74. (1947)
3' 30"
For: piano. *Dedication:* For Cindy.
Score: Ditson, 1949. BU HU NEC
Score: Bradley, 1981.

R2.133 Petite pastorale, Op. 40. (1936)
2'
For: piano. Versions for chamber
orchestra, Op. 40a (1940), and high
school orchestra, Op. 40b (1941),
withdrawn. Version for organ titled
Little Pastorale, Op. 40c.
Score: Summy, 1941. BU

R2.134 Petite suite, Op. 118. (1963) 4'
For: recorder(soprano) or flute,
recorder(alto) or flute, harpsichord or
piano. *Movements:* Prelude; Pavane;
Passepied.
Score: reprod. of ms. BPL BU
Score: Berandol, 1975. BCM HU NEC
Parts: Berandol, 1975. BCM

R2.135 Piano Solos for Young People,
Op. 79. (1947-48) 16'
Contents: Summer Afternoon; Plantation
Moods; Night Song; Puck; Dreaming.
Later version titled Moods, Op. 79b.
Score: Summy, 1949.
Score: Summy, 1949 (published
separately). BPL (Nos. 2 and 4) BU

[Piano Solos for Young People, Op. 79a. No. 5, Day's End]
R2.136 Day's End. (1955) 3' 30"
Score: Presser, 1956. BrU BU

R2.137 Pierrot, Op. 15a. 1'
For: Soprano and piano. *Text:* Sara Teasdale. Earlier version, Op. 15 (1931), withdrawn.
Score: Galaxy, 1943.

Piping down the Valleys Wild. *See* Songs to Children, Op. 76. No. 3, Piping down the Valleys Wild.

Plain Water. *See* Chants d'Auvergne, Op. 117a. No. 1, L'Aio de ròsto.

Plantation Moods. *See* Piano Solos for Young People, Op. 79.

R2.138 Poem, Op. 31. (1934) 3' 25"
For: horn and piano. *Dedicated to:* James Stagliano.
Score: C. Fischer, 1937. BCM BPL BrU HU MIT
Part: C. Fischer, 1937. BCM

R2.139 Poem, Op. 31a. (1940) 3'
For: viola and piano.
Score: C. Fischer, 1945. BCM BU NEC
Part: C. Fischer, 1945. BCM

R2.140 Poem, Op. 31b. (1946) 3'
For: horn or viola, harp, string orchestra. 1 movement.
Score & parts: C. Fischer. Rental.
Score: reprod. of ms. BU

R2.141 Poeme, Op. 20. (1932) 3'
For: piano. 1 movement. Version for violin, violoncello, harp, Op. 20a, withdrawn.
Score: J. Fischer, 1945. BU
Score: Bradley, 1981.

[Polytonal Etudes, Op. 116]
R2.142 Five Polytonal Etudes. (1961-64) 10'
For: piano. *Contents:* Sparks; Mood; Games; Chorale; Chase.
Score: ms. in composer's hand; available from composer.

[Polytonal Etudes, Op. 116. No. 1, Sparks]
R2.143 Sparks. (1961) 1' 30"
For: piano.
Score: J. Fischer, 1969.

[Polytonal Etudes, Op. 116. No. 4, Chorale]
R2.144 Chorale. (1964) 2' 30"
For: piano.
Score: Bradley, 1981.

Praise Ye the Lord. *See* Songs to Sing. No. 1, Praise Ye the Lord.

Prayers of Steel. *See* Sketches of the City, Op. 26. No. 3b, Prayers of Steel.

R2.145 Prelude and Toccata, Op. 43. (1936-37) 7'
For: chamber orchestra(2-2-2-2; 2-2-2-0; timp; str). *Dedicated to:* Howard Hanson. Winner of Juilliard Publications Award (1941). *First performed:* Apr. 29, 1937. Rochester Philharmonic Orchestra, Howard Hanson, conductor.
Score & parts: available from composer.
Score: Kalmus (for the Juilliard Foundation), 1941. BPL BU HU NEC
Score & parts: available from composer.
Reel: Oct. 23, 1958; WGBH-FM, Boston. Boston Symphony Orchestra, Richard Burgin, conductor. BU

R2.146 Prelude to Spring, Op. 10. (1931) 5'
For: chamber orchestra. Withdrawn.

[Preludes on Old Southern Hymns, Op. 90]
R2.147 Eight Preludes on Old Southern Hymns. (1950) 20' 30"
For: organ. Source: from *The Sacred Harp*, 1902 edition. *Contents:* My Soul Forsakes Her Vain Delight; Thou Man of Grief Remember Me; David, the King Was Grieved and Moved; On Jordan's Stormy Banks I Stand; Alas! And Did My Savior Bleed? Fight on, My Soul; Do Not I Love Thee, O My

Lord? Once More, My Soul, the Rising Day.
Score: Gray, 1952. BCM BPL BU HU NEC

[Preludes on Old Southern Hymns, Op. 112]
R2.148 Six Preludes on Old Southern Hymns, Op. 112. (1960) 11' 35"
For: organ. Source: from *The Sacred Harp*, 1902 edition. *Contents:* By Babel's Streams We Sat and Wept; How Happy Are the Souls Above; Though the Morn May Be Serene; Hail! Ye Sighing Sons of Sorrow; Mercy, O Thou Son of David; Hark! The Jubilee Is Sounding. *Dedicated to:* David Craighead.
Score: Gray, 1963. BPL BU HU NEC
Reel: Feb. 4, 1962; Pasadena Presbyterian Church, Pasadena, Calif. David Craighead. BU

Priere. *See* Sonata, Piano, Op. 17. No. 2a, Priere.

R2.149 The Prophet, Op. 110. (1960) 73'
For: narrator, Alto, Baritone, chorus(mixed), orchestra(4-3-4-3; 4-3-3-1; timp, perc; hp(2), cel, org; str).
Oratorio. *Text:* Kahlil Gibran. *Contents:* Part I (Prologue: The Coming of the Ship; On Love; On Marriage; On Children); Part II (On Joy and Sorrow; On Reason and Passion; On Pain); Part III (On Teaching; On Beauty; On Death; Epilogue: The Farewell). *First performed:* Feb. 23, 1977; Symphony Hall, Boston. William Cavness, narrator; Eunice Alberts, alto; Mac Morgan, baritone; Boston University Chorus and Boston University Symphony Orchestra, Gardner Read, conductor.
Score & parts: available from composer.
Score: reprod. of ms. BU

Puck. *See* Piano Solos for Young People, Op. 79.

[Quartet, Strings]
R2.150 String Quartet No. 1, Op. 100. (1957) 22'

4 movements. *Commissioned by:* Kindler Foundation. *First performed:* Jan. 6, 1958; Washington D.C. Classic String Quartet.
Score & parts: reprod. of ms. BU

R2.151 Quiet Music, Op. 65. (1946) 9' 30"
For: string orchestra. 1 movement.
First performed: May 9, 1946; Washington D.C. National Gallery Orchestra, Richard Bales, conductor.
Score: reprod. of ms. BU
Score: Seesaw, 1971.

R2.152 Quiet Music, Op. 65a. (1950) 9' 30"
For: organ.
Score: Abingdon, 1963. BPL BrU BU HU NEC

[Quintet, Op. 47]
R2.153 Piano Quintet. (1937-45) 21'
For: string quartet, piano. 1 movement. Later version titled Music for Piano and Strings, Op. 47a.
Score & parts: reprod. of ms. BU
Reel: Boston University. Edith Stearns, piano; Boston Fine Arts Quartet.

R2.154 The Reveille, Op. 89. (1950) 7'30"
For: chorus(TTBB), piano, snare drum. Withdrawn. Version for chorus(SATB), piano, snare drum, Op. 89a (1957), also withdrawn.

R2.155 The Reveille, Op. 89b. (1965) 7' 30"
For: chorus(SATB), wind ensemble(bassoons(2), trumpets(4), horns(4), trombones(4), tuba), timpani, percussion, organ. 1 movement. *Text:* Bret Harte. *First performed:* Mar. 28, 1963; Boston University. Boston University Brass Choir and Boston University Choral Art Society, Gardner Read, conductor.
Score & parts: Seesaw, 1971.
Score: ms. in composer's hand. BPL
Score: reprod. of ms. BU

River Night. *See* Songs for Baritone, Op. 68 and Op. 68a. No. 2, River Night.

Sarabande. *See* Suite, Op. 33a. No. 3, Sarabande; Arr.

[Satirical Sarcasms, Op. 29]
R2.156 Three Satirical Sarcasms. (1934-35) 6'
For: piano. *Contents:* Ironical March; Is It a Waltz?; Eccentric Dance.
Score: reprod. of ms. (separate mss). BU
Score: Seesaw, 1971. BU
Score: Seesaw, 1971 (published separately). BU

[Satirical Sarcasms, Op. 29a]
R2.157 Three Satirical Sarcasms. (1941) 6'
For: orchestra(3-3-3-3; 3-3-3-1; timp, perc; pf; str). *Contents:* Ironical March; Is It a Waltz?; Eccentric Dance.
Score & parts: available from composer.
Score: reprod of ms. BU

R2.158 Saw You Never in the Twilight, Op. 6a. 3' 30"
For: Alto, chorus(SATB), piano or harp. *Text:* Cecil F. Alexander. Version for soprano and piano, Op. 6 (1930), withdrawn.
Vocal score: Ditson, 1942. BU

R2.159 Scherzino, Op. 24a. (1949) 5'
For: woodwind quintet. 1 movement. Earlier version, Op. 24 (1933), withdrawn.
Score: Southern-NY, 1953. BPL BrU BU HU NEC
Parts: Southern-NY, 1953. BU

R2.160 Scherzotic Dance, Op. 37. (1935) 3'
For: piano. 1 movement.
Score: Summy, 1941. BU

R2.161 Sea-Scapes, Op. 46. (1937-40) 5'
For: harp. *Contents:* Sea-Murmurs; Sea-Spray.

Score: reprod. of ms. BU
Score: Seesaw, 1971. BU

R2.162 A Sheaf of Songs, Op. 84. (1949-50) 9'
For: Mezzo Soprano and piano. Withdrawn, but published separately. Version of Nos. 2 and 3 titled Songs for Voice and Woodwind Quintet, Op. 84b.

[A Sheaf of Songs, Op. 84. No. 1, At Bedtime]
R2.163 At Bedtime. (1949) 3' 30"
For: Mezzo Soprano and piano. *Text:* Irene Beyers.
Score: Southern-NY, 1951. BU

[A Sheaf of Songs, Op. 84. No. 2, Sister Awake]
R2.164 Sister Awake.
For: voice and piano. *Text:* Thomas Bateson. Version for voice and woodwind quintet in Songs for Voice and Woodwind Quintet, Op. 84b.
Score: reprod. of ms. BPL
Score: in *Songs*, reprod. of ms. BU

[A Sheaf of Songs, Op. 84. No. 3, The Lamb]
R2.165 The Lamb.
For: voice and piano. *Text:* William Blake. Version for voice and woodwind quintet in Songs for Voice and Woodwind Quintet, Op. 84b.
Score: in *Songs*, reprod. of ms. BU

[A Sheaf of Songs, Op. 84. No. 4, It Is Pretty in the City]
R2.166 It Is Pretty in the City. (1950) 1' 30"
For: Mezzo Soprano and piano. *Text:* Elizabeth Coatsworth.
Score: Southern-NY, 1952. BU NEC

[A Sheaf of Songs, Op. 84a. No. 1, At Bedtime]
R2.167 At Bedtime. (1949) 3' 30"
For: chorus(SSA) and piano. *Text:* Irene Beyers.
Vocal score: reprod. of ms. BU
Vocal score: Southern-NY, 1951. BCM BU NEC

[A Sheaf of Songs, Op. 84a. No. 2,
Sister Awake]
R2.168 Sister Awake. (1954) 1'
For: chorus(SSA) and piano. *Text:*
Thomas Bateson. Version for voice and
woodwind quintet in Songs for Voice
and Woodwind Quintet, Op. 84b.
Vocal score: J. Fischer, 1954. BPL BU
Vocal score: Lawson-Gould, 1980. BU

[A Sheaf of Songs, Op. 84a. No. 3,
The Lamb]
R2.169 The Lamb. (1954) 3'
For: chorus(SATB) and piano. *Text:*
William Blake. Version for voice and
woodwind quintet in Songs for Voice
and Woodwind Quintet, Op. 84b.
Vocal score: J. Fischer, 1954. BU

A Shepherd Lone Lay Fast Asleep. *See*
Chants d'Auvergne, Op. 117a. No. 7,
Le Pastrassou (English).

Shepherd's Song. *See* Chants
d'Auvergne, Op. 117a. No. 2, Bailero.

R2.170 Sinfonia da chiesa, Op. 61b.
(1969) 11'
For: trumpets(2), horn, trombone, tuba,
organ. *Movements:* Intrada; Canzona;
Ricercare. Versions for piano and for 2
pianos titled Sonata da chiesa, Op. 61
and Op. 61a, respectively. *First
performed:* Feb. 3, 1970; Trinity Church,
Boston. Boston University Brass
Quintet, George Faxon, organ; Gardner
Read, conductor.
Score: reprod. of ms. BU
Score: Henmar, 1972. BPL BrU BU HU
MIT NEC T
Parts: Henmar, 1972. BPL BU MIT NEC
T

Sister Awake. *See* A Sheaf of Songs,
Op. 84 and Op. 84a. No. 2, Sister
Awake and Songs for Voice and
Woodwind Quintet, Op. 84b.

R2.171 Sketches of the City, Op. 26;
Symphonic Suite. (1933) 15' 45"
For: orchestra(4-3-3-3; 4-3-3-1; timp,
perc; hp(2), cel; str). Text: after poems

by Carl Sandburg. *Movements:* Fog;
Nocturne in a Deserted Brickyard;
Prayers of Steel. Winner of Juilliard
Publications Award (1938). *First
performed:* Apr. 18, 1934; Rochester,
N.Y. Rochester Civic Orchestra, Howard
Hanson, conductor.
Score & parts: available from
composer.
Score: Kalmus (for the Juilliard
Foundation), 1938. BPL BrU MIT NEC
Score: Kalmus (for the Juilliard
Foundation), 1959. BU HU

[Sketches of the City, Op. 26. No. 3b,
Prayers of Steel]
R2.172 Prayers of Steel. (1958) 4'
For: band. Earlier version, Op. 26, No.
3a (1937), withdrawn.
Score: available from composer.
Reel: Boston University. Boston
University Symphonic Band, Lee
Chrisman, conductor.

R2.173 Snowflakes: A Caprice, Op. 9.
(1931)
For: piano. Withdrawn.

R2.174 Soliloquy, Op. 25. (1933-34) 7'
Withdrawn.

R2.175 Sonata brevis, Op. 80. (1948)
14'
For: violin and piano. 3 movements.
First performed: Dec. 27, 1958;
Brandeis University. Robert Koff, violin
and Martin Boykan, piano.
Score & part: reprod. of ms. BU
Score: Seesaw, 1971. BU
Reel: Jan. 30, 1966; University of
California, Los Angeles. Stanley
Plummer, violin and Natalie Limonick,
piano. BU
Reel: Mar. 2, 1977; Boston University;
in *Omnibus: Music of the 20th Century,
Concert 3.* Roman Totenberg, violin and
Edith Stearns, piano. BU

R2.176 Sonata da chiesa, Op. 61. (1945)
11'
For: piano. *Movements:* Intrada;
Canzona; Ricercare. Version for brass

quintet and organ titled Sinfonia da chiesa, Op. 61b.
Score: reprod. of ms. BU
Score: Seesaw, 1971. BU

R2.177 Sonata da chiesa, Op. 61a. (1947) 11'
For: pianos(2). Version for brass quintet and organ titled Sinfonia da chiesa, Op. 61b.
Score: reprod. of ms. BPL
Score: Seesaw, 1971. BU
Reel: Boston University. Karin and Ingrid Gutberg. BU BU

[Sonata, Piano, Op. 17]
R2.178 Sonata in C Minor. (1932-33) Withdrawn.

[Sonata, Piano, Op. 17. No. 2a, Priere]

R2.179 Priere. (1949) 4'
For: organ.
Score: Lorenz, 1950.

[Sonata, Piano, Op. 27]
R2.180 Sonata in A Minor. (1933-35) 24'
Withdrawn.

[Sonata, Piano, Op. 27. No. 3a, Capriccio]
R2.181 Capriccio. (1934) 4' 30"
Score: in *U.S.A., Vol. 2; Compositions for Piano by Contemporary American Composers,* Leeds, 1946-49. HU

R2.182 Sonatina: Hommage a Mozart, Op. 78. (1948-49) 12'
For: piano. Withdrawn.

R2.183 Song Heard in Sleep, Op. 88. (1950) 7' 30"
For: Soprano, Tenor, piano. *Text:* William Rose Benet.
Score: reprod. of ms. BU

R2.184 Song Heard in Sleep, Op. 88a. (1953) 7' 30"
For: chorus(SATB) and piano. *Text:* William Rose Benet.

Vocal score: Lawson-Gould, 1958. BPL BU

Song of the Spinner. *See* Chants d'Auvergne, Op. 117a. No. 3, Lo Fiolaire.

R2.185 Songs for a Rainy Night, Op. 48. (1938-40) 9'
For: Baritone and piano. Withdrawn, but published separately.

[Songs for a Rainy Night, Op. 48. No. 1, Nocturne]
R2.186 Nocturne. (1938) 2' 30"
For: voice(medium) and piano. *Text:* Frances Frost.
Score: Associated, 1946. BPL BU

[Songs for a Rainy Night, Op. 48. No. 2, All Day I Hear]
R2.187 All Day I Hear. (1939) 3'
For: Baritone and piano. *Text:* James Joyce.
Score: Boosey & Hawkes, 1950. BCM BPL NEC

[Songs for a Rainy Night, Op. 48. No. 3, I Hear an Army]
R2.188 I Hear an Army. 3' 30"
For: voice and piano. Withdrawn.

[Songs for a Rainy Night, Op. 48a. No. 1, Nocturne]
R2.189 Nocturne. (1953) 2' 30"
For: chorus(SSAA) and piano. *Text:* Frances Frost.
Vocal score: Associated, 1968. BPL BU NEC

[Songs for a Rainy Night, Op. 48a. No. 2, All Day I Hear]
R2.190 All Day I Hear. (1953) 3'
For: Alto or Baritone, chorus(SATB), piano. *Text:* James Joyce.
Vocal score: reprod. of ms. BPL NEC
Vocal score: in *Songs James Joyce,* reprod. of ms. BU

[Songs for a Rainy Night, Op. 48b]
R2.191 Three Songs for a Rainy Night. (1940) 9'
For: Baritone and orchestra(4-4-4-4;

4-3-3-1; timp, perc; hp; str). *Contents:*
Nocturne (Frances Frost); All Day I
Hear (James Joyce); I Hear an Army
(James Joyce). Version for baritone
and piano, op. 48, withdrawn.
Score: reprod. of ms. BU

[Songs for Baritone, Op. 68]
R2.192 Three Songs for Baritone. (1946)
10' 30"
For: Baritone and piano. *Contents:*
Lullaby for a Dark Hour (Alfred
Kreymborg); River Night (Frances Frost);
As I Walked through the Meadows (Old
English traditional).
Score: available from composer.

[Songs for Baritone, Op. 68. No. 1,
Lullaby for a Dark Hour]
R2.193 Lullaby for a Dark Hour. (1946)
3'
For: Baritone and piano. *Text:* Alfred
Kreymborg.
Score: Boosey & Hawkes, 1950. BU

[Songs for Baritone, Op. 68. No. 2,
River Night]
R2.194 River Night.
For: Baritone and piano. *Text:* Frances
Frost.
Score: reprod. of ms. BU
Score: in *Songs,* reprod. of ms. BPL

[Songs for Baritone, Op. 68. No. 3,
As I Walked Through the Meadows]
R2.195 As I Walked Through the
Meadows.
For: Baritone and piano. *Text:*
traditional.
Score: in *Songs,* reprod. of ms. BPL
Score: reprod. of ms. BU

[Songs for Baritone, Op. 68a. No. 2,
River Night]
R2.196 River Night. (1954) 5'
For: chorus(SATB) and piano. *Text:*
Frances Frost.
Vocal score: Lawson-Gould, 1958. BPL
BU NEC T

[Songs for Voice and Woodwind
Quintet, Op. 84b]

R2.197 Two Songs for Voice and
Woodwind Quintet. (1949) 4' 45"
Contents: The Lamb (William Blake);
Sister Awake (Thomas Bateson). For
later versions see A Sheaf of Songs,
Op. 84 and Op. 84a, No. 2 and No. 3.
Score: reprod. of ms. BU
Score: J. Fischer, 1954. Rental.

Songs of the Auvergne. *See* Chants
d'Auvergne, Op. 117.

R2.198 Songs to Children, Op. 76.
(1947-49) 10' 30"
For: Mezzo Soprano and piano.
Contents: Lullaby for a Man-Child (Jean
Starr Untermeyer); The First Jasmines
(Rabindranath Tagore); Song of
Innocence (William Blake). Later
version, Op. 76a, for Mezzo Soprano,
flute, harp, string quartet, withdrawn.
Score.

[Songs to Children, Op. 76. No. 1,
Lullaby for a Man-Child]
R2.199 Lullaby for a Man-Child. 4' 30"
For: voice(medium) and piano. *Text:*
Jean Starr Untermeyer. Later version
for chorus(SSA) and piano, Op. 76b,
withdrawn.
Score: Galaxy, 1957. BPL BU HU NEC

[Songs to Children, Op. 76. No. 2,
The First Jasmines]
R2.200 The First Jasmines.
For: voice and piano. *Text:*
Rabindranath Tagore.
Score: in *Songs,* reprod. of ms. BU

[Songs to Children, Op. 76. No. 3,
Piping down the Valleys Wild]
R2.201 Piping down the Valleys Wild.
(rev. 1949) 1' 30"
For: voice(medium) or voice(low) and
piano. *Text:* from *Songs of Innocence*
by William Blake.
Score: Galaxy, 1950. BU HU NEC

R2.202 Songs to Sing, Op. 131.
(1974-78) 8' 30"
For: chorus(SATB). Withdrawn.

[Songs to Sing. No. 1, Praise Ye the Lord]
R2.203 Praise Ye the Lord, Op. 131, No. 1. (1974) 3'
For: chorus(SATB). *Text:* Bible, O.T., Psalm 148.
Vocal score: Lawson-Gould, 1976. NEC

[Songs to Sing. No. 2, As White as Jade]
R2.204 As White as Jade, Op. 131, No. 2. (1974) 2' 30"
For: chorus(SATB) and piano. *Text:* Vail Read.
Vocal score: Silver-Burdett, 1975.

[Songs to Sing. No. 3, Da capo]
R2.205 Da capo. (1978) 3'
For: chorus(SATB). *Text:* Norma Farber.
Vocal score: reprod. of ms.

R2.206 Sonoric Fantasia, No. 1, Op. 102. (1957-58) 13' 30"
For: celeste, harp, harpsichord. 1 movement. *First performed:* Oct. 29, 1960; New York City. Composer's Forum.
Score: reprod. of ms. BU
Score: Presser, 1971. BPL BU HU L MIT NEC
Reel: Boston University. Ingrid Gutberg, celeste; Ann Nisbet Cobb, harp; Joel Spiegelman, harpsichord. BU
Reel: Mar. 30, 1966; University of California, Los Angeles. Henrietta Pelta, celeste; Marjorie Call, harp; Malcolm Hamilton, harpsichord. BU

R2.207 Sonoric Fantasia, No. 2, Op. 123. (1965) 12' 25"
For: violin and orchestra(1-1-1-1; 1-1-1-0; perc, hp; str). 1 movement.
Commissioned by: Cultural Foundation of Boston, 1965, for Roman Totenberg.
First performed: Feb. 26, 1966; Boston University; Boston Winterfest. Roman Totenberg, violin; Boston University Symphony Orchestra, Gardner Read, conductor.
Score: ms. in composer's hand. BPL
Score: reprod. of ms. BU
Score: Presser, 1967.
Reel: Feb. 27, 1966; Hynes Auditorium, Boston. Roman Totenberg, violin; Boston University Symphony Orchestra, Gardner Read, conductor. BU

R2.208 Sonoric Fantasia, No. 2, Op. 123a. 12' 25"
For: violin and piano. 1 movement.
Score: Presser, 1967.
Score & part: Presser, 1974. BPL
Score: Presser, 1974. NEC

R2.209 Sonoric Fantasia, No. 3, Op. 125. (1968) 6'
For: flute/piccolo/flute(E-flat) /flute(alto)/flute(bass), harp, percussion(3)(glockenspiel, vibraphone, xylophone, triangle, woodblocks(3), tamtams(3), snare drum, tenor drum, tambourine, sizzle cymbal, suspended cymbal, gong). 1 movement.
Commissioned by: Robert Austin Boudreau for the American Wind Symphony. *First performed:* June 20, 1968; Pittsburgh, Pa. American Wind Symphony, Robert Boudreau, conductor.
Score: reprod. of ms. BCM BU
Score: Seesaw, 1972. BPL BU HU L NEC

R2.210 Sonoric Fantasia, No. 4, Op. 133. (1975) 15' 30"
For: organ and percussion(timpani, bongos, tom-tom, large suspended triangle, large suspended cymbal, large tamtam, windchimes, crotales). 1 movement. *Dedicated to:* Elizabeth Sollenberger. *First performed:* Apr. 5, 1976; Trinity Church, Boston. Elizabeth Travis Sollenberger, organ and Neil Grover, percussion.
Score: reprod. of ms. BU
Score: C. Fischer, 1979. HU

R2.211 Sound Piece, Op. 82. (1949) 5' 45"
For: brass ensemble(trumpets(4), horns(4), trombones(3), baritone, tubas(2)), timpani, percussion(snare drum, gong, cymbal, bass drum). 1 movement. *First performed:* May 11, 1949; Boston University. Boston University Brass Choir, Gardner Read, conductor.
Score: ms. in composer's hand. BU

Score: King, 1950. BCM Be BU HU NEC
Parts: King, 1950. BCM BU NEC
Reel: Dec. 1, 1977. Boston University
Brass Ensemble, Roger Voisin,
conductor. BU

Spider-Monkeys. *See* Driftwood Suite,
Op. 54. No. 3, Spider-Monkeys.

R2.212 Spiritual: Christmas Plantation
Song, Op. 63. (1945) 8'
For: double bass and piano. *Dedicated
to:* Jacques Posell.
Score: Witmark, 1948. BU HU NEC
Part: Witmark, 1948. BU

R2.213 Spiritual: Christmas Plantation
Song, Op. 63a. (1945) 8'
For: violoncello and piano.

Score: Witmark, 1948.

Star in the East. *See* American
Folksongs. No. 1, Star in the East.

The Storke. *See* A Christmas Ballad,
Op. 129.

R2.214 Suite, Op. 21. (1933)
For: harp. Withdrawn.

[Suite, Op. 21. No. 4a, Gavotte]
R2.215 Gavotte. (1941) 4'
For: orchestra(high school).
Condensed score: C. Fischer, 1943. BPL

R2.216 Suite, Op. 33a. (1937) 12'-13'
For: string orchestra. *Contents:* Prelude;
Scherzetto; Sarabande; Rondo. Version
for string quartet, Op. 33 (1935),
withdrawn. *First performed:* Aug. 5,
1937; CBS, New York City. CBS
Concert Orchestra, Charles Adler,
conductor.
Score: reprod. of ms. BU

[Suite, Op. 33a. No. 3, Sarabande;
Arr.]
R2.217 Sarabande. (1940) 3' 30"
For: piano. *Dedication:* To Vail [
Read].

Score: Art Publications, 1942. BCM BPL
BU NEC

R2.218 Suite, Op. 81. (1948-49) 22'
For: organ. *Contents:* Preamble; Scherzo;
Aria; Toccata. Version for orchestra,
Op. 81a (1951-57), withdrawn. Winner
of First Prize, American Composers
Contest (Pennsylvania College for
Women), 1950. *First performed:* Sept.
25, 1950; Pittsburgh, Pa. Julian
Williams.
Score: Witmark, 1951. BPL BU HU MIT
NEC
Score: Transcontinental, 1971.

R2.219 Suite of Dances, Op. 12. (1931)
5'
For: piano. Withdrawn.

[Suite of Dances, Op. 12a. Gavotte]
R2.220 Gavotte. (1931) 2'
For: orchestra. Withdrawn.

R2.221 Suite of Inventions, Op. 14.
(1931-32) 4'
For: piano. Withdrawn.

Summer Afternoon. *See* Piano Solos
for Young People, Op. 79.

R2.222 Symphony, No. 1, Op. 30, A
Minor. (1934-36) 38'
For: orchestra(3-3-3-3; 4-3-3-1; timp,
perc; hp(2), cel; str). 4 movements.
Dedication: To my mother. Awarded
First Prize, American Composers
Contest (New York Philharmonic
Symphony Society), 1937. *First
performed:* Nov. 4, 1937; New York
City. New York Philharmonic, Sir John
Barbirolli, conductor. Version for
4-hand piano, Op. 30a (1940),
withdrawn.
Score: reprod. from ms. BPL
Score: Affiliated, 1939. BPL BU HU
Score: American Music Edition, 1960.
Reel: recording of first performance.
BU

R2.223 Symphony, No. 2, Op. 45, E-Flat
Minor. (1940-42) 25' 45"

For: orchestra(3-3-3-3; 4-3-3-1; timp, perc; hp; str). 3 movements. Awarded First Prize, Paderewski Fund Competition, 1943). *First performed:* Nov. 26, 1943. Boston Symphony Orchestra, Gardner Read, conductor. Version for 4-hand piano, Op. 45a (1942-43), withdrawn.
Score: ms. in composer's hand. BPL
Score: reprod. of ms. BU
Score & parts: Associated, 1945. Rental.
Reel: recording of first performance.

R2.224 Symphony, No. 3, Op. 75. (1946-48) 25'
For: orchestra(3-3-3-3; 4-3-3-1; timp, perc; pf; str). 3 movements. *First performed:* Mar. 2, 1962; Pittsburgh, Pa. Pittsburgh Symphony Orchestra, William Steinberg, conductor.
Score & parts: Belwin. Rental.
Score: reprod. of ms. BPL BU
Study score: Colombo, 1969. BPL NEC
Study score: Colombo, 1970. BrU BU HU MIT
Reel: recording of first performance. BU

R2.225 Symphony, No. 4, Op. 92. (1951-59) 25'
For: orchestra(3-3-3-3; 4-3-3-1; timp, perc; str). 2 movements. *First performed:* Jan. 30, 1970; Cincinnati, Ohio. Cincinnati Symphony Orchestra, Erich Kunzel, conductor.
Score & parts: available from composer.
Score: reprod. of ms. BU
Reel: recording of first performance. BU

Tally-Ho! *See* Easy Pieces. No. 3, Tally-Ho!

R2.226 The Temptation of St. Anthony: A Dance Symphony, Op. 56. (1940-47) 31' 30"
For: orchestra(3-3-3-3; 4-3-3-1; timp, perc; hp, cel; str). Symphonic poem. Prelude and 4 scenes suggested by the novel of Gustave Flaubert. *First performed:* Apr. 9, 1953; Chicago, Ill. Chicago Symphony Orchestra, Rafael

Kubelik, conductor. Version for 2 pianos, Op. 56a (1948), withdrawn.
Score: reprod. of ms. BU
Reel: recording of first performance. BU

R2.227 Theme with Variations, Op. 16. (1932) 4'
For: piano. Withdrawn.

This New Day. *See* American Hymns. New Day.

R2.228 Though I Speak with the Tongues of Men, Op. 109. (1960) 10'
For: chorus(SATB) and organ. *Text:* Bible, N.T., Corinthians I:13.
Vocal score: Abingdon, 1965. BU HU NEC

R2.229 Threnody, Op. 66. (1946) 5'
For: flute and piano. 1 movement. *Dedicated to:* David Van Vactor.
Score & part: Witmark, 1948. BCM BrU MIT NEC
Score: Witmark, 1948. BPL BU HU
Score: Seesaw, 1971.

R2.230 Threnody, Op. 66a. (1946) 5'
For: flute, harp, string orchestra. 1 movement. *First performed:* Oct. 21, 1946. Joseph Mariano, flute; Eastman-Rochester Symphony Orchestra, Howard Hanson, conductor.
Score & parts: Seesaw, 1971.
Score: reprod. of ms. BU

R2.231 To a Skylark, Op. 51. (1939) 6' 25"
For: chorus(SSATB). *Text:* Percy Bysshe Shelley. *Dedicated to:* Ildebrando Pizzetti.
Vocal score: Associated, 1945. BU

R2.232 To a Skylark, Op. 51a. (1978)
For: chorus(SATB). *Text:* Percy Bysshe Shelley.
Vocal score: reprod. of ms. BU

R2.233 Toccata giocosa, Op. 94. (1953) 7' 15"
For: orchestra(2-2-2-2; 4-2-3-1; timp, perc; hp; str). 1 movement.

Commissioned by: Louisville Orchestra.
First performed: Mar. 13, 1954;
Louisville, Ky. Louisville Orchestra,
Robert Whitney, conductor.
Score & parts: Presser, 1967. Rental.
Score: Templeton, 1954. BU
Disc: Louisville Orchestra LOU 545-5,
1955. Louisville Orchestra, Robert
Whitney, conductor. BCM BrU HU MIT
NEC NU W

R2.234 Touch Piece, Op. 85. (1949) 8'
30"
For: piano.
Score: reprod. of ms. BU
Score: Seesaw, 1971. BU

The Toy Parade. *See* Marches for
Children, Op. 95 and Op. 95a. No. 2,
The
Toy Parade.

The Toy Soldiers' March. *See* Easy
Pieces. No. 1, March of the Tin
Soldiers.

R2.235 Tryste Noel (Nativity Song), Op.
59. (1949) 5'
For: Alto, chorus(SATB), organ(ad lib.).
Text: Louise Imogen Guiney.
Vocal score: Gray, 1949. BU

'Twas in the Moon of Wintertime. *See*
Jesous Ahatonhia, Op. 87.

Under Western Skies. *See* Motion
Picture Music, Op. 1. No. 45a, Under
Western Skies.

The Unknown God. *See* Nocturnes, Op.
23 and Op. 23a. No. 2, The Unknown
God.

R2.236 Variations on a Chromatic
Ground, Op. 121. (1964) 4' 30"
For: organ. *Dedicated to:* Anthony
Newman.
Score: McLaughlin, 1966. BPL BU HU
MIT NEC

R2.237 Vernal Equinox, Op. 96. (1955) 8'
30'
For: orchestra(2-2-2-2; 4-3-3-0; timp,
perc; hp, cel; str). 1 movement.
Commissioned by: Brockton Orchestral
Society. *First performed:* Apr. 12, 1955;
Brockton, Mass. Brockton Symphony
Orchestra, Moshe Paranov, conductor.
Score: reprod. of ms. BU
Disc: GBYSO, 1970. Greater Boston
Youth Symphony Orchestra, Walter
Eisenberg, conductor. WCRB
Reel: Boston University Symphony
Orchestra, Gardner Read, conductor.

Viens par le pre. *See* Chants
d'Auvergne, Op. 117a. No. 11,
Passo pel prat.

R2.238 Villon, Op. 122. (1965-67) 180'
For: voices, chorus, tape,
orchestra(3-3-3-3; 4-3-3-1; timp, perc;
hp; str). Opera in 3 acts. *Text:* adapted
from *The Other Heart* by James
Forsyth.
Score & parts: available from
composer.
Score: reprod. of ms. BU
Vocal score: reprod. of ms. (labelled
Op. 122a). BU

When Moonlight Falls. *See* Nocturnes,
Op. 23 and Op. 23a. No. 1, When
Moonlight Falls.

R2.239 Where Corals Lie, Op. 49. (1937)
6'
For: chorus(SSATBB) and piano. *Text:*
Richard Garnett. *Dedicated to:* Sadie M.
Rafferty and the Evanston Township
High School Chorus. Versions for
chorus and 2 pianos and for 2 pianos,
Op. 49b, withdrawn.
Vocal score: FitzSimons, 1938. BU

R2.240 Where Corals Lie, Op. 49a. 6'
For: chorus(SSAA) and piano. *Text:*
Richard Garnett. *Dedicated to:* Sadie M.
Rafferty and the Evanston Township
High School Chorus.

Vocal score: FitzSimons, 1938. BPL BU HU

A White Blossom. *See* Nocturnes, Op. 23 and Op. 23a. No. 3, A White Blossom.

You Can Dig My Grave. *See* American Folksongs. No. 2, You Can Dig My Grave.

ARRANGEMENTS OF WORKS BY OTHER COMPOSERS

R2.241 In festo transfigurationis domini. 7' 30"
For: trumpets(2), horn, trombone, tuba. Original by Giovanni Pierluigi da Palestrina.
Score & parts: Colombo, 1971. BU

R2.242 Laudate Dominum in tympanis. 5' 30"
For: brass ensemble. Original by Giovanni Pierluigi da Palestrina.
Score: Colombo, 1971. BU
Parts: Belwin, 1971. BU

R2.243 Prelude and Fugue in B Minor. 12'
For: orchestra(4-3-3-3; 4-3-3-1; timp; str). Original by Johann Sebastian Bach.

R2.244 Prelude, Adagio, and Fugue. (1943) 9'
For: string orchestra. Original by Padre Martini.
Score: reprod. of ms. BU

R2.245 Rose of Sharon. 5'
For: chorus(SATB). *Text:* from *The Sacred Harp*. Original by William Billings.
Vocal score: Lawson-Gould, 1959. BPL BU HU

R2.246 Vital Spark of Heav'nly Flame. 3' 50"
For: chorus. Anthem. Original from *The Sacred Harp*, 1850 edition.
Vocal score: Abingdon, 1963. BPL BU
Vocal score: Lawson-Gould, 1978. HU NEC

R3 RONALD M. RIVERA

Born September 4, 1949, in New Orleans, La. Moved to Boston area 1972. *Education:* studied counterpoint and harmony with Russell Smith (Louisiana State University, 1971). *Related activities:* Assistant Director, Boston School of Electronic Music (1972-73); currently designing electronic musical instruments. BPL

WORKS

R3.1 Pie Fisher Enters the Magic Land of Quazoll. (1972-73) 17'
For: tape. Suite. *First performed:* July 1973; Workshop for New Music, Stafford's in the Fields, Chocorua, N.H. *Tape:* available from composer.

R4 CURTIS ROADS

Born May 9, 1951, in Cleveland, Ohio. Moved to Boston area 1980. *Education:* B.A. (University of California, San Diego, 1976); studied percussion with L. Werntz (1961-67); electronic music composition with Morton Subotnick (California Institute of The Arts, 1972-74); computer music with Iannis Xenakis (Indiana University, Bloomington, 1972) and G.M. Koenig (Instituut voor Sonologie, Utrecht, The Netherlands, 1978). *Related activities:* percussionist; worked at the Experimental Music Studio, University of Illinois, Urbana (1970-71), recording studios in Madison, Wis. (1971-72), Electronic Music Studio of the Centre Americain, Paris, France (1973); elected Associate Fellow of the Center for Music Experiments, University of California, San Diego (1977); Visiting Scholar, Structured Sound Synthesis Project, University of Toronto (1979); co-founder and Vice President, Computer Music Association, San Francisco, Calif. (1979); designed the composing language CL (1977); editor of *Computer Music Journal* (1978-); compiler of the *Proceedings of the 1978 International Computer Music*

Conference (1979) and the *Proceedings of the 1977 International Computer Music Conference* (1980); editor and contributor of articles to *Computer Music* (1982); co-author of *Computer Music Tutorial* (forthcoming); Research Associate, Experimental Music Studio, Massachusetts Institute of Technology (1980-); Artistic Co-Director, New England Computer Music Association (NEWCOMP, 1980-). MIT

WORKS

R4.1 Cirrus. (1973)
For: woodwinds and percussion or tape. Written for WHA-FM, Madison, Wis. Version for tape realized and mixed at WHA-FM, Madison, Wis. *Commissioned by:* United States Department of Health, Education and Welfare. *First performed:* September 1973; WIBA-FM, Madison, Wis. (tape version). *Score. Tape.*

R4.2 Colligation 1. (1973) 16' 10"
For: tape(electroacoustic). Score generated by Nova 1200 MC-1 computer program; realized at the California Institute of The Arts Analog Studios; remixed at the Village Recorder, Los Angeles, Calif. *First performed:* Jan. 1974; California Institute of The Arts. *Score. Tape.*

R4.3 Colligation 2, No. 1. (1974) 19'
For: tape(electroacoutic). Score generated by Nova 1200 MC-2 computer program; realized at the California Institute of The Arts Analog Studios; remixed at the Village Recorder, Los Angeles, Calif. *First performed:* Mar. 1974; California Institute of The Arts. *Score. Tape.*

R4.4 Construction. (1976) 13' 50"
For: tape(electronic). Realized at the University of California, San Diego, Mandeville Center for the Arts Electronic Music Studios; remixed at the Village Recorder, Los Angeles, Calif. *First performed:* May 1976; University of California, San Diego. *Score. Tape.*

R4.5 Field. (1981) 12'
For: tape(computer). Sounds generated at the MIT Experimental Music Studio. *Tape.*

R4.6 nscor. (1980) 8' 45"
For: tape(computer). Sounds generated at the University of California, San Diego, Center for Music Experiment; Instituut voor Sonologie (Utrecht, The Netherlands); University of Toronto Structured Sound Synthesis Project; MIT Experimental Music Studio; remixed at Suntreader Studios, Sharon, Vt. *First performed:* Oct. 1980; Varese, Italy.
Reel: MIT
Reel: Feb. 13, 1981; Wellesley College. W

R4.7 Objet. (1977) 14'
For: tape(electronic and computer). Sounds computed on the Burroughs B6700 computer system, realized at the University of California, San Diego, Mandeville Center for the Arts, Electronic Music Studios; remixed at American Zoetrope Recording, San Francisco, Calif. *First performed:* Sept. 1978; Bilthoven, The Netherlands; International Gaudeamus Musicweek. *Tape.*

R4.8 Plex. (1981)
For: tape(computer). Score generated using PROCESS/ING computer program at the University of California, San Diego; sounds generated at the MIT Experimental Music Studio. *Score.*

R4.9 (Prototype). (1975) 8'
For: tape(computer). Sounds computed on Burroughs B7600 computer system; digital-to-analog conversion at the University of California, San Diego, Center for Music Experiment; remixed at the Village Recorder, Los Angeles, Calif. *First performed:* May 1975; University of California, San Diego.

Score.
Reel: MIT

R4.10 3-S. (1972) 13' 34"
For: tape(string textures). Strings of the California Institute of The Arts Orchestra, Gerhard Samuel, conductor. Realized at the California Institute of The Arts Analog Studios; remixed at ID Studios, Hollywood, Calif. *First performed:* June 1973; 1750 Arch Street, Berkeley, Calif. *Score. Tape.*

R4.11 3-Space. (1976) 25'
For: tape. Film music. Structural film (16 mm, color with sound) realized in collaboration with Joanna Kiernan and Sandra Tabori. *First performed:* June 1977; University of California, San Diego. *Film.*

R4.12 Textwork. (1975-76) 11' 27"
For: speaker and tape(computer). Sounds computed on the Burroughs B6700 computer system; realized at the University of California, San Diego, Mandeville Center for the Arts, Electronic Music Studios; remixed at the University of California, San Diego, Center for Music Experiment. *First performed:* Oct. 1980; San Francisco, Calif. *Tape.*

R4.13 (untitled). (1973) 20' 5"
For: synthesizers(electronic)(3) and tape(4-channel). Live concert event. Composed in collaboration with J.P. Taylor and R. Cohen. Generated by two Nova 1200 computer programs. *First performed:* May 1973; California Insitute of The Arts. *Tape.*

R4.14 Wait. (1971) 10' 22"
For: voice and tape(electronic). Vocals by William Barnes. Realized at the University of Illinois, Urbana, Experimental Music Studio. *First performed:* Mar. 1971; University of Illinois, Urbana. *Tape.*

R4.15 work-in-progress. (1981)
For: saxophone and tape(computer). Score. *Tape.*

R5 E. AMELIA ROGERS

Born August 1, 1954, in Ashtabula, Ohio. Moved to Boston area 1978. *Education:* studied composition with Henry Brant, Louis Calabro, Vivian Fine, Marta Ptsazynska (Bennington College, B.A., 1976); Theodore Antoniou, David Del Tredici, John Thow (Boston University, M.M., 1981); conducting with Vincent La Silva (Juilliard School, 1977-78). *Related activities:* composer-in-residence and coordinator of theory progam, Boston University Tanglewood Institute (1979, 1980); Administrative Manager, MIT Experimental Music Studio, (1981-). MIT

WORKS

R5.1 Centrifuge. (1980) 9'
For: oboe and harp. *First performed:* Apr. 10, 1980; Boston University. Debra Carr, oboe and Faye Seemans, harp. *Score & parts:* reprod. of ms. MIT *Reel & cassette:* recording of first performance; available from composer.

R5.2 Fanfare. (1974) 1'
For: trumpets(3) and percussion. *First performed:* Aug. 30, 1974; Aspen, Colo. Francis Bonney, Edward Carroll, Steve Erickson, trumpets; Charles Wilkinson, timpani.
Score: reprod. of ms.; available from composer.

R5.3 Greenhouse. (1980) 7'
For: chorus(SATB). *Text:* Nina Shuessler. *First performed:* May 15, 1980; Longy School of Music. Longy Chamber Singers, Tom Hall, conductor.
Vocal score: reprod. of ms. MIT *Reel & cassette:* recording of first performance; available from composer. *Reel and cassette:* May 25, 1980; Sanders Theatre, Harvard University. Longy Chamber Singers, Tom Hall, conductor; available from composer.

R5.4 Her Room. (1979) 3' 40"
For: chorus(SSA). *Text:* Nina Shuessler. *First performed:* July 14, 1979; Lenox,

Mass.; Boston University Tanglewood Institute. Leonard Atherton, conductor.
Vocal score: reprod. of ms.; available from composer.
Reel & cassette: recording of first performance; available from composer.

R5.5 A Mad Teaparty. (1976) 7'
For: flute, clarinet(bass), marimba, violin, orchestra(2-1-2-2; 2-4-1-0; perc; str). Concerto. *First performed:* Mar. 20, 1976; North Bennington, Vt. Sage City Symphony, Louis Calabro, conductor.
Score: reprod. of ms.; available from composer.
Reel & cassette: recording of first performance; available from composer.

[Movements]
R5.6 Three Movements. (1975) 18'
For: string quartet. *First performed:* June 4, 1975; Bennington College. Joanna Jenner and James Yannatos, violins; Jacob Glick, viola; Barbara Mallow, violoncello.
Score & parts: reprod. of ms.; available from composer.
Reel & cassette: recording of first performance; available from composer.

[Poems by Emily Dickinson]
R5.7 Three Poems by Emily Dickinson. (1976) 9' 20"
For: Mezzo Soprano, Baritone, chorus(SATB), percussion(timpani, glockenspiel, tom-toms(tuneable)(4), snare drum, suspended cymbal). *First performed:* Apr. 21, 1976; Bennington College. Carol Kino, mezzo soprano; Richard Frisch, baritone; Louis Calabro, percussion; Amelia Rogers, conductor.
Score: reprod. of ms.; available from composer.
Reel & cassette: recording of first performance; available from composer.

R5.8 Quartet for an Alma Mater. (1979) 9'
For: horn, piano, harpsichord, percussion(marimba, finger cymbals, temple blocks, flexatone). *First*

performed: May 20, 1979; Hirshberg Gallery, Boston. Maria Lattimore, horn; Sarah Tenney, percussion; Kit Young, piano; Sheila Lloyd, harpsichord.
Score & parts: reprod. of ms.; available from composer.
Reel & cassette: recording of first performance; available from composer.
Reel: Apr. 10, 1980; Boston University. Nancy Bennet, horn; Nancy Farley, piano; Catherine Coombs, harpsichord; Robert Jurkscheit, percussion; available from composer.

R5.9 Quension. (1979) 14'
For: trumpet and percussion(2)(timpani, vibraphone, bass bow, marimba, temple blocks(2 sets), woodblock, guiro, suspended cymbal, maracas, tom-toms(tuneable)(5)). *First performed:* Apr. 10, 1980; Boston University. Edward Carroll, trumpet; Neil Grover and Lawrence Dash, percussion.
Score: reprod. of ms. MIT
Reel & cassette: recording of first performance; available from composer.

R5.10 Sonata. (1976) 16'
For: viola and piano. 3 movements.
First performed: Apr. 21, 1976; Bennington College. Jacob Glick, viola and Lionel Nowak, piano.
Score: reprod. of ms.; available from composer.
Reel & cassette: recording of first performance; available from composers.

R5.11 Strike Four. (1975) 4'
For: string quartet. *First performed:* Nov. 17, 1975; Bennington College. Concord String Quartet.
Score & parts: reprod. of ms.; available from composer.
Reel and cassette: recording of first performance; available from composer.

R5.12 Syzygies. (1976) 14'
For: piano and tape. *First performed:* Apr. 21, 1976; Bennington College. Amelia Rogers, piano. *Tape.*

Reel & cassette: recording of first performance; available from composer.

R5.13 The Yellow Wallpaper. (1979-81) 75′
For: Soprano, Mezzo Soprano, Baritone, chorus(S(3)-M S(3)-A(2) with ampliflication & tape delay), flute(piccolo, alto), oboe(English horn), trumpet (piccolo trumpet), trombone, percussion(2), violoncello, double bass. Chamber opera in one act. *Libretto:* adapted from novella by Charlotte Perkins Gilman. *First performed:* Aug. 7, 1980; Berkshire Music Festival, Tanglewood (Scene III). Members of the Boston University Tanglewood Institute and Berkshire Music Center, Stefan Kozinski, conductor.
Score & parts: reprod. of ms.
Reel & cassette: recording of first performance; available from composer.

R6 PETER ROW

Born September 25, 1944, in Boston. *Education:* B.M., M.M., D.M.A. (Prayag Sangit Samiti, Allahabad, India, 1965-73); studied sitar with Gokul Nag and Nikhil Banerji. *Awards:* Prayag Sangit Samiti, Gold Medal (1969), Prayag Sangit Samiti, Silver Medal (1971), John D. Rockefeller III Fund Grant (1971-73), Smithsonian Institution Grant (1979). *Related activities:* ethnomusicologist; member of the faculty of New England Conservatory; composer of music in the improvisatory North Indian classical tradition. None of his music exists in written form. NEC

R6.1 Rag Khamaj.
For: sitar and tabla. *Movements:* Masitkhani Gat; Rezakhani Gat; Jhala; Sawal Jawab.
Cassette: Nov. 5, 1978; New England Conservatory. Peter Row, sitar and Robert Becker, tabla. NEC

R6.2 Rag Purya Kalyan.
For: sitar. *Movements:* Alap; Jor; Jhala.

Cassette: Nov. 5, 1978; New England Conservatory. Peter Row.

R6.3 Raga Ahir Bhairav.
For: sitar, tambura, tabla. *Movements:* Alap; Masitkhani Gat; Rezakhani Gat; Jhala; Sawal Jawab.
Tape: Brandeis University. WGBH

R6.4 Raga Kirwani.
For: sitar and tabla.
Cassette: Nov. 9, 1976; New England Conservatory. Peter Row, sitar and Pandit Shashi Nayak, tabla. NEC

R6.5 Raga Ragesri Pancham.
For: sitar. *Movements:* Alap; Jor; Jhala.
Cassette: Nov. 9, 1976; New England Conservatory. Peter Row. NEC

R6.6 Ragmala in Bhairavi.
For: sitar and tabla.
Cassette: Nov. 5, 1978; New England Conservatory. Peter Row, sitar and Robert Becker, tabla. NEC

R6.7 Tala Pancham Sawari.
For: tabla lahara and sitar ragma.
Cassette: Nov. 9, 1976; New England Conservatory. Pandit Shashi Nayak, tabla and Peter Row, sitar. NEC

R6.8 Tala Tintal.
For: sitar and tabla. *Movements:* Masitkhani Gat with Improvisations; Rezakhani Gat with Improvisations; Jhala; Sawal Jawab.
Cassette: Nov. 9, 1976; New England Conservatory. Peter Row, sitar and Pandit Shashi Nayak, tabla. NEC

R7 GEORGE A. RUSSELL

Born June 23, 1923, in Cincinnati, Ohio. *Education:* Wilberforce University High School (1940-43); studied composition with Stefan Wolpe (1949). *Awards:* Outstanding Composer Award (*Metronome*, 1958); *Downbeat* five star reviews (1958, 1959, 1963, 1971); Composer Award (*Down Beat*, First Place, 1961); Oscar du Disque de Jazz (1961); Guggenheim Grants (1969, 1972);

National Endowment for the Arts Fellowship (1976); National Music Award (1976); National Endowment for the Arts Jazz Fellowships (1979, 1980, 1981). *Related activites:* jazz performer; writer/arranger for Benny Goodman, Earl Hines, Dizzy Gillespie, Artie Shaw, and others; author of *The Lydian Chromatic Concept of Tonal Organization* (1953); founded the George Russell Sextet (1960); panelist for the National Endowment for the Arts Jazz Fellowship (1975); member of the faculty of New England Conservatory (1969-). NEC

WORKS

R7.1 All about Rosie. (1957) 12'
For: jazz group. Based on motif from Alabama black children's song game. 3 movements. *Commissioned by:* Brandeis University Festival of Fine Arts. *First performed:* 1957; Brandeis University, Festival of Fine Arts.
Score: Margun, nyp.
Disc: in *Outstanding Jazz Compositions of the 20th Century*, Columbia C2S 831. BCM
Disc: in *Gerry Mulligan Presents a Concert in Jazz*, Verve V 8415. Gerry Mulligan and others.
Disc: in *Modern Jazz Concert*, Columbia WL 127, 1958. George Russell and others. HU
Cassette: Dec. 17, 1975; New England Conservatory. NEC Afro-American Orchestra, George Russell, conductor. NEC
Cassette: Dec. 16, 1976; New England Conservatory. Members of NEC Afro-American Music Department, George Russell, conductor. NEC
Cassette: Apr. 25, 1978; New England Conservatory. NEC Jazz Ensemble, George Russell, conductor. NEC
Cassette: Apr. 24, 1979; New England Conservatory. NEC Jazz Ensemble, George Russell, conductor. NEC
Cassette: Apr. 10, 1980; New England Conservatory. NEC Big Band, George

Russell, conductor. NEC
Cassette: Apr. 26, 1981; New England Conservatory. NEC Big Band, George Russell, conductor. NEC

R7.2 Ballad of Hix Blewitt. (1956) 3' 15"
For: saxophone(alto), trumpet, piano, guitar, double bass, drums. Jazz sextet.
Music: Russ-Hix.
Disc: RCA Victor LPM 1372, 1957. George Russell and His Smalltet.
Disc: in *The Jazz Workshop*, RCA Victor LPM 2534, 1962. Reissue of LPM 1372, 1957.
Cassette: Mar. 1, 1977; New England Conservatory; in *Jazz Workshop Series*. Members of NEC Afro-American Music Department. NEC
Cassette: Apr. 24, 1979; New England Conservatory. NEC Jazz Ensemble, George Russell, conductor. NEC
Cassette: Apr. 10, 1980; New England Conservatory. NEC Big Band, George Russell, conductor. NEC
Cassette: Apr. 26, 1981; New England Conservatory. NEC Big Band, George Russell, conductor. NEC

R7.3 Big City Blues. 12' 39"
For: jazz band.
Music: Russ-Hix.
Disc: in *New York, N.Y.*, Decca DL 9216/79216, 1959 (date recorded). George Russell and His Orchestra.
Disc: in *New York, N.Y. and Jazz in the Space Age*, MCA 2 4017, 1973. George Russell and His Orchestra. NEC W
Cassette: May 12, 1973; New England Conservatory; in *A Festival of Contemporary American Music*. NEC Afro-American Music Ensemble, Jaki Byard, conductor. NEC
Cassette: Dec. 17, 1975; New England Conservatory. NEC Afro-American Orchestra, George Russell, conductor. NEC
Cassette: Apr. 26, 1981; New England Conservatory. NEC Big Band, George Russell, conductor. NEC

R7.4 A Bird in Igor's Yard. (1949)
For: clarinet and jazz band.
Commissioned by: Buddy De Franco.
Music: Beechwood.
Disc: in *Cross Currents*, Capitol M
11060, 1972. Buddy De Franco and His
Orchestra. NEC
Cassette: Jan. 30, 1978; New England
Conservatory. Roland Rizzo, clarinet;
Hypertension Band, Hankus Netsky,
conductor. NEC

R7.5 Blues in Orbit. 7' 24"
For: trumpet, trombone,
saxophone(alto), saxophone(tenor),
piano, double bass, drums. Jazz septet.
Music: Russ-Hix.
Disc: in *The Stratus Seekers*, Riverside
RLP 412/9412, 1962 (date recorded).
George Russell Septet.
Disc: in *Svengali*, Atlantic SD 1643. Gil
Evans and others.
Disc: in *1, 2, 3, 4, 5, 6extet*, Riverside
RS 3043. George Russell and Septet.

Chromatic Universe. *See* Jazz in the
Space Age.

R7.6 Concerto for Billy the Kid. (1956)
4' 42"
For: saxophone(alto), trumpet, piano,
guitar, double bass, drums. Jazz sextet.
Music: Russ Hix.
Disc: RCA Victor LPM 1372, 1957.
George Russell and His Smalltet.
Disc: in *The Jazz Workshop*, RCA Victor
LPM 2534, 1962. Reissue of LPM 1372,
1957.

[Concerto, Guitar]
R7.7 Concerto for Self-Accompanied
Guitar. (1962) 9' 25"
Music: Russ-Hix.
Disc: in *The Essence of George Russell*,
Sonet SLP 1411-1412, 1971. Rune
Gustafsson. NEC

[Concerto, Guitar, Double Bass, Jazz
Band]
R7.7.5 Concerto for Guitar and Bass.
Cassette: Apr. 26, 1981; New England

Conservatory. NEC Big Band, George
Russell, conductor. NEC

[Concerto, Guitars(2) and Band]
R7.8 Concerto for Two Guitars. (1962)
Cassette: Apr. 25, 1978; New England
Conservatory. Ron Berman and Eric
Charry; NEC Jazz Ensemble, George
Russell, conductor. NEC
Cassette: Apr. 10, 1980; New England
Conservatory. NEC Big Band, George
Russell, conductor. NEC

R7.9 Cubano Be/Cubano Bop. (1947?)
For: jazz band. *Commissioned by:* Dizzy
Gillespie.
Music: Robbins.
Disc: in *The Greatest of Dizzy Gillespie*,
RCA Victor LPM 2398, 1947 (date
recorded).
Disc: in *Dizzy Gillespie and His
Orchestra*, Vol. II, RCA 731068, 197-.
Dizzy Gillespie and His Orchestra. NEC
Cassette: Dec. 16, 1976; New England
Conservatory. Members of NEC Afro-
American Department, George Russell,
conductor. NEC

R7.10 The Day John Brown Was
Hanged. (1956)
For: saxophone(alto), guitar, double
bass, drums(2). Jazz quintet.
Commissioned by: Hal McKusick.
Music: Russ-Hix.
Disc: in *Jazz Workshop*, RCA Victor
LPM 1366, 1957. Hal McKusick Quartet
and George Russell, drums.

R7.11 D.C. Divertimento. (1962) 9' 14"
For: trumpet, trombone,
saxophone(tenor), piano, double bass,
drums. Jazz sextet. *Commissioned by:*
Broadcast Music, Inc. for International
Jazz Festival (First), Washington, D.C.,
1962.
Music: Russ-Hix.
Disc: in *The Outer View*, Riverside RM
440/RS 3016, 1962 (date recorded).
George Russell Sextet. NU W
Cassette: Apr. 25, 1978; New England
Conservatory. NEC Jazz Ensemble,
George Russell, conductor. NEC
Cassette: Apr. 24, 1979; New England

Conservatory. NEC Jazz Ensemble, George Russell, conductor. NEC
Cassette: Apr. 10, 1980; New England Conservatory. NEC Big Band, George Russell, conductor. NEC

Dimensions. *See* Jazz in the Space Age.

R7.12 Electronic Sonata for Organ (No. 1) . (1969)
Music: Russ-Hix.
Disc: Flying Dutchman FDS 122, 1968 (date recorded). George Russell.
Disc: Sonet SLP 1409, 1968 (date recorded). George Russell.

R7.13 Electronic Sonata for Souls Loved by Nature. (1968) 60'
For: jazz sextet or jazz band and tape. 3 movements. *First performed:* 1969; Oslo, Norway.
Music: Russ-Hix.
Disc: Flying Dutchman, FDS 124 (jazz sextet version).
Disc: in *The Essence of George Russell,* Sonet SLP 1411-1412, 1971 (jazz band version). George Russell, conductor. NEC
Cassette: Jan. 22, and May 2, 1970; New England Conservatory; in *A Jazz Workshop.* George Russell, director. NEC
Cassette: Jan. 25, 1975; New England Conservatory; in *Electric Weekend.* NEC Uptown Dues Band. NEC
Cassette: Apr. 24, 1979; New England Conservatory (excerpts). NEC Jazz Ensemble, George Russell, conductor. NEC

R7.14 Electronic Sonata for Trumpet. (1981)

Events. *See* Living Time. Events.

R7.15 Ezz-thetic. (1948) 5'-9'
For: jazz group. *Commissioned by:* Lee Konitz. *Dedication:* To the late Ezzard Charles.
Music: Russ-Hix.
Disc: in *Ezz-thetic,* Prestige 116, 1951 (date recorded). Lee Konitz and others.

Disc: in *Max Roach Plus Four,* Trip 5522, 1956 (date recorded). Max Roach and others.
Disc: RCA Victor LPM 1372, 1957. George Russell and His Smalltet.
Disc: in *Ezz-thetic,* Riverside RLP 375, 1961 (date recorded). George Russell Sextet.
Disc: in *The Jazz Workshop,* RCA LPM 2534, 1962. Reissue of LPM 1372, 1957.
Disc: in *Ezz-thetic,* Prestige 7827, 1973. Reissue of Prestige 116, 1951. NEC
Disc: in *Outer Thoughts,* Milestone M 47027, 1975. George Russell Sextet. HU NEC
Disc: in *Ezz-thetics,* Riverside 9375, 1975. Reissue of Riverside RLP 375, 1961. MIT
Cassette: May 8, 1971; New England Conservatory; in *A Festival of New England Composers Past and Present.* NEC Jazz Ensemble, Gunther Schuller, conductor. NEC
Cassette: Dec. 17, 1975; New England Conservatory. NEC Afro-American Orchestra, George Russell, conductor. NEC
Cassette: Dec. 16, 1976; New England Conservatory. Members of NEC Afro-American Music Department, George Russell, conductor. NEC
Cassette: Mar. 1, 1977; New England Conservatory; in *Jazz Workshop Series.* Members of NEC Afro-American Music Department. NEC
Cassette: Apr. 25, 1978; New England Conservatory. NEC Jazz Ensemble, George Russell, conductor. NEC
Cassette: Apr. 24, 1979; New England Conservatory. NEC Jazz Ensemble, George Russell, conductor. NEC
Cassette: Apr. 26, 1981; New England Conservatory. NEC Big Band, George Russell, conductor. NEC

R7.16 Fellow Delegates. (1956) 5' 38"
For: saxophone(alto), trumpet, piano, guitar, double bass, drums. Jazz sextet.
Music: Russ-Hix.
Disc: RCA Victor LPM 1372, 1957. George Russell and His Smalltet.
Disc: in *The Jazz Workshop,* RCA Victor

LPM 2534, 1962. Reissue of LPM 1372, 1957.

R7.17 Freein' Up. (1965) 12' 44"
For: trumpet, trombone, saxophone(tenor), piano, double bass, drums. Jazz sextet.
Music: Russ-Hix.
Disc: in *The George Russell Sextet at the Beethoven Hall*, BASF MC 25125, 1973. George Russell Sextet. HU NEC NU W
Disc: in *The George Russell Sextet at the Beethoven Hall*, SABA SB 15059. George Russell Sextet.

R7.18 A Helluva Town. (1958) 5' 1"
For: jazz bamd.
Music: Russ-Hix.
Disc: in *New York, N.Y.*, Decca DL 9216/79216, 1958 (date recorded). George Russell and His Orchestra.
Disc: in *New York, N.Y. and Jazz in the Space Age*, MCA 2 4017, 1973. George Russell and His Orchestra. NEC W

R7.19 Jack's Blues. (1955) 3' 44"
For: saxophone(alto), trumpet, piano, guitar, double bass, drums. Jazz sextet.
Music: Russ-Hix
Disc: RCA Victor LPM 1372, 1957. George Russell and His Smalltet.
Disc: in *The Jazz Workshop*, RCA LPM 2534, 1962. Reissue of LPM 1372, 1957.

R7.20 Jazz in the Space Age. 42' 19"
For: jazz band. *Movements:* Chromatic Universe--Part 1; Dimensions; Chromatic Universe--Part 2; The Lydiot; Waltz from Outerspace; Chromatic Universe--Part 3.
Music: Russ-Hix.
Disc: in *Jazz in the Space Age*, Decca DL 9219/79219, 1960 (date recorded). George Russell and His Orchestra. HU
Disc: in *New York, N.Y. and Jazz in the Space Age*, MCA 2 4017, 1973. George Russell and His Orchestra. NEC W
Disc: in *Ezz-thetics*, Riverside RLP 375, 1961 (date recorded). George Russell Sextet.

Disc: in *Ezz-thetics*, Riverside RLP 9375, 1975. Reissue of Riverside RLP 375. MIT
Cassette: Dec. 16, 1976; New England Conservatory. Members of NEC Afro-American Music Department, George Russell, conductor. NEC
Cassette: Apr. 10, 1980; New England Conservatory. NEC Big Band, George Russell, conductor. NEC

R7.21 Knights of the Steamtable. (1956) 2' 32"
For: saxophone(alto), trumpet, piano, guitar, double bass, drums. Jazz sextet.
Dedication: To the countermen of Local 1199, Retail Drug Workers.
Music: Russ-Hix.
Disc: RCA Victor LPM 1372, 1957. George Russell and His Smalltet.
Disc: in *The Jazz Workshop*, RCA LPM 2534, 1962. Reissue of RCA LPM 1372, 1957.

R7.22 Listen to the Silence. (1971) 45' 40"
For: Bass, chorus(SATB), jazz ensemble(fender bass, double bass, guitar(electric), organ, piano(electric), trumpet, saxophone(tenor), timpani).
Text: from *Bury My Heart at Wounded Knee* by Dee Brown; The Mark by Maurice Nicoll; *Duino Elegies* by Rainer Maria Rilke; *Newseek Magazine*, Feb. 2, 1971; *The New York Times*, July 8, 1970. *Commissioned by:* Norwegian Cultural Fund for the 1971 Kongsberg International Jazz Festival. *First performed:* June 26, 1971; Kongsberg, Norway. Daniel Windham, bass; Oslo Konservatoriet Chorus; members of NEC Chorus, Arnuv Hegstad, conductor.
Music: Russ-Hix.
Disc: Concept Records CR 002, 1973. Recording of first performance. NEC
Cassette: Apr. 10, 1980; New England Conservatory. NEC Big Band, George Russell, conductor. NEC

R7.23 Living Time. Events I-VIII. (1972) 45'
For: jazz band. *Commissioned by:* Columbia Records.

Music: BMI.
Disc: in *The Progressives*, Columbia CG 31574 (Event V).
Disc: Columba KC 31490, 1972. Bill Evans, piano and electric piano; George Russell Orchestra, George Russell, conductor.
Cassette: Apr. 25, 1978; New England Conservatory. NEC Jazz Ensemble, George Russell, conductor. NEC
Cassette: Apr. 26, 1981; New England Conservatory. NEC Big Band, George Russell, conductor. NEC

[Living Time. Events IX-XV]
R7.24 Events IX-XV.
For: saxophone(soprano)/saxophone(tenor), piano, guitar, double bass, percussion. Jazz quintet.

R7.25 Livingstone I Presume. (1955) 3′ 25″
For: saxophone(alto), trumpet, piano, guitar, double bass, drums. Jazz sextet.
Music: Russ-Hix.
Disc: RCA Victor LPM 1372, 1957. George Russell and His Smalltet.
Disc: in *The Jazz Workshop*. RCA Victor LPM 2534, 1962. Reissue of LPM 1372, 1957.

R7.26 A Lonely Place. (1962) 7′ 18″
For: trumpet, trombone, saxophone(alto), saxophone(tenor), piano, double bass, drums. Jazz septet.
Music: Russ-Hix.
Disc: in *The Stratus Seekers*, Riverside RLP 412/9412, 1962 (date recorded). George Russell Septet.
Cassette: Apr. 24, 1979; New England Conservatory. NEC Jazz Ensemble, George Russell, conductor. NEC
Cassette: Apr. 10, 1980; New England Conservatory. NEC Big Band, George Russell, conductor. NEC

R7.27 Lydia and Her Friends. (1965) 6′ 53″
For: trumpet, trombone, saxophone(tenor), piano, double bass, drums. Jazz sextet.

Music: Russ-Hix.
Disc: in *The George Russell Sextet at the Beethoven Hall*, BASF MC 25125, 1973. George Russell Sextet. HU NEC NU W
Disc: in *The George Russell Sextet at The Beethoven Hall*, SABA SB 15059. George Russell Sextet.
Cassette: Mar. 7, 1972; New England Conservatory; in *An Evening of Contemporary Music*. Roger Rosenberg, tenor saxophone; Stanton Davis, trumpet; Gary Valente, trombone, Gary Peterson, piano; Albert Weatherby, double bass; James Mitchell, drums. NEC
Cassette: Mar. 23, 1972; New England Conservatory. Roger Rosenberg, tenor saxophone; Stanton Davis, trumpet; Gary Valente, trombone; George Russell, piano; James Carroll, double bass; James Mitchell, drums. NEC

R7.28 Lydian Lullaby. (1955)
For: saxophone(alto), guitar, double bass, drums. Jazz quartet.
Commissioned by: Hal McKusick.
Music: Russ-Hix.
Disc: in *Jazz Workshop*, RCA Victor LPM 1366, 1957. Hal McKusick Quartet.

R7.29 Lydian M-1. (1955)
For: jazz ensemble. *Commissioned by:* Teddy Charles.
Music: Russ-Hix.
Disc: in *The Teddy Charles Tentet*, Atlantic 1229, 1956 (date recorded).

The Lydiot. *See* Jazz in the Space Age.

R7.30 Manhattan-Rico. (1958) 10′10″
For: jazz band.
Music: Russ-Hix.
Disc: in *New York, N.Y.*, Decca DL 9216/79216, 1958 (date recorded). George Russell and His Orchestra. HU
Disc: in *New York, N.Y. and Jazz in the Space Age*, MCA 2 4017, 1973. George Russell and His Orchestra. NEC W
Cassette: Dec. 17, 1975; New England Conservatory. NEC Afro-American

Orchestra, George Russell, conductor. NEC

R7.31 May in December.
For: jazz group. *Text:* Hix Blewitt.
Music: Russ-Hix.

R7.32 Miss Clara. (1956)
For: trumpet, trombone, saxophone(alto), saxophone(baritone), guitar, double bass, drums. Jazz septet.
Commissioned by: Hal McKusick.
Disc: in *Jazz Workshop*, RCA Victor LPM 1366, 1957. Members of the Hal McKusick Octet.

R7.33 New Donna. (1960) 8' 18"
For: trumpet, trombone, saxophone(tenor), piano, double bass, drums. Jazz sextet.
Music: Russ-Hix.
Disc: in *Stratusphunk*, Riverside RLP 341/9341, 1960 (date recorded). George Russell Sextet.

New York, N. Y. Suite. *See* Big City Blues; East Side Medley (in Arrangements section); A Helluva Town; Manhatta-Rico; Manhattan (in Arrangements section).

R7.34 Night Sound. 3' 55"
For: saxophone(alto), trumpet, piano, guitar, double bass, drums. Jazz sextet.
Music: Russ-Hix.
Disc: RCA Victor LPM 1372, 1957. George Russell and His Smalltet.
Disc: in *The Jazz Workshop*, RCA Victor LPM 2534, 1962. Reissue of LPM 1372, 1957.

R7.35 Now and Then. (1965) 14' 7"
For: jazz band.
Music: Russ-Hix.
Disc: in *The Essence of George Russell*, Sonet SLP 1411-1412, 1971. George Russell, conductor. NEC
Cassette: May 12, 1973; New England Conservatory; in *A Festival of Contemporary American Music*. NEC Afro-American Music Ensemble, Jaki Byard, conductor. NEC
Cassette: Dec. 16, 1976; New England

Conservatory. Members of NEC Afro-American Music Department, George Russell, conductor. NEC
Cassette: Apr. 26, 1981; New England Conservatory. NEC Big Band, George Russell, conductor. NEC

R7.36 Odjenar. (1949)
For: saxophone(alto), trumpet, piano, guitar, double bass, drums. Jazz sextet.
Music: Russ-Hix.
Disc: in *Ezz-thetic*, Prestige 116, 1951 (date recorded). Lee Konitz and others.
Disc: in *Ezz-thetic*, Prestige 7827, 1973. Reissue of Prestige 116, 1951. NEC

R7.37 Oh Jazz, Pò Jazz. (1965) 11' 29"
For: trumpet, trombone, saxophone(tenor), piano, double bass, drums. Jazz sextet.
Music: Russ-Hix.
Disc: in *The George Russell Sextet at the Beethoven Hall*, BASF MC 25125, 1973.
  George Russell Sextet. HU NEC NU W
Disc: in *The George Russell Sextet at the Beethoven Hall*, SABA SB 15059. George Russell Sextet.
Cassette: May 8, 1971; New England Conservatory; in *A Festival of New England Composers Past and Present*. NEC Jazz Ensemble, Gunther Schuller, conductor. NEC
Cassette: Dec. 16, 1976; New England Conservatory. Members of NEC Afro-American Music Department, George Russell, conductor. NEC

R7.38 Othello Ballet Suite.
Commissioned by: Norwegian TV for the ballet *The Net*.
Disc: Sonet SLP 1409, 1971. W

R7.39 The Outer View. (1962) 10' 3"
For: trumpet, trombone, saxophone(tenor), piano, double bass, drums. Jazz sextet.
Music: Russ-Hix.
Disc: in *The Outer View*, Riverside RM 440/RS 3016, 1962 (date recorded). George Russell Sextet. NU W
Disc: in *Outer Thoughts*, Milestone M 47027, 1975. George Russell Sextet. HU

NEC
Cassette: Apr. 24, 1979; New England Conservatory. NEC Jazz Ensemble, George Russell, conductor. NEC

R7.40 Pan-Daddy. (1962) 5' 47"
For: trumpet, trombone, saxophone(alto), saxophone(tenor), piano, double bass, drums. Jazz septet.
Music: Russ-Hix.
Disc: in *The Stratus Seekers*, Riverside RLP 412/9412, 1962 (date recorded). George Russell Septet.
Disc: in *Outer Thoughts*, Milestone M 47027, 1975. George Russell Septet. HU
NEC

R7.41 Round Johnny Rondo. (1956) 3' 25"
For: saxophone(alto), trumpet, piano, guitar, double bass, drums. Jazz sextet.
Music: Russ-Hix.
Disc: RCA Victor LPM 1372, 1957. George Russell and His Smalltet.
Disc: in *The Jazz Workshop*, RCA Victor LPM 2534, 1962. Reissue of LPM 1372, 1957.

R7.42 The Sad Sargeant. (1956) 3' 25"
For: saxophone(alto), trumpet, piano, guitar, double bass, drums. Jazz sextet.
Music: Russ-Hix.
Disc: RCA Victor LPM 1372, 1957. George Russell and His Smalltet.
Disc: in *The Jazz Workshop*, RCA LPM 2534, 1962. Reissue of LPM 1372, 1957.

R7.43 The Stratus Seekers. (1962) 6' 52"
For: trumpet, trombone, saxophone(alto), saxophone(tenor), piano, double bass, drums. Jazz septet.
Music: Russ-Hix.
Disc: in *1, 2, 3, 4, 5 6extet*, Riverside RS 3043. George Russell Septet.
Disc: in *The Stratus Seekers*, Riverside RLP 412/9412, 1962 (date recorded). George Russell Septet.
Disc: in *Outer Thoughts*, Milestone M 47027, 1975. George Russell Septet. HU
NEC
Cassette: Apr. 26, 1981; New England

Conservatory. NEC Big Band, George Russell, conductor. NEC

R7.44 Stratusphunk. (1958) 6' 03"
For: trumpet, trombone, saxophone(tenor), piano, double bass, drums. Jazz sextet.
Music: Russ-Hix.
Lead sheets: in *The Lydian Chromatic Concept of Tonal Organization for Improvisation*, 1953.
Disc: in *Cross Section: Saxes*, Decca DL 9209/79209, 1956 (date recorded). Hal McKusick Sextet.
Disc: in *The Dynamic Sound of J.J. with Big Band*, RCA Victor LPM 3350, 1958 (date recorded). J.J. Johnson and others.
Disc: in *Stratusphunk*, Riverside RLP 341/9341, 1960 (date recorded). George Russell Sextet.
Disc: in *Out of the Cool*, Impulse AS 4, 1961. Gil Evans Orchestra. NEC
Disc: in *Outer Thoughts*, Milestone M 47027, 1975. George Russell Sextet. HU
NEC
Cassette: Dec. 20, 1970; New England Conservatory. NEC Jazz Ensemble, Carl Atkins, conductor. NEC
Cassette: Dec. 17, 1975; New England Conservatory. NEC Afro-American Orchestra, George Russell, conductor. NEC
Cassette: Dec. 16, 1976; New England Conservatory. Members of NEC Afro-American Music Deprtment, Geroge Russell, conductor. NEC
Cassette: Mar. 1, 1977; New England Conservatory; in *Jazz Workshop Series*. Members of NEC Afro-American Music Department. NEC
Cassette: Apr. 25, 1978; New England Conservatory. NEC Jazz Ensemble, George Russell, conductor. NEC

R7.45 Swingdom Come. (1960)
For: trumpet, trombone, saxophone(tenor), piano, double bass, drums. Jazz sextet.
Music: Russ-Hix.
Disc: in *George Russell Sextet at the*

Five Spot, Decca DL 9220/79220, 1960 (date recorded). George Russell Sextet.

R7.46 Takin' Lydia Home. (1965) 2' 05"
For: trumpet, trombone, saxophone(tenor), piano, double bass, drums. Jazz sextet.
Music: Russ-Hix.
Disc: in *The George Russell Sextet at the Beethoven Hall*, BASF MC 25125, 1973. George Russell Sextet. HU NEC NU W
Disc: in *The George Russell Sextet at the Beethoven Hall*, SABA SB 15059. George Russell Sextet.

R7.47 Theme. (1961)
For: trumpet, trombone, saxophone(tenor), piano, double bass, drums. Jazz sextet.
Music: Russ-Hix.
Disc: in *George Russell Sextet in K.C.*, Decca DL 4183/74183, 1960 (date recorded). George Russell Sextet.

R7.48 Things New. (1960) 6' 52"
For: trumpet, trombone, saxophone, piano, double bass, drums. Jazz sextet.
Music: Russ-Hix.
Disc: in *Stratusphunk*, Riverside RLP 341/9341, 1960 (date recorded). George Russell Sextet.

R7.49 Thoughts. (1961)
For: trumpet, trombone, saxophone(tenor), piano, double bass, drums. Jazz sextet.
Music: Russ-Hix.
Disc: in *1, 2, 3, 4, 5, 6extet*, Riverside RS 3043. George Russell Sextet.
Disc: in *Ezz-thetics*, Riverside RLP 375, 1961 (date recorded). George Russell Sextet.
Disc: in *Outer Thoughts*, Milestone M 47027, 1975. George Russell Sextet. HU NEC
Disc: in *Ezz-thetics*, Riverside RLP 375, 1975. Reissue of RLP 375, 1961. MIT

R7.50 Volupte. (1964) 12' 09"
For: trumpet, trombone, saxophone(tenor), piano, double bass, drums. Jazz sextet.

Music: Russ-Hix.
Disc: in *The George Russell Sextet at the Beethoven Hall*, BASF MC 25125, 1973. George Russell Sextet. HU NEC NU W
Disc: in *The George Russell Sextet at the Beethoven Hall*, SABA SB 15059. George Russell Sextet.
Cassette: Apr. 10, 1980; New England Conservatory. NEC Big Band, George Russell, conductor. NEC

Waltz from Outer Space. *See* Jazz in the Space Age.

R7.51 West of Benchazi. (1949)
For: jazz group.
Music: Beechwood.

R7.52 Witch Hunt. (1956) 3' 48"
For: saxophone(alto), trumpet, piano, guitar, double bass, drums. Jazz sextet.
Music: Russ-Hix.
Disc: in *The Jazz Workshop*, RCA Victor LPM 1372, 1957. George Russell and His Smalltet.
Disc: in *The Jazz Workshop*, RCA LPM 2534, 1962. Reissue of LPM 1372, 1957.

R7.53 Ye Hypocrite, Ye Beelzebub. (1956) 3' 48"
For: saxophone(alto), trumpet, piano, guitar, double bass, drums. Jazz sextet.
Music: Russ-Hix.
Disc: in *The Jazz Workshop*, RCA Victor LPM 1372, 1957. George Russell and His Smalltet.
Disc: in *The Jazz Workshop*, RCA LPM 2534, 1962. Reissue of LPM 1372, 1957.

ARRANGEMENTS OF WORKS BY OTHER COMPOSERS

R7.54 Au Privave.
For: trumpet, trombone, saxophone(tenor), piano, double bass, drums. Jazz sextet. Original by Charlie Parker.
Disc: in *The Outer View*, Riverside RM 440/RS 3016, 1962 (date recorded). George Russell Sextet. NU W
Disc: in *Outer Thoughts*, Milestone M

47027, 1975. George Russell Sextet. HU NEC

R7.55 Beast Blues.
For: trumpet, trombone, saxophone(tenor), piano, double bass, drums. Jazz sextet. Original by Carla Bley.
Disc: in *George Russell Sextet at the Five Spot*, Decca DL 9220/ 79220, 1960 (date recorded). George Russell Sextet.

R7.56 Bent Eagle.
For: trumpet, trombone, saxophone(tenor), piano, double bass, drums. Jazz sextet. Original by Carla Bley.
Disc: in *Stratusphunk*, Riverside RLP 341/9341, 1960 (date recorded). George Russell Sextet.
Disc: in *Outer Thoughts*, Milestone H 47027, 1975. George Russell Sextet. HU NEC
Cassette: Mar. 1, 1977; New England Conservatory; in *Jazz Workshop Series*. Members of NEC Afro-American Music Department. NEC
Cassette: Apr. 25, 1978; New England Conservatory. NEC Jazz Ensemble, George Russell, conductor. NEC
Casette: Apr. 10, 1980; New England Conservatory. NEC Big Band, George Russell, conductor. NEC

R7.57 Dance Class.
For: trumpet, trombone, saxophone(tenor), piano, double bass, drums. Jazz sextet. Original by Carla Bley.
Disc: in *George Russell Sextet at the Five Spot*, Decca 9220/79220, 1960 (date recorded). George Russell Sextet.

R7.58 East Side Medley. 8'
For: jazz band. *Movements:* Autumn in New York (original by Vernon Duke); How about You (original in *Babes on Broadway* by Burton Lane and Ralph Freed).
Disc: in *New York, N.Y.*, Decca DL 9216/79216, 1959 (date recorded). George Russell and His Orchestra. HU

Disc: in *New York, N.Y. and Jazz in the Space Age*, MCA 2 4017, 1973. George Russell and His Orchestra. NEC W
Cassette: Dec. 17, 1975; New England Conservatory. NEC Afro-American Orchestra, George Russell, conductor. NEC

R7.59 End of a Love Affair.
For: saxophone(alto), trumpet, piano, guitar, double bass, drums. Jazz sextet. Original by Edward C. Redding.
Disc: in *Cross Section: Saxes*, Decca DL 9209/79209, 1956 (date recorded). Hal McKusick Sextet.

R7.60 Honesty.
For: trumpet, trombone, saxophone(tenor), piano, double bass, drums. Jazz sextet. Original by Dave Baker.
Disc: in *Ezz-thetics*, Riverside RLP 375, 1961 (date recorded). George Russell Sextet.
Disc: in *Ezz-thetics*, Riverside RLP 9375, 1975. Reissue of RLP 375, 1961 (date recorded). MIT
Disc: in *Outer Thoughts*, Milestone M 47027, 1975. George Russell Sextet. HU NEC

R7.61 Kentucky Oysters.
For: trumpet, trombone, saxophone(tenor), piano, double bass, drums. Jazz sextet. Original by Dave Baker.
Disc: in *Stratusphunk*, Riverside RLP 341/9341, 1960 (date recorded). George Russell Sextet.
Cassette: Mar. 1, 1977; New England Conservatory; in *Jazz Workshop Series*. Members of NEC Afro-American Music Department. NEC

R7.62 Kige's Tune.
For: trumpet, trombone, saxophone(alto), saxophone(tenor), piano, double bass, drums. Jazz septet. Original by Al Kiger.
Disc: in *The Stratus Seekers*, Riverside RLP 412/9412, 1962 (date recorded).

George Russell Septet.
Cassette: Mar. 1, 1977; New England
Conservatory; in *Jazz Workshop Series*.
Members of NEC Afro-American Music
Department. NEC
Cassette: Apr. 25, 1978; New England
Conservatory. NEC Jazz Ensemble,
George Russell, conductor. NEC
Cassette: Apr. 24, 1979; New England
Conservatory. NEC Jazz Ensemble,
George Russell, conductor. NEC

R7.63 Lambskins.
For: trumpet, trombone, saxophone,
piano, double bass, drums. Jazz sextet.
Original by David Lahm.
Disc: in *Stratusphunk*, Riverside RLP
341/9341, 1960 (date recorded). George
Russell Sextet.

R7.64 Lord Go Lightly on a Lonely
Man.
For: jazz band. Original by Lec
Genesis.
Cassette: Apr. 26, 1981; New England
Conservatory. NEC Big Band, George
Russell, conductor. NEC

R7.65 Lunacy.
For: trumpet, trombone,
saxophone(tenor), piano, double bass,
drums. Jazz sextet. Original by Dave
Baker.
Disc: in *George Russell Sextet in K.C.*,
Decca DL 4183/74183, 1960 (date
recorded). George Russell Sextet.

R7.66 Lydia in Bags Groove.
For: trumpet, trombone,
saxophone(tenor), piano, double bass,
drums. Jazz sextet. Original by Milt
Jackson.
Disc: in *The George Russell Sextet at
the Beethoven Hall*, BASF MC 25125,
1973. George Russell Sextet. HU NEC
NU W
Disc: in *The George Russell Sextet at
the Beethoven Hall*, SABA SB 15059.
George Russell Sextet.

R7.67 Lydia 'round Midnight. 6' 30"
For: trumpet, trombone,
saxophone(tenor), piano, double bass,

drums. Jazz sextet. Original by
Thelonious Monk.
Disc: in *Ezz-thetics*, Riverside RLP 375,
1961 (date recorded) (titled 'Round
Midnight). George Russell Sextet.
Disc: in *The George Russell Sextet at
the Beethoven Hall*, BASF MC 25125,
1973. George Russell Sextet. HU NEC
NU W
Disc: in *The George Russell Sextet at
the Beethoven Hall*, SABA SB 15059.
George Russell Sextet.
Disc: in *Outer Thoughts*, Milestone M
47027, 1975. George Russell Sextet. HU
NEC
Disc: in *Ezz-thetics*, Riverside 9375,
1975 (titled 'Round Midnight). Reissue
of RLP 375. MIT
Cassette: Mar. 1, 1977; New England
Conservatory; in *Jazz Workshop Series*
(titled 'Round Midnight). Members of
NEC Afro-American Music Department.
NEC

R7.68 Lydia's Confirmation.
For: trumpet, trombone,
saxophone(tenor), piano, double bass,
drums. Jazz sextet. Original by Charlie
Parker.
Disc: in *The George Russell Sextet at
the Beethoven Hall*, BASF MC 25125,
1973. George Russell Sextet. HU NEC
NU W
Disc: in *The George Russell Sextet at
the Beethoven Hall*, SABA SB 15059.
George Russell Sextet.

R7.69 Manhattan. 10' 32"
For: jazz band. Original in *Garrick
Gaieties* by Richard Rogers and Lorenz
Hart.
Disc: in *New York, N.Y.*, Decca DL
9216/79216, 1958 (date recorded). George
Russell and His Orchestra. HU
Disc: in *New York, N.Y. and Jazz in
the Space Age*, MCA 2 4017, 1973.
George Russell and His Orchestra. NEC
W
Cassette: Dec. 17, 1975; New England
Conservatory. NEC Afro-American
Orchestra, George Russell, conductor.
NEC

R7.70 Moment's Notice.
For: trumpet, trombone, saxophone(tenor), piano, double bass, drums. Jazz sextet. Original by John Coltrane.
Disc: in *George Russell Sextet at the Five Spot*, Decca DL 9220/79220, 1960 (date recorded). George Russell Sextet.

R7.71 Nardis.
For: trumpet, trombone, saxophone(tenor), piano, double bass, drums. Jazz sextet. Original by Miles Davis.
Disc: in *Ezz-thetics*, Riverside RLP 375, 1961 (date recorded). George Russell Sextet.
Disc: in *Outer Thoughts*, Milestone M 47027, 1975. George Russell Sextet. HU NEC
Disc: in *Ezz-thetics*, Riverside 9375, 1975. Reissue of RLP 375, 1961 (date recorded). MIT

R7.72 121 Bank Street.
For: trumpet, trombone, saxophone(tenor), piano, double bass, drums. Jazz sextet. Original by Dave Baker.
Disc: in *George Russell Sextet at the Five Spot*, Decca DL 9220/79220, 1960 (da te recorded). George Russell Sextet.

R7.73 Rhymes.
For: trumpet, trombone, saxophone(tenor), piano, double bass, drums. Jazz sextet. Original by Carla Bley.
Disc: in *George Russell Sextet in K.C.*, Decca DL 4183/74183, 1960 (date recorded). George Russell Sextet.
Cassette: Apr. 26, 1981; New England Conservatory. NEC Big Band, George Russell, conductor. NEC

'Round Midnight. *See* Lydia 'round Midnight.

R7.74 Sandu.
For: trumpet, trombone, saxophone(tenor), piano, double bass, drums. Jazz sextet. Original by Clifford Brown.
Disc: in *George Russell Sextet in K.C.*, Decca DL 4183/74183, 1960 (date recorded). George Russell Sextet.

R7.75 Sippin' at the Bells.
For: trumpet, trombone, saxophone(tenor), piano, double bass, drums. Jazz sextet. Original by Miles Davis.
Disc: in *George Russell Sextet at the Five Spot*, Decca DL 9220/79220, 1960 (date recorded). George Russell Sextet.

R7.76 Stereophrenic.
For: trumpet, trombone, saxophone(alto), saxophone(tenor), piano, double bass, drums. Jazz septet. Original by Dave Baker.
Disc: in *The Stratus Seekers*, Riverside RLP 412/9412, 1962 (date recorded). George Russell Sextet.

R7.77 Tune Up.
For: trumpet, trombone, saxophone(tenor), piano, double bass, drums. Jazz sextet. Original by Miles Davis.
Disc: in *George Russell Sextet in K.C.*, Decca DL 4183/74183, 1960 (date recorded). George Russell Sextet.

R7.78 War gewessen.
For: trumpet, trombone, saxophone(tenor), piano, double bass, drums. Jazz sextet. Original by Dave Baker.
Disc: in *George Russell Sextet in K.C.*, Decca DL 4183/74183, 1960 (date recorded). George Russell Sextet.

R7.79 You Are My Sunshine.
For: trumpet, trombone, saxophone(tenor), piano, double bass, drums. Jazz sextet. Original by Jimmy Davis.
Disc: in *The Outer View*, Riverside RM 440/RS 3016, 1962 (date recorded). George Russell Sextet. NU W
Disc: in *The George Russell Sextet at the Beethoven Hall*, BASF MC 25125, 1973. George Russell Sextet. HU NEC

NU W
Disc: in *The George Russell Sextet at the Beethoven Hall*, SABA SB 15059. George Russell Sextet.
Disc: in *Outer Thoughts*, Milestone M 47027, 1975. George Russell Sextet. HU NEC
Cassette: Mar. 1, 1977; New England Conservatory; in *Jazz Workshop Series*. Members of NEC Afro-American Music Department. NEC
Cassette: Apr. 24, 1979; New England Conservatory. NEC Jazz Ensemble, George Russell, conductor. NEC

R7.80 You're My Thrill.
For: saxophone(alto), trumpet, piano, guitar, double bass, drums. Jazz sextet. Original by Jay Gorney and Sidney Clare.
Disc: in *Cross Section: Saxes*, Decca DL 9209/79209, 1956 (date recorded). Hal McKusick Sextet.

R7.81 Zig-Zag.
For: trumpet, trombone, saxophone(tenor), piano, double bass, drums. Jazz sextet. Original by Carla Bley.
Disc: in *The Outer View*, Riverside RM 440/RS 3016, 1962 date recorded). George Russell Sextet. NU W
Disc: in *Outer Thoughts*, Milestone M 47027, 1975. George Russell Sextet. HU NEC

R8 ROBERT RUTMAN

Born 1931 in Berlin, Germany. Moved to Boston area 1975. *Related activities:* inventor of musical instruments (single string steel cello, bow chimes, buzz chimes); founder of and performer with the U.S. Steel Cello Ensemble; sculptor; painter. CPL

[Bitter Suites; Side 1]
R8.1 Bitter Suites.
For: steel cello and bow chimes(2).
First performed: 1978. Robert Rutman, steel cello; Suzanne Bresler and David Zaig, bow chimes.
Disc: Rutdog Records 1009, 1979.

Robert Rutman, steel cello; Suzanne Bresler and David Zaig, bow chimes. MIT

[Bitter Suites; Side 2]
R8.2 Bitter Suites.
For: bow chimes(4). *First performed:* 1978. Steve Baer, Jim Van Denakker, Rex Morril, Robert Rutman.
Disc: Rutdog Records 1009, 1979. Steve Baer, Jim Van Denakker, Rex Morril, Robert Rutman. MIT

R8.3 Buzz Off.
For: wood buzz chime. *First performed:* Oct. 1979. Robert Rutman.

S1 JOHN A. SCHEMMER (Tony)

Born August 5, 1946, in New York City. Moved to Boston area 1968. *Education:* B.A. (Yale University, 1968), New England Conservatory, Berklee College of Music. *Related activities:* composer-in-residence, Composers' Festival (University of Maine, Farmington, 1978). BkPL

WORKS

S1.1 Berceuse. (1979) 1'
For: piano. *Dedicated to:* Nola Keene Breglio.
Score: reprod. of ms.; available from composer.

S1.2 Fantasy on a Theme of Ralph Vaughan Williams. (1971) 13'
For: organ.
Score: reprod. of ms.; available from composer.

S1.3 Hark the Herald. (1980) 3'
For: brasses and organ or piano(4-hands). Arrangement of Hark the Herald Angels Sing.
Score & parts: reprod. of ms.; available from composer.

[Lieder]
S1.4 Six Lieder. (1970)
For: voice and piano.
Score: available from composer.

S1.5 Melody for Sopranino Sax. (1980) 2'
For: saxophone(sopranino) or oboe or flute.
Score: reprod. of ms.; available from composer.

[Occasional Songs]
S1.6 Eight Occasional Songs. (1972)
Text: Tony Schemmer.
Score: reprod. of ms.; available from composer.

S1.7 Octet. (1978-80) 28'
For: flute, oboe, clarinets(in A)(2), horn, bassoon, guitar(amplified), piano. 4 movements. *Dedicated to:* Philip and Patricia Morehead. *First performed:* July 16, 1978; Rockport Opera House, Rockport, Me. (1st movement). Tony Schemmer, conductor.
Score & parts: reprod. of ms.; available from composer.
Reel & cassette: available from composer.

S1.8 Phaust. (1978) 170'
For: voices(6), chorus, orchestra(2(pic, afl)-0-2(tsax, &bcl), asax, tsax, bsax-0; 0-2-2-0; perc(2); pf, org, gt(amp), db(amp); str). Opera in two acts and a prologue. *Libretto:* Tony Schemmer.
First performed: Apr. 4, 1980; Sanders Theatre, Havard University. Cheryl Cobb, Keith Kibler, James Maddalena, Raymond Sepe, Valerie Walters; Philip Morehead, conductor.
Score & parts: reprod. of ms.; available from composer. Rental.
Vocal score: reprod. of ms.; available from composer. Rental.
Chorus parts: reprod. of ms.; available from composer. Rental.
Reel & cassette: recording of first performance; available from composer.

[Pieces]
S1.9 Five Pieces for Piano. (1976) 12'
Contents: Theme; Humoresque; Fugue; Dream; Finale.
Score: reprod. of ms.; available from composer.

Reel & cassette: available from composer.

S1.10 Prelude. (1970) 12'
For: organ and trumpet(optional).
Dedicated to: Daniel Carney and Holly Gardiner Burnes. *First performed:* Sept. 12, 1970; Christ Church, Gardiner, Me. Tony Schemmer, organ.
Score & part: available from composer.

S1.11 Recessional. (1972) 10'
For: organ. *Dedicated to:* Robert Warren and Mia Savoia Steiner.
Score: available from composer.

S1.12 The Ringmaster. (1970) 70'
For: Soprano and piano. Song cycle.
Text: Nan Proctor Mason. *First performed:* Aug. 1970; The Barn, Quaker Hill, Pawling, N.Y. Elsa Jean Davidson, soprano and Tony Schemmer, piano.
Score: available from composer.

S1.13 Sonata for Oboe and Piano. (1981) 18'
For: oboe or clarinet or saxophone(soprano) and piano.
Movements: Allegro; Sandor's Ballad; Omaggio a Django; Finale. *Dedicated to:* Ann Bajart Schemmer.
Score & parts: reprod. of ms.; available from composer.
Reel & cassette: available from composer.

[Standards for Piano]
S1.14 Ten Standards for Piano. (1979) 18'
Contents: Sphinx; Last Laugh; Waltz on B; Sea Monstre; Blues on B; Wonderboy; East-West Divine; Neighborhood 3/4; Getting Started; Da Capo.
Score: reprod. of ms.; available from composer.

S2 MARTIN MAX SCHREINER

Born July 21, 1950, in Springfield, Mass. Moved to Boston area 1980.

Education: studied composition with Philip Bezanson and Robert Stern (University of Massachusetts, Amherst, B.M., 1976). *Related activities:* clarinetist, saxophonist; music copyist; teacher. CPL

WORKS

S2.1 Celestial Fanfare. (1975) 1'
For: flute and clarinet.
Score: reprod. of ms.

S2.2 A Head with My Eyes. (1978) 5'
For: Soprano, clarinet, piano. *Text:* Rene Dupont. *First performed:* 1979; Springfield, Mass. Michele Eaton, soprano; Martin Schreiner, clarinet; Pamela Weeks, piano.
Score & part: reprod. of ms.

S2.3 Introductory and Fugue. (1973) 5'
For: Soprano, lute or guitar, clarinet.
First performed: 1974; University of Massachusetts, Amherst.
Score: reprod. of ms.

S2.4 Prelude and Fugue. (1974) 4' 30"
For: horn. *First performed:* Feb. 18, 1975; University of Massachusetts, Amherst. Ellen Donahue.
Score: reprod. of ms.

[Sonata, Piano]
S2.5 Piano Sonata. (1979) 18'
3 movements. *First performed:* May 1981; New School of Music, Cambridge, Mass. Karen Sauer.
Score: reprod. of ms.
Reel & cassette: available from composer.

[Songs of Departure]
S2.6 Four Songs of Departure. (1978) 9'
For: Soprano and flute. *Text: Rihaku;* English translation by Ezra Pound.
Contents: Taking Leave of a Friend; Leave-Taking Near Shoku; Separation on the River; The City of Choan. *First performed:* Nov. 21, 1978; Springfield Technical Community College. Michele Eaton, soprano and Joanna Karb, flute.
Score: reprod. of ms.

S2.7 Spring Pools. (1980) 3'
For: piano.
Score: reprod. of ms.

S2.8 Three for Seven. (1975; rev. 1980) 10'
For: oboe, clarinet, clarinet(bass), bassoon, horn, trumpet, trombone(bass). 3 movements. *First performed:* 1977; University of Massachusetts, Amherst.
Score & parts: reprod. of ms.

S2.9 Waltz. (1976) 2' 30"
For: piano.
Score: reprod. of ms.

S3 GUNTHER SCHULLER

Born November 22, 1925, in New York City. Moved to Boston area 1967. *Education:* studied harmony with T. Tertius Noble (St. Thomas Choir School); also studied flute and horn. *Awards:* Brandeis University, Creative Arts Award (1960), National Institute of Arts and Letters Award (1960), Guggenheim Grants (1962, [1963?]), College Band Directors' National Association, North Central Division, Original Composition Award (1963), Darius Milhaud Award for best film score (1964), ASCAP-Deems Taylor Award (1970), Alice M. Ditson Conductor's Award (Columbia Univeristy, 1970), Grammy Award for Best Chamber Music Performance (1973), American Academy and Institute of Arts and Letters (member, [1980?]), honorary degrees from Northeastern University (1967), University of Illinois (1968), Colby College (1969), Williams College (1975), Rutgers University (1980), Cleveland State University (1981). *Related activities:* conductor, broadcaster, educator, author, editor, administrator; guest conductor of the orchestras of Boston, Cleveland, New York, Chicago, the New England Conservatory Ragtime Ensemble, BBC Symphony, Berlin Philharmonic and others; horn player, New York City Ballet Theater Orchestra (1943); co-principal horn, Cincinnati

Symphony Orchestra (1943-45) and Metropolitan Opera Orchestra, New York City (1945-49); coined the term "Third stream" to describe the synthesis of contemporary Western art music and various types of ethnic music and jazz (1957), and is associated with the style as a composer; conducted and organized concert series Twentieth Century Innovations sponsored by the Carnegie Hall Corporation (1963-65); hosted radio program, *Contemporary Music in Evolution* for WBAI, New York City and *Changing Music* for WGBH-FM, Boston (1973); author of *Horn Technique* (1962) and *Early Jazz: Its Roots and Musical Development* (1973); reconstructed works of Charles Ives, Scott Joplin, Kurt Weill; served on the faculties of Manhattan School of Music (1950-63), Yale University (1964-67); New England Conservatory (1967- ; President, 1967-77); teacher, conductor, administrator (Berkshire Music Festival, Tanglewood, 1963- ; artistic director, 1971-). NEC

WORKS

S3.1 Abstraction. (1960) 5'
For: saxophone(alto), guitar, percussion, string quartet, double basses(2). Jazz nonet.
Score: MJQ, 1966. BPL HU
Disc: in *Jazz Abstractions*, Atlantic SD 1365, 1961. Ornette Coleman, alto saxophone; Jim Hall, guitar; Scott Lafaro and Alvin Brehm, double basses; Sticks Evans, drums; Contemporary String Quartet. HU NEC
Cassette: May 8, 1971; New England Conservatory; in *A Festival of New England Composers Past and Present*. Carl Atkins, alto saxophone; NEC Jazz Ensemble, Gunther Schuller, conductor. NEC

S3.2 Adagio. (1953) 5'
For: flute, violin, viola, violoncello.
First performed: Nov. 30, 1958; Carl Fischer Concert Hall, New York City;

New York Flute Club concert. James Politis, flute; Marion Hersh, violin; Ralph Hersh, viola; John Pastore, violoncello.
Score & parts: Margun.

S3.3 American Triptych, a Study in Textures. (1964-65) 14'
For: orchestra(3(pic)-3(Ehn)-3(bcl)-3(cbsn); 4-3-3-1; timp, perc(3), glock, vibra; hp; str). *Movements:* Alexander Calder's Four Directions; Jackson Pollock's Out of the Web; Stuart Davis's Swing Landscape. *Commissioned by:* Association of Women's Committees for Symphony Orchestras. *First performed:* Mar. 1965; New Orleans, La. New Orleans Philharmonic, Gunther Schuller, conductor.
Score: Associated, 1966. BCM BPL BU HMA HU MIT NEC UMB
Parts: Associated, 1966. Rental.

S3.4 Aphorisms. (1967) 14'
For: flute, violin, viola, violoncello. 5 movements. *Commissioned by:* Carleton College. *Dedication:* In Memory of George Edwin Black. To Carleton College. *First performed:* May 12, 1976. Robert Cole, flute; members of the Lenox Quartet.
Score: Associated, 1979. NEC
Parts: Associated, 1979.
Cassette: Mar. 8, 1976; New England Conservatory. Sharon Zuckerman, flute; Michael Bogetti, violin; Gillian Rogell, viola; Kathleen Luger, violoncello. NEC
Cassette: Oct. 17, 1977; New England Conservatory. John Heiss, flute; Daniel Stepner, violin; Aaron Picht, viola; Bruce Coppock, violoncello. NEC

S3.5 Atonal Jazz Study. (1948) 5'
For: jazz ensemble(flute, clarinet, saxophone(alto), saxophone(tenor), saxophone(baritone), horns(2), trumpet, trombone, tuba, percussion, piano, double bass).
Score & parts: Margun.

S3.6 Automation. (1962) 7'
For: instrumental ensemble(flute, oboe,

saxophone(alto), saxophone(tenor), saxophone(baritone), horns(2), trumpet, trombone, tuba, drums, piano, double bass). Film music.
Score & parts: Margun.

[Bagatelles]
S3.7 Five Bagatelles. (1964) 15'
For: orchestra(2(&pic)-1(&Ehn)-2(&bcl)-2(&cbsn); 4-3-3-1; timp, perc(3-4), vibra; hp, pf; str).
Commissioned by: Fargo-Morehead Symphony Orchestra. *First performed:* Mar. 22, 1964. Fargo-Morehead Symphony Orchestra, Gunther Schuller, conductor.
Score & parts: Associated. Rental.
Disc: Louisville Orchestra LS 686, 1968. Louisville Orchestra, Jorge Mester, conductor. BCM BrU BU HU HUm MIT NEC W

S3.8 Blumenstrauss (The Bouquet). (1941) 2'
For: Soprano and piano. *Dedication:* To my mother.
Score: Margun, 1979. NEC

The Bouquet. *See* Blumenstrauss.

S3.9 Capriccio. (1960) 15'
For: tuba and orchestra(1-1-2(bcl)-0; 2-0-1-0; hp; str(8-0-3-2)). 3 movements.
Commissioned by and dedicated to: Harvey Phillips. *First performed:* 1962; New York City; in 20th-Century Innovations Series. Harvey Phillips, tuba; Gunther Schuller, conductor.
Score & parts: Mentor, 1960.
Cassette: Mar. 1, 1970; New England Conservatory. Harvey Phillips, tuba; Boston Philharmonia, Gunther Schuller, conductor. NEC

S3.10 Capriccio stravagante. (1972) 19'
For: orchestra(3-3-4-3; 4-4-3-1; timp, perc; hp, cel, pf; str). *Commissioned by:* San Francisco Symphony Association in celebration of the 60th anniversary of the San Francisco Symphony. *First performed:* Dec. 6, 1972; San Francisco, Calif. San Francisco Symphony

Orchestra, Seiji Ozawa, conductor.
Score & parts: Associated, 1972. Rental.

S3.11 Colloquy. (1968) 20'
For: pianos(2) and orchestra(3(pic)-3(Ehn)-3(bcl)-3(cbsn); 4-3-3-1; timp, perc(6); hp, cel; str). *First performed:* June 6, 1968; Berlin, West Germany. Joseph Rollino and Paul Sheftel, pianos; Berlin Philharmonic Orchestra; Gunther Schuller, conductor.
Score & parts: Associated. Rental.
Pf. red: Assocated. NEC

S3.12 Composition for Carillon. (1962) 8'
3 movements. *Commissioned by:* Daniel Robbins. *First performed:* June 27, 1962; University of Chicago; Summer Quarter Carillon Recitals.
Score: Margun.

[Composition for Carillon; Arr]
S3.13 Composition for Carillon. 8'
For: harpsichord or organ. 3 movements.
Score: Margun.

[Composition for Carillon; Arr]
S3.14 Composition for Carillon. 8'
For: organ, glockenspiel, vibraphone or marimba, chimes. 3 movements.
Score & parts: Margun.

S3.15 Composition in Three Parts. (1963) 15'
For: orchestra(4(pic)-3-4(Ebcl, bcl)-3; 4-4-3-1; timp, perc(4); hp, pf; str).
Commissioned by: Minneapolis Symphony. *Dedicated to:* Stanislaw Skrowaczewski. *First performed:* Mar. 29, 1963. Minneapolis Symphony, Gunther Schuller, conductor.
Score & parts: Associated. Rental.

S3.16 Concertino. (1959) 19'
For: jazz quartet(vibraphone, piano, double bass, drums) and orchestra (2(pic2)-2-2-2; 2-3-2-0; perc; str). 3 movements. *First performed:* Jan. 2, 1960; Baltimore, Md. Modern Jazz Quartet; Baltimore Symphony Orchestra, Herbert Grossman, conductor.

Score: MJQ, 1961. HU NEC T W
Parts: Associated (orchestra). Rental.
Parts: MJQ, 1961 (solo). W
Disc: Atlantic SD 1359, 1961. Modern Jazz Quartet; Stuttgart Radio Orchestra, Gunther Schuller, conductor. HU MIT NEC W

[Concertino. Passacaglia; Arr.]
S3.17 Passacaglia. 7'
For: jazz quartet(vibraphone, piano, double bass, drums) and band. Written for the Modern Jazz Quartet. *First performed:* 1959; University of Illinois, Urbana-Champaign.
Score & parts: MJQ.

[Concertino. Progression in Tempo]
S3.18 Progression in Tempo. 6'
Music: MJQ.

[Concerto, Contrabassoon]
S3.19 Concerto. (1978)
For: contrabassoon and orchestra(2(pic2)-2(&Ehn2) -2(&bcl,&cbcl)-3(cbsn); 4-4-3-1; perc; str). 4 movements. *Commissioned by:* National Symphony Orchestra. *First performed:* Jan. 1979. Lewis Lipnick, contrabassoon; National Symphony Orchestra, Mstislav Rostropovich, conductor.
Music: Associated.

S3.20 Concerto da camera. (1971) 16'
For: orchestra(1-1-1(bcl)-1; 1-1-1-0; perc(2); hp, cel, pf; str). *Commissioned by:* Eastman School of Music for its 75th anniversary. *First performed:* Apr. 24, 1972; Eastman School of Music. Gunther Schuller, conductor.

[Concerto, Double Bass]
S3.21 Concerto. (1968) 16'
For: double bass and orchestra(0(pic, afl)-1(&Ehn)-1(&Ebcl)-1(&cbsn); 1-1-2-0; cel; str(4-0-4-4)). 6 movements.
Commissioned by: Koussevitzky Music Foundation (Library of Congress). Written for Gary Karr. *First performed:* Jan. 27, 1968; New York City. Gary Karr, double bass; New York

Philharmonic, Gunther Schuller, conductor.
Score & parts: Associated, 1978. Rental.
Pf. red: Associated, 1978. BU HU NEC

[Concerto, Horn, No. 1]
S3.22 Concerto No. 1. (1943-44) 18'
For: horn and orchestra(3(pic)-3(Ehn)-3(bcl)-3(cbsn); 4-3-3-1; timp, perc; hp, cel; str). 2 movements. *First performed:* Apr. 7, 1944. Gunther Schuller, horn; Cincinnati Symphony Orchestra, Eugene Goossens, conductor.
Music: Margun. Rental.

[Concerto, Horn, No. 2]
S3.23 Concerto No. 2. (1977) 20'
For: horn and orchestra(3(pic)-3(Ehn)-3(bcl)-3(cbsn); 4-4-4-1; timp, perc; hp, cel, pf; str).
Commissioned by: Mario di Bonaventura.
First performed: Feb. 12, 1977; Budapest, Hungary. Ferenc Tarjanyi, horn; Budapest Philharmonic Orchestra, Mario di Bonaventura, conductor.
Score & parts: Associated, 1977. Rental.

[Concerto, Orchestra, No. 1]
S3.24 Concerto (Gala Music). (1966) 25'
For: orchestra(3(pic)-3(Ehn)-3(bcl)-3(cbsn); 4-4-3-1; timp, perc; hp(2), cel, pf, org; str). *Commissioned by:* Chicago Symphony Orchestra. *Dedicated to:* Jean Martinon and the Chicago Symphony Orchestra in celebration of its 75th anniversary. *First performed:* Jan. 20, 1966; Chicago, Ill. Chicago Symphony Orchestra, Gunther Schuller, conductor.
Score & parts: Associated, 1966. Rental.

[Concerto, Orchestra, No. 2]
S3.25 Concerto No. 2. (1976) 22'
For: orchestra(4-4(oboe d'amore, Ehn)-5(Ebcl, asax, bcl, cbcl)-4(cbsn2); 4-4-4-1; timp, perc(6); hp, cel, pf; str). 3 movements. *Commissioned by:* National Symphony Bicentennial Commission. *First performed:* Oct. 12, 1976; Washington, D.C. National Symphony Orchestra, Antal Dorati,

conductor.
Score: Associated, 1976.
Parts: Associated, 1976. Rental.

[Concerto, Piano]
S3.26 Concerto. (1962) 20'
For: piano and
orchestra(3(pic)-3(Ehn)-3(bcl)-3(cbsn);
4-3-3-1; timp, perc(3); hp; str). 3
movements. *Commissioned by:* Mr. and
Mrs. Harris K. Weston for Jeanne
Rosenblum Kirstein. *First performed:*
Oct. 26, 1962. Jeanne Kirstein, piano;
Cincinnati Symphony Orchestra, Max
Rudolf, conductor.
Score & parts: Schott, 1968. Rental.
Pf. red: Schott/Associated, 1968. MIT
NEC

[Concerto, Trumpet and Chamber
Orchestra]
S3.27 Concerto. (1979)
4 movements. *Commissioned by:* Gerard
Schwarz and supported by a Ford
Foundation Grant. *First performed:* Aug.
25, 1979; Jefferson, N.H. Gerard
Schwarz, trumpet; White Mountains
Festival Orchestra, Gunther Schuller,
conductor.
Score & parts: Associated.

[Concerto, Violin]
S3.28 Concerto. (1975-76) 22'
For: violin and orchestra(4(pic4)-2(&Ehn)
-4(asax,bcl2)-2(&cbsn); 4-4-4-1; timp,
perc; hp, cel, pf; str). 3 movements.
Commissioned by: Eastman School of
Music for Zvi Zeitlin. *First performed:*
Aug. 25, 1976; Zvi Zeitlin, violin;
Lucerne Festival Orchestra, Gunther
Schuller, conductor.
Score & parts: Associated, 1976. Rental.
Pf. red: Associated.

[Concerto, Violoncello]
S3.29 Concerto. (1945; rev. in progess)
18'
For: violoncello and orchestra(3-3-3-3;
4-3-3-1; perc; hp, cel; str).
Score: Margun.

S3.30 Consequents. (1969) 17'
For:

orchestra(2(pic2,afl)-2(Ehn)-2(Ebcl)-2(cbsn);
4-4-4-1; perc; str). 4 movements.
Commissioned by: New Haven
Symphony Orchestra. *First performed:*
Dec. 16, 1969; New Haven, Conn. New
Haven Symphony Orchestra, Gunther
Schuller, conductor.
Score & parts: Associated, 1970. Rental.

S3.31 Contours. (1955-58) 23'
For: orchestra(1-1-2(bcl)-1; 1-1-1-0;
perc(2); hp; str(7-6-5-4-2)). *Movements:*
Entrata; Capriccio; Partita; Lamento;
Chiusa. *First performed:* Dec. 31, 1959;
Cincinnati, Ohio. Cincinnati Symphony
Orchestra, Gunther Schuller, conductor.
Study score: Schott, 1960. BPL BU HU
T
Disc: Odyssey Y 34141, 1976.
Contemporary Chamber Ensemble,
Arthur Weisberg, conductor. BCM BU
HU HUm MIT NEC

S3.32 Contrasts. (1961) 15'
For: woodwind quintet and
orchestra(3(pic, afl)-3-3(Ebcl,
bcl)-3(cbsn); 3-3-3-1; timp, perc(7); hp,
pf; str). 2 movements. Written for the
Donaueschingen Festival of
Contemporary Music, West Germany.
Dedicated to: Heinrich Strobel. *First
performed:* [Nov. 1961?] Southwest
German Radio Orchestra of
Baden-Baden, Hans Rosbaud, conductor.
Score & parts: Associated, 1961
(orchestra). Rental.
Parts: Associated, 1961 (solo). NEC

S3.33 Conversations. (1959) 10' 30"
For: string quartet and jazz
quartet(vibraphone, piano, double bass,
percussion). Third stream music. *First
performed:* Sept. 25, 1959; New York
City. Modern Jazz Quartet and Beaux
Arts Quartet, Gunther Schuller,
conductor.
Score: MJQ, 1960. BPL HU NEC W
Disc: in *Third Stream Music*, Atlantic
SD 1345, 196-. Modern Jazz Quartet.
BU HU NEC NU W

Criss-Cross. *See* Variants on a Theme
of Thelonius Monk.

S3.34 Curtain Raiser. (1960) 2'
For: flute, clarinet, horn, piano.
Score & parts: Margun, n.d.

S3.35 Deai (Encounters). (1978)
For: voices(7) and
orchestras(3)(1(offstage): Sopranos(2),
Mezzo Soprano, Tenor, Baritones(2),
Bass; 2-2-2(bcl)-2; 2-2-2-0; perc; hp;
str); 2(offstage): (2(pic)-2(Ehn)-2-2);
2-2-1-0; tri; cel; str); 3(onstage):
3(&pic)-3(&Ehn)-2(&bcl)-3(&cbsn); 5-4-3-2;
timp, perc, glock, mar, vibra; hp(2), cel,
pf; str). 3 conductors. *Commissioned by:*
Boston Symphony Orchestra. *First
performed:* Jan. 17, 1978; Tokyo,
Japan. Boston Symphony Orchestra,
Toko Gakuen School of Music
Orchestra, Seiji Ozawa and Gunther
Schuller, conductors.
Scores & parts: Associated, nyp.

S3.36 Densities, No. 1. (1962) 4'
For: clarinet, harp, vibraphone, double
bass. *First performed:* Mar. 14, 1963;
New York City. Eric Dolphy, clarinet,
and others.
Score: MJQ, 1968. HU
Parts: MJQ, 1962.
Disc: in *Dedicated to Dolphy*,
Cambridge CRS 1820, 1967. Bill Smith,
clarinet; Gloria Agostini, harp; Harold
Farberman, vibraphone; Richard Davis,
double bass. NEC

S3.37 Diptych. (1964) 8'
For: horn, trumpets(2), trombone, tuba,
band. 2 movements. *Commissioned by:*
New York Brass Quintet under the
sponsorship of the Cornell University
Music Department. *Dedicated to:* New
York Brass Quintet. *First performed:*
Mar. 22, 1964; Ithaca, N.Y. New York
Brass Quintet; Cornell University Band,
William Campbell, conductor.
Score: Associated, 1971. BU HU MIT
Parts: Associated, 1971. BU

[Diptych; Arr.]
S3.38 Diptych. 8'
For: trumpets(2), horn, trombone, tuba,

orchestra(3(&pic)-2(&Ehn)-
2(&bcl)-3(&cbsn); 4-2-2-1; timp, perc,
glock; hp; str). *First performed:* Mar.
30, 1967; Boston, Mass. Armando
Ghitalla and Roger Voisin, trumpets;
James Staglione, horn; William Gibson,
trombone; Chester Schmitz, tuba;
Boston Symphony Orchestra, Erich
Leinsdorf, conductor.
Score & parts: Associated. Rental.

Django. *See* Variants on a Theme of
John Lewis (Django).

S3.39 Double Quintet. (1961) 12'
For: woodwind quintet, trumpets(2),
horn, trombone, tuba. 3 movements.
Commissioned by and dedicated to:
University of Southern California,
Friends of Music. *First performed:* Jan.
1962; Festival of Contemporary Music.
Gunther Schuller, conductor.
Score & parts: reprod. of ms. NEC
Score & parts: Associated, 1962. Rental.
NEC
Reel: Apr. 3, 1980; Boston University;
in *Omnibus: Music of the 20th Century,
Concert 4.* Theodore Antoniou,
conductor. BU
Cassette: Dec. 7, 1971; New England
Conservatory; in *An Evening of
Contemporary Music.* Tibor Pusztai,
conductor. NEC
Cassette: Apr. 19, 1973; New England
Conservatory. NEC Repertory Wind
Ensemble, Michael Walters, conductor.
NEC
Cassette: May 1, 1975; New England
Conservatory. NEC Repertory Wind
Ensemble, Michael Walters, conductor.
NEC
Cassette: Mar. 23, 1978; New England
Conservatory. NEC Repertory Wind
Ensemble, Michael Walters, conductor.
NEC
Cassette: Feb. 27, 1979; New England
Conservatory; in *The Enchanted Circle.*
Theodore Antoniou, conductor. NEC
Cassette: Mar. 13, 1980; New England
Conservatory. NEC Repertory Wind
Ensemble, Michael Walters, conductor.

S3.40 Dramatic Overture. (1951) 10'
For: orchestra(3(pic)-3(Ehn)-3(bcl)-3(cbsn);
4-3-3-1; timp, perc, glock, vibra; hp(2),
cel/pf; str). 1 movement. *Dedicated to:*
Leon Barzin. *First performed:* Aug.
1954; Darmstadt, West Germany;
Internationale Ferienkurse fuer neue
Musik. Frankfurt Radio Orchestra,
Ernest Bour, conductor.
Score: Associated, 1951.
Score: Associated, 1979. BU HU MIT
NEC
Parts: Associated, 1951. Rental.
Disc: Louisville Orchestra LS 666, 1966.
Louisville Orchestra, Robert Whitney,
conductor. BrU BU HU HUm MIT NEC
W (1966) 14'
Cassette: Dec. 3, 1969; New England
Conservatory. NEC Symphony
Orchestra, Leon Barzin, conductor. NEC

S3.41 Duets for Unaccompanied Horns.
(1962)
Score: Oxford, 1962. Be BU HU T

S3.42 Duets for Unaccompanied Horns,
Nos. 1 and 3.
Disc: in *Horn of Plenty*, Crystal S 371,
1976. Calvin Smith and William Z.
Semberg. MIT

S3.43 Duo Sonata. *See* Sonata,
Clarinets (2) .

[Early Songs]
S3.44 Six Early Songs. 18'
For: Soprano and orchestra(3-3-4-3;
4-2-2-1; perc; hp, cel, pf; str). *Text:*
LiPo; German paraphrases by Klabund.
Contents: Die Kaiserin (The Emperess);
Im Boot (In a Boat); Die ferne Floete
(The Distant Flute); An der Grenze (At
the Border); Der Silberreiher (The Silver
Heron); Der Fischer im Fruehling (The
Fisherman in Spring). *First performed:*
1973; New York City. Eleanor Steber,
soprano; NEC Symphony Orchestra.
Score: Margun, n.d.
Parts: Margun. Rental.
Vocal score: Margun, 1976. HU MIT NEC
Cassette: May 8, 1975; New England
Conservatory (Im Boot). Roosilawati
Hidajat, soprano and Louise Costigan,

piano. NEC
Cassette: May 8, 1975; New England
Conservatory (Die Silberreiher). Isabel
Shattuck, soprano and unidentified
pianist. NEC

Encounters. *See* Deai.

S3.45 Episodes. (1964) 7'
For: clarinet. *Dedicated to:* Bill Smith.
First performed: Sept. 1964; Venice,
Italy; La Biennale di Venezia. William
Smith.
Score: Associated, 1979. BU HU NEC

[Etudes]
S3.46 Five Etudes. (1966) 14'
For: orchestra(3(pic)-3-2-2; 4-3-3-1;
timp, perc(4), glock, vibra; hp, pf; str).
Commissioned by: Greater New Haven
Youth Orchestra. *First performed:* Mar.
19, 1967; New Haven, Conn. Greater
New Haven Youth Orchestra, Gunther
Schuller, conductor.
Score: Associated, 1971. BPL BU HU
NEC
Parts: Associated. Rental.

S3.47 Fanfare. (1962) 1'
For: trumpets(4) and trombones(4). *First
performed:* Nov. 20, 1963; Madison,
Wis. Members of the Madison Civic
Symphony Orchestra, Roland Johnson,
director.
Score & parts: Margun, n.d.

S3.48 Fanfare for St. Louis. (1968) 6'
For: timpani, percussion, wind
ensemble(flutes(3), oboes(3), clarinets(3),
bassoons(3), horns(4), trumpets(4),
trombones(3), tuba). *Commissioned by
and dedicated to:* Eleazar Carvalho and
the St. Louis Symphony Orchestra for
the opening of Powell Symphony Hall.
First performed: Jan. 24, 1968; St.
Louis, Mo. St. Louis Symphony
Orchestra, Eleazar Carvalho, conductor.
Score: Margun.
Parts: Margun. Rental.

S3.49 Fantasia concertante. 9'
For: trombones(3) and orchestra(2-2-3-3;

4-3-0-1; perc; hp; str).
Score: MJQ.

[Fantasy, Harp]
S3.50 Fantasy. (1959) 6'
First performed: Israel. Sonya Kahn.
Score: Associated, 1959. BPL
Score: Associated, 1969. BU HU
Cassette: Feb. 27, 1979; New England
Conservatory; in *The Enchanted Circle.*
Cynthia Price. NEC
Cassette: Apr. 29, 1980; New England
Conservatory; in *The Enchanted Circle.*
Cynthia Price. NEC

S3.51 Fantasy Quartet. (1958) 6' 20"
For: violoncellos(4). *First performed:*
Apr. 8, 1960; Carnegie Recital Hall,
New York City. Laszlo Varga, Jules
Eskin, Michael Rudiakov, Sterling
Hunkins.
Score: MJQ, 1968. HU
Parts: MJQ.
Disc: Composers Recordings CRI 144,
1961. Laszlo Varga, Jules Eskin,
Michael Rudiakov, Sterling Hunkins. BPL
BrU BU HU MIT NEC T W

[Fantasy, Violoncello]
S3.52 Fantasy [Op. 19] (1951) 9'
Dedicated to: Laszlo Varga. *First
performed:* 1952; WNYC-FM, New York
City. Laszlo Varga.
Score: Rongwen, 1960. BU HU NEC
Disc: Gasparo GS 101, 1975. Roy
Christensen. MIT NEC W

S3.53 The Fisherman and His Wife.
(1970) 60'
For: voices, chorus, orchestra(1(pic,
afl)-1(Ehn)-1(Ebcl, bcl, asax,
barsax)-1(cbsn); 2-1-1-1; perc(2); elec gt,
hp, cel/pf, elec org; str). Opera for
children in 13 scenes. *Libretto:* John
Hoyer Updike, after the fairy tale by
Wilhelm Grimm and Jacob Grimm.
Commissioned by: Junior League of
Boston. *First performed:* May 1970;
Boston. Boston Opera Company.
Score: Associated.
Parts: Associated.
Vocal score: Associated, 1970. NEC

S3.54 Five Pieces for Five Horns.
(1952) 11' 30"
First performed: 1953; Macmillan
Theater, Columbia University;
International Society for Contemporary
Music.
Score & parts: Bruzzichelli, 1965. BPL
BrU BU MIT NEC
Study score: Bruzzichelli, 1965. HU
Reel: Nov. 13, 1980; Boston University;
in *Omnibus: Music of the 20th Century,
Concert I.* Jean Rife, John Farr,
Timothy Kerwin, Michael Schwartzberg,
Sylvia Alimena. BU

S3.55 The Five Senses. (1967) 60'
For: jazz ensemble(flute,
clarinet/saxophone(alto)
/saxophone(baritone), horn, trumpet,
trombone, tuba, drums, guitar, double
bass). Ballet for television.
Score: ms.

Gala Music. *See* Concerto, Orchestra,
No. 1.

Die Heimsuchung. *See* The Visitation.

[Hommages]
S3.56 Trois Hommages. (1942-46) 9'
For: horn or horns(2) and piano.
Movements: Intermezzo (Hommage a
Frederick Delius); Pavane (Hommage a
Maurice Ravel); Chanson (Hommage a
Darius Milhaud).
Score & parts: Margun, 1979. HU NEC

Hudson Valley Reminiscences. *See*
Soundscapes.

[Invenzioni]
S3.57 Tre Invenzioni. (1972) 20'
For: instrumental ensemble(piccolo,
English horn, clarinet(Eb), clarinet (in
A), clarinet(bass), saxophone(alto),
bassoon, contrabassoon, trumpet,
trombone, baritone, tuba, percussion,
harpsichord, piano). *Movements:*
Capriccio; Chorale; Toccata.
Commissioned by: Fromm Foundation.
First performed: Aug. 8, 1972;
Berkshire Music Center, Tanglewood;

Contemporary Music Festival. Bruno
Maderna, conductor.
Score & parts: Associated, 1972.
Disc: Odyssey Y 34141, 1976.
Contemporary Chamber Ensemble,
Arthur Weisberg, conductor. BCM BU
HU HUm MIT NEC

S3.58 Journey into Jazz. (1962) 15′
For: narrator, jazz
quintet(saxophone(alto),
saxophone(tenor), trumpet, double bass,
drums), chamber orchestra(1-1-1-1;
1-1-0-0; perc; hp; str). *Text:* Nat
Hentoff. *Commissioned by:* Broadcast
Music, Inc. *Dedication:* For my children,
Edwin and George. *First performed:*
May 1962; Washington, D.C.; First
National Jazz Festival. Ray Reinhardt,
narrator; National Symphony Orchestra,
Gunther Schuller, conductor.
Score: Associated, 1967. BU HU NEC
Parts: Associated.
Disc: in *Jazz Journey*, Columbia CL
2247/CS 9047, 1964. BrU

S3.59 Journey to the Stars. (1962) 15′
For: orchestra(1(pic)-0-2(bcl)-1; 2-2-2-2;
timp, perc(2); hp, cel/pf; str). Film
music. *Movements:* First Three Minutes′
Contemplation of Spaceflight; Moon
Sequence; Sun Sequence; Mars
Sequence; Saturn Sequence; Beyond the
Milky Way; Our Own Galaxy into
Intergalactic Space. *Commissioned by:*
Cinerama, Boeing Company, United
States Science Exhibit. Written for
Seattle World Fair, 1962, to accompany
Spacearium film. *First performed:* Dec.
1, 1962 (concert version). Toledo
Orchestra, Gunther Schuller, conductor.
Score & parts: Associated, 1962. Rental.

S3.60 Eine Kleine Posaunemusik. (1980)
For: trombone and orchestra. 5
movements. *Commissioned by:* John
Swallow. *First performed:* July, 1980;
Norfolk, Conn.; Yale Summer Music
Festival. John Swallow, trombone;
Arthur Weisberg, conductor.
Score & parts: Associated, nyp.
Cassette: May 7, 1981; New England
Conservatory. John Swallow, trombone;

NEC Wind Ensemble, Frank L. Battisti,
conductor. NEC

S3.61 Lifelines. (1960) 7′
For: flute, guitar, percussion.
Parts: Associated, 1960.

S3.62 Lines and Contrasts. (1960) 10′
For: horns(16). 2 movements. Written
for the Horn Club of Los Angeles.
First performed: Oct. 23, 1960; Los
Angeles, Calif. Los Angeles Horn
Ensemble.
Score & parts: Margun.
Disc: in *New Music for Horns*, Angel S
36036, 1970. Horn Club of Los
Angeles, Gunther Schuller, conductor.
HU MIT NEC

S3.63 Little Brass Music. (1963) 5′
For: trumpet, horn, trombone, tuba.
Score & parts: Mentor, 1967. BCM HU
NEC
Reel: Jan. 19, 1976; Boston University.
Members of the Empire Brass Quintet.
BU
Cassette: Mar. 20, 1977; New England
Conservatory. Members of the Empire
Brass Quintet. NEC

S3.64 Little Fantasy. (1957) 4′
For: orchestra(1-1-1-1; 2-1-1-0; timp,
perc; str(minimum 3-2-2-1-1)). Children′s
music. *First performed:* Apr. 7, 1957;
Englewood N.J. Salomon Concert
Orchestra, Lester Salomon, conductor.
Score & parts: Margun. Rental.

S3.65 Meditation. (1963) 6′
For: band. *Commissioned by:* Edward
Benjamin Restful Music Fund. Winner
of College Band Directors National
Association, North Central Division,
Original Composition Award (1963).
First performed: Mar. 7, 1963;
Greensboro, N.C. Grimsley High School
Symphony Band.
Score & parts: Associated, 1963. NEC
Score: Associated, 1955. NEC
Score: Associated, 1965. HU
Cassette: Mar. 11, 1972; New England
Conservatory. Massachusetts Youth

Wind Ensemble, Frank L. Battisti, conductor. NEC

S3.66 Meditations. (1960) 4'
For: Soprano and piano. *Text:* Gertrude Stein. *Dedication:* To Freddy and Florence. *First performed:* Dec. 19, 1963; New York City. Antonia Lavanne, soprano and Howard F. Rovics, piano.
Score: E.B. Marks, 1964.
Score: in *New Vistas in Song*, E.B. Marks, 1967. BPL NEC W

[Moods]
S3.67 Five Moods. (1973) 8'
For: tubas(4). *Commissioned by:* Harvey Phillips. *Dedication:* In memory of William Bell. *First performed:* May 25, 1973; Indiana University; in First International Tuba Workshop.
Score: Associated, 1976. BU HU NEC
Parts: Associated, 1976. BU NEC
Disc: Crystal S 221, 1976. New York Tuba Quartet. NEC

[Movements, Flute and String Orchestra]
S3.68 Movements. (1962) 14'
Movements: Progression; Sequences; Retrogression. *Commissioned by:* City of Dortmund, West Germany and the Dortmund Chamber Orchestra. *First performed:* May 29, 1962; Dortmund, West Germany. Hans Juergen Moehring, flute; Dortmund Chamber Orchestra, Hans Herbert Joeris, conductor.
Score & parts: Associated. Rental.
Pf. red: Associated, 1961.

S3.69 Movements for Flute and String Trio. *See* Adagio.

S3.70 Museum Piece. (1970) 19'
For: early music ensemble(recorders(sopranino)(2), recorders(soprano) (2), recorders(alto)(2), flute(Renaissance bass), shawms(soprano)(2), shawms (alto)(2), shawm(bass), krumhorns(alto)(3), krumhorn(tenor), racket(bass), cornetti(2), viole da gamba(3), lutes(2), harpsichord, regal, triangle, drum) and orchestra(2(pic, afl)-2(Ehn)-2(&bcl)-2; 3-2-2-1; timp, perc; cel/pf; str).
Movements: Rustic Shimmerings; A Play of Sonorities (Duets and Trios); Serenades; Canzon da sonar. Written in celebration of the centennial of the Museum of Fine Arts, Boston. *First performed:* Dec. 11, 1970; Symphony Hall, Boston. NEC Collegium Musicum; Boston Symphony Orchestra, William Steinberg, conductor.
Score: Associated. Rental.
Parts: Associated. Rental. NEC

S3.71 Music for a Celebration. (1980) 6'
For: chorus, audience, orchestra.
Commissioned by: Women's Symphony Orchestra League. *First performed:* Sept. 26, 1980; Springfield, Mass. Springfield Symphony Orchestra, Robert Gutter, conductor.
Score & parts: Associated.

S3.72 Music for Brass Quintet. (1961) 12'
For: horn, trumpets(2), trombone, tuba. 3 movements. *Commissioned by:* Elizabeth Sprague Coolidge Foundation (Library of Congress). *First performed:* Jan. 13, 1961; Washington D.C. New York Brass Quintet.
Score & parts: Associated, 1962. BCM Be BU HU HUm MIT NEC
Disc: Composers Recordings CRI 144, 1961. New York Brass Quintet. BrU BU HU MIT NEC T W
Cassette: Nov. 29, 1976; New England Conservatory. NEC Brass Quintet. NEC
Cassette: Jan. 21, 1980; New England Conservatory; in *The Enchanted Circle*. New York Brass Quintet. NEC
Cassette: Mar. 12, 1980; New England Conservatory. NEC Scholarship Brass Quintet. NEC

Music for Carillon. *See* Composition for Carillon.

Music for Violin, Piano and Percussion. *See* Symbiosis.

S3.73 Music from Yesterday in Fact. (1963) 12'
For: jazz quintet(trumpet, saxophone(alto), drums, piano, double bass), flute, clarinet(bass), horn, violin, violoncello.
Score & parts: Margun.

Music to Journey to the Stars. *See* Journey to the Stars.

S3.74 Night Music. (1962) 4' 54"
For: clarinet(bass), guitar, double basses(2), drums. Jazz quintet.
Score: MJQ, 1963. HU
Parts: MJQ, 1962.
Disc: in *Dedicated to Dolphy,* Cambridge CRS 1820, 1967. William Smith, bass clarinet; Jim Hall, guitar; Richard Davis and George Duvivier, double basses; Mel Lewis, drums. NEC

[Nocturnes]
S3.75 Three Nocturnes. (1973) 16'
For: orchestra(3(pic)-3(Ehn)-3(bcl)-3(cbsn); 4-3-3-1; timp, perc(5); hp, cel, pf; str).
Commissioned by: Sinfonia Foundation (Phi Mu Alpha) for its 75th anniversary.
First performed: July 15, 1973; National Music Camp, Interlochen, Mich. World Youth Orchestra, Gunther Schuller, conductor.
Score & parts: Associated, 1973. Rental.

S3.76 O Lamb of God. (1941) 3'
For: chorus(SSAATTBB) and organ(optional). Anthem.
Vocal score: Margun, 1979. NEC

S3.77 O Spirit of the Living God. (1942) 2' 30"
For: chorus(SSAATTBB) and organ(optional). Anthem.
Vocal score: Margun, 1979. NEC

S3.78 Octet. (1979)
For: clarinet, bassoon, horn, string quartet, double bass. 4 movements.
Commissioned by: Chamber Music Society of Lincoln Center. *First performed:* Nov. 2, 1979; New York City. Chamber Music Society of

Lincoln Center.
Score & parts: Associated.

Passacaglia. *See* Concertino. Passacaglia; Arr.

S3.79 Perpetuum mobile. (1948) 4'
For: horns(4)(muted) and bassoon or tuba.
Score & parts: Margun, 1948.

S3.80 Poems of Time and Eternity. (1972) 13'
For: chorus(SATB), flute/piccolo, clarinet, bassoon, horn, violin, viola, violoncello, piano. *Text:* Emily Dickinson. Written for tour of NEC Chorus. *First performed:* Aug. 1972; Avignon, France. NEC Chorus, Lorna Cooke deVaron, conductor.
Score & parts: Margun.
Disc: Crest Records, 1980 (last movement omitted). Hartt Chamber Singers; Hartt Contemporary Players.
Cassette: May 2, 1973; New England Conservatory. NEC Chorus, Lorna Cooke deVaron, conductor. NEC

S3.81 The Power within Us. (1971) 25'
For: Baritone, narrator, chorus, orchestra(3-2(Ehn)-2(bcl)-3(cbsn); 4-3-3-1; timp, perc; hp, pf, org; str). Oratorio.
Text: English words translated from *La relacion de Alvar Nunez Cabeza de Vaca.*
First performed: Mar. 11, 1972; Atlanta, Ga. Larry Bogue, baritone; John D. Burke, narrator; Georgia Senior High School All-State Chorus; Georgia Senior High School All-State Orchestra, Gunther Schuller, conductor.
Score: Associated, 1978. BU HU NEC
Parts: Associated, 1978. Rental. *Vocal score.*

Progression in Tempo. *See* Concertino. Progression in Tempo.

[Quartet, Double Basses]
S3.82 Quartet. (1947, 1959) 19'
3 movements. *First performed:* 1960; Carnegie Recital Hall, New York City. Alvin Brehm, Bob Gladstone, Orin O'Brien, Fred Zimmerman.

Study score: Bruzzichelli, 1965. HU NEC
Parts: Bruzzichelli, 1965. BU NEC
Disc: Turnabout TVS 34412, 1971.
James Carroll, Arnold Craver, Sam
Hollingworth, Clifford Spohr. BrU BU
HU MIT NEC
Cassette: Apr. 29, 1974; New England
Conservatory. Edwin Barker, Jack
Cousin, Alan Nagel, Barbara Schultz.
NEC
Cassette: May 6, 1974; New England
Conservatory. Edwin Barker, Jack
Cousin, Alan Nagel, Barbara Schultz.
NEC

[Quartet, Strings, No.1]
S3.83 String Quartet No.1. (1957) 18'
3 movements. *Commissioned by:* Fromm
Foundation. *First performed:* Mar. 1957;
University of Illinois,
Urbana-Champaign; in Festival of
Contemporary Arts. Walden Quartet.
Study score: Universal, 1958. Be BPL
HU MIT NEC
Parts: Universal.
Disc: University of Illinois CR 5, 1957.
Walden Quartet. BrU HU
Disc: Golden Crest NEC 115, 1977.
Composers String Quartet. MIT NEC W

[Quartet, Strings, No. 2]
S3.84 String Quartet No. 2. (1965) 14'
3 movements. *Commissioned by:* Iowa
University String Quartet.
Score: Associated.
Parts: Associated, 1965.
Disc: New World NW 212, 1978.
Emerson String Quartet. BCM HU MIT
NEC T W

[Quintet, Woodwinds]
S3.85 Woodwind Quintet. (1958) 15'
3 movements. *Commissioned by and
dedicated to:* New York Woodwind
Quintet. *First performed:* Cologne,
West Germany; West German Radio.
New York Woodwind Quintet.
Score: Associated/Schott, 1968. BPL BU
HUm MIT T W
Parts: reprod. of ms. NEC
Parts: Associated/Schott, 1968. MIT
NEC W

Disc: Concert Disc M1229/CS 229,
1963. New York Woodwind Quintet. BU
HU HUm NEC W
Disc: in *The Avant Garde Woodwind
Quintet in the U.S.A.*, Vox SVBX 5307,
1977. Dorian Quintet. BU MIT NEC W
Cassette: Dec. 15, 1975; New England
Conservatory. NEC Scholarship
Woodwind Quintet. NEC

[Recitative and Rondo, Violin and
Orchestra]
S3.86 Recitative and Rondo. (1953) 11'
For: violin and
orchestra(2-3(Ehn)-3(bcl)-3(cbsn); 4-3-3-1;
perc; hp, pf; str). 2 movements. *First
performed:* July 16, 1967; Ravinia
Festival. Victor Aitay, violin; Chicago
Symphony Orchestra, Seiji Ozawa,
conductor.
Score & parts: Associated. Rental.

[Recitative and Rondo; Violin and
Piano]
S3.87 Recitative and Rondo, Op. 21.
(1953) 11'
First performed: Oct. 23, 1953; New
York City. Gabriel Banat, violin and
Artur Balsam, piano.
Score & part: Associated.

[Renaissance Lyrics]
S3.88 Six Renaissance Lyrics. (1962) 15'
For: Tenor, flute, oboe, violin, viola,
violoncello, double bass, piano.
Contents: Sonnet 87 (William
Shakespeare); Noche oscura (Juan de la
Cruz); Unter den Linden (Walther von
der Vogelweide); Sonnet 126 (Petrarch);
Continuation des amours (Pierre de
Ronsard); O notte, O dolce tempo
(Michelangelo Buonarroti). *First
performed:* Aug. 1, 1962; Berkshire
Music Center, Tanglewood. Charles
Bressler, tenor; New York Chamber
Soloists, Melvin Kaplan, conductor.
Score: Associated, 1979. BU HU
Parts: Associated, 1979. BU
Cassette: Feb. 27, 1979; New England
Conservatory; in *The Enchanted Circle*.
Kim Scown, tenor; Theodore Antoniou,
conductor. NEC

S3.89 Sacred Cantata. (1966) 20'
For: chorus(SATB) and chamber
orchestra(1-1-0-1; 1-1-1-0; perc(2); org;
str(1-0-0-1-1)). *Text:* Bible, O.T., Psalm
98. *Commissioned by:* American Guild
of Organists. *First performed:* June
1966; Atlanta, Ga. American Guild of
Organists Annual Convention. Schola
Cantorum of New York and the Atlanta
Symphony, Hugh Ross, conductor.
Score & parts: Associated. Rental.
Score: reprod. of ms. NEC
Vocal score: Associated, nyp.

S3.90 Schreie der Raben. (1946) 2'
For: Soprano and piano.
Score: Margun.

[Shakespearean Songs]
S3.91 Five Shakespearean Songs. (1964)
15'
For: Baritone and
orchestra(2(&pic)-2(&Ehn)
-2(&bcl)-2(&cbsn); 4-3-3-1; timp, perc;
hp, pf; str). *Text:* William Shakespeare.
Commissioned by: Canadian
Broadcasting Corporation. *First
performed:* Nov. 22, 1964. Larry Bogue,
baritone; CBC Symphony Orchestra,
Gunther Schuller, conductor.
Score & parts: Associated, 1964. Rental.

S3.92 Shapes and Designs. (1969) 14'
For: orchestra(3(pic)-3(Ehn)-3(bcl)-3(cbsn);
4-3-3-1; perc; hp, cel/pf; str).
Movements: Intersecting Triangles;
Links; Arcs; Wedges. *Dedicated to:*
Arthur Winograd and the Symphony
Society of Greater Hartford. *First
performed:* Apr. 26, 1969; Hartford,
Conn. Hartford Symphony Orchestra,
Gunther Schuller, conductor.
Score & parts: Associated, 1969. Rental.

[Sonata, Clarinet, Horn, Piano]
S3.93 Sonata. (1941) 13'
Score & parts: Margun.

[Sonata, Clarinets(2)]
S3.94 Duo Sonata. (1948-49) 12'
For: clarinet and clarinet(bass). 3
movements. *First performed:* Nov.
1954; Macmillan Theater, Columbia

University; in Composers Forum. Jack
Kreiselman, clarinet and Sidney Keil,
bass clarinet.
Score: Associated, 1976. BU HU NEC
Reel: Feb. 24, 1980; Boston University;
Alea III Concert. Julie Vaverka, clarinet
and Diane Heffner, bass clarinet. BU
Cassette: Feb. 27, 1979; New England
Conservatory; in *The Enchanted Circle*.
Robert Annis, clarinet and William
Wrzesien, bass clarinet. NEC

[Sonata, Oboe and Piano]
S3.95 Sonata. (1948-51) 22'
Dedicated to: Josef Marx. *First
performed:* Feb. 1952; New York City.
Josef Marx, oboe and Russell Sherman,
piano.
Score & part: McGinnis & Marx, 1960.
HU HUm MIT NEC
Disc: Desto DC 7116, 1971. Ronald
Ariah Roseman, oboe and Gilbert
Kalish, piano. BU HU MIT NEC
Disc: Composers Recordings, nyp.

S3.96 Sonata serenata. (1978)
For: clarinet, violin, violoncello, piano.
Movements: Impromptu; Elegia (In
memoriam Joe Venuti); Romanza; Rondo
giojoso. *Commissioned by:* Ambassador
and Mrs. George J. Feldman for the
Aeolian Chamber Players. *First
performed:* Sept. 28, 1978; New York
City. Aeolian Chamber Players.
Score & parts: Associated.

[Soundscapes]
S3.97 Four Soundscapes (Hudson Valley
Reminiscences). (1974) 15'
For: orchestra(3(afl,pic2,
&pic(offstage))-2(&Ehn)-3(bcl)-3(cbsn);
4-3-3-1; timp, perc, glock, mar, vibra;
hp, cel/pf, pf(offstage); str). *Movements:*
A Day on the River (Hommage to
Ives); Nocturnal Diversions; Peace and
Plenty (after Inness); Scherzo fantasque
(after Washington Irving). *Commissioned
by:* Hudson Valley Philharmonic
Orchestra. *Dedication:* To the memory
of Pierre Monteux. *First performed:*
Mar. 2, 1975; Poughkeepsie, N.Y.
Hudson Valley Philharmonic Orchestra,
Gunther Schuller, conductor.

Score & parts: Associated, 1974. Rental.
Score: Associated, 1978. BU HU NEC

S3.98 Spectra. (1958) 22'-25'
For: orchestra(4(pic, afl)-4(Ehn2)-4(Ebcl, bcl)-4(cbsn); 4-3-3-1; perc(4); hp; soli str(7-5-4-3-2), tutti str(2-2-8-9-7)).
Commissioned by: Dimitri Mitropoulos and the New York Philharmonic.
Dedicated to: Dimitri Mitropoulos. *First performed:* Jan. 1960; New York City. New York Philharmonic, Dimitri Mitropoulos, conductor.
Score: Associated/Schott, 1964. BrU BU HU NEC
Parts: Associated/Schott, 1964. Rental.

S3.99 Studies, Horn.
Score: Oxford, 1962. BPL HU

[Studies on Themes of Paul Klee]
S3.100 Seven Studies on Themes of Paul Klee. (1959) 20'
For:
orchestra(3(pic2)-3(Ehn)-3(bcl)-3(cbsn); 4-3-3-1; timp, perc(4), glock, xylo; hp, pf; str). *Movements:* Antike Harmonien (Antique Harmonies); Abstraktes Trio (Abstract Trio); Kleiner blauer Teufel (Little Blue Devil); Die Zwitschermaschine (The Twittering Machine); Arabische Stadt (Arab Village); Ein unheimlicher Moment (An Eerie Moment); Pastorale. Sponsored by a Ford Foundation Grant and written for the Minneapolis Symphony.
Dedicated to: Antal Dorati. *First performed:* Nov. 27, 1959; Minneapolis, Minn. Minneapolis Symphony, Antal Dorati, conductor.
Score & parts: Universal. Rental.
Score: Universal, 1962. HU NEC W
Study score: Universal, 1962. Be BrU BU HU MIT NEC
Disc: Mercury MG 50282/SR 90282, 1961. Minneapolis Symphony , Antal Dorati, conductor. HU HUm
Disc: RCA Victor LM/LSC 2879, 1966. Boston Symphony Orchestra, Erich Leinsdorf, conductor. BrU BU HU MIT NEC NU W
Disc: International Contemporary Music

Exchange ICME 1, 1974. Reissue of excerpts from RCA Victor LSC 2879, 1966. BCM
Disc: Mercury Golden Imports SRI 75116, 1980. Minneapolis Symphony, Antal Dorati, conductor. MIT

S3.101 Study in Textures. (1967) 7'
For: band. *Commissioned by:* Kappa Kappa Psi and Tau Beta Sigma. *First performed:* Aug. 1967; Fort Worth, Tex.; Kappa Kappa Psi National Convention. National Intercollegiate Symphonic Band, Gunther Schuller, conductor.
Score: Associated, 1971. BU HU MIT
Parts: Associated, 1971.

S3.102 A Study in Texture (Orchestra).
See American Triptych.

S3.103 Suite. (1945) 7'
For: chamber orchestra(2-2-2-2; 2-1-1-0; str).
Score & parts: Margun. Rental.

S3.104 Suite for Woodwind Quintet. (1945) 6'
Movements: Prelude; Blues; Toccata.
Score & parts: McGinnis & Marx, 1958. BCM HU NEC
Disc: Orion ORS 79345, 1979. Pacific Arts Woodwind Quintet. MIT
Cassette: Dec. 12, 1975; New England Conservatory. NEC Chamber Wind Ensemble. NEC
Cassette: Feb. 2, 1977; New England Conservatory. NEC Scholarship Woodwind Quintet. NEC

S3.105 Symbiosis: Music for Violin, Piano and Percussion. (1957) 18'
For: dancer(optional), violin, piano, percussion. 4 movements.
Commissioned by: Joseph Malfitano.
First performed: Oct. 6, 1957; New York City. Maria Maslova, dancer; Joseph Malfitano, violin; Russell Sherman, piano; Walter Rosenberger, percussion; Gunther Schuller, conductor.
Score & part: reprod. of mss. NEC
Score & part: Associated, 1957. NEC
Score & part: Associated, 1981.

S3.106 Symphonic Study. (1947-48) 9'
For: orchestra(6(pic2, afl)-5-3(bcl)-2;
6-4-4-1; timp, perc; hp, cel; str) or
(3-3-3-3; 4-3-3-1; timp, perc; hp, cel;
str). *First performed:* May 1949;
Cincinnati, Ohio. University of
Cincinnati College-Conservatory
Orchestra, Roland Johnson, conductor.
Score & parts: Associated. Rental.

S3.107 Symphonic Tribute to Duke
Ellington. (1955) 40'
For: jazz duo(drums and double bass)
and orchestra(3(pic)-2-2(bcl)-3(cbsn);
4-3-3-1; timp, perc; hp, pf; str).
Commissioned by: Thor Johnson. *First
performed:* Aug. 19, 1976; Berkshire
Music Center, Tanglewood. Gunther
Schuller, conductor.
Score & parts: Margun.

S3.108 Symphony. (1965) 22'
For:
orchestra(3(pic2)-2(&Ehn)-2(&bcl)-3(cbsn);
4-4-3-1; timp, perc; hp, pf; str). 4
movements. *Commissioned by:* Dallas
Public Library, Fine Arts Department
for the Dallas Symphony Orchestra.
First performed: Feb. 19, 1965; Dallas,
Tex. Dallas Symphony Orchestra,
Donald Johanos, conductor.
Score: Associated, 1971. MIT
Parts: Associated. NEC
Disc: Turnabout TVS 34412, 1971.
Dallas Symphony Orchestra, Donald
Johanos, conductor. BrU BU HU MIT
NEC

S3.109 Symphony for Brass and
Percussion, Op. 16. (1949-50) 18'
For: timpani, percussion, brass
ensemble(trumpets(4), horns(6),
trombones(3), baritones(2), tuba or
baritone, tubas(2)). 4 movements. Later
version titled The Traitor. *First
performed:* 1950; New York City;
International Society for Contemporary
Music concert. Leon Barzin, conductor.
Score: Malcolm, 1959. BCM Be BPL HU
T
Parts: Malcolm. BCM
Disc: in *Music for Brass*, Columbia CL
941, 1957. Jazz and Classical Music

Society Brass Ensemble, Dimitri
Mitropoulos, conductor. NEC
Disc: in *Classics for Brass*, Argo ZRG
731, 1973. Philip Jones Brass
Ensemble, Elgar Howarth, conductor. BU
NEC
Reel: May 7, 1975; Boston
Conservatory. Boston Conservatory
Brass Ensemble, Chester Roberts,
conductor. BCM
Cassette: Mar. 15, 1972; New England
Conservatory. NEC Symphony
Orchestra, Tibor Pusztai, conductor.
NEC
Cassette: Mar. 19, 1974; New England
Conservatory. NEC Repertory Wind
Ensemble, Michael Walters, conductor.
NEC
Cassette: Apr. 26, 1977; New England
Conservatory. NEC Repertory Wind
Ensemble, Michael Walters, conductor.
NEC
Cassette: Dec. 8, 1977; New England
Conservatory. NEC Wind Ensemble,
Frank L. Battisti, conductor. NEC
Cassette: Mar. 30, 1978; New England
Conservatory. NEC Wind Ensemble,
Frank L. Battisti, conductor. NEC
Cassette: Mar. 13, 1980; New England
Conservatory. NEC Repertory Wind
Ensemble, Michael Walters, conductor.
NEC.

S3.110 Symphony for Organ. (1981) 30'
Commissioned by: House of Hope
Presbyterian Church, St. Paul, Minn.
First performed: Nov. 8, 1981; House
of Hope Presbyterian Church, St. Paul,
Minn. Clyde Holloway.

S3.111 Tear Drop. (1967)
For: instrumental ensemble(flute,
clarinet/saxophone(alto)/saxophone
(baritone), horn, trumpet, trombone,
tuba, guitar, double bass, drums).
Written for television film.
Score & parts: Margun.

S3.112 Threnos. (1963) 17'
For: oboe and
orchestra(3(pic2)-3(Ehn)-3(bcl)-2(&cbsn);
3-4-3-1; timp, perc(4); hp; str).
Dedication: In memoriam Dimitri

Mitropoulos. *First performed:* Nov. 29, 1963; Cologne, West Germany. Lothar Faber, oboe; West German Radio Orchestra, Witold Rowicki, conductor. *Score & parts:* Associated, 1963. Rental.

S3.113 The Traitor. (1954?) Dance music. *Commissioned by:* Connecticut College. Earlier version titled Symphony for Band and Percussion, Op. 16. *First performed:* Aug. 19, 1954; New London, Conn.; American Dance Festival.

S3.114 Transformation. (1957) 6' *For:* jazz ensemble(flute, clarinet/saxophone(tenor), bassoon, horn, trombone, harp, vibraphone, drums, piano, double bass). *Commissioned by:* Brandeis University Festival of Fine Arts. *First performed:* June 6, 1957; Brandeis University.
Score: Margun, 1956.
Parts: Margun.
Disc: in *Outstanding Jazz Compositions of the 20th Century*, Columbia C2L 31. BCM
Disc: in *Modern Jazz Concert: Brandeis Jazz Festival*, Columbia WL 127, 1958. BrU
Reel: Nov. 13, 1980; Boston University; in *Omnibus: Music of the 20th Century, Concert I*. Boston University Collegium in Contemporary Music, Gunther Schuller, conductor. BU
Cassette: in *Modern Jazz Concert: Brandeis Jazz Festival*, Columbia WL 127, [1957?]. NEC
Cassette: May 19, 1976; New England Conservatory. NEC Contemporary Music Ensemble, Gunther Schuller, conductor. NEC

S3.115 Trio. (1948) 11' *For:* oboe, horn, viola. 3 movements. *First performed:* 1948; New York City. Josef Marx, oboe; John Dijanni, viola; Gunther Schuller, horn.
Score & parts: Associated, 1975. BrU BU HU MIT NEC
Disc: in *Music for Oboe*, Composers Recordings CRI SD 423, 1980. James

Ostryniec, oboe; Noah Chaves, violin; David Bakkegard, horn. MIT NEC T W

S3.116 Triplum I. (1967) 17' *For:* orchestra(3(pic)-3(Ehn)-3(bcl)-3(cbsn); 4-3-3-1; timp, perc, mar, xylo; hp, cel, pf, org; str). 3 movements.
Commissioned by: Lincoln Center Fund for Festival '67. *Dedicated to:* New York Philharmonic and Leonard Bernstein. *First performed:* June 28, 1967; New York City. New York Philharmonic, Leonard Bernstein, conductor.
Score & parts: Associated. Rental.
Disc: in *Bernstein Conducts Music of Our Time*, vol. 2, Columbia MS 7052, 1967. New York Philharmonic, Leonard Bernstein, conductor. BrU BU HU NEC W

S3.117 Triplum, No. 2. (1975) 20' *For:* orchestra(3-3(&Ehn)-2(in A)-2(&cbsn); 4-3-3-1; timp, perc(3); hp, cel, pf; str). 3 movements.
Commissioned by: Baltimore Symphony Orchestra. *First performed:* Feb. 26, 1978; Baltimore, Md. Baltimore Symphony Orchestra, Sergiu Comissiona, conductor.
Score & parts: Associated, 1975. Rental.

S3.118 Triptych. (1976) 22' *For:* organ. *Commissioned by:* American Guild of Organists. *First performed:* June 24, 1976. Old West Church, Boston. Yuko Hayashi.
Score: Associated, 1981.

S3.119 Twelve by Eleven. (1955) 8' *For:* flute, clarinet/saxophone(tenor), bassoon, horn, trombone, piano, vibraphone, drums, double bass. Jazz nonet. *First performed:* Nov. 19, 1955; Town Hall, New York City. Modern Jazz Quartet and unidentified chamber ensemble; Gunther Schuller, conductor.
Score & parts: MJQ, 1955.
Score: MJQ, 1966. HU

S3.120 Variants. (1960) 18" *For:* jazz quartet(vibraphone, piano,

double bass, drums) and orchestra (2-1-3(bcl)-3(cbsn); 4-3-3-1; timp, perc(2); hp; str). Ballet. *Choreography:* George Balanchine. *Commissioned by:* New York City Ballet. *First performed:* Jan. 4, 1961. New York City Ballet; Modern Jazz Quartet; New York City Ballet Orchestra, Gunther Schuller, conductor.
Score: MJQ, 1964, 1972. HU MIT NEC
Parts: MJQ. Rental.

S3.121 Variants on a Theme of John Lewis (Django). (1960) 10'
For: jazz septet(flute, flute/saxophone(alto), vibraphone, guitar, piano, double basses(2), drums) and string quartet. *First performed:* May 16, 1960; New York City. Robert Di Domenica, flute; Eric Dolphy, flute/saxophone; Eddie Costa, vibraphone; Bill Evans, piano; Barry Galbraith, guitar; Contemporary String Quartet.
Score: MJQ, 1966. BPL BU HU NEC
Disc: in *Jazz Abstractions*, Atlantic SD 1365, 1961. Robert Di Domenica, flute; Eric Dolphy, saxophone; Jim Hall, guitar; Eddie Costa, vibraphone; Bill Evans, piano; Scott Lafaro, and George Duvivier, double basses; Sticks Evans, drums; Contemporary String Quartet.

S3.122 Variants on a Theme of Thelonious Monk (Criss-Cross). (1960) 15'
For: flute, saxophone(alto), saxophone(alto)/flute/clarinet(bass), vibraphone, guitar, piano, double basses(2). Jazz octet; third stream music. *First performed:* May 16, 1960; New York City. Robert Di Domenica, flute; Eric Dolphy, flute and alto saxophone; Ornette Coleman, alto saxophone; Eddie Costa, vibraphone; Barry Galbraith, guitar; Bill Evans, piano; Sticks Evans, drums; Contemporary String Quartet; unidentified double basses.
Score & parts: Margun, 1960.
Disc: in *Jazz Abstractions*, Atlantic SD 1365, 1961. Eric Dolphy and and Robert Di Domenica, flutes; Ornette Coleman, alto saxophone; Jim Hall, guitar; Eddie

Costa, vibraphone; Bill Evans, piano; Sticks Evans, drums; Contemporary String Quartet; Scott Lafaro and George Duvivier, double basses. NEC
Cassette: Nov. 12, 1975; New England Conservatory; in *Misterioso; Third Stream Recompositions of the Blue-Note Repertoire of Thelonius Monk*. Members of NEC Third Stream Department. NEC

S3.123 Vertige d'Eros. (1945) 30'
For: orchestra(3(pic,afl)-2(&Ehn) -3(bcl2)-2(&cbsn); 4-3-3-1; timp; hp(2), cel, pf; str). *First performed:* Oct. 14, 1967; Madison, Wis. Madison Symphony Orchestra, Roland Johnson, conductor.
Score: Margun.
Parts: Margun, 1945. Rental.

S3.124 The Visitation (Die Heimsuchung). (1966) 180'
For: voices, chorus, jazz septet(clarinet, saxophone(alto), trumpet, trombone, piano, double bass, drums), orchestra(3(pic, afl)-3(Ehn)-3(Ebcl, bcl)-3(cbsn); 4-3-3-1; timp, perc; cel, hpsd/pf; str). Opera in 3 acts.
Libretto: Gunther Schuller, after a motif by Franz Kafka. *Commissioned by:* Hamburg State Opera. *First performed:* Oct. 12, 1966; Hamburg, West Germany. Hamburg State Opera. Gunther Schuller, conductor.
Score & parts: Associated.
Vocal score: Associated, 1967. BrU BU HMA HU HUm MIT NEC W *Libretto:* Associated, 1967. NEC W
Reel: 1967. San Francisco Opera Company, Gunther Schuller, conductor. HU

[The Visitation. Suite]
S3.125 Suite from The Visitation. 41'
For: orchestra(3-3-3(Ebcl, bcl)-3; 4-3-3-1; timp, perc; hp, cel, pf; tape; str).
Score & parts: Associated. Rental.

Yesterday in Fact. *See* Music from Yesterday in Fact.

ARRANGEMENTS

Allegretto sombreoso. *See* Set, No. 1. Incantation.

Das alte Jahr. *See* The Old Year.

Ann Street. *See* Set, No. 2. Ann Street.

At Sea. *See* Set, No. 3. At Sea.

S3.126 Balkan Hills Schottische. 4' 30"
For: instrumental ensemble(violins(9), flutes(4), piccolo, accordion, piano, guitars(4), banjo, drums, double basses(3)). Folk dance music, American.
Score & parts: in *Country Dance Music*, Margun, 1976. NEC
Disc: in *Country Fiddle Band*, Columbia 33981, 1976. NEC Country Fiddle Band, Gunther Schuller, conductor. HU NEC

S3.127 The Battle of Trenton. 14'
For: orchestra(2-2-2-2; 2-2-2-0; perc; hpsd(optional); str). Original by James Hewitt.
Score: Margun.
Parts: Margun. Rental.

S3.128 Bethena: A Concert Waltz. 4' 40"
For: instrumental ensemble. Ragtime music. Original by Scott Joplin.
Score & parts: Belwin-Mills.
Disc: in *More Scott Joplin Rags*, Golden Crest CRS 31031, 1974. NEC Ragtime Ensemble, Gunther Schuller. BU HU MIT NEC

S3.129 Brass Transcriptions, Vol. 1.
For: trumpets(2), horns(2), trombone.
Contents: Merce! grido piangento (Carlo Gesualdo); Madrigale (Leone Leoni); Gloria (Guillaume Dufay).
Score & parts: Margun.

S3.130 Brass Transcriptions, Vol. 2.
For: trumpct, horns(3), trombones(2).
Contents: Morro lasso (Carlo Gesualdo); Madrigale (Giovanni Gabrieli); Solo e pensoso (Luca Marenzio); Lamentation (John Dowland).
Score & parts: Margun.

S3.131 Brass Transcriptions, Vol. 3.
For: (maximum)trumpets(2), horns(3), trombones(3). *Contents:* Ayre (Matthew Locke); 5 Bransle (Michael Praetorius); Missa (Bartolomeo Spontone); E ben ragione (Giuseppe Caimo); Al marmorar (Giovanni Gastolei).
Score & parts: Margun.

S3.132 Brass Transcriptions, Vol. 4.
For: (maximum)trumpets(2), horns(2), trombones(2). *Contents:* 2 Ricercari (Andrea Gabrieli); Motet (Giovanni Maria Nanino); Scioglio omai (Jacopo Perti); Latin Ode (Cipriano de Rore).
Score & parts: Margun.

Calcium Light Night. *See* Set, No. 1. Calcium Light Night.

S3.133 Canzona a sei.
For: trumpets(2), trombones(2), violins(2), viola. Original by Giovanni Gabrieli.
Score & parts: Margun.

S3.134 Cataract Rag.
For: instrumental ensemble. Ragtime music. Original by Robert Hampton.
Disc: in *The Road from Rags to Jazz*, Golden Crest CRS 31042, 1975. NEC Ragtime Ensemble, Gunther Schuller, conductor. BU MIT NEC

S3.135 Charleston Rag. 4'
For: chamber orchestra(1-0-1-0; 0-1-1-1; drs; pf; str). Ragtime music. Original by Eubie Blake.
Score & parts: Margun.
Disc: in *The Road from Rags to Jazz*, Golden Crest, CRS 31042, 1975. NEC Ragtime Ensemble, Gunther Schuller, conductor. BU MIT NEC

S3.136 Chorale. 1'
For: trumpets(2), horn, trombone. From Cantata No. 60 by Johann Sebastian Bach.
Score & parts: Margun.

S3.137 Chromtimeldtune. (1962) 7'
For: orchestra(0-1-1-1; 1-1-1-1; pf;

str(3-1-1-1-1)). Reconstructed from original manuscripts of Charles Ives.
Score: MJQ, 1963. BPL NEC
Parts: MJQ. Rental.
Disc: Columbia MS 7318, 1970. Gunther Schuller, conductor. BU MIT NEC

[Combination March, Band]
S3.138 Combination March. 3'
Original by Scott Joplin.
Score: Margun, 1975. NEC
Parts: Margun.
Disc: in *Footlifters; a Century of American Marches*, Columbia M 33513, 1975. W

[Combination March, Orchestra]
S3.139 Combination March. 2' 30"
For: orchestra(3-2-3-2; 4-2(optional; cor2)-3-2-1;perc(3), glock; str). Original by Scott Joplin.
Score & parts: Margun.

Creole Eyes. *See* Ojos criollos.

S3.140 Devil's Dream. 3' 30"
For: instrumental ensemble(violins(9), flutes(5), accordion, guitars(3), banjos(2), washboard, drums, double basses(3)). Folk dance music, American.
Score & parts: in *Country Dance Music*, Margun, 1976. NEC
Disc: in *Country Fiddle Band*, Columbia 33981, 1976. NEC Country Fiddle Band, Gunther Schuller, conductor. HU NEC

S3.141 Euphonic Sounds: A Syncopated Novelty. 4' 5"
For: instrumental ensemble. Ragtime music. Original by Scott Joplin.
Score & parts: Belwin-Mills.
Disc: in *More Scott Joplin Rags*, Golden Crest CRS 31031, 1974. NEC Ragtime Ensemble, Gunther Schuller, conductor. BU HU MIT NEC

S3.142 Fischer's Hornpipe. 3'
For: instrumental ensemble(violins(9), flutes(5), piano, guitars(5), banjo, washboard or drums, double basses(3)). Folk dance music, American. Original by Johann Christian Fischer.
Score & parts: in *Country Dance Music*,

Margun, 1976.
Disc: in *Country Fiddle Band*, Columbia 33981, 1976. NEC Country Fiddle Band, Gunther Schuller, conductor. HU NEC

S3.143 Flop-Eared Mule. 3'
For: instrumental ensemble(violins(9), flutes(4), piccolo, accordion, piano, guitars(4), banjo, washboard, double basses(3)). Folk dance music, American.
Score & parts: in *Country Dance Music*, Margun, 1976.
Disc: in *Country Fiddle Band*, Columbia 33981, 1976. NEC Country Fiddle Band, Gunther Schuller, conductor. HU NEC

S3.144 The Gen'l Slocum. 5'
For: orchestra(4(pic)-3(Ehn)-3(barsax)-4; 4-4-3-1; timp, perc; pf; str). Symphonic poem. Reconstructed from original manuscripts of Charles Ives.
Score: Associated.
Parts: Associated.
Cassette: May 9, 1971; New England Conservatory; in *A Festival of New England Composers Past and Present*. NEC Symphony Orchestra, Gunther Schuller, conductor. NEC

S3.145 Grandpa's Spells.
For: instrumental ensemble. Original by Jelly Roll Morton.
Disc: in *The Road from Rags to Jazz*, Golden Crest CRS 31042, 1975. NEC Ragtime Ensemble, Gunther Schuller, conductor. BU MIT NEC

S3.146 Harlem Rag.
For: instrumental ensemble. Ragtime music. Original by Thomas Turpin.
Disc: in *The Road from Rags to Jazz*, Golden Crest CRS 31042, 1975. NEC Ragtime Ensemble, Gunther Schuller, conductor. BU MIT NEC

S3.147 Heliotrope Bouquet.
For: instrumental ensemble. Original by Louis Chauvin.
Disc: in *The Road from Rags to Jazz*, Golden Crest CRS 31042, 1975. NEC Ragtime Ensemble, Gunther Schuller, conductor. BU MIT NEC

Incantation. *See* Set, No. 1. Incantation.

The Indians. *See* Set, No. 2. The Indians.

S3.148 Instrumental Transcriptions, Vol. 1.
For: instruments(3). Works originally by Antoine Busnois, Matheus e Perusio, Solage, Grimace.
Score & parts: Margun.

S3.149 Instrumental Transcriptions, Vol. 2.
For: instruments(3). Works originally by Solage, Anthonella de Caserta, [Philipoctus de Caserta] Adam de la Halle, Heinrich Isaac, Johannes Ockeghem.
Score & parts: Margun.

S3.150 Instrumental Transcriptions, Vol. 3.
For: instruments(4). Works originally by Guillaume de Machaut, Solage, Johannes Ockeghem, Anthonella de Caserta, Johannis Cesaris, Heinrich Isaac.
Score & parts: Margun.

S3.151 Instrumental Transcriptions, Vol. 4.
For: instruments(5-7). Works originally by Josquin Depres, Guillaume de Machaut, Adam de la Halle.
Score & parts: Margun.

S3.152 Instrumental Transcriptions, Vol. 5.
For: flute/recorder, oboe, English horn or clarinet or bassoon. Originally Due capricci a tre by Johann Vierdanck; Due corenti, and Balletto by Biagio Marini.
Score & parts: Margun.

S3.153 Kitten on the Keys.
For: instrumental ensemble. Ragtime music. Original by Zez Confrey.
Disc: in *The Road from Rags to Jazz*, Golden Crest CRS 31042, 1975. NEC

Ragtime Ensemble, Gunther Schuller, conductor. BU MIT NEC

S3.154 Larry O'Gaff. 2' 29"
For: instrumental ensemble(violins(9), flutes(5), accordion, piano, guitars(5), drums, tambourine, double basses(3)). Folk dance music, American.
Score & parts: in *Country Dance Music*, Margun, 1976. NEC
Disc: in *Country Fiddle Band*, Columbia 33981, 1976. NEC Country Fiddle Band, Gunther Schuller, conductor. HU NEC

The Last Reader. *See* Set, No. 2. The Last Reader.

A Lecture. *See* Set, No. 1. A Lecture.

Like a Sick Eagle. *See* Set, No. 1. Like a Sick Eagle.

Luck and Work. *See* Set, No. 3. Luck and Work.

S3.155 A Mexican Serenade. *See* Solace.

S3.156 Millers Reel. 2' 32"
For: instrumental ensemble(violins(9), flutes(4), piccolo, piano, guitars(5), spoons or drums, double basses(3)). Folk dance music, American.
Score & parts: in *Country Dance Music*, Margun, 1976. NEC
Disc: in *Country Fiddle Band*, Columbia 33981, 1976. NEC Country Fiddle Band, Gunther Schuller, conductor. HU NEC

S3.157 Money Musk. 2' 18"
For: instrumental ensemble(violins(9), flutes(4), piccolo, guitars(3), banjos(2), drums, double basses(3)). Folk dance music, American.
Score & parts: in *Country Dance Music*, Margun, 1976. NEC
Disc: in *Country Fiddle Band*, Columbia 33981, 1976. NEC Country Fiddle Band, Gunther Schuller, conductor. HU NEC

The National Anthem. See Star Spangled Banner.

The New River. *See* Set, No. 1. The New River.

S3.158 Ojos criollos (Creole Eyes).
For: instrumental ensemble. Ragtime music. Original by Louis Moreau Gottschalk.
Disc: in *The Road from Rags to Jazz*, Golden Crest CRS 31042, 1975. NEC Ragtime Ensemble, Gunther Schuller, conductor. BU MIT NEC

S3.159 The Old Year. 5'
For: chamber orchestra. From Das Alte Jahr vergangen ist by Johann Sebastian Bach.
Music: ms.

S3.160 On the Road to Boston. 3' 30'
For: instrumental ensemble(piccolo, flutes(5), violins(9), piano, guitars(5), drums, double bass(3)). Folk dance music, American.
Score & parts: in *Country Dance Music*, Margun, 1976. NEC
Disc: in *Country Fiddle Band*, Columbia 33981, 1976. NEC Country Fiddle Band, Gunther Schuller, conductor. HU NEC

S3.161 L'Orfeo. 120'
For: voices, chorus, baroque orchestra. Opera. Original by Claudio Monteverdi.
Score & parts: Margun. Rental.

S3.162 Over the Waves. 5' 30"
For: instrumental ensemble(violins(9), flutes(5), piano, guitars(4), banjo, drums, xylophone, double basses(3)). Folk dance music, American. Original by Juventino Rosas.
Score & parts: in *Country Dance Music*, Margun, 1976. NEC
Disc: in *Country Fiddle Band*, Columbia 33981, 1976. NEC Country Fiddle Band, Gunther Schuller, conductor. HU NEC

S3.163 Pastime Rag, No. 4: A Slow Drag.
For: instrumental ensemble. Ragtime music. Original by Artie Matthews.
Disc: in *The Road from Rags to Jazz*, Golden Crest CRS 31042, 1975. NEC

Ragtime Ensemble, Gunther Schuller, conductor. BU MIT NEC

S3.164 Pleasant Moments. 4'
For: cornet and chamber orchestra(1-0-2-0; 2-0-1-0; perc(trap set); pf; str(1-0-1-1-0)). Original by Scott Joplin.
Score & parts: in *Cornet Favorites*, Margun.
Disc: in *Turn of the Century Cornet Favorites*, Columbia M 34553, 1977. Gerard Schwarz, cornet; Columbia Chamber Ensemble, Gunther Schuller, conductor. HU

S3.165 Prelude, No. 8. 3' 30"
For: instrumental ensemble(flute, oboe, saxophone(alto), saxophone(baritone), horn, trumpet, tromone, tua, drums, piano, double bass). From *The Well-Tempered Clavier* by Johann Sebastian Bach.
Score & parts: Margun.

[Prelude and Fugue, Brasses]
S3.166 Prelude and Fugue, No. 22. 7'
For: trumpets(2), horn, trombones. From *The Well-Tempered Clavier* by Johann Sebastian Bach.
Score & parts: Margun.

[Prelude and Fugue, No. 22, Instrumental Ensemble]
S3.167 Prelude and Fugue, No. 22. 7'
For: instrumental ensemble(flute, oboe, saxophone(alto), saxophone(baritone), horn, trumpet, trombone, tuba, drums, piano, double bass). From *The Well-Tempered Clavier* by Johann Sebastian Bach.
Score & parts: Margun.

Premonitions. *See* Set, No. 3. Premonitions.

S3.168 Ragtime Nightingale. 5'
For: chamber orchestra(1-1-1-1; 1-1-1-1; dr; pf; str). Original by Joseph Lamb.
Score: Margun, 1976. NEC
Parts: Margun, 1976.
Disc: in *The Road from Rags to Jazz*, Golden Crest CRS 31042, 1975. NEC

Ragtime Ensemble, Gunther Schuller, conductor. BU MIT NEC

S3.169 Royal Palace. 45'
For: voices, dancers, orchestra(3(pic)-2-2(asax)-3; 4-2-2-1; timp, perc, glock, xylo; hp, cel, pf; (offstage: perc, bells, glock; hp, cel, pf); str). Opera. Original by Kurt Weill; reconstructed in collaboration with Noam Sherrif. *First performed:* Oct. 5, 1968; San Francisco, Calif. San Francisco Opera.
Score & parts: Universal.
Reel: 1971; Holland Festival. HU

S3.170 Sarabande.
For: double basses(4). From Suite No. 6 for Unaccompanied Violoncello by Johann Sebastian Bach.
Parts: Margun.

S3.171 Saraband and Gigue.
For: horns(3). From Suite No. 6 for Unaccompanied Violoncello by Johann Sebastian Bach.
Parts: Margun.

The Se'er. *See* Set, No. 1. The Se'er.

S3.172 Set, No. 1. 18'
For: instrumental ensemble. *Contents:* The Se'er; A Lecture; The New River; Like a Sick Eagle; Calcium Light Night; Incantation (Allegretto sombreoso). Reconstructed from manuscripts of Charles Ives.
Score & parts: Presser. Rental.
Disc: Columbia MS 7318, 1970. Gunther Schuller, conductor. BU HUm MIT NEC
Cassette: Mar. 1, 1970; New England Conservatory. Boston Philharmonia, Gunther Schuller, conductor. NEC

[Set, No. 1. Calcium Light Night]
S3.173 Calcium Light Night.
For: piccolo, oboe, clarinet, bassoon, trumpet, trombone, percussion(2), piano. Original by Charles Ives.
Score & parts: Presser. Rental.

[Set, No. 1. Incantation]
S3.174 Incantation (Allegretto sombreoso). 3'
For: flute, English horn, violins(3), piano. Original by Charles Ives.
Score & parts: Peer/Presser. Rental.

[Set, No. 1. A Lecture]
S3.175 A Lecture. 4'
For: flute, clarinet, bassoons(2), snare drum, string quartet, double bass. Original by Charles Ives.
Score & parts: Associated/Presser. Rental.

[Set, No. 1. Like a Sick Eagle]
S3.176 Like a Sick Eagle. 3'
For: flute, English horn, violin, viola, violoncello, double bass. Original by Charles Ives.
Score & parts: Presser. Rental.

[Set, No. 1. The New River]
S3.177 The New River. 2'
For: instrumental ensemble(flute, clarinets(2), saxophone(baritone), trumpets(2), trombone, tuba, percussion, violins(4), double bass, piano). Original by Charles Ives.
Score & parts: Presser. Rental.

[Set, No. 1. The Se'er]
S3.178 The Se'er. 3'
For: clarinet, horn, trombone or saxophone(tenor) or baritone, cornet, drums, piano. Original by Charles Ives.
Score & parts: Associated/Presser. Rental.
Cassette: Nov. 2, 1972; New England Conservatory. NEC Wind Ensemble, Frank L. Battisti, conductor. NEC

S3.179 Set, No. 2. 8'
For: instrumental ensemble. *Contents:* The Indians; Ann Street; The Last Reader. Reconstructed from manuscripts of Charles Ives.
Score & parts: Presser. Rental.
Disc: Columbia MS 7318, 1970. Gunther Schuller, conductor. BU HUm MIT NEC

[Set, No. 2. Ann Street]
S3.180 Ann Street. 3′
For: flute, trumpet in C, trombone, glockenspiel, piano. Original by Charles Ives.
Score & parts: Presser. Rental.

[Set, No. 2. The Indians]
S3.181 The Indians. 3′
For: trumpet in C, Indian drum, string quartet, double bass, piano. Original by Charles Ives.
Score & parts: Associated/Presser. Rental.

[Set, No. 2. The Last Reader]
S3.182 The Last Reader. 2′
For: flutes(2), trumpet in C, string quartet, double bass. Original by Charles Ives.
Score & parts: Presser. Rental.

S3.183 Set, No. 3. 11′
For: instrumental ensemble or orchestra. *Contents:* At Sea; Luck and Work; Premonitions. Reconstructed from manuscripts of Charles Ives.
Score & parts: Presser. Rental.
Disc: Columbia MS 7318, 1970. Gunther Schuller, conductor. BU HUm MIT NEC

[Set, No. 3. At Sea]
S3.184 At Sea. 3′
For: English horn, horn(optional), celeste, piano or glockenspiel, violins(3). Original by Charles Ives.
Score & parts: Peer/Presser. Rental.

[Set, No. 3. Luck and Work]
S3.185 Luck and Work. 4′
For: flute, English horn, percussion, piano, violins(3), viola, violoncello, double bass. Original by Charles Ives.
Score & parts: Presser. Rental.

[Set, No. 3. Premonitions]
S3.186 Premonitions. 4′
For: orchestra(1-1(&Ehn)-1(in A)-1; 3-1-1-1; perc; cel; str). Original by Charles Ives.
Score & parts: Presser. Rental.

S3.187 Silver and Gold Two-Step. 4′
For: instrumental ensemble(violins(9), flutes(3), piccolos(2), accordion, guitars(5), drums, double basses(3)). Folk dance music, American.
Score & parts: in *Country Dance Music*, Margun, 1976. NEC
Disc: in *Country Fiddle Band*, Columbia 33981, 1976. NEC Country Fiddle Band, Gunther Schuller, conductor. HU NEC

S3.188 Solace: A Mexican Serenade. 4′ 55″
For: orchestra. Original by Scott Joplin.
Score & parts: Belwin-Mills. ·
Disc: in *More Scott Joplin Rags*, Golden Crest CRS 31031, 1974. NEC Ragtime Ensemble, Gunther Schuller, conductor. BU HU MIT NEC

S3.189 Sonata pian e forte.
For: English horn, bassoon, trumpets(2), trombones(2), violin, viola, violoncello. Original by Giovanni Gabrieli.
Score & parts: Margun.

S3.190 Spem in alium nonquam habui. 11′
For: trumpets(16), horns(8), trombones(16), double basses(4). Original by Thomas Tallis.
Score: Margun.
Parts: Margun. Rental.

[Star Spangled Banner]
S3.191 The National Anthem. 2′
For: chamber orchestra.
Score & parts: MJQ.
Disc: Colpix CP 448, n.d. Orchestra U.S.A., Gunther Schuller, conductor. NEC

S3.192 The Stars and Stripes Forever.
For: chamber orchestra(1-1-1-1; 1-1-1-1; perc(trap set); pf; str(1-1-1-1-1)). Original by John Phillip Sousa.
Score & parts: Margun.

S3.193 Steamboat Waltz. 3′ 15″
For: instrumental ensemble(violins(9), flutes(5), accordion, piano, guitars(4), banjo, drums, double basses(3)). Folk

dance music, American.
Score & parts: in *Country Dance Music*, Margun, 1976. NEC
Disc: in *Country Fiddle Band*, Columbia 33981, 1976. NEC Country Fiddle Band, Gunther Schuller, conductor. HU NEC

S3.194 Treemonisha.
For: voices, chorus, orchestra. Opera. Original by Scott Joplin. *First performed:* May 23, 1975; Houston, Tex. Houston Grand Opera, Gunther Schuller, conductor.
Score & parts: Dramatic. Rental.
Disc: Deutsche Grammophon 2530 620/2707 083, 1976. Houston Grand Opera, Gunther Schuller, conductor. HUm MIT NEC W

[Treemonisha. Suite]
S3.195 Treemonisha. 40'
For: orchestra(1-1-2-1; 2-2-1-1; perc; hp, pf; str).
Score & parts: Dramatic. Rental.

S3.196 Tribute to Rudy Wiedoeft. (1978)
For: saxophone and band. *Movements:* Saxophobia; SAXARELLA; Valse Erica. Original by Rudy Wiedoeft. *First performed:* Dec. 11, 1978; Milwaukee, Wis. Ted Hegvick, saxophone; Gunther Schuller, conductor.
Score & parts: Big Three.

S3.197 Valzer poetici. 11'
For: orchestra(3-3-3-2; 4-2-3-1; perc; hp; str). Original by Frederick Shepherd Converse.
Score: Margun.
Parts: Margun. Rental.

S3.198 Wall Street Rag. 3' 50"
For: instrumental ensemble. Original by Scott Joplin.
Score & parts: Belwin-Mills.
Disc: in *More Scott Joplin Rags*, Golden Crest CRS 31031, 1974. NEC Ragtime Ensemble, Gunther Schuller, conductor. BU HU MIT NEC

S3.199 When the Saints Go Marchin' In.

Folk music, American.
Score & parts: MJQ.

S3.200 Woodwind Quintet Transcriptions, Vol. 1. (1945-55)
Contents: Sextet, Op. 71 (Ludwig van Beethoven); Notturno, Op. 40 (Gabriel Faure); Menuet from String Quartet, K. 421 (Wolfgang Amadeus Mozart); Prelude in E Flat Major, Op. 23, No. 6 (Sergei Rachmaninoff); Scherzo from String Quartet, Op. 41, No. 1 (Robert Schumann); Scherzo from Midsummer Night's Dream (Felix Mendelssohn). Arranged for the Metropolitan Woodwind Quintet.
Score & parts: Margun, 1980. MIT

S3.201 Yale-Princeton Football Game. 5'
For: orchestra(4(pic)-3(Ehn)-3(barsax)-4; 4-4-3-1; timp, perc; pf; str). Original by Charles Ives.
Score & parts: Associated. Rental.

S3.202 Yamekraw. 10'
For: orchestra(3(pic)-3(Ehn)-3(bcl)-3(cbsn); 4-3-3-1; timp, perc; hp; str). Original by James P. Johnson.
Score: ms.

S4 ROBERT SELIG

Education: Mus.B., Mus.M. (Northwestern University, 1961, 1962); doctoral studies (Boston University, 1966-67); studied composition with Donald Martino, Ernst Krenek, Gardner Read, Anthony Donato. *Awards:* Berkshire Music Center, Fellowship (1968), Guggenheim Grants (1971, 1977), American Music Center Composer Assistance Program (1975), Massachusetts Council on the Arts and Humanities, Artist Fellowship Program (1975), Martha Baird Rockefeller Fund for Music Grant (1976), Paderewski Fund commission (1980). *Related activities:* songwriter for United Artists Corporation (1964-66); composer-in-residence, Eastern Music Festival (1982); member of the faculty

of New England Conservatory (1968-).
NEC

WORKS

S4.1 After the Ice. (1981) 22' 50"
For: Soprano and piano. *Text:* poems
by Richard Moore and Alfred, Lord
Tennyson. *Contents:* The Streams;
Survivors; Flower in the Crannied Wall;
Ask Me No More; After the Ice; All in
All; Wind. *Commissed by:* Paderewski
Fund. *First performed:* Dec. 8, 1981;
New England Conservatory; in
Enchanted Circle. Cheryl Cobb, soprano
and Cristina Gerling, piano.
Cassette: recording of first
performance. NEC

S4.2 Athena.
For: Mezzo Soprano and string
orchestra.

S4.3 Chicago: Three Portraits of a City.
For: chamber orchestra.

S4.4 Chocorua. (1972) 35'
For: voice, chorus, chamber orchestra.
Opera in 1 act. *Libretto:* Richard Moore.
Commissioned by: Fromm Foundation
and Berkshire Music Center,
Tanglewood.
Score & parts: Margun. Rental.
Reel: May 9, 1975; WGBH-FM, Boston.

S4.5 Concerto. (1969) 28'
For: rock group and orchestra.
Commissioned by: Eastern Music
Festival. *Dedicated to:* Gunther Schuller.
First performed: Eastern Music Festival,
Greensboro, N.C. Eastern Philharmonic
Orchestra, Sheldon Morgenstern,
conductor.
Score & parts: reprod. of ms. NEC
Score & parts: Margun. Rental.
Cassette: May 9, 1971; New England
Conservatory; in *A Festival of New
England Composers Past and Present.*
Donald Pate, double bass; Leonard
White, III, drums; Webster Lewis,
organ; Marcus Fiorello, guitar; NEC
Symphony Orchestra, Gunther Schuller,
conductor. NEC

Cryptic Portraits. *See* Sonata.

Flight into Fury. *See* Orestes.

S4.6 Islands (Mist in the Valley). (1968)
15'-17'
For: chorus(SSAATBB) and chamber
orchestra(1-1(Ehn)-1-0; 1-0-0-0; str). 1
movement.
Score & parts: Margun, 1981. Rental.

S4.7 Mirage. (1967) 3' 23"
For: trumpet and string orchestra. 1
movement. *Dedicated to:* Armando
Ghitalla.
Score & parts: Margun. Rental.
Disc: Cambridge CRS 2823, 1970.
Armando Ghitalla, trumpet; Chamber
Orchestra of Copenhagen, John
Moriarty, conductor. BCM BrU BU HU
NEC W

Mist in the Valley. *See* Islands.

S4.8 Music for Brass Instruments.
For: trumpets(2), horn, trombone, tuba.
Cassette: Mar. 20, 1977; New England
Conservatory. Empire Brass Quintet.
NEC

S4.9 Orestes: Flight into Fury. (1970) 7'
For: trumpet and piano. 1 movement.
Music: Margun.
Cassette: Mar. 2, 1971; New England
Conservatory; in *An Evening of
Contemporary Music.* James Simpson,
trumpet and Yasuo Watanabe, piano.
NEC

S4.10 Pometacomet, 1676 (Symphony
No. 1) . (1974-75) 21'-23'
For: band. 1 movement. *Dedication:* To
the memory of Dwight and Helen
Shepler; To Frank Battisti. *First
performed:* Nov. 5, 1975; New England
Conservatory. NEC Wind Ensemble,
Frank L. Battisti, conductor.
Score & parts: Margun. Rental.
Reel: 1976. WGBH
Cassette: recording of first
performance. NEC
Cassette: Feb. 26, 1976; New England

Conservatory. NEC Wind Ensemble, Frank L. Battisti, conductor. NEC

Portraits of a City. *See* Chicago.

S4.11 Quartet: The Three Seasons of Autumn. (1971)
For: voice, flute, violoncello, percussion. *First performed:* Feb. 2, 1973; Jordan Hall, Boston. Collage.
Cassette: recording of first performance. NEC

S4.12 Quintet, Woodwinds and Horn.

S4.13 Reflections from a Back Window: Six Terra Cotta. (1980) 16' 45"
For: piano. *Movements:* Up and Around, Over and Under; Blues from a Back Window; Another Way; Outdoor Pop Rock; From a Widow's Walk (Some Dark Thoughts); Festive Fantasy. *First performed:* Dec. 8, 1981; New England Conservatory; in Enchanted Circle. Christopher Oldfather.
Cassette: recording of first performance. NEC

S4.14 Rhapsody for Three Players. (1970) 8'
For: flute, violin, clarinet(bass). 1 movement.
Score: Margun.

Seasons of Automn. *See* Quartet.

S4.15 Sonata: Three Cryptic Portraits. (1977) 21'
For: piano. 3 movements. *First performed:* Dec. 8, 1980[*sic*]; New England Conservatory; in Enchanted Circle. Alys Terrien-Queen.
Score: Margun. NEC
Cassette: recording of first performance.
Cassette: Dec. 8, 1981[*sic*]; New England Conservatory; in *Enchanted Circle.* Alys Terrien-Queen. NEC

S4.16 Sonata, Violin.

[Songs]
S4.17 Three Songs to Texts of D. H. Lawrence.
For: Baritone, winds, piano.

S4.18 Survival Fragments. (1976) 10'
For: Soprano and piano. *Text:* Richard Moore. *Contents:* The Stars; The Gem; Leaves at Night; Abroad; Struggle; Branches.
Score: Margun.
Cassette: Feb. 26, 1978; New England Conservatory. Elizabeth Parcells, soprano and Christopher Oldfather, piano.

S4.19 Symphony for Woodwind Quintet. (1971) 20'
3 movements.
Score & parts: Margun.
Cassette: Apr. 27, 1970; New England Conservatory; in *An Evening of Contemporary Music.* Robert Stallman, flute; David Seaton, clarinet, Timothy Valentine, oboe; Michael Johns, horn; Kazuyoshi Asno, bassoon. NEC

Symphony No. 1. *See* Ponetacomet, 1676.

Terra Cotta. *See* Reflections from a Back Window.

S4.20 Variations for Brass Quintet. (1967) 15'
For: trumpets(2), horn, trombone, tuba. 10 movements.
Score & parts: Margun.
Cassette: Dec. 8, 1981; New England Conservatory; in *Enchanted Circle.* NEC Scholarship Brass Quintet. NEC

S5 HAROLD SHAPERO

Born April 29, 1920, in Lynn, Mass.
Education: studied composition with Nicolas Slonimsky (Boston, 1936-37), Ernst Krenek (Malkin Conservatory, 1937), Walter Piston (Harvard University, 1938-41), Paul Hindemith (Berkshire Music Center, Tanglewood,

1940-41), Nadia Boulanger (Longy School of Music, 1942-43). *Awards:* George Arthur Knight Prize (Harvard University, 1938), Rome Prize Fellowship (American Academy in Rome, 1941, 1948), Naumburg Fellowship (1942), John Knowles Paine Travelling Fellowship (Harvard University, 1943), Gershwin Prize (B'nai B'rith, 1945), Joseph H. Bearns Prize (Columbia University, 1946), Guggenheim Grants (1947-48), Fulbright Fellowship (1948-49), Senior Fulbright Program grant (1962). *Related activities:* composer-in-residence, American Academy in Rome (1970-71); currently, director, Brandeis University Electronic Music Studios; member of the faculty of Brandeis University (1950-). BrU

WORKS

S5.1 America Variations. (1981; rev. in progress) 20'
For: piano. 1 movement.
Score: ms.

[Baritone Songs]
S5.2 Four Baritone Songs. (1942) 8'
For: Baritone and piano. *Text:* e.e. cummings. *Contents:* Buffalo bill's defunct; little man; i go to this window; jimmie's got a goil. *First performed:* Apr. 23, 1965; Buffalo, N.Y. Larry Bogue, baritone and Harold Shapero, piano.
Score: reprod. of ms.

S5.3 Concerto. (1952-1980; rev. in progress) 28'
For: orchestra(2(&pic)-2(&Ehn) -2(&bcl)-2(&cbsn); 4-3-3-1; timp, perc; hp, pf; str). 3 movements. *Score.*

S5.4 Credo. (1954) 8'
For: orchestra(2(&pic)-2-2-2; 2-2-2-1; timp; str). Theme and 2 variations.
Commissioned by: Louisville Orchestra.
First performed: Oct. 19, 1955; Louisville, Ky. Louisville Orchestra, Robert Whitney, conductor.
Score: Southern-NY, 1966. BPL BrU HU
Parts: Southern-NY. Rental.

Disc: Louisville Orchestra LOU 56-5, 1956. Louisville Orchestra, Robert Whitney, conductor. BrU BU HU HUm NEC W

S5.5 Functional Music for the TV Film Woodrow Wilson. (1958) 25'
For: orchestra. *Commissioned by:* CBS News and Prudential Life Insurance Company. *First performed:* 1958; New York City. Television recording orchestra, Alfredo Antonini, conductor.
Score & parts: ms.

S5.6 Hebrew Cantata. (1954) 27'-30'
For: Soprano, Alto, Tenor, Baritone, chorus(mixed), flute, trumpet, violin, harp, organ. *Text:* Jehuda Halevi, in Hebrew (romanized) and English.
Movements: All the Stars of Morning; Beside an Apple Tree; Rarest Beauty; The Heritage of the Lord; Stars of the World; A Servant of God; Slaves of Time; Until Night and Day Shall Cease.
Commissioned by: American Jewish Tercentenary. *Dedication:* To the memory of Dr. Simon Rawidowicz.
First performed: 1958; University of California, Los Angeles. Gregg Smith Singers.
Score: Southern-NY, 1966. BPL BrU HU
Reel: recording of first performance.

[Hebrew Songs]
S5.7 Two Hebrew Songs. (1973) 17'-18'
For: Tenor and piano. *Contents:* They Who Sow at Night (S. Shalom); Will There Yet Come Days of Forgiveness and Grace (Louis Goldberg).
Commissioned by: Cantor Jack Kessler, Temple Beth Shalom, Saxonville, Mass. for the 25th anniversary of Israel. *First performed:* 1973; Temple Beth Shalom, Saxonville, Mass. Jack Kessler, tenor and Harold Shapero, piano. *Score.*

[Hebrew Songs; Arr.]
S5.8 Two Hebrew Songs. (1973) 17'-18'
For: Tenor, piano, string orchestra.
Contents: They Who Sow at Night (S. Shalom); Will There Yet Come Days of Forgiveness and Grace (Louis Goldberg).
First performed: Mar. 8, 1980; Sanders

Theatre, Harvard University. Kim Scown, tenor; Lisa Goldman, piano; Harvard Chamber Orchestra, Leon Kirchner, conductor.
Score & parts: ms.
Reel: recording of first performance.

S5.9 Lyric Dances. (1955-80; rev. in progress) 30'
For: orchestra(2(&pic)-2(&Ehn) -2(&bcl)-2(&cbsn); 2-2-2-1; timp, perc; hp, pf; str). *Commissioned by:* New York City Center Ballet.
Score & parts: ms. (revised version).

S5.10 Nine-Minute Overture. (1940) 9'
For: orchestra(2(&pic)-2(&Ehn)-2(&Eb cl)-2; 4-3-3-1; timp, perc; pf; str). Awarded Rome Prize Fellowship (American Academy in Rome), 1941. *First performed:* 1941; New York City. CBS Symphony Orchestra, Howard Barlow, conductor.
Score & parts: Southern-NY. Rental.
Tape: recording of first performance.

S5.11 On Green Mountain. (1957) 10'-11'
For: instrumental ensemble(flute, clarinet, saxophone(alto), saxophone(tenor), bassoon, horn, trumpet, trombone, harp, guitar, piano, drums). Chaconne after Claudio Monteverdi. 1 movement. *Commissioned by:* Brandeis University Festival of Fine Arts, 1957. *Dedicated to:* Gunther Schuller. *First performed:* 1958; Brandeis University.
Score & parts: Southern-NY. Rental.
Disc: in *Outstanding Jazz Compositions of the 20th Century*, Columbia C2L 31. BCM
Disc: in *Modern Jazz Concert: Brandeis Jazz Festival*, Columbia WL 127, 1958. BrU

[On Green Mountain; Arr.]
S5.12 On Green Mountain. (1957-80) 10'-11'
For: orchestra(2(pic)-2-2-2; 2-3-3-0; timp, perc(2), vibra; hp, gt, bgt, pf; str). Chaconne after Claudio Monteverdi. 1 movement. *Commissioned by:*

Foundation for New Music, Los Angeles, Calif. *Dedicated to:* Jack Elliott.
Score & parts: reprod. of ms; available from composer.

S5.13 Partita in C. (1960) 20'-22'
For: piano and orchestra(1(pic)-1(Ehn)-1-1; 1-1-1-0; timp(3), perc, glock, vibra, xylo; hp; str). *Movements:* Sinfonia; Ciaccona; Pastorale; Scherzo; Aria; Burlesca; Cadenza; Esercizio. *Commissioned by:* Ford Foundation Concert Artist Program. *First performed:* 1961; Detroit, Mich. Seymour Lipkin, pianist; Detroit Symphony Orchestra, Paul Paray, conductor.
Score & parts: Southern-NY. Rental.
Disc: Louisville Orchestra LS 674, 1967. Benjamin Owen, piano; Louisville Orchestra, Robert Whitney, conductor. BCM BrU BU HU HUm MIT NEC W

[Pieces]
S5.14 Three Pieces in C Sharp. (1969) 15'
For: tape(piano and Buchla synthesizer). 3 movements. Written in collaboration with Hannah Shapero. *First performed:* 1970; Brandeis University.

Pieces for Three Pieces. See Three Pieces for Three Pieces.

[Psalms]
S5.15 Two Psalms. (1952) 7'-8'
For: chorus(SATB). Text: Bible, O.T., Psalms 146, 117, 100. *Movements:* Lauda; Jubilate. *Dedicated to:* Irving Fine. *First performed:* 1953; Berkshire Music Center, Tanglewood. Tanglewood Festival Chorus.
Vocal score: Southern-NY, 1953. BrU HU

[Quartet, Strings, No. 1]
S5.16 String Quartet No. 1. (1947) 19' 46"
4 movements. Awarded the Rome Prize Fellowship (American Academy in Rome), 1948. *Dedicated to:* Walter Piston. *First performed:* 1947;

Dartmouth College. Juilliard String Quartet.
Study score: Southern-NY, 1958. BPL BrU BU HU MIT
Parts: Southern-NY, 1958. BrU MIT
Disc: Columbia ML 5576/MS 6176, 1960. Robert Koff and Paul Bellam, violins; Walter Trampler, viola; Charles McCracken, violoncello. BPL BrU BU HU MIT NEC

S5.17 Serenade in D. (1945) 30'
For: string orchestra. 5 movements. Awarded the Joseph H. Bearns Prize (Columbia University), 1946. *Dedicated to:* Nadia Boulanger. *First performed:* Mar. 7, 1981; Brandeis University. Brandeis Chamber Orchestra, David Hoose, conductor.
Score & parts: Southern-NY. Rental.
Study score: Southern-NY, 1959. BPL BrU BU HU MIT
Disc: MGM E3557, 1957. Arthur Winograd String Orchestra, Arthur Winograd, conductor. BU HU MIT NEC

S5.18 Sinfonia in C Minor. (1948) 10'
For: orchestra(2(&pic)-2-2-2(&cbsn); 4-2-3-0; timp; str). *Commissioned by:* Houston Philharmonic Orchestra. *First performed:* 1948; Houston Philharmonic Orchestra, Efrem Kurtz, conductor. Originally titled The Travelers Overture.
Score & parts: Southern-NY. Rental.

[Sonata, Piano]
S5.19 Sonata in F Minor. (1948) 30'
3 movements. *Commissioned by:* Boosey & Hawkes. *First performed:* 1949; Museum of Modern Art, New York City. Beveridge Webster.
Score: Southern-NY, 1964. BCM BPL BrU HU

[Sonata, Piano. Nos. 1-3]
S5.20 Three Sonatas for Piano. (1944) 27'
Dedicated to: Arthur Berger and Alexei Haieff. *First performed:* 1944. New York City; League of Composers. Harold Shapero.
Score: G. Schirmer, 1944. BPL BU HU
Disc: New Editions 1, 195- (Sonata No.

1). Bernhard D. Weiser. BrU HU HUm NEC
Disc: Concert Disc CS 217, 1960 (Sonata No. 1). Frank Glazer. BCM BrU NEC
Disc: Decca DL 10.021/710.021, 1960 (Sonata No. 1). Sylvia Marlowe, harpsichord. BrU W

[Sonata, Piano(4-Hands)]
S5.21 Sonata. (1941) 15'-16'
3 movements. *Dedication:* For L.B. (Leonard Bernstein) and H.S. (Harold Shapero). *First performed:* 1941; Museum of Fine Arts, Boston. Leonard Bernstein and Harold Shapero.
Score: Affiliated Musicians, 1953. BrU BU HU
Disc: Columbia ML 4841, 195-. Harold Shapero and Leo Smit. BCM BrU BU HU MIT W
Disc: Columbia AML 4841, 19--. Reissue of Columbia ML4841, 195-.

[Sonata, Trumpet(in C) and Piano]
S5.22 Sonata. (1940) 10'
2 movements. *Dedicated to:* Aaron Copland. *First performed:* 1941; Berkshire Music Center, Tanglewood.
Score: Southern-NY, 1956. BCM BPL BrU HU
Disc: in Contemporary Music For Trumpet, Redwood ES 4, 1977. Marice Stith, trumpet and Stuart W. Raleigh, piano. HU

[Sonata, Violin and Piano]
S5.23 Sonata. (1942) 15'
3 movements. *Dedicated to:* Paul Makowsky. *First performed:* 1943; New York City. Fredell Lack, violin and Harold Shapero, piano.
Score: Southern-NY, 1954. BrU BU HU
Cassette: Nov. 11, 1981; New England Conservatory. Donald Armstrong, violin and Vytas J. Baksys, piano. NEC

S5.24 Symphony for Classical Orchestra. (1947) 40'
For: orchestra(2(&pic)-2-2-2(&cbsn); 2-2-2(&btrb)-0; timp; str). 4 movements.
Commissioned by: Koussevitzky Music Foundation (Library of Congress).

Dedicated to: Serge Koussevitzky Music Foundation in the Library of Congress and to the memory of Serge and Natalie Koussevitzky. *First performed:* 1948; Symphony Hall, Boston. Boston Symphony Orchestra, Leonard Bernstein, conductor.
Score & parts: Southern-NY. Rental
Study score: Southern-NY, 1965. BCM BPL BrU HU MIT W
Disc: Columbia ML 4889, 1954. Columbia Symphony Orchestra, Leonard Bernstein, conductor. BCM BrU HU HUm NEC W
Disc: Composers Recordings CRI SRD 424, 1979. Reissue of Columbia ML 4889, 1954. BrU BU MIT NEC T W

S5.25 Three Pieces for ˙Three Pieces. (1939) 10′
For: flute, clarinet, bassoon.
Movements: Classical; Oriental; Contrapuntal. *First performed:* 1939; Harvard University. Harvard Music Club Concert.
Study score: Southern-NY, 1967. BCM BrU HU
Parts: Southern-NY, 1967. BCM BPL HU

Three Pieces in C Sharp. See Pieces.

Travelers Overture. See Sinfonia in C Minor.

[Trio, Strings]
S5.26 String Trio. (1938)
For: violin, viola, violoncello. 3 movements. *First performed:* Apr. 23, 1965; State University of New York, College at Buffalo. Paul Zukofsky, violin; Jean Dupouy, viola; Edward J. Humeston, violoncello.
Score & parts: reprod of ms.
Reel: recording of first performance.

S5.27 Variations in C Minor. (1947) 18′-20′
For: piano. 1 movement. *First performed:* Jan. 1, 1948; Jordan Hall, Boston. Harold Shapero.
Score: Southern-NY, 1962. BCM BrU HU

S6 SEYMOUR SHIFRIN

Born February 28, 1926, in New York City; died September 27, 1979. Moved to Boston area 1966. *Education:* B.A., M.A. (Columbia University, 1947, 1949); studied composition with William Schuman (1942-45), Otto Luening (1947-49), Darius Milhaud (1951-52). *Awards:* Seidl Fellowship (1947-48), Joseph H. Bearns Prize (Columbia University, 1950), Fulbright Fellowship (1951-52), Fromm Foundation Prize (1953), Guggenheim Grants (1956, 1959), National Institute of Arts and Letters Award (1957), Brandeis University, Creative Arts Award (1958), Copley Foundation Award (1961), Horblit Award (Boston Symphony Orchestra, 1963), Koussevitzky International Recording Awards (1970, 1972), Naumburg Recording Award (1970), National Endowment for the Arts grant (1978?). *Related activities:* served on the faculties of Columbia University (1949-50), City College of The City University of New York (1950-51), University of California, Berkeley (1952-66), Brandeis University (1966-79). The composer's musical estate is held by the Yale University Music Library. BrU

WORKS

S6.1 Cantata to Sophoclean Choruses. (1955-57) 40′
For: chorus(SATB) and orchestra(2-2-2-2; 4-3-4-0; timp, perc; cel, pf; str). *Text:* from *Oedipus Rex* and *Antigone* by Sophocles; tra nslated by William Butler Yeats and Dudley Fitts, respectively. *Contents:* Lament for Oedipus; Ode; Paen; Ode.
Score: Peters, 1976. BrU
Parts: Peters, 1976. Rental.
Reel: Apr. 9, 1979; Wellesley College (Lament for Oedipus). Sarah Gray, piano; Nancy Cirillo and Diane Cataldo, violins; Gillian Rosenbaum, viola; Joel Moerschel, violoncello. W

[Cantos]
S6.2 Four Cantos. (1950) 6'
For: piano.
Score: in *New Music* vol. 23, no. 4,
New Music Edition, 1950. BrU BU HU L
NEC
Score: Merion, 1958.

S6.3 The Cat and the Moon. (1949) 5'
For: Soprano and piano.
Score: American Composers Alliance.

[Chamber Symphony]
S6.4 Kammer-Sinfonie. (1952-53) 20'
For: orchestra(1-0-2(&bcl)-0; 2-0-2-0;
str(6-6-4-4-0)). 3 movements.
Study score: Litolff, 1960. BrU HU UMB
W
Parts: Litolff. Rental.

S6.5 Chronicles. (1970) 30'
For: Tenor, Bass, Bass Baritone,
chorus(mixed), orchestra(2(pic)-2-2(bcl)-2;
2-2-2-1; timp, perc; pf; str). Cantata.
Text: Bible, O.T. *Contents:* Chronicles 1:
1-3; Chronicles 22:7-10; Isaiah 60:18;
Isaiah 55:1, 12, 13; Job 10:1, 3-8, 18,
20, 21; Job 28:7, 8, 12, 14, 15; Job
33:15-17. *Commissioned by:* Temple
Emmanuel of San Francisco on the
occasion of the 120th anniversary of
its founding. *Dedication:* To my parents
on the 50th anniversary of their
marriage. *First performed:* Oct. 27,
1976; Symphony Hall, Boston;
International Society for Contemporary
Music, World Music Days. Seth McCoy,
tenor; Gregory Reinhart, baritone; David
Arnold, bass baritone; NEC Chorus;
Lorna Cooke deVaron, conductor;
Boston Symphony Orchestra, Seiji
Ozawa, conductor.
Score: Peters, 1971. BrU
Parts: Peters, 1971. Rental.

S6.6 Composition for Piano (Fantasy).
(1950) 14'
Score: ms.

Concert Piece. *See* Konzertstueck.

S6.7 Duettino.
For: violin and piano.
Score: Merion, 1972. NEC

S6.8 Duo.
For: violin and piano. (1965-69) 12' 1
movement. *Dedicated to:* Rose Mary
Harbison.
Score: Peters, 1973. BrU BU HU MIT
NEC T
Reel: Apr. 9, 1979; Wellesley College.
Nancy Cirillo, violin and Charles Fisk,
piano. W

[Early Songs]
S6.9 Two Early Songs. (1947) 6'
For: Soprano and piano.
Score: American Composers Alliance.

Fantasy. *See* Composition for Piano.

S6.10 Give Ear, O Ye Heavens. The
Song of Moses. (1959) 3'
For: chorus(SSAATTBB) and organ.
Text: Bible, O.T., Deuteronomy 32: 1-4.
Vocal score: Peters, 1960. BrU HU W

S6.11 In eius memoriam. (1967-68) 6'
For: flute, clarinet, violin, violoncello,
piano. 1 movement.
Score: Peters, 1976. BPL BrU BU HU
MIT NEC W
Parts: Peters, 1976. W
Disc: in *New American Music for
Chamber Ensemble*, Nonesuch H 71351,
1978. Boston Musica Viva, Richard
Pittman, conductor. BrU BU MIT NEC W
Reel: Oct. 11, 1977 [1979?] Longy
School of Music. Boston Musica Viva,
Richard Pittman, conductor. WGBH

Kammer-Sinfonie. *See* Chamber
Symphony.

S6.12 Konzertstueck (Concert Piece).
(1959) 8'
For: violin. 3 movements. *Dedicated to:*
Austin Reller.
Score: Litolff, 1960. BrU HU MIT W

[Last Songs]
S6.13 5 Last Songs. (1979)
For: Soprano and piano or orchestra.
Orchestration completed by Martin
Boykan.
Score: American Composers Alliance.

[Lullaby, Violin]
S6.14 Lullaby.
Score: Merion, 1972. NEC

[Lullaby, Voice and Piano]
S6.15 Lullaby. (1966)
Score: American Composers Alliance.

S6.16 A Medieval Latin Lyric. (1954) 2'
For: chorus(mixed).
Vocal score: American Composers
Alliance.

S6.17 The Modern Temper: A Dance.
(1959) 6'
For: piano(4-hands). *Commissioned by:*
Peggy Salkind and Milton Salkind for
the Composers Forum (San Francisco,
Calif.).
Score: Litolff, 1961. BrU HU W

S6.18 Music for Orchestra. (1948) 9'
Score: American Composers Alliance.

S6.19 The Nick of Time. (1978) 20'
For: flute, clarinet, percussion, piano,
violin, violoncello, double bass. Written
for Speculum Musicae; supported by a
National Endowment for the Arts
Grant.
Score: Mobart, nyp.

S6.20 No Second Troy. (1953) 4'
For: Soprano and piano.
Score: American Composers Alliance.

S6.21 The Odes of Shang. (1962) 17'
47"
For: chorus(mixed), piano,
percussion(played by members of
chorus: maracas, claves, castanets,
sandpaper blocks, cow bells(4), large
suspended cymbal, small suspended
cymbal, hand cymbal, hollow
woodblock, glockenspiel, Japanese
windchimes, Indian bells(2),
tablas(3)(high, medium, low), low
pitched drum). *Text:* two poems from
*The Classical Anthology Defined by
Confucius* by Ezra Pound. *Commissioned
by:* Berkeley Chamber Singers.
Score: Peters, 1974. BrU
Disc: New World NW 219, 1977.
University of Michigan Chamber Choir;
members of University of Michigan
Symphony Orchestra, Thomas Hilbish,
conductor. BCM BU HU HUm MIT NEC
T W
Tape: May 7, 1971; New England
Conservatory; in *A Festival of New
England Composers Past and Present*,
NEC Chorus, Lorna Cooke deVaron,
conductor. WGBH(reel) NEC(cassette)
Cassette: May 9, 1979; New England
Conservatory. NEC Chorus, Lorna Cooke
deVaron, conductor. NEC

[Pieces]
S6.22 Drei Stuecke. (1958) 18'
For: orchestra(3(pic,
afl)-3(Ehn)-3(bcl)-3(cbsn); 4-3-3-1; timp,
perc, glock, xylo; hp, cel; str). 3
movements. *Commissioned by:* Richard
Rodgers and Oscar Hammerstein, II for
the League of Composers and the
International Society for Contemporary
Music. Recipient of the Naumburg
Recording Award (1970) and the
Koussevitzky International Recording
Award (1972).
Score & parts: Litolff, 1959. Rental.
Study score: Litolff, 1959. BrU HU MIT
NEC W
Disc: Composers Recordings CRI SD
275, 1971 (titled Three Pieces for
Orchestra). London Sinfonietta,
Jacques-Louis Monod, conductor. BrU
BU HU HUm MIT NEC W

S6.23 Play for the Young.
For: violin and violoncello.
Score: Merion, 1972. NEC

[Quartet, Strings, No. 1]
S6.24 Streichquartett. (1949) 17'
1 movement.

Study score: Bote & Bock, 1961. BrU
HU NEC

[Quartet, Strings, No. 2]
S6.25 String Quartet No. 2. (1962) 18'
3 movements. *First performed:* Nov. 4,
1962; University of California, Berkeley.
Lenox Quartet.
Score: Peters, 1977. BPL BrU MIT T W
Parts: reprod. of ms. NEC
Parts: Peters, 1977.

[Quartet, Strings, No. 3]
S6.26 String Quartet No. 3. (1965-66)
13'
Commissioned by: Koussevitzky Music
Foundation (Library of Congress).
Dedication: To the memory of Serge
and Natalie Koussevitzky.
Score: Peters, 1974. BPL BrU HU MIT
NEC
Parts: Peters, 1974. NEC

[Quartet, Strings, No. 4]
S6.27 String Quartet No. 4. (1966-67)
18'
3 movements. Recipient of
Koussevitzky International Recording
Award. *Commissioned by and dedicated
to:* Fine Arts Quartet.
Score: Peters, 1973. BrU MIT NEC T W
Parts: Peters, 1973. MIT
Disc: Composers Recordings CRI 358,
1976. Fine Arts Quartet. BrU BU HU
MIT NEC T W

[Quartet, Strings, No. 5]
S6.28 Quartet No. 5. (1971-72) 17'
Commissioned by and dedicated to:
Stanley Quartet.
Score: Peters, nyp.

S6.29 A Renaissance Garland. (1975)
For: Soprano, Tenor,
recorder(soprano/alto/tenor/bass), lute,
viol(tenor/bass), percussion(small drum,
tambourine, triangle, tuned bells).
Contents: Sonnet (Sir Thomas Wyatt);
Ballad (anon.); An Excellent Sonnet of
a Nymph (Sir Philip Sidney); Sonnet
(William Shakespeare). *Commissioned
by:* Boston Camerata. *Dedication:* For
Mir.

Score: reprod. of ms.
Study score: Mobart, 1979. BrU BU.
Parts: Mobart, 1979. Rental.

S6.30 Responses. (1973) 9'
For: piano. 5 movements.
Score: Peters, 1978. BrU BU MIT
Disc: Composers Recordings CRI SD
461, 1981. Robert Taub. BrU BU HU
MIT NEC
Cassette: Nov. 22, 1976; New England
Conservatory. Russell Sherman. NEC
Cassette: Apr. 10, 1979; New England
Conservatory. Lois Shapiro. NEC
Cassette: Apr. 26, 1979; New England
Conservatory. David Evans. NEC

S6.31 Ripeness Is All. (1976)
For: Soprano and guitar. *Dedication:* To
Milton Babbitt on his 60th Birthday.
Score: American Composers Alliance.

S6.32 Satires of Circumstance. (1964)
17'
For: Mezzo Soprano, flute/piccolo,
clarinet, violin, violoncello, double
bass, piano. *Text:* Thomas Hardy.
Contents: Waiting Both; The
Convergence of the Twain; What's
There to Tell? *Dedicated to:* Paul
Fromm. Recipient of Koussevitzky
International Recording Award (1970).
Score & parts: reprod. of ms. NEC
Score: Peters, 1971. BCM BrU HU MIT
NEC T W
Parts: Peters, 1971. BrU BU HU NEC
Disc: in *Spectrum: New American
Music*, vol. 2, Nonesuch H 71220, 1969.
Jan De Gaetani, mezzo soprano;
Contemporary Chamber Ensemble,
Arthur Weisberg, conductor. BCM BrU
BU HU MIT NEC W
Reel: May 23, 1975. WGBH
Reel: Oct. 11, 1977 [1979?] Longy
School of Music. D'Anna Fortunato,
soprano; Boston Musica Viva, Richard
Pittman, conductor. WGBH

S6.33 Serenade. (1954) 20'
For: oboe, clarinet, horn, viola, piano.
3 movements. *Commissioned by:*
Juilliard School for its 50th
anniversary festival. *First performed:*

Feb. 17, 1956; New York City.
Score: reprod. of ms. NEC
Score: Litolff, 1958. BPL BrU HU MIT NEC
Disc: Composers Recordings CRI 123, 1958. Melvin Kaplin, oboe; Charles Russo, clarinet; Robert M. Cecil, horn; Ynez Lynch, viola; Harriet Wingreen, piano. BrU BU HU MIT NEC T W

S6.34 Sonata. (1948) 15'
For: violoncello and piano.
Score: American Composers Alliance.

Song of Moses. *See* Give Ear, O Ye Heavens.

S6.35 Spring and Fall. (1953) 3'
For: Soprano and piano.
Score: American Composers Alliance.

Stuecke fuer Orchester. *See* Pieces.

S6.36 Trauermusik. (1956) 10'
For: piano.
Score: Litolff, 1960. BrU HU W

S6.37 Trio. (1974) 11'
For: violin, violoncello, piano. 1 movement. *Dedicated to:* Francesco Trio. *First performed:* Jan. 20, 1975; San Francisco, Calif.; San Francisco Chamber Music Society. Francesco Trio.
Score: Mobart, 1976. BrU HU MIT NEC T W

S6.38 Waltz. (1977) 1' 30"
For: piano.
Score: in *Waltzes by 25 Contemporary Composers*, Peters, 1978. BrU MIT NEC W

S7 GREGORY SILBERMAN

Born October 29, 1953, in Witchita, Kan. Moved to Boston area 1974.
Education: B.M., M.M. (New England Conservatory); studied improvisation with Ran Blake; jazz piano with Jaki Byard; classical piano with Margaret Chaloff; composition with Avram

David. *Related activities:* manager of Ran Blake; coordinator of New England Conservatory Third Stream Studies Department; member of the faculties of Harvard University and New England Conservatory Extension Division (1980-). NEC

WORKS

S7.1 Beginning. (1977) 3'
For: piano. *Dedicated to:* Madame Margaret Chaloff. *First performed:* May, 1977; Windsor, Conn. Gregory Silberman.
Lead sheets: ms. in composer's hand.

S7.2 Maria Teresa. (1981) 5'
For: piano. *Dedicated to:* Maria Teresa Tannozzini.
Score: ms. in composer's hand.

S7.3 Victoria. (1979) 5'
For: piano, double bass, drums or pianos(2). *First performed:* Mar. 8, 1980; Fanueil Hall Marketplace, Boston. Gregory Silberman, piano; Joe Link, drums; Peter Bouteneff, double bass.
Score: Margun, 1981.
Disc: Soul Note SN 10, 1981. Ran Blake and Jaki Byard; pianos.
Cassette: May 1981; Teatro Ristori, Verona, Italy. Ran Blake and Jaki Byard, pianos.

S7.4 Wedding March. (1981) 5'
For: piano, double bass, drums.
Dedicated to: Dorothy Colman Wallace.
First performed: June 1981; Boston. Gregory Silberman, piano and Peter Bouteneff, double bass.
Score: ms. in composer's hand.
Cassette: recording of first performance.

S8 SHEILA SILVER

Born October 1946, in Seattle, Wash. Moved to Boston area 1971. *Education:* B.A. (University of California, Berkeley, 1968); M.F.A., Ph.D. (Brandeis University, 1974, 1976); studied composition with Arthur Berger, Jacob Druckman, Erhard Karkoschka, Gyoergy Ligeti, Harold Shapero, Seymour Shifrin. *Awards:* George Ladd Prix de Paris (University of California, Berkeley, 1969-71), Abram L. Sachar International Fellowship (Brandeis University, 1974-75), Internationaler Wettbewerb fuer Komponistinnen (Mannheim, West Germany, Second Prize in Chamber Music, 1975), West Coast Fromm Foundation Prize (Finalist, 1975), Indianapolis Symphony Orchestra Competition (Finalist, 1977), Radcliffe Institute Fellowship (1977-78), Rome Prize Fellowship (American Academy in Rome, 1978-79), Berkshire Music Center commission (1979), League-ISCM National Composers Competition (Winner, 1981). *Related activities:* pianist; contributor of articles to various journals; served on the faculties of Phillips Exeter Academy, Exeter, N.H. (1976-77), Brandeis University (1977), State University of New York at Stony Brook (1979-). BrU

WORKS

S8.1 Canto. (1979) 30'
For: Baritone and instrumental ensemble(oboe/English horn, trumpet, trombone, percussion(3), viola, violoncello, double bass). *Text:* Ezra Pound. *Commissioned by:* Berkshire Music Center, Tanglewood. *First performed:* Aug. 1979; Berkshire Music Center, Tanglewood. David Hamilton, baritone; Theodore Antoniou, conductor. *Score & parts:* reprod. of ms.; available from composer.

S8.2 Chariessa. (1978) 17'
For: Soprano and piano. Song cycle. *Text:* Sappho, translated by Mary Ethel Barnard. *First performed:* Radcliffe College. Karen Komar, soprano and Sheila Silver, piano.
Score: reprod. of ms. BCM
Reel: May 16, 1978; Boston Conservatory. Karen Komar, soprano and Sheila Silver, piano. BCM

[Chariessa; Arr.]
S8.3 Chariessa. (1980)
For: Soprano and orchestra(2(pic)-2(&Ehn)-2(&bcl)-2; 2-2-2-0; perc(2); hp; str). *First performed:* July 1981; Rome, Italy. RAI Orchestra.
Score & parts: reprod. of ms.; available from composer.

S8.4 Dynamis. (1978) 8'
For: horn. Written for David Hoose. *First performed:* June 1979; American Academy, Rome, Italy. David Hoose. *Score:* ms.

S8.5 Ek Ong Kar. (1981) 13'
For: chorus(SATB) or chorus(women). *Text:* Mantra(Sikh).
Vocal score: reprod. of ms.; available from composer (both versions).

[Elisabethan Songs]
S8.6 Two Elisabethan Songs. (1981) 8'
For: chorus(SATB). *Contents:* When Daisies Pied (William Shakespeare); Cherry Ripe (Thomas Campion).
Vocal score: reprod. of ms.; available from composer.

S8.7 Fantasy Quasi Theme and Variation: Inspired by the Piano Variations of Aaron Copland. (1980) 7' *For:* piano. *First performed:* Mar. 1981; National Gallery of Art, Washington, D.C. Claudia Stevens. *Score:* reprod. of ms.; available from composer.

S8.8 Galixidi. (1976) 20'
For: orchestra(3(pic)-2(Ehn)-3(Ebcl, bcl)-2(&cbsn or cbcl); 4-2-3-1; perc(5-6); hp; str). *Commissioned by:* Seattle Philharmonic Orchestra. Finalist, Indianapolis Symphony Orchestra Competition, 1977. *First performed:* Mar. 1977; University of Washington. Seattle Philharmonic Orchestra, Jerome Glass, conductor.
Score & parts: reprod. of ms.; available from composer.

S8.9 Ode to Julius. (1972) 12'
For: pianos(2) and percussion. *First performed:* May 1972; Brandeis University. Margaret Ulmer and George Fisher, pianos; Jeff Hankin, percussion. *Score:* reprod. of ms.; available from composer.

S8.10 Past Tense. (1973) 13'
For: instrumental ensemble(flute, clarinet, clarinet(bass), bassoon, horn, harp, violin, viola, violoncello, double bass, percussion). Finalist, West Coast Fromm Foundation Prize, 1975. *First performed:* Mar. 1974; Los Angeles, Calif. William Kraft, conductor.
Score & parts: reprod. of ms.; available from composer.

[Quartet, Strings]
S8.11 String Quartet. (1975) 25'
Doctoral thesis. Awarded Second Prize in Chamber Music, Internationaler Wettbewerb fuer Komponistinnen (Mannheim, West Germany), 1975. *First performed:* Nov. 1976; Mannheim, West Germany. Assmann Quartet.
Score & parts: reprod. of ms.; available from composer.
Score: University Microfilm, 1976. BrU

S8.12 Quarthym. (1971) 7'
For: recorder(alto). *First performed:* Nov. 1971; Stuttgart, West Germany. Brigitte Koerber.
Score: ms. in composer's hand.

S8.13 Theme and Variations. (1980) 6'
For: vibraphone and bows(2).
Score: reprod. of ms.; available from composer.

S9 EZRA SIMS

Born January 16, 1928, in Birmingham, Ala. Moved to Boston area 1958. *Education:* B.A., Mathematics (Birmingham-Southern College, 1947); studied composition with Hugh Thomas, G. Ackley Brower (Birmingham Conservatory, 1945-48); Quincy Porter (Yale University, B.M., 1952); Darius Milhaud, Leon Kirchner (Mills College, M.A. 1956). *Awards:* Margaret Lee Crofts Fellowship (Tanglewood, 1960), Raphael Sagalyn Prize (Tanglewood, 1960), Guggenheim Grant (1962), Cambridge Arts Council Grants (1975, 1976), National Endowment for the Arts Fellowships (1976, 1978), Martha Baird Rockefeller Fund for Music Grant (1977), Massachusetts Council on the Arts and Humanities, Artist Fellowship Program (1979). *Related activities:* contributor of articles on microtones and related entries to *The Harvard Dictionary of Music*, 2nd ed. and reviews to *Boston After Dark* and *Ballet Review* (New York); member of the staff, Eda Kuhn Loeb Music Library, Harvard University (1958-62, 1965-74); observer and composer at Electronic Music Studio, NHK, Tokyo, Japan (1962-63); music director of New England Dinosaur (1968-); member of the faculty of New England Conservatory (1976-78); president of Dinosaur Annex (1977-). NEC

WORKS

S9.1 Abalone Co. *See* Clement Wenceslaus
Lothaire Nepomucene, *Prince Metternich (1773--1859) IN MEMORIAM.*

S9.2 Aeneas on the Saxophone. (1977) 2'
For: Soprano, Mezzo Soprano, Tenor, Baritone, clarinet, clarinet(bass), horn, trombone, viola, double bass. Microtonal music (18-note scale, 72-note equal temperament). 1 movement. *Text:* from *Drayneflete Revisited* by Osbert Lancaster.
Dedicated to: The memory of James Waring. *First performed:* Jan. 16, 1978; First and Second Church, Boston. Dinosaur Annex, Rodney Lister, conductor.
Score & parts: American Composers Alliance, 1978. HU
Reel: recording of first performance. WGBH

S9.3 After Lyle, or Untitled. (1975)
For: tape. Dance music; musique concrete. *Choreography: Fragments of a Garden* by Toby Armour. *Commissioned by:* Toby Armour. *First performed:* Apr. 1975; Wheelock College. New England Dinosaur. *Tape.*
Cassette: May 2, 1977; New England Conservatory; in *Enchanted Circle* (titled Untitled, or After Lyle). NEC

S9.4 Air from Cunegonde [Version 1]. (1980)
For: voice(high) and piano. Written in collaboration with Richard Busch. Piano part different from entry below.
Score: American Composers Alliance.

S9.5 Air from Cunegonde [Version 2]. (1980)
For: voices(high)(2) and piano. Written in collaboration with Richard Busch. Piano part different from entry above.
Score: reprod. of ms. NEC

S9.6 Alec. (1968)
For: tape. Musique concrete; dance music. *Choreography: Visions at the Death of Alexander* by Toby Armour. *Dedicated to:* Toby Armour. *First performed:* Nov. 1968; Charles Street Meeting House, Boston. Toby Armour and dancers.
Tape: available from composer.

S9.7 All Done from Memory. (1980)
For: violin. Microtonal music (18-note scale, 72-note equal temperament). 1 movement. *Commissioned by and dedicated to: Janet Packer. First performed:* Jan 18, 1981. First and Second Church, Boston; Dinosaur Annex concert. Janet Packer
Score: reprod. of ms. NEC
Score: American Composers Alliance. HU
Tape: recording of first performance.

S9.8 -- And, As I Was Saying,.... (1979)
For: viola or violin. Microtonal music (18-note scale, 72-note equal temperment). *Commissioned by:* Aaron Picht. *First performed:* June 1979;

Institute of Contemporary Art, Boston; Dinosaur Annex concert. Aaron Picht, viola.
Score: reprod. of ms. (version for viola). W
Score: reprod. of ms. (version for violin). NEC
Score: American Composers Alliance (both versions). HU

S9.9 Antimatter: Three Dances for Toby. (1968)
For: tape. Collage; dance music. *Choreography:* Toby Armour. *Commissioned by and dedicated to:* Toby Armour. *First performed:* June 1968; Charles Street Meeting House, Boston. Toby Armour and dancers. *Tape.*

[Arabesques]
S9.10 12 Arabesques.
For: violoncello and piano.
Score & part: American Composers Alliance.

S9.11 Behold Icarus. (1975)
For: tape. Collage; musique concrete; dance music. *Commissioned by:* Johnny Seitz and Carla Montagno. *First performed:* May 1975; Joy of Movement Center, Cambridge, Mass. Johnny Seitz and Carla Montagno, dancers. *Tape.*

S9.12 The Bewties of Fute-Ball [Version 1]. (1974)
For: chorus(children)(5-part), recorders(optional), piano(optional), percussion(optional)(metal idiophones). *Dedicated to:* Lyle Davidson and his class. *First performed:* May 1977; First and Second Church, Boston. Cambridge Chorale; Scott Wheeler, conductor.
Score: American Composers Alliance. HU
Parts: American Composers Alliance.
Reel: recording of first performance.

S9.13 The Bewties of Fute-Ball [Version 2]. (1974)
For: chorus(SSATB), flute(optional), oboe(optional), horn(optional),

trombone(optional), pianos(2)(optional), percussion(optional)(metal idiophones). *Dedicated to:* Lyle Davidson and his class.
Score: American Composers Alliance. HU
Parts: American Composers Alliance.

Bricklayers. *See* 5 Toby Minutes Plus 49.5".

S9.14 Brief Glimpses into Contemporary French Literature. (1958; rev. 1978)
For: Countertenors(4) and piano. *Text:* David Stacton. *Dedicated to:* John Herbert McDowell. *First performed:* 1975 (earlier version), Jan. 16, 1978 (later version); Boston. Dinosaur Annex.
Score: reprod. of ms. NEC
Score: American Composers Alliance. HU
Reel: recording of first performance. WGBH

S9.15 Buechlein for Lyon. (1962)
For: piano. *Dedication:* For the edification, amusement, and instruction of my landlord. *First performed:* 1962; New York City; Music in Our Time Concerts (partial performance). Lawrence H. Smith.
Score: American Composers Alliance. HU

S9.16 Cadence: The Dedication of the Music Room [Version 1] (1976) 30" *For:* piano(4-hands). 1 movement. *Dedicated to:* Rodney and his. *First performed:* Jan. 16, 1978; First and Second Church, Boston; Dinosaur Annex concert. Rodney Lister and Scott Wheeler.
Score: ms. in composer's hand.
Reel: recording of first performance. WGBH
Reel: Jan. 17, 1978; WGBH-FM, Boston; Live Performance Program. Dinosaur Annex. WGBH

S9.17 Cadence: The Dedication of the Music Room [Version

2] (1976) 30" *For:* piano(4-hands). 1 movement. *Dedicated to:* Scott and his. *First performed:* Jan. 16, 1978; First and Second Church, Boston; Dinosaur Annex concert. Rodney Lister and Scott Wheeler.
Score: ms. in composer's hand.
Reel: recording of first performance. WGBH
Reel: Jan. 17, 1978; WGBH-FM, Boston; Live Performance Program. Dinosaur Annex. WGBH

S9.18 Cantata III. (1962)
For: Mezzo Soprano and percussion. Microtonal music (quarter-tones). *Text:* collage. *Commissioned by and dedicated to:* Cathy Berberian.
Score: American Composers Alliance. HU

Cantata 1960. *See* Songs, Tenor and Orchestra.

Cantata on Chinese Poems. *See* Chamber Cantata on Chinese Poems.

S9.19 Cat's Cradle: Incidental Music to the Sacrament according to the Books o Bokonon. (1969)
For: chorus, flutes(2), clarinets(2), trumpet, trombone, percussion. Dance music. *Text:* from *Cat's Cradle* by Kurt Vonnegut. *Commissioned by:* Ina Hahn. *First performed:* 1969; Loeb Drama Center, Harvard University. Ina Hahn Dance Company.
Score: ms.

S9.20 Celebration of Dead Ladies. (1976)
For: voice, flute(alto), basset, clarinet(in A), viola, violoncello, percussion. Microtonal music (18-note scale, 72-note equal temperment). *Text: Song for the Clatter Bones* by James Stephens. *Dedicated to:* Aaron Copland.
Score: American Composers Alliance. HU

S9.21 Chamber Cantata on Chinese Poems. (1954) 8' 45"

For: Tenor, flute, clarinet/clarinet(bass), viola, violoncello, harpsichord or piano. *Text:* Chinese proverbs (anon.) and poems by Wang Wu-Shih, Ch'u Kuang-Hsi, Su Shih, Wang Wei, Su T'ing, Li Po, P'ai Yu Ch'en. *First performed:* 1959; Donnell Library, New York City; Composer's Forum. Earl Rogers, tenor.
Score & parts: Merion. Rental.
Score: American Composers Alliance. HU
Disc: Composers Recordings CRI 186, 1964. Richard Conrad, tenor; Daniel Pinkham, conductor. BU HU HUm MIT NEC T W

S9.22 Chanson d'aventure: Nou Sprinkes the Sprai. (1951; rev. 1975) 3'-4'
For: Tenor and keyboard. *Text:* anon.
First performed: 1951; New Haven, Conn. (earlier version). Robert Mackinnonit, tenor and Albert Fuller, harpsichord. Jan. 1976; First and Second Church, Boston; Dinosaur Annex concert (later version). Raymond Hardin, tenor and Rodney Lister, piano.
Score: American Composers Alliance. HU
Reel: recording of first performance (later version). WGBH
Reel: Jan. 17, 1978; WGBH-FM, Boston; Live Performance Program (later version). Dinosaur Annex concert. Raymond Hardin, tenor and Rodney Lister, piano. WGBH

S9.23 Clement Wenceslaus Lothaire Nepomucene, Prince
Metternich (1773-1859) IN MEMORIAM. (1970) *For:* tape. Collage; musique concrete; dance music. *Choreography: Abalone Co.* Toby Armour.
Commissioned by: Toby Armour. *First performed:* July 1970; Parker 470, Boston. Toby Armour and dancers.
Tape: available from composer.

S9.24 Collage XIII: The Inexcusable. (1977)
For: tape. Dance music. 1 movement.
First performed: Mar. 1977; Illinois Wesleyan University. Jane Plum and dancers.
Tape: available from composer.

S9.25 Come Away. (1978)
For: Mezzo Soprano, flute(alto), clarinet, viola, horn, trombone, double bass. Microtonal music (18-note scale, 72-note equal temperment). *Contents:* Songs and Ayres XXIII (Thomas Campion); Lullaby in The Woman Hater; (Francis Beaumont and John Fletcher); After the Visit (Thomas Hardy); Songs and Ayres XVII (Thomas Campion); Death Carol in When Lilacs Last in the Dooryard Bloomed (Walt Whitman). Supported by a National Endowment for the Arts Composer/Librettist Fellowship. *Dedicated to:* Toby Armour.
First performed: Mar. 1978; Institute of Contemporary Art, Boston. Laurel Stavis, mezzo soprano; members of Dinosaur Annex, Scott Wheeler, conductor.
Score: reprod. of ms. NEC W
Score: American Composers Alliance. HU
Reel: 1980; First and Second Church, Boston. Dinosaur Annex.

[Come Away. Lullaby]
S9.26 Lullaby. (1979)
For: Soprano and viola or violin (2 alternate viola accompaniments, 1 alternatively for violin). Microtonal music (18-note scale, 72-note equal temperament). *Text:* from *The Woman Hater* by John Fletcher. *Dedicated to:* Jean Hakes.
Score: American Composers Alliance. HU

S9.27 Commonplace Book or A Salute to Our American Container Corp. (1969)
For: tape. Musique concrete. *First performed:* Jan. 1973; Museum of Fine Arts, Boston; Music Here and Now.
Tape: available from composer.

[Cradle Songs]
S9.28 Three Cradle Songs. (1958-77)
For: Mezzo Soprano, clarinets(2), guitar. *Text:* traditional. *First performed:* Jan. 16, 1978; First and Second Church,

Boston; Dinosaur Annex concert. Laurel Stavis, mezzo soprano; Diane Heffner and Jennifer Gilman, clarinets; Jan Wissmuller, guitar.
Score: American Composers Alliance. HU
Reel: recording of first performance. WGBH
Reel: Jan. 17, 1978; WGBH-FM, Boston; Live Performance Program; Dinosaur Annex concert. Laurel Stavis, mezzo soprano; Diane Heffner and Jennifer Gilman, clarinets; Jan Wissmuller, guitar. WGBH

Dancers for Toby. *See* Antimatter.

The Dedication of the Music Room. *See* Cadence.

S9.29 Dreams for Sale. (1970)
For: Mezzo Soprano, Baritone, piano.
Text: from *Dreams for Sale, a Commercial Entertainment* by Arthur Williams. *First performed:* Sept. 30, 1979; First and Second Church, Boston; Dinosaur Annex concert. Lorna Cooke deVaron, mezzo soprano; Ezra Sims, baritone; Scott Wheeler, piano.
Score: American Composers Alliance.
Reel: recording of first performance. WGBH

S9.30 The Duchess of Malfi: Toby Armour Her Toy. (1969)
For: tape. Musique concrete; dance music. *Choreography: Loomerie* by Toby Armour. *Commissioned by and dedicated to:* Toby Armour. *First performed:* Aug. 1969; The Cubiculo, New York City. Toby Armour, dancer.
Tape: available from composer.

S9.31 Elegie nach Rilke. (1976) 13'
For: Soprano, flute, clarinet, violin, viola, violoncello. Microtonal music (18-note scale, 72-note temperament).
Text: from *10th Duino Elegy* by Rainer Maria Rilke. *Contents:* ...Oh aber gleich darueber...; Nur die jungen toten...; Aber dort, wo sie wohnen; Und urr, die an steigendes glueck sehnen...

Commissioned by: Goethe Institute (Boston) for Boston Musica Viva.
Dedicated to: The memory of Lois Ginandes. *First performed:* Nov. 16, 1976; Longy School of Music. Elsa Charlston, soprano; Boston Musica Viva, Richard Pittman, conductor.
Score: reprod. of ms. NEC W
Score & parts: American Composers Alliance. HU
Disc: Composers Recordings CRI 377, 1977. Elsa Charliston, soprano; Boston Musica Viva, Richard Pittman, conductor. BU HU MIT NEC W
Reel: recording of first performance. WGBH

S9.32 Elina's Piece.
For: tape. Musique concrete; dance music. *Choreography: Hard Edge* by Elina Mooney. *Commissioned by:* Elina Mooney. *First performed:* Nov. 1970; The Cubiculo, New York City. Elina Mooney and Christopher Beck, dancers.
Tape: available from composer.

S9.33 Ethnic Disco w/Quotes.
For: tape. Dance music. *Commissioned by:* Toby Armour. *First performed:* New England Dinosaur.
Tape: available from composer.

S9.34 5 Toby Minutes Plus 49.5". (1971)
For: tape. Collage; musique concrete; dance music. *Choreography: Bricklayer* Toby Armour. Includes Two Toby Minutes I. *Commissioned by:* Toby Armour. *First performed:* Dec. 1971; Wheelock College. New England Dinosaur. *Tape.*

Flourish. *See* Quartet, Oboe and Strings. Flourish.

[Folksongs]
S9.35 Two Folksongs. (1958) 5' 30"
For: Baritone and piano. *Text:* traditional. *Contents:* Charles Guiteau; Streets of Laredo. *First performed:* 1972; Carnegie Recital Hall, New York City. Robert Kuehn, baritone and

Stephen Mayer, piano.
Score: American Composers Alliance.
HU
Reel: Jan. 16, 1978; First and Second Church, Boston; Dinosaur Annex concert. Gilbert High, baritone and Rodney Lister, piano. WGBH
Reel: Jan. 17, 1978; WGBH-FM, Boston; Live Performance Program: Dinosaur Annex. Gilbert High, baritone and Rodney Lister, piano. WGBH

Fragments of a Garden. *See* After Lyle.

S9.36 A Frank Overture, Four Dented Interludes. And Coda. (1969)
For: tape. Collage; musique concrete; dance music. *Choreography: Spookride* by James Waring. *Commissioned by:* Toby Armour. *First performed:* Mar. 1969; Massachusetts Institute of Technology. Toby Armour and dancers. Included in More Overture and Another Interlude.
Score: American Composers Alliance. HU
Tape: available from composer.

From an Oboe Quartet. *See* Quartet, Oboe and Strings. From an Oboe Quartet.

[Grave Dance, Piano]
S9.37 Grave Dance. (1958) 8'
First performed: 1978; Boston; Dinosaur Annex concert. Rodney Lister.
Score: American Composers Alliance. HU

[Grave Dance, Piano and Strings]
S9.38 Grave Dance. (1975) 8'
For: violins(2), violin or viola, violoncello, piano. *First performed:* Jan 16, 1978; First and Second Church, Boston; Dinosaur Annex concert. Janet Packer and Mary Crowder Hess, violins; David Allcott, viola; Chase Morrison, violoncello; Rodney Lister, piano.
Score & parts: American Composers Alliance. HU
Reel: recording of first performance. WGBH

Reel: Jan. 17, 1978; WGBH-FM, Boston; Live Performance Program: Dinosaur Annex. Janet Packer and Mary Crowder Hess, violins; David Allcott, viola; Chase Morrison, violoncello; Rodney Lister, piano. WGBH

S9.39 Ground Cover. (1972)
For: tape. Collage; musique concrete; dance music. *Choreography:* Toby Armour. *Commissioned by:* Toby Armour. *First performed:* 1972; Theatre for the New City, New York City. Deborah Lee.
Tape: available from composer.

Hard Edge. *See* Elina's Piece.

Hemorrage. *See* --including the--

Homage to Gene Krupa. *See* Summer Piece.

Hopes and Fears. *See* Lion at the Door.

I Breathe When I Sleep. *See* Twenty Years After.

S9.40 In Memoriam Alice Hawthorne. (1963-67) 9' 30"
For: narrator, Tenor, Baritone, horn, clarinets(2)(E-flat), clarinets(contrabass)(2), marimbas(2). Microtonal music (inflections of sixth- and quarter-tones). *Contents:* Introduction and Litany; A Passion; Antiphon and Coda. *Text:* The Gashlycrumb Tinies; The Object Lesson; The Listing Attic, The Nursery Frieze by Edward Gorey. *Dedicated to:* Arthur Williams. *First performed:* 1977; Dinosaur Annex concert. Ezra Sims, narrator; Eric Culver, conductor.
Score: American Composers Alliance. HU
Parts: American Composers Alliance.
Reel: Jan. 16, 1978; First and Second Church, Boston. Lorna Cooke DeVaron, narrator; Dinosaur Annex, Scott Wheeler, conductor. WGBH
Reel: Jan. 17, 1978; WGBH-FM, Boston; Live Performance Program. Ezra Sims,

narrator; Dinosaur Annex, Scott
Wheeler, conductor. WGBH

Incidental Music to the Sacrament
according to the Books
of Bokonon. *See* Cat's Cradle.

S9.41 --including the--
For: tape. Collage; musique concrete;
dance music. *Choreography: Hemorrhage*
by Kevin Dewey. *Commissioned by:*
Kevin Dewey. *First performed:* Nov.
1970; Massachusetts College of Art,
Boston. Goule mecanique.
Tape: available from composer.

The Inexcusable. *See* Collage XIII.

S9.42 Interlope. (1971)
For: tape. Collage; musique concrete;
dance music. *Choreography:* Toby
Armour. *Movements:* Distraction with
Boings; Greater Marches Than These;
And Overtures. *Commissioned by:* Toby
Armour. *First performed:* Dec. 1970;
Parker 470, Boston. New England Dance
Theatre.
Tape: available from composer.

Kubla Khan. *See* Music for the Kubla
Khan of Coleridge, I [-II].

S9.43 Landscape II: 7 July 70 (Parker
470). (1970)
For: tape. Musique concrete; dance
music. *Choreography:* Toby Armour.
Commissioned by: Toby Armour. *First
performed:* July 1970; Parker 470,
Boston. Toby Armour.
Tape: available from composer.

S9.44 Lion at the Door. (1969)
For: voice(medium). Dance music. *Text:*
Vera Nemchinova. *Choreography: Hopes
and Fears* by Aileen Pasloff. *First
performed:* Mar. 1969; Harvard
University. Toby Armour and dancers.

S9.45 Longfellow Sparrow: An Outdoor
Piece for Late Afternoon. (1976)
For: wind ensemble(flutes(5),
clarinets(5), trumpets(3), trombones(3)).

Microtonal music (18-note scale,
72-note temperament). *Commissioned
by:* Cambridge Arts Council.
Score: American Composers Alliance.
HU

Loomerie. *See* The Duchess of Malfi.

Lullaby. *See* Come Away. Lullaby.

S9.46 McDowell's Fault or The Tenth
Sunday after Trinity. (1968)
For: tape. Collage; dance music.
Choreography: Toby Armour.
Commissioned by: Toby Armour.
Dedicated to: John Herbert McDowell.
First performed: Aug. 1968; Second
Church of Boston. Toby Armour and
dancers.
Tape: available from composer.

S9.47 Madame Mim's Work Song.
(1975) 2'
For: Soprano and piano. *Text:* from *The
Sword in the Stone* by T.H. White.
Dedicated to: Toby, Adam and Micaela
Schneider. *First performed:* 1975; Sir
James Matthew Barrie Junior School,
London, England. Rodney Lister,
conductor.
Score: American Composers Alliance.
HU
Reel: 1976; First and Second Church,
Boston. Barbara Winchester, soprano
and Rodney Lister, piano.
Reel: Jan. 16, 1978; First and Second
Church, Boston; Dinosaur Annex
concert. WGBH

S9.48 Masque. (1955)
For: chamber orchestra. Withdrawn.

S9.49 Mass. (1955)
For: chorus(SSAATTBB). *Text:* Proper of
the Latin Mass. *Dedicated to:* Hugh
Thomas.
Vocal score: American Composers
Alliance. HU

S9.50 Midorigaoka. (1978) 15'
For: violins(2), violas(2), violoncello.
Microtonal music(18-note scale, 72-note

temperament). 1 movement.
Commissioned by: Kijima Masataka.
Dedicated to: Kijima Masataka, Oda
Makoto, Mori Kazu, Mizuno Ayako.
First performed: Feb. 1979; Tokyo,
Japan; ISCM Music Days. Noda
Teruyuki, conductor.
Score & parts: American Composers
Alliance. HU
Reel: recording of first performance.

S9.51 More Overture and Another
Interlude. (1970)
For: tape. Collage; musique concrete;
dance music. *Choreography: Spookride
II* by James Waring. 2 movements
(includes A Frank Overture, Four
Dented Interludes. And Coda; and 6
Waltzes by Fryderyck Franciszek
Chopin). *Commissioned by:* Pennsylvania
Ballet. *First performed:* Oct. 1970;
Philadelphia, Pa. Pennsylvania Ballet.
Tape: available from composer.

S9.52 Mugs McGhee's Last Song. (1970)
For: Mezzo Soprano, piano, page
turner. *Text:* from *Dreams for Sale, A
Commercial Entertainment* by Arthur
Williams. *First performed:* Apr. 1970;
The Open Space, New York City.
Arlene Rothlein, mezzo soprano.
Score: American Composers Alliance.
Reel: recording of first performance.
Reel: Jan 16, 1978; First and Second
Church, Boston; Dinosaur Annex
Concert. Lorna Cooke deVaron, mezzo
soprano and Scott Wheeler, piano.

S9.53 Museum Piece. (1972)
For: tape. Collage. *Commissioned by:*
Carol Beckwith. Written as an
accompaniment for display of New
Guinea artifacts collected by Carol
Beckwith and mounted with
photographs made by her, at the
Museum of Fine Arts, Boston, June
1972.
Tape: available from composer.

S9.54 Music for Sakoku. (1963)
For: tape. Musique concrete; incidental
music for the play by Oda Makoto.

Additional instrumental music
composed by Yumi Takahashi.
Commissioned by: NHK-TV, Tokyo,
Japan. *First performed:* Apr. 1963;
NHK-TV, Tokyo, Japan.
Tape: available from composer.

S9.55 Music for the Kubla Khan of
Coleridge, I. (1958)
For: speaker, gamelan, instrumental
ensemble. *Text:* Samuel Taylor
Coleridge.
Score: ms. in composer's hand.

S9.56 Music for the Kubla Khan of
Coleridge, II.
For: speaker and tape. Collage. *Text:*
Samuel Taylor Coleridge.
Tape: available from composer.

S9.57 Music for The Ticklish Acrobat.
(1957)
For: oboe, celeste, xylophone.
Withdrawn.

S9.58 Music for The Trojan Women.
(1955)
For: chamber orchestra. Withdrawn.

S9.59 Musica varia breviculaque sive
Phenomena, ad usum Musicae
Vivae Bostoniensis. (1981) 18' *For:*
flute, clarinet, violin, viola, violoncello.
1 movement. *Commissioned by:* Boston
Musica Viva with a grant from the
Massachusetts Council on the Arts and
Humanities. *Dedicated to:* Elizabeth
Mallinckrodt.
Score & parts: American Composers
Alliance. HU

Nou Sprinkes the Sprai. *See* Chanson
d'aventure.

Now Is the Hour in the Wild Garden
Grown Blessed. *See* Real Toads.

S9.60 Octet for Strings.
For: violins(4), violas(2), violoncellos(2).
Microtonal music (inflections of sixth-
and quarter-tones).
Score & parts: Merion, 1965. HU

An Outdoor Piece for Late Afternoon.
See Longfellow Sparrow.

S9.61 The Owl and the Pussycat. (1975)
For: Bass, harmonica(chromatic),
guitar(electric). Dance music. *Text:* from
the poem by Edward Lear.
Choreography: Toby Armour.
Commissioned by: Cambridge Arts
Council. *First performed:* Dec. 1975;
Massachusetts Institute of Technology.
Mark Kazanoff, bass/chromatic
harmonica; John Lehmann-Haupt, guitar;
New England Dinosaur.
Score: American Composers Alliance.
HU

A Passion. *See* In Memorian Alice
Hawthorne.
Withdrawn as a separate work.

S9.62 Pastorale. (1970)
For: tape. Musique concrete; dance
music. *Choreography:* Toby Armour.
Commissioned by: Toby Armour. *First
performed:* June 1970; The Cubiculo,
New York City. Toby Armour, Bruce de
St. Croix, Jan Houston, dancers.
Tape: available from composer.

Phenomena. *See* Musica varia
breviculaque sive Phenomena, ad usum
Musicae Vivae Bostoniensis.

Prince Metternich (1773-1859) IN
MEMORIAM. *See* Clement Wenceslaus
Lothaire Nepumucene, Prince Metternich
(1773-1859) IN MEMORIAM.

[Quartet, Oboe and Strings]
S9.63 Oboe Quartet. (1971-75)
For: oboe, violin, viola, violoncello.
Movements: Flourish; II Variations; From
an Oboe Quartet.
Score & parts: American Composers
Alliance.

[Quartet, Oboe and Strings. Flourish]
S9.64 Flourish. (1975)
For: oboe, violin, viola, violoncello.
First performed: Mar. 1976; Old South
Meeting House, Boston. Dinosaur

Annex.
Score: American Composers Alliance.
HU
Parts: American Composers Alliance.
Reel: recording of first performance.

[Quartet, Oboe and Strings. From an
Oboe Quartet]
S9.65 From an Oboe Quartet. (1971)
For: oboe, violin, viola, violoncello.
Microtonal music (inflections of sixth-
and quarter-tones). May be performed
alone, or preceded by II Variations, as
II and From an Oboe Quartet.
Dedicated to: Bert Lucarelli. Computer
realization at the Artificial Intelligence
Laboratory, Massachusetts Institute of
Technology, 1971.
Score: American Composers Alliance.
HU NEC
Parts: American Composers Alliance.
Tape: recording of computer realization;
available from composer.

[Quartet, Oboe and Strings. II
Variations]
S9.66 II Variations. (1973)
For: oboe, violin, viola, violoncello.
Microtonal music (18-note scale,
72-note equal temperament). May be
performed alone, or preceding From an
Oboe Quartet, as II and From an Oboe
Quartet. *Dedicated to:* Rodney Lister.
First performed: May 1974; Museum of
Fine Arts, Boston. Ken Roth, oboe;
Janet Packer, violin; David Schreiber,
viola; Deborah Thompson, violoncello.
Score: American Composers Alliance,
1973. HU NEC
Parts: American Composers Alliance.

[Quartet, Strings, No. 1]
S9.67 String Quartet. (1959)
Dedicated to: Quincy Porter. *First
performed:* 1960; New York; Music in
Our Time. Beaux Arts Quartet.
Score & parts: American Composers
Alliance.
Score: reprod. of ms. HU NEC
Reel: 1965; University of Alabama.
Atlanta Symphony Quartet.

Quartet, Strings, No. 2. (1961). *See* Sonate Concertante.

Quartet, Strings, No. 2. (1962). *See* String Quartet, No. 2 (1962).

[Quartet, Strings No. 3] (1962) 25′
S9.68 Third Quartet.
For: string quartet. Microtonal music (quarter-tones). 3 movements. *Commissioned by:* Endicott Memorial Foundation. *Dedicated to:* Lenox Quartet. *First performed:* 1965; Carnegie Recital Hall, New York City. Lenox Quartet.
Score: American Composers Alliance, 1964. HU NEC
Parts: American Composers Alliance, 1964.
Disc: Composers Recordings CRI 223 USD, 1968. Lenox Quartet. BrU BU HU HUm MIT NEC W

S9.69 Real Toads. (1970)
For: tape. Musique concrete; dance music. 1 movement. *Choreography: Now Is the Hour in the Wild Garden Grown Blessed* by Cliff Keuter. *Commissioned by:* Cliff Keuter. *Dedicated to:* Marianne Moore. *First performed:* 1970; Manhattan School of Music. Cliff Keuter and dancers.
Tape: available from composer.

S9.70 Ruminations. (1980) 10′
For: instrument (melody)(3-1/2 octave range). Microtonal music (18-note scale, 72-note equal temperament). 1 movement. *Dedicated to:* Harry Sparnay.
Score: American Composers Alliance.

The Sacrament according to the Books of Bokonon. *See* Cat's Cradle.

Sakoku. *See* Music for Sakoku.

A Salute to Our American Container Corp. *See* Commonplace Book.

A Scale Exercise. *See* String Quartet No.2 (1962). A Scale Exercise.

S9.71 Second Thoughts. (1974)
For: double bass or double basses and tape(optional). Microtonal music (inflections of sixth- and quarter-tones). *Commissioned by:* Alan Nagel. *First performed:* Feb. 1974; New England Conservatory. Alan Nagel and Barbara Schultz, double basses; with double bass trio and tape.
Score: American Composers Alliance.

7 July 70 (Parker 470). *See* Landscape II.

S9.72 Sextet. (1981) 20′
For: clarinet(in A), saxophone(alto), horn, violin, viola, violoncello. Written for Kenneth Radnofsky and the Dinosaur Annex. *Dedicated to:* Margaret Lee Crofts.
Score & parts: American Composers Alliance.

S9.73 Slow Hiccups. (1975)
For: recorders(soprano)(2) or recorders(alto)(2) or instruments (melody)(equal)(2). *First performed:* 1976; Peabody School, Cambridge, Mass. Kathy Matasy and Lawrence Scripp, clarinets.
Score: American Composers Alliance.

S9.74 Slow Hiccups [title printed upside down and backwards] (1975) *For:* recorders(soprano)(2) or recorders(alto)(2) or instruments(melody)(equal)(2). *First performed:* 1976; Peabody School, Cambridge, Mass. Kathy Matasy and Lawrence Scripp, clarinets.
Score: American Composers Alliance. HU

[Sonata, Violoncello and Piano]
S9.75 Sonata. (1957)
1 movement. *First performed:* 1959; Donnell Library, New York City; Composer's Forum. Seymour Barab, violoncello and Gilbert Kalish, piano.
Score & parts: American Composers Alliance. HU

S9.76 Sonate concertante. (1961)
For: oboe, viola, violoncello, double
bass and/or string quartet. Microtonal
music (quarter-tones). *Contents:* 5
Sonatine (for oboe, viola, violoncello,
double bass); 5 Sonate (for string
quartet). Each may be performed
separately. *Dedicated to:* Darius
Milhaud. *First performed:* 1961; New
York City; Music in Our Time. Ralph
Shapey, conductor.
Score: Merion, 1960. HU
Parts: Merion, 1960.
Reel: rehearsal for first performance.

Sonate, String Quartet. *See* Sonate
concertante.

Sonatine, Oboe and Strings. *See* Sonate
concertante.

[Sonatine, Piano]
S9.77 Sonatine. (1957)
3 movements. *Dedicated to:* Emi
Sawada. *First performed:* 1957 or 1958;
KPFA-FM, Berkeley, Calif. James
Workman.
Score: American Composers Alliance,
1961. HU
Reel: Jan. 16, 1978; First and Second
Church, Boston. Scott Wheeler. WGBH

S9.78 Song. (1980)
For: Mezzo Soprano, clarinet, viola.
Microtonal music (18-note scale,
72-note equal temperament). *Text:* W.H.
Auden. *Dedicated to:* Cathy Berberian.
First performed: Mar. 6, 1981;
Somerville Public Library. Mary Ann
Sego, alto; Anne Black, viola; Ian
Greitzer, clarinet.
Score & parts: American Composers
Alliance.
Score: reprod. of ms. NEC
Tape: recording of first performance.

[Songs, Alto and Viola]
S9.79 Five Songs. (1979) 14'
Microtonal music (18-note scale,
72-note equal temperament). *Contents:*
Dirge (Thomas Nashe); To His Winding
Sheet (Robert Herrick); Come, Sleep

(John Fletcher); Recitative (John Ford);
Away, Delights (John Fletcher); Death,
Be Not Proud (John Donne). *Dedication:*
For Janice Meyerson and Aaron Picht.
Score: reprod. of ms. NEC W
Score: American Composers Alliance.
HU

[Songs, Tenor and Orchestra]
S9.80 Three Songs (Cantata 1960).
For: Tenor and
orchestra(2(pic)-2-2(E-flat, bass)-2;
2-2-0-0; glock, vibra; pf; str). *Text:*
from the poems of Andrew Marvell,
Robert Herrick, Ben Jonson. *First
performed:* [1960?], Bennington
College (2nd and 3rd songs). Earl
Rogers, tenor.
Score: American Composers Alliance.
HU

S9.81 Sonia-Piece. (1970)
For: flute and tape. Microtonal music
(quarter-tones). A realization of *The
Composer Game* by John Herbert
McDowell. Written in collaboration with
John Herbert McDowell. *First
performed:* Mar. 1970; Massachusetts
Institute of Technology. Sonia
Guterman, flute.
Score: reprod. of ms.

[Spencer-Lieder]
S9.82 Sieben Spencer-Lieder. (1960)
For: Soprano and keyboard. *Text: Zany
Zoo* by Sylvia Spencer. *First
performed:* 1960; Living Theater, New
York City. Ann Bowers, soprano and
Randolph Mickelson, harpsichord.
Score: American Composers Alliance.
HU

Spookride. *See* A Frank Overture, Four
Dented Interludes. And Coda.

Spookride II. *See* More Overture and
Another Interlude.

S9.83 String Quartet No. 2 (1962)
(1974) 31'
For: flute, clarinet, violin, viola,
violoncello. Microtonal music (18-note

scale, 72-note equal temperament). 5 movements. *Commissioned by:* Boston Musica Viva. *Dedication:* To Nicolas Slonimsky that he (or, rather, Baker's) may be less in error. *First performed:* Feb. 24, 1976; Longy School of Music. Boston Musica Viva, Richard Pittman, conductor.
Score & parts: American Composers Alliance, [197-?]
Score: reprod. of ms. NEC W
Disc: Composers Recording CRI 377, 1977. Boston Musica Viva, Richard Pittman, conductor. BU HU MIT NEC W
Reel: recording of first performance. WGBH
Reel: Oct. 11, 1977. Boston Musica Viva, Richard Pittman, conductor. WGBH

[String Quartet No. 2 (1962). A Scale Exercise]
S9.84 A Scale Exercise for String Quartet No. 2 (1962). (1974)
For: flute, clarinet, violin, viola, violoncello. Microtonal music (18-note scale, 72-note equal temperament).
Score: American Composers Alliance. HU

S9.85 String Quartet No. 2 (1962): A Vade mecum to Its
Scales and Harmonic Organization. (1974) *Text:* reprod. of ms. NEC W
Text: American Composers Alliance.

S9.86 Study. (1972-73)
For: violin, viola, violoncello, in any combination of 1 to 3 instruments, equal or unequal voices. Microtonal music (18-note scale, 72-note equal temperament).
Score: American Composers Alliance. HU

S9.87 Summer Piece: Homage to Gene Krupa. (1970)
For: tape. Musique concrete; dance music. *Choreography:* James Waring. *Dedicated to:* Gene Krupa. *First performed:* 1970; Indian Hill School, Stockbridge, Mass.
Tape: available from composer.

S9.88 Tango Variations. (1971)
For: tape. Collage; musique concrete. *First performed:* Jan. 1973; Museum of Fine Arts, Boston; Music Here and Now.
Tape: available from composer.

S9.89 The Temptations at the Siege of Air and Darkness. (1975)
4 movements. *For:* voices, piano, instruments(unspecified)(optional). *Text:* from *The Sword in the Stone* by T.H. White. *First performed:* May 1975; Heathland School, London, England (4th movement). Rodney Lister, conductor.
Score: American Composers Alliance. HU
Reel: Jan. 16, 1978 (4th movement); First and Second Church, Boston. Dinosaur Annex. WGBH

The Tenth Sunday after Trinity. *See* McDowell's Fault.

S9.90 Thirty Years Later. (1972)
For: tape. Musique concrete.
Commissioned by: James Waring.
Tape: available from composer.

title printed upside down and backwards. *See* Slow Hiccups.

Toby Armour Her Toy. *See* The Duchess of Malfi.

Toby Minutes I[-III]. *See* Two Toby Minutes I[-III]

Toby Minutes Plus 49.5". *See* 5 Toby Minutes Plus 49.5"

S9.91 Le Tombeau d'Albers. (1959)
For: orchestra(2(pic)-2-2(bcl)-2(cbsn); 4-2(in C)-3-1; timp, xylo, sarons; hp; str). 2 movements.
Score: American Composers Alliance. HU

S9.92 Twenty Years After, or I Breathe When I Sleep. (1978) 10'
For: violin and clarinet. Microtonal music (18-note scale, 72-note equal temperament). 1 movement. *Dedication:*

For Janet and Kathy. *First performed:*
Oct. 1978; Institute of Contemporary
Art, Boston. Janet Packer, violin and
Kathy Matasy, clarinet.
Score: reprod. of ms. NEC
Score: American Composers Alliance.
HU
Reel: Sept. 30, 1979; First and Second
Church, Boston; Dinosaur Annex
concert. Janet Packer, violin and Ian
Greitzer, clarinet. WGBH

II and From an Oboe Quartet. *See*
Quartet, Oboe and Strings. II
Variations.

S9.93 Two for One. (1980)
For: violin and viola. Microtonal music
(18-note scale, 72-note equal
temperament). *First performed:* Mar. 6,
1981; Somerville Public Library. Janet
Packer, violin and Anne Black, viola.

S9.94 Two Toby Minutes I. (1971)
For: tape. Collage; musique concrete;
dance music. *Choreography:* Toby
Armour. Included in 5 Toby Minutes
Plus 49.5".

S9.95 Two Toby Minutes II. (1971)
For: tape. Collage; musique concrete;
dance music. *Choreography:* Toby
Armour.

S9.96 Two Toby Minutes III. (1971)
For: tape. Collage; musique concrete;
dance music. *Choreography:* Toby
Armour.

II Variations. *See* Quartet, Oboe and
Strings. II Variations.

Untitled, or After Lyle. *See* After Lyle.

Visions at the Death of Alexander. *See*
Alec.

Waiting for the Moon. *See* When the
Angels Blow Their Trumpets.

S9.97 Wall to Wall. (1972)
For: tape. Collage; musique concrete.

First performed: 1972; Museum of Fine
Arts, Boston; Music Here and Now.
Tape: available from composer.

S9.98 The Walrus and the Carpenter.
(1975)
For: speaker and woodblocks(6). Dance
music. *Text:* from *Alice's Adventures in
Wonderland* by Lewis Carroll.
Choreography: Toby Armour.
Commissioned by: Cambridge Arts
Council. *First performed:* Dec. 1975;
Massachusetts Institute of Technology.
New England Dinosaur.

S9.99 Warts and All. (1969)
For: tape. Collage; dance music.
*Choreography: The Game Man and the
Ladies* by Cliff Keuter. *Commissioned
by:* Cliff Keuter. *First performed:* 1969;
New York City. Cliff Keuter and
dancers.
Tape: available from composer.

S9.100 What God Is Like to Him I
Serve?
For: chorus(SATB). *Text:* Anne
Bradstreet. *Dedicated to:* Hugh Thomas.
First performed: 1976;
Birmingham-Southern College.
Birmingham-Southern College Choir,
Hugh Thomas, conductor.
Vocal score: American Composers
Alliance. HU

S9.101 When the Angels Blow Their
Trumpets: Gospel Song for Three
Actors. (1976) 3'
For: Soprano, Alto, Tenor. Incidental
music for *Waiting for the Moon* by
Arthur Williams. *First performed:* Jan.
1977; Theatre for the New City, New
York City.
Score: American Composers Alliance.
HU
Reel: Jan. 16, 1978; First and Second
Church, Boston; Dinosaur Annex
concert. WGBH

S9.102 Where the Wild Things Are.
(1973)
For: tape. Collage; musique concrete;

dance music. *Choreography:* Toby Armour. *Commissioned by:* New England Dinosaur. *First performed:* Oct. 1973; Wheelock College. New England Dinosaur.
Tape: available from composer.

S9.103 Yr obedt servt. (1977) 10'
For: instrumental ensemble(clarinets(4), violins(2), viola, violoncello, double bass, trombone, guitar, marimbas(2)). 1 movement. *First performed:* Jan. 16, 1978; First and Second Church, Boston. Dinosaur Annex, Scott Wheeler, conductor.
Score & parts: American Composers Alliance.
Reel: recording of first performance. WGBH
Reel: Jan. 17, 1978; WGBH-FM, Boston; Live Performance Program. Dinosaur Annex. WGBH
Cassette: Apr. 10, 1978; New England Conservatory; in *Enchanted Circle.* Dinosaur Annex, Scott Wheeler, conductor. NEC

S9.104 Yr obedt servt II. (1981)
For: clarinets(2), violin, violoncello, chamber orchestra(1(&afl)-0-0-2; 2-0-2-0; mar(2); str(4 or 5-2-1-1)). Microtonal music (18-note scale, 72-note equal temperament). *Dedicated to:* The memory of J.S. (1865-1957).
Score: American Composers Alliance. HU
Parts: American Composers Alliance.

S10 ROBERT B. SIROTA

Born October 13, 1949, in New York City. Moved to Boston area 1973. *Education:* studied composition with Richard Hoffmann, Joseph R. Wood (Oberlin College Conservatory of Music, B.M., 1971); Leon Kirchner, Earl Kim (Harvard University, Ph.D., 1979); Nadia Boulanger. *Awards:* Long Island Composers' Alliance Competition (Winner, 1973), WGBH-Boston Musica Viva Recording Prize (1979), Holtkamp International Organ Composition Competition (Honorable Mention, 1979),

National Endowment for the Arts Composer/Librettist Fellowship (1980), Watson Foundation Grant. *Related activities:* currently on the faculty of Boston University and Director, Young Artist Composers Program, Boston University Tanglewood Institute. BU

WORKS

Adagio. *See* Scherzo and Adagio.

S10.1 Bontshe the Silent. (1978) 40'
For: Mezzo Soprano, Bass, chamber orchestra(1(pic)-1(Ehn)-1(bcl)-1(cbsn); 1-1-1-0; perc(2); hp, pf; str(1-1-1-1-1)). Chamber opera in 3 scenes. *Libretto:* Robert Burns Shaw from the story by Isaac Loeb Peretz. Thesis, Harvard University, 1979. Winner of National Endowment for the Arts Composer/Librettist Fellowship (1980). *First performed:* Feb. 27, 1980; Boston University. Sondra Gelb, mezzo soprano; Stephen Hicks, bass; ensemble from the Boston University Collegium in Contemporary Music, Robert Sirota, conductor.
Score: ms. in composer's hand. HU
Reel: recording of first performance. BU

Chorale Preludes. *See* Lenten Chorale Preludes.

S10.2 Concerto for Saxophone. (1981) 20'
For: saxophone and orchestra(2-2-2(&bcl2)-2(&cbsn); 3-2-2-1; perc(2); hp; str). *Commissioned by and dedicated to:* Rikki Stone.
Score: ms. in composer's hand.

S10.3 Concerto Grosso. (1981) 12'
For: chamber orchestra(1(pic/afl)-1(Ehn)-1-1; 1-1-1-0; perc; pf; str(1-0-1-1-1)). 1 movement. *Commissioned by:* Alea III. *Dedicated to:* Theodore Antoniou. *Score & parts.*

S10.4 Epigrams. (1972) 11'
For: flute. 9 movements. *Dedicated to:* Lynn Schubert. *First performed:* May 7,

1972; Oberlin, Ohio. Lynn Schubert.
Score: ms. in composer's hand.
Reel: Feb. 27, 1980; Boston University;
in *Composers' Profile Concert.* Rose Ann
Dennison.

Etudes. *See* Pieces, Piano.

S10.5 Fantasy. (1975) 9'
For: violoncello and piano. Winner of
WGBH-Boston Musica Viva Recording
Prize (1979). *Dedicated to:* Norman
Fischer. *First performed:* May 22, 1976;
Harvard University. Norman Fischer,
violoncello and Robert Sirota, piano.
Score: ms. in composer's hand.
Tape: WGBH.

S10.6 Gloria. (1972) 12'
For: chorus and chamber
orchestra(2-2(&Ehn)-1-1; 2-2-1-0; timp;
pf; str). Winner of Long Island
Composers' Alliance Competition, 1973.
Dedicated to: Nadia Boulanger. *First
performed:* Mar. 2, 1974; Huntington,
N.Y. Nassau Community College Select
Choir; Huntington Symphony Orchestra,
Seymour Lipkin, conductor.
Score: ms. in composer's hand.

S10.7 Jeux. (1974) 6'
For: organ(3-manual). 4 movements.
First performed: Apr. 6, 1974;
Memorial Church, Harvard University.
Victoria R. Sirota.
Score: ms. in composer's hand.

[Lenten Chorale Preludes]
S10.8 Two Lenten Chorale Preludes.
(1978-79) 9'
For: organ. *Movements:* Herzliebster
Jesu; An Wasserfluessen Babylon. *First
performed:* Mar. 25, 1979; East
Northport, N.Y. Victoria R. Sirota.
Score: ms. in composer's hand.

S10.9 Night Echoes I. (1974) 6'
For: organs(2). *Commissioned by:* Trinity
Church, Boston. *First performed:* Nov.
25, 1974; Trinity Church, Boston.
Victoria R. Sirota.
Score: ms. in composer's hand.

S10.9.5 Night Echoes II. (1975) 7'
For: organ and tape(pre-recorded
organ). 4 movements. *First performed:*
Aug. 13, 1975; Methuen, Mass. Victoria
R. Sirota.
Score: ms. in composer's hand.

[Pieces, Organ]
S10.10 Four Pieces for Organ. (1975) 7'
4 movements. *Commissioned by:*
Bozeman-Gibson and Co. Organ
Builders. *First performed:* June 1, 1975;
East Northport, N.Y. Victoria R. Sirota.
Score: ms. in composer's hand.

[Pieces, Piano]
S10.11 Three Pieces for Piano.
(1973-79) 12'
First performed: Apr. 18, 1979;
Portsmouth, N.H. Robert Sirota.
Score: ms. in composer's hand.
Reel: Dec. 1, 1976; Boston University
(titled Two Etudes). Robert Sirota. BU

S10.12 Prelude for Harpsichord. (1981)
3'
1 movement. *Dedicated to:* Lauren
Shohet. *First performed:* Mar. 5, 1981;
Concord, Mass. Lauren Shohet. *Score.*

[Quartet, Strings]
S10.13 String Quartet. (1980) 14'
2 movements. *First performed:* Apr. 23,
1980; Brookline Library, Brookline,
Mass.
Score: ms. in composer's hand.

S10.14 Scherzo and Adagio. (1980) 14'
For: string orchestra or string quartet.
Commissioned by: Chamber Orchestra
of the Commonwealth. *First performed:*
Feb. 15, 1980; Longy School of Music.
Chamber Orchestra of the
Commonwealth, Roger Davidson,
conductor.
Score: ms. in composer's hand.
Reel: Feb. 27, 1980; Boston University
(Scherzo). Alexander Romanul and Brett
Allen, violins; George Pascal, viola;
Michael Romanul, violoncello. BU

S10.15 Songs and Spells. (1981) 19'
For: chorus and instrumental
ensemble(flute/piccolo, oboe, clarinet,
bassoon, horn, trumpet, trombone,
percussion(2), piano, violins(2), double
bass). *Text:* William Shakespeare. *First
performed:* Aug. 21, 1981; Berkshire
Music Center, Lenox, Mass. Leonard
Atherton, conductor.
Score: ms. in composer's hand.

S10.16 Toccata. (1979) 8'
For: organ(3-manual). Received
Honorable Mention, Holtkamp
International Organ Composition
Competition (1979). *First performed:*
Feb. 18, 1979; Old West Church,
Boston. Victoria R. Sirota.
Score: ms. in composer's hand.

S11 LEO SNYDER

Born January 1, 1918, in Boston.
Education: studied composition with
Francis Judd Cooke (New England
Conservatory, B.M., M.M). *Related
activities:* pianist; lecturer; critic for
WBUR-FM, WBCN-FM, *Listen Magazine*;
member of the editorial board of
Opera Guide, Boston; served on the
faculties of New England Conservatory
(1952-56), Boston University (1956-67),
Northeastern University (1967-). NU

WORKS

S11.1 The Book of Americans. 60'
For: chorus and chamber orchestra.
Children's opera or cantata; contents
may be presented individually or in
various combinations. *Text:* Rosemary
Carr Benet and Stephen Vincent Benet.
Contents: Colonial Times; Revolutionary
Times; The Time of Lincoln; Expansion
by Land and Sea.
Vocal score: Leeds, 1962. NEC NU

S11.2 The End Is Coming.
For: Tenor, trumpet, horn, trombone.
Text: Thomas Carey and Leo Snyder.
Written for the Northeastern University
Brass Trio. *First performed:* summer,

1981. Peter Cody, tenor; Northeastern
University Brass Trio.

S11.3 Love Is a Language.
For: Soprano and piano. Song cycle.
Text: poems by Norma Farber. *First
performed:* Oct. 1980; Northeastern
University. Elena Gambulos, soprano
and Donald Palumbo, piano.
Disc: Sounds of Northeastern, 1981.
Elena Gambulos, soprano and Donald
Palumbo, piano.

S11.4 Overture 200.
For: chamber orchestra. Sponsored in
part by Northeastern University and the
City of Boston. *First performed:*
Northeastern University. Northeastern
University Symphony Orchestra, David
Sonnenschein, conductor.

S11.5 Permutations. (1980)
For: flute and piano. Suite. *Movements:*
Chaconne; Quasi di Lontano; Caprice.
Dedicated to: Robin Hendrich. *First
performed:* Mar. 5, 1981; Northeastern
University. Robin Hendrich, flute and
Henry Weinberger, piano.

S11.6 The Princess Marries the Page.
For: Soprano,. Tenor, Baritones(2),
chamber chorus, chamber orchestra,
piano. Opera in 2 acts. *Text:* Edna St.
Vincent Millay. *First performed:* May
1979; Northeastern University. Elena
Gambulos, soprano; Wayne Rivera,
tenor; Robert Honeysucker and Rene de
La Garza, baritones; unidentified
chamber chorus and orchestra; William
Merrill, piano; Donald Palumbo,
conductor.

S12 JOHN STEWART

Born November 27, 1945, in Dothan,
Ala. Moved to Boston area 1964.
Education: University of New Mexico
(1962-64); studied composition with
Robert Cogan (New England
Conservatory, B.M., 1968); Earl Kim,
Leon Kirchner (Harvard University, M.A.,
1972); Lukas Foss; conducting with
Frederick Prausnitz, John R. Ferris,

John Aldis, Eric Ericson, Norman Luboff; piano with Leo Juffer and Luise Vosgerchian; voice with Joan Heller. *Related activities:* served on the faculties of various music schools in the Boston area; choral director, Concord Academy (1973-77); composer-in-residence, Charles River Creative Arts Program, Dover, Mass. (1975-76); member of the faculty of the New England Conservatory (1977-). NEC

WORKS

S12.1 Apollonius of Tyana: A Dance, with Some Words. (1977) 30'
For: woodwind quintet and actors(2). Dance music. 12 movements. *Text:* after Charles Olson. *Commissioned by and dedicated to:* Cantilena Quartet. *First performed:* 1977; Concord Academy. Cantilena Quartet.
Cassette: Apr. 9, 1979; New England Conservatory; in *The Enchanted Circle* (concert version). Cantilena Quintet. NEC

S12.2 Chamber Piece I. (1963) 12'
For: English horn, viola, string quartet. 1 movement. *First performed:* 1963; Albuquerque, N.M.
Score & parts: reprod. of ms.

S12.3 Chamber Piece II. (1968) 15'
For: violin, clarinet, violoncello, horn. 1 movement. *First performed:* 1969; Harvard University.
Score & parts: reprod. of ms.

[D.H. Lawrence Songs]
S12.4 Three D.H. Lawrence Songs. (1979) 5'
For: voices(2)(equal or unequal), or chorus(mixed), or chorus(SA) or chorus(TB). Optional instrumental doubling of the performer's choosing; score presents two parts, from which the above possibilities are only suggestions. Aleatoric music. 3 movements.
Score: reprod. of ms.

S12.5 Four-Hands. (1970)
For: piano(4-hands). 1 movement. *First performed:* 1970; Harvard University.
Score: ms. in composer's hand.

S12.6 Meeting. (1965) 5'
For: Soprano or Tenor and piano. Song cycle. 2 movements. *Text:* Stephen Spender. *First performed:* 1965; Jordan Hall, Boston. Richard Conrad, tenor and Carl Davis, piano.
Cassette: Nov. 15, 1978; New England Conservatory. Joan Heller, soprano and John Felice, piano. NEC

S12.7 Pie Jesu. (1964)
For: chorus(SATB). *Text:* liturgical. *First performed:* 1971; Harvard University. Harvard Graduate Chorale, Gerald Moshell, conductor.
Vocal score: reprod. of ms.

S12.8 Pieces. (1966) 9'
For: oboe, viola, guitar. 3 movements. *First performed:* 1966. New England Conservatory. Robert Deutsch, oboe; unidentified violist; Robert Paul Sullivan, guitar.
Score: reprod. of ms.

S12.9 Responsibilities. (1971) 10'
For: Baritone, piano, violoncello, horn, guitar. Song cycle. 1 movement. *Text: A First Confession* and *Responsibilities* by William Butler Yeats. *First performed:* 1971; Harvard University.

S12.10 Song of the Musicians. (1971; rev. 1979) 6'
For: Soprano, flute, flute(alto), guitar or Soprano and piano. *Text:* from the play *Calvary* by William Butler Yeats. Version for soprano and piano recomposed from version for soprano, flutes, guitar. *First performed:* 1980; New England Conservatory. Paula Messac, soprano and Todd C. Gordon, piano.

S12.11 The Windhover. (1971) 10'
For: chorus(mixed), woodwind quintet, trumpet, trombone, double bass. 1

movement. *Text:* Gerard Manley Hopkins. Master's thesis, Harvard University, 1972. *First performed:* 1971; Harvard University. Harvard Graduate Chorale.
Score: reprod. of ms. HU

S13 TISON STREET

Born May 20, 1943, in Boston, Mass. *Education:* studied composition with David Del Tredici and Leon Kirchner (Harvard University, B.A., M.A.). *Awards:* John Knowles Paine Travelling Fellowship (Harvard University, 1965-66), Naumburg Recording Award (1972), National Institute of Arts and Letters Award (1973), Rome Prize Fellowship (American Academy in Rome, 1973), Massachusetts Council on the Arts and Humanities, Artist Fellowship Program (1977), National Endowment for the Arts Grant (1978), Brandeis University, Creative Arts Award (1979), Guggenheim Grant (1981), Fromm Foundation commission, Kindler Foundation commission, Koussevitzky Music Foundation (Library of Congress) commission. *Related activities:* violinist; composer-in-residence, Marlboro Music Festival (1964-66, 1972); member of the faculty of Harvard University (1979-). HU

WORKS

S13.1 Adagio in E-Flat. (1977) 14'
For: oboe and string orchestra(8-8-6-4-2).
Score & parts: Associated, 1980.
Pf. red: Associated.

S13.2 Arias. (1978) 13'
For: violin and piano.
Score & part: available from composer.

S13.3 Chords from the Northeast. (1976) 10'
For: piano.
Score: available from composer.

Come, Holy Spirit. *See* Sacred Anthems.

S13.4 Gradus ad Parnassum. (1976) 2'
For: piano.
Score: available from composer.

S13.5 John Major's Medley. (1977) 13'
For: guitar.
Score: available from composer.

Leave, Then, Thy Foolish Ranges. *See* Sacred Anthems.

S13.6 Montsalvat. (1980) 8'
For: orchestra(2-2-2-2; 2-2-2-0; perc(2), glock, vibra; hp; str).
Score & parts: available from composer.

Nearer, My God to Thee. *See* Sacred Anthems.

S13.7 Odds and Ends from So Much Depends: a Collection of Pieces and Songs. (1963-72) 16'
For: Soprano, Tenor, piano, string quartet. *Contents:* The Red Wheelbarrow (William Carlos Williams); My Country, 'Tis of Thee; He Who Hath Glory Lost (James Joyce); Threefold Amen.
Score & parts: available from composer.

[Pieces]
S13.8 Three Pieces. (1977) 8'
For: viols(4)(treble(2), tenor, bass) and harpsichord(2-manual).
Score & parts: available from composer.

[Quartet, Strings]
S13.9 String Quartet, 1972. (1972) 11' 45"
1 movement. *Dedicated to:* Leon Kirchner. *First performed:* Mar. 26, 1973; Sanders Theatre Harvard University. Composers String Quartet. Recipient of Naumburg Recording Award, 1972 and Rome Prize Fellowship (American Academy in Rome), 1973.
Study score: G. Schirmer, 1974. BrU BU HU MIT
Parts: G. Schirmer.

Disc: Composers Recordings CRI SD 305, 1973. Concord String Quartet. BrU BU HU MIT NEC W

[Quintet, Strings]
S13.10 String Quintet, 1974. (1974) 12' 30"
For: violins(2), violas(2), violoncello.
Commissioned by: Fromm Foundation in conjunction with the Berkshire Music Center, Tanglewood. *First performed:* summer, 1974; Berkshire Music Center, Tanglewood.
Music: G. Schirmer.
Disc: Composers Recordings CRI SD 381, 1977. Concord String Quartet and Marcus Thompson, viola. BrU BU HU MIT NEC W

[Sacred Anthems]
S13.11 Three Sacred Anthems. (1973)
For: chorus. *Contents:* Come, Holy Spirit; Leave, Then, Thy Foolish Ranges; Nearer, My God to Thee.
Vocal score: G. Schirmer, 1974 (also issued separately).

[Trio, Strings]
S13.12 String Trio. (1963) 8'
For: violin, viola, violoncello. 1 movement.
Score & parts: available from composer.
Reel: Apr. 5, 1976; Boston University. Joseph Silverstein, violin; Walter Trampler, viola; Leslie Parnas, violoncello. BU

S13.13 Variations. (1964) 7'
For: flute, guitar, violoncello. Theme and 5 variations. Master's thesis, Harvard University, 1971. *Dedication:* In memoriam V.P.
Score & parts: G. Schirmer, 1977. MIT NEC
Score: reprod. of ms. HU.

S13.14 Variations on a Ground. (1981) 12'
For: organ and orchestra(2-2-2-2; 0-3-0-0; timp(2); str).

Score & parts: available from composer.

S14 MARIE STULTZ

Born April 13, 1945, in San Antonio, Tex. *Education:* B.M.E., M.M. (Southern Methodist University, 1967, 1972); studied composition with Robert Sirota (Boston University) and John Heiss (New England Conservatory). *Related activities:* founder of the North Parrish Treble Chorus; music director, North Parrish Choral Society; currently co-music director, The Old North Church, Marblehead, Mass. and voice instructor. W

WORKS

S14.1 Fireside Amusements. (1980) 10'
For: chorus(SA), flute, piano. *Text:* nursery rhymes. *Contents:* The Man in the Moon; Horseshoe Nail; Old Mother Goose. *Dedicated to:* Jacquelyn, Valerie and Melissa Forgione. *First performed:* Apr. 1980; John T. Berry Rehabilitation Center, North Reading, Mass. North Parrish Treble Chorus.
Score: reprod. of ms. W
Reel: recording of first performance (Nos. 1 and 3). W

[Japanese Lyrics]
S14.2 Three Japanese Lyrics. (in progress) 10'
For: Bass and harp. *Text:* Grace James. *Contents:* Music of My Lute; The Little House; The Wine Is Sweet.
Commissioned by and dedicated to: Daniel Pantano.
Music: ms.

S14.3 King Jesus Is Born. (1979) 4'
For: chorus(children)(SA) and piano. Anthem. *Text:* Marie Stultz.
Commissioned by: North Parrish Choral Society for the fifth anniversary of the Treble Chorus. *Dedicated to:* North Parrish Treble Chorus. *First performed:* Dec. 1979; Andover, Mass. North Parrish Treble Chorus.

Vocal score: reprod. of ms. W
Parts: available from composer. Rental.

S14.4 Missa illuminare. (in progress)
For: chorus(SATB). Mass. *Dedicated to:*
Barbara Bruns, St. Michael's Church.
Sketches: ms.

S14.5 Nancy Girl. (1980) 3'
For: chorus(SATB). *Text:* nursery rhyme.
Dedicated to: Nancy Ferretti. *First
performed:* Apr. 1980; John T. Berry
Rehabilitation Center, North Reading,
Mass. North Parrish Choral Society.
Vocal score: reprod. of ms. W
Reel: recording of first performance.

S14.6 Serenade: The Silver Swan. (in
progress)
For: clarinet and organ. *Movements:*
Dusk; The Lover's Meet and on the
Streets; The Dance; The Frustration of
Parting; The Peace of Dawn as the
Lovers Remain. *Dedicated to:* Richard
Stultz and Kathy Rideout.
Score: ms.; available from composer.
Rental.

Some Say That Ever 'gainst that
Season. *See* Winter on Avon. Some
Say That Ever 'gainst that Season.

S14.7 Song of Jubilation. (1980) 6'
For: chorus(SATB), voices(treble) or
Soprano, organ. Motet. *Text:* adapted
from the Bible, N.T., Matthew.
Commissioned by: Old North Church,
Marblehead, Mass. *Dedicated to:* Dr.
Randall Niehoff and the Old North
Church. *First performed:* Apr. 12, 1981;
Old North Church, Marblehead, Mass.
Old North Church Junior and Senior
Choirs.
Vocal score: reprod. of ms. W

S14.8 Suite Nativitaet. (1980) 14'
For: chorus(SATB), chorus(SA),
instrumental ensemble(flute, oboe,
clarinet, timpani, chimes, triangle,
strings(5-part)). Text: 14th and 15th
century German carol tunes.
Movements: Maria durch ein Dornwald
ging; Wachet auf; Susani; O laufet ihr

Hirten; Quem pastores Laudavere;
Gloria. *Commissioned by:* North Parrish
Choral Society for a performance
funded by the Massachusetts Council
on the Arts and Humanities. *Dedicated
to:* The Reverend Dennis and Karin
Kohl. *First performed:* Dec. 7, 1980;
South Church, Andover, Mass. North
Parrish Choral Society and North
Parrish Treble Chorus.
Score & parts: reprod. of ms.; available
from composer. Rental.
Study score: reprod. of ms.; available
from composer. Rental.
Vocal score: reprod. of ms.; available
from composer. Rental.
Tape: recording of first performance.
Tape: Dec. 14, 1980; St. Margaret's
Church, Burlington, Mass. North Parrish
Choral Society and North Parrish
Treble Chorus.

S14.9 The Tethered Colt. (1980) 15'
For: chorus(unison) and piano. Operetta
in 1 act. *Text:* Marie Stultz.
Commissioned by: Old North Church,
Marblehead, Mass. *Dedicated to:* Old
North Church Junior Choir. *First
performed:* 1980; Old North Church,
Marblehead, Mass. Old North Church
Junior Choir.
Vocal score: reprod. of ms.; available
from composer. Rental.
Cassette: recording of first
performance.

[The Tethered Colt; Arr]
S14.10 The Tethered Colt. (1980) 15'
For: voices(treble)(2),
chorus(children)(2-part), piano. Operetta
in 1 act. *Text:* Marie Stultz. *First
performed:* April 12, 1981; Marblehead,
Mass. St. Michael's Church Youth Choir.
Vocal score: reprod. of ms. available
from composer. Rental.

S14.11 Winter on Avon. (in progress)
25'
For: Soprano, Tenor, Bass,
chorus(SATB), instrumental
ensemble(flute, oboe, clarinet, bassoon,
harp, timpani, strings(5-part)). Cantata.
Text: William Shakespeare. *Movements:*

Prologue; Who Sees His True Love;
Under the Greenwood Tree; Some Say
That Ever 'gainst that Season; Greasy
Joan; The Winter Wind. *Dedicated to:*
Hart and Carol Leavitt. *First performed:*
Dec. 13, 1981; Winchester, Mass. North
Parrish Choral Society.
Score & parts: ms.; available from
composer. Rental.
Vocal score: ms.; available from
composer. Rental.

[Winter on Avon. Some Say That
Ever 'gainst that Season]
S14.12 Some Say That Ever 'gainst
that Season.
For: chorus(SATB). Cantata excerpt.
Text: William Shakespeare.
Vocal score: reprod. of ms. W

S14.13 The Worthy Gift. (1980) 15'
For: voices, chorus(SA), trumpets(2),
recorders(2), harpsichord, viola da
gamba, bells, hand drum, finger
cymbals. Operetta in 2 acts. *Libretto:*
based on the story *Why the Chimes
Ring*; 15th century carols; *The Play of
Herod*. *Commissioned by:* Old North
Church, Marblehead, Mass. *Dedicated to:*
The Junior Choir, Old North Church.
First performed: Dec. 23, 1980;
Marblehead, Mass. Old North Church
Junior Choir.
Score & parts: reprod. of ms; available
from composer.
Chorus parts: reprod. of ms.; available
from composer.

ARRANGEMENTS OF WORKS BY OTHER COMPOSERS

S14.14 Lo, How a Rose E'er Blooming.
(1979) 3'
For: chorus(SA) and piano. Christmas
music. *Text:* traditional. Original by
Michael Praetorius. *Dedicated to:* North
Parrish Treble Chorus. *First performed:*
Dec. 1979; South Church, Andover,
Mass. North Parrish Treble Chorus,
Richard Stultz, piano.
Vocal score: reprod. of ms.; available
from composer. Rental.

Cassette: recording of first
performance; available from composer.

S14.15 Magnificat. (1979) 9'
For: chorus(SATB), trumpets(2),
harpsichord, strings(5-part). Original by
Johann Pachelbel.
Score & parts: reprod. of ms.; available
from composer.
Choral parts: Presser.

S14.16 Remember O Thou Man. (1978)
8'
For: chorus(SATB), chorus(SA),
recorders(2) or flutes(2), regal or organ,
hand drum, strings(4-part). Original by
Thomas Ravenscroft. *First performed:*
Dec. 1978; St. Theresa's Church, North
Reading, Mass. North Parrish Choral
Society and North Parrish Treble
Chorus.
Score: reprod. of ms.; available from
composer. Rental.
Reel: recording of first performance.

S14.17 Wachet auf. (1979) 5'
For: chorus(SA) and strings(5-part).
Text: traditional. Original by attributed
to Philipp Nicolai. *First performed:*
Dec. 1979; North Reading, Mass. North
Parrish Treble Chorus.
Vocal score & parts: reprod. of ms.;
available from composer.

S15 DONALD SUR

Born February 1, 1935, in Honolulu,
Hawaii. Moved to Boston area 1968.
Education: studied composition with
Seymour Shifrin (University of
California, Berkeley, A.B., 1956); Earl
Kim, Roger Sessions (Princeton
University, M.F.A., 1962); Colin McPhee
(University of California, Los Angeles),
Earl Kim (Harvard University, Ph.D.,
1972). *Awards:* Ford Foundation Grant
for study of Asian music (1965),
Bohemians Prize (New York Musicians
Club, Harvard University, 1969),
National Endowment for the Humanities
Grants (1976, 1978), Old Dominion
Award (Massachusetts Institute of

Technology, 1972), Van Deiman Foundation (University of Toronto) grant. *Related activities:* served on the faculty of the Massachusetts Institute of Technology (1971-74). HU

WORKS

[Bagatelles]
S15.1 Five Bagatelles. (1957) 5'
For: piano. 5 movements. *First performed:* 1961; Princeton, N.J. Phyllis Rappeport.
Score: Composers Collaborative, 1981. Rental.

S15.2 Catena I. (1961) 3' 30"
For: flute, mandolin, marimba, bongos. 1 movement. *First performed:* 1961; Princeton, N.J.
Score & parts: Composers Collaborative, 1981. Rental.
Cassette: Oct. 30, 1976; New England Conservatory; in *ISCM World Music Days, 1976.* Collage. NEC

S15.3 Catena II. (1962) 2'
For: flute, mandolin, viola, bongos. 1 movement. *First performed:* 1962; Princeton, N.J.
Score & parts: Composers Collaborative, 1981. Rental.
Cassette: Oct. 30, 1976; New England Conservatory; in *ISCM World Music Days, 1976.* Collage. NEC

S15.4 Catena III. (1976) 7'
For: flute, clarinet(bass), violin, violoncello, percussion(2). 1 movement. *Commissioned by:* National Endowment for the Arts. *Dedicated to:* Nicola LeFanu. *First performed:* Feb. 1, 1976; Jordan Hall, Boston. Collage.
Score & parts: Composers Collaborative, 1976. Rental.
Cassette: Oct. 30, 1976; New England Conservatory; in *ISCM World Music Days, 1976.* Collage. NEC

Interval Forms. *See* Piano Fragments.

[Intonations]
S15.5 Two Intonations. (1975) 7'

For: piccolo, oboe, concertina, cimbalom, violas(3), violoncello, percussion. 2 movements. *First performed:* 1975; Sanders Theatre, Harvard University. Speculum Musicae.
Score & parts: Composers Collaborative, 1981. Rental.

S15.6 Piano Fragments. (1966) 7'
For: piano. 15 movements. Winner of the Bohemians Prize (New York Musicians Club, Harvard University, 1969). *First performed:* 1967; Seoul, Korea. Chung-Haing Lee. Originally titled Interval Forms. Written under pseudonym Eternal Gloves.
Score: Composers Collaborative, 1981. Rental.

S15.7 Raindrops under the Eaves. (1965) 7'
For: percussion(Korean). 1 movement. *First performed:* 1965; Seoul, Korea. Members of the Korean Classical Music Institute.
Score & parts: Composers Collaborative, 1981. Rental.

S15.8 Red Dust. (1967) 15'
For: percussion(27 instruments), conch, trumpet(Korean). *First performed:* 1967; Seoul, Korea. Members of the Korean Classical Music Institute and KBS Orchestra.
Score & parts: Composers Collaborative, 1981. Rental.

S15.9 The Sleepwalker's Ballad; an Accompanied Recitative. (1962-72) 20'
For: Soprano and instrumental ensemble(flute/piccolo, oboe, clarinet, clarinet(E-flat), contrabassoon, horn, percussion(2)(marimba, vibraphone, bongos, maracas, claves, quijada(jawbone or LP vibra-slap), skillet(small cast-iron skillet struck with hardwood mallets), guiro, ilukere(African horsetail swisher), cowbell), harpsichord, violin, viola, violoncello. 1 movement. *Text:* Federico Garcia Lorca (translated by Stephen Spender and J.L. Gili). Doctoral thesis, Harvard University, 1972. *First*

performed: 1972; Massachusetts Institute of Technology. Bethany Beardslee, soprano and Speculum Musicae.
Score: HU
Score & parts: Composers Collaborative, 1981. Rental.

S15.10 Symbols. (1954) 2′ 38″
For: voice(high) and piano. *Text:* William Butler Yeats. *Contents:* Parnell; Gratitude to the Unknown Instructors; Symbols; Three Movements. Song cycle.
Score: ms. in composer's hand.

S15.11 Il Tango de Trastevere. (1977) 7′
For: double basses(4). 1 movement. *Commissioned by:* National Endowment for the Arts. *Dedicated to:* Donald Palma and Pat Tabors. *First performed:* 1977; Minneapolis, Minn. Times Square Basstet.
Score & parts: Composers Collaborative, 1978. Rental.

T1 PASQUALE TASSONE

Born April 21, 1949, in Italy. Moved to Boston area 1958. *Education:* B.M.Ed. (Lowell University, 1972); Accademia Musicale Chigiana, Siena, Italy (1981); studied composition with John Adams, Hugo Norden (Boston Conservatory, 1978); Sandro Gorli, Giacomo Manzoni (Conservatorio di Musica G. Verdi, Milan, Italy, 1981); Franco Donatoni. *Awards:* Harvey Gaul Composition Contest (First Prize, 1978), New Music for Young Ensembles Contest (Honorable Mention, 1979). *Related activities:* teacher, Arlington, Mass. public schools. BCM

WORKS

T1.1 An American Ritual. (1978) 5′
For: orchestra(2(&pic)-2(&Ehn)-2-2; 4-2-2-1; timp, perc, vibra; str). 1 movement. Written for Arlington High School Orchestra. *First performed:* Apr.

1978; University of Massachusetts, Amherst; in Massachusetts State Conference of Music Educators. Arlington High School Chamber Orchestra.
Score: reprod. of ms.
Cassette: available from composer.

T1.2 Chroma. (1979) 11′
For: band. 1 movement. *First performed:* May 1979; Massachusetts Institute of Technology. MIT Concert Band, John Corley, conductor.
Score: reprod. of ms.
Cassette: available from composer.

T1.3 Dialogue. (1977) 4′
For: wind quintet. 1 movement. *First performed:* May 1978;· Boston Conservatory.
Score: reprod. of ms. BCM
Cassette: available from composer.

T1.4 Folksong Overture (for Young Players). (1980) 5′
For: orchestra(2-1-2-1; 2-2-2-1; perc, pf(optional); str(0-0-0-0-0)). *First performed:* Arlington public school orchestra.
Score & parts: Kendor, 1980.

T1.5 Mass in Honor of St. Ann. (1976)
Commissioned by: St. Ann's Choir, Littleton, Mass. *First performed:* May 1976; St. Ann's Church, Littleton, Mass.
Score: reprod. of ms.
Cassette: available from composer.

T1.6 Passacaglia (for Young Players). (1977) 3′-4′
For: orchestra(2-1-2-0; 2-2-2-1; timp, perc(optional); str). 1 movement. *First performed:* Apr. 1978. Arlington public school orchestra.
Score & parts: Kendor, 1978.

T1.7 Piaculi poenae.
For: band. Withdrawn.

T1.8 Projections.
For: band. Withdrawn.

T1.9 Psalm 21: Unto Thee Lift I up My Eyes. (1978) 5'
For: chorus(SATB). First prize, Harvey Gaul Composition Contest, 1978.
Vocal score: reprod. of ms.

T1.10 Psalm 123.
For: chorus and organ or piano. Withdrawn.

T1.11 Scambio. (1979) 5'
For: saxophone(alto) and piano. 1 movement.
Score: reprod. of ms.
Cassette: available from composer.

T1.12 Suite for Solo Clarinet. (1977) 5'
1 movement. *First performed:* Dec. 1977; Boston Conservatory.
Score: reprod. of ms. BCM
Reel: available from composer.

T1.13 Suite for Wind Trio. (1979) 6' 30"
For: flute, clarinet, bassoon. 1 movement. Honorable mention, New Music for Young Ensembles Contest, 1979. *First performed:* Mar. 1981; New York City.
Score: reprod. of ms.
Cassette: available from composer.

Tribute to Bartok. *See* Unknown Memory (Tribute to Bartok).

T1.14 Unknown Memory (Tribute to Bartok). (1981) 5'
For: violin, clarinet, piano. *First performed:* Aug. 31, 1981; Siena, Italy.
Score: reprod. of ms.; available from composer.
Cassette: available from composer.

Unto Thee Lift I up My Eyes. *See* Psalm 21: Unto Thee Lift I up My Eyes.

T1.15 Variations on a Theme of Praetorius. (1980) 13'
For: band. 1 movement.
Score: reprod. of ms.

T2 IVAN TCHEREPNIN

Born February 5, 1943, in Paris, France. Moved to Boston area 1960. *Education:* early training in piano and composition with parents; studied composition with Leon Kirchner and Randall Thompson (Harvard University, B.A., 1964, M.A., 1969); electronic music with David Tudor and Karlheinz Stockhausen; conducting with Pierre Boulez. *Awards:* Belaieff Prize (1961), Brookline Library Music Association Composers Award (1964), George Arthur Knight Prize (Harvard University, 1966), John Knowles Paine Travelling Fellowship (Harvard University, 1965), ASCAP Awards (Standard) (1968-82). *Related activities:* served on the faculties of San Francisco Conservatory of Music (1967), Stanford University (1967, 1970-72), Harvard University (1969-70; director of electronic music studio, 1972-). HU

WORKS

T2.1 Les Adieux. (1971) 42'
For: voices(2),electronics/light boards(4), instrumental ensemble(flute/piccolo, clarinet, bassoon, trumpet, horn, trombone, piano, harp, percussion(2), viola, violoncello, double bass).
Dedicated to: Howard Hersh. *First performed:* May 1972; San Francisco, Calif. San Francisco Conservatory New Music Ensemble, Howard Hersh, director.

T2.2 Alternating Currents, I (from AC-DC). (1967) 20'
For: percussion(8), tape recorders(2 or more), ring modulators(4) (with accessories). *Dedicated to:* Christian Wolff. *First performed:* 1967; Harvard University.

T2.3 Beethoven's Late Quartet. (1968) 30'
For: string quartet, birds, radio announcer(live or recorded), amplitude modulators. Written for KPFA-FM,

Berkeley, Calif. *Dedicated to:* Anthony Groffo. *First performed:* 1968; KPFA-FM, Berkeley, Calif. *Score & parts. Tape.*

T2.4 Beginnings. (1963) 5'
For: piano. *Dedicated to:* Sandra Prutting. *First performed:* 1963; Harvard University. Ivan Tcherepnin.
Score: ms.

T2.5 Cadenzas in Transition. (1963) 12' 30"
For: flute, clarinet, piano. 1 movement. Winner of Brookline Library Music Association Composers Award (1964). *Dedicated to:* Leon Kirchner. *First performed:* 1963; Brookline Public Library.
Score: reprod. of ms. BrPL
Score & parts: Belaieff, 1964. HU
Reel: recording of first performance. BrPL

[Christmases]
T2.6 Three Christmases. (1970-72) 8'
For: pianos(2). *Movements:* Silent Night Mix; Piece sans titre; Alleluia.
Score: Belaieff, 1976 (also titled Drei Stuecke fuer zwei Klaviere). HU BPL

[Christmases. Silent Night Mix]
T2.7 Silent Night Mix. (1970)
For: pianos(2).
Score: in *Soundings*, vol. 1, Garland, 1972. H

T2.8 Cloud Music. (1978) 10'
For: tape. Film music. Soundtrack for *Sky Piece*, a film made by Alfred Guzzetti at the Carpenter Center, Harvard University.

Clouds. *See* Globose floccose. Clouds.

[Concerto]
T2.9 Oboe Concerto. (1980)
For: oboe, band, harp, percussion. *First performed:* June 1981; Pittsburgh, Pa. American Wind Symphony Orchestra.
Score & parts.

T2.10 Entourages sur un theme russe. (1962) 9'
For: horn, Ondes Martenot(optional), piano, percussion. 2 movements. Winner of Belaieff Prize, 1961. *First performed:* Aug. 1962; Academie Internationale d'Ete, Nice, France.
Score & parts: Belaieff, 1970. HU

Fetes. *See* Variations on Happy Birthday. Fetes.

T2.11 Flores musicales. (1979; rev. 1980)
For: oboe, violin, violoncello(optional), psaltery, synthesizer, electronics.
Movements: Overture (P'tite P'tite); The Violin Ghost; Grand Fire Music; High in the Woods; Concatenations. *Dedicated to:* Peggy Pearson. Later version includes violoncello part for Yo-Yo Ma. *Commissioned by:* Omnibus Series, Boston University. *First performed:* Nov. 29, 1979; Boston University; Omnibus series. Peggy Pearson, oboe; David Gable, violin; Ivan Tcherepnin, Serge synthesizer and electronics. Later version first performed: July 1980; Harvard University. Yo-Yo Ma, violoncello; other unidentified performers. *Score & parts.*
Disc: in *Electric Flowers*, Composers Recordings SD 467, nyp.
Reel: recording of first performance. BU

[Flores musicales. Grand Fire Music]
T2.12 Grand Fire Music. (1966) 18'
For: tape. *Tape.*

T2.13 Flute Fancy. (1978) 4'
For: flute and electronics. Film music. Soundtrack for *The Changing Forest*, a film made by Janet Mendelsohn for the United States Department of the Interior. *Sketch.*

T2.14 Globose floccose. (1973) 17' 30"
For: string quartet, brasses(5), electronics, tape. *First performed:* Dec. 1973; Harvard University; Fromm

Foundation concert.
Score: Belaieff, nyp

[Globose floccose. Clouds]
T2.15 Clouds.
For: tape. *First performed:* Dec. 1973;
Harvard University; Fromm Foundation
concert. *Tape.*

Grand Fire Music. *See* Flores musicales.
Grand Fire Music.

T2.16 Light Music with Water. (1970)
30'-35'
For: instrumental ensemble(brasses(5),
string quartet, woodwind quintet, harp,
percussion(3)), strobe
lights(sound-activated)(4), tape.
Commissioned by: San Francisco
Conservatory of Music. *First
performed:* 1970; San Francisco
Conservatory of Music. San Francisco
Conservatory New Music Ensemble.
Parts & perf. dir: ms. *Tape(sound
effects).*

Movements-Mediations. *See* Work
Musik.

T2.17 Mozartean Suite. (1962) 8'
For: flute, clarinet, bassoon. *First
performed:* 1962; Dunster House,
Harvard University.
Score: ms.

T2.18 One, Two, Three for KQED.
(1970) 8'
For: tape. *First performed:* KQED-FM,
San Francisco, Calif. *Tape.*

T2.19 Peelings. (1975) 7'
For: tape. Film music; collage. Film by
Len Gittelman.
Tape: 1975; Cambridge, Mass.

[Pieces]
T2.20 Two Pieces. (1967) 8'
For: piano. *Movements:* Reminiscence;
Melody. *Dedication:* To my parents.
First performed: 1979; New England
Conservatory. Tanya Bartevian.
Score: ms.

T2.21 Pieces from Before. (1958-62) 9'
For: piano. *Movements:* For Christmas;
Valse; Vernal Equinox; Riding the
Clouds. *First performed:* 1962; Harvard
University.
Score: Belaieff, 1965. HU NEC

T2.22 Post Office. (1968) 3'
For: tape. Film music; collage. Film
made by Derek Lamb at the Carpenter
Center, Harvard University.
Tape: 1968; Carpenter Center, Harvard
University.

T2.23 Reciprocals. (1962) 9'
For: flute, clarinet, bassoon. *First
performed:* 1962; Academie
Internationale d'Ete, Nice, France.
Score & parts: ms.

T2.24 Reverberations. (1968) 12'
For: tape. *First performed:* 1970;
Stanford University. Alea II. *Tape.*

[Rings, String Quartet]
T2.25 Rings. (1969) 15'
For: string quartet and ring modulator.
Live electronic modulation of string
quartet music. *First performed:* 1969;
Harvard University.
Score & parts: ms.

[Rings, Tape]
T2.26 Rings. (1966) 20'
Tape.

T2.27 Santur Opera. (rev. 1977) 60'
For: santur and electronics. *First
performed:* 1977; The Kitchen, New
York City. First staged performance:
Nov. 1980; Festival d'Automne, Paris,
France. Earlier version titled Santur
Tales.
Tape: (Santur Tales).

T2.28 Sarina at Two. (1977) 2'
For: tape. *First performed:* 1977;
KPFA-FM, Berkeley, Calif. *Tape.*

T2.29 Set, Hold, Squelch and Clear.
(1976) 60'
For: oboe, frequency follower,
synthesizer(Serge). Later version for

orchestra titled La va et le vient. *First performed:* Feb. 1976; Merce Cunningham Performance Space, New York City. *Score. Tape.*

Silent Night Mix. *See* Christmases. Silent Night Mix.

T2.30 Sombres lumieres. (1964) 4'
For: flute, guitar, violoncello. *Commissioned by:* Pielage family. *Dedication:* A la memoire de Erik Pielage. *First performed:* 1965; Harvard University.
Score: Belaieff, 1970. HU

T2.31 Sommermusik fuer Blechblaeser. (1970) 24'
For: trumpets(2), horns(2), trombone, tuba. Aleatoric music. *Movements:* Descents; Ascents; Interlude 1; Differences; Interlude 2; Interlude 3; A Walk Through the Woods; Finale. *Dedicated to:* "Coco" Woodworth. Originally titled Summer Brass. *First performed:* 1972; Harvard University.
Score: Belaieff, 1971. BU HU

[Songs]
T2.32 Five Songs. (1979?)
For: alto, flute, flute(alto), Delta T, electronics. *Commissioned by:* WFMT-FM, Chicago, Ill. *First performed:* WFMT-FM, Chicago, Ill. *Score.*
Disc: in *Electric Flowers*, Composers Recording SD 467, nyp.

Stuecke fuer zwei Klaviere. *See* Christmases.

T2.33 Suite progressive pentatonique. (1959) 5'
For: flute, violoncello, timpani. *Dedicated to:* Hsien Ming Tcherepnin (my mother). *First performed:* 1959; Academie Internationale d'Ete, Nice, France.
Score: ms.

T2.34 Summer Nights. (1980)
For: piano. *Dedicated to:* Luise Vosgerchian. *First performed:* 1980; Harvard University. Luise Vosgerchian. *Score.*

Summerbrass. *See* Sommermusik fuer Blechblaeser.

T2.35 U.S.A. Film. (1975) 17' 30"
For: tape. Film music; collage. Film made by Eric Martin. *Dedicated to:* Eric Martin. *Tape.*

T2.36 La Va et le vient. (1978) 17'
For: orchestra. *Commissioned by:* Lucerne International Music Festival. *Dedication:* To the memory of Alexander Tcherepnin and the newborn Stefan Tcherepnin. Earlier version, for oboe, frequency follower, Serge synthesizer, titled Set, Hold, Squelch and Clear. *First performed:* 1978; Lucerne International Music Festival. Basel Radio Symphony Orchestra, Ivan Tcherepnin, conductor.
Score & parts: ms.
Reel: recording of first performance. HU

T2.37 Valse perpetuelle (The 45 R.P.M.). (1977) 3' 53"
For: piano. *Commissioned by:* C.F. Peters Corp. *First performed:* Art Institute, Chicago, Ill. John Cobb.
Score: in *Waltzes by 25 Contemporary Composers*, Peters, 1978. BrU MIT NEC W
Disc: Nonesuch D 79011, 1981. John Cobb. MIT

[Variations on Happy Birthday]
T2.38 Twelve Variations on Happy Birthday. (1970-77) 20'
For: piano. *First performed:* Mar. 1980; Brooklyn, N.Y. Joseph Kubera. *Score.*

[Variations on Happy Birthday. Fetes]

T2.39 Fetes. (1975) 12'
For: piano.
Score: Belaieff, 1978. HU

T2.40 Watergate Suite. (1972-73) 7'
For: tape. *First performed:* summer,
1974; Darthington, England. *Tape.*

T2.41 Wheelwinds. (1966-67) 14'
For: flutes(2)/piccolo, flute(alto), oboe,
English horn, clarinet, clarinet(E-flat),
clarinet(bass), bassoon. *Dedicated to:*
Leon Kirchner. Master's thesis. *First
performed:* 1967; Harvard University.
Score & parts: Schott, 1967. HU
Score: ms. HU
Score: Ars Viva, 1971. HU

T2.42 Work Musik. (1965) 8'
For: clarinet, horn, guitar(electric),
violoncello. *Dedicated to:* Henri
Pousseur. Winner of the George Arthur
Knight Prize (Harvard University), 1966.
Originally titled Movements-Mediations.
Score & parts: ms.
Score: ms. HU

T3 NICHOLAS CHRIS TGETTIS

Born September 1, 1933, in Salem,
Mass. *Education:* studied composition
with Donald Smith, Francis Judd
Cooke, Carl McKinley (New England
Conservatory, B.M., 1960); Daniel
Pinkham, Joseph Block, Gardner Read,
Hugo Norden, (Boston University, M.M.,
1969); Franz Reizenstein, (London,
England). *Awards:* Brookline Library
Music Association Composers Award
(First Prize). *Related activities:* pianist;
member of the faculty of various area
public schools; composer-in-residence,
CETA Art Colloquium, Salem, Mass.
NEC

WORKS

T3.1 Anncone. (1980) 5'
For: string orchestra. 1 movement.
Dedicated to: Rita Dyer. *First
performed:* Feb. 15, 1981; Salem High
School Auditorium, Salem, Mass.
Salem Philharmonic Orchestra, Alan F.

Hawryluk, conductor.
Score & parts: ms. in composer's hand;
available from composer.

[A Cappella Choruses]
T3.2 Three A Cappella Choruses. (1979)
8'
For: chorus. *Contents:* Procne; Leasure;
Rise Up My Love. *First performed:*
1979; Clifton Lutheran Church,
Marblehead, Mass. North Shore Chorale.
Vocal score: ms. in composer's hand;
available from composer.

T3.3 Appollo #8 - Fantastic Voyage.
(1980)
For: orchestra(2-2-2-2; 4-3-3-1; perc; hp;
str).
Score: ms. in composer's hand;
available from composer.

[Blossom Poems]
T3.4 Two Blossom Poems. (1978) 3'
For: piano.
Score: ms. in composer's hand;
available from composer.

T3.5 Bowforte String Quartet. (1978)
Score & parts: ms. in composer's hand;
available from composer.

T3.6 Brother Russell. (1973)
For: tubas(5) or brasses(5).
Score & parts: ms. in composer's hand;
available from composer.

T3.7 Cape Ann Suite. (1966) 19'
For: string orchestra. *Movements:*
Prelude; Lady Arbella; Roger Conant
and the Planters; Mount Ann;
Thanksgiving.
Score: Helicon, 1976. NEC
Parts: Helicon.

T3.8 Celebration of the Eucharist.
(1978) 27'
For: chorus(SATB). *Text:* Bible, O.T.,
Bible, N.T., selected other texts. *First
performed:* 1978; Beverly Baptist
Church, Beverly, Mass. North Shore
Chorale, Steven Denson, conductor.
Vocal score: Helicon, 1980. NEC

T3.9 Clown Waltz. (1973)
For: orchestra(2-2-2-2; 2-2-3-1; perc; str).
Score & parts: ms. in composer's hand; available from composer.

T3.10 Clowns: Symphonic Poem After a Painting of Robert Owen. (1971) 17'
For: orchestra(2(&pic)-2(&Ehn)-2(&bcl)-2(&cbsn); 4-2-3-1; timp, perc(2), str).
Score: ms. in composer's hand; available from composer.

[Duets]
T3.11 Twelve Duets for Treble Instruments. (1974)
Score: reprod. of ms.; available from composer.

T3.12 Fantasia on When Jesus Wept. (1975) 9'
For: Soprano, Alto, Tenor, Bass, chorus(SATB), string quartet. 1 movement. *Text:* William Billings.
Parts: ms. in composer's hand.

[Humoresques]
T3.13 Three Humoresques. (1979)
For: piano.
Score: ms. in composer's hand.

T3.14 Incident at Salem Bridge - 1775. (1975) 55'
For: voices, narrator, chorus, orchestra(2-2-2-2; 2-2-3-1; timp, perc, bells; str). Cantata.
Score & parts: ms. in composer's hand; available from composer.

T3.15 Isaiah, Chapter 53. (1971) 30'
For: Soprano, Alto, Tenor, Bass, chorus(SATB), orchestra(2(&pic)-2(&Ehn)-2-2; 2-2-3-1; timp, perc(2); str). Cantata.
Score: ms. in composer's hand; available from composer.

T3.16 Liturgy of Peace. (1975)
For: chorus(SATB) and organ. Withdrawn.

T3.17 Madrigal for Spring. (1979) 6'
For: chorus(SATB) and piano. 1 movement. *Text:* Ariana Marchello.
Vocal score: ms. in composer's hand; available from composer.

T3.18 Night Freight. (1976) 6'
For: pianos(2). 1 movement. *Dedicated to:* Wayne L. Garry. *First performed:* Hellenic College. L. Owyang and J. Kroner.
Score: reprod. of ms. NEC

T3.19 Old South Point 1668. (1974) 16'
For: piano. Sonata. 1 movement. *First performed:* June, 1976; Emmanuel College. L. Owyang.
Score: ms. in composer's hand; available from composer.

T3.20 Pani Zofia: Polonaise. (1977) 6'
For: orchestra(2-2-2-2; 4-2-3-1; perc; hp; str). 1 movement. *First performed:* Feb., 1979; Salem, Mass. Salem Philharmonic Orchestra, Alan Hawryluk, conductor.
Score & parts: available from composer.

[Pantomime Dances]
T3.21 Five Pantomime Dances. (1974)
For: piano and dancer.
Score: ms. in composer's hand; available from composer.

T3.22 Pergamas: Pictoral Symphony. (1976)
For: orchestra(2-2-2-2; 4-2-3-1; perc; str).
Score: ms. in composer's hand; available from composer.

T3.23 Petite suite. (1976)
For: flute and piano.
Score & part: available from composer.

[Quartet, Strings]
T3.24 String Quartet. (1979)
Score & parts: available from composer.

[Quartet, Strings, C]
T3.25 String Quartet in C. (1976)
Score & parts: available from
composer.

[Quartet, Strings, D]
T3.26 String Quartet in D. (1976)
Score & parts: available from
composer.

[Quartet, Strings, F]
T3.27 String Quartet in F. (1976)
Score & parts: available from
composer.

[Quartet, Strings, G]
T3.28 String Quartet in G. (1976)
Score & parts: available from
composer.

T3.29 Quintet for Brass. (1972)
Score & parts: available from
composer.

[Quintet, Woodwinds, 1976]
T3.30 Woodwind Quintet. (1976) 17'
Movements: Overture; Song; Waltz;
Finale. *First performed:* May, 1977;
Worcester, Mass. Seven Hills Quintet,
Paul Tennent, director.
Score & parts: ms. in composer's hand.

[Quintet, Woodwinds, 1981]
T3.31 Woodwind Quintet. (1981) 11' 5"
2 movements.
Music: available from composer.

T3.32 Rhapsody. (1973) 26'
For: piano and orchestra(2-2-2-2;
0-0-0-0; timp, perc(2); pf; str).
Score: ms. in composer's hand;
available from composer.

T3.33 Sappho. (1976) 75'
For: Soprano, Alto, chorus(SSAA),
dancers, orchestra(2-2-2-2; 2-2-3-1;
perc; hp; str). Chamber opera in 4
tableaux. *Contents:* Exile; Exhaltation to
Aphrodite; Return; Prayer to Aphrodite.
First performed: Higgins School,
Peabody, Mass. Michael Lamy,
conductor.

Score & parts: ms. in composer's hand;
available from composer.

T3.34 Scherzo. (1979)
For: piano and orchestra(2-2-2-2;
2-2-2-2; timp; str).
Score: ms. in composer's hand;
available from composer.

[Sonata, Piano (Classic)]
T3.35 Piano Sonata - Classic. (1979)
Score: available from composer.

[Sonata, Piano (Fantasy)]
T3.36 Piano Sonata - Fantasy. (1979)
Score: available from composer.

[Sonata, Piano (Suite)]
T3.37 Piano Sonata - Suite. (1979)
Score: available from composer.

T3.38 Sonatina. (1966)
For: piano.
Score: Brandon.

[Songs]
T3.39 Three Songs. (1973) 16'
For: Soprano and
orchestra(2-2(&Ehn)-2-2; 4-3-3-1; timp;
hp; str). *Text:* Anna Della Monica.
Score: available from composer.

T3.40 Street Suite. (1980)
For: clarinet and bassoon.
Score: available from composer.

T3.41 Toccata. (1980)
For: piano.
Score: ms. in composer's hand;
available from composer.

[Touch Pieces]
T3.42 Three Touch Pieces. (1977)
For: piano.
Score: ms. in composer's hand;
available from composer.

[Trio, Oboe, Clarinet, Bassoon]
T3.43 Trio for Woodwinds.
Winner of Brookline Library Music
Association Composers Award, First
Prize.

[Trio, Piano, Clarinet, Violin]
T3.44 Trio. (1973)
Score & parts: available from composer.

T3.45 The Villa: Symphonic Poem after Byron. (1970) 9'
For: orchestra(2(&pic)-2(&Ehn)-2(&bcl)-2(cbsn); 4-2-3-1; timp, perc(2); hp; str).
Score: available from composer.

[Vocal Pieces]
T3.46 4 Vocal Pieces. (1970)
Contents: Amen; Alleluia; Long Long Ago; Salutations to the Dawn.
Score: Brandon.

[Vocal Pieces, Voice and Flute]
T3.47 Four Vocal Pieces. (1975)
For: voice, chorus(SSA), chorus(SATB), flute, piano. *Contents:* With Pipe and Flute; The Piper; To a Flute Player; The Flute Player.
Score & parts: available from composer.

[Vocal Settings]
T3.48 Five Vocal Settings of Poems. (1980) 13'
For: voice, chorus(SATB), piano, string orchestra. *Text:* Robert Haiduke.
Contents: Edge of Sea; Mountains; Mirage; Witch's Brew for Halloween; La Valse.
Score & parts: available from composer.

[Waltzes]
T3.49 Three Waltzes. (1972)
For: piano.
Score: available from composer.

[Woodcuts]
T3.50 Three Woodcuts. (1977)
For: piano. *Movements:* Poseidon; Pegasus; Athena.
Score: available from composer.

T4 RANDALL THOMPSON

Born April 21, 1899, in New York City.

Education: studied composition with Archibald T. Davison, Edward Burlingame Hill, Walter Spaulding (Harvard University, B.A., 1920, M.A., 1922) and Ernest Bloch. *Awards:* Francis Booth Prize (Harvard University, 1918); George Arthur Knight Prize (Harvard University, 1920), Rome Prize Fellowship American Academy in Rome, 1922-25), Guggenheim Grants (1929, 1930), honorary doctorates (University of Rochester, 1933; University of Pennsylvania, 1969), Elizabeth Sprague Coolidge Award for Services to Chamber Music (1941), Cavaliere Ufficiale a Merito della Repubblica Italiana (1959), Harvard Glee Club Medal, Signet Society Medal. *Related activities:* author of *College Music* (1935); served on the faculties of Wellesley College (1927-29, 1936), University of California, Berkeley (1937-39), Curtis Institute of Music (Director, 1939-41), University of Virginia, Charlottesville (1941-45), Princeton University (1945-48), Harvard University (1948-65; Walter Bigelow Rosen Professor of Music, 1951-65).
HU

WORKS

T4.1 All on a Summer Eve: Song. (1917)
For: violin or violoncello and piano. Suggested by a text by Everett Glass.
Score: ms. in composer's hand. HUh
Part(violoncello): ms. in composer's hand. HUh

T4.2 Allegro in D Major. (1918)
For: piano.
Score: ms. in composer's hand. HUh

T4.3 Alleluia. (1940) 5'
For: chorus(SATB). *Dedicated to:* Berkshire Music Center, Serge Koussevitzky, director. *First performed:* 1940; opening exercises of the first summer of the Berkshire Music Center, Tanglewood.
Score: reprod. of mss. HUh NEC

Score: E.C. Schirmer, 1940. BrU HUm
MIT NEC
Score: E.C. Schirmer, 1968. Be BCM BPL
HU
Disc: GIA Records EL 19; also EL 100.
Peloquin Chorale, C. Alexander
Peloquin, conductor.
Disc: Key 12. Howard University Choir.
Disc: Decca M541, 194-. Fleet Street
Choir, T.B. Lawrence, conductor.
Disc: Vox PL/PLP 7750, 1952. Vienna
State Academy Chamber Chorus,
Ferdinand Grossman, conductor. HU
NEC
Disc: Cambridge CRS 403, 1957.
Harvard Glee Club; Radcliffe Choral
Society, G. Wallace Woodworth,
conductor. BU HU HUm L
Disc: Music Library MLR 7085, 1957.
Catawba College Choir, Robert Weaver,
conductor. W
Disc: Fellowship FR1/FS 1, 1961.
Singing City Choir of Philadelphia,
Elaine Brown, conductor. HU
Disc: Harvard Glee Club FH-RT, 1965
(date of recording). Harvard Glee Club;
Radcliffe Choral Society, Randall
Thompson, conductor. HU
Disc: RCA LM/LSC 7043, 1966. Massed
choruses from the First International
Choral Festival, G. Wallace Woodworth,
conductor.
Disc: Music Library 6996, 1967.
Stanford University Choir, Robert
Weaver, conductor. W
Reel: Apr. 23, 1965; Sanders Theatre,
Harvard University. Harvard Glee Club;
Radcliffe Choral Society, Randall
Thompson, conductor.
Reel: Mar. 5, 1972; Trinity Church,
Boston. HU
Reel: Apr. 28, 1974; Lincoln-Sudbury
High School, Sudbury, Mass. Randall
Thompson, conductor. HU
Reel: May 5, 1974; Christ Church,
Cambridge, Mass. Randall Thompson,
conductor. HU

[Alleluia; Arr.]
T4.4 Alleluia. 5'
For: chorus(SSAA).
Vocal score: E.C. Schirmer, 1968. HU W

Amen, Alleluia. *See* Requiem. The
Leave Taking. Amen, Alleluia.

[Amens, Chorus(4-part)]
T4.5 Two Amens. (1927)
Vocal score: in Fragments notebook;
ms. in composer's hand. HUh

[Amens, String Quartet]
T4.6 Amens. (1971)
Wedding music.
Score: in Music Book, 1970-71; ms. in
composer's hand. HUh
Score: in Wedding Music; ms. in
composer's hand. HUh

T4.7 Americana; a Sequence of Five
Transcripts from Americana
Set to Music. (1932) 18'11" *For:*
chorus(mixed) and piano. *Text:* from *The
American Mercury.* Contents: May Every
Tongue (SATB); The Staff Necromancer
(SSATTB); God's Bottles (SSAA
unaccompanied); The Sublime Process
of Law Enforcement (SATB);
Loveli-Lines (SSAATTBB). *Commissioned
by:* League of Composers. *Dedicated to:*
A Capella Singers of New York. *First
performed:* April 3, 1932; New York
City; League of Composers concert.
Randall Thompson, conductor.
Score & parts: E.C. Schirmer. Rental.
Vocal score: ms. in composer's hand.
HUh
Vocal score: E.C. Schirmer, 1932. BCM
HU HUm L NEC T UMB
Vocal score: E.C. Schirmer, 1960
(reissue of 1932 ed.). BCM
Reel: Feb. 9, 1979; New England
Conservatory. NEC Chorus, Lorna Cooke
deVaron, conductor. WGBH
Cassette: May 9, 1979. New England
Conservatory (Nos. 1, 2, 3, 5). NEC
Chorus, Lorna Cooke deVaron,
conductor. NEC

[Americana; Arr]
T4.8 Americana; A Sequence of Five
Transcripts from Americana
Set to Music. (1932) 18' 11" *For:*
chorus(SATB) and orchestra. *Text:* from
The American Mercury. Contents: May
Every Tongue; The Staff Necromancer;

God's Bottles; The Sublime Process of Law Enforcement; Loveli- Lines. *First performed:* 1940. Los Angeles Philharmonic Orchestra, Alfred Wallenstein, conductor.
Score & parts: E.C. Schirmer, 1932. Rental.
Score: E.C. Schirmer.
Disc: New World NW 219, 1977. University of Michigan Chamber Choir; University of Michigan Symphony Orchestra, Thomas Hilbish, conductor. BCM BU HU HUm MIT NEC T W
Reel: June 10, 1973; Meadville, Pa. Allegheny Choir; Allegheny Orchestra, Randall Thompson, conductor. HU

[Americana. God's Bottles]
T4.9 God's Bottles. (1932)
For: chorus(SSAA). *Text:* from *The American Mercury.*
Vocal score: ms. in composer's hand (includes piano reduction for rehearsal).
Disc: Concert Hall CHC 52, 1950? Randolph Singers, David Randolph, conductor. NEC

T4.10 Antiphon. (1971)
For: chorus(SATB). *Text:* George Herbert.
Vocal score: in *Two Herbert Songs*, E.C. Schirmer, 1971. BPL HU L

T4.11 Aria pensee.
For: Baritone and piano. *Text:* P. H. R.; lyrics for *The Millionaire.* From *L'Avenir Degonfle* by M. Contretemps.
Score: ms. in composer's hand. HUh

T4.12 Ballad. (1926)
For: voice(low) and piano. *Text:* Elizabeth Ann Moses.
Score: mss. in composer's hand. HUh

T4.13 The Battle of Dunster Street. (1953)
For: piano. Incidental music. 3 movements.
Score: ms. in composer's hand. HUh

T4.14 The Best of Rooms. (1963)
For: chorus(SATB). *Text:* Robert Herrick.

Vocal score: ms. in composer's hand. HUh
Reel: Palm Sunday, 1963; Evanston, Ill. Randall Thompson, conductor. HU

T4.15 Bitter-Sweet. (1970)
For: chorus(SATB). *Text:* George Herbert. *Dedicated to:* Katie. *First performed:* Oct. 25, 1970; New York City. Church of the Incarnation Choir, Thomas Dunn, director.
Vocal score: in Music Book, 1970-71; ms. in composer's hand. HUh
Vocal score: in *Two Herbert Songs*, E.C. Schirmer, 1971. BPL HU L

T4.16 The Boats Were Talking. (1925)
For: piano. *Dedicated to:* Leopold and Edie.
Score: ms. in composer's hand. HUh
Score: E.C. Schirmer, 1980. HUh

The Butterfly That Stamped. *See* Solomon and Balkis.

T4.17 Canon.
For: voices(medium)(3). *Text:* Bible, O.T., Psalm 121.
Score: ms. in composer's hand. HUh

T4.18 Canon. (1927)
For: Soprano and Baritone. *Contents:* The Lover in Winter Plaineth for Spring; Felices ter (*Carminum I:13* by Horace); Inscription pour une statue de l'amour; Rima; Mein.
Score: mss. in composer's hand. HUh

The Carol of the Rose. *See* The Place of the Blest. The Carol of the Rose.

Choose Something Like a Star. *See* Frostiana. Choose Something Like a Star.

Chorale Prelude. *See* A Psalm of Thanksgiving. Nun danket.

[Chorale Preludes]
T4.19 Twenty Chorale Preludes, Four Inventions and a Fugue.

For: organ.
Score: E.C. Schirmer, 1970. BPL HU

[Chorale Preludes. Herr, ich habe missgehandelt]
T4.20 Herr, ich habe missgehandelt. (1959)
For: organ.
Score: in Music Book, Jan. 9-Mar. 19, 1959; ms. in composer's hand. HUh
Score: in *Twenty Chorale Preludes, Four Inventions and a Fugue,* E.C. Schirmer, 1970. BPL HU

[Chorale Preludes. Meine Seele erhebt den Herren]
T4.21 Mein Seele erhebt den Herren. (1959)
For: organ. Version with melody in pedal and version with canon at the octave.
Score: in Music Book, Jan. 9-Mar. 19, 1959; mss. in composer's hand. HUh
Score: in *Twenty Chorale Preludes, Four Inventions and a Fugue,* E.C. Schirmer, 1970. BPL HU

[Chorale Preludes. Wer nun den lieben Gott laesst walten]
T4.22 Wer nun den lieben Gott laesst walten. (1959)
For: organ.
Score: in Music Book, Jan. 9-Mar. 19, 1959; ms. in composer's hand. HUh

T4.23 A Concord Cantata. (1975) 22'
For: chorus(SATB) and orchestra(2(&pic)-2-2-2; 2-2-3-1; timp, perc; str). *Contents:* The Ballad of the Bridge (Edward Everett Hale); Inscription (A. French); The Gift Outright (Robert Frost). *Commissioned by:* Concord Bicentennial Committee. *Dedicated to:* The Townspeople of Concord, Massachusetts, 1775-1975.
First performed: May 2, 1975; Concord, Mass. Concord Chorus; Nashua Symphony, Willis Traphagen, conductor and Edward Gilday, director.
Score & parts: E.C. Schirmer. Rental.
Vocal score: ms. in composer's hand. HUh
Vocal score: ms. in composer's hand

(The Gift Outright). HUh
Vocal score: E.C. Schirmer, 1975. BCM BPL BU HU

T4.24 Discipleship. (1926)
For: voice(low) and piano. *Text:* Merle St. Croix Wright.
Score: in Five Songs; ms. in composer's hand. HUh
Score: in Songs, 1925-26; ms. in composer's hand. HUh

Divertimento for Strings. *See* Trio for Three Double Basses.

Do You Remember an Inn, Miranda? *See* Tarantella.

T4.25 Doubts. (1926)
For: voice(low) and piano. *Text:* Eleanor Dougherty.
Score: in Songs, 1925-26; ms. in composer's hand. HUh

T4.26 Drought. (1925)
For: voice(low) and piano. *Text:* Merle St. Croix Wright.
Score: in Five Songs; ms. in composer's hand. HUh
Score: in Songs, 1925-26; ms. in composer's hand. HUh

T4.27 The Echo Child. (1927)
For: voice(medium) and piano. *Text:* Mary Ely Baker. *Dedication:* For M.E.B.
Score: mss. in composer's hand. HUh
Score: in Five Songs; ms. in composer's hand. HUh
Score: in *New Songs for New Voices,* Harcourt-Brace, 1928. HU
Disc: RCA Victor VM 789.

T4.28 The Eternal Dove. (1968)
For: chorus(SATB). *Text:* Joseph Beaumont. Written for volume compiled in honor of Professor G. Wallace Woodworth by the Department of Music, Harvard University. *Dedicated to:* G. Wallace Woodworth. *First performed:* May 17, 1970; Cambridge, Mass. Harvard University Choir, John R. Ferris, director.
Vocal score: ms. in composer's hand.

HUh
Vocal score: reprod. of ms. HUh
Vocal score: E.C. Schirmer, 1971. BPL
HU
Vocal score: in *Words and Music: The
Composer's View*, Department of Music,
Harvard University, 1972. BPL HU NEC
W

T4.29 Fare Well. (1973)
For: chorus(SATB). *Text:* Walter de la
Mare.
Vocal score: E.C. Schirmer, 1973. BPL
HU
Vocal score: E.C. Schirmer, 1974.
Reel: Mar. 4, 1973; Merrick, N.Y. St.
John's Lutheran Church. HU
Reel: May 22, 1974; Boston
Conservatory. Boston Conservatory
Chorale, William A. Seymour,
conductor. BCM

T4.30 A Feast of Praise. (1963) 15'
For: chorus(SATB), trumpets(2), horns(2),
trombones(2), tuba, harp, or
chorus(SATB) and piano. Cantata. *Text:*
Bible, O.T., Baruch 3:34; Bible, O.T.,
Psalm 81:3; Bible, O.T., Psalm 47:5-7.
Contents: The Stars in Their Watches;
Nocturne; God Is Gone Up with a
Shout. *Commissioned by:* Stanford
University, Department of Music.
Dedicated to: Harold Schmidt. *First
performed:* Aug. 11, 1963; Stanford,
Calif. Stanford Summer Chorus, Randall
Thompson, conductor.
Vocal score: E.C. Schirmer, 1963. BPL
HU
Reel: n.d.; University of Tennessee,
Knoxville. Randall Thompson, conductor.

Felices ter (2-voice setting). *See*
Canons.

Felices ter (4-voice setting). *See* Odes
of Horace. Feleice ter.

[Frostiana]
T4.31 Frostiana; a Sequence of Seven
Choruses. (1959) 25'
For: chorus(mixed) and piano. *Text:*
from *You Came Too* and *Steeple Bush*

by Robert Frost. *Contents:* The Road
Not Taken (SATB); The Pasture (TBB);
Come in (SAA); The Telephone
(SAATTBB); A Girl's Garden (SAA);
Stopping by the Woods on a Snowy
Evening (TBB); Choose Something Like
a Star (SATB). *Commissioned by:* The
Town of Amherst, Mass. for its 200th
anniversary of incorporation.
Dedication: To the townspeople of
Amherst, Massachusetts on their
two-hundredth birthday, 1759-1959. *First
performed:* Oct. 18, 1959; Amherst,
Mass. J. Heywood Alexander, piano;
Amherst Bicentennial Choir, Randall
Thompson, conductor.
Vocal score: E.C. Schirmer, 1960. Be
BPL HU NEC
Vocal score: E.C. Schirmer, 1960 (The
Road Not Taken). NU
Reel: 196-; Brookline, Mass. NEC
Chorus, Randall Thompson, conductor.
HU
Reel: Oct. 13, 1972; Harvard Musical
Association. HU
Reel: Apr. 28, 1974; Lincoln-Sudbury
High School, Sudbury, Mass. Randall
Thompson, conductor. HU
Reel: May 22, 1974; Boston
Conservatory (selections). Boston
Conservatory Chorale; William A.
Seymour, conductor.
Cassette: Apr. 18, 1978; New England
Conservatory. NEC Repertory Chorus,
David Carrier, conductor (Nos. 1 and 7).
NEC

[Frostiana; Arr.]
T4.32 Frostiana. (1965) 25'
For: chorus(SATB) and orchestra(2-2-2-2;
4-1-0-0; perc; hp; str). *Text:* from *You
Came Too* and *Steeple Bush* by Robert
Frost. *Contents:* The Road Not Taken;
The Pasture; Come In; The Telephone;
A Girl's Garden; Stopping by the
Woods on a Snowy Evening; Choose
Something Like a Star. *Dedication:* To
the townspeople of Amherst,
Massachusetts, 1759-1959.
Score: ms. in composer's hand. HUh
Score: E.C. Schirmer, 1975. BPL HU
Parts: E.C. Schirmer, 1975. Rental.

Disc: Harvard Glee Club, FH-RT, 1965
(date of recording). Harvard Glee Club;
Radcliffe Choral Society;
Harvard-Radcliffe Orchestra, Randall
Thompson, conductor. HU
Reel: Apr. 23, 1965; Sanders Theatre,
Harvard University. Harvard Glee Club;
Radcliffe Choral Society;
Harvard-Radcliffe Orchestra, Randall
Thompson, conductor. HU

[Frostiana. Choose Something Like a
Star; Arr.]
T4.33 Choose Something Like a Star.
For: chorus(women)(4-part) and piano.
Text: Robert Frost.
Vocal score: E.C. Schirmer, 1971.

T4.34 Fuga a tre. (1977)
For: instrument(unspecified).
Score: ms. in composer's hand. HUh

Fugue in C Major. *See* Chorale
Preludes.

The Garment of Praise. *See* Requiem.
The Garment of Praise.

T4.35 The Gate of Heaven. (1959)
For: chorus(SSAA).
Sketches: in Music Book, Jan. 9-Mar.
19, 1959; ms. in composer's hand. HUh
Vocal score: E.C. Schirmer, 1961. NEC

[The Gate of Heaven; Arr]
T4.36 The Gate of Heaven.
For: chorus(SATB).
Vocal score: E.C. Schirmer, 1961.
Reel: May 1959; Hollins College.
Hollins College Chapel Choir. HU
Reel: Palm Sunday, 1963; Evanston, Ill.
Randall Thompson, conductor. HU

[The Gate of Heaven; Arr]
T4.37 The Gate of Heaven.
For: chorus(TTBB).
Score: E.C. Schirmer, 1961.

The Gift Outright. *See* A Concord
Cantata.

T4.38 Glory to God in the Highest.
(1958) 1' 56"

For: chorus(SATB). *Text:* Bible, N.T.,
Luke II:14. *Dedicated to:* Harold C.
Schmidt.
Vocal score: E.C. Schirmer, 1958. BCM
BPL HU
Disc: Columbia M 34134, 1976. Mormon
Tabernacle Choir, Jerold D. Ottley,
conductor. BCM
Reel: May 5, 1974; Christ Church,
Cambridge Mass. Randall Thompson,
conductor. HU

The God Who Gave Us Life. *See* The
Testament of Freedom; Arr.

God's Bottles. *See* Americana. God's
Bottles.

Good Tidings from the Meek. *See*
Requiem. The Triumph of Fate. Good
Tidings from the Meek.

T4.39 Grand Street Follies. (1926)
For: voices, pianos(2), horn, percussion.
Incidental music.
Score: ms. in composer's hand (lost).

The Happy Shore. *See* Love Songs. The
Happy Shore.

T4.40 The Heavens Declare. (1926)
For: voice(low) and piano. *Text:* Merle
St. Croix Wright.
Score: in Five Songs; ms. in
composer's hand. HUh
Score: in Songs, 1925-26; ms. in
composer's hand. HUh

Herbert Settings. *See* Antiphon;
Bitter-Sweet.

Herr, ich habe missgehandelt. *See*
Chorale Preludes. Herr, ich habe
missgehandelt.

T4.41 A Hymn for Scholars and Pupils.
Version 1. (1973) 5'
For: chorus(SAA) and chamber
orchestra(1-0-0-0; 0-2-1-1; org;
str(1-1-1-1-1) or 1-0-0-0; 0-2-0-0; org;
str(1-1-1-1-0). *Text:* An Hymn for
Schollars and Pupils by George Wither.
Dedicated to: Elizabeth and Carlton

Sprague Smith. *First performed:* June 8, 1973; Washington, Conn. Wykeham Rise School Choir.
Score & parts: E.C. Schirmer. Rental.
Score: ms. in composer's hand. HUh
Vocal score: ms. in composer's hand. HUh
Reel: recording of first performance. HU

[A Hymn for Scholars and Pupils. Version 1; Arr.]
T4.42 A Hymn for Scholars and Pupils. (1973)
For: chorus(SAA), flute, piano. *Text: An Hymn for Schollars and Pupils* by George Wither. *Dedicated to:* Elizabeth and Carlton Sprague Smith.
Vocal score: E.C. Schirmer, 1975. BPL HU
Part: E.C. Schirmer, 1975. BPL HU

T4.43 A Hymn for Scholars and Pupils. Version 2. (1973?)
For: chorus(SATB) and instrumental ensemble(flute, trumpets(in C)(2), trombone, tuba, organ, strings). *First performed:* Nov. 11, 1973; Raleigh, N.C.; North Carolina Music Educators Association concert.
Vocal score: reprod. of ms. HUh

T4.44 I Wan' My Friends. (1925)
For: voice(low) and piano. *Text:* Merle St. Croix Wright. Later titled Spiritual.
Score: in Five Songs; ms. in composer's hand (titled Spiritual). HUh
Score: in Songs, 1925-26; ms. in composer's hand. HUh

T4.45 Indianola Variations. (1918)
For: pianos(2). 7 variations. Variations 2, 4, 5 by Leopold Damrosch Mannes.
Score: mss. in composer's hand. HUh

Inventions. *See* Chorale Preludes.

T4.46 Jabberwocky. (1951)
For: piano. Ballet. *Choreography by:* Varney Thompson.
Score: ms. in composer's hand. HUh

T4.47 Jazz Poem. (1927-29)
For: piano and orchestra. *Dedication:* To M.W.T.
Sketches: ms. in composer's hand. HUh
Score & parts: E.C. Schirmer. Rental.
Pf. red: ms. in composer's hand. HUh
Part(piano): ms. in composer's hand. HUh

T4.48 Katie's Dance. (1969)
For: [flute?].
Score: ms. in composer's hand. HUh

T4.49 The Lark in the Moon. (1938)
For: chorus(mixed). Folk song, English.
Score: ms. in composer's hand. HUh
Score: E.C. Schirmer, 1940 (includes piano reduction).

T4.50 The Last Invocation. (1922)
For: chorus(SSATTB). *Text:* Walt Whitman.
Score: mss. in composer's hand. HUh

T4.51 The Last Words of David. (1949) 4'
For: chorus(SATB) or chorus(TTBB) and orchestra (2(&pic)-2(&Ehn)-2(&bcl)-2(&cbsn); 4-3-2(&btrb)-1; timp, perc; hp; str). *Text:* Bible, O.T., 2 Samuel 23:3-4.
Commmissioned by: Boston Symphony Orchestra for Serge Koussevitzky in honor of the 25th anniversary of his directorship. *Dedicated to:* Serge Koussevitsky. *First performed:* Aug. 12, 1949; Berkshire Music Center, Tanglewood. Berkshire Music Center Chorus; Boston Symphony Orchestra, Serge Koussevitzky, conductor.
Score: mss. in composer's hand. BU HUh
Score: E.C. Schirmer, 1950. HU
Parts: E.C. Schirmer, 1950. Rental.
Vocal score: E.C. Schirmer, 1950. BCM BPL BU NU
Disc: Golden Crest CR/S 4032, n.d. Walter Ehret Chorale, Walter Ehret, conductor. BCM BU
Disc: Vox VX 25590/STVX 425590. West Point Chapel Choir.
Disc: Carillon LP 122, [1961]. Harvard

Glee Club, Elliot Forbes, conductor.
HUm
Disc: Austin 6241, 1963. Baylor Bards, Martha Barkema, conductor.
Disc: Harvard Glee Club FH-RT, 1965 (date of recording). Harvard Glee Club; Radcliffe Choral Society; Harvard-Radcliffe Orchestra, Randall Thompson, conductor. HU
Reel: Palm Sunday, 1963; Evanston, III. Randall Thompson, conductor. HU
Reel: Apr. 23, 1965; Sanders Theatre, Harvard University. Harvard Glee Club; Radcliffe Choral Society; Harvard-Radcliffe Orchestra, Randall Thompson, conductor. HU
Reel: Nov. 5, 1972; Harvard University. Harvard University Choir, John R. Ferris, conductor. HU
Reel: Apr. 28, 1974; Lincoln-Sudbury High School, Sudbury, Mass. Randall Thompson, conductor. HU
Reel: May 5, 1974; Christ Church, Cambridge. Randall Thompson, conductor. HU

The Leave Taking. *See* Requiem. The Leave Taking.

The Light of Stars. *See* Love Songs. The Light of Stars.

T4.52 Little Prelude. (1935)
For: piano. Children's music.
Score: C. Fischer, 1936.

T4.53 The Lord Is My Shepherd. (1962)
For: chorus(SSAA) and organ or piano, or chorus(SATB) and organ or harp or piano. *Text:* Bible, O.T., Psalm 23.
Vocal score: ms. in composer's hand. HUh
Vocal score: E.C. Schirmer, 1964 (version for chorus(SSAA)). BPL
Vocal score: E.C. Schirmer, 1966 (version for chorus(SATB)). HU
Reel: Apr. 16, 1967; Town Hall, New York City. State University of New York, College at Oneonta, Women's Glee Club, Charles Burnsworth, conductor. HU

Love Is Like a Wind upon the Water.
See Love Songs. Siciliano.

[Love Songs. The Happy Shore]
T4.54 Five Love Songs. The Happy Shore. (1978)
For: chorus(SATB) and string quartet or piano. *Text:* Edmund Spencer.
Vocal score: ms. in composer's hand. HUh
Vocal score: E.C. Schirmer, 1978.

[Love Songs. The Light of Stars]
T4.55 Five Love Songs. The Light of Stars. (1919)
For: Soprano, Alto, Tenor, Bass. *Text:* Henry Wadsworth Longfellow.
Score: E.C. Schirmer, 1980.

[Love Songs. The Passenger]
T4.56 Five Love Songs. The Passenger. (1957)
For: Baritone and chamber orchestra or piano. *Text:* Mark Antony De Wolfe Howe.
Score & parts: E.C. Schirmer (version for chamber orchestra). Rental.
Score: ms. in composer's hand (version for piano). HUh
Score: E.C. Schirmer, 1980 (version for piano).
Reel: Feb. 14, 1969; University of South Florida. Jerold Reynolds, baritone and unidentified pianist. HU

[Love Songs. Siciliano]
T4.57 Five Love Songs. Siciliano (Love Is Like a Wind upon the Water) (1978)
For: Baritone and piano. *Text:* Love Is Like a Wind upon the Water by Philip H. Rhinelander. *Commissioned by:* Rocky Mountain Ridge Music Center, Estes Park Colo., as a bequest in memory of Tell Ertl.
Score: E.C. Schirmer, 1980.

[Love Songs. Two Worlds]
T4.58 Five Love Songs. Two Worlds.
For: chorus(SATB) and piano. *Text:* Edmund Waller.
Vocal score: reprod. HUh
Vocal score: E.C. Schirmer, 1977.

Lullaby. *See* The Nativity according to Saint Luke. Lullaby.

T4.59 Mass of the Holy Spirit.
(1955-56) 34'
For: chorus(SATB). *Movements:* Kyrie; Gloria (SSAATTBB); Credo; Sanctus (SAATTBB); Hosanna; Benedictus; Agnus Dei. *Dedicated to:* Choir of St. Stephen's Church, Providence.
Sketches: ms. in composer's hand. HUh
Vocal score: ms. in composer's hand. HUh
Vocal score: E.C. Schirmer, 1956. HU
Vocal score: E.C. Schirmer, 1957 (movements also available separately). BPL HUm NEC
Disc: Cambridge CRS 403, 1957. Harvard Glee Club; Radcliffe Choral Society, G. Wallace Woodworth, conductor. BU HU L HUm
Reel: Cambridge CRS 403, 1957. Harvard Glee Club; Radcliffe Choral Society, G. Wallace Woodworth, conductor. HU
Reel: Dec. 12, 1972; Boston Conservatory. Boston Conservatory Chorale, William A. Seymour, conductor. BCM
Reel: Jan. 21, 1973; Boston Conservatory. Boston Conservatory Chorale, William A. Seymour, conductor. BCM
Reel: May 22, 1974; Boston Conservatory (Benedictus). Boston Conservatory Chorale, William A. Seymour, conductor. BCM
Reel: Dec. 9, 1976; St. Cecilia's Church, Boston. Boston Conservatory Chorus, Sterling P. Cossaboom, director. BCM

T4.60 Mazurka. (1926)
For: piano.
Score: ms. in composer's hand. HUh

T4.61 The Mirror of St. Anne, an Antiphonal Setting in Inverse Contrary Imitation.
(1972) *For:* choruses(SATB)(2). *Text:* Isaac Watts. Original version but issued earlier as Fanfare and St.

Anne's in Ode to the Virginian Voyage. *Vocal score:* E.C. Schirmer, 1972.

Mein Seele erhebt den Herren. *See* Chorale Preludes. Meine Seele erhebt den Herren.

Music Book, July 29, 1953-Jan. 16, 1954. *See* Odes of Horace. Felice ter; Veritas.

Music Book, Jan. 9-Mar. 19, 1959. *See* Chorale Preludes; The Gate of Heaven; The Nativity according to Saint Luke. Selections.

Music Book, 1970-71. *See* Amens, String Quartet.

T4.62 My Master Hath a Garden. (1927)
For: voice(medium) and piano. Children's music. *Text:* anon.
Score: ms. in composer's hand. HUh
Score: in *Four Songs for Children*; ms. in composer's hand. HUh
Score: in *New Songs for New Voices*, Harcourt-Brace, 1928. HU
Score: in *Two Songs*, E.C. Schirmer, 1938. BPL
Disc: RCA Victor VM 789.
Reel: Feb. 14, 1969; University of South Florida. Jerold Reynolds, baritone and unidentified pianist. HU
Reel: May 5, 1974; Christ Church, Cambridge, Mass. Lydia Snow, soprano and unidentified pianist. HU

T4.63 The Nativity according to Saint Luke. (1961) 100'
For: voices(12), chorus(SATB), chorus(children), chamber orchestra (1-1-1(Bb/A)-1; 1-1-0-0-; timp, perc, church bells; organ; str(1-1-1-1-1)). Oratorio. *Text:* Bible, N.T., Luke, and Mary's Lullaby by Richard Rowlands.
Contents: Zaccharias and the Angel; The Annunciation; The Naming of John; The Apparition; The Adoration; The Song of Simeon. *Dedication:* In honor of the 200th anniversary of the dedication of Christ Church, Cambridge, 1761-1961.
First performed: Dec. 1961; Christ

Church, Cambridge, Mass.
Sketches: ms. in composer's hand. HUh
Score: ms. in composer's hand. HUh
Score: E.C. Schirmer, 1961. HU
Parts: E.C. Schirmer, 1961. Rental.
Vocal score: ms. in composer's hand.
HUh
Vocal score: E.C. Schirmer, 1961. HU
Vocal score: E.C. Schirmer, 1962. BCM
BPL MIT
Disc: Festival Arts S 2693-2695, 1963.
Randall Thompson, conductor. HU
Reel: recording of first performance.
HU

[The Nativity according to Saint Luke.
Selections]
T4.64 *For:* church bells.
Score: in Music Book, 1959; ms. in
composer's hand. HUh

[The Nativity according to Saint Luke.
Lullaby]
T4.65 Lullaby. (1961)
For: Soprano, chorus(SATB)(optional),
piano.
Reel: May 5, 1974; Christ Church,
Cambridge, Mass. Lydia Snow, soprano
and unidentified pianist. HU

T4.66 Noel. (1947)
For: chorus(SATB).
Vocal score: ms. in composer's hand.
HUh

T4.67 Now I Lay Me down to Sleep.
(1947)
For: chorus(SSA). Motet. *Text:* from *The
New England Primer* (1784).
Vocal score: E.C. Schirmer, 1954.

Nun danket. *See* A Psalm of
Thanksgiving. Nun danket.

O Venus, regina cnidi paphique. *See*
Odes of Horace. O Venus, regina
cridi paphiquc.

T4.68 Ode to the Virginian Voyage.
(1956-57)
For: chorus(SATB) and orchestra or
piano. *Text:* Michael Drayton. *Contents:*
Sinfonia; You Brave Heroic Minds;

Earth's Only Paradise; Fanfare and St.
Anne's (Rectus et Inversus); In Kenning
of the Shore; And in Regions Far; They
Voyages Attend; Finale: Go and
Subdue. Fanfare and St. Anne's
originally for choruses(SATB)(2); later
published under title The Mirror of St.
Anne. *First performed:* May 13, 1957;
Williamsburg, Va. College of William
and Mary Choir; Norfolk Civic Chorus;
Norfolk Symphony Orchestra, Edgar
Schenkman, conductor.
Score & parts: E.C. Schirmer. Rental.
Score: mss. in composer's hand. HUh
Vocal score: E.C. Schirmer, 1957. HU
NEC
Vocal score: E.C. Schirmer, 1958. BPL
Disc: 1957; Technichord Recording
Service. Recording of first
performance. HU
Reel: recording of first performance.
HU
Reel: Nov. 17, 1957. Stanford
University Chorus; Stanford University
Orchestra, Sandor Salgo conductor. HU
Reel: Apr. 23, 1965; Sanders Theatre,
Harvard University. Harvard Glee Club;
Radcliffe Choral Society;
Harvard-Radcliffe Orchestra, Randall
Thompson, conductor. HU

T4.69 Odes of Horace. (Nos. 1-5, 1924;
No. 6, 1953)
For: chorus(mixed) and orchestra or
piano. *Text:* Horace. *Contents:* O Venus,
regina cnidi paphique (I, 30; SSATTBB);
Vitas hinnuleo me similis, Chloe (I, 23;
SATB); Montium custos nemorumque,
Virgo (III, 22; SATB); Quis multa
gracilis (I, 5; TTBB); O fons bandusiae,
splendidior vitro (III, 13; SSATBB);
Felices ter (I, 13; SATB).
Score & parts: E.C. Schirmer. Rental.
Score: ms. in composer's hand (Nos.
1-5). HUh
Vocal score: ms. in composer's hand
(Nos. 1-5). HUh
Vocal score: in Music Book, July 29,
1953-Jan. 16, 1954; ms. in composer's
hand (No. 6). HUh
Vocal score: E.C. Schirmer, 1932 (Nos.
1-5). BPL HU L
Vocal score: E.C. Schirmer, 1956 (No. 6).

BPL HU
Disc: Orion ORS 75205, 1975? (No. 6).
HU

[Odes of Horace. Selections]
T4.70 Odes of Horace. (1924)
For: chorus(mixed) and piano. *Text:*
Horace. *Contents:* Vitas hinnuleo me
similis, Chloe (I, 23; SATB); Mentium
custos nemorumque, Virgo (III, 22;
SATB); O fons bandusiae, splendidior
vitre (III, 13; SSATBB).
Disc: Vox PL 7750, 1952. Vienna State
Academy Chamber Chorus, Ferdinand
Grossman, conductor. HU NEC
Disc: Harvard Glee Club FH-RT, 1965
(date of recording). Sanders Theatre,
Harvard University. Harvard Glee Club;
Radcliffe Choral Society, Randall
Thompson, conductor. HU

Odes of Horace. Selections. *See also*
Symphony No. 1.

The Passenger. *See* Love Songs. The
Passenger.

T4.71 The Passion according to Saint
Luke. (1964-65) 92'
For: voices, chorus(SATB), orchestra.
Oratorio. *Text:* Bible, N.T., Luke: 19, 22,
23. *First performed:* Mar. 28, 1965;
Symphony Hall, Boston. Handel &
Haydn Society.
Sketches: ms. in composer's hand. HUh
Sketches: reprod. of ms. HUh
Score & parts: E.C. Schirmer. Rental.
Vocal score: ms. in composer's hand.
HUh
Vocal score: reprod. of composer's ms.
HUh
Vocal score: E.C. Schirmer, 1965. BPL
Libretto: HUh
Reel: recording of first performance.
HU

T4.72 The Peaceable Kingdom. (1936)
15' 44"
For: chorus(mixed). Cantata. *Text:* Bible,
O.T., Isaiah. *Contents:* Say Ye to the
Righteous; Woe unto Them; The Noise
of a Multitude (SATB); Howl Ye

(SATB)(2); The Paper Reeds by the
Brooks; But These Are They That
Forsake the Lord (SATB)(2); For Ye
Shall Go Out with Joy(SATB); Have Ye
Not Known? (SATB); Ye Shall Have a
Song (SATB)(2). *Commissioned by:*
League of Composers for the Harvard
Glee Club and the Radclifffe Choral
Society.
Vocal score: mss. in composer's hand
(except Nos. 6, 7, 9). HUh
Vocal score: E.C. Schirmer, 1936
(movements also available separately).
BPL BU HU HUm L T UMB
Vocal score: E.C. Schirmer, 1963. MIT
NU
Disc: Music Library MLR 7065, 195-.
San Jose State College A Cappella
Choir, William Erlenson, director. HU
HUm NU
Disc: RCA Victor, 195-. BrU
Disc: Omega 811, 1958. Vassar College
Glee Club; MIT Glee Club, Klaus
Liepmann, conductor. MIT
Disc: Fellowship Records FR 1, 1960.
Singing City Choir of Philadelphia,
Elaine Brown, director. HU
Disc: Lyrichord LL 124/LLST, 1964.
Whikehart Chorale, Lewis R. Whikehart,
conductor. BCM BrU BU HU W
Disc: Harvard Glee Club FH-RT, 1965
(date of recording). Harvard Glee Club;
Radcliffe Choral Society, Randall
Thompson, conductor. HU
Disc: Orion ORS 76228, 1976.
Pepperdine University A Cappella
Chorus, Lawrence E. McCommas,
conductor. HU NEC
Reel: 1961. Harvard Freshman Glee
Club; Radcliffe Freshman Chorus,
Randall Thompson, conductor. HU
Reel: Palm Sunday, 1963; Evanston, Ill.
Randall Thompson, conductor. HU
Reel: Apr. 23, 1965; Sanders Theatre,
Harvard University. Harvard Glee Club;
Radcliffe Choral Society, Randall
Thompson, conductor. HU
Reel: Apr. 28, 1974; Lincoln-Sudbury
High School, Sudbury, Mass. Robert
Wentworth, conductor. HU
Reel: May 16, 1974; Boston
Conservatory (selections). Boston

Conservatory (selections). Boston
Conservatory Chorale, Brian O'Connell,
conductor. BCM
Reel: May 22, 1974; Boston
Conservatory (selections). Boston
Conservatory Chorale, William A.
Seymour, conductor. BCM
Reel: May 9, 1979; Boston
Conservatory (selections). Boston
Conservatory Chorus, Phillip Steinhaus,
conductor. BCM
Cassette: Dec. 13, 1977; New England
Conservatory. NEC Chorus, Lorna Cooke
deVaron, conductor. NEC

The Pelican. *See* The Place of the
Blest. The Pelican.

T4.73 Pierrot and Cothurnus; Prelude.
(1922) ·
For: orchestra(2-2(&Ehn)-2-2(&cbsn);
4-3-0-0; timp, perc; hp; str). Suggested
by *Aria da capo*, a play in one act by
Edna St. Vincent Millay.
Score: ms. in composer's hand. HUh

T4.74 The Piper at the Gates of Dawn;
Symphonic Prelude. (1924)
For: orchestra(2(&pic)-2(&Ehn)
-2(&bcl)-2(&cbsn); 4-3-3-1; timp, perc;
hps(2), cel, pf; str). Suggested by the
chapter in *The Wind in the Willows* by
Kenneth Grahame. *Dedicated to:* Mrs.
Felix Lamond.
Sketch: ms. in composer's hand. HUh
Score: ms. in composer's hand. HUh
Score: reprod. of ms. HUh
Reel: May 8, 1971; Eastman School of
Music. HU

T4.75 The Place of the Blest. (1969) 26'
For: chorus(SSAA) and chamber
orchestra(1-1-1-1; 0-0-0-0; str(1-1-1-1-1)).
Cantata. *Text:* Robert Herrick. *Contents:*
The Carol of the Rose; The Pelican
(Richard Wilbur); The Place of the
Blest; Alleluia. *Commissioned by:* St.
Thomas Church, New York City, in
honor of the 50th anniversary of the
founding of St. Thomas Choir School.
Dedicated to: Choir School of St.
Thomas Church, William Self, Organist
and Master of the Choir. *First*

performed: Mar. 2, 1969; St. Thomas
Church, New York City. St. Thomas
Church Boys Choir, George Bragg,
conductor.
Score & parts: E.C. Schirmer, 1971.
Rental.
Score: mss. in composer's hand. HUh
Score: reprods. of composer's mss.
HUh
Score: E.C. Schirmer, 1971. BPL
Vocal score: E.C. Schirmer, 1971. BPL
HU
Vocal score: E.C. Schirmer, 1971 (No. 1).
Vocal score: E.C. Schirmer, 1971 (No. 2).
Reel: recording of first performance.
HU
Reel: May 2, 1969. Texas Boy's Choir.
HU
Reel: n.d. Christ Church Choir. HU

T4.76 Prairie Home. (1951)
For: voice(medium) and piano.
Score: reprod. of ms. HUh

T4.77 A Psalm of Thanksgiving.
(1966-67)
For: chorus(SATB),
chorus(children)(2-part),
orchestra(2-2-2-2; 2-2-2-0; timp, perc;
hp; str) or organ or piano. Cantata.
Text: Bible, O.T., Psalm 107. *Contents:*
Chorale Prelude, Nun danket (based on
the chorale by Johann Crueger); Psalm.
Commissioned by: Mrs. Lucy B. Lemann.
Dedicated to: Dr. Maurice
Fremont-Smith. *First performed:* Nov.
15, 1967; New England Conservatory.
NEC Chorus; children's chorus; NEC
Symphony Orchestra, Randall
Thompson, conductor.
Sketch: ms. in composer's hand
(chorale, for organ). HUh
Score & parts: E.C. Schirmer. Rental.
Score: ms. in composer's hand. HUh
Vocal score: ms. in composer's hand.
HUh
Vocal score: E.C. Schirmer, 1967. NEC
Vocal score: E.C. Schirmer, 1970. BPL
HU
Disc: Fassett Recording Studio, 1967.
NEC Chorus; children's chorus; NEC
Symphony Orchestra, Randall
Thompson, conductor. HU

Reel: recording of first performance.
HU

T4.78 Pueri hebraeorum; Antiphonal.
(1927)
For: choruses(SSAA)(2).
Vocal score: ms. in composer's hand.
HUh
Vocal score: E.C. Schirmer, 1928. BPL
Disc: in *Twentieth Century Compositions
for Treble Voices,* Copeland Sound
Studios CSS 5544, n.d. University of
North Carolina Choir, Richard Cox,
conductor.
Reel: Palm Sunday, 1963; Evanston, III.
Randall Thompson, conductor. HU

[Quartet, Strings, No. 1, D minor]
T4.79 String Quartet· in D Minor. (1941)
29'
4 movements. *Dedicated to:* Elizabeth
Sprague Coolidge. *First performed:* Oct.
30, 1941; Coolidge Auditorium, Library
of Congress, Washington D.C. Coolidge
Quartet.
Study score: C. Fischer, 1948. BPL BU
HMA HU HUm T
Parts: reprod. of ms. L
Parts: C. Fischer, 1948. HU HMA NEC
Disc: Decca (England) M 541, [195-?].
Disc: Concert Hall CHS 1092. Guilet
String Quartet. HU
Reel: Oct. 13, 1972. Tanglewood
Quartet. HU

[Quartet, Strings, No. 2, G Major]
T4.80 String Quartet No. 2 in G Major.
(1967) 25'
Movements: Prelude; Air and Variations;
Adagio; Allegro con brio. *Commissioned
by:* Harvard Musical Association. *First
performed:* April 17, 1967; Harvard
Musical Association. Brandeis
University Quartet.
Sketches: ms. in composer's hand. HUh
Score: ms. in composer's hand. HUh
Study score: E.C. Schirmer, 1972. BPL
BrU HU
Parts: E.C. Schirmer, 1972. HU L
Disc: Fassett Recording Studio, 1967.
Brandeis University Quartet. HU
Reel: recording of first performance.

HU
Reel: May 7, 1967; Wellesley College.
Brandeis University Quartet. W

T4.81 Quintet. (1920)
For: flute, clarinet, viola, violoncello,
piano. 2 movements. Winner of George
Arthur Knight Prize (Harvard University,
1920). *Dedicated to:* Leopold D.[
amrosch] Mannes.
Score & parts: ms. in composer's hand.
HUh

T4.82 Requiem; a Dramatic Dialogue in
Five Parts. (1957-58) 80'
For: choruses(SATB)(2) and string
ensembles(2)(optional; duplicating voice
parts). *Text:* Bible. *Contents:*
Lamentations; The Triumph of Faith;
The Call to Song; The Garment of
Praise; The Leave Taking. *Commissioned
by:* University of California, Berkeley
for the dedication of new music
building. *Dedicated to:* Univeristy of
California Chorus, Edward B. Lawton,
conductor. *First performed:* May 22,
1958; Berkeley, Calif.
Score & parts: E.C. Schirmer. Rental.
Vocal score: E.C. Schirmer, 1963. BPL
HU
Disc: Technichord Limited Edition TC
15, RC 15/16, 1959. Harvard Glee Club;
Radcliffe Choral Society, Elliot Forbes,
conductor. HU HUm

[Requiem. The Garment of Praise]
T4.83 The Garment of Praise. (1958)
For: choruses(SATB)(2) and string
orchestra.
Score & parts: E.C. Schirmer. Rental.
Vocal score: E.C. Schirmer, 1963. NEC

[Requiem. The Leave Taking. Amen,
Alleluia]
T4.84 The Leave Taking. (1958)
For: choruses(SATB)(2).
Vocal score: E.C. Schirmer.

[Requiem. The Leave Taking. Thou
Hast Given Him]
T4.85 Thou Hast Given Him. (1958)

For: choruses(SATB)(2).
Vocal score: E.C. Schirmer.

[Requiem. The Leave Taking. Ye Were Sometimes Darkness]
T4.86 Ye Were Sometimes Darkness (Walk as the Children of Light). (1958)
For: choruses(SATB)(2).
Vocal score: E.C. Schirmer.

[Requiem. The Triumph of Fate. Good Tidings from the Meek]
T4.87 Good Tidings from the Meek. (1958)
For: choruses(SATB)(2).
Vocal score: E.C. Schirmer.

The Road Not Taken. *See* Frostiana.

T4.88 Rosemary. (1929)
For: chorus(SSAA) or chorus(SSA). *Text:* from *Tiger Joy* by Stephen Vincent Benet. *Contents:* Chemical Analysis; A Sad Song; A Nonesense Song; To Rosemary on the Methods by Which She Might Become an Angel. *Dedicated to:* Gerald Reynolds and the Women's University Glee Club of New York.
Vocal score: ms. in composer's hand. HUh
Vocal score: E.C. Schirmer, 1958. BPL HU L

T4.89 Scherzino. (1920)
For: flageolet, violin, viola. *First performed:* Dec. 14, 1920; New York City. Leopold Damrosch Mannes, flageolet; Leopold Godowsky, violin; Rieber Johnson, viola.
Score & parts: ms. in composer's hand. HUh

T4.90 Scherzo in F Major. (1921)
For: piano.
Score: ms. in composer's hand. HUh

T4.91 Scherzo in G Minor. (1921)
For: piano.
Score: ms. in composer's hand. HUh

T4.92 Septette. (1917)
For: flute, clarinet, string quartet, piano. 2 movements. *First performed:* June 3, 1917 (first movement).
Score: ms. in composer's hand. HUh

T4.93 Serenade in Selville. (1920)
For: Bass and piano. *Text:* Robert Cameron Rogers.
Score: ms. in composer's hand. HUh

T4.94 The Ship Starting. (1922)
For: Soprano and piano. *Text:* Walt Whitman.
Score: ms. in composer's hand. HUh
Score: in Tapestry; ms. in composer's hand. HUh
Part(voice): ms. in composer's hand. HUh

[The Ship Starting; Arr.]
T4.95 The Ship Starting. (1922)
For: Soprano and orchestra(2(&pic)-2-2-2(&cbsn); 4-2-3-0; timp, perc; hps(2); str).
Score: ms. in commposer's hand. HUh

Siciliano. *See* Love Songs. Siciliano.

T4.96 Solomon and Balkis (The Butterfly That Stamped). (1942) 43'
For: voices(5), chorus(SA), orchestra(1-1-1(Bb/A)-1; 2-2-0-0; timp, perc(2); str). Opera in 1 act. *Text:* adapted from *The Just So Stories* by Rudyard Kipling. *Commissioned by:* League of Composers and the Columbia Broadcasting System, Inc. *First performed:* Mar. 29, 1942; WABC-FM, New York City and its affiliates (concert version). Howard Barlow, conductor. First stage performance: Apr. 14, 1942; Lowell House Dining Hall, Harvard University. Harvard University Orchestra; Radcliffe Choral Society, Malcom Holmes, conductor.
Score & parts: E.C. Schirmer. Rental.
Score: reprod. of composer's ms. (with revisions in composer's hand). HUh
Vocal score: ms. in composer's hand. HUh
Vocal score: E.C. Schirmer, 1942. BPL HU HUm NEC T
Reel: May 27, 1970; Lighthouse Music

School, New York City (version for soloists and piano). Lena Morasse, Kathleen McGarth, Mark Kator, Joseph Parinello, soloists; and others; Frances Mains, piano; Richard Krause, director. HU

T4.97 Some One. (1927)
For: voice(medium) and piano. *Text:* Walter de la Mare. Children's music.
Score: in *Four Songs for Children*; ms. in composer's hand. HUh
Score: in *New Songs for New Voices*, Harcourt-Brace, 1928. HU
Disc: RCA Victor VM 789.

[Sonata, Piano, C Minor]
T4.98 Piano Sonata in C Minor. (1922-23)
3 movements. *Dedicated to:* Felix Lamond.
Score: ms. in composer's hand. HUh

[Sonata, Piano, G Minor]
T4.99 Piano Sonata. (1922)
1 movement.
Score: ms. in composer's hand. HUh

T4.100 Song after Sundown. (1935)
For: piano.
Score: C. Fischer, 1936.

Songs, 1925-26. *See* Discipleship; Doubts; Drought; The Heavens Declare; I Wan' My Friends; White Moth at at Twilight.

Songs (Five). *See* Discipleship; Drought; The Heavens Declare; I Wan' My Friends; White Moth at Twilight.

Songs (Four) for Children. *See* My Master Hath a Garden; Some One; Velvet Shoes; The Wild Home Pussy.

T4.101 Southwind. (1926)
For: voice(low) and piano. *Text:* Elizabeth Ann Moses.
Score: ms. in composer's hand. HUh
Spiritual. *See* I Wan' My Friends.

T4.102 Spring. (1920)
For: voice(high) and piano. *Text:* from *Songs of Innocence* by William Blake.
Dedicated to: Mrs. Richards.
Score: ms. in composer's hand. HUh
Score: reprod. of ms. HUh

T4.103 The Straw Hat. (1926)
For: piano. Incidental music.

T4.104 Suite. (1940) 13' 30'
For: oboe, clarinet, viola. 5 movements. *Dedicated to:* Bertrand H. Bronson.
Score: E.C. Schirmer, 1941. HMA HU HUm
Parts: E.C. Schirmer, 1941. BPL HMA HU HUm
Disc: Unicorn UNLP 1029, 1956. Louis Speyer, oboe; Pasquale Cardillo, clarinet; Joseph de Pasquale, viola. BrU HU
Disc: Crystal S 321, 1979. Peter Christ, oboe; David Atkins; clarinet; Alan de Veritch, viola. MiT NEC

T4.105 Suite for Piano. (1924)
Dedication: To Leopold Damrosch Mannes because he wrote 2/3 of the subject, and therefore the greater part of this suite as well as one of his own--one week in Roma.
Score: ms. in composer's hand (with annotation in the hand of Leopold Damrosch Mannes). HUh

T4.106 Symphony No. 1. (1924-29) 30'
For: orchestra(2(&pic)-2(&Ehn)-2(&bcl)-3(cbsn); 4-2-3-1; timp, perc; hp, org; str). 3 movements. Adapted from settings of Odes of Horace: Poscimur (I, 22) for chorus(SATB) and orchestra (1st movement, 1924-25) and Vides ut Alta (I, 9) for chorus(SATB) (2nd and 3rd movements, 1925). *Dedicated to:* Howard Hanson. *First performed:* Feb. 20, 1930; Rochester, N.Y. Rochester Philharmonic Orchestra, Howard Hanson, conductor.

Sketches: ms. in composer's hand (2nd & 3rd movements). HUh
Score & parts: C. Fischer. Rental.
Score: mss. in composer's hand (original versions). HUh
Score: Birchard, 1931. BPL HU
Disc: Angel S 37315, 1978. Utah Symphony, Maurice Abravanel, conductor. BU HU MIT NEC
Reel: May 9, 1971; NEC Symphony Orchestra, Gunther Schuller, conductor. HU
Cassette: May 9, 1971; New England Conservatory; in *A Festival of New England Composers Past and Present.* NEC Symphony Orchestra, Gunther Schuller, conductor. HU NEC

T4.107 Symphony No. 2. (1931) 27′ 32″
For: orchestra(3(pic)-2(&Ehn)-3-3; 4-3-3-1; timp; str). 4 movements.
Dedicated to: M.W.T. *First performed:* Mar. 24, 1932; American Composers' concert. Rochester Philharmonic Orchestra, Howard Hanson, conductor.
Sketch: ms. in composer's hand. HUh
Score & parts: C. Fischer. Rental.
Score: ms. in composer's hand. HUh
Score: Birchard, 1932. BPL HU HUm NEC
Disc: American Recording Society ARS 45, 195-. American Recording Society Orchestra (i.e.,Vienna Symphony Orchestra), Dean Dixon, conductor. BCM HU MIT NEC W
Disc: Desto D 406/DST 6406, 1964. Vienna Symphony Orchestra, Dean Dixon, conductor. BU HU MIT
Disc: Columbia MS 7392, 1970. New York Philharmonic, Leonard Bernstein, conductor. BU HU HUm NEC

T4.108 Symphony No. 3. (1949)
For: orchestra(3(pic)-3(Ehn)-2-2(&cbsn); 4-3-3-1; timp, perc(3); str).
Commissioned by: Alice M. Ditson Fund of Columbia University. *First performed:* May 15, 1949; New York City. CBS Symphony Orchestra.
Sketch: ms. in composer's hand. HUh
Reel: recording of first performance. HUh

T4.109 Tapestry. (1925)
For: voice and piano. *Text:* William Douglas.
Score: ms. in composer's hand. HUh

Tapestry. *See also* The Ship Starting.

T4.110 Tarentella (Do You Remember an Inn, Miranda?). (1936-37)
For: chorus(TTBB) and piano. *Text:* Hilaire Belloc. *Dedicated to:* Yale Glee Club, Marshall Bartholomew, director.
Vocal score: ms. in composer's hand. HUh
Vocal score: E.C. Schirmer, 1937. Ber BPL BU

T4.111 The Testament of Freedom; A Setting of Four Passages from the Writings of Thomas Jefferson. (1943) 24′ *For:* chorus(TTBB) and piano or orchestra(2-2-2-2; 4-3-3-1; timp, perc; str). *Text:* A Summary View of the Rights of British America (1744) (No. 1), Declaration of Causes and Necessity of Taking up Arms (1775) (Nos. 2 and 3), Letter to John Adams (1821) (No. 4). *Contents:* The God Who Gave Us Life; We Have Counted the Cost; We Fight Not for Glory; I Shall Not Die without a Hope. *Dedicated to:* University of Virginia Glee Club, in memory of the Father of the University. *First performed:* Apr. 13, 1943 (version for chorus and piano). University of Virginia Glee Club; Randall Thompson, piano; Steven Tuttle, conductor.
Score: E.C. Schirmer, 1971. BPL BrU
Study score: E.C. Schirmer, 1944. Be BPL BrU BU HU NEC
Parts: E.C. Schirmer. Rental.
Vocal score: E.C. Schirmer, 1944. BrU HU NEC
Disc: Mercury Wing SRW 18113. Eastman School of Music Choir; Eastman- Rochester Symphony Orchestra, Howard Hanson, conductor.
Disc: Pfeiffer 8777. Pfeiffer College Concert Choir, Richard Brewer, conductor.
Disc: Columbia XP333/8, 1943.

Recording of first performance.
Disc: RCA Victor
DM1054/M1054/VM1054, 1945. Harvard
Glee Club; Boston Symphony Orchestra,
Serge Koussevitzky, conductor.
Disc: Mercury MG 40000, 195-. Eastman
School of Music Choir; Eastman-
Rochester Symphony Orchestra, Howard
Hanson, conductor. HU HUm NEC
Disc: ASCAP CB 162, 1954 (3rd
movement). University of Pittsburgh
Men's Glee Club, David G. Weise,
conductor. BCM HU NEC W
Disc: Mercury MG 50073, 1956.
Eastman School of Music Choir;
Eastman- Rochester Symphony
Orchestra, Howard Hanson, conductor.
BU W
Disc: in *Music for Democracy*, Omega
811, 1958. Vassar College Glee Club;
MIT Glee Club, Klaus Liepmann,
conductor. MIT
Disc: Eastman Rochester Archives ERA
1007, 197-. Eastman School of Music
Choir; Eastman-Rochester Symphony
Orchestra, Howard Hanson, conductor.
BPL BU
Disc: Angel S 37315, 1978. Utah
Chorale; Utah Symphony, Maurice
Abravanel, conductor. BU HU MIT NEC
Reel: MAY 22, 1974. Boston
Conservatory. Boston Conservatory
Chorale, William A. Seymour,
conductor. BCM

[The Testament of Freedom; Arr.]
T4.112 The Testament of Freedom.
(1960) 24'-27'
For: chorus(TTBB) and band. *Text:* A
Summary View of the Rights of British
America (1744) (No. 1), Declaration of
Causes and Necessity of Taking up
Arms (1775) (Nos. 2 and 3), Letter to
John Adams (1821) (No. 4) by Thomas
Jefferson. *Contents:* The God Who Gave
Us Life; We Have Counted the Cost;
We Fight Not for Glory; I Shall Not
Die without a Hope. Arr. by John
Corley in collaboration with the
composer. *First performed:* Oct. 22,
1960; Massachusetts Institute of
Technology. MIT Concert Band; MIT

Glee Club, Randall Thompson,
conductor.
Score: E.C. Schirmer, 1961. HU
Parts: E.C. Schirmer, 1961. Rental.
Disc: in *Music at M.I.T. Centennial
Album*, M80P 4379/84, 1961 (No. 1).
MIT Glee Club; MIT Concert Band,
Klaus Liepmann, conductor. HUm MIT
NU
Reel: recording of first performance.
HU

[The Testament of Freedom.
Selections; Arr.]
T4.113 The Testament of Freedom.
(1943) 24'
For: chorus(TTBB) and piano(4-hands).
Contents: The God Who Gave Us Life; I
Shall Not Die without a Hope.
Vocal score: ms. in composer's hand.
HUh

Thou Hast Given Him. *See* Requiem.
The Leave Taking. Thou Hast Given
Him.

T4.114 Torches. (1920)
For: Soprano, viola, piano. Incidental
music. *Text:* Raesbeck.
Score: Brentano, 1920.

T4.115 Trio for Three Double Basses
(Divertimento for Strings).
For: double basses(3) or violoncellos(3)
or violas(3). 4 movements. *Dedicated
to:* Serge Koussevitzky. *First
performed:* 1949; Harvard Club,
Cambridge, Mass; dinner to honor
Serge Koussevitzky and members of
the Boston Symphony Orchestra.
George Moleux, Willis Page, Henry
Freeman.
Score: E.C. Schirmer, 1972. BPL HU
Parts: E.C. Schirmer, 1972. HU

T4.116 A Trip to Nahant; Fantasy.
(1954) 24'
For: orchestra(2(pic)-2-2-2;
4-2-2(&btrb)-0; perc, glock; hp, cel; str).
Symphonic poem. 1 movement.
Commissioned by: Koussevitzky Music
Foundation (Library of Congress).

Dedication: To the memory of Serge and Natalie Koussevitzky.
Sketch: ms. in composer's hand. HUh
Score & parts: C. Fischer. Rental.
Score: ms. in composer's hand. HUh
Score: reprod. of composer's ms. HU
Reel: Apr. 3, 1955. Philadelphia Orchestra, Eugene Ormandy, conductor. HU
Reel: Jan. 21, 1957. Boston Symphony Orchestra, Charles Munch, conductor. HU

The Triumph of Fate. *See* Requiem. The Triumph of Fate.

Two Worlds. *See* Love Songs. Two Worlds.

T4.117 Varied Air. (1921-22)
For: piano. Appears to be second movement of an unidentified composition for piano; first movement lost. *Dedicated to:* Mrs. Frances L. Groves.
Score: mss. in composer's hand. HUh

T4.118 Velvet Shoes. (1927)
For: voice(medium) and piano. *Text:* Elinor Hoyt Wylie. Children's music.
Score: in *Four Songs for Children*; ms. in composer's hand. HUh
Score: in *New Songs for New Voices*, Harcourt-Brace, 1928. HU
Score: in *Two Songs*, E.C. Schirmer, 1938. BPL L
Score: E.C. Schirmer, 1965 (reissue of 1938 ed.). L
Disc: RCA Victor VM 789.
Disc: RCA LCT 1158. Povla Frijsh, soprano and Celius Dougherty, piano.
Disc: Yaddo Festival 8A.
Disc: in *Art Songs*, Town Hall TH 002, 1962. MIT
Disc: Music Library MLR 7105, 1965. W
Disc: in *When I Have Sung My Songs: The American Art Song, 1900-1940*, New World NW 247, 1976. Povla Frijsh, soprano and Celius Dougherty, piano. BU MIT NEC
Reel: Feb. 14, 1969; University of South Florida. Jerold Reynolds, baritone. HU

[Velvet Shoes; Arr.]
T4.119 Velvet Shoes.
For: chorus and piano. Children's music. *Text:* Elinor Hoyt Wylie.
Vocal score: E.C. Schirmer, 1960. NEC

T4.120 Veritas. (1954)
For: Baritone and piano. *Text:* Mark Antony De Wolfe Howe. *Dedication:* To the muses.
Score: ms. in composer's hand. HUh
Score: reprod. of composer's ms. HUh
Part(voice): in Music Book, Jan. 1954; ms. in composer's hand. HUh

Walk as the Children of Light. *See* Requiem. The Leave Taking. Ye Were Sometimes Darkness.

A Wedding in Rome. *See* Wedding Music.

T4.121 Wedding Music.
For: string quartet. Suite. 8 movements. Originally titled A Wedding in Rome.
Score: ms. in composer's hand. HUh
Reel: 1971. HU

Wedding Music. *See also* Amens, String Quartet; Bitter-Sweet.

Wer nun den lieben Gott laesst walten. *See* Chorale Preludes. Wer nun den lieben Gott laesst walten.

T4.122 White Moth at Twilight.
For: voice(low) and piano. *Text:* Merle St. Croix Wright.
Score: ms. in composer's hand. HUh
Score: in Five Songs; ms. in composer's hand. HUh
Score: in Songs, 1925-26; ms. in composer's hand. HUh

T4.123 The Wild Home Pussy. (1927)
For: voice(medium) and piano. *Text:* Emma Rounds. Children's music.
Score: in *Four Songs for Children*; ms. in composer's hand. HUh
Score: in *New Songs for New Voices*, Harcourt-Brace, 1928. HU
Disc: RCA Victor VM 789.

T4.124 The Wind in the Willows. (1924) *For:* string quartet. *Movements:* River Bank; Toad, Esq.; The Wild Wood. *Score:* mss. in composer's hand (Nos. 1 & 2). HUh

The Wind in the Willows. *See also* The piper at the Gates of Dawn.

Ye Were Sometimes Darkness. *See* Requiem. The Leave Taking. Ye Were Sometimes Darkness.

ARRANGEMENTS OF WORKS BY OTHER COMPOSERS

T4.125 A Book of Songs by Erskine Wood, with Accompaniments for Piano by Randall Thompson. *For:* voice and piano. *Contents:* The White Seal's Lullaby (Rudyard Kipling); O Mistress Mine (William Shakespeare); Ariel's Fairy Song (William Shakespeare); Ariel's Sea Dirge (William Shakespeare); Sigh No More, Ladies (William Shakespeare); A Summer Lullaby; An Indian Lullaby; Ballade des dames des temps jadis (Francois Villon); Love, Ere Love Flies beyond Recall (Justin Huntly McCarthy); Gunga Din (Rudyard Kipling); Little Erskine's Baby Song. *Score:* G. Schirmer, 1922.

T4.126 Cold on ye Mountain. (1952) *For:* Tenor and chorus(TBB). Carol by P.H.R. *Vocal score:* reprod. of ms. HUh

V1 NICHOLAS VAN SLYCK

Born October 25, 1922. *Education:* Philadelphia Conservatory of Music; studied composition with Walter Piston (Harvard University, B.A., M.A.); piano with George Reeves; conducting with Henry Swoboda. *Related activities:* pianist; conductor; Vice President, Massachusetts Music Teachers Association; member, Cambridge Arts Council; conductor, Harvard Chamber Orchestra (1946-48); founder and conductor, Dedham Chorus (1954) and

Quincy Orchestra (1962-67); conductor, Merrimack Valley Philharmonic Orchestra (1967-); compiler and editor of the piano anthology *Looking Forward* (1981); served on the faculties of Milton Academy (1948-49) and Harvard University Graduate School of Education (1965-68); Director, South End Music Centre of Boston (1950-62), Longy School of Music (1962-76), New School of Music, Cambridge, Mass. (1976-). BPL

WORKS

Aeons. See Concerto, Piano.

V1.1 Ambush and Chase. (1960) 5' *For:* chamber orchestra(2-2-0-0; 0-1-1-0; timp; str). 1 movement. *Commissioned by:* Kalman Novak and Adventures in Music. *First performed:* Apr. 1, 1961; Lexington, Mass. *Score:* ms.

V1.2 Anniversaries. (1960-80) *For:* piano. *Dedicated to:* Trudi Van Slyck.

[Anniversaries. Overtones of the Orient]
V1.3 Overtones of the Orient. (1976) *For:* piano. *Score:* in *Looking Forward*, General Music, 1981.

[Anniversaries. Twighlight Way]
V1.4 Twighlight Way. (1968) *For:* piano. *Score:* in *Looking Forward*, General Music, 1981.

V1.5 Arboretum musicorum. (1961) 8' *For:* recorders(4) and percussion. *Movements:* Tropical; Marine; Night-Blooming Cereus; Evergreen. *Commissioned by:* American Recorder Society, Boston Chapter. *First performed:* Apr. 29, 1962; Second Church, Boston. American Recorder Society, Boston Chapter. *Score:* ms.

V1.6 Ascensiontide.
For: chorus.
Vocal score: reprod. of ms. L

[Cadenzas]
V1.7 Twelve Cadenzas: Preludes in All Keys in a Brilliant Style. (1966) 17'-18'
For: piano.
Dedicated to: Mary di Scipio. *First performed:* Oct. 23, 1966; Simsbury, Conn. Mary di Scipio.
Score: ms.
Reel: May 10, 1976; Longy School of Music. Trudi Van Slyck.

Canon. *See* Inventions.

[Capriccii]
V1.8 Three Capriccii. (1957) 9'
For: piano. *Dedicated to:* Trudi Salomon. *First performed:* Mar. 1961; Boston Conservatory. Nicholas Van Slyck.
Score: ms.

[Celebrations]
V1.9 Two Celebrations. (1970-73) 4'
For: chorus(SATB), trumpets(2), trombones(2). *Text:* Bible, O.T.. *Contents:* The Lord is King; Psalm 154. *First performed:* May 14, 1976; Longy School of Music. Longy School Chorus.
Score & parts: Amherst Press, 1974. L

V1.10 Chamber Concerto. (1954) 15'
For: trumpet, timpani, string orchestra. 3 movements. *Dedicated to:* Jacob Knuttenen. *First performed:* Apr. 1955; Milton Academy. Members of the Milton Academy faculty, Nicholas Van Slyck, conductor.
Score & parts: ms.

V1.11 Chamber Music. (1953) 12'
For: pianos(2). *First performed:* Feb. 1954; Brookline Public Library. David Bacon and Nicholas Van Slyck.
Score: reprod. of ms. BkPL
Reel: recording of first performance. BkPL

V1.12 Check-Mates. (1980) 10'
For: violin, viola, piano. 8 movements

based on Czechoslovakian folk tunes.
Score & parts: General Music.

V1.13 Chronicle of Life. (1961) 20'
For: Soprano, Bass, chorus(SATB), chamber orchestra(0-2-0-0; 2-0-0-0; hp; str). Cantata. *Text:* Nicholas Van Slyck. *Contents:* Childhood; Youth; Maturity; Old Age. *Commissioned by and dedicated to:* Belmont Community Chorus and Dedham Choral Society. *First performed:* May 27, 1962; Ames School, Dedham, Mass. Belmont Community Chorus and Dedham Choral Society, Nicholas Van Slyck, conductor.
Score & parts: ms.
Vocal score: ms.
Reel: recording of first performance.
Reel: 1964; Jordan Hall, Boston. Cecelia Society, Kalman Novak, conductor.

V1.14 Concert Music. (1954) 19'
For: piano and orchestra(2-2-2-2; 4-2-3-1; perc(3); str). 4 movements. *Dedicated to:* Richard Perry. *First performed:* Nov. 1957; Lily Dumont, piano; L'Orchestre de la Suisse romande, Kalman Novak, conductor.
Score & parts: ms.
Reel: Apr. 26, 1962; Jordan Hall, Boston. Nicholas Van Slyck, piano; Civic Symphony Orchestra of Boston, Kalman Novak, conductor.

V1.15 Concertino. (1970) 15'
For: violoncello and orchestra(2-2-2-2; 2-2-2-0; timp; str).
Score: ms.

[Concerto, Flute, Violin, Harpsichord, String Orchestra]
V1.16 Concerto. (1959) 15'
Dedicated to: Melville Smith. *First performed:* June 17, 1961; Boston Common, Boston. Nicholas Van Slyck, harpsichord; Cambridge Festival Orchestra, Eleftherios Eleftherakis, conductor.
Score: ms.
Reel: 1962; Sanders Theatre, Harvard University. Melville Smith, harpsichord;

Longy Festival Orchestra, Kalman Novak, conductor.

[Concerto, Piano]
V1.17 Concerto (Aeons). (1979) 30'
For: piano and orchestra(2-2-2-2; 4-3-3-1; timp, perc; str). 2 movements. *Commissioned by and dedicated to:* Trudi Van Slyck. *First performed:* Apr. 27, 1980; Salem, N.H. Trudi Van Slyck, piano; Merrimack Valley Philharmonic Orchestra, Nicholas Van Slyck, conductor.
Score & parts: ms. in composer's hand.

[Concerto, Piano, No. 2]
V1.18 Piano Concerto No. 2. (1957) 30'
For: piano and orchestra(2(&pic)-2-2(bcl)-2(cbsn); 4-2-3-1; timp, perc; str). 3 movements. *Dedicated to:* My parents.
Score: ms.

V1.19 Dialogo concertato. (1968) 10'
For: piano and organ. 1 movement. *Dedicated to:* Marcel Dupre. *First performed:* Mar. 5, 1969; Episcopal Divinity School, Cambridge, Mass. Nicholas Van Slyck, piano and David Pizarro, organ.
Score: ms.

V1.20 Dialogues. (1952) 17'
For: pianos(2). 3 movements. *Dedicated to:* David Bacon. *First performed:* Apr. 30, 1953; South End Music Center, Boston. David Bacon and Nicholas Van Slyck.
Score: ms.
Reel: Nov. 16, 1961; Brookline Public Library. BkPL

V1.21 Diferencias sobre La follia. (1966) 9'
For: harpsichord. 1 movement. *Dedicated to:* Irma Rogell.
Score: ms.

[Diferencias sobre La follia; Arr.]
V1.22 Diferencias sobre La follia. (1966) 9'

For: organ. 1 movement. *Dedicated to:* Irma Rogell. *First performed:* Aug. 9, 1967; Methuen, Mass. David Pizaro.
Score: ms.

V1.23 Divertimento No. 1. (1947-48)
For: chamber orchestra(1-1-1-0; 1-0-0-0; pf; str). *Commissioned by:* Radcliffe Drama Club. *First performed:* 1947; Cambridge, Mass. Harvard Chamber Orchestra, Nicholas Van Slyck, conductor.
Score: ms.

V1.24 Divertimento No. 2. (1948)
For: chamber orchestra(2-2-2-2; 1-0-0-0; str). *Commissioned by:* Radcliffe Drama Club. *First performed:* 1948; Cambridge, Mass. Harvard Chamber Orchestra, Nicholas Van Slyck, conductor.
Score: ms.

V1.25 Duet Cycle. (1967) 25'
For: Soprano, Baritone, piano. Song cycle. *Text:* based on nine early English poems.
Score: ms.

V1.26 Duo capriccioso. (1974) 10'
For: piano(4-hands). Variations. *First performed:* Oct. 16, 1974; WGBH-FM, Boston. Trudi Van Slyck and Nicholas Van Slyck.
Score: ms.
Reel: recording of first performance. WGBH
Reel: Jan. 1976; Longy School of Music. Trudi Van Slyck and Nicholas Van Slyck.

[Elegies]
V1.27 Four Elegies. (1970) 8' 30"
For: Baritone or Mezzo Soprano and piano. *Text:* early English poems. *Contents:* Eight O'Clock; Crying of Water; What the Bullet Sang; O Mortal Folk. *First performed:* Jan. 19, 1972; Northeastern University. Emmily Romney, mezzo soprano and William Merrill, piano.
Score: reprod. of ms.

V1.28 Encore March. (1969) 6'
For: orchestra(2(&pic)-2(&Ehn)
-2(&bcl)-2(&cbsn); 4-3-3-1; timp, perc;
str). *Commissioned by:* Harvard
University Class of 1944. *Dedicated to:*
Boston Pops. *First performed:* June 9,
1969; Symphony Hall, Boston. Boston
Pops, Nicholas Van Slyck, conductor.
Score & parts: ms.
Reel: recording of first performance.
WCRB

V1.29 Fanfare for Percussion. (1963) 2'
For: xylophone, triangle, cymbal, snare
drum, bass drum, timpani. *First
performed:* Jan. 1964; Quincy, Mass.
Members of the Quincy Orchestra,
Nicholas Van Slyck, conductor.
Score & parts: ms.

Fantasia numerica. *See* Sonata,
Bassoon.

V1.30 Finger-Paints. (1958)
For: piano. Children's music.
Score: reprod. of ms. (Nos. 1-17). L
Score: General Music, 1980.

V1.31 Forest Music. (1977) 18'
For: horn and piano. *Movements:*
Graveside; In the Forest; Nocturnal
Chase; Final Ceremony. *Dedicated to:*
Richard Greenfield. *First performed:*
May 24, 1979; Arlington, Mass. Richard
Greenfield, horn and Trudi Van Slyck,
piano.
Score: ms.

V1.32 Fugue Cycle. (1968) 30'
For: organ. 12 fugues.
Score: ms.

[Fugue Cycle; Arr.]
V1.33 Fugue Cycle. (1968) 30"
For: pianos(2). *First performed:* Apr. 25,
1968; Boston Center for Adult
Education. Trudi Van Slyck and
Nicholas Van Slyck.
Reel: recording of first performance;
available from composer.

Fuguetta. *See* Inventions.

V1.34 Gabriel's Sounds. (1980) 12'
For: timpani, percussion, brass
ensemble(trumpets(3), horns(4),
trombones(3), tuba). *Movements:* Bold as
Brass; Bare Bones; Horns of a
Dilemma; Windscale 12.
Score: ms.

V1.35 Gardens of the West. (1973) 20'
For: piano. Suite. *Movements:* Fantasie;
Spirit of Busoni; Elegy for Electric
Piano; Meditation on the Art of Fugue.
Dedicated to: Trudi Van Slyck. *First
performed:* Oct. 16, 1974; WGBH-FM,
Boston. Trudi Van Slyck.
Score: ms.
Reel: recording of first performance.
WGBH

V1.36 Hear the Sound of the Modes.
(1972) 3'
For: chorus(SATB) and flute. *Text:*
Nicholas Van Slyck. 1 movement.
Dedicated to: Longy School Chorus.
Vocal score: General Music, 1974. L

Improvisation. *See* Mysteries.

In Three Dimensions. *See* Sonata,
Piano, No. 5.

V1.37 In Two Parts. (1958)
For: piano.
Score: in *New Scribner Music Library*,
vol. I: Beginners, Scribner's, 1964.

Intermezzo. *See* Inventions.

V1.38 Introduction and Thirty Variations
on a Theme of Franz Schubert. (1969)
45'
For: piano. Theme by Franz Peter
Schubert. *Dedication:* In memoriam:
Richard Perry. *First performed:* Apr.
1974; Cambridge, Mass. Nicholas Van
Slyck.
Score: ms.

[Inventions]
V1.39 Nine Inventions. (1969) 10'
For: piano. *Movements:* Prelude; Gigue;
Canon; Burlesca; Passacaglia;
Intermezzo; Cantus; Scherzo; Fuguetta.

Dedicated to: Trudi Salomon.
Score: ms.
Score: in *Looking Forward*, General Music, 1981 (Canon, Fuguetta, Intermezzo, Passacaglia).

Irma's Toye for Harpsichord. *See* Suite, Harpsichord, No. 2.

V1.40 Journey in Song. 20'
For: chorus(children) and piano. *Text:* Nicholas Van Slyck.
Vocal score: General Music, 1975.

V1.41 Judgement in Salem. (1974) 25'
For: Soprano, Alto, Tenor, Bass, piano, snare drum. *Text: Salem Farms* by Henry Wadsworth Longfellow. *First performed:* Nov. 16, 1975; Essex Institute, Salem, Mass. Cambridge Quartet and others.
Score: ms. in composer's hand.
Score: General Music, 1975.
Reel: 1979; Gretchen d'Armand, soprano; Pamela Gore, alto; Jerry Hadley, tenor; John d'Armand, bass; Philip Morehead, piano.

V1.42 Laments and Processional Music. (1960) 9'
For: piano(left-hand). *First performed:* Feb. 5, 1967; Belmont Public Library, Belmont, Mass.
Score: ms.
Reel: recording of first performance.

V1.43 Lamentations of Jeremiah. (1961-81) 60'
For: Baritone, choruses(2), woodwinds, brasses, percussion. *Text:* Bible, O.T., Lamentations I:i-v.
Score: ms.

V1.44 Legend of Sleepy Hollow. (1963) 25'
For: chamber orchestra(1-C 1-1; 1-0-0-0; timp; str). Ballet music. 3 movements. *Commissioned by:* Diamond Junior High School, Lexington, Mass. *First performed:* Apr. 17, 1964. Nicholas Van Slyck, conductor.

Score: ms.
Reel: recording of first performance.

V1.45 Metamorphoses No. 1; Free Variations on a Twelve-Tone Row. (1962) 19'
For: piano. *Dedicated to:* Trudi Salomon. *First performed:* Mar. 1964; Boston Center for Adult Education. Trudi Salomon.
Score: General Music, nyp.
Reel: 1966; Trudi Salomon.

V1.46 Metamorphoses No. 2; Free Variations on a Twelve-Tone Row. (1963) 14'
For: piano. *First performed:* Feb. 1964; Boston Conservatory. Nicholas Van Slyck.
Score: ms.

V1.47 Metamorphoses No. 3. (1964) 25'
For: organ. *Commissioned by and dedicated to:* David Pizaro. *First performed:* Oct. 27, 1965; New York City. David Pizarro.
Score: ms.

V1.48 Music for Christmas. (1953) 7'
For: chorus(SATB) and organ or chamber orchestra(2-0-0-0; 1-0-0-0; str). 3 movements. *Commissioned by:* Milton Academy. Dec. 12, 1953. Milton Academy Chorus, Howard Abell, conductor.
Vocal score: ms.

[Mysteries]
V1.49 Seven Mysteries. (1977) 16'
For: piano. *Movements:* Turbulence; Chorale; Improvisation; Will O' the Wisp; Meditation; Barcarolle; Anatomy of the Dance. *Dedicated to:* Trudi Van Slyck. *First performed:* July 9, 1978; Falmouth, Mass. Trudi Van Slyck.
Score: ms.
Score: in *Looking Forward*, General Music, 1981 (Improvisation and Will O' the Wisp).
Cassette: 1978; Arlington Town Hall, Arlington, Mass. Trudi Van Slyck.

Night-Blooming Cereus. *See* Sonata, clarinet.

V1.50 Noel. (1966) 1'
For: flute and piano. *Dedicated to:* Lorrie Van Slyck.
Score: ms.

V1.51 Octet. (1962) 20'
For: flute, clarinet, horn, violin, viola, violoncello, timpani, piano(additional strings optional). 3 movements.
Commissioned by: Wellesley College.
First performed: Apr. 1963; Wellesley College.
Score: ms.

An Order of Intervals. *See* Sonata, Piano, No. 4.

Overtones of the Orient. *See* Anniversaries. Overtones of the Orient.

V1.52 Pairs. 12'
For: clarinets(2) or flute and clarinet.
Score: Southern-Tex, 1979.

V1.53 Pantomime. (1970) 21'
For: piano(4-hands). *Dedicated to:* Trudi Salomon. Apr. 18, 1971; Harvard, Mass. Trudi Van Slyck and Nicholas Van Slyck.
Reel: 1974; WGBH-FM, Boston. Trudi Van Slyck and Nicholas Van Slyck. WGBH
Reel: Jan. 1976; Longy School of Music. Trudi Van Slyck and Nicholas Van Slyck.

Passacaglia. *See* Inventions.

V1.54 Passamezzo antico. (1952) 6'
For: trumpets(2), horn, trombone, tuba.
First performed: 1963; Boston. Boston Brass Quintet.
Score & parts: Southern-Tex, 1972. L

V1.55 Passing Parade for Symphonic Winds. (1973) 4' 30"
For: band. *Dedicated to:* George Perrone. *First performed:* 1974; Framingham, Mass. South Framingham

High School Band, George Perrone, conductor.
Score: ms.

V1.56 Pianists Workshop. (1954-56)
For: piano. *Dedicated to:* Margaret Moreland and Richard Perry. *First performed:* Apr. 1955. Massachusetts Institute of Technology. Richard Perry.
Score: ms.
Score: in *Looking Forward*, General Music, 1981 (excerpts).

V1.57 Piano Partners. (1977-80)
For: pianos(2). *Dedicated to:* Trudi Van Slyck.
Score: General Music, 1981.

[Pictures]
V1.58 Four Pictures: Suite. (1958) 16'
For: piano. *Movements:* Seascape; Gravescene; Nightscene; Portrait R.P.
Dedicated to: Trudi Salomon. *First performed:* Feb. 1959; RIAS-Radio, Berlin, East Germany. Trudi Salomon.
Score: ms.
Reel: recording of first performance.
Reel: 1959; available from composer.
Reel: Dec. 2, 1959; Brookline Public Library. Trudi Salomon. BkPL

V1.59 Portrait. (1965) 6'
For: piano. 1 movement. *Commissioned by:* Concerts in the Home. *Dedicated to:* Lynne Bixler for her wedding. *First performed:* June 12, 1965; Boston. Sylvia Patrick.
Score: ms.

V1.60 Prelude & Fugue (for Tongue-in-Cheek). (1972) 5'
For: chorus(SATB), timpani, vibraphone.
Text: Nicholas Van Slyck.
Vocal score: General Music, 1973. L

V1.61 Quartet. (1959) 24'
For: clarinet, violin, violoncello, piano. 3 movements. *Dedicated to:* Anita Van Slyck. *First performed:* Dec. 1959; Jordan Hall, Boston. Sherman Friedland, clarinet; William Hibbard, violin; unidentified cellist; Nicholas Van Slyck, piano.

Score & parts: ms.
Reel: May 1961; Sanders Theatre, Harvard University. Philip Viscuglia, clarinet; Eleftherious Eleftherakis, violin; Nell Novak, violoncello; David Bacon, piano.

[Quartet, Strings]
V1.62 String Quartet (1954) 17'
Dedicated to: Anita Van Slyck.
Score & parts: ms.

V1.63 Quintet. (1967) 30'
For: string quartet, piano. *First performed:* May 22, 1975; Robbins Library, Arlington, Mass; in Robbins Library Concert Series. Longy String Quartet; Trudi Van Slyck, piano.
Score & parts: ms. in composer's hand.

V1.64 Rain Song. (1974) 4'
For: Soprano, Alto, Tenor, Bass, guitar. *Text:* Nicholas Van Slyck.
Vocal score: General Music, 1974.

V1.65 Rhythm Rounds. (1958) 6'
For: chorus(SATB). *Text:* Nicholas Van Slyck. *First performed:* June 1958; New England Conservatory. South End Music Center faculty and students, Nicholas Van Slyck, conductor.
Vocal score: General Music, 1969. L

[Ritornelles]
V1.66 Six Ritornelles: Rondos in Chamber Style. (1966) 15'
For: piano. *Dedicated to:* Trudi Van Slyck. *First performed:* Feb. 5, 1967; Belmont, Mass. Nicholas Van Slyck.
Score: ms.
Score: in *Looking Forward*, General Music, 1981 (No. 2).
Reel: recording of first performance.

[Romances]
V1.67 Six Romances. (1967) 10'
For: voice(low) and piano. *Text:* John Fletcher, John Dryden, Robert Herrick, and others. *First performed:* Apr. 1, 1968; Mt. Holyoke College. Calliope Shenas.
Score: ms.

V1.68 Sea Drift. (1965) 22'
For: Soprano and piano. Song cycle.
Text: Walt Whitman. *Dedicated to:* Olga Averino. *First performed:* Feb. 22, 1966; Longy School of Music. Penny Colwell, soprano and Nicholas Van Slyck, piano.
Score: ms.
Reel: Feb. 5, 1967; Belmont, Mass. Penny Colwell, soprano and Nicholas Van Slyck, piano.

V1.69 Sin tono. (1956)
For: guitar and guitars(2). *Movements:* Suite; 8 Studies; Sonostinata. *Dedicated to:* Guy B. Simeone.
Score: ms.

[Sonata, Bassoon]
V1.70 Sonata (Fantasia numerica). (1960) 12'
4 movements. *Dedicated to:* Tom Elliot.
First performed: Feb. 1, 1961; Jordan Hall, Boston. Tom Elliot.
Score: General Music, 1976.

[Sonata, Clarinet]
V1.71 Sonata (Night-Blooming Cereus). (1958) 12'
5 movements. *Commissioned by and dedicated to:* Sherman Friedland. *First performed:* May 1959; Jordan Hall, Boston. Sherman Friedland.
Score: ms.

[Sonata, Clarinet and Piano]
V1.72 Sonata. (1947) 12'
3 movements. *Dedicated to:* Don Mischara. *First performed:* 1947; Harvard University. Aaron Johnson, clarinet and Nicholas Van Slyck, piano.
Score: ms.

[Sonata, Flute]
V1.73 Sonata. (1957) 8'
3 movements. *Dedicated to:* Elinor Preble. *First performed:* May 28, 1959; Museum of Science, Boston. Elinor Preble.
Score: General Music, 1976.

Sonata, Harpsichord. *See* La Tomba di Scarlatti.

[Sonata, Piano, No. 1]
V1.74 Sonata. (1947) 15'
3 movements. *Commissioned by and dedicated to:* Noel Lee. *First performed:* Feb. 1948; Jordan Hall, Boston. Noel Lee.
Score: ms.

[Sonata, Piano, No. 2]
V1.75 Piano Sonata No. 2. (1948) 17'
3 movements. *Dedicated to:* Cynthia Bishop. *First performed:* Mar. 1949; Jordan Hall, Boston. Cynthia Bishop.
Score: ms.
Reel: Apr. 25, 1956; Brookline Public Library. BkPL

[Sonata, Piano, No. 3]
V1.76 Sonata No. 3. (1952) 11'
1 movement. *Dedicated to:* John Bavicchi. *First performed:* Apr. 12, 1953; Cambridge, Mass. Nicholas Van Slyck.
Score: ms.

[Sonata, Piano, No. 4]
V1.77 An Order of Intervals. (1954-55) 16'
3 movements. *First performed:* Nov. 1956; Andover, Mass. Klaus Goetze.
Score: ms.

[Sonata, Piano, No. 5]
V1.78 In Three Dimensions. (1956) 17'
Dedicated to: Klaus Goetze. *First performed:* May 1957; Cambridge, Mass. Trudi Salomon.
Score: ms.
Reel: 1958. Trudi Salomon.

[Sonata, Piano, No. 6]
V1.79 Sonata, No. 6. (1959) 22'
4 movements. *Dedicated to:* Lily Dumont. *First performed:* June 15, 1960; Judson Hall, New York City. Nicholas Van Slyck.
Score: ms.
Reel: Nov. 17, 1963; WCRB-FM, Waltham, Mass. R.G. Sturges.

[Sonata, Violin]
V1.80 Sonata. (1952) 15'
Dedicated to: Hellmut Wohl. *First performed:* May 1955; New England Conservatory. Jan Bobak.
Score: ms.

[Sonata, Violoncello]
V1.81 Sonata. (1954) 16'
Movements: Chaconne; Interrupted Serenade; Rondo.
Score: ms.

[Sonata, Violoncello and Piano]
V1.82 Sonata. (1966) 19'
Dedicated to: Virginia and David Bacon. *First performed:* Feb. 5, 1967; Belmont Public Library, Belmont, Mass. Hannah Sherman, violoncello and Margaret Rohde, piano.
Score: ms.
Reel: recording of first performance.

[Sonatas, Violin and Piano]
V1.83 Four Sonatas. (1956-65)
Contents: No. 1 in D; No. 2 in D; No. 3 in E; No. 4 in G. *Dedicated to:* Wolf Wolfinsohn. *First performed:* Apr. 1961; Judson Hall, New York City. Ayrton Pinto, violin and Nicholas Van Slyck, piano.
Score: ms.

[Sonatina, Clarinet and String Orchestra]
V1.84 Sonatina. (1948) 8'
Dedicated to: Aaron Johnson. *First performed:* May 1948; Sanders Theatre, Harvard University. Aaron Johnson, clarinet; Harvard Chamber Orchestra, Nicholas Van Slyck, conductor.
Score: ms.

[Sonatina, Recorders(2)]
V1.85 Sonatina. (1959) 3'
Score: ms.

[Sonatinas, Piano]
V1.86 Six Sonatinas. (1956-68)
Contents: No. 1 in C; No. 2 in D; No. 3 in A; No. 4 in G; No. 5 in E; No. 6 in F. *Dedicated to:* Alice Procter; Ruth Jaeger; Natalie Werbner; Trudi

Salomon.
Score: ms.
Score: in *Looking Forward*, General
Music, 1981 (Nos. 2 and 5).

V1.87 Stretching Exercises and Other
Studies.
For: piano.
Score: in *Looking Forward*, General
Music, 1981 (excerpts).

[Suite, Harpsichord, No. 1]
V1.88 Suite. (1970) 7'
Movments: Prelude; Air; Forlane;
Toccata. *Dedicated to:* Betty Burroughs.
First performed: Dec. 1971; WCRB-FM,
Waltham, Mass. Irma Rogell.
Score: E.C. Schirmer, 1970. BPL HU L

[Suite, Harpsichord, No. 2]
V1.89 Irma's Toye for Harpsichord, 2d
Suite. (1972) 3' 30"
Movments: Prelude; Allemand;
Saraband; Gigue. *Dedicated to:* Irma
Rogell. *First performed:* 1974; New
York City.
Score: ms.

[Suite, Piano(4-Hands)]
V1.90 Suite. (1968) 10'
Movments: Prelude; Dirge; Finale;
Postcript.
Score: ms.

[Suspensions]
V1.91 Five Suspensions, for Elementary
Tone Control.
For: piano. Children's music.
Score: reprod. of ms. L

V1.92 Symphonic Paraphrase. (1960) 22'
For: orchestra(2-2-2-2; 4-2-3-1; timp,
perc; str). *First performed:* Dec. 1960;
Sanders Theatre, Harvard University.
Cambridge Civic Symphony, Nicholas
Van Slyck, conductor.
Score: ms.
Reel: reocrding of first performance.

V1.93 Symphonic Paraphrase No. 2.
(1966) 17'
For: orchestra(2-2-2-2; 4-2-3-1; timp,

perc; str). *Dedicated to:* Quincy
Symphony Orchestra. *First performed:*
Apr. 5, 1967; Quincy Orchestra,
Nicholas Van Slyck, conductor.
Score: ms.
Cassette: Mar. 7, 1976; Andover, Mass.
Merrimack Valley Philharmonic
Orchestra. Nicholas Van Slyck,
conductor.

[Textures]
V1.94 Six Textures. (1973) 13'
For: pianos(2). *First performed:* Apr.
1974; Longy School of Music. Trudi
Van Slyck and Nicholas Van Slyck.
Score: ms.
Reel: Robbins Library, Arlington, Mass.
Trudi Van Slyck and Nicholas Van
Slyck.

Three Can Play. *See* Twelve for Three.

V1.95 Toccata. (1967) 2'
For: piano(left-hand).
Score: ms.

V1.96 La Tomba di Scarlatti: 3 Short
Sonatas for Harpsichord. (1965) 10'
Dedicated to: Irma Rogell. *First
performed:* Apr. 8, 1965; Jordan Hall,
Boston. Irma Rogell.
Score: ms.

[A Touch of the Times]
V1.97 Music for the Movie A Touch of
the Times. (1949)
For: flute, oboe, clarinet, violin, viola,
violoncello, piano. *Commissioned by:*
filmmaker. *First performed:* 1950;
Kenmore Theatre, Boston. Members of
the Boston Symphony Orchestra,
Nicholas Van Slyck, conductor.
Score: ms.

[A Touch of the Times; Arr.]
V1.98 Music for the Movie A Touch of
the Times. (1949)
For: pianos(2).
Score: ms.

V1.99 Twelve for Three: 12 Pieces for
Trio. (1973) 15'

For: woodwinds(3) or strings(3) or clarinets(3). *Dedicated to:* Commonwealth Chamber Players. Originally titled Three Can Play. *Score & parts:* Southern-Tex, 1976. *Reel:* May 1974; Boston. Commonwealth Chamber Players.

Twighlight Way. *See* Anniversaries. Twighlight Way.

V1.100 Variations. (1947) 16'
For: piano and orchestra(2-2-2-2; 3-0-0-0; str). 1 movement. *Dedicated to:* Russell Locke. *First performed:* Mar. 1947; Sanders Theatre, Harvard University. Noel Lee, piano; Harvard University Orchestra.
Score: ms.

V1.101 Virtuoso Chorus (4 Etudes for Chorus). (1975) 10'
For: chorus(SATB) and piano. *Text:* Nicholas Van Slyck. *Contents:* Warm-Up; Rhythm; Humming; Dynamics. *Dedicated to:* Judy; Dick; Jane; Olga.
Vocal score: General Music, 1975.

V1.102 Water Nymph. (1977) 3' 30"
For: Soprano, flute, piano. *Text:* Roden Berkeley Wriothesley Noel.
Commissioned by and dedicated to: Mary McEwen. *First performed:* Nov. 20, 1977; Lincoln, Mass. Mary McEwen, soprano; and others.
Score: ms.

Will O' the Wisp. *See* Mysteries.

V1.103 Wintertime. (1960) 4' 30"
For: pianos(2). 1 movement. *Dedicated to:* Jean McCawley. *First performed:* Milton, Mass. Jean McCawley and Nicholas Van Slyck.
Score: ms.

V1.104 With Twenty Fingers. (1970-71)
For: piano(4-hands). *Movements:* Easy (Not Difficult at All); Not So Easy (Not So Difficult); Not Easy at All (Easy/Difficult). *Dedicated to:* Trudi Salomon.
Score: General Music, 1973. BPL L

ARRANGEMENTS OF WORKS BY OTHER COMPOSERS

V1.105 Der Kunst der Fuge (Art of the Fugue). (1972) 100'
For: piano(4-hands). Original by Johann Sebastian Bach.
Score: ms.
Reel: Oct. 7, 1976; Goethe Institut, Boston. Trudi Van Slyck and Nicholas Van Slyck.

V1.106 Pachelbel's Canon. (1977) 4' 30"
For: chorus(SSATTB) and piano. Original by Johann Pachelbel.
Vocal score: General Music, 1977.

V2 BARRY LLOYD VERCOE

Born July 24, 1937, in Wellington, New Zealand. Moved to Boston area 1971.
Education: Mus. B. (University of Auckland, New Zealand, 1959); Diploma, Teaching (Teachers College, Auckland, New Zealand, 1960); B.A., Mathematics (University of Auckland, New Zealand, 1962); A.Mus.D. (University of Michigan, 1968); studied composition with Ross Lee Finney (University of Michigan, 1962-65); computer music with Godfrey Winham (Princeton University, 1968-70).
Awards: Rockefeller Foundation grant (1966), Ford Foundation Contemporary Music Project for Creativity in Music Education (1967-68), Princeton National Fellowship (1968-69), Massachusetts Council on the Arts and Humanities, Artist Fellowship Program in Music Composition (1975), National Endowment for the Arts Grant for music composition (1978). *Related activities:* systems analyst, Applied Data Research Corp. (1969-70); member of the Executive Committee, American Society of University Composers (1971-73); established the MIT Experimental Music Studio (1973); Conference Chairman, First International Conference on Computer Music (1976); U.S. Advisor, UNESCO Joint European Studies Commission on Technology and the Arts (1977-78); developed the MUSIC 360 language for synthesizing

sound on IBM computers (1968-70) and the MUSIC-11 system for digital processing of audio on PDP-11 minicomputers (1976-80); author of *An Interpreting Compiler for ALMA Code, User's Manual* (1973); *The MUSIC 360 Language for Digital Sound Synthesis: Reference Manual* (1973), *Man-Computer Interaction in Creative Applications* (1975), *The MUSIC-11 Language for Digital Sound Synthesis: Reference Manual* (1978); served on the faculties of Oberlin College (1965-67), Seattle-Tacoma School System (composer-in-residence, 1967-68), Yale University (1970-71), Massachusetts Institute of Technology (1971-). MIT

WORKS

V2.1 Dialogue. (1968) 4'
For: trumpet and tape.
Score: University Microfilms, 1969.

V2.2 Digressions. (1968) 15'
For: choruses(mixed)(2), tape(computer), orchestra. *Text:* Veni Creator Spiritus; The Earth Grown Like the Moon from *Songs of the Slums* by Toyohiko Kagawa. *Commissioned by:* Music Educators National Conference for its 1968 Biennial Convention. *First performed:* Feb. 1968; Seattle Opera House, Seattle, Wash. Barry Vercoe, conductor.
Vocal score: Elkan-Vogel, 1969. MIT
Disc: Crest Records MENC, 1968.

[Masefield Poems]
V2.3 Two Masefield Poems. (1958, 1968)
For: chorus(SATB). *Text:* John Masefield.
Vocal score: reprod. of ms.

V2.4 Metamorphoses. (1965) 11'
For: orchestra(1-0-1-1; 1-1-1-0; perc(2); str). *First performed:* Mar. 1967; Cincinnati, Ohio. Cincinnati Symphony Orchestra, Max Rudolf, conductor.
Score: University Microfilms, 1969.

[Negro Poems]
V2.4.5 Five Negro Poems. (1967) 6'
For: chorus(SATB), flute, piano.
Contents: Nativity (Aquah Laluah); Jazz Poem (Carl W. Hines, Jr.); Where Have You Gone? (Mari E. Evans); The Rebel (Mari E. Evans); Who Knows? (A.L. Milner-Brown). *First performed:* Dec. 1967; Tacoma, Wash. Clover Park High School Choir, Wilbur Elliot, conductor.
Score: reprod. of ms. MIT
Disc: Crest Records.

V2.5 Setropy: A Fantasy. (1964) 5'
For: clarinet and piano. *First performed:* Feb. 1964; Midwest Composers' Symposium.
Score: reprod. of ms. MIT

V2.6 Synapse. (1976) 6'
For: viola and tape(computer). Realized at the MIT Experimental Music Studio. Written for Marcus Thompson. *First performed:* Feb. 27, 1976; Massachusetts Institute of Technology; American Society of University Composers Convention. Marcus Thompson.
Score: reprod. of ms. MIT *Tape.*
Disc: in *Computer Generations*, Composers Recordings CRI 393, 1978. BrU BU HU MIT NEC W

V2.7 Synthesism. (1968) 4' 35"
For: tape. Computer music. Realized at the Princeton University Computer Center. *First performed:* Feb. 1971; Carnegie Recital Hall, New York City.
Disc: in *Computer Music*, Nonesuch H 71245, 1970. BU HU MIT NEC

V3 ELIZABETH HENDRY VERCOE

Born April 23, 1941, in Washington D.C. *Education:* B.A. (Wellesley College, 1962); studied composition with Ross Lee Finney (University of Michigan, M.M., 1963), Leslie Bassett (1964-65); Gardner Read (Boston University, Mus.A.D., 1978); musicology with Louise Cuyler (1965) and Gustave Reese (1965). *Awards:* Boston University,

School for the Arts, Composition Department, Student Composition Contest (First Prize, 1978), Hubert Weldon Lamb Prize in Composition (Wellesley College, 1978), Pi Kappa Lambda (1978), WGBH-Boston Musica Viva Competition (Winner, 1979), Ohio State School of Music Competition (Winner, 1980), Gedok Festival (Mannheim, West Germany) Award (1981), Meet the Composer Grant (1981). *Related activities:* pianist; music writer for WUOM-FM (1965-66); Kodaly Institute Research Assistant (1972); music critic, *Concord Journal* (1979-); adjudicator, Brookline Library Music Association Composers Award (1978), and Wellesley Choral Society Young Performers Competition (1980); served on the faculties of Westminster Choir College (1969-71) and Framingham State College (1973-74). W

WORKS

V3.1 Balance. (1974) 20'
For: violin and violoncello. 3 movements. *First performed:* Apr. 16, 1975; Brunswick, Me. Bowdoin College Contemporary Music Festival. Aeolian Chamber Players.
Score: Arsis, 1978. MIT W
Cassette: Apr. 26, 1978; Brookline Public Library. Janet Packer, violin and Chase Morrison, violoncello.

V3.2 Children's Caprice. (1963)
For: orchestra. Master's thesis, University of Michigan. *First performed:* 1963. Arlington Civic Symphony.

V3.3 Concerto. (1977) 29'
For: violin and orchestra(2-2-2-2; 4-2(in C)-3-1; timp(4), perc(2); hp; str). 3 movements. Doctoral thesis, Boston University.
Score & parts: University Microfilms.

V3.4 Fanfare. (1981) 1' 30"
For: trumpets(3) and timpani.
Commissioned by: Wellesley College for the inauguration of Nannerl Overholser

Keohane, eleventh president of the College. *First performed:* Sept. 18, 1981; Wellesley College. Members of the MIT Concert Band, John Corley, conductor.
Score: reprod. of ms. W

V3.5 Fantasy. (1975) 10'
For: piano. *Dedicated to:* Evelyn Zuckerman. *First performed:* Dec. 13, 1976; New England Conservatory. Evelyn Zuckerman.
Score: Arsis, 1978. MIT T W
Disc: Coronet LPS 3105, 1980. Rosemary Platt. MIT T
Reel: Feb. 13, 1981; Wellesley College. Vivian Taylor. W
Cassette: recording of first performance. NEC
Cassette: Dec. 13, 1976; New England Conservatory. Evelyn Zuckerman.

[Gratitudes]
V3.6 Six Gratitudes. (1978) 9'
For: piano. *Movements:* Hommage to Chopin; To Debussy; To Ravel; To Hindemith; Ives' Cage and Mine; To Samuel Barber. *Dedicated to:* Clara Lyle Boone. *First performed:* Nov. 5, 1978; President's House, Massachusetts Institute of Technology. Elizabeth McCrae.
Score: American Composers Alliance.

V3.7 Herstory I: A Song Cycle. (1975) 22'
For: Soprano, vibraphone, piano. *Contents:* Noon Walk on the Asylum Lawn (Anne Sexton); Her Kind (Anne Sexton); Side By Side (Adrienne Cecile Rich); For a Child: The Crib (Adrienne Cecile Rich) and Morning Song (Sylvia Plath); Mirror (Sylvia Plath); Old (Anne Sexton); Sleep (Elizabeth Bishop). Winner of WGBH-Boston Musica Viva Competition. *First performed:* Mar. 24, 1977; Brookline Public Library. Delores Corley, soprano; Paul Pitts, vibraphone; Dale Stark, piano.
Score: American Composers Alliance, 1978? W
Cassette: Feb 3, 1981; WGBH-FM, Boston. Boston Musica Viva. WGBH

V3.8 Herstory II: Thirteen Japanese Lyrics. (1979) 20'
For: Soprano, piano, percussion(percussion may be handled by soprano and pianist or by a third performer). *Text:* from *One Hundred Poems from the Japanese*, translated by Kenneth Rexroth; authors given as titles of movements. *Contents:* Lady Murasaki Shikibu; Interlude 1; Lady Kasa; Cont. Lady Kasa; Lady Otomo No Sakanoe; Lady Suo; Lady Horikawa; Lady Ukon; Lady Otomo No Sakanoe; Interlude 2; Lady Akazome Emon; The Mother of the Commander Michitsuna; The Poetess Ono No Komachi; Lady Shikibu; Lady Shikibu. Finalist in the Politis Composition Prize (Boston University), 1980. *First performed:* May 9, 1980; Boston University; Alea III concert. Elizabeth Van Ingen, soprano; Janice Weber, piano; Patrick Hollenbeck, percussion.
Score: American Composers Alliance.
Reel: recording of first performance. BU

V3.9 Pasticcio: Pattern and Imagery from Paul Klee. (1965) 10'
For: violoncello and piano. *Movements:* Dance of the Grieving Child; Night Flutterer; Reflective; Lady Demon; Mask of Fear. *First performed:* Feb. 22, 1965; Ann Arbor, Mich. Carol Young, violoncello and Rebecca West, piano.
Score: American Composers Alliance.
Cassette: Nov. 1975; Boston University. Joan Esch, violoncello and Elizabeth Vercoe, piano.

V3.10 Persona. (1980) 12'
For: piano. *Commissioned by and dedicated to:*, Vivian Taylor. Funded in part by a Meet the Composer Grant and by Smith College. *First performed:* Mar. 27, 1981; New York City. Vivian Taylor.
Score: reprod. of ms. W
Score: American Composers Alliance.
Reel: Apr. 5, 1981; Wellesley College. Vivian Taylor. W

[Riddles from Symphosius]
V3.11 Eight Riddles from Symphosius. (1964)
For: voice(medium) and piano. *Text:* Richard Wilbur. *Contents:* Hobnail; Mother of Twins; Onion; The Chick in the Egg; Stairs; River and Fish; Chain; Saw. *First performed:* Apr. 22, 1964; University of Michigan. Lois W. Alt, alto and Elaine Friedman, piano.
Score: reprod. of ms. W

V3.12 Sonaria. (1980) 6'
For: violoncello. Received Unanimous Honorable Mention, Felipe Gutierrez Espinosa International Competition, 1980.
Score: American Composers Alliance.

[Studies]
V3.13 Three Studies. (1973) 3'
For: piano. *Movements:* Mirrors; Daydream; Fugue. *First performed:* Nov. 18, 1975; Boston University. Andrew Kraus.
Score: Arsis, 1978. MIT W
Cassette: recording of first performance.

V4 JOHN VOIGT

Born June 26, 1939, in Boston, Mass. *Education:* B.A., English (Boston State College, 1968); M.S., Library Science (Simmons College, 1972). *Related activities:* author of *Jazz Music in Print*, contributor of articles to the Wilson Library Bulletin and publications issued by Olympia Press; Librarian, Berklee College of Music (1970-). Be

WORKS

V4.1 Bingo: A Game of Chance. (1980) Duration variable.
For: bingo caller and double basses(5). Aleatoric music.
Parts & tape: Hornpipe.
Disc: Baker Street Studios BSS 101, 1978. John Voigt, double basses and unidentified bingo caller. MIT

V4.2 Finally One Day. (1980) 7'
For: voice(female), xylophone, double
bass. *Text:* John Voigt.
Score: Hornpipe, 1980.

A Game of Chance for Contrabass
Quintet. *See* Bingo: A Game of Chance.

V4.3 On an Experiment Seeking Favour
and Love. (1980) 6'
For: double bass.
Score: Hornpipe, 1980.

V4.4 On an Experiment Seeking Favour
and Love II. (1980) 6'
For: double bass and electronics(any
electronic modification device or
instrument).
Score: Hornpipe, 1980.
Cassette: Hornpipe, 1980.

V4.5 Slum Settings. (1978) 19'
For: narrator and double basses(5).
Text: Nether City by John Voigt.
Disc: Baker Street Studios BSS 101,
1978. Unidentified narrator and John
Voigt, double basses. MIT

V4.6 Stardust. (1980) 6'
For: double bass and radio(AM)(tuned
to an easy-listening station softly).
Variations.
Score: Hornpipe, 1980.

W1 BETSY WARREN

Born in Boston. *Education:* A.B., A.M.
(Radcliffe College); studied composition
with Walter Piston, Nadia Boulanger,
Aaron Copland; attended seminars
given by Bela Bartok. *Related activities:*
singer (uses name Betsy Frost). BPL

WORKS

W1.1 Air for Ann. (1978)
For: violin and piano.
Score: ms.

W1.2 The American Group.
For: Soprano and piano. *Contents:*
Sound the Trumpet; The Quiet Room;

The Magnet; The Rain Journey. *First
performed:* Apr. 13, 1977; Cambridge
Musical Club, Cambridge, Mass. Betsy
Frost i.e. Betsy Warren, soprano and
Reginald Boardman, piano.
Score: ms. *Tape.*

Anthology for Chorus SA or Duet. *See*
Fair Haven.

W1.3 The Appletree Madrigals. (1978)
For: chorus(SSAA) and pianos(2). *Text:*
Ruth Whitman. Written for the
centenary of Radcliffe College. *First
performed:* Mar. 1980; Sanders Theatre,
Harvard University. Radcliffe College
Choir. *Vocal score. Tape.*

W1.4 Ask If You Damask Rose Be
Sweet.
For: chorus.
Vocal score: E.C. Schirmer, 1974?

W1.5 Consort.
For: flute(baroque) and harpsichord.
Score & part: Wiscasset. BPL

W1.6 Dieu vous gard'. (1975)
For: Tenor, string quartet, double bass.
Text: Pierre de Ronsard. *First
performed:* Apr. 13, 1977; Cambridge
Musical Club, Cambridge, Mass.
(performed under the title String
Quartet with Tenor). Benjamin Cox,
tenor; Adeen Zeitlin and Margaret
Dusenberry, violins; Elizabeth S. Lowell,
viola; Ruth Belvin, violoncello; Justin
Locke, double bass.
Score: ms. *Tape.*

W1.7 Duet. (1974) 4'
For: flute(baroque) and harpsichord.
First performed: Oct. 16, 1974;
Cambridge Musical Club, Cambridge,
Mass. Natalie Palme, tenor recorder
and Naoko Hague, harpsichord.
Score: ms.
Score: Wiscasset, 1981. *Tape.*

[Duets, Flutes(2)]
W1.8 Five Duets. (1977)
Score: ms.

[Duets, Saxophones]
W1.9 Duets for Two Saxophones. (1975)
4'
For: saxophone(soprano) and
saxophone(alto). 3 movements. *First
performed:* Apr. 13, 1977; Cambridge
Musical Club, Cambridge, Mass. Alan
Klingaman, soprano saxophone and Carl
Lafky, alto saxophone.
Score: ms.
Score: Wiscasset, 1981 (titled For Two
Saxophones). BPL *Tape.*

[Duets, Sopranos]
W1.10 Five Duets. (1975)
For: Sopranos(2) and piano. *Contents:*
Lucy Locket; Pussy Cat; Taffy Was a
Welshman; "To Bed to Bed" Says
Sleepyhead; When Good King Arthur
Ruled His Land. *First performed:* Apr.
13, 1977; Cambridge Musical Club,
Cambridge, Mass. Lily Kinas and
Jessica Locke, sopranos; Georgeann
Peterson, piano.
Score: ms. *Tape.*

[Duets, Violin and Viola]
W1.11 Four Duets. (1942)
Score: ms.

W1.12 Ecclesiastes III. (1975)
For: Sopranos(2) and keyboard. *Text:*
Bible, O.T., Ecclesiastes 3:1-4, 8.
Score: ms.

W1.13 Fair Haven (Anthology for
Chorus SA or Duet).
For: chorus(SA) or Soprano and Alto.
Score: E.C. Schirmer, 1949.
Score: Wiscasset, n.d.

W1.14 Fantasy. (1978)
For: harp. 2 movements. *First
performed:* Feb. 20, 1979; The College
Club, Boston. Cynthia Price.

Five Poems in Five Minutes. *See* Five
Songs in Five Minutes.

W1.15 Five Songs in Five Minutes.
For: chorus(SATB). *Text:* David
Thompson Watson McCord. *Contents:*

Oz; Knotholes; Corinna; Queer; Trouble
with Pies.
Vocal score: ms. (titled, Five Poems in
Five Minutes).
Vocal score: Wiscasset, 1980. BPL *Tape.*

For Two Saxophones. *See* Duets,
Saxophones.

W1.16 Fugue and Postlude. (1974) 3'
For: harpsichord. *First performed:* Oct.
16, 1974; Cambridge Musical Club,
Cambridge, Mass. Naoko Hague.
Score: ms.

W1.17 Jonah. (1981)
For: Baritone and string quartet. *Text:*
Bible, O.T., Jonah.
Score: ms.

W1.18 Jubilee Hymn. (1977)
For: chorus(SATB). *Text:* Betsy Warren.
Written for the 25th year of the reign
of Queen Elizabeth II.
Vocal score: ms.

W1.19 Impromptu. (1979)
For: piano.
Score: ms. in composer's hand.

W1.20 Missa brevis. (1976) 9'
For: chorus(SATB). *Text:* Mass (Revised
Anglican). Written to commemorate the
50th anniversary the laying of the
foundation stone of Christ Church
Cathedral, B.C., Canada.
Vocal score: ms.

W1.21 Night Watch in the City of
Boston. (1975)
For: Soprano, Tenor, Bass,
chorus(SATB), orchestra(1-1-1-1; 0-1-0-0;
str). Cantata. *Text: Night Watch in the
City of Boston* by Archibald MacLeish.
Contents: Overture; Old Colleague; A
Law School Boy; What City Wit?; City
of God; Interlude; Lead Me; City of
Man; City of the Famous Dead; The
Darkness Deepens; Show Me the City.
Score: reprod. of ms. BPL
Score: Wiscasset, 1981. BPL HMA

Parts: Wiscasset. Rental.
Vocal score: Wiscasset, 1981. BPL

Nursery Rhymes. *See* Duets, Sopranos.

W1.22 Octet. (1977) 9'
For: oboes(2), clarinets(2), horns(2), bassoons(2).
Score & parts: ms.

[Piece, Flute and Piano]
W1.23 Piece.
Score: ms. in composer's hand.

[Piece, Violoncellos(4)]
W1.24 Piece. (1978)
Score: ms.

W1.25 Psalm. (1974) 4'
For: Soprano and flute or recorder.
Text: Bible, O.T., Psalm 121 and Bible, O.T., Psalm 33. *First performed:* Oct. 16, 1974; Cambridge Musical Club, Cambridge, Mass. Betsy Frost, soprano and Natalie Palme, alto recorder.
Score: ms.
Score: Wiscasset, 1981. BPL *Tape.*

[Quartet, Saxophones]
W1.26 Saxophone Quartet. (1977)
For: saxophone(soprano), saxophone(alto), saxophone(tenor), saxophone(bass).
Score: ms.
Score: Wiscasset, 1981.
Parts: Wiscasset, 1981. BPL

[Quartet, Strings]
W1.27 String Quartet, No. 1. 11' 30"
First performed: Feb. 20, 1979; The Chromatic Club, Boston. Commonwealth Chamber Players.
Score: ms.
Score: Wiscasset, 1981.

[Quartet, Strings(3) and Piano]
W1.28 Quartet. (1978)
For: violins(2), violoncello, piano.
Score & parts: ms.

Quartet, Strings and Tenor. *See* Dieu vous gard'.

[Quartet, Tubas]
W1.29 Quartet. (1977)
Written for horn players of the orchestra of Covent Garden.
Score: ms.

[Quartet, Violins]
W1.30 Quartet. (1980)
3 movements.
Score: ms.
Score: Wiscasset, 1981.

[Quartet, Viols]
W1.31 Quartet. (1974) 4'
For: viols(treble)(2), viol(tenor), viols(bass). 2 movements. *First performed:* Oct. 16, 1974; Cambridge Musical Club, Cambridge, Mass. Carol Lewis and Judy Cochran, treble viols; Louise Treitman, tenor viol; Karen Larsen, bass viol.
Score & parts: ms.

W1.32 Redstart. (1981)
For: voice and piano. *Text:* Emily McFarland.
Score: ms.

W1.33 Ride a Cock Horse. (1975)
For: piano.
Score: ms.
Score: Wiscasset.

W1.34 The Rose and the Ring. (1980) 90'
For: Soprano, Mezzo Sopranos(2), Alto, Tenor, Baritone, Basses(2), chorus, orchestra(1-1-1-1; 0-1-1-0; timp; str). Chamber opera in three acts. *Text:* William Makepeace Thackeray.
Score: reprod. of ms. BPL
Score & parts: Wiscasset. Rental.
Vocal score: Wiscasset. Rental.

[Sonata, Clarinet, Horn, Piano]
W1.35 Sonata. (1975) 9'
3 movements.
Score: ms.

[Sonata, Flute and Harp]
W1.36 Sonata. (1976)
3 movements. *First performed:* Feb. 20, 1979; The Chromatic Club, Boston.

Dana Wood, flute and Cynthia Price, harp.
Score: ms. *Tape.*

[Sonata, Viol(Bass) and Piano]
W1.37 Sonata. (1977)
3 movements. *First performed:* Apr. 13, 1977; Cambridge Musical Club, Cambridge, Mass. Justin Locke, bass viol and Steven Drury, piano.
Score: ms. *Tape.*

[Sonata, Violin and Piano]
W1.38 Sonata. (1977) 7'.
4 movements.
Score: ms.

Songs for Soprano and Piano. *See* The American Group.

String Quartet with Tenor. *See* Dieu vous gard'.

W1.39 Suite. (1977; rev. in progress) 10'
For: piano. 4 movements. *First performed:* Feb. 20, 1979. The Chromatic Club, Boston. Ralph Richey.
Score: ms. *Tape.*

Suite for Recorders. *See* Trio, Recorders.

W1.40 Suite for Soprano and Bass. (1976)
For: instruments(unspecified)(2) or flute and violoncello. 6 movements.
Score: ms.

W1.41 Theme and Variations for Four Brass Instruments. (1975) 4'
For: trumpets(2), horn, tuba or trombone.
Score & parts: ms.

[Trio, Flute, Oboe, Piano]
W1.42 Trio. (1978)
1 movement.
Score & parts: ms.
Score & parts: Wiscasset, 1981.

[Trio, Recorders]
W1.43 Trio (Suite). (1975) 5'
For: recorders(tenor)(2) and recorder(bass). *Movements:* Nobile; Senz 'affanno; Delicato. *First performed:* Apr. 13, 1977; Cambridge Musical Club, Cambridge, Mass. Joseph Dyer, Natalie Palme, David Ruhl.
Score: ms.
Score: Wiscasset, 1981. *Tape.*

[Trio, Recorders(2) and Viol]
W1.44 Trio. (1974) 6'
For: recorder(tenor), recorder(contrabass), viol(bass). 3 movements. *First performed:* Oct. 16, 1974; Cambridge Musical Club, Cambridge, Mass. David Ruhl, tenor recorder; Natalie Palme, great bass recorder; Karen Larson, bass viol.
Score: ms.

W1.45 Wedding Gift. (1979)
For: oboe, viola, piano. 2 movements.
Score: ms.

W2 CLIFFORD M. WEEKS

Born April 15, 1938, in Spring Valley, N.Y. Moved to Boston area 1959. *Education:* Professional Diploma (Berklee College of Music, 1962), B.M., M.M. (Boston Conservatory, 1963, 1975); Certificate of Advanced Graduate Study (Boston State College, 1977); graduate studies in Afro-American Music (New England Conservatory); studied compositon with Richard Bobbitt and Avram David; arranging with Everett Longstreth and Herb Pomeroy; trombone with Ron Barron and John Coffey. *Awards:* Omega Man of the Year (1972), Black Educators Alliance Award (1976). *Related activities:* arranger for professional artists; trombonist; vocal coach; instructor of piano, arranging, composition, trombone; conductor. Be

WORKS

W2.1 Divertimento. (1962)
For: orchestra. Withdrawn

W2.2 The King. (1975) 17'
For: narrator, chorus(SATB),
orchestra(2(&pic)-2(&Ehn)
-2(&bcl)-2(&cbsn); 4-3-3-1; timp(4), perc,
glock; hp; pf; str). Oratorio. *Text:* based
on the life and teachings of Martin
Luther King Jr., from books by Laron
C. Bennett and Robert Hoyt; poem by
Barbara Powers. *First performed:* Jan.
1976; Boston Symphony Orchestra
Youth Concert Series. Walt Sanders,
narrator; chorus of students and
faculty of the Boston Public Schools;
Fine Arts Chorale of Weymouth;
members of the Boston Symphony
Orchestra.
Score: reprod. of ms. BCM

W2.3 The Man of the Mountain. (1963)
For: orchestra. Withdrawn.

W2.4 Motet in the Style of Josquin
des Prez. (1961)
For: chorus(SATB). Withdrawn.

W2.5 Scherzo in the Style of Clifford
Weeks. (1962)
For: oboe and piano. Withdrawn.

W2.6 Songs in the Style of Ravel.
(1962)
For: voice and piano. Withdrawn.

[Stage Band Compositions and
Arrangements]
W2.7 Four Stage Band Compositions
and Arrangements.
For: jazz band. *Movements:* Right On Lil
Ethel; Bossa Me; One for Shelley; Villa
Cordobes.
Music: Berklee Press, 1976.

W2.8 Triptych. (1964) 6'
For: tuba and piano. 3 movements.
Score: Robert King, 1971. Be
Disc: RPC Records. Karl Megules, tuba
and Bernie Leighton, piano.

ARRANGEMENTS OF WORKS BY OTHER COMPOSERS

W2.9 Along Came Betty. (1961)
For: jazz band. Original composed by
Benny Golson.
Score: in *A Tribute to Benny Golson.*
Jazz in the Classroom, vol. 5. Berklee,
1961. Be
Disc: in *A Tribute to Benny Golson.* Jazz
in the Classroom, vol. 5. Berklee, 1961.

W3 EDGAR WEISS

Born November 18, 1947, in Stamford,
Conn. Moved to Boston area 1970.
Education: B.M. (Berklee College of
Music); studied composition with John
Bavicchi, William Maloof, Jeronimas
Kacinskas, Herb Pomeroy. *Related
activities:* trombonist; arranger;
television producer; served on the
faculties of Berklee College of Music
(1970-80), Northeastern University
(1980-). NU

WORKS

W3.1 Duet Cycles on Rhythm. (1980-81)
2'-3'
For: instruments(unspecified)(wind). 6
movements.
Parts: ms.

W3.2 Flossin'. (1981) 7'-8'
For: jazz band. Variations. 1 movement.
Commissioned by: Northeastern
University Rocky Road Jazz Band. *First
performed:* 1981; Boston.
Score & parts: ms.

W3.3 Ida's Energy. (1975) 3'
For: piano. Variations. *Dedication:* In
memory of Ida Crockin of Norfolk, Va.
First performed: Feb. 27, 1975; Berklee
College of Music. Robert DeGrout.
Score: ms.

W3.4 Mila's.
First performed: 1973; New England
Conservatory. A.A. Cohen.

W3.5 Modogenesis. (1971) 18'
For: trombone(with mutes) and
percussion(timpani(4), tom-toms(3),
snare drum, suspended cymbal,

woodblock, vibraphone, xylophone). 3 movements. Written in collaboration with Ron Delp. *First performed:* 1971; Berklee College of Music. Edgar Weiss, trombone and Ron Delp, percussion. *Score & parts:* Seesaw, 1972.

W3.6 Nunc pro tunc. (1979) 8′ 30″
For: brass ensemble(trumpets(4), trombones(4), horns(4)) and percussion (timpani(2), tom-toms(5), vibraphone, snare drum, bass drum, suspended cymbal, triangle). 4 movements. *Commissioned by:* Arlington Philharmonic Society. *First performed:* 1979; Lexington, Mass. Members of the Arlington Philharmonic. *Score & parts:* ms.

W3.7 Parish or Perish. (1970) 3′
For: Tenor and piano. *Text:* based on the poem by Edgar Weiss. *First performed:* 1972; Berklee College of Music. Brian O'Connell, tenor. *Score:* ms.

W4 WILLIAM SCOTT WHEELER (SCOTT)

Feb. 24, 1952, in Washington D.C. Moved to Boston area 1973. *Education:* Berkshire Music Center, Tanglewood (1975); studied composition with Lewis Spratlan, Donald Wheelock (Amherst College, B.A., 1973); Arthur Berger, Harold Shapero (Brandeis University, M.F.A., 1978); Oliver Messiaen. *Related activities:* pianist; conductor; Music Director, Cambridge Chorale (1976-78); music coordinator, pianist and conductor, Dinosaur Annex music ensemble (1976-); member of the faculty of Emerson College (1978-). BPL

WORKS

W4.1 A Babe Is Born. (1979) 3′
For: chorus(mixed). *Text:* anon. *Dedicated to:* Emerson College Chorus. *First performed:* Dec. 1979; Church of the Covenant, Boston. Emerson College Chorus, Scott Wheeler, conductor.

Vocal score: ms. in composer's hand.
Reel: recording of first performance.

W4.2 Calamity Rag. (1979) 4′
For: piano. *Dedicated to:* Willa Rouder. *First performed:* Oct. 1979; Emerson College. Scott Wheeler. *Score:* ms. in composer's hand.

W4.3 Chanson singeresse. (1978) 4′
For: piano. *Dedicated to:* Wendy Wheeler and Patrick Pedonti. *First performed:* June 1978; Darien, Conn. Scott Wheeler. *Score:* ms. in composer's hand.

W4.4 Green Geese. (1977) 3′
For: piano. *Dedicated to:* Willa Rouder. *First performed:* Sept. 1978; Edgartown, Mass. Willa Rouder. *Score:* ms. in composer's hand. *Cassette:* recording of first performance.

W4.5 Grey Gardens. (1977) 7′
For: piano(4-hands). *Dedicated to:* Rodney Lister. *First performed:* Sept. 30, 1977; First and Second Church, Boston; Dinosaur Annex concert. Scott Wheeler and Rodney Lister. *Score:* ms. in composer's hand. *Reel:* recording of first performance. WGBH *Reel:* Feb. 7, 1979; WGBH-FM, Boston; *Live Performance Program: Brave New Music.* Dinosaur Annex. WGBH *Cassette:* Sept. 1979; First and Second Church, Boston; Dinosaur Annex concert. Scott Wheeler and Rodney Lister.

W4.6 Oranges and Lemons. (1978) 8′
For: voice and piano. *Contents:* Housekeeping Song (Arthur Williams); A Waist (Gertrude Stein); The King of China's Daughter (Dame Edith Sitwell). *Dedication:* To Mrs. Margaret Lee Crofts; To Barbara Winchester. *First performed:* Oct. 3, 1978; Institute of Contemporary Art, Boston; Dinosaur Annex concert. Barbara Winchester, soprano and Scott Wheeler, piano.

Score: ms. in composer's hand.
Reel: recording of first performance.

W4.7 Pas de malheur. (1978) 4'
For: trumpet and harp. *Dedicated to:*
Jeff and Dawn Myers. *First performed:*
Apr. 1979; Isabella Stewart Gardner
Museum, Boston. Peter Kertzner,
trumpet and Martha Moor, harp.
Score: reprod. of ms.

W4.8 Peter Quince at the Clavier.
(1976) 5'
For: chorus(mixed) and piano. *Text:*
Wallace Stevens. *Commissioned by:*
Singers, Ltd, Darien, Conn. *Dedicated
to:* Alice Myers and Singers, Ltd. *First
performed:* May 1976; Darien, Conn.
Singers, Ltd, Alice Myers, conductor.
Vocal score: ms. in composer's hand.
Reel: recording of first performance.

W4.9 Peter Quince at the Clavier.
(1977) 5'
For: chorus(women) and piano. *Text:*
Wallace Stevens. *First performed:* May
1977; First and Second Church, Boston.
Cambridge Chorale, Scott Wheeler,
conductor.
Vocal score: ms. in composer's hand.
Reel: recording of first performance.

W4.10 Piece for Five Players. (1975) 7'
For: English horn, clarinet, trumpet,
viola, double bass. *First performed:*
May 1975; Brandeis University. Scott
Wheeler, conductor.
Score: ms. in composer's hand.
Reel & cassette: recording of first
performance.

W4.11 Portrait. (1980) 2'
For: clarinet.
Score: ms. in composer's hand.

W4.12 Sextet. (1973) 10'
For: flute, clarinet, horn, violin, double
bass, piano. 3 movements. *First
performed:* May 1973; Amherst College.
Scott Wheeler, conductor.
Score: ms. in composer's hand.
Reel & cassette: recording of first
performance.

[Short Piano Pieces]
W4.13 Three Short Piano Pieces. (1974?)
Withdrawn.

W4.14 Singerie. (1979) 5'
For: violin, clarinet, piano. *First
performed:* May 19, 1980; First and
Second Church, Boston. Members of
Dinosaur Annex.
Score: ms. in composer's hand.
Reel: recording of first performance.

W4.15 Sweet Cream. (1978) 8'
For: violins(2), viola, piano. *First
performed:* Apr. 1978; First and Second
Church, Boston. Members of Dinosaur
Annex.
Score: ms. in composer's hand.

W4.16 To the Owl. (1978) 4'
For: Soprano, flute, clarinet,
violoncello. *Text:* Alfred, Lord
Tennyson. *Dedicated to:* Arthur Berger.
First performed: May 1978; Isabella
Stewart Gardner Museum, Boston.
Barbara Winchester, soprano and
mernbers of Dinosaur Annex.
Score: ms. in composer's hand.
Reel: recording of first performance.

W5 ROBERT WINFREY

Born June 14, 1933, in Atlanta, Ga.
Moved to Boston area 1971. *Education:*
studied composition with Kemper
Harreld, Willis Laurence James
(Morehouse College, B.A., 1954); Hary
R. Wilson (Teachers College, Columbia
University, M.A., 1960); organ with Seth
Bingham; piano with Mary Barber.
Awards: Tangley Oaks Fellowship
(Columbia University, 1968), Harvard
University Kuumba Singers Creative
Arts Award (1973), Rollins Griffith
Memorial Award, (1979). *Related
activities:* organist, pianist, arranger,
teacher, school administrator; served
on the faculty of the University of
Massachusetts, Boston; currently
Minister of Music, Bethel Baptist
Church, Roxbury, Mass.; Director of
Kuumba Singers, Harvard University and
of the All-City Chorus of the Boston

Public Schools; Coordinator of Creative Arts, African-American Institute, Northeastern University; Assistant Headmaster in Charge of Music, Roland Hayes Division of Music, Boston Public Schools. Be

WORKS

W5.1 Let's Build a City. (1972)
For: voice and piano. Written for Southern Christian Leadership Conference of Boston for their Save Our Cities Exposition at Hynes Auditorium, 1972. *Score.*

[Let's Build a City; Chorus and Orchestra]
W5.2 Let's Build a City.

[Let's Build a City; Chorus and Piano]
W5.3 Let's Build a City.
For: chorus(2-part) or chorus(SATB) and piano. Version for chorus(SATB) also performed under title Let's Build a Nation.
Vocal score: G. Schirmer, 1977 (both versions).

W5.4 A Nation's Prayer Hymn. (1977)
For: chorus(SATB) and piano. *Text:* Robert Winfrey. Written for performance in the House of Representatives commemorating the 200th anniversary of passage of the resolution authorizing the flag of the United States of America. *First performed:* June 14, 1977; Washington, D.C. Boston Public Schools All-City Chorus; Charles Sego, piano; Robert Winfrey, conductor. *Vocal score.*

W6 JAN WISSMULLER

Born December 11, 1948, in Trenton, Mich. *Education:* studied composition with John Harbison (Massachusetts Institute of Technology), John Weinzweig (University of Toronto), Earl Kim (Harvard University). *Related activities:* currently on the faculty of Boston University. BU

WORKS

W6.1 Chamber Music, Book I. (1977) 14'
For: Mezzo Soprano and piano. 6 movements. *Text: Chamber Music* by James Joyce. *First performed:* Mar. 1977; Harvard University. Beverly Morgan, mezzo soprano and Leslie Amper, piano.
Score: reprod. of ms.
Reel: recording of first performance.

W6.2 Clausula, Dissembled. (1975) 4'
For: tape. 1 movement. *First performed:* 1975; Toronto, Ont. *Tape.*

W6.3 Cocktails for Eight. (1974) 12'
For: flute, trumpet, trombones(2), harp, percussion, viola, violoncello. *First performed:* 1974; Toronto, Ont.
Reel: recording of first performance.

W6.4 Dinosaur Waltzes. (1980) 7'
For: clarinet(bass) and double bass. 1 movement. *Commissioned by:* Dinosaur Annex. *Dedicated to:* Kathy and Mort. *First performed:* Oct. 17, 1980; First & Second Church, Boston. Kathy Matasy, bass clarinet and Morton Cahn, double bass.
Score: reprod. of ms.
Reel: recording of first performance.

W6.5 Kassandra. (1980) 25'
For: Soprano and instrumental ensemble(flute, oboe, clarinet, bassoon, percussion(2), piano, harp, violin, violoncellos(3), double basses(3)). 1 movement. *Text:* Aeschylus. Thesis, Harvard University.
Score: reprod. of ms. HU
Study score: reprod. of ms.

W6.6 Leda; Suite for Ballet. (1975) 20'
For: chamber orchestra(0-1-1(& asax)-1; 1-0-0-0; perc(4); pf; str). 5 movements.
Score: reprod. of ms.

W6.7 Little Trio. (1978) 7'
For: flute, violin, violoncello. 1 movement. *Commissioned by:* River School Quartet. *First performed:* Oct.

19, 1978; Boston University; in
Omnibus: Music of the Twentieth
Century. Catherine Craver, flute; John
Daverio, violin; Timothy Allcott,
violoncello.
Reel: recording of first performance.
BU

W6.8 Puppet Music. (1976) 8'
For: mandolin, guitar,
instruments(children's). 1 movement.
Commissioned by: Puppet Showplace.

W6.8.5 Trio. (1977) 12'
For: clarinet, violin, violoncello. 3
movements. *Commissioned by:* Dinosaur
Annex. *First performed:* Jan. 1978;
Harvard University. Kathy Matasy,
clarinet; Janet Packer, violin; Chase
Morrison, violoncello.
Reel: recording of first performance.
Reel: Mar. 11, 1978; Harvard University.
Harvard Group for New Music. HU

W6.9 The Twa Corbies/The Three
Ravens. (1979) 6'
For: Mezzo Soprano, Baritone, piccolo,
oboe, trombone, piano, mandolin,
violin. 1 movement. *Text:* anon.
Commissioned by: Dinosaur Annex. *First
performed:* Sept. 30, 1979; First &
Second Church, Boston. Barbara
Winchester, mezzo soprano; Sanford
Sylvan, baritone; Nan Washburn,
piccolo; Barbara Knapp, oboe; Robert
Pilkington, trombone; Rodney Lister,
piano; Jan Wissmuller, mandolin; Janet
Packer, violin; Scott Wheeler,
conductor.
Reel: recording of first performance.

Y1 JAMES YANNATOS

Born March 13, 1929, in New York
City. Moved to Boston area 1964.
Education: studied composition with
Paul Hindemith, Quincy Porter (Yale
University); Ernst Bacon (Syracuse
University); Hugo Weisgall (Cummington
School of the Arts); Nadia Boulanger
(Paris); Luigi Dallapiccola (New York
City); Darius Milhaud (Aspen Music
School); Philip Bezanson (University of

Iowa, Ph.D.); conducting with Leonard
Bernstein and William Steinberg; violin
with Ivan Galamian and Hugo
Kontschak. *Awards:* Alice M. Ditson
Conductor's Award (Columbia
University), Bay Foundation Grant,
Fondation des Etats-Unis Harriet Hale
Woolley Scholarship, Fulbright
Fellowship. *Related activities:* violinist;
conductor; Director of Harvard-Radcliffe
Orchestra (1964-); served on the
faculties of Grinnell College (1961-63),
University of Hawaii (1964-69), Harvard
University (1969-). HU

WORKS

Y1.1 All about Mice: Variations on
Hickory, Dickory, Dock. (1967) 7' 30"
For: orchestra(2-2-2-2; 4-3-3-1; perc(3-4);
str). *Commissioned by:* New Jersey
Symphony Orchestra. *First performed:*
1967; New Jersey. Version for
children's concert indicated by cuts in
the score.
Score & parts: Sonory. Rental.
Reel: University of Illinois. Illinois
Youth Orchestra. HU

Y1.2 American Rituals. (1975) 18'
For: orchestra and tape(electroacoustic).
Tape consists of recorded choral and
electronic effects. *Commissioned by:*
Sage City Symphony. *First performed:*
Mar. 1975; Bennington, Vt.
Score & parts: Sonory. Rental.
Reel: Mar. 1976; Harvard University.
Reel: Mar. 1977; Hartt College of
Music.

Y1.3 Bits and Pieces. (1976) 4' 30"
For: string quartet or string orchestra.
Movements: Prelude; Dance; Blues;
Contrasts; Unities. *Commissioned by:*
Greenwood Camp. *First performed:*
summer, 1976; Cummington, Mass.
Score & parts: Sonory, 1978. HU L

Y1.4 The Brag. (1976) 3'
For: voice(medium) and piano. *Text:*
Mark Twain [Pseud. of Samuel
Clemens]. *First performed:* 1976;

Williamsburg, Va.
Score: Sonory, 1981. HU

Y1.5 Celebrations for a City. (1977) 25'
For: chorus(SATB), chorus(children),
wind ensemble, band(optional).
Instrumentation varies with occasion.
Text: Bible and James Yannatos.
Commissioned by: Cambridge Arts
Council. *First performed:* 1977;
Cambridge, Mass. Cambridge High
School Chorus; Cambridge High School
Band; children form Cambridge public
schools; Harvard University Winds.
Score & parts: Sonory. Rental.
Vocal score: Sonory (excerpts).

Y1.6 Cycles, a Musical Entertainment.
(1974) 15'
For: Soprano, narrator, flute, clarinet,
piano, percussion, viola, violoncello,
double bass. *Contents:* Voices Emerging;
The Flood Revisited: Irreverency I;
Cycle: Space, Time, Cosmos; Cheers:
Irreverency II. *Text:* Bible, O.T.,
Genesis and other sources.
Commissioned by: Collage. *First
performed:* Mar. 1974; Boston, Mass.
Score & parts: American Composers
Alliance.
Disc: Sonory S 4628, 1976. Collage;
James Yannatos, conductor. HU MIT
NEC T W
Reel: Mar. 31, 1974; Museum of Fine
Arts, Boston. Collage. HU

[Dances]
Y1.7 Three Dances. (1950) 6'
For: violin and piano. *First performed:*
1950; Toronto, Canada; CBC broadcast.
Score: Sonory.

Y1.8 Duo. (1956) 11'
For: violin and piano. 2 movements.
Dedication: To Nyia. *First performed:*
Mar. 1979; New York City. Valerie
Kuchment, violin and Eric Steumacher,
piano.
Score & part: Sonory, 1981. HU
Reel: recording of first performance.

Y1.9 Eight Miniatures for Ten Fingers.
(1977) 4'
For: piano.
Score: Sonory, 1978. HU MIT

[Epigrams, Voice and Piano]
Y1.10 Five Epigrams. (1961) 4' 30"
For: voice(high) and piano. *Text:* Morton
Marcus. *First performed:* 1962; Grinnell,
Iowa. Nyia Yannatos, soprano and
Richard Howe, piano.
Score: Sonory, 1981. HU

[Epigrams, String Quartet]
Y1.11 Five Epigrams. (1961) 4' 30"
Dedicated to: Lenox Quartet. *First
performed:* 1964; Grinnell, Iowa. Lenox
Quartet.
Study score: Associated, 1966. BPL HU
NEC
Parts: Associated, 1966. BPL HU

[Episodes]
Y1.12 Seven Episodes. (1963) 7' 30"
For: horn, trumpets(2), trombone,
trombone or tuba, percussion(optional).
Score & parts: American Composers
Alliance.

Y1.13 Fanfare and Variations: A Dance
Overture. (1966) 10'
For: orchestra(2-2-2-2; 4-2-2-0; perc(3-4);
str). *First performed:* 1967; Baltimore,
Md. Baltimore Symphony Orchestra.
Score & parts: Sonory. Rental.

Y1.14 Fantasy. (1960) 12'
For: viola and piano. 2 movements.
First performed: 1961; Iowa City, Iowa.
James Yannatos, viola and Leonard
Klein, piano.
Score & part: Sonory.

Love. *See* Mini-Cycle II.

Y1.15 Madrigals.
For: flute or violin and viola. *Dedicated
to:* Sam and Debbie Bruskin.
Score: Sonory, 1981. HU

Y1.16 Many Ways to Look at a Woman. (1962) 10'
For: chorus(SATB). Cantata.
Commissioned by: Grinnell College.
First performed: 1962; Grinell, Iowa. Grinnell College Choir.
Score: Sonory.

Y1.17 Miniatures. (1980) 8'
For: instrument(treble), instrument(bass), piano, or instrument(unspecified) and piano. 8 movements.
Score & parts: Sonory, c1981. HU

Miniatures for Ten Fingers. *See* Eight Miniatures for Ten Fingers.

Y1.18 Mini-Cycle I: Moods. (1968) 5'
For: voice(high) and piano. *Text:* Martin Robbins. *Contents:* Spring; Playground; Seascape; Notes before a Recital. *First performed:* 1972; Boston, Mass. Joan Heller, soprano and Christopher Kies, piano.
Score: in *West Coast Review*, vol. 5, no. 2 (Oct. 1970).
Score: Sonory, 1981. HU
Disc: Sonory S 4628, 1976. Joan Heller, soprano and Christopher Oldfather, piano. HU MIT NEC T W
Reel: Mar. 1973; Harvard University. Joan Heller, soprano and Christopher Kies, piano. HU.
Cassette: Mar. 27, 1973; New England Conservatory; in *An Evening of Contemporary Music.* Joan Heller, soprano and Christopher Kies, piano. NEC

Y1.19 Mini-Cycle II: Love. (1969)
For: voice(high) and piano. *Text:* James Vincent Cunningham. *First performed:* 1972; Boston, Mass. Joan Heller, soprano and Christopher Oldfather, piano.
Score: American Composers Alliance.
Score: Sonory, 1981. HU
Reel: Mar. 1973; Harvard University. Robert Gartside, tenor and Gerry Moshell, piano. HU

Moods. *See* Mini-Cycle I: Moods.

Y1.20 Oedipus. (1960) 40'
For: Baritone (or narrator), chorus (or narrator), dancers, orchestra (2-2-2-2(&cbsn); 4-3-3-1; timp, perc, xylo; hp, pf; str). Ballet. *Libretto:* James Yannatos; based on *Oedipus Rex* by Sophocles. *Contents:* Prologue; Scene I; Entr'acte; Scene II; Scene III; Epilogue. Doctoral thesis. *First performed:* 1963; Chatauqua, N.Y. Chautauqua Youth Orchestra.
Score: reprod. of ms. HU
Reel: Harvard University.

Orpheus and Euridice. *See* Suite for Orpheus and Euridice.

[Pentatonic Choruses]
Y1.21 Three Pentatonic Choruses. (1980) 5'
For: chorus(SATB). *Text:* poems by children.
Score: Sonory, 1981. HU

Y1.22 Polarities. (1973) 12'
For: percussion(3) and brass ensemble(horns(4), trumpets(3), trombones(3), tuba). 3 movements.
Commissioned by: Harvard University Science Center. *First performed:* 1973; Cambridge, Mass. Members of the Harvard-Radcliffe Orchestra.
Score & parts: Sonory.

Prayers from the Ark. *See* Prieres dans l'arche.

Y1.23 Prieres dans l'arche (Prayers from the Ark). (1965) 9'
For: Soprano and chamber orchestra(1-1-1-1; 1-1-1-0; str(1-1-1-1-0)).
Text: Carmen Bernos de Gaztold.
Contents: Priere du coq; Priere du chat; Priere du papillon; Priere de la tortue; Priere de l'alouette; Priere du petit cochon. *Dedicated to:* Nyia, Dion and Kalya. *First performed:* 1965; Cambridge, Mass. Chloe Owen, soprano; Harvard-Radcliffe Orchestra.
Score: ms. HU
Score & parts: Sonory. Rental.
Disc: Sonory S 4628, 1976. Lucy Shelton, soprano; John Kirk, flute;

Peggy Pearson, oboe; David Satz, clarinet; Thomas Stephenson, bassoon; Kenneth Pullig, trumpet; Cynthia Brown, horn; Michael Gisser, trombone; Robert Manero and Stephen Hefling, violins; Aaron Picht, viola; Joan Esch, violoncello; Barry Boettcher, double bass; James Yannatos, conductor. HU MIT NEC T W
Reel: May 7, 1965; in *A Tape of Vocal and Instrumental Music* by James Yannatos (selections). HU

[Prieres dans l'arche; Arr.]
Y1.24 Prieres dans l'arche.
For: Soprano and piano. *Text:* Carmen Bernos de Gaztold. *Contents:* Prieres du coq; Priere du chat; Priere du papillon; Priere de la tortue; Priere de l'alouette; Priere du petit cochon.
Score: Sonory.
Reel: Mar. 1973; Harvard University (Priere du chat and Priere du coq). HU

Y1.25 Puzzles. (1973) 15'
For: instruments(treble)(3) or instruments(bass)(3). 17 movements.
Parts: Sonory, 1981. HU

Y1.26 Quartet, Strings, No. 1. (1959) 15'
4 movements. *First performed:* 1960; Iowa City, Iowa. Graduate students.
Music: Sonory.

Y1.27 Quartet, Strings, No. 2. (1965-67) 25'
6 movements. *Commissioned by:* Grinnell College. *First performed:* 1967; Grinnell, Iowa. Lenox Quartet.
Music: Sonory.

Y1.28 The Rocket's Red Blare. (1970) 120'
For: voices, chorus, orchestra(1-1-1(& asax)-1; 1-1-1-0; perc(2); cel, org; str). Opera in 2 acts. *Text:* James Yannatos.
First performed: 1971; Harvard University. Harvard-Radcliffe students.
Score & parts: Sonory. Rental.
Reel: May 1971; Harvard University. Chalyce Brown, Joan Heller, Ervin

Buice, Ivan Oak, Peter Kazaras; other vocal soloists; chorus and orchestra, James Yannatos or Philip A. Kelsey, conductor. HU

Y1.29 Romance. (1953) 3'
For: violin and piano. *First performed:* 1953; San Antonio, Tex.
Score: Sonory.

Y1.30 Serenade. (1981) 10'
For: violin, viola, violoncello.
Score & parts: Sonory.

[Settings of e.e. cummings]
Y1.31 Three Settings of e.e. cummings. (1967) 8'
For: chorus. *Contents:* Buffalo Bill's; The Rose; In Just. *Dedication:* For G. Wallace Woodworth. *First performed:* 1976; Harvard University. Harvard Graduate Chorale.
Score: Associated, 1972. HU
Score: in *Words and Music: The Composer's View*, Department of Music, Harvard University, 1972. BPL HU W

Y1.32 The Silence Bottle. (1973) 25'
For: Sopranos(3) or children, Baritone, clarinet, bassoon, piano, percussion, double bass. Children's television opera in 2 acts. *Text:* Martin Robbins.
Score & parts: Sonory. Rental.
Reel: May 1971; Loeb Drama Center, Harvard University.

[Sillies]
Y1.33 Four Sillies. (1973) 4'
For: chorus(SATB) or chorus(SA) or chorus(TB). Children's songs. *Text:* poems by children.
Score: Sonory, 1980. HU
Reel: Mar. 1973; Lowell House, Harvard University. HU
Reel: in *A Collection of Vocal and Instrumental Music* by James Yannatos. HU

Y1.34 Silly and Serious Songs.
For: chorus, piano, percussion(optional), autoharp(optional). *Text:* by children. Four books and teacher's manual.

Commissioned by: Bay Foundation.
Score: Sonory, 1980. HU
Cassette: 1980. Charlene
Fagelman-Morse, Barbara Kunhardt, and
Marie Anagnostopoulos (Books I-IV).
HU

Y1.35 Sonata, Clarinet and Piano. (1962)
12'
4 movements. *First performed:* 1963;
Iowa City, Iowa.
Score & part: American Composers
Alliance.
Disc: Sonory S 4628, 1976. Thomas
Hill, clarinet and Laurence Berman,
piano. HU MIT NEC T W
Reel: HU

[Sonata, Violoncello]
Y1.36 Sonata for Solo Cello. (1978) 15'
3 movements. *First performed:* Mar.
1979; New York City. Leopold
Teraspulsky.
Score: Sonory, 1978. HU MIT

[Songs]
Y1.37 Three Songs. (1959) 7'
For: voice(medium) and string quartet.
Text: James Yannatos. *First performed:*
1959; Paris, France. Australian String
Quartet.
Score: ms. HU
Score: Sonory, 1981.

Y1.38 Sounds of Desolation and Joy.
(1978)
For: voice(medium). *Text:* collage of
excerpts from the poetic writings of
Edwin Arlington Robinson, Dante,
William Shakespeare, Charles Pierre
Baudelaire, Thomas of Celano, Francois
Villon, Walt Whitman, Emily Dickinson,
Johann Wolfgang von Goethe.
Commissioned by: Lucy Shelton.
Score: Sonory, 1981. HU

Y1.39 Suite for Orpheus and Euridice.
(1981) 20'
For: orchestra(1-1-1-1; 2-0-0-0; perc(1-2);
str). *Movements:* Overture; Pas de deux;
Duets; Finale (Overture).
Score & parts: Sonory. Rental.

Y1.40 Suite for Six. (1968) 15'
For: flute, clarinet(bass), bassoon, horn,
percussion, double bass. Suite. 6
movements. *First performed:* 1969;
Harvard University; Fromm Foundation
concert.
Score & parts: American Composers
Alliance.

Y1.41 To Form a More Perfect Union.
(1976) 85'
For: voices(7), chorus(SATB),
instrumental ensemble(flute, clarinet/
saxophone, trumpet, percussion, piano,
guitar/harmonica, viola, double bass).
Oratorio in 2 acts. *Libretto:* Martin
Robbins. *Commissioned by:* Phi Beta
Kappa. *First performed:* Williamsburg,
Va.
Score & parts: Sonory. Rental.

Variations on Hickory, Dickory, Dock.
See All about Mice.

[Variations on Sur le pont d'Avignon]
Y1.42 Five Variations on Sur le pont
d'Avignon. (1980) 3'
For: violin and piano.
Score & part: Sonory, 1981. HU

Y1.43 Voices and Reverberations. (1972)
15'
For: string orchestra and tape(optional).
Concerto. 3 movements. *First
performed:* 1973; Hanover, N.H.
Harvard-Radcliffe Orchestra.
Score & parts: Sonory.
Reel: Apr. 1973; Harvard University.
Harvard-Radcliffe Orchestra, James
Yannatos, conductor. HU

Z1 ARLENE ZALLMAN

Born September 9, 1934, in
Philadelphia, Pa. Moved to Boston area
1976. *Education:* studied composition
with Vincent Persichetti (Juilliard
School) Luigi Dallapiccola (Florence,
Italy), George Crumb (University of
Pennsylvania. M.A.). *Awards:* Fulbright
Fellowship, MacDowell Colony
Fellowship, Marian Freschl Prize for
Vocal Composition (Juilliard School),

National Endowment for the Arts Grant. *Related activities:* pianist; currently on the faculty of Wellesley College. W

WORKS

Z1.1 Analogy. (1971) 4' 38"
For: flute. *First performed:* 1972; New Haven, Conn.
Score: reprod. of ms. W
Cassette: Oct. 17, 1976; Wellesley College. W

Z1.2 Ballata. (1960) 2'
For: Tenor and piano. *Text:* Petrarch.
Score: reprod. of ms. W

Z1.3 Focus. (1967) 8'
For: chamber orchestra(1(pic)-0-1(Ebcl)-1; 0-1-0-0; perc(2); pf; str(4)). Dance music.
Commissioned by: Douglass College, Department of Dance. *First performed:* 1967; Douglass College.
Score: reprod. of ms. W

Z1.4 From The Greek Anthology. (1965)
For: speaker and piano. Text: from *The Greek Anthology*, translated by Dudley Fitts. *Movements:* Dedication of a Mirror (Plato); Hektor of Troy (Archias); Her Voice (Meleager); To Heliodora (Meleager); The Lost Bride (Antiphanes); On Mauros the Rhetor (Palladas); The Lyf So Short (Palladas).
Score: ms.
Cassette: Oct. 17, 1976; Wellesley College. W

Injury. *See* Sonnet XXXIII.

Z1.5 Kyrie. (1966) 3'
For: chorus(SATB).
Vocal score: reprod. of ms. W

Z1.6 The Locust Tree in Flower. (1969) 5'-6'
For: Soprano, Alto, Tenor, Bass, chorus(SATB). *Text:* a cycle of poems selected from works of William Carlos Williams. *Dedicated to:* George Crumb.

First performed: 1972; Oberlin, Ohio.
Vocal score: reprod. of ms. W

Z1.7 Le Malade imaginaire. (1974)
For: voice, flute, oboe, trumpet, horn, violin, viola, violoncello, harpsichord.
Text: Jean Baptiste Moliere. *Contents:* Prologues; Musical Interludes; Opera Scene. *Commissioned by:* University of Texas, Austin, Department of Drama.
First performed: 1974; University of Texas, Austin.
Score: ms.

[Le Malade imaginaire. Selections]
Z1.8 Suite from Le malade imaginaire of Moliere. (1974) 8'
For: piano or harpsichord, or harpsichord, flute, violoncello.
Movements: Prelude; Chaconne. *First performed:* Oct. 17, 1976; Wellesley College. W
Score.
Cassette: recording of first performance. W

Z1.9 19 gennaio 1944. (1960) 8'
For: chorus(SATB). *Text:* Salvatore Quasimodo. *Dedicated to:* Maria Maughelli.
Vocal score: reprod. of ms. W

Z1.10 Per organo di Barberia. (1975) 3'
For: Soprano and violoncello. *Text:* Sergio Corazzini. *First performed:* Oct. 17, 1976; Wellesley College. Bethany Beardslee, soprano and Helen Harbison, violoncello.
Score: ms.
Cassette: recording of first performance. W

[Pieces]
Z1.11 Five Pieces for Solo Clarinet. (1961) 4'
First performed: 1961; Florence, Italy.
Score: reprod. of ms. W

[Preludes, Piano]
Z1.12 Three Preludes. (1978-80) 5'
Contents: Burning; Kaleidoscope; Corridor. Funded by a National

Endowment for the Arts Grant. *Dedicated to:* John Willenbecher; my daughter Minna. *First performed:* Nov. 1, 1981; Massachusetts Institute of Technology. Vivian Taylor. *Score:* reprod. of ms. W

Z1.13 Racconto. (1965) 6'-7'
For: piano. *First performed:* 1966; New York City. Abraham Stokman. *Score:* reprod. of ms. W
Cassette: Oct. 17, 1976; Wellesley College. Victor Rosenbaum. W
Cassette: Oct. 20, 1976; New England Conservatory. Victor Rosenbaum. NEC

Z1.14 Serenade. (1980-)
For: violoncello. *Movements:* Soliloquium; Dance. *Commissioned by and dedicated to:* Joan Esch. Funded in part by a Meet the Composer Grant and a grant from Smith College. *First performed:* Feb. 15, 1981; Smith College. Joan Esch. *Score:* reprod. of ms. W
Reel: Apr. 5, 1981; Wellesley College. Joan Esch. W

[Songs from Quasimodo]
Z1.15 Three Songs from Quasimodo. (1975) 7'-8'
For: Soprano, flute(alto), violoncello, piano. *Text:* Salvatore Quasimodo. *Contents:* Gia la pioggia; Oboe sommerso; Ed e subito sera. *First performed:* Oct. 1976; Wellesley College. Bethany Beardslee, soprano, Elinor Preble, flute; Helen Harbison, violoncello; Charles Fisk, piano. *Score:* reprod. of ms. W
Cassette: recording of first performance. W

Z1.16 Sonnet XVIII. (1957)
For: Soprano and piano. *Text:* William Shakespeare. *First performed:* 1958; Juilliard School. *Score:* reprod. of ms. W

Z1.17 Sonnet XXXIII, Injury. (1979) 3'
For: Baritone, horn, piano. *Text:* William Shakespeare. *First performed:* Feb. 1981; Wellesley College. Sanford

Sylvan, baritone; David Hoose, horn; Lois Shapiro, piano. *Score & part:* reprod. of ms. W

Z1.18 Sonnet CXXVIII, the Virginal. (1979-80) 3'
For: Baritone and piano. *Text:* William Shakespeare. *Dedicated to:* Bethany Beardslee. *First performed:* Nov. 1980; Wellesley College. Sanford Sylvan, baritone and Lois Shapiro, piano. *Score:* reprod. of ms. W

Z1.19 Temples at Paestum. (1962) 4'
For: piano. *Score:* ms.

Z1.20 Toccata. (1978-79) 12'
For: piano. Funded by a National Endowment for the Arts Grant. *Dedicated to:* Victor Rosenbaum. *Score:* reprod. of ms. W

Z1.21 Tramonto. (1960) 3'
For: flute. *First performed:* 1962; New York City. Paul Dunkel. *Score:* reprod. of ms. W

Z1.22 Variations. (1977) 12'-13'
For: violin, clarinet, piano. *First performed:* 1978; Smith College. *Score:* reprod. of ms. W

The Virginal. *See* Sonnet CXXVIII.

Z1.23 Willow Poem. (1970-) 3'
For: Alto, clarinet(E-flat), horn, viola, guitar. *Text:* William Carlos Williams. *First performed:* Nov. 3, 1978; Wellesley College. Mary Westbrook-Geha, mezzo soprano; Aline Benoit, clarinet; Llewellyn Humphreys, horn; Nancy Cirillo, violin; Louis Arnold, guitar. *Score & parts:* reprod. of ms. W
Reel: recording of first performance. W
Cassette: recording of first performance. W

Z1.24 Winter. (1972) 4'
For: Soprano and piano. *Text:* William Carlos Williams. *First performed:* Alice

Tully Hall, New York City. Bethany
Beardslee, soprano and Yehudi Wyner,
piano.
Score: reprod. of ms. W

ARRANGEMENTS OF WORKS BY OTHER COMPOSERS

Z1.25 Sonata for Orchestra. Third
Movement. (1976)
Original by Godfrey Winham;
completed after the composer's death
by Arlene Zallman.
Score: ms.

APPENDIX: ADDITIONAL COMPOSERS

This register includes composers for whom there is insufficient information to enable them to be included in the bibliography proper. Among the individuals whose names appear below are some who did not respond to correspondence, some whose responses lacked adequate detail, and some who could not be located. Except for the names of composers, information from this register does not appear in either index.

RICHARD ALLEN
God's Trombones; for trombones(2) and instruments(variable). --Two Preludes; for piano.

RONALD ARNATT
Prelude on Lift High the Cross; for organ (1962, 2'). --Short Mass for the People; for chorus(unison) and organ.

GARY BURTON
Four Mallet Studies. --Six Unaccompanied Solos; for vibraphone.

JOHN ARTHUR BYARD (JAKI)
Alan's Got Rhythm. --Aluminum Baby. --A Basin Street Ballad. --Bass Ment Blues. --The Big Box. --Bird's Mother. --Blues Backwards and Forwards. --Cappy. -- Cast Away. --Cats Cradle Conference Rag. --Chandra. --Chromatics; for pianos(2) (1981). Written in collaboration with Ran Blake. --Cinco y quatro. --D.D.L.J. -- Denise. --Diane's Melody. --Distance. --European Episode. --Falling Rains of Life. --Flight. --Freedom Together. --Gallery. --Garnerin a Bit. --Geb Piano Roll. --Genoa to Pescara. --Go to Hell. --Hazy Eve. --Here to Hear. --The Hollis Stomp. --I Don't Care. --J.B.S. Slow Blues. --Jaki's Spanish Tinge. --Journey to Brussels. --Lilting. --Mellow Septet. --Mrs. Parker of K.C. --New Orleans Strut. --Night Leaves. --No. 251. --Nocturne; for double bass. --Ode to Bird. -- Ode to Charlie Parker. --Ode to Prez. --Olean Visit. --On the Spot. --One Note. -- Out Front. --P.C. Blues. --Pete and Thomas. --Prelude; for pianos(2). Written in collaboration with Ran Blake. --Ray's Blues. --Sasagapo. --Searchlight. -- Seasons. --Serenity. --Sonata; for pianos(2). Written in collaboration with Ran Blake. --Spanish Tinge. --Stay. --Strolling Along. --Sunshine. --There Are Many Worlds. --Think It Over. --Tillie Butterball. --To Milan Lions. --To My Wife. --A Toodle oo Toodle oo. --Top of the Gate Rag. --Trendsition Ziljian. -- Tribute to the Ticklers. --Twelve. --II V I. --Waltz of the Dues Payers. -- Waste.

DAVID CARNEY
Duo Concertante; for viola and piano (1977). --Two Marian Antiphons; for chorus, violins(2), viola, violoncello, trumpets(2), horn, trombones(2).

JOEL COHEN
Sabbath Evening Service; for Baritone or Cantor, chorus(mixed), organ. -- Three Choruses from the Song of Songs by Phineas Newborn.

MARIO DI BONAVENTURA
Pavane pour un enfant gate; for piano

(1955). --Suite; for Mezzo Soprano and string orchestra.

JEFF FRIEDMAN
Image #4. --Portrait of Duke in Blue. --Three Etudes; for trombone (1979).

JULIUS GAIDELLIS
Sonata in E Minor; for violin and piano (1951).

PETER GEORGE GANICK
Approximate Music; for piano (1968). --Before the Dawn; for voice and piano (1967). --Bubble Gum Music; for piano (1968). --Cavaty Sonata; for piano (1971). --Curzon; for pianos(2) (1971). --Duet; for oboe and bassoon (1971). --Duo; for flute and piano (1972). --Durations; for clarinet, clarinet(in A), clarinet(alto), clarinet(bass), violins(2), viola, violoncello. --Eight Short Trios; for recorder(soprano), recorder(alto), recorder(tenor) (1970). -- Element Pieces; for flute and violin (1969). --Essay on Three Sonatas; for piano (1972). --Fifteen; for oboe (1968). --Five Pieces; for violin and piano (1969). --Five Short Pieces; for piano (1970). --Four Sketches; for violin and piano (1970). --Friendly Music #1; for piano (1968). --Future Sonata; for flute (1973). --The Garden; for chorus(SATB) (1968). --Improvised Piece; for pianos(4) (1971; 14'). --Invocation; for trumpet/trumpet(in C) and piano (1966-67). --Islands; for pianos(2) (1971). --Kleine Saetze; for recorders(soprano)(2), recorder(alto), recorder(tenor) (1968). --Melodies; for flute (1971; unfinished). --#8.11; for recorder(alto) (1972 or 1973). -- Octam #1.5; for instrumental ensemble (1971). --Octet; for clarinets(4), violins(2), viola, violoncello (1971). --Octet; for recorders(8) (1972 or 1973). --Octet No. 2; for Alto, flutes(2), clarinet, viola, violoncello, double basses(2) (1973). --Piano Pieces (1967). --Piano Solo Piece for Priscilla (1973). --Piece; for baritone and string quartet (1968-69). --Piece; for oboe and piano (1969).

--Piece; for piano (1971). --Piece; for string quartet (1969). --Piece for Katy; for piano (1971). --Piece for Nine Instruments; for flutes(2), oboes(2), violins(2), viola, violoncello, double bass (1971; unfinished). --Piece for One Performer; for double bass (1969). --Piece #1; for piano (1970). --Piece #2; for piano (1970). --Quartet; for flute, violin, violoncello, piano (1968). --Quartet; for oboe, English horn, violin, viola (1973; unfinished). --Quintet; for violin, clarinets(2), oboe, bassoon (1974). --Quintet; for woodwinds, trombone, guitar(electric) (1969). --Quintet for the Primavera Recorder Consort; for recorders(soprano)(2), recorders(bass)(2), recorder(great bass) (1972). -- Rhythmic Exercise; for instrument(unspecified) (1968). --Sentences; for string quartet (1968). --Seven Piano Pieces (1967). --Short Piano Piece (1970)-- Six Pieces; for bassoon (1968). --Six Pieces; for flutes(2) or recorders(2) (1969). --Six Poems by Larry Eigner; for Soprano, Mezzo Soprano, flute, oboe, clarinet, bassoon, trombone, guitar, electric bass, piano (1970-71; unfinished). --Sketch; for recorder(alto) (1972-73). --Small Quartet; for oboe, saxophone, violin, piano (1968). --Solo Pieces; for flute (1971). --Sonata in the Style of Mozart; for piano (1970). --Sonata No. 1; for flute and piano (1968). --Sonata No. 2; for flute and piano (1969). --Songs; for guitar (1971). --String Quartet #1. --String Quartet #3; for viola and violoncellos(3) (1969). --System; for recorder(alto)/recorder(tenor) (1969). --Three Pieces; for recorder(alto) (1972-73). --Three Rock Songs Revisited; for voice and piano (1969). Trio; for flute, oboe, bassoon (1968). -- Trio #1; for oboe, violin, bassoon (1967; rev. 1971). -- Trio #2: Alternation; for violin, violoncello, piano (1968). --Trio #3; for violins(2) and viola (1970). --Trio #4; for violin, guitar, violoncello (1971). --Trio #5; for clarinet(bass), saxophone(tenor), trombone (1971). --Twelve-Tone Music; for violin (1969). --Two Popular Songs; for voice and guitar or keyboard (1970). --Two Short Trios; for boe, clarinet, saxophone(soprano) (1970). --Viola Solo: Melodid Pertaskatedt (1972 or 1973). --Viola Solo #2 (1973). --Water Music; for wind ensemble(oboes(4), bassoons(3), trumpets(2), tuba) (1973). --Wedding Songs; for tape and piano (1970).

MICHAEL GIBBS
And on the Third Day. --Antique. --Arise, Her Eyes; for vibraphone, guitar, double bass, drums, chamber orchestra; jazz music. Written in collaboration with S. Swallow. --By Way of a Preface; for vibraphone, guitar, double bass, drums, chamber orchestra; jazz music. -- Canticle I. --Canticle II. --Childhood. --Deluge. --Family Joy Oh Boy. -- Fanfare. --Fantasia; for band; jazz music. --Feelings and Things. --Fly Time Fly. --Four or Less. --From My Diary 19-14; for voice and orchestra. --Inside In. -- Interviews; for orchestra. --Intimate Reflections; film music. --Intrude. --June the Fifteenth 1967. --Just Ahead. --Laughing Man, Blue Comedy; for band. -- Liturgy. --Madame Sin; film music. --Melanie. --Model Cities Program; for voice and accompaniment. --Nocturne vulgaire; for vibraphone, guitar, double bass, drums, chamber orchestra; jazz music. In collaboration with S. Swallow. -- Nonsequence. --Panther Pauseballet. --Pense; for band. --Phases; for vibraphone, guitar, double bass, drums, chamber orchestra; jazz music. -- The Rain before It Falls; for vibraphone, guitar, double bass, drums, chamber orchestra; jazz music. --Second Thoughts; for band. -- Secrets; film music. --Skinny Dip; for band. --Six Improvisatory Sketches. --Some Echoes; for jazz band. --Some Shadows; for jazz band. --The Start of Something Similar. --Sweet Rain. --Tanglewood '63. --Three; for vibraphone, guitar, double bass, drums, chamber orchestra; jazz music. --Throb;

for vibraphone, guitar, double bass, drums, chamber orchestra; jazz music. -- Triple Portrait. --Tunnel of Love. --Turn of the Century. --Unfinished Sympathy.

JAMES P. GIUFFRE (JIMMY)
Abstract No. 1. --Affinity. --Afternoon. --Alternation. --Angles. --Appaches. -- Big Boy. --The Big Deep. --Big Girl. --Big Pow Wow. --Big Top. --The Bird. -- Blues. --Blues Day. --Blues in the Barn. --Brief Hesitation. -- A Bright Moon. --The Butterfly. --Call of the Centaur. --Celebration. --The Chanting. --Chirpin Time. --Clarinet. --Clarinet Quintet No. 1. --Creme de Menthe. --Cricket Song. --Cry Want. --Dancin Pants. --Deep People. --Dervish. --Dichotomy. -- Discovery in a Landscape. --Divided Man. --Down Country. --A Dream. --Dripping Water. --Drive. --The Duke You Say. --Easy Lady. --The Easy Way. --Egypt. Elephant. --Emphasis. --Empty Rooms. --Enter Ivory. --Eternal Chant. --Evolution. -- Feast Dance. --Fine. --The Five Ways. --Flight. --Flute Song. --Footsteps. -- Four More. --Four Mothers. --Four Others. --Frappe. -- From Then to Then. --Fugue. --Fun. --The Gamut. -- Goosegrease. --Gotta Dance. --Green Country. --Happy Man. --Hex. --I Don't Wanna Resign. --I Got Those Blues. --I Hear Red. --An Impression. --Indian Club. -- Legend of the Haunted Waters. --Life's Music. --The Listening. --The Little Boy. -- --Little Melody. --Little Orphan Annie. --Lovely Willow. --Man Alone. --Many a Man. -- Moanin Blues. --Mobiles. --Montage. --Moonlight. --Mosquito Dance. --Motion Eterne. --Music in Marble Halls. --Naiades; for clarinet choir. --New York Blues. --Night Dance. -- Ode to Switzerland. --Off Center. --Om. --One Score and Eight Horns Ago. --Orb. -- Ornothoids. --Out of Somewhere. --Pace. --Passage to the Veil. --Pastoh Presseny. -- The Pesky Serpent. --The Pharoah. --Phoenix. --Piece; for clarinet and string orchestra. --Pony Express.

--Primordial Call. --Princess.
--Problems. --Propulsion. -- Punkin.
--Quadrangle. --Quest. --Ray's Time.
--Remember. --Rhythmspeak. --River
Chant; film music. --Sad Time.
--Safari. --Saturday Night Dance.
--Scootin About. --Sighet Sighet. --A
Simple Tune. --Sing Song. --Slave
Song. --Smiles. --Snake. --Solo. --
Somp'm Outa Nothin. --La soncalli.
--Song of the Wind. --Sonic. --Space.
-- Spanish Flames. -- Spanish Flower.
--Spasmodic. --The Story. --Suite for
Germany. --Suspensions. -- The
Swamp People. --Syncopate. --Take a
Bow. --That's the Way It Is. --That's
True That's True. --Three Bars in One.
--Threewee. --Threshold. --Tibetan Sun.
--Tide Is In. --Time Enough. --Time
Machine. --Trance. --Tree People.
--Trudgin. --Two for Timbuctu. --Two
Kings of Blues. --Uncharted. --Used to
Be. --Venture. --The Waiting.- Whirrrr.
--Yggdrasill. --You Know.

MIKE GOODRICK
Quartet No. 1; for saxophones(alto)(2),
saxophones(tenor)(2),
saxophone(baritone) (1965). --Ring; for
jazz group.

GRACE WARNER GULESIAN
Ballet of Bacchus; for orchestra?--Ballet
of Nubi; for orchestra?--Black Oxen; for
chorus(TTBB) and piano (1941). --A
Brittany Love Song; for voice and
piano (1928). --Cape Cod Anne;
operetta (1944). --Colonnade Row; for
Mezzo Soprano and piano. --Cuban
Serenade; for voice and piano (1935).
--Dick Whittington: A Musical
Extravaganza in Prologue and Three
Acts (1932). --Dodja, the Mystic;
operetta. --Down Where the
Waterlillies Grow; for voice and piano.
--Dream Hours; for voices(women)(3)
and piano (1934). --Dream Ships
Sailing; for chorus(SAB) and piano
(1941). --Dreamland Hands; for voice
and piano (1942). -- Fantasy: Two
Moods in E Minor; for violin and
piano. --The Fog; for voice and piano

(2 versions). --Glimpses; for voice and
piano. --Green Branches Swaying; for
chorus(SA) and piano (1941). --Green
Branches Swaying; for chorus(SSA)
(1941). --Hail, Boston University; for
chorus and orchestra. --The Healing
Presence; for voice and piano. --A
Heap O' Livin'; for voice (medium) and
piano (1929). --The Hollyhocks; for
chorus(women) and piano (1934). --A
Honeymoon in 2,000; for voices,
chorus, piano. --The House and the
Road; for voice(medium) and piano
(1924). --The House by the Side of the
Road; for voice (high) or
chorus(women)(3-part) and piano (1927).
--The House by the Side of the Road;
for chorus(SATB) (1927). --How
Beautiful the Night; for voice and
piano. -- Hymn to America; for chorus
and piano (1930). --Hymn to America;
for chorus(woman)(3-part). --I Saw God
Wash the World; for voice and piano.
--I'd Like to Play a Kettle Drum; for
voice and piano (1937). --The Joker;
for bassoon and piano. --The March of
Youth; for chorus(unison) and
piano(optional) (1935). --Night Winds;
for voice and piano (1935). -- One
Golden April Morning; for voice and
piano (1928). --The Parrot; for voice
and piano (1928). --Pretty Is Fragile;
for voice and piano. --Princess Marina;
operetta (1932). --Revery; for voice and
piano. --Roadside Birches; for voice
and piano (1933). --The Sea Hath Its
Pearls; for voice(high) and piano (1927).
--Sea Magic; for voice and piano
(1933). -- Singing Brook; for voice and
piano. --Songs of the East; for voice
and piano (1939). --Spring Interlude;
for voice and piano (1930). --Spring
Voices; for voice (medium) and piano
(1933). --Summer Night; for
chorus(SSA) or chorus(SATB) and piano
(1929). --Take Me Back to Boston; for
voice and piano (1923). --The Tom Cat;
for voice(low) and piano (1928).
--Unafraid; for voice and piano (1967).
--Washington; for voice and piano
(1935). --Young April; for voice(high)
and piano (1934).

DONALD HARRIS
Fantasy; for violin and piano or orchestra (1956, 1957; 7' 30"). -- For the Night to Wear; for Mezzo Soprano and instrumental ensemble[?] (1978; 8' 15"). --Ludus I; for instrumental ensemble (flute, oboe, clarinet, horn, bassoon, violins(2), viola, violoncello, double bass) (1966; 8' 25"). --Ludus II; for flute, clarinet, violin, violoncello, piano (1973; 10' 28"). --On Variations; for chamber orchestra (13' 30"). -- Piano Sonata (1957; 13'). --String Quartet (1965; 9' 35"). --Symphonie en deux mouvements (1959-63; 16').

ANDREW W. JAFFE
Abebe Kilkile; for soprano and jazz orchestra (1976). --Atlanta; for jazz group. --Ballad 21; for jazz group. --Bedroom Eyes; for jazz group. --Blue Collards; for jazz group. -- Blues for Cannonball Adderley; for jazz group. --Blues for Nothing; for jazz group. --Chalkdust Blues; for jazz group. --Dersu; for jazz group. -- Dig Wee Just; for jazz band. --Don't Worry; for jazz group. --Doxology; for jazz group. --Etudes; for oboe. -- Green Lines; for jazz group. --Hearing Is Believing; for jazz group. --Histology; for jazz group. -- I Wish It Would Happen to You; for jazz group. --Integrity; for jazz group. -- Iron Country Curtains; for jazz group. --It Must've Been Something I Wrote; for jazz group. --Kate's Caper; for jazz group. --The Keeper; for jazz group. -- Let Your Wife Take Care of That; for jazz group. --Let's Make a Deal; for jazz group. --Medley on the Moods of Cannonball Adderley; for jazz band. --Meet Me Outside; for jazz group. --Next to Nothing; for jazz group. -- Orchestral Dance Suite; for jazz orchestra. --Personology; for jazz group. -- Petty Obstacles; for jazz group. --Pieces; for oboe and piano. --Preludes; for piano. --Recount; for jazz group. --Samba de Saudade; for jazz group. --San Tomas; for jazz group. --A Scent of Man; for jazz group. --The Scorpion; for jazz group. --Sic Vita; for Soprano, violin,

woodwind quintet. --Sideways Blues; for jazz group. --Something Old, Something New; for jazz group. --Spare Change; for jazz group. --Steve Biko; for jazz group. --String Quartet. --Symbolic Interaction; for jazz group. --The System; for jazz group. --That Sound; for jazz group. -- Thelonious' Intoningus; for jazz group. --Theme for the New Sixties; for string quartet and jazz group(4). --Things Ain't What They Oughtta Be; for jazz group. --Time Out; for jazz group. --Tommy Twelve-Tones; for jazz group. -- Transition; for jazz group. --Transition; for jazz group. --Tuesday Night at the Blues; for jazz group. --What's Up Front; for jazz group. --Whole Town; for jazz group. --Woodie's Goodies; for jazz group.

CHARLES KLETZSCH
Audubon; chamber opera. --Duet; for Tenor, Baritone, guitar, organ. --Gesualdo; chamber opera. --Jefferson; chamber opera. --Piano Sonata. --Rip Van Winkle; chamber opera. --Symphony. --The Three Bears; chamber opera. --Two Duets; for piano and chamber organ.

ROBERT J. LURTSEMA
Butterfly Music; for flutes, clarinets, harps; film music (1976). --Faggoten, but Not Gone; for bassoons(4); ballet. --Julia Child and Company; for bassoons; television music.

KENNETH MacKILLOP
Three Songs on Poems by Millay; for Soprano and piano.

WILLIAM MALOOF
Gloria; for chorus. --In Celebration. --A Song for the Twentieth Century; for chorus(TTBB), winds, percussion; cantata. --Three Shakespearean Sonnets; for voice and flute. --Vocalise.

JAMES MANN
Kaleidophone (1973). --Sextet for

Winds; for clarinets(2), bassoons(2), horns(2) (1974).

DAVID NOLTE PATTERSON
The Celery Flute Player; for piano (1971; 10'). --Chantier; for violin and piano (1971: 7'). --Combine; for organ (1977; 12'). --Differences; for voices(6) and tuba (1963; 5'). -- Herrick Songs; for voice and piano (1963; 4'). --Music for Piano (1959; 11'). --Pied Beauty; for performers(amplified), tintinnabula, tape (1976).- -Winter Birds; for trumpets(3) (1970; 2'). --Wolfslopes; for tape (1975; 4'). -- Woodwind Quintet (1963; 2'). --The Woolworth Philodendron; for percussion(4) and tape (1968; 7').

BOB PILKINGTON
Close Encounters: Variations on a Theme by John Williams; for jazz group (instrumentation variable). --Excursions II; for jazz group (instrumentation variable).

CONRAD POPE
At That Hour; for Mezzo Soprano, flute, clarinet, violin, viola, violoncello, piano (1977). --Concert of Ensembles; for violin and violoncello (15'). --Joys; for Baritone and instrumental ensemble(flute, saxophone(tenor), horn, trombone, percussion(4), violin, viola, violoncello, double bass) (1971). --Rain; for Alto, clarinet, violin, violoncello, piano (1976). --Sonata; for violoncello (1972; 12'). --String Trio; for violin, viola, violoncello (1970).

JEROME ROSEN
Concerto; for clarinet and orchestra. --Concerto; for synket and orchestra (1968). --String Quartet No. 1 (1952-53; 20' 50"). --Calisto and Melibea; opera. --Sonata; for clarinet and violoncello (1950).

VICTOR ROSENBAUM
Four Duos; for flute and viola (4'). --Love Comes Quietly; for Soprano, flute, viola (2'). --Magic: Two Songs on Texts of Thomas Wolfe; for Soprano and piano (5'). --Mazurka and Pavane; for piano (3'). --Piece for Piano (3'). --The Shepherd Boy's Song; for chorus(women), violin, viola, piano (7'). --Suite; for piano (10'). --The Three-Faced; for Soprano and piano (1' 30"). --Variations; for violin, viola, violoncello (10'). --With Rue My Heart Is Laden; for chorus(SATB) (3').

ALLAN SCHINDLER
Opener 1976. --String Sextet; for violins(2), violas(2), violoncellos(2)? --Visionary; for flute, clarinet, bassoon, violin, harp, tape (1977).

MICHAEL SCOTT
Another Dream; for jazz group (instrumentation variable). --Backwards Bop; for jazz group (instrumentation variable). --A Birthday Wish; for jazz group (instrumentation variable). --Broken Glass; for jazz group (instrumentation variable). --Good Space; for jazz group (instrumentation variable). --Isle La La Motte; for jazz group (instrumentation variable). --Kelly's; for jazz group (instrumentation variable). --The Lady Amalthea; for jazz group (instrumentation variable). --Mithril; for jazz group (instrumentation variable). --Mood of the Blues; for jazz group (instrumentation variable). --An Old Fashioned, Kansas City Blues; for jazz group (instrumentation variable). --On the Kansas Side; for jazz group (instrumentation variable). --Travelin' Light; for jazz group (instrumentation variable). --Woods and Hills; for jazz group (instrumentation variable).

WILLIAM TESSON
Psalm I; for voices and brass (1967).

NEWTON WAYLAND
Alice in Wonderland. --The Bat Poet; for Mezzo Soprano, piano, percussion. -- Beauty and the Bachelor. --Beauty and the Beast. --Catch a Rainbow; incidental music. --Eight Fatal Songs;

for Mezzo Soprano and saxophone(tenor) or bassoon. -- The Emperor's New Clothes. --Fannee-Doolee, from Zoom; for voice. --Feeling Free. --Five Commercial Songs; for Soprano, Baritone, piano, drum set, bassoon or double bass. --Flying, from Zoom; for voice; television music. --Including Me. --Men from Mars, from Zoom; for voice; television music. -- Nova. Theme; television music. --Pinocchio. --Ubbi-dubbi, from Zoom; for voice; television music. The Village. -- The Virgin Island Experience. --What's My Thing; for orchestra. --Wind in the Willows. --Zoom. Theme; television music.

JACK WEAVER
Greenwood Haven (12'). --Quartet for Synthesized Voices (11').

HERMAN WEISS
Cantata II. Postcards; for Mezzo Soprano, clarinet, violin, piano (1974).

JOHN TOWNER WILLIAMS
Bachelor Father, Bachelor Flat; television music (1961). --Because They're Young film music (1960). --Black Sunday. --The Chase, from M Squad. --Checkmate; television music. --Chrysler Theater. Theme; television music. --Cinderella Liberty; film music (1973). -- Close Encounters of the Third Kind; film music. --Conrack. --Convoy. --The Cowboys (1972). --Daddy's Gone a-Hunting (1967). --David Copperfield; television music. --Diamond Head; film music. --The Discovery, from M. Squad. --Dracula; film music. --Earthquake; film music. --The Eiger Sanction; film music. --Elegy for Strings. --The Empire Strikes Back; film music. --The End, from M Squad. --Essay for Strings; for string orchestra; television music (9' 30"). --Family Plot; film music (1976). --Fanfare for the Commonwealth (1980). --Fitzwilly; film music. --Flute Concerto. --The Fury; for orchestra (1978). --G.E. Theatre.

Theme; television music. --Gidget Goes to Rome; film music. -- Gilligan's Island. Theme; television music. --Guide for the Married Man; film music (1967). --Heaven's Gate. --Heidi; television music. -- How to Steal a Million; film music (1966). --I Passed for White (1960). --Images (1972). --Jane Eyre (1970). --Jaws; film music. --Jaws II; film music. --John Goldfarb, Please Come Home; film music (1964). --Jubilee 350 Fanfare (1980). -- The Killers (1964). --Kraft Playhouse. Theme; television music. --Land of the Giants; television music. --Legend. --The Long Goodbye; film music. -- Lost in Space. --The Missouri Breaks; film music. --1941. --None but the Brave (1965). --Not with My Wife You Don't; film music. --Paper Chase; film music (1973). --Penelope; film music. --Pete 'n Tillie (1972). -- Piano Sonata (1951). --Poseidon Adventure; film music (1972). --The Raiders of the Lost Ark; film music. --The Rare Breed; film music. --The Rievers; film music. --Secret Ways (1961). --Sinfonia; for winds. --Sinfonietta; for band (17'). --Star Wars; film music. --The Story of a Woman (1970). --Sugarland Express; film music. --Superman; film music. --Symphony No. 1. --Symphony No. 4. --Tales of Wells Fargo; television music. --The Towering Inferno; film music. --Valley of the Dolls; film music. --Violin Concerto. --Your Cheatin' Heart.

PHILLIPS ELDER WILSON, JR. (PHIL)
Another Balance; for jazz band. --Apples; for jazz band. --Basically Blues; for jazz band. --Big Jesus Diesel; for jazz group (instrumentation variable). -- Breath of Fresh Air; for jazz band. --Buttercrunch; for jazz band. --By the Time I Get the Kleenex; for jazz band. --Camel Driver; for jazz band. -- Flight of the Sackbutts; for trombones(9) and jazz group (instrumentation variable). --Gobble Rock; for jazz band. --The Great Bat; for jazz band. --High on Life; for jazz group (instrumentation variable). --Hills

and Valleys; for jazz band. --It Mostly
Bees that Way, Sigmond Floyd; for
jazz band. --Mother England; for jazz
band. --Myra Breckenridge.
--Outrageous Mother; for jazz band.
--Piano Fortress; for jazz band. --Red
Flannel Hash; for jazz group
(instrumentation variable). -- These Are
the Days; for jazz band. --Three
Friends; for jazz band. --Today's Blues;
for jazz band. --Who Done It; for jazz
group (instrumentatio1 variable).
--Witch Doctor; for jazz group
(instrumentation variable). --Woe Whoa;
for jazz band.

GERTRUDE PRICE WOLLNER
After Paul Draper; ballet (1944).
--Allegro; for oboe and bassoon (1950).
-- Cello Sonata; for violoncello (1946).
--A Dance to My Daughter; for piano.
-- Exaggerated Impressions; for strings
and percussion (1950). --Impressions of
Tour of Old Marblehead; for piano
(1951). --Music for Caesar and
Cleopatra; incidental music. --Music for
The Scarlet Letter. --Music, Narration,
Pantomime, Dance; television music.
--Poem by Tagore (1957). --Quartet; for
English horn, violin, viola, violoncello
(1950). --Reed Drum; dance music
(1940). --Suite; for string orchestra
(1950). -- These August Nights; for
voice and piano (1935). --Trio; for
violin, clarinet, violoncello (1958). --We
Catch Fish, from We Do Things; for
voice, flute, clarinets(2), bassoon,
violins(2), viola, violoncello, double
bass.

DANN C. WYMAN
Easements; for piano (9'). --Sonata; for
viola and piano (11').

INDEX OF NAMES AND TITLES

All references are to item numbers. Except for composers' names, the Appendix is not indexed. Alphabetization is word-by-word. The filing order for punctuation is: apostrophes, parentheses, commas, hyphens, periods. Words with punctuation following, file after words without. Numerals file in order before words.

From the Sea and the
    Mirror, L7.12
From Winter, C2.7
Fromm Fellowship Players,
    P6.195
Fromm Foundation, A4.34,
    A5.31, B4.5, B10.9,
    C4.1, C9.2, D5.13,
    H2.14, H5.11, H9.40,
    K4.8, K4.20, L4.5,
    L5.2, M6.9, M10.60,
    M10.62, M11.23, S3.57,
    S3.83, S4.4, S13.10,
    Y1.40
Fromm Foundation
    commission, D5, H2,
    S13
Fromm Foundation Prize,
    A4, E3.23, H5, S6.
    See also West Coast
    Fromm Foundation Prize
Fromm, Herbert, F8, F8.4,
    F8.5, F8.9, F8.14,
    F8.15, F8.18, F8.26,
    F8.55, F8.83
Fronmeyer, Myra, L9.16
Frontiers, E3.8
Frost, Betsy, W1.2, W1.25
Frost, Frances, R2.105,
    R2.186, R2.189,
    R2.191, R2.192,
    R2.194, R2.196 Frost,
    Robert, B13.50,
    B13.59, P10.29, T4.23,
    T4.31, T4.32, T4.33
Frostiana, T4.31, T4.32,
    T4.33
Frothingham, Eugenia, F9.
    See also Lombard,
    Eugenia
Fry, Pat, L6.4
Fuchs, Joseph, B4.8,
    P7.14
Fuga canonica, N2.13
Fugue & Chorale, C1.4
Fugue and Postlude, H6.7,
    W1.16
Fugue Cycle, V1.32, V1.33
Fugue on a Victory Tune,
    P7.22
Fugue or Voluntary,
    P6.226
Fugue pour quatuor a
    cordes sur un sujet de
    Fenaroli, P7.23
Fulbright Fellowship, B4,
    C8, L2 L5, M6, P1, P5,
    P6, S5, S6, Y1, Z1
Fulbright-Hays grant, B7
Fulbright Program Grant,
    see Senior Fulbright
    Program Grant
Fulginitti, Anthony,
    B1.11
Full Moon in March, H2.16
Fuller Foundation
    Tri-College Electronic
    Music Grant, K5
Fuller, Albert, S9.22
Fuller, R. Buckminster,
    M4.2

Fulmer, Mimi, A3.6
Fulmer, Mrs. Robert,
    A3.6
Fun 'n' Games, O1.16
Fun for Two, P11.37
Fun to Play, P11.38
Functional, J3.7
Functional Music for the
    TV Film Woodrow
    Wilson, S5.5
Funk Dumplings, H3.10
Furies, L9.7
Furies of Complexity,
    D3.14
Furtwangler, F., A5.90
Fusco, Tony, B9.35
Fusion, B9.16
Fussell, Charles, D9.7,
    J1
Fyr on Flode, M5.9

G.B.T., H3.11
G.F.P., P2.9
G. Schirmer, Inc., D6.76
Gable, David, T2.11
Gaboudikian, Sylva,
    B3.27, B3.50, B3.61
Gabriel's Sounds, V1.34
Gabriele, Linda, D8.20
Gabrieli, Andrea, S3.132
Gabrieli, Giovanni,
    S3.130, S3.133, S3.189
Gabrielli Quartet, D2.89
Gaidellis, Julius, App
Gaelic Blessing, P4.30
Gaelic Song, P11.39
Gage, Irwin, G4.4
Gaigai, Efrain, B2.2
Gaignard, Hymeld, H7.14
Gaita, Lucille, H4.42
Gajewski, Piotr, H7.10
Galactic Novae, R2.60
Galamian, Ivan, Y1
Galaxy, M10.30
Galbraith, Barry, S3.121,
    S3.122
Galbraith, George
    Starbuck, B13.75
Galimir Trio, H9.23
Galixidi, S8.8
Gallery (for Young
    Musicians), G3.11
Gambulos, Elena, L11.8,
    L11.9, S11.3, S11.6
Game Man and the Ladies,
    S9.99
Game of Chance, O1.17,
    V4.1
Game of Fifths, P10.9
Gamelan, E1.32
Games, A5.42
Ganick, Peter George, App
Ganz, Rudolf, F3
Garber, Harvey, H9.6
Garcia Lorca, Federico,
    H9.16, K4.4, S15.9
Garden Abstract, B8.18
Garden of Artemis, P6.60
Garden of Delight, B5.67
Gardens of the West,
    V1.35

Gardini, Nelli, F3
Gardner, Isabella
    Stewart, E1.55, E1.68,
    E1.80
Gardner, Kay, M5.5
Gargarian, Gregory, G1
Garick, Richard, B9.16
Garlands, B4.14
Garment of Praise, T4.83
Garnett, Richard, R2.239,
    R2.240
Garrett, Margo, A3.1,
    B4.30
Garrigue, Jean, H8.3
Gartside, Robert, G4.11
Garvey's Ghost, B5.68
Gary Symphony Orchestra,
    P4.127
Gary, Hobart Jude, O1.59
Gascoigne, George, C4.15
Gastagnetta, Grace,
    D6.109, D6.110
Gastolei, Giovanni,
    S3.131
Gate of Heaven, T4.35,
    T4.36, T4.37
Gathering Place, F5.8
Gathering Song, P4.31
Gauger, Thomas, M13.23
Gaul Composition Contest,
    see Harvey Gaul
    Composition Contest
Gavotte, R2.215
Gay, Gudrun, H10.77,
    H10.125
Gay, John, A5.9
Gay, Paul, G2, G2.1,
    G2.6, G2.9, G2.11
Gaylin, David, F4.33
Gaztold, Carmen Bernos
    de, Y1.23, Y1.24
Gebrauchsmusik, or, TV
    '67, O1.18
Gedok Festival (Mannheim,
    West Germany) Award,
    V3
Gedok Festival (Mannheim,
    West Germany)
    Honorable Mention,
    G3.13
Gelb, Sondra, S10.1
Gen'l Slocum, S3.144
Genesis, A1.8
Genesis, Lec, R7.64
Genet, Jean, D8.2
Gentle Air, M1.11
George Arthur Knight
    Prize (Harvard
    University), M9, M9.1,
    S5, T2.42, T4, T4.81
George Gershwin Medley,
    P2.18
George Ladd Prix de Paris
    (University of
    California, Berkeley),
    C9, K3, K4, S8
George Russell Sextet at
    the Beethoven Hall,
    R7.17, R7.27, R7.37,
    R7.46, R7.50, R7.66,
    R7.67, R7.68, R7.79

P7.66, S3.19, S3.25, S3.58

National Teachers Award, H11

Native Village, B3.33

Nativity according to Saint Luke, T4.63, T4.64, T4.65

Naturally "D", E5.3

Nature's Driving Force, L1.150

Naughty Necklace, K2.57

Naumburg Chamber Music Award, H2.25, K3.19, K4, M6

Naumburg Foundation, H2.20, H2.25, K4.17, K4.19, M6.19, M10.22

Naumburg Recording Award, K4.1, D5, L5, P7.68, S6.22, S13.9

Naumburg fellowship, S5

Nautilus, M5.14

Navajo Wildlands, F7.9

Nayak, Pandit Shashi, R6.4, R6.7, R6.8

Nayiri Choral Group, B3.5, B3.8, B3.9, B3.20, B3.30, B3.35, B3.40, B3.63

Nayiri Orchestra, B3.5, B3.20

Nayirian Choral, B3.5, B3.35, B3.61

Nayirian Songs, B3.25, B3.33, B3.49, B3.58, B3.59

Neale, J.M., D4.172

Neapolitan Day, C13.79

Negri, Ada, C13.10

Negro Poems, V2.4.5

Neidlinger, Buell, C4.11, C4.14

Neiger, Millard, B1.12

Neihardt, John G., F4.4, F4.17, F4.20, F4.23

Nelson, Mary Jane, L6.9

Nelson, Ron, K5

Nemchinova, Vera, S9.44

Nenikikamen, A5.63

Neoclassic Pieces, D2.70

Nesbit, Catherine, M5.9

Net, R7.38

Nether City, V4.5

Netherlands Vocal Ensemble, A5.104

Netherworld, L1.151

Netsky, Hankus, B5.10, N1

Never Can Say Goodbye, B5.106

Never on Sunday, B5.107

Neville, Constance, F2.16, F2.17

New American Music for Chamber Ensemble, S6.11

New American Music for Chamber Ensembles, H5.21

New Born, D6.106

New Boston Saxophone Quartet, H7.13

New Boston Wind Quintet, H8.11

New Creation Suite, H3.14

New Dances, A4.17

New Day, L1.152, R2.9

New Donna, R7.33

New England Chamber Opera Group, E1.17, E1.33, E1.34, E1.35

New England Civic Ballet, B1.68

New England Conservatory, *see also* NEC; Chadwick Medal, Pi Kappa Lambda Annual Competition for Seniors and Graduates

New England Conservatory Concerto Competition, H1

New England Conservatory of Music Faculty Composers, C8.17, C8.18, D8.5, M10.41

New England Conservatory, Composition Award, B8.18

New England Dance Theatre, S9.42

New England Dinosaur, S9.3, S9.33, S9.34, S9.61, S9.98, S9.102

New England Dinosaur Dance Theatre, E1.57

New England Primer, T4.67

New England Sketches, P7.30

New England Women's Chorus, O1.42

New England Women's Symphony, M5.5, O1.42

New Events, E4.10

New Events: Boston Composers of the '70s, C8.14, E4.19, K5.3

New Hampshire Philharmonic, G2.6, G2.9

New Haven Symphony Orchestra, M6.7, R2.36, S3.30

New Haven Youth Orchestra, S3.46

New Hymns, B8.30

New Jersey State Council on the Arts Grant in Composition, M4

New Jersey Symphony Orchestra, Y1.1

New Madrigals, H10.65

New Moods, A6.2

New Music, S6.2

New Music Trio, E3.7

New Music for Horns, S3.62

New Music for Piano, B4.12, B4.12

New Music for the Armenian Divine Liturgy, J1.6

New Music for the Piano, K3.1

New Music for Young Ensembles Contest, T1.13

New Music: A Quarterly of Modern Compositions, P7.34

New Orleans Philharmonic, S3.3

New River, S3.177

New School of Music, M9.8

New Scribner Music Library, V1.37

New Songs for New Voices, T4.27, T4.62, T4.97, T4.118, T4.123

New Sounds for the Young Pianist, O1.30

New Union Prayerbook, K2.29

New Venture, L1.153

New Vistas in Song, D6.147, K3.11, S3.66

New Year's Prayer, F8.45

New York Brass Quintet, P6.163, S3.37, S3.72

New York Camerata, H2.10

New York Chamber Soloists, S3.88

New York City Ballet, S3.120

New York City Ballet Orchestra, S3.120

New York City Center Ballet, S5.9

New York City Opera, D6.177, K4.8

New York High School of Music and Art students, D6.76

New York Music Critics Circle Award, D6.177, D6.182, K4.15, K4.16, P7.12, P7.46, P7.66

New York Musicians Club Prize, *see* Bohemians Prize

New York Philharmonic, B4.15, D6.130, K1.11, K3.3, K4.1, K4.12, P7.22, P7.50, R2.222, S3.21, S3.98, S3.116

New York Philharmonic Society Contest, *see* American Composers Contest

New York Port Authority, D6.66

New York Profiles, D6.107

New York State Bar Association, H2.15

New York State Council on the Arts, D5.1, M6.6

New York State Council on the Arts Meet the Composer Grant, E1.21, K5, M8

New York State Council on the Arts commission, E3

Now Every Child That
    Dwells on Earth, G5.7
Now I Lay Me down to
    Sleep, T4.67
Now Is the Hour in the
    Wild Garden Grown
    Blessed, S9.69
Now and Then, R7.35
Now the Trumpet Summons
    Us Again, P6.126
Nowak Lionel, R5.10
Nowe Welcome, Somor,
    L7.21
Nowels, Lynn, C6.3
Noyes, Alfred, B1.61,
    D4.14
nscor, R4.6
Nun danket Fantasy, E1.28
Nunc dimittis, H2.23,
    P4.9
Nunc pro tunc, W3.6
Nunca, nunca, C13.80,
    C13.81
Nuns Fret Not, L7.22
Nuova guitarra, A6.3

O Be Joyful in the Lord,
    P6.83
O Beautiful My Country,
    P6.127
O Blessed Trinity, P4.84
O Come Let Us Sing, H4.22
O Come, All Ye Faithful,
    D6.34
O Haupt voll Blut und
    Wunden, P4.15
O Heav'nly Father, H10.17
O Lamb of God, S3.76
O Lord God, to Whom
    Vengeance Belongeth,
    P6.128
O Lord, My God, P6.231
O Mistress Mine, G5.8
O Pensive Dove, M7.12
O Sacred Head, Sore
    Wounded, P4.15
O Sing Unto the Lord,
    L10.1
O Sing unto the Lord,
    D6.113
O Sing unto the Lord a
    New Song, P7.40
O Spirit of the Living
    God, S3.77
O viso dolce, C13.82
O'Brien, Corey, F4.10
O'Brien, Orin, S3.82
O'Casey, Sean, A5.44
O'Connell, Brian, H4.7,
    K1.13, K1.26, P9.3,
    W3.7
O'er Yonder in the Wood,
    R2.18
OP Overture, A5.69
Oakes, Dana, F4.3, F4.19
Oaks, Brian, M9.9
Oasis, L1.157
Oath of Hippocrates, L3.5
Oberle, Freya, B8.15

Oberlin College
    Contemporary Chamber
    Ensemble, C7.6, C7.6
Objet, R4.7
Occasional Songs, S1.6
Occhi dolorosi, C13.83
Ocean, B8.43
Ockeghem, Johannes,
    S3.149, S3.150
October, C13.84
October 1968, F4.55
October Night, M10.39
Octopus Wrecks, L4.15
Oculus non vidit, H10.18,
    H10.66
Odds and Ends from So
    Much Depends, S13.7
Ode, B12.30, C5.5, M13.11
Ode for Small Orchestra,
    D7.7
Ode to Antranig, the
    Hero, B3.34
Ode to Julius, S8.9
Ode to the Virginian
    Voyage, T4.68
Odes of Horace, T4.69,
    T4.70
Odes of Snang, S6.21
Odjenar, R7.36
Odoni, Eleni, B5.122
Odysseus' Theme, H6.13
Odyssey, A5.29
Oedipus, A5.66, Y1.20
Oedipus at Colonus, A5.67
Oedipus Rex, S6.1, Y1.20
Of Crows and Clusters,
    D6.114
Of Dark and Bright, C1.12
Of Obedience, K4.13
Of the Father's Love
    Begotten and Unto Us a
    Boy Is Born, F3.10
Oh, *see also* O
Oh Jazz, Po Jazz, R7.37
Oh, Fair Is the Wind,
    P11.67
Ohanian, David, C11.11
Ohio State School of
    Music Competition, V3
Ohio State University,
    P6.3
Oi Tai Buvo, K1.13
Ojos criollos, S3.158
Oken, Pam, P2.27
Oklahoma City Junior
    Symphony Orchestra,
    A4.5
Oklahoma City Symphony
    Orchestra, A4.14,
    A4.17, A4.19, A4.29,
    A4.32, H9.6, H9.16
Ol' Man River, B5.111
Old C, E1.70, E1.71,
    E1.72
Old Court Dance, R2.51
Old Dominion Award
    (Massachusetts
    Institute of
    Technology), F2, S15

Old Entertainment for
    Amusing Oneself Now,
    B12.17
Old Little Man, F8.46
Old Man's Touch, L1.158
Old Music Box, C13.85
Old North Church Junior
    and Senior Choirs,
    S14.7
Old North Church Junior
    Choir, S14.9, S14.13
Old North Church,
    Marblehead, Mass.,
    S14.7, S14.9, S14.13
Old North Singers, H10.11
Old South Church Choir,
    M7.13
Old South Point 1668,
    T3.19
Old Tom Again, H9.3
Old Year, S3.159
Olden Pieces, B8.31
Oldfather, Christopher,
    D8.1, M3.2, S4.13,
    Y1.19
Oliphint, Bernadine,
    A4.37
Oliver, John, K2.2, K2.3,
    K2.31, M10.80
Olsen, Robert, F7.19
Olson, Charles, C8.1,
    S12.1
Omega Man of the Year, W2
Omernick, Kenneth, P4.31
Omnibus Series, Boston
    University, T2.11
On a Bright Sunny
    Morning, P11.68
On a Theme by B.G.,
    L1.159
On an Experiment Seeking
    Favour and Love, V4.3,
    V4.4
On Either Side [E,K,]
    1980, F4.25
On Green Dolphin Street,
    B5.113
On Green Mountain, S5.11,
    S5.12
On Parade, R2.50
On Seven Winds, G3.11
On Stage, D6.115, D6.116
On Stage Blues, L1.160
On Stage Everybody, L3.6
On the Borderland, C13.88
On the Dispute About
    Images, P6.129
On the Move, L1.161
On the Road, P11.69
On the Road to Boston,
    S3.160
Once Upon a Time, C13.86
One Flew over the
    Cuckoo's Nest, A5.68
One for You, P11.70
One Man's Jazz Journey,
    L1.162
1' 24", O1.2
One More Time, P2.10
One Thousand, Two
    Hundred, F4.26

Parcells, Elizabeth, A1.18, M6.20
Parhelion, E1.74
Parini, Giuseppe, C13.19
Parish or Perish, W3.7
Parisonatina al'dodecafonia, M6.21
Parisot, Aldo, M6.21
Parke, Rod, H10.8
Parker, Charlie, E5.115, R7.54, R7.68
Parker, Louise, A4.40
Parkers Mood, B5.115
Parkside Contemporary Players, F2.7
Parmet, Marc, L7.4
Parodies, A5.75
Parody-Fantasia, H2.11
Parrot, Lalon, E1.16
Parson, Larry R., P6.34
Parsons, William, F2.2, F2.5
Part-Songs on Children's Texts, C12.5
Partita, B4.19, N2.20, P6.132, R2.127
Partita on a Theme by Lowell Mason, N2.19
Partita on Baruch Haba, F8.49, F8.50
Partita on the Lourdes Hymn, P4.87
Partridge in a Pear Tree, P6.133
Party for My Ghoul Friend, B13.45
Pas de malheur, W4.7
Pasloff, Aileen, S9.44
Passacharlia, C10.11
Passacussion, H4.24
Passage of Three Times, F2.14
Passamezzo antico, V1.54
Passenger, T4.56
Passing Parade, V1.55
Passion according to Saint Luke, T4.71
Passion of Judas, P6.134, P6.135, P6.136, P6.137
Passionsmusik uber die Sieben Worte Jesu Christi am Kreutz, P6.232
Passiontide Chorales, H3.34
Passo pel prat, R2.27
Past Tense, S8.10
Pastel, L1.166
Pasticcio, V3.9
Pastiche, F1.4
Pastime Rag, S3.163
Pastoral, P6.138
Pastorale, D4.119, L1.167, L8.3, M13.12, M13.13, S9.62
Pastorale on the Morning Star, P6.139
Pastorale Revisions, B11.7
Pastore, John, S3.2
Pastrassou, R2.24, R2.25

Pater noster, D2.74, D2.75, P6.140
Patmagrian, Rudolph, E3.20
Patrick, Sylvia, V1.59
Patt, David, P9.7
Patterson, Alfred Nash, M7.13, P7.38
Patterson, David Nolte, App
Patterson, Jennifer, K2.2, K2.3, K2.32, K2.47, K2.79, K2.81, K2.95
Patton, Paul, F4.43, F4.56
Paulu, Catherine, A4.1
Paulu, Norman, A4.1
Pavese, Cesare, H10.38
Payne, John, D6.151
Pea Soup, B13.46, B13.47
Peace, A5.76
Peace and Brotherhood through Music, K2.61
Peaceable Kingdom, T4.72
Pearlman, Martin, P1, P1.2, P1.3, P1.4
Pearson, Duke, H3.29
Pearson, Mark, H7.19
Pearson, Peggy, M11.9, T2.11
Pease, Ted, B13, P2, P2.1 P2.3, P2.4, P2.5, P2.7, P2.8, P2.9, P2.11, P2.13, P2.15, P2.17.5, P2.20, P2.22, P2.24, P2.27, P2.29, P2.30, P2.32, P2.34, P2.36
Peelings, T2.19
Peirce, Margaret, P4.41
Peisch, Stephen, P3
Peller, Robin, F6.2
Peloquin Chorale, P4.7, P4.9, P4.34, P4.41, P4.52, P4.63, P4.82, P4.109, P4.121, P4.129, P4.134
Peloquin, C. Alexander, P4, P4.7, P4.9, P4.16, P4.22, P4.24, P4.28, P4.34, P4.41, P4.46, P4.54, P4.68, P4.77, P4.82, P4.87, P4.96, P4.97, P4.101, P4.108, P4.118, P4.119, P4.126, P4.129, P4.130
Penderecki, Krzysztof, M5
Penetration, A6.4
Penfield Elementary School Chorus, E1.40, E1.86
Penfield High School Chorus, E1.78
Penitential Rite, P4.61
Pennsylvania Ballet, S9.51
Pennsylvania College for Women, R2.218

Pennsylvaniana Suite, R2.130, R2.131
Penny Candy, B13.48
Pentad, N2.22
Pentatone, P11.73
Pentatonic Choruses, Y1.21
Pentatonic Kyrie, H10.69
People and Players Street Theater Company, H3.15
Pepe, Carmine, J1
Peppler, Jane, M5.23
Per organo di Barberia, Z1.10
Peregrinations, C12.6
Peretz, Isaac Loeb, S10.1
Pergamas, T3.22
Peri Massone, H10.105
Periander, A5.77
Period Pieces, E1.75
Perkins, Frank, B5.155
Perlman, Itzhak, K3.3
Permutations, B12.16, B12.17, S11.5
Permutations. Juggler, B12.18
Perpetuum mobile, S3.79
Perrone, George, V1.55
Perry, Richard, V1.56
Persichetti, Vincent, B2, Z1
Persona, V3.10
Personae, B8.33
Personalities, B5.116, B5.117, B5.118, B5.119
Personals, A4.18
Personent hodie, H10.19
Perti, Jacopo, S3.132
Perturbations, L2.14
Peru, Composer Laureate, E4
Perusio, Matheus e, S3.148
Pesah Lanu Sha-ar, F8.6
Peter Quince at the Clavier, W4.8, W4.9
Peter, Lily, D6.111
Peters, C. F., Corp., I2.37
Peters, Robert, P4.38
Petersen, Reinhard, A5.42
Peterson, Barbara, M5.6
Peterson, Georgeann, W1.10
Peterson, Oscar, B5
Petite berceuse, R2.132
Petite pastorale, R2.133
Petite suite, R2.134, T3.23
Petite valse de la bonne bourse, C7.10
Petrarch, S3.88, Z1.2
Petrassi, Goffredo, B7
Petrie, Asenath, K2.64
Peyton, Malcolm, L7, L7.2, N1, P5, P5.14, P5.17, P5.18
Pfleger, Augustin, P6.232
Phaedra, L11.5
Phantasia, see also Fantasy

Small Pieces, B8.40
Smart, Christopher,
    L7.13, L7.24, L7.32,
    P6.142
Smart, Gary, B11.2
Smicrope, Robert, E2
Smit, Leo, B4.8, B4.19
Smith College, V3.10,
    Z1.14
Smith College Orchestra,
    P11.7, P11.19
Smith, Bob, L6.9
Smith, Craig, C12.3, H2.8
Smith, Donald, T3
Smith, Edward Lucie, see
    Lucie-Smith, Edward
Smith, Fenwick, M11.21
Smith, Gordon, B9.9
Smith, Hopkinson, H10.111
Smith, Lawrence H.,
    B4.21, S9.15
Smith, Linda, P6.210
Smith, Lois, K3.15
Smith, Rand, E3.3
Smith, Ray, L6.12
Smith, Russell, R3
Smith, Warren Story, F9
Smith, William, S3.45
Smithsonian Institution
    Grant, R6
Smoke after Smoke, B5.147
Smylie, Dennis, M6.6
Snap Shot, J3.11
Snider, Ernest, A4.24
Snyder, Clarence, F3.4,
    F3.6, F3.26, F3.39,
    F3.41
Snyder, Gary, H2.15,
    H2.17, H8.6
Snyder, Leo, S11, S11.2
Sobalvarro, Valentina,
    B1.59, B1.60
Society for Vocal Chamber
    Music, B12.27
Soderblom, Kenneth, A4.24
Sofas, Anna, B2.3
Soft Falls the Sounds of
    Eden, F2.15
Sokol, Thomas, P6.195
Sokoloff, Nikolai, D6.107
Solace, S3.188
Solage, S3.148, S3.149,
    S3.150
Soldier Boy, Soldier,
    A4.27
Solemne Musicke, N2.25
Soliloquies, M1.20
Soliloquy, B8.41, B8.42,
    B8.43, B8.44, B8.45,
    B8.46, B8.47, B8.48,
    B8.49, B8.50, B8.51,
    D2.97, D5.18, F9.11,
    L1.203, P12.24
Soliloquy and Sorcery,
    H4.33
Soliloquy for Contrabass,
    D2.97
Solinski, Josef, B5.136
Solitaire, B5.148
Sollberger, Harvey, M6.6

Sollenberger, Elizabeth
    Travis, P6.218, R2.210
Solo, K5.16
Solo Piece, E5.4
Solomon and Balkis, T4.96
Solomons Dance Company,
    see Gus Solomons Jr.
    Dance Company
Solstice, L1.204, L9.15
Solti, Georg, D5.12
Sombres lumieres, T2.30
Some Changing Times 5/4,
    L1.205
Some One, T4.97
Some Say that Ever
    'gainst That Season,
    S14.12
Somebody's Coming, D6.165
Sometime Buster's Strut,
    D3.4, D3.5
Sometimes It Takes a
    While, L1.206
Sometimes in Winter,
    G5.27
Sometimes the Soul,
    P6.184
Sommermusik fur
    Blechblaser, T2.31
Sommerset Carol, C14.5
Sonaria, V3.12
Sonata after Essays for
    Piano, D8.20
Sonata brevis, R2.175
Sonata concertante, K2.74
Sonata da Requiem, P6.185
Sonata da chiesa, R2.176,
    R2.177
Sonata Fantasy, F3.40
Sonata pian e forte,
    S3.189
Sonata serenata, S3.96
Sonate Concertante, S9.76
Sonatine antique, H11.2
Sonatine classique, C7.13
Sonetto di Petrarca,
    D6.147
Song after Sundown,
    T4.100
Song for Kathleen, P11.94
Song for Spooner, P12.26
Song for a Big Evening,
    F3.41
Song for the Bells,
    P6.189
Song for the Clatter
    Bones, S9.20
Song Heard in Sleep,
    R2.183, R2.184
Song of Affirmation,
    D6.148
Song of Daniel, P4.122,
    P4.123
Song of Exploration,
    B12.27, B12.28,
    B12.29, B12.30
Song of Hope, P4.117
Song of Isaiah, E3.20
Song of Jeptha's
    Daughter, P6.190
Song of Jubilation, S14.7
Song of Miriam, F8.73

Song of Moses, S6.10
Song of Ruth, E1.63
Song of Solomon, E1.64
Song of Songs, F8.64
Song of Songs Songs,
    H10.103
Song of Thanksgiving,
    P4.124
Song of the Magi, D4.142
Song of the Mockingbird,
    G5.14
Song of the Musicians,
    S12.10
Song of the Open Road,
    D6.149
Song of the Pilgrim,
    B3.48
Song of the Spinner,
    R2.21
Song of the Troubadour,
    B3.49, B3.50
Song of Truth, D2.116
Song of Zachary, P4.125
Song on Song (Oblong),
    H10.104
Song to the Light, K1.23
Song's End, D6.151
Song, 3 Views, P1.5
Songbook I, H10.105
Songs (on e.e.
    cummings), O1.40
Songs after Poems by
    William Blake, L9.16
Songs after Sonnets of
    Conrad Aiken, B1.63
Songs and Spells, S10.15
Songs by American
    Composers, P6.183
Songs for a Rainy Night,
    R2.186, R2.187,
    R2.189, R2.190, R2.191
Songs for a Requiem,
    L9.12
Songs for Children,
    T4.62, T4.97, T4.118,
    T4.123
Songs for Elementary and
    High School Students,
    B3.51
Songs for Kindergarden,
    B3.52
Songs for Young and
    Grown-up Children,
    D4.143
Songs from a Dozen
    Fantasies from Dunkin
    Donuts, B9.35
Songs from Ecclesiastes,
    P6.191
Songs from Quasimodo,
    Z1.15
Songs from Shakespeare,
    P5.16
Songs from The Princess
    of Alfred Tennyson,
    G4.22
Songs from Twelfth Night,
    D8.25
Songs from Walt Whitman,
    P5.17
Songs of Abelard, D6.152

St. Gertrude School of Music, P4.1

St. Gertrude School of Music Choir, P4.1

St. James Methodist Church Choir, B12.1, B12.7

St. Jean de Brebeuf, R2.87

St. John's Church Choir, O1.4, O1.33

St. John, Dominique, B5.181

St. Joseph College, P4.127

St. Joseph Symphony Orchestra, D4.116

St. Louis Symphony Orchestra, D5.7, S3.48

St. Mark's School, P6.169

St. Mary's Seminary, P4.55, P4.120

St. Michael Church, P4.3, P4.105, P4.122

St. Michael Church Choir, P4.3

St. Michael's Church Youth Choir, S14.10

St. Patrick Cathedral Choir, P4.52

St. Paul's Cathedral, F8.57

St. Paul's Cathedral Choir, F8.57

St. Peter's Abbacy, P4.19

St. Peter's Lithuanian Choir, K1.10

St. Sahag St. Mesrob, Medal, B3

St. Thomas Church, T4.75

St. Thomas Church Boys Choir, T4.75

Staatliche Hochschule fur Musik und Darstellende Kunst (Stuttgart, West Germany) Ensemble Neue Musik, A5.12

Stabat Mater, P6.195

Stacton, David, S9.14

Stage Band Compositions and Arrangements, W2.7

Stage Parodies, D6.161

Stages, M10.74

Staglione, James, S3.38

Stahlman, Barbara, B1.61

Stand on Guard, K2.79

Standards for Piano, S1.14

Stanford Summer Chorus, T4.30

Stanford University, Department of Music, T4.30

Stanger, Russell, M13.8

Stanley Quartet, K4.16, P7.48, S6.28

Stanton Award, see Harris Stanton Award

Star, C13.105, C13.106, C13.107, D5.22, E1.87

Star and Pulsar Discovered Waltzing, P6.149

Star at Christmas, D4.144, D4.145

Star in the East, R2.5

Star Light, L1.217

Star Loss, L1.218

Star Shone Out, D4.146

Star Spangled Banner, S3.191

Star-Tree Carol, P6.196

Stardust, V4.6

Stark, Dale, V3.7

Stark, Lucien, A4.21

Starr, Kenneth, F3.22, F3.40

Stars and Stripes Forever, S3.192

Stars Fell on Alabama, B5.155

Starshine, M5.15

Stasys Santraras, B1.24

State University of New York, College at Potsdam Chorus, D6.61

State University of New York, College at Potsdam, Crane School of Music, D6.124, D6.149

State University of New York, Stony Brook University Orchestra, F6.4

Stautner, John, H3.13

Stautner, Kim, H3.13

Stavis, Laurel, L7.9, S9.25, S9.28

Steamboat Waltz, S3.193

Stearns, Edith, M13.13

Stearns, Peter Pindar, M4

Steber, Eleanor, S3.44

Stecchetti, L., C13.84

Stecher, Melvin, P7.10

Stedry, Patricia, H2.2

Steel Drum Man, L1.219

Steelman, Lee, B12.19, B12.27

Steese, Ruth, E1.40, E1.86

Steffes, Mary Jo, O1.13, O1.28

Stein, Gertrude, E1.38, E1.39, E4.38, M11.19, M11.25, P1.5, S3.66, W4.6

Stein, Warren, M5.2

Steinberg, William, P7.14, R2.224, S3.70, Y1

Stellar Visions, L1.220

Stellar World, L1.221

Stephens, James, S9.20

Stepner, Daniel, H5.7

Steppin' Lively, N1.8

Steps, M10.75

Stepton, Rick, M2

Stereophonic Suite, P8.7

Stereophrenic, R7.76

Stern Grove Festival Association, D5.3

Stern, Lisa, L8.3

Stern, Robert, D9, J1, S2

Stern, Wendy, C2.5

Steumacher, Eric, Y1.8

Stevens, Claudia, S8.7

Stevens, Lee, F4.49, F4.53

Stevens, Susan, C8.16

Stevens, Wallace, B2.3, B2.8, B7.1, P1.5, W4.8, W4.9

Stevenson, Robert Louis, H1.10

Stewart, Bradley, P8.4

Stewart, John S12

Stewart, Susan, O1.55

Stewart, William, P5.14

Stichomythia, A5.94, A5.95

Stillness, F5.26

Stimmung der Abwesenheit, A5.18

Stingley, Mark, A3.1

Stith, Marshall, O1.55

Stock, David, M10.44

Stockhausen, Karlheinz, A5, D2, F1.2, T2

Stokman, Abraham, Z1.13

Stokowski, Leopold, C8.6, M13.15, P6.163

Stoltzman, Richard, M10.3, M10.10, M10.11, M10.29, M10.42, M10.84

Stomper, Paul, E5.6

Stone, D3.24

Stone Is Rolled Away, D4.147

Stone and Earth, C9.15

Stone, Rikki, S10.2

Stone, Susan, K2.4, K2.70

Stoneciphering, B5.156

Stonehill College, P4.64

Storke, R2.32

Stout, Alan, A1

Straley, Leslie, H10.76

Stramm, August, M11.1, M11.4

Stranger, F8.75

Stranger, Russell, M13.1

Strata, M6.40

Stratford Shakespeare Festival, C10.14, C10.16

Stratti, C4.24

Stratus Seekers, R7.5, R7.26, R7.40, R7.43, R7.62, R7.76

Stratusphunk, B5.157, R7.33, R7.44, R7.44, R7.48, R7.56, R7.61, R7.63

Strauss, Marjorie, L10.17

Strauss Prize, see Richard Strauss Prize

Stravinsky, Igor, C7.6

Straw Hat, T4.103

Strayhorn, Billy, B5.99, P2.26

Tabori, Sandra, R4.11
Taffel, Ann, H8.14
Tagore, Rabindranath,
    F7.23, R2.198, R2.200
Tails of Woe, B4.2
Takahashi, Yumi, S9.54
Take Me Out to the Ball
    Game, B13.77
Take One; Third Stream
    Jazz, B5.17, B5.85,
    B5.105, B5.111,
    B5.140, B5.142,
    B5.150, B5.156,
    B5.169, B5.176, B5.192
Take Two; Third Stream
    Jazz, B5.17, B5.85,
    B5.105, B5.111,
    B5.140, B5.142,
    B5.150, B5.156,
    B5.169, B5.176, B5.192
Taki, Rentaro, B5.89
Takin' Lydia Home, R7.46
Taking Charge, F1.7
Tala Pancham Sawari, R6.7
Tala Tintal, R6.8
Tale of Glory, D4.31,
    D4.31.5
Talent Associates, D6.179
Tall Kentuckian, D6.164,
    D6.165, D6.166
Taller To-day, L7.30
Talley Felt the Rain,
    A1.5
Talley, Lynne, F9.15
Tallis, Thomas, S3.190
Tally-Ho, R2.49
Tampa Arts Council,
    D6.58, D6.60
Tangeman, Nell, D6.106,
    E3.21
Tenglewood Awards, *see*
    Bernstein Fellowship;
    Margaret Grant Award;
    Raphael Sagalyn Prize
Tanglewood Festival
    Choir, P6.195
Tanglewood Festival
    Chorus, A5.17, S5.15
Tanglewood Festival of
    Contemporary Music,
    see Berkshire Festival
    of Contemporary Music
Tangley Oaks Fellowship
    (Columbia University),
    W5
Tango Variations, S9.88
Tango alla canonica,
    L7.31
Tango de Trastevere,
    S15.11
Tanner, Rich, M2.2
Tape Study, K5.22, K5.23
Tape.intervention, C6.6
Tapestry, T4.109
Tarantella, R1.14
Tarentella, T4.110
Tarjanyi, Ferenc, S3.23
Tarnow, Brent, M5.18
Tarot, O1.49
Tarr, Edward, O1.11
Tartars, C13.109

Tartini, Giuseppe, E1.104
Tasgal, David, H10.76
Tashi, M10.29, M10.79
Tashi Quartet, M10.79
Tassone, Pasquale, T1
Taste and See, P4.102
Tatragoms Bride, C6.20
Tau Beta Sigma National
    Sorority, D6.152,
    S3.101
Taube, Werner, A5.42
Taylor, Deems, *see* Deems
    Taylor Award
Taylor, Edward, H10.105
Taylor, J.P., R4.13
Taylor, Jane, D5.22
Taylor, Meshack, A4.24
Taylor, Vivian, A4.24,
    A4.30, R1.1, R1.10,
    V3.10, Z1.12
Tchaikovsky, Piotr
    Ilyich, C13.122
Tcherepnin, Ivan, A1,
    T2, T2.4, T2.11, T2.36
Tcheskinoff, Michelle,
    B3.16, B3.17, B3.19,
    B3.29
Tchiakowski, Michael, G8
Tchitouni, B3.9, B3.21,
    B3.35
Tcholakian, Violet, B3.26
Te Deum, C3.27, D4.148,
    H4.39, H4.40, P4.126,
    P4.127, P6.201
Te Deum laudamus, F3.45
Te luci ante, K1.26
Tea for Two, B5.162
Teacher of the Year, L3
Tear Drop, S3.111
Tears, C2.13
Teasdale, Sara, P11.110,
    R2.137
Teddy Charles Tentet,
    R7.29. *See also*
    Charles, Teddy
Teeter, B3.56
Teilhard de Chardin,
    Pierre, P4.38
Teixeira, T., P2.22
Tekeyan, Vahan, B3.3,
    B3.24, B3.36, B3.41,
    B3.44
Telecommunications,
    A5.101
Telemann, Georg Philipp,
    G3.16, G3.17, G3.18
Tema nuovo e vecchio,
    H4.41
Temianka, Henri, K4.24
Temperaments, G1.25
Tempest, F8.66, M4.8,
    M9.2
Temple Anshe Emet, F8.3
Temple Emanu-El, F8.58
Temple Emanu-El Chorus,
    F8.9
Temple Emmanuel, S6.5
Temple in Brooklyn, D1.20
Temple Israel Chorus,
    F8.57

Temple Ohabei Shalom
    Chorus and Orchestra,
    F8.15
Temples at Paestum, Z1.19
Temptation of St.
    Anthony, R2.226
Temptations at the Siege
    of Air and Darkness,
    S9.89
*Ten Fanfares by Ten
    Composers*, P7.19
Tennessee State
    University Band, A4.25
Tennent, Paul, T3.30
Tenney, Sarah, M10.12,
    R5.8
Tennyson, Alfred, Lord,
    B8.3, D6.117, D7.6,
    F6.1, G4.22, M1.22,
    S4.1, W4.16
Tent, E1.91
Tenth Sunday after
    Trinity, S9.46
Teraspulsky, Leopold,
    Y1.36
Terpsichore, L2.31
Terre des hommes, P4.71
Terrien-Queen, Alys,
    S4.15
Teruyuki, Noda, S9.50
Tessera, H6.19, M11.29
Tesson, William, F5, G2,
    App
Testament of Freedom,
    T4.111, T4.112, T4.113
Tethered Colt, S14.9,
    S14.10
Tetralogue, F6.6
Tetreault, Mark, M3.4
Text Settings, M10.80
Texts, J3.13
Textures, V1.94
Textwork, R4.12
Tgettis, Nicholas Chris,
    T3
Thackeray, William
    Makepeace, D6.179,
    W1.34
Thank God It's Friday,
    L7.32
Thank We the Lord, D4.149
Thanksgiving Song, D4.150
That Comfortable Groove,
    L1.231
That Lonely Place, L1.232
That Precious Blanket,
    K2.81
Thatcher, Howard, N2
    S14.10
Theater Piece on Sayings
    of Confucius, O1.50
Theiman, Alexander, F9.6
Theme, R7.47
Theme and Variations on
    the Blues, L1.233
Themes, J2.8
Theodorakis, Mikis,
    B5.122, B5.164,
    B5.176, B5.177, B5.178
There Is Sweet Music
    Here, M1.22

INDEX OF GENRES AND MEDIA OF PERFORMANCE

All references are to item numbers. The Appendix is not indexed. Alphabetization is word-by-word. The filing order for punctuation is parentheses, commas and slashes.

Bass, Piano, C13.11, C13.19, M6.39, T4.93
Bass, Piano, Soprano, K2.70
Bass, Tenor, H10.64
Bass, Tenors(2), Violoncello, H10.22
Basses(2), Altos(2), Sopranos(2), Tenors(2), F2.3, H8.3
Basses(3), Altos(4), Sopranos(4), Tenors(4), C4.7
Basset, Clarinet(in A), Flute(Alto), Percussion, Viola, Violoncello, Voice, S9.20
Basset Horn, Clarinet(Bass), Clarinets(2), M6.5
Bassoon, B8.48, D2.94, H10.115, M10.74
Bassoon(Optional), Chorus(SSA), Double Bass(Optional), Organ or Piano, Violoncello(Optional), P6.119
Bassoon, Alto, Bass, Celeste, Clarinet, Flute, Percussion, Soprano, Tenor, Trombone, Trumpet, O1.28
Bassoon, Baritone, Children or Sopranos(3), Clarinet, Double Bass, Percussion, Piano, Y1.32
Bassoon, Baritone, Clarinet(E-flat), Flute(Alto), Trumpet, O1.14
Bassoon, Baritone, Horn, Percussion(2), Vibraphone, Violin, O1.15
Bassoon, Chamber Orchestra, Clarinet, Flute, Oboe, Violin, B4.29
Bassoon, Chorus(Children)(2-part), Piano, H5.2
Bassoon, Chorus(SATB), Clarinet, Double Bass, Flute, Viola, Violins(1 or 2), Violoncello, P7.38
Bassoon, Chorus(SATB), Clarinet, Flute, Harpsichord, Piano, Viola, Violin, Violoncello, Voices, C1.1
Bassoon, Chorus(SATB), Clarinet, Flute/Piccolo, Horn, Piano, Viola, Violin, Violoncello, S3.80
Bassoon, Clarinet, T3.40
Bassoon, Clarinet or Saxophone, Double Bass, Flute, Oboe, Percussion, Piano, Trumpet, Violoncello, C11.6
Bassoon, Clarinet(Bass), Double Bass, Flute, Horn, Percussion, Y1.40
Bassoon, Clarinet(Contrabass), Flute, Oboe, Piccolo, B8.57
Bassoon, Clarinet(in A), Flute(Alto), Viola, Violin, Violoncello, D2.15
Bassoon, Clarinet, Clarinet(Bass), Clarinet(E-flat), English Horn, Flute(Alto), Flutes(2)/Piccolo, Oboe, T2.41
Bassoon, Clarinet, Clarinet(Bass), Flute, Soprano, L9.12
Bassoon, Clarinet, Clarinet(Bass), Horn, Oboe, Trombone(Bass), Trumpet, S2.8
Bassoon, Clarinet, Cornet, F1.9
Bassoon, Clarinet, Double Bass, Flute, Oboe, Soprano, Tenor, Viola, Violin, Violoncello, G4.23
Bassoon, Clarinet, Double Bass, Flute, Oboe, String Quartet, P7.16

Bassoon, Clarinet, Double Bass, Horn, Oboe, Percussion, Piano, Trumpet, A5.96
Bassoon, Clarinet, Double Bass, Horn, String Quartet, S3.78
Bassoon, Clarinet, Flute, L10.11, O1.57, P7.34, S5.25, T1.13, T2.17, T2.23
Bassoon, Clarinet, Flute, Oboe, B1.25, B4.26, H4.33, H5.6
Bassoon, Clarinet, Flute, Oboe, Percussion Ensemble, String Orchestra, L6.2
Bassoon, Clarinet, Flute, Oboe, Piano, B1.30
Bassoon, Clarinet, Flute, Oboe, Piano, Synthesizer(Arp String), Tape, Vibraphone, L6.19
Bassoon, Clarinet, Flute, Oboe, String Quartet, M10.60
Bassoon, Clarinet, Flute, Piano, Viola, Violin, Violoncello, B4.28
Bassoon, Clarinet, Flute, Trumpets(2), Voice, F4.8
Bassoon, Clarinet, Flute/Piccolo(Optional), Horn, Oboe/English Horn(Optional), M6.9
Bassoon, Clarinet, Flute/Piccolo, Horn, Tenor, B6.4
Bassoon, Clarinet, Flutes(2), Horn, Oboe, Percussion, Soprano or Tenor, Trombone, Tuba or Trombone(Bass), P9.5
Bassoon, Clarinet, Flutes(2), Oboe, Piano, Trombone, Trumpets(2), C13.53
Bassoon, Clarinet, Harpsichord, Soprano, Viola, C2.12
Bassoon, Clarinet, Horn, Piano, Viola, Violin, Violoncello, K1.21
Bassoon, Clarinet, Oboe, B12.34, T3.43
Bassoon, Clarinet, Oboe, Percussion(2), Piano, Piccolo, Trombone, Trumpet, S3.173
Bassoon, Clarinet, Oboe, Soprano, Viola, Violin, Violoncello, D9.11
Bassoon, Clarinet, Oboe, Speakers(2), B8.24
Bassoon, Clarinet, Piano, Tenor, Violin, Violoncello, B7.2
Bassoon, Clarinet/Clarinet(Bass), Flute/Piccolo, Horn, Oboe/English Horn, Trumpet, R2.111
Bassoon, Clarinet/ Saxophone(Tenor), Double Bass, Drums, Flute, Horn, Piano, Trombone, Vibraphone, S3.119
Bassoon, Clarinets(2), Double Bass, Flute, Piano, Violin, Violoncello, B8.11
Bassoon, Clarinets(2), Flute, Harp, Viola, L10.15
Bassoon, Clarinets(2), Flute, Horn, Oboe, C13.107
Bassoon, Clarinets(2), Percussion(2), Violin, Violoncello, M10.40
Bassoon, Clarinets(in A)(2), Flute, Guitar(Amplified), Horn, Oboe, Piano, S1.7

Chorus(Men)(3-part), Chorus(Treble),
    Organ, Timpani, Trumpets(3), P4.76
Chorus(Men)(3-part), Congregation,
    Orchestra, P4.119
Chorus(Men)(3-part), Organ or Piano,
    Timpani, P4.39
Chorus(Men)(4-part), Cantor,
    Congregation, Organ, Timpani,
    Trombones(2), Trumpets(2), P4.123
Chorus(Men)(4-part), Harpsichord,
    Tenor, H6.21
Chorus(Men), Band, Narrator, Soprano,
    H4.8
Chorus(Men), Baritone, Bass, Brass
    Ensemble, Tenor, P7.3
Chorus(Men), Clarinet, Clarinet(Bass),
    Horns(2), Piano, Trumpet, C9.5
Chorus(Men), Double Bass, Flute,
    Guitar, Horn, Percussion,
    Vibraphone, P6.118
Chorus(Men), Organ, C13.101
Chorus(Men), Organ, Timpani,
    Trombones(2), Trumpets(2), Tuba,
    P4.16
Chorus(Mixed), B1.4, E1.52, E4.1,
    F8.28, F8.29, F8.82, G6.2, G7.1,
    G7.3, G7.7, H2.22, K4.25, L2.12,
    L2.13, L2.35, L7.11, L7.15, L7.36,
    M8.15, M10.18, P4.33, P4.35, P4.86,
    P6.66, P6.136, P6.145, S6.16, S12.4,
    T4.49, W4.1,
Chorus(Mixed)(Optional),
    Bands(5-part), Bells(20),
    Handbells(Optional), Orchestra,
    E1.12
Chorus(Mixed), Alto, Bass, Guitar or
    Piano, Soprano, Tenor, P6.129
Chorus(Mixed), Alto, Bass,
    Percussion(2), Soprano, String
    Quartet, Tenor, H2.30
Chorus(Mixed), Baritone, Bass, Mezzo
    Soprano, Soprano, Tenor, P6.135
Chorus(Mixed), Baritone, Clarinet,
    Double Bass, Percussion, Piano,
    Saxophone(Tenor), Violin,
    Violoncello, H2.15
Chorus(Mixed), Bass, Bass Baritone,
    Organ, Tape, Tenor, P6.174
Chorus(Mixed), Bells, Celeste, Double
    Basses(2), Percussion, Pianos(2),
    P4.7
Chorus(Mixed), Brasses(9), Percussion,
    C10.7
Chorus(Mixed), Brasses, Cantor,
    Congregation, Organ, Timpani, P4.122
Chorus(Mixed), Brasses, Congregation,
    Organ, Percussion, Speaker, Voice,
    P4.89
Chorus(Mixed), Brasses, Timpani, P4.92
Chorus(Mixed), Cantor, Organ, F8.5
Chorus(Mixed), Chamber Orchestra,
    P4.43
Chorus(Mixed), Chimes, Double Bass,
    Harp, Organ, Timpani, P4.117
Chorus(Mixed), Chimes, Harp, Soprano,
    P4.129

Chorus(Mixed), Chorus(SSA),
    Chorus(Treble Unison)(Optional),
    Organ, P6.83
Chorus(Mixed), Chorus(Spoken), P5.4
Chorus(Mixed), Chorus(Unison) or
    Soprano, Organ, D4.132
Chorus(Mixed), Clarinet, Double Bass,
    Harp, Narrator, Organ, Viola,
    Voices(5), P6.134
Chorus(Mixed), Congregation, P4.101,
    P4.130
Chorus(Mixed), Congregation,
    Orchestra, Organ, P4.126
Chorus(Mixed), Dancers(Optional),
    Narrator, Orchestra, Voices, D6.11
Chorus(Mixed), Double Bass, Trombone,
    Trumpet, Woodwind Quintet, S12.11
Chorus(Mixed), Guitar or Piano,
    P6.110, P6.193
Chorus(Mixed), Handbells, Organ, L7.14
Chorus(Mixed), Harp, Tenor,
    Violoncello, Woodwinds(5), F8.78
Chorus(Mixed), Instrumental Ensemble,
    Organ, Tenor, P4.38
Chorus(Mixed), Instrumental Ensemble,
    Speaker, P4.121
Chorus(Mixed), Instruments(8), H3.15
Chorus(Mixed), Keyboard, C3.12
Chorus(Mixed), Orchestra, D6.26,
    M11.30, P4.19, P6.92
Chorus(Mixed), Orchestra or Piano,
    T4.69
Chorus(Mixed), Orchestra(Unspecified),
    A6.2
Chorus(Mixed), Orchestra, Soprano,
    P6.195
Chorus(Mixed), Orchestra, Voice, P4.46
Chorus(Mixed), Orchestra, Voices,
    D6.164
Chorus(Mixed), Organ, G7.4, P4.91,
    P6.137
Chorus(Mixed), Organ or Piano, P6.159
Chorus(Mixed), Organ or
    Piano(Optional), P6.73
Chorus(Mixed), Organ or Piano,
    Soprano, P6.195
Chorus(Mixed), Organ(Optional), P6.162
Chorus(Mixed), Organ, Timpani,
    Trombones(3), Trumpets(3), Tuba,
    P4.113
Chorus(Mixed), Organ, Voice, P4.42
Chorus(Mixed), Organ, Woodwinds,
    P6.140
Chorus(Mixed), Percussion, Piano,
    S6.21
Chorus(Mixed), Piano, D6.126, T4.7,
    T4.31, T4.70, W4.8
Chorus(Mixed), Soprano,
    Tape(Optional), P6.175
Chorus(Mixed), Tape, P6.76, P6.87
Chorus(Mixed), Timpani(Optional),
    Trombones(2), Trumpets(2),
    Tuba(Optional), P6.159
Chorus(SA), D4.42, D4.128, P6.14,
    W1.13
Chorus(SA) or Chorus(TB), Y1.33

Chorus(SA) or Chorus(TB), Organ,
    Trumpets(3), P6.201
Chorus(SA), Bassoons(2), Harp or
    Piano, Oboes(2), Soprano, P6.108
Chorus(SA), Chorus(SATB), D4.137,
    D4.155
Chorus(SA), Chorus(SATB), Hand Drum,
    Recorders(2) or Flutes(2), Regal or
    Organ, Strings(4-part), S14.16
Chorus(SA), Chorus(SATB), Instrumental
    Ensemble, S14.8
Chorus(SA), Chorus(SATB), Piano,
    D4.137, D4.155
Chorus(SA), Congregation, Organ,
    Timpani, Trombones(3), Trumpets(2),
    P4.106
Chorus(SA), English Horn, Flute, Oboe,
    Strings, P5.8
Chorus(SA), Flute, Piano, S14.1
Chorus(SA), Hand Drum, Piano,
    Recorder, Snare Drum, G3.11
Chorus(SA), Handbells, Piano or Organ,
    D4.30
Chorus(SA),
    Instruments(Unspecified)(Optional),
    P6.94
Chorus(SA), Orchestra, O1.42
Chorus(SA), Orchestra or Piano, D6.154
Chorus(SA), Orff Instruments, Piano,
    P10.12
Chorus(SA), Organ, D4.24, P4.47
Chorus(SA), Organ, Violin(Optional),
    F3.27
Chorus(SA), Piano, D4.15, D4.87,
    D4.90, D4.136, D6.28, H10.22.5,
    P10.21, S14.14
Chorus(SA), Piano or Organ, D4.31,
    D4.123
Chorus(SA), String Quartet, F3.26
Chorus(SA), Strings(5-part), S14.17
Chorus(SAA), Chamber Orchestra, T4.41
Chorus(SAA), Flute, Piano, T4.42
Chorus(SAA), Organ, B13.4
Chorus(SAATTB), H10.19
Chorus(SAB), B13.50, B13.55, D4.25,
    D4.31, D4.34, D4.38, D4.48, D4.55,
    D4.60, D4.74, D4.88, D4.100, D4.147
Chorus(SAB), Guitar, Handbells,
    Harpsichord, Recorder, G3.3
Chorus(SAB), Organ, D4.41, P4.4, P4.36
Chorus(SAB), Organ or Piano, B13.25,
    D4.31.5
Chorus(SABar), Baritone, Piano or
    Organ, D4.9
Chorus(SAT), D4.150
Chorus(SATB), A1.10, A2.3, A5.37,
    A5.89, B1.15, B1.45, B3.9, B3.15,
    B3.31, B3.35, B3.40, B3.63, B12.1,
    B12.7, B12.14, B13.31, B13.37,
    B13.49, B13.56, B13.65, B4.31,
    B8.30, B8.36, C10.1, C10.14, C12.3,
    C12.5, C6.14, D2.2, D2.74, D2.85,
    D2.118, D3.1, D3.19, D3.22, D4.3,
    D4.18, D4.20, D4.21.5, D4.33, D4.43,
    D4.47, D4.52, D4.59, D4.77, D4.80,
    D4.81, D4.97, D4.104, D4.108,
    D4.118, D4.153, E1.78, E3.18, E3.19,
    F3.18, F5.7, F5.9, F5.14, F5.25,
    F7.2, F7.4, F7.5, F7.10, F7.24,
F7.26, F8.39, F8.40, F8.45, F8.56,
G5.2, G5.3, G6.14, G7.8, H4.26,
H10.10, H10.11, H10.18, H10.20,
H10.23, H10.24, H10.28, H10.30,
H10.57, H10.62, H10.63, H10.65,
H10.69, H10.73, H10.127, H10.128,
J2.3, J3.3, K1.1, K1.13, L7.8
L11.12, M5.3, M7.10, M7.12, M8.10,
M10.80, M11.34, M11.35, O1.4, O1.60,
P4.2, P4.6, P4.13, P4.45, P4.53,
P4.83, P4.90, P4.93, P4.97, P4.100,
P4.125, P5.2, P6.18, P6.45, P6.84,
P6.90, P6.127, P6.141, P6.147,
P6.148, P6.223, P12.15, P7.40, R2.5,
R2.8, R2.9, R2.18, R2.21, R2.22,
R2.27, R2.32, R2.62, R2.100, R2.105,
R2.203, R2.205, R2.232, R2.245,
R5.3, S5.15, S8.5, S8.6, S9.100,
S12.7, S14.4, S14.5, S14.12, T1.9,
T3.8, T4.3, T4.10, T4.14, T4.15,
T4.28, T4.29, T4.36, T4.38, T4.66,
V1.65, V1.101, V2.3, W1.15, W1.18,
W1.20, Y1.21, Y1.33, Z1.5, Z1.9
Chorus(SATB) or Chorus(Equal Voices),
    Cantor, Double Bass, Organ or
    Brasses, Timpani, P4.54
Chorus(SATB) or Chorus(Unison), Organ
    or Piano, H3.26
Chorus(SATB) or Congregation, Organ,
    Percussion, Trombones(2),
    Trumpets(3), P4.112
Chorus(SATB)(Optional), Piano,
    Soprano, T4.65
Chorus(SATB), Alto or Baritone, Piano,
    R2.190
Chorus(SATB), Alto or Baritone, Piano
    or Organ, D4.7
Chorus(SATB), Alto, Bass, Orchestra,
    Soprano, Tenor, A5.83, G6.1
Chorus(SATB), Alto, Bass, Soprano,
    String Quartet, Tenor, T3.12
Chorus(SATB), Alto, Bass, Soprano,
    Tape, Tenor, P6.72
Chorus(SATB), Alto, Bass, Soprano,
    Tenor, Z1.6
Chorus(SATB), Alto, Cantor or
    Baritone, Organ, Soprano, Tenor,
    P6.167
Chorus(SATB), Alto, Harp, R2.158
Chorus(SATB), Alto, Organ(Ad Lib.),
    R2.235
Chorus(SATB), Alto, Piano, R2.158
Chorus(SATB), Alto, Piano, Soprano,
    D4.141
Chorus(SATB), Band, H4.40
Chorus(SATB), Band(Optional),
    Chorus(Children), Wind Ensemble,
    Y1.5
Chorus(SATB), Band, Chorus(Children),
    D6.59
Chorus(SATB), Band, Orchestra, M1.1
Chorus(SATB), Band, Organ(Ad Lib.),
    P6.3
Chorus(SATB), Baritone, Chamber
    Orchestra, P4.29
Chorus(SATB), Baritone, Horn, Soprano,
    Tenor, D6.105
Chorus(SATB), Baritone, Mezzo Soprano,
    Percussion, R5.7

Clarinet(Bass), Chorus, Double Bass,
    Piano, B7.1
Clarinet(Bass), Clarinet, A1.3, H7.21,
    S3.94
Clarinet(Bass), Clarinet(Alto),
    Clarinets(2), M8.29
Clarinet(Bass), Clarinet(E-flat),
    Clarinet(in A), Marimba, Viola,
    Violin, Violoncello, L7.38
Clarinet(Bass), Clarinet,
    Clarinet(E-flat), Crotales, Mezzo
    Soprano, Piano, L7.16
Clarinet(Bass), Clarinet, Dancers,
    Percussion, Violoncello, K2.52
Clarinet(Bass), Clarinet, Double Bass,
    Flute, Saxophone(Soprano), Tam-tam,
    Viola, Violin, Violoncello, B8.37
Clarinet(Bass), Clarinet, Flute,
    Flute/Piccolo, Harp, Percussion(4),
    Soprano, Viola, Violoncello, B8.2
Clarinet(Bass), Clarinet, Flute, Horn,
    Oboe, Soprano, Tenor, Trombone,
    Trumpet, P5.3
Clarinet(Bass), Clarinet, Flute, Oboe,
    Percussion, Piccolo,
    Saxophone(Soprano), Tape, M10.61
Clarinet(Bass), Clarinet, Flute,
    Viola, Violin, Violoncello, H9.39
Clarinet(Bass), Clarinet,
    Flute/Piccolo, Viola, Violin,
    Violoncello, H2.27
Clarinet(Bass), Clarinet, Flutes(2),
    Viola, Violin, Voices(6), C9.11
Clarinet(Bass), Clarinet, Percussion,
    Piano, Soprano, Speaker(Female),
    Speaker(Male), Tenor, Viola, Violin,
    Violoncello, J3.11
Clarinet(Bass), Dancers(3), Guitar,
    Percussion, L2.34
Clarinet(Bass), Double Bass, W6.4
Clarinet(Bass), Double Bass, Flute,
    Percussion, H4.43
Clarinet(Bass), Double Bass, Flute,
    Percussion, Piano, Violin,
    Violoncello, Voice(High), D2.19
Clarinet(Bass), Double Bass, Flute,
    Trumpet, Viola, C9.3
Clarinet(Bass), Double Basses(2),
    Drums, Guitar, S3.74
Clarinet(Bass), Flute, Harp, Piano,
    Violin, Violoncello, M12.5
Clarinet(Bass), Flute, Marimba,
    Orchestra, Violin, R5.5
Clarinet(Bass), Flute, Oboe,
    Violoncello, C4.23
Clarinet(Bass), Flute, Percussion(2),
    Violin, Violoncello, S15.4
Clarinet(Bass), Flute, Trumpet, Viola,
    Violin, Violoncello, M10.44
Clarinet(Bass), Flute, Violin, S4.14
Clarinet(Bass), Harp, Oboe, L4.11
Clarinet(Bass), Organ, Trumpet, B8.1
Clarinet(Bass), Piano, B5.2
Clarinet(Bass), Piano, Soprano,
    Violoncello, M10.72
Clarinet(Bass), Tape, C5.5
Clarinet(Bass), Tape(Computer), K5.16
Clarinet(Bass), Trumpet, Violoncello,
    B8.53
Clarinet(Bass), Violin, M10.32

Clarinet(Bass)/ Basset
    Horn/Saxophone(Soprano)/
    Saxophone(Tenor)
    /Clarinet(Contrabass), M10.75
Clarinet(Bass)/ Clarinet, Bassoon,
    Flute/Piccolo, Horn, Oboe/English
    Horn, Trumpet, R2.111
Clarinet(Bass)/ Clarinet,
    Chorus(SATB), Percussion, Piano,
    Trombone, Violoncello, E3.1
Clarinet(Bass)/ Clarinet, Double Bass,
    Flute/Flute(Alto), Horn, Tenor,
    Viola, Violin, H6.23
Clarinet(Bass)/ Clarinet, Flute,
    Harpsichord or Piano, Tenor, Viola,
    Violoncello, S9.21
Clarinet(Bass)/ Clarinet, Flute,
    Soprano, Viola, Violin, Violoncello,
    H9.2
Clarinet(Bass)/ Clarinet,
    Flute/Piccolo, Piano, Violin,
    Violoncello, H2.19
Clarinet(Bass)/ Clarinet, Mezzo
    Soprano, Viola, Violin, Violoncello,
    L4.17
Clarinet(Bass)/ Clarinet/
    Saxophone(Soprano), Flute/Piccolo/
    Flute(Alto), Oboe/English Horn,
    Piano, M10.27
Clarinet(Bass)/ Flute/Saxophone(Alto),
    Double Basses(2), Flute, Guitar,
    Piano, Saxophone(Alto), Vibraphone,
    S3.122
Clarinet(Bass)/ Saxophone(Baritone),
    Bassoon, Drums, English Horn, Piano,
    Saxophone(Alto), Saxophone(Soprano)/
    Saxophone(Tenor) or Flute, P2.23
Clarinet(Contrabass), Bassoon, Flute,
    Oboe, Piccolo, B8.57
Clarinet(Contrabass)/Clarinet,
    Saxophone(Soprano), Violoncello,
    M10.33
Clarinet(E-flat), Alto, Guitar, Horn,
    Viola, Z1.23
Clarinet(E-flat), Baritone, Bassoon,
    Flute(Alto), Trumpet, O1.14
Clarinet(E-flat), Bassoon, Clarinet,
    Clarinet(Bass), English Horn,
    Flute(Alto), Flutes(2)/Piccolo,
    Oboe, T2.41
Clarinet(E-flat), Clarinet(Bass),
    Clarinet(in A), Marimba, Viola,
    Violin, Violoncello, L7.38
Clarinet(E-flat), Clarinet,
    Clarinet(Bass), Crotales, Mezzo
    Soprano, Piano, L7.16
Clarinet(E-flat), Clarinet,
    Clarinet(in A), English Horn, Flute,
    Oboe, Trumpet(Muted), Vibraphone,
    Violin, F4.57
Clarinet(in A), Basset, Flute(Alto),
    Percussion, Viola, Violoncello,
    Voice, S9.20
Clarinet(in A), Bassoon, Flute(Alto),
    Viola, Violin, Violoncello, D2.15
Clarinet(in A), Clarinet(Bass),
    Clarinet(E-flat), Marimba, Viola,
    Violin, Violoncello, L7.38
Clarinet(in A), Clarinet,
    Clarinet(E-flat), English Horn,

683

Clarinet, Clarinet(Bass), Double Bass,
Flute, Saxophone(Soprano), Tam-tam,
Viola, Violin, Violoncello, B8.37
Clarinet, Clarinet(Bass), Flute,
Flute/Piccolo, Harp, Percussion(4),
Soprano, Viola, Violoncello, B8.2
Clarinet, Clarinet(Bass), Flute, Horn,
Oboe, Soprano, Tenor, Trombone,
Trumpet, P5.3
Clarinet, Clarinet(Bass), Flute, Oboe,
Percussion, Piccolo,
Saxophone(Soprano), Tape, M10.61
Clarinet, Clarinet(Bass), Flute,
Viola, Violin, Violoncello, H9.39
Clarinet, Clarinet(Bass),
Flute/Piccolo, Viola, Violin,
Violoncello, H2.27
Clarinet, Clarinet(Bass), Flutes(2),
Viola, Violin, Voices(6), C9.11
Clarinet, Clarinet(Bass), Percussion,
Piano, Soprano, Speaker(Female),
Speaker(Male), Tenor, Viola, Violin,
Violoncello, J3.11
Clarinet, Clarinet(E-flat),
Clarinet(in A), English Horn, Flute,
Oboe, Trumpet(Muted), Vibraphone,
Violin, F4.57
Clarinet, Cornet, Drums, Horn, Piano,
Saxophone(Tenor) or Trombone or
Baritone, S3.178
Clarinet, Dancers(4), Flute,
Percussion, Piano, Viola, Violin,
Violoncello, M10.45
Clarinet, Dancers(Optional),
Flutes(2), Violoncello, B12.12
Clarinet, Double Bass, Drums, Piano,
L1.73
Clarinet, Double Bass, English Horn,
Trumpet, Viola, W4.10
Clarinet, Double Bass, Flute(Alto),
Horn, Mezzo Soprano, Trombone,
Viola, S9.25
Clarinet, Double Bass, Flute, Guitar,
Piano, Trumpet, Vibraphone, Violin,
D2.23
Clarinet, Double Bass, Flute, Harp,
Marimba, G4.2
Clarinet, Double Bass, Flute, Harp,
Oboe, Tenor, Violas, Violoncellos,
D6.5
Clarinet, Double Bass, Flute, Harp,
Soprano, Trumpet, Vibraphone, Viola,
L7.22
Clarinet, Double Bass, Flute, Horn,
Piano, Violin, W4.12
Clarinet, Double Bass, Flute,
Narrator, Percussion, Piano,
Soprano, Viola, Violoncello, Y1.6
Clarinet, Double Bass, Flute,
Percussion, Piano, Soprano, Violin,
Violoncello, B9.34
Clarinet, Double Bass, Flute,
Percussion, Piano, Violin,
Violoncello, S6.19
Clarinet, Double Bass, Flute, Piano,
Soprano, Violin, Violoncello, B10.3
Clarinet, Double Bass, Flute, Piano,
Violoncello, F5.30

Clarinet, Double Bass, Flute/Piccolo,
Mezzo Soprano, Piano, Violin,
Violoncello, S6.32
Clarinet, Double Bass, Flutes(2),
Speaker, Trumpets(2), F4.10
Clarinet, Double Bass, Harp,
Vibraphone, S3.36
Clarinet, Double Bass, Piano, F5.1,
F5.12, F5.21
Clarinet, Double Bass, Piano, Violin,
L7.17
Clarinet, Double Bass, Soprano,
Violin, L7.5, L7.6
Clarinet, Double Bass, Violin, L7.34
Clarinet, Drums, Guitar, Oboe, Piano,
Saxophones(2), Trombone, B5.29
Clarinet, English Horn, Flute, Harp,
Percussion(2), Pianos(2), Soprano,
Viola, B8.23
Clarinet, English Horn, Orchestra,
Violin, Violoncello, H4.5
Clarinet, Flute, B1.14, C12.1, D2.29,
S2.1, V1.52
Clarinet, Flute(Alto), Harp, Mezzo
Soprano, Percussion, Viola,
Violoncello, M11.4
Clarinet, Flute, Guitar, Percussion,
Soprano, Viola, Violin, K5.1
Clarinet, Flute, Harp, Percussion,
K5.8
Clarinet, Flute, Harpsichord, B12.26,
F4 48
Clarinet, Flute, Harpsichord,
Oboe/English Horn, Percussion,
Violin, Violoncello, P6.111
Clarinet, Flute, Harpsichord, Soprano,
Violoncello, B12.27
Clarinet, Flute, Horn, Oboe,
Violoncello, E3.13
Clarinet, Flute, Horn, Piano, S3.34
Clarinet, Flute, Horn, Piano(4-hands),
Soprano, Trombone(Bass), Trumpet,
Vibraphone, P12.6
Clarinet, Flute, Horn, Piano, Timpani,
Viola, Violin, Violoncello, V1.51
Clarinet, Flute, Mezzo Soprano, Piano,
Violin, Violoncello, H5.21
Clarinet, Flute, Oboe, H10.106
Clarinet, Flute, Oboe, Percussion,
Soprano, Violin, Violoncello, K3.8
Clarinet, Flute, Oboe, Percussion,
Soprano, Violoncello, K3.7
Clarinet, Flute, Oboe, Piano, Viola,
Violin, Violoncello, V1.97
Clarinet, Flute, Oboe, Soprano, Viola,
Violin, Violoncello, C9.2
Clarinet, Flute, Oboe, Viola, Violin,
Violoncello, M10.41
Clarinet, Flute, Oboe, Violin, H10.107
Clarinet, Flute, Oboe/English Horn,
Piano, Viola, Violin, Violoncello,
H10.34
Clarinet, Flute, Percussion, H5.1
Clarinet, Flute, Percussion(2), Piano,
Viola, Violin, Violoncello, L2.14
Clarinet, Flute, Percussion, Piano,
H5.5

Clarinet, Flute, Percussion, Piano,
  Soprano, Tape, Violin, Violoncello,
  D8.1
Clarinet, Flute, Percussion, Piano,
  Soprano, Viola, Violoncello, H2.26
Clarinet, Flute, Piano, F5.10, L6.21,
  T2.5
Clarinet, Flute, Piano,
  Saxophone(Alto), A6.4
Clarinet, Flute, Piano, Soprano,
  Viola, M9.10
Clarinet, Flute, Piano, Soprano,
  Viola, Violin, Violoncello, D8.19
Clarinet, Flute, Piano, Trombone,
  Trumpet, Viola, F4.19
Clarinet, Flute, Piano, String
  Quartet, T4.92
Clarinet, Flute, Piano, Viola,
  Violoncello, T4.81
Clarinet, Flute, Piano, Violin,
  C12.10, M1.4
Clarinet, Flute, Piano, Violin,
  Violoncello, F7.17, S6.11
Clarinet, Flute, Piano, Violins(2),
  Violoncello, K2.69
Clarinet, Flute, Piano, Violoncello,
  H5.16
Clarinet, Flute, Piano/Celeste,
  Soprano, Trumpet, Viola, Violin,
  M9.3
Clarinet, Flute, Saxophone(Alto),
  M8.31
Clarinet, Flute, Soprano, J3.12
Clarinet, Flute, Soprano, Viola,
  Violin, Violoncello, S9.31
Clarinet, Flute, Soprano, Violoncello,
  W4.16
Clarinet, Flute, Trombone, Trumpet in
  C, P12.22
Clarinet, Flute, Trumpet, F4.53
Clarinet, Flute, Viola, K1.8
Clarinet, Flute, Viola, Violin,
  Violoncello, S9.59, S9.83, S9.84
Clarinet, Flute, Violin, H2.12
Clarinet, Flute, Violin, Violoncello,
  Voices, H10.1
Clarinet, Flute, Violoncello, K1.9
Clarinet, Flute, Wind Ensemble, B1.7
Clarinet, Flute/Piccolo, Oboe,
  Percussion(2), Soprano, Violin,
  Violoncello, K3.5
Clarinet, Flute/Piccolo, Oboe,
  Soprano, Violin, Violoncello, C6.3
Clarinet, Flute/Piccolo, Percussion,
  Piano, Violoncello, M10.43
Clarinet, Flutes(2), J2.8
Clarinet, Guitar(Bass)(Optional),
  Percussion, Piano, L6.1
Clarinet, Guitar(Electric), Horn,
  Violoncello, T2.42
Clarinet, Guitar, Horn, Trombone,
  Trumpet, Vibraphone, Violin,
  Violoncello, D2.18
Clarinet, Guitar or Lute, Soprano,
  S2.3
Clarinet, Harp, Soprano, Viola,
  Violoncello, H9.21
Clarinet, Harp, Violin, B1.79
Clarinet, Horn, Oboe, Piano, Viola,
  S6.33

Clarinet, Horn, Piano, F4.55, S3.93,
  W1.35
Clarinet, Horn, Piano, Violin,
  Violoncello, H10.31
Clarinet, Horn, Violin, Violoncello,
  S12.3
Clarinet, Horns(2), Oboe, Percussion,
  Trombones(2), Viola, D6.7
Clarinet, Jazz Band, R7.4
Clarinet, Lute or Guitar, Soprano,
  S2.3
Clarinet, Marimba, H4.35
Clarinet, Marimba, Vibraphone, F1.10
Clarinet, Mezzo Soprano, Percussion,
  Piano, Soprano, Tenor, P1.5
Clarinet, Mezzo Soprano, Piano,
  Violin, L7.12
Clarinet, Mezzo Soprano, Viola, S9.78
Clarinet, Oboe, B4.6
Clarinet, Oboe, Organ, Trombone,
  Trumpet, B12.23
Clarinet, Oboe, Percussion(2),
  Piccolo, Soprano, Violin,
  Violoncello, K3.6
Clarinet, Oboe, Viola, T4.104
Clarinet, Orchestra, B8.9, M10.3
Clarinet, Orchestra, Trumpet, Violin,
  A5.24
Clarinet, Organ, S14.6
Clarinet, Percussion, Soprano,
  Violoncello, M12.1
Clarinet, Percussion, Viola, G1.19
Clarinet, Percussion, Violoncello,
  L2.36
Clarinet, Piano, A4.31, B4.7, B8.14,
  B9.8, C11.3, C12.7, D6.44, D6.57,
  F2.9, F5.5, K2.26, M2.3, M8.9,
  M10.84, N2.6, N2.11, N2.31, V2.5
Clarinet, Piano, Saxophone(Alto),
  Saxophone(Tenor), Voice, B5.122
Clarinet, Piano, Soprano, S2.2
Clarinet, Piano, Soprano, String
  Quartet, K1.7
Clarinet, Piano, Tenor, Trombone,
  Viola, Violoncello, A4.2
Clarinet, Piano, Trombone, B5.54
Clarinet, Piano, Trombone, Tuba, M3.4
Clarinet, Piano, Viola, B1.78, F4.54,
  H8.9, M10.37
Clarinet, Piano, Violin, B1.79,
  B12.35, L7.3, T1.14, T3.44, W4.14,
  Z1.22
Clarinet, Piano, Violin, Violoncello,
  L6.13, M10.79, S3.96, V1.61
Clarinet, Piano, Violoncello, B1.80
Clarinet, Soprano, E3.4
Clarinet, Soprano, Violoncello, B12.28
Clarinet, String Orchestra, V1.84
Clarinet, String Quartet, D8.15,
  G1.11, H6.16, M10.29, M10.42, N2.12
Clarinet, Tape, F4.22, P6.65
Clarinet, Trombone(Bass), E5.1
Clarinet, Trombone, Violin, B1.12
Clarinet, Trumpet, Violoncello, D2.122
Clarinet, Viola, F4.13, M7.19, N2.2
Clarinet, Viola, Violin, Violoncello,
  M6.26
Clarinet, Violin, S9.92
Clarinet, Violin, Violoncello, W6.8.5
Clarinet, Violoncello, D9.10

Double Bass, Bongos, Trumpet, Voices(2 or 3), P4.73

Double Bass, Brasses, Cantor, Chorus(SATB), Congregation, Organ, Timpani, P4.60

Double Bass, Brasses, Chorus(SATB), Congregation, Organ, Percussion, P4.58

Double Bass, Brasses, Chorus(SATB), Organ, Percussion, P4.111

Double Bass, Cantor, Chorus(SATB) or Chorus(Equal Voices), Organ or Brasses, Timpani, P4.54

Double Bass, Celeste, Electric Bass, Guitar, Organ, Percussion, Piano, H4.16

Double Bass, Celeste, Mezzo Soprano, Piano, Trombone, Trumpet, Tuba, Vibraphone, Violin, Violoncello, F2.7

Double Bass, Chamber Orchestra, Drums, Narrator, Saxophone(Alto), Saxophone(Tenor), Trumpet, S3.58

Double Bass, Chimes, Chorus(Mixed), Harp, Organ, Timpani, P4.117

Double Bass, Chorus(Men), Flute, Guitar, Horn, Percussion, Vibraphone, P6.118

Double Bass, Chorus(Mixed), Clarinet, Harp, Narrator, Organ, Viola, Voices(5), P6.134

Double Bass, Chorus(Mixed), Trombone, Trumpet, Woodwind Quintet, S12.11

Double Bass, Chorus(SATB), Drum, Flute, Harp, Trombone, Trumpet, Voices, Xylophone, P4.44

Double Bass, Chorus(SATB), Drums, Flute, Guitar, Piano, B13.53

Double Bass, Chorus, Clarinet(Bass), Piano, B7.1

Double Bass, Clarinet(Bass), W6.4

Double Bass, Clarinet(Bass), Flute, Percussion, H4.43

Double Bass, Clarinet(Bass), Flute, Percussion, Piano, Violin, Violoncello, Voice(High), D2.19

Double Bass, Clarinet(Bass), Flute, Trumpet, Viola, C9.3

Double Bass, Clarinet, Clarinet(Bass), Flute, Saxophone(Soprano), Tam-tam, Viola, Violin, Violoncello, B8.37

Double Bass, Clarinet, Drums, Piano, L1.73

Double Bass, Clarinet, English Horn, Trumpet, Viola, W4.10

Double Bass, Clarinet, Flute(Alto), Horn, Mezzo Soprano, Trombone, Viola, S9.25

Double Bass, Clarinet, Flute, Guitar, Piano, Trumpet, Vibraphone, Violin, D2.23

Double Bass, Clarinet, Flute, Harp, Marimba, G4.2

Double Bass, Clarinet, Flute, Harp, Oboe, Tenor, Violas, Violoncellos, D6.5

Double Bass, Clarinet, Flute, Harp, Soprano, Trumpet, Vibraphone, Viola, L7.22

Double Bass, Clarinet, Flute, Horn, Piano, Violin, W4.12

Double Bass, Clarinet, Flute, Narrator, Percussion, Piano, Soprano, Viola, Violoncello, Y1.6

Double Bass, Clarinet, Flute, Percussion, Piano, Soprano, Violin, Violoncello, B9.34

Double Bass, Clarinet, Flute, Percussion, Piano, Violin, Violoncello, S6.19

Double Bass, Clarinet, Flute, Piano, Soprano, Violin, Violoncello, B10.3

Double Bass, Clarinet, Flute, Piano, Violoncello, F5.30

Double Bass, Clarinet, Flute/Piccolo, Mezzo Soprano, Piano, Violin, Violoncello, S6.32

Double Bass, Clarinet, Flutes(2), Speaker, Trumpets(2), F4.10

Double Bass, Clarinet, Harp, Vibraphone, S3.36

Double Bass, Clarinet, Piano, F5.1, F5.12, F5.21

Double Bass, Clarinet, Piano, Violin, L7.17

Double Bass, Clarinet, Soprano, Violin, L7.5, L7.6

Double Bass, Clarinet, Violin, L7.34

Double Bass, Clarinet/Clarinet(Bass), Flute/Flute(Alto), Horn, Tenor, Viola, Violin, H6.23

Double Bass, Clarinet/Saxophone(Tenor), Drums, Piano, Trumpet, L1.45

Double Bass, Clarinet/Saxophone(Tenor), Horn, Percussion, Violin, H6.8

Double Bass, Clarinets(2), Flute, Percussion, Piano, Timpani, Trumpets(2), Violin, H9.19

Double Bass, Clarinets(2)/Clarinets(Bass)(2), Horns(2), Percussion, M5.17

Double Bass, Contrabassoon, Percussion, H7.5

Double Bass, Cymbal, Flutes(2), Piano, Snare Drum, G3.8

Double Bass, Dancer/Narrator, Harp, Tape, Trombone, Violin, G1.17

Double Bass, Dancers(4)(Optional), M4.10

Double Bass, Drums(2), Guitar, Saxophone(Alto), R7.10

Double Bass, Drums, Flugelhorn, Guitar, Saxophone(Alto), Saxophone(Baritone), Saxophone(Tenor), Trombone, P2.28

Double Bass, Drums, Flute, Guitar, Piano, Saxophone(Alto), Saxophone(Tenor), Trumpet, B13.47

Double Bass, Drums, Flute, Saxophone, Woodwind Ensemble(24), M10.36

Double Bass, Drums, Guitar, Orchestra, Saxophone(Alto), Trumpet, F1.5

Double Bass, Drums, Guitar, Piano, Saxophone(Alto), Saxophone(Baritone), Saxophone(Tenor), Trombone, Trumpet,

Flute(Alto), Electric Bass,
    Guitar(Electric), Harp, Mezzo
    Soprano, Percussion(2),
    Piano(Electric), Viola, L5.3
Flute(Alto), Flute, Guitar, Soprano,
    S12.10
Flute(Alto), Harp, Percussion,
    Soprano, R2.66
Flute(Alto), Organ, M13.12
Flute(Alto), Piano, M13.13
Flute(Alto), Piano, Soprano,
    Violoncello, Z1.15
Flute(Alto)/ Flute, Baritone, Piano,
    Soprano, Tape, D8.20
Flute(Alto)/ Flute,
    Clarinet/Clarinet(Bass), Double
    Bass, Horn, Tenor, Viola, Violin,
    H6.23
Flute(Alto)/ Flute/Piccolo,
    Clarinet/Clarinet(Bass)/
    Saxophone(Soprano), Oboe/English
    Horn, Piano, M10.27
Flute(Baroque), Harpsichord, W1.5,
    W1.7
Flute(Optional), Chorus(SATB),
    Keyboard, Oboe(Optional),
    Recorder(Optional),
    Trumpet(Optional), D4.91
Flute(Optional), Chorus(SSATB),
    Horn(Optional), Oboe(Optional),
    Percussion(Optional),
    Pianos(2)(Optional),
    Trombone(Optional, S9.13
Flute(Optional), Clarinet(Optional),
    Double Bass(Optional), Guitar
    (Optional), Percussion(2)(Optional),
    Piano, Voice(Medium), A5.60
Flute(Optional), Piano, P10.9
Flute, Actress/Mezzo Soprano,
    Clarinet, Percussion, Viola, Violin,
    Violoncello, M11.1
Flute, Alto or Baritone, Cantor,
    Chorus, Organ, F8.69
Flute, Alto, Bass, Bassoon, Celeste,
    Clarinet, Percussion, Soprano,
    Tenor, Trombone, Trumpet, O1.28
Flute, Alto, Clarinet, Horn,
    Percussion, Pianos, Sopranos(2),
    Violin, Violoncello, M12.2
Flute, Alto, Delta T, Electronics,
    Flute(Alto), T2.32
Flute, Alto, Piano, Viola, Violin,
    Violoncello, L11.5
Flute, Baritone, Chorus(SSATB), Organ,
    K2.21
Flute, Baritone, Clarinet, Oboe,
    Viola, Violoncello, D6.80
Flute, Bassoon or Horn or Violoncello,
    Piano, C13.112
Flute, Bassoon, Chamber Orchestra,
    Clarinet, Oboe, Violin, B4.29
Flute, Bassoon, Chorus(SATB),
    Clarinet, Double Bass, Viola,
    Violins(1 or 2), Violoncello, P7.38
Flute, Bassoon, Chorus(SATB),
    Clarinet, Harpsichord, Piano, Viola,
    Violin, Violoncello, Voices, C1.1
Flute, Bassoon, Clarinet, L10.11,
    O1.57, P7.34, S5.25, T1.13, T2.17,
    T2.23

Flute, Bassoon, Clarinet or Saxophone,
    Double Bass, Oboe, Percussion,
    Piano, Trumpet, Violoncello, C11.6
Flute, Bassoon, Clarinet(Bass), Double
    Bass, Horn, Percussion, Y1.40
Flute, Bassoon, Clarinet(Contrabass),
    Oboe, Piccolo, B8.57
Flute, Bassoon, Clarinet,
    Clarinet(Bass), Soprano, L9.12
Flute, Bassoon, Clarinet, Double Bass,
    Oboe, Soprano, Tenor, Viola, Violin,
    Violoncello, G4.23
Flute, Bassoon, Clarinet, Double Bass,
    Oboe, String Quartet, P7.16
Flute, Bassoon, Clarinet, Oboe, B1.25,
    B4.26, H4.33, H5.6
Flute, Bassoon, Clarinet, Oboe,
    Percussion Ensemble, String
    Orchestra, L6.2
Flute, Bassoon, Clarinet, Oboe, Piano,
    B1.30
Flute, Bassoon, Clarinet, Oboe, Piano,
    Synthesizer(Arp String), Tape,
    Vibraphone, L6.19
Flute, Bassoon, Clarinet, Oboe, String
    Quartet, M10.60
Flute, Bassoon, Clarinet, Piano,
    Viola, Violin, Violoncello, B4.28
Flute, Bassoon, Clarinet, Trumpets(2),
    Voice, F4.8
Flute, Bassoon, Clarinet/
    Saxophone(Tenor), Double Bass,
    Drums, Horn, Piano, Trombone,
    Vibraphone, S3.119
Flute, Bassoon, Clarinets(2), Double
    Bass, Piano, Violin, Violoncello,
    B8.11
Flute, Bassoon, Clarinets(2), Harp,
    Viola, L10.15
Flute, Bassoon, Clarinets(2), Horn,
    Oboe, C13.107
Flute, Bassoon, Clarinets(in A)(2),
    Guitar(Amplified), Horn, Oboe,
    Piano, S1.7
Flute, Bassoon, Oboe, L3.9
Flute, Bassoon, Piano, D8.27
Flute, Bassoon, Viola, G4.24
Flute, Bassoons(2), Clarinet, Double
    Bass, Snare Drum, String Quartet,
    S3.175
Flute, Bongos, Mandolin, Marimba,
    S15.2
Flute, Bongos, Mandolin, Viola, S15.3
Flute, Celeste, Clarinet, Harp,
    Percussion, Soprano, Viola, Violin,
    Violoncello, M9.7
Flute, Celeste, Clarinet, Soprano,
    Viola, Violoncello, M9.2
Flute, Chamber Orchestra,
    Loudspeakers, Projections(Optional),
    Tape, A5.45
Flute, Chorus(Men), Double Bass,
    Guitar, Horn, Percussion,
    Vibraphone, P6.118
Flute, Chorus(SA), English Horn, Oboe,
    Strings, P5.8
Flute, Chorus(SA), Piano, S14.1
Flute, Chorus(SAA), Piano, T4.42
Flute, Chorus(SATB), V1.36

717

Piano, Clarinet, Double Bass, Flute,
    Narrator, Percussion, Soprano,
    Viola, Violoncello, Y1.6
Piano, Clarinet, Double Bass, Flute,
    Percussion, Soprano, Violin,
    Violoncello, B9.34
Piano, Clarinet, Double Bass, Flute,
    Percussion, Violin, Violoncello,
    S6.19
Piano, Clarinet, Double Bass, Flute,
    Soprano, Violin, Violoncello, B10.3
Piano, Clarinet, Double Bass, Flute,
    Violoncello, F5.30
Piano, Clarinet, Double Bass,
    Flute/Piccolo, Mezzo Soprano,
    Violin, Violoncello, S6.32
Piano, Clarinet, Double Bass, Violin,
    L7.17
Piano, Clarinet, Drums, Guitar, Oboe,
    Saxophones(2), Trombone, B5.29
Piano, Clarinet, Flute, F5.10, L6.21,
    T2.5
Piano, Clarinet, Flute, Horn, S3.34
Piano, Clarinet, Flute, Horn, Timpani,
    Viola, Violin, Violoncello, V1.51
Piano, Clarinet, Flute, Mezzo Soprano,
    Violin, Violoncello, H5.21
Piano, Clarinet, Flute, Oboe, Viola,
    Violin, Violoncello, V1.97
Piano, Clarinet, Flute, Oboe/English
    Horn, Viola, Violin, Violoncello,
    H10.34
Piano, Clarinet, Flute, Percussion,
    H5.5
Piano, Clarinet, Flute, Percussion(2),
    Viola, Violin, Violoncello, L2.14
Piano, Clarinet, Flute, Percussion,
    Soprano, Tape, Violin, Violoncello,
    D8.1
Piano, Clarinet, Flute, Percussion,
    Soprano, Viola, Violoncello, H2.26
Piano, Clarinet, Flute,
    Saxophone(Alto), A6.4
Piano, Clarinet, Flute, Soprano,
    Viola, M9.10
Piano, Clarinet, Flute, Soprano,
    Viola, Violin, Violoncello, D8.19
Piano, Clarinet, Flute, Trombone,
    Trumpet, Viola, F4.19
Piano, Clarinet, Flute, String
    Quartet, T4.92
Piano, Clarinet, Flute, Viola,
    Violoncello, T4.81
Piano, Clarinet, Flute, Violin,
    C12.10, M1.4
Piano, Clarinet, Flute, Violin,
    Violoncello, F7.17, S6.11
Piano, Clarinet, Flute, Violins(2),
    Violoncello, K2.69
Piano, Clarinet, Flute, Violoncello,
    H5.16
Piano, Clarinet, Flute/Piccolo,
    Percussion, Violoncello, M10.43
Piano, Clarinet,
    Guitar(Bass)(Optional), Percussion,
    L6.1
Piano, Clarinet, Horn, F4.55, S3.93,
    W1.35
Piano, Clarinet, Horn, Oboe, Viola,
    S6.33

Piano, Clarinet, Horn, Violin,
    Violoncello, H10.31
Piano, Clarinet, Mezzo Soprano,
    Percussion, Soprano, Tenor, P1.5
Piano, Clarinet, Mezzo Soprano,
    Violin, L7.12
Piano, Clarinet, Saxophone(Alto),
    Saxophone(Tenor), Voice, B5.122
Piano, Clarinet, Soprano, S2.2
Piano, Clarinet, Soprano, String
    Quartet, K1.7
Piano, Clarinet, Tenor, Trombone,
    Viola, Violoncello, A4.2
Piano, Clarinet, Trombone, B5.54
Piano, Clarinet, Trombone, Tuba, M3.4
Piano, Clarinet, Viola, B1.78, F4.54,
    H8.9, M10.37
Piano, Clarinet, Violin, B1.79,
    B12.35, L7.3, T1.14, T3.44, W4.14,
    Z1.22
Piano, Clarinet, Violin, Violoncello,
    L6.13, M10.79, S3.96, V1.61
Piano, Clarinet, Violoncello, B1.80
Piano, Clarinet/Clarinet(Bass),
    Flute/Piccolo, Violin, Violoncello,
    H2.19
Piano, Clarinet/Clarinet(Bass)/
    Saxophone(Soprano), Flute/Piccolo/
    Flute(Alto), Oboe/English Horn,
    M10.27
Piano, Clarinet/ Saxophone(Tenor),
    Double Bass, Drums, Trumpet, L1.45
Piano, Clarinets(2), Double Bass,
    Flute, Percussion, Timpani,
    Trumpets(2), Violin, H9.19
Piano, Clarinets(2), Double Basses(2),
    Flute, J2.5
Piano, Countertenors(4), S9.14
Piano, Cymbal, Double Bass, Flutes(2),
    Snare Drum, G3.8
Piano, Dancer, T3.21
Piano, Dancer(Optional), Percussion,
    Violin, S3.105
Piano, Dancer, Drums, Saxophone(Alto),
    Speakers(3), Trumpet, Violin,
    Violoncello, A4.24
Piano, Dancers, K2.52, K2.57, K2.71
Piano, Dancers(6 or More), K2.46
Piano, Double Bass(Ad Lib.), Flute,
    Oboe, String Quartet, C3.5
Piano, Double Bass, Drums, M3.14,
    S7.3, S7.4
Piano, Double Bass, Drums, Flute,
    Guitar, Piano, Saxophone(Alto),
    Saxophone(Tenor), Trumpet, B13.47
Piano, Double Bass, Drums, Guitar,
    Saxophone(Alto),
    Saxophone(Baritone),
    Saxophone(Tenor), Trombone, Trumpet,
    L1.10, L1.16, 11.37, L1.44, L1.59,
    L1.85, L1.134, L1.137
Piano, Double Bass, Drums, Guitar,
    Saxophone(Alto),
    Saxophone(Baritone), Trombone,
    Trumpet, P2.19, P2.21
Piano, Double Bass, Drums, Guitar,
    Saxophone(Alto), Trumpet, R7.2,
    R7.6, R7.16, R7.19, R7.21, R7.25,
    R7.34, R7.36, R7.41, R7.42, R7.52,
    R7.53, R7.59, R7.80

Piano, Flute, Horn, Saxophone(Tenor),
    Trombone, Trumpet, N1.6
Piano, Flute, Horn, Soprano, P10.16
Piano, Flute, Horn, Violin, D8.12,
    F4.28
Piano, Flute, Mezzo Soprano,
    Violoncello, H2.6
Piano, Flute, Oboe, L7.19, W1.42
Piano, Flute, Oboe, Viola, Violin,
    Violoncello, B9.14
Piano, Flute, Soprano, P6.192, V1.102
Piano, Flute, Soprano, Violin,
    Violoncello, A3.5
Piano, Flute, String Quartet, P11.32
Piano, Flute, Tape, D8.16
Piano, Flute, Viola, H8.14
Piano, Flute, Violin, D2.39, M9.8
Piano, Flute, Violoncello, A1.20,
    B9.23, C7.16, D6.175, H10.101
Piano, Flute, Voice, F4.14, O1.31
Piano, Flute/Piccolo, Instrumental
    Ensemble, Soprano, Violin, M10.62
Piano, Flutes(2), J2.4
Piano, Flutes(2), Horn, Trumpet,
    Violin, G5.11
Piano, Guitar, Percussion, H3.7
Piano, Guitar, Violin, B4.32
Piano, Guitar, Violin, Violoncello,
    L9.14
Piano, Guitar, Voice, B8.35
Piano, Harp, Mezzo Soprano, String
    Quartet, P11.9
Piano, Harp, Trombone, F4.39
Piano, Harp, Violoncellos(4), C2.1
Piano, Harp, Voice, B5.5
Piano, Harpsichord, Horn, Percussion,
    R5.8
Piano, Harpsichord, Saxophone(Alto),
    B12.11
Piano, Horn, Mezzo Soprano or
    Baritone, M5.20
Piano, Horn, Ondes Martenot(Optional),
    Percussion, T2.10
Piano, Horn, Snare Drum, Trumpet,
    B8.26
Piano, Horn, Soprano, B1.72
Piano, Horn, Violin, C13.50, C13.112,
    H10.102, O1.19
Piano, Horn, Violin, Violoncello, H6.7
Piano, Horn, Violoncello, L9.19, O1.29
Piano, Horns(2), Vibraphone(Optional),
    Viola, Violin, Violoncello, F4.45
Piano, Instrument(Bass),
    Instrument(Treble), Y1.17
Piano, Instrumental Ensemble,
    Saxophone, A1.4
Piano, Instruments(8), Percussion,
    C7.2
Piano,
    Instruments(Unspecified)(Optional),
    Voices, S9.89
Piano, Jew's Harp, Violin, A4.7
Piano, Lights, Soprano(High),
    Violin(con sordino), K3.14
Piano, Mezzo Soprano or Soprano,
    Violoncello, P10.20
Piano, Mezzo Soprano, Page Turner,
    S9.52
Piano, Mezzo Soprano, Violin, F3.29,
    P5.17

Piano, Narrator(Optional), B13.1,
    B13.7, B13.9, B13.58
Piano, Narrator, Voice, K2.40
Piano, Oboe, Soprano, C7.12
Piano, Oboe, Viola, W1.45
Piano, Oboe, Violin, Violoncello,
    A5.81
Piano, Oboe, Voice, H10.33
Piano, Orchestra, A1.21, B5.13, K2.59,
    K3.4, K4.14, S5.13, T3.32, T3.34,
    T4.47, V1.14, V1.100
Piano, Orchestra, Violin, A5.30
Piano, Percussion(2), B1.81
Piano, Percussion(3), Soprano,
    Violins(2), Violoncellos(2), E4.36
Piano, Percussion, Soprano, V3.8
Piano, Percussion, Soprano, Timpani,
    Wind Ensemble, M8.22
Piano, Percussion, Winds(9), A5.21
Piano, Piano(4-hands), L10.3
Piano, Saxophone(Alto), Soprano,
    Trombone, Trumpet, Violin,
    Violoncello, A4.37
Piano, Saxophone(Soprano),
    Violoncello, M10.56
Piano, Soprano, String Quartet, Tenor,
    S13.7
Piano, Soprano, Tenor, B3.22, B3.27,
    R2.183
Piano, Soprano, Vibraphone, V3.7
Piano, Soprano, Viola, T4.114
Piano, Soprano, Violin, C9.10, E3.20,
    F3.29
Piano, Soprano, Violoncello, L9.10,
    P10.20
Piano, Speaker(Female), Violins(2),
    K3.18
Piano, Speaker(Optional), B13.2
Piano, String Orchestra, R2.108
Piano, String Orchestra, Tenor, S5.8
Piano, String Quartet, H2.24, K1.18,
    M7.17, P7.48, R2.153, S9.38, V1.63
Piano, String Quartet, Voice, C13.31
Piano, String Quartet, Voice(Low),
    C13.39
Piano, Strings(2), Voices(4),
    Woodwinds(5), F8.14
Piano, Tape, R5.12
Piano, Tape(Computer), B11.4
Piano, Tape(Live), E1.105, E1.106
Piano, Tape, Violin, E1.94
Piano, Tom-tom, Vibraphone, Viola,
    H8.5
Piano, Trombones(3), H4.32
Piano, Trumpet, Violins(2),
    Violoncello, H10.52
Piano, Trumpets(2), F5.22
Piano, Viola, Violin, V1.12
Piano, Viola, Violin, Violoncello,
    B12.21, P7.41
Piano, Viola, Violins(2), M8.30, W4.15
Piano, Violin or Viola, Voice(High),
    C13.81
Piano, Violin, Violoncello, B1.82,
    B3.16, B3.17, B4.33, B7.3, B10.9,
    C13.3, C13.7, C13.48, C13.50,
    C13.87, C13.111, C13.112, C13.113,
    C14.3, E3.24, F8.79, G4.25, H2.32,
    K2.35, K2.89, K3.19, K4.24, M1.6,

733

Soprano, Bassoon, Flutes(2),
    Percussion, Piano, Trumpet,
    Violins(2), H8.6
Soprano, Bassoons(2), Chorus(SA), Harp
    or Piano, Oboes(2), P6.108
Soprano, Bassoons(2), Chorus(SA),
    Oboes(2), Piano, P6.108
Soprano, Bells, Chamber Orchestra,
    Horn, D5.20
Soprano, Brass Ensemble, Chorus(SATB),
    Percussion(2), Timpani, P6.12
Soprano, Brasses, Choruses(2), Tape,
    E1.6
Soprano, Celeste, Clarinet, Flute,
    Harp, Percussion, Viola, Violin,
    Violoncello, M9.7
Soprano, Celeste, Clarinet, Flute,
    Viola, Violoncello, M9.2
Soprano, Celeste, Flutes(3),
    Pianos(2), M9.4
Soprano, Celeste, Percussion(3),
    Timpani, Wind Ensemble, M8.13
Soprano, Chamber Orchestra, A3.7,
    C1.15, H2.14, L4.16, Y1.23
Soprano, Chamber Orchestra, Tenor,
    H10.2
Soprano, Chimes, Chorus(Mixed), Harp,
    P4.129
Soprano, Chorus(Children)(3-part),
    Harp, String Quartet, P10.3
Soprano, Chorus(Mixed), Orchestra,
    P6.195
Soprano, Chorus(Mixed), Organ, D4.132
Soprano, Chorus(Mixed), Organ or
    Piano, P6.195
Soprano, Chorus(Mixed),
    Tape(Optional), P6.175
Soprano, Chorus(SATB), D4.29, D4.146,
    H10.12, L11.6, P6.146
Soprano, Chorus(SATB)(Optional),
    Piano, T4.65
Soprano, Chorus(SATB), Countertenor or
    Mezzo Soprano(Ad Lib.),
    Guitar(Electric),
    Saxophone(Soprano),
    Saxophone(Soprano)/
    Saxophone(Tenor), D5.16
Soprano, Chorus(SATB), Harp, String
    Orchestra, G6.5
Soprano, Chorus(SATB), Orchestra,
    B3.25, D7.14
Soprano, Chorus(SATB), Organ, D4.85,
    D4.149, S14.7
Soprano, Chorus(SATB), Organ, Trumpet,
    F7.3
Soprano, Chorus(SATB), Piano, D7.15
Soprano, Chorus(SATB), Piano or Organ,
    D4.53, D4.58, D4.66, D4.121, D4.138
Soprano, Chorus(SSA), D4.172
Soprano, Chorus(SSAATTBB), Orchestra,
    F3.7
Soprano, Chorus, Flute, Harpsichord,
    Tenor, Viola, O1.63
Soprano, Chorus, Orchestra, Tenor,
    P4.82
Soprano, Chorus, Trumpets(3),
    Violoncello, G4.8
Soprano, Clarinet, E3.4
Soprano, Clarinet(Bass), Piano,
    Violoncello, M10.72

Soprano, Clarinet, Clarinet(Bass),
    Flute, Flute/Piccolo, Harp,
    Percussion(4), Viola, Violoncello,
    B8.2
Soprano, Clarinet, Clarinet(Bass),
    Flute, Horn, Oboe, Tenor, Trombone,
    Trumpet, P5.3
Soprano, Clarinet, Clarinet(Bass),
    Percussion, Piano, Speaker(Female),
    Speaker(Male), Tenor, Viola, Violin,
    Violoncello, J3.11
Soprano, Clarinet, Double Bass, Flute,
    Harp, Trumpet, Vibraphone, Viola,
    L7.22
Soprano, Clarinet, Double Bass, Flute,
    Narrator, Percussion, Piano, Viola,
    Violoncello, Y1.6
Soprano, Clarinet, Double Bass, Flute,
    Percussion, Piano, Violin,
    Violoncello, B9.34
Soprano, Clarinet, Double Bass, Flute,
    Piano, Violin, Violoncello, B10.3
Soprano, Clarinet, Double Bass,
    Violin, L7.5, L7.6
Soprano, Clarinet, English Horn,
    Flute, Harp, Percussion(2),
    Pianos(2), Viola, B8.23
Soprano, Clarinet, Flute, J3.12
Soprano, Clarinet, Flute, Guitar,
    Percussion, Viola, Violin, K5.1
Soprano, Clarinet, Flute, Harpsichord,
    Violoncello, B12.27
Soprano, Clarinet, Flute, Horn,
    Piano(4-hands), Trombone(Bass),
    Trumpet, Vibraphone, P12.6
Soprano, Clarinet, Flute, Oboe,
    Percussion, Violin, Violoncello,
    K3.8
Soprano, Clarinet, Flute, Oboe,
    Percussion, Violoncello, K3.7
Soprano, Clarinet, Flute, Oboe, Viola,
    Violin, Violoncello, C9.2
Soprano, Clarinet, Flute, Percussion,
    Piano, Tape, Violin, Violoncello,
    D8.1
Soprano, Clarinet, Flute, Percussion,
    Piano, Viola, Violoncello, H2.26
Soprano, Clarinet, Flute, Piano,
    Viola, M9.10
Soprano, Clarinet, Flute, Piano,
    Viola, Violin, Violoncello, D8.19
Soprano, Clarinet, Flute,
    Piano/Celeste, Trumpet, Viola,
    Violin, M9.3
Soprano, Clarinet, Flute, Viola,
    Violin, Violoncello, S9.31
Soprano, Clarinet, Flute, Violoncello,
    B4.35, W4.16
Soprano, Clarinet, Flute/Piccolo,
    Oboe, Percussion(2), Violin,
    Violoncello, K3.5
Soprano, Clarinet, Flute/Piccolo,
    Oboe, Violin, Violoncello, C6.3
Soprano, Clarinet, Guitar of Lute,
    S2.3
Soprano, Clarinet, Harp, Viola,
    Violoncello, H9.21
Soprano, Clarinet, Mezzo Soprano,
    Percussion, Piano, Tenor, P1.5

Tenor, Chorus, Orchestra, Soprano,
    P4.82
Tenor, Clarinet, Clarinet(Bass),
    Flute, Horn, Oboe, Soprano,
    Trombone, Trumpet, P5.3
Tenor, Clarinet, Clarinet(Bass),
    Percussion, Piano, Soprano,
    Speaker(Female), Speaker(Male),
    Viola, Violin, Violoncello, J3.11
Tenor, Clarinet, Double Bass, Flute,
    Harp, Oboe, Violas, Violoncellos,
    D6.5
Tenor, Clarinet, Mezzo Soprano,
    Percussion, Piano, Soprano, P1.5
Tenor, Clarinet, Piano, Trombone,
    Viola, Violoncello, A4.2
Tenor, Clarinet/Clarinet(Bass), Double
    Bass, Flute/Flute(Alto), Horn,
    Viola, Violin, H6.23
Tenor, Clarinet/Clarinet(Bass), Flute,
    Harpsichord or Piano, Viola,
    Violoncello, S9.21
Tenor, Double Bass, Flute, Oboe,
    Piano, Viola, Violin, Violoncello,
    S3.88
Tenor, Double Bass, String Quartet,
    W1.6
Tenor, Flute, Guitar, P6.120
Tenor, Flute, Harpsichord, Viola Da
    Gamba, D8.25
Tenor, Flute, Keyboard, Soprano, H10.9
Tenor, Flute, Violoncello, L11.3
Tenor, Harp, H2.17
Tenor, Harp, Horn, Percussion(2),
    Vibraphone, Viola, Xylophone, L2.2
Tenor, Harpsichord, Violoncello, B12.5
Tenor, Horn, Trombone, Trumpet, S11.2
Tenor, Instrumental Ensemble, Soprano,
    R2.76
Tenor, Instruments(5), Soprano, L7.13
Tenor, Instruments(7), C9.13
Tenor, Keyboard, S9.22
Tenor, Lute, Percussion,
    Recorder(Soprano/Alto/Tenor/Bass),
    Soprano, Viol(Tenor/Bass), S6.29
Tenor, Oboe, Organ, Soprano, Violin,
    H10.8
Tenor, Orchestra, D7.6, M5.5, S9.80
Tenor, Organ, E1.61, K2.73
Tenor, Organ or Piano, K2.16
Tenor, Organ or Piano or Tape, E1.63,
    E1.64
Tenor, Organ, Soprano, K2.50
Tenor, Organ, Sopranos(2), P6.235
Tenor, Piano, B4.30, C13.1, C13.2,
    C13.10, C13.29, C13.100, C13.119,
    E1.68, H10.74, H10.104, M5.6, M7.20,
    P6.133, P6.144, P6.157, P6.183,
    S5.7, S12.6, W3.7, Z1.2
Tenor, Piano, Soprano, B3.22, B3.27,
    R2.183
Tenor, Piano, Soprano, String Quartet,
    S13.7
Tenor, Piano, String Orchestra, S5.8
Tenor, Soprano, H10.66
Tenor, Soprano, String Quartet, F8.64
Tenors(2), B8.31, H10.37

Tenors(2), Altos(2), Basses(2),
    Sopranos(2), F2.3, H8.3
Tenors(2), Bass, Violoncello, H10.22
Tenors(2), Flute, Horn, Oboe, Piano,
    Soprano, Violoncello, H10.39
Tenors(3), Altos(3), L2.4
Tenors(4), Altos(4), Basses(3),
    Sopranos(4), C4.7
Theater Music, see Musical Comedies;
    Stage Works
Third Stream Ensemble, B5.23
Third Stream Group, B5.70, B5.167
Third Stream Music, B5.1, B5.10,
    B5.11, B5.12, B5.17, B5.22, B5.24,
    B5.28, B5.29, B5.30, B5.31, B5.32,
    B5.53, B5.63, B5.76, B5.77, B5.78,
    B5.83, B5.84, B5.85, B5.105, B5.111,
    B5.116, B5.117, B5.118, B5.119,
    B5.122, B5.135, B5.140, B5.141,
    B5.142, B5.143, B5.144, B5.150,
    B5.156, B5.165, B5.166, B5.166,
    B5.169, B5.170, B5.171, B5.172,
    B5.173, B5.176, B5.179, B5.180,
    B5.181, B5.182, B5.192, S1.122,
    S3.33,
Timpani(4), Band, M13.9
Timpani(4), Orchestra, M13.8
Timpani(4), Piano(4-hands), M13.10
Timpani(Obbligato), String Orchestra,
    C1.8
Timpani(Optional), Chorus(Mixed),
    Trombones(2), Trumpets(2),
    Tuba(Optional), P6.159
Timpani(Optional), Chorus(SATBB),
    Organ, Trombones(2)(Optional),
    Trumpets(2)(Optional), F3.45
Timpani, Alto, Bass, Chorus(Women) or
    Chorus(Men), Organ, Percussion(Ad
    Lib.), Soprano, Tape, Tenor, P6.11
Timpani, Bass Baritone, Narrator,
    Percussion, Pianos(2), Tenor, P6.32
Timpani, Brass Ensemble, Chorus(SATB),
    Percussion(2), Soprano, P6.12
Timpani, Brass Ensemble, Gong, M8.28
Timpani, Brass Ensemble, Percussion,
    M8.7, R2.211, S3.109, V1.34, W3.6
Timpani, Brass Ensemble,
    Percussion(2), P7.4
Timpani, Brass Ensemble,
    Percussion(3), P7.19
Timpani, Brass Ensemble,
    Percussion(4), B1.70
Timpani, Brass Ensemble,
    Percussion(9), Piano, H9.18
Timpani, Brasses, Cantor,
    Chorus(Mixed), Congregation, Organ,
    P4.122
Timpani, Brasses, Cantor,
    Chorus(SATB), Congregation, Double
    Bass, Organ, P4.60
Timpani, Brasses, Cantor,
    Chorus(SATB), Organ, P4.23
Timpani, Brasses, Cantor, Chorus,
    Congregation, Organ, Percussion,
    P4.32
Timpani, Brasses, Chorus(Mixed), P4.92
Timpani, Brasses, Chorus(SATB),
    Congregation, Harp, P4.105

Trombone(Bass), Horn, Trumpets(2), Tuba, H9.35, H9.36, H9.37
Trombone(Bass), Horns(2), Trombone, Trumpet, B9.27
Trombone(Bass), Piano(Optional), E5.3
Trombone(Bass)/Percussion, A4.16
Trombone(Bell Only), Garden Hose, Trombone, P8.7
Trombone(Optional), Chorus(SSATB), Flute(Optional), Horn(Optional), Oboe(Optional), Percussion(Optional), Pianos(2)(Optional), S9.13
Trombone(Optional), Slides, Trumpet(Optional), String Quartet, B9.16
Trombone(Tenor), Percussion(2), Saxophone(Tenor), Violins(3), G1.5
Trombone, Actor, Projection Equipment, Screen(9x12), Speaker(Female), Television Camera, Trumpets(2), Violins(2), Violoncellos(2), K3.15
Trombone, Alto, Bass, Bassoon, Celeste, Clarinet, Flute, Percussion, Soprano, Tenor, Trumpet, O1.28
Trombone, Alto, Bass, Horn, Organ or Piano, Soprano, Tenor, Trumpets(2), P6.58
Trombone, Band, Clarinet, Trumpet, A4.35
Trombone, Band, Horn, Trumpets(2), Tuba, S3.37
Trombone, Baritone, Clarinet, Clarinet(Bass), Double Bass, Horn, Mezzo Soprano, Soprano, Tenor, Viola, S9.2
Trombone, Baritone, Mandolin, Mezzo Soprano, Oboe, Piano, Piccolo, Violin, W6.9
Trombone, Baritone, Piano, L2.6
Trombone, Bass Baritone, Double Bass, Horn, Viola, Violoncello, P5.18
Trombone, Bassoon, Clarinet, Flutes(2), Horn, Oboe, Percussion, Soprano or Tenor, Tuba or Trombone(Bass), P9.5
Trombone, Bassoon, Clarinet, Flutes(2), Oboe, Piano, Trumpets(2), C13.53
Trombone, Bassoon, Clarinet, Oboe, Percussion(2), Piano, Piccolo, Trumpet, S3.173
Trombone, Bassoon, Clarinet/ Saxophone(Tenor), Double Bass, Drums, Flute, Horn, Piano, Vibraphone, S3.119
Trombone, Celeste, Double Bass, Mezzo Soprano, Piano, Trumpet, Tuba, Vibraphone, Violin, Violoncello, F2.7
Trombone, Chorus or Voice, Double Bass(Optional), Saxophones(2), Trumpet, H3.18
Trombone, Chorus(Mixed), Double Bass, Trumpet, Woodwind Quintet, S12.11
Trombone, Chorus(SATB), Chorus(Unison)(Optional) or Congregation, Horn, Organ,

Percussion(2), Tenor, Timpani, Trumpets(2), P6.55
Trombone, Chorus(SATB), Clarinet/Clarinet(Bass), Percussion, Piano, Violoncello, E3.1
Trombone, Chorus(SATB), Double Bass, Drum, Flute, Harp, Trumpet, Voices, Xylophone, P4.44
Trombone, Chorus(SATB), Horn or Trumpet, Piano(Optional), Trombone(Bass) or Tuba, Trumpets(2), B1.1
Trombone, Chorus(SATB), Horns(2), Narrator, Trombone(Bass), Trumpets(2), Tuba, A4.18
Trombone, Chorus(Unison)(Optional), Horn, Trumpets(2), Tuba, P6.151
Trombone, Chorus, Clarinets(2), Flutes(2), Percussion, Trumpet, S9.19
Trombone, Chorus, Horn, Organ, Percussion, Trumpets(2), Tuba, D7.4
Trombone, Clarinet, Clarinet(Bass), Flute, Horn, Oboe, Soprano, Tenor, Trumpet, P5.3
Trombone, Clarinet, Cornet, Drums, Horn, Piano, S3.178
Trombone, Clarinet, Double Bass, Flute(Alto), Horn, Mezzo Soprano, Viola, S9.25
Trombone, Clarinet, Drums, Guitar, Oboe, Piano, Saxophones(2), B5.29
Trombone, Clarinet, Flute, Piano, Trumpet, Viola, F4.19
Trombone, Clarinet, Flute, Trumpet in C, P12.22
Trombone, Clarinet, Guitar, Horn, Trumpet, Vibraphone, Violin, Violoncello, D2.18
Trombone, Clarinet, Oboe, Organ, Trumpet, B12.23
Trombone, Clarinet, Piano, B5.54
Trombone, Clarinet, Piano, Tenor, Viola, Violoncello, A4.2
Trombone, Clarinet, Piano, Tuba, M3.4
Trombone, Clarinet, Violin, B1.12
Trombone, Conceptual Artist, Instruments(Unspecified), P9.4
Trombone, Dancer/Narrator, Double Bass, Harp, Tape, Violin, G1.17
Trombone, Double Bass, Drums, Flugelhorn, Guitar, Saxophone(Alto), Saxophone(Baritone), Saxophone(Tenor), P2.28
Trombone, Double Bass, Drums, Guitar, Piano, Saxophone(Alto), Saxophone(Baritone), Saxophone(Tenor), Trumpet, L1.10, L1.16, L1.37, L1.44, L1.59, L1.85, L1.134, L1.137
Trombone, Double Bass, Drums, Guitar, Piano, Saxophone(Alto), Saxophone(Baritone), Trumpet, P2.19, P2.21
Trombone, Double Bass, Drums, Guitar, Saxophone(Alto), Saxophone(Baritone), Saxophone(Tenor), Trumpet, P2.24, P2.36

Saxophone(Baritone), Trombone,
P2.19, P2.21
Trumpet, Double Bass, Drums, Guitar,
Saxophone(Alto),
Saxophone(Baritone),
Saxophone(Tenor), Trombone, P2.24,
P2.36
Trumpet, Double Bass, Drums, Guitar,
Saxophone(Alto),
Saxophone(Baritone), Trombone, R7.32
Trumpet, Double Bass, Drums, Piano,
Saxophone(Alto), L1.116, L1.259
Trumpet, Double Bass, Drums, Piano,
Saxophone(Alto),
Saxophone(Baritone), Trombone, P2.14
Trumpet, Double Bass, Drums, Piano,
Saxophone(Alto),
Saxophone(Baritone)/ Clarinet,
Saxophone(Tenor), L1.60, L1.216
Trumpet, Double Bass, Drums, Piano,
Saxophone(Alto), Saxophone(Tenor),
Trombone, R7.5, R7.26, R7.40, R7.43,
R7.62, R7.76
Trumpet, Double Bass, Drums, Piano,
Saxophone(Alto)/ Clarinet, L1.80,
L1.87, L1.158, L1.173, L1.185,
L1.234
Trumpet, Double Bass, Drums, Piano,
Saxophone(Alto)/ Clarinet,
Saxophone(Baritone),
Saxohone(Tenor), Trombone, L1.15,
L1.38, L1.78, L1.100, L1.112,
L1.113, L1.118, L1.130, L1.131,
L1.132, L1.133, L1.187, L1.233,
L1.261
Trumpet, Double Bass, Drums, Piano,
Saxophone(Alto)/ Clarinet,
Saxophone(Baritone), Trombone,
L1.40, L1.63, L1.92, L1.202
Trumpet, Double Bass, Drums, Piano,
Saxohone(Alto)/ Clarinet, Trombone,
L1.71
Trumpet, Double Bass, Drums, Piano,
Saxophone(Tenor), Trombone, R7.11,
R7.17, R7.27, R7.33, R7.37, R7.39,
R7.44, R7.45, R7.46, R7.47, R7.49,
R7.50, R7.54, R7.55, R7.56, R7.57,
R7.60, R7.61, R7.65, R7.66, R7.67,
R7.68, R7.70, R7.71, R7.72, R7.73,
R7.74, R7.75, R7.77, R7.78, R7.79,
R7.81
Trumpet, Double Bass, Drums, Piano,
Saxophone(Tenor)/ Clarinet, L1.19,
L1.20, L1.21, L1.22, L1.25, L1.51,
L1.56, L1.72, L1.75, L1.76, L1.89,
L1.101, L1.102, L1.115, L1.26,
L1.148, L1.150, L1.152, L1.157,
L1.179, L1.183, L1.190, L1.191,
L1.206, L1.224, L1.225, L1.227,
L1.229, L1.238, L1.250, L1.257
Trumpet, Double Bass, Drums, Piano,
Saxophone, Trombone, R7.48, R7.63
Trumpet, Double Bass, Drums,
Saxophone(Alto), Trombone, L1.174
Trumpet, Double Bass, Drums,
Saxophone(Tenor)/ Clarinet, L1.98,
L1.129, L1.221
Trumpet, Double Bass, Flute, Narrator,
Percussion, Trombone, H3.21

Trumpet, Double Bass, Flute, Oboe,
Voice, F4.4
Trumpet, Double Bass, Guitar,
Percussion, Piano, Saxophone, H3.10
Trumpet, Double Bass, Guitar,
Percussion, Saxophone, H3.11, H3.16
Trumpet, Double Bass, Horn,
Speaker/Conductor, Trombone, Viola,
Violin, F4.35
Trumpet, Double Bass, Horn, Trombone,
Viola, Violin, F4.34
Trumpet, Double Bass, Percussion,
Saxophone, H3.17
Trumpet, Euphoniums(2), Flutes(2),
Violin, F4.3
Trumpet, Flugelhorn, Jazz Band,
Saxophone(Alto), L1.31
Trumpet, Flugelhorn, Rhythm Section,
Saxophone(Alto),
Saxophone(Baritone),
Saxophone(Tenor), Trombone, G5.18
Trumpet, Flute, Harp, Percussion,
Trombones(2), Viola, Violoncello,
W6.3
Trumpet, Flute, Harpsichord, Horn,
Oboe, Viola, Violin, Violoncello,
Voice, Z1.7
Trumpet, Flute, Horn, F4.29, Trumpet,
Flute, Horn,
Instruments(Unspecified), Piano,
F4.49,
Trumpet, Flute, Horn, Piano,
Saxophone(Tenor), Trombone, N1.6
Trumpet, Flute, Mandolin, Marimba,
Oboe, Percussion, Violin, H7.27
Trumpet, Flutes(2), Horn, Piano,
Violin, G5.11
Trumpet, Guitar, Percussion, Trombone,
Violin, P3.7
Trumpet, Harp, W4.7
Trumpet, Horn, Piano, Snare Drum,
B8.26
Trumpet, Horn, Tenor, Trombone, S11.2
Trumpet, Horn, Trombone, E5.5, G2.11,
P6.212, P8.9
Trumpet, Horn, Trombone, Trumpet in C,
Tuba, C2.11
Trumpet, Horn, Trombone, Tuba, S3.63
Trumpet, Horn, Trombone, Tuba,
Woodwind Quintet, H7.28
Trumpet, Horns(2), Trombone,
Trombone(Bass), B9.27
Trumpet, Horns(3), Trombones(2),
S3.130
Trumpet, Jazz Band, L1.182
Trumpet, Mezzo Soprano, String
Orchestra, B1.21
Trumpet, Organ, G3.16, G3.17, H3.34
Trumpet, Organ or Piano, C13.65
Trumpet, Organ, Soprano,
Voices(Men)(8), H6.1
Trumpet, Organ, Tape, P6.131
Trumpet, Oscillator, H10.51
Trumpet, Percussion(2), R5.9
Trumpet, Piano, B5.67, C2.8, H10.93,
P8.10, S4.9
Trumpet, Piano, Saxophone(Alto),
Soprano, Trombone, Violin,
Violoncello, A4.37

753

Viola, A4.36, D2.128, E3.5, F2.18,
   M1.11, M10.59, M10.83, M13.3, N2.22,
   P5.10, P7.27, R2.139, Y1.14
Viola Da Gamba, Flute, Harpsichord,
   Tenor, D8.25
Viola Da Gamba, Handbell, Violin,
   P6.185
Viola or Violin, S9.8
Viola or Violoncello, Piano, M1.11,
Viola(Ad Lib.), Chorus(SATB), Organ(Ad
   Lib.), R2.24, R2.25
Viola(Ad Lib.), Chorus(SATB), Piano,
   R2.19
Viola(Optional), Alto, English
   Horn(Optional), Oboe(Optional),
   Soprano, Violin(Optional), P6.96
Viola(Optional), Double
   Bass(Optional), Organ, Violins(2),
   Violoncello, P6.186
Viola, Actress/Mezzo Soprano,
   Clarinet, Flute, Percussion, Violin,
   Violoncello, M11.1
Viola, Alto, L9.16, S9.79
Viola, Alto, Clarinet(E-flat), Guitar,
   Horn, Z1.23
Viola, Alto, Flute, Piano, Violin,
   Violoncello, L11.5
Viola, Alto, Piano, Violin,
   Violoncello, C1.10
Viola, Baritone, Clarinet,
   Clarinet(Bass), Double Bass, Horn,
   Mezzo Soprano, Soprano, Tenor,
   Trombone, S9.2
Viola, Baritone, Clarinet, Flute,
   Oboe, Violoncello, D6.80
Viola, Bass Baritone, Double Bass,
   Horn, Trombone, Violoncello, P5.18
Viola, Basset, Clarinet(in A),
   Flute(Alto), Percussion,
   Violoncello, Voice, S9.20
Viola, Bassoon, Chorus(SATB),
   Clarinet, Double Bass, Flute,
   Violins(1 or 2), Violoncello, P7.38
Viola, Bassoon, Chorus(SATB),
   Clarinet, Flute, Harpsichord, Piano,
   Violin, Violoncello, Voices, C1.1
Viola, Bassoon, Chorus(SATB),
   Clarinet, Flute/Piccolo, Horn,
   Piano, Violin, Violoncello, S3.80
Viola, Bassoon, Clarinet(in A),
   Flute(Alto), Violin, Violoncello,
   D2.15
Viola, Bassoon, Clarinet, Double Bass,
   Flute, Oboe, Soprano, Tenor, Violin,
   Violoncello, G4.23
Viola, Bassoon, Clarinet, Flute,
   Piano, Violin, Violoncello, B4.28
Viola, Bassoon, Clarinet, Harpsichord,
   Soprano, C2.12
Viola, Bassoon, Clarinet, Horn, Piano,
   Violin, Violoncello, K1.21
Viola, Bassoon, Clarinet, Oboe,
   Soprano, Violin, Violoncello, D9.11
Viola, Bassoon, Clarinets(2), Flute,
   Harp, L10.15
Viola, Bassoon, English Horn,
   Trombones(2), Trumpets(2), Violin,
   Violoncello, S3.189
Viola, Bassoon, Flute, G4.24

Viola, Bassoon, Flutes(3), Horn,
   Trumpets(2), Voice, F4.9
Viola, Bassoon, Violin, Violoncello,
   H9.22
Viola, Bongos, Flute, Mandolin, S15.3
Viola, Celeste, Clarinet, Flute, Harp,
   Percussion, Soprano, Violin,
   Violoncello, M9.7
Viola, Celeste, Clarinet, Flute,
   Soprano, Violoncello, M9.2
Viola, Celeste, Violoncello, L6.18
Viola, Chimes, F2.6
Viola, Chorus(Mixed), Clarinet, Double
   Bass, Harp, Narrator, Organ,
   Voices(5), P6.134
Viola, Chorus, Flute, Harpsichord,
   Soprano, Tenor, O1.63
Viola, Clarinet, F4.13, M7.19, N2.2
Viola, Clarinet(Bass),
   Clarinet(E-flat), Clarinet(in A),
   Marimba, Violin, Violoncello, L7.38
Viola, Clarinet(Bass), Double Bass,
   Flute, Trumpet, C9.3
Viola, Clarinet(Bass), Flute, Trumpet,
   Violin, Violoncello, M10.44
Viola, Clarinet(in A), Horn,
   Saxophone(Alto), Violin,
   Violoncello, S9.72
Viola, Clarinet, Clarinet(Bass),
   Double Bass, Flute,
   Saxophone(Soprano), Tam-tam, Violin,
   Violoncello, B8.37
Viola, Clarinet, Clarinet(Bass),
   Flute, Flute/Piccolo, Harp,
   Percussion(4), Soprano, Violoncello,
   B8.2
Viola, Clarinet, Clarinet(Bass),
   Flute, Violin, Violoncello, H9.39
Viola, Clarinet, Clarinet(Bass),
   Flute/Piccolo, Violin, Violoncello,
   H2.27
Viola, Clarinet, Clarinet(Bass),
   Flutes(2), Violin, Voices(6), C9.11
Viola, Clarinet, Clarinet(Bass),
   Percussion, Piano, Soprano,
   Speaker(Female), Speaker(Male),
   Tenor, Violin, Violoncello, J3.11
Viola, Clarinet, Dancers(4), Flute,
   Percussion, Piano, Violin,
   Violoncello, M10.45
Viola, Clarinet, Double Bass, English
   Horn, Trumpet, W4.10
Viola, Clarinet, Double Bass,
   Flute(Alto), Horn, Mezzo Soprano,
   Trombone, S9.25
Viola, Clarinet, Double Bass, Flute,
   Harp, Soprano, Trumpet, Vibraphone,
   L7.22
Viola, Clarinet, Double Bass, Flute,
   Narrator, Percussion, Piano,
   Soprano, Violoncello, Y1.6
Viola, Clarinet, English Horn, Flute,
   Harp, Percussion(2), Pianos(2),
   Soprano, B8.23
Viola, Clarinet, Flute, K1.8
Viola, Clarinet, Flute(Alto), Harp,
   Mezzo Soprano, Percussion,
   Violoncello, M11.4
Viola, Clarinet, Flute, Guitar,
   Percussion, Soprano, Violin, K5.1

Violin, Clarinet, Flute/Piccolo, Oboe,
    Soprano, Violoncello, C6.3
Violin, Clarinet, Guitar, Horn,
    Trombone, Trumpet, Vibraphone.
    Violoncello, D2.18
Violin, Clarinet, Harp, B1.79
Violin, Clarinet, Horn, Piano,
    Violoncello, H10.31
Violin, Clarinet, Horn, Violoncello,
    S12.3
Violin, Clarinet, Mezzo Soprano,
    Piano, L7.12
Violin, Clarinet, Oboe, Percussion(2),
    Piccolo. Soprano, Violoncello, K3.6
Violin, Clarinet, Orchestra, Trumpet,
    A5.24
Violin, Clarinet, Piano, B1.79,
    B12.35, L7.3, T1.14, T3.44, W4.14,
    Z1.22
Violin, Clarinet, Piano, Violoncello,
    L6.13, M10.79, S3.96, V1.61
Violin, Clarinet, Trombone, B1.12
Violin, Clarinet, Viola, Violoncello,
    M6.26
Violin, Clarinet, Violoncello, W6.8.5
Violin, Clarinet/Clarinet(Bass),
    Double Bass, Flute/Flute(Alto),
    Horn, Tenor, Viola, H6.23
Violin, Clarinet/Clarinet(Bass),
    Flute, Soprano, Viola, Violoncello,
    H9.2
Violin, Clarinet/Clarinet(Bass),
    Flute/Piccolo, Piano, Violoncello,
    H2.19
Violin, Clarinet/Clarinet(Bass), Mezzo
    Soprano, Viola, Violoncello, L4.17
Violin, Clarinet/ Saxophone(Tenor),
    Double Bass, Horn, Percussion, H6.8
Violin, Clarinets(2), Double Bass,
    Flute, Percussion, Piano, Timpani,
    Trumpets(2), H9.19
Violin, Clarinets(2), Mezzo Soprano,
    Viola, Violoncello, P5.16
Violin, Clarinets(3), Mandolin,
    Soprano, Viola, Violoncello, M9.12
Violin, Dancer(Optional), Percussion,
    Piano, S3.105
Violin, Dancer, Drums, Piano,
    Saxophone(Alto), Speakers(3),
    Trumpet, Violoncello, A4.24
Violin, Dancer/Narrator, Double Bass,
    Harp, Tape, Trombone, G1.17
Violin, Double Bass, English Horn,
    Flute, Viola, Violoncello, S3.176
Violin, Double Bass, Flute, Oboe,
    Piano, Tenor, Viola, Violoncello,
    S3.88
Violin, Double Bass, Flute,
    Percussion, Piano, Saxophone(Alto),
    Viola, C4.17
Violin, Double Bass, Flute, Trumpet in
    C, G5.10
Violin, Double Bass, Guitar,
    Vibraphone, D1.3
Violin, Double Bass, Horn,
    Speaker/Conductor, Trombone,
    Trumpet, Viola, F4.35
Violin, Double Bass, Horn, Trombone,
    Trumpet, Viola, F4.34

Violin, Double Bass, Piano, Viola,
    Violoncello, C11.8
Violin, Double Bass, Viola,
    Violoncello, C5.8
Violin, Double Bass, Viola,
    Violoncello, Woodwind Quintet, K1.12
Violin, Electronics, Oboe, Psaltery,
    Synthesizer, Violoncello(Optional),
    T2.11
Violin, Euphoniums(2), Flutes(2),
    Trumpet, F4.3
Violin, Flageolet, Viola, T4.89
Violin, Flute, D2.39
Violin, Flute, Harpsichord, Horn,
    Oboe, Trumpet, Viola, Violoncello,
    Voice, Z1.7
Violin, Flute, Harpsichord, String
    Orchestra, V1.16
Violin, Flute, Horn, Piano, D8.12,
    F4.28
Violin, Flute, Horn, Violoncello, E3.8
Violin, Flute, Mandolin, Marimba,
    Oboe, Percussion, Trumpet, H7.27
Violin, Flute, Oboe, Piano, Viola,
    Violoncello, B9.14
Violin, Flute, Piano, D2.39, M9.8
Violin, Flute, Piano, Soprano,
    Violoncello, A3.5
Violin, Flute, Viola, Violoncello,
    D8.13, H9.23, K1.3, S3.2, S3.4
Violin, Flute, Violoncello, B8.4,
    C9.16, N1.7, W6.7
Violin, Flute/Piccolo, Instrumental
    Ensemble, Piano, Soprano, M10.62
Violin, Flutes(2), Horn, Piano,
    Trumpet, G5.11
Violin, Guitar, Percussion, Trombone,
    Trumpet, P3.7
Violin, Guitar, Piano, B4.32
Violin, Guitar, Piano, Violoncello,
    L9.14
Violin, Handbell, Viola Da Gamba,
    P6.185
Violin, Harmonium, Violoncello, C13.7
Violin, Harp, A4.38
Violin, Harp, Percussion(3), Soprano,
    Viola, Violoncello, L5.9
Violin, Harpsichord, B12.9, P6.13
Violin, Harpsichord or Piano, P6.172
Violin, Harpsichord, Oboe, A4.1,
    H10.91
Violin, Harpsichord, String Orchestra,
    P6.26
Violin, Horn or Violoncello, Piano,
    C13.50, C13.112
Violin, Horn, Piano, H10.102, O1.19
Violin, Horn, Piano, Violoncello, H6.7
Violin, Horn, Viola, H6.22
Violin, Horn, Viola, Violoncello,
    H9.24
Violin, Horns(2), Piano,
    Vibraphone(Optional), Viola,
    Violoncello, F4.45
Violin, Jew's Harp, Piano, A4.7
Violin, Mezzo Soprano or Soprano,
    Organ or Piano, F3.29
Violin, Mezzo Soprano, Piano, P5.17
Violin, Oboe, H10.119
Violin, Oboe, Organ, Soprano, Tenor,
    H10.8

Violins(4), Violas(2),
    Violoncellos(2), L2.32, L2.33, S9.60
Violoncello, B2.1, B8.15, B8.46,
    B9.25, B9.26, D3.15, H10.109, M4.3,
    M4.7, M4.9, M6.21, M6.41, P5.11,
    S3.52, V3.12, Z1.14
Violoncello or Violin or Viola, Piano,
    M1.11
Violoncello(Amplified),
    Organ(Electric), Saxophone(Tenor),
    H2.10
Violoncello(Optional),
    Bassoon(Optional), Chorus(SSA),
    Double Bass(Optional), Organ or
    Piano, P6.119
Violoncello(Optional), Electronics,
    Oboe, Psaltery, Synthesizer, Violin,
    T2.11
Violoncello, Actress/Mezzo Soprano,
    Clarinet, Flute, Percussion, Viola,
    Violin, M11.1
Violoncello, Alto, L2.7
Violoncello, Alto, Clarinet, Flute,
    Horn, Percussion, Piano,
    Sopranos(2), Violin, M12.2
Violoncello, Alto, Flute, Piano,
    Viola, Violin, L11.5
Violoncello, Alto, Piano, Viola,
    Violin, C1.10
Violoncello, Alto, Violin, B1.75
Violoncello, Baritone, Chorus(Mixed),
    Clarinet, Double Bass, Percussion,
    Piano, Saxophone(Tenor), Violin,
    H2.15
Violoncello, Baritone, Clarinet,
    Flute, Oboe, Viola, D6.80
Violoncello, Baritone, Guitar, Horn,
    Piano, S12.9
Violoncello, Bass Baritone, Double
    Bass, Horn, Trombone, Viola, P5.18
Violoncello, Bass, Chorus(SATB),
    Continuo, Sopranos(2), Tenor,
    Violas(2), P6.232
Violoncello, Bass, Harpsichord, H10.49
Violoncello, Bass, Tenors(2), H10.22
Violoncello, Basset, Clarinet(in A),
    Flute(Alto), Percussion, Viola,
    Voice, S9.20
Violoncello, Bassoon, Chorus(SATB),
    Clarinet, Double Bass, Flute, Viola,
    Violins(1 or 2), P7.38
Violoncello, Bassoon, Chorus(SATB),
    Clarinet, Flute, Harpsichord, Piano,
    Viola, Violin, Voices, C1.1
Violoncello, Bassoon, Chorus(SATB),
    Clarinet, Flute/Piccolo, Horn,
    Piano, Viola, Violin, S3.80
Violoncello, Bassoon, Clarinet or
    Saxophone, Double Bass, Flute, Oboe,
    Percussion, Piano, Trumpet, C11.6
Violoncello, Bassoon, Clarinet(2),
    Percussion(2), Violin, M10.40
Violoncello, Bassoon, Clarinet(in A),
    Flute(Alto), Viola, Violin, D2.15
Violoncello, Bassoon, Clarinet, Double
    Bass, Flute, Oboe, Soprano, Tenor,
    Viola, Violin, G4.23
Violoncello, Bassoon, Clarinet, Flute,
    Piano, Viola, Violin, B4.28

Violoncello, Bassoon, Clarinet, Horn,
    Piano, Viola, Violin, K1.21
Violoncello, Bassoon, Clarinet, Oboe,
    Soprano, Viola, Violin, D9.11
Violoncello, Bassoon, Clarinet, Piano,
    Tenor, Violin, E7.2
Violoncello, Bassoon, Clarinets(2),
    Double Bass, Flute, Piano, Violin,
    B8.11
Violoncello, Bassoon, English Horn,
    Trombones(2), Trumpets(2), Viola,
    Violin, S3.189
Violoncello, Bassoon, Viola, Violin,
    H9.22
Violoncello, Celeste, Clarinet, Flute,
    Harp, Percussion, Soprano, Viola,
    Violin, M9.7
Violoncello, Celeste, Clarinet, Flute,
    Soprano, Viola, M9.2
Violoncello, Celeste, Double Bass,
    Mezzo Soprano, Piano, Trombone,
    Trumpet, Tuba, Vibraphone, Violin,
    F2.7
Violoncello, Celeste, Viola, L6.18
Violoncello, Chamber Orchestra, M8.1
Violoncello, Chamber Orchestra,
    Clarinets(2), Violin, S9.104
Violoncello, Chorus(Mixed), Harp,
    Tenor, Woodwinds(5), F8.78
Violoncello, Chorus(SATB),
    Clarinet/Clarinet(Bass), Percussion,
    Piano, Trombone, E3.1
Violoncello, Chorus(SATB),
    Clarinets(2), Flute, Horn, Oboe,
    Timpani, H4.22
Violoncello, Chorus(SATB),
    Harpsichord, Oboe, G5.8
Violoncello, Chorus(SATB), Percussion,
    Piano, Speakers(3), E3.9
Violoncello, Chorus(Women), Clarinet,
    Percussion, H6.9
Violoncello, Chorus, Soprano,
    Trumpets(3), G4.8
Violoncello, Cimbalom, Concertina,
    Oboe, Percussion, Piccolo,
    Violas(3), S15.5
Violoncello, Clarinet(Bass),
    Clarinet(E-flat), Clarinet(In A),
    Marimba, Viola, Violin, L7.38
Violoncello, Clarinet(Bass), Double
    Bass, Flute, Percussion, Piano,
    Violin, Voice(High), D2.19
Violoncello, Clarinet(Bass), Flute,
    Harp, Piano, Violin, M12.5
Violoncello, Clarinet(Bass), Flute,
    Oboe, C4.23
Violoncello, Clarinet(Bass), Flute,
    Percussion(2), Violin, S15.4
Violoncello, Clarinet(Bass), Flute,
    Trumpet, Viola, Violin, M10.44
Violoncello, Clarinet(Bass), Piano,
    Soprano, M10.72
Violoncello, Clarinet(Bass), Trumpet,
    B8.53
Violoncello, Clarinet(in A), Horn,
    Saxophone(Alto), Viola, Violin,
    S9.72
Violoncello, Clarinet, Clarinet(Bass),
    Dancers, Percussion, K2.52

Violoncello,
    Clarinet/Clarinet(Contrabass),
    Saxophone(Soprano), M10.33
Violoncello, Clarinets(2), Mezzo
    Soprano, Viola, Violin, P5.16
Violoncello, Clarinets(3), Mandolin,
    Soprano, Viola, Violin, M9.12
Violoncello, Costumes(Lighted), Harp,
    Tape(Live), E1.90
Violoncello, Dancer, Drums, Piano,
    Saxophone(Alto), Speakers(3),
    Trumpet, Violin, A4.24
Violoncello, Double Bass, B8.33,
    C4.11, M7.9
Violoncello, Double Bass(Optional),
    Organ, Viola(Optional), Violins(2),
    P6.186
Violoncello, Double Bass, English
    Horn, Flute, Percussion, Piano,
    Viola, Violins(3), S3.185
Violoncello, Double Bass, English
    Horn, Flute, Viola, Violin, S3.176
Violoncello, Double Bass, Flute, Oboe,
    Piano, Tenor, Viola, Violin, S3.88
Violoncello, Double Bass, Oboe, Viola,
    S9.76
Violoncello, Double Bass, Piano,
    Viola, Violin, C11.8
Violoncello, Double Bass, Viola,
    Violin, C5.8
Violoncello, Double Bass, Viola,
    Violina, Woodwind Quintet, K1.12
Violoncello, Flute, E2.1, H5.14,
    H10.110, W1.40
Violoncello, Flute or Violin, Piano,
    C13.112
Violoncello, Flute(Alto), Piano,
    Soprano, Z1.15
Violoncello, Flute, Guitar, S13.13,
    T2.30
Violoncello, Flute, Harp, B9.17
Violoncello, Flute, Harp, Percussion,
    Trombones(2), Trumpet, Viola, W6.3
Violoncello, Flute, Harp, Soprano,
    B12.6
Violoncello, Flute, Harpsichord,
    B12.24, D7.3, F8.13, Z1.8
Violoncello, Flute, Harpsichord, Horn,
    Oboe, Trumpet, Viola, Violin, Voice,
    Z1.7
Violoncello, Flute, Harpsichord,
    Soprano, B12.16, B12.19
Violoncello, Flute, Horn, Mezzo
    Soprano, Oboe, Viola, H10.50
Violoncello, Flute, Horn, Oboe, Piano,
    Soprano, Tenors(2), H10.39
Violoncello, Flute, Horn, Violin, E3.8
Violoncello, Flute, Mezzo Soprano,
    Piano, H2.6
Violoncello, Flute, Oboe, B1.76
Violoncello, Flute, Oboe, Piano,
    Viola, Violin, B9.14
Violoncello, Flute, Percussion, Voice,
    S4.11
Violoncello, Flute, Piano, A1.20,
    B9.23, C7.16, D6.175, H10.101
Violoncello, Flute, Piano, Soprano,
    Violin, A3.5
Violoncello, Flute, Tenor, L11.3
Violoncello, Flute, Timpani, T2.33

Violoncello, Flute, Viola, A5.103,
    B1.77
Violoncello, Flute, Viola, Violin,
    D8.13, H9.23, K1.3, S3.2, S3.4
Violoncello, Flute, Violin, B8.4,
    C9.16, N1.7, W6.7
Violoncello, Guitar, Piano, Violin,
    L9.14
Violoncello, Harmonium, Violin, C13.7
Violoncello, Harp, Percussion(3),
    Soprano, Viola, Violin, L5.9
Violoncello, Harpsichord, F4.52
Violoncello, Harpsichord, Soprano,
    B12.18
Violoncello, Harpsichord, Tenor or
    Bass Baritone, B12.5
Violoncello, Horn, Oboe/English Horn,
    Tape(Computer), Viola, C6.6
Violoncello, Horn, Piano, L9.19, O1.29
Violoncello, Horn, Piano, Violin, H6.7
Violoncello, Horn, Viola, Violin,
    H9.24
Violoncello, Horns(2), Piano,
    Vibraphone(Optional), Viola, Violin,
    F4.45
Violoncello, Keyboard, Viola, H10.100
Violoncello, Mezzo Soprano or Soprano,
    Piano, P10.20
Violoncello, Oboe, Piano, Violin,
    A5.81
Violoncello, Oboe, Viola, Violin,
    H9.25, S9.63, S9.64, S9.65, S9.66
Violoncello, Orchestra, M7.4, P7.77
Violoncello, Organ, Soprano, Viola,
    C9.6
Violoncello, Percussion(2), Soprano,
    Violin, K3.9
Violoncello, Percussion, Violin, L6.17
Violoncello, Percussion, Violin, Wind
    Ensemble, K4.3
Violoncello, Piano, B3.29, B4.10,
    B8.5, B9.4, B12.4, C3.20, C13.102,
    D6.55, F1.3, G4.16, L2.3, L4.4,
    L9.9, M8.19, P7.18, P11.2, P11.51,
    P2.213, S9.10, S10.5, T4.1, V3.9
Violoncello, Piano, Saxophone(Alto),
    Soprano, Trombone, Trumpet, Violin,
    A4.37
Violoncello, Piano,
    Saxophone(Soprano), M10.56
Violoncello, Piano, Soprano, L9.10,
    P10.20
Violoncello, Piano, Trumpet,
    Violins(2), H10.52
Violoncello, Piano, Viola, Violin,
    B12.21, P7.41
Violoncello, Piano, Violin, B1.82,
    B3.16, B3.17, B4.33, B7.3, B10.9,
    C13.3, C13.7, C13.48, C13.50,
    C13.87, C13.111, C13.112, C13.113,
    C14.3, E3.24, F8.79, G4.25, H2.32,
    K2.35, K2.89, K3.19, K4.24, M1.6,
    M9.5, N2.15, O1.59, P7.74, P7.75,
    P11.104, S6.37
Violoncello, Piano, Violin or Viola,
    Violins(2), S9.38
Violoncello, Piano, Violins(2), W1.28
Violoncello, Recorders(3), Viola,
    Violin, D6.138

Winds(14 or More), English Horn,
    Percussion(3), Trumpets(3), F4.33
Winds, Harp, Soprano, G4.22
Wood Buzz Chime, R8.3
Woodblocks(6), Speaker, S9.98
Woodwind Ensemble(24), Double Bass,
    Drums, Flute, Saxophone, M10.36
Woodwind Ensemble, Brasses(5),
    Cassette Choir, Laser Projections,
    Tape, E1.96
Woodwind Ensemble, Violoncello, F4.12
Woodwind Quintet, A1.14, A4.8, B1.34,
    B1.43, B1.44, B9.28, B12.23.5, C5.2,
    D2.93, G2.14, H2.25, H7.14, H8.11,
    K1.19, K5.15, L2.17, L10.14, M5.14,
    M8.25, M10.64, N2.10, N2.17, N2.20,
    P7.49, R2.159, S3.85, S3.104,
    S3.200, S4.12, S4.19, T3.30, T3.31
Woodwind Quintet, Actors(2), S12.1
Woodwind Quintet, Chorus(Mixed),
    Double Bass, Trombone, Trumpet,
    S12.11
Woodwind Quintet, Chorus(SATB), M8.3
Woodwind Quintet, Chorus, Harp, D7.1
Woodwind Quintet, Double Bass, Viola,
    Violin, Violoncello, K1.12
Woodwind Quintet, Horn, Trombone,
    Trumpet, Tuba, H7.28
Woodwind Quintet, Horn, Trombone,
    Trumpets(2), Tuba, S3.39
Woodwind Quintet, Orchestra, S3.32
Woodwind Quintet, Piano, D8.17, R2.72
Woodwind Quintet, Soprano, D8.29
Woodwind Quintet,Trombone, Trumpet,
    C13.103
Woodwind Quintet, Voice, R2.197
Woodwind Quintets(2), Percussion,
    R2.107
Woodwinds(3), C13.121, R1.15, V1.99
Woodwinds(4), C13.122
Woodwinds(4) or Brasses(4), C13.123,
    C13.124
Woodwinds(5), Chorus(Mixed), Harp,
    Tenor, Violoncello, F8.78
Woodwinds(5), Piano, Strings(2),
    Voices(4), F8.14
Woodwinds, Baritone, Brass,
    Choruses(2), Percussion, V1.43
Woodwinds, Brasses, Percussion, M3.9
Woodwinds, Chorus(Mixed), Organ,
    P6.140
Woodwinds, Percussion, R4.1

Xylophone, Bassoon, Double Bass,
    Instruments(Treble)(3), O1.8
Xylophone, Chorus(SATB), Double Bass,
    Drum, Flute, Harp, Trombone,
    Trumpet, Voices, P4.44
Xylophone, Chorus(TTBB), M7.22
Xylophone, Clarinets(2), Viola, M5.18
Xylophone, Double Bass, Voice(Female),
    V4.2
Xylophone, Harp, Horn, Percussion(2),
    Tenor, Vibraphone, Viola, L2.2

COMPOSERS IN THE BOSTON COMPOSERS PROJECT

A1   John C. Adams
App   Richard Allen
A2   Nicholas Altenbernd
A3   Martin Amlin
A4   T.J. (Thomas Jefferson) Anderson, Jr.
A5   Theodore Antoniou
App   Ronald Arnatt
A6   Reed Alden Augliere

B1   John Bavicchi
B2   Larry Thomas Bell
B3   Hampartzoum Berberian
B4   Arthur Victor Berger
B5   Ran Blake
B6   Peter Herbert Bloom
B7   David John Boros
B8   Roger Bourland
B9   Hayg Boyadjian
B10   Martin Boykan
B11   Martin Brody
B12   Roslyn Brogue
B13   Marjorie L. Burgess
App   Gary Burton
App   Jaki (John Arthur) Byard

C1   Curt Cacioppo
C2   Michael Page Carnes
App   David Carney
C3   Alastair K. Cassels-Brown
C4   Robert Ceely
C5   Basil Chapman
C6   Peter Child
C7   Timothy Vincent Clark
C8   Robert David Cogan
C9   Edward Cohen
App   Joel Cohen
C10   John Cook
C11   Francis Judd Cooke
C12   Richard Cornell
C13   Silvio Coscia
C14   John Crotty

D1   John Gennaro Damian
D2   Avram David
D3   Lyle Davidson
D4   Katherine K. Davis
D5   David Del Tredici
D6   Norman Dello Joio
D7   Donald E. Denniston
App   Mario Di Bonaventura

D8	Robert Di Domenica
D9	John F. Duesenberry
E1	Paul Earl
E2	Barbara J. Engel
E3	David M. Epstein
E4	Pozzi Escot
E5	Thomas Gregory Everett
F1	Peter R. Farmer
F2	Martin Farren
F3	Nancy Plummer Faxon
F4	(Alan) John Felice
F5	Anthony J. Ferrazano (Anthony Zano)
F6	Thomas E. Flaherty
F7	James Forte
App	Jeff Friedman
F8	Herbert Fromm
F9	Eugenia Frothingham
App	Julius Gaidellis
App	Peter George Ganick
G1	Gregory Mark Gargarian
G2	Paul Gay
App	Michael Gibbs
App	Jimmy (James P.) Giuffre
G3	Victoria M. Glaser
G4	John Goodman
App	Mike Goodrick
G5	William Gottshall
G6	Rouben Gregorian
G7	Robert Gronquist
App	Grace Warner Gulesian
G8	Lance F. Gunderson
H1	Reginald W. Hache
H2	John Harbison
App	Donald Harris
H3	Mark S. Harvey
H4	Peter Peabody Hazzard
H5	John C. Heiss
H6	W. Newell Hendricks
H7	James A. Hoffmann
H8	Alfred Hoose
H9	John Huggler
H10	Nicholas D. Humez
H11	Leslie H. Hurwitz
App	Andrew W. Jaffe
J1	Leon Janikian
J2	Gloria Jasinski
J3	Kevin Jones

K1	Jeronimas Kacinskas
K2	Minuetta Kessler
K3	Earl Kim
K4	Leon Kirchner
App	Charles Kletzsch
K5	Shirish Korde
L1	John La Porta
L2	Otto E. Laske
L3	Henry Lasker
L4	Thomas Oboe Lee
L5	Fred Lerdahl
L6	Erik Lindgren
L7	J. Rodney Lister
L8	Gregory Livingston
L9	Ruth Lomon
L10	Harriet Agda Lundberg
App	Robert J. Lurtsema
11	Sally Lutyens
App	Kenneth MacKillip
M1	Edward J. Madden
M2	Joseph Makholm
App	William Maloof
M3	Joseph Gabriel Maneri
App	James Mann
M4	John David Mann
M5	Pamela J. Marshall
M6	Donald Martino
M7	James McCullough
M8	Thomas J. McGah
M9	Douglas McGilvra
M10	William Thomas McKinley
M11	Joyce Mekeel
M12	Marjorie Merryman
M13	Malloy M. Miller
N1	Hankus Howard Netsky
N2	Hugo Norden
O1	Linda Ostrander
App	David Nolte Patterson
P1	Martin Pearlman
P2	Ted (Frederick) Pease
P3	Stephen Peisch
P4	C. Alexander Peloquin
P5	Malcolm C. Peyton
App	Bob Pilkington
P6	Daniel Pinkham
P7	Walter Hamor Piston
P8	Stephany King Plsek
P9	Thomas J. Plsek

App	Conrad Pope
P10	Leila Pradell
P11	Alice McElroy Procter
P12	Kenneth Pullig
R1	Dianne Goolkasian Rahbee
R2	Gardner Read
R3	Ronald M. Rivera
R4	Curtis Roads
R5	E. Amelia Rogers
App	Jerome Rosen
App	Victor Rosenbaum
R6	Peter Row
R7	George A. Russell
R8	Robert Rutman
S1	Tony (John A.) Schemmer
App	Allan Schindler
S2	Martin Max Schreiner
S3	Gunther Schuller
App	Michael Scott
S4	Robert Selig
S5	Harold Shapero
S6	Seymour Shifrin
S7	Gregory Silberman
S8	Sheila Silver
S9	Ezra Sims
S10	Robert B. Sirota
S11	Leo Snyder
S12	John Stewart
S13	Tison Street
S14	Marie Stultz
S15	Donald Sur
T1	Pasquale Tassone
T2	Ivan Tcherepnin
App	William Tesson
T3	Nicholas Chris Tgettis
T4	Randall Thompson
V1	Nicholas Van Slyck
V2	Barry Lloyd Vercoe
V3	Elizabeth Hendry Vercoe
V4	John Voigt
W1	Betsy Warren
App	Newton Wayland
App	Jack Weaver
W2	Clifford M. Weeks
W3	Edgar Weiss
App	Herman Weiss
W4	(William) Scott Wheeler
App	John Towner Williams

App   Phil (Phillips Elder) Wilson, Jr.
W5   Robert Winfrey
W6   Jan Wissmuller
App   Gertrude Price Wollner
App   Dann C. Wyman

Y1   James Yannatos

Z1   Arlene Zallman